BOUND: THE COMPLETE COLLECTION

BOOKS 1 TO 4

SHANDI BOYES

Edited by
MOUNTAINS WANTED PUBLISHING

Illustrated by
SSB COVERS & DESIGN

By: Shandi Boyes
Editing: Mountains Wanted Publishing
Photographs: Shutterstock Account
Cover Designer: SSB Designs

DEDICATION

To the readers who inspire me every day to write.

Shandi xx

WANT TO STAY IN TOUCH?

Facebook: facebook.com/authorshandi

Instagram: instagram.com/authorshandi

Email: authorshandi@gmail.com

Reader's Group: bit.ly/ShandiBookBabes

Website: authorshandi.com

Newsletter: https://www.subscribepage.com/AuthorShandi

ALSO BY SHANDI BOYES

Perception Series

Saving Noah (Noah & Emily)

Fighting Jacob (Jacob & Lola)

Taming Nick (Nick & Jenni)

Redeeming Slater (Slater and Kylie)

Saving Emily (Noah & Emily - Novella)

Wrapped Up with Rise Up (Perception Novella - should be read after the Bound Series)

Enigma

Enigma (Isaac & Isabelle #1)

Unraveling an Enigma (Isaac & Isabelle #2)

Enigma The Mystery Unmasked (Isaac & Isabelle #3)

Enigma: The Final Chapter (Isaac & Isabelle #4)

Beneath The Secrets (Hugo & Ava #1)

Beneath The Sheets(Hugo & Ava #2)

Spy Thy Neighbor (Hunter & Paige)

The Opposite Effect (Brax & Clara)

I Married a Mob Boss(Rico & Blaire)

Second Shot(Hawke & Gemma)

The Way We Are(Ryan & Savannah #1)

The Way We Were(Ryan & Savannah #2)

Sugar and Spice (Cormack & Harlow)

Lady In Waiting (Regan & Alex #1)

Man in Queue (Regan & Alex #2)

Couple on Hold(Regan & Alex #3)

Enigma: The Wedding (Isaac and Isabelle)

Silent Vigilante (Brandon and Melody #1)

Hushed Guardian (Brandon & Melody #2)

Quiet Protector (Brandon & Melody #3)

Bound Series

Chains (Marcus & Cleo #1)

Links(Marcus & Cleo #2)

Bound(Marcus & Cleo #3)

Restrain(Marcus & Cleo #4)

Psycho (Dexter & ??)

Russian Mob Chronicles

Nikolai: A Mafia Prince Romance (Nikolai & Justine #1)

Nikolai: Taking Back What's Mine (Nikolai & Justine #2)

Nikolai: What's Left of Me(Nikolai & Justine #3)

Nikolai: Mine to Protect(Nikolai & Justine #4)

Asher: My Russian Revenge (Asher & Zariah)

Nikolai: Through the Devil's Eyes(Nikolai & Justine #5)

Trey (Trey & K)

K: A Trey Sequel

The Italian Cartel

Dimitri

Roxanne

Reign

Mafia Ties (Novella)

Maddox

Demi

Rocco

Clover

Smith

RomCom Standalones

Just Playin' (Elvis & Willow)

Ain't Happenin' (Lorenzo & Skylar)

The Drop Zone (Colby & Jamie)

Very Unlikely (Brand New Couple)

Short Stories

Christmas Trio (Wesley, Andrew & Mallory -- short story)

Falling For A Stranger (Short Story)

Coming Soon

Skitzo

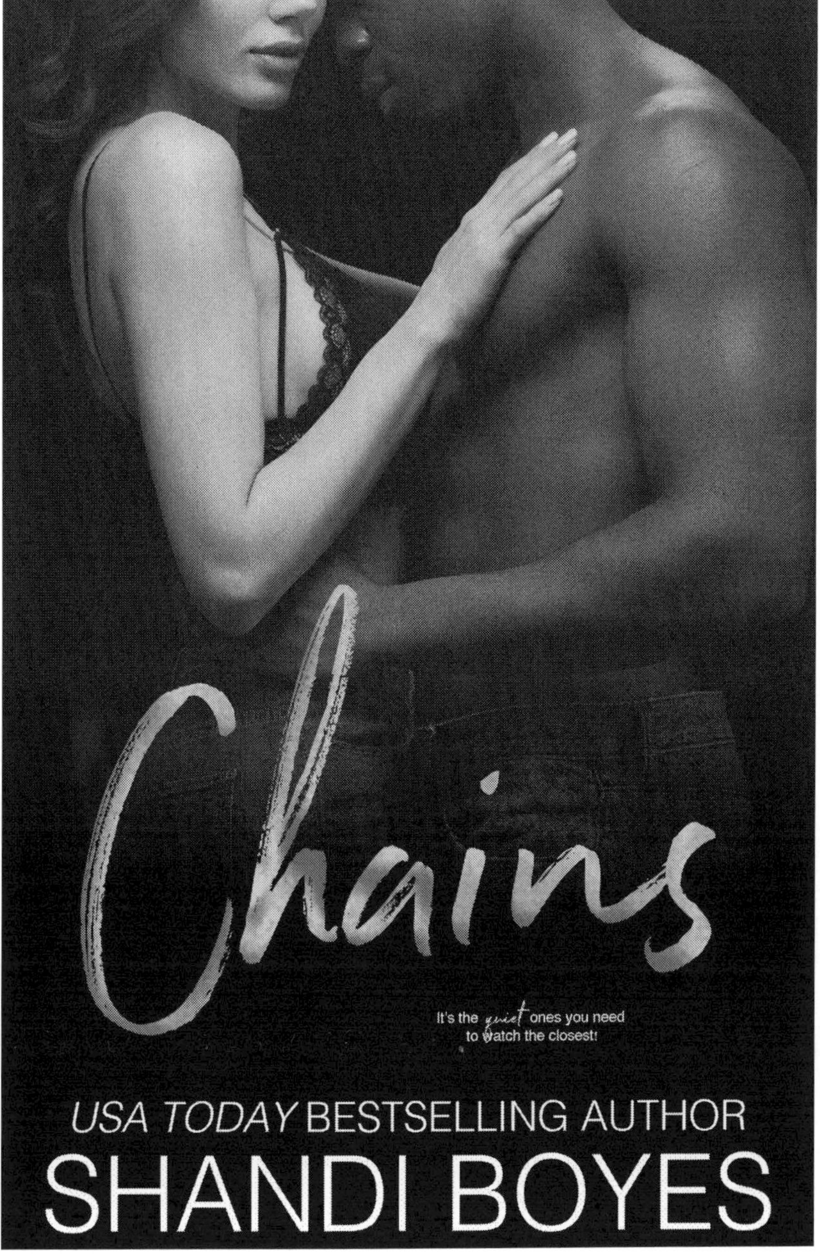
Chains
It's the quiet ones you need
to watch the closest!
USA TODAY BESTSELLING AUTHOR
SHANDI BOYES

PROLOGUE

"Hold the elevator," I shout at the top of my lungs. My words are weak, hampered by the sob sitting at the back of my throat dying to break free.

Through a clog of people standing in the middle of the bustling foyer, I notice a black suit-covered arm shooting out to hold the elevator doors open for me. Gratitude replaces some of the panic scorching my veins, thankful I won't be stuck bawling my eyes out in a crowded space.

I run my hands across my cheeks to ensure my tears haven't spilled before pushing through the throng of people gawking at me with sympathy. I'm sure I look like a total wreck. The well-presented package I put together every day has been decimated, replaced with an ashen face and desolate eyes. I don't need to look in the mirror to know my eyes are red and brimming with tears and that my natural tan coloring is faded and washed out. I felt the blood drain from my face the moment I took the call that broke my heart.

Forty minutes ago, I took a phone call no woman ever wants to receive—a call that shattered my world with four little words, "There's been an accident."

Everything blurred in an instant. My entire world was upended. I can't remember how I made it to Jamaica Hospital in Queens. I think I drove here, but if I was asked to place my hand on a Bible and swear to it, I wouldn't be able to testify that was what happened. My mind is shut down, my heart beyond shattered. The only reason my legs are moving is because they're being encouraged by hope, a hope that not every nightmare I've had is coming to fruition at once. A hope that was also delivered with four short words: "Tate is in ICU."

More tears threaten to trickle down my cheeks as the words spoken to me forty minutes ago play on repeat. They add unfixable cracks to my already shattered heart, drowning out the doctor calls being announced over the hospital paging system. With my mind distracted on keeping my body upright, I neglect to notice the small lip at the entrance of the elevator. I fall forward at a faster rate than my heartbroken mind can register, sending me and my Manolo Blahnik shoes ungracefully tumbling into the elevator car.

"Careful," says a deep and manly voice from above.

His warning comes too late. My fall is so brutal, the stranger's clutch on the tops of my arms doesn't stop my knees hitting the tiled floor with an almighty bang. Pain rockets through my body, producing a whimper of protest from my parched lips and adding more tears to my already drenched eyes.

Ignoring the pain of my grazed knees, I crawl forward so I can hide my mortified face in the corner. I need a few minutes to gather my composure before I face the next heartbreaking chapter of my story.

Through the shrilling of the pulse in my ears, I hear the stranger ask, "What floor?"

"Trauma unit, please," I push out, my voice as low as the beat of my heart.

The elevator chugs to life, launching my stomach into my throat. I suck in deep breaths as I fight through the torrent of pain silently asphyxiating me. *This is by far the worst day of my life.*

My manic breaths have me stumbling onto a unique scent not often registered in a hospital: the smell of freshly laundered linen. After running my hand under my nose to remove the contents spilling from it, I drift my eyes to the refreshing scent. Through a volley of tears threatening to drop, my eyes scan a handsome African-American man wearing dark trousers and a buttoned-up shirt. He is standing near the elevator panel, eyeing me through a set of unbelievably thick lashes. Although my vision is blurred by my teary eyes, I can't miss the concern pumping from his alluring green gaze.

"Are you okay?" he questions, his voice commanding but full of unease.

The simplicity of his question breaks the dam of moisture in my eyes. My head flops forward as a broken howl tears through my quivering lips. I gave it my best shot to hold in my devastation, but I'm not strong enough anymore. I am beyond broken.

Before I can register what's happening, I am thrust off the floor and surrounded by warmth. As I hiccup through an infinite number of tears, the unnamed man holds me to his firm chest and whispers into my hairline. With my pulse ringing in my ears, I can't hear a word he is speaking, but I know he is comforting me. His whole composure impels reassurance. The heat of his breath on my temple and the warmth of his body curved around mine, simmers the shakes hampering my petite frame. He makes me completely forget I'm trapped in the depths of hell. The whole scenario is something you'd expect to see in a sappy 90s romantic movie starring Tom Hanks and Meg Ryan. It's cringeworthy and unoriginal, but heartfelt and endearing at the same time. I'm not usually into clichés, but I'm willing to set aside my idiosyncrasy to accept the comfort of a stranger on my darkest day.

When the ding of the elevator announces its arrival to the trauma unit, disappointment unwillingly registers on my face. I bite on the inside of my cheek, hoping it will stop my tears long enough to thank the stranger for his comfort. After running the back of my hand across my cheeks, I pull back from his chest. I take a minute so my rattled brain can contemplate an appropriate response. While staring at his slow-thrusting chest, I notice two large wet patches on his shirt. I cried so hard the lightweight material clings to his skin, exposing more of his rich chocolate skin.

My hunched posture straightens when he cups my jaw. His hand swallows half of my face as he uses the pad of his thumb to remove my tears. His touch scorches my cheek, and for a fraction of a second, he makes me forget where I am. He is standing so close, the sweetness of his breath fans my dry lips. I want to look at him, but I won't. I've always been a hideously ugly crier. I am sure today is no different.

Once all my tears are cleared, the stranger places his fingers under my chin and slowly raises my downcast head. A sharp gasp expels from his lips when my head is lifted high enough that my long, dark brown locks fall from my face, fully exposing me. I bounce my eyes around the interior of the elevator, seeking anything but his gaze. Clearly, my concerns about my appearance are warranted by his gasping-in-shock response.

"Look at me."

He keeps his hand hovering just under my chin. He is not quite touching me, but is close enough my body is on high alert. My chest rises and falls three times before my eyes follow the prompts of my blurry brain. Just as his razor-sharp jawline, decadent plump lips, and the tip of his straight, defined nose come into view, my name is called.

Snapping my head to the side, I locate my younger sister, Lexi, standing in the corridor. Tears are flooding her cheeks, and her eyes look lifeless and hollow. She is shaking so much, I'm confident she is on the verge of collapse. I rush to her and scoop her into my arms. Her tears trickling down my neck are absorbed by the collar of my cashmere jumper when she burrows her head under my chin.

"They're gone," she whispers painfully, her low voice breaking my heart even more.

"It's okay. It will be okay," I assure her as the ghastliness of the situation slams back into me, hammering me enough I struggle to breathe.

I run my trembling hand down Lexi's hair in a soothing manner. "We will always have each other. No matter what happens, we will get through this."

While pressing a kiss to her temple, her freshly washed hair triggers the briefest memory. As my heart rate climbs, I swing my eyes to the left. My breath hitches in my throat when I catch the quickest glimpse of a pair of unique green eyes peering at me.

"Thank you," I mouth to the blurred man standing in the elevator.

Even with my nearsightedness hindering my vision, I don't miss the curt nod of his head before the elevator doors snap shut.

1

Four Years Later...

"Calm your farm. They don't have legs, so they haven't just up and left town. They have to be here somewhere."

I stop digging my hand into our lumpy two-seater couch and swing my eyes to my sister, Lexi. She wears the "we're about to be homeless if I turn up to work late again" look better than me. Her long brown locks are twisted in a sideways French braid, and her hours of coughing this morning have given her cheeks a vibrant red hue. Looking at her in her fluffy pink pig slippers and Ms. Sunshine pajamas doesn't give any indication to the gauntlet of pain her weary body ran through this weekend.

Lexi is sick. I don't mean she drank too much on the weekend and is feeling the effects of it sick, I mean sick-sick. She has cystic fibrosis, the one sickness that can be easily hidden by her bright smile and gorgeous face. Even though we have a five-year age gap, people often mistake us as twins. We have the same dark, stormy eyes from our mother, thick, wavy hair from our father, and the wit of our youngest brother, Tate.

If you were to scroll back through generations of records of the Garcias from Montclair, New Jersey, locate a photo of any female within the 20-25 year age category, you will find a replica of Lexi and me. We are the very epitome of the Garcia genes.

I stop searching for my keys and crank my neck to our family portrait hanging above the brick and mortar fireplace. Heat blooms across my chest when I lock my eyes with my mom sitting in the middle of the painting, surrounded by her three children. If I disregard the faded edges of the oil paint my father used to create his masterpiece that's been hanging on the wall the past fifteen years, I could pretend I was looking in the mirror. That's how similar I look to my mother.

I take a moment to remember a lady who smelled like fresh flowers and had a heart bigger than my daddy's boots before I continue with my hunt to find my felonious keys. My breathing halts when the coolness of metal graces the tips of my fingers.

Screwing up my nose, I slip my hand deeper into the badly-in-need-of-an-upgrade couch. From the crazy beat of my heart and the way a beading of sweat has mottled Lexi's forehead, anyone would swear I was searching for Blackbeard's treasure, not a set of keys to a family sedan that's as old as me.

"Ah ha!" I squeal in excitement when my finger loops around an icy metal material.

Agitation spurs on my annoyance when a broken spring is the only thing that emerges from my in-depth frisk of the saggy couch.

Gritting my teeth, I throw my head back and close my eyes, vainly trying to stifle the scream bubbling up my chest.

My efforts are utterly pointless when Lexi asks, "Are these what you're looking for?"

After cracking my eyes open, I snap my head to the side. An ear-piercing squeal emits my lips when I discover my car keys dangling on Lexi's finger.

"If I find out you were hiding them this entire time, I'll forget my detour to the pharmacy this afternoon," I threaten, snatching the keys out of her hands. Although I was aiming for my tone to come out playful, it has an edge of bitchiness to it. I've never been a morning person, so a Monday following a long weekend is the worst of the worst.

"Forget the pharmacy. You need to visit the optometrist," Lexi fires back, her voice as vicious as the angry snarl marring her beautiful face. "They were sitting in the exact spot you put them Friday night: on the entranceway table."

While grumbling about my annoying nearsightedness, I tug on my coat, sling my satchel over my shoulder, then twist a thin scarf around my neck. I hate winter in general, but I hate it even more since its early arrival gave Lexi a bad case of pneumonia three weeks ago. She was so sick I was certain she would end up in the hospital. Considering that's an expense neither of us can afford, I'm being extra cautious to ensure I don't get the slightest sniffle. Something as simple as a mild cold could be catastrophic for Lexi.

"Thank you," I express, accepting a travel mug of steaming hot chocolate from Lexi. "I'll be home a little late tonight, so don't worry about dinner for me. I'll grab a soup on my way past Donovan's."

She nods while pacing to the front door. I increase my already brisk pace when chilly air blasts into our cozy three-bedroom home. October always brings windy conditions to our hometown, but with a drastic drop in temperatures this month, the wind is brisker than normal. Locals are so wary we'll be hit by another freak snowstorm like we did in October 2011 that the hardware store sold out of rock salt this weekend.

I'm just about to gallop down the front stairs of our patio when I remember I need to remind Lexi about the special parcel arriving today. She is nearly as forgetful as I am nearsighted. Being extra cautious not to slip on the warped wood lining our patio, I spin around to face Lexi.

"I know, the courier is arriving at 10 AM, electrician will be here by 11." White air from the crisp fall morning puffs out of her blue-tinged lips.

My mouth twitches as I prepare to speak, but Lexi beats me. "I know, Cleo. It's cheaper to run than our last system." She peers down at me with her big chocolate eyes, tears welling in them. "I promise I won't hesitate to use it if I am feeling cold."

She hates when I baby her, but her illness isn't something she will simply get over. There is no cure for cystic fibrosis. Eventually, it will take her from me, leaving me all alone. Anything I can do to keep that from happening any earlier than it has to, I will do. Even eating reheated broth and pretending it's chicken soup so I can afford to buy the medication she needs to breathe without wheezing. That's how much I love my sister.

"I wasn't going to say anything about the new heating system," I lie, waving my hand in the air like I'm shooing away my overbearing mother. "I just wanted to wish you luck for your date today," I continue, ensuring my voice has an extra hint of sappiness. "It's not every day you get to have lunch with a world-renowned surgeon."

"Up and coming world-renowned surgeon," Lexi corrects, her dour mood picking up. "And just for clarity: the whole 'gifted hands' thing they refer to when discussing surgeons doesn't always correspond to their title."

After gagging to fake repulsion, I tilt into her side and press a quick kiss on her cheek. My mothering instincts kick into overdrive when I feel how cold her face is.

"One time." I hold my index finger into the air to enhance my statement. "Free rein on my entire wardrobe."

I see Lexi's excitement winding up from her stomach to her white cheeks. "Even the dresses Sasha gave you during your internship?"

I twist my lips before nodding. Her squeal is brittle enough I won't need salt to crack the ice sleeting the sidewalk this winter. Her girly scream will decimate even the thickest ice.

After returning my gesture of a peck on the cheek, Lexi bolts into our modest clapboard house, slamming the front door behind her. I release a deep breath, grateful my ploy to get her into the warmth of our home worked without a tinge of hesitation. I have no doubt the loss of another dress from my rapidly dwindling designer collection will be worth the sacrifice to keep her warm.

Blowing air onto my blue-tinted fingertips, I trudge to my 1994 baby-poo-brown Buick Century coupe. She was a good car... back in 1994 when my parents drove her off the sales lot. Now she has more rust than original paint-work and a big dent in the quarter back panel from Lexi's inability to see our mailbox that's been in the same location the past twenty years of her life.

While snubbing the self-pity party encroaching me, I push my key into the broken lock on my driver's side door and slide inside. With the heater on the blink the last four years, the steering wheel is as frozen as my hands. To say the past four years have been shit would be a major understatement. There aren't enough derogatory words in the dictionary to illustrate how my last four years have been.

My dreary mood picks up when it only takes three cranks of the engine before my old girl's motor finally kicks over.

"I know, Honey. It's been a tough few months," I mumble when she coughs and wheezes as much as Lexi's lungs did over the weekend.

Pretending I didn't call my car a nickname, I reverse out of the driveway and make the short trip to the train station. Even though I only live sixteen miles from work, with tolls and outrageous fuel costs, it's more economical for me to catch the train.

Miguel, my regular station officer and friend, greets me with a broad grin when he notices my car pulling into the parking lot only three short blocks from my home. Returning his smile, I pull into the vacant spot he points out for me.

"How is the darling Cleo today? Did you have the chance to try out that recipe I gave you last week?" Miguel questions after opening my driver's side door and taking my satchel from my grasp.

I curl out of my car and pace toward the booth he will sit in for the next nine hours. "Not yet, but I have the ingredients written down. I'm hoping to cook it for Thanksgiving for Lexi and me." *If I can afford to.*

"That will be lovely, Cleo. My wife will be honored." I don't need to glance into his eyes to know they are relaying the truth. I heard it in his honest words.

I stop pacing and peer up into Miguel's glistening eyes. "How is Janice? Is the tumor shrinking?"

Janice and Miguel have been married for nearly thirty years. They live two blocks from my home and were good friends of my parents. Late last year, Janice was diagnosed with a rare tumor at the base of her skull. Doctors aren't optimistic, but that hasn't stopped Miguel and his youngest son, Jackson, researching possible medical trials for Janice to participate in.

The moisture in Miguel's eyes grows before he shakes his head. "But it isn't growing. So that's something."

"It is," I reply, loving his optimism.

When I spot my train chugging over the tracks on the horizon, I accept my satchel from Miguel, lean in and press a kiss onto the side of his cheek, then skedaddle to the Montclair Heights platform.

Warm air from the train's engine soothes the chill running down my spine from the brisk winds seeping through my thin coat.

Just as I enter the train car, Miguel calls my name. A smile creeps onto my face when he shouts, "I'm still looking for a wife for my eldest son, Preston. A six-year gap is nothing for a girl as smart as you."

"I'll keep that in mind if things don't work out between Jackson and Lexi," I reply, still smiling. Jackson is the gifted up-and-coming surgeon Lexi is going on a date with today. "Besides, most people can only handle one Garcia at a time. I would hate to bombard you."

"Bombard? It would be my pleasure..." The remainder of Miguel's sentence is drowned out when the train doors snap shut.

My eyes remain planted on a smiling Miguel as the train car clatters down the track. Once he is nothing but a speck on the horizon, I move along the crammed aisle with the hope of finding an empty seat. My efforts are pointless. The commuter train is bursting at the seams. Suit-clad men and affluent-looking ladies mingle with Montclair University students and retirees going to spend their day gazing at New York's famous landmarks.

Then there are people like me. The lower-class citizen hoping one day to claw her way to middle class. Forget upper class. I don't need any more designer threads or a house worth millions of dollars. All I want is enough money to afford both my sister's medication and food. If I can supply those two things without scrimping and scrounging every week, I will happily live in the middle-class status.

Fifty minutes—and numerous elbows later—myself and half the population of Montclair merge into Penn Station. A sense of vibrancy hits me the instant I meld into the sea of people clogging the mid-Manhattan sidewalks.

I love the vivacity of New York. It doesn't matter if you're poorer than dirt or richer than Donald Trump, this city doesn't judge. My prospects of being mugged are just as high as the lady standing next to me dressed head to toe in Chanel. *She even smells like Chanel.*

Not wanting to look tattered standing next to the nicely scented lady, I undo the buttons on my jacket and run my hands down my white blouse and black pleated skirt. Even though the past two years my bank account has never stepped over double figures unless it's payday, I am proud of the condition I've kept my Zimmerman ivory lace top and vintage black A-line skirt I was gifted by a work colleague five years ago.

Like all freshly graduated journalism students, I prayed for the pinnacle of internships: Global Ten Media, one of the largest and most profitable media companies in the country. Imagine my surprise when I was not only accepted to intern at Global Ten, but I was also hand-selected to work alongside Sasha Linter, head personal assistant to Viktor Brimmington, Chief Financial Officer of Global Ten Media.

After completing my twelve-month internship, I was offered an extremely lucrative position in the entertainment arm of Global Ten. With my salary nudging towards six figures and mind-boggling perks thrown into the deal, I was set—destined for greatness until I, along with every other entertainment chief in the state, ran a month-long story on the number one singer in the country doing a stint in rehab when he was actually fighting for his life in the intensive care unit of his hometown hospital.

That blunder saw my position downgraded from chief investigative reporter in the entertainment division of Global Ten Media to the lady who ensures the obituaries have a flair of dignity and respect instilled in every announcement. It was a hard and harrowing fall from grace. I didn't think anything would come close to the knock I took when I discovered my desk was moved to the equivalent of a dark and dingy dungeon.

I was wrong.

That hit was nothing compared to the massive knock my life took four short weeks later when my parents and youngest brother were killed in a traffic accident.

When the chill of 2015 blew into the city a month earlier than usual, Montclair locals were left scrambling to prepare for the icy conditions. While wrangling with the boiler in the basement of our family home, I didn't consider calling my dad to warn him of the conditions. They were returning from a two-week long visit to my mom's hometown in Brazil and were not prepared for the icy conditions they were returning to.

When they hit a section of black ice on the highway, my dad's car veered into oncoming traffic. My parents were killed on impact. Tate held on for ten days. With my dad recently being laid off, and our family health plan expired, I not only had to submit their obituaries to the local paper, I also had to write them. It was a horrific year I would give anything to forget.

After checking my memories didn't cause sentimental tears to well in my eyes, I step to the edge of the street as I wait for the pedestrian light to illuminate. Although I will never forget my parents and Tate, I've shed enough tears to last me a lifetime, and I truly believe I don't have any left.

2

"Oh my god! Are you frigging kidding me?" I screech at the top of my lungs when one of the thousand yellow taxis lining the street hits a puddle in front of me, saturating not just me and my designer blouse, but the two people standing beside me as well.

I ball my hands into tight fists, barely suffocating the squeal rumbling up my chest as my eyes drop down to my now ruined blouse. The ivory coloring has been replaced with a mottled mess, similar to the way Lexi's plate looks after eating Grandma G's barbequed skewers covered in rich gravy.

Inwardly cursing at my seemingly bad luck today, I hug my coat in tight and cross the road as per the flashing man indicates. Within a few mere feet, I enter my office building. Global Ten Media is a mecca of a building that rises well above the clouds floating in the air. With its crisp steel panels and multi-hued glass, it's a timeless architectural work of art that adds to the beauty of mid-Manhattan. It's just a pity its insides don't match its outsides. Global Ten Media is a severely depressing place to work.

My day goes from bad to shit when my rummage through my oversized handbag fails to locate my employee swipe card I need to gain access to the secure foyer of my office building. With the owner of Global Ten Media's wealth in the billions, security in this facility is very tight. A security team in the hundreds, a bulletproof glass atrium, and motion cameras scanning every nook and cranny of the space ensure Global Ten Media is one of the most secure locations in the state.

Exhaling my anger in a deep sigh, I pace to the security counter to gain a visitor pass. With my knack for losing things, I have three spare employee ID cards in the top drawer of my desk, but I can't access them without first getting into the bulletproof lobby of my building.

Acting like he doesn't know I've worked here for the past three years,

Richard, the head security officer at Global Ten requests to see my photo ID. Gritting my teeth at his leering grin, I hand him my license.

"Your license is expired," he says, his tone as conceited as his cocky attitude.

"I am aware of that," I snap. Last month, I had to pick between putting gas in my car or paying my license renewal. I chose gas.

My brow arches high into my hairline when Richard takes his time appraising my license. My annoyance can't be helped. We do this same routine a minimum of once a month. Richard's cockiness never eases, and neither does my bitchiness. I'm not usually a snarky type of person, but when Richard arranged a date with both Mischa from Accounting and me for the same night at the same restaurant, my usually carefree attitude became nonexistent around him. I love a man who holds confidence, but there is a massive difference between commanding respect and just plain being an outright asshole. Richard is an asshole.

"Are we done?" I keep my eyes front and center, refusing to look at Richard's snickering work buddies eyeing our interaction with glee all over their faces.

Richard hands me back my license. I place it into my purse before sauntering to the secondary entrance of my office building, grateful Richard's taunts have been kept to a minimum today.

My brisk strides stop when Richard declares, "I have to frisk you before I can let you enter the foyer, Cleo."

Blood roars to my ears, no doubt accentuating my already tanned cheeks with a vibrant red glow. "You need to frisk me?" I spin on my heels to face the smirking, arrogant, pompous prick. I don't care that he has a face women fantasize about while bringing themselves to climax, he is still an asshole.

Not at all intimidated by my glare, Richard nods. "We have some very important dignitaries in the building today. With all the cutbacks Human Resources is making, I don't want to give them a reason to fire me," he snickers.

I cock my brow and glare into his eyes. "And wasting time frisking an *employee* of the company isn't a concern of yours?"

The smug grin on his face enlarges. "Not at all. I'm simply doing my job, Cleo." My skin crawls from the way my name rolls off his tongue in a long, creepy purr. "I am sure management will commend me for doing my job to the best of my ability."

Acting like I can't feel the eyes of a dozen spectators, I stand still as Richard runs the metal detector gun over my well-worn coat. Although my coat is tattered and faded, it would cost far more to replace than I can afford. So, until it's no longer wearable, it will remain my favorable coat.

I'm not surprised when the metal detector squeals while moving over the midsection of my jacket. "It's the metal buckles on my coat," I assure him when I spot suspicion building in his eyes.

Richard bows his brow, rudely ignoring my guarantee. Biting on the inside of my cheek to stop the incessant rant escaping my lips, I undo the buckles of my jacket and sling it over the security desk at my side. Richard's snickering counterparts' slight chuckle breaks into hearty laughter when they notice my puddle-stained blouse and drenched skirt.

"Assholes," I mutter under my breath.

Straightening his spine, Richard extends to his full height. His tall height and vast frame shadow my five-foot-five stature, but I don't back down. I stand tall and proud, just like the woman my mother taught me to be. *Pride doesn't cost you a damn thing.*

Richard scrubs his hand over the scruff on his chin as his sullied eyes drink in every inch of my skin. Once he has finished his avid and uncalled-for glance, he lifts his hands to my shoulders.

"You touch anywhere inappropriate, being unemployed will be the least of your problems," I warn when his hands glide off my shoulders as he begins frisking me. I may appear like a little Latin lover with curvy hips and ample breasts, but the knocks of life have hardened my skin so men like Richard may agitate me, but they don't scare me.

After sliding his hand over my midsection, Richard crouches down to search the lower half of my body. My teeth grit when his new position puts him in direct line of my thrusting breasts. Agitation swirls in my stomach when he stares at my chest for several uncomfortable seconds before lifting his heavy-hooded gaze to me.

"You don't need to be worried about me giving you a sneaky touch-up, Cleo. I don't need to put my hands on you. The visual alone is entertaining enough."

Confused by his confession, my brows stitch. I am utterly clueless as to what his statement refers to. When Richard fails to ease my curiosity, I follow the direction of his heavy-hooded gaze. My heart twists when my eyes zoom in on my erratically panting chest. With my saturated blouse clinging to my soaked white cotton bra, I look like I've turned up to work minus a few essential pieces of clothing.

Mortified that my light brown nipples are on display for the world to see, my hands snap up to cover my chest. The room feels like it's closing in on me when my inconspicuous sweep of the area registers at least half a dozen pairs of eyes gawking at me.

"Are we done?" I question through clenched teeth as I return my eyes to Richard.

"Yes, we are done." His tone is mocking. "I can't see anything dangerous on you." He tilts toward my side to ensure I am the only one to hear his last words. "Other than your mighty fine tits. They're a danger to any man."

With blood rushing to my cheeks, I snatch my coat off the security desk and race to the bulletproof divider separating the foyer from the public galley. I hear Richard and his arrogant colleagues laughing and spouting lewd comments with every step I take.

When the buzzer of the security bell sounds through my ears, I push open the heavily weighted door. I stop frozen halfway into the foyer when a saying my mom always quoted rings through my ears. "Take a stand for yourself by refusing to let others steal your joy, Cleo. Only those who allow themselves to be ridiculed are ridiculed."

Incapable of ignoring my mother's advice, I spin on my heels and saunter back to Richard standing at the side of the security desk. I lift my chin high, my smile bright and inviting. The gleam in Richard's blue eyes grows with every step I take. He rubs his hands together as his heavy-hooded gaze lowers to take in my bouncing bosoms. When I stop in front of him, he slowly drags his eyes up my body. His gaze is derogatory, and it makes my skin crawl. While licking his lips, he rocks on his heels like he has the world at his feet—like nothing can bring him down.

The glint of arrogance brightening his face is snuffed when I raise my knee and ram it into his groin. His pupils widen to the size of saucers, and the color drains from his face. When he stumbles on his feet, I guide him toward a set of chairs lining the galley. Well, I really shouldn't say guide. I more shoved him into the seat. The two security officers watching the exchange between Richard and me sit slack-jawed and mute, neither reprimanding or encouraging me. It wouldn't matter even if they did. I'm too far gone serving justice to stop and consider their recommendations anyway.

Patting Richard on the shoulder like a teacher giving a student advice, I say, "Ice may help, but from what I felt, don't leave it on there too long. You don't want any more shrinkage than you already have."

Richard swallows several times in a row before nodding, his head bobbing up and down like a bobblehead toy. Happy he has accepted my advice, I spin on my heels and pace back to the security partition. I can feel numerous sets of eyes staring at me, but I don't look back. I took a stand, and I am damn proud of myself.

My high-chin composure cracks the instant I enter the empty elevator. Holy shit! I can't believe I did that. I could get fired. Or even worse, sued for workplace harassment. That's the last thing I need. I can barely afford Lexi's medication as it is, let alone living off welfare. I can't believe I acted so foolishly.

Although this was bound to happen eventually, I wish I chose a more appropriate time of the year to teach Richard a lesson. Between wood for the furnace, electricity, and warmer clothing, winter is the most expensive time in my household. We only made it through last year as Lexi got a part-time job that melded with her school schedule. Although she has offered to do the same this year, with her already having a severe bout of pneumonia, I can't risk sending her into the germ-infested world more than she already is.

Pushing my panic to the side, I press the button on the elevator dashboard for the basement. *I wasn't joking when I said my desk is now in a dungeon.* Just before the elevator doors fully snap shut, a suit-covered arm stops them. My pulse quickens as the faintest memory of the stranger who offered me comfort four years ago creeps to the surface of my blurry mind. Although my memories of that day are best described as hazy, the man's comforting green eyes have often popped up in my dreams the past four years. They have been my only salvation in a life of torment.

Disappointment slashes me open when a man with inky black hair, a heart-cranking face, and irises as dark as his well-fitting suit enters the elevator car. His well-put-together package makes my disheveled composure even more noticeable. Smiling at his curious glance at my drenched attire, I take a step backward, moving out of his line of sight. In the quietness of our gathering, the sloshing of water in my ankle boots is easily distinguishable.

"Bad morning?" The hairs on my nape prickle from the deep roughness of his voice.

"It could be worse." My tone relays the truth of my statement.

It could get a whole heap worse if my fire-breathing supervisor hears of my run-in with Richard this morning. Calling my boss a bitch is putting it nicely. There aren't enough derogatory words in the world to describe her. And with her fondness for Richard—*and every other male employee at Global Ten*—my inability to ignore Richard's daily taunt could be a very costly mistake.

The rest of our ride in the elevator is made in silence. I'm too busy categorizing the life necessities of my budget to hold a conversation. The suit-clad gentleman doesn't appear to be bothered by my silence. Don't get me wrong. He eyes me with curiosity, but his glare isn't strong enough to push my worry away from working out my expenditures if I find myself standing at the end of the unemployment line.

When the elevator dings, announcing it has arrived in the basement, I adjust my coat to ensure it's hiding my erect nipples from the freezing air-conditioned temperature on my floor before gesturing for the gentleman to exit before me. I want to pretend I am acting cordially, but, in reality, I just want to use his well-built frame to hide my caught-in-the-rain look from as many people as possible until I can dash into the bathroom halfway down the hallway.

The suit-clad stranger smiles a grin that sends blood rushing to the surface of my skin, nearly drying my soaked blouse with its furious heat. "Ah, this isn't my floor."

When he gestures for me to exit, I pace out of the elevator and spin around to face him. "You do know there aren't any more floors below this one? It's only up from here," I point out, my voice relaying my shock that a man as astute-looking as him doesn't know the inner workings of an elevator.

The smile on the stranger's face grows. "I am well aware of that. Thank you."

When he leans over to push his desired floor on the elevator panel, his suit jacket gapes open. His well-fitting business shirt exposes cut lines of a ridged stomach and stiff pecs. I hold his gaze, confused about why he appears familiar, but I'm confident we've never met. I never forget a face.

Just before the elevator doors close, he locks his dark eyes with me and mutters, "It was a pleasure riding with you, Cleo."

3

Shock gnaws my stomach as I stand mute in the corridor. Although my normal self-awareness is blinded by worry, I'm certain I didn't offer an introduction to my elevator companion. *Or did I?*

When the shriek of the 10 AM alarm sounds through my ears, my concerns about the mysterious stranger vanish as I scramble to my seat. Just like a bunch of primary school kids hearing the school bell, hysteria breaks out on my floor. The coffee room goes from a bustling hive of activity to becoming emptier than my wallet after paying Lexi's school fees this semester, and the conversation being held around the water cooler switches from talking about the latest episode of *The Walking Dead* to discussing expenditures and cost-saving strategies. Today's response is nothing out of the ordinary. We all know what the dreaded 10 AM alarm means: the witch is flying her broom into her office.

Wearing my mud-stained shirt with pride, I briskly saunter past Thomas and Kate from Classifieds and slip into my office chair. I scoot down low in my seat so only the top of my head can be seen over the partition separating my "office" from the hallway. With adrenaline still heating my blood from my exchange with Richard, I've lost any trust I had for my logically thinking head.

My heart rate slows to a third of its normal speed as my eyes track my boss making the short fifteen-pace walk from the elevator to her office—yes, I've counted. For every step she takes, the quietness of the room intensifies. I'm not even game to breathe for the fear she will hear my lungs expanding. I'm not the only one scared of my boss. Even her deputy, Martin, who has twenty-seven years of experience in journalism fears her. That's how terrifying she is.

Only once her office door slams shut does the usual hum of activity awaken in the dead quiet space. I exhale the breath I am holding in before gasping in another. My lungs wheeze in appreciation, grateful to be filled with fresh air. That's when reality smacks back into me about how foolish my behavior was this morning. Without her medication, Lexi can barely breathe. So as much as I dislike my job and the people surrounding me, I will do everything in my power to keep it. I'll even side with the devil if I have to.

Setting my guilt to the side, I wiggle up in my seat and swing my eyes around my dingy space. When I am satisfied the coast is clear of prying eyes, I sneak out of my cubicle and make a beeline for the bathroom. Even if my boss doesn't hear about my confrontation with Richard, my disheveled appearance alone gives her a reason to dismiss me. Only last month, Barbara from Personal Ads was demoted to coffee girl just because her dark gray pea coat didn't match her nearly black slacks.

Any concerns about being fired are left for dust when I spot my appearance in the full-length mirror in the women's restroom. You can't be concerned about something when it's a certainty. Not only is every inch of my breasts on display, so are my areolas and capable-of-cutting-diamonds nipples. The thin material I am wearing as a shirt looks like a sheet of saran wrap. It's completely see-through.

Always being resourceful, I yank my shirt off my head and dig out a laundry bar wrapped in a zip lock bag from my oversized purse. After scrubbing the brown streaks the puddle made to my blouse, I twist the nozzle on the hand dryer fixed to the wall and commence drying it. Thankfully, renovations to the rest of the building haven't reached the basement yet, or I would have been left stranded.

It takes approximately twenty minutes for my blouse to go from ringing wet to slightly damp. When I slip it back over my head, I appraise myself in the mirror. Although my nipples could use an industrial strength Band-Aid to hide their budded appearance, thankfully, the rest of my breasts are concealed by the now murky brown/ivory-colored material.

Happy I've diverted the possibility of being arrested for public indecency, I leave the bathroom with more spring to my step than I entered. My chirpy attitude drains to the soles of my boots when my nearsighted gaze locks in on a flurry of black sitting in my office chair. My pulse rings in my ears when I recognize the jet-black coloring of the woman's hair sitting behind my desk. It's my boss — the devil herself.

"Delilah, umm... can I help you?" I ask, stopping at the edge of my cubicle.

Delilah joined our department approximately two years ago. Rumors circulated throughout the mill that she was seconded to her position to whip our department from a money pit to a profitable entity of the Global Ten Media Group. Although we've seen a growth in the number of advertisements placed in our department, that has more to do with the bad flu epidemic that swept through the community than Delilah's placement. Although nothing concrete has been discovered, numerous long-standing department members argue that she was sent to the dungeon with the same decree as the rest of us. She must serve her sentence in the depths of hell for her treachery to the media mega-giant: Global Ten Media.

Delilah drifts her beady dark eyes to me. "Chloe, so glad you could *finally* join me."

I don't bother correcting her on calling me the wrong name. I've done it numerous times the past two years. Nothing has changed. And there is nothing wrong with being called Chloe anyway. It's better than Delilah's surname. Although, I will admit, even though her last name is hideous, it suits her. Delilah Anne Winterbottom. Perfect for a cold ass bitc...

My inner monologue stops when Delilah suddenly rises from my chair, startling me. Smirking at my skittish response, she runs her hands down the expensive-looking midnight black pantsuit that's tailored to accentuate her fit mid-to-late thirties body. If you could look past the lines on her face from years of scowling, Delilah could be classed as attractive. Her glossy hair is cut in a fierce bob that sits a little longer on the left. She has bright, dark eyes and peachy lips. It's just a pity her insides display she is the spawn of Satan.

"Let's walk." Not waiting for me to reply, Delilah saunters down the narrowed corridor.

It takes approximately ten paces for my inquisitiveness to get the better of me. "If this is about Richard..."

My sentence trails off when Delilah interrupts, "Who is Richard?"

I wait for her to press the elevator call button before shrugging my shoulders. "Umm... just a client wanting to book bulk obituaries." I stray my eyes to the ground, ensuring Delilah won't see the deceit in them. I've often been told my eyes are the gateway to my soul, so I'm not willing to risk one sideways glance from her to call me out as a fraud.

When the elevator arrives at our floor, Delilah glides her hand across the front of her body, gesturing for me to enter before her. My knees clang together as I step into the empty space. Politeness is not a strong point for Delilah—hell, I don't even know if she understands the word—so I am somewhat surprised by her sudden cordial behavior.

My heart drops from my chest when Delilah enters the elevator and hits the button for the very top floor. Clearly, her performance of acting unaware of Richard's identity was an Oscar-worthy act. That's the floor management is located on, specifically Human Resources.

Pleas for clemency sit on the tip of my tongue, but no matter how many times I try to fire them out of my mouth, my lips refuse to relinquish a single word. Although Delilah scares me more than I'd care to admit, that isn't the reason I'm not falling to my knees and begging for forgiveness. Pride has always been a strong point of mine. Today is no different.

Delilah's fear-provoking demeanor proves just as solid when we enter the management level of my office building. As we pace through the bright and airy space, the room falls into resolute silence. I've often wondered what it felt like to be a man walking on death row. Now I know.

When we reach a large oak door in the bottom right hand corner of the space, Delilah locks her eyes with me. "If you screw this up, don't bother clearing out your desk," she warns.

Not giving me the chance to reply, she knocks three times before pushing down the brass handle and swinging open the double-width door. The brightness of the mid-morning sun beaming in the floor-to-ceiling windows causes me to squint my eyes. We are so high in the sky, clouds float past the jaw-dropping New York skyline showcased in all its glory by the gigantic corner office. It's the type of view that would inspire painters to paint. It's enchanting and breathtaking, and it makes me fall in love with the city even more.

The view changes from breathtaking to soul-stealing when the black leather chair facing the window pivots around. Air traps halfway in my lungs when my eyes run over the gentleman I shared the elevator with earlier. Upon spotting my shocked expression, his lips crimp in the corners, exposing a tiny set of dimples on his top lip I didn't notice earlier.

"Cleo, Delilah, I'm glad you could join us. Please take a seat."

Noticing he said "us," I shift my eyes in the direction he is gesturing for us to sit. A pretty blonde lady in her late forties is seated in one of the three large rolled arm chairs across from the enormous wooden table the unnamed gentleman is sitting behind. With her head angled to the side, she rakes her light green eyes down my body not once, not twice, but three times.

Ignoring the twisting in my stomach, I plunk down in the seat Delilah nudged her head at. My brash movements are unladylike and missing the grace held by the blonde eyeing me with zeal. Once Delilah takes the last remaining chair left vacant, the unnamed man with pulse-racing good looks shifts his eyes to the blonde. His gaze is wide and edgy. "Thoughts?"

Suspense crackles the air as the blonde scoots to the edge of her chair. "She is perfect. Curvy and innocent-looking but with a hint of vivacity the clients will love."

"Her hostility this morning?" he queries, his lips quirked with intrigue.

The blonde appears unfazed by his concern. "Doormats are out. They want a challenge, someone who doesn't follow all the rules," she responds, her voice quickening with each syllable she speaks.

Unease spreads across my chest as I tilt to Delilah's side. "Who are they talking about?"

She shushes me using nothing but an evil glare. I slouch deeper into my chair so I can sneakily watch the situation unfold while fiddling with the chipped polish on my nails. The two unnamed attendees and Delilah continue their conversation as if they didn't request my attendance. They discuss protocols for undertaking such an investigation, monetary values I could only pray to have written on a check in my name, and how it could be the story of the century.

Although I'm interested in their conversation, my ears only prick when Delilah says, "If the sanction you're referring to is Chains, you will never get in. Rights to invite new members are only bequeathed to members who have been exclusively in the club for a year. Security is tight, but the identities of those who attend is even tighter. I'm not saying I don't understand your interest in breaking this story. If you could get in, the results would be immense. Rumors are that they have judges, DA's, movie stars, and numerous politicians in that *highly* exclusive group, but the likelihood of securing an invitation are zero to none."

For the quickest second, the stern mask Delilah frequents daily slips, exposing a side I've never seen of her when the unnamed suit-clad man says, "We have an invitation. It may have cost me half of my shares in my foreign equity company, but we have an invitation."

The room feels like it's closing in on me when he turns his eyes to me and mutters, "And Cleo is our way in."

I straighten my spine when Delilah swings her narrowed gaze to me. The wrinkles on her top lip deepen when she runs her eyes down my half-presentable frame. "Perhaps after a day at the spa and a makeover with Clint." Her words come out in a hiss, and they are tainted with disdain.

"No," the unnamed man responds, holding his hand in the air like he is stopping traffic. "Leave Cleo how she is. She is perfect just like that. She has a unique look men in that industry crave. Someone they can mold into their ideal mate while bringing her to heel."

An average person may construe his declaration as a compliment. I do not. With an edgy gleam brightening his sable-colored eyes and a smirk that sets my pulse racing, my first response is alarm, not glee.

Incapable of ignoring the tension thickening the air, I squeak out, "Can someone please explain to me what's going on?"

Seconds feel like hours as I return the imprudent stare of three pairs of unique eyes staring at me. The tension hanging in the air is so thick, it's physically hard for me to breathe.

Just when I think my question will never be answered, the blonde pipes up, "Do you value your position at Global Ten Media, Cleo?"

"Yes, very much so," I reply without pause for consideration. It's purely for the weekly paycheck and less-than-stellar health coverage, but I keep that snippet of information to myself.

"Well, if you play your cards right, your position here will not only be guaranteed for the remainder of your life, but Mr. Carson has also generously offered for you to join his team as a lead investigative reporter for the New York Daily Express," the blonde continues, gesturing her hand to the man seated across from me.

My excitement is too vast for me to register that she just called the mysterious dark-haired man Mr. Carson—the owner of Global Ten Media. I'm too shocked to register anything. The man I rode the elevator with while wearing a saran wrap shirt is the owner of the entire company I work for. *Jesus Christ! How am I not getting fired right now?*

Snubbing my dropped-jaw expression, the blonde continues, "You will be given your own office space on the seventy-third floor, an executive assistant, and your salary will be in the six-figure range."

I sit stunned, mute and wide-eyed. I try to force my mouth to say something, but nothing comes out — not even a squeak.

"Chloe," Delilah barks a short time later, her tone clipped.

"Cleo," I correct, loathing that my mouth chooses now to cooperate.

Snarling, Delilah sneers, "So what do you say, *Cleo?* Are you interested in joining the investigative team of the New York Daily Express?"

Unable to speak from the excitement drying my throat, I bob my chin. I've been waiting for this day for years—from the very moment I fell from grace.

Delilah smiles a grin that does nothing to settle the jitters in my stomach. "Wonderful. Then let's get this wrapped up," she demands, bouncing her eyes between Mr. Carson and the unnamed blonde. "With Cleo being an integral part of my team, I am requesting to be brought in on this investigation on a consultation basis. With your strict schedule to get this to print before any other media outlet, I will ensure a satisfactory timeframe is maintained."

They continue negotiating for several minutes. I sit in silence as pieces of paper are passed across the table for Delilah to sign. From the way Delilah is handling all the correspondence, anyone would swear she is my guardian, not the supervisor of my department.

Their excited chatter dulls when, numerous heart-clutching minutes later, I murmur, "What are you wanting me to do when I join this team?"

Although my words come out clear, they are crammed with suspicion. My mother always said, "If something is too good to be true, it most likely is." This seems too good to be true.

"I have a bachelor's in media relations with a concentration in investigative journalism. I was the top of my class three out of my four years of college, and I interned with the best journalism department on this side of the country. I have the skills needed for the job, but why the sudden switch in departments? I've been in the dungeon so long, even I'm starting to forget why I was sentenced there."

A stretch of terse silence crosses between us. It's thick and skin-crawlingly uncomfortable. After holding a private conversation with Mr. Carson only utilizing her eyes, Delilah turns her gaze to me. As she glances at me, she tries to soften the harsh lines of her face. It's a fruitless effort. Even the world's best collagen can't hide years of scowling.

"We need you to go undercover at an exclusive club in lower Manhattan," she advises, glaring into my eyes with a look that holds an equal amount of both demand and plea.

Hearing an "and" hanging in the air, I verbalize it.

"And do anything necessary to uncover the story," Mr. Carson fills in. Propping his elbows onto his desk, he braces his backside on the edge of his chair. "If this story breaks, Cleo, your name will forever be associated with it, thus not only meaning someone as wealthy as me will have a hard time signing your checks, but it will be a struggle keeping you exclusively with the Global Ten entity."

Excitement heats my blood. "Okay. That sounds wonderful. But you still haven't answered my question. You kind of skedaddled around it."

Ignoring Delilah's irate scowl burning a hole in the side of my head, I ask, "What *exactly* do you want me to do in this club, Mr. Carson?"

Several seconds of terse silence stretches between Mr. Carson and me as we undertake an intense stare-down. Although he has pulse-racing good looks that would boil any woman's blood, that isn't the reason I'm sweating. It's the indecisiveness in his eyes causing my biggest concern.

Our teeth-gritting showdown ends when he drops his eyes to the top drawer of his desk and pulls out an embossed envelope. Re-locking his eyes with me, he slides the elegant document across the table. I run my hands down the front of my skirt, not wanting to stain the pristine-looking paper with my grubby fingers. The wild beat of my heart merges into dangerous territory when I grasp the lightweight document in my hand. The article is extremely thin, soft as tissue paper, and elegantly scrolled with gold-foiled print. On first impressions alone, I assume it's an invitation to an elaborate wedding more than a party being held in lower Manhattan.

My eyes scan over the document, noticing nothing out of the ordinary to a standard invitation... until I hit the disclosure statement at the bottom.

"Since the BD/SM scene includes a wide range of activities involving a negotiation transfer of power between consenting partners, the bottom/submissive will be required to fill in a questionnaire before the commencement of any scenes. All limits and fears will be carefully discussed before the bottom/submissive can perform in any BD/SM scenes. This will ensure a safe, sane and consensual evening for all involved."

My eyes bug, and my jaw muscle slackens. Any words I try to force out my gaped mouth come out as dust fragments by the time they have been dragged through my bone-dry throat.

Sensing my speechless composure, Mr. Carson assures me, "You're not in any form obligated to attend this party in the matter stated at the bottom of the invitation. All we want is a pair of eyes in the room, Cleo."

"In a room with a group of men who want to beat me for pleasure?" I strangle out, my words hoarse.

"Cleo," Delilah spits out, her voice a malicious snarl.

I turn my shocked eyes to her. With my usually calm composure lost, today her evil glare has no effect on me whatsoever.

"You can't seriously expect me to do this?" I blubber, my words shockingly stern.

Delilah's silence speaks volumes. That's exactly what she expects me to do.

"I am not being subjected to torture just so you can get a fancier office," I sneer, my voice a cross between a whisper and a growl.

My glaring stare-down with Delilah ends when the unnamed blonde balances on the very edge of her chair and locks her eyes with me. "Your ideas about the BDSM community are vastly different than what it actually is. Anyone in the community knows it is the submissive who truly holds the greatest power."

"Then *you* do it," I snap. I'm not normally so confrontational, but my mind is spiraling so much that my first response is resistance. "If you have such a *vast* understanding of the BDSM community, why don't you go undercover?"

Not speaking, the blonde stands from her seat. Her movements are so agile and sharp, even Delilah jumps in surprise. Curling her hand around my wrist, she yanks me from my seat. For a lady whose frame is slightly smaller than mine and who is a good two to three inches shorter, she has a lot of guts. The dizziness spiraling in my stomach grows when she drags me across the room to stand in front of a full-length dressing mirror with an expansive wool trench coat hanging off the wrought iron frame.

As we stand side by side, I take in our unique differences: her pale, nearly translucent skin against my sun-kissed tan, her doe-shaped blue eyes compared to my large brown oval eyes. How her waif-thin frame looks sickly standing next to my rounded hips and ample breasts. With her hair the color of the sun beaming in the floor-to-ceiling windows, we couldn't be any more opposite if we tried. My hair is as dark as my massively dilated pupils.

"Stop using the personal side of your brain, Cleo, and start thinking with a rational investigative reporter head," the blonde mutters, peering at me in the mirror. "If you were Mr. Carson, and you had the opportunity of breaking the story of the century, who would you choose to send undercover? Me or you?"

Before I can fire a single syllable from my mouth, she continues speaking. "Don't tell me what your gut is telling you. I only want to hear what the business side of your brain is thinking."

"That's different," I mumble while taking in my glassy eyes and panicked face. "This doesn't feel like business. This feels personal."

She shakes her head, denying my claims. "Nothing in business is personal unless you let it become that way. As Mr. Carson said, we only need eyes in the room. Nothing more."

She takes a step back and slips in to stand behind me. Grasping my chin, she lifts my head high in the air. "Look at that face, Cleo. That's a face that will not only break the story of the century. It's the face that will ensure your sister's final years are lived in comfort."

The air sucks from my lungs, her words physically winding me. From the remorseful gleam in her eyes reflecting in the mirror, I know she felt the direct impact her words had to my heart, but her eyes also expose that our exchange is nothing more than a business transaction to her. There is nothing personal about it.

"That was low," I mumble, my words barely a whisper.

"Yes, it was," she admits, nodding. "But it was also the truth. Mr. Carson personally selected you for this assignment as he knows there won't be a story without you. So, if I have to occasionally issue a hit below the belt to get our message across, that's what I will do. That's how imperative a story like this is to our company."

The way she says "our" makes me wonder what her connection with Global Ten Media is.

The room falls into silence as I contemplate a response. As I said earlier, I will do everything in my power to ensure my sister's every want, need and desire are taken care of. But can I do this? Can I set aside my personal feelings and run purely on the instincts of my astute mind?

Inhaling a nerve-clearing breath, I shift my eyes to Mr. Carson. "I accept the position you're offering."

The tightness in his shoulders clears away as relief washes over his face. His carefree attitude doesn't last long when I say, "On one condition."

Delilah slices her hand through the air, preparing to cut off my attempts at negotiations. Thankfully, Mr. Carson ignores her, his eyes never moving from mine.

"And what is that condition, Cleo?"

The hammering of my heart echoes through my voice when I negotiate, "Even if this story never breaks, or I am let go from your company, you agree to pay my sister's medical and school expenses for the remainder of her life."

My pulse is so furious, it drowns out most of Delilah's incessant rant about my ungratefulness, and how I should feel privileged a man with Mr. Carson's integrity would bestow such an honor upon me. Even catching portions of her belligerent tirade doesn't impact me in the slightest. There is only one person in the world I allow to tilt the axis of my moral compass. She is the person I promised to take care of when she was left in my custody at the tender age of seventeen: my sister, Lexi. For her, nothing is below me—not even accepting an invitation to a seedy BDSM club in lower Manhattan.

I don't know how many seconds pass as Mr. Carson reflects on my statement, but it feels like hours have ticked by before he nods.

"Yes?" I stammer out, wanting to ensure my nearsightedness doesn't have me mistaking a shake as a nod.

"Yes," Mr. Carson acknowledges, filling me with both gratefulness and trepidation.

4

"I don't care if TMZ is reporting that Elvis is eating a cheeseburger at McDonalds, your ass *will* be sitting in the backseat of the limo by 9 PM sharp. Do you understand me?" Delilah roars down the phone.

Her voice is so loud, she gains the attention of Lexi lying on the two-seater sofa in the middle of our cramped living room. She is having another bad day. Her skin is clammy and beaded with sweat, and she has spent the last two hours coughing up more mucus than a normal person would create in a lifetime.

Twisting my body away from Lexi, I whisper, "This isn't a ploy to get out of our agreement, Delilah. Lexi isn't well. Can't we change the invitation so I can attend the next party?"

"No!" I jump from her abrupt response. "It's not brunch at a country club. These events aren't held on a weekly schedule. Who knows when the next one might be," she snarls viciously.

"Does it matter? Without an invitation, the likelihood of another media company breaking the story before us is extremely unlikely. And, besides, what's a few more weeks on an invitation that has taken years to get?" I argue.

"Can your sister wait weeks?" Delilah doesn't wait for me to get over the first punch to my stomach before she issues another. "Or are the icy winds blowing into your poorly insulated house knocking more time off her already thin schedule?"

Spotting my worried expression, Lexi lifts herself from the couch. Guilt consumes me when I notice the ratty mess her shirt is in. Moth holes dot the hemline, and the previous vibrant red coloring is now murky and dull from too many wash cycles. With our winter clothing budget going toward a new heating system I had installed in Lexi's room and our washing machine on the blink, our cold-weather wardrobes are severely limited.

I pace to the linen closet to yank down a blanket for Lexi. "I only agreed to do this because Mr. Carson said he would pay Lexi's medical bills." I drop my voice to ensure Lexi won't hear the remainder of my sentence. "I have not yet seen a dime of that money. She is sick, Delilah. She needs a nebulizer I can't afford."

Smiling to ease the worry on Lexi's face, I wrap the blanket around her shoulders, then pace out of the living room.

"You won't be able to afford anything if your ass isn't in that limousine at 9 PM sharp!" Delilah snarls. The sound of her leather office chair creaks down the line. I'm not at all surprised to discover she is still at the office late on a Saturday afternoon. "Last warning, Chloe. If you fail to arrive at the party at the designated time on the invitation, don't bother arriving to work Monday morning."

Before I have the chance to respond—or correct her for calling me the wrong name—Delilah disconnects the call. I take a few moments standing frozen in the middle of the foyer, racking my tired brain about why I ever agreed to such a ludicrous request. My mother always said, "Never dance with fire unless you plan on getting burned." I haven't even gotten close to the fire yet, and my toes are already charred.

I've spent the last two weeks in my brand-new office researching the world I am set to enter tonight. Although in-depth research into the BDSM community has eased some of the uncertainty swirling my stomach, it hasn't completely smothered it. From the information I have unearthed, in a properly hosted party, I will not be touched or manhandled in any way unless I give prior consent. It's just my eyes I'm hazy about. Some images you can never wash from your mind, no matter how much you wish you could.

My pity party for one stops when the sound of our doorbell jingles in my ears. My eyes instinctively shoot to Lexi. With our tight budget and even tighter sisterly bond, Lexi and I rarely venture out on the weekends or invite guests over, so I am somewhat surprised by an impromptu visitor.

With a fragile Lexi shadowing me, I pace to my front door. My curiosity is piqued when I peer out the peephole and notice Luke, ex-boyfriend and pharmacist from our local pharmacy, standing on the stoop of the stairs. He has a large cardboard box in one hand and his other hand is gripping his coat in close to his neck, vainly trying to keep the brisk winds seeping into his blazer.

After unlocking the deadbolt, I swing open the door. The tip of my nose burns when the below chilly temperatures grace it with their presence.

"Hey, Luke, how are you?" I query, my voice relaying my uncertainty. "Are you lost?"

When I notice Luke's bottom lip is a hue of blue and quivering, I gesture for him to enter the warmth of the foyer. It may not be elegant and grand like the house he lives in, but at least it's warm.

Luke scrubs his boots on the bristled mat stationed at the front door before entering. Heat blooms across my chest when his eyes eagerly absorb my modest home. The warmth isn't from shame. It's pride. Nothing but admiration is beaming from Luke's bright gaze.

"Nice place you have here, Cleo."

The heat rises from my chest to my cheeks. "Thank you."

A stretch of awkward silence passes between us. Lexi doesn't help alleviate the situation at all. She just stands to the side of the foyer with her eyes bouncing between Luke and me.

When the silence becomes too great for me to ignore, I mumble, "Is there something... did you need... Ah, what are you doing here, Luke?" That's about as gracious as I get — no country club politeness in this household. My abruptness is nothing new for Luke. He dealt with it plenty of times during our two-year relationship in high school.

The rudeness clutching my throat loosens its grip when Luke's smirk becomes a full smile. "Sorry, Cleo, I just realized I've known you for nearly ten years, dated you for two, but have never been inside your house."

The thick stench of awkwardness returns stronger than ever when Lexi mutters, "You've seen inside her panties but not her house?" She locks her shocked eyes with mine. "Nice one, Sis. I knew there was a hussy in there somewhere."

Forget tiptoeing around the edge of the fire. Living with Lexi is the equivalent of dancing in the middle of the raging flames, one scorching moment after another. Unable to stand my furious glare for a moment longer, Lexi excuses herself from our gathering before toddling off to her room.

Once she enters her bedroom at the end of the hall, I swallow down the bitter bile in the back of my throat and return my eyes to Luke. "Well, now you've seen it," I squeak out, embarrassment dangling off my vocal cords. "And... *now you can go*?" The unease in my voice makes what should be a strong declaration sound more like a suggestion.

Nothing against Luke, he was a great boyfriend, wonderful friend, and talented in the bedroom, but my priorities have changed since high school. Unlike Luke and our numerous combined friends, I grew up—quickly. My life is not about flirty weekends and how many shots I can down in a night. My focus must remain on ensuring my budget and my sister's health are maintained, not my social calendar.

"Ouch," Luke mutters, dragging my focus back to him. "I'd heard rumors you'd changed, Cleo. Never would have believed it if I hadn't seen it for myself."

I try to think of a comeback, but I'm honestly at a loss for words. I was the epitome of Ms. Popular in high school. I was the head cheerleader, crowned prom queen during our senior year, and voted most likely to succeed.

All I achieved the past seven years is two school loans I can't afford, skyrocketing insurance premiums, and a seemingly bad attitude. I wouldn't say I am a negative person, but after enduring knock after knock the past four years, things are starting to creep up on me.

My eyes stray from the ground when the warmth of a hand runs down my arm. I'm shocked when I lift my eyes and discover only Luke still standing in the foyer. I thought Lexi had rejoined our gathering. I honestly had no clue it was Luke issuing the kind gesture. Although our breakup was amicable, I was the one who started the process, so I'm somewhat surprised by his jovial nature.

My pulse quickens when Luke locks his eyes with mine. "You've got to stop being so damn proud, Cleo. We are a community here in Montclair. We help our own."

His statement causes tears to sting my eyes. "I know," I mutter, nodding.

There is no use denying what he is saying. Montclair is my hometown, and if I weren't so stubborn, I know the locals would help us. But Lexi and I aren't the only ones struggling. Many homes in our area are up for foreclosure, so I can't cry wolf because I'm struggling to make ends meet. We may not have every necessity we need, but we have a roof over our heads. That's more than some people in our community have.

"In saying that," Luke says, stepping closer to me. "If you had told me how much Lexi needed this, I would have delivered it weeks ago." He keeps his deep tone low to ensure Lexi won't hear him. He knows she doesn't need any guilt added to the baggage she is already carrying.

My eyes bounce between Luke's light green gaze when he hands the large box he is grasping to me. Incapable of reading the signs his eyes are relaying, I pry open the box. I gasp in a shocked breath when my eyes absorb the state-of-the-art nebulizer and air filter sitting next to a six-month supply of Lexi's medication. Seeing all the essential things she needs to breathe with ease sitting in one little box causes a flood of emotions to slam into me. As a tear rolls down my cheek, I throw my arms around Luke's neck and hug him tightly.

"Hey, easy there," he croons, pulling me in tighter. "I'm just the delivery guy, Cleo. I'm not the one who deserves your thanks."

I pull back and peer into his eyes. "Who?" I want to say more, but the gratefulness sitting on my chest makes it hard for me to breathe let alone talk.

"He didn't leave a card. All he wanted me to say was 'you do know there aren't any more floors below this one? It's only up from here.'" Confusion clouds Luke's bright eyes. It mimics my gaze to a T.

It takes a few moments for the recognition of the quote to dawn on me. When it does, both relief and anxiety overwhelm me. That was the only thing I said to Mr. Carson the day we rode the elevator together. I have to hand it to him: he is smart. Just when I was tempted to back out of our agreement, he dangles a carrot in front of my face and lures me right back in. It displays how he went from a struggling New Jersey boy to billionaire before he reached the age of 30.

After swearing that I'll contact him if I require any assistance, I walk Luke to his Jeep parked at the curb.

"I don't know what the first half of his saying referred to, but I do agree with the second part," Luke says, cracking open his car door. Our weekends driving it on the beach caused the rusty hinges to give out a squeak in protest to his firm swing. "When you've hit rock bottom, there is only one way you can go. That way is up."

A grin curls on my lips when he leans over and presses a kiss to the side of my mouth. I remember when the whiskers on his chin couldn't even cause a shadow in the midday sun. Now, a few hours after shaving his cut jaw is shadowed in darkness.

"I miss you guys," I mumble before I can stop my words.

Luke, Chastity, and Michael were my very best friends in high school. I didn't think anything would shatter our close connection. At eighteen you don't consider how much work goes into maintaining a scholarship at one of the top schools in the country, or how every penny you earn will go towards helping your parents pay the second mortgage they put on their family home to set you up in a private dorm off campus. It wasn't until my parents passed did I realize how much of a burden I had placed on them. Although I knew my apartment was expensive, I thought I'd have years to thank them for the struggles they endured. Their trip to Brazil was supposed to be one gift of many. Little did I know it would be the only one they would receive from me to thank them for being the best parents a child could ask for.

Luke grins a lazy smirk that sets my pulse racing and dampens my somber thoughts. "As we do you, Cleo. There is no rat pack when one is missing."

Ignoring the way his rough and rugged voice prickles the hairs on my nape, I ask, "I'll see you soon?"

Luke tries to hold in his excitement. He fails. The corners of his lips curl, and his eyes flare with excitement.

"I hope so." Leaning in, he places another kiss on the edge of my mouth before climbing into his jeep.

My stomach swirls as I stand on the curb, watching Luke's car disappear into the horizon. You know that giddy feeling you get before you walk down the stairs after spending four hours getting ready for prom? That's how I'm feeling right now. I don't know if it's from being awarded thousands of dollars' worth of medical equipment for Lexi, Luke's two innocent pecks, or that I'm about to go and get glammed up for a night at a BDSM club. But no matter what the reason is behind my sudden new lease on life, I'm going to grasp it with both hands. The past four years have been my lowest, so I'll cherish every giddy feeling I get.

5

Cold winds whip up under my trench coat when I step into the blacked-out sedan idling at the curb of my house. I don't miss the curious glances of Mr. and Mrs. Rachet peering out their lace curtains from the home across the street. Their gaped-mouth reaction isn't surprising. Although our street is positioned in the middle of a beautiful tree-lined suburb, it isn't every day you spot an overpriced light gray Bentley parked on the curb.

With my hands shaking with nerves, it takes me several attempts to get the seatbelt to latch into place. Closing my eyes, I calm the mad beat of my heart and repeat the mantra I've cited numerous times this evening: tonight's event is no different than the many other undercover stints I've done for Global Ten Media in the past.

My reassurance doesn't help in the slightest.

Even when camping out with the paparazzi for a sneaky picture of Ben Affleck when the nanny-affair scandal erupted, I didn't feel as scandalous as I do now. It probably has something to do with the fact I'm barely wearing anything under my well-worn coat.

Within twenty minutes of Luke leaving, another impromptu visitor arrived on my doorstep. This time, the caller was unknown to Lexi and me. The unease twisting my stomach into a nasty mess wound up to my throat when I accepted the flimsy white box held together with an elaborate red bow from the unnamed caller. Any chance of keeping my heart away from coronary failure was lost when I ripped off the bow and dug my hand into layers of delicate tissue paper to unveil an outfit I would be wary wearing to bed let alone in public.

The ear-piercing squeal Lexi emitted when I held up the rose-colored I.D. Sarrieri hotel slip dress sent her into a ten-minute coughing fit. Her flabbergasted reaction mimicked mine to a T. From my year of interning under Sasha,

I knew the value of the dress clutched in my hand was more than our quarterly electric bill.

From the note scrawled inside a small white gift card, Mr. Carson perceived my intentions of sacrificing the pricey garment for the greater good—once it was desecrated at the BDSM club tonight.

One night, then do with it as you please, was all he wrote inside the gilded card the negligée was delivered with.

It isn't just the silky-smooth negligee subtly gracing my sweat-slicked skin that has my heart hammering my ribs. It's the fact Mr. Carson selected the perfect size garment to house my bountiful curves. How could a man who only peered at me for mere minutes divulge enough information to know my rounded hips and busty breasts didn't have a chance in hell of squeezing into a size 2?

Snubbing the unease gurgling in my stomach, I wrangle my seatbelt into place. As the Bentley rolls down my long street, I snag my compact out of my clutch purse, wanting to ensure the sprinkling of rain I dodged while dashing out of my house didn't ruin the bold curls Lexi placed in my hair this afternoon. When she spotted the card from Mr. Carson, she read it more as an invitation than an assignment. Happy for her to read the message how she saw fit, I didn't correct her misguided optimism.

After adding a sheen of lip gloss to the nude palette on my face, I place my compact back into my clutch and turn my eyes to the scenery whizzing by. It doesn't matter how many times I've viewed Montclair's culturally rich landscape, it never fails to amaze me. It's a mesmerizing town full of treasured memories. A place I hope one day to raise my own family.

With the late hour, it doesn't take as long to reach lower Manhattan as I would have liked. As the Bentley glides to a stop behind a phantom Rolls Royce, I slip a large sequined mask over my wide eyes. Nerves overpower my efforts to tie the satin straps to the back of my head, but I continue with my mission, not willing to risk having my photo snapped by a group of curious onlookers lurking at the side of the dimly lit club.

Although Mr. Carson is anticipating tonight's gathering will unearth some huge names in the BDSM community, my hopes were dashed the instant I discovered the event was a masked party. I've never believed you need to see someone's face to know their true intentions—even the most guarded people can be stripped bare with the right words—but when your assignment is to unearth their identities, physical masks add another layer to an already complicated mission.

Breathing out my tension, I finish securing my mask over my face before surveying the area. With a bank of affluent cars stretched as far as the eye can see, the normally bland environment has gained a handful of nosey spectators. Although my intuition tells me they are most likely residents shocked by the sudden bombardment of wealth in a less-than-stellar part of Manhattan, my first year at Global Ten Media taught me to never run with a theory before thoroughly evaluating it.

When the Bentley pulls onto the curb at the front of a club that looks like its doors closed centuries ago, the driver lowers the privacy partition and gestures with his head for me to exit. One glance into his glassy dark eyes causes a barrage of nerves to hammer into me. I sit frozen, not speaking or moving. I don't even blink.

It feels like my frozen stance lasts hours, but it's mere seconds. It was only long enough for me to remember that exposing a scandalous bit of skin is a small price to pay to have Lexi's medical expenses paid in full. There is nothing I wouldn't do for my sister—nothing at all.

Rolling my shoulders, I clutch the Bentley's door handle and swing it open. The cold breeze blowing in from the west does nothing to ease the heat creeping up my neck. I've slid halfway out of the back of the Bentley before reality dawns.

Drifting my massively dilated eyes to the driver, I ask, "What time will you return to collect me?"

"When you're ready to leave, I will be ready."

His admission does nothing to ease the panic scorching my veins. "How?" I mutter, my one word displaying I didn't believe a single word he spoke. "How will you know when I'm ready to leave?"

He locks his impressively dark eyes with me. For the first time tonight, the swirling of my stomach gets a moment of reprieve when he declares, "I will know, Cleo. I will be ready."

"Okay. Good," I stumble out before continuing my mission of exiting the Bentley.

Nippy winds blast my face when I step onto the cracked sidewalk. Other attendees waiting to enter the premise eye me with curiosity, but none approach me. The vast range of people is surprising. Clearly, all attendees have wealth I could only dream of achieving, but even with their faces hidden behind masks, the range in age and appearance varies greatly. Some are tall, while others wouldn't reach my chin, and the width of the attendees is also diverse.

When the flash of a camera hinders my vision, I snap my eyes to the side, silently praying the paparazzi are unaware of tonight's event. The dangerous beat of my heart simmers when I spot the faces hidden behind the lens. Thankfully, the curious onlookers are nothing but a group of teen boys more interested in capturing photos of the cars than the occupants inside.

Shaking off my nerves, I pace into the foyer of the building, acting like I am about to watch a Broadway show, not an all-out orgy. The inside of the rundown building does not match the outside. Chandeliered ceilings, priceless paintings, and rugs that would only look better positioned in front of a raging fire make the space scream of wealth and importance.

The only thing stopping me from believing I am in the middle of a bustling Broadway studio is when the patrons in front of me remove their thick wool coats and Burberry leather gloves. Although most the women's bodies are covered with silky sleepwear like I am wearing under my jacket, it's the shocking sight of a collar and lead curled around one woman's delicate neck that causes my slack-jawed expression.

As the gathering of people grows, the swell of the crowd forces me toward a marble check-in station. For every step I take, the unease in my stomach intensifies. Any chance of settling my nerves is left for dust when the lady standing in front of me hands her invitation to the hostess before lowering onto all fours.

Holy moly, I mumble to myself when she enters a set of thick velvet curtains by crawling at the heels of her male partner. When portions of the scantily dressed people inside the club seep through the gaped curtain, I snap my eyes away, spin on my heels and flee. The only thing that slows my frantic escape is when my panicked gaze locks in on a pair of dark eyes entering the single glass door I am heading toward. Even with a majority of his face covered with a plain black mask, I know who he is—I never forget a face. It's the driver of my Bentley.

I stand frozen for a beat, unsure if I am coming or going. When the hostess aims to gather my attention, the sable-haired man in the navy pinstripe suit sneakily gestures his head to the hostess. With my hands fisted at my side, I shake my head. My movements are so frantic it looks like I have a nervous twitch.

Spotting my stubbornness, the demand in the stranger's eyes grows, mimicking every man in the foyer gawking at me with zeal. When he once again nudges his head to the hostess, I grit my teeth and stand my ground. I was wrong earlier. This is way above my paygrade.

When the Bentley driver fails to acknowledge the threat in my silent stance, I head for the door. My brisk steps end when the faintest murmur of "Lexi," rings through my ears. Just hearing her name instantly halts my hasty retreat. Images of the pain her eyes held when she told me about our parents' accident flash before my eyes. It's the same pain her eyes hold every time she gasps for air when she is struggling through a coughing attack.

My back molars grind when I swing my eyes to the suit-clad man. Although he peers straight ahead, seemingly not noticing me, he can't fool me. I can feel the heat of his gaze, and I can also see the twitching smirk his conceited lips fail to hide. He knows he has me over a barrel. I didn't just make a deal with the devil two weeks ago. I foolishly gave away my hand. They not only know Lexi is my weakness. They know she is my *only* weakness.

After inhaling and exhaling three deep breaths, I roll my shoulders, swivel around and saunter to the pretty hostess standing at the counter of the now nearly empty foyer. She accepts my invitation with an inviting smile and twinkling eyes, a complete contradiction to the greeting I issue her. Mine is nowhere near as pleasant as hers.

"Can I take your coat?" she questions, raising her pretty blue eyes to me.

Noticing that she asked, didn't demand, I hug my coat close to my body. "The air is a little chilly. I'd prefer to keep it if I can?"

She seems taken aback, but I hold my ground, pretending I'm not the slightest bit concerned she may deny my request.

When her silence becomes too great to ignore, I sneer, "Is there a problem with me keeping my coat?" I keep my voice firm, remembering that my hours of research uncovered that not only are there male Doms in this lifestyle, there are strong-willed female ones as well.

With my head held high in the air and my nose pointed down at the white-washed young woman's face, I increase my stare.

Relief consumes me when she quickly mumbles, "No ma'am, not at all. The air does have a nip to it."

She places my invitation into a locked box at her side before gesturing with her hand for me to enter the velvet curtains. In an instant, my high-chinned composure slips. My knees wobble with every step I take towards a previously unventured world. The further I move away from the reception desk, the more the faint hum of music replaces the pulse shrilling in my ears. After one final breath to rid my body of nerves, I push through the curtains.

Shock is the first thing that consumes me, closely followed by intrigue. I was expecting to see a mass of naked bodies humping and grinding against each other. Although the outfits the partygoers are wearing would be best described as skimpy, there are more covered torsos than completely naked ones. Multihued lights and soft, ambient music gives the vibe more of a sophisticated club feel than a raging orgy-fest. Booths line the outer walls and soft, sheer curtains shackled to the ceiling lend the space an elegant feel instead of industrial. If there weren't weird fetish attire on over half of the patrons, I wouldn't be able to tell the difference between this club and a standard dance club I frequented back in my college days.

The further I encroach into the club, the more various "scenes" I researched online are unearthed. Heat creeps across my cheeks when a gathering of three in the bottom left-hand corner of the vast space gains my attention. With some type of leather gag in her mouth, the lady who crawled into the club earlier is slouched over her partner's knee while another man wearing a weird leather taped vest pays dedicated attention to a region of her body that shouldn't be displayed in public.

With my eyes planted on the floor, I pretend I didn't witness what I just witnessed as I continue with my mission to find an inconspicuous hiding place. My efforts to remain undetected falter when I crush into a group of men standing at the edge of the room. I can barely see as it is, let alone in a club where dim lighting makes my usually poor eyesight even worse.

The situation goes from curious to downright awkward when the man in the middle of the trio eyes me with more interest than a man of his age should. His being older than my deceased grandfather doesn't stop his degrading ogling of my body. Smiling to mask my disgust, I make a beeline to a topless waitress balancing bottles of water on a silver tray. With stifling temperatures from having so many red-blooded people in the one space added to my coat-covered body, it's the perfect recipe for a sweat-producing disaster.

On the way to the waitress, I catch the impish watch of numerous club spectators. Their gazes make my stomach sick with anxiety. I've never felt so nauseous. Acting like I can't feel my knees clanging together, I straighten my spine and glide across the room while giving myself a stern lecture on being a grown woman who can party with the best of them.

"This is just a college party," I mutter to myself. "And they're wearing the same amount of clothing my girlfriends and I wore at those so-called parties."

Accepting a bottle of water from a smiling blonde waitress with an uncovered chest, I scan my eyes across the room, seeking an ideal research station. As Albert Einstein said, "Condemnation without investigation is the highest form of ignorance." So, until I've had a chance to assess the situation thoroughly, I shouldn't be issuing a judgment.

It takes approximately ten minutes aimlessly wandering around the affluent surroundings for me to find the perfect vantage point in the dimly lit club. There is a bar at the very back of the room that sits higher than the gathering of people mingling below, thus not only keeping me out of the radar of the men who want to mold me into the ideal submissive, but it also gives me a prime view of the entire club.

While pacing towards the bar, I realize my initial assessment about the gleam brightening the eyes of the patrons peering at me is not one hundred percent accurate. Not all their gazes are filled with lust. Some are interested, while others are crammed with suspicion. I can't blame their motives. I've arrived with a poor attitude and a closed mind. My reaction can't be helped, though. I would be acting the same way if you threw me in a clown costume and demand I make animal puppets. When you're thrown into something you're not accustomed to, it often comes with a nasty side dish of apprehension.

"What can I get you?" questions a deep voice the instant I plop my backside onto a polished barstool at the end of a long wooden bar.

Clutching my chest to ensure my heart remains in my chest cavity, I swing my eyes to the bartender wiping the sparkling countertop. The endeavor to keep my heart in its rightful spot becomes challenging when the bartender locks his unique brownish-black eyes with me.

The rugged grittiness of his voice sends goosebumps racing to the surface of my skin when he warns, "Unless you want a group of men charging in your direction, you might want to wipe that doe-eyed look out of your eyes right now."

He stops wiping the glistening countertop and raises his eyes to peer past my shoulder. Following his gaze, I notice the trio of men I bumped into earlier are watching me with a covetous gaze. Women of all ages will tell you that being eyed with zeal is nothing out of the ordinary when attending a function this late on a Saturday night, but there is something different about their avid gazes. It causes my pulse to quicken with an equal amount of excitement and concern. I don't know if my peculiar reaction stems from feeling conflicted sitting amongst people whose lifestyle choices are vastly contradicting from mine, or because I didn't realize how judgmental I was until tonight. I would say my response is a little bit of column A and a dash of column B.

My moral pendulum swings toward column A when the bartender roughly mutters, "They can smell a newcomer from a mile away."

Swallowing down the bile crawling up my esophagus, I drift my eyes back to him. "That obvious?"

The bartender smiles a grin that makes my heart beat a little faster. "If the way you're clasping your coat isn't enough of an indication of your newbie status, then the scent leeching from your pores is a surefire indication."

Even hearing his jesting tone doesn't stop me from sniffing myself. *I certainly don't smell any different.*

Plopping an unopened bottle of chilled water down in front of me, the bartender says, "I'm giving you an hour before you go racing out those doors." He nudges his head to a set of concealed emergency doors on my left, ensuring I am aware of the closest viable exit.

My fighting spirit emerges as I ask, "What makes you so sure I'm going to flee? I'm not as naïve as half the women in this club."

His smile grows, and it does wicked things to my libido. "That's the majority of your problem..." He leaves his sentence open, waiting for me to fill in the gaps.

"Cleopatra," I fill in. *What? I was running on empty. My brain is too busy calculating the distance from the bar to the exit that it doesn't have time to conjure up a believable alias.*

"Cleopatra?" he mutters, enunciating my name in a long, throaty purr.

He props his elbows onto the countertop and tilts in close to me. "Doms love the brats even more than the naïve virgins romance books told you they like."

"What? Why?" Shock is evident in my voice from seeing the truth beaming from his slanted gaze. "Don't they want pure, untouched women?" My research may have been a little cliché, but not having anything concrete to work with, I relied on the facts displayed in front of me.

The bartender chuckles. "Not at all." His words are straight to the point. No pussy-footing around for him. "To a true Dom, there is only one thing better than being awarded power in the bedroom." He pauses, soundlessly building the suspense. "It's being handed the power from an equally powerful counterpart. That's the ultimate reward."

I want to act ignorant, like I don't know what he is referring to, but my research into the BDSM community the past two weeks ensures I can't play that card. What he is saying is true. One article noted with an increase in members to the BDSM society the past five years, older participants are seeking newer, more challenging projects.

Noticing my inability to issue a comeback, the bartender sets the timer on his watch, winks cockily, then moves to serve patrons standing at the other end of the bar. Just as his attitude portrays, he walks with a swagger that bolsters his boastful attitude.

Masking the panic on my face with a neutral expression, I swivel in my chair to face the congregation of people mingling in the poorly lit space. For every minute that ticks by on the clock, the room becomes noticeably smaller, and the patrons' clothing becomes optional. As the temperature rises, so do the various "scenes" being played throughout the club. Some skits seem innocent enough. Others... they put the late night shows I witnessed Lexi flicking past last Saturday night to shame.

With numerous sexual acts being played out before my eyes, and the unashamed gazes of men and women of all ages, I've been struck with a severe bout of nausea. Don't get me wrong, I've been eyed with ardor before, but this is different. The people eyeballing me aren't watching me with the usual attraction. They are looking at me as if I am a commodity, not a person.

Hoping to lessen the swishy movements of my stomach, I chug down the entire bottle of water the bartender set down in front of me twenty minutes ago. It does nothing to settle my flipping stomach. It's beyond suppressing.

When the flashing disco lights add to the wooziness inflicting my head, I slip off my seat and scan the room, seeking a washroom sign amongst the scantily clad group. *Perhaps splashing some cool water onto my face will help calm the panic scorching my veins?*

Like a poorly scripted B grade movie, I tumble off my stool and bump into the gentleman seated next to me. If I wasn't immersed in a debauched world I don't belong in, it would be a perfect time for me to stumble into the man of my dreams. Unfortunately, this is no romance novel.

When the man I bumped into unexpectedly runs the back of his hand down the red hue marring my cheeks, his shoes nearly have a meeting with the two bottles of water I guzzled down the past forty minutes. The dark-haired stranger stares into my eyes with a predatory smirk on his face to ensure I can't misread his intentions. Accepting my apologies for bumping into him with a smile is not on his agenda.

His unambiguous gaze strangles any of my attempts to investigate this environment thoroughly before passing judgment. It isn't just reading his true objective that has me swinging the axe before checking the wood pile. It's the fact he is silently propositioning me all while ignoring the woman kneeling at his feet, fawning for his attention. His gaze makes me feel sick, and it causes regret to spread through me.

Gritting my teeth to keep the contents of my swishing stomach in their rightful place, I race toward the exit the bartender gestured to earlier. Splashing water on my face for a situation like this would be nothing but a woeful waste of time. Even with keeping my eyes fixated on the exit door, my vision is bombarded with images no amount of wine will ever replace. A woman hangs from a steel beam like contraption with nothing but rope as clothing, while a man's back is marked with the sting of a leather flogger.

The coolness of the bar lock on the heavily weighted exit door gives relief to my overheated skin when I push down and throw open the door.

"Forty-three minutes and fifteen seconds," the bartender hackles when I charge into the alley. "You lasted longer than I predicted."

6

Refreshing winds sneak through the cracks of my coat as I stumble into the alley. While gasping in harsh breaths to ward off a panic attack quickly surfacing, I fiddle with the buttons on my trench coat. My body is so overheated I feel like I'm going to pass out at any moment. Slinging my coat off my shoulders, I lean against the outer wall of the club and continue with my endeavor to calm the torrent of emotions pumping into me. I've never been more overwhelmed, over-stimulated and overly panicked in my life. That environment was... I don't have any words to express it. Wrong. Tantalizing. Intriguingly weird. If my mouth would cooperate with the prompts of my brain, those are some of the words I could use to describe it.

Although flabbergasted, I will say one thing: if this is people's idea of a fun Saturday night, I either need to get out more often or lock myself in my room and never leave. With the crazy beat of my heart, the latter seems the more plausible option.

After giving myself a few moments to settle down, I gather my coat in my arms and push off the brickwork. With a stream of yellow taxis on nearly every street in Manhattan, I'm sure it won't take me long to flag one down. Just before I pass the door I tumbled out of five minutes ago, bright lights beam down the narrow alleyway, hindering my vision. With one hand grasping the large steel door to steady my swaying, I lift my other one to shelter my eyes. Relief spreads across my chest when I spot the light gray Bentley I rode in earlier gliding towards me.

When it comes to a stop beside me, I fling open the back door and slide into the backseat.

"Oh my god, thank goodness you are here. This entire... *situation* isn't for me."

I freeze like a statue when a deep and highly manly voice says, "I'm sorry to hear that. Perhaps you should reconsider the answers you provided in your questionnaire. Ensuring you're partnered with the correct companion is the most imperative step in this... *situation."*

Only turning my eyes for the fear of snapping my neck from an abrupt movement, I rest them with a man seated in the seat across from me. My loosened jaw muscle drapes even lower when my eyes lock in on one of the most mesmerizing pairs of green eyes I've ever seen. Even behind a silver mask, the effervescence of his dazzling gaze cannot be hidden. His eyes are wondrous, and they soon have me trapped in a trance.

Following the natural intuition of my body, I angle the top half of my frame to face the mystery companion. My new position awards me with more exquisite features: rich, flawless chocolate skin, straight defined nose, a rigid jawline void of a single hair, and a mouthwatering body encased in a black suit with silver pinstripes. The vision is ravishing, completely smothering the storm brewing in my stomach by replacing it with the potent desire of lust.

Just as eagerly as I absorb him, the mystery stranger angles his head to the side and rakes his eyes down my body. His perusal is long and heart-strangling, and it causes every nerve ending in my body to activate. The heat of his avid gaze makes me completely forget that I'm meeting him wearing nothing but a sheer slip of satin and an even more meager pair of panties. When he returns his eyes to my face, my trancelike state intensifies. His gaze is primal and strong, and it sets my pulse racing.

"Who did your questionnaire partner you with?" he queries, the husky roughness of his voice adding to the giddiness clustering in my tingling core.

"Questionnaire?"

The temperature in the cabin of the Bentley turns roasting when the stranger smirks a devilishly delicious smile. It isn't an inviting or invigorating smile, more of an intriguing grin.

"All subs are issued a questionnaire at the start of proceedings. Were you not given one?" he queries, peering straight into my eyes.

"Umm... no." I sheepishly shake my head.

He slopes his head to the side and peers at the steel door of the club, attempting to conceal the angry storm growing in his eyes with an impervious look. He miserably fails. My hands twitch, dying to smooth out the wrinkle of concern peeking out of his silver mask. Thankfully, since I'm stuck in a lusty haze, my hands remain fisted at my sides.

"All subs must be issued a questionnaire. It's protocol," the stranger mutters, more to himself than me.

Not giving me the chance to form a response to being instantly dismissed as a submissive, he releases the latch on his seatbelt and scoots across the seat, filling the minor portion of space between us. The hairs on the nape of my neck prickle when his intoxicating smell graces my senses. Body wash, freshly washed linen, and a spicy aftershave hit a few of my hot buttons, rendering me even more mute than his entrancing green eyes.

As his eyes drink in my flushed neckline, lust rages low in my stomach. I've met many intriguing men in my life, but the aura beaming from this man, he's just... *whoa!* He has a sense of familiarity about him—like I've seen him before—but with his face concealed by a large mask, I can't one hundred percent testify to that. His mystery boosts the excitement caking my skin with a fine layer of sweat.

When he tilts in close to me, I pant in a surprised breath when the intensity of his eyes hit me full-force. In the dimly lit Bentley, they appear almost mint green in coloring. They are the most exquisite and unique pair of eyes I've seen. The panic roaring through my body earlier no longer exists as I roam my eyes over the magnificent creature sitting in front of me. My eyes go frantic, wanting to ensure every unique quality of his mask-covered face is absorbed and compartmentalized before they lose the chance.

His perusal of me is just as thorough. His eyes burn into my skin, heating every nerve ending in my body with his powerful gaze. An overwhelming sense of desire scorches through me, forcing my thighs to squeeze together. Acting on the impulses of my lust-driven heart, my tongue darts out to moisten my lips. Although the prompts of my body are absurd, if he is going to kiss me, I refuse for his plump, inviting mouth to brush against a pair of bone-dry lips that his jaw-dropping looks incited.

Embarrassment unlike anything I've ever felt swallows me whole when he quietly mutters, "Although tempting, cavorting with a member of Chains is not permitted without the sub first filling in a questionnaire." He is sitting so close to me, his liquor-scented breath bounces off my famished lips.

Mortified he read the silent prompts of my hankering heart so accurately, I sheepishly raise my eyes to his. A parcel of air expelled from his mouth fans my flushed cheeks when he locks his eyes with mine. I hold his gaze as the gleam in his eyes switches from confident to confused. He watches me in silence for several minutes, his eyes bouncing between mine, his breathing low.

The hairs on my nape bristle to attention when he stretches out his arm so the back of his fingers can run down my cheek. His briefest touch sends tingles dancing across my face before zooming to the lower half of my body.

The brutal slap my ego took minutes ago fades when he whispers, "I've never wanted to break the rules as much as I do right now."

I peer into his eyes, returning his covetous gaze while also silently pleading for him to throw caution to the wind. Sometimes the best things can only be achieved by taking a chance.

Several minutes pass with us sitting so close to each other we share the same breath. The silence fills the cabin of the Bentley with enchanting sexual tension.

When he leans in even closer, I close my eyes and perk my lips. My breathing shallows to a pant and time comes to a standstill. When a buzzing sensation zaps my left shoulder, I pop open my eyes. Mortified realization smacks into me hard and fast when he adjusts the spaghetti strap of my negligée. He wasn't tilting in so our lips could become acquainted, he was leaning across to ensure my heavy bosoms remained in their rightful place.

Even with his briefest touch causing a spark to stimulate every nerve in my body, my humiliation grows tenfold. Not only does he not want to kiss me, he wants to ensure every inch of my skin remains covered while in his presence. *Ouch!* That's a second brutal slap my ego never expected to endure tonight.

Burying my pride in a deep pit in the middle of my stomach, I stumble out, "I'm sorry for the intrusion. I mistook your vehicle for another. It was a mistake. One of many I've made thus far tonight." Embarrassment hinders my vocal cords, making my words come out huskier than normal.

Ignoring the tense shake encroaching my body, I reach for the silver door handle and yank it open. Excitement thrums my veins when my rushed movements force his hand to brush the skin on the side of my knee.

"I hope you have a pleasant evening." Cringing that he is about to enter a BDSM establishment, I fling open the back passenger door and start to leave the Bentley.

Before I fully exit, the stranger's hand darts out to snag my wrist. His simplest touch surges a rush of desire to my throbbing sex. It's so potent, my thighs squeeze together to lessen its effect. I sit frozen and mute halfway out of his vehicle, shocked his meekest touch could cause such a fervent response out of me, but also intrigued.

"Don't let the unknown frighten you. If you face something you fear head on, you'll realize the unknown isn't frightening. It's the known."

I take a few moments absorbing his statement. Although I do agree with a majority of it, I can't comprehend why he would believe knowledge is frightening. Knowledge is power. It's the one thing that costs nothing to have, but it's worth more than anything.

"Knowledge is power." I twist my neck to peer into his eyes. "It isn't frightening."

"It is when a man doesn't know how to use it." He returns my staggered stare. "Knowledge is useless unless it's attached to an action. Just because you know something does not mean it can be done. Action is power. Knowledge is a given."

I try to think of a comeback, but I'm left a little stumped. I've never held an intellectual debate with a man while wearing a satin slip and more makeup than I've ever worn, let alone with a man who has turned my normally astute brain to puree by doing nothing more than holding my hand.

"Knowledge may only be a given for you, but it's vital to me. It's what tells me I shouldn't be having this conversation in an alleyway with a man about to enter a BDSM club while wearing an outfit that does nothing to represent the strong and independent woman I am."

I expected my words to rile him up. It has the complete opposite effect. The spark in his eyes grows as does the smirk etched on his face. "Secondhand knowledge is the reason you've closed your mind to new possibilities. You're allowing others to influence your decisions instead of evaluating them for yourself."

I stare at him, wholly stumped.

Spotting my shocked expression, he says, "Tonight is your first time in a BDSM club."

I attempt to reply, but he continues speaking, making me realize he didn't ask a question, he was stating a fact.

"These events aren't held for people new to the lifestyle. Yes, you can have couples interested in certain aspects of BDSM, but that rarely steps over the line of using a set of fluffy handcuffs or issuing open-hand spankings during sexual exchanges."

My insides tighten when he reaches the last half of his sentence.

"Considering you've been sitting across from me the past ten minutes, and no one has exited the club looking for you, I am assuming you arrived here alone?"

This time, since his tone alludes to a question, I nod. My sex aches when a relief dashes through his heavy-hooded gaze.

Staring into my eyes, he asks, "Can you tell me the last time you saw a solo ballroom dancer perform?"

My brows furrow as I shake my head. "I never have," I reply.

"Exactly," the stranger confirms, his dark brow slanting higher than the silver mask on his face. "Chains is a club designed for you to interact with or without a partner, but when you turn up solo, you're to be paired with someone suitable to ensure you experience the club the right way."

My confusion increases tenfold. I am completely and utterly confused.

"If you were to turn up to a ballroom dancing class without a partner, the instructor would pair you with someone they believe matches your level of skill and experience, would they not?" he questions my confused expression.

Not needing to deliberate on a response, I dip my chin.

"That's what the questionnaire at Chains is for. To make sure you're paired with the right partner," he elaborates.

Although I can see the direction he is attempting to take our conversation, my confusion doesn't ease in the slightest. "But what does that have to do with our conversation?"

"You arrived what..." he stops talking to rake his eyes over my body, "less than an hour ago. Am I correct?"

While nodding, I tug my coat in close to my body to hide its reaction to his quick glance.

"Did you talk to anyone in that time?" he questions, peering into my eyes. I swear, his eyes have the ability to completely stop the beat of my heart. They are so entrancing.

I nearly shake my head before my interaction with the bartender filters into my mind.

"I talked to one man," I admit, my voice louder than I was hoping, startling not just me and the mysterious stranger, but his driver as well. "He was very nice. Pleasant even." *Compared to the many other not-so-pleasant men in the room.*

A new type of excitement scorches my veins when the dark-haired stranger's jaw gains a tick from my confession. From his reaction alone, I surmise he didn't expect me to answer this way. He seems to be able to read me so well, he knew I fled the party without interacting with any of the attendees.

"This man you spoke to, did he request to peruse your questionnaire before approaching you? Or attempt to discuss why you didn't have one?" His tone is gruff and menacing.

The tick in his jaw extends to his hard-lined lips when I shake my head. I've read plenty of romance novels that display dominant man as possessive and jealous, but that cliché doesn't usually extend to Doms. His reaction proves my research may have not been accurate.

"No, but we never really had the chance to talk. It was all *business* for him," I answer, my tone mocking and full of deceit.

I don't know why I am purposely goading him. Perhaps it's the fact I love seeing the possessive spark in his eyes flaring brighter with every moment I sit across from him?

"*Business?*" His voice is so low it's nearly a growl.

"Yeah. He was *very* busy. Quick too." I purposely wait, letting him stew a little before adding on, "The members of Chains are *extremely* demanding. If you know the owner, can you have a word with him or her on my behalf?"

He stares into my eyes, his mesmerizing gaze answering my question without a word seeping past his lips.

"They really need more bar staff. That poor guy was run off his feet."

The conceitedness stretched across my face from making the unnamed stranger jealous turns to panic when he returns to his side of the bench seat, opens the back driver's side door and exits the vehicle. His movements are so quick, he extends his hand to aid me out of the Bentley before I can swallow the hard lump in my throat.

"Why don't we go and have a word with the owner together? I'm sure he will be more than willing to hear your suggestion in person," he mutters.

"Oh… that's not necessary," I stammer out, my words croaky. "He's probably a very busy man."

"I'm sure he isn't as busy as the bar staff." His words are as dangerous as the mouthwatering cut of his jawline.

7

Not giving me a chance to object, the stranger curls his hand around mine and paces to the stainless steel door I stumbled out mere minutes ago. The soft hum of voiceless music overtakes the thump of my pulse in my ears when he throws open the door and we step inside the dimly lit club. Just like earlier, numerous eyes swing in my direction. This time, it's not only male eyes I've gained the attention of. There are just as many female gazes watching every movement the mysterious stranger and I make. Their moods perk up as they glance at him hopefully. From the way they are eyeing us with so much interest, anyone would swear we were the ones performing on stage, not the lady with a giant black ball stuffed in her mouth.

I twist my coat around my wrists before pulling it to my chest. With the mysterious stranger's hand warming my back, the front of my body is noticeably cool. Keeping my head front and center, I sneakily shift my eyes sideways. Shock gnaws at my chest. Although we are surrounded by scantily clad and completely naked bodies, the green-eyed man has his eyes firmly planted on me. His avid gaze heats every inch of my skin—from the tips of my toes to the roots of my sweat-drenched hair.

"I've never been into exhibitionism, but if you keep looking at me like that, I may reconsider," the stranger mumbles, ensuring I am aware my sneaky glance didn't go unnoticed.

Shockwaves of arousal pump through me like liquid ecstasy. The brittle roughness of his words equally shock and excite me. I'm shocked because of the location we are entering – I assumed exhibitionism would be high on his list of priorities – and excited because his threat means I'm not the only one allowing lust to steer away my inhibitions.

Smirking at my glazed-eyed response, the masked man continues to move through the vast gathering of people. When they see us coming, the crowd parts, giving us a clear path to a long, dark corridor positioned next to the bar I hid at earlier. For every step I take, the sweat misting my skin thickens. I don't know if it originates from the way everyone seems to know the masked man, or because my body failed to shut down its longing. Whatever it is, my body's prompts are shocking and somewhat intimidating, even more so because of the unethical environment.

The distress gnawing my chest drops to my stomach when the bartender notices our approach. "Oh, now I understand why your name is Cleopatra. A queen for the king," he jests, winking playfully. "Maybe next time you can be Bonnie and I'll be Clyde."

Although I can't miss his jeering tone, his playful banter is lost on the mysterious stranger. His hand stiffens on my back, and for the first time in minutes, his eyes move away from me. The belligerent smile etched on the bartender's mouth is wiped right off his face when the stranger connects his thin-slit eyes with his. Although he doesn't speak a word, his gaze must be threatening enough, because the bartender swallows harshly before curtly nodding. When he paces down the polished bar to serve patrons at the other end, his steps are shaky and lacking the confidence they held earlier.

"He was only playing," I assure him, my words barely heard over the soft hum of music playing from the speakers above our heads.

My eyes rocket to the stranger when he mutters, "Do you like knife play, Cleo?"

My brain didn't register his question. It's too busy prompting my body to breathe through the panic scorching my veins that he knows my name. The color drains from my face as my lungs squeal about the shortage of oxygen.

My panic only recedes when the stranger drops his eyes to mine. Although shrouded by a lifetime of secrets, they have an open honesty to them. He doesn't know me, he just shortened the alias I gave the bartender. *I hope.*

"Knife play?" I question, endeavoring to return our conversation to neutral territory. Well, as neutral as it can be in a BDSM club.

When we reach the end of the corridor, the stranger removes his hand from my back, triggering my body to scream in disgust. Before I have the chance to voice an objection to his lack of contact, my disappointment is replaced with nerves when my eyes take in the word "manager" engraved on the tinted glass door. I was hoping his threat to talk to the manager was just a ploy to get me back inside the club. Apparently, I was mistaken.

"Knife play is often referred to as blood play," he responds, swinging open the half-glass door. "Those are the types of scenes that interest a man like Matthew."

I peer into his eyes, ensuring he can spot my confusion. I don't have the faintest clue what he is referring to.

"Matthew is not just a bartender at Chains, Cleo, he is also an invited guest," he explains to my bemused expression before guiding me into the office. "You may have taken your conversation with him as friendly. He did not. He is networking for a new sub."

Even with shock bubbling my veins, my body fails to display its surprise at his admission. My eyes are too busy categorizing every inch of the large office we've just entered. Black polished bookshelves line four walls. They are brimming with a broad range of books, from classic first editions worth thousands of dollars to the latest rom-com releases. A thick glass desk with black iron legs sits in the middle of the space, illuminated by the chain-link chandelier shackled to the ceiling.

As I remind my body to breathe, I step further into the space. My lips quirk when I notice the theme of the expansive office is a chain-link design. The furniture is not the type you'd find in any retail store. This is custom made. With its elegant lines and quality material, it appears more like a piece of art than furniture. If I hadn't noticed the inclusion of painted BDSM scenes adorning the walls, I could have mistaken this place for that of an extremely wealthy businessman, not a seedy BDSM club manager.

"Whose office is this?" I query, spinning around to face the mysterious stranger.

When I neglect to find him standing next to me, my neck snaps to the side. My movements are so abrupt, the muscles in my neck squeal in protest. The rapid beat of my pulse surges into unknown waters when my eyes lock in on the mystery stranger sitting in a large leather chair behind the only desk in the room. He has removed his suit jacket and rolled up the sleeves of his crisp business shirt, exposing the cut lines of his muscular arm, but, unfortunately, the mask concealing his face remains in place.

Swallowing a brick lodged in the middle of my throat, I garble, "This is your office? You're the manager of Chains?"

The corners of his lips tug high, excitement at my flabbergasted response is all over his concealed face. He shouldn't look so pleased. He is the man I am here to take down. The one person who knows the name of every face mingling outside his office doors. He holds the key I need to unlock the story that could change the course of my career. *He should not be smiling.*

He leans forward, dragging the cuffs of his shirt even higher on his heavily veined arms. "I don't manage Chains, Cleo, I own it," he informs me. The roughness of his voice sends a chill down my spine. With the vast range of emotions pumping into me, I don't know if it's a good or bad chill.

When he gestures for me to sit in the seat across from him, my first instinct is to shake my head and bolt. But, for some reason unbeknownst to me, I push off my feet and saunter to him. The dangerous beat of my heart turns calamitous the closer I get to him. As if his body and soul-stealing facial features aren't enough to contend with, his eyes, my gosh, they totally squash any shrewdness I hold. They have the ability to render me speechless and turn my brain to mash. *Clearly—as I'm standing in the middle of a BDSM club acting like I'm meeting the President, and I haven't even seen the uncovered version of his eyes yet.*

When I take the seat across from him, the still unnamed man removes a five-page document from a concealed drawer on his left. Like he is aware of the power his eyes have over me, his entrancing gaze never once wavers from mine. While holding his gaze, I catch the rise and fall of my heavy bosoms. The movements of my chest undoubtedly prove I am breathing, but the tightness spread across my torso says otherwise. I feel like I am drowning, not in a pool of despair but in a pool of lust. This man exhibits such animalistic traits I have no doubt he'd be remarkable in bed. He is confident without being overly cocky, like he knows of his sexual prowess, and he doesn't need to shamelessly flaunt it, but there is also an unknown edge to him that's just as intriguing. *A complex man I'd give anything to spend a few hours unraveling.*

The sound of a pen scratching on paper gathers my attention from the wicked thoughts of him flaunting his sexual abilities in morally unethical ways.

With his eyes now glancing down at the sheets of paper, the masked man says, "Name, Cleo. Age..."

He stops talking and lifts his eyes to me. My spine turns as solid as a rod when he runs his heavy-hooded gaze down my body in a long perusal.

"Twenty-five," he murmurs, returning his gaze to the sheet in front of him.

I can't hide my surprise that he correctly guessed my age from one glance at my body.

"Physical capabilities?" He doesn't wait for me to reply before he mutters, "Physically capable."

I squeeze my thighs together to lessen the manic throb between my legs from the assuredness in his voice.

Any chance to ease the intense tingle flies out the window when he raises his eyes to me and asks, "Submissive's safe word?"

I sit in silence, muted, aroused and confused. From my research online, you only require a safe word if you intend to be involved in a physical activity. Considering I have no intention of doing anything of that nature in this type of establishment, I never took the time to ponder a safe word.

Every muscle in my body tightens when he utters, "We will come back to that one."

Dropping his eyes to the paper, he continues. "Name the Dom/top is to be called during scenes?"

Once again, he doesn't wait for me to answer, he just writes something down.

With my inability to leash my curiosity, I sit on the edge of my chair and adjust my position so I can peer at the name scribbled across the sheet. *Master Chains,* I mumble to myself.

"Who is Master Chains?" I query, my words coming out surprisingly strong considering the circumstances I find myself in.

Both excitement and fear holds me captive for several heart-clutching seconds when the most devastating smile I've ever experienced spreads across the masked man's face. If his smile didn't answer my question, the truth beaming from his eyes is a surefire indication.

Ignoring the excitement heating my blood, I slouch deeper in my chair and pull my coat into my chest, ensuring *Master Chains* won't notice my budded nipples. Considering the man across from me in a stranger—and enjoys extracurricular bedroom antics—my body's reaction to his smile is utterly ridiculous. I've never acted so moronic in my entire life.

The situation goes from difficult to downright awkward when he mimics my slouched position before questioning, "Bondage?"

Unsure what he wants for an answer, I shrug my shoulders.

"Have you ever participated in any form of bondage?" he elaborates, the deep rasp of his voice calm, almost soothing.

I briskly shake my head.

"Handcuffs? Rope? Have you had your hands bound behind your back with a tie or some form of restraint?"

The throb between my legs amplifies with every word he speaks. With a hint of embarrassment, I once again shake my head. Although Luke and I were together for two years, we only had sexual contact the last six months of our relationship. His bedroom abilities were great, and he made it hard for any man following him to steal his limelight, but our adventures never extended beyond altering our position, so it was comfortable in his Jeep. And although I've slept with men since Luke, I was never with them long enough for sexual preferences to be discussed.

The unnamed man's heavy brow arches above his mask. He appears shocked by my response.

The stunned expression on his face morphs onto mine when he asks, "Do you like to be spanked, Cleo?"

Hoping to mask my shock with humor, I reply, "Do you enjoy making strangers squirm in their seats, *Master Chains*?" I drawl out his alias in a long and highly inappropriate purr, my desire to goad him nearly as urgent as my wish to unmask his handsome face.

"Depends."

"On what?" I hold his gaze, my interest in discovering his answer unable to be concealed.

He smiles a grin that sets my pulse racing. "On whether or not you enjoy being spanked."

Warm slickness coats my panties. Even hearing a jeering undertone in his timbre doesn't dampen my eagerness the slightest. I am hot, needy and on the verge of combusting.

"Do you want to spank me?" I try to keep my tone neutral. My attempts are borderline.

The smile on his face grows, as does the lust raging in his eyes. "That... amongst many other things."

The coils in my stomach wind so tight, I physically squirm in my seat. My reaction surprises me. I've handled the direct approach some men use numerous times before, but none have caused me to shamelessly writhe in my seat. I'm wiggling around so much, I look like a child busting to use the bathroom.

"You don't even know me," I barely whisper when the entirety of the situation overwhelms me. "How could you possibly know what you want to do to me?"

I suck in a surprised breath when he locks his eyes with mine and says, "I only needed one glance into your eyes, because eye contact is what causes your--"

"Soul to catch on fire," I interrupt, saying a verse my dad quoted many times during his twenty-five-year marriage to my mom. "There is no greater way to see someone's true self than looking at their soul through their eyes."

He nods and smiles, seemingly pleased with my response. Until this day, I never understood my dad's favorite quote. Now I do. I fully understand. Because the instant the stranger locked his eyes with mine, a furious blaze raged through my soul, charring it for life. Don't get me wrong, even with half of his face concealed by a mask, the stranger is ridiculously handsome, but there is something about his eyes that tell me not to be fooled by his outer package. His insides are just as temptingly dangerous as his attractive outer layer.

Our fire-sparking stare down ends when he mutters, "So, Cleo, let me ask you again, do you like being spanked?" His voice is deeper and much more rugged this time around.

"Not particularly," I sputter out, shockingly maintaining his gaze.

With how potent the lust is raging though my veins, I'm surprised I haven't thrown my head back, snapped my eyes shut, and gotten lost in the throes of ecstasy. The only reason I haven't is because the nagging voice in the back of my head is warning me to hold my cards close to my chest.

"The only time I've been spanked was when I was naughty. Thankfully, that was not very often in my childhood," I disclose, not the slightest bit embarrassed admitting I was the beloved golden child of my family.

The moisture in the middle of my legs grows when Master Chains' lips tug into a wry smirk. "You will only get spanked when you're naughty here too, Cleo," he mutters, his voice so low I'm certain he didn't expect me to hear him. "Unless you like that type of thing," he continues. This time, there is no doubt he wanted me to hear him.

After glancing into my eyes long enough the satin material of my slip sticks to my skin, he drops his gaze back to the document in his hand. "These next set of questions require you to rate them 1 to 5, one being a definite no, five being a yes, please," he explains.

I lick my dry lips before nodding. I don't know why I'm continuing with this bizarre exchange, but try as I may, I can't tear myself away from our conversation. Some may say it's purely my investigative skills flourishing, but I know that isn't the case. Although this lifestyle is intriguing, and there would be no better way to uncover it than to associate with the man responsible for bringing it to fruition, that isn't what is keeping my backside planted in my seat. It's the intrigue of the man seated across from me. My desire to unmask him is even more voracious than my wish to bring this scandalous story to every news outlet in the country.

My ability to pretend this exchange is nothing but a business transaction is lost when the stranger questions, "Anal sex?"

8

My mouth gapes, and my eyes bulge, but remarkably, I squeak out. "Two."

I should be nervous. I should be feeling all types of grievance for continuing a conversation on a world I essentially know nothing about. But my curiosity is encouraging me to trek into a wrong, yet tantalizing discussion with the mysterious masked man.

The stranger marks my response on the sheet of paper before asking, "Asphyxiation?"

In shock, I stare at him, unresponsive and wide-eyed. He revels in my flushed appearance. His eyes flare in excitement, and his lips tug in the corners. This as cliché as they come, but this man's aura screams sex. His eyes are a decoy, the perfect asset to lure unknowing victims out of the shadows, before his deep, cultured voice ensnares the last of their reservations. He is incredibly appealing and undoubtedly dangerous.

A small voice of reason inside me breaks through the lust haze his entrapping eyes created. "What were the numbers again?" I strive to keep my attention on the task at hand, and not the way his eyes have small flecks of brown around the cornea.

"One for a definite no, five for a yes, please," he responds, his voice not altering the slightest, seemingly unruffled by the zapping current crackling between us.

"Two," I squeak out again, my words not as confident as I hoped.

The anxiety curled around my throat intensifies with every question he asks. "Abrasion? Age Play? Anal plugs? Arm adhesives?"

For the next ten questions, my responses rarely alter from a shaky one or two, but one leaves me utterly flabbergasted.

"Umm... can you repeat that? I'm fairly certain I didn't hear you right."

The contents of my stomach lurch into my throat when he repeats, "Animal play."

I glare at him, beyond mortified. *He has sex with animals?*

Spotting the repulsion on my face, he mutters, "It's not what you're thinking. Animal play is for people who like to be collared. Or crawl on all fours. Some even occasionally bark."

Flush heats my cheeks as images of the lady lowering herself onto her knees earlier this evening flashes before my eyes.

"Oh. Sorry," I mumble, my words so shaky they are nearly unintelligible.

Although I can tell by his eyes that my inexperience amuses him, they also reveal his hesitation. Clearly, he doesn't deal with BDSM rookies often.

We sit across from each other in silence for several moments. Nothing but the sound of my heart thrashing against my ribs is audible. For the first time in my life, I'm at a loss for words. The good manners my mother raised me with are telling me to issue the stranger an apology, but my shocked state due to our peculiar gathering has rendered me speechless.

Since my mouth refuses to cooperate, I issue him my regret by using my eyes. I've always believed apologies are nothing but meaningless words unless you see remorse in the eyes of the person issuing the apology. *I can only hope he sees mine.*

Reading the silent apology brimming from my eyes, the tightness of the stranger's jaw loosens, and the width of his eyes returns to their normal girth. He scoots across his chair, sitting on the very edge before locking his eyes with mine. "This really is your first time at a club like this, isn't it?" When I nod, he adds, "And every question you've answered thus far has been the truth?"

I once again nod, my face hot with embarrassment. He throws his pen onto the desk before sinking into his chair. The metal hinges give out a squeak, enhancing the pin-drop silence that has encroached us. He sits, staring at a door on his right. I also remain quiet, unsure exactly what to say in a baffling situation like this. I tried to come here tonight with an open mind, but, obviously, that didn't occur.

After numerous heart-strangling seconds, the stranger returns his eyes to me. "Can I show you something?" For the first time tonight, his voice doesn't hold the same amount of assertiveness it usually wields.

Still mute, I bob my head.

The sluggish beat of my heart, strangled with remorse, gets a moment of reprieve when he pushes back from his desk, walks around it, then holds his hand out in offering. His chivalry catches me off guard. I fumble like a giddy school girl while placing my coat on his desk and standing from my seat before accepting his kind gesture. A surge of awareness scorches through my veins when he curls his hand around mine. His touch is warm and stimulating, and just like earlier, it causes the hairs on my body to bristle to attention.

Pretending I'm unaffected by the spark of lust firing between us, I allow the stranger to guide me to the door he's been staring at the past five minutes. Glancing into my eyes with a gleam I can't recognize, he slips his empty hand into the pocket of his trousers. My pulse thrums in my neck when he pulls out an antique-looking silver key, the type you'd expect to find hanging out of a treasure chest. The clunking of a heavy lock sounds through my ears when he twists the key into the hole. My lungs take stock of their oxygen levels when he lowers the steel handle and swings open the door.

He flicks on a light switch at his left. It takes several moments for the overhead lighting to illuminate the black room. When it does, I gulp in a shocked breath. When I joke to people that I work in a dungeon, I am certain this is what they imagine. A chain contraption I've never seen before hangs from the ceiling, sex instruments and apparatuses I am accustomed with but have never used cause a rush of heat to my cheeks, and the feeling of being in an environment I don't belong in overwhelms me.

Putting on my investigative journalism cap, I pace deeper into the room, appraising it with both the business and personal side of my brain. Even to a BDSM novice like me, it's clear this area is some sort of playroom. It has a manly feel to it, but it's also cold and sterile with the inclusion of black leather and silver chains on nearly every surface.

My eyes rocket to the unnamed man standing in silence outside the door when I spot a flogger draped over a leather studded chaise in the middle of the room. Unlike the flogger the man earlier tonight was being whipped with, this one doesn't have leather tassels attached to the end. It has chain-links, chains that look incredibly painful.

"Chains? Your instrument of choice is chains?"

He remains quiet, assessing me in great detail. I return his stare, seeking answers to my question in his forthright eyes. My outward demeanor displays both my disgust and arousal. Don't ask me how it's possible to have two vastly contradicting responses, but that's precisely what I am dealing with right now. His eyes appear just as conflicted as mine.

Sensing my opposing viewpoints, the stranger pushes off the doorjamb and paces towards me. I don't know whether my judgment is impaired by confusion, but even his walk commands more attention in this room. Snubbing the swirling of my stomach, I hold his gaze as he strides to me. His gaze is primitive and strong, and it enhances the beads of sweat sliding down my back.

The temperature in the room becomes unbearable when he stops in front of me. I stray my eyes to the ground, no longer capable of ignoring the pull his soul-stealing eyes have over me.

"Don't fear the pleasure you can get from pain," he mutters, his tone low and crackling with sexual tension as he lifts my chin back into its original position. "Pain has a reason it was added to pleasure."

"Says the man dishing out the punishment," I mumble before I can stop my words.

Unaffected by my callous snarl, he runs his index finger along my forehead, removing a strand of hair stuck to my sweat-slicked skin. "You fear the unknown."

I shake my head, denying his claim. "No. People only fear the unknown when they are incapable of achieving what they want."

He smiles, seemingly pleased by my response. "Exactly. So, what did you want to achieve by coming here tonight, Cleo?"

The hairs on my arms bristle, my body choosing its own response to the way my name rolls off his tongue in a long, seductive purr.

When I remain quiet, he says, "People's views of this lifestyle are often tainted and starkly contradicting to what it is."

I scan my eyes over the room. "Not from what I am seeing. This is pretty much what I envisioned when I have nightmares about being tortured."

"I acknowledge your concerns, but that does not mean I have to agree with them." His tone is stern, yet understanding. "The people in this club are no different than yourself, Cleo. They just express themselves in a manner you're not accustomed to. That doesn't make them weird or different. It makes them real. And if you sat back and thought about it, you'd realize it also makes them courageous."

Pushing aside the fact he is excluding himself from his assessment, I say, "This is normal to you?" I wave my hand across the room that hasn't relinquished its firm hold on my stomach. "Turning up to your place of employment with your face concealed is normal to you?"

He stares into my eyes, not the slightest bit fazed by the disdain in my voice. "Yes. This is *normal* to me. But despite what you believe, the people in this club do not cover their faces solely to hide themselves. They conceal themselves to ensure they are truly seen. Imagine how different the world would view beauty if it were only seen through the soul of a person's eyes."

I try to compile a response, but I am honestly at a loss for words. He took beliefs I've been raised with and twisted them in a way that gives them a whole new meaning. I've often said beauty is skin deep. His response replicates my sentiments exactly.

A few minutes pass in silence. I wouldn't say it was any more confronting than the prior thirty minutes we've spent together. It more appears as if he is giving me time to absorb the enormity of his statement.

Once he is happy I've taken in his wisdom, he questions, "What do you want to do, Cleo? Stay and open your mind to the possibility of learning something new? Or leave and continue to wonder if your views are misguided and ill-advised?"

I shrug my shoulders. This is the first time in my life I truly don't know what to do. Intrigue is a potent power that can baffle even the most brilliant minds.

"What do you think I should do?" My voice is low and embarrassed that I'm leaving an imperative decision in the hands of a stranger.

"You, and only you, can make that decision. Contrary to what you have been told, nothing is *ever* forced in this industry," he replies with his mesmerizing eyes dancing between mine.

The unease twisting my stomach gets a moment of reprieve when I see the honesty in his eyes. Although it doesn't lessen my trepidation, it simmers it enough that I feel comfortable taking my time to deliberate a decision.

While roaming my eyes around the playroom, which doesn't look as stark and uninviting as it did mere minutes ago, I take a few moments contemplating a response to his question. Half of my time is spent returning the stranger's lusty stare, while the other half categorizes all the scary, nerve-surging events that have occurred tonight. The man standing before me intrigues me, more than any man before him, but is that solely based on where I met him? Who can honestly say they've held a conversation with a man who owns a secret BDSM club while standing in the middle of his playroom? Perhaps I have done as Delilah and her counterparts requested? Maybe I am only looking at this from a business standpoint?

Oh, who am I kidding? I am not standing in this room contemplating my fate to break a story. I am here solely because the green-eyed man's notable stature refuses to relinquish me from its firm hold. Considering where we met and our interactions thus far, expecting to envision any morally right response is an absolutely ludicrous notion.

With my heart thrashing against my chest, I return my eyes to the still unnamed man. "I want to go home? This lifestyle isn't for me?" My jittering voice makes my words come out more like questions than demands.

For the quickest second, a flare of disappointment flashes through the stranger's eyes before he shuts it down quicker than it arrived. It was so fast, if I wasn't trapped in his trance, I may have missed it.

Before I have the chance to recant my statement, he says, "Then let's get you home," his tone the lowest I've heard.

In silence, he guides me out of the room, gathers my coat from the table, and leads me out of his office. Just like earlier, my stomach swirls when we reach the main part of the club. Except this time, it isn't just the various scenes playing throughout that have my stomach twisted in knots. It's the feeling I am making a huge mistake. It's the same unease I got the day my parents and little brother were involved in their car accident.

Before I can gather why I am having such a peculiar feeling for a stranger, we enter the vacant foyer at the front of the club. The palpable tension between us intensifies in the emptiness of the space. When he moves away from me, regret surges through my veins.

He gathers a small white envelope from behind the unmanned check-in station, then paces back towards me. His sweltering green eyes fringed by thick black lashes never once leave mine as he spans the distance between us. His avid gaze makes me feel alive, desired even.

"In case your curiosity gets the better of you," he states, handing the envelope to me.

Never being one to leash my curiosity, I attempt to tear open the envelope. He places his hand over mine, foiling my endeavors. "I said only *if* you're curious. Are you curious, Cleo?"

A small voice inside me screams a resounding, "Yes," but my astute brain swallows down its absurd response with a brisk shake of my head.

Disappointment flares in his stranger's eyes. He isn't the only one disappointed. The entire evening has my libido at the pinnacle of sexual exhilaration, all to be crashed by the inhibitions cited by my socially acceptable-striving brain.

"Okay. Then it was a pleasure meeting you, Cleo," the stranger bids me farewell, holding out his hand in offering.

A jolt of adrenaline ignites the lower half of my body when he presses a kiss to the top of my hand. I yank my hand out of his embrace, startled by the response of my body. I breathe deeply, struggling not to lured into his enticing trap as my eyes check my hand for scorch marks. His touch was so blistering, I was sure there would be a welt.

Smiling at my seemingly skittish response, the masked man gestures his head to the door I stumbled in nearly two hours ago. "The doorman will summon a taxi for you."

"Thank you, but that isn't necessary, I have someone available to take me home." I inwardly sigh, grateful my voice didn't come out with the shake hampering my curvy frame.

My brows scrunch when a hazy cloud forms over the stranger's bright gaze. It's one I've only seen once so far tonight. It was when I was goading him in the back of the Bentley.

Spotting my confused expression, he mutters, "Envy slays itself with its own arrows."

With that, he runs the back of his hand down my cheek. A little groan involuntarily escapes me before I can shut it down. He pulls his hand away and takes a step backward, as if he too felt the current his touch inspired. Not speaking a word, he spins on his heels and walks into a world where I don't belong without a backward glance.

I stand frozen for a moment. My mind is hazy, my body on high alert. It's only after numerous minutes of silent deliberation does the reason why his eyes seem so familiar smack into me hard and fast. My heart rate surges with unease as my mind drifts back to a moment in time I'll never forget. A moment that both haunts and appeases me. The time a stranger comforted me during my darkest day.

"It can't be him," I mutter under my breath, certain the owner of a BDSM club wouldn't offer a stranger comfort out of the goodness of his heart. *Surely not.* The people in this industry are sick and demented human beings who get off on punishing those beneath them. *Aren't they?*

Certain the debauched environment I'm standing in is weakening my perception, I pivot on my heels and head for the door. The little voice inside me screams for me to stop, but I don't listen. Although intrigued beyond comprehension by the masked man, I plan on pushing one of the most bizarre and unusual nights I've ever had into the background of my mind, where I intend for it to stay for eternity.

I just need my heart to read the memo my brain wrote.

9

The air is sucked from my lungs when I walk into my office Monday morning. It isn't just Delilah sitting in my office chair that has me gasping for air, it's the images of the unnamed man flashing across my screen that have me choked. Since Delilah and Mr. Carson are so engrossed in absorbing each sordid image flicking across the monitor, they fail to notice me sneaking up behind them. From the images of the masked man alone, I can easily derive that these pictures were taken on Saturday night. What I can't fathom is how they were captured. With the lack of pixelation and graininess to the images, it's clear they were not obtained by a long-range camera. They almost look as if they were snapped by someone sitting intimately close to the unnamed man. Like they were captured without his knowledge.

The bagel slathered in cream cheese I scarfed down on the train to work threatens to resurface when the images flick to a set of pictures taken in the back of a light gray Bentley. Any prospect of keeping my one-night-only appearance at a BDSM club a secret is left for dust when I catch my wide-eyed expression in the reflection of the dark tinted windows. Even with my image not being as clear as the green-eyed stranger, it's clear enough that there is no denying it's me sitting in the back seat of the Bentley.

When the room swirls around me, I reach out to grasp my office chair, wanting to ensure I don't go tumbling to the floor as I fight for my lungs to fill with air. My abrupt movement gains me the attention of Delilah and Mr. Carson.

"Chloe, so glad you could *finally* join us," Delilah snarls, her eyes lifting to the clock that shows I have arrived fifteen minutes before my scheduled start time. "I've been updating Mr. Carson on the progress of your investigation."

Mr. Carson shifts his eyes to me. His dark brows stitch when he takes in my white cheeks and massively dilated eyes. "Are you okay, Cleo?" he questions, his tone revealing his concern.

I shake my head. "Where did you get the images from?"

Mr. Carson braces his hip on the corner of my desk, his surprised expression growing the longer I glare into his murky eyes. "There was a pen tip-sized camera installed in one of the beads of your negligée," he informs me, his words as jutted as the hard lines in Delilah's top lip. "You were aware of this, Cleo. Delilah told me you were mindful of our requirement to digitally document your investigation into Chains."

Before a single denial can escape my lips, Delilah abruptly stands from her chair. "Yes, Cleo was aware of the camera. She is just a little frazzled by the events of the weekend," she exclaims, her loud voice ricocheting off my office walls.

Glowering at me, Delilah curls her arms around Mr. Carson's shoulders and guides him to my office door. The heavy groove between her manicured brows deepens when Mr. Carson yanks away from her embrace. His stern eyes issue her his reprimand for touching him without a word seeping from his lips. Once Delilah has absorbed every malicious torrent of his silent scold, Mr. Carson swings his eyes to me. The fury in his eyes softens when he takes in my wide eyes and flushed cheeks.

"Were you aware of the hidden camera, Cleo?" he questions, peering into my eyes.

I nearly shake my head. The only thing that stops me is the irate scowl Delilah gives me from behind Mr. Carson's shoulder. Her silent threat is just as effective as the one Mr. Carson issued her. It's heart-clutching and stern, and it renders me speechless.

If her vicious glare isn't enough to render me mute, her mouthed, "Lexi," is as effective as duct tape to my mouth.

Unable to speak through my dry, gaped mouth, I pitifully nod. Some may construe my reply as cowardice, but that response would only be from people who have not handled the wrath of an angry Delilah Winterbottom. I'd rather have my day with the devil than spar against a woman as evil as her.

Mr. Carson locks his eyes with mine, no doubt trying to gauge my true response. Neither agreeing with or denying my declaration, he says, "You appear to have made some solid contacts in Chains Saturday night. If you keep up this caliber of work, you won't have to rely on any man to supply your sister's medical care."

And there it is: the below-the-belt hit I was waiting for. His remark could be construed as a compliment. I do not see it that way. His comment not only ensures Delilah will continue being my puppeteer, but it also guarantees he maintains the upper hand. He may seem genuinely nice and somewhat intriguing, but like every other man I've met in a high-power position, he didn't get there by playing nice. Just like the gaze of several men at Chains, I am nothing but a commodity to him.

Once Mr. Carson's broad frame slips into the elevator on my floor, Delilah closes my office door and swivels around to face me. Heat creeps up my neck and curls around my throat from her malicious stare.

"When I spoke to you Sunday morning, you gave me the impression you didn't make any contacts Saturday night." Not giving me a chance to reply, she continues speaking, "You're a silly little girl if you believe you have control over *anything* that happens in this building."

She paces closer to me, nostrils flaring, fists clenched. "You and the lowlifes in the basement may be fine living out your career down there, but I guarantee you, the presidential suite at the Ritz Carlton will feel like the dungeon by the time I am finished with you if you *ever* lie to me again." Her words come out in a long hiss, vicious and full of threat.

I swallow several times in a row, attempting to cool the fire burning in my throat.

Delilah tugs on the hem of her designer pantsuit before bending her knees so we meet eye to eye. "Do you understand what I am saying to you, *Chloe?"* She doesn't attempt to hide the fact she knows she is calling me the wrong name.

"Loud and clear," I reply through clenched teeth. I straighten my spine. Each millimeter I gain unleashes more of my Garcia fighting spirit. "But let me get one thing straight," I continue, my tone as vicious as the one she was using earlier. "If you *ever* hide a camera in my clothing again without my knowledge, when I fall from grace, I'll take you to the depths of hell right alongside me."

My threat doesn't deter Delilah's resting bitch face the slightest. If anything, it strengthens it.

"Duly noted." Her tone is mocking and full of lies. "Lucky for me, I have a bank account that can sustain the fall from grace. Do you, Cleo?"

Her malice-packed smile tells me she already knows my reply. She has researched me just as much the past two weeks as I have her. From what reports I gathered on her, she doesn't need to work to maintain the elaborate lifestyle she has been living since the day she took her first breath. She is here purely to torture the poor bastards who don't have any other option but to work for the man. *That man being Mr. Carson.*

Happy I have heeded her warning, Delilah saunters to my door. Her head is held high, her steps overly dramatic. Just before she exits, she cranks her neck back and peers at me. "I want the man in the Bentley's name, occupation, marital status and how many digits are in his bank account by the end of the month."

I shake my head. "I can't. That's impossible. There are no scheduled parties for Chains in the near future, and I don't have those types of contacts. My invitation was one-time only," I reply.

I also have an irrepressible desire to protect him from your vindictive claws, but I keep that snippet of information to myself.

"Name. Occupation. Marital status. And how many digits are in his bank account by the end of the month," she repeats, pausing dramatically between each request. "Or find yourself positioned at the end of a very long unemployment line."

I hold in my frustrated squeal until Delilah exits my office. Even with my door shut, I'm certain three floors down heard my malicious tirade on the evil witch. God, I wish I was smart enough to deny their requests weeks ago. Nothing worth having ever comes easily. That should have been a clear indication on how this assignment was going to unravel.

Slinging off my torn jacket, I hang it on the coat rack in the corner of my office, then slump into my chair. A puff of air whizzes out of my nose when I take in the ridiculously large space. My desk alone would be worth more than my annual salary I earned writing obituaries.

While absorbing the freshly cut floral arrangement in the Cartier vase on my desk, I rack my brain about how I can get out of this predicament with an employment status still attached to my name. Honestly, I don't even care if it's a position based in the dungeon, as long as it pays something, I'll happily accept it.

No matter how many ways I approach it, the same answer pops up. If I want to remain employed, I must investigate the masked man. Attempting to switch off the personal side of my brain, I click through the pictures of the unnamed man sprawled across my computer monitor. Even through a screen, his pulse-racing good looks and soul-stealing eyes still render me speechless. Although our time together was one of the oddest I've had with the opposite sex, he hasn't steered far from my thoughts the past two days. Not just because of his panty-drenching attractiveness, but because the more my astute brain tried to rationalize with my lust-driven heart that the man in the elevator is not the same man I met at Chains, my heart refuses to listen. It's certain he is the same man.

Even if he isn't the kind stranger from the elevator, I'm still shocked by the impression the masked man made on me Saturday night. I always assumed a dominant man was controlling and manipulative. He showed my representation wasn't entirely accurate. When I said I wanted to go home, he respected my decision. Disappointment may have flared in his eyes, but he never once voiced his concerns. That's a quality not many men hold, let alone a man in a powerful position.

A few minutes tick by on the clock as I recall the events of my weekend with the masked stranger. When the final moments I spent with him surface, my eyes rocket to my tattered coat. I placed the envelope he gave me in my pocket before sliding into the back of the taxi his doorman summoned. Annoyed at the Bentley driver's claim he would be waiting for me being nothing but a pipedream, I completely forgot about the envelope until now.

Pushing back from my desk, I stroll to my coat rack. My heart is thrashing against my chest, my eyes wide. Ignoring the shake of my hand, I delve it into the coat pocket. Panic scorches my veins when my hand comes out empty not even two seconds later. Harshly grabbing my jacket, I dig my hand into the opposite pocket. It's just as empty as the first. A fine layer of sweat slicks my skin when I search every nook and cranny of my coat, vainly trying to secure a document that could guarantee my employment status.

I stand still, muted and confused when my avid search fails to find the envelope. I was sure I put it in there. My frozen state only ends when my cell phone vibrates on my desk. Since my sister is the only one who has my number, I rush to my desk and snag my phone off the top. The terror thickening my blood thins when I drop my eyes to the phone screen and read.

Lexi: *If I log into this website, is there a possibility I'll see your snatch? Even if the possibility is slight, I still want a warning.*

Laughing to ward off my confusion, I sit in my office chair and type my reply.

Me: *What website? And for future reference, my snatch has rarely seen daylight, let alone a camera lens. P.S – Snatch is a nasty word, I much prefer something like lady garden or beaverville.*

Any worries about being unemployed by this afternoon are pushed to the background of my mind when an image flashes up onto my phone screen. It's the envelope I've spent the last thirty minutes searching for. It's attached to another message from my deviant sister.

Lexi: *Unless your S.N.A.T.C.H is hairy with two buck teeth at the front, you can't call it a beaver. P.S – This is the envelope I was referring to. P.P.S – I already peeked inside. P.P.P.S - If you ever visit a place like that again without me, you won't need to worry about a stranger spanking you. I'm sure I can find a wooden paddle here somewhere.*

My eyes bulge at the last half of her message. With how strict the security was at Chains, I assumed the envelope wouldn't have any identifiable marks on it, so how does she know where it came from?

Me: *Angry?*

It feels like hours pass before a reply finally pops up on my screen.

Lexi: *Ah, no. Jealous. I want a Christian Grey.*

My dainty laugh quickly fills the expansive space of my office.

Me: *I hate to tell you this, but the closest you'll get to finding Christian at that establishment would be dating a man the age of his grandfather.*

Ignoring the deceit darkening my blood, I lift my cold canister of hot chocolate to my mouth as I wait her reply. Although none of the men inside the club sparked an interest out of me, the owner most certainly did. If the caliber of men at Chains matched its owner, I'm sure it would be inundated with attendees willing to pay any price to enter its tightly shut doors.

Speckles of brown spit cover the screen of my computer monitor when my cell phone suddenly rings, startling me. While dabbing up the stains of hot chocolate from my cream skirt with a tissue, I swipe my finger across the screen of my phone.

"I'll take whatever I can get," Lexi says down the line, not bothering to offer a greeting. "If you date Christian's grandfather, you're bound to meet Christian at some point."

"Then you will just steal him from Anastasia with a few bats of your eyelashes and a cunning smirk?"

Lexi laughs. It's husky and exposes the rough weekend she had. "No. I'll just borrow him for a few years, then Ana can have him back."

Although Lexi's tone is joking, it causes a stabbing pain to hit the middle of my chest. I know as well as anyone that Lexi is living on borrowed time, but it doesn't make it any easier to acknowledge.

Pretending she can't feel the sentiment pouring out of me, Lexi asks, "So how long have you been leading this double life? Journalist by day, BDSM madam at night."

I sink deeper into my chair. "It's an undercover assignment I'm supposed to be working on," I confess, no longer capable of keeping secrets from the woman who is more like a best friend than a sister.

Lexi gasps, seemingly surprised.

"I was hand selected by Mr. Carson himself."

"Oh la la," she croons. "Is that who sent you the slip?"

Even knowing she can't see me, I nod. "Yep," I reply, the one word drawn out dramatically. "He wouldn't want the lead investigator of the New York Daily Express turning up to an assignment looking shabby."

Lexi sighs heavily down the line. "*Please.* You could wear a paper bag, and it would look like you were draped in diamonds."

"Only because their scan of my body wouldn't drop any lower than my bosoms."

Minutes pass with nothing but the sound of Lexi's laugh shrilling down the line. God, it's a beautiful thing to hear. I cherish every single one as I know one day I'll never hear it again.

When her laughter starts playing havoc with her overworked lungs, she says, "I love you and your impossible big rack, Cleo the Creep."

"Not as much as I love you and your monstrous tatters, Lexi the Leech," I reply as a broad grin stretches across my face.

After issuing our farewell in a more cordial manner, I lower the phone from my ear. Just before I switch it off, I hear Lexi calling my name.

"Yeah." I push the phone back to my ear.

"If it was a person at this club that caused you to come home with more life in your eyes than you've had since Tate passed away, don't treat it like an assignment. Treat it as if it's an adventure."

Guilt hangs heavy on my heart. "It's not that simple, Lexi. For one, I don't belong in that lifestyle. And two, I could lose my job if I don't hand in this assignment by the end of the month."

"So?" she replies, her tone abrupt and clipped.

That's fine for her to say, she wasn't the one counting measly pennies from our childhood piggy bank last month to pay the electric bill.

Lexi sighs heavily. "I'm the one living on borrowed time, Cleo. Not you. Stop worrying about everyone else and for once put yourself first."

Stealing my chance to reply, she disconnects the call.

10

While placing freshly laundered clothes into my drawers, the quickest flash of white gathers my attention. Although there is only the smallest portion of the pristine document sticking out from a pile of bills, I know exactly what it is. It's the envelope the masked man handed me two weeks ago. He told me to only open it if I was curious. Although he has rarely left my thoughts the past two weeks, my curiosity has never reached the level it is now.

With the most scandalous of all political scandals unearthed earlier this week, Mr. Carson has seconded all investigative journalists at Global Ten Media onto the story dividing the nation. I won't lie. Relief consumed me the instant he relieved me of my investigation into Chains.

Although I turned up to work and did my job to the best of my ability every day the past two weeks, my heart wasn't in the investigation. Not just because the digital security at Chains is the tightest I've ever seen, but because I knew the instant the story broke, I was not just exposing the men and women who value Chains' exclusivity clause, but the man behind the helm as well. The person who opened my eyes to the possibility not everyone who attends BDSM parties are evil and sadistic, they are humans as well. And quite possibly they could hold the traits of a man who would give a stranger comfort in her moment of need.

Granted, my research into the BDSM community has never gone as far as it did two weeks ago, but I've been broadening my horizons. Don't get me wrong, I haven't spent my weekends tied to someone's bedposts or had my backside spanked until it's red raw, I've just been interacting with members of the community in a non-physical element—via online chat forums. Although I've had to take down a small handful of creeps, I've also met some lovely people. Surprisingly, the careers of those involved in the BDSM lifestyle differ greatly. I've spoken to a school teacher, a single dad, an emergency room doctor, and even a handful of stay at home moms.

Although I kept my career title out of our conversations, for the most part, I was forthright on why I was talking to them. I explained that their lifestyle was something placed on my radar, and that I was researching to see if it was a fit for me. Other than the three unsolicited dick pics that popped up, the information I've been given has been beneficial in my investigation.

Did it ease my curiosity on the identity of the unknown man? Not at all. But I feel like I understand him a little more now than I did during our exchange two weeks ago. Does that mean our gathering would have ended differently if I'd done more thorough research before we met? I doubt it. Although my curiosity remains piqued, I don't believe the BDSM lifestyle is for me. *If only I could say the same thing about the masked stranger.*

I change into a pair of fluffy pajamas and refill my glass of wine before snuggling under my thin feather down quilt. While sipping on the fruity wine in my glass, I log into my Kindle account. With Lexi's date spilling into the early hours of the morning, I'll continue my motherly stalk from the comfort of my bed. What better way to do that than with a bottle of aromatic wine and the latest new release from my all-time favorite author?

Thirty minutes and numerous missed lines later, I rest my kindle on my knees and swing my eyes to the envelope. Even with the engrossing words of a romance novel sucking me into a fictional world, my attention remains focused on the envelope. It's been glaring at me from across the room the past half an hour, begging for curiosity to eat me alive. *Clearly, the late hour has made me a little batty.*

Unable to harness my inquisitiveness for a second longer, I peel back my pink ruffled-edge quilt and pad toward my desk. A last-minute change of heart sees me logging into my outdated computer and firing up my email account. I gasp in a surprised breath when my computer dings, announcing I have one new email. In haste, I click on the attachment. My eyes skim the screen at a rate too quick for my brain to register. After exhaling the nerves jangling in my throat, I re-read the email. A dash of excitement thickens my blood when I spot the invitation from Luke, inviting Lexi and me to his twenty-seventh birthday party in a few weeks' time.

I return Luke's email, accepting his invitation before slumping into my chair and flicking my eyes to my bedside table. I sigh when I notice the time. It's a little after one AM. I'm glad Lexi's date is going well, but I am beyond exhausted. Endeavoring to keep my eyelids from drooping, I play a few games of solitaire on my computer. The entire time I am playing, the envelope from Chains calls my name on repeat.

When its efforts become too great for me to ignore—or for me to pretend I'm sane—I yank the envelope from its inconspicuous hiding place and rip it open. Just like the invitation I handed the hostess two weeks ago, this paper is super thin and elaborately gilded. Unlike the invitation, it's void of a lengthy disclosure statement. All it has is a website address and a pin code.

Adopting a nonchalant approach, I type the web address into the search engine of my browser and hit enter. I swear, I've never seen my internet provider work so fast before. The website pops up before a single qualm can filter through my overworked brain. The website formatting is basic: nothing but a plain black screen with a silver chain filling the edges.

Snubbing the shake of my hands, I click my mouse cursor into the security access box and type the 24-digit code listed on the paper. Following the prompts on the screen, I pretend I'm downloading the latest movie on Passionflix. The only time I stop to think of what I am doing is when an arrow pops up on the screen.

Following the direction of the arrow, my confused gaze locks in on a flashing red dot at the top of my monitor. I jump out of my skin when a computerized voice says, "Smile," before a clicking noise booms out of my ancient speakers. I sit slack-jawed and muted, shocked my computer snapped my picture without my consent.

My panic dulls from an out-of-control boil to a feeble simmer when a message flashes across the monitor, disclosing that the image was taken for security purposes and that all files are stored on a secure server even the world's best hacker couldn't infiltrate. *Like that helps the panic scorching my veins.*

Setting aside my churning stomach, I navigate through the website, seeking any clues that may assist in my investigation if the case into Chains is reopened.

"Yeah, keep telling yourself that, Cleo," I mumble under my breath.

There is only one man's identity I am here to seek out. It isn't the gentleman with a creepy porn star mustache and slicked back hair that pops up on video chat within seconds of me joining the private chat room of Chains. It's the unnamed man with the mesmerizing green eyes.

Thirty minutes later, I haven't unearthed anything more compelling than the information I obtained in the private chat rooms I've been mingling in the past two weeks. Although Chains members' names are displayed in alphabetical order, just like the username I chose, all clients are utilizing an alias of some kind. And the small handful of members who have photos attached to their accounts either have their faces covered by a mask, or they are concealed by a shadow.

I don't know whether to be disappointed or happy my scan of the members' faces failed to find a man with piercing green eyes and an alluring smile. I should run with happy, appreciative he isn't out trolling BDSM websites for a new submissive. *Unless he already has one?*

Unwarranted jealousy crackles through me, spurring an epidemic of emotions to consume me—confusion being the most potent of them all. I have no reason to be jealous of a man I don't know, but there is no doubt it's anger bristling my blood pressure. It's so strong, it's almost blinding.

Shutting down my unwarranted jealousy as nothing more than a bout of idiocy, I conclude that Chains' website was a waste of thirty minutes. With a twisted heart, I drag my mouse cursor to the logout button in the bottom right hand corner of my monitor. While hovering my mouse over the button, a new messenger window pops up. My heart lurches into my throat when it displays who is in the process of typing a message: *Master Chains.*

Although I'm two seconds away from logging out, no matter how much my rational brain encourages me to push the logout button, my hand refuses to comply with its demands. Before I have the chance to register my disgust that I'm having a heart versus mind battle over a man I have no right to be conversing with, a message pops up on my monitor.

Master Chains: *Curious?*

I consider not typing a response. The only reason I do is when I notice "seen at 1:43 AM" displayed at the bottom of the message screen. I may be treading into shark-infested waters, but the polite manners handed down from my parents make my decision less difficult.

For how many objections are running through my mind, I waste no time responding.

Cleopatra: *More like bored.*

The tightness clutching my heart loosens when I read his reply.

Master Chains*: If this is where you end up when you're bored, I wish I weren't so intriguing two weeks ago.*

Smiling that he remembers me, I type my response.

Cleopatra: *Don't go out in the wind, your tickets might blow off.*

Time stands still as I await his message.

Master Chains*: If I am going to be classed as weird, I may as well do it with confidence.*

My girlish laugh bounces around the room as my fingers fly wildly over my keyboard.

Cleopatra: *So you're admitting you are weird?*

Even with my tone aiming for playful, anticipation for his response still hangs thickly in the air.

Master Chains: *I said "classed as weird," not "I am weird." There is a difference.*

Any concerns lingering in the back of my mind that I'm interacting with an owner of a BDSM clubs vanish as I type a response to his witty remark. There is nothing but silly giddiness fluttering in my stomach.

Cleopatra*: That sounds like something only a weirdo would say.*

His reply returns in an instant.

Master Chains: *Precisely...*

An inane grin stretches across my face as butterflies take flight in my stomach.

Cleopatra: *You're so weird.*

Master Chains: *Says the expert on what is and isn't weird.*

For the first time in weeks, I throw my head back and laugh.

When a set of headlights flash into my room, my eyes rocket to the alarm clock on my bedside table. The muscles in my jaw loosen when I notice the time displayed. Quicker than a blink of an eye, an entire hour has passed. Honestly, I have no clue how to describe what Master Chains and I have talked about the past sixty minutes. It was an odd interaction of witty banter, corny jokes, and a handful of flirty messages between two people who should have nothing in common, but just gobbled up an hour of precious time via an internet chat.

Just like our impromptu get together two weeks ago, it has been an exciting and eye-opening experience. For the past hour, I truly forgot the stigma attached to Master Chains' lifestyle. I interacted with him as if he is a man, not a Dom attached to a paradoxical universe I know nothing about.

My attention shifts to my bedroom window when the sound of a car door closing booms through my ears. *Lexi must be home from her date.*

Setting aside the feeling of regret curtailing my regular breathing pattern, my fingers gently tap on my keyboard.

Cleopatra: *My sister has just returned home from a date. I should probably go.*

I won't lie, I'm hoping he begs me to stay. The past hour has been unlike anything I've ever experienced. I enjoyed it so much, I'm not willing to let it end just yet.

Disappointment consumes me when he replies.

Master Chains: *Okay. It was nice talking to you, Cleo.*

Cleopatra: *You too. This was fun... although slightly weird.*

Master Chains: *I thought we already established this? Weird is my specialty.*

The heavy sentiment of regret on my chest weakens from his reply. Even though he is technically a stranger, I can hear the playful tone of his words. Perhaps that is why the past hour flew by so quickly? Within a matter of minutes, we both had an understanding of our personalities. I'm forthright, cheeky and have a bizarre desire to goad him. He has an edge of mysteriousness, accepts my attempts at inciting him with a sense of maturity, and he makes me forgot the heavy slate of worry I've been carrying the past four years. For the past hour, I was merely Cleo, a twenty-five-year-old New Jersey native talking to a man who can make her heart beat faster with nothing more than black words typed on a white screen.

Smiling, I type the perfect response to his message.

Cleopatra: *A wise man once told me being yourself doesn't make you weird or different, it makes you courageous. So, wear your weirdness with pride, Master Chains.*

A raging fire combusts in my core when I read his reply.

Master Chains: *Considering it's the only thing I am wearing, I guess it must do.*

Like he can sense my frozen-in-lust stance his message instigated, another message closely follows his womb-combusting one.

Master Chains: *Goodnight, Cleo.*

I scrape my teeth over my bottom lip as I reply. It takes all my strength to type my three word response.

Cleopatra: *Goodnight, Master Chains.*

I stare at the monitor for several moments, hoping it will announce he is typing another message. Unfortunately, all I see is a blank message box. Swallowing down my uncalled-for disappointment, I push away from my desk and go hunt for Lexi.

After consuming two glasses of the wine Lexi brought home from her date and gorging on the orange poppy seed pudding she picked up at an all-night diner, I head back to my room, beyond exhausted. Even though it's a bitterly cold fall night, warmth is blooming across my chest. Not just because Lexi's date with Jackson went even better than the first five they've had, but because of my communication with Master Chains.

While relaying our exchange to Lexi, I realized how beautiful it was for him to spend an hour of his time with me just to kill my boredom. The last time we spoke, I was close-minded and unable to see the man behind the industry he worked in. Tonight strengthened my belief about evaluating a person before judging them. Although I will never fully understand the metaphor, I didn't truly see Master Chains until I didn't see him.

The heat spreading across my chest inflames when my quick scan of my computer monitor has me stumbling upon a message that was not there earlier. I scramble across the room, tripping over a pair of jeans sprawled on the floor on my way. Excitement slicks my skin with sweat when I read his message.

Master Chains: *This may be pretentious of me, or perhaps even weird, but would you care to do what we did tonight all over again? Say 10 PM tomorrow?*

A childish smile etches onto my mouth as my fingers work the keyboard like a pro. My message is delivered before a single gripe is cited by my astute brain.

Cleopatra: *I'll bring the boredom, you bring the weirdness. See you tomorrow at 10 PM sharp.*

11

"I'm coming!" I shout from the hallway before entering my room. "Between work and a train derailing, I've only just walked in the door," I continue notifying my computer, like it will magically type what I'm saying and send it to Master Chains waiting on the other end.

Just as it has been every night the past two weeks, the message box on my computer monitor displays the same greeting.

Master Chains: *I brought the weirdness. Did you bring the boredom?*

Wanting to ensure he doesn't disappear before I've changed into some comfortable clothing, I drag my hand across the keyboard and hit send. My reply is gibberish, but it sends a clear message to Master Chains that I am here. I could sit down and type a proper response, but considering our conversations extend into the wee hours of the morning, I would prefer to get comfortable before commencing our one-on-one chat.

"Have you eaten tonight?" Lexi startles me from her protective post in the hallway between our rooms.

While sliding down the zipper of my A-line business skirt, my spare hand digs into my oversized purse. A groan tears from Lexi's hard-lined lips when I produce a protein bar I purchased on my dash from my office building to Penn Station.

"Really?" Lexi's brows arch high into her hairline. "A protein bar? That's your idea of a nutritious meal?"

Grateful the overbearing mother baton I've been wielding the past four years has been passed to Lexi, I nod. Lexi laughs, shakes her head dismissively, then leaves my room. We've had similar interactions the past two weeks. She always responds in the same manner. I guess this is her way of showing she is here if I need her, but she is choosing not to meddle in my private affairs.

I want to say I've done the same for her in regards to her prospering relationship with Jackson. Unfortunately, that isn't true. For years, I've lived vicariously through my sister's love life, so even a heart-stopping kinship with Master Chains hasn't dampened my eagerness in her relationship in the slightest. With Lexi needing to cram many years of living into her shortened lifespan, I want to ensure she cherishes every moment. If that can only be achieved with a bit of sisterly meddling, I'm willing to get my hands a little dirty. Because if anyone deserves to be swept off their feet by a prince on a white horse, it is Lexi.

Striving to ignore the sentimental tears looming in my eyes, I throw my hair into a messy bun, crack open my protein bar, and sink into my office chair. When I catch my reflection in the duchess mirror on my left, I'm not surprised to see excitement has heated my blood, enhancing my already tanned cheeks with a vibrant hue, and my eyes are wide and bright.

Although our conversations have blatantly stepped over a level acceptable for pen pals, nothing Master Chains and I have discussed the past two weeks has made me feel uncomfortable. Giddy. Intrigued. Horny. Those are words I would use to describe our hours together online. Me and the mysterious dark-haired man only known as Master Chains talk about everything: the news, my dragon boss, our plans for the upcoming festive season. The only thing we haven't discussed is what led to our nightly chats. If I push aside that one small point, the budding relationship we are building is one of the closest I've had since my high school days. I don't know if it's because I'm hiding behind a computer monitor, but I am myself around Master Chains. His appreciation for my witty banter has me exposing sides of my personality I haven't seen since my tragic loss four years ago. Somehow, he gets me, which is ludicrous considering I don't even know his real name.

Heat spreads across my cheeks when I read Master Chains' latest message.

Master Chains: *If that's a code you want me to decipher, I would hate to tell you, I don't have the patience for riddles.*

My fingers glide over the keyboard at a record pace.

Cleopatra: *For some reason, I highly doubt that. You seem to have a lot of patience. It's nearly saint-like.*

My message isn't a total lie. Although we've only communicated via the internet, I've witnessed many sides to Master Chains the past two weeks. He is a little bossy, extremely forthright, kind and understanding, and he has a slight dash of patience. My theory is mainly based on the patience he has shown me the past two weeks. He can hold a flirty conversation without pushing for it to go to the next level. He is the only guy I've spoken to exclusively online who didn't demand a more tangible form of communication at the end of our first conversation.

Although I would love to hear his deep, manly voice again, it's guaranteed I won't make the move to push our relationship in that direction. I'm not just protecting my heart, I'm protecting my employment status. To me, our relationship doesn't cross any of the invisible lines I drew in the sand regarding my investigation into Chains last month. It may slightly blur them—or even fill them in a little—but it certainly doesn't cross them.

My eyes drop to my screen when I notice a new message flag flashing on the screen.

Master Chains: *Saint is a word not in my vocabulary.*

Cleopatra: *Then maybe you should add it? Master Saint has a nice ring to it—even my blasted eardrums agree.*

His reply is almost instant.

Master Chains: *Blasted eardrums?*

I exhale a deep breath.

Cleopatra: *L.O.N.G story... One I'd rather tackle after a steamy shower. Desecration is best discussed with a clean slate.*

My challenging week had one final hurdle I had to leap over before I was granted escape to the wonderment of a weekend. I had a two-hour sit down with Delilah. Pleasant is not a word I will ever use to describe that lady. Even with Mr. Carson requesting for our department's focus to remain on the political scandal covering every front page in the country, Delilah demanded an update on my investigation into Chains—and she wanted it last week.

Guilt made itself comfy in the middle of my chest during our meeting, but no information I handed Delilah had me double-guessing my friendship with Master Chains. As requested during our initial meeting in Mr. Carson's office, I keep my personal and business lives separate. Nothing I mentioned during our longwinded meeting included the private conversations I've held with Master Chains.

Although Master Chains works in an industry that leaves a bitter taste in my mouth when people mention it, the past two weeks taught me that doesn't mean he is a horrid person. What he said the night in his playroom is true. He is just a regular person... but in a weirder, kinkier type of way.

As I throw my arms into the air to stretch out a tiresome week, another message pops up on my computer screen.

Master Chains: *Where were you tonight, Cleo? You're over an hour late.*

Even through a typed message, I can't miss the concern in his voice.

Cleopatra: *Slaying a fire-breathing dragon one witty line at a time.*

His reply arrives in an instant.

Master Chains: *Was it a female or male dragon?*

My lips quirk as the noise of keys tapping sounds through my ears.

Cleopatra: *Does it matter either way? As long as the dragon was slayed, and the princess was saved, the gender of the dragon shouldn't be of any concern.*

My breathing shallows as I await his reply. I stated earlier I've witnessed many sides of Master Chains the past two weeks, but this is a side I have yet to witness. Rarely do our conversations mention an outside party. Usually, the focus remains solely on us.

Master Chains: *Maybe not to mere mortals, but for weirdos like me, the gender, orientation, and intention of the fire-breathing dragon you were wrestling late on a Friday night is something I want to know. Desperately.*

The beat of my heart climbs to a never-before-reached level as I type a reply.

Cleopatra: *How desperate?*

For how quickly Master Chains responds, I swear he intuited my reply.

Master Chains: *Desperate enough my hands are twitching.*

My brows stitch as confusion etches onto my face.

Cleopatra: *What does desperation and twitching hands have in common?*

The instant I hit the enter button, the reasoning behind his message smacks into me. It excites me more than I'd care to admit. Leaving my hang-ups about exactly whom I am conversing with, my fingers fly recklessly over the keyboard.

Cleopatra: *I'm sorry, spanking or any other sexual activities must first be discussed between the Dom and submissive in lengthy detail before such tasks can be undertaken. It's protocol.*

Even knowing I shouldn't be riling him up, I can't help it. What the bartender said is right. I truly am a brat.

I brace my elbows on my desk when his reply flashes up on the screen. His message is short—six small words, but I have to read it three times in a row, certain my tired brain isn't understanding it correctly.

Master Chains: *What's your cell phone number?*

This time, my reply takes me a little longer to type.

Cleopatra: *I don't think that's a good idea. Have we reached the talking on the phone stage of our friendship yet?*

Panic, mixed with a strong sense of excitement makes my stomach a horrid mess as I await his response.

Master Chains: *You can either give it to me, or I'll have someone in my IT department find it for me.*

I should be appalled by his response, but for some reason unbeknownst to me, I'm not. Nothing but unbridled excitement is blazing through my veins, clouding my perception. Clearly, since I reply:

Cleopatra: *Please disregard every derogatory name I've called you the past two weeks. You're not at all weird. You are a creepy stalker. I can't believe I got them mixed up. They are two entirely different entities.*

I push send before I lose the nerve.

Master Chains: *You're approximately five seconds away from finding out exactly how creepy I am.*

Adrenaline pumps through my heart so fast I fear it will burst out of my chest.

Cleopatra: *Is that a threat, Master Chains?*

All noise surrounding me ceases to exist as I glare at the monitor, eagerly anticipating his reply.

Master Chains: *A threat is something issued when it isn't a guarantee. So, no, Cleo, that was not a threat.*

I graze my teeth over my bottom lip as I contemplate a response. I'm genuinely at a loss on how to reply. Numerous times the past week I've typed out a similar request, only to delete it before I hit send. Courage has never been a weak point for me, but there is something about this man that has me acting differently than I usually would. I don't know if it's because every conversation we've had makes me giddy or because I truly know nothing can come from our bizarre connection. Not just because I was assigned to investigate his club, but because we live entirely different lifestyles. Although I've always believed opposites attract, that logic can only stretch so far before it would eventually snap. Wouldn't it?

In an apparent response to my internal battle, another message from Master Chains pops up on my monitor.

Master Chains: *You stood in the middle of my playroom with your face as white as a ghost, and your eyes panicked, yet that hasn't stopped us talking the past two weeks. Don't you think we're past sexting?*

My throaty laugh bounces off the stark walls of my room and jingles in my ears.

Cleopatra: *Sexting? If the past two weeks have been your idea of sexting, you need to up your game, Mister.*

My lips form into an O when I hit send. I really should stop and consider my responses before hitting the enter button. The logical side of my brain knows our conversations have hit a point of being unacceptable for friends, but my lust-driven heart is too focused on its goals to listen to its morally right counterpart. It's beyond saving when it comes to this man.

Master Chains: *Master. And hence the point in me asking for your number... I'm trying to "up my game."*

My fingers fly over the keyboard so fast, I'm certain I've just broken the Guinness Book of World Records for the fastest typing speed.

Cleopatra: *Up your game or whisper wicked thoughts into my ear, Master Chains?*

Jesus, where did that naughty vixen emerge from?

The angry scold of my astute mind blurs into the background when I read Master Chains' next message.

Master Chains: *Grrrr <<< That's me growling. If we were talking, I wouldn't have to type it out.*

I punch my cellphone number into the message box so fast, my fingers threaten to go on strike. What? I'm not a complete idiot. Who wouldn't want to hear a man with pulse-racing good looks growling over the phone? Furthermore, I'm an adult who can shut down our friendship the instant it steps over a level no longer acceptable.

I roll my eyes skywards. "Yeah, sure you can, Cleo," I reprimand myself.

My eyes rocket to the side when my cellphone vibrates and rings on my bedside table not even ten seconds later. Pushing back from my desk, I stand from my chair and pace to my phone. My heart is thrashing wildly against my chest, and a crazy throb has clustered low in my stomach.

After wiping the sweat coating my palms on my stretchy yoga pants, I swipe my finger across the screen of my phone advising I have a private number calling me.

"Hello," I greet, my voice husky with both arousal and excitement.

"Cleo."

His deep and rugged voice sends a shiver of excitement down my spine. I don't know why, but for the past two weeks, I didn't hear his voice with the same amount of authority it commands in real life. I shouldn't be surprised, though. You can't express anything via a computer program, let alone the raspy roughness of an alluring male voice.

The first question fired off Master Chains' tongue sets alarm bells ringing in my ethical brain, "Are you seeing anyone, Cleo?"

Three long heartbeats pass before I stammer out, "Not right now."

"Does that mean you're seeking a relationship?" he queries, his words low and thigh-shakingly dangerous.

Even hearing a range of emotions in his voice doesn't help gauge his true feelings. I can't tell if he is angry right now? Curious? Jealous? Is he just being nosy? Or is he genuinely interested in my reply?

I guess there is only one way to find out.

"Maybe..." I breathe out slowly, my voice high in uncertainty.

Five minutes pass without a syllable escaping Master Chains lips. I'm so convinced our call has disconnected, I pull my phone away from my ear every twenty seconds to check the timer is still counting down. It is.

I lick my dry lips before asking, "Is me wanting to date a problem for you?"

Disappointment slashes me open when he replies not even two seconds later. "No." My freshly cut wounds stop gushing blood when he mutters, "Yes. No. I don't know." His words are as ruffled as my composure.

My jittering hands make it hard for me to keep my phone pressed to my ear. "If it makes you feel any better, between work and talking to you every night, I barely have time to shower, let alone date."

"There is a difference between not having the time and not wanting to make the time. Saying you are 'too busy' is just an excuse. If dating is something you truly want to do, you'll make the time for it," Master Chains responds, his deep voice teeming with antagonism.

I stand frozen in the middle of my room, replaying his words over and over again in my head. No matter how many times I hear it, I come to the same conclusion: he sounds jealous.

"Maybe at this stage of my life, I don't want to date," I reply, my high voice exposing my excitement to his unwarranted jealousy. There has only been one man on my mind the past month. Him. It's nice to know I'm not the only one harboring confusion regarding our bizarre kinship.

The swiftness of Master Chains' reply shocks me. "You just said you want to date. Now you're saying you don't want to. It's either one of the other, Cleo, which one is it?" he asks, his tone clipped.

"Jesus, did someone wake up on the wrong side of the bed? Why are you so moody? You asked me a question, I answered as honest as I could. Do I want to date? Yes, I do. Does that mean I'm going to drag myself around Manhattan like a floozy desperate to get a ring on her finger? No, it doesn't. Unlike you and your lifestyle, normal people don't have a pre-drawn questionnaire to fill out to make sure they are partnered with the right person. Thus, not only making dating hard, it also means it sucks!" I snarl down the line.

Clearly, Master Chains isn't the only one having a bad day. My mood is just as woeful as his.

"Maybe if those normal people you mention in every conversation had a questionnaire like the one at Chains, you wouldn't have such a hard time finding a suitable man to date." His tone is calmer than mine and more direct.

I gasp in a shocked breath, stunned at the bluntness of his reply.

Gritting my back molars together, I sneer, "Oh, believe me, Master Chains, if I truly want to date, I'll have no troubles finding a fitting suitor. Actually, this conversation is enticing me to jump back onto the dating bandwagon. As riveting as our conversations have been, there are some key elements missing only face-to-face contact can achieve."

Apparently, my desire to goad him over the phone is just as potent as it is in person.

My breathing turns labored when he mutters, "You should count your lucky stars we are talking over the phone, Cleo. My hands have never twitched so much."

I try to fire a smart-ass remark off my tongue, but no matter how much my mouth moves, not a single noise seeps from my lips — not even a grunt. My body is too engrossed in calming the fiery rage burning in my stomach to hold a conversation, let alone one with a man whose voice hits every one of my hot buttons.

Reading the silent prompts of my body like he intimately knows me, Master Chains drops his deep voice to a seductive purr while muttering, "From the breath you just took, I'm going to mark down a five in the spanking column of your questionnaire."

"You still have that?" I push out. The arousal curled around my throat makes me sound like I'm in the throes of an earth-shattering climax.

My ears prick when I hear the ruffling of paper. Although embarrassed he can hear the rapid pants of my breath, I like this new element of our kinship, the one that includes background noises. I've often wondered what he was doing in the process of our messaging. Was he at Chains, or surrounded by family and friends? With nothing but the soft exhalations of his breath sounding down the line, I can imagine he is in a similar environment to me—a quiet spot in the comfort of his home.

Master Chains' deep timbre drags me back to the present when he says, "I carry your questionnaire with me everywhere I go."

A rustle of air parts my lips. "You do?"

He waits a beat before replying. "No, I don't. But I heard flattery gets you everywhere."

The muscles in my cheeks groan in protest from the sudden incline of my smile. "You better watch out, Master Chains. My corny metaphors are rubbing off on you."

"That isn't what I want you to rub against me," he growls down the line, causing every fine hair on my body to stand to attention.

His playful banter forces me to ask, "Is this the way it will be every time we talk? You whispering wicked thoughts into my ear?"

God, I hope he says yes.

"Depends." He draws out the one word as if it's an entire sentence.

The swiftness of my reply displays my eagerness. "On what exactly?"

Master Chains waits until the suspense thickening the air becomes murderous before saying, "On how long it takes us to finish your questionnaire."

I've barely caught my breath from the raw huskiness of his voice when he asks, "Blindfolds? Beatings? Being bitten?"

It takes a lot of effort, but I push out, "Are we really going down the questionnaire road again?"

"Yes," he replies, his stern voice unwavering. "You said it yourself, Cleo. Spanking or any other sexual preferences must first be discussed between the Dom and his sub in lengthy detail before such tasks can be undertaken. It's protocol. I would hate to break protocol."

"If protocol is truly a concern of yours, shouldn't you be the one answering the questionnaire?" My voice is back to its usual self, friendly with a hint of cheekiness. "How come I've been automatically designated as the submissive? Because I can sure as hell tell you, if anyone is going to be flogged with the chain flogger you have in your playroom, it won't be me."

Blood surges to my pussy when the manly growl I wanted to hear earlier tears through my eardrums. It's rugged and drawn out, and it sends my libido into unchartered waters.

"Does that mean you've been thinking about my playroom, Cleo?"

Even knowing I should shut down this conversation before it ventures into a situation not acceptable for a budding friendship, I brazenly whisper, "Maybe."

"And?" he growls in a low, raspy tone.

Although we are talking on the phone, I swear I can feel the heat of his breath on my neck.

"And what?" I fill in when he fails to expand on his question.

He waits four heartbeats before asking, "Does that mean you're curious about this... lifestyle, Cleo?"

I swear, I nearly fall into orgasmic bliss from the way he growls "lifestyle." I take a few moments considering a reply before stammering out, "No."

He releases a sharp, disappointed breath, forcing me to say, "Yes. No. I don't know."

My response mimics the reply he gave when I asked if me dating bothered him. Obviously, I'm not the only baffled by our peculiar friendship.

"Well since we are both harboring confusion in regards to what we want to achieve from our acquaintance, why don't we get the formalities out of the way first, then we can work on the confusion," Master Chains suggests.

"I'm not confused," I argue, my tone shockingly strong. "I know *exactly* what you want from this acquaintance."

I hear Master Chains adjust his position, but he doesn't utter a word.

Wanting to coerce a reaction out of him, I declare, "You want to fuck me, Master Chains." I stun myself with the crudeness of my statement.

My brain doesn't have the chance to register its disgust before Master Chains replies, "Fuck is not a word I'd use to describe what I want to do to you, Cleo." His words are strong and seemingly unaffected by my lack of dignity. "Devour. Worship. Possess. Those are more suitable words for what I want to do to you."

Just like the night we met, his words make me hot and needy. But, thankfully, this time he is unable to see my reaction to the frankness of his reply. Although, I'm sure the quickening of my breaths jingling down the line gives away my excitement, he can't see the childish squirming I'm doing to lessen the throb between my legs.

I don't know how much time passes before Master Chains asks, "So, Cleo, let me ask you again. Blindfolds? Beatings? Being bitten?"

Enough time passes that the insane pulse between my legs simmers to a dull ache, but it isn't long enough for me to regain my shrewdness. Obviously, since I ask, "What was the number scale again?"

12

"Happy Birthday, Cleo."

The rough huskiness of Master Chains' voice drawing out my name causes every nerve in my body to activate. My breathing turns labored as a feverous wildfire takes hold in my sex. Just like we did the weeks following our first internet conversation, for the past two weeks, Master Chains and I have continued with our nightly discussions. But now, instead of interacting via a computer, we talk on the phone—every day.

I should be embarrassed admitting this out loud, but I'm not. My conversations with Master Chains have led to many self-induced, mind-blowing orgasms the past two weeks. I thought our chat messages were risqué, they are *nothing* compared to our phone conversations. They are just... *whoa!* They blow my mind. The sound of his voice alone quickens my pulse, let alone the vast range of libido-bolstering words that come out of his sinfully wicked mouth.

Don't get me wrong, we don't just discuss sex when we talk. We talk about anything and everything that crosses our minds. But his voice is so deliciously seductive even the most mundane conversation is ten times better when spoken by him.

Sauntering deeper into my room, I reply, "Thank you."

The shortness of my reply is unable to conceal my slurred words. After drinking half a bottle of the decadent wine Master Chains gifted me for my birthday, I may be slightly tipsy—if not drunk. I've always been a cheap drunk, rarely getting past two glasses before the welcoming alcoholic buzz warms my veins. *Obviously, tonight is no different.*

It feels like an eternity passes before Master Chains asks, "Did you drink the entire bottle by yourself, Cleo?"

"No," I reply, but the childish hiccup parting my lips weakens my statement. "Although, the half a bottle I drank has me slightly adrift from tipsy and well on my way to being drunk."

If I've learned anything the past two weeks, it's that I can't lie to Master Chains. No matter how many times a little white lie sat on the tip of my tongue, begging to be released, my mouth refused to relinquish it. I don't know why, but I have a feeling even if I were to lie to him, he'd tell, so why bother?

"Do you have a glass of water beside your bed as stated on the gift tag?"

I nod. "Check!"

"Headache tablets?"

"Sure do," I reply, pulling back the covers of my bed.

"Did you eat before drinking?"

"Uh huh," I answer, nodding.

"Would you care to be my sub?" he groans in a low, pussy-shaking growl.

Standing frozen at the side of my bed, I demand for my lungs take in air as I strive to ignore the little voice inside of me screaming "yes" on repeat. My lungs follow the commands of my body, but no matter how much air they gulp in, it doesn't feel like enough. The room is strangled of oxygen since the heady aroma of lust is thick in the air. Giddiness clusters in my mind just as rampantly as a tingling sensation gathers in my stomach. I am breathless, panicked, and incredibly turned on.

I only start breathing again when Master Chains says, "I'm being facetious, Cleo. You were overly obliging, so I thought I'd test the waters. I would have hated to miss the opportunity to have you shackled to the St. Andrews Cross in my playroom if you had had a change of heart."

The pulse in my soaked sex goes from a leisured canter to a brisk gallop when the image of me bound and at his complete mercy flashes before my eyes.

Blaming my body's disturbing response to his tease on the alcohol, I say, "The instant I have a change of heart, you'll be the first to know." My words are strangled from the arousal curled around my throat.

"That sounds like a challenge, Cleo. Are you challenging me?" Master Chains growls, his voice gritty and spine-tinglingly delicious.

It's the fight of my life to say, "No. That was merely a fact, not a challenge."

My frozen stance resumes when Master Chains' wicked growl sounds down the line. It's panty-wetting good and sets my pulse racing. Softly sighing at my lack of dignity around him, I slip into my bed and nuzzle into my comforter. It isn't as warm and inviting as Master Chains' flirtatious invitation, but it's better than nothing.

After rolling on to my side to lessen my woozy head, I ask, "Can I ask you something, Master Chains?"

I hear him adjusting his position before he simply replies, "Anything."

His response doesn't surprise me. He has been nothing but forthright with me since the first night we spoke. He expressed his desires for me in a confidence most men lack, but he did it in a way that didn't make my skin crawl. If I'm being honest, his approach made me wish I could step outside the lines I deem acceptable for our friendship. Every minute I talk to him adds another minute of doubt to my muddled brain. He has me thinking dangerous thoughts—*reckless thoughts*. But no matter how many times I try to shut down the friendship I know has branched into hazardous territory, I can't do it. Talking to him is the highlight of my day, so how can I be expected to give that up?

Hearing my name breathed heavily down the line returns my focus to the present.

"Sorry, I kind of spaced out there for a minute," I say, explaining the reason behind my absence.

"Spacing out I can handle. You falling asleep... not so much. With you trekking across New York today, we've barely had a chance to talk as it is."

Master Chains' reply strengthens the giddiness the half a bottle of wine caused to my head. It also proves I'm not the only one cherishing our daily talks. I'm glad I have a similar effect on him. It may be a bizarre and weird sensation, but it's still there nonetheless.

"Ask your question, Cleo, before the alcohol takes hold," Master Chains requests, the smooth command of his voice enhancing the knowledge of his statement.

After scraping my teeth over my bottom lip, I ask, "Have you ever hurt anyone? In your playroom?"

My eyes bulge. The alcohol lacing my veins must be making me more brazen than normal. Although we've discussed many topics the past four weeks, I usually strive to keep our conversation away from the BDSM lifestyle. But after enduring a day that can only be described as perfect, my interest in unveiling the man with the molten lava voice is becoming as desperate as my lungs' desire to breathe.

Master Chains waits a beat before answering, "Yes."

Air whooshes out of my mouth in a brutal grunt, amplifying my dizzy state.

"But only because my sub wanted me to," he explains, his words as fast as my pants of breath. "I'm not a sadist, Cleo. I would never hurt a sub unless she indicated an interest in that type of play. I don't instill pain for my own pleasure, I issue it to entice it."

"Pain for pleasure? That doesn't make any sense." My words come out slurred with an equal amount of alcohol and confusion.

"It doesn't have to make sense to you, Cleo. Just like your sexual preferences may not suit every native New Jersey girl, the preferences of a sub vary greatly. It's the compatibility of the Dom and his sub that should be your greatest concern, not what they do behind closed doors. Contrary to what society tells you, what happens between them is no one's business but theirs."

I take a moment to consider his reply before saying, "But what if a Dom shows an interest in someone who doesn't want to be hurt? Would he just coerce her or him to change their mindset?" Although my questions allude to Doms in general, the uncertainty in my words reveals who my questions are really directed at: us.

"A BDSM relationship isn't molding someone to be whom you want them to be." Master Chains's quicken voice displaying he knows whom my questions are referring to. "It's about understanding someone's differences and appreciating them."

"Appreciating them? Or power tripping them? Isn't a BDSM lifestyle just a ruse for a modern man cave? A place where men can bang their chests and be the king of their castle without giving two hoots about the poor defenseless slaves entrenched under them?" I argue before I can stop my words.

"A slave is a person with no power or rights," Master Chains retaliates, his voice void of the snarkiness mine is holding.

"A slave is a person who must legally obey his master, *Master Chains,*" I sneer, my voice cracking with emotion, hating that he doesn't crave a normal relationship like me. "Slaves don't have any power, as it's taken away from them, just like it's taken away from submissives."

"No, Cleo, that's where you're wrong." Although I can't see him, I can imagine him shaking his head. "A sub does *not* have their power taken away from them. They give it, fully, willing and able. When they entrust their rights, their desires, and themselves to another, it's given as a gift, not taken."

"Why would they do that? Why would anyone in the 21st century give up their power?"

"Because they understand the importance of power to a man who had none." The pain in his voice startles me. "The transfer of power between a Dom and his sub is a gift, Cleo. A treasured gift. It's not something ever stolen."

Regret curls around my throat, tightening more and more as his reply plays on repeat in my hazy mind. Even with the buzz only alcohol can create hindering my perception, I couldn't miss the pain in his words. They sliced through me like brittle shards of glass, cutting and disfiguring my heart so it's as ugly as my callous and baseless words. I called him to thank him for his kind generosity today, and all I ended up doing is arguing about a world I know nothing about using fictitious information obtained by others. I thought I was a broad-minded person. Clearly, I am not.

"I'm sorry," I force out through a sob. "I shouldn't have pushed..." *I'm just scared to death of how you make me feel.* "It's been a long day, and I'm letting my tiredness speak on my behalf--"

"Cleo, stop," Master Chains demands, interrupting my apology.

My body jumps to his command. I smack my lips together and level out my breathing. For several seconds, nothing but my pants of breath sound down the line as I struggle to keep my conflicting emotions at bay. Our conversation was heated, but full of intrigue, and it has my emotions sitting on edge.

"It's your birthday, please don't cry," Master Chains pleads softly, proving his uncanny ability to read my emotions by hearing nothing but the pants of my breath. Considering most of our interactions have only been over the phone, I find that astounding.

"Why don't we save our discussion of the complex neuroses of a Dom and his sub for a day you're not celebrating?"

The gentleness of his words make my endeavor not to cry nearly unwinnable, but I give it my best shot. I bite hard on the inside of my cheek as my eyes drift to the large bouquet of red roses sitting on my bedside table—one of many birthday gifts from Master Chains to me.

"Tell me what you did today?" Master Chains requests, his voice a soft purr that drags my focus away from a complex issue too complicated for my tipsy brain.

My teeth scrape over my bottom lip before I answer, "I had an adventure. One of the best days of my life."

"Until we meet again," Master Chains corrects, his tone playful and deep. Even the demand in his voice can't stop a huge smile spreading across my face.

"Until we meet again," I agree, allowing the alcohol warming my veins to speak on behalf of my heart.

I hear Master Chains' cheeks rising over the phone, pleased at my agreeing response. He has dropped several hints the past month about us meeting. I've never taken his bait until now. Just interacting with him is a careless move on my part, but he makes me so wild and reckless that I refuse to consider the repercussions our friendship could cause to both our lives.

"In my playroom?" he suggests, his voice laced with sexual ambiguity.

I giggle quietly. "Keep dreaming." I offer him the same response I've given every day the past two weeks.

Master Chains chuckles a pussy-tingling laugh. "Lucky I'm an optimist determined to make my dreams come true."

I roll my eyes while adjusting my position. My annoyed response is a complete lie. I'm far from annoyed, more like grateful we've managed to steer our conversation back in the direction it usually follows: flirty and friendly.

"That's the problem with optimists, they think they changed the world. Little do they know it was the realist who did all the work," I jest, my brows inching into my hairline.

"Spoken like a true pessimist," Master Chains growls candidly.

I screw up my nose and stick out my tongue.

His rough groan causes the hairs on my neck to prickle. "There are much better things you could be doing with your tongue than immaturely sticking it out."

"Yeah... but it wouldn't be as much fun," I reply, my voice tainted with laughter.

"Oh, baby, I assure you it would be ten times better."

"Is that a challenge, Master Chains?" I quote, mimicking the deep tone he used earlier.

"No, Cleo, that wasn't a challenge. It was a guarantee," he breathes out heavily, forcing my thighs to squeeze together. "And unless you're determined to discover I am a man of my word, you better tell me about this adventurous day you had before I jump on the first flight to New Jersey to prove it to you firsthand," he continues, pretending he is unaware of what my day entailed.

His response is an utter lie. He knows exactly what I did today, as he planned the entire thing. Although the diamond pendant dangling around my neck is one of the most dazzling I've seen, that isn't the reason I love it. It was the journey I undertook to discover it that was the most awarding. A simple text message started a day unlike anything Lexi and I have ever experienced. We went on a treasure hunt across New York using nothing but the clues Master Chains sent me.

It all started with a riddle.

Master Chains: *New York City is being terrorized by monkeys who escaped the zoo. Hurry Cleo, the people of Manhattan are counting on you.*

It took Lexi and me approximately ten minutes to discover what the riddle was referring to: the Manhattan Mayhem Room. With nothing but time on our hands—and Master Chains not replying to my calls—we drove to the location stated in the riddle. We were greeted by the hostess of Manhattan Mayhem Room with a single red rose and an hour-long experience of their reality escape game. It was a thrilling and addictive morning.

Upon exiting, the hostess handed me a printed card. From the impressive cursive and the elegant gilded paper, it didn't take a genius to realize the message was written by Master Chains. It read:

Since the monkeys have returned to the zoo,
why don't you go watch one scratch his head too?

I didn't need to ask Lexi if she wanted to continue with the game Master Chains instigated. The inane grin etched on her face gave her reply. She was just as eager as me. And thus, our day continued. For every location we visited, we received a single red rose and another clue. We stopped by classic New York landmarks we've seen many times, and ones we've always wanted to visit but never had the chance.

Our final location was Steven Kirsch's jewelry store on W 46th street. That was the first time doubt entered my mind the entire day. What Master Chains did for me today was beautiful and heartfelt, but I had already taken advantage of his generosity, so I wasn't willing to accept something of great monetary value as well.

When I informed Lexi of my reservation, she dragged me through the single glass door like a woman on a mission. My god, for a little petite Latin lady, she has the strength of ten gladiators.

My plan to leave without the gift Master Chains purchased for me was left for dust when the shopping assistant showed me what Steven Kirsch had personally designed for me. It was a white gold pendant shaped into a chain link. The small half carat perfectly cut brilliant diamond suspended in the middle of the link gave the manly design a feminine touch. It was simply striking and so unique I couldn't resist picking it up and slipping it around my neck, where it has stayed the past four hours.

"Then I drank half a bottle of wine and gorged on cake like it was calorie free." I finish the story Master Chains already knows. "It was sugary and delicious, and it made me wonder if your lips would taste just as sweet."

I snap my mouth shut, mortified I said my private statement out loud. I've had many reckless thoughts about Master Chains the past six weeks, but I've never once carelessly blurted them out.

The panic roaring through my veins dulls when Master Chains' virile laugh barrels down the line. It's a beautiful noise that pushes aside every reservation lingering in the back of my mind. Not just the ones that popped up today, but every one I've had since the day we met.

"Note to self, a tipsy Cleo is the most honest of them all," he snickers down the line, his commanding voice choked with laughter.

With my hand hovering over the budded peaks of my nipples his laughter incited, I say, "I don't know how to lie to you. You seem to have this magic hold over me that ensures I speak nothing but the truth when it comes to you."

"Hmmm," he murmurs down the line. "If that was the case, Cleo, you wouldn't have denied my advances weeks ago in my playroom. Instead of listening to your wants, you allowed the philosophies of others to guide your decision."

"That's not true," I reply with a brief shake of my head. "I'm not a sheep. I make my own decisions."

Master Chains coughs to clear his throat before saying, "The first thing members of this lifestyle overcome are people's misguided mindsets. They learn that at one stage, every relationship has a stigma attached to it, whether it's religion, age, gender or because their sexual desires don't follow the line deemed acceptable by society. Even Adam and Eve were frowned upon at one stage."

"Preaches the man who conceals his face in the one place he should feel the most comfortable," I blurt out, my words muffled by a soft moan rippling through my lips.

"Throwing a man into the unknown ensures he will come out more determined than ever," Master Chains replies.

Before I can demand clarification on his statement, he continues speaking, "You wanted me that night in Chains, but you were too blinded by the public's concept of normal to act on it."

I remain quiet, unable to negate his accurate statement. What he is saying is true. Even being immersed in an environment unlike anything I've ever imagined, I wanted him—*badly*—but I refused to act on the prompts of my body, believing my moral compass was pushed off-kilter from the demoralizing acts I witnessed the hour prior.

My inability to deny Master Chains' account of the night we met commences the first stretch of silence our conversations have had the past two weeks. Normally, we only pause for bathroom breaks or when Lexi immaturely snatches my cell out of my grasp before tearing through our house like a three-year-old with me snapping at her heels, demanding the return of my phone.

Although a gap of silence is a rare occurrence for us, it doesn't feel awkward. It enhances our bizarre connection and allows my body to begin shutting down from a thrilling, yet exhausting day.

A short time later, I hear the sound of sheets ruffling before Master Chains breathes out, "You know that would feel better if I were doing it."

I freeze for a minute, confused by his comment. It's only during another period of silence does the reasoning behind his statement become clear. Without realizing what I am doing, I'm rolling my erect nipple between my thumb and finger. I assumed the zapping of ecstasy tingling down my spine was from Master Chains' sultry laugh, I had no clue it was because I was stimulating myself while listening to his rugged pants of breath rustling down the line.

I snap my hands away from my chest, appalled at my deplorable behavior. My panic soars when the entirety of the situation dawns on me. *How did he know what I was doing?*

My tired eyes bounce around my room. Shock and panic are smeared over my face. Ever since I had the surveillance camera placed in the bead of my negligée, I've been mindful of my personal security. I've never felt as violated as I did that morning in my office. Not even when being propositioned at an exclusive BDSM club.

Failing to find anything of suspicion in my room, I return my focus to my cell pushed up against my ear. "How did you know what I was doing?" I cringe, loathing that I just admitted I was touching myself. "Not that I was doing *that*," I splatter out, making me grimace more.

A large tiger-like yawn breaking free from my mouth nearly drowns out Master Chains' reply, "Your breathing gives away your excitement, Cleo. You were panting heavier than normal."

"Maybe I fell asleep?" I reason, saying anything to lessen the embarrassment heating my cheeks. "I am extremely tired."

"Because it's your birthday, I'll let your lie slide," Master Chains informs, his deep voice lowering to a husky purr that entices my breathless state. "It would be wise not to test my patience tomorrow, Cleo."

Another stretch of silence descends upon us, once again void of any awkwardness. It just enhances our undeniable sexual connection while also adding to the tiredness drooping my eyelids.

The fatigued expression marring my face switches to anticipation when Master Chains mutters, "Don't stop what you were doing on my behalf, Cleo." His voice sounds labored, like he too is struggling with conflicting viewpoints. "Sometimes the best way to learn how you can please someone is by pleasing yourself."

"I'm fairly sure that's something only a desperate person would say." My words come out strangled with need. They are breathless and evidently display my heightened state of arousal. "Are you desperate, Master Chains?"

"Desperate to touch you," he growls down the line, and I hear the quickening of his pulse in his words. "To lick, caress and bite you. To see your skin turn pink under the hand."

My back arches from the sheer hunger displayed in his deep tone. I try to think of a witty comeback to switch the direction of our conversation to a more respectable territory, but my attempts come up short. My senses are too heightened by Master Chains' confession to form a rational thought, and the alcohol warming my blood is encouraging my recklessness.

"Do you want to come, Cleo?" Master Chains' voice sends a shiver of excitement down my spine. "To end your birthday reveling on the high of an orgasm?"

I take a second to consider a response before moaning, "Yes." I've tiptoed too far into the haze of orgasm to register the aftermath my confession may have. Nothing but the chase of climax is on my mind.

"Do you want me to help you come?" The animalistic roughness of his voice tightens every muscle in my body.

"Yes, please, Master Chains," I practically beg as my eyes flick to my bedroom door to ensure it's closed. I don't know why I'm being so modest. I just asked a stranger to help me orgasm. I don't think modesty has a place in my personality anymore.

I scissor my legs together when Master Chains' throaty groan sounds down the line. I've never heard anything as provocative in my life.

The sound of a chair being dragged across a wooden floor booms into my ears before Master Chains says, "If you follow every command I give, I will let you come."

My lungs saw in and out as I bob my chin. "Okay."

"Every command, Cleo. No hesitation," he warns, his tone commanding.

"I understand," I advise, panting.

"Good girl," he says, pleased.

With my eyes snapped shut, I follow the instructions Master Chains recites down the line. I slither my hand over my quivering stomach, stopping just above the rim of my daisy-printed panties. My heart rate kicks up a notch when I dip my fingers inside the waistband of the cotton material. I'm still inches away from the area aching for release, but I'm panting, hot, and on the verge of ecstasy. Master Chains' voice alone is enough to have me sitting on the edge of a very steep cliff, let alone the wicked things he is whispering in my ear.

"You are not to touch your clit, Cleo. You are too sensitive, and I don't want this to be over yet," Master Chains instructs, his voice stern and tempting.

While slipping two fingers between the folds of my pussy to coat them with wetness, I dip my chin. I'm shocked by my brazenness. I didn't even flinch when the warmth of my arousal graced my fingertips. *What's this man doing to me?*

At the request of Master Chains, I open my eyes before sliding my fingers inside of my clenching core. We moan in sync, a rough, thunderous groan that strengthens my excitement when my fingers push in deeper.

"Tell me what it feels like, Cleo. Are you wet? Tight?"

"Uh huh," I force out, my two short words drowned by a breathless grunt. "It's snug and warm." *And would feel ten times better if it were your fingers.*

Master Chains' rough groans force my fingers to pump into me faster. I raise my backside off my bed and rock my hips in a rhythm matching the thrusts of my fingers. My mind is shut down, my body overwhelmed by the chase of climax. With my other hand, I press my cell closer to my ear, loving the fast pants of Master Chains' breaths coming down the line. He sounds like his own orgasm is building as rapidly as mine, and it adds to my excitement.

In an embarrassingly short period of time, the familiar tightening of an impending climax spreads across my core. The walls of my vagina clamp around my fingers, and my pussy grows wetter.

"I'm close," I warn, my entire body quaking.

The scent of my arousal mingles with the cool fall air when I kick the duvet off my legs, my body too overheated with desire to need the warmth of a blanket. My knees shake when I use the pad of my palm to add pressure to my throbbing clit. It sends a jolt of ecstasy to my drenched core.

"Oh god," I grunt over and over again, too stuck in the trance of climax to garble more coherent words.

"Not yet," Master Chains shouts down the line. "Do not come, Cleo. Do you understand me?"

"Oh... please... I'm so close." My words are separated by desperate moans, my need to come blinding me.

"Control the desire, Cleo. Enjoy the sensation of being in the current without being swept away by it," Master Chains demands, his clipped tone ensuring my body jumps to his command.

I lick my dry lips before slowing the grinding of my fingers. The tingle spreading from my core to my budded nipples remains strong, but the haze of climax isn't as powerful.

"Good girl," Master Chains praises, noticing my breaths have decreased. "Enjoy the feeling—the sensation. Take your time exploring your beautiful body without racing to the finish line."

While listening to Master Chains whisper in my ear, I take in the way my vagina massages my fingers with every plunge I do. How there is a little nub at the end of my cervix that spasms when my fingertips brush past it, and how there isn't a drug in the world that could replicate the high I get during sexual activities. I also close my eyes and think about the man with the entrancing green gaze and more-than-tempting body.

I don't know how much time passes before Master Chains finally says, "Use your shoulder to hold your cell to your ear so your other hand can play with your clit."

Eagerly, I nod before doing as instructed. The slickness coating my sex dampens when the pad of my thumb rolls over the throbbing hood of my clit. I release a throaty moan, expressing everything my body is feeling without a word seeping from my lips.

"Start slow, Cleo. Gentle rolls and soft flicks. Work your body until you feel like you are about to combust, then stop."

I groan and disappointment sears through me.

"Soon, Cleo. Very soon," Master Chains promises.

As my fingers pump in and out of my soaked sex, I roll, tweak and flick my clit with my thumb. I build up my excitement to the point of snapping three times before Master Chains finally gives me permission to come.

"Prepare yourself, Cleo. It will be unlike anything you've ever felt," he warns.

He wasn't lying.

I scream a glass-shattering squeal when the most life-altering orgasm I've ever experienced shreds through me. I thrust and buck against the mattress, my mind hazed with lust, my body heightened beyond belief. Dizziness clusters in my mind as my entire body quakes. My orgasm is powerful, strong, and so blinding, I fail to notice my phone has slipped away from my ear.

It takes several long and tedious minutes for the shakes of climax to dissipate. My orgasm is welcomed and long, but utterly draining. Ashamedly, it's the strongest orgasm I've ever had, not just self-induced.

After running the back of my hand across my sweat-beaded forehead, I secure my cell off my pillow and push it against my ear.

The tingles still causing havoc with my libido intensify when Master Chains whispers, "Happy Birthday, Cleo."

It's the struggle of my life to reply, "Thank you, Master Chains."

13

Feeling my cell phone vibrating in my pocket, I attempt to interrupt Mrs. Collard, Miguel's ninety-six-year-old legally deaf grandmother. When she fails to acknowledge my attempts to interrupt her reciting the pumpkin biscuit recipe she used to make the rock-hard brick sitting untouched on my plate for the fifth time, I inconspicuously slip my phone out of my dress pocket and peer down at the screen.

The girly giggle rippling through my lips gains me the attention of Miguel and his oldest son, Preston, who are refilling their drinks at a small bar in Miguel's living room. With Lexi and Jackson's relationship blossoming nicely, Miguel's wish for us to have a combined Thanksgiving like our family did years ago was granted. It not only gave me the chance to cook the secret family recipe Miguel's wife Janice shared with me months ago, but it also gave Miguel the opportunity to set me up with his eldest son, Preston.

Preston is a wonderful man. Just like his youngest brother, he works in the medical field. His conversations are intelligent, and his looks are top shelf, but he is missing one element I seem to be craving the past eight weeks: the intrigue of mystery. Now, if I were being fair I would admit it isn't Preston's fault he has failed to secure my attention. That blame solely lies with the gentleman who just sent me a GIF of Tinker Bell being spanked.

Snubbing Lexi's curious glance peering at me over her wine glass, I reply to Master Chains' text.

Cleo: *She doesn't look very impressed.*

Agitated excitement makes me restless as I await his reply.

Master Chains: *That's because she hasn't reached the good part yet.*

Cleo: *Good part?*

Time slows to a snail's pace as I impatiently wait for my phone to buzz, indicating it has received a new message.

Master Chains: *Sweet sex is nice, Cleo, but being taken hard and fast after being spanked is even nicer.*

I curve my knees inwards before adjusting my position, wanting to ensure no one sees the flash of heat creeping up my neck from his reply. Even receiving numerous messages like this one the past two weeks hasn't dampened their effect in the slightest. They are still as core-tingling as ever.

Just as we did the weeks following our first conversation, Master Chains and I have continued with our nightly discussion. Although we now text numerous times throughout the day as well. I like to pretend my little slip-up the night of my birthday didn't alter my relationship with Master Chains, but that would be a lie. Although our conversations are still fun and flirty, the sexual vibe cracking between us has most certainly ramped up a notch. Our relationship has always been bizarre, but we've now reached the fevered pitch of oddly compelling. I shouldn't be surprised, though. What Master Chains planned for my birthday was out of this world—it was the most kindhearted thing anyone has done for me—so I shouldn't have expected the day to end on anything but an awe-inspiring high.

A ghost of a smile cracks my lips when an ideal response to Master Chains' text pops into my head. My fingers fly wildly over the screen of my phone so my brief taps drown out the silence encroaching me.

Cleo: *I guess that's something I'll have to take your word on. I have no experience being fucked after a spanking.*

Like he has done several times the past six weeks, Master Chains intuits my reply. His message arrives at the same time mine was received.

Master Chains: *If I have it my way, that won't be a concern of yours much longer, Cleo.*

A shudder runs the length of my spine when I recall the seductive way my name rolled off his tongue after our heated exchange two weeks ago. Well, if I am being honest, not all my spine-tingling response is from remembering the way he says my name. Some of it's from his assumption we will be meeting soon. Although the subject of us meeting has been discussed many times the prior six weeks, Master Chains' efforts have been bolstered since my birthday. I don't know if his eagerness stems from our heated exchange or because he has stated numerous times he is returning home this week after an extended stint on the west coast of the country.

My focus shifts back to the present when my phone vibrates in my hand.

Master Chains: *Was that a pause of contemplation or commiseration?*

Cleo: *More like condemnation!*

His reply pops up in an instant.

Master Chains: *Don't be too hard on your heart. It's the sensible one. It's the only one not denying its desires.*

My mouth gapes, shocked he read the hidden statement in my text. I wasn't condemning him or his suggestion, I was condemning my body's reaction to his playful text. You'd think the effect his wicked words create would dampen since we've been talking for weeks. They haven't. Not the slightest. I don't think months or years will ever change the outcome his words create on my body. And don't get me started on his sultry could-melt-chocolate voice. My apprehensions are at my weakest when we talk. Thank god today we've reverted to texting each other. It may be the only chance I have left to maintain my shrewdness when it comes to him and my woozy-with-wine brain.

The only reason we've relapsed to messaging each other today is because we are in the attendance of Thanksgiving functions and didn't want to be rude to those who invited us. I'll be honest, I miss hearing his voice. I've spent the last three hours glancing at the clock, calculating how much time I need to wait once dessert is served before I can excuse myself without being rude.

Is that bad of me to say? Should I be ashamed to admit I'm missing a man whose real name is still a mystery to me? The little voice inside me says no, it doesn't believe you need to see someone in the flesh to have a connection with them, but my rational head knows I am wading into muddy waters. I only met Master Chains as I was investigating a BDSM club he owns, so believing I have any type of connection with him should be utterly absurd. *Shouldn't it?*

Swallowing down the overcooked glazed duck creeping up my esophagus from my silent thoughts, I shut down my cell and slide it into the pocket of my oversized purse. With my heart the heaviest it's been the past eight weeks, I accept the glass of chardonnay Preston is holding out for me.

"Boyfriend troubles?" Preston questions, nudging his head to my handbag I just placed my phone in.

My heart squeezes in my chest. "Umm... no," I reply with a brisk shake of my head. "Just an acquaintance checking in."

Preston's lips quirk. He seems genuinely surprised by my response. "That wasn't the same person you've been texting all afternoon?"

I lift my eyes to his, taking in the crispness of his buttoned-up shirt, the five o'clock shadow on his rigid jaw, and his straight and defined nose on the way. A sense of familiarity overcomes me when I lock my eyes with his glistening baby blues.

"Yeah, it was," I answer honestly, sick of the constant lies spilling from my lips the past six weeks.

The mask of shock on Preston's handsome face intensifies. "So is the pained look in your eyes because your stomach is having a disagreement with Grandma's biscuits, or is it twisted up over the man your mind hasn't wandered from the entire night?"

Shock gnaws at my chest. I've never had someone read me so easily before. Well, excluding Master Chains. He doesn't even need to see my face to know what I am thinking. He can read my emotions by hearing nothing but the sounds of my breath over a cell phone.

"I'm guessing it's the guy you've been secretly texting all night," Preston continues when he spots the chaotic range of emotions expressed by my forthright eyes.

"Am I that readable?" I attempt to quip.

The remorse in my words defeats my effort to be playful. I'm not remorseful over my confusing relationship with Master Chains, I'm regretful at my lack of politeness. Miguel and his family invited me into their home for

Thanksgiving, and I've shown my gratefulness by spending the entire time on my phone. My mother would be rolling in her grave at my appalling behavior.

Preston laughs a scrumptious chuckle that eases the heaviness of guilt sitting on my chest. "Your distraction was just a wee bit obvious." He expands his index finger and thumb to emphasize his response.

"Sorry," I apologize, beyond revolted by my lack of manners. "I swear I am not normally so rude."

"You have nothing to be sorry about, Cleo. Your distraction means no one has noticed my own disinterest in grandma's burnt turkey," he jests with a waggle of his brows.

Heat spreads across my chest. This is the Preston I remember from my childhood years. Although he isn't as vocal as his younger brother, he has a welcoming and forthcoming side.

My brow cocks into my hairline. "Is your *distraction* anyone I know?" I drawl out overdramatically, more than happy to steer our conversation away from my rude behavior. "Because you know as well as I do, if your father discovers you're not dating a Montclair local, you're *not* dating."

For the first time in the years I've known him, Preston's cheeks get a hue of pink. My heart rate kicks into overdrive. I've never met a man who blushes before.

By the time Preston shares the details of his newly flourishing relationship, hours have ticked by on the clock. I'm glad I managed to rein in my rudeness long enough to appreciate the kind gesture Miguel and Janice instilled by inviting us for Thanksgiving dinner. Tonight proved why they were such close friends of my parents': they are wonderful people who have raised two very smart and well-mannered men.

"Thank you so much for inviting us, I had a wonderful time." I lean in to press a kiss to Miguel's cheek, the sentiment of my words unable to be missed.

"The pleasure was mine, dear Cleo, let's hope another four years doesn't go by before we do it all again," he responds, returning my gesture.

"It won't, I promise," I vow before issuing the same farewell to Janice.

After bidding farewell to Preston and Jackson with a brisk wave, I slide into the driver's seat of my baby-poo brown Buick. With Lexi's goodbye to Jackson taking a little longer than I anticipated, I pull my phone out of my purse and fire it up. The lazy beat of my heart kicks up a gear when the screen illuminates I've missed six text messages from Master Chains and even more unanswered calls.

Through a trembling heart, I decide to read his messages before tackling my full voicemail. His first two messages follow a similar path as the ones we've been exchanging a majority of the day. They are playful and flirty, and clearly show we've stepped over the line acceptable for friends. The middle two texts allude to his annoyance at my failure to reply to his messages. They are crammed with palpable tension and send my heart rate rocketing. The last two messages... they abundantly prove his creepy stalking skills have flourished the past few weeks. They are somewhat concerning, to say the least.

I'd like to say I am surprised by his reaction, but that would be a lie. It doesn't take a genius to assume a man with a commanding aura like Master Chains has a possessive vibe attached to his personality. I've used it numerous times the past few weeks when taunting him. Even knowing I shouldn't goad a man like Master Chains, I can't help it. There is something about him that makes me act young and reckless, and unfortunately, along with that recklessness comes the desire to make him jealous. I won't lie, my confidence skyrocketed every time he reacted to one of my teases. It's a dangerous game I shouldn't be participating in but can't help but love. It's kind of like candy. You know it isn't good for you, but you don't stop eating it until every delicious piece is devoured.

Acting purely on the instincts of my guilt-riddled heart, I scroll down my list of my contacts, hit Master Chains' name, and lift my phone to my ear.

He answers not even two seconds later, "One of my drivers will collect you tomorrow afternoon," he says, not bothering to issue a greeting.

"It's Cleo," I reply, assuming he has mistaken my number as another caller.

"I am well aware of that," he informs me, his deep tone clipped and brimming with tension.

A sense of unease washes over me. Although I anticipated his cold response to my lack of contact the past four hours, something still seems off-kilter with his abrupt replies. Not once has he exerted anger towards me the past six weeks—not even when we tackled controversial issues like his need to have control in the bedroom, or how he hasn't had a relationship outside of the usual Dom/sub liaison affiliated with the BDSM lifestyle. So, to say I'm somewhat shocked by the invisible anger radiating down the line would be an understatement—a major one.

"What are you doing?" I ask when the pants of his breath increase. He sounds like he is running a marathon.

"Packing," Master Chains snaps.

A tense stretch of silence passes between us, crammed with palpable friction. My mind is too scrambled trying to work out where he is going to uphold an intellectual conversation. He has only just returned home yesterday, so I'm shocked—and perhaps a little devastated—he is packing again so soon.

I push my phone in close to my ear when a male voice I don't recognize breaks through the sound of feet stomping down a set of stairs.

"Tell Cameron I want to be in the air in an hour, I want to touch down in New York no later than dawn," I hear Master Chains instruct his male caller.

"Yes, Sir. Your car is waiting out front as per your request," responds a mature male voice.

When the silence makes the shrilling of my pulse noticeable, I mumble, "You're coming to New York?" I'm sure he can hear the hammering of my heart in my voice.

"Yes, Cleo, I am coming to New York," Master Chains responds, his voice gruff and loaded with annoyance I haven't dealt with the prior eight weeks.

When a vehicle door slamming shut sounds down the line, closely followed by the noise of tires rolling over asphalt, reality smacks into me.

"You're coming to New York now?!" I squeal in surprise.

My eyes rocket to the clock in the dashboard of my car. It displays it's a little after 2 AM.

I hear muffled static like a cell being connected to Bluetooth before Master Chains tersely replies, "Yes."

"Why?" I practically scream while striving to overlook the way his clipped replies aren't just sending my heart rate into overdrive. My libido has also gone into meltdown mode.

"You wanted me to react, Cleo. I'm reacting." The serene calmness of his low tone doesn't match his response.

I balk as my mouth gapes open and closed, but not a peep escapes my lips, my mouth refusing to relinquish another lie from my indecisive brain. Although I'd like to plead innocence, I can't. After hearing Preston talk about the dates he and his new flame have been on, I was struck with a severe case of envy, which in turn, pushed me into idiocy territory. I want to have a picnic in Central Park before taking a ride in the back of a horse-drawn carriage.

I try to tell myself I don't want my relationship with Master Chains to go any further than pen pals using modern technology to our benefit, but that isn't true. I ignored his calls as I wanted to force a reaction out of him, because if he didn't react, I'd know the bizarre feeling that twists in my stomach every time I think of him is nothing but foolish hope—*hope that I'm not completely insane.*

My lips quiver as I begin to speak, "I'm sorry for not returning your calls. What I did was immature and uncalled for, but it doesn't require you to fly to New York at 2 AM. Why don't we take tonight to calm down, then we will talk about this like adults tomorrow?" I suggest, my words as weak as my apology.

The heavy regret on my chest lightens when Master Chains replies, "Talking is one of the many things we will do this weekend." My heart hangs halfway between my chest and my stomach when he continues, "Because I very much look forward to hearing your reasoning for taunting me in person."

"In person?" I strangle out, my words choking past the lump his declaration rammed in my throat.

"Yes, Cleo, in person." He sounds calm and put together—a stark contrast to the hyperventilating composure his response caused me.

"You're going to need to fill me in. I'm a little lost."

Pretending he can't hear the deceit in my comment, Master Chains explains, "You're spending the weekend with me at my property in New York."

"Ah... no, I'm not," I reply, briskly shaking my head. "I have commitments, work, plans with..."

My voice trails off when I fail to find another excuse to issue him. The only plans I have this long weekend is catching up on the episodes of *The Walking Dead* I missed the past six weeks talking to him, striving not to fall into a food-induced coma from eating the truckload of carbs Janice sent us home with tonight, and if I'm brave, Lexi and I may tackle the Black Friday sales. My plans are no different than any other single American girl.

Master Chains' thigh-quivering growl returns my focus to him. "Just a word of warning, Cleo: if you lie to me in person, some form of punishment will be issued."

Shockingly, blood surges to the lower region of my body from his threat. I writhe in my seat as a range of ways he could punish me filter through my dirty mind. They all involve the leather studded chaise in his playroom and his big manly hand.

Hearing the quickening of my breaths, Master Chains asks, "Curious, Cleo?" His voice is not as calm as it was earlier. It's more gruff and tainted with sexual tension.

It takes a mammoth effort, but I force out, "No."

The pulse in my soaked sex reaches never-before-achieved levels when Master Chains grinds out, "Strike one. You don't want to know what the repercussions will be when you reach three."

The air is forced from my lungs in one painfully long grunt. *What the hell is wrong with me?* I am being coerced into spending my weekend with a man I don't know, all because I didn't answer his messages in a timeframe he finds suitable, yet, my body gets turned on by his malicious threats. I'm stronger than this, and I am sure as hell no one's submissive.

I stop squirming in my seat at the same time the passenger side door opens and Lexi slides inside my car. Snubbing her curious glance taking in my wide-eyed expression, I whisper down the phone. "I didn't ignore your messages to force you to react. I simply wanted a few hours to bask in the glory of solitude."

I grow more winded when Master Chains growls, "Strike two. If you wanted solitude, you should have done it without a man gazing in your eyes like you were a present sitting under his Christmas tree waiting to be unwrapped."

My eyes bulge. "What the hell are you talking about?" My words are laced with an equal amount of sexual exhilaration and utter shock.

I jump out of my skin when my cell buzzes unexpectedly, announcing I've received a new text. When I pull my phone down from my ear, air traps in the back of my throat, choking me with anxiety. My lungs strain for breath as my eyes drink in two of the three pictures Master Chains forwarded to me. From the red long-sleeve jersey dress I purchased specifically for Miguel's Thanksgiving function, I can easily deduce that these images were taken of me tonight, but the inclusion of Preston in every picture is another foolproof indication.

The reasoning behind Master Chains' switch in composure becomes apparent when I flick to the last picture. With Preston's head angled away from the prying photographer snapping our picture unaware, and my chin tucked into his neck to ensure I could hear him over the music playing, we appear as if we were in an intimate tryst.

"It isn't as it seems," I mutter down the line, pushing aside the fact someone has grossly invaded my privacy. "Preston is a friend. Nothing more."

Several moments pass in uncomfortable silence before Master Chains mutters, "I very much look forward to hearing you tell me that in person tomorrow, Cleo."

14

After making the short four-block trip home, I pace into my room and sit on the edge of my bed, where I remain in silence for several moments, dumbfounded. I'm at a complete loss about what has occurred tonight. Yes, I taunted Master Chains, hoping he would react, but I didn't expect it to go to this level. Furthermore, I never expected to have my privacy so badly invaded. Who in the world would take secret pictures of me with Preston, then forward them to Master Chains? It truly doesn't make any sense. What benefit would they get out of making Master Chains jealous?

Like a truck crashing into a brick wall, reality crashes into me.

I'm going to kill her.

Pushing off my bed, I charge out of my room, my speed unchecked as I search our modest three-bedroom home for any signs of my meddling sister. I find her sitting in the den talking on her cell phone five minutes later. Spotting the fury beaming from my eyes, she advises her caller she needs to go and promises to call them later. I don't wait for her to disconnect her call before I snatch her cell out of her hand and scroll to her messages. The air in my lungs is brutally removed when I discover three identical pictures matching the ones Master Chains forwarded me sitting in the sent box of her messages.

"Are you kidding me?!" I scream, twisting her cell phone around so she can see the pictures of Preston and me sprawled across the screen. "Do you have any idea what you've done? He isn't just jealous about your ridiculous messages, he is coming here—tonight!"

The fear in Lexi's eyes is masked by exhilaration when she processes my declaration. "Chains is coming here?" Her high tone abundantly proves she has no qualms about meddling in my private affairs. "To see you?"

"Yes!" I reply, throwing my arms up in the air. "When I called to apologize for my childish behavior, I discovered he was in the midst of packing. If that wasn't already shocking enough, imagine discovering he was packing because he assumed I was ignoring his messages due to my getting cozy with another man!"

I feel my anger growing from the tips of my toes to my face when the excitement blazing in Lexi's eyes turns blinding. "Come on, Sis, you have to admit, his reaction is hot. He's coming here because he wants to stop you playing tongue wars with anyone but him. That's fucking hot."

"That's *not* hot, it's childish!" I sneer, my low voice successfully hiding the deceit in my reply. Even though I am beyond ropeable, excitement is still quickening my pulse.

Lexi glares at me like I've grown a second head. "What woman doesn't love a brooding, temperamental, jealous man?"

"The woman investigating him!" I shout, my face reddening with anger.

"*Was* investigating," Lexi corrects. "Your assignment regarding Chains ended *weeks* ago—the instant you started talking to him."

"And if they decide to reopen it?" I cock my hip and spread my hands across my waist. "What happens then?"

Lexi shrugs. "We'll cross that bridge when it comes."

"It isn't that simple," I shout, throwing my hands into the air.

"Yeah, it is. If the case gets reopen, you cite bias," she suggests, like she has taken some time considering my predicament.

"The job of a journalist is *not* to stamp out bias. We're supposed to *manage* it."

"Then manage it!" Lexi yells, her scratchy voice relaying she is close to having a coughing fit. "You knew from the moment you returned Chains' first message you were creating a conflict of interest between your personal life and work life, yet, you still sent it, and thousands of messages since."

"That doesn't change the facts, Lexi. You had no right to do what you did! No right at all." The anger in my voice isn't as high strung as it was when I first walked into the den. It's been strangled by the truth in Lexi's replies. I knew my relationship with Master Chains was tiptoeing in a dangerous minefield, but no matter how many times I tried to shut it down, I couldn't.

"I did what I did as I knew you would never work up the courage to do it," Lexi enlightens me as she stands from the couch. "It's time for your relationship with Chains to move forward. I helped you do that."

I hold her gaze, my lips twitching, my fists clenched at my side. "The pace of our relationship wasn't your decision to make. And even if for some insane reason it was, who's to say this is what I wanted?"

"Your six-hour-long conversations you've had with him every night the past month," Lexi fires back, her voice rising in anger. "The combined hours of your conversations are triple the amount of time I've spoken to Jackson in our entire relationship. We've been together for over two months, I've studied every groove of his body, and I've slept with him more times than I can count, but do you see us burning the candle at both ends talking for six hours every night?"

Not waiting for me to reply, she continues speaking, "No, you don't, as most people realize when they've reached the next step in their relationship." She locks her determined eyes with mine. "You've reached the next step."

"Did you ever stop to think we only communicate over the phone as the ability to hold an intellectual conversation is the only thing we have in common?" I query, my brows becoming lost in my hairline. "Compatibility is much more than just holding a conversation, Lexi."

While crossing her arms over her chest, Lexi glares into my eyes. Her narrowed gaze calls out my deceit without a single word escaping her hard-lined lips. She knows me well enough to know every vicious word fired off my tongue is a complete lie.

"This isn't what I wanted, Lexi. Not like this," I continue to argue, my Garcia stubbornness not allowing me to back down from our disagreement. "I wanted us to take the next step when we were ready, not because we were forced to."

Needing to leave the room before she spots the indecisiveness in my eyes, I spin on my heels and enter the hallway.

My brisk strides down the corridor stop when Lexi yells, "It isn't nice having your whole life planned out for you, is it?!"

I take three calming breaths before pivoting around to face her. The fury turning my blood black dissipates when I see the pain etched on her beautiful face. Her eyes are red and brimming with tears, and her lips are quivering.

"I've had that my whole life, Cleo. What I can do. What I can eat. What I can wear. I even get told how to breathe," she whispers, her voice relaying she is on the verge of tears. "First by Mom, then by you."

"That's because we love you, Lexi, we only want the best for you." The heavy sentiment in my voice bolsters my statement.

Lexi nods in agreeance. "As I do for you too, Cleo. That's why I did what I did. Just as you have done every day of my life, I'm pushing you to live your life to the fullest."

The angry tension firing between us becomes a distant memory when she moves to stand in front of me. "If only you could see the way your face lights up when you talk about him, Cleo, then you'd understand why I'm begging you not to run away from this like every other relationship you've had. You want this—*you need this*—you're just too scared to admit it."

"It's not that," I reply, running my index finger across my cheek to ensure no tears have fallen from my eyes. "Even if I wasn't scared about how crazy he makes me feel, we are from two different worlds. I don't even know his real name, Lexi. He is practically a stranger."

Lexi shakes her head. "I don't believe that, not for a single minute. Our walls are paper thin. I've heard you talking to him many times the past month. You know him, and he knows you—the real Cleo, not the one you think is socially acceptable."

Even with a surge of blood gushing to my heart from her declaration, I continue to argue. "You don't understand. What we have isn't normal. He isn't... *normal*."

Guilt overwhelms me, making it hard for me to breathe when the last sentence is forced out of my mouth. I've spent weeks debating with Master Chains my ability to make my own informed decision, yet I'm still judging him because he owns a BDSM club, instead of the man presented to me every night.

Lexi runs her hand down my arm before locking her glistening eyes with mine. "Thank god for that, as the last thing you need is someone normal. Normal is predictable. Normal is boring. Normal is living your life without a single adventure. Nobody wants normal, Cleo. I sure as hell don't, and neither should you."

"I'm no expert, but I'm fairly certain it isn't normal to get incredibly turned on at the idea of being spanked," I spit out before I can stop my words.

"It isn't?" Lexi recants, her voice high and void of its earlier emotions. After looping her arm around mine, she walks down the corridor, dragging me with her. "I sure as hell hope Jackson doesn't catch on to your ideas of what is and isn't normal, because spankings are one of my favorite things."

I gasp in a shocked breath as my wide eyes rocket to Lexi. She glares at me with her manicured brows waggling. I bump her with my hip, which sends her beautiful laugh into the night air. I shouldn't be surprised by her admission. She has always been the wild child of our family. I'm not. I'm the safe, guarded sister who dreams of long walks on the beach and soft, gentle lovemaking.

The little voice inside me roars to life, vehemently denying every statement I just made. It stomps its feet like a five-year-old and crosses its arms over its chest. I'm so goddamn confused. Logically, I know just talking to a man in the BDSM lifestyle is frowned upon. But Master Chains' logic of not caring about the opinions of others is rubbing off on me. Nothing but silly giddiness consumes me when I think about him. Shouldn't something like that be explored instead of ignored?

Wanting to change the tempo of our conversation before I hear reason to my reckless thoughts, I keep my voice friendly and composed while saying, "You know how there are certain things you can never erase from your mind?"

Lexi nods, a little overeagerly.

"The vision of Jackson spanking you is one of those things," I mutter, faking a gag. "The next time you want to share details of your sex life, can you issue a warning first? I'm having a hard enough time keeping down the charcoaled turkey as it is."

Lexi's infectious laugh fills the space, instantly erasing any leftover anger harbored in the back of my mind.

"Okay, I promise to issue a warning about all future sex discussions... on one condition," she barters, spinning around to face me.

A smile cracks onto my mouth when I see the cheekiness beaming from her eyes. She truly is the most annoying, opinionated and beautiful young lady I've ever met.

My smile sags the instant she mumbles, "Give Chains a chance. If you meet him and hate him, we'll never mention his name again."

"And what if I have the opposite reaction? What if he is everything I've wished for and more?" I ask, expressing my true concerns for the first time this evening.

Lexi grasps both of my hands in hers and squeezes them tightly. "Then you grab ahold of him and never let go."

"And my job?" I barely whisper. "What happens to that?"

Lexi peers at me with a set of eyes much wiser than her twenty-one years. "You go back to writing about people who lost their lives instead of living yours as if it has already ended."

15

"Cleo Garcia?"

Hugging my dressing gown tightly to my body, I dip my chin to the male caller standing on the stoop of my stairs. With the clock only just hitting 8 AM and it being Black Friday, I'm somewhat ill-prepared for guests.

"Sign here please," he instructs, twisting a steel clipboard around to face me.

After scribbling my name across the courier delivery strip, the blond-haired man tears out the receiver's copy of the delivery confirmation form and hands it to me with a plain white envelope.

"Thank you," I stutter out, confusion in my tone as I shut the door.

With the early winter chill left outside, I loosen my grip on my dressing gown and rip open the thin envelope. Before my eyes can skim the six-page document, I spot Lexi staggering out of her room. Her eyes are puffy, and she has a large drool stain on her left cheek.

"Did I hear a male voice?" she queries, her voice groggy from just waking up.

"Yeah, it was a courier driver delivering this document," I reply, nudging my head to my hands.

Shock morphs onto Lexi's face, mimicking mine to a T. As she slowly trudges towards me, I drop my eyes to the document. The longer my eyes scan the official-looking paperwork, the more my empty stomach rumbles. It isn't grumbling due to lack of nutrients, it's protesting about the blank non-disclosure agreement the courier just delivered.

Upon spotting the contempt on my face, Lexi's pace quickens. "What is it?" She stops beside me. The smell of her Roxy perfume filters into my nostrils when she leans across my body so she can peruse the document.

"This is your idea of normal," I mumble, the fast rate of my heart relayed in my voice. "Master Chains requires me to sign a non-disclosure agreement before we can meet today."

"No shit," Lexi squeals, her eyes bugging out of her head. "I told you he was *loaded*." She emphasizes the last word of her sentence with a shameful flair money-hungry trophy wives use.

"More like insane if he thinks I'll sign this," I interrupt, my tone lowering as anger boils my veins. "Not only can I not legally sign this form, I morally refuse to."

"You have to sign it," Lexi debates, removing the document from my hand. "If you don't sign it, you can't spend the weekend with Chains."

I shrug my shoulders. "Exactly. No skin off my nose," I lie.

I barely catch Lexi's dropped-jaw expression as I spin on my heels and stride to my bedroom.

"Cleo, we discussed this last night. I thought we came to an agreement?" Lexi bickers, shadowing me into my room.

"That was before he slapped me with an NDA," I interject, padding to my bed. "If you think I'm going to spend a weekend with a man who requires me to sign a contract before we can officially meet, you don't know me very well. That document is not just rude, pretentious and arrogant, it undermines every conversation we've had the past six weeks."

"How?" Lexi disputes, her eyes watching me like a hawk as I hunt for my cell phone in the overnight bag I stupidly packed in haste this morning.

Failing to find my cell amongst the mountain load of clothes I packed, I twist my body to face Lexi. "Because it represents that every word he spoke was a lie."

Lexi stares at me, her confusion growing tenfold.

"If he was being honest, don't you think it's a little too late for a non-disclosure agreement?"

"No." Lexi shakes her head. "He is protecting his identity, Cleo, not himself. In his industry, it's a smart thing for him to do."

The way she defends him makes me wonder if last night was the first time she's had contact with Master Chains.

"And who's protecting me?"

"Me," Lexi replies without pause for consideration. "Do you truly think I'd encourage you to meet him if I thought he was dangerous? I might be desperate for you to start living, but I'd never put you in danger."

She uncrosses her arms and pushes off her feet. "Stop looking for an excuse to get out of this meeting. You want this, you're just frightened by what that means."

I scoff, feigning innocence. Lexi arches her brow, silently calling out my deceit. She knows exactly what I'm feeling. I barely slept a wink last night as my stomach was a horrid mess of excitement and unease. I do want this, I just don't want the messiness associated with it. If I had met Master Chains under different circumstances, I wouldn't hesitate to meet him. But considering I only met him as I was investigating his club makes the unease gurgling in my stomach wind up my throat.

Pulling her cellphone out of the pocket of her fluffy robe, Lexi hands it to me. "Instead of getting yourself all worked up, call him and explain your concerns about the NDA. If he doesn't understand your hesitation, don't go and see him. Simple."

Ignoring the feeling of disappointment pumping into me, I accept the cell from Lexi, dial Master Chains' number I know by heart, and push her phone to my ear. My brows scrunch when I get an automated response saying the number is no longer in service. Acting like I am unaware of the workings of cell phone service, I scroll to the messages Lexi sent him last night and type a short message requesting for him to call me. The same automated response about his number no longer being in service is received via text not even two seconds later.

Lexi's confused eyes track me as I cross the room and log into the Chains website. The already dangerous beat of my heart kicks up a gear when I discover a big red cross next to Master Chains' online account. His profile has been stripped of any information, and his shadowed profile picture has been replaced with the standard inactive account one you find on all social media sites.

"What the hell?" I mumble, my confusion boosting by the second. "His account has been revoked."

A blinding smile stretches across Lexi's tired face. "I guess he doesn't need an online persona when the real Master Chains is about to be unveiled."

Panicked excitement engulfs me. Spotting my flabbergasted appearance, the smug look on Lexi's face grows. "Does that mean you have to tell him in person you have no intention of signing his NDA?"

Barely holding in my flipping stomach, I reply, "Yeah, I guess that's what I must do."

Lexi's eyes flare, and exhilaration beams out of her. Fighting not to let her excitement rub off on me, I force a fake snarl onto my face. Lexi doesn't buy my attempts at acting unaffected. She knows as well as I do, I don't have a chance in hell of listening to my astute brain when I am in Master Chains' presence. The odds of me backing out of our agreement in person is just as unlikely as me not meddling in Lexi's love life. They are slim to none.

Approximately six hours later, I am sitting in the back of a silver Jaguar as it rolls towards the Brooklyn Bridge. Nervous butterflies flutter in my stomach and a misting of sweat coats my forehead. Snubbing the handkerchief hanging out of a pocket of the overnight bag Lexi placed on the seat next to me, I secure one of the tissues from the middle console of the Jaguar to dab the sweat off my face.

"Just in case you change your mind," Lexi jested while placing my bag next to me.

My eyes open wide in shock when the Jaguar veers off the road just before we hit the Brooklyn Bridge. It comes to a stop at an underpass a few streets back. The rise and fall of my chest intensifies when a high-class BMW pulls in next to us not even ten seconds later. I exhale a deep breath to calm the nerves running rampant through my body. It does nothing to ease the panic scorching me alive. I am a quivering bag of nerves.

The skittish tension making my skin a clammy mess gets a moment of reprieve when a fierce looking middle-aged gentleman clambers out of the BMW and paces towards my stationary vehicle. Not speaking, he opens the back passenger door and slides into the seat next to me. Wanting to ensure his wide frame has enough room, I remove my overnight bag from the seat and place it on my lap. My nerves have me jittering so much, my bag physically shakes.

After wiping a thick layer of sweat from the top of his brow, the man mutters, "NDA."

"Excuse me?" I mumble, unsure if he is talking to me or the driver. Considering he hasn't looked at either of us—let alone issued a greeting—I can't be sure whom he is speaking to. "Are you talking to me?"

The buttons on his dark blue business suit struggle to conceal the rigid bumps of his stomach when he adjusts his position to face me. My heart smashes against my ribs when his desolate eyes glare into mine. If this man is setting out to intimidate me, he is doing a mighty fine job.

"The NDA that was delivered to you this morning, Cleo, where is it?" he snarls.

Shocked by his rudeness, my lips thin in grimness, but not a syllable expels from my stunned mouth. When my eyes unwittingly drop to the white envelope sitting between us, he follows my gaze. I balk when his hand delves out to snatch the envelope off the dark gray leather bench.

After placing the document under the crook of his arm, he hands a single yellow post-it note to the Jaguar driver before exiting the vehicle.

"Oh... I didn't sign it," I stammer out.

My words are too late. The Jaguar door is brutally thrown closed, and it commences rolling off the curb before the first word escapes my lips.

With my heart in my throat, I scoot to the edge of my seat and lock my shocked gaze with the pair of blue eyes peering at me in the rearview mirror. "Excuse me, I need to speak to the gentleman at the bridge. Can you please take me back to him?" I point to the large brute of a man talking into his cellphone at the side of the BMW to emphasize my request.

"No," the driver replies, his voice slurred with a heavy accent I don't recognize. "We go to this address." He taps his finger onto the post-it note stuck to his steering wheel.

"I don't want to go to that address. I need you to either take me back to the gentleman in the BMW or take me home."

"No," he repeats, "we go to this address." He taps on the post-it note so hard, the Jaguar's horn sounds into the late afternoon air.

"Sir, please, you need to understand what I'm saying. If you don't take me back to that man so I can explain I didn't sign the forms he just took, your position could be compromised." My next sentence comes out in a flurry when the driver commences rolling up the privacy partition between us. "I'll pay you double the rate they are paying if you will just take me back to the man at the bridge."

I plead to my reflection in the tinted glass window for twenty minutes before I give in to the fact I'm not going anywhere other than the address listed on the post-it note. Slouching in defeat, I pull my cellphone out of my pocket to send Lexi a message on my kidnapped status.

Me: *Thanks to you, I've been kidnapped. Send help. I'm trapped in the back of a Jaguar as it weaves through the streets of Tribeca.*

Lexi: *Your GPS has been tracked, and a SWAT team is on high alert. At first signs of an orgasm, a group of tall, dark, and drool-worthy armed men will arrive to rescue you from such treachery! Do not fear, Cleo, your virtue will not be sacrificed for the greater good.*

Even with nervous butterflies fluttering in my stomach, a giggle topples from my lips when I read her reply. I don't know why I'm shocked by her response. There has only been one time I've seen Lexi serious: the months following our parents' and little brother's death. I lost a lot of sleep those months wondering if she would ever recover from our loss. It was a challenging time for everyone involved, but it seemed to hit Lexi harder than anyone.

It was only after enduring one of the hardest discussions we ever had did I realize what her worries pertained to. Lexi wasn't just grieving our devastating loss, she was suffering the effects of guilt. Unlike me, her guilt wasn't attached to her grief. It was because the morning after Tate's wake she realized, one day, I'll be left all alone. I've never loved my sister more than I did that day. She wasn't worried about CF taking her away in the prime of her life, all she cared about was leaving me alone. That selflessness was what made me pledge to do everything in my power to ensure her final years are her best. I've strived for that goal every day since.

After wiping under my eyes to ensure no sneaky tears spilled, I respond to Lexi's message.

Me*: I'm not sure dark, drool-worthy men will help save my virtue, but thanks for the offer.*

Lexi: *You are so hard to please, Cleo. First, you're fighting off a man whose voice sounds like it could melt chocolate, now you're denying the help of a group of core-clenching SWAT members. What's wrong with you?*

My mouth gapes as suspicion runs wild through my veins.

Me*: How do you know what Master Chains' voice sounds like?*

The noise of traffic, beeping horns, and the angry slurs of road-raging motorists fade into the background as I await Lexi's reply.

With how much time passes, I am certain she isn't going to respond.

Just as I am about to hit the call button at the top of my message screen, another text from Lexi finally pops up.

Lexi: *We may have spoken previously. But I don't have time to discuss that now, Jackson is about to drive under a bridge... I may lose you... C..l..e..o, are you there? You're. . .breaking up...*

My fingers punch into my phone so hard I'm shocked I don't break the screen.

Me: *You can't fake static interruptions via a message, Lexi!*

Lexi: *Like hell I can't. My big sister taught me I can do anything I set my mind to.*

I grit my teeth.

Me: *Lexi...*

Lexi: *Bye Cleo. I'm switching off my phone now...*

I stare at my cell for several moments, struggling to find an appropriate response. Although my suspicions ran high this morning that she'd been in contact with Master Chains, I pushed it to the background of my mind. Not because I wasn't curious what they talked about, but because I didn't want to run the risk of Lexi finding out about my conversation with Jackson.

I wasn't joking when I disclosed my meddling in Lexi's love life. As her guardian, it's my job to ensure her dates are given the same lecture Luke got from my dad when we first began dating. Although my sermon on the rules of dating a Garcia woman was minus the sweat-producing panic my dad's instilled in Luke, it still had Jackson trembling in his boots.

My heart leaps out of my chest when my phone unexpectedly vibrates in my hand.

Lexi: *I'm not switching off my phone. If an emergency does occur, call me. Until then, let down your hair, push out your monstrous rack and go and have some fun! P.S: I want all the juicy details. P.P.S: opening your heart doesn't mean you have to open your legs, but it's a lot more fun if you do!*

My anger dampens slightly.

Me: *I'm restricting your cable access the instant I get home.*

Lexi: *Meh! Like that will help.*

The uncertainty curled around my heart loosens its firm grip when Lexi's next message comes through.

Lexi: *I love you, Cleo the Creep, and if you'd just give people the chance to see the Cleo I see, the entire world would love you too. Stop listening to everyone around you. Just breathe and be yourself, then everything will turn out fine!*

My heart bursts when I read her last sentence. That's a quote our mother always said to us. She was such a beautiful woman. She never judged, yelled at, or ridiculed us. She just encouraged us to be who we wanted to be, not what society classed as acceptable. *God, I miss her.*

For how long it takes for me to type my reply, anyone would swear I was writing an essay instead of a simple three-word text.

Me: *Okay. I'll try.*

16

Forty minutes and numerous messages later, the Jaguar pulls into an isolated driveway at the end of a narrow road. The crazy beat of my heart surges to a new level when a black wrought iron gate chugs open, exposing an architectural wonder of steel and glass. The curved design of the stainless steel roof softens the hard lines of the white brick pillars holding up the monstrous dwelling, and the floor-to-ceiling windows bounce a multihued beam of light onto the large in-ground pool positioned in front of the spectacular residence.

Dragging my eyes from the wonderment in front of me, I send a final message to Lexi.

Me: *I'm here. Wish me luck.*

Her message returns in an instant.

Lexi: *You don't need it, but I'll give it to you anyway. Good luck! Bye xx*

Me: *Bye xx*

After placing my cell in the front pocket of my overnight bag, I peer out the heavily tinted window. The view switches from magnificent to awe-inspiring when my eyes lock in on a blur of black standing at the front of two large double doors. Disdain for my nearsightedness twists in my chest when my poor vision hinders my endeavor to unveil the face of the person standing in wait. I don't need 20/20 vision to know who is waiting for me, though. From his build alone, I can easily distinguish it's a man, but it's the energetic spark surging through my body that reveals his true identity: it's Master Chains.

After taking a few deep breaths to clear the panic smeared across my face, I curl out of the door the driver is holding open for me. I issue my disdain for his earlier ignorance with a nasty stink eye before I commence walking up the platform-like stairs. The shake of my knees becomes more apparent with every step I take to the blotch of black standing in front of me.

The further I encroach, the more my vision improves—as does the crackling of energy.

"Holy shit," I mumble under my breath when three long blinks clear my vision enough I can see the face of the man waiting to greet me.

"Holy fucking shit," I murmur, louder this time when it dawns on me why his face is so recognizable. He isn't just the ridiculously handsome owner of an exclusive BDSM club in lower Manhattan, nor the man who hasn't strayed from my thoughts the past eight weeks. He is a member of one of the most successful bands in the world. A man worth millions and millions of dollars. He is Marcus Everett, bassist of Rise Up.

"Cleo," Marcus greets in his deep timbre when I stop in front of him, sending a flurry of goosebumps to the surface of my skin.

"Hi," I squeak out, my voice so high it sounds like I haven't hit adulthood yet.

I'm not just shocked to discover Master Chains is a very well-known man, I'm stunned at our bizarre connection. It was the story I ran on the lead singer of Marcus's band being in rehab when he was fighting for his life in ICU that caused my fall from grace four years ago. For months, I blamed Rise Up for being the catalyst of events that destroyed my life. It was only after discovering their publicist was fired for issuing false reports to the media on Noah's whereabouts did I realize the demise of my career wasn't Rise Up's fault. It was the lady behind the helm of their publicity, a woman whose identity I'm still striving to uncover to this date.

My focus reverts back to the present when Marcus places his hand under my chin and lifts my downcast face. I gasp in greedy breaths when the intensity of his eyes hits me full-force. My god, they are truly mesmerizing. I thought they were impressive on the numerous front page spreads he has been on the past four years of his success, but nothing compares to seeing them in real life.

Marcus's eyes scan my face as if he is memorizing each individual pore on my skin. "You are just as I remembered," he murmurs more to himself than me. "I'm glad you came, Cleo. I was concerned the NDA would scare you away," he says, glancing into my eyes.

"Oh...umm ...I..." I roll my eyes at my inability to form an entire sentence. I'm a grown woman for crying out loud, not some teenage girl crushing over a sexy rock star. He is still a man, for goodness sake. *A very handsome, panty-melting man, but still a man nonetheless.*

I wave my hands across the front of my body, physically pushing away my nerves. "In regards to the NDA..." I stammer out before a stunning middle-aged Latina lady appears at his side, interrupting me.

"Do you require anything else, Mr. Everett?" she questions, her beautiful accent on full display.

The heat on my cheeks cools when Marcus removes his scorching eyes from my face to lock them with the lady standing at his side. "No, thank you, Aubrey. Everything is perfect. You are free to go."

The smile on Aubrey's face expands when she is awarded with Marcus's breathtakingly beautiful smile. "Yes, Sir, thank you." She bows her head and steps backward.

The quickest flash of agitation blazes through Marcus's eyes from Aubrey's response before he shuts it down quicker than it arrived. Once Aubrey climbs into the passenger seat of the Jaguar I just exited, it pulls out of the driveway and disappears into the rapidly setting sun, leaving only two living souls in the entire property: Marcus and me.

Oh, shit, this isn't good.

"They're coming back, aren't they?"

The heat spreading through my body intensifies when Marcus places his hand on the curve of my back and guides me into his residence without a peep from his deliciously plump lips. While my eyes bug in awe at the wonderment of his property, he undoes the three buttons on my coat. Although the foyer is decorated in a neutral palette of white veined tiles and sleek furnishings, it still thrusts his wealth in my face. If I weren't already skeptical, this space undoubtedly proves we are on opposing ends of the financial scale. I'm standing in a foyer that screams wealth wearing a tatty coat, while Marcus melds into the opulent surroundings in a dark suit tailored to showcase every spectacular ridge of his panty-drenching body.

After guiding my jacket off my shoulders, Marcus places it and his suit jacket in a concealed coatroom on his right. While pacing back to me, his eyes lower to drink in my whimsical Adrianna Papell dress. This was the very first dress Sasha awarded me with during my internship. It has remained my favorite since that day. With its rounded neckline and free-flowing skirt, it gives a hint of my voluptuous curves without being inundated by them, and the white satin printed material adds an edge of sexiness to the seemingly plain design. I've always felt like royalty any time I've worn this dress. Even more so when I am eyed with the zeal Marcus is awarding me with right now.

Stopping in front of me, Marcus rakes his eyes along the length of my body before locking them with me. He is standing so close, the tips of my budded nipples connect with his light blue dress shirt with every inhalation I take. No thoughts pass through my mind as I return his lusty stare. My brain has once again become mush in his presence.

Just as the tension in the air becomes so dense storm clouds form on the horizon, Marcus asks, "Are you hungry?"

From the way his voice is laced with sexual innuendo, I can't tell if his question is truly about food. I don't know if my confusion stems from being stuck in the haze of lust, or because I am literally braindead from staring into his entrancing eyes too long.

My horrified eyes snap down to my stomach when a loud grumble sounds from it, my body choosing its own response to his question. The embarrassment slicking my skin with a fine layer of sweat gets a pardon when the corners of Marcus's lips tug high before the most dazzling smile graces me with its presence.

"I'll take that as a yes," he mutters, his deep tone unable to hide the laughter in his voice.

While biting on the inside of my cheek, I nod. I am famished, but not all my desires are associated with food. Attraction is too tame of a word to describe what I'm feeling standing across from Master Chains in the flesh. The extreme sexual connection we've been building the past eight weeks is nothing compared to the palpable tension bouncing between us now. It's so explosive it crackles in the air.

The pleas of my hungry stomach are pushed to the background of my mind when Marcus runs his index finger down the sliver of silk draped over my shoulder. He straightens the strap of my dress. His meekest touch sends a scorching pulse to my soaked sex, urging me to squeeze my thighs together. I am equally appalled and excited by my body's response to his touch and incredibly turned on.

After ensuring the strap is in its rightful spot, Marcus locks his eyes back with me. "While we eat, we have a few matters we need to attend to."

"I thought we covered everything with the questionnaire?" I jest with a weak waggle of my brows.

I inwardly sigh, grateful my moronic trance is slowly lifting. There is no bigger turn-off than a grown woman shamefully fawning over a man. Yes, Marcus is an attractive man who makes my mouth salivate, but if I want any chance of keeping our bizarre kinship on an even playing field, I need to rein in the childish prompts of my body by occasionally using its more astute counterpart: my brain.

"We did, but there were a few things the questionnaire didn't elaborate on," Marcus responds as his beautiful eyes dance between mine, holding me captive with both intrigue and wonderment.

"Then why don't we get the formalities out of the way now, then we can enjoy our meal in peace? Tension and food don't mix well," I suggest. "Furthermore, with how much my stomach is twisting, I don't think putting food in there would be a wise idea."

My gaze stops mimicking the movements of Marcus's eyes when he unexpectedly questions, "Did you kiss Preston, Cleo?"

I step backward and gasp in an exasperated breath. With my mind a blurred mess of confusion the past twelve hours, I completely forgot what lead to our impromptu meeting.

"No," I answer with a brief shake of my head. Trying to work out how Marcus knows Preston's name makes what should be a confident statement come out sounding unsure.

I release the breath I am holding in when Marcus continues with his interrogation, verifying he perceived the honesty in my eyes. "Did you want to?" He peers straight into my shocked gaze, his demeanor calm.

Not trusting my voice to relay the honesty of my reply, I shake my head. Either not seeing my response, or choosing to ignore it, Marcus continues staring into my eyes, silently demanding a response.

"No," I eventually mutter when the tension thickening the air becomes too great to ignore.

The tightness in his shoulders physically relaxes as a spark of relief filters through his ageless eyes. Every second we stand across from each other in silence lures me deeper into what is certain to be dangerous territory. Pussy-clenching, will-never-view-sex-in-the-same-light-again, but still dangerous nevertheless.

Shaking my head to release myself from the invisible pull his eyes stimulated, I say, "Since we are sharing, I have a question for you." My words sound forced due to the exhilarating unease wrapped around my throat.

Marcus watches me for a long moment, studying me in-depth before he curtly nods, agreeing to my cross-examination.

Ignoring the hunger for friction against my skin, I ask, "Was last night the only time you've had contact with my sister?"

Bile creeps up my esophagus when Marcus abruptly responds, "No." He gives me a few moments to absorb his statement before he continues, "Lexi contacted me the morning following our first phone conversation, then again this morning."

"And?" I question when he fails to elaborate on his response.

I prick my ears, wanting to ensure I can hear him over the mad beat of my heart when he says, "Both conversations contained the same warning: if I didn't treat you right, there would be repercussions for my actions."

My brows stitch. "That doesn't sound like Lexi."

His lips curl into a wry smirk. "Well, she said it more along the lines of, 'If you fuck with my sister, I'll fuck you over,'" he quotes, his expression deadpan.

I lean forward and burrow my head into the deep groove in the middle of his chest, praying he won't see the humiliation smearing my face. *That sounds exactly like something Lexi would say.*

Embarrassment is the last thing on my mind when Marcus's manly smell engulfs my senses. Just like the quick whiff I caught in the back of the Bentley, he smells freshly showered, spicy, and intoxicating. I nuzzle my cheek in harder against his firm chest, hoping to get enough of his scrumptious scent imbedded onto my skin to last me a lifetime. A scent is often the strongest tie to a memory. I love the way the faintest aroma of my mom's perfume causes a flurry of memories to bombard me. Now I've just added another spicy scent to my sensory palette—one I'm certain I've smelled before.

I suck in a sharp breath as recollection dawns in my blurry mind. That's the same scent I smelled that day in the elevator. I'm certain of it. Unashamed, I lean in again and take another long sniff of Marcus's invigorating smell. The crazy current zapping through my body stills as muted shock registers its intention. It's indisputably the same smell—there is no doubt in my mind.

Before my brain can catalog the commands of my heart, Marcus places his hand under my chin and raises my head. Time comes to a standstill as his movements mimic those made on that eventful night four years ago. His touch calms the torment twisting in my stomach and clears my mind of any thoughts. This time, instead of bouncing my eyes away when he releases a deep sigh, I connect my disarrayed eyes with his. Even with his eyes veiled by lust and his lips tugged at the corners, I can confidently say he is the same man from that night in the elevator.

While dancing his truth-exposing eyes between mine, Marcus mutters, "I should have kissed you that night." Every word spoken is done with a brush of his thumb over my exposed collarbone. "Would have saved me weeks of torture."

"By handing it to me," I mumble before smacking my lips together, mortified at my inability to think before I speak.

I've dreamt of this exact day many times. My response to discovering the identity of the mysterious stranger in the elevator was more cordial and graceful in my dreams. Heck, even my thoughts about how I was going to interact with Master Chains were more refined than the tactless behavior I just displayed.

A dash of euphoria runs through me, shoving my embarrassment to the side, when Marcus growls before leaning intimately toward me. As if his tempting growl was already spiking my libido, his impressive stature sends a knee-clanging chill of excitement down my spine.

Endeavoring to keep the miniscule snippet of dignity I have left, I take a retreating step. Marcus angles his head to the side, cocks his brow, then takes a step forward. Pretending I can't feel the zapping of energy between us growing instead of decreasing as I am aiming for, I take another step back. Seeing my defiance as a challenge, Marcus stares straight into my eyes as he steps forward. He has the gaze of a man on the hunt, and it sets my pulse racing.

In silence, we continue our routine until my back splays on a polished concrete pillar at the side of the foyer. Marcus stands so close to me I can't tell where my body ends and his begins. My breathing pattern alters as excited panic heats my blood. I'm barely holding it together as it is, but having him standing so near is squashing every reservation I've ever had about our incompatibility.

When he curls his hand around the curve of my jaw, my traitorous tongue darts out to moisten my lips. His eyes drop to track the path my tongue takes, the hunger growing in them with every second that passes.

The warmth of his breath bounces off my newly slicked lips when he mutters, "What would you prefer, Cleo, me hand it to you, or you continuing to handle it yourself?"

Ignoring the way his manly voice causes the hairs on my nape to prickle, I ask, "Whatever do you mean?"

The smugness on his face grows, right alongside my rampant horniness. Giddiness clusters in my head, making me dizzy and whimsical. I should have realized our flirty banter would be just as powerful in person as it's over the phone. The tenseness surging between us is fire-sparking.

"How many times did you touch yourself after we've talked?" Marcus queries, his words strong and determined, a complete contradiction to my body's reaction to his highly insensitive question. My knees are wobbling so badly, if he didn't have me pinned to the pillar, I would have buckled to the floor by now.

"I don't have the faintest clue what you're referring to," I stammer out, my voice relaying the hammering of my heart. "I don't do *that.*"

I draw in a lung-filling gulp of air when he places his leg between my quaking thighs. The fire raging in my belly grows. Our conversation already has me forgetting what planet I live on, so having part of his body near an area begging for his attention is pushing me into full-blown moronic mode.

The breath I've just gulped in is fiercely forced back out when Marcus tugs my bottom lip away from my menacing teeth. The taste of copper fills my tongue when I run it along the seam of my stinging mouth. Shockwaves jolt through me. I was having such an out-of-body experience I didn't realize I was chewing on my lip so harshly.

After guiding his thumb along the path my tongue just took, Marcus connects his eyes with me. "If I didn't believe you're around five seconds from fleeing, I would call strike three. But since I am feeling generous, I'll let your little lie slide."

After he drinks in my flushed cheeks and wide eyes, he says, "I don't just know you touched yourself after we talked, Cleo, I also know you screamed my name every time you came."

Jesus, who is this man? How the hell can he read me so easily?

Not willing to back down without a fight, I mumble, "Who said I was thinking about you? Maybe I was--"

My words stop when Marcus pushes his index finger against my lips. "Think before you speak, Cleo. You only have one strike left, use it wisely. The repercussions of your lies could be endless."

"And what repercussions will you serve for your lies?" I query, ignoring the way his finger causes my lips to tingle.

I can see his confusion growing, spreading across his face like a tidal wave of misunderstanding. "I haven't lied, so I have no concerns of ramification."

"Then why ask me to sign an NDA?" Disappointment is conveyed in my tone.

His entrancing eyes bounce between mine. "It's a commitment of confidentiality. Not just for me, but for you as well. NDAs are not uncommon in my lifestyle," he replies, his words as confident as the agreement we are discussing. "If you had concerns regarding the NDA, why did you sign it?"

"I didn't," I disclose, my words low and crammed with worry about how he'll respond to me not signing the NDA.

The heavy brows sitting above his mint green eyes slant in confusion. "My lawyer called me an hour ago. He has your signed NDA locked in the safe in his office."

His last sentence comes out slower than his first when he notices me shaking my head. "If your lawyer is the man I met under the Brooklyn Bridge, he never gave me the chance to speak, let alone advise I had some reservations I needed cleared up before I would sign the agreement."

"Reservations? What possible reservations could you have about an NDA? They are pretty straightforward."

"The fact they are pretentious, arrogant, and intimidating," I fire back, sending my voice bouncing off the stark white walls and shrilling into my ears. "If you truly want to know someone, it can be done without slapping a legal document in their face. Real men don't hide behind legal propaganda. They know what they want and go for it without getting lawyers involved."

Marcus balks as if my words physically slapped him. "*Real men?* You think me asking you to sign an NDA doesn't make me a real man?"

The arrogance pumping from his eyes sends my libido rocketing to the next galaxy, but it doesn't stop me from nodding.

"If I wasn't a *real man*, Cleo—" The pants of my breath increase from the seductive way my name rolls off his tongue "—that night at Chains, I would have taken you over the chaise in my playroom like your eyes were begging me to do."

"A *real man* would have said 'fucked over the chaise in my playroom,'" I mock, hating that my ability to goad him hasn't diminished in person.

"I don't fuck, baby, I decimate," Marcus growls in a low and highly intimidating tone. "By the time I'm done with you, you won't even recognize yourself."

My pupils widen as a furious wildfire combusts in my heavy stomach. I've never been more turned on or intimidated in my life. How can six simple words snarled in arrogance cause such a vehement response from me? *I don't fuck, baby, I decimate.* Jesus, they are just as effective the second time around, even hearing them in my own voice.

"Flattery may get your everywhere, but intimidation gets you nowhere," I mutter, my weak tone relaying the uncertainty of my reply.

I'm truly at a loss about which way to take this conversation. Half of me wants to kiss the arrogance right off his face, where the other half wants to teach him a lesson like I did to Richard months ago—with a hard knee to his balls. I'm so baffled by the opposing set of emotions hammering into me. I truly feel like I am two different people when I am with him.

"Lucky for me, intimidation intrigues you enough your feet refuse to move," Marcus replies as the egotism in his eyes grows.

"I am here because you intrigue me, not because you intimidate me," I disclose, unable to tear my eyes away from his heavy-hooded gaze.

My pulse quickens when Marcus steps even closer, not leaving an ounce of air between us. His new position ensures I can feel every rock-hard inch of his six-foot height and muscular frame. "Intimidation scares girls, but intrigues women," he quotes, staring down at me with a hungry gaze.

"You think intimidation intrigues me?"

I throw my head back and release a shameful moan when he rocks his hips forward, dragging his thick rod along my heated core. "No, Cleo, I think intimidation turns you on and that's what intrigues you."

"You've only known me for a matter of weeks, you can't possibly believe that gives you enough insight into who I am," I stumble out breathlessly.

"I know you well enough to confidently say your mouth speaks on behalf of your brain, your eyes express the pleas of your heart, and your body is the most revealing of them all. It not only expresses the sentiments of both your mind and your heart, it discloses your desires. The ones you are intimidated by."

Holding his gaze, I admit, "It isn't intimidation that turns me on." My breathless words shamefully expose my aroused state. "It's you, *Master Chains*. Your eyes, your sinful mouth, the sound of your voice. Those are the things that brought me to climax when I touched myself after our conversations, not intimidation."

He stares at me, chest thrusting, eyes blazing. I maintain his heart-stuttering gaze, allowing my heart to win this round in the tormented heart versus mind battle I've been struggling through the past two months.

We stand as one for several moments. Even if I couldn't feel every inch of his delicious body pressed against mine, my body's awareness of his closeness would still be paramount. It can seek out its mate in a crowd of millions. Only now do I realize it wouldn't matter how many objections my brain cited, this was never going to be a fair fight. Logic and common sense don't stand a chance against a man who holds the commanding appeal Master Chains has, because lust is truly the most potent poison to an ethical mind.

My eyes rocket to Marcus when he mutters, "I don't know whether I want to kiss the indecisiveness out of your eyes, Cleo, or spank it out." The deep manliness of his voice tracks through my veins like liquid ecstasy.

I lick my lips, giving my brain time to conjure an appropriate response. It's a pointless endeavor since I disclose, "If you play your cards right, I might let you do both."

Before the entire sentence can escape my lips, Marcus seals his mouth over mine.

17

Marcus growls a long, menacing groan when my mouth cracks open at the request of his tongue. Feeding off weeks of torturous foreplay, I scrape my fingernails over his clipped afro before sliding my tongue along the length of his. The dizziness wreaking havoc with my stability earlier turns calamitous when the intoxicating flavors of his mouth overwhelm my taste buds. He tastes manly and sweet with a hint of expensive whiskey.

When I drag my tongue along the roof of his mouth, the intensity of our kiss switches pace. Marcus weaves his fingers through my wavy locks before tugging my head back roughly. I gasp, incredibly turned on by his dominant hold. Giving in to the command of his skilled kiss, I relinquish my mouth to his. He awards my submissiveness by rocking his hips forward, allowing me to discover I'm not the only one aroused by our tantalizing kiss. His cock is firm, hard, and struggling to be contained in his dark blue trousers.

As our tongues duel in a core-clenching showdown, I run my hands down the ridges of his back. I don't need to see him naked to confidently declare he has an amazing body. He is tall, but not gigantic, slender with a smattering of muscles in all the right places, and from what I feel braced against my heated core, well-equipped.

The more our kiss evolves, the louder the purrs rumbling up my throat become. If his kisses are anything to go by, his abilities in the bedroom will be out of this world. His kiss is strong, dominant and as captivating as his personality. It's above and beyond what I dreamed the past eight weeks. It's truly breathtaking.

Listening to the pleas of my heaving lungs, I throw my head back and gasp in some quick breaths. Taking advantage of my new position, Marcus drags his lips away from my tingling mouth to place a succession of bites and sucks on my exposed neckline. After sinking his teeth into the skin near my collarbone, his tongue lashes out to soothe it. My breaths are greedy and rampant, shamefully displaying my enhanced state of arousal.

Marcus's fingers roll my budded nipple, making it impossible to catch my breath. Even through my satin dress and a padded bra, the twists and turns of his fingers cause me to writhe and buck against him. Shameful pleas for "more" roll off my tongue with every tweak. I thrash against him, willing him to go further, pushing him to give me more.

A whimpered moan simpers from my lips when his painful twist of my nipple sends a raging current to my soaked sex. My eyes snap open, and my breathing turns ragged as I fight through the frantic flow of desire scorching my veins. I am both shocked and turned on by my body's response to his aggressiveness.

"Your nipples are extremely responsive," Marcus growls against my neckline. "Nipple clamps will increase their sensitivity even more."

Ignoring the pleas of my brain to seek clarification on nipple clamping, I thrust my chest out, urging him to repeat the action. A stronger, more potent current rockets to my sex when he twists my nipple again, a little harder than the first time. I unashamedly writhe against him, my mind shut down, my body heightened beyond reproach. Nothing but the race to climax is on my mind.

Lost in the throes of ecstasy, I curl my legs around Marcus's waist and reacquaint our lips. I kiss him with all my might, striving to make him forget the callousness of my earlier words. He returns my kiss with just as much passion, a mind-stimulating blur of nibs, sucks and lashes of his delectable tongue.

I'm so entranced by his kiss, I don't register him moving us until the hardness of the pillar is replaced with the soft comfort of a deluxe couch. While matching the movements of Marcus's tongue stroke for stroke, I work on the buttons standing between me and his rock-hard body.

When the last button of his shirt is undone, I tear my mouth away from his. The dampness in my panties grows when my eyes drink in every delicious inch of his uncovered torso. Just as I had expected, his body is mind-spiraling: rippled abs, smooth, lickable pecs, and two bulges of muscles sitting on his shoulders all women love to sink their nails into when in the haze of climax. He is *P.E.R.F.E.C.T.*

The core-clenching visual of a shirtless Marcus is stripped from my vision when he unexpectedly flips me over. A tinge of modesty encroaches me when the hem of my skirt glides up my freshly shaven thighs to gather around my waistline. My doubt doesn't linger for long when Marcus runs his hand along the seam of my satin panties clinging to my soaked sex.

"You're drenched," he growls in a raspy groan.

With my head buried in the couch and my ass thrust in the air, his gifted hands work me into a frenzy. He plays my body as well as he plays the bass guitar in his chart-topping group, with a dominant confidence not many men embrace. Indescribable moans trickle from my O-formed mouth when his long strokes trigger more wetness to pool between my legs. I wriggle and buck uncontrollably, my body silently pleading for more.

My knees scrape across the expensive-looking couch when an unexpected slap stings my left butt cheek. "Stop wiggling so much," Marcus demands.

His commanding and stern voice bolsters my excitement, which in turn increases my wriggling. When a second slap hits the area still tingling from its first punishment, I cry out. It isn't a painful cry, more a cross between turned on and confused. The sting rocketing through my body is oddly arousing, but painful enough I follow his command and stop wriggling.

"Good girl," Marcus praises, his tone strangled by lust.

Panting to lessen my desire to climax, I twist my neck to the side when a strange scraping noise sounds through my ears. My pulse quickens when my eyes zoom in on Marcus's thick leather belt being dragged through the loops of his suit pants. Panic overtakes some of my unbridled horniness when images of what he may be planning to do with that belt bombard me.

I suck in nerve-calming breaths as my body pleads with my brain not to pass judgment before evaluating the situation. *Perhaps he is just removing his belt to ease his trousers down his thighs?*

Any possibility of my brain listening to the pleas of my body are left for dust when Marcus mutters, "Safe word, Cleo? I need to know your safe word."

Paralyzed by an equal amount of fear and arousal, I shake my head. Seemingly not noticing my silent rejection, Marcus adjusts my position. He alters the angle of my hips so I am erotically exposed to him before tethering my hands behind my back with his leather belt. The coolness of the material is refreshing to my overheated skin, and the tightness of the restraint is constricting but not painful.

"You need less clothes," Marcus mutters while running his hand up my thigh, his touch warm and inciting. "But that will have to wait. I've grown impatient."

My breathing quickens when his hand reaches my aching-with-desire core. He pinches the hood of my throbbing clit before rolling the bud between his talented fingers and thumb. My grunts turn wild as confusion clouds me. I am so conflicted. I shouldn't be enjoying this. I should be demanding for him to untie me this very instant. But I am so aroused, even my astute brain has shut down. It can't focus on anything but the sheer brilliance that Marcus has me precariously dangling on the edge of orgasmic bliss by doing nothing more than spanking my ass and stroking my pussy through my panties. *God—if it didn't feel so good, I'd be calling myself a hussy.*

When Marcus slides my panties away and slips his finger inside me, all coherent thoughts vanish. "I knew we put a five down on spankings for a reason. You're saturated. Did you enjoy being spanked, Cleo?"

My muscles pull taut as every nerve in my body begs for release. "Yes," I breathe out heavily, unashamed and on the brink of combusting.

"Yes, what?" Marcus questions, increasing the tempo of his thrusts.

The shaking of my thighs echoes in my voice when I stammer, "Yes, Master Chains."

Pleasure ripples through me when Marcus growls a pleasing moan at my submissive response. When the lunges of his finger increase, so does the rock of my hips. I moan and rock, moan and rock over and over again until every fine hair on my body bristles with awareness of a lingering climax. A beading of sweat dots my forehead, and every muscle in my body is aching, but I don't slow my pace, I meet Marcus thrust for thrust.

My sways turn frantic when Marcus switches from one finger to two. I buck against him so uncontrollably the sofa feet jump along the thick wool carpet. I purr long, husky moans, loving the way his fingers are stretching me wide as he grinds them in and out of my drenched sex.

"Safe word, Cleo," Marcus demands again, his voice raising to ensure I can hear him over the frantic moans ripping from my mouth.

As one of his hands works me into an incoherent, blubbering mess, the other one slithers up the planes of my stomach before curling around my throat. His mouth swallows my throaty moans when he forces my head back and seals his lips over mine. His tongue assaults my mouth at the same frenzied pace his fingers fuck me.

I must be mad. I'm fully clothed, bent over a couch in an unknown location with a man I only officially met thirty minutes ago straddled over me, defiling me like no man has ever done before, and I'm the most turned on I've ever been. *Stuff mad, I'm a genius.*

"Oh god," I purr, when Marcus moves his lips away from my mouth to nibble on my earlobe.

"Safe word," he demands again before sinking his teeth into the flesh of my ear.

My legs shake as my stomach muscles firm. I am sweating, panting, and on the verge of combusting. My mind is in lockdown mode, my body fully relinquished to the man commanding every inch of it.

"Safe word," Marcus growls again, his stern tone snapping me out of the trance his talented fingers have me trapped in.

Sweat trickles down my inflamed cheeks when I shake my head. "No," I push out breathlessly. "No safe word. We don't need one."

"Without a safe word, I won't let you come," Marcus warns, his words gravelly and spine-tinglingly delicious.

His threat doesn't faze me in the slightest. The walls of my vagina clench around his fingers as the shimmers of an earth-shattering orgasm come to life. By the time I give him a safe word, my orgasm will have already reached fruition.

My body screams blue murder when Marcus withdraws his fingers in one fell swoop. Before I have the chance to announce a protest, he exerts another slap to my left butt cheek. This one is even harder than the first two. I throw my head back and call out, appreciating the sting of warmth spreading across my backside.

"Safe word?" Marcus commands again while rubbing his palm over the blistering burn on my bottom.

"Pineapple," I mumble, my perception garbled by arousal. "My safe word is pineapple."

"Pineapple?" Marcus confirms, his voice relaying his uncertainty.

When I bob my head, he slips his fingers back into my throbbing core and increases his thrusts. He plunges into me so deep, he hits the sweet spot inside. He works my body like he knows every inch of me intimately, like he has studied every depth of me inside and out. I'm so wet, the insides of my thighs are glistening with my arousal, and his fingers slide into me without any hindrance.

I rock back and forth, forcing his fingers to plunge into me faster—harder. My mind is spiraling, I am out of control. Nothing but incoherent grunts part my parched lips.

"Now, Cleo!"

Aroused by his command, satisfied screams shrill into the cool night air as a blistering of fireworks detonate before my eyes. I quiver and shake, and my entire body pulls taut as a feverish orgasm overtakes me. The rough grunts tearing from Marcus's mouth increase the length of my climax, pushing it from fire-sparking to earth-shattering.

When the manic throbs controlling my body become overwhelming, I back off my thrusts against Marcus's hand. I feel like I am spiraling out of control, like I'm nearly on the verge of collapse. My muscles have never ached so much in my life.

Sensing my desire to slow down the blinding lust running rampant through my veins, Marcus removes his fingers from my quivering core. With one of his hands gripping my hip, he glides his slick fingers through the swollen lips of my pussy and occasionally toys with the bud of my clit. His gentle touch tethers me down enough I can enjoy the revitalizing shimmer sparking through my body without disordered rebellion twisting in my stomach.

Several minutes pass before every mind-hazing tremor of my orgasm has been exhausted. My climax was long and welcomed, completely shredding me of any energy I had left.

I am so drained, I don't realize we have company until it's too late.

18

It takes me stumbling backward and landing on my ass with a sickening thud before I realize the deep voice sounding through my eardrums is coming from an intercom attached to the wall of Marcus's sunken living room. We are still alone.

"Jesus, Cleo, don't hurt yourself," Marcus pleads, like he isn't the man who just spanked my backside until it's red and burning.

After adjusting my position to conceal my dripping core, I shift my eyes to Marcus standing at the side of the room. I watch him for several moments, absorbing all his silent prompts. His brows are beaded with sweat, his hands are fisted at his side, and his pants are well-extended at the crotch. He looks angry, confused and incredibly aroused. His expression mimics mine to a T. Well, except the angry part.

The dampness making my panties a sticky mess grows when he scrubs his hand over his hairless jaw. The evidence of my arousal is still glistening on his fingers. It's a rapid reminder of what we were in the process of doing before we were interrupted.

After taking in the grainy image of a man's face on the security monitor, Marcus turns his eyes to me. My heart falls from my chest when I see the apprehensive mask on his face. The only thing that stops disappointment from fully consuming me is my inability to register if his indecisiveness stems from wanting to ignore his impromptu caller or not wanting to mix business with pleasure.

Even if I weren't trapped in the haze of lust, I'd still recognize the face beaming out of Marcus's security panel. It doesn't take a genius to identify who a set of heart-thumping dimples on a soul-stealing face belong to. It's the lead singer of Marcus's band: Noah Taylor.

"Come on, Marcus, open up, we know you're home," Noah grins into the monitor, pushing the intercom buzzer a few times for good measure. "Hawke had Hunter trace your cell."

Marcus murmurs something under his breath. He is so quiet I miss what he said. After pushing a button on his security panel, he paces back to me still sprawled on the floor. His commanding walk complements the demand emitting from his heavy-hooded gaze. He walks with a sense of importance, but not in an arrogant, pompous way you'd expect a man of his stature to hold.

After tugging my dress down to a respectable level, he connects his eyes with mine while uncoiling my bound wrists. His silent stare deepens the intense connection between us, making it feel more personal than just a physical attraction. It's raw and real, and it causes my heart to shudder.

I plead with my lungs to breathe when the veracity of our exchange filters into my spent brain. For that short instance on the couch, I truly let go. I was so caught up in the moment, I never once stopped to assess the barriers I've been placing between us the past eight weeks. Nothing was on my mind. Not a single darn thing.

Dropping his thick leather belt to the side with a clunk, Marcus carefully inspects the small red welts circling my wrists. "Does it hurt?"

I shake my head. "Not in a bad way." Shockingly, it feels nice wearing his marks.

He runs his thumbs over the indentations before lifting and locking his eyes with me. Unease spreads through me like a wildfire when I see a dark cloud of concern dimming his entrancing eyes. The thrumming of exhilaration pumping through my veins slows as my worried eyes bounce between his. I hate that he is harboring uncertainty about our encounter when I'm feeling nothing but elation.

Noticing I've spotted his distress, the uncertainty in Marcus's eyes softens before a smirk forms on his kiss-swollen lips. His attempts at acting impassive curtail some of the regret slicing through me, but it doesn't completely vanish.

Remaining silent, he stands from his crouched position before brushing the wrinkles from his clothing. Once all the creases our tryst on the couch caused have been cleared, he drops his eyes to me. They don't look as barren as they did mere seconds ago. The corners of my lips crimp when he extends his hand in offering to assist me off the floor. The instant his hand curls around mine, the beat of my heart turns tempestuous, and it makes me wish I didn't see the quickest glimpse of a black stretch limousine rolling to a stop at the front of Marcus's property.

Instinctively, my hand darts up to flatten my disheveled hair. I'm not prepared for guests, let alone integral ones in Marcus's life such as his bandmates. My hair is a knotted mess from his firm hold, my lips are swollen from our kisses, and evidence of my climax is glistening on the inside of my thighs.

Heat extends across my lower back when Marcus spreads his hand on the base of my spine and guides me out of his living room. Priceless paintings and smooth, crisp lines lead the way to a long hallway on our right. My legs are wobbling with the aftereffects of climax, making my steps down the elegant hall rickety. Have you ever tried to walk after an energy-draining orgasm? It's nearly impossible.

Gratefulness replaces some of the anxiety plaguing me when Marcus opens a door halfway down the corridor. "You can clean up in here while I get rid of my guests," he mutters, nudging his head to the pristine guest bathroom.

Sick gloom spreads across my chest, making it hard for me to breathe. Discovering the reason for the apprehension in his eyes hits me harder than I am expecting, knocking me off-balance. Marcus grips the tops of my arms, thankfully halting my ungraceful topple to the floor. Even mad that I'm good enough to fondle on his couch, but not good enough to meet his bandmates doesn't stop an electric current surging up my arm from his firm hold.

Gritting my teeth at the opposing set of viewpoints pumping into me, I pull out of Marcus's grasp and take a step away from him. I feel dirty, ashamed—and quite frankly—used.

"I can go if you want me to," I suggest, loathing that my voice comes out shaky.

Marcus's eyes rocket to mine as his jaw muscle tightens so firmly it nearly snaps. "You want to leave?"

I shake my head. "No. I just don't want to interrupt your normal flow," I reply, grateful my voice comes out sounding as it normally does, friendly, but composed. "I understand our meeting was unplanned, so I'm not expecting you to have a clear schedule." *Or hide me in a bathroom like a dirty secret,* but I keep that snarky comment to myself.

The confusion on Marcus's face intensifies with every word I utter, as does the anger in his seemingly frank eyes. When he stares down at me, nostrils flaring, eyes blazing, I begin to wonder if I said my silent thoughts out loud. The sound of a car door closing booms into the uncomfortable silence surrounding us, breaking our tense stare down.

"Look, forget I said anything. I'll just hide out in here until your guests leave," I mumble.

My brisk pace into the washroom halts when Marcus's arm darts up to brace against the doorframe. I inhale a sharp breath when his abrupt movement causes his intoxicating scent to invade my nostrils. As his panty-melting eyes bore into mine, he presses the palm of his opposite hand to the other side of my head, once again trapping me between him and an unmovable object.

I close my eyes and count to three before reopening, hoping to calm my nerves screaming in excitement. Any composure my deep breaths awarded me with vanishes the instant I lock my eyes with Marcus's narrowed gaze.

"Do you think I'm embarrassed of you?"

God—why does it hurt just hearing him suggest he is embarrassed of me?

"Answer me, Cleo."

I shrug. "Why else would you want to get rid of your guests?"

My body fails to breathe when he leans in intimately close to my side and mutters, "Because I want to finish what I started," into my ear. "I want to *possess* every inch of your body, then I want to do it again with you bound and gagged in my playroom."

I shudder as the aftershocks of my orgasm quiver through my weary body. *Or is it a new climax?* I can't tell. I'm fairly sure it's a new one when a shameful moan topples from my O-formed mouth from Marcus sinking his teeth into my earlobe. My thighs meet when his tongue exonerates his bite with a pain-erasing lick.

Once the sting of his teeth is a distant memory, Marcus's mouth drops to pay dedicated attention to my exposed neck. His nips on my neck aren't as painful as the one to my ear, but they are strong enough to add to the wetness slicking my panties. They have me sucking in air like I've just ran a marathon, and I can't help but feel I'm being lured into a trap by his skillful mouth.

I'm so immersed in the chase of climax, I don't notice the ringing of Marcus's doorbell until he pulls away from my neck. I try to hold in my annoyance from the loss of his contact, my attempts fall short. An annoyed whimper parts my lips before my brain has the chance to register its arrival.

Satisfied with my shameful response, a sinful smirk etches onto Marcus's kiss-swollen mouth. "There will be plenty of time for that," he mutters, running his fingers along my neckline like he is erasing the marks his mouth made to my skin.

Once he is happy he has soothed the love bites on my neck, he locks his eyes with mine. My god, his eyes are beautiful... and so very familiar. How could I have ever doubted he was the same man in the elevator? I know I've seen his face splashed across the front pages of gossip magazines for years, but the feeling of familiarity I got when we first met was much deeper than the bizarre connection a fan gets with their idols. I know he is famous, I know he has more money than I could ever wish for, and I know he has a fascination with kink, but there is something more—much, much greater—that draws me to him. I just hope I can work out what it is before his overbearing aura swallows me whole.

Marcus runs his index finger down the crinkles in my nose from my confused expression, dragging my attention back to him. When I lock my eyes with his, he says, "Five minutes, Cleo. If you aren't out of this washroom in five minutes, I'll come find you."

"And?" I say when his sentence sounds unfinished.

His commanding gaze holds me captive as he mutters, "And I will show you how disobedience requires discipline."

The threat in his words sends a shiver down my spine. Before I can ask exactly what discipline he is referring to, the sound of the doorbell ringing is replaced with fists banging on glass. Their knocks are so hard, I can imagine the glass warping from the undiluted pounding.

"Five minutes," Marcus warns again.

When I nod, he places a kiss on the edge of my mouth before spinning on his heels and ambling to the door. Even watching him walk away from me is a riveting experience. His steps are gracious, yet full of command, and it showcases his spectacular backside in the brightest light.

19

I wait until Marcus's retreating frame is no longer in view before stepping into the bathroom. As I pace toward the large double sink and full-length mirror on the far wall, I absorb my flushed face, wide eyes, and kiss-swollen lips. The heavy swell of my breasts, still engorged with desire, bounce against my chest with every step I take. I've never seen myself like this before. Don't get me wrong, I've seen my aroused face in the mirror before, but not like this. I don't just look aroused. I look happy. Taken. *Claimed.*

The width of my pupils grows when I spin around and peer over my shoulder. Shockwaves jolt through my body when I raise the hem of my dress and notice a large red handprint marking nearly my entire left butt cheek. I should be appalled Marcus marked my skin. I should be marching out of this bathroom and demanding an apology for being handled so roughly. But the only thought passing through my lust-crazed head is how can I get a matching mark on the opposite side of my bottom.

What the hell is wrong with me? I am not a submissive. I am a strong-willed and determined young lady. I don't have a submissive bone in my entire body. *Do I?*

After taking a few moments to store away my concerns for a more appropriate time, I use a washcloth stored under the double vanity to clear away the evidence of my arousal glistening on my thighs. As the warm material scratches my delectable skin, the events of the last forty-five minutes run through my mind. Although shocked at discovering Master Chains' true identity, that wasn't the most shocking part of my evening. And no, it isn't what you're expecting.

I'm not surprised by Marcus's dominance. If I hadn't met him entering a BDSM club, the dominating personality he displayed the past eight weeks was all the indication I needed to know he was going to be controlling in the bedroom. My biggest surprise—the one that leaves me utterly flabbergasted—is my body's response to his aggressiveness. I'm not submissive, but that didn't stop my body from enjoying every spank, painful grip and twist he inflicted upon it. It relished it. *It loved it.* That's why I'm so damn confused. Is it possible a feminist can be turned on by being controlled in the bedroom? If you had asked me before my interaction with Marcus tonight, I would have said no. Now, I'm not so sure.

A deep chuckle barreling down the hallway draws my focus away from my conflicting internal quarrel. Not willing to discover Marcus's idea of punishment, I finish clearing the smears of climax off my leg before running my fingers through my ratted hair. After dabbing the sweat off my face with an extremely soft hand towel, I hang it on the edge of the vanity and pace to the door. I inhale courage-building breaths before pulling open the door.

The sound of chatter filters through my ears the instant I step into the hallway. Clearly, Marcus's endeavor to "get rid of his guests" was ineffective. Following the noise, I pace down the hall and round the corner. The first person I notice as I approach the sunken living room is Marcus standing near an attached bar at the side. The sleeves of his dress shirt have been rolled up to his elbows, and the crinkles our tumble on the couch created are barely seen with his shirt tucked back into his well-fitting trousers. The buttons are realigned and appear untouched. With his hair clipped close to his scalp and his lips already plump and inviting, he appears unaffected by the intermission to our heart-cranking gathering.

The only thing that gives it away is his leather belt sprawled on the floor next to the couch we were making out on. It's slithered between the legs of two extremely attractive brunettes who are eyeing me with suspicion. I'm not surprised by their reaction. I probably look a little weird frozen at the side of the living room, not moving or speaking. *Oh god—I hope they don't think I'm a deranged stalker.*

Following their shocked gaze, Marcus's grip firms on the decanter of whiskey in his hand. After having a quiet word with the blond man standing at his side, he sets down the decanter and paces toward me. My pulse quickens with every prowling step he takes. It isn't just the spark of lust firing in his eyes sending my heart rate skyrocketing, it's the pin-drop silence surrounding us. It appears I'm not the only one stunned into silence. My reaction can be expected, I'm standing mere feet from one of the world's most prolific bands, but what's their excuse for their muted composure?

"Breathe, Cleo," Marcus demands softly when he stops to stand in front of me.

My body jumps at the clipped command in his voice by inhaling a lung-filling gulp of air. The endeavors of my struggling lungs double when Marcus weaves his fingers through mine and guides me towards the beautiful group of specimens staring at me. Their faces are washed with confusion, their mouths gaped and hanging.

"Cleo, these are my band members, Slater, Noah, and Nick," Marcus introduces, pointing to a set of faces I've seen many times the past four years splashed across entertainment magazines. "And this is Emily, Jenni, and Kylie," he continues introducing. "Everyone, this is Cleo. My ..."

Marcus's bandmates fail to notice he doesn't finish his sentence. They are too stunned to do anything but stare. I noticed, but I'm still reveling in the high of climax, and so speechless at the caliber of beauty in front of me, my brain hasn't had the chance to convey its thoughts.

When the silence shifts from unsettling to downright uncomfortable, I run my hands down the flare of my dress before lifting them to my face. There must be a massive blemish on me somewhere the floor-length mirror in the restroom failed to point out.

I jump out of my skin when a deep voice on my left yells, "Marcus, you dog! Now your disappearing act last night makes sense." The voice is coming from Slater, the handsome blond man Marcus was speaking with earlier. He is the drummer of Rise Up.

With a grin on his face that exposes his cheeky personality, Slater struts towards us. "So you're the one who's had Marcus's panties in a twist the past month," he says, peering into my eyes.

While accepting the hand he is holding out in offering, I shrug my shoulders. "Whatever do you mean?" I force out, my words not as strong as I am hoping. "He'd have to be wearing panties before I could twist them up." I inwardly sigh when my voice comes out with the edge of playfulness I was aiming for.

My spirited response loosens Marcus's tight grip on my hand and causes Slater to throw his head back and laugh.

And just like that, the awkwardness plaguing our gathering is lost.

After accepting greetings from Nick and Noah in the form of a handshake, I am welcomed into the Rise Up family by Jenni and Emily with kisses to my cheek and tight hugs. Kylie's greeting still warms my heart, but it's a little more reserved than her predecessors. *Thank god.*

"You'll eventually get used to them," Kylie mumbles in my ear while giving me a brief hug. "They are a little heavy on the PDA, but they are wonderful people."

"Thanks," I reply, returning her gesture. Pulling back from her embrace, I drop my eyes to the tiny curve in her belly. "How long until you're due?"

"Twenty torturous weeks," Slater mumbles, his words muffled by the slice of pizza he is shoving into his mouth—pizza my grumbling stomach didn't know we had until now. "This baby isn't as willing to submit to the jam donut negotiation I made with Penelope."

Heat blooms across my chest from the glimmer Slater's eyes got when referring to his daughter. Although I've heard rumors Slater and Kylie want to keep their three-year-old daughter, Penelope, out of the spotlight, I've seen numerous paparazzi snaps of her. That's the one part I don't like about my job: the sleazy underhanded tactics some reporters will stoop to for a story. To me, the band members of Rise Up are fair game. They knew when they chose their career path that they would be targeted by the paparazzi, but I don't believe that logic should extend to their children.

"Speaking of children, where are they?" My brow archs into my hairline. With Marcus being the only member of Rise Up not in the family way, it's rare to see the band minus their mini counterparts.

"With the band just returning from a six-week press tour, the grandparents were chomping at the bits to get their mitts on them," Emily explains before her light brown eyes drift across the room to Noah, who playfully winks at her. "So we decided to take advantage of their eagerness with a weekend visit to New York."

"In other words, Slater was so desperate to know who Marcus was sneaking off to talk to every night, we used our naughty weekend privileges to find out," Kylie pipes up.

My hands itch to cover my inflamed cheeks, but they remarkably remain in place. Mainly because of Marcus's firm grip.

"Hey, don't go putting this all on me. You guys were just as interested in discovering why Marcus up and left town in the middle of Thanksgiving as I was," Slater grumbles, hooking his thumb to his bandmates, who don't attempt to deny his claims. "We only just got home, and Marcus was flying out the following morning at 2 AM. We all smelled a rat. I was the only one brave enough to go after it."

My heart thrashes against my chest when Slater locks his dark eyes with me. "Now we know where the smell is coming from."

Before he can spot my flaming cheeks his admission instigated, Slater connects his gaze with Kylie and mutters, "And don't worry, baby, I've got your naughty weekend covered. Didn't you see the big pool Marcus has out front?"

My confusion grows when Noah utters, "It's nearly winter."

"Pftt, do you think that will stop me?" Slater replies, his tone dead serious.

When everyone in the room laughs, I stand awkwardly out of place, either not privileged to understand their private joke, or completely missing the punchline. Either way, their laughter is so contagious, I can't help the smile that curls on my lips.

My confusion increases tenfold when Marcus pulls me to his side before muttering, "Remind me tomorrow to get my pool drained."

By the time the three large pizzas the band brought have been demolished, four hours have ticked by on the clock. Just from spending the last few hours with the integral members of Rise Up, I can confidently say any rumors circulating about the band dismantling are complete and utter lies. Within minutes of being introduced to them, I stopped seeing them as multi-platinum-selling artists. They are nothing more than a group of friends from a little unknown town in the state of Florida. Their bond is as strong as their unique personalities.

I place my empty wineglass onto the coffee table in the living room when Slater takes the empty seat next to me. Sensing my need of a refill, Marcus's pulse-racing eyes lock with mine. He silently questions if I'd like another without a word spilling from his lips. A flurry of giddiness inundates me. He has done the same thing numerous times this evening. He intuited my desires without a syllable needing to leave my mouth.

Not wanting to interrupt his conversation with Noah and Nick, I shake my head to his silent question. His attentiveness combined with my earlier orgasm already makes me lightheaded, let alone adding more alcohol into the mix.

"So," Slater drawls out, over-enunciating the short word in a long and rugged drawl. "What's the deal with you and Marcus?"

I pop my feet under my bottom and swivel my torso to face Slater. "I think you have our roles confused," I jest while taking in the way the lightness of his clipped hair makes his brown eyes pop off his face. Slater is a ruggedly handsome man, slightly larger in build than Marcus but of a similar height.

When he peers at me, confused, I add, "Shouldn't I be probing you for information? You've known Marcus a lot longer than me."

"Yeah, but the shit I'd be sharing would be no different than his Wikipedia profile. You've got the good *stuff*. The secret *stuff.*" He waggles his brows in a suggestive manner. "The *stuff* only someone who has his panties in a twist would know."

Masking my surprise that Marcus's enigmatic personality is just as strong with men who have known him for years, I say, "Oh, I didn't realize you swung *that* way."

Slater's brow cocks, and his face goes deadpan. "What way?"

"*That* way," I jest, peering into his eyes with a jeering expression stretched across my face.

It takes Slater a few moments to get the hidden innuendo in my cheeky response. When he does, his cheeks whiten and pupils dilate. "What the fuck?!" he roars, gaining the attention of everyone surrounding us. "I do *not* swing *that* way thank you very much."

"Why else would you want to know Marcus's sexual prowess unless you were planning on using it?"

When Slater gags loudly, five sets of eyes gawking at us return to their earlier conversation. Clearly, his childish reaction is nothing out of the ordinary for them. The only pair of eyes that remain steadfast on us is Marcus. I don't need to take my eyes off Slater's repulsed face to know he is watching us. I can feel the heat of his gaze burning into me, searing me from the inside out as it has numerous times the past four hours.

Before tonight I never understood the saying, "Eye contact is more intimate than words could ever be." Now I do. I fully understand. I've heard more words expressed by Marcus's eyes the past four hours than I've heard from his mouth the last six weeks. Every glance he has directed at me has felt like a silent promise, a guarantee that he too is counting down the seconds until it's just him and I in his sprawling mansion once again.

Doing anything to stop me embarrassingly squirming in my chair, I return my focus to Slater. "Well if *that* isn't your thing, why do you want to know about Marcus's *secret* business?"

"Do you want me to be honest? Or sugarcoat it in a way Jenni and Emily appreciate?" Slater's tone is the most serious I've heard come out of his mouth tonight.

"I'd prefer honesty over sweetness any day." *Perhaps that's why I loved Marcus's dominance so much?*

"Alright, but don't say I didn't warn you," Slater warns, his voice a unique mix of humor and caution. "For years, I thought Marcus was either a virgin or into some fucked-up kinky shit."

Wow—the virgin part I wasn't expecting. But the fucked-up kinky shit pretty much hits the nail on the head when it comes to Marcus and his sexual proclivities.

Slater slouches deeper into the luxurious couch before drifting his eyes to Marcus. "In the beginning, I was certain my virgin theory was solid, but a saint wouldn't resist the temptations thrown at him every week the past four years. Being the only single guy in the band, Marcus could have pussy on a platter..."

Slater keeps talking, but I don't hear his words over the unwarranted jealousy ringing in my ears. I know I have no right to be jealous—Marcus isn't mine—but I can't stop the wave of possessiveness smashing into me. It grows and winds and twists in my tummy until the pizza I consumed at dinner is sitting in the back of my throat, begging to be released.

It's so strong, I dart my hand up to clutch my throat, trying to keep the contents of my stomach from seeing daylight. The instant my fingertips brush the skin on my neck, a flurry of memories bombard me. Images of Marcus kissing and caressing my neckline outside the bathroom come rushing to the forefront of my mind, overtaking the horrid images of him and scandalously clad groupies making out in the wings of the many stages he has graced in his illustrious career.

Fighting not to let him see my suspicion, I connect my fearful eyes with Marcus. Just as he has done every time I've sought his gaze across the room, he twists his head to the side and returns my ardent stare. Not speaking a word, my truth-seeking eyes silently interrogate him, asking a set of questions I'd never be game to articulate out loud. *Is this something you do every time you return home? Do you have a different woman waiting for you in every city you visit? Am I the only one who feels the ridiculous connection between us?*

Marcus's gaze is so commanding, his silent response never alters. "No. No. No."

My attention diverts from Marcus when the heat of a hand encloses over mine. "Hey, you alright?" Slater questions, his voice low and brimming with concern. "You look a little unwell."

Mine and Slater's necks crank to the side in sync when a low and simmering growl sounds over the gleeful hum of chatter filling the space. Marcus's jaw is tense, and his eyes are transfixed on mine and Slater's connected hands. His gaze remains stagnant until I tear my hand away from Slater's tight clutch. After bouncing his narrowed gaze between Slater and me for numerous terrifying seconds, Marcus returns to his conversation with Noah and Nick.

"Holy fucking shit," Slater murmurs under his breath, his voice low and overdramatized. "That noise did *not* just come out of Marcus's mouth."

Unaware if he is asking a question or stating a fact, I remain quiet. I don't think I'd be able to talk even if I wanted to. Marcus's manly growl has me frozen in place with desire. I can't speak nor move.

Slater stares at Marcus for several minutes, his face amused, his eyes bright. After running his hand along the scruff of his chin, he shifts his focus to me. The longer he studies me, the closer his brows join.

His perusal is so long and terrifying, I am expecting something much more unsettling to come out of his mouth than, "Do you have any plans on the fifteen of December?"

20

The bristling of energy firing between Marcus and me is so dense, the air is infused with the pungent aroma of lust. From the moment he curled his hand around mine and commenced guiding me through his vast residence, an electric current has been surging up my arm nonstop. After bidding farewell to Marcus's bandmates, we've spent the last two hours like an ordinary couple on a date. The only difference between us and any other first-date couple is that our time was void of the usual awkwardness you'd expect. Because we've been communicating the last six weeks, we sidestepped the standard first date discomfort. Favorite foods, pet peeves and minutes of uncomfortable silence have already been achieved, leaving nothing but a clean slate.

Although the sexual connection between us is abundant, it isn't the only connection we have. Marcus is an extremely intelligent man. Conversing with him on any level is an inspired event, but doing it in person is truly mesmerizing. His seemingly bossy, kind-hearted, and opinionated personality displayed to me the past six weeks was replicated tonight, just in a more compelling, earthshattering way. Visually seeing him express himself enhances his commanding voice. It was an invigorating, spine-tingling, and if I am being honest, arousing experience.

Marcus has all the attributes you want in a man. He is devilishly good-looking, has charisma, charm and wit, and he portrays a sense of confidence that not only assures you will be thoroughly taken care of in the bedroom, but that you will also never forget the experience. His only downfall is every conversation we've held includes the words submissive, discipline, and last, but not at all least, safe word.

I don't know about you, but the fact Marcus needs to hear any other word than "stop" to know I've reached my limit sends warning alarms off in my head. Don't get me wrong, I knew from the instant I met Marcus in the alley of Chains he would never be a man to sprinkle rose petals over a four-poster bed while Chopin played softly in the background. I didn't arrive here expecting hearts and flowers, but I also didn't envision a cold and sterile feeling during our interactions either. How can a man who exudes so much raw sexual energy not exert that same feeling while discussing his sexual ambitions? Why does he treat sex like it's a business transaction instead of an act of pleasure?

My thoughts stray from analyzing the inner workings of a complex man when Marcus's deep timbre sounds through my ears. Shifting my eyes to him, my breath traps in my throat. From the way his jaw is ticking and the thinness of his eyes, anyone would swear he heard my inner monologue.

Swallowing down the unease twisting my stomach, I say, "Sorry, I kind of spaced out for a minute."

He nods, accepting my pitiful excuse, but my assurance does nothing to lessen the twitch in his razor-sharp jawline.

While walking the length of the elegant hallway in the top level of his house, Marcus gives me a general rundown on the layout of his property. "Powder room, gym, media room and spare guest bedroom," he advises, pointing to a door corresponding to each location.

He places my overnight bag on the floor just outside a set of large double doors before delving his hand into his trouser pocket. My heart rate climbs when he produces a silver key similar to the one he used to unlock the door of his playroom in Chains. I stand frozen in lust when he slides the key into the lock and twists the handle.

Shock—and a dash of disappointment—consume me when he swings open the door, revealing a bright, airy room with a large white four-poster bed covered by a rose-printed bedspread. A highly inappropriate giggle seeps from my lips before I have the chance to shut it down. My response can't be helped. Although it isn't exactly what I was envisioning earlier, it's pretty darn close.

Hearing my quiet laughter, Marcus drops his gaze to me. He takes a few seconds absorbing my raised cheeks and glistening eyes before asking, "Is there something you find amusing?"

"No," I reply, shaking my head. "It just isn't what I was expecting for your bedroom."

"This isn't my bedroom." Marcus's response is direct and straight to the point.

"It isn't?" The disappointment in my tone can't be missed.

Marcus shakes his head. "My room is down the hall and to the left."

I twist my neck in the direction he is pointing. "What's on the right?" I ask when I notice the hallway splits in two at the end.

Remaining quiet, Marcus gathers my bag and paces deeper into my room. Just when I think he isn't going to answer my question, he mutters. "It's my playroom."

My eyes bug. "You have a playroom in your house?"

"Yes," Marcus answers.

"Why?"

My heart falls from my chest when he says, "Because I need... *more*, Cleo."

"More than we did on the couch?" I ask while silently praying he says no.

My prayers go unanswered when he says, "Yes. What I did earlier was wrong. I shouldn't have done it."

His words physically impact me, pushing my confidence to a level I've never experienced before. *It's a dark and very lonely place.* Fighting against my wobbly legs, I pace deeper into the room and sit on the edge of the bed. I feel sick. Actually, I feel disgusting. How could I have misread things between us so badly? I was certain his eyes were revealing just as much excitement as mine. I've never read someone so poorly before.

I'm so immersed in keeping in the contents of my stomach, I don't notice Marcus crossing the room until he is crouched down in front of me. He places his fingers under my chin and lifts my head. He peers into my eyes, his face washed with confusion. I can tell the exact moment he reads the prompts in my eyes. He intakes a sharp breath, and his pupils dilate.

"It was nothing you did, Cleo," he explains, his voice smeared with uncertainty. "It was me. I lost control. I did things I've never done before. Things I'm ashamed of."

The confusion in my eyes grows tenfold. I am completely and utterly gobsmacked.

Marcus scrubs his hand over his tired eyes before admitting, "I've never *interacted* with a sub outside of a playroom."

"I'm not your submissive, Marcus," I interrupt, my words garbled by the nausea swishing in my stomach.

He nods, agreeing with my admission. "That's another mistake I made." The regret in his eyes doesn't match his statement. If he is trying to ease the conflict tearing my heart in two, he is doing a terrible job.

"Maybe I should go," I suggest, standing from the bed. "Maybe the only mistake you made was bringing me here."

"No!" Marcus pleads, his voice growing louder. "Give me a chance to work out a way to explain this to you in a manner a *normal* person would understand."

Grief makes itself comfortable in the middle of my chest from the pained way he said "normal." I had no idea he was taking my taunts on his weirdness the past eight weeks literally. If I did, I would have stopped being so narrow-minded and expressed my confusion on his sexual preferences with more diligence. He has been open and upfront with me for weeks, and I returned his candidness with hurtful jokes I'm sure he's heard many times before.

Breathing out my guilt, I wrap my hand around his and sit back on the edge of the bed. "Give it to me straight, Marcus. Don't worry about hurting my feelings or sugarcoating it, just hit me with honesty."

He takes a few moments glancing into my eyes, gauging the truth in my request before saying, "Because I've only had Dom/sub relationships the past four years, all sexual contact was done in a playroom situation, the one place I have complete control. Tonight, I struggled because I wanted to exert that same level of control over you, but I couldn't."

His confession surprises me. He was already displaying command I've never experienced, so it has me wondering how much dominance does he instill in his playroom?

"I've blatantly defended the transfer of power in a BDSM lifestyle as a choice. Tonight, I took away your choice."

I glare at him, shocked and confused. "You didn't take anything away from me. Not anything I didn't want to give."

"Yes, I did. I should have never interacted with you without first knowing your safe word, and I most definitely shouldn't have forced you to give me one. That's not the way things in this lifestyle work. The transfer of power is a gift, not a rule. There is just something about you, Cleo. You make me reckless, and quite frankly, I don't like it."

An inappropriate smile stretches across my face before I have the chance to stop it. My response can't be helped. I've had many heedless thoughts about Master Chains the past two months. It's nice knowing I'm not the only one harboring confusion about our bizarre connection.

I lift and lock my eyes with Marcus. "Doesn't your recklessness make you wonder if there is something more between us than just a Dom/sub relationship?"

"Yes," he admits, curtly nodding, "But that isn't something I want."

Although I can appreciate his honesty, my smile is wiped straight off my face. "Why?"

"Because I need the power, Cleo. I need the control. Tonight proved that. You have no idea how hard it was for me to hold back. Dominance is who I am, I can't just switch it off."

"So you need to hurt me to get pleasure?" I ask with my brows scrunched together, confusion in my tone.

"No," he answers, shaking his head, "I'm not a sadist, Cleo. I just need the control and the trust that comes along with a Dom/sub relationship. There, I know the boundaries and the rules. I can't offer the same amount of assurance outside of that."

I sit muted for several minutes, unsure how to respond to his affirmation. I'm glad he has continued being truthful, but it doesn't make it any easier to swallow. He isn't the only one who needs more. I want the affection that comes from a partnership—the cuddling after sex, the dates that lead to a night of lovemaking. I want someone who doesn't look at me as if I am lesser than he is. I get that enough in my everyday life. I don't need it in my personal life.

Marcus catches my eye for the briefest second, pushing my doubts to the very background of my mind. Clearly, since I ask, "Theoretically, what would a Dom/sub relationship involve?"

Over the next ten minutes, Marcus gives me a general rundown on how his previous D/s agreements worked. For the most part, I listened attentively, but occasionally, I interrupted him to get an explanation on BDSM jargon I was not familiar with. It was an informative and eye-opening discussion that eased some of my curiosity while also increasing it.

It wasn't just the vast range of information I was bequeathed that added to my confusion, it was my reaction to his admissions. I was expecting uncertainty to be the greatest emotion I'd be handling during our discussion, but it wasn't. It was jealousy. Even with Marcus not interacting with his previous subs in any form until they signed a legally binding contract didn't diminish the vehement jealousy consuming me. I hated the idea of him being with anyone—*hated it*!

The only thing that eased the furious rage blackening my blood was when Marcus advised why the band acted so shocked this evening. Not once in the thirteen years they've known each other have they met anyone associated with Marcus's personal life. Until tonight, he kept his business and personal life at opposing ends of the field. I am the very first person to meld them together.

My focus shifts from staring into space when Marcus stands from the bed. "I've given you a lot to consider, Cleo, so why don't I give you some time to actually deliberate?"

Not waiting for me to reply, he strides to the door. Just before he exits, I call his name. He pauses halfway through the door for four long heartbeats before swinging his eyes to me. The expression on his face mimics mine perfectly. He is just as confused, aroused, and conflicted as I am.

"Have you ever considered the possibility of having the best of both worlds?" I query as my eyes dance between his.

His throat struggles to swallow before he replies, "If you'd asked me two months ago, I would have said no."

Not elaborating on his response, he spins on his heels and exits my room.

21

By the time I wake the following morning, the sun isn't even hanging in the sky yet. With most of my night spent tossing and turning, my temples are throbbing, and my eyes are presenting the effects of a restless night. I am so incredibly confused as to what happened last night. I can smell Marcus's cologne in my hair, feel where he has been inside me, but the area that races every time I think about him hasn't beaten the same since he stalked out of this room.

For weeks, I tried to convince myself that my attraction to Master Chains was nothing more than craving something I couldn't have. But that isn't true. Yesterday proved that. The more I battled my desires, the stronger my feelings grew. Have you ever tried to deny the pleas of your heart? It's harder than refusing to let your eye blink. It's impossible. That should mean something, shouldn't it?

That's why I stopped fighting my attraction yesterday. I gave in to the desires of my body and heart. Our steam-filled tryst on the couch was perfect, even my astute brain has a hard time finding a flaw, so why can't Marcus look past his need to dominate me? Why can't he see our encounter for what it was? An intense connection between two red-blooded humans.

Realizing I'll never get the answers I need here, I throw off the rose-printed bedspread and trudge to the attached bathroom of my suite. Even with my mind scrambled with confusion, it can't miss the invigorating tightness only an ego-bolstering orgasm can cause to weary muscles. It's a blissful reminder of the cruel and tormented night I had.

When I reach the pristine bathroom, I undo the latch of my dress I slept in and let it drop to the floor. In silence, my desecrated panties closely follow it. As I step into the large double-sized shower, the quickest glimpse of my marked bottom in the vanity mirror freezes both my feet and my heart. Just like the past six weeks, the pleas of my heart and brain are on disparate sides, neither willing to back down on their stern beliefs. My body... that's an entirely different story. It doesn't give two hoots about the pleas of my brain nor my heart. It just wants Marcus.

My heart rate quickens when I recall what Marcus said to me yesterday, "I know you well enough to confidently say, your mouth speaks on behalf of your brain, your eyes express the pleas of your heart, and your body is the most revealing of them all. It not only expresses the sentiments of both your mind and your heart, it discloses your desires, the ones you're intimidated by." *He truly can read me like no man before him.*

My love of a long, steaming shower is forgotten when I am bathed and dressed in less than three minutes. With my desire to find Marcus more compelling than my urge to wrangle my hair into a presentable state, I throw it into a messy bun on the top of my head before exiting my room.

The cuff on my ripped jeans drags along the polished wooden floor as I search each of the rooms located on the lower level of Marcus's residence. When I fail to locate him, I gallop back up the curved stairwell. While gliding through the impressive gym and twelve-seater media room, I roll up the sleeves of my paisley-print long-sleeve shirt. With the heating in the house set to a sweltering temperature, my body is overheated and slicking with sweat.

My tornado speed through Marcus's residence slows when I walk past a cracked open door that was closed last night. It's the door opposite his bedroom, the room that had me tossing and turning until the wee hours of this morning: his playroom.

With my teeth grazing my bottom lip, I knock on the door with a silver key dangling out the lock. "Marcus? Are you in there?"

I prick my ears, seeking any signs of life. When I neglect to find any, I push open the door. Nerves spread across my chest as my eyes roam uncontrollably around the room. Although it's void of the same dark, dingy feeling Marcus's playroom at Chains has, there is no doubt this is his playroom. It isn't just the variety of floggers on the wall that gives it away, it's the studded leather chaise that featured in my fantasies the past eight weeks, and a weird cage-like contraption in the middle of the space.

Allowing my inquisitiveness to get the better of me, I pace deeper into the room. As my eyes drink in a wood cross contraption bolted to a wall on my right, I run my fingers over the leather chaise. Flashes of Marcus spanking me yesterday rush to the forefront of my mind when the coolness of the leather graces my fingertips. I could image how tantalizing heated skin from being spanked would feel when placed onto the cool smoothness of his chaise.

My aimless wandering around Marcus's playroom ends when a shimmering of white captures my attention. After checking I am still alone, I move toward the wooden chest tucked under a matching set of drawers. The closer I get, the more my heart rate climbs. I don't need a PhD in BDSM to know what the small pearl-like balls the size of marbles are. I'm just grateful they look unused.

My desire to open the wooden chest slips from my grasp when I notice a pile of paperwork sitting on top of the only set of drawers in the room. Angling my head to the side, I scan my eyes over the document.

My heart lurches into the back of my throat when I read the first line under 1.0.0 of the contract. "Submissive agrees to give power to Dom/Master for the agreed period of time as stated in this contract."

That's one of the biggest dilemmas a night of contemplation was unable to erase. What happens to me once Marcus has had his fill? Will I be disregarded and forgotten as easily as his last submissives were? Will he just move on and find another sub the following week? Those thoughts are more sickening to me than the idea of being whipped with the metal flogger I saw in his playroom at Chains. I hate the thought he could lose interest in me as quickly as he gained it. I guess that's why he so adamantly declared last night that a relationship between a Dom and his sub is not about love. It's purely about a sexual connection.

The mad beat of my heart steps toward coronary territory when a deep voice unexpectedly sounds into the room. "What are you doing in here, Cleo?"

Clutching my chest to ensure my heart remains in its rightful spot, I swing my eyes to the left. With an impressive frame filling the doorway, the small sheen of light illuminating the room fades, aiding my nearsightedness. I don't need a light to identify the man standing by the door, though. My quickening pulse and the bristling of the hairs on my nape is the only indication I need to distinguish the shadowed stranger.

"You scared me, Marcus." I saunter closer to him.

With his frame no longer blocking the light beaming into the room, my poor eyesight has no troubles spotting him. My steps stop as rampant horniness clusters low in my stomach. I demand my lungs to breathe as I watch a rivulet of sweat roll off Marcus's firm pec before weaving through the bumps of his abs. Once the bead of sweat has been absorbed by the dark blue coveralls he is wearing unclipped, I slowly raise my eyes to his, taking in every cut muscle on his glistening torso on the way. The throb of my pussy switches from barely controlled to manic when I notice a length of chain around his neck. The links are loosely coiled around the impressive muscles sitting on top of his shoulders before draping down the deep groove in the middle of his chest. *I've never seen such an erotic visual in my life.*

My hand darts up to clutch my chain link pendant when I notice one of his chain links is positioned in the exact spot my pendant sits. They are nearly identical in size and coloring. When I lock my eyes with Marcus, the shift in the air between us is so great, my knees buckle.

"What are you doing?" I ask when my inquisitiveness gets the better of me, my words coming out in a long, breathless moan.

"You shouldn't be in here." He steps deeper into the room.

"Why?" Disappointment rings in my tone. "You want to show me the real you. Why not do it in a place you feel most comfortable?" Gratefulness spreads through me that my tone didn't come out with the usual snarkiness it holds when I taunt him.

"This isn't a game, Cleo. This isn't a place you enter to ease your curiosity. This is a place you come once it no longer exists."

"It's a little hard to ease my curiosity about a world I know nothing of if I can't first enter it," I argue, my voice stern yet pleading. "You say you need more. Well, so do I. More information. How can you expect me to understand your desires if you're not willing to explain them in a way I can understand them?"

His stares at me with blazing eyes. His jaw muscle is tense, his fists balled. After what feels like an eternity, he pushes off his feet and saunters deeper into the room. With his entrancing eyes locked on me, he unravels the chains draped around his neck. I watch him with eagerness when he unscrews a U bolt at the top of the cage-like contraption in the middle of the room and attaches the chain he was wearing to the end. The muscles in his cut arms flex when he yanks down hard on the chain, ensuring it stays in place. Happy it didn't budge an inch under his rough pull, he paces to a large oak wardrobe on his right.

My barely-put-together composure is placed under pressure when Marcus removes a padded leather chair from the top shelf of the cupboard. I'll be the first to admit I am a novice when it comes to sexual apparatuses, but I can still recognize what he is clasping. It's a sex swing. It isn't your typical-looking sex swing, though. It's much sturdier than the ones my internet research into the BDSM community unearthed. This one has chains weaved throughout the padded design and looks like it could hold the weight of twenty people.

After attaching the seat to the steel cage, Marcus turns his eyes to me. "I made this for you," he practically growls. "I drew up its design the night you left Chains with the intention of claiming you in it."

"You made it for me?" My words come out ditzy and make me want to cringe, but my flabbergasted response can't be helped. He not only made a sex swing for me, he wanted to claim me as his from the night we met.

Marcus stares into my eyes before nodding. He doesn't need to speak for me to know the words he really wants to say. *This is me, Cleo. The real Marcus. The one you're intimidated by. The one you're too scared to admit you're turned on by. The one you want to dominate and control you.* Okay, maybe the last sentence was my inner monologue, not Marcus's.

Following the demands of my body, I push off my feet and head towards Marcus. The warning growl simpering through his hard-lined lips nearly halts my steps, but I push on, determined to prove there is something greater between us than just a Dom/sub relationship. Not just to him, but to me as well. And if I am being honest, I'll also admit I'm incredibly aroused at the idea he made a sex swing for me. From its technical design and the pure sturdiness of it, this isn't something he just whipped up overnight. This took time. Time a busy man like him doesn't have.

For every step I take, the sexual tension between us thickens. The pungent aroma of lust filtering through my nose strengthens my strides while also increasing the wetness between my legs. Marcus holds my gaze, his eyes silently warning me that I'm skating on thin ice. His whole composure screams of dominance, and it has me the most aroused I've ever been.

By the time I stop in front of him, the reasoning behind my original endeavor has been lost. Nothing but the desires of my body are at the forefront of my mind.

"Show me how it works," I request, my voice displaying the plea associated with it. I will be beyond devastated if he walks away from me now.

Marcus tilts his head to the side and eyes me for several moments, appraising the true response from my forthright eyes. *I want you to claim me—badly!* I can see his ambiguity winding up from his stomach to his entrancing eyes. For the first time, the confident shield he wears like armor doesn't appear as shiny as usual.

Just when I think he is going to deny my request, he commands, "Remove your jeans."

22

I comply with Marcus's request, removing my jeans at a rate quicker than their skintight design is accustomed to. I peel them off my quaking thighs before kicking them to the side. With his eyes connected with mine, Marcus gathers my jeans, folds them, then places them on top of the set of drawers housing his Dom/sub contracts. I swallow several times in a row when he pivots back around to face me. The indecisive Marcus I was dealing with mere minutes ago has vanished, replaced by a man whose aura demands respect. My shoulders instinctively roll when his eyes drop to take in my thrusting chest. He assesses every inch of me in a long, dedicated sweep, like he is categorizing each individual piece of me as if they are prized treasures.

The unease burning my veins simmers when Marcus mutters, "You can keep your shirt... for now."

When he strides towards me, I close my eyes and draw in some deep breaths. My heart is racing, and my knees are curved inwards. I am both nervous and excited. My eyes pop back open as I taste the sweetness of his breath on my lips. The air from my lungs rushes out in urgency when I find myself glancing straight into a set of determined eyes. It comes charging back in when Marcus reaches between my legs and snaps my panties off my body.

He stares at me, studying my reaction to his aggression. I feel nothing but dizziness, my head woozy with the potent desire of lust. The corners of his lips tug in the corner, no doubt pleased at my submissive response. His lewd smirk boosts the wetness puddling between my thighs, and it forces me to squirm on the spot. My hands twitch to touch him, but I keep them fisted at my side, remembering I'm not the one calling the shots.

Like he can sense my desire, Marcus reaches out and secures my hands in his. He runs them over his sweat-glistening torso and down the bumps of his abs before stopping at the bulge in the crotch of his overalls. My breathing kicks up a notch when I feel how hard and thick he is. He wants me to know how aroused he is. He wants to assure me I'm not the only one being ruled by my libido, and that he is just as attracted to me as I am him.

After running my hand down the length of his rod, Marcus shoots his other hand out to clutch the bottom of my shirt. He waits until I've secured an entire breath before he slowly raises the hem and pulls it over my head. My nipples bud, and the scent of my arousal lingers in the air.

He holds my gaze for several terrifying moments before he drops his eyes to my exposed breasts. I snubbed the tight restraints of a proper bra as my shirt has a built-in one. After giving both of my breasts an equal amount of attention by using nothing but his soul-captivating eyes, he lowers his gaze to my glistening sex. I swear, I nearly combust into ecstasy when his tongue delves out to replenish his dry lips. I should be ashamed by how wet I am. I'm so drenched, I can feel dampness on my thighs. But I'm not embarrassed or ashamed. From the way Marcus is looking at me, I feel nothing but desired.

He truly is a Master. He has me sitting on the edge of ecstasy, and he hasn't even touched me yet. That's remarkable... and slightly concerning. If he has so much power over my body using nothing but his eyes, imagine how intense it will be when he actually touches me?

I guess I'm about to find out since he is reaching towards me.

Goosebumps prickle my skin when he curls his arms around me and dips me backward.

"Oh god," pants from my mouth when the coolness of leather graces the heated skin on my backside.

Maintaining a quiet approach, Marcus adjusts my position so I'm nestled deep into the padded seat of the swing. Soft leather hugs the curves of my body while the double-stitched edge digs into the nape of my neck. My new position exposes every inch of my throbbing core to Marcus's more-than-avid eyes. I'm poised in front of his half-dressed form as naked as the day I was born, but not a snippet of indignity encroaches me. I squeeze my legs together to lessen the scandalous throb. My efforts are fruitless when Marcus slides his hand up my thighs to pry them apart.

"If you move them again, I will spank you," he warns, his tone low and bristling.

When my knees join to ease the excitement his threat instigated, he snaps out, "With the cane."

That instantly halts my childish squirms. *I can't imagine how that could ever be pleasant?* After peering at me beneath a set of incredibly long lashes, Marcus moves around the cagelike contraption, adjusting the thick chains shackled inside the pen before untethering the leather cuffs at the side of my head.

Agitated excitement sears through me when I realize what the cuffs are for. They will bind me to this chair—willingly! They ensure I'm not just going to be unable to move. I will be at the complete mercy of Marcus. That's why he designed this swing, so I would be under his complete control. I won't be able to move without his assistance, let alone steer the direction of our exchange. *Why do I find the idea of that incredibly arousing?*

Within minutes, my legs are suspended midair, and my wrists bound above my head. The small chains woven through the leather seat are draped across my breasts and positioned in a crisscross pattern down my stomach. The urge to squeeze my legs together grows when Marcus adjusts the chains so they form an X above my glistening sex. The coolness of the material gives relief to my overheated skin, while also adding a naughty edge to an already wicked exchange.

Keeping his eyes on the task at hand, Marcus asks, "What's your safe word, Cleo?"

I lick my dry lips before answering, "Pineapple."

"Say it again," he demands. The command in his voice gains the attention of my slicked sex.

"Pineapple," I breathe out heavily.

After shackling the chains draped between my legs to the seat of the swing, Marcus lifts his eyes to me. My pulse quickens when I see the command beaming from them. He is in full control and loving every minute of it.

"If at any stage you feel uncomfortable, say your safe word, Cleo. It will immediately stop what we are doing."

I dip my chin, acknowledging I understand. I may be a BDSM novice, but I've researched this lifestyle, and I believe I now have a broad understanding of why a safe word is needed during exchanges of power like this.

"But don't use your safe word haphazardly. Because the instant you say it, our play session immediately ends, and it will not start back up."

While grazing my teeth over my bottom lip, I nod. "I understand."

The heat racing to the surface of my skin inflames when Marcus runs his index finger across my collarbone before trailing it down my erratically thrusting chest. He gently tweaks the bud of my right nipple, twisting and rolling it until it's stiff and puckered. He plays with my nipple for mere seconds, but it feels like hours. His skills are impressive. He's barely touched me, and I'm panting, wet, and dying for release.

Once he has my nipple painfully sitting on edge, he switches his devotion to my left breast. "You're very responsive to touch. I like that," he declares with a wicked gleam in his eyes.

When my left nipple is as hard as my right, his finger slowly traces the chain pattern crisscrossing my stomach. My muscles tighten with every millimeter he gains towards my aching-with-desire sex. My head flops back, and my eyes shut when he runs the back of his hand down my glistening mound.

"You're drenched," he growls out, his voice raspy. "And you haven't even gotten to the good part yet."

Before I can request an explanation, I'm suddenly flipped over. A frightened squeal emits from my lips when I freefall towards the hardwood floor of the playroom. I attempt to hold out my arms to soften the blow, forgetting that they are restrained at the side of my head.

Suddenly, my panic switches to excitement when the coolness of metal hits areas of my body inflamed and throbbing. I gasp in a quick breath before releasing it in a low throaty moan. The chains weaved in the leather swing aren't just stopping me from plummeting to the rigid floor, they are rubbing against erogenous zones of my body, predominately, my pounding clit and tweaked nipples.

My concerns of falling to my death are pushed aside as I writhe in my seat, trying to increase the pressure of the chain link on my aching clit. My frantic breaths level, and my body prepares for climax when my thrusts against the chain spur a surge of anticipation to cluster through me. The odds of me descending into orgasmic bliss matures when a firm slap hits my right butt cheek. Marcus's hit is so hard, even the thick padding in the chair can't take away from its fiery sting.

"Do not come, Cleo," Marcus demands, his voice stern and commanding. "Until I say the word, you're not to come. Do you understand me?"

I squeak out, "Yes."

"Yes, what?" he asks while adjusting the chains provocatively draped around my sex so they produce the perfect pressure to my throbbing clit.

"Yes, Master Chains."

Marcus slithers his hand down my thigh before cupping my pussy. His movements increase the pressure on my clit, while the heat of his hand expands my excitement. My chin quivers as I fight with all my might not to let the throes of ecstasy overwhelm me. My attempts nearly become unwinnable when Marcus slips two fingers inside my quivering core.

With the chain links painfully pinching my nipples and clit, and his fingers grinding into me at a frantic pace, I grunt incoherently and lose all cognition. My breathing pans out as my body prickles with awareness of a pending orgasm. The rush of desire is frantic, overwhelming me.

"Please," I beg shamefully, no longer capable of holding in the silent screams of my body. "Please, Master Chains. I want to come. I need to come."

"Need and want are two very different things, Cleo. Which one is it?" He quickens the thrusts of his fingers, driving me to the edge even more.

I call out as the signs of an earth-shattering orgasm surface. Goosebumps prickle my skin as my body shakes uncontrollably.

"I *want* to come," I grunt, my words barely recognizable. "But I *need* you to make me come."

"Good girl."

With his other hand, Marcus grabs the edge of the swing and yanks it towards him. My thighs quake when his fingers plunge into me even deeper. He is so deep, I can feel the tips of his fingers brushing my cervix. Sweat gathers between my breasts before rolling down my torso and dripping on the floor near Marcus's bare feet. As his fingers grind in and out of me on repeat, I feel the storm of climax rolling in. It's angry and full of torment, and dying to break free.

"Now, Cleo!" Marcus roars, his loud voice enhancing the shakes hampering my body. "Come now!"

I pop my eyes open as pure, unbridled wildness scorches through me. I grunt and moan, my muscles pulling taut as an intense orgasm inflicts every inch of me. Marcus continues stimulating me, taking me to the very brink of sanity by using nothing but his talented fingers.

"Stop. Oh, god, please stop. It's too much. Too strong. I can't handle it," I beg when the most awe-inspiring orgasm I've ever endured continues to pummel into me.

"If you truly want me to stop, say your safe word, Cleo," Marcus replies. His voice sounds exerted, like he is enduring the throes of orgasm right alongside me.

The roughness of his tone intensifies the strength of my climax. My ankles push against the cuffs curled around them before my body gives in to the upwelling of desire striving to overtake it. I stop thrashing against the restraints holding me firm, shut my eyes, and let the bliss of orgasm sweep me away.

My core tightens as waves of pleasure roll over me. Tingles race from my budded nipples to my quivering thighs. My orgasm is powerful, long, and utterly exhausting.

"Good girl," Marcus praises, his words barely heard over my long, winded grunts.

I've barely emerged from the clouds of climax when Marcus flips the sex swing back over. I inhale my first full breath in over twenty minutes when the pressure of the chains is alleviated from my chest. My eyes flutter open and closed as an extreme bout of tiredness overwhelms me. I'm panting and hot, both from arousal and the shock of our intense exchange. Blinking to ward off sleep, I take in numerous lung-filling gulps of air to calm the mad beat of my heart.

The heat burning me from the inside out grows when my eyes stumble upon a breathtaking visual. I was so immersed in the paroxysm of climax, I didn't notice Marcus had removed his overalls. Mesmerized by the deliriously handsome specimen standing in front of me, I run my tongue along my parched lips as my eyes scandalously drink him in. He has such an amazing body. Firm and hard, and so very masculine. It's like God designed him only using the best parts: slender hips, banging guns, tight, firm pecks, and rippled abs that hit every one of my hot buttons.

The struggles of my heaving lungs double when my eyes drop to Marcus's thick, jutted penis. I suck in deep breaths as I stare at his naked package unashamed. I knew from what I felt earlier his cock would be impressive. I just didn't realize it would be *that* impressive. It's long and mouthwateringly thick. If I wasn't bound to a sex swing like an out-of-control nymph, I'd be tempted to measure its sheer girth with my tongue. I'm certain one long lick would never be enough.

A low moan escapes me when I return my gaze to Marcus. The corners of his plump lips are tugged high, and his eyes are dark and commanding. I thought the standing ovation orgasm he awarded me with would be the end of our encounter. It isn't. His forthright eyes reveal it wasn't the conclusion of our event. It was just the beginning.

He isn't even halfway done with me yet.

23

Swallowing to relieve my parched throat, I lower my thrilled eyes to Marcus's cock inching towards me. While gripping the base of his impressively thick shaft, he glides it through my shimmering sex, coating himself with the residue of my climax. The position of the sex swing is the perfect height, allowing our pelvises to connect without any hindrance. Nothing at all is between us. Not a single thing.

I moan a low, simpering groan when the head of his cock flicks the bud of my swollen clit. "You make me reckless, Cleo," Marcus grinds out through clenched teeth. "You make me irresponsible and careless," he continues before dipping the tip of his engorged shaft into my drenched sex.

The walls of my vagina clench around him, urging him in deeper, silently pleading for more. My wishes are left unanswered when he pulls his cock out until it's bracing against my heated core.

"I don't know whether I should punish you for making me reckless or punish myself?" Marcus breathes heavily, his words strained and husky.

"As long as that punishment doesn't involve sexual deprivation, I can handle anything you want to dish," I reply, shocked I can articulate anything with how tightly arousal is curled around my throat.

"Be careful what you wish for, Cleo," Marcus warns before gripping the edge of the sex chair and dragging it forward with an ardent thrust.

I snap my eyes shut and erotically scream when his wide cock impales me in one fluid thrust. Tears prick my eyes as my body fights through the pain of taking a man as well-endowed as Marcus. I can feel all of him. Every glorious inch. Although I love being filled by him, I'm glad he awarded me with a pussy-soaking climax before we reached this stage of our exchange or my pussy may have never recovered.

My sex grows wetter when a muffled growl tears from Marcus's lips. "You feel so good," he hisses through clenched teeth. He closes his eyes for a second, like he is rejoicing the moment. I can understand his response. I too am beyond excited.

After cracking his eyes back open, Marcus tilts his head to the side and watches me, reading the prompts of my body like a true master. He waits until my nostrils stop flaring and my pupils have returned to their normal width before he glides his cock back out of my weeping pussy. Even with a stinging burn hampering me, the walls of my vagina hug his cock, coercing him to stay. My silent pleas fall on deaf ears when he drags his cock out until his glistening knob is resting against my swollen cleft.

Before disappointment has the chance to rear its ugly head, Marcus jerks his hips forward, once again filling me to the brim. A crackling of energy zaps up my spine when the head of his cock slams into my cervix. It's painful enough to enhance the sexual responses of my body, but not painful enough to be intolerable. *I don't think anything he could do to me would ever be intolerable.*

"Remember the rules, Cleo," Marcus grunts when he registers the signal of pain crossing my face. "If you need me to stop, say your safe word."

I shake my head. "I don't want you to stop," I confess quickly, panicked he will stop. "It's painful, but it's not a normal type of pain. It's...It's--"

"The feeling of being thoroughly *claimed*," Marcus fills in when I fail to find a word to describe what I am feeling.

"Yes," I agree, nodding. A whimpered moan spills from my lips when his cock flexes at my confession, stretching me more.

Since the discomfort shooting through my uterus has eased to a dull ache, Marcus withdraws his cock while muttering, "Yes, what?"

"Yes, Master Chains," I splatter out in a breathless grunt, my brain too busy trying to work out how to keep him inside of me to articulate a more confident response.

For the next ten minutes, Marcus continues with the same routine of entering me quickly before stilling his movements. With every thrust he does, the tingle of an approaching orgasm overtakes the tenderness stinging my core, but no matter how many times I plead with him for more, he doesn't increase the speed of his pumps. He just watches me carefully, studying every expression crossing my face.

Only once he is happy the pain rocketing through me has been replaced with pleasure does he speed up his pace. He grinds in and out of me with controlled precision, like a man who knows how to drive a woman wild. *Like a man who knows how to fuck.* The muscles in his cut body flex and contract with every pump he does. Just watching the way he moves so fluidly is a riveting experience, one I could watch for hours.

Over time, the familiar tingle of ecstasy races down my spine as my skin flushes with arousal. My pants shift from soft moans to incoherent grunts. When sex strums in a rhythm matching Marcus's perfect thrusts, I close my eyes and pray for the bliss of orgasm to carry me away.

"Keep your eyes open," Marcus demands, increasing the pace of his pumps.

As the sound of skin slapping skin filters through my ears, I weakly pry my eyes back open.

"Good girl," Marcus commends as droplets of sweat glide down his temples. "This time, we will come together. Do you understand, Cleo? You're not to come before me."

Unable to speak through my dry, parched throat, I shake my head.

Marcus throws his hips forward, grinding into me harder, almost uncontrollably. "If you come before me, you will be punished, Cleo," he warns, his low tone threatening.

"It's not that," I force out, my voice husky and exhausted. "I can't come during sex. I've never been able to come during sex." Embarrassment dangles on my vocal cords.

Confusion registers on Marcus's face for the quickest second before he shuts it down faster than it arrived. I curl my hands around the chains attached to the cuffs on my wrist when he moves one of his hands off my hip to toy with my clit. He rolls and pinches the firm bud until it tightens so firmly, it nearly snaps.

But, unfortunately, it still isn't enough.

There must be something seriously wrong with me if I can come from being stimulated by fingers, but not by a man with a mouthwatering cock. I don't know if it's a mental issue or not, but I've always been this way. Not once in my entire adult life have I come during sexual intercourse.

"You need more."

I feel hollow when he suddenly withdraws and stalks to the corner of the room. My pupils widen to the size of dinner plates when he stops in front of the wall housing enough whips and floggers to make any Dom proud. While keeping his eyes locked on my exhausted face, he clasps a long bamboo cane in his hand. I exhale a deep breath as panic envelops me. The idea of being beaten with a cane scares me.

Reading the silent prompts of my body, Marcus moves his hand to the cat o' nine tails sitting next to the cane. My body registers the same amount of concern, but it isn't as strong as its response to the cane. When he clutches the small black leather riding crop in his hand, I inhale a deep breath as my knees attempt to curve inward. It doesn't look anywhere near as frightening as the cane and the cat o' nine tails.

"Riding crop it is," Marcus mutters to himself, pacing towards me.

My safe word sits on the tip of my tongue when I see the dominant command radiating from his beautiful eyes. But no matter how many times I try to fire it off my tongue, my mouth refuses to relinquish it. That probably has something to do with the fact it's too busy hanging open from witnessing the glorious visual of Marcus completely naked from head to toe. *My god—I've never seen a man scream sex as much as he does.*

"What's your safe word, Cleo?" Marcus questions again, easing the uncertainty thumping in my chest.

Swallowing harshly, I confirm, "Pineapple."

While running the end of the riding crop across my sweat-misted chest,

Marcus asks, "Do you trust me?"

Before I can answer, he flicks the riding crop on the bud of my right nipple, his tap a direct hit.

"Yes," I cry out as excitement takes hold of every nerve ending in my body.

"Yes, what?" he growls before inflicting another perfectly placed flick to my left nipple.

"Yes, Master Chains," I pant out, my nostrils flaring, my entire body on high alert.

Every fine hair on my body bristles to attention when he trails the riding crop down my sweat-soaked stomach in a long slithering pattern like a snake weaving its way through the desert sand. I throw my head back and moan a long, hungry grunt when the riding crop sends a spasm of painful pleasure rocketing through my sex from his precise hit on my clit.

Before I've come down from the high his strike instigated, Marcus slams his cock back into me. "Grip the chains and don't let go until I say so." He nudges his head to the chains above my bound wrists, his voice labored. "When I give you permission to let go, you can come."

Nodding, I do as instructed, appreciating his confidence in his ability to make me wild enough with desire that I will come during sexual intercourse. When I grip the chains, my heaving bosoms thrust into Marcus's face, and he takes me even deeper. He drives into me so hard, he bottoms out at my cervix before he draws his cock back out. He fucks me so hard and fast, nothing but the sound of frantic grunts and breathy moans are heard for the next several minutes.

My entire body quivers as the signs of an orgasm shimmer to life. "Oh god," I grunt, my words barely audible.

I grip onto the chains so hard, it's painful, but my body doesn't cite an objection. It's blinded by lust, unable to concentrate on anything but the man pounding into me at a breakneck pace. Sweat beads at Marcus's temples before rolling down his rich chocolate skin. He gives it his all, taking me to the very edge of orgasmic bliss, I can taste it on the tip of my tongue.

As he increases his thrusts, Marcus says, "Let go of the chains, Cleo."

Following his command, I let go of the chains. I fall back into the leather chair at the exact moment the riding crop flicks my clit three times. His strikes are skilled and precise, hitting the exact spot he intended without a smidge of hesitation.

"*Ohh...* I'm ..."

I throw my head back and yell as a wave of pleasure spreads through me, starting at the center of my core and sweeping through my entire body. Marcus's cock jolts inside me, throbbing and pulsing with every squeeze of my pussy as ecstasy awakens in my body. I shudder and shake, my body loving the ability to milk his cock. My pussy squeezes around his densely veined shaft, begging to feel the warmth of his cum mixed with mine.

Marcus pumps into me four more times, thrusting harder and faster with every plunge until my name leaves his mouth in a painful groan and the hotness of his cum coats the walls of my clenching sex.

24

Groaning a long, tedious grunt, I slowly flutter my eyes open. I jackknife into a half-seated position when the unfamiliarity of a room greets me. Unlike the room I awoke in this morning, this one is manly and stark with pristine white walls and black-trimmed edges. The bed I'm lying in stands in the middle of the vast space, and artistic black and white retro paintings line the walls. The thick black drapes block out a majority of the sun, but not enough I can't tell it's hanging well into the sky.

After inhaling a deep breath to settle the dizziness clustering in my head, I swing my legs off the bed. My face grimaces when my weary muscles scream in protest from my sudden movements. If my entire body wasn't rejoicing in the revitalizing shimmer of the two earth-shattering orgasms Marcus awarded me with, I may have listened to the objections of my muscles with more diligence. But since it's more a pleasurable pain than a hurtful one, I'm going to push its complaints to the side and enjoy it for what it is. *Bliss.*

I throw my arms above my head and have a stretch as my eyes turn to look at the rumpled bed. If waking up alone wasn't already enough of an indication that I slept alone, the fact the left side of the bed is smooth and unwrinkled is a surefire sign Marcus placed me in the bed before leaving the room. I'll be honest, I don't recall exactly what happened after our exchange. I remember climaxing harder than I've ever climaxed, and Marcus unbuckling the restraints tied around my wrists and ankles, but everything after that's a little fuzzy.

I didn't realize sex could be so exhausting. I swear, I used every muscle in my body when I came. I probably collapsed from exhaustion before Marcus even lifted me out of the swing.

My body shudders just thinking about our time together. That entire experience was just...*whoa!* Like...*wow!* With the stigma attached to playrooms, I thought any time spent in one would be torturous and fear-provoking. It wasn't. Not even close. Don't get me wrong, I'm sure not every Dom is like Marcus. If they were, the BDSM lifestyle would be inundated with novices wanting to join the fun.

Ignoring the niggle in the back of my head warning me that Marcus went easy on me because it was my first time in the playroom, I pace toward a stack of shelves concealed behind the wall the bed is pushed up against in the hope of finding some clothes to cover my naked frame. With how pristinely clean the rest of Marcus's property is, I'm not surprised by the sparkling condition of his expansive walk-in closet. Expensive dress shirts, designer trousers, and custom-made suits line the entire back wall. They are color coordinated, going from light gray to midnight black. Even the polished shoes sitting beneath them are sorted by shading.

While running my hand across the high threadcount material used in Marcus's dress shirts, I move to a stack of white undershirts in the middle of the space. Images of the exchanges between Marcus and me flash before my eyes when his freshly laundered scent emits from the stack of shirts into my nostrils. After plucking one shirt out from the pile, I lift it to my nose and inhale deeply.

"Oh. My. God. I don't think I've ever smelled anything as delicious."

My heart leaps into my chest when a deep voice says, "I have."

I swing my eyes to the side in just enough time to watch Marcus prowl across the room. There are mere feet between us, but it seems to take him forever to reach me since everything has slowed to a snail's pace. When he stops in front of me, he inhales a deep and unashamed whiff of air through his nostrils before releasing it in a low groan. My thighs squeeze together, alerting me to my nakedness.

After quickly throwing Marcus's shirt over my head, I shift on my feet to face him. "My perfume is--"

"It isn't your perfume I'm smelling," he interrupts, his voice husky and rough. "It's you."

If I were wearing any panties, the rough ruggedness of his voice would have decimated them.

He cups the edge of my jaw in his hand before locking his eyes with mine. "Your scent matches your beauty to perfection—as sweet as your angelic face and as sinful as your tempting body."

If I didn't see the truth in his eyes, I would have denied his claims. But even seeing the honesty in his panty-melting gaze doesn't stop heat from creeping across my cheeks. Who wouldn't be flustered receiving a compliment like that from a deliriously handsome man who screams sex and sensuality? Flattery may be its own form of evil, but I have no qualms accepting it in small doses.

Marcus watches me for several moments, absorbing me in silence, assessing every inch of my soul. "How are you feeling?" he questions, like he hasn't already read the truth from my eyes.

I smile. "Good. A little sore, but good."

"That can be expected," he explains while removing a strand of hair stuck to my forehead. "Even though the swing is designed to take your weight, your muscles naturally pull taut to aid in the suspension. It's not as trusting as your mind."

I want to ask him how he knows that, but I won't, because I don't want to think about him doing anything like what we did with anyone but me.

Marcus bounces his eyes between mine before dropping them to the lower half of my body. "And down there? Any pain, redness or swelling?"

"Nope," I reply, briskly shaking my head, praying it will ward off any embarrassment associated with his question. "It's perfectly A-Okay."

He connects his eyes back with me. "Did you check?"

No. "Yes," I lie as the redness of his compliment blazes into embarrassment.

Marcus sees straight through my lie. "Oh, Cleo, that was strike three. Now you must be punished."

I swallow as alarmed excitement burns through me. I'd be lying if I said I wasn't interested in what his punishments will entail.

While rolling up the cuffs on his light gray business shirt, Marcus strides to a white ottoman sitting in the middle of his dressing room. My pulse quickens when he sits on the edge of the ottoman before locking his eyes with mine.

With a nudge of his head, he summons me. "What do you say, Cleo? Three spanks for three lies?" he questions with his dark brow slanted high. "I would say that's a fair agreement, wouldn't you?"

I don't answer him. I can't. I'm frozen in place with desire.

Smirking, Marcus once again summons me with a gesture of his head. "Defiance will only make matters worse, Cleo." His voice slithers through me like liquid ecstasy, adding to the heat between my legs. "Once a punishment has been issued, it must be delivered. There is no cause for delay."

Pretending it isn't utterly absurd for a grown woman to be punished like a child, I push off my feet and pad towards him. The hankering in his eyes forces me to roll my shoulders back and swing my hips. The seductive movements of my body switch my regular walk to a provocative prance, intensifying the strength of the electric current zapping between us. It also makes me feel desired and sexy.

Once I'm within reaching distance, Marcus seizes my wrists and yanks me down until I am sprawled across his splayed thighs. When the breeze of the inducted air-conditioning cools my heated core, I become more aware of my exposed state. A rough groan tears from Marcus's mouth when he lifts the hem of his shirt. I draw in deep breaths, attempting to calm the cluster of lust tingling in my core as he caresses and gropes the globes of my ass with gentle squeezes and rubs.

When he moves his hand away from my backside, I grit my teeth and prepare for a hard blow. Surprisingly, the first one barely registers, it's nothing more than a playful tap. He puts a little more grunt behind the second one, but it still only entices excitement out of me. The third one... that one is the firmest of them all, but it still isn't strong enough to erase my eagerness.

The reasoning behind Marcus's gentle approach becomes apparent when he mutters, "Goddamn it, Cleo, why didn't you tell me I'd marked your skin yesterday?"

He doesn't give me a chance to respond before he stands from the ottoman and strides into the bathroom, taking me with him. After placing me onto my feet near the long marble counter, he rummages through his vanity. While he seeks god-knows-what, I drift my eyes around the opulent space. This bathroom is gigantic, nearly the size of most living areas. A large egg-shaped bath sits in the middle of the space, and a double rainforest shower is nestled in the far righthand corner. The glass medicine cabinet Marcus is rummaging through spreads across nearly the entire wall, and there are four sinks instead of the usual two.

Shrugging off my confusion on why anyone would need four sinks, I return my eyes to Marcus, who is pacing towards me with a bottle of aloe vera in his hand.

"This will ease the burn," he advises, passing the lotion to me. "If you had told me last night, I would have given it to you then. I can't take care of you if you don't tell me you're in pain, Cleo."

I hate the unease in his words. "Sorry. Everything was a little frantic, so a small sting to my backside wasn't my utmost priority."

I assumed my confession would ease the torrent of pain pumping through his eyes. It didn't. If anything, it made it grow.

"I promise to tell you from now on," I stammer out, saying anything to lessen the uncomfortable friction between us, while also praying there will be another time.

Thankfully, this time, my confession has the effect I am aiming for. The hurt in Marcus's eyes dissipates, revealing more of the commanding allure they generally hold.

"Okay. Good," he mutters while walking to the door. "Shower, then meet me downstairs for breakfast."

My body tightens in exhilaration, loving the clipped command of his voice.

His brisk strides stop when I ask, "Do you want to join me for a shower?"

The dampness slicking my skin moves to the lower half of my body as I await his reply. I'm shocked by the boldness of my suggestion, but incredibly proud I managed to listen to the pleas of my body without first stopping to evaluate them.

Marcus doesn't turn around to acknowledge me. He simply utters, "No. I can't trust myself around you. Particularly when you're naked."

With that, he exits the bathroom, closing the door behind him.

25

Forty-five minutes later, I bounce down the stairwell of Marcus's elaborate home wearing a burgundy one-shoulder dress. Although not as pricey as the dress I wore last night, this is still one of my favorite dresses. The impeccable threadcount of the wool material aids the aloe vera lotion soothing the sting in my backside, and the elegant cut showcases my voluptuous curves in a pleasing light.

When I round the corner of the large, airy kitchen, the first person I notice is Marcus. He is seated on one of the four stools tucked under the granite island counter of the well-equipped space. I prop my shoulder on the doorjamb of the kitchen, not wanting to interrupt his call, while also giving my eyes the opportunity to drink in his delicious suit-covered body. I still can't believe the stranger in the elevator four years ago and the man I met at a BDSM club two months ago is the man sitting before me now. I guess I shouldn't be surprised. Marcus has two very opposing personalities depending on what situation he is in. Around his bandmates and in public, he is Marcus: the quiet, reserved bassist of Rise Up. With me, he is Master Chains: a dominant, sexy lover who seems to know my body better than I do. It truly is the best of both worlds. I'm tempted to pinch myself just to ensure I'm not dreaming.

Excitement stirs my blood when the heat of a gaze gathers my attention. I was so occupied thanking my lucky stars for Marcus, I didn't realize he had finalized his call. After he finishes absorbing every inch of my body with as much detail as I bestowed upon him, he locks his panty-wetting gaze with mine.

"Hi," I mumble, glancing into his hypnotizing eyes.

I should be embarrassed he busted me ogling him, but I'm not. Mere hours ago he had me strapped in a sex swing in the middle of his playroom. I don't even understand the meaning of the word embarrassed anymore.

"Hi," he greets back, his lips curving into a sultry smirk. "Come and eat breakfast."

I skip into the room, my mood as playful as the cheeky gleam in Marcus's gaze from me rolling my eyes at his commanding tone.

"No reprimand for eye rolling?" I ask, exposing my love of erotic romance novels may have misguided my beliefs on the BDSM lifestyle.

The lusty smile on Marcus's face grows as he pulls out a stool for me. "An occasional eye roll outside of the playroom I can handle. But I'd be cautious doing it inside that domain." He leans toward me and breathes into my ear, "Unless you want to be spanked."

My body tightens, beyond aroused by his frisky tease, but I ignore its prompts, deciding the pleas of my stomach are more important than the desires of my heart. Once I take my seat, Marcus hands me a coffee cup full to the brim with steamy hot chocolate. My mouth salivates when I spot two white marshmallows floating in the rich goodness.

"How did you know I like marshmallows in my hot chocolate?" I blow on the steamy liquid, then take a sip. It's the perfect temperature, but at the exact moment it hits my taste buds, it reminds my stomach it hasn't been fed in over sixteen hours.

Pushing a plate of cream cheese-coated bagels to me, Marcus says, "It's my job to know your every want, need and desire, Cleo."

"I thought that was only in the bedroom?" I jest, plucking a bagel off the plate and popping a large piece into my mouth.

I moan softly, loving the savory flavor engulfing my taste buds. I've always had a healthy appetite, but it's even more rampant after my session in the playroom with Marcus this morning. I take another large bite of the bagel. It tastes just as delicious the second time around.

While taming my hunger pains, I scan my eyes over the large eat-in kitchen we are seated in. Just like the rest of Marcus's house, it's extremely modern with crisp lines and smooth surfaces. The latest appliances grace every surface, and not a dust bunny can be seen. The elegance of the room still thrusts his wealth into my face, but the more time I spend with him, the less concerned I am about our vastly contradicting bank balances. I'm not here for financial gain.

A large chunk of bagel traps halfway down my throat when my inquisitiveness has me stumbling onto something even more scandalous than the number of calories I'm consuming at a record-setting pace.

After swallowing the trapped bagel, I ask, "What's that?" pretending I haven't recognized the set of papers sprawled across the countertop.

Marcus places his half-empty mug of coffee onto the glistening kitchen counter before gathering the documents into a neat stack. His Adam's apple bobs up and down as his attention diverts to the Dom/sub contract he is grasping. "I thought we should settle some formalities before we continue with our weekend."

I stop chewing since the once delicious bagel now tastes like it's been laced with arsenic. It's as poisonous as the sick gloom spreading through my chest.

I force the remainder of the bagel past the solid lump in my throat before mumbling, "What type of formalities?"

"I want you to be my sub, Cleo," Marcus replies candidly, glancing at the papers. Missing my slack-jawed expression, he advises, "With our sexual compatibility being so strong, I adjusted the terms on your contract to a six-month agreement, instead of the usual three I've stipulated on previous contracts." His voice is confident, like I should be pleased he is awarding me double the amount of time his previous subs received. I'm not pleased. I'm disgusted.

Since he isn't looking at me, he fails to read the fury reddening my face as he continues explaining the terms of the pre-drawn contract. "Rise Up leaves on a world tour in three months' time, so I added an appendix to your contract to include the provisions of international travel."

"You want me to go on tour with you?"

When Marcus nods, I sneer, "I work, Marcus. You know this."

Nodding, he flicks over the document to a hand-written appendix added to the bottom of page six. "That's why I added this amendment to the contract this morning. As well as a clothing and living allowance, your income will be supplemented by me for the period of time stated on the contract," he explains, his calm composure not matching the life-altering conversation we are undertaking.

"During the first half of the contract, we will be based either here or at my residence in Florida, but the final three months will be at hotels chosen by my record company. If you don't find the accommodation suitable for your needs, we can move to a new location or discuss a monetary value for compensation."

The bagel I've only just forced down creeps back up my esophagus as his words ring on repeat in my ears. It doesn't matter how many times I hear it, I reach the same conclusion every time: he thinks I'm a prostitute.

"You want to pay me to sleep with you?" I ask, my brow cocked, my jaw hanging.

Marcus keeps his gaze on the contract while replying, "No. I'm compensating you for being my sub, not paying for services."

Black fury rages through my veins when my silent demands for him to make eye contact with me fall on deaf ears. During my research into the BDSM community, I heard it's not uncommon for Doms to request no eye contact from their subs, but this is ridiculous. If he had no qualms glancing into my eyes during our exchange in his playroom this morning, why can't he look at me now?

"And what happens once the contract ends, Marcus? What happens then?" My high voice is unable to conceal my anger at being disrespected like this.

Marcus takes his time configuring a response before muttering, "What do you mean?"

"What happens to me? You just simply move on to another sub, but what happens to me?" I query, banging my open palm on the middle of my thumping chest. "Perhaps I might get lucky and find another money-foolish Dom to take care of me once you've had your fill? Or maybe I should jump from Dom to Dom now until I find one willing to extend my contract from the 6-month one you're offering to a full year."

Marcus's furious growl doesn't have half the effect on me it normally does. My body is too boiling with anger to listen to any absurd prompts of my lust-driven heart.

No longer hungry, I place my half-eaten bagel onto the plate and shift my eyes to the side. With a range of emotions pumping into me, I need to look at anything but the man who is the catalyst of my problems, even more so since he is refusing to make eye contact with me. It seriously feels like this weekend has been one giant step forward, two mammoth steps back with him. Every time I think I'm making headway in our odd connection, he is quick to remind me this is nothing more than a Dom / sub relationship to him.

No longer capable of ignoring my swirling stomach, I push back from the granite countertop and slip off my seat. Before I have the opportunity to move away, Marcus's hand darts out to seize my wrist. "You haven't eaten nearly enough to sustain your appetite until lunch."

He can't be serious, can he? How can he expect me to sit down and eat with a man who refuses to look at me, let alone one who wants to sign over my God-given rights to him for a stipulated amount of time?

"You need to eat, Cleo," Marcus demands, his voice as commanding as ever.

I lick my dry lips before snapping, "I'm not hungry."

I keep my gaze front and center, refusing to let him see he has me on the verge of tears.

"Even if you're not hungry, you need to refuel your muscles that were exhausted in the swing," he argues, his composure calm and seemingly unaware of the emotional wreck standing beside him.

Gritting my teeth, I drift my eyes to his, too hurt to conceal my devastation for a moment longer. When Marcus notices the glossy sheen in my wide gaze, he murmurs under his breath before abruptly standing from his chair. His movements are so quick he sends his barstool toppling over. Its brutal crash to the tiled floor is barely audible when he curls his arms around my back and draws me into his chest.

When his familiar smell lingers in my nostrils, my fight not to cry is virtually unachievable, but I give it my best shot. Tears are something I reserve for my darkest days, and although the range of emotions I've been dealing with the past eight weeks has seen my moods swing from inspiring highs to devastating lows, it isn't even a tenth of the pain I felt four years ago when my parents and Tate passed away—not in the slightest.

After inhaling a deep breath to calm my nerves, I take a step backward, pulling out of Marcus's embrace. When I connect my eyes back with his beautiful green irises, it makes what I am about to say ten times harder.

"I want to go home."

26

The worry Marcus's eyes held when he discovered he'd marked my skin is nothing compared to the anxiety they are holding now.

"I'll never be who you need me to be," I mumble before I chicken out. "I like you, Marcus, I like you a lot, but I can't help but feel you only want me to be your sub. You're treating me like I'm some kind of disposable plaything instead of a real woman."

It feels like a big ugly knife is stabbed into my chest when he doesn't attempt to deny my claims. I stand frozen for a moment, still debating with myself about what I was hoping my confession would achieve. I pick at the lint on my dress, then fiddle with the cuff before I eventually realize I'm just delaying the inevitable. I'll never fully submit, and Marcus will never want anything more from me than to be his sub.

I count to ten before locking my eyes with his. Now, I wish I didn't. His eyes will forever be my weakness. They cause my doubts to waiver without a word needing to spill from his lips. Not able to ignore the pull of his alluring eyes, I drop my disarrayed gaze to his chest and try to force some sort of goodbye out of my mouth. My lips twitch, but not a syllable escapes them.

Disturbed by my lack of self-esteem in his presence, I pivot on my heels and pace out of the kitchen. Just before I enter the hall, Marcus wraps his broad arms around my waist. I can feel his heart smashing against his ribs when he draws me to his heated torso. My body is aroused, stimulated by his closeness. It truly doesn't care how angry he makes me, all it cares about is how good he makes it feel.

"I know this is new to you. I know it's daunting and scary," Marcus murmurs into my hairline, his voice barely a whisper. "But you're letting your fears lead your desires, instead of dancing with them."

When I attempt to spin around to face him, he tightens his grip on my wrist, refusing my request. I grit my teeth, hating that he won't let me see his forthright eyes. If he has nothing to hide, why won't he make eye contact with me?

"Would you listen to yourself? You tell me to dance with my fear, but you won't even face yours head on. If you were being honest with yourself, you'd admit I'm not the only one scared. You're just as frightened as me."

A rustle of air parts Marcus's lips, fanning the misting of sweat on my neck his firm hold caused. Silence encroaches us, amplifying the quiet tick of his jaw. It's a torturous and teasing time. My body relishes the heat of him curved around me, but my heart is locked down and confused. My brain... don't even ask.

It feels like eternity passes before Marcus mutters, "You make me reckless." The calm neutrality of his voice sets my nerves on edge, but it doesn't lessen the vehement anger pumping through my blood.

I smack my back molars together before snarling, "Yeah, well, you make me mad."

Marcus tightens his grip around my waist, foiling my attempt to pull away from him. Awareness of his nearness sizzles through my veins and stills my movements, my body too exhausted to fight the man who took it to the brink hours ago.

Happy he has subdued my attempts to flee, Marcus asks, "Mad enough you want to leave?"

"Yes!" When he expels a harsh breath like my confession sucker-punched him, it forces me to say, "No. I don't know. You confuse me, Marcus!"

"Self-judgment can confuse you, but emotions never lie. What's your heart telling you, Cleo?"

"That I need more than a stipulated amount of time on a contract," I admit, my tone low, equally panicked and angry at what his response may be. "What we did yesterday and today was beautiful, but I don't want to feel worthless the instant it's over."

His fingers flex against my hip. "I made you feel worthless?"

My hair clings to the five o'clock shadow on his chin when I shake my head. "No."

His relieved breath rustles the hairs clinging to my sweat-soaked neck. "Then tell me what's wrong, Cleo. I can't fix your concerns if I don't understand them."

My heart melts a little from his confession. He could have just brushed off my worries without a second thought, but he didn't. That alone lessens some of the unease twisting in my stomach.

I take a minute to contemplate how I can explain my concerns in a way it won't sound clingy. It's an extremely long minute. "I don't believe love is a necessity for a sexual relationship, but I don't think it should be cold and lacking of any emotion either."

"So you believe our exchange lacked warmth?" Marcus probes, eager to understand my concerns.

"Not necessarily," I reply, my words shaking with nerves. "During sexual contact, I feel desired. It's how I felt after it that's my greatest concern."

"So you enjoyed our time in the playroom?"

My heart rate kicks up a notch as I nervously reply, "Yes." *Very much so.*

His tight hold around my waist loosens. "So what happened between now and then that changed your mind?"

I try to spin in his arms. He once again denies my attempts.

"You asked me weeks ago to open my mind to the possibility of seeing things from a different prospective," I say, pretending I can't feel the hammering of his heart on my back. "I did that this morning in your playroom. I pushed aside the opinions of others and tried to see your world in a new light. It was beautiful—truly it was. But the moment I wanted to cherish for eternity will be forever tainted now."

"Why, Cleo?" he queries, sounding confused.

"Because you took something beautiful and made it hideously ugly by judging our exchange for our sexual compatibility," I bark, my words cracking off my tongue like a whip.

"It was not about that at all." The strength of his words ensure I hear the truth in his reply. "It was about opening your mind to the possibility not everything you believe is true. You have needs and desires you're too afraid to admit you have, Cleo. The playroom let you voice who you truly are."

I try to defend his false claims, but I'm left a little stumped. I loved our time together in the playroom. It went above and beyond anything I could have wished for. But I can't stand the to and fro feeling associated with it. Why can't that experience extend beyond those doors without the need to sign a contract?

"You went to Chains seeking something, Cleo. Until you stop allowing the opinions of others to consume you, you'll never find what you went there looking for," Marcus declares, his commanding tone softening with understanding.

I desperately want to tell him I was only at Chains on assignment, but I can't. Something deep inside me won't let my mouth relinquish the truth. I don't know if my hesitation stems from being afraid he will no longer be a part of my life, or because for some stupid reason, I believe my assignment was the universe's way of bringing us together. Some may say the connection we have was built on a lie, but that isn't true. The buzzing sensation that consumes me when he is close was just as strong in the elevator four years ago as it was in the backseat of the Bentley. *Clearly, I'm the only one harboring unexplainable feelings regarding our incontestable connection.*

"Don't be afraid of the unknown, Cleo. Conquer it," Marcus mutters into my hairline, taking my silence as deliberation on his request.

"I'm not afraid, Marcus," I reply, my voice relaying the pain shredding my heart in two. "And I'm also not your submissive. I would have never agreed to come here if I knew it was on the premise of you signing me on as your sub."

Marcus coughs to clear his throat before replying, "A D/s contract is nothing more than a way of laying down a set of boundaries both parties agree to. It's a smart thing to do at the beginning of any relationship, as it means there will be less chance of disappointment when it ends."

My heart clenches in my chest. Our relationship hasn't even started yet, and he is already preparing for it to end. That hurts.

"By laying boundaries at the start of our relationship, there will be *no* relationship," I scold as my anger returns stronger than ever. "A sexual relationship may just be an emotionless transaction to you, Marcus, but it means more than that to me. I can't just switch off my emotions like you, I have a heart."

"As do I, Cleo."

"Clearly not. All you want is a sub to play silly games with," I snarl as hurt overtakes the anger in my voice. "That's one thing I will never be, so why don't we just cut our losses and pretend we never met?"

Using his loosened grip to my advantage, I pull away from him and charge for the hallway. My brisk movements cause the first tear to roll down my cheek. Before I can brush it away, my wrists are snatched. In less than the time it takes for me to blink, I'm trapped between the hallway wall and a hot, brooding hunk of a man.

Marcus stands so close to me I can feel every vein in his body working hard to contain the anger pumping out of him in invisible waves. His hot breath hits my flushed cheeks as his furious green eyes bore into mine.

"Let me go, Marcus," I demand. The scent of the bagel I was eating earlier bounces off his lips and filters into my nose.

"No." He leans in deeper, stealing my ability to breathe and think.

I thrash against him, fighting with all my might to break free. All I end up achieving is more wetness between my legs, my body choosing its own ridiculous response to his closeness. I've never felt more ashamed of my lust-driven heart than I do now. Yes, Marcus is gorgeous and seems to know me and my body better than any man before him, but the responses of my body are absurd. I'm angry, goddammit! I'm not supposed to get aroused while angry.

"What do you want from me, Marcus?!" I shout, my words forced through a sob in the back of my throat. "Tell me what you want or let me go!" I scream as I thrust against him. My heart is beyond broken, my mind, scrambled.

"I want you!" he yells, his short reply unable to conceal his anger. "In my playroom. In my bed. Over my knee so I can spank the sass right out of you. You think you're confused, Cleo? Try being me. I've never wanted this. I've never carried a sub out of my playroom and put her in *my* bed. I've never introduced her to *my* bandmates. I've never wanted to mark every inch of her skin so everyone knows she is *mine*. I want that with you. I want *you*!"

My wailing stops, closely followed by the beat of my heart. Although I had hoped he would reply this way, I truly didn't expect him to. Perhaps I'm not the only one jolted by the breakneck speed of our connection? Maybe he is just as confused as me?

"Then do that." I bounce my eyes between his.

"I can't," he snarls through clenched teeth, his words barely a whisper.

"Why?" Shock is evident in my tone. "Why can't you?"

Three long breaths rattle through Marcus's chest before he replies, "I need the control. I need the power. I don't know how to give that up."

The raw edginess in his voice cuts through me like brittle glass. He sounds both angry and confused. The urge to forget our entire argument consumes me when I see the chaotic cloud brewing in his beautiful eyes. Although his alluring irises are obscured with palpable tension, they are still his biggest ally, because they show him as the man he is: both Master Chains and Marcus.

The chaos in his eyes dulls from a raging tornado to a summer storm when I say, "You don't have to give up your power or control. You said dominance is a part of who you are. I don't want you to change, Marcus, I just want you to understand how it feels for the person on the other end of that contract."

He peers at me, his confusion growing by the minute. "How can I do that?"

A ghost of a smile cracks onto my lips, grateful he is opening up to the possibility of changing the stringent set of rules he's been following the past four years.

"You just have to open your eyes to the prospect not everything is as it seems," I quote, referring to something he has said to me many times the past six weeks. "Sometimes you have to take people at face value, Marcus, not by a set of rules they are forced to follow."

"My dad has always said 'rules stop idiotic people making heedless mistakes,'" he mutters, his eyes flaring with an array of emotions I can't decipher.

"Do you want to know one of my dad's favorite quotes?"

Marcus's brows join. He appears more fretful now than he did earlier when he noticed my tears. After his chest rises and falls, he nods.

"There is an exception to every rule." I fist his dress shirt nervously in my hand before mumbling, "Maybe I'm your exception?"

"Exception? I don't think you could ever be classed as an exception, Cleo." Marcus's voice is stern but calm at the same time. "You're too disobedient to be classed as anything more than a brat."

Just like every minute I've spent with him, I act before I consider the repercussions of my actions. A heady grunt parts Marcus's lips when I jab my fingers into his ribs. He jerks, surprised by my fierce response. He isn't the only one shocked. My mouth is gaped, and my eyes are wide. *I really need to think before I act.* He has me sprawled against a wall in his residence at his complete mercy, and I just struck him. *I'm a complete idiot.*

Before panic can make itself known, a hearty chuckle parts from Marcus's plump lips. His rapturous laugh slides through my veins like molten lava, activating every one of my hot buttons. It's such a beautiful thing to hear in the middle of the strangling situation we've faced the past twenty minutes. In no time at all, it switches the energy zapping between us from a heated debate to a heightened conversation between two people who know each other well —*intimately well.*

After regaining his composure, Marcus drops his amused eyes to me. In an instant, the tension in the air shifts from tense to tantalizing. The humor in his gaze fades as his eyes darken with desire. The crackle of attraction firing between us bristles the hairs on my arms, making me needy and hot. How can he not see the unique bond we have is greater than a D/s relationship? He must be blind. It's so bright, I'm sure they could see it from space.

My concern about Marcus not noticing the sparks firing between us fades when he mutters, "Tell me what I need to do to make this happen, Cleo. I can't guarantee I can cross off every item on your list, but that doesn't mean I'm not willing to try."

My lips curl upwards, pleased with his response. "You want to compromise with me?"

Marcus shakes his head. "A compromise is an agreement where neither party gets what they want. This is a negotiation."

"I'm pretty sure negotiating and compromising are the same thing," I reply, my tone playful.

"Not in my industry, it isn't," Marcus argues, shaking his head.

I assume he is referring to his BDSM lifestyle, until he continues talking. "By compromising, Rise Up would have taken the first contract extension offered to ensure our label was managed by Cormack. By negotiating, we not only kept Cormack as our manager, we also secured a larger cut of royalties and a bigger percentage of any advertising campaigns we undertook the past two years. Compromise and negotiation are two very different things."

"Okay, so how does this work?" I quirk my brows, my earlier bad mood a distant memory. Even though tension still hangs thick in the air, it also has a hint of understanding mingling throughout it.

"We lay our cards on the table until we reach an amicable decision we are both happy with," Marcus answers, his aura as commanding as ever.

I don't know why, but I get the feeling this won't be a fair fight. It probably has something to do with the fact my defenses have already weakened from peering into his gorgeous eyes the past ten minutes.

Shaking off my unease, I say, "Alright, let's negotiate. What's your first offer, Master Chains? What's the one thing you want the most out of this negotiation?"

"You," he answers without pause for consideration.

Now I have no doubt this won't be a fair fight.

Smirking at my flushed expression, Marcus asks, "What's your counterbid, Cleo?"

I quirk my lips, pretending I am considering a reply. I don't need time to deliberate, though. I already know what I require for our relationship to move forward. I'm just worried about what his response will be once he discovers my terms.

Deciding there is only one way to unearth his reaction, I say, "I'm happy to fulfil your request with one stipulation."

Marcus's smirk enlarges to a full smile, no doubt satisfied with my response. "And what's that stipulation, Cleo?" The cultured smoothness of his voice makes my stomach quiver.

Pushing aside my heart's desire to sign the D/s contract mere feet from us, I negotiate, "I want the contract taken off the table."

When a flare of panic blazes through Marcus's eyes, I add, "For now. I'm not asking for it to be removed indefinitely, I just don't want it thrusted in my face every two seconds this weekend. We barely know each other, Marcus. For all you know, you may be chomping at the bits to get rid of me by tomorrow afternoon. Forty-eight hours straight with a Garcia woman is a hard limit for any man."

The heaviness on my chest lightens when Marcus softly mutters, "Maybe for a foolish man."

It feels like the sun circles the earth five times before Marcus says, "I agree with your stipulation, but only with adding one of my own."

My teeth graze over my bottom lip as I wait for him to continue. "I need control, Cleo. This is something I cannot negotiate on. If this condition is not agreed upon, I will not continue with our negotiations."

Panic squeezes me, stealing my ability to breathe even more than Marcus's well-formed body pushed up against me. Just the thought of our relationship ending makes me feel sick. Although I was threatening the exact same thing mere minutes ago, a little voice in the back of my head was praying he would come after me. If he hadn't, who knows what I would have ended up doing.

With my jaw tight with worry, I ask, "How much control are we talking?"

Marcus remains quiet, which fuels my worry more. The only thing that eases the swishing movements of my stomach is his eyes. Although they still have the same command they have always held, there is a small smidge of confusion dampening their appeal.

Just when I think he will never answer me, Marcus says, "I need full control in the playroom."

His response doesn't shock me whatsoever. Any man with a dominant command like Marcus would have a hard time giving that up, so I never considered requesting for that term to be revoked during our negotiations.

Although not shocked by Marcus's first statement, his follow-up sentence surprises me. "But I'm willing to try and rein in my need for control outside of that domain."

I don't have a chance in hell of stopping the smile dying to stretch across my face, so I set it free. This is a huge step for him to take. It feels like he just leaped us over all the barriers standing between us. *Well, nearly all of them.*

Spotting my glaring grin, Marcus mutters, "I said I would try, Cleo. That's not a guarantee it will happen."

Shrugging my shoulders, I say, "Just the fact you offered is already a step in the right direction."

I fist his shirt more firmly before pulling him closer to me. When the thickness of his cock braces against my heated core, my playful statement comes out sounding more needy than I am aiming for. "Besides, I've never had a problem with your need for control. I like your domineering personality, just as much as you like my goading one."

A whizz of air parts Marcus's lips, silently denying my interpretation of our odd connection. "Your desire to tease me is one of your many quirks I plan on straightening out in my playroom."

Hearing the playfulness in his tone stops panic from engulfing me. I'd like to say my body also had a neutral response to his tease. It didn't. Just the thought of entering his playroom again has my pulse quickening, and don't get me started on the response from the lower extremities of my body.

Marcus places his hand on the curve of my jaw, shifting my focus from my wicked thoughts to him. The heat of his hand strips away the icy barrier that's been dividing us the past thirty minutes, and the hunger in his eyes makes my stomach knot with thrilled anticipation. I've never had my values severely waver like they do when I take in his beautiful features. His plump, delicious lips, straight, defined nose, and eyes so powerful their heat and hunger spur on my reckless desires. They provoke me to be daring—*to be me.* The real Cleo, not the socially acceptable one I've been hiding behind the past four years.

Locking my eyes with Marcus, I say, "I accept the terms you're requesting, Master Chains."

"No counterbid, Ms. Garcia?" he replies as his morally corrupt eyes drift between mine, his pleasure at me agreeing to his terms beaming out of him in invisible waves.

My teeth catch my bottom lip as I consider his question. My mind is completely blank. The only thing I hope to gain from our agreement is the man standing in front of me. Considering that was crossed off at the very beginning of our negotiations, I can't think of a single thing to counterbid.

Warm dampness forms in the middle of my legs when Marcus saves my lower lip from my menacing teeth before his thumb tracks the groove of my top lip. His touch is brief, but strong enough to annihilate any lingering doubt in the back of my mind that I'm treading into dangerous waters.

"I have one final request."

Marcus cocks his brow as his eyes demand further explanation without a word leaving his plump lips.

"That we seal our deal in a more *pleasant* way then the usual handshake most deals are agreed upon," I elaborate, shocking myself with my brazen request.

My breathing lengthens when Marcus's deliriously sinful-looking lips incline closer to mine. "I accept the terms of your agreement without the need for an added stipulation." The warmth of his breath on my hungry lips forces my knees to curve inwards.

"Do we have an agreement, Cleo?"

I drift my eyes between his while nodding. "Yes."

"Yes, what?" he growls in a way that makes my knees shake.

Lost in a lust haze, I reply, "Yes, Master Chains."

Marcus's smiling eyes are the last thing I see before the skill of his kiss clears away the mess our heated conversation caused to my muddled brain.

27

"Are you ready, Cleo?" Marcus firms his grip on my hip.

Snubbing the way his fingers digging into my skin force my heart to skip a beat, I bob up and down my head.

"Keep your chin low and your eyes on your feet," he warns again before lowering a New York Yankee's cap down low on my brow.

Noticing the nervous sweat beaded there, he says, "Remember, you asked for this."

"I know." My words come out jittery and low. "Doesn't make it any less nerve-racking though."

Marcus chuckles softly, easing the uncertainty burrowing a hole in my stomach. "You want to know the real Marcus. This is my life."

I exhale a nerve-clearing breath before nodding. Although what Marcus says is true, I had no clue a simple request over breakfast would have me entering a second previously un-ventured world in less than twelve hours.

Before I got fully caught up kissing a man who makes me feel like life didn't exist before him, my stomach announced its rampant hunger. Not wanting to relinquish Marcus's delicious lips from mine, I continued to nibble and suck on his coffee-flavored mouth. My ploy was working... until the grumbles of my stomach grew louder. Incapable of pretending he didn't hear the pleas of the starving hole in my stomach, Marcus pulled his lips away from mine, guided me back into the kitchen, and forced me to eat.

While devouring the plate of bagels under Marcus's watchful eye, we continued with our negotiations—although it was a little more risqué than our first and void of the earlier tenseness. Marcus's stipulations followed a similar path to his earlier ones: he needed control, power, and me. Mine were a little less demanding than his. I just wanted him—the real Marcus.

It was that confession that saw us driving an hour into the city and standing in the alley we are at now. Marcus believes this location will show him as the real man he is. I guess I am about to find out.

After another nerve-clearing breath, I say, "Alright. Let's do this."

I gag, loathing that my words come out shaky. I've been in the media industry for a little over five years. If I can't handle the press by now, I'll never get the hang of it.

Smiling, Marcus pulls me in to his side, then steps out of the alleyway and onto the sidewalk. In a matter of seconds, a swarm of paparazzi bombards us. The oversized Hollywood glasses covering my eyes do nothing to diminish the bright flashes of camera bulbs coming from all directions. With Marcus's highly recognizable face, I knew it wouldn't take long for the paparazzi to track him down. Pictures of any Rise Up members are still highly lucrative even years into their success.

Tugging my cap down low, I lean tighter in to Marcus's side as he weaves us through the gauntlet of paparazzi.

"Marcus, this way!" screams one paparazzi.

"Do you wish to comment on recent rumors of a Rise Up rift?"

"Where is the rest of the band? Will they be joining you at the grand opening?"

The questions continue coming hard and fast as Marcus guides me towards a black steel door at the side of a converted warehouse. He doesn't speak a word. Not even when he is rudely probed about his sexual orientation or whether he and last year's Grammy winner, Wesley Heart, had a bisexual relationship with the bassist of Big Halo.

I'd like to say I'm shocked by the aggressiveness of the paparazzi, but unfortunately, I'm not. I witnessed their tactics firsthand my inaugural year at Global Ten Media. Although the laws have changed, the drive to give the public what they crave hasn't dampened the slightest. I'm not defending the paparazzi, I'm simply stating they use any tactics available to them to give the public what they crave: their much-loved celebrities.

I will say one thing, though, it was a whole lot less unsettling on the other side of the lens. By the time Marcus cracks open the large steel door, I've been elbowed, had my ear drum nearly burst, and asked my own set of derogatory questions pertaining to Marcus and his sexual proclivities. The only good thing about being bombarded by the media is that it prompted me at some stage this weekend to inform Marcus of my career title. Even though I'm concerned about what his reaction will be—as he and his bandmates have a clear love/hate relationship with the media—it isn't something I can keep hidden from him.

I just hope Marcus understands legally and ethically, I can't disclose any information pertaining to my actual position. Although I want to be honest, the confidentiality clause included in my employment contract has me weary on what information I can share. If I were to disclose restricted information to the wrong person, I could be fired. Or even worse—sued! Considering that's something I can't afford, I need to be diligent in how I approach this prickly situation.

Once we scurry through the thick steel door, it slams shut, blocking out the paparazzi and their endless questions. While Marcus assists me in removing my coat, my eyes drift around the large space. Exposed brick and thick black beams feature predominately in the open space. A commercial-sized stainless kitchen sits in the far lefthand corner and several long corridors weave off the vast area.

Not noticing our presence, a small group of builders sitting at a makeshift table in the middle of the room continue consuming the cut sandwiches and steaming cups of coffee served to them by a pretty African American lady.

After hanging our coats on a rack at the side of the foyer, Marcus pulls open a glass door with "Links" etched into it and gestures for me to enter.

"Links? As in chain links?" I ask, curiosity in my tone as I glide past him to enter the main room of the warehouse. The smell of fresh paint lingers into my nose, only just overtaking Marcus's delicious aroma I caught on my way past his suit-clad body.

Marcus smiles a grin that sets my pulse racing. "Links is a conglomerate of Chains. Kind of like its sister company."

I tack my brows in close while my disarrayed eyes bounce around the area. I'm utterly confused. Why would Marcus conceal his face while entering Chains, but turn up to Links without a disguise? Although he ensured my eyes and face were concealed from the press, he didn't even wear a cap. That truly doesn't make any sense.

Clasping the chain link given to me on my birthday between my thumb and finger, I tilt toward Marcus's side and whisper, "Is this another BDSM club?" I keep my voice low, ensuring the pretty sable-haired lady eyeballing us from afar won't hear me.

Marcus laughs a muscle-clenching chuckle. "No, Cleo." He shakes his head. "This is not a BDSM club. It's a shelter for victims of domestic violence. The profits from Chains' first year of trading allowed me to purchase this old recreation center from the county. With the help of three anonymous donors, I had the building remodeled so it can sleep one hundred occupants comfortably."

He doesn't need to elaborate on who the three anonymous donors where. His sparkling eyes tell the entire story. They are his bandmates: Noah, Nick and Slater.

"This will be the rec/dining room." He points to a hall on our right. "Down the end of the hallway is the sleeping quarters and washroom facilities. The configurations range from single rooms to ones that hold up to eight guests."

Tears prick in my eyes from the pride radiating in his voice. This is clearly a project very close and dear to his heart.

I spin on my heels to face him, my movements a little wobbly in my stiletto heels. "So how is this a sister company of Chains?" I query. Although I understand the capital to start this project came from Chains, it doesn't explain their correlation.

Marcus takes a moment to consider his reply before saying, "People often mistake the BDSM lifestyle with violence. They don't see the transfer of power between a Dom and a sub as a choice, they think it's something taken from them."

I nod. I had similar misguided assumptions, so I'm not surprised by his response.

"Although Chains practices the sane, safe, and consensual rules many BDSM members follow, the same can't be said for all members of our community." His jaw muscle tightens as his eyes darken with anger.

"Just like every community, the BDSM lifestyle has a handful of bad seeds ruining the image of the entire community," I fill in, reading the response from his eyes.

"Yes," Marcus answers, the fury in his eyes softening. "Chains was a part of a pledge I made to a friend three years ago. She wanted a place people could go play in safety. Links is part of our combined pledge. It's a place where people who have had their safety compromised can seek shelter."

"So Links is only for members of the BDSM society?" I ask with an arched brow.

Marcus shakes his head. "No. Links is for anyone affected by domestic violence. Just some of their care will be handled by associates of the BDSM community. The stigma attached to this lifestyle extends further than being ridiculed by people not understanding someone having different sexual preferences than them. It's seen members fired from their workplace, or their children ridiculed at school. Our vision is to use Links as a way to break the taboo in this lifestyle. Most of the people who contributed to bringing Links to life and ensuring its success are part of the BDSM community."

My first response to his admission is shock, but it only lasts as long as it takes for me to recall the many professionals I spoke to during my two-week investigation into the BDSM lifestyle. The caliber of expertise was astounding. One was a world-renowned heart surgeon who preferred to leave the tough decisions he makes every day in his industry at work, which is why he is a submissive. Every decision about his sexual pleasure was left in the capable hands of his Domme. All he had to do was sit back and relax, and entrust that his Domme would take care of him.

An intrusive question sits on the tip of my tongue, but I'm unsure of how I can ask it without it coming out sounding judgmental, so I keep my mouth shut.

"You won't learn about the real me if you don't ask questions, Cleo," Marcus says, once again intuiting my needs by hearing nothing but the sounds of my breath.

I chew nervously on my bottom lip before blurting out, "You defend the lifestyle choices of your members so vehemently, but I've never once read a report linking you to the lifestyle."

"That isn't a question," he snaps, his clipped tone sending a shiver down my spine.

After licking my dry lips, I ask, "You defend the lifestyle choices of your members so vehemently, but I've never once read a report linking you to the lifestyle. Why?"

He locks his forthright eyes with mine. "Although I believe people shouldn't be judged on their sexual preferences or orientation, my beliefs don't extend to members of my family," he answers, his face expressionless.

"Oh." His honesty blindsides me, and I can't think of a more appropriate response. "That's sad."

Marcus scoffs. "More like ill-advised, arrogant, and narrow-minded," he murmurs more to himself than me.

"That too," I agree, nodding. "It's unfortunate they can't see you for who you really are." I arch my brow. "It's quite an intriguing visual."

Marcus's lips curve sardonically. "Listen to you defending the BDSM lifestyle. There may be hope for me yet."

I roll my eyes before playfully slapping him on the chest. He bands his arms around my back and draws me in so he can nibble on my lips. I melt into his embrace, loving every playful nib and suck he makes. You would swear our argument this morning was months ago. It was swept to the side as quickly as our kiss heats up.

Before I can get carried away in the sensuality of Marcus's kiss, an ear-piercing scream roars through my eardrums. The squeal is so loud my heart leaves my chest, and Marcus pulls away from our embrace to crank his neck to the side. Following his gaze, I spot the lady who was earlier serving sandwiches glaring at us. With one hand spread across her hip and the other clasping a coffee pot, her massively dilated eyes bounce between Marcus and me. Her stunned reaction deepens dramatically the longer she takes in our huddled embrace. She looks shocked, distressed, and confused. *Oh, god—I hope she isn't one of Marcus's previous subs.*

The likelihood of the bagels I scarfed down an hour ago resurfacing grows when Marcus intertwines our hands before pacing towards the dark-haired beauty. His tug on my arm ensures I fall in step behind him, even though my feet want to stay planted. While battling to settle my swishing stomach, I take in the rapidly approaching stranger.

The smile she directs at Marcus is bright and confident, but her stance portrays more intimacy than a general business associate would hold when greeting a fellow colleague. She has beautiful rich African American skin, a small button nose, and plump lips. Her makeup palette is so natural I wouldn't be surprised if she was wearing nothing more than a neutral lip-gloss. Her eyes are hazel in color and stand out against her sable-colored hair, which is trimmed close at the edges but is long enough on the top to give it a sexy mussed appearance. She is young and gorgeous, and has the type of beauty that makes me green with envy.

Her gaze narrows as she assesses me, studying every inch of me as avidly as I did her. She starts at my panicked face, taking in the slight shimmer of powder I dusted on my nose on the car trip over and my rosy-colored lips. After absorbing my unruly hair twisted into a French braid, she lowers her eyes down my body. Her perusal is long and heart-strangling, and it coats my skin with nervous perspiration.

The insecurity plaguing me gets a moment of reprieve when she returns her glistening eyes to me, and I spot the gleam of approval in them. My nerves tingle. I shouldn't be pleased I've secured her seal of approval, but for some reason I am.

The logic behind my relieved response is made apparent when Marcus stops in front of the unnamed lady and says, "Cleo, this is my baby sister, Serenity."

My heart warms from the pride glowing out of Serenity's eyes from Marcus's introduction.

"Serenity, this is Cleo, my... " Marcus's words trail off into silence.

If Serenity didn't throw her arms around my neck and hug me tightly, I may have been tempted to kick Marcus in the shins for his failure to give me a title for the second time in less than twenty-four hours. I guess I should be grateful he didn't introduce me as his submissive. *I'd rather have no title than that one.*

"It's so wonderful to meet you, Cleo," Serenity says, pulling back from our embrace. Her gleeful eyes bounce between mine for several moments before she mutters, "Wow, you're as gorgeous as Marcus described."

I balk, stunned Marcus told her about me. He mentioned previously his family isn't welcoming of his BDSM lifestyle, so I'm shocked I came up during his conversations with his sister. I wonder how he introduced me to her then?

Not registering the shock on my face, Serenity weaves her arm around the crook of my elbow and gives me a guided tour of Links. Although Marcus follows closely behind us, he remains quiet, allowing his sister to express his sentiments on the charity he established from the ground up with his bare hands. The pride in her voice is easily distinguishable. She is just as proud of her brother as I am.

This is an extremely early call, but if the little thud I get in my chest every time I think about Marcus is love, it's been thudding a little faster since we arrived at Links. Coming here had the exact effect Marcus was aiming for. I got to know him—the real Marcus Everett—not the millionaire recording artist or BDSM club owner—him! The man who has no qualms spending millions of dollars to give victims of domestic violence shelter during their roughest days. The man whose briefest touch sends a flurry of excitement to both my core and my heart.

"We have last minute touch-ups happening on the murals today, then the furniture arrives on Wednesday, all ready for the grand opening next Saturday," Serenity explains when our tour returns to the rec room it started in.

"Wow, that sounds like a lot of work." Although the space has been perfectly remodeled, it's void of a single item of furniture. How can she possibly have enough hands on deck to assemble one hundred beds in that short amount of time, let alone all the other mammoth tasks she has been explaining the past thirty minutes?

Serenity's head bobs up and down as her eyes take in the space. "It is, but it will be worth it. There are men, women and children sleeping in the alleyway waiting for this facility to open." She places her hand onto my arm and tilts toward my side. "Between me and you, if regulations weren't so strict, I wouldn't have to hide them in the alleyway every time an inspector arrived unannounced."

Oh, my god, she is a sweetheart. Although now I can recognize the similarities between her and Marcus, the past thirty minutes have exposed that their personalities are on opposing ends of the spectrum. Serenity is bubbly and full of life. Marcus seems reserved and somewhat shy in the presence of others. Don't get me wrong, his aura still demands respect, but he doesn't need to express it with words.

The one way Marcus and Serenity are identical in every way is their hearts. By combining Marcus's vision and bank balance with Serenity's go-get-'em personality and determined work ethic, victims of domestic violence will have a place to call home until they can get back onto their feet. That's a beautiful thing to do—celebrity or not.

"Well, if there is anything I can do to help, please don't hesitate to ask," I offer, my tone exposing the honesty of my statement.

Serenity's eyes bug, "Really?"

When I nod, she asks, "Can you handle a ladle?"

I smile before once again nodding.

"Great! Because we could really use some help serving food in the kitchen next Saturday. If you're free, I wouldn't turn down a volunteer."

I shift my eyes to Marcus to gain his approval. This project is his baby, and I don't want to step on his toes by attaching myself to it without his permission. That could just make this incredibly awkward if things don't work out between us this weekend.

While Marcus's forthright eyes give me permission to accept Serenity's request, he walks over and joins our conversation. Ignoring the way his fingers interlocking with mine causes my breathing to shallow, I return my eyes to Serenity and say, "Sure. I'd love to help. I could bring my little sister as well?"

Serenity dances on the spot, revealing she is closer in age to Lexi than me and Marcus. "Do you have a younger brother too?" she questions, waggling her brows in a suggestive manner. "If he looks anything like you, I sure could put him to good use." Her tone is drenched with sexual innuendo.

Although I can hear the playful mirth in her question, it doesn't stop a jab of pain hitting the middle of my chest. Tate was a wonderful young man whose life got cut way too short. He was a senior in high school and the much-loved quarterback for the Montclair Mounties. His loss didn't just impact my family, it impacted the entire community.

"Umm... I did. He and my parents were killed in a traffic accident four years ago," I enlighten her, my voice cracking with emotions.

Marcus's grip on my hand tightens as the large smile on Serenity's face sags. "I'm so sorry," she apologizes, her eyes full of regret. "Oh my goodness, Cleo. I feel so bad being disrespectful like that."

"Please don't apologize. It's fine. You didn't know." I wave off her concerns with a sweep of my empty hand.

My attempts at defusing the situation are woeful. Serenity is stunned into silence, and Marcus is peering at me with concern. The uncomfortable silence continues as I search for something to say to ease the discomfort depriving the air of oxygen. Before a single thing is discovered, a man in a crisp black suit at the side of the room requests Serenity's assistance. I take a relieved breath, grateful for the interruption.

While squeezing mine and Marcus's conjoined hands, Serenity locks her eyes with me. "Let me take you to lunch next week as a form of apology."

"It's not needed, truly, Serenity," I reply, hating that I've made her feel remorseful.

"Please, Cleo," she begs, peering at me with a pair of big hazel eyes. "You will be doing me a favor. With all my girlfriends being back home, I don't have anyone to hang with in New York. It's getting lonely eating by myself every day."

I highly doubt her reply. She has the type of aura that instantly makes you want to befriend her. But since I dislike the spark of remorse in her eyes, I nod.

"But I'm paying," I say, wanting to ensure she knows I'm only agreeing to dine with her under the presumption we are eating as friends, not because she owes me an apology.

"A free lunch! Yay!" Serenity claps her hands together before pressing a quick kiss to my cheek.

"You take good care of this one, Marcus. I really like her," she says to Marcus before mimicking our farewell with a peck to his cheek.

After giving our hands one final squeeze, Serenity saunters to the man requesting her attention. The seductive sway of her petite hips doesn't go unnoticed by the men devouring homemade sandwiches like they have never been fed.

The smile their sneaky glances caused grows when Marcus moves to stand in front of me. After tucking a felonious hair behind my ear, he locks his striking eyes with mine. "Why didn't you tell me about your parents and brother?"

My left shoulder lifts into a wee shrug. "There was never an appropriate time."

We've talked about many things the past six weeks, but siblings, careers, and our vastly contradicting bank balances never came up. It also isn't the best starting point for a blossoming relationship. Usually all it achieves is hours of awkward uncomfortableness and a string of sympathies I've heard many times the past four years.

"I still wish you would have told me, Cleo. I don't like secrets." Although you could construe his words as a scold, the softness in his eyes doesn't relay that. He isn't angry, he is compassionate.

Marcus's eyes stop dancing between mine when a man in his mid-twenties wearing a paint-splattered shirt stands beside him. "Hi…ah…Marcus. I'm a huge fan of yours. When Jimbo said we were working on one of your projects I thought he was pulling my leg," he says, his deep voice accentuated with an Australian accent. "Would it be too much if I snapped a quick photo with you to show my sisters back home?" He drifts his eyes between Marcus and me as if he is requesting my permission as well.

When Marcus nods, I accept the cell phone from the unnamed man and take multiple shots of him and Marcus together. After handing the stranger back his phone, he requests to introduce Marcus to the remaining four men seated around the table. I move to the side of the room, happy to watch Marcus interact with his fans without invading their space. It's not often you get a chance to meet an idol one-on-one, so I don't want to take anything away from their experience.

The happiness beaming out of the men when Marcus offers them his hand to shake forces a huge smile on my face. They clumsily stumble out of their chairs before accepting his offer. I bet my starstruck face yesterday was similar to the expressions their faces are holding now.

The heat sluicing my veins from seeing Marcus in his element doubles when I secure his utmost devotion from across the room. Even though he converses with the unnamed men for the next ten minutes, his eyes rarely leave mine. His gaze is primitive and strong, and it forces my eyes to stray to the ground on numerous occasions. Giddy nervousness envelops me as heat rises to my cheeks. I'm shocked by my body's response to his avid stare. My personality could never be described as shy or timid, but I'm certain that's the foreign feeling pumping through me right now. *Or maybe it's the feeling of being desired?*

When Marcus finishes autographing an old electric bill found dumped on the floor by one of the tradesman, he heads in my direction. His steps are predatory and full of command, adding to the dampness pooling between my legs. I force my lungs to secure a deep breath, feeling the need to replenish them before they lose the ability to secure an entire breath.

The prompts of my body are spot on when Marcus drapes his arm around my waist and pulls me to stand in front of him. He is just as aroused as I am, his cock hard and thick against my lower back.

"That could have ended disastrously," he mutters, his hot breath fanning my sweat-slicked neck. "Imagine the influx of questions about my sexuality if the paparazzi discovered I got hard while talking to male fans."

Before I can ask what caused his aroused state, Marcus says, "I didn't think anything could top the visual of your face in the middle of ecstasy, Cleo. But your smile... Jesus. It made me instantly stiff. I know you make me reckless, but I didn't know you had that type of power over me."

I grind my backside along the length of his rod, thanking him for his compliment with a touch of the friskiness it awarded me with. Marcus's rough groan sends the aroma of lust into the air. It's heavy and thick, a seductive mix of our combined scents. I can't hold back my excitement. I grind against him again, more firmly this time around.

Marcus's lips brush the shell of my earlobe when he enticingly mutters, "Naughty girls get punished, Cleo. Do you want to be punished?"

I pant in anticipation, my mind spiraling with endless possibilities when one of Marcus's hands flattens on my stomach so he can draw me in closer to him. My new position allows me to feel how excited he is about the prospect of punishing me as well.

"The idea of being punished turns you on." He isn't asking a question, he is stating a fact. "I can feel the heat of your pussy through layers of clothes."

I don't respond to his admission. I just grind against him once more. Sexual tension bursts through me when his manly scent invades my senses. He smells fresh and clean, but intoxicatingly virile at the same time. My nostrils flare as I fight the desire to grind against him again since our closeness has gained us the inquisitive stares of the tradesman. It's a tough fight. I'm desperate for him, my hunger blatantly displayed by my flushed face and wide eyes.

"Why did you have to buy a house an hour out of the city?"

My knees crash together when Marcus sinks his teeth into my shoulder blade. My moan is only just concealed by the sound of chairs scraping across the hardwood floor, signaling the end of the workers' lunch break. I weakly wave to the tradesmen bidding us farewell with a dip of their chins and friendly smiles.

"Can we leave too?"

"Are you growing impatient, Cleo?" Marcus's commanding tone is unable to conceal that I'm not the only one eager.

"Yes," I respond, my one word needy. "I've waited eight weeks to taste your cock. I don't think I can wait a moment longer."

"Jesus, Cleo." His grip tightens around my waist so firmly it's almost painful. "When you say things like that, I want to take you hard and fast until nothing but pleas for forgiveness spill out of your filthy little mouth."

"That's the point. I want you to *fuck* me—hard and fast." I nearly do a jig on the spot, I'm so stoked I managed to articulate my body's desires without a single smidge of hesitation.

The heat of Marcus's cock scorches my back when he rocks his hips forward, dragging his thickened shaft along the ridges of my spine. "I'm not above clearing the room, Cleo," he warns, his voice strained. "If that's what it will take to ensure your every desire is met."

His admission dampens my excitement somewhat. Serenity has been working nonstop on this project the past month. I can't let my inability to harness my unbridled horniness set her schedule back for even a minute.

Snubbing the screaming protests of my body, I spin on my heels and face Marcus. His eyes are wide with lust, and he is breathing harder than normal. It makes what I am about to say ten times harder.

"I can't let you do that." The uncertainty of my words weakens what should be a confident statement. "But I can let you do me... *in around an hour.*"

Marcus's lust-filled eyes bounce between mine for several minutes. It's the first time I've ever noticed a tinge of hesitation in them. The more he takes in my flushed expression, the darker his eyes become with desire.

My pulse thrums when he mutters, "Get your coat. I have a hotel room two blocks from here."

28

Even being bombarded by paparazzi on our way to the hotel can't dampen my excitement. Perspiration is misting my skin, and stupid butterflies are fluttering in my stomach. I keep my cap-covered head down low and follow Marcus as he weaves through the nosy reporters and wide-eyed New Yorkers crammed on the bustling sidewalks. I'm not the only one eager. I can feel Marcus's excitement thrumming through his hand curled around mine. I won't lie. It makes me giddy knowing he has the same uninhibited attraction to me as I do him.

The nerves twisting my stomach switch to excitement when we enter the revolving glass door of an elegant hotel in lower Manhattan. With the door manned by a group of beefy security personnel, the two-block paparazzi chase comes to an end the instant we slip inside. As Marcus guides me through the expansive foyer, my eyes shoot in all directions, eager to absorb each beautiful feature.

A gorgeous silk-pleated panel covers the entire back wall of the foyer, dark-veined wood panels line the walls in a checked design, and the floor is done with gray tile in an asymmetrical pattern. The three large round chandeliers dangling from the ceiling bounce multihued beams of light onto the dark coloring, softening the starkness of its design. It's a beautiful space that screams of modernity and wealth.

Shock registers on my face when Marcus forgoes the usual check-in process most guests must endure when first arriving at a hotel. He heads straight for the bank of silver elevators tucked behind the concierge desk. Upon entering, he dips his chin in greeting to the elderly elevator attendant before moving to the back of the crowded car. I'm tempted to ask why he neither checked in or advised the elevator attendant of his floor number. But then I realize, we are from two very contrasting worlds. This type of process is probably nothing out of the ordinary for a man as wealthy as Marcus.

A thrill of excitement courses through me when Marcus tugs me to his side. His firm grip on my hip adds to the throb between my legs. The temperature in the elevator car becomes roasting as the potent scent of lust permeates the air.

I can barely contain my excitement when Marcus murmurs into my ear, "Remove your panties. I want nothing in my way when we arrive at my room."

My knees violently crash together as my eyes rocket to his. I'm practically panting to control the excitement thickening my blood. Although I am incredibly aroused by his request, I shake my head. The elevator is brimming with hotel guests. I'm not talking one or two, I'm talking over a dozen.

Marcus's alluring eyes burn into mine as he mutters, "It was not a request, Cleo. Remove your panties or be punished." His commanding eyes strengthen his statement, but they don't faze me in the slightest. For some inane reason, the idea of being punished by him sounds more like a treat than a penance. Even more so since he doesn't have access to the scary torturous instruments in his playroom.

Spotting the defiance brightening my dark eyes, Marcus leans in intimately close and whispers, "Do you want to come, Cleo?"

The hotness of his breath on my ear spurs on a new type of excitement, the one only he can muster: the anticipation of orgasming during sex.

I nod, unashamed.

"Then remove your panties. Or I will withhold your ability to climax indefinitely."

The command in his voice causes my thighs to tremble. Fighting past my shaking legs, I lean into the corner of the elevator, slither my hands under my skirt and grasp the band of my satin panties. Using Marcus's frame as a shield, I slide the damp material down my quaking thighs before kicking them to my side. The wetness between my legs grows, loving the edge of naughtiness in our exchange. Just the thought of being caught has the veins in my neck strumming.

The scent of my arousal filters through my nose when Marcus gathers my panties from the ground by pretending he is tying the laces on his shoe. My thighs push together as I feel the heat of his breath on my right kneecap. He is mere inches from my dripping core.

Keeping his eyes front and center, Marcus slips my panties into his pocket before extending to his full height. Even with his crotch mostly covered by his suit jacket, I know he is hard. The pleats of his trousers are fully extended, and the zipper is jutted out as it struggles to contain his impressive manhood. I lick my lips, hoping to God my brazen request in Links is about to be fulfilled. When I squirm on the spot, fighting hard to ease the throb between my legs, evidence of my excitement extends to my upper thighs. I've never felt more scandalous or desired in my life.

My squirming comes to a stop when an unexpected smack hits my right butt cheek. I bite on my bottom lip to hold in my excited moan before drifting my eyes to Marcus. He faces the front of the cart, seemingly unaware of the blaze his smack caused to my thumping sex. Although he concealed his slap with an impromptu cough, the unexpected noise still gains us the attention of numerous sets of eyes.

Ignoring the inquisitive stare from the lady standing next to Marcus, I lean toward his side and murmur, "What was that for?"

He doesn't answer me. He simply smiles a wickedly delicious smirk that sets my pulse racing. Squeezing my knees together, I divert my eyes to the elevator dashboard, silently praying it will arrive at our floor before I embarrassingly combust into ecstasy without being touched. For every floor the elevator takes, the excitement vexing my libido grows and the number of occupants in the car decreases. In no time at all, it's just Marcus, me and the elevator attendant left.

Before my lust-hazed brain can register the elevator's arrival at the very top floor, Marcus grips my hand and steps into the empty corridor. The elevator doors have only just snapped shut when he curls his arms around my back, dips me, and seals his lips over mine. His tongue plunges into my mouth with a sense of urgency, like he couldn't wait a moment longer to kiss me.

Clearly, that's the case when he pulls his lips away from mine and murmurs, "I couldn't wait a second longer."

He grips my hand in his and paces towards a set of doors at the end of the long corridor, his steps urgent. The instant we enter a massive room, I pounce. My hands go frantic, trying to figure out a way to remove his jacket and trousers at the same time. I need the heat of his flesh against mine, and I need it now.

My endeavor to remove Marcus's clothes is left for dust when he throws his arm across the entranceway table, sending all the contents on top scattering onto the floor with a clatter. Placing his hands under my arms, he lifts me to sit on the solid wooden table. Before I can comprehend what's happening, the flare of my skirt is bunched around my waist, and Marcus burrows his head between my legs.

I call out when his tongue runs along the cleft of my pussy before it plunges inside. I clench my thighs around his head, I'm so close to climax I can taste it. He devours my pussy with a set of greedy licks and playful nibs until the tension in my sex coils so tightly, I can no longer hold back.

"Oh god, I'm going to come," I grunt, my words barely coherent. "Can I please come, Master Chains?" I ask, knowing the desires of my body are no longer controlled by me. Their sole rights belong to the man who can have me teetering on the edge of orgasmic bliss by simply speaking.

Gratitude scorches through me when Marcus murmurs, "You can come."

The vibration of his deep voice against my soaked sex is the final push I need to freefall over the edge. With his teeth grazing my clit, Marcus's name tears from my throat in a grunted moan as I get lost in the throes of ecstasy. My nails bend harshly into the muscles on his shoulders as every nerve in my body fights through a blinding orgasm. I quiver and shake against his tongue, my mind shut down, my body overwhelmed by the shimmers of climax.

Once every climatic shudder has been exhausted, Marcus places one last lash of his tongue onto my clit before he raises his head. His mouth is glistening with evidence of my arousal, and his eyes are wide and bright.

"Ever since the day you fell onto your knees in the elevator, I've been dying to taste you."

My heart squeezes in my chest, beyond exalted he remembered our very first meeting. "You remember that day?"

Marcus toys with the bud of my clit before slipping two fingers into my wet core. "You thought I forgot?"

My breaths quicken to match the pace of his fingers pumping into me. With my pussy still throbbing with the aftermath of a toe-curling orgasm, it doesn't take long for his talented fingers to work me into a frenzy.

"Answer me, Cleo."

My muscles tense in anticipation from the clipped command of his voice. "No," I reply, shaking my head, sending droplets of sweat flinging off my inflamed cheeks. "I just didn't realize I was so memorable."

I tighten my grip around his neck when his fingers flick the little nub inside me that drives me wild. The familiar tingle of ecstasy grows with every dedicated thrust of his fingers. My body coils tightly, preparing for another release. I snap my eyes shut when the fiery warmth spreading through me becomes too much to bear. I personally know Marcus's skill level in the bedroom, but I am still shocked by how quickly he has my next orgasm building.

"Open your eyes," Marcus demands, his voice stiff. "I want you to see what your ecstasy-riddled face does to me."

I slowly flutter my eyes open and am awarded with the glorious visual of Marcus removing his erect cock from the tight restraint of his trousers. His suit pants drop to the floor with a flutter before his other hand works his boxers down his splayed thighs. His cock is so thick, the veins weaving up his long shaft are throbbing with need, and the tip is glistening with pre-cum. His balls are pulled in close to his body, preparing for imminent release. Just the sight of him finger fucking me with his trousers gathered around his ankles shifts my race to climax from a frantic pace to a desperate dash. I need to climax even more than I need to breathe.

I reach out to touch Marcus's thick cock, only to have my hands snapped away. I pout. I'm dying to feel the heat of his flesh in my hand and to taste him in my mouth. My disappointment doesn't last long when Marcus grinds his fingers into me deeper, ensuring his fingertips brush the sensitive nub inside me with every pump he does. I rock my hips forward, meeting his rhythm thrust for thrust. All thoughts vanish as a blistering of stars form before my eyes. My body quakes as a second orgasm shimmers to life.

"Now, Cleo!" Marcus demands, plunging his fingers into me at a frantic speed. "Come now!"

The desire to snap my eyes shut overwhelms me when the intensity of my orgasm hits full fruition. I grunt and moan, battling the sensation roaring through every inch of my spent body.

"Eyes on me, Cleo," Marcus demands. "Watch what you do to me. Watch how reckless you make me."

A guttural moan tears through my lips when my eyes snap to him in just enough time to see the first jet of cum rocket out of his engorged knob. The hotness of his seed pumps out of him in raring spurts, coating my throbbing pussy and landing halfway up my stomach. I moan even louder, loving the possessive vibe sparking the air. I did that. Me. My face in the middle of ecstasy was the only thing needed to make him cum. That's a highly thrilling and addictive experience, and it hurtles my orgasm to a never-before-reached level.

It feels like hours pass before my body stops shaking with the effects of climax. My muscles are weary, and every inch of my body is slicked with sweat. After removing my coat from my shoulders, Marcus locks his lust-crazed eyes with me.

"You were the first woman to fall to her knees in front of me," he admits, his alluring eyes bouncing between mine. "I always had the desire for power in the bedroom, but it was that day that catapulted my needs to the next level."

"What?" I ask, certain my sexually satiated brain isn't registering what he is saying accurately. "What are you saying? I'm the reason you became—"

"Master Chains," he fills in.

He waits a moment, giving me a chance to fully absorb his confession. I honestly don't know what to think. I'm flattered. Obviously. But I'm also a little unsure. His lifestyle choice is my biggest cause of concern, so to discover I'm the reason he entered into that lifestyle is a little unsettling.

"Should I be flattered or upset?" I ask Marcus, my brain too exhausted to decipher the whirlwind of emotions pumping into me.

He bounces his captivating eyes between mine for several heart-stuttering seconds before saying, "No matter which journey life takes, you always end up where you are supposed to be. This is my life, Cleo, so even if you didn't fall in the elevator all those years ago, I truly believe this is who I would have eventually become."

My heartbeat slows to a gentle flutter when he cups the edge of my jaw. "Just like I truly believed I would eventually find you again. Whether it was ten years or four, I knew one day I would find you."

My eyes burn from the sudden influx of tears in them. He's been looking for me this entire time? That's crazily beautiful. I'll be the first to admit the speed of our relationship is crazy, but that doesn't lessen the intensity of it. Marcus knows me. Master Chains knows me. And I know him—both sides of him.

"Will you please kiss me, Master Chains?" I request, dying for any part of his body to be on mine.

Smiling, Marcus seals his mouth over mine. I can taste myself on his lips. It's a tangy and sharp flavor I've never experienced before. I lap it up, loving all the firsts I've been experiencing this weekend. My first time in a playroom.

My first time climaxing during sex. And my first time falling in love. I thought I loved Luke, but only now do I realize it isn't the same feeling I get when I am with Marcus. At the time, my relationship with Luke was heartwarming, but it didn't utterly consume me like Marcus does. He is on my mind all the time. Even before I knew his real name.

After banding his arms around my waist, Marcus pulls me off the entranceway table and moves deeper into the large suite. I grind my pussy against his crotch, loving that every grind increases his cock's thickness. The softness of high threadcount bedding graces my back when Marcus lays me on the kingsize bed in the middle of the suite. His mouth captures my breathy moan when he pins me to the bed, my body relishing the weight of him pressed against me.

We kiss for several minutes until nothing is on my mind but cherishing every delicious inch of the man in front of me.

With his knee keeping my shuddering thighs apart, Marcus undoes the buttons of his business shirt. The warm wetness between my legs grows when his delicious body is seductively freed from the tight restrictions of his clothing. He takes his time, building the sexual tension firing between us until it reaches a fevered pitch. My pussy clenches when his crisp blue business shirt gapes open, exposing inches of his rigid stomach.

While pulling off his blue striped tie, Marcus asks, "What's your safe word, Cleo?"

"Pineapple," I murmur, my body heightened beyond approach.

A girly squeal emits from my lips when he steps back from the bed and unexpectedly flips me over. A thrill of anticipation follows the path my zipper takes when he unlatches the hook of my dress and slides down the fastener until it's sitting in the small of my back. I hear his breathing hitch up a notch when my dress falls off my shoulders and crinkles around my knees pressed into the mattress. My heavy breasts fall forward when his talented fingers make quick work of my satin bra. He dumps it on the floor next to his removed trousers before cupping my soaked sex.

"You're drenched, Cleo," Marcus grinds out, his voice deep and tempting. "Have you been a bad girl?"

Unashamedly, I dip my chin. "Yes."

Fiery heat spreads across my naked backside when he exacts a painful spank to my right butt cheek. "Yes, what?"

"Yes, Master Chains," I stammer out, my words unable to conceal my pleasure.

My mind spirals with possibilities when the softness of silk lowers over my eyes. After fastening his tie to the back of my head, Marcus runs his hand down the curve of my back. My knees scrape across the bedding when he adjusts the curve of my hips, erotically staging me for his visual pleasure.

A violent shudder courses through me when I feel the heat of his breath against the puckered hole of my rear as he asks, "What's your safe word, Cleo?"

It's the fight of my life to murmur, "Pineapple."

29

The buzz of a cell phone distracts the enticing visual of Marcus shaving in front of the vanity mirror of his hotel suite. It's fascinating watching the man who drove me to the brink of ecstasy more times than I can count doing something so domesticated. I don't know what I was expecting, but I'm certain a man as wealthy as Marcus wouldn't need to shave his face if he didn't want to. He could just summon someone to do it for him. That's why I find it so refreshing to discover he maintains a lot of power in regards to his personal life. Not just in his playroom, but in every walk of his life. I guess it's all part and parcel of him needing to be in control.

Ignoring the pleas of my tired muscles, I roll out of the bed I'm sprawled on and pace to my handbag left dumped on the floor. I've spent the last twenty minutes struggling to regain the use of my sexually satiated muscles so I can join Marcus for a shower before we make the hour trip back to his residence. I swear, muscles I didn't know existed are hurting.

After yanking open the zipper of my handbag, I pull out my cellphone. A faint smile cracks onto my lips when I read the message displayed on the screen.

Lexi: *Just checking in to ensure you haven't died of sexual exhaustion.*

After checking Marcus's location, I return Lexi's text.

Me: *Before today, I would have never believed there was such a thing as death by sexual gratification.*

Lexi's reply is almost immediate.

Lexi: *Do share!*

My laugh fills the space, gaining me the attention of Marcus, who is wiping shaving cream from his cut jawline. From the hungry gleam in his eyes, no one would know he came four times already today. He looks as hungry for sexual relief as ever.

When his eyes drop to my phone, I jingle it in my hand. "Just Lexi checking in," I inform him, my tone breathy from his compelling stare.

Marcus's plump lips curl into a smirk. "When you're done, join me in the shower," he demands, nudging his head to the large double shower my near-sightedness displays as nothing but a blur of white. Although Marcus's voice is as commanding as ever, it couldn't hide the plea in his words. He wants me as badly as I want him.

Once I nod, agreeing with his request, Marcus enters the bathroom, closing the door behind him. I drop my eyes to my phone to begin typing a reply to Lexi. Halfway through my false vow of saintly virtue, my cell buzzes, announcing my battery is low.

"Oh, bugger," I mumble to myself. I delete my original longwinded reply to Lexi and send a much simpler one.

Me: *My phone is about to go dead. I'll update when I get home.*

I send thanks to God for Lexi when I read her reply.

Lexi: *I placed a charger in your purse yesterday morning. Now you have no excuse for keeping me on tender hooks.*

I laugh while typing.

Me: *Can't talk, just about to have a shower with a handsome, droolworthy man whose rich chocolatey voice is one of his lesser attributes.*

I attach a cheeky winking emoji to my message. Lexi's reply is instant.

Lexi: *Cleo!!*

Before I can reply, my phone shuts down. My rummage through my handbag only awards me with a USB charger. While racking my brain for a solution to my situation, my eyes scan the room. Like the stars are aligning in my favor, my examination of the vast space has me stumbling onto a MacBook Air sitting beneath a stack of papers on a small dressing table in the corner of the room.

I pace towards the Mac, silently praying it will have enough power to give my battery some type of charge until I can fully charge it at Marcus's property. With Lexi's medical condition, I've never allowed my battery to run flat. More times than not, a cellphone is the most valuable asset in an emergency situation.

After plugging my phone into the Mac, I hit the power button. Gratefulness pumps into me when the screen on the Mac instantly fires up. Happy it has adequate power to charge my cell, I place it on the dressing table and move towards the bathroom, more than eager to join Marcus in the shower. My brisk strides stop, closely followed by the beat of my heart, when the screen on the Mac fully illuminates.

"What the hell?" I mumble under my breath while pacing back to the Mac, my steps shaky.

My rickety stride has nothing to do with the effect of multiple muscle-weary orgasms, and everything to do with the live image being streamed on the monitor of the Mac. My eyes frantically scan the screen, wanting to ensure my exhausted brain isn't misreading the visual displayed before me. This can't possibly be what my eyes are relaying. There must be some type of mistake.

My heart falls from my chest when my avid assessment reaches the same conclusion time and time again: a live feed from my bedroom is being streamed on the laptop monitor. I may have believed it was an old video if it wasn't for the I.D Sarrieri hotel slip Mr. Carson purchased for me sitting packaged on my bed. After removing the felonious hidden camera, I placed the slip up for Auction on eBay last week. It sold the day of Thanksgiving. I only packaged it for delivery yesterday morning, moments before the NDA from Marcus was delivered.

My hand darts up to my mouth. I feel sick—incredibly sick. Not trusting my legs to keep me upright, I sit on the chair in front of the dressing mirror. This can't be true. What benefit would someone get from putting a camera in my bedroom? And why would they plant a laptop in Marcus's hotel room?

My blank stare at the monitor has me stumbling onto more evidence of my gross invasion of privacy. A document sitting in the bottom lefthand side of the screen has been saved under my name. It looks like an email saved to the desktop. Snubbing the shake of my hands, I glide my finger over the touchpad on the MacBook Air and click on the file.

It's lucky my stomach is empty. If it weren't, the violent heaves racking through my body would have seen the Mac's keyboard covered with vomit by now. After taking a moment to settle my squishy stomach, I scan my eyes over the email document.

"Dear Mr. Everett, Please find attached the background search you requested for Cleo Garcia of 160 Valley Road, Montclair, NJ 07042. I hope this search is to your satisfaction. Harry Closter."

I feel sick—horribly sick. My stomach twists as violently as my heart when the reality of the situation dawns on me. This Mac wasn't planted in Marcus's room. This is his computer. I don't give my heart the chance to plead with my brain to stop and rationally consider the facts. I just click on the attachment at the bottom of the email without a single thought passing my mind.

Just as my brain suspected, the form places the final nail in Marcus's coffin. My name, date of birth, address, negative bank balance, and employee status are displayed in a neat bullet point format. Its plain and stark presentation is vastly contradictory to the blatant fury raging through my blood right now.

As I scroll down, the situation gets worse. Pages and pages of the online journal I kept as part of my grieving process filters onto the screen. Lexi's therapist suggested for her to write down her thoughts she didn't want to voice out loud. I thought it was a brilliant idea, so I did exactly that the past four years. I wrote down my fears, my pain, and my desire to meet the man who offered me comfort in my hour of need. These words were not meant to be seen by anyone but me—they are sacred.

I guess one good thing has come from my privacy being so horribly invaded. It proves Marcus doesn't know me at all. He couldn't tell I was on the brink of climax by hearing the pants of my breath or know I was on the verge of crying because of one spoken word. He only knew because he's been spying on me this entire time! The date on the email ensures there is no misconception. It's dated the morning following our first communication on the Chains website.

No longer capable of holding in my fury, I grit my teeth, slam the Mac screen closed, and send it hurling across the room. It crashes into the wardrobe before grumbling to the floor. Its deformed and mangled appearance matches the sentiments of my heart to a T. How could I have been so stupid?! Why was I so blinded with lust, I couldn't see what this weekend was really about? A stupid game between a power-craving Dom and the belittled sub beneath him.

Hot, salty tears burn my eyes, but I refuse to let them fall. He does *not* deserve my tears. *He does not deserve me!* My entire body shakes with anger as I stand from my seat and snag my dress off the floor. I angrily yank it over my head before pulling my arms through the long sleeves. I don't bother securing the latch at the back, I'm too angry to care about the opinions of others. I just want to get out of here. I just want to go home.

While running my fingers through my hair to settle the disheveled mess, my eyes scan the room for Marcus's trousers. *I am not leaving this room without my panties.* My privacy may have been grossly invaded, but I still have my pride. I also refuse to let him have a single piece of me—even if it's something as measly as a scrap of satin.

I race to the other side of the bed when a portion of Marcus's dark slacks peeks out from the other side of the bed. The view of the twisted bedsheets intensify the swishy movements of my stomach. I shift my eyes away, refusing to look at a place I felt worshipped mere minutes ago. *How stupid was I?*

The pocket in Marcus's trousers rip when I roughly yank them open, seeking my panties. For the first time in five minutes, I secure an entire breath when a silky smoothness graces the tips of my fingers. I wipe under my eyes to ensure no rogue tears have fallen before sliding my panties up my thighs and slipping into my stilettos.

The instant the flare of my dress hits my knee, my body's awareness of Marcus activates. I take in a nerve-calming breath before lifting my eyes from the ground. Just as my body intuited, Marcus is standing in the doorway of the bathroom. He has a white towel wrapped around his drenched hips, and his brow is arched high. Time slows to a snail's pace when he rakes his eyes down the length of my body, absorbing my clothed form.

When he shifts his eyes to the MacBook Air sprawled halfway across the floor, my eyes follow his movements. A dash of panic mingles with the anger lacing my veins when I notice my cellphone is still tethered to the Mac. Although my bank balance has slightly improved the past eight weeks, I can't afford to replace my phone if it's as broken as the Mac. I have four years of catching up bills before my money can go towards luxury expenses.

Swallowing away my worry, I return my eyes to Marcus. Fury blackens my blood and flushes my face when I see the truth beaming from his eyes. He knows what I saw on his Mac. His eyes tell me the entire story. Snarling, I issue him a wrathful stare. I've never been so angry in my life. It feels like it's burning me alive.

"*Cleo...*" His voice comes out in a warning, like I'm the one who invaded his privacy. "I can explain."

Angrily shaking my head at his failure to refute my silent accusation, I bob down to grab my cellphone off the floor. My yank is so rough it snaps the USB charging cord in half. After gathering my handbag off the bed where I dumped it, I make a beeline for the door.

Marcus beats me to it.

He dives over the bed and flattens his back against the hotel suite door before I even get one foot into the entranceway. His ninja-like moves forced the towel around his hips to slip, leaving him as naked and exposed as I feel. I'm so angry, my body doesn't even request for me to look down.

"Move," I sneer through clenched teeth, my tears threatening to fall at any moment.

Marcus stares straight into my eyes before shaking his head. His stance is as determined as the strong gleam beaming from his eyes.

"Move!" I scream again as the first tears topple from my eyes.

I angrily brush them away, loathing that they are making me look weak. I am not weak. I can't say the same about the so-called man in front of me. Marcus moves with such agility, he has me wrapped up in a firm hold before I can comprehend what's happening. I thrash against him, hating that my body's first response was to melt into his embrace. The instant his familiar scent was detected my body forgot the rage scorching my veins. *He is the reason my heart is being torn in two, so why is my body craving his touch?*

"Let me go!" I yell, hoping my startled cries will alert another hotel guest on our floor to my distress.

Marcus firms his grip. "Not until you give me the chance to explain," he responds, his words pleading.

"What's there to explain? You spied on me! No further explanation needed!"

I continue fighting, not willing to give this man another second of my time. He has already had more than he deserves. My heart smashes against my ribs as my lungs fight to secure an entire breath. My mind is shut down, my heart beyond repair.

"I told you you make me reckless, Cleo. I warned you that I can't control myself around you," Marcus says, his tone confused.

Even hearing the pain in his words doesn't stop my wailing. I kick my arms and legs out wildly, ensuring the heels on my stilettos connect with his shins. He doesn't deserve my sympathy. I showed him a side of me no one has ever seen. I gave him pieces of me I'll never get back, and this is how he repays me.

When his fingers cause a sting of pain to rocket to my core, our time together in his playroom comes rushing to the forefront of my mind. It's a cruel and twisted reminder of the rollercoaster of emotions I've been dealing with the past twenty-four hours. I thought the longest day I'd ever endured was the day my parents were killed. It wasn't. Today has felt like an eternity. A horridly beautiful day that saw my heart expand so much, it had no other choice but to shatter.

The only good thing that comes from being bombarded with memories of Marcus's playroom is that it reminds me of the one word that will instantly halt his campaign. The one word he promised would ensure our exchange would end the instant I said it.

"Pineapple," I murmur, hiccupping through the stream of tears rolling down my face. "Pineapple," I repeat, ensuring there is no way he couldn't hear my request.

Marcus's grip around my waist firms before he finally lets go and takes a step back. I keep my gaze locked on the tiled floor for several moments, gasping in breaths like it's my last chance to breathe. After brushing the tears off my cheeks in one fell swoop of my hand, I lift my disarrayed gaze to Marcus. The torment in his eyes replicates mine to a T. They are full of despair and regret.

But even knowing he is hurting doesn't stop me from saying, "Goodbye, Marcus."

When he steps towards me, I hold out my hand and shake my head. "Please don't make me say my safe word again. You said once it's used, there is no going back, the scene is ended. Show me you're a tenth of the man I thought you were by being a man who keeps his word."

Marcus's nostrils flare as his eyes bounce between mine. I can see he wants to say something, but thankfully, not a sound seeps from his lips. It takes my brain screaming at my body for me to push off my feet and walk past him. The tears welling in my eyes grow when his familiar freshly showered smell hits my senses, but I keep my gaze forward, refusing to look at the man who so grossly broke my trust.

"*Cleo*...please," Marcus murmurs when I lower the door handle and swing open the door.

I don't stop. I continue with my endeavor to reach the bank of elevators at the end of the hall. If I don't leave now, I may say something I can never take back. The heat of Marcus's gaze warms my back the entire way. It never once wavers until I step into the elevator car several minutes later. After dipping my head in greeting to the elevator attendant, I move to the far corner of the empty car.

The instant the doors snap shut, I crumble to the ground and howl.

30

Throwing my keys into the glass bowl on the entranceway table of my home, I pace deeper into the foyer. I honestly don't recall how I got here. I'm fairly certain I caught the train, but I can't one hundred percent testify to that. My body has gone into autopilot mode. I'm exhausted, hurt and heartbroken.

Lexi's perfume engulfs my nasal cavities when I am unexpectedly wrapped up in a pair of strong arms. "Oh my god, Cleo. Are you okay? Did he hurt you?"

When she pulls back from our embrace, her eyes go wild, scanning every inch of my face and body for any physical signs of injury. She won't find any. All my damage is internal—it can't be seen by the naked eye.

Lexi's warm hand takes the chill out of my cheek when she cups my jaw and glances into my eyes. "I've been calling you the past two hours," she advises, her calm words not holding the same panic her forthright eyes are.

Her admission shocks me. *Maybe I didn't take the train straight home?*

Lexi licks her dry lips before saying, "Chains called hours ago to tell me you were coming home. I've been trying to reach you ever since."

Just hearing his name amplifies the stabbing pain hitting the middle of my chest. "My phone is dead," I advise, my voice so flat I don't even recognize it.

I suddenly stiffen. "I need a shower."

Cold sweat clings to my skin as I close my eyes. I can smell Marcus on me. In my hair, on my skin, inside of me. I shiver as my lips thin in grimness.

"I *really* need to take a shower," I murmur, my words relaying my utter desire. I've never felt more dirty.

"Okay." Lexi slowly breathes out. "You go and grab a shower while I make you a glass of tea. You look exhausted."

She runs the back of her hand down my cheek, her eyes growing more concerned by the minute. I want to tell her what happened, but I can't right now. I'm having such a hard time processing it all that I can't be expected to relay the information to a third party.

Leaning in, I press a kiss to Lexi's temple, silently thanking her for the sympathies her dark eyes are transmitting before trudging to our shared bathroom. I take my time in the shower, ensuring every inch of my skin is free of Marcus's scent. I wash my hair, shave my legs and scrub my skin until it's red and raw.

By the time I walk out of the bathroom, we are out of hot water and my dour mood isn't as rampant as it was earlier. Don't construe my statement the wrong way. I am still fiercely angry. I'm just not wallowing in self-pity anymore. Marcus might have played me for a fool, but that charade is now over.

My switch in mood has a lot to do with a saying my mom always quoted to Lexi and me at the beginning of our teen years, "Instead of wiping away your tears, wipe away the people who created them."

That's exactly what I am going to do.

And I know the very first place to start.

After wrangling my hair into a messy bun, I pace into my bedroom. From the determination of my strides, no one would be the wiser to the pain shredding my heart. I stop to stand in the middle of my room for several seconds, wanting to ensure Marcus can see his betrayal has had no effect on me whatsoever. From the angle of the livestream on the Mac, it doesn't take a genius to realize the webcam in my computer was the source of the bug. I wouldn't be shocked to discover it's been streaming since the day I logged into the chains website weeks ago.

Once I am satisfied Marcus has spotted my determination, I saunter to my desk, yank my computer out of the wall and dump it into the waste receptacle at the side of our house, removing the trash from my life as if it's nothing but rubbish.

I feel invigorated and free, like nothing can bring me down... until I spot the chain link pendant dangling around my neck in the full-length mirror of my room. That's all it takes for a flood of tears to bombard my eyes. *How could such an awe-inspiring day turn into a clusterfuck in a matter of minutes?*

While battling to keep my tears at bay, horrid shudders wreak havoc with my body. When they become too great for me to bear, I crash onto my bed and burrow my head into my pillow. He will not break me. I am stronger than this. Tears are reserved for my darkest days.

Lexi finds me five minutes later huddled in a ball in the middle of my bed. Not speaking, she places a glass of chamomile tea onto my bedside table and crawls into my bed. She curls her body around mine and whispers reassurances in my ear on repeat. Most follow along a similar path—she is going to kill Master Chains.

As the pain in the middle of my chest grows, minutes on the clock tick by. Utterly exhausted from an emotionally draining weekend, the weight of my eyelids becomes too much for me to ignore. With the heat of Lexi's body heating my back, and her kind words warming my heart, I soon fall asleep.

By the time I wake the next morning, the sun is already hanging high in the sky. I lift my arms out of my comforter and take a long stretch. My muscles are still pulled taut from the exertion of sexual activities. It's a vindictive reminder of the day I endured yesterday.

My neck cranks to the side when I hear the padding of feet sounding down the hall. Lexi stands at my bedroom door with a mug of coffee in one hand and my cellphone in the other. She looks as exhausted as I feel. She stayed with me the majority of the night, not even leaving my side when Jackson arrived to whisk her away on a romantic date. Her dedication and love helped to soothe the hideous scars Marcus's betrayal caused to my heart.

Lexi paces two steps into my room. "I know this is the last thing you need," she says, nudging her head to my cellphone clasped in her hand. "But this has been ringing nonstop."

Immaturely, I roll my eyes and release an exasperated breath. "You'll have to show me how to block his number from calling me."

My eyes snap to Lexi when she says, "It isn't Chains who has been calling."

The beat of my heart kicks into overdrive, and shock smears my face. I guess I shouldn't be surprised, though. I was nothing more to Marcus than a silly little sub to play games with. His demoralizing games strengthen my belief of why he wanted me to sign an NDA. He would hate for any other naïve young lady to discover the tricks he is playing. It wouldn't be as much fun if they were prepared for having their hearts torn from their chests.

I scrub my hand over my tired eyes when Lexi sits on the edge of my bed. "Who is it, then?" My voice is husky with both tiredness and from the number of tears I shed last night.

Lexi doesn't answer me. She simply hands me my phone. The swirling of my stomach kicks up a notch when my eyes drop to the screen. Lexi was right. This is the last thing I need. Before I can comprehend why I have eighteen missed calls from Delilah, my cellphone vibrates and rings in my hand.

Clutching my chest to ensure it remains in place, I swipe my finger across the screen and push my phone to my ear. Although wrangling an irate Delilah is more than I'm up for this Sunday morning, I'm too intrigued about why she is calling me with such urgency to ignore my inquisitiveness.

"Chloe, we need you in the office by noon," Delilah snarls, not bothering to issue a greeting.

"It's Sunday," I mumble, my groggy voice incapable of hiding my shock. "And my name is Cleo by the way," I snap out, sick of being so disrespected.

A deep growl barrels down the line before Delilah barks, "When the story of the century is on the verge of breaking, it doesn't matter if it's Sunday or Christmas Day. If you're not in this office by noon, *Cleo*, don't bother arriving on Monday."

My pulse quickens, more from her declaration of the story of the century about to be broken than her snarky tone.

"What story?"

"The investigation into Chains has been reopened. Mr. Carson wants the story headlining every media outlet in the country before Christmas."

With that, Delilah disconnects the call...

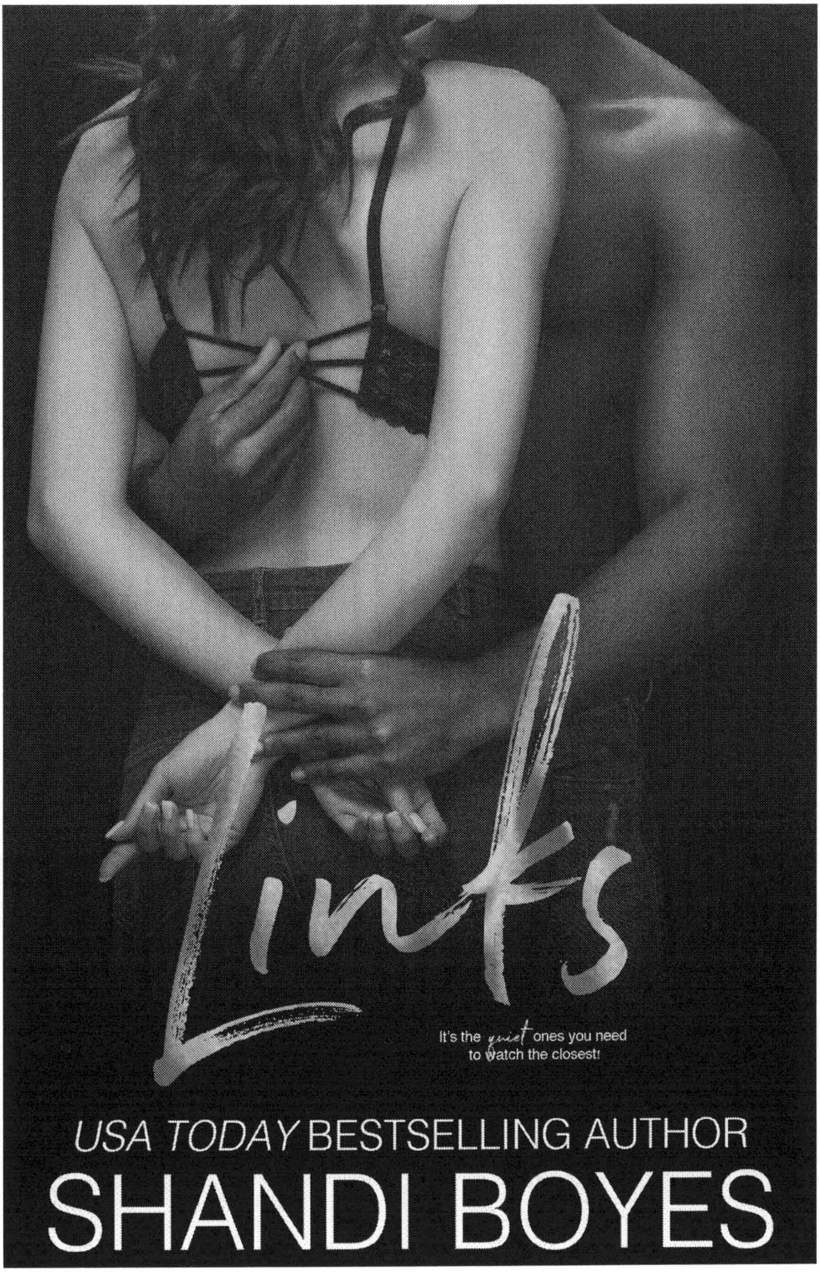
Links
It's the quiet ones you need
to watch the closest!
USA TODAY BESTSELLING AUTHOR
SHANDI BOYES

1

I love my home. This is the place my story began. Nervous butterflies fluttered my parents' stomachs when they walked through these very doors twenty-six years ago with a slightly jaundiced screaming bundle of pink. I took my first steps here, said my first words, and kissed my first boyfriend on the porch out front. Just yesterday, there was no other place I felt more secure, safe, and welcome than my family home. Marcus stole that joy from me. He stripped away my security, leaving me vulnerable and exposed.

I hate that.

I hate that a man who's only known me a matter of weeks has so much power over me he can change my perception so considerably. I hate that even while showering, my eyes scan the small, dingy space for signs of a hidden camera. I hate that no matter how much I scrub my skin, I can still smell him on every inch of my body. But more than anything, I hate that I can't hate him for making me feel weak, helpless, and exposed. Hate is a wasted energy—nothing good ever comes from it. So, as much as I want to hate Marcus for breaking my trust and grossly invading my privacy, I don't. I may despise him and loathe that I foolishly believed things would be different between us, but I don't hate him. Hate is easy. Love is complicated.

If I stepped back and evaluated the entire picture, I would have realized weeks ago this day was bound to happen. My relationship with Marcus built at such a breakneck speed, there was no other option for it but to crash and burn. I was hoping we would break the stigma attributed to instalove, but the only thing that ended up broken was my trust, and, unfortunately, my heart.

I can't believe how much has changed in such a short time. Yesterday, I was basking in the high of two mind-blowing orgasms. Today, I'm waking up with a hollow space where my heart used to belong. But no matter how glum I feel, I will survive this. I'll come out of it bigger and better. Because it isn't what we have in value that defines us, it's how well we rise after falling that shows our true spirit.

More determined than ever, I switch off the faucet and step out of the shower recess. My muscles pull taut, still suffering the effects of a sexually adventurous weekend. Pretending my aching joints are from a night of dancing, I snag a towel from under the leaking sink and commence patting myself dry. The stiff board-like material scratches my delicate skin, but I keep my chin high, refusing to compare the stark confines of my bathroom to the luxurious one I used yesterday.

There is no comparison, anyway. No amount of Italian marble and priceless granite can equal the memories of a family bathroom. I can still recall in crystal clear detail watching my father bathe Tate for the first time in the vanity sink of this very bathroom. I was six and in complete awe of the little boy who was so eager to join the world, my mother gave birth hunched over a wooden chair in our formal dining room. I was already wide-eyed from Lexi joining our family only eleven months earlier that I didn't think anything could top it.

I was wrong. So very, very wrong.

I was always an inquisitive child, but inquisitiveness grew tenfold after watching Tate enter the world. It wasn't the wonderment of birth that had me intrigued, it was watching the dynamic between my mother and father. My mom was understandably panicked, she didn't want to give birth at home. She was frantic, screaming and saying things I'd never heard leave her mouth before. Do you know what my dad did? He rested his forehead against her sweat-drenched one and stared into her eyes. He said nothing. Not a single word. Within ten seconds, the panic marring my mother's face cleared, and the determination in her eyes rampantly grew with every second that ticked by.

I was spellbound. I thought my dad was a wizard, and he'd placed a spell on my mom using mythical powers. It was only as the years went on, and I watched them more and more, did I realize what he'd done that day. He silently requested her trust. Even beyond panicked and in an immense amount of pain, my mom gave it to him. It's days like today I realize what I saw was magic. It was just minus the smoke and mirrors many people use to lure you into their trap. My father loved my mother, and she loved him. There is no greater illusion than loving someone wholeheartedly.

After running my fingers under my eyes to ensure no sneaky sentimental tears spilled, I pad to the vanity mirror. Gripping the edge of the cracked porcelain sink in a white-knuckled hold, I release a longwinded breath before raising my eyes to the foggy mirror. A broad set of wrinkles line my forehead when I spot my reflection in the mirror. A twenty-minute shower did nothing to ease the dark circles plaguing my hollow eyes. My naturally tanned skin looks splotchy, and my pupils are swamping my cornea, making my eyes appear nearly black in color.

"There is no bigger dampener to a woman's beauty routine than having her heart torn out of her chest," I mumble to my disheveled reflection.

Blowing an unruly hair from the front of my eye, I set to work on removing hours of restless sleep no amount of primping will ever erase. I cake a dense layer of concealer onto the rings around my eyes before cracking open my compact powder. Fire engine red lipstick adds an edge of sexiness to my kiss-swollen lips while the shimmer in my gold-flecked eyeshadow compliments the red hue gracing my cheeks. Although I spent a majority of my night struggling to contain my sniffles, a stranger will be none the wiser to my dour weekend activities. From the outside, I look well put together. *If only I could say the same thing about my insides.*

Once I've placed my cosmetics back into my makeup bag, I trudge into my room to get dressed. With Jackson collecting Lexi for a family outing to Fosterfields Living Historical Farm nearly an hour ago, my house is eerily quiet. Not a peep can be heard. I felt sorry for Jackson when he was wrangling Lexi into the passenger seat of his truck. He believed Lexi's desire not to attend the Collard's yearly outing was solely based on not wanting to leave me alone. It wasn't. Lexi is the very epitome of a modern-day woman, one who has champagne taste on a beer budget. The idea of being surrounded by farm animals is more frightening to Lexi than battling the crazies at a 90% off flash sale at Bloomingdales.

Smiling at Lexi's pleading face when Jackson carried her to his car while wailing over his shoulder, I pace to my wardrobe. Because the weather cooled overnight, I dress in a thick woolen skirt and a long-sleeve pleated cream blouse. After zipping my knee-high black boots, I turn to face the mirror. Although my insides are bristling with betrayal, my outside appearance matches the socially acceptable Cleo I've put together every morning for the past four years. I am as fraudulent as ever.

Disappointed and regretful, I turn away from the phony glancing at me in the mirror. This weekend, for the first time in years, I snubbed the need to be socially accepted. There was only one man's attention I wanted, so I gave it my all and went after what I wanted. Foolishly, I thought Marcus liked me for me, so that's what I gave him—the real Cleo—not the fake one I've presented most of my adult life.

I thought Marcus was my reward for my new approach to life. He brought me to the pinnacle of ecstasy with charm, wit, and incredible talent in the bedroom. For hours, I lived in a bubble of bliss, a place far away from the reality I've been living the past four years. It was beautifully serene... until his deceit stripped it all away.

Gritting my teeth at my stupidity in believing I was special to Marcus, I snag my cracked cellphone off my bedside table, shove it into the pocket of my skirt and amble to the door. When I catch sight of the time on the clock halfway down the hall, my quick strides increase. It's nearly 11 AM. The last thing I need added to the muddled mess of my life is an unemployment status.

Although shocked by Delilah's request for my attendance today, I'm not wholly stumped by it. In the world of journalism, a sense of urgency isn't a necessity, it's a requirement. Typically, the push to get a story broadcasted is based on two facts: another media company is about to break the story, or the story is soon to be nonexistent. Considering the latter probabilities are sitting at zilch, the more plausible reason would be another media company has caught wind of the scandalous activities occurring right under their noses a minimum of once a month the past two years.

It took Mr. Carson sacrificing a majority share of his foreign equity company to get an invitation to Chains, so I'm flabbergasted another media company had the gall to put up the same collateral. Although being investigated is never a walk in the park, this whole endeavor could be a silver lining for Marcus. While the media vies to break the story of the century, Chains pockets a mindboggling amount of money. If I didn't know Chains' profits go toward funding Links, I would have said it was a brilliant marketing move on Marcus's behalf.

I'm not surprised by the media's interest in this story. By keeping his guest list top-secret, Marcus created intrigue, which in turn encourages curiosity. And since there is no thinner veil than that of anonymity, the stakes are dangerously high in a world that can't comprehend the word "privacy."

That's why Marcus's breach of my trust hurts so much. I thought he understood the value of privacy. The discretion guaranteed to the members of Chains is the very apex of his business. It's the reason his club is so successful. So why didn't he extend that same level of respect to me?

My pace slows even more as a bitterly cold chill runs the length of my spine. For the quickest moment, I forgot my place. In Marcus's industry, I am nothing more than a commodity. A slave stripped of her rights, my sole purpose in life to obey my master. *Aren't I?*

Honestly, if you had asked me the same question prior to discovering Marcus was spying on me, I would have vehemently denied that a sub is a slave with no power. This weekend was an eye-opening experience, one I would have never been brave enough to venture into without the help of Master Chains. It taught me not everything you read is true, sometimes even a thoroughly researched article can be filled with misconceptions and bias when it's written by someone outside of an industry.

It also demonstrated what my mother always preached, "Be who you are, not what you think someone wants you to be."

That would be a whole heap easier to do without a knife being stabbed in my chest.

2

With gloomy storm clouds putting a damper on the day, my commute to New York wasn't as hair-raising as usual. Although the train was still packed with riders, it wasn't the usual mix of commuters I've come to expect the last five years. The stiff, robotic, professionally clad regulars were replaced with a rousing blend of tourists and locals excited about spending their Sunday in the wonder of New York. Despite the drizzly conditions, their enthusiasm was electric, a stark contrast to the foyer I am entering.

I spent the entire commute to New York trying to clear some of the muddled mess of confusion in my brain. Forty minutes of deliberation gained me an additional forty minutes of chaos.

Being Sunday, an eerie quietness prickles the hairs on my arms when I walk into the bulletproof foyer of Global Ten Media. Other than a small handful of security officers mingling in the vast space, the area is void of its usual hum of activity. My already brisk pace quickens when I spot the time on the large art deco clock on the far wall. I only have ten minutes before I surpass the deadline set by Delilah this morning.

As my hand delves into my oversized clutch to obtain my employee ID, I catch the impish gleam of Richard standing at the side of the foyer. This is the first time I've seen him since our disastrous run-in three months ago. Although I was curious as to his whereabouts, I never voiced my interest. Showing interest only raises curiosity—something I already have in abundance.

"Cleo," Richard greets me, his tone as haughty as always. "Can I help you with anything?"

Smiling, I shake my head while scanning my employee ID into the security panel. Gratefulness pumps into me when the security light switches from red to green. Thankfully, my inclusion in the New York Daily Express team means my security rights were adjusted to include twenty-four-seven access, or I would have required Richard's assistance to enter the secure facility.

After placing my ID back into my clutch, I glide across the polished marble floors. I can feel Richard's eyes tracking me the entire time, but my outward appearance doesn't give any indication I've spotted his insolent stare. I keep my head held high, refusing to let an arrogant man like Richard believe he has me startled.

As I wait for the elevator car to arrive at my floor, I take in my wide-eyed expression in the mirrored doors. My eyes are dull and lifeless, and the blemish on my cheeks gives away my confused state. I exhale harshly, wishing I could fast forward into the future so I could see how this all pans out. Maybe then I'd have a chance in hell of settling some of the confusion fogging my brain.

When the elevator dings, announcing its arrival to my floor, I step into the elevator car. I immediately suck in a desperate gulp of air, alarmed by another presence in the car. The panic bristling my scalp eases when I discover whom I am riding with.

"Hi, Keira. How are you?" I greet, pacing deeper into the elevator.

I arch a brow in suspicion when she fails to acknowledge my greeting or exit the elevator. *If she rode the elevator to the foyer, why isn't she disembarking?*

Spotting my contemptuous expression, Keira explains, "I boarded on floor fifty-eight not realizing the elevator was going down." She gestures her dainty hand to the elevator dashboard. "What level?"

"Seventy-three, please," I reply, my tone void of the suspicion it was holding earlier.

After pushing my desired floor, Keira spins on her heels to face me. Her abrupt movements infuse the air with the slight aroma of vanilla. It's a refreshing scent that soothes some of the irritation twisting my stomach. Keira is a beautiful young lady in her mid-twenties. She has long, straight blonde hair that hangs halfway down her back and ageless facial features. She has timeless beauty, the type that would suit any generation.

"How long have you been working at Global Ten?"

Although we haven't formally met, the news around the water cooler is that Keira is employed as an undergrad in the financial arm of Global Ten. Considering no one outside of the journalism division of Global Ten works weekends, I'm somewhat surprised she is working on a Sunday.

"A little over two months," Keira replies, sighing softly.

"And already working a long weekend? I don't know whether to applaud you or issue a warning," I jest, my tone friendly.

Keira's laugh quickly fills the space. It's full of poise and elegance, just like its owner. "To be honest, I haven't worked that out either. I'm not even sure this industry is for me yet."

My lips purse. "A career in media not your first choice?"

Keira shakes her head. "No. My career aspirations never involved prying into people's lives, nor their trash receptacles," she discloses, her pitch snarky.

Ignoring the way her remark dented my ego, I ask, "Then, why do it? If a career in media isn't your preference, why not find something that is?"

Keira shrugs. "My family is more receptive to this role than my initial choice."

My heart squeezes when I hear the disappointment in her low tone. It's an unfortunate world we live in when social acceptance is valued higher than happiness. It doesn't just happen with career choices either. It's in everyday life. Like every interracial couple, my parents endured a diverse range of obstacles thrown their way. Unfortunately, most of them came from integral members of their family. That was the reason I understood Marcus's logic of keeping his interest in the BDSM lifestyle hidden from his family. Going against a socially judging world is already challenging, let alone when the most important people in your life don't support your lifestyle choices. My parents had each other for support. Marcus could have had me if he hadn't invaded my privacy.

"What about you? Have you always wanted to be a journalist?" Keira drifts my focus back to the present.

A faint smile cracks onto my lips. "Yes. I've always loved reading. It didn't matter if it was the latest romance novel or the sports pages of my local newspaper, I gobbled up anything in print. But my passion for writing flourished when a small piece I wrote on my high school football team winning state was published by my local paper. I don't know what was more exciting, seeing my name in print or receiving my first paycheck for something I'd written."

"I bet it was seeing your name in print?" Kiera intuits with her manicured brow arched high.

"Yeah, it was," I reply honestly, still smiling. "It was an amazing thing to see."

Remembering the proud words my mother said to me that day, I lock my eyes with Keira and say, "That would have never happened if I weren't doing something I loved. Just like you will never realize your dreams in a position you have no passion for. If your passion isn't in the media industry, Keira, find what is and strive to achieve it. It's your life, make the most of it."

Keira watches me in silence for several moments, absorbing my suggestion with more thought than I'd perceived. Her attentive stare plunges the elevator car into silence. I wouldn't necessarily say it's unpleasant, more like she needs a few moments to compile a response. Not wanting her to feel uncomfortable, I float my eyes to the elevator dashboard to watch its ascent.

We climb twelve floors before Keira finally breaks the silence. "Mr. Carson chose well when he selected you as the lead investigator for the story on Chains."

Masking my surprise she is aware of the investigation into Chains, I reply, "Thanks." My tone is low as I struggle to accept her praise. "But I'm fairly certain it wasn't my journalism skills that got me the job."

I roll my shoulders and jiggle my chest to enhance my statement. After numerous juvenile comments from Delilah the past two months, I'm convinced my placement on the New York Daily Express team was solely based on some areas of my body, not my high distinction from NYU.

"Don't sell yourself short, Cleo," Keira implores, glancing straight into my eyes, her gaze forthright. "Although your *assets* are very impressive, I don't believe that's the sole reason Mr. Carson hired you. I've heard rumors the head of media was pushing for this story the past twelve months. It was only after seeing the way you handled Richard did Mr. Carson agree to the investigation."

I grimace when the entirety of her statement is absorbed by my spent brain. I'd been wondering the past two months if Mr. Carson's interest in me began after my altercation with Richard—clearly, my assumptions were correct. There is just one thing unclear.

"Why would physically harming someone lead to career advancement?" My high tone is smeared with disbelief.

Keira shrugs. "I don't know, maybe Mr. Carson wanted someone strong enough to endure the BDSM lifestyle in its full light?" Her voice is void of the disdain most people carry when discussing BDSM lifestyle choices.

I tilt my head to the side and bow my brow. "What do you mean 'in its full light?'"

Hearing the snip of panic in my tone, the brightness of Keira's blue eyes grows. "To see both sides of the spectrum. You're a feminist with submissive traits. It's a brilliant choice by Mr. Carson. I'm quite impressed. He chose someone with enough guts to deeply emerge herself into the lifestyle without being overwhelmed by it."

"I'm not in the BDSM lifestyle, Kiera," I reply, my tone high as panic surges through me.

Keira screws up her nose as if she isn't buying my reply. "Maybe not yet, but you have the qualities of a submissive. It will only be a matter of time before a Dom changes your mindset, or you'll stop judging yourself on the sane, safe and consensual desires your body craves."

Misreading the alarm tainting my face as disgust, Keira stammers out, "Being dominated doesn't make you weak, Cleo. It just means you think outside the box of what society deems as normal. People from all walks of life enjoy kink, just not many are willing to admit it."

"Do you like being dominated?" I question, my voice barely a whisper since it was coerced through the guilt curled around my throat. I've always been an inquisitive person, but it's never had this edge of prying attached to it.

She taps her manicured index finger on the side of her nose. "Discretion is a highly valued commodity in any walk of life, Cleo," she tsks me with a jeering tone. "That's why I am imploring you to write the story on Chains the way in which you see it."

"And how am I *supposedly* seeing it?" After an emotionally tiring weekend, I'm physically exhausted, which means, unfortunately, I'm taking my anger out on the wrong person.

My snarkiness doesn't faze Keira in the slightest. "From a person intrigued by the BDSM lifestyle, but not guided by society's opinion of it. I'm not asking you to act on your desires, Cleo. I'm just encouraging you to push aside your misconceptions and write what you see." Her last sentence comes out in a hurry since the elevator has arrived at my floor.

Pacing out of the elevator, I stand at the side of a large white pillar to conceal myself from prying eyes. "What makes you so sure my stigma about the BDSM lifestyle doesn't match those deemed acceptable by society?"

Keira's manicured brow arches into the air, but not a word spills from her lips. Just like I've been told time and time again, she read the truth from my eyes.

Swallowing down the unease creeping up my esophagus that I'm about to expose my most lethal hand, I say, "Global Ten Media doesn't want a story on the *consenting* exchange of power between a Dom and his sub. They want to exploit the men and women who value Chains' confidentiality clause, not only making a mockery out of these 'people from all walks of life' you are referring to—" I use air quotes to enhance her quoted statement. "—they will destroy the lives of hundreds of people, some who are completely unaware they are associated with such an industry."

I snap my mouth shut, subjugated and mute. Overwhelmed by the catalyst of emotions pumping into me, my usual astuteness is vanquished, leaving nothing but a lecturing idiot debating the rights of members in a community I claim to have no association with.

Keira's determination isn't deterred by my malicious tirade. If anything, it appears to have strengthened it. "That fighting spirit is the exact reason I'm imploring you to write the truth, Cleo. You have the courage to write a story based on facts, not the misguided opinions of others. Any journalist can write a gossip piece crammed with half-truths and glossy pictures. A true journalist knows there is no cream without first churning the milk."

I stand frozen for a beat, unsure of how to reply. I'm shocked and somewhat confused. Although I agree with what Keira is saying, I don't appreciate being bombarded like this. I am also ill-prepared. I brushed Keira off as nothing more than a pretty face. Little did I know there was the heart of a warrior hidden behind her saintly features.

Sensing my inability to issue a comeback, Keira continues to wow me with her grit. "There are two sides to every story, Cleo: the truth and what the public are told. The only thing left to decide is if you're a reporter who writes inspiring pieces, or a pop-culture writer who sugarcoats the facts to meet societal norms."

With that, she spins on her heels and walks down the corridor, stealing my chance to reply.

3

Pretending I've failed to catch Delilah's furious wrath, I glide into the conference room on the top floor of Global Ten Media and take a seat at the end of the oak table. With my run-in with Keira buying into precious time I didn't have, I've arrived nearly ten minutes late. Plopping my oversized handbag onto the floor beside me, I secure one of the many manila folders sitting in the middle of the large table. My heart rate kicks into overdrive when my quick head count of the employees attending the impromptu meeting sits at thirteen. Mr. Carson is leading the meeting, and there are at least half a dozen faces I recognize from his hand-selected investigative team of the New York Daily Express.

My stomach gurgles. With such a heavy presence of big hitters in the Global Ten conglomerate, my fears that the story on Chains is about to break reaches fever pitch. Although my emotions are still on edge, even my ethically motivated brain agrees something about this case doesn't feel right. Call it intuition or a severe case of idiocrasy, but this entire investigation seems more than just an inclination to keep the public informed of the happenings within their community. It feels personal.

Don't get me wrong, even if I hadn't experienced a small taste of the BDSM lifestyle this weekend, my opinions would remain the same. What Marcus said weeks ago in Chains is true. Just because people choose to express themselves in a way society is unaccustomed to doesn't make them weird or different. So why should their personal choices place a target on their backs? *It shouldn't.*

My attention shifts to the meeting when Delilah pushes back from the table and saunters to the front of the room. From the impish gleam in her eyes, her beady black gaze looks fiercer than normal. When she clicks a button on a small remote in her hand, a projector screen drops down from the ceiling, shading the room from the natural sunlight beaming in from the floor-to-ceiling windows.

"As many of you are aware, Chains has been on the radar of the New York Daily Express for the past year," Delilah says as a copy of the invitation I used to gain access to Chains flashes up on the screen. "With its state of the art security and ability to change its location for each hosted party, it has been a hard scene to infiltrate. Locations are not disclosed until an hour before the party commences, and guests are well rehearsed on keeping their identities private. It was virtually impossible to get in."

Glaring into my eyes with an evil smirk etched on her abhorrent face, Delilah clicks on the remote, bringing up a photo of Marcus in the back seat of the Bentley. "New York Daily Express was the first media company to successfully infiltrate the super-secret society known only as Chains."

My stomach lurches into my throat when her next click on the remote switches the image to one displaying my reflection in the Bentley's heavily tinted windows. Although my face is covered by a black sequined mask, I am clearly identifiable, there is no denying my Garcia genes.

The murmured hum of chatter filtering in the conference room fades to silence when recognition dawns on my colleague's faces. One by one, I gain the inquisitive stares of every pair of eyes in the room. Half peer at me in wonderment, whereas the other half have a vast array of emotions pumping from their eyes. Disgust. Intrigue. Curiosity. That's a small selection of the glares inundating me.

"Although the attendees are masked, we secured a sizeable number of images from the last Chains *gathering,*" Delilah snarls, shifting the attention of the room back to her.

Collective "Ah's" fill the space when Delilah plays a slideshow of the images illegally obtained two months ago. Due to my failure to remove my coat until after I left the premises, every picture features Marcus in some light. Although my memories of that night will never fade, it's uncanny to see them through the lens of a third party.

I felt a connection to Marcus the instant my eyes locked with his in the back seat of the Bentley. These images verify our compelling union. They showcase the way he peered down at me as we weaved through the throng of fetish-wearing patrons, the little groove peeking out of his mask when the bartender riled him up, and the flare of regret sparking his alluring gaze in the seconds leading to our separation in the foyer. Even a person with their eyes as thinly slit as Delilah's wouldn't be able to miss the undeniable connection between us.

My heart twists painfully. Now, more than ever, I need to keep my cards close to my chest. Global Ten Media already has me over a barrel with their knowledge of my love for my sister. Imagine how bad it will be if they discover the feelings I am harboring for the man they are investigating?

My heart twists again—more catastrophic this time. How stupid am I? Marcus grossly invaded my privacy, yet I'm more concerned about protecting him than vindicating him. He should be grateful my parents raised me with integrity because that's the only thing stopping me from disclosing his identity. *That, and a small hope not everything between us is lost.*

Setting aside my heart versus brain quarrel for a more appropriate time, I return my eyes to the projector screen. The slideshow Delilah is presenting gives an intriguing look into the BDSM lifestyle, but it's a one-sided glimpse into a world you could never fully comprehend until you have experienced it. Nothing compares to seeing something in the flesh, much less immersing yourself in it. Although my time in the BDSM world was short, it left a lasting impression. Don't ask me if it's a good or bad impression as I wouldn't be able to answer you.

When the tediously long slideshow comes to an end, the projector screen rises back into place, once again illuminating the room with natural light. The view from the conference room is just as impressive as the one in Mr. Carson's office, but with my mood precariously sitting on the edge of a steep cliff, it doesn't wow me as it did months ago.

After placing the remote onto the conference room table, Delilah intertwines her fingers. She rocks on her heels, her face smug and lacking a single wrinkle. "With our undercover reporter not making the impression we were hoping for, any headway we made in identifying the man in the pictures was squandered as quickly as Mr. Carson's bank balance when he spends a day at the race track."

The room breaks into rapturous laughter, my colleagues seemingly catching onto Delilah's joke. I laugh too, but it's more to hide my gratefulness that Delilah is still unaware of Marcus's identity than being amused at a joke I'm not privileged to understand.

My smile is wiped straight off my face not even two seconds later when Delilah shrieks, "That all changed last night. We not only captured a portion of the man's uncovered face, but we know the location of one of his regular haunts in New York." She projects her voice, ensuring she is heard over the boisterous laughter filling the room.

I swallow several times in a row, attempting to soothe the bile burning the back of my throat. This can't be true. This can't be happening. Not now. Not after everything I've endured this weekend. Marcus's clients don't deserve to have their privacy invaded like this. Even more so because of how much they donate to charity organizations. Does Delilah realize that? Does she know she won't just destroy the lives of the members of Chains by exposing their secret, she will hurt hundreds of victims of domestic violence who rely on Chains' profits to fund the shelter they so desperately need?

The panic boiling my veins dulls to a simmer when Delilah instructs us to open our manila folders. Although the image presented on the front page of the dossier is no doubt Marcus, a stranger wouldn't immediately reach the same conclusion. With a shadow sheltering his alluring eyes, nothing but the sharp cut of his jaw and plump lips are on display. Although Global Ten Media has contacts in high places, I doubt even the world's best facial recognition software would get a decisive match on this grainy and badly pixelated image.

"As you can see in the images, we believe the gentleman arriving at Chains last night is the same man photographed during our undercover investigation. He is of similar build and height—"

"Do you have any images of his face?" I interrupt Delilah, unable to leash my curiosity for a moment longer. I inwardly sigh, grateful my voice comes out sounding inquisitive, not fretful.

Delilah glowers at me, her glare as evil as her scowling face. "Not yet. But after liaising with the PI who captured his photo, we need to act quickly."

"Why?" Mr. Carson questions with his index finger pressed against his lips.

"In the darkness of the night, Chains was moved to another location. We believe they are preparing to host another party in the near future," Delilah answers, her tone reserved.

Mr. Carson scoots to the edge of his seat, his interest growing. My interests are also piqued, but not for the reasons you're thinking. I'm outraged, and if I am being honest, a little devastated Marcus is organizing another party so soon. I know I was nothing but a game to him, but he didn't even wait an entire day before commencing his search for my replacement.

Bile scorches the back of my throat. *He can't replace something he never had.*

Snubbing my inner monologue, I swing my eyes to Mr. Carson when he asks, "Did your investigator tail the movers?"

The scowl Delilah was directing at me clears away when she locks her eyes with Mr. Carson. "Unfortunately, no. With long weekend traffic and—"

"Save your excuses for a man willing to accept them," Mr. Carson scolds, slouching into his chair.

I eye him curiously, unable to determine if the expression on his face is panic or anger. The skin between his eyes is pulled taut, but the corners of his lips are tucked into the side of his mouth. I honestly can't tell if he is smirking or grimacing.

Smiling to mask her annoyance at being abruptly cut off, Delilah returns her focus to the journalists seated around the table. "Turn to page two."

Allowing my inquisitiveness to get the better of me, I flick ahead of my colleagues to pursue each image at a rate faster than Delilah is requesting. The ten plus photos present similar to the first one: they don't give any more indication of Marcus's identity than the one at the start of the dossier. If anything, the first image is the most identifiable one in the entire folder. Other than demonstrating Marcus is a fit African American man in his mid to late twenties, there is no identifiable location in any of the photos, and no distinctive markings on his body that will lead to the discovery of his identity... My inner monologue trails off when I reach the last set of pictures in the folder.

"Oh no," I mumble under my breath. "What did you do, Marcus?"

The last two photos don't show Marcus's face, but they do display the full license plate of the taxi he hired to take him to the Chains warehouse and the profile of his driver's face. It's dated an hour after I left the hotel in lower Manhattan. I know Marcus has said numerous times this weekend that I make him reckless, but I didn't realize it extended this far. From my intensive investigation into Chains the two weeks following our initial meeting, I know Chains utilizes a fleet of limousines from a company whose client records are more guarded than the Oppenheimer Blue diamond. So why did he take a taxi to Chains last night? It truly doesn't make any sense.

The swishing of my stomach catapults to a new level when Delilah informs, "We located the taxi driver shown in the last two images. He confidently confirmed the location where he collected the unidentified man. After spending a majority of my morning pleading with the management of a lower Manhattan hotel, I've been granted access to their entire security feed of the last twenty-four hours."

Delilah pauses, taking time to bask in the glory of the triumphant clap of her colleagues. The only one not cheering her on is me. I feel sick. Not only is Marcus's BDSM identity about to be exposed, so is my treachery to Global Ten Media.

Once the euphoric applause simmers to a faint buzz, Delilah scans her eyes across the room. "Now all we need is a journalist willing to spend the remainder of their long weekend scanning the surveillance images burned onto this drive." She jingles a Global Ten Media USB stick in her hand.

All leftover applause vanishes, replaced with nothing but the sound of tumbleweeds drifting over an isolated country road. Several pairs of eyes stray to the conference table, while others pretend to scan Marcus's dossier. There is only one other time I've heard this room so quiet. It was when the entire wing of the entertainment division of Global Ten was summoned here to discover the aftermath of our blunder on publishing the stories of Noah Taylor's stint in rehab when he was actually in an intensive care unit.

"Come on," Delilah requests, her voice a vicious snarl. "I can't be expected to gain the evidence and comb through it as well. Unlike the rest of you, I have a life."

I sink deeper into my chair, praying to God my presence will be just as unnoticed today as it has been the past five years of my employment at Global Ten Media.

My prayers fall on deaf ears when a deep voice at the side asks, "Cleo, can you do it?"

My eyes—along with numerous others—snap to Mr. Carson sitting at the head of the table.

Stunned by Mr. Carson's request, Delilah scoffs, "No offense, Jack, but this task requires more diligence than a so-called journalist whose knowledge on investigative reporting only extends to looking attractive in a satin slip."

Some of the panic smeared on my face switches to anger when members at the higher end of the table snicker at her bitchy remark. More than half of the people sitting around this table should be suffering the same fate I was handed four years ago. The only reason they aren't is because I sacrificed myself to ensure no one on my team went down with me. My team may have researched, wrote, and edited the articles that went to print, but I was the one who approved the publication order. I thought my decision to cop the blame showed class and maturity. Clearly, the only fool seated around this table is me.

The room falls into resolute silence when Mr. Carson snarls, "Enough!

Contrary to what you muttonheads believe, Cleo is the lead investigator on this case. I personally selected her as she is the best candidate to bring this story to print, so if anyone in this room has a problem with her processing the surveillance tape, I suggest you bring your concerns to me. You all know where my office is."

His confession silences the critics surrounding me and forces my mouth to gape.

Standing from his seat, Mr. Carson puts on his suit jacket before swinging his eyes to me. "Do you have the resources and time to assess the surveillance footage?" he questions me, his tone understanding—almost nurturing.

I pause for a minute, gulping in breaths to calm the panic flaring in my veins. When my delayed response causes Mr. Carson's brows to tack, I nod, spinelessly agreeing with his request.

His eyes soften from my harmonized response. "Good. If the timeline becomes too challenging for you, Cleo, request assistance from anyone in this room."

"Okay," I force out, my word as shaky as my composure.

While skimming his eyes across the room, Mr. Carson warns, "If anyone refuses Cleo's request for assistance, your severance package will be forwarded to you the following morning. Do we have an understanding?"

The collective sighs of "Yes" come out of every dignitary seated around the table—Delilah included.

Happy the soldiers have fallen into line, Mr. Carson dips his chin in farewell before exiting the room.

4

Three brisk taps at my office door distract my attention from the hotel surveillance images I've been perusing the past three days. Cranking my neck to the side, I spot Dexter, IT expert and resident hottie of Global Ten Media, standing in my doorway. He has a cheeky smirk etched on his adorable face, and his broad shoulder is propped on the doorjamb separating my office from the bustling foyer of New York Daily Express.

Smiling, I stand from my seat and pace towards him. My brisk strides slow when Dexter says, "I heard you need my help, Cleo."

When I was seconded to IT to demand a replacement device for Delilah's lagging laptop six months ago, I left looking like a blushing idiot. With a name a little on the geeky side and a job title to match, I never thought I'd come face to face with a real-life Greek God when I was introduced to Dexter. Dark, luxurious hair, a little bit of stubble covering his chiseled chin, ice blue eyes shielded by a set of incredibly thick lashes, and a body that hits a few of my hot buttons all combine to make Dexter an incredibly appealing package. Not quite as appealing as Marcus—but that would be a hard feat for any man to conquer.

I stop frozen halfway between my desk and Dexter. My heart slithers into my churning stomach. I haven't heard hide nor hair of Marcus the past four days, yet he is still on my mind so much I'm comparing him to other men. What's wrong with me? I must be a severely demented person. He is the one who invaded my privacy, but I'm the one on the verge of falling to my knees and begging for forgiveness. This is not the woman my parents raised me to be. I am better than this. I am stronger than this. I am a Garcia woman through and through.

Pushing aside the little voice inside me vehemently denying every statement I just made, my eyes drink in how incredibly tempting Dexter's well-built frame looks in a pair of low-hanging jeans, black commando boots, and a plain V-neck tee.

"Sorry to bother you, I'm just a little stuck on a project I've been working on." I stop to stand in front of him. "Me and computers have never been friends."

Dexter smirks a grin that makes my heart skip a beat. "Lead the way, Cleo. I can't work out your kinks if I don't know what I am handling."

Pretending I didn't hear the cheeky innuendo laced in his question, I gesture for him to enter my office. Smiling at the heat creeping across my cheeks, Dexter pushes off his feet and moseys into the vast space, filling it with the piquant smell of bottled cologne.

After checking the corridor is void of prying eyes, I close my office door and lower the privacy blind. I don't need to peer at Dexter to know I've gathered his inquisitive stare, I can feel it. His gaze is so warm it eases some of the uncertainty swirling my stomach. *If only it could do something to calm the panic blackening my veins.*

Swallowing down the dread creeping up my esophagus, I spin on my heels to face Dexter.

"Top secret project," I mumble, lifting my index finger to my lips.

Dexter nods as if he is buying my explanation, but his forthright eyes still harbor suspicion. With a wave of my hand, I gesture for him to sit in my office chair. When he does, I lean across his body and swivel my mouse to awaken my sleeping monitor.

"Is this the hotel footage Delilah's been hounding you for?" Dexter asks when the screen illuminates, his pitch indicating his curiosity.

Masking my surprise he is aware of Delilah's taxing personality, I say, "Yes. Like everything, she wanted this video processed last week."

A feeble laugh rumbles from Dexter's lips. "She's a bit of a prickly pear."

"Prickly pear is too nice of a description for Delilah," I snarl under my breath. "If it wasn't bad enough she assigned me this task on a long weekend, there seems to be an issue with how the surveillance video downloaded from the hotel's mainframe." My words come out sharp, confidently concealing my lack of computer skills.

"See." I point to the monitor.

Dragging his eyes away from my heaving chest squashed against his shoulder, Dexter locks his blue eyes with my computer screen. I cough to clear the tumbleweeds from my throat before straightening my spine. I didn't realize I was standing so close to him until he pointed it out.

The impious gleam in Dexter's eyes switches to curious when, for a fleeting moment, the video freezes. It's only the quickest nanosecond. If it were being watched by anyone but me, they wouldn't have noticed it, but it's still there nonetheless.

"The pixilation didn't change," Dexter mutters, more to himself than me. "Whoever doctored this tape knows what they are doing." He scrubs his hand over the stubble on his chin as he sinks into my office chair. "Have you located any of the images of the man you're searching for on this video?"

With reluctance, I shake my head. "No. From the photos the PI took, the man Delilah wants identified is easily distinguishable," I reply, my tone low and wary.

When Dexter peers at me with confusion etched on his face, I disclose, "A pocket on his trousers was badly torn."

Sick gloom spread through me when I discovered Marcus had left the hotel in the same suit he arrived in. From what he informed me Saturday, I know he had suits readily available in his suite. The hotel we *occupied* Saturday afternoon is on permanent reservation for him. It's his go-to zone whenever the band is in town for radio events or press tours. Although surprised he'd need a hotel room when he owns a residence within an hour drive of the city, at the time, I didn't put much thought into it. My mind was too stuck in the trance of lust to think about anything but devouring the deliriously handsome specimen in front of me.

I fiddle with the chain link pendant around my neck to appease my nerves before asking, "If the tape has been doctored, is there any way the images can be restored?"

My debilitating head versus heart battle undertakes another round as I await Dexter's reply. My head is praying there won't be a chance in hell the missing footage will be recovered, whereas my heart is hoping every second will be retrieved. It isn't what you're thinking. It doesn't want the footage to expose Marcus and advance my career, it just wants the chance to answer lingering questions. My weekend with Marcus was such a confounding time, I'm starting to wonder if I am remembering it right. Not just the end of our exchange when the curtains closed for the final time—the entirety of it.

"I guess there is only one way to find out." With a determined scowl, Dexter scoots in close to my desk. His fingers tap wildly over the keyboard as a sexy pout forms on his lips.

Remaining quiet, I watch him bring up a black prompt screen and fill it with code. It's fascinating witnessing him in his element, but it does nothing to ease the contempt swishing in my stomach. If I weren't still lost on where my loyalties should lie, I could aid Dexter in his investigation by giving him a timeframe to work with. But since days of deliberating didn't scratch the surface of the confusion muddling my brain, I'll keep my big mouth shut. This surveillance tape could vindicate both Marcus and me, so remaining quiet is the smart thing to do—even if it tilts the axis of my moral compass.

"Whoever doctored this surveillance footage is a genius," Dexter mumbles, his eyes never once moving from the screen.

I nod in agreeance. I've watched the 24-hour long surveillance tape numerous times the past three days. In reverse, slow motion, and even at three times the speed. There is not a single frame on the entire tape that includes Marcus or me. Not even when I fled the hotel with a sheet of tears streaming down my cheeks. It's as if Marcus stripped me from his life even faster than I entered it. I don't know whether I should be offended by his dedication or honored.

"You've got at least twenty minutes of missing footage," Dexter says, snapping my attention back to the present. "Here, here, here and here," he continues, pointing to time periods that match when Marcus and I entered the hotel foyer together, to when we exited separately.

I stand still for a beat, dazed Dexter unearthed the lapse in surveillance so quickly. I heard he was a computer genius, but I didn't realize the gossip was literal.

Once the panic has cleared from my eyes, I ask, "Is there any way to recover the edited footage?"

Dexter holds my gaze for several moments, strangling my heart with deceit and silent pleas. "The person who hacked the server is good. The video plays seamlessly. Even slicing the footage apart doesn't take away its authenticity. To the naked eye, this tape appears legitimate and unedited."

"So how do you know there are missing segments?" I query, my tone a unique mix of intrigue and alarm.

Smiling, Dexter brings up the surveillance footage again. Although he plays it at the same speed he used previously, this time, he leaves the timer splayed across the monitor. "Watch closely," he instructs.

With my heart shrilling in my ears, I tilt in close and lock my eyes with the screen. The silence between Dexter and me is so immense, I can hear his pulse surging through his body. It's as manic as the mad beat of my heart. Before I have the chance to understand why his pulse is beating so fast, the air is forcefully removed from my lungs.

"The timer's out. The last second took longer to click over," I gasp in surprise. The only reason I notice the lapse in time was because my heart thumped twice in the last second instead of its usual one beat.

"Yes." Dexter's short reply is unable to conceal the pride in his tone. "If every minute loses a second, by the time twenty-four hours ticks by, you've got twenty-four minutes of lost footage."

"Wow, that's incredible." I honestly don't know whether I'm in shock or awe right now.

"It is," Dexter agrees.

My wonderment switches to hope. "So the chances of getting the uncut version of this footage is practically non-existent?" I try to keep the glee out of my voice. My attempts are borderline.

Dexter grins a cocky smirk. "If you had asked any other member of my team, I would have said zilch. Luckily, you sought the best man for the job."

My mouth twitches, preparing to speak, but not a single syllable escapes my thin, grim lips.

Taking my stunned expression as excitement, Dexter says, "I know you're under the gun with Delilah, but stuff like this takes time. Even more so because of the caliber of work the person put in while doctoring it."

Removing the USB drive from my computer, Dexter stands from my chair. His tall height and large frame are even more noticeable since I'm shrouded in panic. "If it makes it any easier for you, I'll swing by Delilah's office on my way out and explain the situation," he offers.

Not waiting for me to reply, he paces to my office door. "It may keep her off your back for a few days."

Although I appreciate his attempts to calm the dragon, anxiety is still bubbling my veins. I brought Dexter here hoping he'd tell me there was no hope of recovering the edited footage I knew was missing from the surveillance tape. I had no clue he held the skills necessary to salvage the doctored material. If I did, I might have sought the aid of his colleagues.

My lips are dry, so I lick them before saying, "Thanks for the offer, but nothing will slow down Delilah's eagerness for this footage. Like everything, she wanted this tape processed last week." I'm grateful when my voice comes out as I am aiming: appreciative with a hint of formality.

Dexter jerks his chin up. "Alright, my offer stands if you change your mind, though."

I issue him my gratefulness with a smile before swinging open my office door.

"As soon as I have anything, I'll bring it straight to you," Dexter says, stepping into the corridor.

"Straight to me?" I confirm, my pitch so high there is no mistaking the plea in it.

Smiling, Dexter adds, "Sure... If you're willing to do something for me?"

Muted, I stare into his eyes. I don't need to speak to express my sentiments. My entire composure exposes my willingness to keep the images of Marcus and me kissing in the hotel corridor out of Delilah's grubby mitts.

Identifying my eagerness, Dexter says, "Grab a bite to eat with me."

I balk, utterly flabbergasted. I was expecting a penance for a favor, not a reward. I'm also a little taken aback. Dexter is an incredibly handsome man who appears to have a heart of gold, so why wait until I owe him a favor to ask for a date?

I stand in muted silence for several moments, unsure if I am coming or going. Although tempted by Dexter's offer, I'm not a floozy. I can't jump straight from one relationship to another. Even more so because a man like Dexter doesn't deserve the rebound tag.

I freeze for the second time in under a minute. For one, I'm jumping the gun. Whoever said eating with someone equals a long-term commitment? And two, technically, Marcus and I were never a couple, so that leaves me free to do as I please. *Doesn't it?*

The little voice hidden deep inside me screams a resounding "No." My heart unequivocally agrees with its sentiment. My brain... it's still suffering the devastating effects of the mind-bending weekend to formulate an appropriate response.

Spotting anxiety on my face, Dexter says, "Nothing formal, Cleo. Just two work colleagues grabbing a bite to eat. We can even do lunch if you want?" He shrugs his shoulders, his whole composure screaming carefree and relaxed, a stark contradiction to the wheezing and flushed woman standing beside him.

After a beat, I stammer out, "Alright, but just lunch, nothing fancy."

Grinning at my blemished cheeks, Dexter nods before pacing down the bustling corridor. I don't know why I'm acting so irrational. I'd have lunch with the devil herself if it guaranteed the deleted footage from the surveillance video remains in the right hands.

I wait for Dexter's impressive frame to slip into the elevator on my floor before rolling up the privacy blind on my office window, then I trudge to my desk. My steps are slow, weighed down by the mountain load of guilt sitting on my chest. Although I've reasoned with myself numerous times the past four days that I'm just doing my job, it isn't sitting well with the integrity my parents raised me with.

Even being threatened with unemployment a minimum of ten times, told I'd never work in the media industry again, and assigned the ostracized position of Delilah's PA hasn't eased the guilt plaguing me. I am at my wits end. I've nearly quit three times the past two days alone. The only reason I haven't is because of how badly I need this job. With winter rapidly approaching, I have no choice but to push my personal disdain for Delilah and my confusion about my relationship with Marcus to the back of my mind. My focus must remain on keeping my sister's health my utmost priority.

Let me tell you, it's been a very confusing few days.

Slouching into my office chair, my eyes flick up to the frozen images of the hotel lobby. Considering the only images missing from the surveillance footage is of Marcus and me, I can easily deduce that Marcus arranged to have the tape doctored. The only thing I can't work out is why he would do that? Hiding his face is fathomable, he is famous and highly recognizable. But why did he have the images of me exiting the hotel without him also removed? Other than looking like the many other crazies roaming around New York City, there was no need for him to hide my identity.

While I am being forthright, I will admit, if Dexter does unearth images of Marcus and me, I haven't decided what I'll do with that information yet. Career-wise, it would be ludicrous of me to ignore what could be potentially be the story of the century. Personally, my parents raised me better than that. People will often quote that business is business, your personal life is your personal life, and the two can never mix, but what are you supposed to do when it's already happened? I can't just pretend one never occurred—no matter how much my decimated heart wishes it could.

My wallowing in self-pity comes to an end when my cell phone vibrates on my desk. A faint smile cracks my lips when I notice only forty minutes have passed since Lexi's last call. Lexi has been brilliant the past four days. Although she urges me a minimum three times a day to shove my letter of resignation into a region of Delilah's body that never sees sunlight, she has been a godsend. Don't get me wrong, she is still as stubborn and opinionated as ever, but if I didn't have her witty humor and nonchalant approach to life, I'd probably still be wearing holey pajamas and eating Ben and Jerry's rocky road ice cream from the tub. Or even worse, crumbled into submission from Delilah's wrath.

Propping my backside onto the edge of my chair, I swipe my finger across the screen and lift my phone to my ear. "Miss me already? It's only been forty minutes," I greet her, sassiness resonating in my tone. "And no, I've not yet handed in my resignation. The dragon's two-hour spa appointment this morning has made her more tolerable—barely."

"Four days or forty minutes, what's the difference?" replies a female voice I don't immediately recognize. "And in regards to the dragon, I know a guy who knows a guy who used to be a descendant of a British knight. I could possibly get you his number."

Worry thickens my veins. "Oh... I'm so sorry, I thought you were someone else." My high voice is laced with embarrassment. "Umm... Cleo Garcia, how can I help you?" I greet more formally, grimacing.

"Oh, fancy, I like it," chuckles my female caller, her girly giggle shrilling down the line.

Recognition dawns on the identity of my unnamed caller when she says, "I hope your credit card has a healthy balance, Cleo. After spending my morning assembling furniture, my appetite is rampant."

Smiling at the over-enunciation of her words, I stammer out, "Hey, Serenity. I didn't realize we were scheduled to meet for lunch today."

"We aren't," Serenity interrupts before she directs someone in the background to move a couch to the other side of the room. "But there is so much testosterone at Links, if I don't even it out with some girl time, I'll turn into a guy. And I couldn't think of a better way to do that than take you up on your offer of lunch."

When I remain quiet, she mumbles, "You're free for lunch today? Right?"

"Oh... umm... not really. I'm a little swamped today." I catch my eye roll halfway. Even I heard the deceit in my voice.

Disappointment consumes me when Serenity replies, "You need to practice your blow-offs, Cleo, as that one stunk."

Even knowing she is most likely riling me up, I can't help but react to the rejection in her tone. I've been on the receiving end of so much disappointment lately, the last thing I want is to be the cause of someone's distress.

Swallowing away the uncertainty curtailing my windpipe, I ask, "Do you have any objections to Mexican food?"

5

"So how is the prep at Links going? Are you ready for the grand opening on Saturday?"

Serenity waits for the waiter to fill her wine glass with water before replying, "Yes. It's been a hectic few days, but everything is *finally* settling nicely."

"I'm sure it's perfect," I reply, hating the concern obscuring her striking gaze.

Serenity blows her bangs out of her eyes before saying, "One way or another, we are opening our doors bright and early Saturday morning."

Smiling at her pouty lip, I accept the menu the waiter is holding out for me. My mouth salivates when my eyes scan the delicious assortment of items on the menu. Although Toloache is a little on the pricey side, it's a prime spot for our impromptu lunch date. Not only is it within walking distance of Global Ten Media, but it also serves alcoholic drinks.

After placing my order with the waiter for two lemon drop martinis and a pescado taco, I hand him back my menu. While Serenity places her order, I sip on a glass of chilled water while absorbing the energy thrumming around us. Toloache is a breathtaking restaurant with exposed wooden beams, crisp white tablecloths, and smiling waiters in abundance. Although I chose to dine here purely because it serves cocktails during lunch, its gorgeous interior and the pleasantness of its staff ensures today will not be my only visit.

Handing the waiter back her menu, Serenity locks her big hazel eyes with me. Water traps halfway down my throat when she straight-out asks, "What did he do?"

I peer at her, acting unaware of whom her question refers to.

"Marcus—what did he do?" she queries, not the slightest bit concerned about her intrusive prying. "I was hoping the two to three pounds you've lost since Saturday was from sexual exhaustion, but your double order of martinis left that hope for dust. Women only lose weight for two reasons: either chasing a man or recovering from one. Considering you already snagged Marcus, I'm gathering the latter is a more accurate assessment."

My throat works hard to swallow the water trapped halfway down my esophagus. Once it's been forced into my stomach, I place my glass on the table and lift my eyes to Serenity. "Umm… he didn't really do anything. I've just been busy, that's all. I'm so swamped with work, this is the first sit-down meal I've had all week."

That's only a partial lie. Although I have been extremely busy at work, my lagging metabolism is more due to heartache than conflicting work schedules.

Serenity's perfectly manicured brow bows high into her short, glossy hair. She glares into my eyes, calling out my deceit without a word spilling from her lips. *She couldn't be any more like Marcus if she tried.*

"We... *broke up*." I breathe out slowly, winded by the brutal honesty of my reply.

Serenity gasps in a sharp breath, her chest heaving. "What happened?! You seemed so perfect together. In love, even."

"I wouldn't go that far," I mutter, my voice coming out in a tremor since my heart is a jittering mess. "We're just... umm... not compatible."

Her brows inch together, sending a massive groove of lines across her forehead. "Come on, Cleo, give me some credit. I may not have the best track record when it comes to relationships, but even I could see the connection between you and Marcus, so if you want a chance in hell of people believing your theory on why you broke up, don't start with incompatibility."

Her blatant refusal to buy my explanation sends my nerves into a tailspin. "It's hard to explain," I whisper, striving to lose the attention of the people seated around us eyeballing our exchange with interest.

"Hard to explain or comprehend?" Serenity asks, digging her hand into her purse.

"A bit of both," I exhale in a rush.

After accepting the tissue Serenity dug out of her purse, I dab it under my eyes, ensuring the moisture pooling there hasn't caused my mascara to run. "Something happened. I got angry. When Marcus failed to subdue my anger, I left."

"And?" Serenity asks softly, breaking my heart more with her devastated tone. "What happened then?"

I wait for the waiter to set down my two lemon drop martinis and leave before answering, "And... *nothing*. I left Marcus in his hotel room, returned home, and I haven't heard from him since."

I rub at the gnawing pain in my chest as my words ring on repeat in my ears. This kills me to admit, but not all the agony twisting my heart is based on Marcus's deceit, some of it resonates from his silence. A small part of me was hoping one day he'd show up and demand forgiveness. But as each day passes in silence, my belief that our relationship was nothing but a game to Marcus deepens.

Serenity curls her hand over mine and squeezes it gently. "Do you think there's a chance you could work things out?" she asks as her moisture-filled eyes dance between mine.

I lift one shoulder into an awkward shrug. The heavy groove marring the skin between Serenity's eyes deepens.

"That bad?" she asks. Just like Marcus, her eyes expose she already knows my reply.

"Unfortunately, yes." When she takes a sharp breath, it forces me to add, "No. I don't know. He really confuses me, Serenity."

She tugs at the napkin on her lap, anxiously knotting it around her fingers. "Marcus is a complicated man, Cleo, has been for years. But from the way you were looking at him Saturday, I thought you understood that?"

"I thought I did too," I reply, my voice as brittle as cracked glass. "But I was wrong." My words are so soft, if they hadn't stabbed my heart with pain, I would have never believed I'd expressed them.

Serenity twists in her seat to face me head on. "This will sound a little cliché—"

"Clichés are my life at the moment," I interrupt, grimacing.

Gently smiling, Serenity continues, "I really like you, Cleo. You scream integrity and understanding, and you're also beautiful and kindhearted. You're the ideal woman wrapped up in a kickass package." She locks her glistening eyes with me, ensuring I can't misread the truth in her statement as she hits me with my hardest blow of the week. "Marcus needs someone like you in his corner."

The air is vehemently removed from my body, leaving me winded and breathless. As stupid moisture looms in my eyes, I float them around the room, silently praying no rogue tears will roll down my cheeks. It may make me seem pathetic and weak, but for the last eight weeks, my entire life was wrapped up in the fictional world of Master Chains. Talking to him was the highlight of my day, so I am ashamed to admit, I am struggling to give that up. Even irrefutably angry at Marcus doesn't mean I can't miss him. I miss him—truly I do.

My hand shakes when I reach out for my drink, hoping the refreshing coolness will ease the burn in my throat. With how many times I've fought tears this week, my throat is red, raw and dry. I'm stunned at the number of times I've felt the urge to cry the past four days. I've barely shed a tear in three years, but it feels like all my time lately is spent fighting my pitiful sobs.

After downing half my drink in one giant gulp, Serenity squeezes my hand, silently requesting the return of my focus. I suck in a nerve-cleansing breath before returning my eyes to her.

Regret darkens her eyes, then tears glisten. "I'm sorry for pushing, Cleo," she apologizes, her pleading-for-forgiveness eyes strengthening her admission. "Better than anyone, I know how hard relationships are, so I am in no position to judge. I just don't want you to walk away from something magical because you can't see the man behind the fame. That man you spend your weekend with, that's the real Marcus, not the hoopla you dealt with at Links."

"Marcus's fame isn't the cause of my concern," I blubber out, my tone splintering with remorse.

Serenity stares at me, more confused than ever, her gaze searching for answers in my truth-exposing eyes. When her silence becomes too much for me to bear, I explain, "I can't be with a man I don't trust. A relationship without trust isn't a relationship. It's nothing but destruction."

"Marcus broke your trust?" Serenity asks, her pitch spiked with disbelief.

When I dip my chin, shock spreads across her face. "My brother Marcus?" She sounds confused, like she can't comprehend how he'd ever do something as underhanded as that. "Are you sure?"

"Yes," I reply, fiddling with the hem on my blouse. "I saw the proof first-hand. His laptop at his hotel was streaming live footage of my bedroom, and he had a background search on me saved on the desktop."

Serenity sinks into her chair, her mouth gaped, her eyes wide. "Holy hell," she mumbles, stunned. "The background search I can understand—he has to protect his identity—but the live stream... *God*. I feel sick."

I sit quietly, unsure what to say to ease her turmoil. We plunge into awkward silence crammed with palpable tension. I regret my decision to down an entire lemon drop martini on an empty stomach when it suddenly flips, protesting the drastic shift in the air. Compared to our friendly greeting ten minutes ago, the vibrancy of our rapport has been snuffed out, leaving nothing but tension so thick I could cut it with a knife.

I'm thankful our waiter suddenly arrives at our table, balancing two plates of food in his hands. Although I'm wary of trusting my stomach with food, I'm grateful his presence snaps Serenity out of her confused trance.

"Thank you," I whisper, accepting the aromatic dish he is holding out for me, my rickety voice exposing my rattled composure.

After setting Serenity's order down in front of her, the waiter skedaddles away, the stiffness in the air so great, even he wishes to avoid it. I wait for him to be out of earshot before turning my focus back to Serenity.

"I'm sorry for blurting it out like that. That's the reason I didn't want to say anything. I don't want things to be awkward between us."

Serenity's lips twitch like she is preparing to speak, but I continue talking, thwarting her chance to reply. "I also understand if you don't believe me. Marcus is your brother, you have every right to defend his honor."

Serenity's brows tack as fresh tears form in her eyes. "I believe you, Cleo. I'm just stunned, that's all. From the way Marcus talked about you the past few weeks, I knew you were more than a random acquaintance. I just never fathomed you'd upend his usually remarkable decorum."

Pain grips my heart. "He says I make him reckless," I stumble out, my words low.

Serenity's head bobs up and down. "Clearly, that's the case. Trust me when I say this: Marcus isn't usually like this, Cleo. I've never seen him the way he was with you on Saturday."

Her confession warms my heart and somewhat subdues the weight on my chest.

Serenity regathers my hand in hers, squeezing it so hard, my knuckles crack. "If you can't find it in your heart to forgive Marcus, take comfort in the fact you were special to him. So much so, you made him a little crazy."

My eyes burn from a sudden influx of moisture. "I don't know if I should take that as a compliment or not."

"It was most definitely a compliment," Serenity informs me, giggling softly.

After a beat, she squeezes my hand again before dropping her eyes to the overflowing plate of food sitting in front of her. "It smells so good," she mumbles, her tone quickly changing from dread to its usual friendliness.

"It sure does," I agree, happy to use our meals as a way to relieve the tension.

Smiling, Serenity tears a significant bite out of her taco before chewing eagerly. Following suit, I set to work on devouring my own. My hunger rampantly returns when the first delicious bite graces my taste buds.

Forty minutes later, we've eaten two plates of delicious food, sampled three fruity cocktails suggested by our waiter, and embarked on a less heart-strangling conversation. Although the first fifteen minutes of our gathering was plagued with awkwardness, it undoubtedly pushed aside the barrier that separates strangers from friends, leaving us free to have a fun-filled lunch date.

We talked about everything and anything you could imagine. Serenity's desire to fund a charity similar to Links in her hometown, my overbearing protectiveness of my sister, and Serenity's love of her grandfather. Our conversation flowed as freely as water out of a tap, and anyone would swear I was lunching with a lifelong friend, not a lady I only met four days ago.

When the waiter arrives at our table with the bill, Serenity's hand delves into her clutch. "No. I'm paying, remember?" I chide before handing the waiter my credit card—the only one not maxed out.

Smiling, he bows his head gracefully and retreats to ring up our bill. I wait until he is a reasonable distance away from us before saying, "He's cute ... and he's been eyeing you with zeal our entire lunch break."

Serenity's mouth gapes, "Has he?!" she asks, astonishment in her tone. She adjusts her position so she can drink in his fit body and dimple-blemished smile. "He is cute," she agrees, her lips quirking. "He's also gay."

"No, he's not!" I gasp out dramatically.

My brows shoot up when I spot the waiter's flirty wink to a male patron sitting at the guacamole stand in the middle of the cramped space.

"Oh my god, he is!" I squeal, snapping my eyes back to Serenity. "One, how did you know that? And two, how come he was eyeing you with interest, then?"

Serenity gathers her clutch from the tabletop and stands from her seat. Before she gets the chance to answer my interrogation, the waiter arrives back at our table. I scribble my name on the bottom of the bill before placing my credit card back into my purse. My jaw slackens when the waiter twists the leather wallet to Serenity and requests for her to sign a blank slip of paper. A ghost of a smile cracks onto my lips when Serenity sneakily hands the waiter a bunch of crumpled notes before doing as requested.

"Thank you for your discretion," she praises softly, ensuring only those closest to her will hear her compliment.

Acting like she hasn't spotted my stunned expression, Serenity curls her arm around the crook of my elbow and guides me out of the restaurant. Brisk early winter winds whip up the flare of my skirt when we merge into the dense flow of foot traffic on the cracked sidewalk. Just like every time I'm surrounded by the surreal world of New York, my love for the city grows. There is nothing as intoxicating as the smell of millions of people crammed into one space. *Well, except one man.*

Shutting down my absurd inner dialogue, I spin on my heels to face Serenity. "What was all that about?" I ask, nudging my head to the restaurant doors.

"Fame by association," Serenity advises, her tone low. "In this day and age, just knowing someone famous makes you famous."

"Jeez, if you had told me that earlier, I wouldn't have tipped so high," I jest, saying anything to lessen the worry creeping back into her exquisite hazel eyes. "Your signature alone should have wiped twenty dollars off the bill."

Giggling, Serenity replies, "If you were smart, you should have taken pictures of me stuffing my face. I've heard rumors they sell for 200 bucks a pop."

I pretend to drag her back to the restaurant. "I just realized we forgot to have dessert."

Serenity's hearty giggle awards us a few pairs of curious eyes... and a handful of cell phone lenses. Not wanting our exchange ruined by nosy onlookers, I curl my arms around Serenity's shoulders and draw her into a hug.

"Thank you for lunch, I really needed this," I whisper into her ear. "I hope we get to do it again someday?" The unease of my words makes my voice come out jittery.

Pulling back from our embrace, Serenity locks her eyes with me. "No matter what happens between you and Marcus, you will always be family to me, Cleo. Don't ever doubt that."

Her pledge leaves me breathless and causes tears to loom in my eyes.

"Thank you," I mutter, my overworked brain unable to think of a more suitable reply.

After pressing a kiss to my temple, Serenity makes her way to the curb to flag down a taxi. With her dazzling smile and stellar good looks, not even a second passes before a bright yellow cab stops in front of her.

She curls into the backseat before rolling down the window. "I'll see you Saturday," she says to me, her tone forthright.

"Saturday?" I query, my one word coming out in a flurry since the taxi is pulling away from the curb.

Serenity's lips tug high, exposing a smile that should grace the pages of fashion magazines across the globe. "The opening of Links, remember? You said you'd help."

I follow her taxi as it melds into the clogged traffic of Manhattan. My heart is walloping my ribs, my pupils massively dilated.

"I can't do Saturday. It would be too weird," I shout, projecting my voice over the blasting of horns and noisy engines.

"Marcus won't be there," Serenity assures me, slicing her hand through the air like it's no big deal.

Sidestepping a group of road construction crew members eyeing me with ardor, I race across the street. I look like an idiot jogging in a tight pleated pencil skirt and three-inch stilettos, but my speed remains unchecked. I can handle blisters on my feet, but spending hours in the presence of a man who sends my libido rocketing to the next galaxy by doing nothing but breathing would be biting off more than I can chew. A saint would have a hard time curbing their desires around a man with an alluring personality like Marcus's, much less a woman who is well aware of his sexual prowess.

"Why won't Marcus be there?" I ask when I catch up to Serenity's taxi, my high tone polluted with suspicion. "It's his charity. Shouldn't he be there?"

"He doesn't want the paparazzi scaring away people relying on Links for shelter," Serenity yells, startling an elderly lady walking her poodle so badly, she jumps. After issuing a silent apology to the affluently dressed lady, she adds, "Their comfort is more important to Marcus than getting brownie points from a bunch of strangers."

My steps stop, closely followed by the beat of my heart. That does sound like something Marcus would do. He'd want the victims of domestic violence to feel comfortable at Links, not be steamrolled by paparazzi vying to get a money shot of him.

Snubbing the curious gawk of strangers surrounding me, I spread my hands across my waist and demand my lungs to breathe. If I were being honest, I'd admit not all my breathlessness is from chasing Serenity's taxi a quarter of a mile, it's from having the hope of seeing Marcus again stripped away in one brutal blow. Even harboring debilitating anger doesn't lessen the impact of that realization.

God—why does it have to hurt so much?

I don't know if I'm delusional from a lack of oxygen in my lungs, but I swear the last thing I hear before Serenity's taxi melds into a sea of yellow is, "Don't think, Cleo, just breathe."

6

My galloping feet freeze halfway down the porch stairs when I fail to notice the lace curtain in Mrs. Rachet's living room ruffling. Agitated unease curls around my throat as I take the steps more cautiously. Mrs. Rachet is Montclair's equivalent of the town gossip. Her nose is burrowed so deep in her neighbors' lives, she knows their big-hitting news before they do. I swear, she announced my acceptance at Global Ten Media before the mailman delivered my letter of offer.

I've lived across from Mrs. and Mr. Rachet my entire life, so her snooping is as regular as a trip to the grocery store for me, but I'm still stunned her caliber of nosy-nuancing has failed to catch me sneaking out of my home a little before 5 AM. Although she's always shown a keen interest in my private life, her efforts ramped up a gear after the silver Bentley whisked me away to Chains two months ago. Then it went into full-blown overdrive when Marcus's Jaguar collected me last weekend.

Grinning at the disappointment her 10 AM bridge companions will express when she fails to update them on my every move, I trudge to my baby-poo Buick parked at the side of my house. With winter making an early appearance, the windshield is covered with a thin layer of sleet. I increase my pace, eager to discover if the dewy air will put a dampener on my early morning activities.

Cranking open my car door, I slide into the driver's seat and jab my keys into the ignition. "Please," I pray, peering up at the sagging roof lining.

My shoulders sag in disappointment when my first turn of the key has my engine firing to life. I giggle lamentably while shaking my head, beyond baffled that the one time I want my car to kick up a stink about its old, worn-out engine, it starts on the very first try.

Pretending my unanswered prayer isn't an omen on how the remainder of my day will pan out, I shift my gearstick into reverse and head to Montclair Heights train station. The roads are deserted, giving me a clear run. After pulling into my regular parking spot mere minutes later, I gather my belongings from the passenger seat and make my way to the platform to await the 5:15 direct train to Manhattan.

The station is nearly as desolate as the parking lot, only a handful of tourists and early morning commuters are mingling in the vast space. With Miquel's ticket booth closed until 8 AM, I pace to the electronic terminal outside his booth to purchase a return pass. There is a sheet of paper covering the monitor, advising passengers that a disruption to the internet service the railway company uses means all passengers will ride for free.

Concern twists in my stomach, winding up to the base of my throat. Swallowing down my unease, I pass a smiling police officer on my way to the bench I plan on slumping on to await my usually delayed train.

The gurgling of my stomach grows when a train pulls into the station not even two minutes later. The time is precisely 5:15 AM. I blink several times in a row, ensuring my nearsightedness doesn't have me mistaking my train for another.

Happy the train is the one I am scheduled to catch, I step into the nearly empty car and make my way down the aisle. Acting like I can't feel moisture beading on my nape, I settle into a seat a few rows down from a group of rowdy teens making kissy, gaga faces at me. I swipe at my forehead, removing a thin layer of sweat from my brow before snagging my Kindle out of my oversized purse. Although the teens' lewd comments bristle my spine with annoyance, they are not saying anything I haven't heard before. If my stomach wasn't a vulgar mess of confusion, I could take their snickered remarks as compliments. It's not every day a woman gets told she has an ass so fine she could rival Beyoncé.

Before I can register that the teens' comments are louder because they moved into the seats across from me, the smiling officer from earlier steps into my car. With one hand bracing his gun and a swagger many officers have, his eyes scan the car. His quick skim of the area is compelling enough to have the teen boys hot-footing it to the exit two spaces down from me.

The smell of cologne lingers into my nostrils when the officer pushes off his feet to chase after them, shouting into his police radio on the way past. I sit slack-jawed and muted when he races past the Plexiglas windows of the train so fast he is nothing but a blur.

I swallow rapidly, pushing down the bile surging into my throat when the train doors snap shut, leaving me the sole occupant in the entire car for my direct ride to Penn Station.

With how smoothly my run into New York is going, I expect the butterflies in my stomach to soon be pacified. They aren't. Have you ever heard the saying "the calm before the storm?" That's precisely what this morning feels like. When everything seems too good to be true, it generally is. And although

I could rationalize that the early morning hour is aiding in my carefree commute, my intuition is telling me that isn't the case. I don't just feel a storm brewing, I'm sensing a catastrophic tornado.

Approximately one hour later, and multiple chapters of flawless words read through clattering teeth, I place my Kindle into my purse and exit the train at Penn station. On my walk to the 34th Street Subway Station, my eyes study the scenery. Although it's still early, the city is a hive of activity. Taxi fumes mingle in the air right alongside people hustling around like there aren't enough hours in the day. As I continue on my way, I drink it all in, allowing my love of New York to ease the contempt blackening my heart.

My appreciation of my sister city is so boundless, I am soon walking down the street Links is located on without a single qualm. As I pass the alley Marcus and I stood in last week when he prepared me for the paparazzi onslaught, my eyes scan the street. I don't want it to, but disappointment rears its ugly head when I fail to find a single car worth over $2000 in a half-block radius.

Although my shrewd brain is grateful for Serenity's assurance Marcus wouldn't be here, my heart is disenchanted. Its hope of seeing Marcus again saw me stumbling out of bed at 3 AM this morning so I could put together the perfect "you'll regret the day you ever made a fool out of me" persona. I wasn't aspiring to impress Marcus, I just wanted him to see what he lost by playing me for a fool. *I guess the only fool here is me.*

Shrugging off my stupidity before it dampens my mood, I continue my trek, stopping only once I reach the frosted doors of Links. Since it's still early, the area is void of the paparazzi I handled the last time I stood in this very spot. After pushing through the sandblasted double doors, I sling off my newly purchased winter jacket and place it onto the coatrack at the side. A vibrant hum of activity jingles through my ears when I enter the main rec room. My eyes go crazy, fascinated by the practical furnishings now filling the ample space. All a change from last week, sofas, dining tables, and extensive reading chairs now soften the harsh lines of the converted warehouse, giving it a warm and homey feeling.

I clutch my stomach when the smell of freshly baked goodies lingers in the air. It reminds me of my mom's Sunday afternoon routine when I was in middle school. She would bake for hours on end, ensuring the pantry was stocked with goodies our family consumed throughout the week. I blame her scrumptious cooking for the extra cushioning in my backside.

Remembering Serenity's plea for assistance in the kitchen, I follow the delicious smell floating in the air, pretending I can't feel my thighs shaking with every step I take. I smile a greeting at a group of tradesmen making some last-minute adjustments to a row of tables that will feed thousands before entering a state-of-the-art industrial-sized kitchen at the side of the rec room.

"Wow," I mumble, my mouth gaping. "Even Lexi could cook in a kitchen like this."

Lexi's culinary skills are best described as atrocious. Something as simple as peanut butter on toast is an effort for Lexi. I don't know how many times I've saved our kitchen from a raging inferno the past four years.

As I pace deeper into the bustling hive of activity, my eyes absorb the scene. Large pots of porridge are bubbling on the cooktops, and boxes of fresh fruit and loaves of bread fill every surface. At least two dozen people are preparing the first meal of many to be served by this kitchen.

The sick gloom making my skin a sticky mess eases when I see the vast range of volunteers busily preparing Links' very first meal. The age of the people in attendance varies greatly. There is a man with silver hair and a thick beard who would be easily in his seventies flipping pancakes like he was born to. He is standing next to a young girl just shy of her teen years slicing containers of strawberries to be served with the pancakes. The volunteers' wealth is also on opposing ends of the spectrum. One lady manning the pots of porridge is dripping with diamonds, whereas another lady with ripped jeans and flip-flops is buttering bread rolls by the dozen. Although it's staggering to see people from diverse social strata in the one place, it's endearing to see them set their differences aside so they can come together for a worthy cause. Especially at such a busy time of the year.

My head slants to the side, and I prick my ears when a familiar voice jingles over the soft hum of noise. Stopping in the middle of the space, I scan the room for Serenity. I spot her a few seconds later liaising with a handsome man on my right in his late twenties wearing a well-tailored suit. Although sexual energy is bouncing off them in abundance, they do seem to be in a tiff. It looks heated, and it immediately brings to mind the saying, "Don't mix business with pleasure."

Not wanting to disturb them, I loiter at the side of the kitchen and wait for them to finish. Like a train wreck you can't stop watching, I don't want to intrude on their exchange, but I can't force my eyes to look away from them either. Although they seem like an odd match, there is no denying the chemistry suffocating the air with muggy heat. The sexual energy bristling off them is fire-sparking.

Unlike the suit-clad man and me, Serenity has dressed appropriately in a pair of slim-cut jeans and a plain black tee. A few hair products have mussed her hair into a sexy style, and the refreshing smell of flowers is pumping out of her. She looks casual, hardworking and sexy. The only thing dampening her appeal is the large crease of worry grooved in her forehead.

Although Serenity's down-to-earth look gives off the hint of wealth, the suit-clad man's aura screams of it. He has light mousy brown hair, piercing brown eyes, and a body that showcases a sturdy fitness regime. If his eyes weren't relaying his fondness for Serenity, I could have mistaken his tight jaw and thin-lined lips as unbridled anger, whereas now, I think their exchange is more based on confusion. *Or perhaps even jealousy?*

A good ten to fifteen minutes pass before Serenity huffs while pacing away from the handsome man. Although their exchange appeared strangled by confrontation, it doesn't stop the unnamed man's appreciative glance at Serenity's backside as she saunters away from him. Incidentally, her hips are sashaying a little more than usual as well.

"Everything okay?" I ask, startling Serenity from my stalking post when she glides past me.

Serenity closes her eyes and counts backward from three before spinning on her heels to face me. The heavy groove between her eyes clears away when her gaze meets mine.

"You came!" she squeals, sending her high-pitched voice jingling off the walls and booming into my ears.

"Of course I came," I reply, pretending I didn't spend the last forty-eight hours analyzing the perfect defense to recant my offer of assistance. Although most of my ideas came up stumps, I thought my very final excuse of car trouble was a sure-fire winner. *We all know how that panned out.*

Smiling, Serenity wraps me up in a firm hug. For a woman whose arms are the size of twigs, she doesn't lack any strength. I take a few moments relishing the comfort you can only get from a friendly hug. Once I've had my fill, I pull back from our embrace. Warmth spreads across my chest when I notice our exchange hasn't just eased my swishing stomach, it has also erased the concern from Serenity's eyes.

"Where do you need me?" I ask, my tone relaying my eagerness to be assigned a task. I've always aspired to do charity work, but with my busy work schedule and inability to drag my backside out of bed before 9 AM on weekends, my aspirations have never reached fruition.

Serenity bows a brow. "In that outfit... anywhere but here. If you even get a smidge of a stain on that gorgeous skirt, I'll be cursed by the fashion gods."

Guilt creeps into my veins. I can't believe I was so vain, I put my desire for revenge above the needs of the people relying on Links for shelter. It's time for the selfishness to stop. Right here, right now.

"Give me any task your heart desires. The dirtier, the better," I request with an arched brow.

Pressing her index finger to her lips, Serenity contemplates the perfect chore for me to do. Her big hazel eyes drift around our location as her manicured brows cinch together. I can tell the exact moment an idea pops into her head. Her eyes brighten, and her ruby-colored lips curl into a luscious smirk. Her excitement sets me off balance, and a sick feeling hits my stomach like something awful is about to happen.

"Do you have any experience with the media?" Serenity asks, her girly voice an odd combination of pleading and showy.

"Umm..." *Yes, I do.* "A little?" I wish desperately that I could tell her the truth. That I could stop the endless lies streaming out of my mouth the past two months, but I can't. Not just because I am protecting my sister's life by continuing with this charade, but because when my secrets are divulged, it will be to the man responsible for them, not his baby sister.

Taking my resilient approach as determination to wrangle the media, Serenity curls her arm around the crook of my elbow and drags me out of the industrial-sized kitchen.

My steps are even more rickety than the ones I took thirty minutes ago.

7

Links' grand opening was a phenomenal success. From the instant Serenity cut the red tape in front of a gauntlet of disappointed paparazzi expecting to see Marcus, the stream of people entering the doors has been nonstop. It was both a heartwarming and strangling time. Heartwarming as it is a beautiful thing to witness so many people come together for the greater good, choking as I never fathomed there were so many victims of domestic violence. I've spent half my day gleaming at the smiling faces of the patrons Links is sheltering, where my other half was depleted fighting back tears. I'm not ashamed to admit I lost my battle when a small four-year-old girl thanked me for her second helping of pancakes with a quick squeeze of my thigh. I've never felt as proud as I did in that instant.

At one stage, the flow of foot traffic into Links was so frantic, a state-assigned building inspector threatened to close the doors. I don't know if he had a change of heart because he was overwhelmed by the number of people requiring shelter, or he didn't stand a chance going up against a stubborn Garcia woman and a young lady with the heart of a warrior. Either way, at the end of the day, Serenity and I won our appeal. It was an uphill battle, but the fact he agreed to keep the doors open was a win either way.

Appreciating the extra surge of blood pumping into my heart, I press an impromptu peck to Serenity's cheek and wrap her up in a firm hug.

"It feels good, doesn't it?" she whispers into my ear, returning my embrace.

When she draws away from our little huddle at the side of the rec room, I sweep my hand across my cheeks, ensuring no sneaky tears spilled from my eyes. Happy my face is moisture-free, I nod. "What you did here is a truly magical thing, Serenity. You must be so proud."

"I am," Serenity agrees, her head bobbing up and down. "I've very proud of what Marcus and the members of Chains achieved here today."

My eyes rocket to Serenity, disbelief is smeared all over my face. "Marcus told you about Chains?" I mumble, my words low and tainted with worry that I'm unknowingly sharing guarded secrets.

Serenity takes her time drinking in my blemished cheeks and red-tipped nose before nodding. "Yes." Her one word communicates way more than I could ever express.

"When?"

Marcus only told me last week that no one in his family is aware of his involvement in the BDSM lifestyle, so I'm somewhat surprised by his sudden decision of full disclosure.

Serenity gathers her hand in mine. The crazy thump of her pulse pounds my palm. "I went and saw him after our lunch date on Wednesday."

My nerves prickle, hyper-stimulated by her placid response. I'm wheezing, perspiring, and out of breath, dying for her to feed me more information on their interaction.

Serenity says nothing. Not a single word.

Incapable of harnessing my curiosity for a second longer, I blubber out, "And?"

Serenity's heavy exhalation of air rustles the hair clinging to my sweat-damp neck. "And after I tore into him for breaching your privacy, he told me everything about Chains and its association with Links."

She locks her glistening eyes with mine, they are teeming with tears. "Then he told me about all the mistakes he made with you. I've never seen him so unguarded before, Cleo. If his eyes weren't relaying how much pain he was in, I could have used his disarray to my advantage. But..." She sighs, seemingly unable to finish her reply.

"You can't hurt someone you love even when you're angry at them," I fill in, expressing the real reason I've guarded Marcus's secret the past week. Although I'm so furious at him for breaking my trust, my anger isn't intense enough to curb my desire to protect him.

Breathing out the massive sentiment looming in her lungs, Serenity firms her grip on my hand before nodding. "Yes," she scarcely whispers.

Although Serenity's reply assuaged some of my curiosity, it didn't thoroughly squash it. After scanning my eyes over our location, confirming we are void of prying onlookers, I ask, "How did you handle his confession?"

I wait with bated breath for her answer, praying she handled his involvement in the BDSM lifestyle with the same grace she showed today—with nothing but understanding and respect.

I exhale dramatically when she replies, "Nothing's changed. Despite whatever title he has in that industry—"

"Lifestyle," I correct.

"Lifestyle," Serenity copies, her voice reserved. "Marcus will always be Marcus to me." She lifts her eyes to me, the sentiment in them doubling in size. "Just like you'll always be the woman who made him so reckless he lost all his scruples."

Her voice comes out playful, but it doesn't stop a stabbing pain inflicting the middle of my chest. I rub at the pain while wandering my gaze around the room, doing anything to ignore the tears burning my eyes.

Serenity's grip on my hand turns deadly, warming my snap-frozen heart with the heat pulverizing her veins. "Forgive him, Cleo," she implores. "Then you can both move on from this. You're miserable. He's miserable. Why can't you be miserable together?"

"I can't," I mumble, my words as weak as my reply.

"Why?" Serenity asks, like forgiveness is the answer to everything.

I twist my body to face her, hiding my pale cheeks from the horde of people mingling in Links' rec room. "Because you can't forgive someone who hasn't asked for forgiveness," I reply, sucking in a deep breath that thrusts my chest forward. "I also don't deserve his request for clemency, because I am no better than he is."

Serenity's pupils expand as she gulps in a dramatic breath. Her shimmering eyes dance between mine, seeking clarification on my cryptic declaration. Worried she has the ability to read me as well as her brother, I excuse myself, snatch my purse off the shelf, then make a beeline for the bathroom.

My mad dash down the corridor has me accidentally bumping into a blurred frame standing in the cramped space.

"Sorry."

The smell of vanilla permeates the air as the person I nearly barreled over replies, "Cleo, are you okay?"

Stopping just outside the women's restroom, I lift my eyes to the teaming-with-anxiety voice. I'm taken aback when I spot Keira standing halfway down the corridor. She is dressed casually in a pair of white wool pants and a one-shoulder cashmere sweater. Her hair is pulled off her face, making her appear a few years younger than her twenty-six years, and she is holding a brochure for Links firmly in her hand.

The drama making my skin a sticky mess grows when her wide gaze zooms in on the tears welling in my eyes. "Cleo?" she questions, surprised by my disheveled appearance.

"I'm fine," I mumble, pushing open the washroom door. "I just need a minute. It's a little overwhelming out there."

Exhaling in a rush, I step into the bathroom and quickly shut the door behind me. My first instinct is to scramble for the lock, but, unfortunately, there isn't one. Seeking privacy, I spin on my heels and head for the closest stall. Even someone as nosy as Mrs. Rachet would have a hard time spying on me in there.

After taking care of business and seizing a few moments to calm my nerves, I move to the sink to wash up. I sigh, so grateful the washroom is as deserted as it was when I entered it. When my eyes lift to the vanity mirror, I grimace, repulsed at the reflection looming back at me. The tears I've been struggling to keep at bay most of the day have awarded me with raccoon eyes and massively dilated pupils. The makeup I spent an hour perfecting this morning has sagged off my face, leaving nothing but sweat stains dribbling down my cheeks. My outsides look as wretched as I feel on the inside.

Placing my handbag on the vanity, I soak a paper towel and rub it under my eyes, removing a coating of mascara smeared under there. Once that mess is half-presentable, I drag my fingers through my unruly hair, then set to work on hiding the dark rings plaguing my eyes with a concealer stick from my purse. In no time at all, the fake Cleo I've been presenting to the world the past week is back stronger than ever.

"You've got this," I whisper to my reflection in the mirror. "Today is no different than every other day of your life the past four years. One shit storm after another." I mumble my last sentence.

The go-and-get-them attitude I'm attempting to build gets sideswiped when the screen of my silenced cellphone illuminates in my purse. After storing my concealer stick back into my oversized bag, I dig my cell out. Sick gloom spreads across my chest when I notice I have three voicemail messages from Delilah.

I'd like to say her constant checking in has dampened the past week. Unfortunately, that would be a lie. When I informed her the delay in processing the surveillance tape was because of doctored footage, her desire to identify the masked man at the helm of Chains became more zealous than ever.

"It will be only a matter of time before he makes a mistake, as the cost of hiding isn't as transparent as the man wishing to remain invisible," she has quoted multiple times this week.

Like most of society, Marcus's quest for anonymity bolstered Delilah's campaign to expose him. Her beliefs of anyone's God-given-right for privacy are as ill-guided as her moral compass. Both could use a major overhaul.

Deciding I don't have the strength to deal with Delilah right now, I store my cell phone in the pocket of my skirt, zip up my purse and head out of the washroom. My steps falter halfway across the pristine tiled floor. The beat of my heart quickly follows suit. As I stand frozen in the pine-fragranced room, my scalp prickles with primitive awareness.

Before my muddled brain can decipher the bizarre prompts of my body, the sound of a door handle lowering jingles into my ears. My eyes snap to watch the washroom door creep open millimeter by torturous millimeter. I don't need to see the face of the person entering the restroom to identify him, though. The quickening of my pulse is all the indication I need.

Marcus.

8

Adrenaline surges through my veins when Marcus steps into the women's restroom, shutting the door behind him. My heart kicks into a mad beat, a combination of anxiety and excitement as my eyes rake the length of his body. Even though he is dressed casually in a pair of black jeans, a plain white T, and a baseball cap, he is easily distinguishable. No gimmicks or props could fool my body's awareness of his closeness—*not a single damn thing.*

The attraction between us is still as active as ever, cracking and hissing in the air, but it's been shadowed by deceit so heavy, it's forcefully keeping us apart. I gulp, eradicating a lump in my throat when Marcus removes his baseball cap and places it on the vanity I was standing in front of earlier. My breath hitches in my throat when his stunning green irises are fully exposed. His eyes are restless, and his face looks tired, but even with his outside appearance matching the sentiments of my insides, he is still an incredibly handsome man. The roughness of his unshaven jaw gives his appearance a tempestuous edge, and the hollow bleakness of his eyes makes his alluring green gaze even more compelling. I've never seen a man so beautiful and haunted at the same time.

Holding my gaze, Marcus spans the distance between us. Even with the terseness of our situation, the air is fired with lust so strong, it crackles in the air like a whip lashing a sweat-drenched back. My astute brain screams at me to walk away before my lust-driven heart gets snagged by his fascinating eyes, but I don't budge an inch, my body too engrossed by his commanding aura to do anything. I can barely breathe, let alone order my legs to move.

"Stop," I whisper when the scent of his freshly showered smell engulfs me, teetering my emotions more than the silent pleas for forgiveness from his eyes.

"Please stop," I beg again when he fails to adhere to my initial request.

My last plea comes out in a hurry when the coolness of the tiled washroom wall soothes the overheated skin on my back. I was so rapt by his presence I didn't realize I was cowardly retreating. If it weren't for my purse sitting between us, I'd once again be trapped between an unmovable object and the man who can make my heart rate soar to the next galaxy before stepping to the side to watch it plummet back to reality.

"You can't be in here," I mumble, my voice shaky and crammed with uncertainty. "This is the ladies' washroom. You need to go," I stutter, shamefully using any excuse I can to force him to leave.

"I can't," Marcus mutters, his words as deep as the darkness in his eyes. "I tried to stay away, Cleo, believe me I did, but I can't do it anymore."

I stray my gaze to the floor, incapable of withstanding the lure of his tempting eyes. I can't trust myself around this man. He is my weakness. Furthermore, the pain in his eyes is too raw for me to hold this conversation. For every second I peer into them, my defenses weaken more and more.

"I'll make this right, Cleo. I'll fix the mistakes I made," Marcus informs me, his tone a unique mix of commanding and reserved. "I'm not leaving until you give me the chance to make things right."

His fingers hover just below my downcast chin as he brushes them over my chain link pendant nestled between my collarbones. He isn't quite touching me, but he is close enough awareness sizzles through my body. I don't know whether he is keeping his distance out of fear of how I may react, or because he is aware some of my hairs are bristling for reasons other than passion. Some are blatant fury.

"Tell me how to fix this, Cleo. Show me what to do." His voice is softer and more understanding, and it instigates a restless yearning inside of me. "I'll do anything you want—except give you up."

My lips quiver when I speak. "If that were true, you wouldn't have waited a week to make contact. You would have arrived at my door begging for forgiveness days ago. *Or you would have never let me leave to begin with.*" My last sentence comes out heavily laden with sentiment.

"I made a mistake." The shortness of his response is unable to hide the pain in his voice. "But I am here now trying to make things right. I can't take back the errors I made, Cleo, but I can make you forget they ever happened. Give me the chance to do that. Let me show you how much I need you."

His words impact my heart, striking it with an equal amount of disappointment and grief, but it doesn't stop me from saying, "You're talking nonsense, Marcus. You've only known me a matter of months. You don't need me. What we have is nothing more than an infatuation with one another."

Now he is touching me. His fingers trace the throb in my neck before dropping to trail the collar of my shirt. His touch is only brief but intense enough for a spark of ardor to roar through my body. I try to act unaffected by his meekest contact, but my goosebump-covered arms and shallow breathing give away my deceit.

"This isn't infatuation, Cleo. It's something much, much greater than that." Each word is spoken with a brush of his thumb on my bare collarbone. "Your body knows it. Your heart knows it. It's just self-judgment clouding your perception."

"I'm not the one who is confused, Marcus," I whisper, shaking my head. "Men of your stature are not often told they can't have something, so you're mistaking the signals your brain is relaying. You're not reading them for what they truly are: a man who for once was told no."

My confession stills and silences him. Even though he is no longer touching me, his quietness doesn't have the effect I am aiming for. It enhances the insane sexual connection between us instead of dampening it. Even without personal contact, my body's attention to his closeness is still paramount. There is no use denying my attraction to Marcus. My body yearns for him even when angry and harboring a decimated heart. But he broke my trust. No amount of sexual energy can regain broken trust. *Can it?*

When Marcus's silence becomes too great to ignore, I decide to risk a sneaky glance. I know he hasn't left as my body's alerted response is undeniable, but I've always been overly inquisitive and can't hold back my curiosity for a moment longer.

After exhaling a nerve-cleansing breath, I lift my eyes from the ground. *Now I wish I weren't so darn inquisitive.* Our eye contact is brief, but it's long enough for the earth to shift under my feet. Marcus must feel the change in the air as well, as a hint of a smile graces his lips.

Smirking, he steps closer, caging me in more firmly. He is so near, his sinfully delicious body squashes my purse into my stomach and increases the wetness between my legs. He watches me in silence, categorizing every emotion streaming from my soul-baring eyes. His nearness makes my skin clammy with sweat and sends my pulse skyrocketing. As if his lust-provoking eyes aren't enough to contend with, his well-fitted jeans are incapable of warding off the heat of his body. I am surprised I have wilted under his furious heat.

"I won't give up, Cleo. I'll never stop until you are mine," Marcus mutters, his warm breath bouncing off my dehydrated mouth. "Is your brain strong enough to fight the yearnings of both your heart and your body?"

The predatory gleam in his eyes darkens when my tongue delves out to moisten my lips. My reaction can't be helped. His determination is making me so needy and hot, my mouth is void of a single drop of moisture. I've never felt more desired than I do right now—*or conflicted.*

Sensing my body's response to his closeness, a grin tugs Marcus's full lips high. It sends arousal flowing over me like a rush of warm water. I close my eyes, hoping to conceal my body's betrayal to his wolfish grin. It's a pointless endeavor. Even angry, there isn't a drug in the world strong enough to curb my body's desire for this man.

Marcus buries his head in my neck and inhales deeply. "It only takes one glance," he quotes, his warm breath fanning my neckline. My knees crash together when he licks the shell of my ear before muttering. "You charred my soul from the moment you fell into the elevator, Cleo. I can't misread signs like that."

Wary and heartsick, I snivel, "You broke my trust, Marcus. You invaded my privacy. That's not something I can simply forgive and forget. You played me for a fool. I was nothing but a game to you. A little plaything for you to mess with."

I gasp in greedy breaths when Marcus pulls back from our embrace, easing some of the pressure spread across my chest. The veins in my neck strum when he curls his hand around the curve of my jaw. His touch is warm and inviting, and it adds more cracks to my already depleted heart. How can one man make me feel such opposing emotions? My brain is screaming blue murder at him, loathing that in such a short period of time he broke down its usually guarded perception, whereas my body is prickling with exhilaration, beyond pleased he isn't backing down without a fight. My heart... it's too tangled up with my internal quarrels to articulate a response.

The sweetness of Marcus's breath hits my lips when he growls, "If I weren't fearful of you walking away and never seeing me again, I'd take you over my knee for lying. But since I am standing here as Marcus and not Master Chains, I will let your lies slide. Don't continue to test my patience, Cleo. I am not a patient man."

Pushing aside the way his threat increased the moisture between my legs, I pop my eyes open and maddeningly shout, "I'm lying?!"

When Marcus nods, my teeth grit and anger overtakes some of the aroused blemishes on my cheeks. "How am I lying?" I ask, my pitch ear-piercing.

"You were never a game to me. Not once," Marcus implores, his tone stern and direct.

"You broke my trust! Why should I believe a single thing you say?" My words are weak and expose the conflicting set of emotions pumping into me. I am equally angry and exhilarated by our exchange.

Peering into my eyes, Marcus runs his finger over the curve of my top lip. His tame touch sends a tingle of euphoria dancing across my face, and it fires my heart with hope that not every negative thought I've had about us the past two months is true, that maybe the manic throb my heart gets every time I think about him isn't solely based on infatuation and anger.

Just like they do every time I peer into them, Marcus's beautiful eyes lure me into a trap, tempting me with promises of love, honor, and commitment, while also soothing the irritation his disloyalty prickled.

The frantic speed of my pulse accelerates when I spot a new gleam emerging in his eyes—one deeply embedded and previously unseen. I wouldn't necessarily say it's love, more like panic, or perhaps even fear. My brows scrunch, sending a large indent of wrinkles across my forehead. *Does the thought of me not being in his life scare him?*

"Yes, Cleo," Marcus replies, answering my silent question as his mesmerizing eyes dance between mine. "I will give up everything I have to make this right, but I won't give you up."

"Then why did you do it?" I ask, my voice low and full of anguish. "Why did you invade my privacy?"

My pulse rings in my ears when Marcus stares straight into my eyes and pledges, "Because you make me reckless."

My back molars grind together. "That isn't an excuse for reading my journals, Marcus! They were my private thoughts. Those words weren't for anyone's eyes but mine," I yell, expressing my true anger for the first time.

Although I am irrefutably angry at Marcus's lack of discretion in my private life, most of my anger stems from him reading my journals. I poured my heart and soul into my journals on the assumption they would never be read. They showed a side of me I've never been game to express until my weekend with Marcus.

I thought the inane connection Marcus and I had was based on his ability to intuit my desires without me needing to express them. It was only once I discovered he read my journals did reality smack into me. He didn't know me at all. He was just using the information he'd read in my journals as a way of knocking down my barriers. Knowing he used my private thoughts to his advantage hurts me more than him watching me in secrecy for two months.

My eyes rocket to Marcus when he says, "The first time I laid eyes on your journals was when I picked my Mac off the floor last weekend. And I swear to God, Cleo, I didn't read a single word. Not one."

I return his fervid watch, gauging for any deceit in his forthright eyes. I take a step backward as bewilderment registers its intention. There isn't any deceit in his eyes. How can that be true? If he didn't invade my privacy, why was a background search for me on his computer? Why did his Mac open on a live stream of my bedroom? And, most importantly, why should I believe him?

"And the surveillance camera? What about that?" I question, my anger not as wrathful as earlier after being leashed by his honesty.

Marcus licks his lips as the concern in his eyes grows. "At first, the camera was set up to seek confirmation that you were the girl in the elevator. Deep down inside, I knew you were her, but I wanted to see your unmasked face to be sure. It was only supposed to be one glance, I just couldn't stop myself."

The truth in his statement staggers me. I envisioned him brushing off my concerns under the guise that he is a celebrity, meaning my privacy was revoked for the sake of him keeping his. I didn't expect him to hit me with straight-up honesty.

Taking advantage of my stunned composure, Marcus continues to subdue my anger with honesty. "From the moment I met you, I knew there was something different about you. Not just because you fell to your knees in front of me, but because no matter how many times I told myself I only wanted you to be my sub, nothing followed my usual routine with a new sub."

If his declaration is meant to mollify my curiosity, it hasn't. I'm more confused now than I've ever been. "How is this different? You *wanted* me to be your sub. You had a contract drawn up. The only difference between me and your previous subs is this: I'm *not* your sub, Marcus. I never signed the contract. I will *never* sign it."

A wry grin tugs on Marcus's lips, forcing my heart rate to merge into coronary failure territory. "Your refusal to sign our contract is not what makes our relationship different. Generally, if a sub wishes to forgo signing a formal contract, I move on. No ifs or buts."

Even disgusted by his nonchalant response, my pulse quickens from his declaration.

"The difference this time around is me, Cleo, not you. I don't chase. I don't spend hours conversing on the phone. I don't date. And I most definitely don't put my need for control on the backburner at the request of my sub. But I did for you, Cleo, because I need you, I want you, and I won't stop until I have you again."

"I'll never be your sub, Marcus. I'm not submiss—"

"I don't want you as my sub, Cleo," he interrupts, his deep timbre vibrating my heart out of my chest. "I want you as *mine.*"

My knees curve inwards as a spark of ardor runs rampant through my veins. Spotting the mask of eagerness slipping over my face from the way he growled "mine," a lusty grin tugs on Marcus's lips. His wicked smile is an erotic invitation to my libido. It sends it skyrocketing to a point I can no longer hide. My cheeks flame as the hairs on my nape prickle.

Sensing my weakening defenses, Marcus moves in even closer, leaving not an ounce of air between us.

"I'm going to kiss you, Cleo," he informs me, his minty breath fanning my parted lips. "I'm going to kiss you until last week is forgotten. Then I'll kiss you some more just for the hell of it."

My brain commands for me to walk away before I lose the chance, but my body is too busy demanding my lungs breathe to follow its judicious counterpart's plea. Even knowing he is exploiting my attraction to him doesn't have me packing up stumps. I am beyond saving when it comes to this man.

Like he can sense my internal battle, Marcus mutters, "Self-judgment can confuse you, Cleo, but emotions never lie. Stop letting fear lead your desires. Dance with them instead."

For every millimeter his lips incline toward mine, the battle of my lungs doubles. My heaving lungs aren't my biggest concern, though. It's the conflicting array of emotions pumping through me. I'm wheezy, flushed, and incredibly aroused.

As his breathtakingly flawless eyes coax me into an intangible lure, Marcus mutters, "If you want me to stop, Cleo, you know what to say."

Pineapple.

The fact he reminds me of the one word that will instantly halt his campaign to seduce me eases the panic flaring through my veins. If he were here purely to coerce me back into his bed, he wouldn't have given me an out, he would have steamrolled me into submission by tricking my heart into deceiving my brain.

Just as his lips are about to seal over mine, I mumble, "This isn't a good idea, we still have so much to discuss. I have to..." My words trail off when the most delicious pair of lips I've ever tasted press up against mine.

9

The scent of Marcus's skin and the plumpness of his lips causes a flurry of memories to bombard me. Not just ones from last weekend, but ones that involve the stranger in the elevator and the masked man from the Bentley. It makes me want to forget last week ever happened. To push aside the pain and focus on the recovery.

Acting purely on the instincts of my wildly beating chest, I adjust the tilt of my head and part my lips. Marcus's mouth scarcely catches the throaty growl rumbling up my chest when his tongue delves into my mouth in a long, leisurely lick. Cradling my cheeks in his big, manly hands, he bites, sucks and caresses my lips at a tortuously slow pace, savoring every morsel of my mouth.

I vaguely register my purse falling to the floor before my fingers rake over his clipped afro. I return his kiss with just as much passion, a stimulating mix of playful nips and teasing strokes of my tongue. The longer our kiss, the more urgent it becomes, his bites more painful, the strokes of his tongue more controlled. I draw him in closer, needing more. No, wa*nting* more.

Sensing my desires, Marcus bands his arms around my back and pulls me into his tight, firm body. I purr when his wide cock braces against the aching throb in the middle of my legs. My enthusiastic response spurs him on even more. Cupping my thighs, he guides my legs around his waist. The flare of my skirt bunches around my hips, erotically exposing inches of my creamy white thighs.

Stepping forward, Marcus plasters my back on the cold tiled wall before rocking his hips forward. I arch my back, desperate to feel the thickness of his rod running the seam of my panties. As he kisses me with so much tenderness my heart nearly combusts, he swings his hips in a rhythm matching the strokes of his tongue, a teasing pace crammed with lust, heat, and forgiveness.

A whimper escapes my lips when he unexpectedly pulls his talented mouth away from mine long before I've had my fill. Although our lust-fueled kiss went above and beyond anything I could have hoped for, I still want more—much, much more.

With my fingers pressed on my tingling lips, I slowly flutter my eyes open. The insane beat of my heart kicks into overdrive when my heavy-lidded gaze meets with Marcus's. He appears just as moved by our kiss as I am. His eyes are wide and brimmed with sentiment, and his kiss-swollen lips are formed into a sexy, panty-melting smirk. Just seeing him so unkempt and carefree strengthens my desires to forget last weekend ever happened.

The reasoning behind his unwanted withdrawal comes to light when he drops his eyes to my right hip and mutters, "You're vibrating." His tone is rough and gritty, instigating a wild recklessness within me.

It takes several moments for me to register that not all the shudders wreaking havoc with my body were caused by Marcus's stimulating kiss. Some are from the vibration of my cell phone in my skirt pocket.

Unable to tear my heavy-hooded gaze away from Marcus's memorable eyes, I return his lust-riddled stare while delving my hand into my pocket. It feels like a bucket of ice-cold water is thrown over me when my eyes drop down to the screen of my phone and I discover who is calling me: Delilah.

Sick gloom spreads across my chest, making it hard for me to breathe. I was so caught up in Marcus, I failed to notice her additional two calls the past ten minutes.

I swallow several times in a row, ensuring the swishy contents of my stomach remain in their rightful place before swiveling my hips, requesting to be placed down. With reluctance, Marcus places me on my feet before taking a step backward. My body is furious about the loss of his contact. It isn't the only one disappointed, my heart is also beyond reproach.

After taking a few moments to clear my jittering nerves, I lift and lock my eyes with Marcus. "I need to take this," I murmur, my words strained through the bile sitting in the back of my throat. "It could be important."

Pretending I can't feel his concerned stare focused on me, I bob down and collect my purse from the ground. Just as I am about to sidestep Marcus, his hand shoots out to seize my wrist. His touch sends a surge of electricity bolting up my arm, switching my sluggish heart rate to a calamitous gallop. Remaining quiet, he flattens my palm over his erratically beating chest. My eyes burn from a sudden influx of moisture. Our hearts are beating a similar rhythm. A tormented thump of confliction and love.

"I can't misread signs like that, Cleo."

God—I'm so torn. I want to tell him everything. I want to warn him about the tornado set to wreak havoc in his life so he can prepare for the backlash, but I can't. It isn't just Lexi's health I am protecting, it's our entire livelihood. I am legally bound not to disclose a story to any source. If I break my employment contract with Global Ten Media, they will sue me. I can barely afford to live as it is, let alone pay legal expenses—it would send me bankrupt. Furthermore, my family home has so much sentimental value to me, it's priceless. I can't risk losing it. I just can't.

After clearing the panic from my eyes, I swing them to Marcus. A shiver rockets through me when our eyes connect and hold. The jolt is so forceful, I take a stumbling step backward and gasp in an exaggerated breath. I never understood my dad's logic about eye contact causing your soul to catch on fire. I do now. Because that's all it took. One glance into Marcus's eyes told me he would be worth any sacrifice just to see that look one more time. But can I do this? Can I place my faith in a man who invaded my privacy so I can I save him from a woman set to destroy him?

While returning Marcus's empathy-filled glance, the same answer rings on repeat in my ears: *Yes, I can.* I just need to do it right. I need to be the smart, independent woman my parents raised me to be, and I need to do it now before I lose the courage.

More determined than ever, I lock my eyes with Marcus and say, "I have somewhere very important I need to go."

"Okay," he says, not bothering to check my eyes for deceit. The truth was heard in my strong-willed statement. "Do you want me to come with you?"

"No," I reply, nearly shouting. "This is something I should have done a long time ago. It's also something I need to do alone."

Marcus's brows scrunch as a concerned cloud filters over his eyes. He takes a few moments pondering a response before suggesting, "Alright. Can we meet later?" I can tell by his eyes he wants to say more, but, thankfully, he is striving to rein in his need for control.

Grateful he isn't pushing me, I exhale the breath I'm holding in while nodding. "Can you come to my place around eight?" I ask. My words come out rickety, uneasy about inviting someone as wealthy as Marcus into my humble home.

Like he can sense my apprehension, Marcus fiddles with the shell of my ear. His soft touch calms the uncertainty swirling my stomach.

"The value of a home isn't determined by the possessions inside it, Cleo. It's the memories created there," he mutters, intuiting the reason for my nervous tone.

Shock gnaws at my stomach as I stand mute. *How the hell can he read me so easily?*

He fingers the silver stud in my ear as his eyes dance between mine. "Should I pack an overnight bag? Or just..." His words taper into silence, leaving me to fill in the gaps.

Even hearing the playful jeering in his tone doesn't stop lust raging through me. My palms grow as damp as the heated core between my legs. When I spot an impish gleam in his eyes flaring from my slack-jawed expression, I jab my fingers into his ribs.

"We are *only* talking, Marcus," I inform him, my tone laced with surprising bitchiness. "We have a lot to discuss before anything like *that* will be happening. *If* it ever happens again."

My tone isn't any less bitchy the second time around. I'm not angry at

Marcus, I'm fuming at myself. The instant my body registered the sexual innuendo in his jovial tone, it wanted to forgo any prompts of my astute brain and skip straight to the heavy stuff: the obligatory make up sex.

Marcus's smile grows, arousing my libido once more. "I know." His voice is low and tempting. "Conversing with you is my third favorite thing to do with you."

"Third?" I blubber out before I can stop my words, shock in my tone. "I can gather number one." My eyes roll skyward, the rigidity in the air unable to stifle my need to goad him. "But what's number two?"

Glancing into my eyes to ensure I can't miss the truth in his statement, Marcus replies, "Making you smile."

"Which in turn makes you horny. A win-win for us both." I snap my mouth shut, mortified I said my private thoughts out loud.

Heat creeps across my cheeks like a tidal wave of embarrassment, leaving me breathless and flushed. My hands itch to cover my inflamed face, but I keep them balled at my side, not wanting to give Marcus another weapon in his already overflowing arsenal to use against me.

My stern stature buckles the instant Marcus flutters his fingers down the throb in my throat. His touch is so tantalizing it sends a zap of lust straight to my core. While his enticing eyes soundlessly coerce me, his fingers dip into the collar of my blouse.

"Are you sure you need to leave, Cleo? There is only one situation where I appreciate delayed gratification."

My knees become weak from his self-assurance. He is cocky and confident, but not in an egotistical, pompous type of way. When his finger traces the curve of my top lip, my brain begs for me not to get lured into his trap, but the pull is more than I can bear.

Getting caught up in the moment, I snap my eyes closed and sway towards him. The rollercoaster of emotions I'm riding kicks into high gear when his manly, refreshing smell graces my senses. His scent makes me giddy, and it has my shrewdness severely faltering.

With how potently lust is firing in the air, I'm stunned my body hasn't demanded I fall to my knees and beg Marcus for forgiveness. It doesn't care about the past. It wants to live in the here and now—which happens to include the man standing in front of me. But if I want any chance of accepting the promises his eyes issue me every time he peers at me, I need to make this right.

Swallowing down my disappointment, I take a step to my right, moving away from Marcus's warm, tempting body. My lungs saw in and out, wondering if Marcus will follow the usual steps we dance in these types of situations.

He surprises me when he remains still, watching me cautiously.

"I'll see you tonight," I mumble before making a beeline for the door, stumbling out of the washroom with an undignified clumsiness.

After taking a few moments leaning against the wall in the foyer of Links to gather my composure, I push through the frosted glass doors and wave down a passing taxi. Butterflies cause mayhem in my stomach when the flash of numerous paparazzi lights blind my vision. Clearly, Marcus's incognito disguise has been thwarted.

Seconds later, I slide into the back seat of a cab that stops in front of me and hand the driver the remaining crumpled up bills in my purse.

"Global Ten Media," I request to the dark eyes peering at me in the rearview mirror.

Nodding, the cab driver pulls into the dense flow of traffic. A horn beeps, and I jump, making me realize I am even more nervous than I thought. Even pumped knowing what I am about to do is best for everyone involved doesn't make it any less challenging.

I have no doubt my next meeting will be even more explosive than Marcus's kisses.

10

My steps down the hall of Global Ten Media are shaky and long. I'm clutching freshly printed sheets of paper in my hand so tightly, they have crinkles creased down the middle. Before my parents and Tate passed away, challenging situations never bothered me. I wouldn't say I was an overly confrontational type of person, but if I felt something was unjust, I voiced my opinion on the matter.

That all changed the instant I answered the call that upended my life.

There is no greater loss to a person's confidence than losing someone they love. Everything about me changed the day my parents and Tate were involved in their accident. In more ways than I'd care to admit, I changed. I didn't just lose my family that day. I lost a part of myself.

Books have been my therapy the past four years. Before meeting Marcus, fictional worlds were the only thing that could sweep me away from reality. It was the one place I got caught up in without a single thought passing my mind. In a weird, kinky type of way, Marcus became my fairytale. When I am with him, I get swept away from reality. It's an invigorating and carefree time.

I didn't know how much weight I was carrying on my shoulders until I let it all go in his playroom last weekend. That's one side of the BDSM lifestyle that intrigues me the most. You don't imagine how great it can feel to be relieved of all responsibilities when you're juggling so many, it will only be a matter of time before everything comes tumbling down.

Rolling my shoulders to shake off my anxiety, I raise my fist to Mr. Carson's office door and knock three times. My loud bangs drown out my pulse shrilling in my ears. I suck in a deep breath, ignoring the stuttering of my heart. My brow is beaded with sweat, and my whole body is overheated with nerves. I've spent the last twenty minutes hiding out in my office, building up the courage to do this. I am not just about to risk my reputation as a journalist by confessing my sins to Mr. Carson, I'm also risking my sister's health and our entire livelihood. But even with panic so strong it's making it difficult for me to breathe, I need to do this. It's time to come clean on my relationship with Marcus.

Don't construe my confession the wrong way, I have no intention of outing Marcus's secret. I just need to step away from the investigation into Chains before the lines between morally unethical and illegal become so blurred I can't tell the difference. Although I am nervous about what Mr. Carson's reaction will be, I am confident my ramifications will be minor.

My relationship with Marcus may have stepped over what society deems as appropriate for a journalist and her target, but there is no clause in my contract that states I cannot have a relationship with Marcus. It may hint at it not being in my best interest, but there is no way our interactions thus far will put me in breach of my employment contract with Global Ten Media.

My eyes stray from the ground when a creak of a door sounds through my ears. The width of my pupils grows when my eyes zoom in on the person greeting me. I was expecting Mr. Carson's sable gaze, not a set of eyes belonging to the devil herself.

"Umm... Hi, Delilah," I greet her, my voice exposing my suspicion of why she is in Mr. Carson's office so late on a Saturday afternoon.

My eyes snap to the name plaque on the door, suddenly frantic my baffled mind has me arriving at the wrong office. It doesn't. The plaque clearly states *Mr. Jack Carson – CEO of Global Ten Media.*

Smirking at my skittish response, Delilah glides her hand across the front of her body, soundlessly inviting me in. Her composure is entirely too smug for my liking, which makes my anxiety swell. Swiping at the moisture beading on my brow, I step into the vast space. I can't remember the last time I've been so nervous.

After closing Mr. Carson's door, Delilah crosses the room in six long strides, her steps as rigid as the Botox-treated skin stretched across her forehead. She props her backside on the edge of Mr. Carson's desk, giving the indication she is comfortable making herself at home in his domain, before locking her evil eyes with mine. The arrogance pumping out of her is oppressive, fueling the air with ghastly humidity.

Ignoring the fluttering of nerves in my stomach, I hold her gaze, trying to display I am not intimidated by her. She crosses her arms over her chest, a defiant pose that agitates me more.

Only once the air becomes thick with tension does she sneer, "I was beginning to wonder if you were avoiding me since you failed to return any my calls."

"Ah... umm ..." I roll my eyes, loathing my lack of self-worth around this woman. I am stronger than this. I still, then force my nerves to settle. "It's the weekend, Delilah. I'm entitled to take days off. It's written in my employment contract." I inwardly sigh, grateful my voice comes out sounding as I envisioned: firm, yet professional.

"Many things are cited in an employment contract, Cleo. The most stringent is your agreement to be contactable in the event of a life-altering story," Delilah snaps, her composure as bitchy as ever.

"Unearthing the identities of patrons at a BDSM club isn't a life-altering story, Delilah," I rebut, sneering her name the same way she sneered mine. "They are people, no different than me and you."

"Ha!" Delilah remarks, her loud voice shrilling off the walls before booming into my ears. "And how did you reach that conclusion?" Even though she is asking a question, she continues speaking, not waiting for me to answer her. "Even someone as dimwitted as you wouldn't be stupid enough to believe a single word preached by those sick fucks."

I balk, flabbergasted and stunned. "Sick fucks?" I quote, my words spitting off my tongue like venom. "You don't know a single thing about the BDSM community, yet you feel you have the right to judge the people involved in it?" My words are strong and confident, encouraged by the impressive accomplishments I witnessed time and time again at Links today.

Delilah pushes off the desk and moseys towards me. Her steps are arrogant and dramatic. "They made their bed, sweetheart, now they are about to sleep in the roach-infested bedding," she sneers.

"I'd rather sleep in their infested bedding than with a narcissist like you," I grumble under my breath.

When Delilah's eyes slit, it dawns on me that I said my statement a little louder than I was aiming for. I know it's unwise to react to Delilah's taunts, but I can't help but respond. She grates my nerves more sharply than anyone before her.

"If they don't want society deeming them as disturbing, they should seek better ways to curb their desires," Delilah barks, air quoting when she snarls the word "desires."

I wait a beat to reply, giving myself a few moments to calm down. It's clearly a waste of time when I say, "Judging someone's choices without knowing their reasons doesn't define them, Delilah, it defines you. And from what I'm seeing, it isn't a pretty sight."

Deciding I am better than this conversation, I pivot on my heels and pace to the door. The last thing I need added to my already overbalanced plate is a shouting match with a woman who doesn't have a moral bone in her entire body.

My fast pace to the door stops midstride when Delilah threatens, "You walk out that door, *Chloe*, you keep walking until you reach the unemployment line." Her voice is vicious, matching the wilted black heart sitting in her chest.

Gritting my teeth, I spin around to face her. Delilah glares at me, the expression on her abhorrent face displaying she is stationed for battle. Since this is the umpteenth time she has threatened me with unemployment the past two months, her desolate stare doesn't have the effect she is aiming for. If anything, it makes her even more pathetic.

"You need to come up with a new threat, Delilah, as that one is as luckless as your out-of-date hairstyle."

Delilah's eyes slit in disdain as she hisses in a breath. "Don't underestimate me, little girl. Just because we aren't standing in a dungeon, doesn't mean your stupidity will go unpunished. I don't need a whip to have you kneeling before me," she spits out, her tone menacing.

"Enough, Delilah!" I roar so loud it bellows off the sharp walls of Mr. Carson's office. "I'm sick to death of being ridiculed by you. You're nothing but a degenerate old cow who wouldn't know grace and empathy if they slapped you in the face."

I can see Delilah's anger winding up from her stomach to her throat, but I don't back down. I'm too far gone serving justice to stop and consider the repercussions of my actions. I am at my absolute wit's end with this woman.

"If you had done a single ounce of research on the BDSM community, your ignorance on the matter wouldn't be so high. But instead of doing the job Mr. Carson pays you to do, you act like you're some sort of god, glaring down at the people you *believe* are below you. Newsflash, Delilah: leadership is based on inspiration, not intimidation. And respect is earned, not taken."

Even if I hadn't spent the past two months discussing with Marcus the rights of an individual to choose their own sexual proclivities, my opinion on this matter wouldn't alter. My mom was right: a wise woman makes her own decision. An ignorant woman follows the public opinion.

"Just because something is unknown to you, Delilah, doesn't mean you should fear it."

Delilah scoffs, brushing off my remark with nothing but an evil glare. "I don't fear anything," she snarls, her words spit fired out of her mouth like venom, "let alone sick, vile, bilious men and women who—"

"Save hundreds of lives every year, teach students history, math, and science, and make sandwiches and pump gas. They also breathe the same air as you and bleed the same color blood."

"Blood that's been beaten out of them," Delilah roars, her stern pitch loud enough to rattle my bones.

I take a step back, shock is smeared all over my face. "Only the people interested in that type of play," I defend.

"Play?" Delilah mocks with a malicious smirk etched on her face. "Exactly how far did your *research* go in the *lifestyle*, Cleo?"

Panic rises within me. I was so caught up defending the BDSM community's integrity, I blurted out more than I meant to.

Smirking at my stunned expression, Delilah questions, "How deeply undercover did you go, Cleo? A spank with a paddle? A fuck in a dirty alleyway? Or did you fall to your knees like you have every day of your life the past twenty-six years?"

When I remain, quite a victorious gleam brightens her dark eyes. She knows she has me over a barrel.

Pretending her scornful tirade didn't knock my ego, I continue to plead my case, my Garcia stubbornness not allowing me to back down without a fight. "Over the past two months, I've spoken to lawyers, doctors, at home moms, kindergarten teachers, and grandmothers in the BDSM community. I researched the lifestyle, talked to the community, and opened my mind to the possibility people can have preferences different than the ones society deems acceptable. That doesn't make them sick, Delilah. It makes them real."

Delilah laughs a wicked, witch-like cackle that makes my stomach churn. "Real? The only thing real here is the fact you are in over your head, *little girl,*" she mocks, pacing to stand in front of me. She stands so close, her coffee-scented breath bounces off my hard-lined lips.

"I know your mother has passed, Cleo, but that was after you reached adulthood, so it's no excuse for your ignorance." She continues speaking, stealing my chance to absorb her first below-the-belt hit before she smacks me with another. "Mothers are supposed to raise their children with morals and integrity. Clearly, your mother was as dimwitted as you."

"Take it back," I push out through clenched teeth, my low tone crammed with silent warning that I've reached my quota of being so poorly disrespected. First, she disrespected a man I'm falling in love with, now she is desecrating the memory of a lady who meant the world to me. "My mother was a wonderful woman. You could only hope to be one-tenth of the woman she was."

Viciously snarling, Delilah pinches the material of her pantsuit and crouches down to meet me eye to eye. "Why would I take it back?" Her voice is so soft I can barely hear it. "The truth may be a bitter pill to swallow, even for someone as dimwitted as you, but everything I've said thus far is true."

Blood rushes to the surface of my skin, burning my cheeks with anger when Delilah whispers, "Your mother must be rolling in her grave knowing she raised such a stupid, tactless, waste of space." She hisses her last words slowly, ensuring I don't miss a single ounce of the disdain her words are drenched in.

Before I have the chance to consider the impact of my action, I raise my hand and slap Delilah across the face. The sound of her teeth crunching together booms over the blood roaring in my ears. My slap is so forceful, her head rockets to the side. Although shaken I responded with violence, I am damn proud I finally stood up to the devil's reincarnation.

Cupping her flaming red cheek in her hand, Delilah shifts her eyes back to me. When I spot the fury glaring from her narrowed gaze, I brace, preparing for impact. Instead of striking me as I am expecting, Delilah smiles a grin that adds to the churning of my stomach. It's vindictive and laced with malice.

The reasoning behind her serene approach becomes apparent when a deep voice behind my shoulder says, "What's going on in here?"

Swallowing to eradicate the enormous brick suddenly lodged in my throat, I spin on my heels to face the teeming-with-anger voice. The color in my cheeks drains to my shoes when I come face to face with an irate Mr. Carson. He is standing in the doorway of his office, bouncing his eyes between Delilah and me. From the heavy groove in the middle of his dark brows, I can readily perceive he witnessed me assaulting Delilah.

"It isn't as it seems," I mumble, jittering with nerves. "She provoked me. She's been harassing me for years."

Delilah scoffs loudly, but I don't pay her any attention. I keep my gaze front and center, praying Mr. Carson will see the truth beaming from my eyes.

Some of my silent prayers are answered when Mr. Carson advises, "Global Ten Media has a stringent non-bullying policy, Cleo. If you felt you were being intimidated, we had measures in place you could have utilized to put an end to it."

I nod, advising I am aware of the policy he is referring to. I've perused the anti-bullying document numerous times the past two years when Delilah's taunts became too much for me to bear. Unfortunately, her tirades were protected by virtue of being my supervisor. When I brought up the policy during staff meetings, she often rebutted that she was merely giving me "constructive feedback."

My neck cranks to the side when Delilah sniffles, "Slapping your superior for having an opposing opinion is an exaggerated spectral response, Mr. Carson. Surely the severity of retaliating with violence outweighs an occasionally misread comment."

She keeps her voice low, acting like she is on the verge of tears. I'm not buying her Oscar-worthy performance. I can feel the pompousness beaming out of her in invisible waves. She is loving every snip of tension depriving the air of oxygen.

The dread blackening my veins grows when Mr. Carson asks, "Did you inflict physical harm on Delilah, Cleo?"

Even though his eyes relay he already knows my reply, I answer, "Yes. I did."

I'm hoping my honest response is the first of many.

I'm tired of lying.

After Mr. Carson's eyes drink in the clearly visible handprint on Delilah's left cheek, he drops his gaze to me. The anger in his eyes softens with every second that passes. "Did Delilah physically harm you first?" he questions, his tone low.

I wait a beat, praying he will see the remorse in my eyes before shaking my head. As he thrusts his hands into the pocket of his trousers, disappointment overtakes some of the empathy in his eyes.

"You heard what she said in the conference room last week. That type of remark wasn't a one-off occurrence. She's been tormenting me like that for years."

I'm not remorseful for striking Delilah—she deserved it—I'm regretful for putting Mr. Carson in this predicament. Staff quarrels were the bane of my existence when I was head of the entertainment division at Global Ten Media. More times than not, jealousy was the cause of all the squabbling. But this is different, I'm not jealous of Delilah. How could I possibly jealous of someone with a black heart?

My heart rate spikes. *Perhaps I am not the one who is jealous?*

The smell of Mr. Carson's spicy cologne surpasses the anxiety leaching from my pores when he steps deeper into the vast space. When he stops to stand in front of me, Delilah attempts to speak. Mr. Carson cuts her off with a wave of his hand across the front of his body.

"One battle at a time, Ms. Winterbottom," he snaps, his tone direct.

My optimism that he isn't blinded by Delilah's attractive outer shell sails out the window when he says, "Go and wait for me in the conference room, Cleo. Once I have finished speaking with Delilah, I will call you in."

11

My unassured steps down a darkened alley grind to a stop when a deep voice shouts, "Cleo!"

Listening to the protests of my screaming hip, I place the box I've been juggling the past hour onto the curb at my side before pivoting around to face the undistinguishable voice. My spine straightens with concern when my eyes lock in on a blurry figure briskly charging towards me. It isn't the unapproachable demeanor bouncing off the unnamed man in invisible waves that has my heart rate speeding up, it's his bull-like charge. His speed is unchecked as he races across the isolated street.

Panic tightens around my throat when my nearsightedness clears enough I can see the man's face. Although his first impression was less than stellar last Friday, I never forget a face. It's the man I met under the Brooklyn Bridge: the man who collected my unsigned NDA.

The angry scowl tainting his face with ugliness sends my panic to an all-time high. His stare is enough to make the burliest men shake in their boots, and that isn't taking into consideration the furious mask slipped over his face. I flinch when he abruptly stops in front of me. His movements are so curt, whiskey-scented air blasts my face.

"Do you know how much your stupidity cost me?!" he roars, his words shooting out of his mouth like daggers. "I've been working with Mr. Everett for years, and you're the first whore who didn't sign the NDA."

My first reaction is shock, closely followed by disgust. Who does he think he is to speak to me so disgracefully? And what is it about this weekend? Do I have a massive target on my back requesting to be ridiculed? I'm enduring blow after devastating blow. I knew this morning was the calm before the storm.

But even with my mind still spiraling from my exchange with Delilah, my decorum isn't so jilted I can ignore his callous statement. "Who the hell are you calling a whore?" The anger in my voice is easily distinguishable, even more so because of the dead quiet of the alleyway.

Acting like he didn't hear a word I said, the stranger digs his chubby fingers into the top of my arm and drags me further into the alley, away from the prying eyes of strangers lurking on the sidewalks nearby. I attempt to yank out of his grip. My efforts are utterly pointless. His large width and height aren't for show. It matches his strength to a T. He is too strong for a woman of my stature.

"Let me go!" I scream, thrashing to get out of his firm grip. "You're hurting me."

His vindictive chuckle sends a chill of dread down my spine. "That's what submissives like, isn't it?" he sneers, tightening his clutch on my arm. "Being manhandled and thrown around." His thunderous words vibrate my heart right out of my chest.

"I'm not a sub."

"Yeah, yeah, sweetheart, that's what they all say," he laughs, his tone mocking.

I'm so angry, the spit of his vicious words sizzles when they land on my inflamed cheeks. "If you don't get your hands off me this minute, you'll regret the day you met me," I warn.

My threat increases the corrupt cloud in his dark gaze. He is enjoying every minute of our battle.

A winded grunt parts my lips when he uses his body to pin me to the side of a car halfway down the alley. Even winded, I continue to fight against him, endeavoring to get free. After reinforcing his hold by leaning into me harder, he digs a white envelope out of his trousers pocket before removing a pen from the breast pocket of his suit jacket. With a grunt, he nudges his head to the envelope housing the NDA I refused to sign last Friday night.

"Sign it," he sneers, glowering at me like I'm a piece of dog poo stuck under his shoe.

"No," I reply, issuing him the same corrupt glare he wears.

I kick, wail and scream with all my might, praying one of the many people scrambling past the alleyway will hear my plight and come to my aid. All I end up achieving is more windedness. His large frame is just too big. No matter how hard I fight, he doesn't budge an inch. I don't think a crane could move him.

"Let me go!" I demand again, my voice growing angrier.

"Sign the NDA, and I'll let you on your merry way," he snarls in reply.

He grips my arm so hard, I'm confident I'll have a bruise tomorrow morning. His roughness pushes my Garcia fighting spirit into overdrive. I yank backward to gain some distance between us before raising my knee to his groin. Pain rockets through my body when he foils my attempt of kneeing him by twisting his body to the side. My knee slams into his thigh with brutal force, maiming my body as severely as his cruel words nicked my heart.

Yanking me forward as if I am a ragdoll, the unnamed man brings me to within an inch of his ugly face. The toes of my stilettos skim the asphalt when he suspends me in the air by clutching the front of my shirt. Even with fear sparking every nerve-ending, I shut down the responses of my body, refusing to let him see he has me rattled.

"Sign the NDA, or I'll show you how a real man dominates."

Snarling, I shake my head. "No."

His lips pull high, exposing a gold veneer on his right incisor tooth. "You're either an idiot, or you're so fucked in the head, you think this is foreplay."

He runs his morally corrupt eyes down my body, lingering his heavy-hooded gaze on my thrusting chest so long my skin crawls. His tongue delves out to replenish his dry lips as the anger in his eyes rapidly morphs to lust.

"Do you want to *play*, Cleo?" he jeers, staring into my eyes to ensure I can't miss the sexual innuendo laced in his question.

Anger flames my cheeks. "I'd rather wake up in a pool of vomit than *play* with a man like you!" I scream at the top of my lungs, my cry hoarse from the amount of yelling I've been doing.

Fiery anger spreads through me like liquid acid when he uses his spare hand to backhand me. "Shut the fuck up," he snarls, panicked that our gathering has gained us a few inquisitive stares at the end of the alley.

My teeth crunch together as pain zooms through my right cheek. His hit is so firm, white spots dance in front of my eyes and dizziness consumes me. Even though I should be cowering, his hit angers me more. *Only a coward hits women.*

Blood oozes from my nose when I return my frightened eyes to my attacker. "Is that all you've got?" I mock, acting like I can't feel blood trickling over my lips. "I've had girls hit harder than you."

My stomach launches into my throat when his slimy tongue slithers out to lap up a droplet of blood from my top lip. I buck and wail against him, sickened at the thought of him touching me.

He draws me in more firmly to his body so he can whisper in my ear. "I'm not even getting started yet."

My stomach heaves when the scent of his breath lingers into my nostrils. It's as hideous as his horrid face. When one of his hands creeps along my stomach, slowly inching towards my erratically panting chest, I fight with all my might. I grunt, kick and wail until I am utterly exhausted. Not happy with my continuous disobedience, he pins me to the car with one hand before raising the other into the air, preparing to strike me again. I grit my teeth, bracing for impact. The evil grin on his face grows, no doubt relishing my frightened response.

Just before his hand connects with my throbbing cheek, a commotion sounds behind us. Panicked we are not alone, my attacker cranks his head to the side so fast his muscles shriek in protest. Using his distraction to my advantage, I wildly kick out my leg. A grunt rolls up my aggressor's chest when my perfectly placed kick hits him straight between his legs. The air is forcefully removed from his body as his hands dart down to protect his groin.

"You fucking bitch," he stammers out, his words coerced through his balls, which are now sitting in the back of his throat.

Protecting himself from another blow, he dumps me onto my feet. As the color drains from his face, he glares into my eyes. His gaze exposes that he is bankrupt of a soul. I have no doubt, if given a choice, he'd rear up to strike me again. The only reason he doesn't is because a man shouting at him to get away from me resonates over his furious growl.

"This isn't over, bitch," my attacker sneers before hobbling to a dark blue sedan parked under a dimly lit street light on my left.

As my savior chases the crippled man's quickly retreating frame, I struggle to keep upright. I am so disorientated and confused, I'm having trouble recalling why I'm standing in an isolated alleyway late on a Saturday night. *It is Saturday? Isn't it?*

When my wooziness becomes too great for me to bear, I crumble to the ground. I wince in pain when my knees connect harshly with the asphalt. Although my hit is brutal, it isn't painful enough to stop gratefulness from consuming me. During times like this, I realize one day my Garcia stubbornness will backfire on me.

My blurry gaze drifts to my right when a multihued display of light dances in my eyes. I blink several times in a row to clear my vision. When it clears, I realize my attacker's vigorous shakes forced my cellphone out of my pocket.

After gathering my shattered cell off the ground, I scamper across the alleyway on my hands and knees so I can lean on the side panel of the car I was pinned against mere minutes ago. My temples are drilling my skull, and awful nausea is overwhelming me.

Pretending the rogue tear streaming down my right cheek is a bead of sweat, I pinch the bridge of my nose, vainly trying to stop more blood from staining my ivory-colored shirt. I grimace when my fingertips skim over my top lip. When I run my tongue over the burn to soothe it, the taste of copper fills my mouth.

It feels like hours pass before my savior returns from chasing my assailant's car, but it's most likely only minutes. Fresh tears prick my eyes when a familiar face pops into my peripheral vision. Don't ask if they are happy or frightened tears as I wouldn't be able to answer you.

"Hey, Cleo, are you alright?" Richard questions, his tone low and unsure.

12

I nod, soundlessly answering Richard's question before endeavoring to stand from the ground. My brisk nod makes it feel like my brain is rattling in my head, amplifying my dizziness and making my stomach lurch into my throat. Stumbling, I crash into Richard's firm body.

"Whoa, Cleo, careful. You might be concussed." Richard steadies my swaying movements by gripping the tops of my arms. "Take in some deep breaths while you gather your bases."

"I'm okay... I'm just... umm ... *going home*?" My words are strained through my hand clamped over my mouth to ensure the contents of my stomach remain in my stomach.

After guiding me to sit on an old milk crate, Richard places his hand under my chin and carefully raises my downcast head. "Let me have a look at you," he requests, his tone low—almost caring.

His smooth voice eases some of the uncertainty prickling my spine, but it also convinces me I am not lucid. This helpful savior can't be the same man I kneed in the balls three months ago. That Richard doesn't understand the word empathy. He has the type of personality that would prefer to video someone getting attacked rather than aid in their recovery.

A hiss of air whizzes out my lips when Richard's thumb dabs the top right-hand corner of my mouth. "Sorry," he apologizes as his remorse-filled eyes dance between mine. "The split in your lip is a little deep, but it won't need any stitches. Can you stand?"

Since my mouth is refusing to cooperate, I once again nod, more carefully this time.

Placing his hands under my arms, Richard assists me off the crate. I'm definitely in shock because not a single objection is fired from my brain when he curls his arm around my shoulders and commences guiding me out of the alleyway.

"My box. I need my box," I stammer out, my voice exposing the catalyst of emotions pumping into me—shallow, low, and brimming with confusion.

Remaining quiet, Richard gathers my box with his spare hand before he continues with our journey out of the alleyway. My battered appearance gains the curious glance of many spectators out enjoying their Saturday night, but not a single person questions if I need assistance.

Since my legs are so wobbly, it takes nearly five minutes for us to walk the half block to the parking garage employees of Global Ten Media use. With my mind shut down without a single thought, I allow Richard to guide me into the passenger seat of his truck.

When he secures a seatbelt around my waist, I mumble, "I'm okay, I can find my own way home." The shaking of my voice hinders what should be a strong statement. "Should we call the police?"

Richard doesn't acknowledge my comments. He just places my box next to me on the bench seat before cracking open his glove compartment. His Adam's apple bobs up and down as he removes a wad of cotton and some antiseptic ointment from the small first aid kit housed inside. It's very well, as the instant I blurted out my suggestion, I wanted to take it back. Getting the police involved would only add more tension to an already tense situation.

"This will sting a little," Richard warns while squeezing antiseptic lotion onto the cotton.

A hiss of air whizzes through my clenched teeth when he dabs the cut in my top lip. The pain isn't as fiery as my attacker's hit, but it's still unpleasant. Pretending he can't see the moisture welling in my eyes, Richard issues the same amount of attentiveness to the cuts on my knees. He picks out the small gravel embedded in them before sterilizing the open wounds with antiseptic. I sit still—stunned into silence. I don't know what's more devastating: the fact I was just attacked mere feet from hundreds of spectators who failed to help me, or that Richard is so attentive and kind. Considering muggings are a regular occurrence in New York, I am going to say it's Richard's attentiveness.

After placing a pair of Band-Aids on my gravel-scratched knees, Richard packs up the first aid kit, stores it in the glovebox, then runs around his truck to slide into the driver's seat.

As he fires up the engine, his shifts his eyes to me. "What's your address, Cleo?"

Taken aback by his chivalry and still harboring a foggy brain, I mumble, "160 Valley Road, Montclair."

Richard smiles. "A New Jersey girl, hey? No wonder why you never took any of my crap." His voice comes out friendly, but there is a slight undertone of anger associated with it.

Unsure how to reply, I return his smile. While Richard directs his truck out of the multistory parking garage, I check my reflection in the mirror of his visor. I cringe when my massively dilated gaze takes in my split lip and the large red welt on my right cheek. I pinch my left cheek, hoping a rush of blood to my skin will conceal my assault from Lexi's eagle eye. Her threats to cause ill-harm to Chains rang through my ears a minimum five times a day the past week, so imagine how rampant they will become if she discovers one of his staff assaulted me?

Realizing no amount of pinching will replicate the hit of a man three times my weight, I pop the visor back up and turn my eyes to the scenery whizzing by the window. The more my blurry eyes take in the architecturally interesting apartments on a tree-lined street, the more my confusion grows.

"Where are we going?" I query when it dawns on my spent brain that Richard is driving in the opposite direction of my house.

"I just need to stop by my place for a minute." Richard slides his eyes from the road to me. Spotting my wide-eyed response his reply instigated, he advises, "I left my cell at home this morning. Considering I've never been to Montclair, I figured a GPS wouldn't go astray."

"Oh. Okay," I reply softly, my voice expressing remorse for my suspicious glare.

Approximately ten minutes later, Richard pulls his truck onto the curb outside of a large brick and mortar building. If it weren't for the continuous beep of horns sounding in the background, I'd never believed the bustling hive of New York City is only a measly mile away. Although Richard and I talked the past ten minutes, it was just a standard set of questions a security officer would ask a complainant when investigating an incident. It never went to the level it did months ago when his groin and my knee became acquainted.

Unclasping his seatbelt, Richard sweeps his eyes up and down the poorly lit street. His brows lower down his face as his nose crinkles. "Would you mind coming in with me, Cleo? I really don't feel comfortable leaving you out here alone."

I hesitate, unsure if I should trust Richard's motives. More times than not, if you pull back someone's lambskin exterior, you find nothing but mutton underneath. Richard's face is the first one to pop into my head when metaphors like that are expressed. Up until thirty minutes ago, I've always believed he was a wolf in sheep's clothing. Now... I'm unsure what to think.

Sensing my hesitation, Richard says, "Please, Cleo. After what happened, my gut is telling me I shouldn't leave you out here. It will be a lot safer inside." The plea in his eyes adds strength to his appeal.

Still rattled from my attack and wanting to give Richard a chance to prove my assumptions about him are wrong, I hesitantly nod. The gleam in Richard's eyes grows from my agreeing gesture. After placing my purse under the nook of my arm, I follow him down a well-lit sidewalk. I'm ashamed to disclose my knees clang together with every step I take. Clearly, my attack has me more frightened than I'd care to admit.

Pushing aside my panic as the effects of an exhaustingly long week, my eyes drink in the scenery. Hedged greenery leads the way to an elaborate double-doored entranceway with a chandelier brightening the veined marble tiles. With its postmodern war design being upgraded throughout the centuries, the building is pleasing to the eye. It's a classic apartment that screams of wealth.

"No doorman," I mutter more to myself than Richard when he opens the large French antique door and gestures for me to enter the foyer before him. *I always thought these types of buildings had twenty-four-seven doormen?*

Shrugging off my misconception on the envy bubbling my veins, I shadow Richard into the lobby of his apartment building. My eyes bug in wonderment at the rich vaulted ceilings and high thread count drapes. As we pace to a set of elevator banks in the far-right corner, my astonishment grows. This place is lovely, a priceless architectural wonder that adds to the richness of New York.

When the elevator car arrives at the lobby, Richard glides his hand across the front of his body, suggesting for me to enter before him.

"Umm... I'm going to wait out here." My words come out shaky, riddled with guilt that I'm still judging Richard on our previous exchanges instead of the man who saved me from being assaulted.

Richard's finger traces a cross over his chest. "I swear to God, Cleo, if you're worried I'm going to hurt you, please don't be. I'm not going to touch you. I just don't want you alone right now." He angles his head to the side and arches his brow. "Give me five minutes to grab my phone, then we will be on our way."

Detecting that my apprehensions are swaying in his favor, Richard continues with his plea, "You don't even have to come inside my apartment if you don't want to. You can stand in the corridor. That way, if you're feeling dizzy or unwell, you can just shout out for me."

After licking my parched lips, I step into the elevator. "Alright. But if you try anything fishy, we'll have a re-run of our confrontation three months ago."

Richard's deep chuckle vibrates some of the nerves out of my body. "I promise nothing sinister will happen, Cleo. I learned my lesson the hard way. I'm still recovering from your first punishment. Believe me, I'm not eager to sign up for round two anytime soon."

Ignoring the way his reply hinted at future battles between us, I move to the far corner of the elevator car. The moisture slicking my skin with sweat gets a moment of reprieve when I spot a blinking red light at the top of the elevator dashboard. If that's what I think it is, our every move is being captured by a surveillance camera.

After riding the elevator to floor fifteen, I shadow Richard to apartment 15C.

"Are you sure you don't want to come in?" he asks, shoving a key into the lock.

I shake my head, which intensifies my groggy state. "No, I'm fine out here. I..." My words trail off when I can't come up with a legitimate excuse for not entering his apartment other than me not trusting him. Considering he came to my rescue tonight, I don't think slamming him with distrust would be a nice thing to do.

After swinging open his apartment door, Richard strays his eyes to me. His glare is pulse-racing, and it makes my veins thicken with anxiety. "I'll be out in a minute."

"Okay," I reply, lowering my tone to one more acceptable for a grateful woman.

When Richard slips into his apartment, I float my eyes up and down the isolated hall. For a man who works in security, his apartment is quite swanky. Modern paintings line the walls, and decorative lights give the environment a homely feel. It's different than what I imagined his apartment would look like. It's more inviting than the bare-faced demeanor Richard generally displays.

By the time Richard exits his apartment, nearly ten minutes have passed, and my dizziness has wholly vanished. Although my cheek is still throbbing from the unnamed man's hit, I feel very much like the usual Cleo I present every day.

Thrusting his cell into his pocket, Richard says, "Sorry it took so long, I searched every nook and cranny for it, and where do I end up finding it?"

"On the entranceway table?" I predict, remembering my hunt for my car keys months ago.

Richard throws his head back and laughs. "Yes! How'd you know that?"

I shrug my shoulders. "Good guess?"

After calming his laughter, Richard guides me back to the elevator by placing his hand on the curve of my lower back. It's a standard maneuver most guys use, but it seems weird coming from Richard. His hand doesn't move from the small of my back our entire ride in the elevator, during our stroll through his isolated lobby, or our wander down his dead-quiet street.

The only time his hand isn't warming my back is when he gentlemanly opens the passenger door of his truck for me. "There you go."

"Thank you," I stutter, caught off-guard by his courtesy.

After shutting my door, he jogs around the bed of his truck and slides into the driver's seat.

"I'm fine catching the train home if you could point me in the direction of the nearest train station." My voice hints my suggestion was more of a demand than a proposal. "I don't want to take up any more of your time."

Pretending he didn't hear my suggestion, Richard syncs his phone with the Bluetooth in his car and brings up my home address on the electronic dash-board. Happy he has a general consensus on where he is going, he pulls his truck into the surprisingly quiet street. As his vehicle rolls down the asphalt, I drift my eyes around our surroundings, endeavoring to gather my bases. I must still be disorientated, as I genuinely don't have a clue where I am.

Richard doesn't speak the entire fifty-minute commute to my home. Although uneasy about his quietness, I also appreciated it. It gave me time to put things into perspective, leaving only two assumptions on the table.

Richard's sudden shift in personality is either based on feeling guilty about our numerous improper exchanges the past five years, or he has a hard time separating his work life from his personal life. Considering he still has his taser gun, baton, and handcuffs bound to his hip, I'll say it's the latter.

Removing his foot from the gas pedal, Richard's truck comes to a stop at the curb of my house. "Home without a single drop of blood being shed. See, told you there was nothing to be worried about."

His brows scrunch when his eyes roam over my cut lip. "Sorry. That was a badly timed joke."

Smiling to ease the remorse in his eyes, I say, "That's okay. Bad jokes I can handle. Crude comments... well, you know all too well how I react to those."

Richard grimaces as he pulls on the collar of his shirt. "If it didn't hurt so much, I would have said it was a *ballsy* move for you to make." He waggles his brows suggestively when he chuckles out the word "ballsy."

Laughing, I playfully punch him in his bicep. My measly hit only entices more laughter to rumble up his chest. His chuckle is hearty and full of life, and after the mood-strangling week I've had, it's a nice thing to hear.

I wait for Richard's laughter to die down so he can hear the graciousness in my tone before saying, "Thanks for the ride."

He smiles, exposing a set of wrinkles in the corners of his eyes. "No worries, Cleo. I'm glad to be of service," he replies, his eyes twinkling with honor. "What time do you want me to swing by Monday to pick you up?"

When I stare at him, muted and confused, he mutters, "I know what a stickler you are for turning up to work on time. You haven't been late in over five years. I'd hate for tonight's occurrence to break your record-running streak."

"Oh...umm... that's okay. As of a couple of hours ago, I was put on leave."

Richard's light brows meet his hairline. "You're on leave?" he asks, astonishment in his tone.

"Yep," I reply, nodding.

I don't elaborate on the fact I've been forced to take two weeks leave while the incident of me striking a colleague is investigated. Some things are best left unsaid. And, if I am being honest, I don't want to give Richard any incentive to add our exchange three months ago to the crosses now marking my previously exemplary employment record.

Richard's lips quirk. "It's about time, Cleo. You've been at Global Ten for over five years now, and you've never had a vacation day."

My mouth opens, preparing to dispute his claim, but not a syllable escapes my lips. I can't deny the truth. I have over four months of paid leave accumulated. Furthermore, I'm too stunned to talk. How is it a colleague of mine knows more about my deficient social life than I do?

My attention reverts to Richard when he squeezes my hand. "Let me take you to dinner while you're on leave. We can celebrate your introduction to the world of the living."

Smiling to hide my grimace, I reply, "Thanks, that's really sweet, but not necessary. I'm also more a one-woman, one-man type of girl when it comes to dating."

Richard cocks his brow. "I deserve that," he admits, crassly nodding. "What I did to you and Misha from Accounting was wrong. But I'm not the same man I was back then, Cleo. I've matured."

"In three months?" I argue, arching my brow.

"I'm *trying* to change?" Richard rebuts, his voice as unsure as his facial expression. "Come on, Cleo. I'm offering you a free meal, not requesting you to accompany me to the Christmas ball."

I screw my nose up and immaturely stick out my tongue. My one and only exchange with Richard was at the annual charity ball Global Ten Media hosts every year. Although our kiss was heated, if it wasn't for the mistletoe hanging above my head and a few chardonnays warming my veins, it would have never happened. Richard has always had a vibe that screams "trouble!"

That's one of the reasons I agreed to his request for a date years ago. All naïve girls like the idea of taming a bad boy. It was only once my parents and Tate passed away did I realize I shouldn't be seeking a man to tame. I should be searching for a man who complements me and my daily struggles. Someone who will make me feel whole again.

A touch of a smile graces my lips when the first face that pops into my head is Marcus's. Before everything went south, my weekend with him filled me with hope that he was the man I've been searching for. My beacon set to guide me through the storm until I discovered the rainbow at the end of the darkness. My reward for years of misery.

My attention reverts to the present when Richard runs the back of his hand down my blemished cheeks. "I've never seen you flustered before, Cleo. Not even when we kissed."

The lust in his eyes simmers and boils until it becomes so heated it bubbles over into skin-crawling cockiness.

"It's a nice look for you. One I'd like to see grace your face when you're quivering beneath me."

My earlier dizziness returns full force. This time, it isn't associated with being struck. It's from the bile racing up my esophagus from the impish gleam in Richard's eyes. His heavy-hooded gaze is cocky and blazing with self-assurance. I don't think I've ever seen him look so arrogant. And that's saying something, as arrogance is Richard's middle name.

Mortified he mistook my hued cheeks as fondness for his flirty moves, I throw off my seatbelt and curl out of his car.

"Thanks for the lift," I mumble.

After gathering my belongings from his white leather bench seat, I slam his car door shut. The hinges on his spanking new truck squeal in protest from the power of my throw. Forcing a fake smile on my face, I spin on my heels and scuttle down the cracked path to my home.

"You never gave me an answer about dinner," Richard shouts, stopping my brisk pace midstride.

"Umm... I'll text you later about it," I reply.

I don't bother looking back as I would hate for him to see the uncertainty in my eyes. Just like my entire week, my emotions are on vastly different ends of the playing field. Part of me thinks I should accept his offer of dinner as a way of thanking him for his assistance tonight, whereas the other half is warning me not to trust his motives. Considering my intuition has never steered me wrong in the past, I'm left sitting on the fence, confused and overwhelmed.

13

Richard waits for me to reach the front steps of my home before he starts his truck and drives down the street. When his vehicle is nothing but a speck on the horizon, I climb the six stairs of my front porch. Fear unlike anything I've ever experienced consumes me when I spot a dark figure lurking in the shadows. My heart rate surges as my knees clang together. With my emotions still on edge from a stressful day, I'm more rattled by the impromptu visitor than I care to admit.

Panicked beyond belief, I dump my box onto the floor and delve my hand into my purse, searching for the can of pepper spray I keep in there. The panic scorching my veins dulls when awareness washes over me. The hairs on my body bristle, and my breathing shallows. There is only one man I've met who can cause every hair on my body to stand to attention by doing nothing more than breathing.

Marcus.

"Jesus, Marcus, you scared the poop out of me."

"Sorry, Cleo," Marcus mutters, his tone reserved.

I stand frozen for a minute, startled by the brusqueness of his tone. After taking a moment to breathe out my panic, I shift my eyes sideways. Using the shadow of the poorly lit porch to hide my sneaky glance, I rake my eyes up his body, starting at the tips of his polished black dress shoes to his recently trimmed afro. His hands are thrust into the pockets of his trousers, his jaw taut and ticking. From the way his brows are joined, I can easily deduce he witnessed my exchange with Richard. His complete composure is screaming of jealousy.

My knees curve inward as a rush of gratefulness flows over me. After the brutal day I've had, I needed that boost in confidence. Swallowing to relieve my bone-dry throat, I drop my eyes to my watch. I gasp in a stunned breath when I notice it's a quarter past nine. With my run-in with Delilah and the unnamed man leaving me a jittering mess, I'm over an hour late for our arranged meeting. Knowing Marcus waited in the dark for me so long fills me with hope that we will sail through the crazy storm trying to overcome us, and come out even stronger.

Placing my key into the lock, I swing open my front door and step into the foyer of my home. After gathering my box from the ground, Marcus shadows closely behind me. With my entire house cloaked in darkness, it doesn't take a genius to realize Lexi isn't home. Her afternoon movie date with Jackson must have been more jam-packed with activities than she was anticipating.

I run my hand along the right wall, seeking the light switch. It takes a few seconds for the old tube lighting to flicker on. Once it does, I throw my keys and broken cell into the bowl on my entranceway table before spinning around to face Marcus. My steps are shaky, uneasy about what his reaction will be to my humble home.

I didn't need to worry. After placing my box to the side of the foyer, Marcus's eyes eagerly roam around the space, absorbing my precious family portraits and much-loved knickknacks I've amassed over the years. The admiration beaming out of him in invisible waves grows with every silent second that ticks by.

Smiling, I ask, "Can I take your coat?"

Marcus's hands shoot down to the button of his jacket as he strays his eyes to me. My steps toward him fumble when the inviting gleam in his eyes vanishes, making way for a livid expression I don't recognize. As he frantically assesses my face, the veins in his neck twang and his jaw muscle tenses. The fury blackening his eyes multiples when he spots the mark on my right cheek, then it turns downright murderous when he notices my split lip.

I try to issue him some reassurance that I am fine, but not a peep escapes my lips. My brain is too busy categorizing the angry streaks lining his gorgeous face to form a response. I'm also a little stunned by his reaction. I've never seen a man look so fierce and vulnerable at the same time.

When his gaze drops to my blood-splattered shirt and gravel-scuffed knees, my concern for the man who assaulted me intensifies. Marcus looks set to kill. His nostrils are flaring, and his fists are balled at his side. The efforts of my heaving lungs grow when he locks his eyes back with mine. They are brimming with so much pain, it feels like my chest is being torn in two.

"I'm okay," I stammer out, my words so croaky they are nearly incoherent.

Cautiously ambling towards me, Marcus asks, "Who did this to you, Cleo?"

When his delicious scent engulfs me, I close my eyes and inhale a giant whiff. His freshly laundered scent overtakes the revolting smell of desecration leaching out of me. I didn't realize how dirty I felt until now. I shouldn't be surprised, though. My entire day has been one shit storm after another, a horrifying ten hours I'd give anything to erase from my mind.

Tears prick my eyes when Marcus cups his hands around the curve of my jaw. His touch is gentle—almost featherlike. While his crammed-with-remorse eyes dance between mine, his thumb carefully runs over the split in my top lip.

A tornado of pain brews in his eyes when his dedication moves to my throbbing cheek. From the devastation I see there, I feel confident in saying the red welt on my cheek has morphed into a bruise.

The dam of moisture in my eyes I've been struggling to ignore the past hour nearly breaks when Marcus asks again, "Who did this to you, Cleo? Who hurt you, baby?"

I try to formulate a response, but the only thing that comes out of my mouth is a painful sob. I'm not speechless because I'm injured—my attacker's strike was as pathetic as he is. It's the rawness in Marcus's eyes that's too much for me to bear. It's clawing at my chest, disfiguring my heart even more than his deceit did.

Spotting the inundation of moisture in my eyes, Marcus mutters, *"Cleo..."* His distraught tone adds to the wetness pooling in them.

When the first tear unwillingly rolls down my unmarked cheek, Marcus draws me into his chest. He wraps me up with his warmth, sheltering me from the world with his big, protective body. Unable to contain the overwhelming barrage of emotions hammering into me, I burrow my head into his chest and let my tears flow. Usually, I'd fight the desire to cry, but for now, I am beyond saving. It actually feels good to be relieved of my tears. Like all the tension from a long and exhausting week is being drained from my body with every tear I shed.

Marcus scoops me into his arms before moving through my house like he intimately knows the floor plan. Not bothering to switch on the light, he pads into the living room at the side of the entranceway and sits on my springless couch. His freshly showered scent loiters in my nose when he draws me into his chest and runs his hand down my back. His kindness soothes the shakes impeding my body, while his whispered words of reassurance heal the cracks in my heart. He repeatedly tells me that I am safe and that he won't let anyone hurt me, while occasionally adding in a request to be informed of my attacker's identity, and pleading for me to seek medical attention.

I always thought it would be awkward being comforted by a man I am attracted to. It isn't. It's oddly electrifying. The zing of intimacy between Marcus and me is so strong, I feel like it's tethering us closer together, making us an unstoppable duo. For the past two months, I kept denying the extra thud my heart got any time I thought about Master Chains. Now, I'm too tired to continue with the winless fight. I'm not saying I am in love with Marcus, but I've never felt more alive than I do when I'm wrapped in his arms.

When my tears subside from a steady stream to a slight trickle, Marcus carefully pulls back on my shoulders. The hurt in his eyes is still notable, but it isn't as rampant as it was earlier. The back of his fingers make quick work of the tearstains marring my face, but it does nothing to ease my blemished cheeks. His touch is so electrifying it sends a jolt to my aching core, which only adds to the color reddening my skin.

We sit in silence for several moments, but my body's awareness of his closeness is still paramount. Even if brain-eating zombies were taking over the world, my body's alerted response to Marcus wouldn't change. Just feeling the heat of his gaze watching me cautiously is enough to activate a wild recklessness within me.

When my tongue darts out to replenish my parched lips, the air between us shifts, changing our gathering from being stifled by remorse to being fired with lust. Being extra attentive not to touch my bruised cheek, Marcus cradles my jaw in his hands. His thumb brushes the curve of my lip, his touch so gentle I don't feel the slightest twinge of pain.

The thin material of my shirt is unable to hide my response to the tenderness of his touch. My nipples bud and strain against the thin ivory material. I can tell the exact moment Marcus registers my body's excited response to his meager touch. I feel him grow beneath me, his cock becoming so thick, his trousers struggle to contain its growth.

"Please kiss me," I whisper, my desire too rampant to be thwarted by modesty.

When his eyes relay his hesitation, I incline my mouth toward his. "Wash it all away. Make me forget today ever happened." I quote part of the pledge he made to me earlier today.

Marcus's lips were the reason fantasies were created, so I'm more than willing to use them to drag me out of the nightmare I'm currently trapped in.

"*Cleo...*" he grinds out through clenched teeth.

"Please," I whimper while swiveling my hips, ensuring he is aware I know of his wavering constraint. "I need you, Marcus."

My confession clears some of the indecisiveness from his eyes, but it doesn't entirely erase it. Incapable of warding off my desires, I take matters into my own hands. As my breathing shallows, I lean in intimately close to his side. My breath bounces off his deliciously fragrant skin when I place a succession of featherlike kisses along the edge of his jaw. Marcus surprises me by remaining still, neither denying or encouraging my defiance.

Lust heats the air as my mouth slowly inches towards a set of lips I am dying to feel on mine. Our kiss in the washroom was mere hours ago, but with the tenseness of my day, it feels like months have passed.

Just as my lips brush against Marcus's, a commotion sounds through my ears. Marcus balks before he withdraws from our embrace. Ignoring the desire to stomp my feet like a child, I swing my eyes to the noise. Lexi and Jackson are clumsily stumbling in the front door. Their bodies are interlocked as their tongues duel in a fire-sparking showdown.

The scenario switches from cute to creepy when Jackson positions Lexi's skirt-covered backside on the entranceway table in our foyer, rushing memories of Marcus doing a similar thing to me last week to the forefront of my mind.

Bile forms in my throat when a throaty moan expels from Lexi's mouth. Repulsed at the idea of watching my sister in a compromising situation, I cough, announcing they have an audience. Quicker than a match igniting, Lexi yanks away from Jackson. Her eyes are wide and raging with lust, and her cheeks are a vibrant hue of pink. Annoyed at the interruption, a hiss of annoyance escapes her kiss-swollen lips.

The peeved gleam brightening her eyes is snuffed when she takes in my tear-stained cheeks. I've always been a hideously ugly crier. Clearly, today is no different.

Time comes to a standstill as Lexi's eyes bounce between Marcus and me. For every second that ticks by on the clock, the tightness of Lexi's jaw firms. Jackson appears just as muted. I don't know if his quiet response is because he got caught with his pants down—*literally*—or because my sobbing face repulses him.

Deciding there is only one way to find out, I stand from the couch, lock my fingers with Marcus's, and pace toward them. I get halfway into the foyer when my steps stop midstride, my brisk pace cut off by Lexi's rueful snarl. Although she'd never admit it, she is as nearsighted as me, meaning she didn't comprehend the reason for my tears until the entranceway light highlighted my bruised face.

"Oh, hell no," she snarls, glaring at Marcus.

Stealing my ability to offer an introduction, she pushes off the table and storms down the hall. Her speed is so quick, she is nothing but a blur. Confused by her odd response, my eyes glide to Jackson. He is just as baffled as me. His eyes are wide, his jaw muscle weak.

Once again, I don't know where his confusion stems from. Is he reeling from being caught in a heated moment? My disheveled appearance? Or Lexi's sudden decision to flee? When his dark brow bows upon seeing Marcus, I realize all my assumptions were wrong. His dazed response isn't about Lexi or me, Marcus's presence prompts it. I shouldn't be surprised by his reaction, not only does Marcus have a highly recognizable face, but Lexi also has a poster of Rise Up in her room. It may be faded and warn, but it's been thumbtacked to the wall since their first album dropped on the Billboard charts over five years ago.

Smiling at Jackson's slack-jawed expression, I finalize the last steps into the foyer. "Marcus, this is Lexi's... *boyfriend*, Jackson." I introduce. I stammered on Jackson's title as Lexi believes giving relationships a formal title is "crass."

"Jackson, this is Marcus, my..." I purposely trail my words off to silence.

The veins in my neck twang when Marcus slants his head to the side and arches a brow. The corner of my mouth tugs high as his eyes silently demand a reason for his lack of title. Although he's trying to be playful, the hurt clouding his mesmerizing eyes dampens his efforts.

Holding his gaze, I wordlessly issue a reply to his question: *Payback's a bitch, Mister.*

Like he heard my inner dialogue, Marcus's lips twitch as he struggles to hold in his panty-wetting smirk. His concealed smile is a wicked invitation to my libido, making it surge to a never-before-reached level. Not wanting to be busted shamefully squirming on the spot, I glide my eyes back to Jackson. The last thing I need supplementing the already tense air is more awkwardness.

Remaining quiet, Jackson continues gawking at Marcus. His mouth gapes open and closed as if he is attempting to speak, but not a syllable escapes his lips. He looks like a stunned mullet. I can understand his response. I've had sex with Marcus, and I still feel like a flabbergasted idiot every time I'm in his presence. I wonder if somewhere down the line I'll be just as giddy about his attention as I am now? From the way my body is still responding to our near kiss, I don't doubt it.

The awkwardness of our gathering gets a moment of reprieve when Marcus pulls me into his side and presses a kiss to my temple. With the stress of my week, his small gesture has more impact on my rattled composure than I could ever express. It doesn't feel like a gesture a Master would make to his sub. It feels more personal—endearing even.

"You look exhausted, Cleo, let's get you showered and in bed," Marcus suggests, his warm breath ruffling the hairs clinging to my sweat-drenched neck.

Guided by the desires of my body, I bid farewell to Jackson with a dip of my chin before pivoting on my heels. I hear Marcus and Jackson exchange pleasantries before the tapping of Marcus's shoes catches up to my ears. When his heavy steps are complemented by the sound of tiny feet padding down the hall, I raise my eyes from the tiled ground.

Fear overwhelms me, stealing my ability to breathe when my eyes lock in on Lexi standing at the entrance of the hallway. "Jesus Christ, Lexi, what the hell are you doing?" I mutter, my high words filled with dread.

An abrupt parcel of air leaves Marcus's mouth when I say, "Put down the gun, Lexi."

14

Not taking my eyes off the revolver rattling in Lexi's clenched fist, I position myself between Lexi and Marcus. Although I'm certain she is only using the gun to scare Marcus, she is shaking so much I can't risk the chance of her accidentally pulling the trigger and harming him. More quickly than a blink, Marcus grips my elbow and drags me to stand behind him. I protest his protective stance, knowing Lexi will never hurt me, but Marcus is too strong for me to compete against. For the quickest moment, the furious mask on Lexi's face slips, revealing panic. She appears baffled by Marcus's protectiveness of me.

Placing his hands out in front of his body, Jackson cautiously approaches Lexi. "Put the gun down, Lex," he pleads, his tone a stark contradiction to the fear permeating out of him in invisible waves.

Removing one of her hands from the gun, Lexi swipes away a tear tracking down her ashen cheek before shaking her head. "He messed with the wrong family when he hurt my sister," she justifies herself to Jackson, her words as shaky as the gun pointed at Marcus's chest.

Anxiety engulfs me when Lexi drifts her eyes to Marcus and snivels, "I warned you what would happen if you hurt her."

"Yes, you did," His tone is so calm, no one would suspect the dangerous situation he is in. "You made your intentions very clear."

"Then why did you do it?!" Lexi yells, her loud voice startling me so much I jump. "Why did you hit my sister?"

Before I have the chance to negate her false assessment of the situation, Jackson uses Lexi's distraction to his advantage. He charges for her, crossing the room quicker than a heartbeat. Gripping the barrel of the gun, he raises it into the air, then pulls Lexi into his body. They stumble a few feet down the hallway before they hit the floor with a sickening thud. A frightened squeal emits from my lips when the gun is suddenly discharged. In the cramped surroundings, the noise is nearly deafening.

Panic roars to the surface of my skin, coloring it a vibrant red as my eyes frantically search their bodies for any visible injuries. My fear vanishes when Lexi springs to her feet and charges for Marcus. I stagger backward, frightened by the menacing scowl etched on her face. I've never seen her so furious.

A harsh puff of air leaves her mouth when Jackson curls his arm around Lexi's tiny waist and yanks her backward. He grabs her in just enough time that her wildly flung fist fails to connect with Marcus's sharp jawline.

"Goddammit it, Lex, do you have any idea who you are attacking?" Jackson asks, his words breathless as he struggles to keep ahold of Lexi, who is madly thrusting in his arms.

"I don't give a shit who he is!" Lexi retaliates, wailing even more. "He is a dead man, that's who he is!"

"Lexi, stop. Please stop," I beg, grateful my mouth is finally cooperating with the prompts of my brain. "Marcus didn't hit me. He would *never* hurt me. My injuries aren't from him."

Noticing my confession has lowered the volume on Lexi's wailing, I continue with my attempt to subdue her. "You remember that guy I told you about last week? The one I met under the Brooklyn Bridge?"

Lexi freezes as her big worldly eyes meet mine. "The brute of a man who couldn't fit in the backseat?" she asks, her words coerced through a sob sitting in the back of her throat.

Nodding, I reply, "Yes."

I step out from behind Marcus's protective stance and pace closer to Lexi. Since Lexi's blinding rage has simmered, and she is no longer brandishing a weapon, Marcus doesn't put up a protest. "He did this to me. Not Marcus."

I thought my confession would snuff the anger pumping out of Lexi. It didn't. If anything, the tornado of rage in her eyes grows more rampant. Sweat beads her temples as her face flashes with fury.

Shifting her narrowed gaze back to Marcus, she snarls, "So you didn't beat Cleo, you just had one of your goons do it for you."

Marcus balks, utterly flabbergasted. His jaw muscle quivers as he turns his confused eyes to me. "Who is she talking about, Cleo?" he asks me, his tone low and brimming with uncertainty.

Hating the panic in his eyes that my attack is his fault, I'm tempted to pretend the identity of my attacker is unknown. The only reason I don't is because Marcus is peering straight into my eyes. I can't lie to him as it is, let alone when he is accessing my soul from the inside out.

My lips are cracked with dryness, so I lick them before replying, "The guy who collected the NDA last Friday is the same man who attacked me tonight." The hammering of my heart resonates in my low tone. "He wasn't pleased when he discovered I failed to sign the NDA. I got the opinion my stupidity compromised his position."

A heavy groove indents the middle of Marcus's dark brows as his cheeks pale. He looks like he's about to be ill at any moment.

Or go on a warpath.

"My lawyer?" Marcus asks. His tone harbors so much anger, I feel the heat of his words to the soles of my feet. "The man who attacked you was my lawyer?"

My mouth gapes as shock registers its intention. I've never been one to stereotype, but I'm still stunned the man who assaulted me is a lawyer. Although he was wearing an expensive suit and crocodile shoes, he seemed more like a mafia hitman than a lawyer. I'm also stunned a man with as much intelligence as Marcus would hire a person with soulless eyes to represent him. Marcus knows as well as anyone that a person's eyes are the windows to their soul.

Marcus's intoxicating scent lingers in my nostrils when he stops to stand in front of me. With his eyes planted on me, he digs his hand into his pocket to produce his cell phone. My face cools when the heat of his gaze drops to the screen of his cell. His brows knit as his fingers tap wildly over the screen. He appears as if he is searching for something—or someone.

My already dangerous heart rate accelerates when he spins the screen around to face me. It isn't the image of a man in his mid-sixties displayed that has my heart walloping my ribs, it's the dark bleakness rapidly building in Marcus's eyes. With a stream of unreadable emotions filtering through them, they don't hold the same command as usual. Don't get me wrong, they still cause an upwelling of desire to consume me, they just appear a little lost as well.

"Is this the man who attacked you, Cleo?" Marcus asks me, his tone reserved.

A whizz of air parts his lips when I shake my head. He looks relieved, and if I am not mistaken, reassured. His thankful response doesn't last long when I advise, "He isn't the man who collected my NDA."

My eyes float to the side when Jackson relieves Lexi from his firm grip. I watch her cautiously, knowing firsthand how quick her reaction times are. When it comes to protecting her family, Lexi responds with the swiftness of a cobra strike. One of her ex-boyfriends discovered that the hard way when he taunted Tate in the front of half their peers at school. He never lived down the day he was beaten by a girl before being dumped by the exact same girl.

"Cleo said he was really big, at least double her width and a few inches taller." Lexi stops to stand next to me, her eyes fixated on Marcus. "He had sandy brown hair tussled to the side and dark brown eyes."

The panic swishing my stomach stills as gratefulness consumes me. Although Lexi's emotions are still teetering on the edge of a very steep cliff, I can also see her anger has cleared enough to know Marcus means me no harm.

"Can you recall any more features of the man who assaulted you tonight, Cleo?" Jackson asks, stopping at Lexi's side. "What he was wearing? Any identifiable marks?"

I nod a little overeagerly. "He has a gold veneer on his right incisor tooth, and he was wearing crocodile-printed shoes."

I can tell the instant recognition of my attacker's identity registers on

Marcus's face. The sound of knuckles popping boom into the silence when he clenches his fists into balls and his teeth grind together as he works his jaw side to side.

"Who is he?" I ask Marcus, my curiosity piqued.

Before he can answer me, the front door of our home is kicked in, and two uniformed police officers race into the foyer. Their unexpected arrival warps the weathered wood on my front door so much, wood splinters shower the tiled floor.

I jump out of my skin when their screamed demand, "Get on the ground!" roars through my ears.

With the barrel of their guns pointed at Marcus and Jackson, two male officers dexterously move toward our huddled gathering at the side of the living room. When a third officer with sparkling hazel eyes enters my home, her eyes immediately rocket to Marcus. She stares at him like she knows him. Not in a way a standard fan would react when confronted with their idol—like she *knows* knows him—intimately.

On the barked demands of her superior officer, she moves to the dumped gun sitting at the end of the hall. Once she has kicked the loaded revolver out of harm's way, she devotes the attention of her weapon to me. Ignoring the screaming protests of the male officers for him to remain still, Marcus moves to stand in front of me, once again protecting me from the line of fire. Although his protectiveness quells some of my anxiety at his connection with the female officer, it adds to the officer's startled expression.

Her dark brows slant as her eyes frolic between Marcus and me for many heart-strangling seconds. Some of the panic prickling my spine eases when Marcus's stern gaze is enough to have her adjusting the tilt of her gun so it no longer points at his chest.

Unable to ignore the screamed prompts of the male officers for a moment longer, I hold my hands out in front of my body and drop to my knees. The heaviness on my chest alleviates somewhat when Lexi and Jackson follow suit. It would have entirely cleared away if Marcus didn't remain standing.

Not wanting his naturally engrained dominance to cause him harm, I slip my hand into his clenched fist. Feeling the mad beat of my pulse pounding his palm, he drops his eyes to me.

"Please," I mouth, my weak tone expressing I am once again on the verge of tears.

The utter confusion in Marcus's eyes grows tenfold. I can't tell if it's stubbornness or confusion delaying his usually receptive demeanor, but it takes me soundlessly pleading into his eyes for nearly a minute before he finally succumbs.

The instant Marcus's knees hit the hard tiled floor, the two male officers charge for him. They push him onto his stomach, cuff him, read him his rights, then drag him out of my house before a single protest can escape my lips.

15

"As I've stated numerous times the past two hours: the gun was fired accidentally. No one was in any danger."

When the eyes of the male officer questioning me slit in disdain, I shake my head in disbelief before my hands dart up to rub my throbbing temples. Halfway there, I realize not all the throb is from a headache I've had since Marcus was carted away from my house in the back of a marked police car hours ago.

After saying a private prayer, I peer over my shoulder. Gratefulness pumps into me when I see Marcus entering the foyer of my home. He spots me in an instant, sitting on the lumpy two-seater couch in my living room. As he weaves through the crime scene unit swamping my modest home, my eyes go frantic, searching every inch of him for any damage. Other than a tempestuous edge of danger beaming out of him, he appears unharmed.

Tears prick my eyes as I suck in a relieved breath. I've been panicked out of my mind the past two hours. No matter how many times I asked to be informed on Marcus's whereabouts, no one fulfilled my request. The nerves making my skin a clammy mess relax when Marcus takes the empty seat next to me, and envelopes my hand in his. His eyes assess me with just as much vigor as I did him. His attentive stare alleviates the pain gnawing my chest and warms my heart.

Once he is satisfied I haven't been harmed, he transfers his gaze to the officer who has been questioning me the past two hours. "Goodbye," he says, dismissing him with an authority that makes my pulse race.

The officer attempts a reply, but Marcus continues talking, denying him the chance. "This investigation is closed. Mr. Gottle is waiting for you outside."

The officer's throat works hard to swallow as his eyes drift to the foyer of my home. With my front door left hanging on its hinges, he has no trouble spotting a man with an angry scowl standing on the landing of my porch. His gaze looks as displeased as the officers did when I refused to press charges on Lexi and Marcus.

Not speaking, the officer stands from his chair, gathers his belongings, and leaves the living room. The CSI officers who have been trudging through my house the past two hours soon follow suit. For how many police officers are on scene, anyone would swear there was a mass murder discovered in my house, not a simple misfiring of a gun.

Before I have the opportunity to ask Marcus who Mr. Gottle is, an attractive lady of Asian descent in her mid-thirties settles into the chair across from us. The fierceness of her black eyes and flawless skin is accentuated by the smooth lines of her well-tailored navy-blue pantsuit. After placing a leather briefcase on the ground next to her pump-covered feet, she removes an iPad from a pouch inside.

Smiling, she lifts her pretty eyes to me. "Hi, Cleo, my name is Shian. I am an FBI agent from the New York Field Office," she greets us, her tone friendly.

A scratch impinges my throat as my nerves catapult to a new level. *Why would the FBI be brought in on this case?*

"Is this the man who assaulted you tonight?" Shian queries, nudging her head to the switched-on iPad in her hands.

I swallow to relieve my scorching throat before accepting the iPad she is holding out for me. After scrubbing my hand over my tired eyes, I drop them to the black and white mugshot presented on the screen. Anger bubbles my veins when the abhorrent face of my attacker reflects back at me. Although my emotions are still on edge from a stressful week, I have no doubt he is the same man who attacked me.

"Yes. That's him," I confirm to Shian, nodding.

My confession tightens Marcus's jaw muscle so much it nearly snaps, and his grip on my hand also firms. His anger snowballs until it reaches fever pitch. It's so strong I swear steam is billowing out of his ears.

"Who is he?" Although I'm interested in discovering the identity of the man who attacked me, I am beyond exhausted, rattled by the mass upheaval in my life the past week, much less the past two hours.

With New Jersey firearm laws being some of the strictest in the state, I've spent a majority of the last two hours wrangling a mountain load of paperwork in the attic, seeking my dad's Firearm Purchaser Identification Card he used to buy the gun Lexi fired. After a spate of robberies in the area, years ago, my dad thought a firearm was the only opinion left to keep his family safe. When my mom had other ideas, the gun was stored in the safe bolted to the floor of their walk-in-closet. Tonight was the first time it's been removed since that day.

When Shian attempts to answer my question, Marcus sweeps his hand across the front of his body, cutting her off. After sending a quick text on his cell, he places it into his pocket and locks his eyes with mine. "The man who attacked you was a bodyguard for my band a couple of years ago."

"How long ago?" Shian interrogates, her interest piqued. She keeps her gaze bouncing between me and Marcus while she secures a small, lined notepad out of her breast pocket, preparing to jot down any information Marcus relays.

Keeping his eyes fixated on me, Marcus answers, "Around two years." He carefully brushes a loose strand of hair away from my temple before continuing, "The studio let him go after he got a little rough-handed with some female fans." His eyes drift between the bruise on my cheek and the small cut in my lip as he mutters, "I was unaware he was an associate of my lawyer. If I had known, I would have never had him collect your NDA."

"I know," I enlighten, not requiring any more information than what his forthright eyes are relaying. "You don't have to explain it to me."

Shocked by my unruffled reply, Marcus recoils, like my response physically shunted him. Clearly he was expecting me to react poorly to his confession. I lift my hand to rub at the heavy groove between his eyes. The anxiety playing havoc with his beautiful gaze fades from my caring gesture.

Although he hasn't directly said it, I know he harbors unnecessary guilt over my assault. I can feel it deep in my bones. He doesn't need to feel guilty. He may be a man of many talents, but that doesn't mean he needs to take responsibility for the actions of those surrounding him. Especially the actions of a man old enough to know better.

Like it does every time we are together, the vibrancy of the room quickly shifts from tense to teasing as I once again become trapped by Marcus's alluring eyes. His gaze makes me needy and hot, and I shamefully writhe in my seat. I am practically panting, my hunger for him incapable of being leashed.

The fire is doused when Shian coughs, demanding our attention. Mortified, I slide my eyes back to Shian to issue her a silent apology. I can't believe the power Marcus has over me. Only he could make me forget we are sitting in a house full of people processing a crime scene. I shouldn't be surprised, though. When he is in my presence, it's as if the entire world no longer exists.

My brows scrunch when I notice the curve of Shian's lips. Although her expression is pulled taut, there is no mistaking the joyful gleam radiating out of her eyes.

Blaming her odd response as a consequence of my childish squirms, I ask, "Is that all you need from me? I am exhausted and in desperate need of a shower."

Smiling, Shian stands from her seat and gathers the iPad from my hands. Once she places it in her suitcase resting on the side of my lumpy couch, her impressive eyes meet mine. "Yes, that's all I need for now, Cleo. I have your contact details if I require any further information."

I sigh. I've requested similar entreaties numerous times the past two hours. Not once was my plea approved. Although astounded Marcus's celebrity status extends to the FBI, I'm happy to use any leverage he has if it means I can crawl into my bed and forget this week ever occurred.

When Shian holds her hand out in offering, I stand from my chair to accept her gesture. Shian's handshake is sturdy and robust, robust enough my teeth clang together when it rattles up my arm.

After gathering her bag, Shian shifts her eyes to Marcus. "I'll coordinate with a contact I have at One PP to have the perp brought in for questioning. With the footage Hunter obtained from the alleyway, it should be an open and shut case."

"Will Cleo be required to testify?"

Shian runs her hand down Marcus's forearm. "We won't know until the perp is brought in, but hopefully not." She turns her pretty eyes to me. "Cleo seems to have enough on her plate, so I'll keep our contact to a bare minimum."

Gratefulness spreads across my chest as relief filters into Marcus's eyes.

"Okay, great." Marcus's short reply is unable to hide his appreciation for Shian's assistance.

"Let me walk you out," Marcus suggests to Shian as he gestures for her to leave the living room before us. "I have a few minor things I need to discuss with you before you leave."

"Thank you," I mouth to Shian, beyond grateful for her assistance.

Shian dips her chin in farewell before sauntering out of the living room, forcefully removing the remaining CSI officers on her way. Marcus waits for her to be out of earshot before floating his eyes to me.

"I'll join you in a minute?"

His deep tone is laced with uncertainty, and I'm unsure if he is asking a question or stating a fact. There is one thing I do know, though. With my nerves still touchy from a stressful week, I don't want to be alone right now. Call me a coward or any other derogative word you like. I won't put up a protest. Until you have been through what I've been through, you can't judge my actions.

Reconnecting my eyes with Marcus, I weakly stammer, "Please don't leave me."

For the quickest second, a flare of emotion blazes through his eyes. It doesn't last long. Only quick enough to assure me I'm not the only one baffled by our bizarre relationship. He is just as confounded as me.

Leaning in, he presses a kiss to my temple before following Shian onto my front porch. After having my house crammed with more officers than I realized Montclair PD had, I take a moment to relish the serene quietness. An aroused smile curls on my lips when I feel the heat of Marcus's gaze on me the entire time. Even though he is shadowed by the darkness of the night, I know he is watching me. There is no mistaking the heat of covetousness.

Stupidly grinning, I push off my feet and head down the hall. My steps are sluggish, weighed down by an exhausting day. It feels like every dramatic event that could happen in my life decided to flood me at once. Although I've been struggling to dig myself out of the woeful hole I've been living in the past four years, I'd rather claw my way out one fingernail at a time. I'm sure it would have been a whole lot less antagonizing that way.

Just before I enter my cramped bathroom, the faintest hum of chatter filters through my ears. Always inquisitive, I stop outside of Lexi's bedroom door and prick my ears. Guilt replaces some of my anxiety when I hear a noise I haven't heard in years: Lexi's quiet snivels. Although frustrated she put everyone's lives in danger this evening, I know she only reacted the way she did because she loves me as fiercely as I love her. I can't be angry at her for that.

Incapable of leaving things on a sour note, I knock on Lexi's door before opening it. "Everything okay?" I ask, popping my head into her room.

Lexi's head pops off Jackson's bare chest. Her eyes are teaming with fresh tears, and her pupils are filling her cornea. "We're fine. Are you?" she queries, her words as brittle as cracked glass.

My heart clenches in my chest. The last time her face matched this level of devastation was when I caught her in my arms outside of the elevator the night of our parents' deaths.

Hating the pain marring her face, I pace into her room while mumbling, "Yes. I'm fine." My voice doesn't come out as assuring as I was aiming for. "Marcus is handling everything."

As Lexi's bottom lip drops into a pout, she scampers across her bed. In no time at all, she slings her arms around my shoulders and hugs me tightly. Her brisk movements infuse the air with her Roxy perfume. I inhale deeply, letting her familiar smell soothe the unease circling my windpipe.

"I'm so sorry," she apologizes, her warm breath tickling my neck. "Please don't be mad. I didn't mean to take things so far. But when I saw the marks on your face, I just... *snapped."*

Tightening my grip around her petite waist, I reply, "It's okay. I understand. I probably would have reacted the same way."

Lexi stiffens in my arms. "Probably?" she fires back, her voice quickly reverting to its usual perkiness. "Do you need a reminder of what you did to Tommy Rudolph when he picked me up an hour late on prom night?"

"That's different," I retort, ignoring the way Jackson's brow cocked from Lexi's admission. "You shouldn't be late for prom. If he didn't want to cop the wrath of my fury, he should have heeded my warning."

Lexi's body shakes as a little giggle bellows out of her. "He was still limping when he collected his Prom King crown."

I don't care if it's something as simple as arriving late for a date or telling her she should dye her hair, when it comes to protecting my sister, nothing stands in my way. Not even the threat of spending time behind bars.

Lexi and I stay huddled in the middle of her room for several minutes. We don't talk, we just offer each other comfort in the best way we know how. I run my hand down her hair, soothing the frazzled pieces into place while savoring her closeness, and she hugs me so tightly, I'll never forget it, even years after she is gone.

Way before I've had my fill, Lexi draws back from our embrace. "Still can't believe you failed to mention Chains is Marcus Everett—the most prolific bass player/music producer the world has ever seen!" She drifts her bugged-out eyes to the Rise Up poster hanging center stage on the far wall of her room.

"Would you look at that face?! Who wouldn't want to lick every inch of that delicious chocolate skin?"

Before I can show my annoyance at her inappropriate question, Jackson pipes up, "There is nothing wrong with white chocolate, Lex. It's extra sweet and gooey, just the way you like it."

Bitter-tasting bile forms in the back of my throat when Lexi chews on her bottom lip while suggestively waggling her brows. I love my sister—truly I do—but there is only so much of Lexi I can handle in one day. Considering this has been one of the longest days of my life, I've reached my quota.

Leaning in, I press a kiss to the edge of Lexi's cheek before ambling to the hall separating our rooms. Any concerns I had entering the room vanish when Lexi's beautiful laughter shrills into my ears on my way out.

"I friggin' love it when you get jealous, Jax," I hear her mutter as I step into the hallway.

After ensuring her door is closed, I make my way to the bathroom, letting my clothes drop where they fall. I take my time in the shower, hoping a good dose of hot water will scrub away a tiresome week.

Once I've shampooed my hair, shaved my legs, and removed the Band-Aids from my knees, I trudge into my bedroom. Feeling overheated with nerves, I dress down in a pair of black stretchy yoga pants and an oversized long-sleeve shirt. Although I'd like to look presentable for Marcus, no amount of designer clothes or makeup will glamorize the gritty conversation we are about to undertake.

It was only during the quietness of my shower did it dawn on me how hypocritical I've been. I got irrevocably angry at Marcus for invading my privacy when I've been doing the same thing to him the past two months. Although I could argue that legally I couldn't inform him about the investigation into Chains, shouldn't my moral obligation to the man I am falling in love with be my utmost priority?

From now on, it will be. *If he will still have me.*

While tying my unruly hair into a low ponytail, my body's primitive awareness of Marcus activates. The hairs on my arms bristle, and my breathing pans out. Spinning on my heels, I find him standing in the doorway of my room. The groove between his eyes is as strong as ever, but the unnerving snip of anger in them has dampened somewhat the past thirty minutes. His commanding stature adds to the sweat caking my skin. I've always found confidence a turn on, but I didn't realize how profound my desires were until I met Marcus.

"Everything okay?"

"It is now." His eyes stare into mine. "You?"

I smile. "I'm fine." *Even more so because you are here.*

I bite on the inside of my cheek, praying it will stop my immature fidgeting when he pushes off his feet and steps into my room, closing the door behind him. Although our sentences are short, they are eerily assuaging. It's like we don't need words to express ourselves. Our eyes speak on our behalf.

The closer Marcus approaches me, the more the crackling of energy in the air amplifies. The sparks firing between us are so prominent, it makes what I am about to say ten times harder.

"I'm a journalist at Global Ten Media."

16

Marcus stares straight at me, his eyes unpretentious and void of any anger. His response isn't what I was anticipating. I expected him to curse and yell, or at the very least demand an apology. I didn't envision such a serene reaction to my confession.

I hold his gaze as he moves to stand in front of me. "We have many things to discuss, Cleo. But we are not doing that tonight," he advises. His commanding tone ensures I can't mistake his statement as a suggestion, it is a demand.

Although I'd appreciate nothing more than crawling into bed and forgetting today ever happened, my inquisitiveness won't let this matter lie. It wants answers, and it wants them now. "Why aren't you angry? You should be mad—really, *really* mad."

Marcus responds to my question with a shrug of his shoulders. I remain quiet, in shock and unable to comprehend what's happening. I thought he'd be cursing the day we met, but he just stares at me with graciousness in his eyes. I know he guards his emotions with an iron fist, but even Mother Teresa could be excused for losing her cool in a situation like this. His laidback response doesn't make any sense. I am utterly baffled as to why he is so calm.

I freeze as realization dawns. "You know. That's why you stayed away. You were testing me, waiting to see if I would expose your secret. You didn't need to worry. Even angry, I had no intentions of—"

Marcus cuts off my belligerent blubbering by pressing his index finger to the curve of my top lip. His touch is gentle enough it doesn't cause any worry to the cut in my lip, but firm enough he can express his desire for me to remain quiet without speaking a word.

"I didn't stay away to test you. I stayed away to protect you."

If his confession is supposed to ease my confusion, it doesn't. I am more confused now than ever. Marcus peers into my eyes, letting his direct gaze speak on his behalf. It's a pointless endeavor. With my brain on the fritz from a grueling week, it's incapable of deciphering the hidden messages his eyes are relaying.

"You're going to need to fill me in, I'm a little lost."

Marcus's lips curl from my daft response. "I plan on doing exactly that..." He bows his brow and stares straight into my eyes while adding on, "tomorrow."

"No! Tomorrow may be too late," I squeal through his finger pushed against my lip, my impatience incapable of waiting until the morning. "You don't understand what I'm saying, Marcus. This isn't some standard celebrity gossip piece. They have surveillance footage of you. They will destroy you. They won't stop until—"

"Cleo!" Marcus growls, startling me so much my body snaps to his command. I smack my lips together and swallow the remainder of my rant. I'm not frightened by the roar of his voice, I'm turned on. I've never heard anything as provocative as the way he growls my name.

"I understand your concern, but we are not discussing this tonight."

The confidence in his eyes appeases my anxiety. He looks confident, poised, and if I'm not mistaken, cocky. He isn't the slightest bit worried about Global Ten Media's investigation into Chains. I don't know if I should applaud his confidence or reprimand him for being an idiot.

Reading the stunned expression on my face for what it is, Marcus smirks before removing his finger from my lips. Even losing his meekest contact doesn't stop tingles dancing across my cheeks. My excitement remains strong, spurred on by the dominance brewing in his heavy-hooded gaze.

When he brushes away a strand of damp hair clinging to my bruised cheek, the tension in the air disperses as quickly as my inhibitions. I nuzzle into his embrace, my unsubtle display of affection telling him how I want the remainder of my day to pan out. A whizz of air whooshes out of Marcus's lips, fanning more heat onto my cheeks. Although he seems startled by my silent propositioning, the fire blazing in his eyes reveals it isn't a bad shock. He is more intrigued than annoyed.

"Would you like something to eat? Or are you ready for bed?"

"Bed," I whisper, my low tone exposing my heightened state.

It isn't that I'm not hungry, I just don't think I should trust my twisting stomach with food.

"Do you need pain medication first?" Marcus asks, his eyes arrested on my lips.

When I shake my head, his thumb carefully assesses the cut on my lip. His attentiveness unclutters any confusion left in my mind about whether I am falling in love with this man. There is no doubt. I am lost to him.

"Are you sure you don't need pain medication, Cleo? Your lip looks painful."

Hating his crestfallen tone, I graze my teeth over the pad of his thumb before sucking it into my more-than-willing mouth, soundlessly informing him

I am more than fine. Marcus's nostrils flare as lust clears the gloom from his eyes. Heat rushes to my cheeks when his trousers fail to contain his excitement at my frisky tease. My body tightens, beyond pleased I provoked a response out of him. Achieving any type of response from a man as tightly reined at Marcus is a feat worthy of celebration.

Arching a brow at my giddy response, Marcus mutters, "I'm glad to see our week apart didn't subdue your desire to goad me."

"There is no chance of that *ever* happening," I tease as a mammoth smile stretches across my face. "I like teasing you nearly as much as you like dominating me."

Smirking, Marcus bobs down and scoops me into his arms. A girly squeal emits from my lips, thrilled my sassiness is about to pay dividends. I cling to his chest as he walks to the other side of my room, his strides long and efficient. Since my room is so small, it only takes him three long paces to reach my bed tucked into the corner of the dingy space.

A tinge of vulnerability scuttles through me when he draws back the thin comforter so he can place me on the lumpy mattress. Any embarrassment heating my cheeks becomes a forgotten memory when his hands move to the buttons on his suit jacket. While staring into my eyes, he slowly undoes the three buttons before shrugging his coat off his well-built body. I don't know if he realizes what he is doing, but his little strip tease is hitting every one of my hot buttons. I'm needy, flushed, and shamefully writhing on the spot. Thankfully, since his body is cloaking my bed with darkness, he can't see my immature squirming.

I can't take my eyes off him when he hangs his jacket over my computer chair before his fingers make quick work of the buttons on his dress shirt. Even something as simple as undressing is an awe-inspiring event when it's done by a man as deliriously handsome as Marcus.

A shameful whimper parts my lips when his crisp blue shirt falls away from his shoulders, exposing inches of his ravishing chocolate skin. Pretending it's the first time they've sampled his mouthwatering assets, my eyes study every delicious inch of his body in great depth.

After Marcus's shirt joins his jacket on the chair, he kicks off his shoes and drops his hands to the belt wrapped around his slim waist. I pant as an endless stream of possibilities slams into me. I remember that belt—*very well.* Hearing the quickening of my breaths, Marcus connects his eyes with mine. My thighs squeeze together when I see the dominance beaming from his heavy-lidded gaze. His eyes are so commanding, they demand my respect, but in a non-arrogant kind of way. In a way that promises the reward for my admiration will be mammoth.

My hope of him washing away a horrifying week with a night twisted in the sheets is left for dead when the command in his eyes switches to liability. The shift in his demeanor is swift and resolute, completed in under a second. It isn't my juvenile squirming that has him backpedaling, it's his eyes drifting over the bruise on my cheek. I wriggled so much, I moved out of the shadow his body was casting, which broadcasted my bruised cheek to his keen eyes.

"Nothing that happened tonight was your fault," I stammer out, my words forced through the lust curled around my throat.

Acting like he didn't hear a word I said, Marcus drops his trousers to the floor with a clatter before slipping between the sheets. I scoot across the bedding, making way for his impressive frame. A smile graces my lips when my backside splays against the outer wall of my room. I never noticed how small my double bed was until now. My breathing picks up when Marcus leans over to switch off the lamp on my bedside table. If he is hoping the dark will mollify the energy bouncing between us, he needs to try another tactic. Even with the room plunged into darkness, my body's awareness of his closeness is still paramount. It can seek out its mate in a crowd of millions.

A zap of lust fires in my core when Marcus orders, "Come here, Cleo."

I try to shut down my eagerness at the command in his tone. I fail. I am beyond saving when it comes to this man. With my teeth grazing my bottom lip, I slide across the sheets. For every millimeter I gain, the pungent aroma of lust intensifies. It's tense and thick, and it sets my pulse racing.

I keep scooting forward until my erratically beating chest competes with Marcus's for every inhalation of air I take. The sweetness of his breath hits my cheeks when he demands me to roll over. After arching a brow in silent suspicion, I do as requested. Heat blooms across my chest when the warmth of his body curls around mine. The softness of my curves caress the hard ridges of his stomach, and my cushy backside is more than pleased to nestle his stiffened shaft.

It's the fight of my life not to rub my backside along his thick cock—one I'm apparently not strong enough to deny since I grind against him not even two seconds later. A hiss of air straining through Marcus's teeth is the only acknowledgment he gives to my frisky tease. He remains completely motionless, not even the sounds of his breaths are audible.

Incapable of leashing my desire to tease him, I grind against him once more. My insides do a little jig when his fingers flex against my hip. His grip is not painful, but it's strong enough to awaken my desires that were late to the party due to excessive tiredness.

A trail of goosebumps follows the path Marcus's fingers make when he gathers my ponytail to the side of my neck, leaving my skin vulnerable and exposed to his ravishing mouth. I gasp in a quick breath, incredibly aroused as the softness of his lips brushes the shell of my ear.

Disappointment sluices my veins when he doesn't respond in the manner I am hoping. "Sleep, Cleo. You need your rest."

Ignoring my childish whine, Marcus runs his hand down the side of my arm, continuing his insistence that I sleep. I don't know why he'd ever believe a rub of my arm would ward off my sexual hunger. Even if I couldn't feel his impressive manhood at the base of my spine, the sheer closeness of his body is enough to instigate a wild carelessness within me.

The more he comforts me, the higher the grin on my face tugs. For a man who exerts confidence in bucket loads and has the sexual prowess to back it up, his movements are stiff—almost robotic. It reminds me of when I first walked into Chains, wide-eyed and open-mouthed. I had a reason for my slack-jawed expression, though. I was being thrust into a world I knew nothing about. But what possible reason could Marcus have for his uneasy response?... my inner monologue trails off as reality dawns.

"Haven't you done this before?"

Marcus stiffens before muttering, "Done what?"

Struggling to contain my giggle at the unsureness of his reply, I ask, "Spooning? Cuddling? Getting frisky with your clothes on? Haven't you done that before?"

For how long he takes contemplating a response, I expect something more substantial to come out of his mouth than a simple, "No."

"Seriously?!" My screech booms around the room. "How is it possible you've never spooned before?"

I'm not calling him out as a liar, I'm just surprised he's never done something as simple as sleep next to a woman before.

My heart melts when Marcus replies, "Like many things, I never had the desire until I met you." If I hadn't heard the truth in his deep timbre, I would have been tempted to negate his claim.

I nuzzle into him deeper, wanting every inch of his skin touching mine. "You better watch out, Master Chains, I'm beginning to wonder if your Dom persona is just a way of hiding the gigantic heart sitting in your chest." I aim for my voice to come out cheeky, but it has a touch more sentiment than I intended.

When Marcus remains quiet, I attempt to roll onto my opposite hip. He firms his grip on my waist, foiling my endeavor. Expressing my annoyance at not being allowed to peer into his candid eyes, I grind against him. This time, I ensure every inch of his thickened shaft presses against me.

My attempts at riling him up backfire when his menacing growl ripples through my body. It's thick and thigh-shakingly delicious, and it adds to the excitement clustered in my heated core. Unbridled hankering overtakes my desire for sleep. I am aching with need, the thirst for climax so intense it feels unquenchable.

Once again, I attempt to roll on my hip. Once again, Marcus foils my attempt.

"Please let me see you," I shamefully beg, my desire to see him blinding any astuteness I have left.

I can feel his heart pounding his ribs, a tormented thud of confliction and desire. "I can't, Cleo. If I hurt you, I'll never forgive myself." The pain in his low words cuts me raw, leaving me exposed and vulnerable for the world to see.

"You would *never* hurt me." The honesty in my tone bolsters my statement. "Besides, you can't hurt someone just by looking at them."

His fingers painfully flex on my hip, sending a rush of pleasure to my tingling core. "If I see your face, I'll want you," he grinds out through clenched teeth.

"Then have me," I reply, my high tone exposing my glee at his inability to control his desires around me. It's also nice knowing I'm not the only one harboring heedless thoughts.

"No," Marcus responds, his tone direct and stern. "You make me reckless, I can't trust myself around you. It was hard enough holding back the desire to dominate last weekend, I don't know if I can do it again after having you in my playroom."

I swear, my heart and panties combust at the same time. "I *want* you to dominate me. I *need* you to dominate me. I also trust that you will *never* hurt me. Dominance is who you are, Marcus, but you've said it yourself, you're not a sadist. You would never hurt me intentionally."

As silence encroaches us, lust rages heavily between us. It isn't the only emotion thickening the air, but considering it is too early in our relationship to express the sensation bristling every hair on my body, I'll keep my focus on the less frightening one. My need for climax.

I'm not the only one aroused. The heat of Marcus's cock gets thicker and more full with every second that ticks by. His excited response deprives the air of life-necessitating oxygen and mists my skin with a fine layer of sweat. When the silence becomes too much for me to bear, another shameful plea sits on the tip of my tongue, ready for imminent release. I only just hold it in when Marcus draws back, leaving enough room for me to roll over.

I fall onto my back and suck in some deep breaths, feeling like it might be my last chance to secure an entire breath. Once my lungs are replenished with oxygen, I crank my head to the side. The prompts of my body are spot on when my eyes lock with Marcus's alluring gaze. Although the room is shrouded in darkness, there is enough light beaming under the crack of my door that I can see his stunning green irises. His eyes steal my ability to breathe, causing a wild yearning to engulf me.

"Please touch me," I shamefully beg, my desire to have him dominate me incapable of being harnessed.

Marcus's nostrils flare as he contemplates my response. His jaw muscle is ticking, and his lips are hard-lined, but they aren't potent enough to snuff the wavering constraint his eyes are exhibiting. Usually, I find his self-control impressive, but today it's just downright frustrating. His playful striptease already had my orgasm hanging on by a thin thread, and that was before he touched me.

Recalling the only instance when his usually strict decorum slipped, I childishly snicker, "I bet Preston wouldn't make me beg." I know my response is immature, but Marcus isn't the only one thrust into idiocy when we are together. I'm just as careless as him.

More quickly than I can blink, the substantial sentiment in the air shifts from teasing to tense. The anger bouncing off Marcus is undeniable. It's so loud it crackles and hisses in the air, activating every nerve in my body. As my breathing levels out, I scissor my legs together, doing anything to weaken the manic throb between them.

Any chance of controlling my excitement sails out the window when Marcus affirmatively mutters, "Remove your clothing, Cleo."

17

I slide my yoga pants down my quaking thighs, my enthusiasm to follow his demand cannot be overlooked. Once I have my pants bunched around my ankles, my hands shoot to the hem of my shirt to pull it over my head. Within a matter of seconds, I am naked, panting, and on the verge of climax.

Dying to feel the heat of Marcus's skin on mine, I reach out to touch him. A grunt of frustration parts my lips when he snaps my hands away.

"No," he mutters, his response direct.

Smirking at the annoyed huff I couldn't stifle, Marcus adjusts my position until I am lying in the middle of the bed. Although his change in position shrouds half his face with darkness, I can't miss the dominance beaming from his lust-filled gaze. Something as tangible as that's unmissable.

"Lift your head," Marcus requests, his deep tone dangerously low.

My eyelashes flutter against the softness of cotton when he drapes my shirt I just removed over my eyes. I thought the room was dark before, it's even more so now with the rich red coloring of the material blocking the hallway light.

Careful not to touch my marked cheek, Marcus ties the sleeves of my shirt into a knot at the back of my skull before lowering my head back onto the pillow. With one of my senses shut down, the rest become more prominent. I prick my ears and pay careful attention to every sound Marcus makes. From the scuffling of bedsheets and the loss of his body heat, I can easily derive he has moved off the bed, but my shirt inhibits me from knowing which direction he went.

When a noticeable click sounds through my ears, the darkness covering my eyes illuminates to a bright red coloring. *He must have turned on my bedside lamp.* I hear his bare feet padding across my room before a second set of clicking noises sounds through my ears. This one is harder for me to decipher. It has a similar noise to the light being switched on, but it isn't as loud.

My brows meet in the middle of my forehead when I hear a scratching sound. It mimics the sound of wood scraping against cardboard? Or perhaps even chalk running down a chalkboard? My confusion clears when the smell of rosewood hits my senses. *He must have lit the scented candle on my dresser.*

My breathing quickens when the mattress dips at my side. I inhale deeply, savoring the smell of his skin mingled with the aroma of rosewood. Although I am blindfolded, I don't need to see Marcus to know every expression crossing his face. I studied him in great depth last weekend, I can imagine them by simply listening to the prompts of his body.

The way his breath hitches when he removes the cover of my duvet to expose my naked form tells me his dark brows are furrowed. When his finger slices the air as he trails it over my budded nipple, I know his bottom lip is tugged into the corner of his mouth. And when he inhales deeply, sucking in the scent of my arousal floating in the air, I know his penis is thick and jutted.

My nipples tighten when he roughly mutters, "Beautiful," while brushing his hand down my glistening sex.

I throw my head back and grunt a hungry moan when he inflicts a back-handed slap to my pussy, arousing my clit with his perfectly placed hit. Memories of the riding crop inflicting a similar type of response rushes to the forefront of my mind. I squirm as more wetness pools between my legs.

I'm so immersed in calming the throb his tap instilled that I don't realize he has moved off the bed until he says, "Fondle your breasts, Cleo. Play with your nipples. Show me how much you *want* me. How badly you *need* me."

I hesitate, delayed by a dash of vulnerability coursing through me. Although I have no problems pleasing myself, I don't generally do it while I have company. Why would I want to? Isn't the whole idea of having a bed companion so you don't have to please yourself?

"Now, Cleo." Marcus's commanding voice sends a shiver of anticipation down my spine.

Unable to stand the idea of him stopping our exchange due to disobedience, I cup my breasts in my hands and squeeze. A zap of energy surges from my nipples to my pussy when a rough groan tears from Marcus's mouth. Its quake is felt through my body, spurring on my desire to please him.

I tweak and roll my nipples, using the sounds of Marcus's provocative grunts to guide my endeavor to unravel him. I want him as unhinged as me. To be so mindless, not a single thought passes through his astute mind when he is with me.

Excitement overtakes every nerve in my body when the sound of cotton being pulled over skin plays through my ears. My breathing quickens, and my fidgeting becomes more apparent. Just the thought of Marcus being naked has me pinching my nipples harder. I moan and tweak on repeat as my need to come surpasses any embarrassment left lingering in the back of my mind.

In a shameful amount of time, my coil is wound so tight, it's on the verge of snapping. I gasp in a surprised breath, astounded I'm on the edge of ecstasy by doing something as simple as toying with my breasts. Typically, more stimulation is required to make me come—*a lot more.*

My body quivers with anticipation when Marcus says, "Play with your pussy, Cleo. Give it the same amount of dedication you gave your nipples."

I slither my hand down the planes of my stomach, the pounding of my clit too intense for me to show any inhibition. A soft purr parts my dehydrated lips when the wetness of my pussy graces my fingertips. The low groan simpering through Marcus's mouth ensures no modesty can be found.

Knowing I relinquished my power to Marcus the instant I begged him to touch me, I wait for him to give me permission before slipping two fingers into my throbbing core. When he does, I thrust my fingers in hard, spurred on by the raspy roughness of his usually smooth voice. The suspense in the air is titillating, fired by the intoxicating aroma of lust and heat.

"Start slow, so the sensation doesn't overwhelm you," Marcus suggests, his voice strained with arousal. "Enjoy your muscles working in sync to please you, but don't get carried away by it."

Nodding, I pump my fingers in and out of my pussy. My speed is fast enough an upwelling of desire awakens within me, but not fast enough I'll be swept away by the current of ecstasy.

"Oh..." I garble when the heat of Marcus's breath cools my overheated core a few minutes later. He is sitting so close to me, every breath he exhales fans my pussy.

"You look as ravishing as I imagined," he groans before the lash of his tongue clears away some of the arousal glistening my fingers.

My knees shake as I fight not the let the excitement of climax carry me away. It's a tortuous feat. I've always been a little eager to reach the finish line, but it's even more prominent when I'm being chased over the line by a man who holds the sexual stamina Marcus does.

"Flushed. Wet. Ravishing," Marcus growls, each word bringing him nearer to an area begging for his attention.

The frantic pace of my fingers grinding into my pussy slows when Marcus sinks his teeth into the sensitive skin of my inner thigh. He marks my body with a succession of painful nips and strong sucks before his tongue exonerates the sting of his touch. I pant, moan, then pant again, adoring the intense tingle racing down my spine.

When the signs of an impending orgasm arouse low in my belly, my pursuit to come turns relentless. I quicken the speed of my pumps, my need to climax so blinding, it overrides any astuteness I have left. My breathing becomes labored, and heat rushes to the surface of my skin.

I can feel my orgasm teetering on the brink, dying to break free, but no matter how fast I sprint to the finish line, my climax doesn't reach fruition.

Suddenly, reality dawns: the rights over my body no longer belong to me.

"Can I please come, Master Chains?" My quivering words showcase my heightened state. "*Please.*"

The urge to cry overwhelms me when Marcus replies, "No." The deepness of his tone ensures my lust-hazed mind can't misread his short reply.

I'm taken aback by his denial of my request, but it doesn't deter my excitement in the slightest. Using the pad of my thumb, I stimulate my clit more, refusing to give up on my quest for climax. I grind my fingers back into my clenching core, my need to come so strong, I'm not above being disobedient.

The harder my fingers pump into my soaked pussy, the quicker Marcus's grunts become. "Is this where you did it? Is this where you came on your birthday while moaning my name?"

The roughness of his voice doesn't allow me to register the entirety of his statement. I'm too trapped in a lusty haze to have cognitive thoughts. My mind is entirely blank, clouded by the chase to climax.

I roll my thumb over my clit, flicking the hardened bud over and over again. Nothing works. My orgasm stays stagnant.

Adjusting my position, I angle my hips, so they face the direction from which Marcus's voice is projecting before speeding up my pursuit. Perhaps if he sees how desperate I am for him to touch me, he will loosen his tight reins?

Disappointment scorches my veins when my silent pleas fall on deaf ears. Not only do I lose the contact of Marcus's breath on my aching core, but the dip of his impressive frame in the mattress is also lost.

"Please... Oh, god, please, Master Chains," I shamefully plead, my climax so close I can taste it on the tip of my tongue. "I *want* to come, but I *need* you to make me come."

Before any more tactless confessions can seep from my parched lips, Marcus grips my hips and drags me to the edge of the bed. The sting of his fingers clutching the curve of my backside adds an exciting element to our already fire-sparking union.

"Yes," I hiss through clenched teeth when he drags his tongue up the seam of my drenched sex.

I thrash against him when he rolls his tongue around the hood of my clit before suckling it into his mouth. I scream, overwhelmed by the strength of his suck. My mind shuts down as my chase to climax hits full fruition.

The lashes of his tongue match the crazy rhythm of my heart, a frantic speed that ensures I could never mistake it as lovemaking. He is fucking me hard and fast with his mouth, using a mind-spiraling combination of speed and excitement.

I fist the sheets in a white-knuckled hold when a tingling sensation spreads across my stomach, growing and strengthening with every lash of his tongue and graze of his teeth.

When stars form in my eyes, I wistfully beg, "Can I please come, Master Chains?" My words are breathless and laced with arousal.

I cry out in disappointment when Marcus replies, "Not yet. I want to be inside you when you come."

I don't have the chance to respond to the first disappointing blow when I'm hit with another. An embarrassing whine ripples through my lips when Marcus moves away from my dripping core. He moves far enough away, I no longer feel the heat of his body, but not far enough that my body's heightened response to his closeness is snuffed.

My disappointment doesn't linger for long when Marcus says, "Put your arms above your head and intertwine your fingers."

Fighting through the upwelling of desire his commanding tone instigated, I follow his orders. A thin, satin-like material binds my hands above my head. Although the restraints are tight, my body pulls taut in anticipation at being at Marcus's complete mercy.

My arms fully extend when Marcus adjusts my position so he can tether my hands to something above my head. From the angle I am at on my bed, I can only assume it's my bedpost. My breathing turns labored when Marcus glides his naked body down mine. Although he isn't technically touching me, I can feel every inch of his heated skin hovering just above mine.

"What's your safe word, Cleo?" he questions. The assertiveness in his voice triggers stupid butterflies to take flight in my stomach. They aren't nervous flutters, they are ones filled with anticipation.

"Pineapple," I mumble groggily, drunk on lust.

"Say it again."

I swallow to soothe my dry throat before muttering, "Pineapple."

I yelp in surprise when something unexpectedly clamps around my puckered right nipple. The sensation is painful, but oddly arousing, increasing the thrumming of my pulse. At first, my hazed mind believes it's Marcus's mouth, but my theory is soon proven unfounded when his teeth graze my opposite nipple.

"What's that?" I ask, my words breathy as I relish in the glorious tugging sensation of the clamp stimulating my nipple.

Marcus remains quiet as he nips, sucks and caresses my left nipple. His attention never diverts until it's standing as firm as its clamped counterpart. The shudders wreaking havoc with my body intensify when my left nipple is secured with the same tight hold my right nipple is aroused by. When my chest expands to secure a much-needed breath, a weird pulling sensation sends jolts of both pleasure and pain down my body. It's oddly ironic that something painful can also be pleasurable.

I call out when Marcus unexpectedly twists the restraint compressing my nipples. Blissful pain surges through my body, thrusting my race to climax to within an inch of the finish line. *One more tweak like that, and I'll be freefalling over the edge.*

"Oh... God... Don't stop," I garble when Marcus loosens his twists. My words are nearly incoherent since they were grunted, not spoken.

Obeying my request, Marcus twists my nipples again. I arch my back and erotically scream, savoring the feeling shredding through my body. Pleas for more sit on the tip of my tongue, but I shut them down when the crest of his cock braces on my aching-with-desire pussy.

With my attention devoted on his thickened shaft, it takes me a few moments to register the removal of my blindfold. I blink several times in a row, adjusting my poor eyesight to the dimly lit room. My pulse races when my vision clears enough I can see the instruments clamped on my nipples. They are clothespin. Standard clothespins I use to hang out my laundry.

My pupils dilate. "What the hell?" *How can clothespins have me sitting on the edge of a climatic cliff?*

The effort to suppress my orgasm is nearly lost when my eyes lock with Marcus's. His lips are curled in a smug smirk, and lust is raging in his eyes. He looks cocky, self-assured, and totally fuckable. If my hands weren't bound above my head, I'd be tempted to kiss the smug look right off his face. Although I don't know how much good it would do. His eyes are dominant and strong like nothing will deter him.

Marcus watches me intensively, his utmost dedication on ensuring not a smidge of pain crosses my face when he releases one of my nipples from the firm clutch of the clothespin. As blood rushes back into the numb bud, an intense wave of pleasure follows its path. I moan, overwhelmed by the heavenly sensation.

Smirking a grin that sets my pulse racing, Marcus snaps off the second clothespin more roughly than the first. I throw my head back and call out, fascinated by the enthralling feeling of both pleasure and pain rocketing through my body. My nipples have always been highly sensitive, but the sensation blindsiding me now is unexplainable. It hurts, but it's also driving me wild with desire.

"Remember your safe word, Cleo. If you want me to stop, say your safe word," Marcus affirms, reminding me I have the power to end our exchange at any time.

"Don't stop," I reply, licking my parched lips. "It feels good—so, so good."

The feverous spark in Marcus's eyes grows when he gathers one of the clothespins resting on my sweat-slicked torso. He stares into my eyes, relaying his intention without a word seeping from his lips. I pant as anticipation blazes through me. My grunts turn feral when Marcus uses his other hand to spread the lips of my pussy before he latches the clothespin onto my aching clit.

"Oh..." I moan loudly, speechless by the tingling feeling pulling my muscles taut.

The idea of a clit being bound by a clothespin doesn't sound appealing, but let me tell you, it's one of the most orgasmic sensations I've ever endured. It's...it's... nearly enough to make me come. My thighs shake as the commencement of an orgasm sparks to life.

"Wait," Marcus demands, his stern tone enough to rein my orgasm back in. "Do not come, Cleo. Do you understand me? Do not come."

"Please... I can't hold it back much longer."

"Control the urge, fight the desire. Then maybe you will learn to do the same thing with me."

Stealing my chance to request further information, Marcus slams his cock into me in one ardent thrust, taking me to the very root. Fiery heat spreads across my stomach as my back arches. I purr, relishing the feeling of being stretched wide by his thickened shaft.

Feeling my pussy clenching around his densely veined cock, Marcus says, "Wait, Cleo. I want us to come together."

I shamefully whine, knowing all too well how controlled he is in the bedroom. He can last hours if he wants to. A highly inappropriately timed smile etches onto my mouth. I can't believe I am whining about his sexual prowess. I should be grateful he can exert such control, not angered by it. I'd much rather be taken to the brink and back for hours than the whole event be over before it has even begun.

I loosen the tightness of my hips, allowing Marcus to thrust into me deeper.

"Good girl," he praises, acknowledging my attempts at following his command.

Peering into my eyes, his tongue laps up a salty bead rolling down the gulley in my chest before his attention reverts to my swollen-with-desire breasts. The bumps of his tongue running over my sensitive nipples shoot pleasing spasms to my throbbing core. I grind my back molars together, loving the welcome sensation, but hating that it thrusts my desire to come back to the forefront of my mind.

After lavishing my breasts with his skillful mouth, Marcus increases the rocking of his hips. My pussy hugs his glorious cock, caressing and milking it with every grind. I watch his muscles constrict and release, riveted by how fluidly he moves his body. Every pump has my excitement growing tenfold. He screws me like a man who intimately knows how to drive me wild with desire because he does.

When the tingling sensation stretching from my pussy to my chest becomes too great to overlook, the shameful pleas from my lips grow louder. "Please, Master Chains. Please."

"If you need me to stop, Cleo, say your safe word," Marcus grunts between pumps.

"I don't want you to stop. I want to come," I push out, unashamed.

Snubbing my appeal, Marcus's pace picks up even more. He fucks me hard and fast, possessing every inch of me both inside and out. I thought the prowess he exerted last week was mystifying. Only now do I realize I didn't even scratch the surface of his dominating skills. I've never been so thoroughly fucked.

"Oh..." I moan when a blistering of stars detonates before my eyes. The veins in my neck thrum as a shiver racks over me.

"Wait, Cleo!" Marcus demands again, his voice strained with lust. "If you come before me, I will punish you."

"You're already punishing me, so what's the difference?"

Growling, Marcus adjusts the position of my hips, allowing him to plunge into me without any hindrance. Fireworks spark low in my stomach when the rim of his knob hits the sweet spot inside me, and his pelvic muscle smacks into the pin secured on my clit. The rhythmic slap of his balls against my drenched core has my orgasm building at a speed greater than I can shut down.

I shift my eyes to the side of my room, doing anything to snub my overwhelming yearning to come. The more I fight, the harder my battle is. I don't have the strength to ignore this man in general, let alone when he is fucking me like I've never been fucked before.

"Look at me, Cleo," Marcus demands, increasing the rocking of his hips, ensuring every pump has the crest of his cock bottoming out at my cervix.

I'm tempted to deny his claim, angered by him withholding my right to climax, but then I remember our exchange in the hotel. How just the sight of my face in the midst of ecstasy was enough to push him over the brink.

My lungs take stock of my oxygen levels before I slowly float my eyes to Marcus. When our lust-provoked gazes lock and hold, the chances of warding off my orgasm become impossible. My body stills as an upwelling of pleasure scorches through me like an out-of-control fire. I quiver and shake while whispering Marcus's name on repeat.

"Goddammit it, Cleo!" Marcus roars, thrusting into me even harder. His angry snarl growls from his chest to his cock, pushing my orgasm to a never-before-reached level.

He pumps into me another four times, his speed furious before the hotness of his seed coats the walls of my clenching pussy. I moan even louder, worshipping the feral groans seething through his clenched teeth as he is lost in the throes of ecstasy. My pussy clamps around his cock, milking every drop of his cum as I shudder beneath him.

My orgasm is long and exhausting, draining me of any energy I had left. I'm barely lucid when Marcus removes his still rigid cock from my swollen pussy, but even being physically shattered doesn't stop me whimpering from the loss of his contact.

A cool breeze sends a flurry of goosebumps rushing to the surface of my skin when Marcus moves off my bed to gather a handkerchief from the breast pocket of his jacket. After cleaning evidence of my arousal glistening on his cock, he turns his attention to me. A husky moan topples from my dry lips when he carefully removes the pin from my throbbing clit. I'm stunned into silence, amazed a standard household instrument could be used in such a sexually-titillating way. *I'll never look at laundry in the same light again.*

Once he has me semi-respectable, Marcus untethers my hands. A ghost of a smile stretches across my weary face when I discover what he used to bind me to my bed. It's the cord from my satin dressing gown I left draped over the full-length mirror in the corner of my room.

Marcus runs his thumbs over the small indentations the satin material made to my wrists. "Does it hurt?"

Unable to speak through my dry, parched throat, I shake my head. His touch is so soothing, the sting of the burn is now a distant memory. Exhausted beyond belief, I roll onto my side, more than eager to catch up on all the sleep I've missed the last nine weeks.

Marcus has other ideas.

Swamping my body with his overbearing heat, he adjusts the tilt of my hips. A shallow moan seeps through my gaped mouth when he enters me sideways, thrusting slowly to ensure he doesn't encounter any hindrance from my sexually satiated body.

Moaning at how well we fit together, I crank my neck back to peer at Marcus. Although his eyes are still as commanding as ever, they also have a touch of susceptibility to them. Actually, upon consideration, I've never seen them so open and raw.

"I warned you, Cleo." His breathing quickens as he slowly picks up the speed of his thrusts. "I told you you'd be punished if you came before me."

"You can't deliver a punishment during a punishment," I argue when it finally dawns on me why he was withholding my climax. He isn't just punishing me for goading him about Preston, he is instilling his dominance at my admission I work at Global Ten.

I call out when an unexpected slap hits my right butt cheek. My eyes snap shut as my body relishes the fiery warmth spreading across my backside.

"Once a punishment has been issued, it must be delivered. There is no cause for delay," Marcus grunts, his low tone as reckless as he makes me feel when he spanks me.

I dig my right knee into the mattress, opening myself up to him more. "I did what I believed was necessary to get what I craved. Now it's your turn to do the same."

His balls slap my pussy as he plunges into me deeper. "Good girl," he mutters, pleased I am accepting his punishment without putting up a fight.

As if I wouldn't agree. I'm not an idiot. The first thing that crossed my mind when he slid his mouth-watering cock back inside me was, "If this is his idea of punishment, I'm going to start being more disobedient."

Like he has done multiple times the past two months, Marcus intuits my private thoughts. "We'll see who is acting smug when she's deprived of orgasming for the remainder of the night."

When he sinks his teeth into the flesh of my shoulder, my first plead for clemency rushes to the tip of my tongue.

18

Groaning a long and tedious grunt, I smack my hand at the person attempting to wake me up. A tired headache is thumping my temples, and my eyes are carrying the effects of a miniscule amount of sleep. Marcus's punishment didn't stop all night. No matter how sincerely I begged, he screwed, hammered, and fucked me six ways from Sunday. He was relentless, not giving an inch until I collapsed from exhaustion. I swear muscles I didn't even know existed are aching. The only good thing that came from our exchange was that his threat of sexual deprivation only lasted half an hour. It's a good thing, or I may have died. Marcus is a machine, his sole purpose to issue pleasure... *and pain.*

Powerless to ignore the pleas of my inquisitive mind, I slowly flutter my eyes open. I squint, adjusting my eyes to the blinding mid-morning sun streaming in my window. With the furnishing covering my window panels in severe need of an upgrade, the room is blanketed with natural lighting. It's so bright, you'd swear my curtains were drawn.

The animated thrill strumming my veins intensifies when my eyes lock in on a ravishing visual. Marcus is crouched at the side of my bed. He is wearing the same suit he had on last night, minus the tight restraints of a jacket. The shadowing on his jaw has grown darker, mimicking the hankering in his eyes, and the sleeves of his dress shirt are rolled to his elbows. Considering his tight afro is wet, I infer he has been awake a lot longer than me. He is already showered and dressed. Giddiness clusters in my head, pleased he feels so welcome in my home he has made himself comfortable.

"Morning," I stammer, my voice croaky with both tiredness and sexual exhaustion.

Marcus's lips curl into a smile. It does wicked things to my libido. "Morning." He moves closer to me so the smell of his freshly brushed teeth mingles with my not-so-fresh breath.

When his teeth nib at my bottom lip, I no longer care about my ghastly morning breath. I purr when he sucks my lip into his more-than-inviting mouth. His touch is gentle but potent enough for excitement to thicken my veins. I slip my hands under his shirt, craving the feeling of his skin against mine. A faint smile cracks on my mouth when the muscles of his abs contract from my meekest touch. He kisses me for several moments, slowly awakening me from my sleepy state. His kiss is lush, deep, and full of affection, and it has my heart swelling even more than my unbridled desire.

Once he is happy I've merged back into the land of living, Marcus pulls back from our embrace. I pout, childishly announcing my disappointment at his withdrawal. His finger twangs my dropped bottom lip.

"I thought you were going to sleep until eternity."

After playfully biting his retreating thumb, I throw my arms out of my bedding and take a big stretch. Every muscle in my body tightens, and not in a good way. I am aching.

"What time is it?" I ask, grimacing at how sore my muscles are.

My body is so tender it reminds of the time Lexi signed us up to be guinea pigs for the Swedish reflexology class at our local university. We thought we'd be pampered for hours on end, we walked away with more injuries than we entered.

My jaw gapes when my sweep of the room has me answering my own question. If the time displayed on my alarm clock is anything to go off, it's well past one.

"Holy hell, why didn't you wake me?!"

Weary muscles become a faint memory when my eyes lock with Marcus's. From the hunger radiating out of his mesmerizing gaze, no one would guess we participated in a marathon lovemaking session mere hours ago. He looks like a man starved of taste, and I'm the only woman capable of quenching his hunger.

"You looked tired... I also liked watching you sleep. I've never done that before either," he admits, his tone low.

The honesty of his confession staggers me. It also has me recalling segments of our fire-sparking encounter last night. Although our night was magical, it prevented me from achieving a solid eight hours of sleep.

Hugging the bedsheets close to my body, I scoot up the lumpy mattress and rest my back against the wooden headboard Marcus had me tethered to last night. The corners of Marcus's full lips tuck into his mouth when I gesture for him to join me. When he sits next to me, the smell of my body wash mixed with his skin filters through my nose. I snap my eyes shut and inhale extravagantly, not the slightest bit concerned Marcus will hear my brazen sniff. I moan loudly. *I've never smelled anything as invigorating as our scents combined.*

After calming my desire to straddle his lap and mingle our scents some more, I pop open my eyes and shift them to Marcus. His eyes tell me he didn't miss my sniff of his tempting smell. They also expose he wasn't bothered by it. Actually, he looks chuffed.

Striving to put the needs of my astute brain above my lust-crazed heart, I say, "A couple of things you said last night confused me."

Marcus's dark brows slant, but he maintains a quiet front.

"When I was...umm... ah..."

No matter how hard I try to fire the words off my tongue, I can't admit out loud that I touched myself. I nearly died coming to terms with the fact I pleased myself while talking to him on the phone, let alone shamelessly doing it in front of him.

When Marcus continues with his silent stance, I shift my eyes to him. His lips are curled into a crass smirk, and an impish gleam is brightening his eyes. Screwing up my nose, I shove my fingers into his ribs. A brutal grunt escapes his mouth before it makes way for his hearty chuckle. My god, his laughter is delicious. Raspy, deep, and so deliriously scrumptious, it flows through my blood like liquid ecstasy. Usually, any type of laughter in the bedroom would have me breaking out in hives, but since it's coming from Marcus, it isn't as nerve-racking as normal.

I wait for his laughter to settle down before asking, "Are you good now? Can I continue?"

"Please." .

I bite on the inside of my cheek, fighting hard to conceal my glee at his playful response. Not once in the past nine weeks have I witnessed this side to Marcus. I'm not going to lie. It gives me great pleasure knowing I get to see a side of him not many people are privileged to see. The man sitting beside me now isn't Master Chains, the dominant, sexy owner of a BDSM club in lower Manhattan, nor Marcus Everett, bassist of a world-dominating rock group. He is a combination of them both, the best bits rolled into one incredibly alluring package.

I shut down the excitement blazing my veins before it overwhelms me. If I want any chance of reconciling the debilitating heart versus mind battle I've been combatting the past two months, I occasionally need to put the desires of my brain above the hankerings of my heart.

After coughing to clear my throat, I ask, "When I was...umm..." My second attempt at admitting to touching myself isn't any easier than my first.

"Pleasuring yourself," Marcus fills in, his tone knee-quakingly low.

"Yep... umm... that, you said some things that didn't make sense," I push on, pretending the heat inflaming my cheeks is not from embarrassment.

Marcus's plump lips tug high, but not a syllable escapes his mouth.

Too tired to continue with the irksome two-step routine we've undertaken many times the past two months, I blurt out, "Last night you acted like it was the first time you witnessed me fondling myself. We both know that isn't true. You saw a very similar thing the night of my birthday—when you awarded me my final gift of the day."

Lust sparks in Marcus's eyes, making them even more core-crunching than normal. If I weren't so interested in settling my confusion, I'd be tempted to see if I could keep the look in his eyes for eternity.

Marcus adjusts his position to face me head-on before asking, "What *exactly* do you remember about the night of your birthday, Cleo?"

The hairs on my nape bristle from his seductive purr of my name, but I push on, more determined than ever to have my confusion settled once and for all. "We talked about BDSM choices, you made me climax, then I fell asleep."

Marcus laughs. "Short and sweet, an approach my impatience has not yet taught me." He stares straight into my eyes, spearing me in place with his primitive gaze. "Think a little harder, Cleo. Recall the actions leading up to the main event."

Remaining quiet, I rack my brain about the day I'll never forget. It was the day that officially saw us stepping over the line acceptable for pen pals. It was also the day I realized I was falling in love with Master Chains, a huge no-no in Marcus's eyes.

From our conversations the prior two months, I reached the conclusion that Marcus has never been in love. When probing him about his previous D/s relationships, he made it very clear that love was not on his agenda. If he felt one of his subs was getting too close, he paid out the remainder of their contract and ceased communication with them.

Pretending I can't feel the contents of my stomach creeping up my esophagus, I mumble, "I know you were watching me that night as you mentioned me sticking out my tongue."

My tone has a bitchy emphasis to it. It doesn't stem from Marcus spying on me. It's because I am afraid the instant he discovers I am falling in love with him, he will end our relationship even more quickly than it started.

Marcus nods, confirming my suspicion. "Yes, I was watching you that night."

I'm taken aback by his honesty. I thought he would have skirted my accusation—or at the very least try to downplay it, but he didn't. He just hit me with straight-up honesty. I can't fault him for that.

"But what do you recall after you stuck out your tongue?" Marcus asks, his entrancing eyes never once leaving mine.

My tongue delves out to replenish my lips. "You saw the way my body reacts to your voice."

Marcus's eyes twinkle in delight, seemingly pleased I find him so appealing. He shouldn't be surprised, no woman in their right mind could deflect his advances. With soul-stealing eyes, a more-than-tempting body, and the carnal stamina of twenty men, I'm forever ruined by him.

"Then?" Marcus continues prompting while gliding his heavy-hooded gaze over my face.

Hating the loss of confidence in his eyes when his spots the bruise on my cheek, I say, "Then you guided me into one of the most climatic experiences I've ever had. I didn't think anything could top it... until I met you in person. You trumped every wish I've ever made."

My confession stills him for just a moment. Not long enough for awkwardness to fill the silence, but long enough to display he heard the sentimentality of my reply.

I drift my eyes away, worried I've shown my hand way too early. My breath snags halfway to my lungs when Marcus runs the back of his fingers down my blemished cheek.

"Don't be too hard on your heart, Cleo. It's the sensible one. It's the only one not denying your desires," he quotes, reciting a text he sent me the night of Thanksgiving.

He grips my chin and raises my downcast head. A gush of air rushes out of his mouth when our eyes lock and hold. It reminds me of his response the first time we met in the elevator all those years ago. It's a heartfelt reminder of a beautifully cruel moment in time.

Warmth blooms across my chest when he utters, "Normally I can identify a tornado a mile away, but even I was blindsided by you."

My heart skips a beat, and my breaths come out in ragged pants, but it doesn't stop me from saying, "That still doesn't explain my confusion. You watched me touch myself on my birthday, so you can't pretend last night was the first time you've seen it."

The little voice inside me breaks into rapturous applause, pleased as punch I managed to discuss sexual proclivities without stuttering like an idiot.

The veins in my neck strum when Marcus's fingers track its furious pulse. He is barely touching me, but he has my entire body on high alert. "It killed me knowing what you were doing and not being able to watch you."

My eyes go frantic, searching every millimeter of his forthright gaze for deceit. I fail to find a pinch of treachery. How can that be? He just said mere minutes ago that he was watching me, but now he is confessing he didn't stay for the main event. That would be like turning up to *ChikaLicious Dessert Bar,* ordering the Bun Chika Bun Bun, then leaving before the waiter serves it to you. Why would he do that? Itdoesn't make any sense... I stop breathing when reality dawns on my satiated brain.

My eyes rocket to Marcus. "The chair scraping across the floor? I heard a chair being dragged within seconds of you agreeing to help me... *come*."

Marcus doesn't speak a word. He doesn't need to. The entire story is relayed by his honest eyes.

"Why didn't you watch me?" I blubber out before I can stop my words.

My brain grumbles in disgust when I sit still, muted and in shock, and if I am being totally honest, a little bit disappointed. This may be wrong of me to say, but I like that I can make Marcus so reckless he loses control. Yes, he spied on me, but imagine being so desired by someone you make them reckless enough to break their usually unbreakable decorum just to capture every morsel of your soul. Knowing I can unravel a man who is as tightly reined as Marcus is a thrilling and highly addictive experience. One I'd line up for time and time again.

Marcus takes his time configuring a response to my blurted-out question. Just like it does every time we are together, the silence increases the sexual connection bouncing between us. It's so heated, if I weren't naked, I'd be kicking off the sheets curled around my body.

After drifting his eyes from staring at a speck of chipped paint on my wall, Marcus locks them with me. "I didn't want to run the risk of losing you before I made you mine."

My heart squeezes, beyond smitten by his response. Here I was worried I was displaying my feelings for him too early, and he goes and outmaneuvers my declaration with one just as compelling.

Lifting my hand, I rub at the heavy groove between his eyes. "This really is all new to you, isn't it?"

"Very much so," he replies, his tone low.

Hating the unease in his words, I lean my cheek on his shoulder and wrap my arms around his waist. My libido awakens when he pulls me across his body so I can sit side-straddled on his lap. Her delayed response was from the exhausting activities she undertook last night. She is still half-asleep with the rest of my weary muscles.

I rest my cheek on Marcus's chest and listen to the mad thump of his heart. Although I'd love to be swept up in a lusty haze, this type of contact is doing wonders to recuperate the severe beating my ego took the past week. Sometimes doing nothing is more rewarding than doing everything.

A small stretch of silence passes between us. I wouldn't necessarily say it's uncomfortable. We both just need a moment to gather our bases before we face the next daunting phase in our heart-stuttering kinship. I'm at a loss as to where we go from here. There are so many things we still need to discuss, but I genuinely don't know where to begin.

Now that I've had a few hours to calm down, I realize how lucky I am Marcus stopped my belligerent tirade last night. If he hadn't, I could have faced severe legal ramifications. Although I can legally inform him of my job title, that doesn't extend to the particulars of my job. In journalism, the desire to keep a story exclusive means anyone working in the industry has a strict set of policies they must adhere to. Me informing Marcus of the investigation into Chains or sharing any knowledge of the information obtained thus far would place me in breach of my contract. So, not only did Marcus save my hide last night, but he also saved my sister's.

I pop my head off Marcus's chest and peer into his eyes. My heart skips a beat when I notice he is watching me intently. "You knew I couldn't divulge any information. That's why you stopped me last night. You were saving me from prosecution."

He runs his fingers down the crinkle his shirt made in my cheek before tucking a strand of my hair behind my ear. He doesn't need to speak to confirm my statement, the truth is relayed in his striking eyes.

"Thank you." I nuzzle deeper into his embrace. "That's the third time you saved me in less than 24 hours."

I peer into his eyes, my desire for him uncontrollable. "How could I ever repay you for your gallantry, Master Chains?" I inwardly sigh when my voice comes out sounding like the sexpot I was aiming for.

The lust in Marcus's eyes grows as his cock thickens beneath me. "Loyalty can only ever be repaid with loyalty, Cleo," he mutters, his eyes arrested on me.

I glance into his mesmerizing gaze as I contemplate an appropriate response. Although the air is heated with lust, there is something much greater crackling between us. It's thick, pungent, and it makes butterflies take flight in my stomach.

Deep down inside, I know there is one thing I could do to display my utter devotion to Marcus: I could sign our BDSM contract. But I can't do that. What I said to Delilah yesterday was true. People in the BDSM lifestyle are no different than her or me. They crave the same thing every red-blooded human wants when seeking a relationship: loyalty, trust, and devotion. I feel like I have already achieved that with Marcus. But there is something I crave more than anything. I want to be loved. And from the conversations I've had with Marcus the past nine weeks, I know that isn't something he is seeking.

Not wanting irrational thoughts to dampen my mood, I pop my head back down on Marcus's chest and listen to the frantic rhythm of his heart. The unease twisting my stomach alleviates when I notice our hearts are beating a similar tempo. A frantic thump of love and confusion. I know it's early. I know it's crazy. But I can't deny the prompts my body gives every time Marcus is in my presence. Not only does he make me feel like life didn't exist before we met, but he also makes me look forward to the future. That's truly remarkable. I haven't felt this hopeful in years. Not even before my parents and Tate passed away.

Marcus runs his hand down my back, drawing me in closer to his tempting body. "Don't let your fears about what may happen stop you from letting it happen, Cleo. If you don't face your fears, you will never find the courage to break through them."

I huff into his chest. "That's easy for you to preach. You're not the one who faces punishment anytime they step out of line," I respond, my words ruffled.

I don't need to look at Marcus to know he is smiling, I can feel it deep in my bones. "You do know there is an easy solution for that, don't you?" he asks, his tone so smooth it prickles every hair on my body.

Pulling away from his chest, I glance into his amused gaze, demanding further explanation.

He runs his index finger down the crinkle in my nose before saying, "Stop being disobedient."

I screw up my nose even more. "Once again, that's easy for you to preach. I'm not obedient, and I hate following the rules. That's why I am surprised you ever wanted me as your sub. Obedience and rule-following are two fundamental qualities for anyone in the BDSM lifestyle. Two factors I am severely lacking."

Marcus stuns me by replying, "A young man only knows the rules, but a wise man knows there is an exception to every rule."

I burrow my head into his chest to hide the obtusely broad grin stretching across my face. That was a quote similar to one I said to him when we discussed the BDSM contract he had drawn up. Although, I suggested I was *his* exception, I didn't realize he took my statement as literal.

"What happened to me being nothing more than a brat?" I mumble into his chest, my tone a mix of sentimental and playful.

Marcus places his hand under my chin and lifts my head. The instant our eyes lock, a flood of emotions hit me at once, making it hard for me to breathe. His eyes impart more information than his mouth ever could. His desire for me. His confusion about our relationship. It's all expressed by his stunning eyes.

Now I know why he wouldn't look at me when he brought up our BDSM contract. He didn't do it because he was treating me as if I was his sub, he did it as he was afraid I'd see the truth in his eyes. That I would discover I wasn't the only one vulnerable and exposed. He is just as startled about our relationship as I am.

I fight hard not to writhe on the spot when blood surges to the lower extremities of my body. I've had many reckless thoughts the past nine weeks —*heedless thoughts.* But nothing compares to the stream of wicked notions bombarding me now. It's lucky we are huddled on my bed in my house far *far* away from the drawer Marcus's BDSM contracts are stored in, as I can't guarantee with the catalyst of emotions pumping into me right now that I wouldn't sign any contract he presented me with.

God—how can one man change beliefs drilled into me by society by doing nothing more than gazing into my eyes? The power Marcus has over me is outstanding—and truly terrifying.

Strengthening my faith that he knows me better than any man before him, Marcus locks his eyes with mine and mutters, "Curious, Cleo?"

I swear the way he growls out my name nearly tumbles me into ecstasy. It's throaty and rough, and it sets my pulse racing. Leaning in, I press my lips against his mouth, allowing my body to speak on behalf of my heart. Marcus's mouth only just catches the throaty groan torn from my throat when he slides his tongue along the seam of my mouth in a slow, toe-curling lick.

Moaning, I part my lips, giving him unrestricted access to my mouth. My heart leaps out of my chest when the buzz of a cellphone shrills into my ears, stopping Marcus's devotion to my mouth before it has even started.

Realizing the buzzing is coming from him, Marcus delves his hand into the pocket of his trousers. His brows tack together when he spots the name of the person calling him. It's the FBI agent I met last night: Shian.

"I have to take this," he informs me, his tone regretful. "She only calls when it's something important." His last sentence is so quiet, I'm not sure he wanted me to hear it.

I scoot across the bed, freeing him from my clingy hold. "You can take it in here, if you'd like?" I offer as I watch him stand from the bed. "I'm starving anyway." *And dying to pee.*

Not waiting for him to reply, I scamper across the bed. Air rustles through Marcus's teeth when the sheet slips away from my body, revealing my naked form to his more than avid gaze. I cockily wink, adoring the boost his keen response is giving my confidence. He eyeballs me as I secure my clothing from the floor and commence getting dressed. I take my time, savoring the bulge in his trousers growing with every second that ticks by.

Once I am dressed, sans underwear, I place a kiss on the side of his mouth and make a beeline for the door. A sassy grin is curled on my lips, smitten by the way his body responded to my frisky tease.

A blood-curdling squeal rolls up my chest when Marcus seizes my wrist and drags me back to him. My nipples bud when my breasts are flattened on the firmness of his pecs, and the heat of his rod digs into my throbbing core. Rampant horniness overtakes my need to pee when he seals his lips over mine. He kisses me like I've never been kissed before. A kiss so tantalizing, my knees grow weak, and my heart can't keep up with the amount of blood pumping through it.

By the time he pulls away, I am thoroughly dizzy and unable to breathe. He stares down at me with wild, reckless eyes as he brushes his fingers down my marked cheek before gently caressing the cut in my top lip. His touch soothes any irritation niggling my small flesh wound from our earth-shaking kiss. It's a nurturing gesture for a man who claims he is unfamiliar with relationships.

"Did I hurt you?" he asks as his eyes float between mine.

Smiling, I shake my head. "No. I'm perfectly A-Okay."

Stretching onto my tippy toes, I press my lips on his kiss-swollen mouth. "Take your call, then come and have some lunch with me," I mutter against his lips. *I nearly said breakfast, but quickly remembered it's late in the afternoon.*

Hearing the underlying bossiness in my tone, Marcus arches his brow. He isn't angry, more amused. A second yelp bellows out of my mouth when he playfully smacks my backside. His slap isn't hard enough to cause pain, it's purely to incite excitement.

"I'll take my call, then I'll eat you for lunch." His tone is as demanding as ever.

A violent shudder courses through me. *Jesus—who knew words alone could make me climax?*

Smirking at my frozen-in-lust stance, Marcus sucks my pouty lip into his mouth, being extra attentive not to agitate my sore lip. After he has me utterly intoxicated by desire, he pulls his lips away from mine, twirls me around, then playfully shoves me towards my bedroom door. I immaturely stomp my feet like a child while crossing the room. My already shaky steps slow when Marcus's hearty laughter jingles into my ears. If given a choice, I'd never leave my room. Not while Marcus is in it.

Just before I exit into the hallway, Marcus calls my name. I take a minute to clear the hunger from my eyes before cranking my neck back to peer at him.

"Even brats have a place in the BDSM lifestyle, if it's something she craves?" he informs me. Although his statement appears to be a testimony, his expression doesn't relay that. It's a question.

His predatory eyes burn into mine, searing my soul from the inside out as he awaits my reply. His gaze makes me needy and hot, and it causes something deep inside me to shift.

Allowing my heart to speak for the first time in years, I nod.

Marcus draws in a quick, sharp breath, seemingly stunned by my response. He isn't the only one surprised. I was expecting my astute brain to announce irritation at my agreeing gesture the instant it occurred, but not a single thought has passed my mind. I guess even it's beyond saving when it comes to this man.

"I'm not agreeing to sign anything," I stammer out, wanting to ensure he didn't mistake my nod as a covenant that I'll be his sub.

Although I will do anything in my power to keep him in my life, I don't want it to be on negotiated terms for a stipulated amount of time. I just want him—unrestrained.

Exhaling a nervous breath, I lock my eyes with Marcus. "I'm opening my mind to the possibility of learning something new. Are you willing to do the same?" I ask, partially quoting a saying he said to me in his playroom at Chains two months ago.

The lusty smile on Marcus's lips tugs higher as reckless yearning rages in his eyes. "Intellectual growth should commence at birth and cease only at death."

A broad grin stretches across my face, pleased as punch he recited a quote from Albert Einstein. That just proves what my heart has always known. Marcus is my other half.

Showing I am the very epitome of a brat, I brazenly whisper, "Then I very much look forward to being taught by the Master of Masters, Master Chains." I drawl out his name in a long, throaty purr.

Winking at the dominance detonating in his eyes, I pivot on my heels and exit the room, stealing his chance to reply. My steps are more buoyant than ever when Marcus's stern growl rumbles down the hall, making my heart shudder right out of my chest while adding to the throb between my legs.

19

"Good morning," I greet, my voice unbelievably sappy as I skip into the kitchen.

Lexi's big brown eyes stop gawking at the toaster to peer at me. She looks like her night was as adventurous as mine. Her wavy hair is frizzed with voluptuous curls and stuck to her head, and her eyes are circled by dark rings. If it weren't for the pillow crinkle on the side of her cheek, I wouldn't have believed she'd slept.

Hearing the water heater kick in, I trudge further into the kitchen. "Who's in the shower?" I ask at the same time the smell of smoke lingers into my nostrils.

Lexi waits a beat before answering, "Jackson." She rocks to and fro on her heels, her mood a stark contradiction to the raging, hormonal woman I was dealing with last night.

Not wanting to know the reason for her sudden shift in demeanor, I continue our conversation like I haven't noticed her change in decorum. "I thought Jackson had a morning shift?"

Lexi tries to hold in her smile, but the twitching of her lips give away her deceit. "He did, he called in sick."

I arch a brow, shocked by her reply. "Is he unwell?"

Lexi throws her head back and laughs. It's rough and curt—just like its owner. "No, Cleo. He is more than fine—believe me!" She suggestively waggles her brows.

Like a light bulb switching on, the reasoning behind Jackson playing hooky clicks in my spent brain. I gag, faking repulsion. Although I'd prefer for Lexi to keep her sex life to herself, I'm also grateful her relationship with Jackson is blossoming nicely. They have grown very close the past three months. So close,

I'm beginning to wonder if my I'm-never-going-to-fall-in-love sister has bitten off more than she can chew.

Giggling at my repulsed expression, Lexi returns her focus to the toaster billowing out thick black smoke. I increase my sluggish strides. With our home insurance not the best it can be, the last thing I need is a fire breaking out in our kitchen.

"Don't do that," I scold when Lexi spears a butter knife into the toaster.

Lexi's beauty may be the epitome of Hollywood glamor, but she has the cooking skills of a twenty-one-year-old bachelor. Something as simple as browning a few slices of bread is above her culinary skills.

"The bread is stuck and burning," Lexi informs me, like I'm unaware why the room is filling with ghastly smoke.

Leaning over her shoulder, I push the release button on the toaster before switching it off at the wall. Lexi jumps in fright when two pieces of charcoal toast pop out of the machine.

"There's a button for that?" she murmurs, more to herself than me. "When did that happen?"

That's all it takes for laughter to rumble up my chest and spill from my lips. My god, I love my sister, but there are days when her ditzy personality surprises even me. Don't get me wrong, Lexi is as smart as she is beautiful, but like a lot of modern-age young adults, common sense is not her strong point.

"Ouch," Lexi whimpers when she grabs the toast out of the toaster and places the slices on a bread plate. The bread is so burnt, it disintegrates from her faint touch. My brow arches when a breathtakingly exquisite smile stretches across her face before she hands the plate to me.

"For me?" I ask, peering at the plate like it's a contagious virus.

"I figured you could use the boost in energy." Her voice is as quirked as her lips. "I don't want you to waste a minute of Chains' stamina."

My lips twitch, attempting to negate her claim, but not a syllable escapes my mouth.

For the quickest second, her cheeky mask falters, exposing a rare emotion she rarely holds: concern. "I'm also trying to make amends for last night. Jackson is buying a new door to be installed, and I'll patch the bullet hole in the hallway." She says her last sentence with a grimace.

Endorphins pump through my veins, beyond thrilled with her sudden maturity. Jackson's personality must be rubbing off on her.

Her new-found maturity doesn't last for long. "My god, Cleo, did you get any sleep last night?" she mumbles.

Not the slightest bit deterred by my bug-eyed expression, she continues, "I was exhausted just listening to you two going at it."

Hoping to dodge the awkwardness that she heard me in a compromising position, I force a smile on my face before accepting the plate from her grasp. Her brows tack when I set the plate down on the kitchen counter and head for the refrigerator.

"You can't eat toast without peanut butter," I mutter, issuing any excuse I can to prevent me eating the equivalent of coals for breakfast. "And that." I point to the mug of steamy hot chocolate sitting at her right.

What Lexi lacks in culinary talent, she makes up for with barista skills. During her three-month stint working at Crazy Mocha Café last winter, she perfected the most delicious, gooey-to-the-soles-of-your-shoes hot chocolate. Seriously, I've never tasted anything better. *Well, except one thing*. But considering I'm mortified my little sister heard me in the throes of ecstasy, calorie-laced hot chocolate will have to curb my insatiable sweet-tooth cravings. *For now*.

After placing two pieces of toast in the toaster, Lexi hands me a mug of hot chocolate. Beaming with excitement, I tiptoe to the pantry to add the mandatory two marshmallows every hot chocolate needs. A groan that should only be expressed in the midst of ecstasy seeps from my lips when the aromatic flavor hits my taste buds.

"Sounds like the noises I heard coming out of your room last night," Lexi mumbles with her brow cocked.

My drink traps halfway in my throat, causing me to cough and sputter. My wheezy response replicates the gasping Lexi usually does when she struggles to fill her lungs with air.

Once I've forcefully swallowed the sugary liquid, I stumble out, "Sorry."

Although my apology is short, the sincerity in my tone relays everything I want to express but am too embarrassed to articulate.

Lexi laughs while mumbling, "Don't apologize. If anything, I should be thanking you. Jackson has never worked so hard in his life. His feathers were already ruffled sleeping under the same roof as a rock star, much less competing against him. I came so many times I lost count!"

It's lucky my stomach is void of any nutrients or I may have barfed by now.

"I don't need to hear anymore," I assure Lexi, sickened at the thought of her sharing any more than she already has. "I'm glad your... *needs* were taken care of, but can we save the details for a later date? A much, much, later date."

The cheeky gleam in Lexi's eyes explodes. "Sure... on one condition," she barters, her manicured brows waggling.

I slant my head to the side and bow my brow, demanding further information. I don't know why I am continuing this conversation, but try as I may, I can't leash my curiosity.

Lexi paces closer to me, her steps dramatic. "You've got to tell me what vitamins Chains is taking. I'll get a special batch ordered for Jackson for Christmas."

Hearing the playfulness in her voice, my dainty laugh jingles around our stuffy kitchen. "From what I've heard the past few months, I doubt Jackson needs help in the bedroom."

Lexi's teeth graze over her bottom lip as hankering sparks in her eyes "No, he doesn't, but I'll never tell him that. Jealousy never felt as good as it did last night."

Mortified by the sexually sated look on her face, I pick up a slice of charcoaled toast and peg it at her head. It slaps the tiled backsplash behind the hotplates before flopping to the kitchen counter. I pout when it leaves a big black smear on the tiles. With Lexi's cleaning skills as lagging as her cooking capabilities, there is only one way that mark will be removed—by me scrubbing it.

The sulking expression on my face changes to shock when Lexi retaliates by throwing the toast back across the room. Unlike me, her throw has perfect aim. It sails through the air like a Frisbee before smacking me on my left cheek. Lexi's boisterous laughter shrills into my ears when a black cloud puffs off my face from her perfectly placed hit.

My mouth gapes as my Garcia fighting spirit emerges. Bobbing down, I snag the crumbling piece of toast in my hand. My quick movements enhance the dizziness still plaguing me from Marcus's breathtaking kiss, but I push it aside, relishing the playful energy bouncing between Lexi and me. We haven't acted this reckless in years, not since we were kids.

Lexi spreads her hands across her cocked hip. Her eyes egg me on, daring me to step out of my comfort zone. Hoping to catch her off guard, I push off my feet and charge for her. The saggy piece of toast is mushed into her face before a single gripe leaves her lips. My childish giggles are barely contained when I notice the huge smear of soot running down her right cheek.

Happy I've exacted my revenge I spin on my heels and race to the other side of the room. My whole body is shuddering with laughter, my mind void of any concern.

"That's it, you're going down," Lexi warms, snatching the loaf of bread off the kitchen counter. Her movements are so rough, she tears open the flimsy packaging.

Squealing, I dodge slices of bread left, right and center while slaying my hands through the air, chopping away at the bread like a ninja in training. The rapturous laughter bellowing out of Lexi and me increases with every childish strike.

When Lexi runs out of bread, she turns her attention to the half-empty bag of marshmallows hanging out of the pantry.

"Not the marshmallows."

Our one-sided food fight turns into a food catching contest when my grumbling tummy kicks up a stink about its lack of nutrients. Marshmallows bounce off my nose, cheek, and chin before tumbling to the floor. When I finally catch one in my mouth, I throw my hands in the air and do a little jig on the spot. My dance moves are an embarrassment to anyone in the profession, but nothing can dampen my eagerness. After spending the night wrapped up in Marcus's warmth, the traumatic ten hours I endured yesterday are nothing more than a forgotten memory.

The marshmallow traps halfway to my stomach when the hairs on my arms bristle, and my breathing pans out. My hideous dance moves stop, closely followed by the beat of my heart. I don't need to turn around to know Marcus is standing in the entranceway of our kitchen, the shit-eating grin stretched across Lexi's face is all the indication I need to know he witnessed my less-than-stellar dance moves.

Glaring at Lexi for not warning me of his arrival, I spin on my heels to face Marcus. He is standing in the entrance to our kitchen. His lips are curled in a panty-drenching smirk, and his eyes are void of the guilt they harbored last night. The happiness warming my chest fades when I notice he is wearing his suit jacket and shoes. I don't need to ask if he is leaving, the expression on his face tells the entire story.

Spotting the disappointment marring my face, Marcus pushes off his feet and moves to stand in front of me. "I have a couple of things I need to take care of," he informs me, lifting his hand to caress my cheek. "I won't be gone long. Only an hour or two at the most."

"Okay," I reply, my brain incapable of a more confident reply after witnessing a snip of deceit brewing in his eyes. His eyes are so forthright, even something as small as a white lie can't be concealed by them.

While peering into my eyes, his gaze intense, his hands cup my jaw so his thumb can stroke my crimson cheeks. The callus on his fingers from playing the bass guitar for years adds a scratchy feeling to his gentle touch. I nuzzle into his hand, wanting to capture enough of his scent on my skin to last me until his return. A primal glint flares in his eyes, no doubt shocked by my loving gesture. My clinginess even surprises me. I'm generally not so needy, but all my inhibitions are null and void when it comes to this man.

"I'll be back soon, Cleo," he murmurs just as his exquisite green irises lift to peer past my shoulder.

In less than a nanosecond, the snip of deceit in his eyes switches to panic. The change in his persona is swift and resolute, completed in under a second. My attention diverts from working out the fear flaring in his eyes when a gasp seeps through my ears. It sounds like someone is choking... or struggling to breathe. My breath snags halfway in my lungs when reality dawns. Snapping my head to the side, I spot Lexi clutching the kitchen counter. Her face is a vibrant pink color, her eyes wide and panicked.

"Breathe, Lexi," I demand, racing to stand at her side.

Grasping the top of her arm, I gently whack her back, hoping to ease some of the mucus blocking her airways. I hit hard enough that she gasps in the occasional wheezy breath, but not one strong enough to entirely clear her airways.

"I need her inhaler," I advise, lifting my panicked eyes to Marcus.

He stands frozen in place, unsure how to react in a situation like this.

"Where is it?" he asks when his astute brain finally kicks in.

I point to the hall. "There is one in the top drawer of my dresser."

Marcus spins on his heels and is halfway down the hall before the entire sentence leaves my mouth. When the pink hue on Lexi's cheeks inflames to a dark red coloring, my panic reaches an all-time high.

"Breathe, Lexi, breathe," I plead, my words as breathless as her heaving lungs.

I can't believe I acted so reckless. I know the benefits of a good dose of laughter to a damaged soul, but for a CF sufferer, too much laughter can be catastrophic. It doesn't matter if it's a faint chuckle or a full-hearted laugh, it almost always triggers a severe coughing attack.

"Jackson," Lexi wheezes out, her words barely audible. "I don't want him to see me like this."

"Shh. It's okay," I assure her, knowing Jackson is mindful of her condition. Our families have been friends for years. They grew up around Lexi's condition. He is also studying to be a surgeon, so he witnesses stuff like this every day.

Lexi's windedness grows right alongside the plea in her eyes. "Please... Cleo." Her two words are separated by long, gasping breaths. "I don't... want him... to see me... like this."

The pain in her begging eyes cripples me. Like many CF sufferers, this is the part she finds the hardest—the sympathy. Other than when she is undergoing CF therapy, you'd be none the wiser to Lexi's condition. It's indeed a silent disease.

"Come on. You can hide in my room," I mumble, the hammering of my heart notable in my tone.

Placing my arm around her shoulders, I guide her out of the kitchen. Her lungs wheeze and sputter with every step we take. When we are halfway down the hall, Marcus sprints out of my room. He looks more rattled now than when Lexi had a gun pointed at him last night. His brow is beaded with sweat, and his cheeks are ashen.

Remaining quiet, he hands me one of the many Ventolin inhalers I have hidden around my house. Snubbing the shake encroaching my hands, I place the inhaler against Lexi's pale lips and press down on the pump. It takes three full pumps for her pupils to constrict to a safe range. Although the inhaler aids in opening her airways, she continues to cough, not stopping until the mucus blocking them clears so her lungs secure adequate oxygen.

Happy she is over the worst, we recommence our journey to my room. Lexi's steps are slow, drained by the fight her body just endured. That's one thing a lot of people don't understand about CF, it's an exhausting disease. It can take hours to recover from a bad coughing fit.

Just before we enter my room, Jackson emerges from the steam-filled bathroom. He has a small towel wrapped around his wet hips and another one drying his shaggy hair. My eyes follow a bead of water rolling down his hairless torso before it glides over the bumps in his abdomen. For a man who spends most of his days indoors, he has a fit and tight body. Not overly large, but the perfect smattering of muscles in all the right places.

The cheeky gleam in his eyes from catching my perverted gaze switches to panic when he spots a frail Lexi cowering at my side. She is hunched down low, using my curvy frame to shelter herself from Jackson's eagle eye. Her endeavors are utterly pointless. Even if we were surrounded by a sea of millions, I have no doubt Jackson would be able to spot Lexi. When he is with her, his eyes inflame with the same spark mine do every time I am in Marcus's presence. Much to Lexi's dismay, he has met his match.

"Lex, are you alright?" Jackson asks, his tone indicating he is already aware of her answer.

The narrow corridor becomes overcrowded when Jackson moves to stand in front of me. My house has always had a cramped feeling, but it's even more noticeable with so many strong personalities in the one space. The smell of shampoo streams into my nose when Jackson crouches in front of Lexi and lifts her low-hanging head. I can tell the instant recognition for Lexi's rattled state dawns on him. He sucks in a sharp breath as panic clouds his usually bright eyes.

"How bad was it this time?"

Lexi's throat works hard to swallow before she forces out, "It wasn't too bad."

A manic tick impinges Jackson's jaw. "Don't lie to me, Lexi!" he yells, his angry voice ricocheting off the stark bland walls and bellowing into my ears. "I can see the pain on your face!"

Tears prick my eyes from the devastation in his tone.

"I'm calling Dr. Spencer. That's your third attack this week," Jackson continues before pivoting on his heels and storming into Lexi's room.

I balk, utterly shocked. As far as I was aware, Lexi hasn't had a coughing fit this bad in months. Not since I started talking to Marcus. She has daily appointments with a CF specialist to ensure episodes like this are as irregular as possible. If it isn't working, why wouldn't she tell me?

When my confused eyes drop to Lexi, she weakly shakes her head. "Please don't," she pleads, her voice husky. "I've had enough lectures from Jackson the past week. I don't need them from you too."

Stealing my chance to reply, she pulls away from me and paces to her room. I stand frozen for a beat, unsure how to respond. This is the first time she's not been upfront about her condition. Typically, she keeps nothing from me, so I am utterly flabbergasted by her concealment.

Seeking answers, I push off my feet and go after her. Marcus foils my attempt.

"He loves her, Cleo. Give him the chance to show her that."

20

Over two hours pass before the creak of Lexi's door booms down the hall. Placing my Kindle on the coffee table, I stand from my lumpy couch and pace towards the hall. The two slices of toast I ate for lunch threatens to resurface when I see the desolate look on Jackson's face as he slowly strides down the hall. His shoulders are deflated, and his eyes have red rims circling them.

"How is she?" I ask when he stops at the coatrack to gather his winter jacket.

After snagging his switched off cellphone out of the pocket of his coat, he spins on his feet to face me. "Good. She's resting."

He peers past my shoulder, seeking Marcus in the empty living room. "Where's Marcus?"

"He had some stuff he needed to take care of," I answer, striving to ignore the swirling of my stomach.

Jackson's lips purse as he nods. "Everything alright?" he questions, reading the unease portrayed by my soul-bearing eyes.

"Yeah, we're fine. He wanted to stay after Lexi's attack, but I convinced him to go. He isn't familiar with CF, so it took me a while to assure him there is no miracle cure for her condition."

Since the last half of my statement was honest, it concealed the deceit in the first half of my reply. Although Marcus didn't elaborate on his sudden emergency, my intuition is telling me something seems off-kilter with him.

"Was it really Lexi's third attack this week?" I ask Jackson, praying I didn't hear him right earlier.

The concern in Jackson's eyes deepens as he nods. "I wanted to tell you, Cleo, but she begged me not to," he advises, his tone inhibited by remorse.

A puff of air escapes my lips, his admission physically winding me. "The

CF specialist? Is it not helping..." My words trail off when I spot Jackson shaking his head.

"She stopped going a couple of weeks ago," he informs me while switching on his cellphone.

I'm not surprised when he scrolls to his contacts, and I see his second most frequently dialed number is Dr. Spencer. He is the CF specialist who suggested Lexi attend daily physio session four months ago.

"Why would Lexi stop attending therapy? If she doesn't attend her attacks will worsen," I mutter, more to myself than Jackson.

"I'm about to find out." Jackson nudges his head to the screen of his phone which has Dr. Spencer's number displayed.

"Dr. Spencer won't give you any information pertaining to Lexi. He can't. That would be a massive violation of patient/doctor confidentiality," I blubber out, my words fired off my tongue so quickly they aren't adequately developed.

Jackson's brow cocks. "Lexi put me on her HIPAA consent forms last month."

I take a step backward as shock registers its intention. I don't know what's more surprising: I was so wrapped up in Marcus, I failed to notice Jackson's importance in Lexi's life, or the fact my little sister may have fallen in love. I think it's a bit of both.

"You love her," I mumble, confirming what Marcus recognized in a matter of seconds.

Jackson takes a moment deliberating a response before he nods. "I do. I really do. But the thought of losing her scares the shit out of me, Cleo. I don't know if I can handle that."

Tears prick my eyes from the dense sentiment of his tone. I try to offer him some reassurance that she isn't going anywhere, but I can't. As much as I wish it weren't true, one day CF will take Lexi away from us. Jackson knows this as well as anyone.

I scrub my hand over my cheek to remove my sneaky tear before Jackson sees it. Although his eyes are fixated on his phone, I have no doubt he saw it. The veins thrumming in his neck stopped pulsing the instant my rogue tear dribbled down my face.

When Jackson squashes his cell to his ear, I excuse myself from our gathering and pad down the hall. I pretend I'm using the bathroom, where, in reality, I just want to check on Lexi. Although Lexi's coughing fits are nothing out of the ordinary for us, today's was a little more daunting. It may just feel that way because of all the shit I've been hammered with the past week, but it doesn't make it any less worrying.

Just like Jackson said, Lexi is resting in the middle of her bed. Her cheeks have returned to their regular coloring, and the frown marring her face has vanished. The only indication of her severe attack is the wheezing of her breaths as she snores softly. She is as beautiful as ever.

Caressing her door to ensure it doesn't give out a creak, I close it and pad to the bathroom. I did need to use the facilities, but my desire to check on Lexi outweighed the screaming protests of my bladder.

Once I've done my business, I wash my hands in the cracked vanity and pace back into the living room. My brisk strides slow when I spot Jackson's defeated posture. His shoulders are hanging low, and his hand is scrubbing over the heavy stubble on his chin. I jump in fright when he unexpectedly punches the wall in front of him, his force so brutal, his fist dents the drywall.

Sensing he has company, he straightens his spine, extending to his full height. His Adam's apple bobs up and down before he cranks his neck to the side. The panic bubbling my veins increases when I see the devastated look in his eyes. Anyone would swear he was just informed CF is an incurable disease.

"Dr. Spencer said Lexi hasn't arrived for an appointment in over a month." His voice is so rough it sounds like it was dragged over a gravel road before leaving his mouth. "She stopped showing up after her health insurance claims were denied two sessions in a row."

I stop frozen halfway down the hall, my brain too busy racking the conditions of our health coverage to follow the prompts of my body. I am absolutely stunned by Jackson's admission. I've always chosen the most comprehensive policy for Lexi's health insurance. Even when the premiums skyrocketed, I copped the expense as her health is my utmost priority.

It doesn't matter how many times I analyze the information Jackson supplied me, it never makes any sense. "That can't be right, Jackson. There must be a mistake. I'd just as soon starve than sacrifice Lexi's health coverage. You know I'd never jeopardize her health by choosing lower coverage."

"I know, Cleo. You don't need to tell me twice," Jackson replies, the honesty in his eyes bolstering his statement. "I'm just relaying to you what Dr. Spencer told me."

Another stretch of silence passes between us. I spend the entire time struggling to work out why Lexi's health coverage would change. It doesn't make any sense. I only updated our premiums last quarter, and nothing in our lives has changed since then ... I stop frozen as blood roars to my ears.

"She wouldn't," I whisper under my breath.

My heart rate spikes to a dangerous level. "Yes, she would," I snarl as anger overtakes every nerve-ending in my body.

I dart to the entranceway table where I left my cellphone last night. My steps are remarkably stable for how potently rage is roaring through my body. Upon discovering my cracked and beyond repair cell, I shift my eyes to Jackson.

"Can you stay with Lexi?" I ask him.

Not waiting for him to reply, I gather my thin winter coat and thrust my arms into the sleeves. This jacket is in even worse shape than the one I left at Marcus's hotel. Its cuffs are as decrepit as the lady I am about to go to battle with.

Once my shuddering frame is covered with my coat, I spin a scarf around my neck and slip into a pair of stilettos I usually wear in summer. I'm halfway out my front door when reality crashes into me: I don't have my car. Intuiting my needs, Jackson's keys sail through the air. I suck in a grateful breath when my nearsightedness doesn't stop me catching them mid-air.

"The hospital pays all my tolls," Jackson shouts as I gallop down the front stairs, intuiting what I am about to do.

Jackson's truck goes shooting out of my driveway approximately five minutes later. My brisk departure was delayed from struggling to adjust his driver's seat. Although frustrated about the delay, it was necessary. I can barely see over the steering wheel, not to mention my inability to reach the brake pedal.

With my mind shut down, I glide Jackson's truck past Montclair Station and continue down Valley Road. Before I know it, I'm circling the multistory parking bay, seeking a free parking spot in the Global Ten Media parking lot. Considering it's a little before three on a Sunday afternoon, it only takes me mere minutes to find a free spot. After parking between a hummer and a sporty BMW, I snag my purse off the seat and slide out of Jackson's truck. While using my coat as shelter from the miserable weather, I dodge my way through native New Yorkers smart enough to grab an umbrella before leaving their residence.

By the time I enter Global Ten Media's foyer, I look like a drowned rat. My hair is damp and clinging to my drenched plain white tee, and my jeans have puddle marks halfway up the calf, but I push on, more determined than ever. My pace is unchecked as I scan my ID in the security system, then make a beeline to the elevator banks. Even gaining the curious glance of the two business-clad riders in the elevator cart doesn't slow my fortitude. I am far from salvage. When it comes to workplace disagreements, I am usually a reasonably placid person. But when I'm forced to protect the people I love, nothing is below me. Not even the possibility of being fired—or even worse, sued!

Delilah's unfortunate receptionist Debbie glances at me, her eyes widening when she notices my tornado-like charge down the elegantly staged corridor. Just like my office, Delilah's workplace has had a drastic uptick in design the past three months. Gone is the ghastly basement office with leaking pipes and mildew smell, replaced with an office space that looks like it should grace the pages of *Home Living*. I'm not at all surprised to discover Delilah is still working late on a Sunday afternoon. You can't have a life if you have no soul.

Ignoring Debbie's advice that Delilah is in a meeting, I swing open her office door. My force is so brutal, her door sails through the air before smashing into the blacked-out privacy glass sheltering her office from the unlucky people working under her supervision.

"You've gone too far this time, Delilah! I may have taken your crap for years, but that shit ends now!"

Hearing my commotion, the large leather chair facing the timeless view of New York swivels to the front. Wearing a midnight black pantsuit and a dark gray ruffled-neck blouse, her small frame is swamped by blackness. *Fitting, considering she is the spawn of Satan.* With a cellphone pushed against her ear, she runs her beady black eyes down the length of my frame. Her gaze is so fierce, the puddle stains on my jeans let off steam.

After advising her caller she will call them back, she locks her slit gaze with me. The pompousness etched on her abhorrent face grows when she notices my split lip. A sturdy concealer and liquid foundation made quick work of the bruise on my cheek, but no amount of makeup can conceal the cut on my mouth.

"*Chloe*, to what do I owe the pleasure?" Delilah slurs her greeting, ensuring I can't miss the incorrect name.

She glares into my eyes, aggravating me with her malicious scowl. Determined to prove her bullying has no effect on me whatsoever, I push off my feet and pace to her desk. The thinness of her eyes grows with every confident stride I take.

"You have ten minutes to fix my sister's health coverage. If you fail to adhere to my request, my next visit will be to Mr. Carson." I cross my arms over my chest, hoisting my erratically panting breasts high into the air. "He made it very clear to me yesterday that your type of intimidation is not acceptable in his company."

Mr. Carson built his company from the ground up with nothing but hard work and honesty. One of the main reasons I wanted to intern at Global Ten Media was because of the values he instilled in his business. He dared to take a risk in an industry he knew nothing about, and within years it was one of the most respected companies in the nation. It was a truly awe-inspiring experience to see a local New Jersey local become so successful. So much so, I gave anything to become a part of it.

For years, Global Ten was known for its integrity, how it chose valor over comfort, and it knew right from wrong. That all changed the instant Global Ten grew too large for one man to helm. With Mr. Carson's role replaced by a twelve-man board, the honor Mr. Carson ingrained into his company slowly slipped. The caliber of stories went from hard-hitting articles based on factual evidence to glossy entertainment pieces blinded by a chokingly hazardous amount of glitter, primarily put there to hide the loosely-based evidence the story was built on.

As the readership Mr. Carson worked so hard to gain dwindled, so did the principles of his company. It went from a vibrant, hip workplace to dull and boring within a year. It has continued its downhill run the past four years. I was hoping Mr. Carson's sudden revival in Global Ten Media's headquarters was the first step to returning Global Ten back to its glory days. Clearly, my entire axis has been off-kilter the past three months, not just my heart.

The corners of Delilah's lips crimp as she struggles to contain her vindictive smirk. "I am sure Mr. Carson will welcome you into his office with open arms, Cleo." Her tone is low and straight to the point. "Would you like me to go with you? Then I can explain to him why I believe your level of health coverage should remain where it is?"

I inwardly gasp, stunned she confirmed my accusation. Usually, she skirts any hostility to her closed-fist governing with blatant lies. She's not once been upfront in the entire time we've worked together. I underestimated this woman. She isn't just the *spawn* of Satan, she *is* Satan.

Taking my stunned silence as agreement, Delilah stands from her chair and walks around her desk. Her head is held high, her nose pointed down. When she stands next to me, I roll my shoulders and extend to my full height, not allowing her nearly six-foot height to swamp my five-foot-five stature.

"Lead the way," I suggest, waving my hand across the front of my body, my tone void of a single snip of hesitation.

Delilah's eyes blaze with contempt. "Give me a few moments to gather some documentation. I'd hate for Mr. Carson to make an ill-informed decision due to lack of evidence."

"What evidence could you possibly have to present? Other than defying his direct order? We had an agreement, Delilah. Global Ten Media was to pay my sister's medical and school expenses for the remainder of her life. Although slapping you was worth a million pennies, it wasn't worthy enough to cease the terms of the agreement I signed with Global Ten three months ago. Unless they want a lawsuit on their hands, they will uphold their end of our agreement."

The condescension in Delilah's eyes grows, as does the pompous smirk carved on her thin lips. She looks like a woman holding a royal flush, little does she know I've already peered at her deck. She has nothing but worthless threats stacking her overused hand.

I jump out of my skin when Delilah unexpectedly shrieks, "Debbie!" Her boisterous roar rockets through my eardrums.

Like magic, Debbie appears at Delilah's side before the ringing of Delilah's loud squeal clears from my ears.

"I need a copy of Cleo's employment contract she signed three months ago," Delilah informs Debbie, her eyes unwavering from mine "Most particularly, section 2.3.2 of her contract."

Delilah waits for Debbie to leave her office before turning her gleaming-with-victory gaze back to me. She glances into my eyes, soundlessly building suspense. The silence makes my skin clammy and my stomach jittery.

Only once the air becomes thick with tension does she say, "Did you bother reading the confidentiality provision of your contract, Cleo? In particular, the indemnification clause?"

Knowing exactly where she is taking our conversation, I nod. "Only a fool would sign a contract without reading the terms."

Delilah steps closer to me, infusing the air with a rich bottled perfume scent. "So you're aware of your legal responsibility for any losses, damages, or expenses, including attorney fees, if you do not adhere to the contract?" Her tone is low—borderline psychotic.

Not waiting for me to reply, Delilah continues speaking, "The repercussions for your failure to adhere to your employment contract will be endless. By the time I'm finished with you, the loss of a few luxuries on your health insurance coverage will be the least of your concerns."

"I haven't breached my contract, Delilah," I respond, shaking my head.

Although last night I disclosed to Marcus I work as a journalist at Global

Ten Media, that information is public knowledge. It does *not* put me in breach of my employment contract.

"I shouldn't be surprised by your failure to thoroughly research a topic, Delilah. You've always had a horrid tendency to jump the gun." I grimace when my words don't come out with the assuredness I am aiming for.

"Cavorting with a man you're investigating may not place you in violation of your contract, but disclosing and tampering with imperative information on a story we are investigating does."

"How have I disclosed or tampered with imperative information?" I retaliate, my pitch rising in anger. "I'd have to know imperative information before I could disclose it. And considering you've spent the last three months treating me as if I am a dumb bimbo without a brain, I don't know a darn thing. My knowledge on the Chains story is as lacking as your grace and dignity. Both are severely overdue for an overhaul."

My rant comes to an end when Delilah sneers, "I know you not only went undercover in the BDSM lifestyle, Cleo, you're immersed in it. As if it isn't disgraceful enough you bowed on your knees, you took it one step further by tampering with classified information. Thus, not only placing your employment status on the line, but also risking your freedom."

I balk, utterly flabbergasted. My lips move as I struggle to issue some type of comeback, but not a peep seeps from my lips. I am wholly stumped for a reply, too confused from deciphering her ill-guided assumptions to formulate a response.

Although I am stunned, that doesn't mean I'll roll over and take every willful blow from Delilah. It's finally time to stand up for myself. And the first person I'll take down is the witch glaring at me in disdain.

"My employee contract clearly states 'the private affairs of an employee should be of no concern to the employer unless they are found to portray the company in a negative light.'"

"Even if I am a part of the BDSM community, Delilah, that does not give you just cause to persecute me. I am well within my rights as a citizen of our great country to participate in any activities I see fit to live a personally fulfilling life."

"You want a quote from your contact?!" Delilah asks, shouting so loud she startles Debbie, who is entering the office. "How about this one? Good sense dictates that you're to steer clear of any groups or activities that will portray Global Ten Media in a compromising role."

She sullenly rakes her eyes down my body, her gaze more derogatory than any I received while on assignment at Chains BDSM Club. It makes my skin crawl and my heart rate quicken.

"Falling to your knees and begging to be beaten certainly detracts from the professional façade you agreed to present by signing your employment contract with Global Ten."

"Professionalism isn't a look, Delilah, it's tact. Something you clearly lack."

Ignoring Debbie's slack-jawed expression, I pivot on my heels and head for the door. For the first time in years, my brain and heart reach an amicable decision. Even battling a war worthy of the history books can't hide the facts. Defending your integrity to a woman who has none is a pointless endeavor. Narcissists don't possess morals.

Just before I exit Delilah's office, I warn, "You have until 4 PM to correct the oversight in my employee contract. If Global Ten Media fails to fulfill the agreement cited in my contract, I will seek the aid of an attorney."

Always wanting the last word, Delilah shouts, "When you're there, have him clarify the legal ramifications for a breach in an employee contract. Particularly how the inability to pay the daily fines sanctioned by the court will result in your remand."

I sling my neck back and glare straight into her eyes. "Tell me one court that will accept misguided intuition as burden of proof?"

"Tell me one BDSM club owner who can afford to go against a multi-billion-dollar company to keep your sorry ass out of jail?" Delilah counters, her voice sadistic. "He must be the most asinine man in the world if he believes you're worth risking everything for. You're no more valuable than a two-dollar hooker."

Although her snarky comment stings my ego, I push on. "Maybe he is foolish enough to believe I am worth the sacrifice. But there will always be another man more foolish than him."

A large crease ruins Delilah's Botox-primed forehead as confusion clouds her nearly black eyes.

"The man who agreed to marry you. There will never be a bigger fool than him," I explain to her puzzled expression.

Delilah's pupils widen, but she fails to issue me a reply. A victorious smirk attempts to etch on my mouth, but I shut it down. Now is not the time to gloat. Although I am confident Delilah doesn't have a leg to stand on, I know from experience she isn't a woman to be underestimated. Just when you think you're out of the firing zone, she produces her final ammunition. It's usually the most lethal of them all.

"If I had discussed or tampered with imperative information on our investigation into Chains with anyone outside of these walls, you'd be well within your rights to cite a breach in my contract. But since nothing like that has occurred, I have no reason to fear prosecution." I inwardly sigh, grateful the hammering of my heart didn't echo in my voice.

Delilah's face turns a vibrant shade of red. I have no doubt anger is blackening her veins, but it doesn't hinder my campaign in the slightest.

"If anyone should be concerned about being witch-hunted by Global Ten Media, it should be you, Delilah, not me. Your name is scribbled alongside mine on every contract I signed. And you can trust me when I say, Global Ten Media's head-chopping starts at the very top rung if they believe their strict policies are not being governed correctly."

"If you think I'll be snared by your idiocy, you have another thing coming," Delilah snarls, her words spitting out of her mouth like venom. "You may have won Mr. Carson over with your poor taste and woeful 'feel sorry for me' storyline, but even he won't put up with such treachery to the company he built from the ground up."

"Just like he won't sit to the side and watch you disgrace the integrity his company's foundation was built on," I fire back.

With that, I exit her office, stealing her chance to reply.

21

After pulling Jackson's truck to the curb of my house, I take a few moments to settle my nerves. Even spending two hours in rush hour traffic hasn't soothed the worry prickling my spine. I've read my employment contract with Global Ten Media numerous times the past three months, so I am confident in saying they have no case against me. But that isn't the cause of my concern. It was what Delilah said about Marcus going up against a billion-dollar company.

Although my relationship with Marcus doesn't put me in breach of my contract, would a jury of my peers see it that way? It's fine to believe honesty always prevails, but when you're in a world where people see lies as rungs on the corporate ladder to success, I must remain vigilant. If I don't keep my I's dotted and my T's crossed, I may unwillingly commit financial suicide. Not just to myself, but Marcus as well.

There is no doubt Marcus is protective of me. The fact he put himself in the line of fire twice in under thirty minutes last night guarantees I'm not mistaken, but that's where my concerns lie. How far would Marcus go to protect me? Would he lose everything he has just to keep me safe? Considering he put his own safety on the line to protect me, the only answer jumping out at me is a resounding yes.

Shutting down Jackson's engine, I exit his truck and trudge up the cracked sidewalk of my house. My pace is slow, weighed down by the uncertainty sitting on my shoulders. I am genuinely at a loss on how to deal with this situation. The simple answer is to walk away from Marcus and pray Delilah never discovers his identity, but that's easier said than done. Just the thought of never seeing Marcus again gnaws at my insides. I also don't see Marcus being a man who will walk away without putting up a fight. The past nine weeks he has expressed his desires for me with confidence many men lack, and I don't see that suddenly going away because I decided to pull the pin on our relationship.

The hum of chatter filters into my ears as I climb the stairs of my front porch. It's an unusual thing to hear. For years, it has only been Lexi and me. Now it feels like we are surrounded by people. Some new. Others old.

The sound of my front door creaking open plunges my house into resolute silence. Not even the sound of a pin dropping can be heard. The quiet amplifies my body's primitive awareness of Marcus. My scalp prickles, and my breathing pans out.

After placing Jackson's keys onto the entranceway table, I stray my eyes to Marcus. They don't need to skim the room to locate him. My body's intuition is the only guide I need to spot him standing at the side of the foyer, silhouetted by the dim lighting of my living room.

Frozen in place, his eyes study every inch of my body, from the roots of my hair to the tips of my toes. His gaze is so powerful, blood rushes to the surface of my skin, making me needy and hot. Once his avid assessment of my body is finalized, his attention turns to my face.

"Cleo."

I don't know why, but his greeting sounds more like a scold than a welcome. He shoves his cellphone into his pocket and heads straight for me.

"Where have you been? You scared us half to death." His tone is a rare mix of bossy and relieved. "You left your cell on the entranceway table. We had no way of contacting you."

"It's broken," I inform him, gesturing my hand to my broken phone.

The scent of freshly laundered clothes loiters in my nose when he draws me into his firm, hard chest. After squeezing the living daylights out of me like he is afraid I am about to vanish, he pulls back and peers into my eyes. The air is drawn from my lungs from the sheer closeness of his handsome face. My god, he is a gorgeous man: plump, decadent lips, perfect facial features, and eyes that set my soul on fire with one passing glance.

Angling his head to the side, Marcus arches his dark brow, expressing that he didn't miss my lust-riddled stare at his gorgeous face. Although he is amused at my inability to rein in my desires around him, his gaze is dominating and strong, the type that would have grown men shaking in their boots. But instead of cowering in fear, my body thrums in anticipation.

It's amazing—*and slightly intimidating*—how Marcus can change my moods so quickly. In less than three heartbeats, I've gone from dreading my future to feeling like I have the entire world at my feet—like nothing can drag me down. How can a man I'm only just unraveling make me so absentminded? I'm not being facetious when I say nothing is on my mind when I am with Marcus. I am completely mindless. No man has ever had that type of power over me. Only Marcus can make me forget the heavy burden I've been carrying on my shoulders the past four years. Only he can award me with so much courage it makes what I am about to do ten times easier.

Balancing on my tippy toes, I seal my mouth over Marcus's decadent lips. A throaty growl rumbles up his chest from my brazenness. He freezes for a second when I nip at his lips, but his naturally engrained dominance soon becomes too great for him to ignore. My knees curve inwards when his tongue slides into my mouth in a long, controlled lick.

Although he dominates the pace of our embrace, I kiss him with all my might, pretending it's my last chance to kiss him, because it very may well be when I tell him we need to cool our relationship until Global Ten's investigation into Chains is over. My kiss expresses everything I wish I could freely tell him, but will most likely never work up the courage to say out loud. I express my fears, desires, and my hope that I could snap my fingers and make the Wicked Witch of the West fly out of town on her evil broom.

Cupping my thighs, Marcus guides my legs around his waist before slipping his hand under the hem of my shirt. I moan, adoring the roughness of his callused fingers scraping across the skin on my back. Each soft stroke of his fingertips firms my excitement more and more.

Stepping forward, Marcus plasters my back on my front door before rolling his hips upwards. A needy moan ripples through my lips when the thickness of his rod runs the seam of my jeans. I grind against him, the desires of my body overtaking the concerns meddling my mind. For just a moment, I forget the world closing in on us and wholly focus on the man who steals the air from my lungs with nothing more than a whisper of my name.

The longer our kiss progresses, the hazier my memories become about why I kissed him to begin with. I wasn't being figurative when I said Marcus makes me forget everything and everyone surrounding us when we are together. I am completely mindless.

Way before I've had my fill, Marcus pulls his scrumptious mouth away from our embrace. While glancing into my eyes, he runs his finger under my bottom lip, clearing away evidence of our lust-driven kiss while checking no irritation was caused to the cut in my mouth. It's the simplest gesture, but it has the biggest impact to my already faltering heart.

I bite on the inside of my cheek, trying to hide the conflicting array of emotions slamming into me before swiveling my hips, soundlessly requesting to be placed down. My efforts are utterly woeful. The instant the first snippet of anxiety passes through my eyes, Marcus spots it. He firms his grip on my thighs, denying my pleas to be put down.

As his brows inch together, his eyes frolic between mine. "Don't let them win, Cleo. You're stronger than you realize."

God—how can he read me so easily?

The reasoning behind Marcus's sudden withdrawal becomes apparent when a voice I immediately recognize hackles, "I take it from your in-depth search, Cleo is uninjured?"

Peering past Marcus's shoulder, I spot Lexi standing at the end of the foyer. She has her shoulder propped against the wall separating the entranceway from the living room. Her manicured brows are waggling, and a massive grin is etched on her adorable face. Embarrassment at being caught grinding up against Marcus like an immature, horny teen doesn't register with my system. I'm too grateful at her healthy-looking appearance to feel anything but glee.

The pain her eyes held during her coughing attack has been replaced with her usual impish gleam, and her breathing appears to be within a safe range.

The chances of her good health remaining intact sail out the window when she locks her eyes with Marcus and says, "You had Cleo nearly crumbling in ecstasy by doing nothing but a measly grind up. You are either a *Master,* or my sister needs to get out more."

My evil death stare glaring at Lexi ends when Marcus throws his head back and laughs. Just like every time I've heard his scrumptious chuckle, it sends my libido haywire. It's husky and deep, a seductive serenade to my throbbing core. His laughter steals my inhibitions even more quickly than his heart-stuttering kisses.

Once his laughter settles down, Marcus's eyes meet mine. The hankering in his heavy-hooded gaze cannot be missed. He glances into my eyes, coercing me into an intangible trap without a word spilling from his lips. I return his devoted stare, my gaze selfish like I've been deprived of peering into his alluring eyes for months.

"I've never been into exhibitionism, but if you keep looking at me like that, Cleo, I may reconsider," Marcus quotes, pushing my libido into unquenchable territory.

I swoon a little from his reply. Not just because I love how easily he can read me, but because I love the way he takes control in the bedroom. I've never been with a man who ensures my every whim is taken care of before his own needs are fulfilled. It's a nice change, one that until two hours ago, I never planned to give up.

I swivel my hips, renewing my pledge to be set down. After tugging my bottom lip away from my menacing teeth, Marcus places me back on my feet. Shockwaves of disappointment pump through me, making it hard for me to breathe. Marcus groans from the loss of my contact as I pace to the coatrack to remove my jacket. Although the air is a little nippy, the nerves making my stomach a horrid mess mean I can forgo a winter coat.

My clammy skin gets extra muggy when I notice two suitcases packed at the side of the living room. One is the suitcase I used when visiting Marcus on Friday, and the other one is from a collection of bags Lexi purchased on sale last year. Although she didn't have a destination in mind, she thought buying luggage was the first step in commencing a love affair with travel. Always eager for her to live her life to the fullest, I encouraged her to spend her hard-earn money on the paisley printed suitcases.

I shift on my feet to face Lexi. "Are you going somewhere?"

Her eyes flick to Marcus for the quickest second before she drifts them back to me. "No." She shakes her head gently. "Jackson has the rest of the week off, but we're just going to hang around here and bask in the silence."

Heavy grooves line my forehead. "Silence?" I mimic, suspicion laced in my tone. "Since when have you enjoyed silence?"

My eyes rocket to Marcus when he explains, "You're coming with me to Ravenshoe, Cleo."

"Ah... no, I'm not," I fire back, my reply mimicking the one I gave him

Thanksgiving night when he demanded my attendance at his residence in New York.

Marcus drops his eyes to an expensive-looking watch on his wrist. "Our plane leaves in an hour, so if you want to check Lexi didn't miss any necessities while packing your bags, do it now before you run out of time," he informs me, acting like he didn't hear a thing I said.

I stand still for a beat, my mouth opening and closing like a fish out of water. It's only when my spent brain processes the entirety of Marcus's statement does my frozen stance thaw. I shift my eyes to my sister, glaring at her with so much anger, steam billows from my ears. I am furious she has once again meddled in my private affairs.

"Don't you dare," Lexi mutters, her tone quivering with unbridled anger. "You've been interfering in my life since I took my first breath!"

I balk, but I come up a little stumped on a reply. I can't deny the truth.

"Ensuring your baby sister lives a fulfilling life isn't meddling, Lexi," I retaliate, my words not coming out as strong as I hoped. "It means I care for you." She attempts to interrupt me, but I keep talking, denying her the chance. "Tell me one time I packed your bags and forced you out of our house against your wishes. If you can, I'll go to Ravens-whatever with Marcus."

I hear Marcus snickering at my reply, but I keep my focus on Lexi, knowing all too well I have her over a barrel. Although my heart is beating triple time at the idea of going away with Marcus, my head has emerged far enough out of his lust haze to know this isn't a good idea. Furthermore, I may have been a little underhanded in my sister-meddling the past four years, but it's never gone to the extremes Lexi is taking it to. This is the second time in a week she has interfered in my private life.

Lexi stares straight into my eyes, her composure unwavering. The confidence beaming from her narrowed gaze sets my nerves on edge. I angle my head to the side and arch a brow, gauging the gleam glowing from her eyes.

Just as recognition dawns, Lexi sneers, "June 2015."

"That was summer camp!"

"So," Lexi responds, her right shoulder lifting into a shrug. "I didn't want to go, but *someone* told me senior camp was a rite of passage into adulthood, and that no teen could forgo the sanction of summer camp." She glares into my eyes, her face mocking.

I huff dramatically. "It was summer camp," I retort again, yelling. "That doesn't count."

"Yeah, it does," Lexi argues while nodding. "You forced me to go to Bumhicksville. Now I'm doing the same thing to you."

I drift my eyes to Marcus, hoping he will back me up. He doesn't. He just smirks, happy to let his little minion do all the heavy lifting in his campaign of forcing me into submission. But he doesn't understand the consequences this could cause him. By associating with me, the chances of his secret being revealed is significantly increased. Thus, not only risking his reputation, but also his illustrious bank balance.

"I can't go with you," I mutter to Marcus, the regret in my tone unmissable.

Marcus fights to hide his disappointment. He fails.

Hating the rejection marring his striking face, I starkly whisper, "They know about us." My voice is riddled with frustration, loathing that I'm allowing a woman like Delilah to dictate our lives.

Marcus shakes his head, the command in his eyes as staunch as ever. "They know nothing, Cleo. Not a single thing," he vows, his deep timbre clear-cut.

I balk, utterly flabbergasted by his confidence. "How can you be so sure? You don't know this woman, Marcus, she is a monster. She won't stop until everyone knows your secret, and I'm living in the gutter." I say my last sentence softly, guaranteeing Marcus won't hear it.

The hairs on my nape prickle when Marcus pushes off his feet and moves to stand in front of me. I gasp in greedy breaths when he peers into my eyes. As I return his ardent stare, my stunned state amplifies. I misread the glint in his eyes. He isn't overly confident or bossy. He's worried. But not about himself. He's concerned about me.

My defenses are knocked out of the park when he says, "If I thought they had a single thing, I wouldn't be here, because I would *never* put you in that predicament." He glances into my eyes, using his honest gaze to bolster his confession.

His eyes float between my marked cheek and cut lip as he mutters, "They are trying to scare you into making a mistake, Cleo. Don't fall into their trap."

My nose tingles as moisture looms in my eyes. "I can't take you down with me, Marcus. I just... can't." *I care about you way too much to let that happen.*

"You have our stories confused. If anyone is taking anyone down, it's me dragging you down, not the other way around," he replies as the corner of his full lips crimps.

I drift my eyes between his. I am more confused than ever.

"The media has been interested in my story for years, way before you stumbled onto your knees in front of me," he advises, his tone as cocky as his facial expression.

If I weren't being strangled with worry, I'd be tempted to wipe the pretentious look off his face. But since my heart is still sitting at the balls of my feet, I leash my goading for a more appropriate time.

"This is different, Marcus. Since I refused to fall to my knees in front of her, Delilah is gunning for blood, and she won't stop until she gets it."

Marcus's eyes flare with anger as his fists ball. I don't know if his anger stems from another person wanting me to kneel before them, or because I'm not taking his assurance I have nothing to worry about at face value.

"I've always been one step ahead of the media, Cleo. That won't change because you work at Global Ten."

"Yes, it will," I interrupt, my voice shaky. "I am legally bound not to discuss any stories Global Ten Media are investigating. If I don't adhere to my contract, they will sue me. I can't afford that. I can barely afford to live as it is." My last sentence comes out in a whisper, ashamed to admit I am drowning in debt.

Marcus's pulse pulverizes my jawline when he cups my face. His thumbs catch my tears before they have the chance to fall. His kind gesture causes more moisture to well in my eyes.

"I would never let that happen to you, Cleo," he vows, confirming my suspicion that he would defend me against prosecution.

Fighting against being snared by his alluring gaze, I mumble, "I can't let you do that. I can't let you fight my battles. This isn't some small press company writing a story full of half-truths. This is one of the biggest media companies in the world. Even a man as wealthy as you would have a hard time going up against them if they sue me."

"Then there's your answer. Don't give them a reason to sue you," Marcus states matter-of-factly, like it's the most natural thing in the world to do.

"And how am I supposed to do that?" I ask, loathing that I'm once again relying on him to make a mammoth decision in my life.

"You come to Ravenshoe as my guest, not as a reporter." Although his tone is stern, his eyes pacify the sting of his words. "We live in the twenty-first century. Money ensures nothing is sacred. So, you can be assured I didn't ask you to come with me to pry confidential information out of you, Cleo. I invited you to my home to show you me, the real Marcus."

Blood gushes into my heart at a faster rate than it can pump it out.

Sensing my wavering constraint, Marcus continues with his ploy. "Your one and only request during our negotiation last week was to know me. I'm trying to uphold my end of our agreement. I can't do that if you defy my every move."

"I do not mean to defy you, Marcus, I just don't want them to destroy you."

His thumbs brush my crimson cheeks as an unidentifiable glint in his eyes grows. "Losing you would gut me more than any story they could muster."

Oh. My. God. My heart just combusted, and every inhibition I've ever had about us vanishes.

"Are you sure this is what you want? This will change everything between us. Not just Global Ten's investigation. *Everything*," I warn, wanting to ensure he understands what this means for our relationship.

If I go home with him, I'll never see our relationship as a standard Dom/sub agreement. If he is hoping we stick to that path, he needs to remove his offer from the table.

Spotting the indecisiveness in his eyes, I say, "If you're doing this because you feel guilty about what happened last night, please don't. You're not responsible—"

My assured speech stops midsentence when Marcus presses his luscious lips against mine. Although I know he is using my attraction to him to his advantage, I can't stop the throaty purr rumbling up my throat when his tongue slides into my mouth in a slow and seductive lick. He samples every inch of my mouth, lapping up any indecisiveness left floating inside. His kiss is so mind-stealing, if I didn't hear the snickering of my baby sister behind me, I'd be tempted to forgo our entire conversation and skip straight to dessert.

After ensuring I am utterly drunk on lust, Marcus pulls his luscious lips away from mine. My shameful whimper causes my sister's small chuckle to break into rapturous laughter. I crank my neck to the side and glare at her, but it doesn't decrease her childish giggles. It increases them. I arch my brow, soundlessly requesting some privacy. Lexi pouts, disappointed by my appeal. My eyes track her shuddering frame as she saunters toward the hallway, her steps dramatically slow.

Incapable of leaving without having the final remark, Lexi jests, "Be sure to text me what vitamins Chains is taking before you leave. I'd hate to miss the opportunity to have my Christmas stocking *stuffed* over and over again while you're away." Her tone is so lewd, not even a saint would miss the innuendo of her request. "Oh, and just a heads up, the entranceway table is a perfect height for settling disagreements on." She locks her devious eyes with Marcus and brazenly winks before exiting the room.

As my eyes rocket to the small wooden table in our foyer, my stomach lurches into my throat. I've never been more pleased for an empty stomach as I am right now.

Marcus draws my attention back to him by tracking his thumb along the throb in my throat. His touch is so tantalizing, Lexi's hyena chuckle bellowing down the hallway fades into the background. In no time at all, I am once again at the complete mercy of Master Chains and his soul-baiting eyes.

"Did that feel like guilt talking, Cleo?" he asks, his voice husky from our hunger-fueled kiss.

Shaking my head, I take a step backward, putting some much-needed space between us before I get snared by his alluring eyes. Seeing my action as defiance, Marcus angles his head to the side before taking a step forward. I hold my hands out in front of my body, advising this isn't a tactic to gain his attention. I genuinely do need space. I can barely breathe when he is in front of me, much less think rationally.

The fire blazing through me combusts when Marcus denies my silent request by taking another step closer to me.

"Stop it," I scold, faking annoyance. I'm not annoyed. I'm far from annoyed. Deep down inside, I'm loving every bit of attention.

Marcus takes another step closer to me. And another. And another. Until the last snippet of air left dangling between us is filled by his impressive frame.

"Defiance only delays the inevitable, Cleo," he mutters, glancing into my eyes.

My god—I forgot how masterful he is. One glance and all coherent thoughts vanish.

"I'm not being defiant, I just need time to think. I can't do that with you right here." I attempt to gesture to the small portion of space between us, but since Marcus is standing so close, I physically can't. "You're too... *beguiling*. I can't think straight when you're close to me."

"You stole the words right out of my mouth, Cleo," he croons, his voice rugged. "That's what you do to me. You have me tangled up in knots, unsure if I'm coming or going. But I must say, I thought that was all part of the process?"

"Process?" I mumble, my brows inching into my hairline.

The unfamiliar glint I spotted in his eyes earlier flares as he replies, "Dating. That's what we are doing, isn't it?"

A highly inappropriately timed smile threatens to etch onto my mouth from the uncertainty smeared in his deep tone. Anyone would swear he is giving a sermon on the sanctity of marriage in a biker bar full of cheating husbands for how uneasy his words are.

Biting on the inside of my cheek to leash my smile, I say, "To be honest, I don't know what the hell this is." I once again attempt to gesture my arm between us. I once again fail. "It's daunting. Scary. Confusing. *Magical.*"

I wasn't meant to say the last word, but I'm glad I did when the most breathtaking, flawless smile I've ever seen etches on Marcus's face. If I didn't already know I am lost to this man, his smile ensures there is no mistake.

"Then let the magic continue, Cleo, in a place where no one will be looking for it," Marcus suggests.

My brows furrow, sending a smattering of wrinkles across my forehead.

"Chains is a New York-based company. No one is looking for its owner in Florida," Marcus advises my bemused expression.

My heart beats triple time. I can't believe I didn't click to this earlier. Is that how Marcus's identity has remained concealed for so long? Because everyone assumes he is a local New Yorker?

I take a moment to consider his suggestion. I come up with the same response time and time again. Although my intuition is telling me to be wary, I've barely lived the past four years, so isn't a little bit of recklessness well overdue? *Yes, it is.*

"Are you sure this is what you want? It won't be a walk in the park."

"The instant you refused to sign our contract, I knew our relationship was never going to be a walk in the park," Marcus interrupts, his tone forthright. "But nothing worth having comes easy."

A snarl curls on my lips. "You should be grateful I didn't sign the contract. Six months with a Garcia woman is a hard limit for any man." I bounce my eyes between his. "Lucky for me, you seem to be determined to discover that the hard way."

I take back my first admission. There is nothing more captivating in the world than Marcus smiling while his mesmerizing eyes blaze with lust. It is like looking at a solar eclipse. You know you shouldn't do it, as your eyes will never recover, but you just can't help but look.

Marcus moves to stand behind me before he flattens his hand on my stomach. I swoon towards him, the hunger for friction on my skin unmissable. Taking advantage of the exposed skin on my neck from my flopped head, he nibbles a trail of kisses from my earlobe to my collarbone.

"I heard what you did to your boss," Marcus discloses, leaning closer to me. A chill of anticipation glides down my back when his lips press up against the shell of my ear. "For someone who says they aren't in the BDSM lifestyle, you sure do defend it a lot."

I try to fire a comeback that I wasn't defending the BDSM lifestyle, I was simply defending the right for people to make their own decisions in regards to their sexual proclivities—BDSM lifestyle or not, but my words stay entombed in my throat when Marcus's teeth tug on my earlobe.

"You don't play fair," I moan, my words barely coherent as I slant my head more to the side, giving him better access to my neck.

"Life isn't fair, Cleo. You just have to take the good and throw out the bad."

The heat of his breath fans my sweat-drenched neck when he draws me back, awarding me the opportunity to feel how aroused he is.

"What happens if the bad is also good?" I mumble, my heightened state projected by my low tone.

My nostrils flare as I gasp in a ragged breath from Marcus's teeth grazing my shoulder. His bite isn't painful, just oddly arousing.

"Then you've got the perfect combination," he groans against my skin before the lash of his tongue eases the sting of his bite.

Once the zing of pain has been replaced with the zap of lust, Marcus mutters, "Spend the week with me, Cleo? Show me the real you. The one no one else gets to see. And in return, I'll do the same."

My heart beats triple time, pleased he is asking me to go away with him instead of demanding my attendance. "I am officially on leave, which means I'm not *technically* investigating any stories for Global Ten Media," I blubber out, working through my concerns out loud.

Marcus's grip on my waist firms, but he maintains a quiet front, neither encouraging or discouraging my thought process. That, in itself, eases some of my anxieties.

I purse my lips. "I've also never been out of the state," I add, my heart using any excuse it can find to convince my brain that this is a good idea.

I feel Marcus's lips curve into a smile on my neck, but his silence remains staunch. After gathering the small snippet of composure I have left from him standing so close, I pull away from our embrace and turn around to face him. The nerves making my skin a sticky mess clear away when my eyes meet Marcus's. His eyes aren't harboring doubts or concerns. They are clear of any encumbrances. All they show is gratitude I am considering his request.

"You want to see me? The real Cleo?" When Marcus nods, I confess, "You've already seen her. You're the only man who has." My declaration comes out unashamed, not the slightest bit confronted that I'm declaring he is the only person who has seen the real Cleo Garcia in a very long time.

"Good. And if I have it my way, I'll be the only man who does."

I sigh as dizziness clusters in my head. "For a guy who doesn't know relationships, you're doing a mighty fine job of making me swoon, Master Chains."

His eyes flare, thrilled by my compliment. "I'm learning. Slowly."

Smiling, I lean in and place a kiss on the edge of his mouth. His dark brows furrow when I spin on my heels and amble down the hall. Compared to twenty minutes ago, my steps aren't weighed down by remorse. They are springy and carefree, much like my attitude which has had a dramatic uptick the past twenty minutes.

My quick strides slow when Marcus's thick, deep voice rumbles down the hall. "Where are you going?" he asks, confusion evident in his tone.

"To pack," I answer, not bothering to spin around. "Supposedly, I have a plane to catch."

When my reply is met with silence, I pivot around to face Marcus. My next step is a little clumsier than the three before it when I see the deliciously scrumptious smile carved on his gorgeous face. Loving my giddy response to his smile, Marcus brazenly winks.

"Ten minutes, Cleo," he warns, his tone as commanding as ever. "Our plane is already on the tarmac waiting for us."

My strides are unstoppable as I continue walking backward. "Has anyone ever told you that you're bossy?"

"Not lately." Marcus's voice is throaty. "The only person I'm striving to impress is usually too busy goading me to inform me of my bossiness."

Although I am excited by his playful banter, I am also eager to erase the cockiness beaming out of him in invisible waves. Stopping halfway down the hall, I say, "Twenty minutes, and I promise not to goad you our entire flight."

Marcus slants his head to the side and cocks a brow. "You want to re-negotiate the terms of our agreement?"

"No," I reply with a shake of the head. "I'm just adding an appendix to our previously arranged agreement."

Marcus smirks. "Alright." He considers my suggestion for a moment before muttering, "Fifteen minutes, and I'll continue to pretend your goading doesn't annoy the hell out of me."

I try to hold in my laughter, but with my entire composure off-skew, my girly giggles jingle down the hall before I can stop them.

"Twenty minutes, and I'll buy you dinner on the way to our flight," I negotiate once my laughter settles down.

"Seventeen minutes, and *I'll* buy *you* dinner," Marcus barters, stepping closer to me.

My brow quirks. "I thought a negotiation was supposed to be about both parties getting what they want?"

"It is." Marcus takes another step closer to me.

I fold my arms under my chest, vainly trying to act unaffected by his prowling steps. It's a pathetic effort.

"How is giving me more time and buying me dinner a good negotiation on your behalf?"

Marcus peers straight into my eyes, his expression deadpan. "I get to make up for the mistakes I made while getting back the curves you lost during our week apart." As he takes another stalking step, his eyes roam appreciatively over my body. "You'll also need to fuel your energy for what I have planned for you."

My knees crash together as lust heats my skin.

Marcus's full lips tug high, smug about my silent response. "Do we have a deal, Ms. Garcia?"

Struggling to clear the eagerness from my voice, I stumble out, "Yes... on one condition."

His prowling steps stop midstride. As he connects his eyes with mine, his dark brow inches higher on his handsome face, interrogating me without a word spilling from his lips.

After I've settled down the wild thrumming between my legs, I barter, "Eighteen minutes, you can buy us dinner on the way and... I get to suck your cock on the plane ride to Florida."

My insides clench in delight when Marcus thrusts his hand out in offering. "You drive a hard bargain, Ms. Garcia, but only a foolish man would turn down an offer like that."

I have no chance of holding in my giddy smile, so I just set it free. After sealing our deal with a shake of our hands, I spin on my heels and race into the hallway. My overworked muscles scream in protest, but a hurricane couldn't slow me down. My excitement is too great to inhibit.

22

Lexi squeals in fright when I barrel into her room, not bothering to knock.

"Over already?" she mocks, her tone thickly doused with wit. "He must have used up all his ammo last night."

I don't bother answering her, my attention is too focused on her bursting-at-the-seams wardrobe to configure an appropriate response.

"Florida is still warm this time of the year, right?" I ask, yanking open the two doors of her closet.

When she nods, I mumble, "Great."

Her eyes bulge when I spread my hands three feet apart, launch them into her closet and pluck as many of her clothes as I can from their hanging spot in one fell swoop.

"Not my vintage Indian hipster dress," Lexi grumbles when she spots her favorite summer dress sitting on top of the twenty or so outfits I harvested from her wardrobe.

My steps out of her room grind to a halt when I see the devastated mask slipping over her face. "I either borrow half your summer wardrobe or stay here. The choice is yours." I perk my lips and pivot on my heels. "I guess I could stay and hang out with you and Jackson the rest of the week. Since I'm on an unknown amount of leave, I've got nothing better to do with my time." My mouth forms into an O as my eyes widen. "We could borrow the *Notebook* from Ms. Rachet. I'm sure I saw it in her collection of DVDs last month."

Lexi dives off the bed, her pace so frantic, she ripples the air. Clasping the tops of my shoulders, she spins me to face the door and barges me towards it.

"I love you, Cleo—so much so, I drew a gun on a man I thought was hurting you—but an entire week of you meddling in my love life is more than I could handle," she groans, reacting precisely as I had hoped.

My mouth gapes when the entirety of her sentence is deciphered by my lust-fuzzy brain. I dig my feet into the carpet, thwarting her attempts to shove me out of her room. Although we have identical features, I'm a little curvier than Lexi and two inches taller, which means her small frame and lack of height has her at a disadvantage.

Huffing, Lexi drops her arms from my shoulders and crosses them over her chest. I adjust my grip on her clothes before turning around to face Lexi. Her eyes are wide and bright, and her lips are curled into a smirk, but I know she is aware of my sudden change in plans. Her eyes are as telling as mine. They are the gateway to her soul.

"Your *love* life?" I ask, my interest highly notable. If her throat didn't work hard to swallow, I wouldn't have believed she heard my question.

"You're in love?" I push on, ignoring her malicious glare warning me against prying into her private affairs. "Come on, Lexi. I'm not leaving until you spill the beans, so you may as well get it over with."

Her glare turns evil, charring my soul from the inside out. But I push on, more determined than ever. "Are you in love?"

Lexi waits a beat before barely whispering, "Yes."

If I didn't see her lips move, I wouldn't have known she'd spoken.

"I love him, goddammit!" She locks her packed-with-panic eyes with me while muttering, "And it's scaring the shit out of me."

I squeal, startling Lexi so much she flinches. Dumping her clothes onto the floor, I charge for her. Her delightful giggle overtakes my girlish squeal when we flop onto her bed before rolling onto the floor with a loud thud.

"I can't believe you didn't tell me," I mutter in shock. I shouldn't be surprised, though. I've been so tied up in Marcus the past two months, I wouldn't have noticed if the world was coming to an end.

"I can't believe you didn't notice," Lexi fires back, her voice void of its earlier panic. "How do you think I recognized the glint in your eyes last week?" She bounces her loved-up gaze between mine. "Because I've been denying the same gleam the past four weeks."

Blood oozes into my heart, beyond smitten my little sister has fallen in love. "Does Jackson know?" I ask, unashamed of my prying.

Lexi's eyes flick to the door, ensuring we are void of any nosy spectators before she shakes her head. "I nearly blurted it last night. I could have been forgiven for that one, though. I don't care if you have a heart made out of stone, when you're riding your third orgasm for the night, anything that leaves your mouth can be excused."

Pretending she didn't just share way too much information, I curl my arms around her shoulders and give her a tight squeeze. "I know this isn't something you wanted, but if it makes you feel any better, you couldn't have picked a more perfect man to fall in love with. Jackson is a wonderful guy. Caring, sweet—"

"Great in the sack," Lexi interrupts while waggling her brows.

Laughing, I reply, "I guess I'll have to take your word on that."

My heart bursts when Lexi's eyes narrow into a scowl. I've never seen her get jealous over a guy before.

I gather the arsenal she is throwing out, storing it for a more appropriate time before saying, "Jackson is a great guy, Lexi. You should tell him how you feel. Then he can reciprocate it."

Lexi takes a moment considering my suggestion. Her lips are pursed into a considerate pout, and her brows are stitched. Heat blooms across my chest when she nods a few minutes later, agreeing with my advice.

"What about you? Are you going to tell Marcus how you feel?" she queries, adjusting her position so she is facing me head on.

I grimace. "Things are a little different between us."

Lexi doesn't need to ask for clarification. Her eyes speak on her behalf.

"The BDSM lifestyle isn't about love, it's about sexual compatibility," I explain, the hammering of my heart echoing in my tone.

"Which you guys have in abundance," Lexi inputs, her tone more heartfelt than usual.

I nod, supporting her assessment. "But Marcus has unambiguous rules stipulated in our contract. Love is notably absent. That isn't part of our agreement."

"I thought you didn't sign the contract?" Lexi probes as her brows inch together.

"I didn't," I respond, my tone low.

Lexi quirks her lips. "So what's the problem? He stayed with you last night knowing you haven't signed the contract. He invited you to go home with him, once again, knowing you haven't signed the contract. I also heard what he said to you out there," she says, nudging her head to her door. "Maybe he wants more than just a contractual agreement as well? Have you ever thought of that?"

"Yes," I whisper. "He just mentioned something about us dating," I admit, chewing on my bottom lip.

Lexi's brows hit her hairline. "Well, there you go."

I grimace. "It was sweet, but I am afraid if he finds out I'm falling in love with him, he will leave. A BDSM lifestyle is all Marcus knows. It's easier for him, and a whole heap less complicated. Once he reached his quota with his previous subs, he moved on without a hesitation."

My heart clenches in my chest. It hurts a lot more admitting your feelings out loud than bottling them up inside.

"Life is complicated, Cleo, you know that better than anyone," Lexi mutters, her voice more mature than her twenty-one years. "Remember what Daddy always said, 'there is an exception to every rule.'" She waits for me to nod before adding on, "When Chains pulled you behind him last night, I saw the fear that crossed his face. You're his exception, Cleo, whether he likes it or not."

After brushing a stupid sentimental tear from my cheek, I place a kiss on Lexi's temple and pull her into my chest. My dad was as wide as he was tall, and he had a heart that matched his size. He was a wonderful man who taught us that love isn't just about flowers, compliments, and regular dinner dates. It's about respect and understanding and putting the needs of others before yourself. That was what I was trying to do with Marcus earlier. I was trying to give him up to save him. But no matter how hard I tried, my selfish heart couldn't let him go.

Lexi and I stay huddled together for several minutes, comforting each other in a way she pretends she despises, but inwardly adores. Once I've secured enough sisterly love to get me through the week, I pull back from our embrace. The tightness crushing my chest eases when I lock my eyes with Lexi. Her gaze is just as cheeky and determined as ever.

"Are you sure you're okay staying here? It doesn't feel right leaving you after your attack this morning."

Lexi gasps out a whine. "Shut up, Cleo," she demands sternly. "I don't need any more lectures on *my* condition. I've had enough. First Jackson, then Chains, now you." She loudly gags, showcasing our variance in maturity isn't just based on our difference in age. "I have an appointment with Dr. Spencer first thing tomorrow morning. Jackson is driving me there himself."

"Okay, good. I'll transfer some money into his account tonight," I blabber while attempting to recall how much Dr. Spencer's appointment cost and praying I'll have enough to cover the expense.

Lexi rolls her eyes. "Jackson doesn't need your money, but even if he did, it wouldn't be necessary. A lady named Debbie called not long before you arrived home. She blubbered something about my health coverage being returned to its previous level?" Confusion is evident in her low tone.

My heart rate surges as my jaw gapes. I did it. I made the Wicked Witch yield.

Not giving me the opportunity to voice my excitement at her admission, Lexi stands from the ground and gathers her clothing left strewn on the floor. My backside protests about sitting on the rock-hard surface when I move to assist her. Although Lexi's eyes put up a protest to me borrowing her clothes, she hands me the extensive collection she amassed from the floor.

"Thank you," I praise, accepting the dresses from her grasp. "For everything," I add, my exhilaration at finally making head waves with both Delilah and Lexi's health portrayed in my high tone.

"You're welcome." Lexi's voice is doused with sentiment, mistaking my praise as thanks for borrowing her clothes. "It's about time you let me contribute to our relationship. As Daddy always said, 'one-sided partnerships never work. They all require a bit of give and take.'"

I hug her with as much gusto as her words awarded me with before heading for the door.

"My cell is broken, so I'll FaceTime you ... a minimum three times a day."

The small smile on my face breaks into a full-toothed grin when Lexi groans at my disclosure. My brisk pace stops halfway out of Lexi's room when the hairs on my arms bristle and my breathing shallows. There is only one person my body responds to in this manner. *Marcus.*

Suppressing the unease creeping up my windpipe, I continue my journey.

Just as my body intuited, I discover Marcus standing right outside Lexi's room. From the way his brows are furrowed and his intensely beautiful eyes are clouded with anxiety, I know he overheard my conversation with Lexi. He looks the most fretful I've ever seen him.

I attempt to fire some reassurance that he doesn't need to be panicked about my declaration of love, but not a syllable escapes my lips. I like to pretend I'll be perfectly fine when it comes time for us to go our separate ways, but, in all honesty, it will kill me. Our week apart saw me at my lowest, I don't know if I will survive it a second time.

Some of the dread thickening my veins gets a moment of reprieve when Marcus questions, "Are you ready, Cleo?"

I stare at him, surprised he still wants me to go with him when he knows I'm breaking one of his most essential rules of a D/s relationship: no falling in love.

A large chunk of the agitation in his eyes vanishes when I bob my head. His pleased response soothes the churning of my stomach.

"Let me grab my cosmetics bag, and I'll be good to go."

Marcus locks his knee-weakening gaze with mine. "Hurry, Cleo, you only have thirty seconds remaining before your agreed time runs over." He steps closer to me, enveloping me in his freshly laundered scent. "If you negotiate a term and fail to adhere to the terms stipulated during the negotiation process, some form of punishment must be issued."

Snubbing the way his threat increased the excitement pooling between my legs, I race into my bathroom to secure my makeup bag. Even though I appear frantic, I'm mentally counting down the remaining thirty seconds of our agreement, guaranteeing there is no chance I will leave this bathroom before the agreed time on our negotiation lapses.

Marcus's presence may make me heedless, but it doesn't make me reckless enough I'd miss out on the opportunity of being awarded one of his punishments.

23

Since no one is expecting to see a world-famous celebrity drive through a local Montclair burger joint, our commute from my home to a private airstrip in New York is done without incident. Although Marcus's flashy-looking car was enough to encourage curious glances in Montclair, once we melded into the sea of millions traveling to New York, his car became one of many high-valued vehicles rolling over the asphalt.

Just like he did last week, Marcus drives us to our location. I find it surprising a man of his stature doesn't have a fleet of drivers at the ready. Don't get me wrong, I'm not complaining. The visual of Marcus driving a high-performance car will incite wicked dreams for years to come. I'm just stunned he doesn't use his celebrity status to its full advantage. Driving in New York is a challenge for even the most skilled drivers. I avoid it at all cost.

Diverting my perverted gaze away from the way Marcus's cut arms flex as he shifts down the gears, I move them to peer out the window. The greasy burger I consumed during the drive feels heavy in my stomach when my eyes lock in on a private jet idling on the isolated tarmac. It's white in color and has extremely dark tinted windows. When Marcus pulls his car a few feet away from the jet, a fleet of men in black suits move out of the airport hangar on my right, their sole focus on Marcus clambering out of his car.

I'm silenced by shock when Marcus throws his keys to one of the men scampering to follow his every command, while another aides in removing his coat. Once the unnamed middle-aged man has Marcus's suit jacket folded over his arm, Marcus moves to my side of his car to assist me out. I blush, incredibly pleased by his chivalry. Our whole scene is the type you'd expect to see in a blockbuster Hollywood movie. It thrusts Marcus's wealth into my face, but in a giddy, I can't help but be excited type of way.

After removing my hazardously packed luggage from the trunk, Marcus's sports car glides into the hangar to be stored until his return. My knees clang together with excitement when we climb the small set of stairs leading us to the galley of the jet. Enthusiasm isn't oozing out of my pores because it's my first time in a plane, much less a private jet. It's because Marcus hasn't relinquished his firm hold on my hand the past ten minutes. I thought the instant we secured the curious gaze of the people surrounding us, he'd be yanking his hand away. He doesn't. He keeps his hand curled around mine, making me feel more valuable than the expensive plane we are entering.

"Wow," I mumble, no longer capable of holding in my excitement. My eyes eagerly drift over the highly polished wooden cabins and pristinely clean galley. "This is beautiful."

After we make our way down the thin aisle, I use my spare hand to fiddle with the buttons on my well-worn winter coat Marcus returned with my luggage. With the heating system set to a scorching temperature, sweat is beading on my nape.

Just outside the open cockpit door, I release my grip on Marcus's hand, wanting to remove my shrugged-off coat bundled around our joined wrists.

"Thank you," I praise when Marcus assists me in removing my coat before handing it to a man standing on his right. My brows scrunch, astonished the pilot has been downgraded to a coat clerk when he stores my jacket into a small closet concealed by his broad shoulders.

"Have all the preflight checks been done?" Marcus asks the man who just housed my coat.

The man nods, sending a strand of blond hair falling into his eyes. "Yes, everything is buttoned up, and the flight is ready for pushback," he answers, handing Marcus a set of papers to peruse.

"Precipitation?" Marcus queries, his eyes remaining arrested on the documents in his hand.

The unnamed man in his early to mid-thirties lifts his shoulder into a shrug. "The aeronautical charts show a little bit of activity around Philadelphia, but nothing that will alter our flight plan."

"Good. I don't want to get stuck in a holding pattern like we did last week." Marcus hands the documents back to the man. "Give me five minutes to get Cleo settled, Cameron, then we will get this bird into the air."

Cameron smiles a blazing grin. "I'll run some last-minute checks while you iron your kinks," he chuckles with a wink.

After slapping Marcus on the back, he strides into the cockpit, his steps boastful and full of assurance. Marcus waits for Cameron to be out of earshot before turning his eyes to me. The instant our eyes lock and hold, the excitement caking my skin with sweat catapults to a new level. Hearing him talk pilot jargon with Cameron was a thrilling experience, but it can't compete with the confident control his eyes are carrying now.

"Do you want a drink? Something to eat?" Marcus questions.

Not waiting for my reply, he signals for the attention of one of the two female flight attendants watching our exchange from afar.

A lanky blonde with vibrant red lipstick arrives at his side like magic. "Yes, Mr. Everett?"

"Can you get Ms. Garcia some reading material from the galley? Perhaps a drink and some light refreshments," Marcus instructs her.

The flight attendant quickly masks her alarm at Marcus's demands, but she wasn't quite fast enough for me to miss her flabbergasted response.

"Yes, certainly, Mr. Everett," she replies, her tone high. She drifts her massively dilated eyes to me. "Is there anything particular you'd like to eat, Ms. Garcia?"

Raising my brow at the way she snarled my name, I shake my head. "If it isn't too much of a bother, a bottle of water would be lovely, Ms..." I leave my sentence, hoping she will fill in the blanks.

She doesn't. She just pivots on her heels and makes her way back to the galley of the plane, her dramatic saunter amplified by the swing of her tiny hips. I turn my eyes back to Marcus. I don't need to ask if he felt the tension teeming out of the sassy blonde, the tick impinging his jaw is all the indication I need that he spotted her uncalled-for bitchiness. I haven't done anything to her—*I don't even know her*—so her rude response is entirely unnecessary.

Suddenly, my breathing halts as an overwhelming bout of nausea spreads through me.

"She isn't an ex-sub of yours, is she?"

My lungs start working again when Marcus utters, "No."

I don't need to check his eyes for deceit, the disgruntled look on his face answers the rest of my silent interrogation. If his facial expression wasn't compelling enough, any doubt left lingering dissipates when he locks his eyes with mine and mutters, "I've never fancied blondes."

Although I should be disgusted by the nonchalance of his reply, I'm not. The two female flight attendants are gorgeous in their own rights, but not once since we entered the plane has Marcus glanced in their direction. The only time his eyes weren't rapt on me was when they were scanning the flight reports Cameron handed him. My confidence has never been so high.

"Maybe you should let her know you're not interested, then she might stop fawning for your attention," I suggest, nudging my head at the blonde standing at the end of the aisle, eyeballing our exchange with jealousy in her narrowed green eyes.

When she notices I've spotted her indiscreet glare, she pushes off her feet and saunters down the aisle. Her grip on the bottle of water so tight, I'm surprised her manicured nails haven't busted the plastic.

"I could talk to her." Marcus draws my focus back to him. "Or I could just show her I'm not interested," he continues as he floats his heavy-lidded gaze between mine.

Before I have the chance to seek clarification on his suggestion, he bands his arms around my back, dips me, then seals his mouth over mine. His mouth has no chance of capturing the girly squeal reverberating up my chest, beyond stoked at his brilliant methodology. Not only does his brazen move stop the blonde in place, it also stops my vehement jealousy from rearing its ugly head.

By the time Marcus pulls away from our embrace, my panties are soaked, and the blonde is nowhere to be found. As his lust-hazed eyes bore into mine, Marcus runs his thumb over my arched brow. He looks cocky and smug, like nothing will bring him down.

Determined to quell his cockiness, I drag his mouth back to mine by the back of his head and reacquaint our lips. I kiss him with everything I have, striving to make him as mindless as he makes me.

"Growing impatient, Ms. Garcia?" He smiles against my mouth.

Ignoring the stern cough attempting to interrupt us, I reply, "Yes. Always."

I kiss him for several more minutes, not the slightest bit concerned we are holding up the flight crew with our heavy PDA.

Only once I'm confident I have him in a tizzy do I regretfully pull away from our embrace. If I don't stop our heated exchange now, it may never end.

"God you make me want to bend the rules," Marcus mutters. "You make me so reckless, Cleo. So goddamn reckless."

I smile, grateful my ploy to unravel him was effective. With his hand on the small of my back, Marcus guides me into the cockpit we are standing next to. "Would you mind sharing your co-pilot position on our flight today, Cameron? I've got a new co-pilot I'd like to test out."

The stunned expression on Cameron's face morphs onto mine when Marcus nudges his head to me.

"W-what?" I stammer out as my excitement is overrun by nerves. "Cameron is the pilot of our flight, isn't he?"

I know I sound like a fumbling idiot, but my reaction can't be helped. My brain is already lacking oxygen from Marcus's soul-stealing kiss that I'm barely standing upright, let alone lucid enough to sort through the confusion bombarding me.

I can barely breathe when Marcus shakes his head. It isn't his denial of my assumption that has me gasping for air, it is the breathtakingly beautiful smile stretched across his face.

Using my shocked state to his advantage, he grips my elbow and directs me toward a flimsy-looking seat at the back of the cockpit. Blood rushes to the surface of my skin when he lowers me into my chair before fiddling with the straps.

"Oh... I don't need to sit in the cockpit. I'm more than happy to sit in the regular seating."

My words stop when Marcus digs his hand between my jean-covered crotch to secure the metal harness sitting between my legs. My pussy pulses as sexual hunger overtakes some of my panic. Hearing my shameful gasps, Cameron strays his eyes from a range of instruments and buttons on the cockpit panel to me. After drinking in my blemished cheeks and massively dilated eyes, he drops his gaze to Marcus, who is crouched between my legs.

"Would you like me to first-pilot our flight today, Marcus?" Cameron queries, the worry in his tone increasing the panic making me a muted mess.

"No, thank you," Marcus responds, his tone direct.

"Are you sure?" Cameron argues, his response as stern as Marcus's. "Cleo is a striking young lady, so the potential of you becoming distracted is immense. I'm already distracted by her, and I'm not trying to keep a plane 30,000 feet in the air."

My eyes rocket to Marcus, who is scowling at Cameron. I don't know if he is glowering at him as he doesn't appreciate being challenged, or because Cameron said I am beautiful.

Reading the silent wrath pumping out of Marcus, Cameron holds his hands out in front of his body. "Alright, you win," he mutters under his breath before taking the seat on the left-hand side of the cockpit. "Just don't say I didn't warn you when we're plunging back to earth in a fiery deathtrap."

I swallow several times in a row, aiming to ease the burn scorching my throat.

After snapping together the latches on my four-point harness, Marcus lifts his eyes to me. The air sucks from my lungs from the sheer closeness of his gorgeous face. My god, this man is handsome—even when scowling. If he hadn't just strapped me into my seat, I'd be tempted to ease the heavy groove between his eyes with another impromptu kiss.

The throb between my legs grows when Marcus gathers the straps of my harness in his hand and yanks them down hard. The pinch of the stiff material on my shoulders adds to the dampness coating my panties. The curve of his lips tells me he didn't miss my soft moan.

"Are you ready, Cleo?"

Any panic left lingering in my mind is shoved to the side when I see the confidence in his eyes. He has proved time and time again the past few days that he won't let anything happen to me, so I am not the slightest bit concerned about Cameron's mumbled statement.

I pant, inconceivably aroused by the dominance in his heavy-hooded gaze. "As ready as I will ever be, Master Chains," I whisper ever so quietly, ensuring there is no chance Cameron would hear me.

The hankering in Marcus's eyes grows tenfold. After running the back of his fingers down my flaming cheek, he stands from his crouched position. I lick my lips when the crotch of his pants is thrust in my peripheral vision. Seeing his trousers struggling to contain his erection reminds me of our earlier negotiations.

"How come you negotiated a term in our agreement you knew you couldn't fulfill?"

Marcus slides into the pilot's seat of the cockpit before turning his eyes to me. Now I know why he seated me behind Cameron. From his position, he will be able to watch me from the corner of his eye the entire flight.

"Even self-chartered pilots need a bathroom break," he responds, his voice sliding through me like liquid ecstasy. "It's a pity you didn't uphold your end of our negotiation. I was very much looking forward to cashing in your guarantee."

Cameron mumbles a reply to Marcus's bold statement, but it's drowned out by the jet's engines roaring to life. The vibration buzzing through my seat adds to the tingle of my soaked sex. Marcus puts on a set of headphones before he cranks his neck to peer above my shoulder. Following his gaze, I find a set of similar-looking headphones hanging on a hook just above my head.

After twisting my hair into a side braid, I slip the headphones over my ears. The thump of my pussy doubles when Marcus's seductive voice sounds through the headphones not even two seconds later.

"Cabin crew, prepare for takeoff," he instructs them.

He fiddles with some instruments in front of him before saying, "Rochester Clearance. Tampa straight one four three ready to copy IFR to Ravenshoe."

A crackle sounds over the line before a female voice replies, "Tampa straight one four three, cleared to Ravenshoe via radar vectors to Clost Island then as filed. Fly runway heading. Climb and maintain thirty-six thousand feet. Expect 89 minutes after departure. Departure on 120.8, squawk 1252."

Marcus recites the information back to the traffic controller before it switches to a recorded message updating him on the current weather conditions.

After a few minutes, the jet judders forward. My eyes go frantic, drifting between Marcus and the tarmac as the plane starts taxiing toward the runway.

"Rochester ground, Tampa straight one four three ready to taxi IFR, with Sierra," Marcus articulates down the line.

"Tampa straight one four three clear whiskey to two-niner," the air controller replies.

As the jet rolls down the tarmac, nothing but static sounds down the line. The silence enhances the crackling of energy filling the air with muggy heat. It's nearly as compelling as the bristling energy that bounces between Marcus and me during bouts of silence.

When we reach the end of a long strip of tarmac, Marcus turns his gaze to me. My brows scrunch when he holds out a sheet of paper. Ignoring the rattle encroaching my hands, I accept the article from his grasp. Electricity zaps up my arms when our fingers touch for the briefest moment. My eyes rocket to Marcus. From the way his eyes are dilated, I have no doubt he too felt the current of electricity surging between us.

"When you're ready, read what's printed on the card," he instructs, his words barely audible through my headphones since he has switched off his mic.

I drop my eyes to the card, noticing it has a set of flight instructions scripted onto it. Just like the man who wrote it, his handwriting is stunning. It's elegant and refined, a true replica of the man who wrote it.

Too excited to express words, I lift my eyes back to Marcus, smile, then nod.

After taking a few moments to settle the nerves in my voice, I recite the instructions written on the card. "Rochester ground, Tampa straight one four three ready for takeoff IFR, runway two-niner."

"Good girl," Marcus mouths when my words come out with a confident decree.

A massive grin stretches across my face. I've never ridden in an airplane before, much less aided in its takeoff.

"Tampa straight one four three, winds two eight zero at fourteen, cleared for takeoff," the air controller announces, agreeing with my request for takeoff clearance.

After giving me a flashy wink, Marcus returns his focus to the tarmac. The pants of my breath double as the jet engines roar to full power. I wring the hem of my shirt around my fingers as we glide down the tarmac at a faster rate than my excitement is building. Our speed increases and increases until the tires of the jet have no other choice but to lift away from the tarmac.

An incredible whoosh hits my stomach when the jet takes off into the clear blue sky. My excitement is so bountiful I can't help but release a little squeal.

"Rochester ground, Tampa straight one four three, two thousand, climbing to thirty-six," Marcus advises with laughter in his voice, his jittery tone telling me he didn't miss my excited squeal.

"Four thousand feet, climbing to thirty-six."

Marcus continues updating the traffic controller of our ascent until we reach 36,000 feet.

Once we are nothing but a little blip in the beautiful blue sky, the female air traffic controller guiding our departure says, "Tampa straight one four three, contact Oakland Centre on 127.8."

"127.8 for Tampa straight one four three, good day," Marcus replies.

Inanely grinning, I fold up the sheet of paper and slip it into pocket of my jeans before swinging my eyes to the awe-inspiring scenery outside. The sky is the bluest I've ever seen. Other than a small smattering of white clouds floating by, it's utterly faultless. I've only ever seen one thing more fascinating in my twenty-six years: Marcus's captivating green irises.

"It so beautiful up here."

"It is," Cameron agrees, his voice as emotion-packed as mine.

The hairs on my arms prickle when Marcus's deep timbre sounds through the headphones. "Have you ever wondered what heaven looks like, Cleo?"

I don't need to look at him to know I have secured his utmost devotion. I feel it in every essence of my soul. As my eyes wander away from the panorama the world's best painter couldn't replicate, I nod. Just as I suspected, Marcus's eyes are steadfast on mine.

"I couldn't think of a better spot to look down on the people I love," he continues, nudging his head to the breathtaking scenery surrounding us. "I think this is as close to heaven as you can get."

"It's perfect." I keep my eyes fixated on Marcus. "You're perfect."

Now I understand why he was so adamant on wanting me to sit in the cockpit. He wanted me to experience this flight in a way like no other. It wouldn't matter if you had a heart as black as Delilah's, you could never look at this pristinely beautiful sky and not think of the people you love. It's too compelling to be brushed off as anything less than miraculous. He knew it would give me a little bit of closure in my grief—*a little bit of peace*.

Overwhelmed by the unexpected emotions streaming through me, a rogue tear glides down my cheek. I quickly brush it away, not wanting Marcus to see it. Although I was quick, I have no doubt he saw it. It isn't just his rapid exhale of air that gives it away, it's the spark of compassion in his eyes.

After ensuring my eyes are moisture-free, I lock them with Marcus. "Thank you." I only mimed two short words, but my soul-baring eyes relay so much more.

Smiling in a way that steals the air from my lungs, Marcus replies, "This is only the beginning."

24

I've barely had time to contain my first lot of excitement when Marcus begins preparing the plane for landing. I've been in complete awe the eighty minutes of our flight, I didn't bother unlatching my seatbelt. I'm not going to lie. My panties are the most saturated they have ever been. I knew from the moment I slid into the back seat of Marcus's Bentley that he would be a man I could marvel at for days. But I had no clue his abilities stretched this far. Tell me one girl you know who hasn't had a fantasy of getting down and dirty with a pilot. Now imagine discovering that pilot is also a dominant rock star?

Yeah, my panties are soaked for a reason.

After landing the plane with the same amount of expertise he flew it with, Marcus removes his headset and clambers out of his seat. I attempt to mimic his movements. I hang my headset on the hook above my head before dropping my hands to my belt. Since excitement is thrumming every nerve in my body, I'm all thumbs, meaning I can't unlatch the harness from its firm grip.

Spotting my pitiful attempts at releasing myself, Marcus stops his post-flight checks with Cameron and moves to assist me.

"Thank you." My enthusiastic praise shamefully exposes my aroused state. I've never been more turned on in my life.

The chances of leashing my unbridled horniness are nonexistent when Marcus connects his heavy-hooded gaze with me. His eyes expose that he is battling the exact same fight.

After cranking his neck to Cameron, Marcus asks, "Are you okay to complete post-flight checks?"

Cameron balks, seemingly stunned by his requests. It's only after his confused eyes dance between Marcus and me does reality dawn.

Smiling, he responds, "Sure. It's nothing I can't handle if you've got plans."

Once my hand is gripped in his, Marcus strolls down the corridor at a faster rate than my legs can move. Although we're moving at a speed faster than light, I don't miss the angry snarl of the pretty blonde flight attendant.

Unable to leash my inner bitch, I cockily wink at her, ensuring she doesn't underestimate what I am planning to do to Marcus the instant we get away from her eagle eye.

You'll be a forgotten memory in under a second.

I plan on imprinting myself onto his soul for eternity.

Warm winds whip up my hair when we descend the six stairs from the flight deck. Just like in New York, a crew of men emerge from a hangar when they spot Marcus moving towards them. Faster than I can blink, a set of keys are thrown through the air. Marcus is handed a pristinely laundered suit jacket, and I'm aided into the passenger seat of a very flashy-looking sports car with its doors hanging high into the air.

It's lucky I am wearing jeans, or the low structure of this car would have indecently exposed inches of my skin. My spine straightens as disappointment consumes me. *If I weren't wearing jeans, this ride could have been an entirely new experience as well.*

Swallowing down my disappointment, I watch Marcus jog around to the driver side and slide into his seat. My heart is fitfully beating in my chest, and my brow is slicked with sweat. I can't remember the last time I was so consumed by such unbridled hankering.

I writhe in my seat, utterly unashamed that my squirms have gained me the inquisitive stares of the men surrounding us. That's truly outstanding. Not once in my twenty-six years have I failed to stop and evaluate the opinions of the people around me.

Identifying the glimmer in my eyes for what it is, Marcus asks, "Growing impatient, Cleo?"

"Whoever created the whole 'delayed gratification notion' should be hung by his testicles."

His laugh slides through my body like molten lava, activating every one of my hot buttons. "What makes you so sure it was a man?"

I shoot him a wry look. "No woman would ever be so cruel. We are nurturers, not sadists."

"I beg to differ. You clearly haven't seen Shian in her element if you believe women can't dish out punishment."

My eyes rocket to him, certain I didn't hear him right. Astonishment mars my face when I spot the honesty in his forthright gaze. Although I am not entirely sideswiped at discovering Shian is a Domme, I'm still in awe that she has enough vigor to fight for what she wants in a very male-dominated field. I can only hope to be as strong-willed as her one day.

Intuiting my inner monologue, Marcus says, "Don't get any ideas, Cleo. Although I'm tempted to have you top me, it will only be while you're riding my cock. I don't plan on switching things up permanently."

The deep rasp of his voice adds to the slickness between my legs. Unable to speak through my parched, gaped mouth, I shamefully nod, approving his assessment of our situation. I have no intention of topping him. What I said last night was true: I love being dominated by him. And I don't have any plans on changing that in the near future.

"Please tell me your house isn't an hour away?"

"Depends," Marcus replies.

I purse my lips. "On what?"

I jump out of my skin when the wing-like doors of Marcus's car are closed. After gathering my heart from the floor, I return my focus to Marcus. Being trapped in a small two-seater vehicle with him makes the sexual chemistry zapping between us even more prominent. It crackles and hisses in the air, overtaking the loud rumble of his engine when he fires up the ignition of his slick sports car.

Marcus's eyes connect with mine. His heavy-lidded gaze spears me in place. "On how much you trust me," he mutters, his voice so lusciously scrumptious. "Do trust me, Cleo?" he breathes out slowly, spurring a set of goosebumps to race to the surface of my skin.

"Yes," I respond immediately, not needing time to deliberate a response. "I trust you."

Smiling a grin that makes the entire world disappear, Marcus devotes his attention to the road in front of him. Gas fumes stream through my nostrils when he plants his accelerator to the floor. The tires of his car fail to gain traction on the tarmac for several moments before we go whizzing towards a side entrance manned by a large black security truck that resembles a tank. When the two burly security officers sitting inside spot Marcus's car rapidly approaching, they scurry to open the chain-link fence they are positioned next to.

After dipping his chin in thanks, Marcus pulls his car onto the highway. I'm thrust into my chair, his speed as out-of-control as my rampant horniness. He weaves his vehicle through the dense flow of traffic surrounding us with the same dominance he exerts in his playroom. It's a confident control that ensures not a smidgen of concern enters my mind, a control that sends my libido skyrocketing.

The reasoning behind his erratic speed comes to light when my vision is suddenly assaulted by flashing lights. I lift my hand, sheltering my eyes from the paparazzi snapping our photo from the backseat of a motorcycle. They veer so close to Marcus's car, I'm afraid they will scratch his pristine paintwork.

The cars streaming past my window blur as Marcus strives to lose the dozen or so paparazzi hot on our tail. He pushes his car to its absolute limit, showcasing its powerful engine in its full light. If I didn't hand my trust to him in the playroom last week, I'd be panicked out of my mind at the speed he is going, but I'm not—*not the slightest*. I have so much faith in him, I know he'd never put my life in unnecessary danger.

Within seconds, the paparazzi give up on their pursuit, the combination of Marcus's driving skills and the grunt of his engine too much for them to contest against. Happy we are void of any pesky intruders, Marcus shifts down the gears as he guides his speedometer back to a safe range. Once he is doing the posted speed limit, he swings his eyes to me.

"You okay?" he checks.

I smile, pleased as punch he is more concerned about me than the thrashing he just gave his no doubt multi-million-dollar car.

"Yes, I am perfectly A-Okay," I reply as my eyes stray from the pretty oceanside scenery to him. "Horny as fuck, but fine nonetheless."

"Jesus Christ, Cleo," Marcus mutters, his tone stern. "If you keep talking like that I'll wash out your filthy little mouth."

My lips crimp as a smile crosses my face. "Please," I tease, my voice throaty. "As long as it's done with your cock."

My thighs quake when Marcus's panty-wetting growl rumbles through my pussy. Drifting his eyes back to the road, his pressure on the gas pedal increases, slowly creeping his speedometer back into forbidden territory. I place my hand on his thigh and squeeze. My giddiness intensifies when his muscles bunch from my meekest touch.

"You do know if you had a driver, this wouldn't be an issue." I stray my eyes from the road to his, wanting to ensure he knows every word I speak is gospel. "I could already have your cock in my mouth if you'd loosen your need for control just a little."

His car hugs the curve in the road as his pressure on the gas pedal increases, but not a squeak oozes from his succulent lips.

Twenty minutes later, we are stumbling up the stairs of a palatial mansion on the outskirts of town. I can hardly hear the sounds of waves tumbling in the distance over the purrs toppling out of my mouth. Although I am interested in perusing the scenery, I can't tear my focus away from Marcus for even a second. Our twenty-minute ride from the private airstrip was crammed with palpable sexual tension. It was so fire-sparking, my orgasm is already teetering on the edge of orgasmic bliss.

My hands are frantic as they strive to strip Marcus of his long-sleeve dress shirt concealing his yummy body from my avid eyes. I'm so dying to feel his skin against mine, I haven't stopped to consider the fact I nearly have him half-naked on the front porch of his home.

I drag my mouth away from Marcus so my eyes can scan the darkened street. "Paparazzi?" I ask, fretful I'm making him so heedless, he hasn't stopped to consider the ramifications.

The stubble on Marcus's chin scratches the delicate skin on my collarbone when he drags his mouth down my jaw to suckle on my neck. "They don't know about this place," he mutters, his warm breath fanning my sweat-drenched neck.

I tear at his shirt, yanking it so roughly, I'm confident I hear buttons popping. Happy I have enough of his ravishing torso exposed to quell my eyes' eagerness to ravish him, I set to work on the belt wrapped around his waist. Marcus has similar ideas as me. He fists the hem of my long-sleeve shirt before whipping it over my head, exposing my erratically panting chest to his more-than-keen gaze. His eyeballs me, like it's the first time he has ever seen me naked.

The coolness of a sizeable Balinese door soothes the overheated skin on my back when I lean against it and thrust out my chest, offering myself to him.

"Yes," I hiss through clenched teeth when his large callus-covered hand creeps up my stomach to cup my breast.

As I frantically yank his black belt through the loops of his trousers, he bestows lavish attention to my aching-with-desire nipples. I pant when he releases my right breast from the tight restraints of my bra by pulling down the satin cup covering it. My nipples bud painfully, engorged by a fresh, salt-infused breeze blowing over my exposed chest.

Marcus's eyes burn into mine, relaying his every attention before his mouth drops to suck my erect nipple into his warm and inviting mouth. I still as an upwelling of desire scorches through me. I don't freeze for long, just long enough to cherish the feeling of being so yearned for, we couldn't achieve the ten paces from his car to the front door of his home without him needing to touch me. I've never felt as desired as I do right now.

As Marcus's tongue slithers around the firm nub of my nipple, his other hand moves to unzip my jeans. He only has the top button undone before his hand is slipping inside my panties. When the tips of his fingers brush the wetness pooling between my legs, his manly groan vibrates straight to my shuddering core.

"So impatient," he murmurs against my breast when I flex my hips up, begging for more direct contact.

When his thumb hovers over my throbbing clit, my hands shoot out to secure a hold on something. His touch is so potent, if I don't tether myself down, I'll float into ecstasy at the first sweep of his thumb on my clit.

Not realizing his front door is unlocked, my firm grab of the large silver door handle triggers the door to swing open. Before I have the chance to register I am falling, my backside and elbows connect with the hard wooden floor in the foyer of Marcus's home, and he lands on top of me with a thud. I grunt as an equal amount of excitement and pain scuttles through my body. Although my backside isn't appreciating the hard knock it just took, my body is too focused on being swamped by Marcus's delicious body to cite an objection to our unpleasant fall.

I grab Marcus's undone tie and yank his luscious lips to mine before his mouth can relay a single worry his eyes are portraying. He hesitates for only a second before he returns my kiss with equal vigor. His tongue slides around my mouth as his thick cock rocks against my heated core. My hands are all over him, touching and caressing every inch of him. I am desperate for him —everywhere.

When I tell him that, before I can comprehend what's happening, he has me flipped over onto my knees with my ass thrust in the air. My bra sags to the floor with a soundless thump before my jeans are roughly tugged down my quaking thighs to pool around my knees. We are both so desperate for each other, our movements are frantic and out of control.

I call out, no longer capable of constraining my excitement when Marcus thrusts into me in one swift motion. My pussy hugs his glorious cock as every nerve-ending in my body bristles. With the hardness of the tiled floor on my knees adding to the intoxicating energy strumming my veins, and Marcus's perfect cock ramming into me at an uncontrolled pace, I'm soon lost to the chase of climax. It's blinding to the extent I don't believe any previously cited *more* is required.

I moan loudly when Marcus twists my ponytail around and around his hand before he tugs my head back roughly. He yanks on my hair at a speed matching the frantic grinding of his cock. The hair pulling is rough enough, my scalp stings from his firm hold, but not rough enough to kill the thrum of excitement making my orgasm race to the finish line.

I lick a bead of sweat off my top lip before begging, "Can I please come, Master Chains?" My pleaded moan is barely heard over the sound of skin slapping skin.

Marcus barely breathes out the word "yes" when my climax hits fruition. I scream as a blistering of beautiful stars detonate before my eyes. I quiver and shake while my pussy squeezes his cock, begging for the opportunity to milk his thickened shaft while in the midst of ecstasy. Before last weekend, my chances of bringing a guy to orgasm while riding my own were impossible. Now, I'm riding the crest of climax with nothing more than a few erotic tugs on my hair while being thoroughly claimed by a mouthwatering cock.

My silent pleas are answered when Marcus takes me to the very base of his cock. He growls out my name in a deep, throaty moan as the hotness of his cum rockets out of his engorged knob. He stills, filling me to the very brim with every magnificent drop of his spawn. His groans are feral—almost animalistic.

With my palms damp from our vigorous activities, I soon lose my grip on the varnished wooden floor. I crumble into a heap on the floor, taking Marcus down with me. Ensuring he doesn't squash me, Marcus slides his still twitching shaft out of my throbbing core before rolling onto his back.

I take a few moments lying sprawled on the floor to gather my breath before drifting my eyes to Marcus. He is peering up at the ceiling, shocked into silence. Small beads of sweat are rolling down his delicious chocolate skin before they are absorbed by the collar of his shirt, and his trousers are bunched around his shoe-covered feet. A sultry smirk curls on my lips, loving that I made him so mindless, he is still pretty much clothed.

Feeling the heat of my smile directed at him, Marcus cranks his head to the side. With his brow arched high, he drinks in my blemished cheeks and sexually satiated eyes.

"What are you doing to me, Cleo? We barely made it in the front door."

My inane grin enlarges. "Once again, if you had a driver, this wouldn't be an issue," I jest, my mood playful.

Marcus groans before throwing his arm over his tired eyes. If I had any energy left, I'd laugh at his unusual response, but I am too sated to absorb the swift change in his personality.

My heart stops beating, and my head cranks to the side when a light switches on above my head. Panic scorches my veins, worried we are about to be busted.

As my hands shoot up to cover my exposed breasts, an elderly male voice queries, "Mr. Everett? Is that you?"

The sound of bare feet padding down a set of stairs rings through my ears as my frightened eyes snap to Marcus. An ill-timed giggle spills from my lips when I spot the panicked mask slipped over his face. I've never seen him so fretful—not even when Lexi had a gun pointed at his chest.

"Yes, Abel, it's me," Marcus answers before scampering onto his feet.

After quickly tucking his cock, which is glistening with evidence of my arousal, into his trousers, he gathers my shirt from the floor and throws it over my head even more quickly than he removed it. I grip the waistband of my jeans huddled around my knees and yank them up my quaking thighs. I've scarcely pulled them past my dripping core when an elderly African American man enters the foyer.

"Oh, I'm so sorry, dear," he mumbles, averting his wide eyes from my disheveled self, which is sprawled across the floor, to a carved wooden pillar on his left.

Embarrassment burns my throat, horrified he is meeting me this way. You can never redo a first impression. After stuffing my bra into the pocket of his trousers, Marcus shoots his hand out in offering to aid me off the floor. Although I am mortified at being caught unaware, silly giddiness is still fluttering in my stomach. My reaction can't be helped. I've never seen Marcus so ruffled. Due to my rough handling of his shirt, he is missing numerous buttons, which means it is gaped open, erotically exposing inches of his scrumptious chest and rock-hard abs, and his trousers are crinkled from being bunched around his thighs during our heated exchange.

His tousled appearance strips him of all the titles he has, leaving nothing but a twenty-eight-year-old man with a mischievous glint in his eyes. He is the untouched Marcus—one I doubt anyone has seen in a very long time.

Curling his hand around mine, Marcus moves us toward the muted man standing at the side of the foyer. My mouth gapes, more in wonderment of Marcus's beautiful property than being busted with my pants down. Since I was so rapt on chasing the thrill of climax, I failed to notice how impressive Marcus's Florida residence is. Just like his New York property, the huge top story of his home is held up with big, wide pillars. But instead of being stark white concrete, they are chunky carved wood. The ceiling is vaulted with a similar grain of the wood, and a thin white mesh material canopied between the pillars softens the hardness of the industrial material. If we had been in the private jet for longer than an hour, I would have sworn Marcus had shipped me away to an overseas continent. His entire home has a gorgeous Balinese feel to it.

My attention diverts from the awe-inspiring residence when I become conscious of the activity we were just undertaking. It isn't the blemished hue on Abel's freckled cheeks prompting my fuzzy brain, it's the small gush of Marcus's cum dribbling into my panties. I squeeze my thighs together, praying to the Lord a wet patch doesn't form on the crotch of my jeans. I knew Hollywood movies were full of crap. I don't know one girl who can have sneaky sex in the middle of a dancefloor and continue dancing minutes later like nothing happened.

"I'm sorry for the intrusion," Abel apologizes, his gaze focused on the woven mat under his feet. "I was not expecting you at such a late hour. I was afraid we had an intruder."

"It's okay, Abel," Marcus acknowledges, accepting his apology with a sincerity in his tone I haven't heard before. "I should have warned you about our late arrival. I got a little caught up convincing my guest I wanted her attendance that common courtesy slipped my mind."

Marcus squeezes my hand, ensuring I can't mistake who was the cause of his distraction. The warmness spreading across my chest grows when Abel lifts his gaze from the ground. His worldly eyes glisten with moisture as he drifts them between Marcus and me. Usually, his type of stare would have my skin crawling, but all I feel is squishy comfort from his prolonged gaze. He has gentle eyes and an aura that tells me he is a wonderful man. If I had to guess Abel's age purely by looking at him, I would say he was in his mid to late fifties, but his eyes give away his true age. I would say it's closer to mid-seventies.

After rubbing the sleep from his eyes with the back of his hand, Abel locks them with Marcus. "Are you going to introduce me to our guest?" he queries, his tone not as apprehensive as the one he was using earlier.

"Yes, sorry." Marcus smiles. Tilting his torso to face me, he introduces, "Abel, I would like to introduce you to Cleo, my girlfriend."

"Girlfriend?" I splutter out, my lungs failing to breathe. I was expecting him to trail off his sentence like he has every other time he has introduced me, but his voice didn't waver in the slightest.

I'm not the only one stunned, Abel looks as flabbergasted as me. As his ageless eyes bounce between Marcus and me, the sheen glimmering in them grows damper.

Not the slightest bit put off by my slack-jawed expression, Marcus continues with his introduction, "Cleo, this is Abel, my..." This time, his words trail off to silence as confusion clouds his penetrating gaze.

I smile, glad I'm not the only one he struggles to give a title to.

"It's a pleasure to meet you, Ms. Cleo," Abel says, soundlessly requesting my attention back to him. "I am Mr. Everett's butler. If you require anything during your stay, please do not hesitate to call me." He holds out his rheumy hand in offering.

I loosen Marcus's grip on my hand so I can accept his kind gesture. "Thank you. I won't be too much of a bother. Hopefully, you won't even notice I'm here."

I grimace when my declaration doesn't come out as confident as I am hoping. Up until a week ago, I wouldn't have said I was a screamer in the bedroom. Now, I'm not so sure. From the pillow crease in Abel's beautifully colored skin, I'm confident my cries of ecstasy were sufficient enough to wake him from his deep slumber.

Abel squeezes my hand as his eyes meet mine. "Now where is the fun in that, Ms. Cleo? Life is about noise, mess, and chaos." He flicks his eyes to Marcus, the heavy sentiment in them undeniable. "He needs to learn that more than anyone."

Denying Marcus the chance to refute his statement, Abel spins on his heels and exits the room. "Breakfast will be served at 7 AM and not a minute past," he informs us before he disappears into the darkness of the night even more quickly than he arrived.

I turn my eyes to Marcus. Stupid giddiness is making my skin a clammy mess. "I like him." I rock on the balls of my feet.

Marcus smiles a grin that causes my heart to skip a beat. "That's because he is as disobedient as you," he replies with laughter in his tone.

He adjusts his position so he is facing me front on. "Would you like a tour?" he asks, nudging his head to the grandeur of his home spread out in front of me.

"Yes, but first I need to use the restroom. I need to wash up." The grimace on my face guarantees he can't mistake what my request is pertaining to.

I'd like to say the vibrant red coloring heating my cheeks is solely based on my embarrassment, but that would be a lie. Most of it's centered on the spark of lust rapidly reforming in Marcus's eyes.

25

Marcus's home is just as beautiful as I imagined. There are four bedrooms all facing the moonlit ocean, 4.5 bathrooms, a huge state of the art kitchen with a bamboo roof and granite counters, and three well-appointed living spaces. As suspected when I first roamed my eyes over his property, a Balinese feel has been incorporated in each room. The house is large in size, but with the furnishings being just as bulky, it doesn't feel airy. It feels inviting.

"I have a studio in a shed at the back of the property," Marcus explains while guiding me down an impressively long hallway with his hand on the curve of my back. "It's positioned next to the garage we pulled in front of earlier."

We stop outside a large wooden door that's an exact replica of the one hanging in his foyer. "And this is the master suite," Marcus advises, swinging open the thick hand-carved door.

I gasp as my eyes drink in the magnificent room. A large king-size bed sits in front of a dark wooden wall that flows up from the richly polished floorboards. The ceiling is done in a pitch roof design, held in place with large sticks of bamboo, and all the linen is a crisp white design. It's stunningly beautiful, enough to render any girl speechless.

My nostrils flare when I step deeper into the space, eager to absorb Marcus's freshly laundered scent wafting in the air. The opulence of his room becomes even more apparent the further I pace inside. Its grandeur was impressive from the doorway, but I didn't comprehend the enormity of the space until I fully immersed myself in it. I could host a party for twenty in this room and still not feel claustrophobic.

My bewilderment increases when I notice a bottle of my favorite perfume sitting on the dresser on the far left-hand side wall. It's positioned next to a gathering of my cosmetics.

Marcus extends my shock by pacing to a set of large wooden drawers at the side of the room. "I had Abel clear some space for you. You can have these two drawers for your personal belongings," he advises, gesturing his hand to the top two drawers. "And there is another set of drawers and a section of hanging space in the walk-in closet for your clothing. Abel does a dry cleaning run every second day, but if you have anything urgent to be done, there is a laundry room downstairs."

Since my mouth is refusing to cooperate with the prompts of my brain, I nod.

Marcus moves to stand next to his gigantic bed. "I noticed the indent in your mattress signaled you prefer sleeping on the left-hand side, but would you mind changing it to the right, as I prefer sleeping on the left?" he asks, peering at me like he hasn't noticed my stunned-mullet composure.

Dumbfounded and mute, I once again nod.

"Good," Marcus replies, pleased by my agreeing gesture.

This could just be my vulnerability talking since I am still reveling in an orgasmic high, but I can barely contain my excitement that Marcus is inviting me to sleep in his room when he has four other unoccupied rooms in his house. Is it just me, or does this feel like a mammoth step in the right direction for our relationship being more than a standard D/s affiliation?

Marcus motions his head to a set of doors hidden behind the wooden wall of his bed. "The bathroom is behind there. It's been stocked with your body wash, shampoo, and conditioner, the only thing Abel couldn't find was the cream you use to remove your makeup. He got the alternative suggested by the pharmacist, but if isn't to your liking we can--"

"I am sure it will be fine," I interrupt, grateful my mouth is finally liaising with my brain. "Everything is perfect, and the tour was wonderful, but aren't you missing a room?" I query, spinning around to face Marcus, my tone incapable of hiding my happiness.

I don't need to expand on my question. His eyes relay that he understands which room I am referring to. His playroom.

"This is my private residence, Cleo," Marcus informs me, his tone low and a little snappish.

"Yes. I understand that," I respond through scrunched brows, alarmed by the sudden change in his tone. "But that doesn't answer my question. This is your residence, so where is your playroom?"

I nearly do a jig on the spot, proud I articulated his sexual tendencies without breaking into hives. My playful mood is reeled in and stored away for a later date when I see an indistinguishable cloud forming in Marcus's narrowed gaze. I watch him for a moment, categorizing every emotion pumping through his forthright eyes. Although his eyes are raw and honest, they do nothing to quell my confusion.

Still dumbfounded at what caused the resolute change in his demeanor, I say, "When discussing the terms of our contract, you said half of our time would be spent at your Florida residence, while the other half would be at hotels assigned by your studio. Correct me if I am wrong, but at one stage in our earlier discussions, you stated you have a clause in your contract that stipulates any sexual contact will only occur in a playroom environment."

Marcus nods, agreeing with my assessment. "That's correct. But this is different. You didn't sign our contract, so the rules cited in that contract no longer apply," he replies guilelessly.

I stand in silence for a minute, too stunned to move forward with our conversation. What does that mean for our relationship? Does my rejection of a legal contract mean we won't have any sexual encounters in his playroom? If so, that stinks.

"I have a playroom, Cleo. It just isn't here," Marcus says, seemingly reading my silent thoughts. "It's in my apartment on Hyde."

Shock gnaws at my stomach as I stand mute. "Your playroom is in another location?"

"Yes." Marcus hesitantly paces toward me. "It's where my subs stayed during the length of our contract."

"So did you stay here while they stayed there?" I continue probing, seeking answers to questions I hope will help settle my confusion. "Or do you only stay here while seeking a new sub?"

"They stayed there while I stayed here," Marcus answers as his eyes flick between mine.

He watches me quietly, seeing my confusion winding up from my stomach to my throat.

"By keeping my personal life and business life in separate locations, it ensured they remained two separate entities. You're the first person to meld them together."

Although I appreciate his honesty, it doesn't stop sick gloom wreaking havoc with my stomach. I saunter to his bed and sit, where I stay for several moments silently contemplating. I'm at a loss on how to continue with our conversation. Don't get me wrong, I am ecstatic he is acknowledging there is a difference between me and his previous subs, but I'm also confused. Is it just me, or does it seem morally wrong he kept his subs hidden away from society like dirty little secrets? Kind of like how our relationship must remain hidden?

"It's not even close to being the same thing, Cleo," Marcus utters, intuiting my inner monologue. "My previous subs understood our agreement. It was clearly outlined so there was no possibility of confusion. And contrary to what you believe, Doms are not the only people in kink seeking a sexually compatible relationship without strings attached. To some subs, the provision of no contact outside of a playroom is just as important as outlining their hard limits."

Confused by his confession, my brows stitch. "So they wanted to be separated from you?" *Who in their right mind wouldn't want to be lavished with Marcus's attention 24/7?*

"Not all of them," Marcus admits. "But they understood if they signed to be my sub, they had to follow through with our agreement as cited. Although I was happy to discuss adding provisions to a contract, my living quarter clause was not negotiable. If they didn't agree to that term, our contract would not go through."

"They?" I stammer out, swallowing harshly. "How many are we talking?"

Marcus arches his dark brow, his stare violent. "Would you like me to ask you how many men you've slept with, Cleo?"

My pulse quickens from the clipped undertone of his voice. It's curt and brisk and should have me quaking in my boots, but with my mind still trapped in an orgasmic high, my stupid body strums in excitement.

Even knowing the number of men I've slept with isn't anything to be ashamed of, I shake my head. Not because I don't want to be honest with Marcus, but because I can't be confident I can stomach his reply if we were to travel down this road. It was also an insulting question for me to ask.

The mattress dips when Marcus takes a seat next to me. Even with my mood a little edgy, I can't deny the current surging between us. Something like that's unmissable.

"I brought you here as I thought it would be the best place to show you the real me, but your responses have me doubting my decision," he mutters uneasily, making me realize he isn't angry, he is unsure. I need to remember this is all new to him as well. This is a learning process for us both.

"Don't doubt your decision. I'm just being stupid. Everything is perfect. It's all perfect." I stand from the bed and pace away from him to give myself a few minutes to reel in my spiraling composure.

"Cleo..." Marcus grinds out, freezing my steps midstride. His tone appeases my anguish way more than his words ever could.

The tap of his feet is so quiet I don't realize he is moving for me until the heat of his body warms my back. "I can't help you understand your issues if you don't explain them to me," he mumbles into my hairline.

The urge to forget the niggling doubts in the back of my mind bombards me when he curls his arms around the front of my body and draws me into him. I lean into his chest and close my eyes, letting the frantic rhythm of his heart soothe my unwarranted irritation. I don't know why I am being so irrational? He invited me into his private sanctuary usually only reserved for him, yet I'm being a catty, emotional cow.

Standing still, I rack my mental calendar. I inwardly huff. Now it all makes sense. Although I still have a few days left until my period is due, I've always had a horrid neurosis of being extra bitchy the week leading up to my cycle.

I gulp, soothing the burn of my throat before saying, "I'm sorry for my crazy moods. I'm due for my period next week, so I'm letting things bug me more than normal."

A suspicious grin curls on my lips when Marcus freezes for the slightest second. Surely this can't be the first time he's dealt with a hormonal woman? Suddenly, my spine straightens. With his subs being housed separately from him, it could quite possibly be the case.

I spin on my heels to face Marcus the best I can in the protective cocoon he has me wrapped in. I keep my focus on the rise and fall of his chest as I attempt to gather back any shrewdness I have left. It's a pointless effort the instant my eyes connect to his. He stares into my eyes, once again turning my brain to mush from his predatory glare. I am needy and hot, and willing to do anything to feel the friction of his skin against mine.

"I don't have any issues, per se, I'm just a little taken aback you don't have a playroom," I blubber out before I can stop my words.

When Marcus's deep growl rumbles through my chest, my pupils widen, and a raging wildfire takes hold in my stomach. It's lucky he has his arms wrapped firmly around my waist, or I may have gone toppling to the floor.

"You're upset because I don't have a playroom?"

I peer up at him sheepishly through a set of long lashes. "I wouldn't say upset, more disappointed," I admit, my tone as shuddering as the pulse between my legs. "I enjoyed our time in your playroom. Very much so."

Relief engulfs his gorgeous green irises as his grip on my waist loosens. His relieved response surprises me.

"Why, what did you think I was upset about?" I ask breathlessly. I'm not breathless because of his tight hold, I'm winded from having his strikingly handsome face so near to mine.

Marcus's eyes glide around the room, stopping momentarily on each item he purchased to make me feel at home. "I thought you were upset about my request for us to share a room."

"God no," I reply, not even thinking. "I love the idea of sharing a room with you." Another declaration of love sits on the tip of my tongue, but I hold it back—barely!

Hating the unease dampening his usually bright eyes, I say, "As I said earlier, forget I said anything. It wasn't me talking, it was the red witch preparing to wreak havoc with my womb in around six days' time."

Marcus screws up his nose as his Adam's apple works hard to swallow. Clearly, he is uncomfortable discussing women's matters.

I fist his ruined dress shirt in my hands and pull him close to me, filling the last portion of space between us with his impressive body. "You do know what this means, though, don't you?"

Marcus's eyes float between mine, his recklessness growing by the minute. "We have six days to work through the crazy sexual tension bouncing between us."

I take a step backward, seductively prancing to the bathroom door he motioned to earlier. Since I still have his shirt clutched in my hand, his movements mimic mine.

"Do you think six days will suffice, Cleo?" Marcus asks me, his voice alone enough to kickstart my chase of climax.

"Not at all," I reply. My hair clings to my sweat-slicked neck when I shake my head. "But I've got a few tricks up my sleeve I can use when our time is up."

I drop my eyes to the extended crotch of his pants before seductively licking my lips. My hunger to taste him in my mouth is unmissable.

A girly squeal rumbles up my chest when Marcus suddenly launches for me. His firm pecs crash into me with enough force, my feet lift from the ground. I'm not concerned I'm going to fall. his grip on my backside ensures there is no possibility of that.

After guiding my legs around his waist, Marcus strides into the bathroom, grinding his hips upwards with every step he takes.

26

A soft groan simpers through my lips as I snuggle into the heavenly soft pillow my head is caressing. I've known for years my mattress was in pressing need of an upgrade, but after sleeping on a bed like a cloud, the first thing I am doing when I return home is purchasing new linens. I'd love to buy a new mattress, but that would be a little more than my budget could stretch.

After pulling my arms out of the comforter, I have a leisurely stretch. The weary muscles I've awoken with the past week aren't as antagonizing as usual. The hour-long soak I had in the tub last night with Marcus made quick work of their tautness. I feel deliriously wonderful. Marcus was so attentive last night. Don't get me wrong, I know from my research into the BDSM lifestyle that a nurturing Dom is just as common as a sadistic one, but last night felt different. He didn't seem as if he was washing my hair because it was part of his role, it appeared as if he was doing it because he wanted to. I swooned nearly as many times as I came last night.

Peeling the heavenly soft high-thread-count sheet off my body, I swing my legs over the edge of the bed. I gag when I see my disheveled appearance in the wooden framed mirror sitting on top of a chest of drawers at the side of the room. I don't know what Marcus sees in me. My hair is a ratted mess, my eyes are plagued with dark rings from my lagging sleep cycle, and the faint bruise on my cheek isn't the only blemish on my skin.

Shrugging off the desire to book Marcus an optometrist appointment, I stand from the bed. My sexually satiated muscles are more noticeable in a standing position. While rubbing the kink in the back of my neck, I saunter into the sizeable walk-in closet positioned behind his floor-to-ceiling headboard. Matching his residence in New York, most of the space is lined with fancy suits and pricey polished dress shoes. I pad to a stack of drawers to secure a pair of Marcus's black running shorts and a plain white undershirt. With my grumbling stomach unable to be contained, my desire to shower and dress more presentably must wait until I have eaten.

Not wanting to startle Marcus too much with my ruffled morning appearance, I head to the bathroom to brush my teeth and hair. An inane grin curls on my lips when I realize he purchased an exact replica of the hairbrush I use at home. I bet that was an interesting endeavor for Abel? I'm sure it's not very often a rock star's butler takes a trip to Walmart.

With my hair pulled into a low ponytail, I exit Marcus's bedroom and saunter down the wooden staircase. My quick strides slow when the heat of the midmorning sun warms my face. My eyes scan the area, seeking any type of clock. I fail to find any.

My endeavor to tell the time from the position of the sun ends when the sickly-sweet smell of pancakes and bacon filters into my nose. I increase my stride, my rampant hunger stronger than ever. Upon entering the kitchen, I discover Abel standing near a large open cooktop, frying bacon and flipping pancakes.

"Good morning, Abel," I greet as my eyes seek Marcus in the vast space.

Abel spins on his heels to face me. "Ms. Cleo, how did you sleep?"

"Well, thank you," I answer, grateful he doesn't seem peeved by my tardiness.

I slip into one of the six stools tucked under the counter when Abel nudges his head, requesting for me to sit. My eyes bulge when he places a large mug of hot chocolate in front of me before moving back to the stove.

"Where is Marcus?" I query, lifting the mug to my lips to blow air on the steamy contents inside.

Abel places four pancakes and numerous strips of bacon onto a plate before answering, "He is working off his breakfast in the gym."

"He's already eaten?" I interrogate, my tone high with disappointment that I once again missed the opportunity to dine with him.

"Yes, Ms. Cleo, many hours ago," Abel replies with laughter in his tone.

With a grin, he nudges his head to the digital clock in the microwave oven. I nearly fall off my chair when I see it's a quarter to twelve. I shouldn't be shocked at the time. The only person who believes the early bird catches the worm is a person who hasn't spent their night in a Marcus Everett lust-inspired trance.

"He did ask me to call him once you were awake, so I better do that," Abel informs me, placing a large plate of food down in front of me.

"Wait," I request loudly, startling him enough he stops strolling to a security intercom at the side of the room.

"Perhaps I can surprise him in the gym once I've eaten?" I mumble, saying anything that will give me a few minutes alone with Abel.

I don't know why, but my intuition tells me Abel could be my greatest ally in unearthing the real Marcus—not the hyped persona the members of Chains and the public know.

Abel connects his big brown eyes with mine. "Mr. Everett does not appreciate disobedience, Ms. Cleo," he informs me. If it weren't for the twinkle in his eyes, I would have thought he was worried about being disciplined.

I purse my lips. "He only told me yesterday 'a young man only knows the rules, but a wise man knows there is an exception to every rule.' Surely you can't get in trouble for following his advice."

Abel runs his hands down the white apron tied around his slim waist while contemplating a response. "It's nearly my lunch break," he mumbles a short time later.

"And it's horribly rude to leave a guest to eat alone," I jest while pulling out the empty stool next to me.

My heart beats faster when the cutest grin I've ever seen stretches across Abel's face. Marcus wasn't joking, Abel is just as bratty as me.

When Abel occupies the seat next to me, I take a sip of my hot chocolate. An inappropriate moan topples from my lips when the scrumptious goodness hits my taste buds.

Abel smiles. "Good?"

"It's delicious. What's that?" I swish the spicy flavor around my mouth. "Nutmeg?"

"It is," Abel confirms, smiling radiantly. "With just a hint of cinnamon."

When Abel hands me a knife and fork from a stack on the kitchen counter, I secure a second fork for him and push my plate to sit between us. He eyes me curiously, seemingly shocked.

"You did say it's your lunch break, and there is plenty of food here for us both," I advise his puzzled expression.

"Ah." Abel's eyes glisten in the midday sun. "I knew you were different from the moment I laid my eyes on you. You have a very kind soul, Ms. Cleo."

I pop a large chunk of pancake in my mouth, hoping to conceal the huge smile his compliment awarded me with.

Abel and I sit in silence for several minutes while consuming our breakfast. Although I am the hungriest I've ever been, there is no doubt Abel's pancakes are the most delicious I've ever eaten. They are fluffy and filled to the brim with sugary goodness, similar to the man sitting next to me. Abel doesn't need to speak to express himself. His worldly eyes share a lifetime of memories without a word needing to be said. He appears to have lived a very fulfilling life.

"Have you known Marcus long?" Abel questions me before popping the last slice of crispy bacon into his mouth.

I swallow my mouthful of pancake before shaking my head. "We talked on the internet for a few months, but I only met him in person last week," I disclose before screwing up my nose. "Well, actually we met a little over four years ago at a hospital in Queens, but it was just a flyby meeting."

"Oh." That is all Abel mumbles, but his eyes show he wants to say so much more.

"Have you worked with Marcus long?" I query, hoping to keep our conversation flowing.

Abel slides off the barstool to put our empty plate in the stainless steel dishwasher. "It will be five years this coming June," he answers as the happy twinkle in his eyes softens. "But I've known him for many years, before he was even out of diapers. You should have seen him when he was a young boy, Ms. Cleo. Big green eyes that were full of mischief."

I smile at the thought of a grubby-faced Marcus. "So you've known his family for a while?"

I pace around the bench to assist him in clearing away the mess he made while making me breakfast. When he tsks me, I say, "You cooked, the very least I can do is help clean."

Abel's narrowed gaze lifts from my empty mug of chocolate to me. He glares into my eyes, warning me to step out of his domain. I angle my head to the side and bow my brow before awarding him my best stubborn Garcia glance. We stand in opposition for several seconds, neither willing to back down.

A victorious grin morphs onto my face when Abel says, "Very well. But if Mr. Everett discovers you washing dishes, I'll tell him it was your penance for refusing to eat breakfast."

My mouth gapes. "You wouldn't dare."

"Oh, yes I would," he replies without pause or delay.

Rolling my eyes, I rinse our used dishes in a sink of bubbly water. "Do you spend much time with Marcus's family anymore?"

Abel accepts the plate I am holding out for him. "Ms. Serenity used to visit weekly before she left to help Marcus in New York. I've missed her weekly visits," he confesses before loading the plate into the dishwasher. "She is coming back this weekend. I am sure she will have plenty of stories to share with me about her time in the city."

"I had lunch with her last week. She is doing very well," I advise, aiming to ease the small bit of pain in his eyes.

My endeavor has the effect I am hoping for. "I am delighted to hear that, Ms. Cleo. She is a good apple, much like Marcus. After everything they've been through, they both deserve to find happiness."

Suddenly, his lips smack together, and guilt rapidly darkens his eyes. He runs his hand down his apron several times in a row before locking his glistening eyes with me. "Please forgive me, I have said too much."

Not wanting to push our conversation into uncomfortable territory, I gently nod while moving to gather the cooking instruments off the stovetop. Once they are rinsed free of oil, I hand them to Abel to stack in the dishwasher. We stand side by side cleaning the kitchen in silence for several moments. It isn't uncomfortable. I just need a moment to contemplate his blurted confession, whereas he needs a few moments to ensure it doesn't happen again.

"I have a younger sister," I inform him a short time later, striving to lessen the tension bristling the air with muggy heat. "Her name is Lexi. She has a beautiful soul, but she is a lot of work."

A gathering of wrinkles spreads across the bridge of Abel's nose when he smiles. "Then you must be sympathetic to Mr. Everett? I grew up with two older sisters, and that was a challenge so I couldn't imagine having three younger sisters to contend with."

"Marcus has three sisters?" I ask, my tone drenched with amazement.

"Oh, yes." Abel paces to the side of the kitchen. "They are as beautiful as their mother."

After drying my hands with a tea towel, I move across the room to join Abel. Warmth blooms in my chest when my eyes drop down to the wooden photo frame he is holding out for me. The young teen in the photo is easily distinguishable. It is Marcus. Although his tightly twisted afro is longer than he wears it now, there is no mistaking his dazzling green eyes. He is just as devilishly handsome in this photo as he is now.

"That's Ms. Annalise and Ms. Celestine," Abel informs me, pointing to two people in the photo I've not yet had the pleasure of meeting. "You already know Serenity."

Annalise is the spitting image of Serenity, all the way down to same eye coloring. Celestine is the youngest of the group, she appears quite a few years younger than her older siblings. Her eyes are brown in color, and her dark, wavy hair hangs halfway down her back. Just like Marcus, his three sisters are incredibly attractive.

"You could meet them next month," Abel says, accepting the picture frame back from my grasp. "If you can convince Marcus to attend the celebration."

"Celebration?"

Abel peers past my shoulder, making sure we are still alone before he opens the top drawer of the study nook we are standing next to. The invitation he passes to me is as elegant as the one Mr. Carson handed me months ago. It has gold script handwritten on paper so thin it crumbles under my touch.

"Marcus is organizing a party for his mother's fiftieth birthday. A wonderful celebration, unlike anything this town has seen. One he doesn't plan on attending."

My brows scrunch, confused by his statement. "Why would Marcus organize a party but not attend?"

Abel places his rheumy hand on my forearm. "That's something only he can tell you." The emotion expressed by his eyes as he peers up at me cuts me raw. He has such a beautiful soul. "It won't be long, Ms. Cleo. He will open up to you. I just know it."

Unable to speak with my heart sitting in my throat, I nod. Although Marcus and I still have a very long way to go, I genuinely believe I was assigned the Chains' investigation as it was the universe's fucked up way of bringing us back together. I've never understood fate, but I know there is a more significant hand at play when it comes to my relationship with Marcus.

"Now go and show him that the man frolicking with you in the foyer last night is the same young man I raised him to be," Abel requests as the sassiness in his eyes grows tenfold. "Just try to do it with your clothes on this time."

My hands itch to cover my heated face, but I keep them fisted at my side, determined not to give Abel the satisfaction of seeing he has me flustered.

Abel's worldly eyes tell me he has lived his best years, but they are the same set of eyes that guarantees he will keep Marcus on his toes for many years to come.

I don't know why, but I get great satisfaction in knowing that.

27

After receiving precise directions to the gym, I press a kiss to Abel's cheek and saunter outside. Gravel crunches under my bare feet as I cross a hedge-lined driveway separating the primary residence from a group of outdoor buildings. With the weather more pleasant than an early New Jersey winter, the hairs on my arms only bristle slightly from the fresh ocean breeze gliding over them. This area of Florida is gorgeous. The ocean background seen over the dense clifftop is as blue as the sky, and the sand lining the beaches is crystal clear.

The winds budding my nipples eases when I step under the alcove of the first building. I am not at all musically inclined, but it doesn't take a genius to know the first structure is the recording studio Marcus mentioned yesterday. If the soundproof booth with a large black microphone isn't a strong enough indication, the musical instruments lining every wall spell it out.

Following Abel's directions, I duck down the corridor separating the studio from the four-car garage and enter the second door on my left. I feel Marcus's presence before I see him. He has his back facing me as he runs on a treadmill in the corner of the room. His shirt has been removed and tucked into the back of his plain black running shorts, and rivulets of sweat are streaming down his cheeks.

I prop my shoulder onto the doorjamb of the gym, happy to undertake my workout less vigorously. I don't need a piece of equipment to complete a strenuous exercise regime. The sight of Marcus's muscles releasing and contracting is enough of a workout for my sexually-motivated body. It mimics his movements, tightening more and more with every lengthened stride he takes.

Way before I've had the chance to inspect every perfect muscle in his ripped body, Marcus's head slings sideway. I straighten my spine, vainly trying to act like I wasn't getting all hot and bothered perving on him. It's a fruitless effort. My wide eyes and hanging jaw gives away my deceit.

"Good morning, Cleo," Marcus greets me, his voice super rough from his laborious activities.

His index finger jabs the speed button on the treadmill, lowering it from a fast run to a brisk walk before it comes to a complete stop. While running a small white towel over his sweat-drenched head, he moves to stand in front of me. I suck in air deeply through my nose, worshipping the smell of sweat on his heated skin. It rushes a flurry of memories into my mind—naughty, wicked memories.

"How did you sleep?" Marcus asks, leaning in to press a kiss on my cheek.

I snap my head to the side, forcing his lips to land on my mouth. "Perfect," I reply, my throaty purr vibrating against his full lips.

"Good," he breathes out seductively before his tongue lashes my mouth, soundlessly requesting access. I give it to him.

We kiss for several moments, savoring in a rare moment of pure silence between us. He caresses my cheeks in his big hands and playfully nibs at my lips. I purr into his mouth, appreciating the tang of his sweat flavoring our kiss His kiss is scrumptious, toe-curling, and sweet, a vast reminder that the man standing before me is Marcus, not Master Chains.

Once he has every morsel of my breakfast left lingering in my mouth taken care of, Marcus pulls away from our embrace. I stare up at him, wide-eyed and in complete awe as he checks our embrace didn't cause any irritation to my split lip. It didn't—not the least. His kiss completely wiped all thoughts from my mind—good and bad.

I never thought it was possible to feel desired when wearing not a smidge of makeup and men's clothing two sizes too big. But I do feel desired—very much so. How could I not when Marcus is glancing into my eyes with more admiration than I've been awarded the past four years? The way he stares at me makes it seem like I am saving him from a life of misery, not the other way around.

"Have you eaten?" Marcus questions, snapping me out of my loved-up haze.

Smiling, I dip my chin.

"Good. Come. I want to show you something."

Not waiting for me to reply, Marcus paces out of the virile-smelling gym. We race across the driveway faster than my legs can move. When my dainty strides hinder Marcus's long ones, he scoops down, curls his arms around my waist, and hoists me over his shoulder. I incoherently grumble, faking annoyance at his caveman hold. It's all for show. I'm idolizing every minute of his carefree attitude. I also get the most spectacular view of his traffic-stopping backside.

A warm sting spreads across my left butt cheek when Marcus awards my firm squeeze of his backside with a playful slap. I giggle wildly and kick out my legs, striving to ignore the tingling of excitement racing down my spine. Even with my ponytail swishing to and fro in front of my eyes, I can't miss the broad grin stretched across Abel's face when he spots Marcus and me entering the foyer of the palatial Everett mansion.

Smiling, Abel waves at me. I wave straight back.

"I'm going to town." Abel projects his voice across the vast space, ensuring Marcus can hear him over my childish giggles. I'm not laughing at our immaturity. I am laughing at the little jig Abel did as we strode by him. For a man who would be hitting close to eighty, he has some smooth moves.

"I'll be back in a few hours, Mr. Everett," Abel continues shouting, his body still grooving.

Marcus raises his other hand in the air—*the one not clutching my backside*—signaling to Abel he heard him.

Only once we stop outside one of the spare bedrooms he showed me yesterday does Marcus place me back on my feet. He waits for the blood that raced to my face from my upside down hold to clear away before he locks his eyes with mine. My lungs take stock of their oxygen levels when I spot the cheeky gleam in his eyes rapidly being replaced with dominance.

He tucks a stray strand of hair behind my ears before digging a silver key out of his running pants pocket. Confusion engulfs me when he places the key into a lock on the door I didn't notice yesterday. It looks new and chunky, and I swear I've seen a similar one to it before. I suck in a lung-filling gulp of air, conscious it may be my last chance to secure an entire breath when he swings open the door. Air traps halfway down my throat when my eyes lock on a large leather chaise positioned in the middle of the room.

As I command for my lungs to breathe, I step into the space that's nearly an exact replica of his playroom in Chains. The bed that was positioned in the middle of the room yesterday has been pushed against the far wall. Its floral bedding has been stripped, replaced with a dark satin material that complements the veins woven throughout the woodgrain base. Floggers, whips, canes, and spanking instruments I don't have a name for line the wall on my right, while the white lace drapes covering the window have been switched to a sun-blocking Venetian blind.

I run my fingers over the brand-new leather chaise, appreciating the coolness of its material on my overheated skin, as my wide eyes take in the rest of the room. Marcus watches me from the doorway but remains completely quiet. He is studying my response as eagerly as I am assessing his newly-formed playroom.

I recognize the Saint Andrew's cross mounted on my right from my research into the BDSM lifestyle, but there is a wooden table-like contraption sitting on my left that I've never seen before. It has a black leather cushioned top, and four leather encased nooks positioned in place by adjustable nubs. It's a sturdy contraption that looks like it could take the weight of three individuals, but its odd angle and the position of the nooks gives the indication it's only designed for one.

"What's that?" I ask Marcus, curiosity in my tone.

My pulse quickens when he pushes off his feet and saunters into the room. His dominance is as prominent as ever, vibrating out of him in invisible waves.

"It's a gift I had made for you."

I can't stop my smile, so I just set it free. "You didn't make this one?"

"No," Marcus answers. "My specialty is chains, not wood." His voice has a hint of playfulness to it, a rarity I didn't expect to hear while standing in his playroom.

He stops beside me before connecting his massively dilated eyes with mine. "It's a spanking bench. Your torso lays over the top, and your feet and hands are supported by the footrests."

You'd think my first reaction would be panic that he had a spanking bench made for me. It isn't. My insides clench in exhilaration.

Endeavoring to rein in my seemingly unquenchable desires when it comes to this man, I move to the various floggers hanging on the sidewall. The excitement tingling in my core turns uncontrollable when my eyes lock in on a black riding crop identical to the one Marcus used on me last week. My knees curve inwards as my pupils dilate.

"How did you get this done in such a short period of time?" I query, my high tone exposing my aroused state.

I am more turned on than shocked. I'm not surprised Marcus had a playroom installed. I am thrilled. I'm just stunned at how quickly it was formed. I guess for people with money, patience is not a requirement?

Marcus commences answering my question with a shrug of his shoulders. "Chains moves the location of its parties every week. This was a minor request for my playroom designer."

My eyes snap to his. "There are playroom designers?"

Marcus nods as his eyes drift around the room. "Because your questionnaire was vague, I asked Clarice to supply a broad range of toys. Once I believe you're ready, we will work out which ones you prefer and remove the ones you don't."

My thighs tremble as my knees crash together, hoping to ease the mad throb building between my legs. I am sweating profusely, my body frantically perspiring to cool my skyrocketing temperature.

I shift my eyes back to what should be seen as a wall of pain, but for some reason, my demented brain is seeing it as a wall of pleasure. Sexual curiosity is eating me alive. I don't just want to know the names of the toys presented in front of me, I want to know what they feel like as well.

Remembering Marcus's request to show him the real Cleo, the one no one else gets to see, I turn my eyes to Marcus and say, "Can we start that experimenting now?"

Marcus's eyes bore into mine, assessing my soul from the inside out. It's a long, heart-strangling stare. The excitement making my skin a sticky mess eases when I spot the indecisiveness in his eyes.

"I'm fine," I mumble, not appreciating the silent interrogation his eyes are relaying. Yes, he knows my body better than anyone before him, but that's second to me. If I say I am fine, I am fine!

Not speaking, Marcus curls his clammy hand around mine and paces to the door we only entered mere minutes ago. Shamefully, I pout, hating that my assurance wasn't potent enough to squelch his concerns. I thought the desire displayed in my eyes would have been the most significant indication of how badly I want this. Although I am a little unnerved about tiptoeing into the BDSM lifestyle again, my excitement easily overpowers my anxiety.

"You requested to see the real Cleo. I'm trying to show you that. I can't do that if you defy my every move," I partially quote, using his own words against him.

The efforts of my heaving lungs turn calamitous when Marcus stops just outside the door. He cranks his neck to me, his stare the most thigh-quakingly delicious scowl I've ever been given. After running his eyes over my disappointed face, he releases his grip on the handle so he can run it over his clipped afro.

"That woman I was in your playroom is me. I've never felt more invigorated and free as I was that morning." Although my body is pleading for his dominance to be unleashed, my words come straight from my heart, as every one I spoke was true. "The man you are in this room is a part of you, Marcus. This is your domain. The one place you feel most comfortable. Share that with me. Let me in. Be my Master."

My breathing turns labored when his eyes lock and hold with mine. His pupils fill his cornea, making his alluring green eyes darker than usual, and the rigid line of his jaw is pulled taut. His gaze is spine-tingling, and it switches my heart rate from a leisured cantor to a gallop.

There he is. The man I've fantasized about every night the past nine weeks.

Master Chains.

28

I pant, incredibly aroused when Marcus moves to close his playroom door, trapping us inside. I forget to breathe when he spins on his heels and slowly prowls back to me. He is mere feet from me, but it feels like the sun swings from the east to the west by the time he is within reaching distance of me.

My nostrils pump when he tugs my elastic out of my hair, freeing my dark locks from their tight restraints. As my hair falls to my shoulders, he grips the hem of my shirt and pulls it over my head. He draws in a sharp breath between his teeth when he discovers I am braless underneath. My nipples bud, pleased to have secured the utmost devotion of his alluring eyes. He stares at me for mere seconds, but it feels like hours. His attentive gaze makes me feel devoted and cherished. It also makes me squirm on the spot.

My plain black running shorts are next to go, pulled down my shuddering thighs without any hindrance. He folds them neatly before placing them on a cabinet at the side of the room. I stand still, frozen in a trance when he begins removing his clothing.

"Jesus Christ," I mutter under my breath, incapable of not reacting to the splendid sight in front of me.

Marcus's muscles are pulled taut from the rigorous activities he undertook earlier, meaning each bump, curve, and plane carved into his mouthwatering body is on full display. His cock is also thick and jutted, but that isn't the most appealing part of his package. It's the dominance beaming from his heavy-hooded gaze. He truly is a Master—pushing my race to climax into the forefront of my mind by doing something as innocuous as undressing.

After gathering something from a set of drawers on his right, he moves back in front of me. I'm tempted to discover what he is holding in his hands, but I can't force my eyes away from his. He has me locked in a trance, drunk on lust.

"What's your safe word, Cleo?" he prompts, peering into my eyes.

I cough to clear the tumbleweeds in my throat before replying, "Pineapple."

"Say it again."

"Pineapple," I repeat more forcefully.

Marcus pauses, soundlessly building the suspense, flaunting his powerful aura in an impressive way. He hasn't even touched me, and I'm the wettest I've ever been. My core won't stop crunching in anticipation as my body begs for him to lose control—to act so reckless, he can't hold back his desires.

I don't know how much time passes gazing into his eyes before he commands me to kneel. His voice is thick and demanding but with a guttural quality from our delay in conversation. Eager to follow his demand, I lower myself onto my knees. The plush carpet hugs my gravel-scraped skin, making what would usually be a painful stance less achy.

"Kneeling is a mark of respect for your Master. Any time you wish to enter my playroom, you must kneel first," Marcus advises me.

When I lift my eyes from the ground, my breathing shallows to a ragged pant. I am face to face with Marcus's primed cock. My first instinct is to reach out and touch him, but I suppress my desires—*barely*—knowing I handed my powers to him the instant I entered this room.

"Do you understand, Cleo?" Marcus questions, put off by my silence.

I lick my lips before nodding, advising I understand his request.

"You're also not to wear any clothes or have your hair pulled up in any way." He carefully clasps my chain link pendant between his thumb and index finger. "And you're to wear this pendant at all times, in and out of this room. It's your collar—a symbol to everyone in our community that you are mine. Do you understand?"

"Yes," I reply, nodding, my mind too dazed by his admission to form a better response.

If my necklace is a symbol of our relationship, does that mean he wanted me to be his before he discovered our sexual compatibility? And before he had our contract drafted?

My internal deliberation is interrupted when something smooth and cold is placed under my chin to lift my head. My knees scrape the carpet when I discover what it is. It is an exact replica of the black riding crop Marcus used on me in the sex swing—although a little more compact.

My core spasms when my eyes meet Marcus's. His gaze is dominant, primitive and robust.

"Yes, what?" he questions, his deep timbre sending a chill of anticipation down my spine.

"Yes, Master Chains," I correct, my words barely a whisper since they were forced through the lust curled around my throat.

Marcus's lips crimp in the corners as he moves the riding crop away from my chin. He trails it down my thrusting chest, weaving it like a snake through a sandy desert before stopping just above my pubic bone.

"Spread your knees wider," he requests while running the tip of the riding crop between the folds of my quaking pussy.

When I do as instructed, he awards my obedience with an ideally placed smack on my aching clit. I close my eyes and call out, loving the painful stimulation awakening every inch of my body. Marcus waits for the fiery warmth engulfing me to calm before taking a step closer to me, propelling his glorious cock into my peripheral vision.

"Put your hands on the balls of your feet, then lean back until your backside is resting on your hands." The deep rasp of his voice is felt by the tips of my toes.

I sigh softly, disheartened I'm moving away from an object I've been dying to taste in my mouth for months. I don't know if Marcus believes my skills in giving head are lacking, or he doesn't like having his cock sucked, but if he keeps denying my request to taste him in my mouth, he'll never discover I have no gag reflex. Don't ask how I found I have no gag reflex, it's a story only those closest to me know—AKA Lexi.

My disappointment doesn't linger for long. Only as long as it takes Marcus to say, "You're going to suck my dick, Cleo, but if at any time you remove your hands, I will withdraw contact, and you will be punished."

Pleasure clusters in my core, ecstatic I'm finally going to taste him. I don't care I can't touch him. Tasting him will be worth the sacrifice. I lick my lips in anticipation as Marcus runs his hand down his cock, stroking it in a slow and tantalizing pace.

After gathering a bead of pre-cum from his swollen knob, he runs his thumb over the cut in my lip, using his arousal to loosen up the tightness of the small scar forming there.

"If you feel pain at any time, tell me." His tone ensures I cannot mistake his comment as a suggestion. It was a demand.

I nod, my eyes arrested on his glorious cock inching toward me.

"Are you ready?" he asks, his tone gruff.

I lick my lips. "Please," I pant.

When he gives me permission, my tongue delves out to lick the bead of salty -goodness glistening on his tip. Marcus's lips part, and he sharply draws in a breath when I suck him into my mouth for the first time. The appreciative moan escaping my lips vibrates his knob when he slowly inches into my mouth. My god—he tastes good. Salty, manly and virile. The perfect combination to drive me wild.

"Open wider, Cleo," Marcus instructs, his hooded gaze heating my face.

The corners of my mouth burn when I part my lips more.

"Good girl."

Since my hands are tucked under my backside, Marcus must control the pace of our exchange. He guides his cock in and out of my mouth as my tongue works on his swollen crown. I suck, lick and graze my teeth over his impressive shaft. When his groans turn gruffer from my tongue running along the dense vein nourishing his cock, I give it more attention with every pump he does.

Sweat beads at my temples as he increases the rocking of his hips. I suck ravenously as he feeds his cock into my greedy mouth. I run my tongue over the sensitive slit, lapping up every morsel of his arousal while peering up at him, coaxing him to lose control.

"Ah. Yes. Just like that," he praises, enticing me even more.

The riding crop drops to the floor with a clatter when he clutches the back of my head. I purr loudly when his painful grip sends a pleasurable tingle racing down my spine. He uses my hair to control his grinds. He pumps in and out of my mouth at a speed fast enough that he thickens with every thrust, but not too fast he loses complete control.

"You're enjoying this," he mutters, weaving his fingers through my hair to tighten his grip. "On your knees, servicing your Master."

"Yes. Oh, god. Yes," I moan in reply. "I've been wanting this for weeks. Months." I peer up at him, my eyelids heavy with lust. "Years."

Air hissing through his teeth is the only reply he gives me. I lavish his cock with attention, worshiping the heavy feeling of him in my mouth. My erotic purrs vibrate on his taut flesh, my excitement at unraveling him unable to be contained. I graze my teeth over his knob as my tongue works on the vein feeding his magnificent erection. I want him unraveled, to be completely mindless.

"You don't just want to suck my cock. You want me at your complete mercy, so you feel like you have control, that you have the power," Marcus grunts as his pumps into my mouth quicken.

I answer him by increasing the power of my sucks. I do love doing this to him, satisfying him with my mouth, I also cherish how uncontrolled I can make him. Seeing how restrained he is when pleasing me is an exhilarating experience, but the sight of him standing above me, feeding his glorious cock into my mouth is just as exhilarating. I adore the way his lips part when I run my teeth over the plush crown of his cock, and how the veins in his neck thrum when I enhance the pressure of my sucks. I love that I can make him so reckless, his sexual hunger is finally placed first.

Reading the response from my forthright eyes, Marcus says, "That will never happen, Cleo. Power play isn't about one partner having more power than the other. It's like ballroom dancing. Both partners have an essential role to play to give the best performance. Both are as important as the other."

His thumb tracks the hollow in my cheek from my greedy sucks. "Contrary to what you believe, you're naturally submissive. You *love* being dominated, you *crave* giving pleasure, and you *relish* the idea of being punished. But instead of trusting me to take care of you, you continually defy me in the hope you will force me to dominate you."

My knees drag across the carpet as my pussy pulses with desire. I can't deny what he said as every word was factual.

"Disobedience may get you punished, Cleo, but not in the way you're hoping. Pain during pleasure is much more enticing than pain solely from being punished."

I whimper when he draws his cock out of my mouth. My insides sigh in disappointment, devastated at the hollow and empty feeling in my mouth.

He peers down at me, his eyes blazing with lust. "Punishment comes in many forms, Cleo. Not all of it is painful. Like now. Your disobedience will only award you with disappointment. Your constant need to goad me is why you can't touch me tonight. It's why I am fucking *your* mouth at *my* pace, in *my* desired position, in *my* playroom."

A sensual moan purrs out my mouth before I can stop it. Sexy dominance beams out of him in invisible waves, but that wasn't the sole cause for my shameful moan. It was what his eyes were relaying. He might have said, "My. My. My." But his eyes were conveying, "Mine. Mine. Mine."

"Do you understand what I am saying, Cleo? From now on, your disobedience will only award you with disappointment."

I glance up at him, my hunger for him unconcealed in my hankering eyes. "Yes, I understand, Master Chains."

His lips curl in a heart-stuttering smirk. "Good girl," he murmurs, bringing his cock back to within reaching distance.

I run my lip down the length of him, continuing with my mission to unravel him, to have my name torn from his mouth as his warm cum spurts onto my tongue. My cheeks hollow painfully when I suck down hard. Marcus's grunts turn feral as his efforts to contain his excitement come undone. He grinds into my mouth so profoundly the crown of his cock hits the back of my tonsils. The veins in his clenched jaw throb when he realizes I have no gag reflex.

"Just as I imagined—if not better," he hisses through clenched teeth.

Before I have the chance to register its arrival, his orgasm takes me by surprise. My eyes widen when cum rockets out of his cock at a faster rate than I can swallow it.

"Take it all, Cleo. Do not spill one drop. Don't stop until you suck me dry."

My eyes widen as I frantically gulp the salty goodness pumping out of him in thick, hot spurts. He tastes so good. Brackish, manly, and 100% Marcus. I moan, exulted I am finally tasting him in my mouth, but struggle to reel in my unbridled hankering.

Marcus's feral grunts make me needy and hot, while the sting of him pulling my hair rushes my need to climax to the forefront of my mind. My mind dangerously spirals out of control as an endless stream of possibilities floods me. I squeeze my thighs together, vainly trying to quell the frantic pulse making my sex a sultry mess. Nothing works. My rampant horniness is too wild to contain.

Incapable of holding back my desires for a moment longer, my hands shoot out to grip the base of Marcus's twitching shaft. I work my hand up and down his pulsating member as my tongue laps up every drop of his spawn. I love his taste so much I don't want to miss a single drop.

A frustrated groan parts my lips when Marcus steps backward, pulling his pulsating cock out of my mouth with a pop. My lust-crazed eyes dart up to his, demanding an explanation for his withdrawal of contact. I am so desperate for him, sexual frustration is bubbling in my veins.

"You were told not to touch me. Disobedience has no place in this room, Cleo. Now you must be punished. There is no cause for delay."

My kneecaps crack back into place when Marcus yanks me off the floor. When my legs curl around his sweat-slicked waist, his erect flesh hangs heavy between my legs. I grind against him, hungry for friction on my skin. Marcus adjusts my position, denying me the opportunity to rub my clit against his engorged knob.

"Disobedience does not equal pleasure."

Before a single gripe can leave my lips, his tongue slides into my mouth, claiming and possessing every inch of me. His dominating kiss makes me feel aroused and incredibly wanted even knowing I am about to be punished.

I wait for panic to make itself known when Marcus places me onto my feet next to the wall housing the finest quality whips, floggers, and spanking apparatuses. It never comes. The lust crackling in the air is too dense for something as weak as fear to enter the equation. I'm not scared, panicked or hesitant. I am hazed with helpless pleasure, ready to submit to my Master.

What I said to Marcus earlier was a lie. This isn't just his domain. It's mine as well.

29

"Did you know about this?" Lexi asks, not bothering to issue a greeting.

The large leather chair in Marcus's office gives out a squeak when I sit down. With my cracked cell phone sitting on the entranceway table of my home in Montclair, I've resorted to using the computer to keep in contact with Lexi the past three days. Although Marcus offered to replace my cell, we've never gotten around to it. We would have needed to leave the private sanctuary of his house for that to happen, and since neither of us were eager to do that, FaceTime became the perfect solution to preserve my sister-meddling.

Today is the first time Marcus and I have been apart the past three days. He left the house only twenty minutes ago to attend an emergency meeting with his band at their record label's head office in Hopeton. With cabin fever making my feet itchy, I initially requested to go with him. When he explained the mass number of paparazzi who swarm Hopeton, I withdrew my request. I prefer watching the clamor from the other side of the camera lens, rather than be inundated with it.

The last seventy-two hours of my life have been a magical, not just my sexual relationship with Marcus, but our entire bizarre kindship. Although our relationship has been built at a reckless speed, our opposing personalities have melded together so nicely, you'd swear we've been a couple for years, not mere days. Our online association was filled with lust and fire-sparking passion, so it was only natural it would follow a similar path when brought into a real-life setting.

Although there have been times where I've felt vulnerable and exposed, I've learned a lot about myself the past three days. I've always trusted Marcus, so my most significant learning curve wasn't about trusting him, it was about trusting my own instincts as well. What Marcus said in his playroom was true.

I've wanted to submit to him for weeks, I was just too worried about society's opinion on my decision that I pushed my desires to the side by using the excuse of equality and feminism.

Not anymore. From now on, I'm going to openly express myself. Does that mean I'll sign a contract with Marcus and become his sub? No, it doesn't. Marcus can pretend all he likes that my bratty personality annoys him, but until his forthright eyes relay the same annoyance, I'll continue being who I am.

"Base to Cleo, are you there?" Lexi's loud voice screeches out of the computer speakers, drawing my attention back to her.

I sink deeper into my chair, the lusty smile on my face telling her where my thoughts wandered to. Lexi sticks her finger down her throat, pretending she is repulsed by the stories my eyes are relaying. I waggle my brows, grateful I'm finally giving her a taste of her own medicine.

"Mrs. Rachet will be devastated you shared your roaring sex life with half of Montclair before she did," Lexi snickers loudly.

Giggling, she twists her phone around to show she is sitting in her CF specialist's bustling waiting room. Usually, I'd break out in hives from having my sex life discussed in public, but I'm too panicked at discovering Lexi is at Dr. Spencer's office to be embarrassed.

With my heart sitting in my chest, I scoot to the edge of my chair. "Why are you at Dr. Spencer's? Is everything okay?" I interrogate, my panic unmissable in my fretful tone.

Not waiting for Lexi to reply, I minimize our FaceTime screen and bring up the latest flight schedule. If she's had another severe attack, nothing will stop me catching the first flight home. I may finally be expressing my desires without pausing to consider society's opinion, but that doesn't mean my love of my sister has diminished. She has, and always will be, my utmost priority. I also made a promise to my mom the day of her funeral, I plan on keeping my promise.

"Did he tell you he was doing this?" Lexi asks, distracting me from securing my credit card out of my purse resting on the desk.

I've only heard her use that voice a small handful of times in her twenty-one years. It's usually when she is overwhelmed with excitement. Come to think of it, the last time I heard her speak in such a way was when Jackson asked her out for the first time.

I drag the mouse across the mousepad, eager to bring up our FaceTime screen. My nerves are so rattled I miss the darn cursor box numerous times. The instant I have Lexi's beaming face projecting out of the monitor, I stammer out. "You're not pregnant, are you?"

Lexi laughs—loudly.

"No!" She freezes as her expression goes deadpan. "God no!" She gags as a shiver racks over her body, like the idea of being pregnant is worse than catching cooties.

"Then what's going on?" I tilt closer to the monitor, wanting to ensure Abel doesn't overhear my latest comment. "Did those special vitamins arrive earlier than expected?"

Lexi chuckles again. This one isn't laced with shocked concern like her earlier one. It's brimming with sexual undertone.

"No. But I've been refreshing the tracking information every hour," she admits with a suggestive waggle of her brows. "Tell Abel I said thanks for the tip on the acai berries. Ever since I added them to Jackson's smoothies, I've been walking bowlegged."

My breakfast gurgles in my stomach, disturbed by Lexi confession. "I'm not sure that was Abel's intention, but I'll be sure to let him know."

My first impression of Abel was highly accurate. Not only is he a wonderful man who has lived an amazing life, he is also my biggest ally in unearthing the real Marcus. Just like my first day here, we've had breakfast together every morning the past three days. He shares stories from when he lived next door to Marcus in a rundown housing project in Ravenshoe, while I give him play-by-play rundowns on Lexi's many quirky antics. We may even occasionally gang up on Marcus to get things our way. Not anything major, usually, just what movies we're going to watch or what we should eat for dinner. I won't lie, it's nice having a sparring partner when wrangling a man as dominant as Marcus. Who knows, maybe one day I will get to top him.

Smiling at my wickedly evil thoughts, I shift my eyes to Lexi. She peers at me through the camera lens, not the least bit intimidated by my demanding stare. The longer we're silent, the more my quintessential need to know everything gnaws at my insides.

"What going on?!" I squeal, no longer capable of holding in my eagerness to discover what has shunted Lexi into silence. She doesn't understand the meaning of quiet, let alone undertaking it.

Lexi waits a beat, annoyingly fostering the suspense depriving the air of oxygen. My ballet flats tap the carpet madly, the tension thickening my veins too great to ignore.

Only once the air turns murderous does Lexi finally mutter, "I've been added to the Kalydeco program."

I freeze as confusion envelopes me. "What?" I ask, certain I didn't hear her right.

We've been trying to get Lexi admitted to the Kalydeco program for years. But with its price tag sitting at over $300,000 a year, it was well out of our budget.

"I'm in," Lexi confirms, nodding so briskly our video stream glitches. "The initial tests Dr. Spencer ran on Monday came back clear. I start the program today."

"Today?!" I squeal, too shocked to say more. My entire body shakes as tears freely glide down my face.

Lexi swipes at a puddle of moisture pooling in her eyes while nodding. "Today!" she roars down the line, scaring the living daylights out of me.

I push back from the desk and stand from my chair. My movements are so abrupt, the large leather chair sails backward until it crashes into the drywall with a thud. I stare at my sister's smiling face for several moments, muted and confused. I don't bother clearing the tears streaming from my eyes. There are too many for me to contend with, so why bother? My heart fitfully pounds my chest as the weight I've been carrying on my shoulders the past four years alleviates.

No longer able to hold in my excitement, I throw my arms into the air and do a happy jig. Lexi joins me, not the slightest bit embarrassed she is shaky her booty in a crammed waiting room. She dances like nobody is watching, her happiness too overwhelming to leash.

I don't know how much time passes before I slump back into my chair. We danced long enough Lexi's cheeks are a vibrant red coloring, and I'm wheezing and out of breath, but not long enough my utter shock has dissipated.

"Can you believe he did this?" Lexi asks.

I shake my head. "No, I can't. I added provisions during our negotiations, but I never knew he'd take it this far."

Her brows scrunch as confusion clouds her moisture-filled eyes. "Negotiations?"

I nod.

Her eyes widen as the color in her cheeks drain. "You negotiated *my* health into *your* deal?"

When I nod again, Lexi grumbles, "That's disgusting."

Stunned by her bizarre response, I explain, "Requesting to have health coverage included in an employment contract isn't unusual. If you negotiate fairly, the terms can work out amicable for both parties. I saw the desperation in Mr. Carson's eyes when he propositioned me to investigate the Chains story, so I went in gung-ho. Obviously, my tactic worked."

My confession doesn't ease the confusion marring Lexi's face. If anything, it intensifies it. "Global Ten Media isn't paying for me to participate in the Kalydeco program," she stumbles out a short time later, her tone reserved.

My lungs struggle to secure an entire breath. "Then who is?" I ask, my eyes dancing between Lexi's candid gaze.

Lexi tilts in close to her cell, filling my computer monitor with her beautifully flustered face. "Chains is," she reveals, her low tone indicating she is concerned what my response will be.

My pupils widen as my pulse comes to a grinding halt. My lips twitch, endeavoring to say something to ease the concern brewing in her eyes, but not a word is fired off my tongue. I am too stunned to articulate anything. Don't get me wrong, it's a good shock, but still shock nonetheless.

My wide eyes lift to the computer monitor when Lexi's name is called. She raises her finger in the air, soundlessly requesting a minute before she devotes her attention back to me.

"I've got to go, Cleo. Dr. Spencer is ready for me," she informs me, glee distinguishable in her voice. "I'll call you the instant I leave his office."

After an impromptu air kiss, Lexi disconnects our chat, leaving me sitting dumbfounded and mute. I slump lower into my chair, shocked into silence.

The Kalydeco program isn't just $300,000 in total. It's $300,000 a year for the remainder of Lexi's life. A drug like this is so beneficial for Lexi, her life expectancy just grew by another ten to fifteen years, so that's millions and millions of dollars. Although Marcus's generosity doesn't surprise me, I am still overwhelmed he did this for Lexi. *I'm overwhelmed he did this for me.*

How could I ever repay him for something so mammoth?

30

Ten minutes later, I am still sitting in Marcus's office, stunned in silence. Although my mind is stuck in a foggy haze, one thing is evidently clear. Strangers may construe Marcus's decision to fund Lexi's treatment as coercing me to be his sub, but I don't see it that way. I've only known Marcus a matter of months, but I know him well enough to say he didn't help Lexi for his own gain, he did it out of the goodness of his own heart.

The first time Marcus gave me access to his office, I stumbled upon some accounting records left strewn on his desk. When I saw Chains' monthly revenue, I nearly fell off my chair. I know the value of privacy is priceless, but the amount people are willing to pay to guarantee it's mind-boggling. But do you want to know something even more shocking? Every month, Chains' profits are distributed to numerous charities close to Marcus's heart—Links being the biggest beneficiary. Marcus doesn't keep a single penny for himself. Not one.

That proves without a doubt that Marcus is as generous as he is dominant. His generosity is one item on a long list of reasons why I've fallen head over heels in love with him. Yes, I love him. I know it's early. I know it's crazy. But I love him. Wildly. Recklessly. Wholeheartedly. I love him.

The sweep of my hand across my cheeks to remove sneaky sentimental tears freezes halfway when the annoying buzz of my FaceTime Messenger App shrieks into my ears. After gathering my heart from the floor, I swivel my seat to face the computer monitor on Marcus's large desk. Eager to discover how Lexi's appointment went with Dr. Spencer, I wiggle my mouse and click my FaceTime app.

Since I'm expecting my caller to be Lexi, I don't check the name of the person requesting to FaceTime me. It's a foolish move on my behalf. Sick gloom spreads across my chest when a face I'm not expecting to see pops up on my computer screen. It's Richard, security officer at Global Ten Media.

After exhaling my nerves with a deep breath, I lock my eyes with Richard's. His facial expression is calm and unemotional, but his eyes are telling an entirely different story. They are stormy with alarm.

"Hi, Richard. Is everything okay?" I ask, distressed by his apparent instability.

He isn't the only one with unpredictable nerves. I've gone from an all-inspiring high to a devastating low in a matter of seconds. The shift in my demeanor has my body shaking so much it appears as if we have a bad connection. We don't. The internet service is so seamless I can see every dark speckle in Richard's icy eyes. His edgy gaze has my anxieties creeping toward a steep cliff, threatening to fall into horrid tension at any moment.

The unpleasant assumptions running rampant through my mind are proven on point when Richard straight out asks, "How do you know Marcus Everett?"

My breath hitches halfway to my lungs. It isn't his failure to issue a greeting that has me gasping for air, it's the concern exhibited by his somber gaze. Although we've only associated at work, I've seen many sides of Richard's personality the past five years. Not once have his eyes held the amount of arrogant apprehension they do now. More times than not, showy cockiness beams out of him in invisible waves.

Although I am stunned by Richard's off-putting demeanor, I act unaware of who his question is referring to. I will forever be in Richard's debt for the assistance he provided me Saturday night, but my desire to protect Marcus outweighs displaying gratitude to a man who has a long way to prove his worth to me.

"Who?" I stammer out, my words as uneasy as Richard's facial expression.

My knuckles whiten from my firm grip on Marcus's chair as I await Richard's reply. It's lucky we are conversing via a computer or the sound of my heart smashing my ribs would give away the deceitfulness of my reply.

Heavy lines of doubt score Richard's smooth forehead. "Marcus Everett—bassist of Rise Up?" he continues to interrogate, not the slightest bit concerned about the intrusiveness of his question. "How do you know him?"

My throat tightens, then burns. "Umm… I don't really know him. Not any more than a standard fan would." My heart falls from my ribcage. Even I heard the deceit in my voice.

Richard glares into my eyes, calling me a fraud without a syllable escaping his lips. I look away from the screen, hating that I'm so transparent. My fighting spirit when battling people like Delilah is without hindrance as my replies are honest and straight from my heart. But I've always found it hard to lie in general, even more so when it's to people who haven't given me a reason to be deceitful. Richard may be an asshole, but he's never given me a reason to lie to him.

"You don't know Marcus?" Richard asks again, dragging my focus back to him.

The instant my eyes connect with his I regret my decision. He may have only said four small words, but his eyes cross-examine me more than his words ever could.

"No," I reply again, peering straight into his eyes, concealing my lie with a rueful glare.

A rock settles in my stomach, hating how easy the lies are flowing from my mouth. But there is no way I'll sit back and watch someone take aim at the man I am in love with without trying to intercept their play.

The heat of Richard's frustrated gaze is so potent it scorches my skin through the computer monitor. "He isn't the man responsible for your attack last week?" he continues to insinuate, his tone having a whip of anger attached to it.

"No," I answer again without pause for delay. Marcus may be harboring guilt for my attack, but I know he isn't responsible for what happened in the alleyway Saturday night.

Richard's head bobs up and down as the confusion in his eyes rapidly morphs to challenging. "So if I were to knock on the door of Marcus's Florida residence, you wouldn't be there?"

A rush of nausea churns my stomach, but I keep my expression neutral, remembering what Marcus said when we arrived here four days ago. No one is aware of this location—not even the scheming paparazzi.

I lift and lock my eyes with Richard's, my determination the strongest it's ever been. "No. I wouldn't be there," I lie, my tone as devious as the smirk etching onto Richard's face.

"Okay," Richard sighs heavily. "I guess we are about to discover if your eyes really are the gateway to your soul, Cleo."

My breathing turns manic when the shrill of a doorbell booms into my ears not even two seconds later. It didn't just come from outside Marcus's office. It sounded through the computer monitor as well... ...

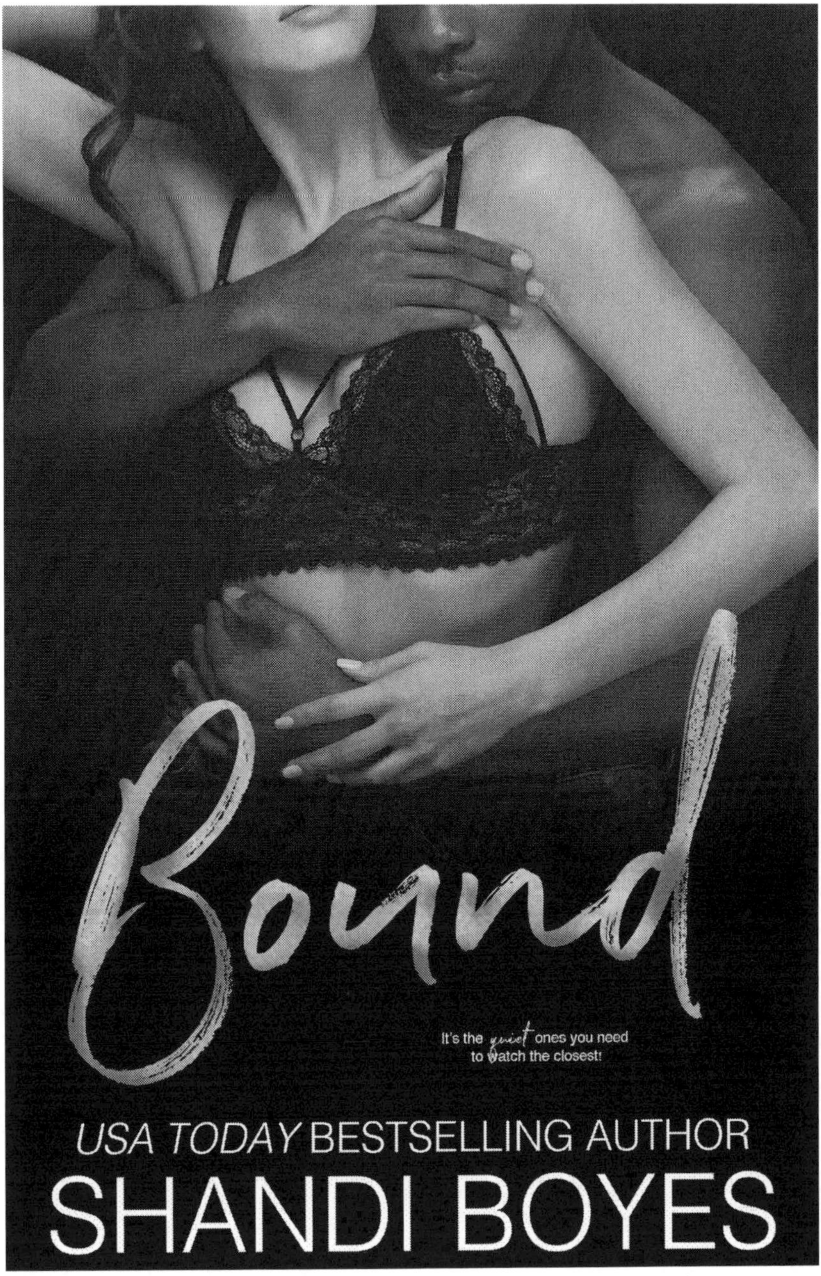
Bound
It's the quiet ones you need
to watch the closest!
USA TODAY BESTSELLING AUTHOR
SHANDI BOYES

1

"Come on, Cleo, open up. I know you're in there."

My eyes snap to the carved wooden door of Marcus's office as sick alarm makes itself known to my stomach. Even with blood roaring in my ears, I can't be mistaken. Richard's deep voice didn't just rumble through Marcus's dead-quiet palatial mansion, it boomed out of the computer speaker as well. He is here. In Florida. Knocking on the door of the man our joint employer is actively investigating. *Goddammit!*

In a tizzy, I drag my mouse across the screen and disconnect my FaceTime chat with Richard. It might seem immature, but when I'm clutching at straws, irrational ideas are the first thing to pop into my head. When the quiet amplifies Richard's repeated requests for entry, my fists firm into balls and a long curse of expletives muffle out my mouth. Why can't anything ever be easy for me? Why can't I catch a break from my miserable existence? *Why did I fall in love with the man I was assigned to investigate?*

The dread making my skin a sticky mess intensifies when Abel's distinctive voice calls out, "Just a minute."

My pupils widen as my breathing turns labored. I completely forgot Abel was here.

"Don't open the door, Abel!" I strive to project my plea through the thick walls positioned between us. Aiming for my voice to come out unrecognizable to Richard, I sound like a lady in her late eighties who smokes three packs of cigarettes a day.

I level my breathing and prick my ears, praying Abel heard my request. When my screamed plea is met with silence, I push off my feet and head for the door. A loud thud booms into the hallway when I throw open the door with so much force it smacks into the drywall, leaving a significant dent.

Pretending I didn't just damage Marcus's property, I race into the corridor separating the open-plan living rooms from the private sleeping quarters.

The entire house is so eerily quiet that nothing but my feet padding against the wooden floor sounds through my ears. When I cut the corner at the end of the hall, my ballet flats fail to gain friction on the highly varnished flooring. I lose control of my footing, sending me crashing into a large wooden side table. My back molars grit when fiery pain rockets through my body, but I continue with my mission, my desire to protect Marcus too strong to allow something as weak as pain to slow me down. For how determined my steps are, you'd be none the wiser to the throbbing ache impinging my right wrist. It's nearly as painful as my horribly twisted heart.

"Don't open the door, Abel," I plead again, more quietly this time since I am near the entrance of Marcus's house.

All the air in my body leaves in a brutal grunt when I enter the main foyer. It isn't my bull-like charge that has me wheezing for breaths, it's realizing my pleas came too late. Abel has already opened the door.

I take a step backward, cowardly hiding behind a thick wooden pillar. Like a missile assigned to its target, Richard spots me in an instant.

"Hello, Cleo," he greets me from his position on the front porch of Marcus's residence, his tone as haughty as ever.

When my head pops out from its conspicuous hiding place, the shit-eating grin on Richard's face turns as blinding as the midday sun. He shrugs off his thick wool business coat as he steps into the foyer, not bothering to wait for an invitation.

"You're good," he says with his eyes arrested on me as he folds his coat over his arm. "For a microsecond, I truly thought my assumptions were wrong. But, here you are, exactly where I suspected you'd be."

He thrusts his other hand into the pocket of his dark blue trousers as his eyes take in the wonderment of Marcus's property. If I weren't consumed by unbridled panic about how he managed to find me, I'd verbalize my annoyance at his failure to acknowledge Abel standing at his side, offering to take his coat. Richard completely snubs him, acting as if he isn't even in the room with us as he saunters further inside.

"What are you doing here, Richard?" My voice is rickety with an equal amount of nerves and anger.

As my Garcia fighting spirit emerges, so does my irritation at having my privacy once again invaded. Even though this property is owned by the man our company is investigating, Richard has no right to arrive here unannounced, much less to interrogate me as if I am under investigation. He isn't even a journalist for crying out loud. He is a security officer.

Richard pretends he didn't hear my question, but I know he did. The tightness of his jaw firmed the instant my mouth opened. Once he's moved far enough into the foyer to unblock the doorway, Abel closes the sizeable Balinese door, then pivots around to face me. From the unease tainting his face, I can tell his spikes are also bristled by Richard's unexpected arrival. It isn't that Abel doesn't appreciate visitors. From the stories he shared, and the way he welcomed me, he usually greets guests with open arms. But he seems confused by Richard's presence. I can understand his response. To someone unaware of Richard's difficult personality, his demeanor can be a little hard to gauge. At first, his no-hesitation approach reveals a man who exudes a lot of confidence. It's only once you peel back his layers do you realize Richard uses his confidence and good looks to shield his less attractive attributes—mainly his lack of personality.

My attention diverts to Richard when a wolf whistle sounds out of his O-formed lips. He is standing at the edge of the entranceway, drinking in the enormity of Marcus's residence. From his vantage point, the opulence of the property is showcased in the most brilliant light. If he didn't already know he was standing in an extremely wealthy estate, the view from the entranceway ensures there is no doubt. The clifftop ocean scenery streaming through the large Constantine doors replicates sights I've only ever seen in movies, and the quality of the furnishings is so refined it almost seems royal.

"Wow, nice place you have here, Cleo," Richard mutters under his breath, his smug tone telling me he knows all too well this isn't my residence. "A little different from your New Jersey home, but I guess we've all been known to splurge when we're not the one footing the bill." He adds a brazen wink to his last sentence.

He gallops down the three steps of the foyer before moseying towards me. His entire composure screams of cocky arrogance, setting my nerves on edge.

"Where's Marcus?" he questions as his icy blue eyes meet mine.

Just hearing Marcus's name strengthens my desire to protect him. I roll my shoulders and stand tall, vainly trying to portray I'm not put off by Richard's unexpected arrival. It's all a ploy. I'm shaking so much on the inside, the glass of milk I consumed at breakfast is churning into butter.

"What are you doing here, Richard?" I repeat, more forcefully this time. I inwardly sigh, grateful my voice comes out with the confident tone I was aiming for. It was determined, yet free of the fear clutching my throat.

The smell of bottled cologne filters through my nose when Richard stops to stand in front of me. "I thought I'd pop in and make sure you're okay. The last time I saw you was when you were attacked in an alleyway, then you up vanished without a trace, leaving everyone baffled."

I crank my head to the side, pulling away from him when he brushes the back of his fingers over my bone-dry lips. Five days have passed since my assault, meaning the split in my mouth is nearly healed, and the bruise on my cheek is nothing more than a faint blemish. There is no reason for him to touch me in the manner he did when completing first aid on my injuries last Saturday.

"As you can see, I'm fine," I inform him, pretending I can't see the anger in his eyes doubling from my rejection. "As for leaving everyone baffled, those important to me know of my location, so your concern is utterly unnecessary."

I peer into Richard's aloof eyes, ensuring he can't miss me calling out his worry as a ruse. You don't travel this far just to check on someone who isn't even the equivalent of a work friend. I can smell a rat from a mile away, and considering the scent of desecration is leeching out of Richard by the bucket load, it doesn't take a genius to realize where the smell is coming from.

"If you were truly concerned about me, you could have just called me or sent me an email, then your worry would have been erased in an instant. You didn't need to travel all the way here to check on me." I fold my arms over my chest, successfully concealing my erratically heaving lungs from his avid gaze before continuing, "So cut the crap, Richard, and tell it to me straight... what are you doing here?"

Richard's eyes flash as the corners of his full lips pull into a broad grin. "There's the Cleo I remember. I was beginning to wonder if the rumors were true."

"What rumors?" I ask with a huff, feigning disinterest.

Hearing a snip of panic in my voice, Abel moves closer to our gathering. His steps are so discreet, I don't even hear the slightest tap of his hard-soled shoes as he spans the distance between us. When his eyes question if he should call Marcus, I shake my head. I don't need backup when it comes to taking down a man like Richard.

I've been battling him for so many years I'm considering putting "arrogant asshole combatant" on my resume as a qualification. I'd also prefer to leave Marcus out of the equation. For all I know, Richard could be running on pure speculation, and he has arrived here solely with the hope I'll slip up and expose Marcus's secret identity. Clearly, he doesn't know me very well. When it comes to protecting the people I love, nothing stands in my way, not even an arrogant man who is five seconds away from having his crotch reintroduced to my knee.

Abel's worldly eyes bounce between Richard and me for several moments before he nods. I can tell by his eyes he wants to say more, but he graciously trusts my intuition. After bidding farewell to Richard with a dip of his chin, he leaves the foyer.

Richard waits a beat before stepping closer to me, bursting the invisible bubble I'd prefer to keep between us. He is so close, a waft of cinnamon lingers into my nose. Considering it has been hours since I ate breakfast, I can only assume the scent is coming from Richard.

Not wanting Abel to get the wrong impression about my relationship with Richard, I take a step backward. Richard may believe we are alone, but I know we aren't. I can feel the warmth of Abel's gaze on my back as he eyeballs our exchange from the wings. Usually, I'd find his intrusive stare annoying, but since it's Abel, my hackles remained sheathed. His prying watch has more of a concerned grandfather vibe than a Nancy-nosey feel.

My jaw muscle tightens when Richard uses my distraction of Abel to his advantage. He runs the back of his fingers down my right cheek in a long, dedicated sweep. Under different circumstances, I could take his gesture as innocent, but the lusty gleam in his eyes ensures I can't mistake it as a friendly gesture. If he is hoping his amorous move will mollify the uncomfortable tension bristling between us, he needs to try another tactic. My heart melts when Marcus does a similar gesture, but coming from Richard, my skin is crawling, and the air grows stuffier.

Don't get me wrong, Richard is a handsome man. He has a well-carved face and fit body that would tempt any woman with a pulse, but over the past five years, I've seen his insides—they are nowhere near as pretty as his exterior.

I exhale a deep breath, eradicating the nerves from my body before locking my eyes with Richard. "Please don't take this the wrong way, as I truly appreciate the assistance you gave me last weekend, but you're way out of line arriving here unannounced and without an invitation."

My already teetering attitude veers to the negative when Richard has the audacity to throw back his head and laugh. I'm not talking a slight chuckle, I'm talking a full-hearted, using-every-inch-of-his-body-laugh. If my heart weren't a conflicted mess, it would be a hard laugh to ignore. It has that contagious quality, one you can't help but laugh along with.

"Unannounced?" Richard jeers. "I figured as much. That's why I got creative with my endeavor to reach you."

My heart leaps out of my chest when he nudges his head to the security panel at the side of the entranceway. The granulated image of Marcus's front gate that usually beams out of the monitor 24/7 has been replaced with a plain black screen.

When my eyes rocket back to Richard, it's the fight of my life to keep my knee in its rightful place. Pompous arrogance beams out of him in despicable abundance. "You tampered with the security system? Are you a complete idiot?! You could be arrested!"

Richard shrugs his shoulders. "It was either that or continue being turned away every hour on the hour by a Wesley Snipes wannabe." His narrowed gaze strays to the side of the room, acknowledging he is also aware Abel is watching us.

Realizing his cover has been blown, Abel steps out of the alcove he was hiding in. As his fierce eyes lock with Richard, he reinforces his stance. Only now do I realize the uncertainty tainting his face earlier wasn't based on worry. It was dislike. Clearly, today isn't the first time Abel has tangled with Richard, as his displeasure is too robust for someone who's just met him. Richard may be the very epitome of a chauvinistic asshole, but it usually takes 2-3 meetings to discover that, even for someone who can read people's personalities with just a sideways glance. There are just two things unclear. Why is Richard so desperate to talk to me? And why has Abel been foiling his attempts?

Drifting my eyes back to Richard, I start at the less confusing issue. "Why have you been trying to reach me?" I ask, bouncing my eyes between his tapered gaze.

Before Richard can answer me, the shrill of a landline telephone rings through my ears. I jump out of my skin, displaying I'm more rattled than I'd care to admit.

Dropping his eyes to his watch, Richard mumbles, "Damn. Global Ten could take a page from their book. Their response time is impressive."

My brows stitch into a frown, confused by his statement, but before I can mutter a response, Richard drifts his eyes to Abel. "Unless you want a swarm of police arriving here in around ten minutes, you might want to answer that."

A dash of hesitation clouds Abel's usually receptive eyes, but his stance remains firm. I can tell by the expression on his face he wants to answer the call, but he doesn't feel comfortable leaving me alone with Richard.

I adjust my position to face Abel front on. "It's okay," I assure him, nodding.

I may have only said two short words, but my eyes offer Abel more assurance than my words ever could. Richard is no doubt a blood-sucking leech, but I don't fear him. Although his taunts the past five years nicked my heart and bruised my ego, they have never once caused me physical harm, so I don't see that changing in the near future.

Abel's hesitation only lasts as long as it takes for his caller to hang up and redial. After issuing a final warning to Richard solely using his eyes, he quickly pivots on his heels and heads for the landline phone stationed in the office nook at the side of the kitchen.

My focus returns to Richard when he says, "Since that's most likely Marcus's security company calling to advise a breach of his security, I better make this quick." He steps closer to me, filling the last portion of air left between us with his imposing frame. "I told you last week I was trying to change. This is me proving to you I'm a changed man. I'm standing here in front of you, being as upfront as I can be, because I figured you of all people would appreciate the honesty."

My lips twitch as a witty comeback attempts to escape my mouth, but no matter how much my tongue tries to fire off a rebuttal, my mouth refuses to relinquish it. My brain is too rapt on reading his forthright gaze to do anything more. Richard's eyes are the frankest I've ever seen them. They not only expose a man who has a sickening amount of confidence, they also reveal he is telling the truth. His naturally engrained arrogance may have me doubting his motives, but he truly believes what he is saying. He thinks he is a changed man.

As Richard's eyes sweep the room to ensure we are still alone, his hand delves into his trouser pocket to produce a folded-up piece of paper. Horrid unease makes it hard for me to breathe when he holds it out for me. Pretending I can't feel my hands shaking a hundred miles an hour, I accept the document from his grasp and unfold it. For every second that ticks by in silence, the air becomes more stifling. You know that feeling you get when your whole world is about to become undone? That's what I am feeling right now. I've only felt like this one time before. It was the day my parents and little brother Tate were involved in their accident.

I take a moment to fill my lungs with oxygen before dropping my eyes to the sheet of paper I'm clutching for dear life. The air I've just sucked in is vehemently removed when my eyes absorb the badly pixelated image. Although the photo is grainy and small, there is no doubt it's a photo of Marcus and me. With my cap-covered head held high as I take in the affluent surroundings of the hotel lobby we are entering, my entire face is exposed.

"Where did you get this?"

Acting like he didn't hear a word I spoke, Richard spins on his heels and heads for the door. His long strides are so efficient, he is halfway across the foyer before my brain registers he is leaving. In a flurry, I push off my feet and follow after him. "Where are you going?" I ask, my high tone displaying my utter bewilderment.

He can't just bequeath me a snippet of information like this then leave me hanging. That's the worst form of torture to a person as inquisitive as me.

Richard cranks his neck back to peer at me. "If my Spidey-senses are right, we have around two minutes before our conversation is interrupted by an old man who doesn't realize he is well past his prime." He nudges his head to Abel slipping down the corridor situated between Marcus's studio and four-car garage.

My heart rate spikes as the hairs on my arms prickle with roused apprehension. *Where is he going?*

Continuing for the door, Richard says, "Considering I traveled here to talk to you in person, I don't fancy doing that while sitting behind bars for trespassing, or even worse, in the hospital with a bullet wound."

I gulp in a shocked breath, startled by his assumption he's about to be injured. Abel may have guarded our conversation with a protective mentality, but he'd never take it to the level Richard is concerned about. *Would he*?

Richard nudges his head to a dark sedan barely visible behind a green hedge sheltering Marcus's property from the road frontage. I discover how Richard gained access to Marcus's estate when I follow the direction of his gaze. There is a heap of industrial-sized wires hanging out of a security panel positioned on the wrought-iron gate. The fear curled around my throat tightens. *Why is Richard so desperate to talk to me, he's willing to risk his freedom to do so?*

"Come with me, Cleo, and I'll tell you everything I know," Richard implores, reading the silent questions streaming out of me.

When he locks his eyes with mine, my defenses waiver. His pleading eyes are persuasive, not only begging for me to give him a chance to prove he is a changed man, but also pleading for me to not believe everything I've been told—to properly evaluate the situation and make my own informed decision. But how can I do that without having time to contemplate? Not taking time to assess things usually leads me into foolish territory, and since I've spent way too much time in that zone the past three months, I'm hesitant to tiptoe toward it once more.

"I can't go with you, Richard," I whisper starkly, shaking my head.

Although my resolve is teetering on a very steep cliff, it isn't rattled enough to place Richard's request above the desires of my heart. I trust Marcus so much, I have faith he will protect us from any storm trying to destroy us. Even one as vicious as Delilah.

For the quickest second, Richard's cocky mask slips, exposing a side of him I've never seen in the five years I've known him—unbridled fear. "Alright, but if anything happens to you or Lexi, don't say I didn't warn you."

"Lexi?" I gasp out in panic, stepping closer to him. "What does this have to do with Lexi?"

Richard doesn't reply, he just slips down the side of Marcus's house and advances towards his vehicle. With the shadows of the arched awnings sheltering his large frame from the multiple security cameras monitoring Marcus's property, he moves undetected through the vast space.

Not taking the time to stop and think, I follow after him, my steps surprisingly quick for how much my thighs are quaking. "Richard, please, if Lexi is in danger, I need to know."

I can't believe I let the desires of my heart lead me so far astray that I've placed over twelve hundred miles between Lexi and me. The furthest I've ever been away from her is an hour. Even Marcus's fancy jet couldn't get me to her in an hour if something terrible were to happen.

A breathless squeal escapes my mouth when Richard splays his hand across my stomach and roughly yanks me back. The sharp edges of Marcus's property scratch the skin on my back when he draws me far enough under the awning to hide my frame from Abel, who is racing toward the house. His speed is so fast, gravel kicks up from his feet, dusting his polished black shoes with icky gray dust. I attempt to call out to him, but with panic curled around my throat, not a syllable escapes my thin grim lips.

The worry making my skin a sticky mess grows when my eyes zoom in on the weapon Abel is carrying. It's a replica of a gun I'd expect to see on a cattle farm or in a war movie. It's large, bulky, and looks like it could cause more harm than the gun Lexi threatened Marcus with.

Once Abel enters the house, Richard turns his eyes to me. "Is that a response you'd expect from a man not concerned about your safety? Or is that how a man who's been lying to you would react? Look closer, Cleo. The people surrounding you aren't who you think they are."

Stealing my chance to negate his false assumptions, Richard hightails it to his car mere feet from us. When he reaches the driver's side door, he stares at me for several moments, begging me to go with him. I stand in the shadows, drifting my eyes between Marcus's house and Richard's vehicle while contemplating. It feels like hours pass as I strive to clear the muddled confusion in my mind, but it's more like seconds. I don't know why I bother taking the time to deliberate. My brain is too fritzed with panic to let rational thoughts congregate.

Pretending I can't hear Abel shouting my name from inside Marcus's residence, I move out of the shadows and dash toward Richard's car. My intuition is screaming blue murder at my stupidity, but the urge to protect my sister far outweighs any concerns thickening my blood. She has, and always will be, my utmost priority, and I'm not below putting myself in danger to ensure she remains safe.

As I slide into the passenger seat of Richard's car, Abel charges out of Marcus's house. For a man in his mid-seventies, he has the core of a man many years younger. Standing in the dust cloud his brisk pace created, he cranks his head to the right before swinging it to the left as he strives to find me amongst the sprawling manicured grounds. My lungs fail to breathe when his eyes lock in on me sitting in the passenger seat of Richard's car. Although the windows are heavily tinted, I have no doubt he has seen me as the concern in his eyes triples the instant he spots me.

The smell of burning rubber streams into my nose when Richard plants his foot on the accelerator and pulls his car away from the curb at a frightening speed. Not the slightest bit hindered by chasing a vehicle with a 1500 horse-power motor under the hood while wearing a fitted black suit and polished dress shoes, Abel pursues us on foot. His speed is so unchecked, he reaches the end of the driveway in two heart-thrashing seconds.

A frightened squeal emits from my lips when the sound of the gun being fired booms into my ears not even two seconds later. Its loud bang echoes down the dead quiet street, rattling my heart straight out of my chest.

"Jesus Christ," Richard mutters under his breath as his panicked eyes bounce between the road and his rearview mirror. "Is he fucking insane? He's shooting at us with a shotgun."

My terrified eyes turn back to Abel standing at the end of Marcus's drive-way. He has his gun braced on his shoulder as his fierce eyes stare down the long barrel. Although my insides are jittering like a hooker on crack, I know I'm not in any danger. Call it intuition or a stupid case of idiocy, but I know Abel would never hurt me. Richard, on the other hand...

My words trail off when a loud bang ricochets down the street for the second time. Noticing the direction of Abel's gun, reality smacks into me.

"He's isn't aiming for us, he's trying to take out your tires."

Wanting to test the accuracy of my assumption, Richard dangerously veers his car down an isolated dirt road on our left. Dust billows around us as his vehicle weaves down the rapidly narrowing track. Just as I suspected, the instant Richard's tires left the pavement, Abel's gun stops firing.

I sink deeper into my seat and sit in silence for several miles, pondering if I just made a careless mistake. Several minutes of deliberation award me with even more confusion. Nothing makes any sense. Why would Richard go to such lengths to talk to me face to face when he could have just spoken to me over the phone? And why did Abel react so fiercely to me leaving with Richard? I'm at a complete loss as to what the hell is going on.

Hoping Richard will be the key to unlocking my confusion, I swing my eyes to him. The concern blackening my blood grows when my impromptu scan of the car's interior has me stumbling onto more evidence of my idiocy. There is an open box of ammunition and a handgun stashed in the console between Richard and me. If that isn't concerning enough, it's sitting on top of a massive pile of polaroid photos. I'm not talking one or two random snaps Richard may have taken during his travels from New York to Florida. I'm talking about hundreds upon hundreds of photos taken from multiple angles, in multiple locations.

I'm in every single image.

2

Watching Richard from the corner of my eye, I unlatch my seatbelt and carefully pull it across my body. The thin black material sliding through the belt mechanism sounds through my ears, closely followed by a noisy clunk when it's latched. I freeze, panicked beyond belief that it has advised Richard of my intended stealth-like moves. It hasn't. Richard's focus remains on the narrowed dirt track we are traveling on.

With the road careening along the glorious coastline of Bronte's Peak, his usual astuteness has vanished. I can't say I don't understand his fascination. The view is so spectacular, if I weren't fearful about being trapped in the confines of a vehicle with a man who's apparently been stalking me for months, I'd also stop to admire the wonderment of Bronte's Peak in all its glory. But since I'm on the verge of a panic attack, I leash my desire and keep my focus on the task at hand—my imminent escape.

After taking a few moments to gather the composure I still hold, I continue with my mission. I clamber to the edge of my seat, sitting so close to the window, my shoulder blade touches the rigid, salt-blasted glass. I take in a lung-filling gulp of air before curling my hand around the door latch. Although Richard's speed is fast enough my body must brace for impact, it isn't fast enough to worry a tumble out of his car will threaten my life.

The air I've only just sucked in is forcefully evicted when my tug on the door handle fails to open the latch. It remains locked—trapping me in the car with Richard.

Gritting my teeth, my eyes scan the area, seeking an alternative exit. There isn't one. Other than crawling over Richard's well-formed torso to scale out the driver's side window, I'm trapped, hostage of a man who has two dozen photos of me sleeping.

Realizing there is only one way out of this car, I creep my hand toward

Richard's gun nestled between us. My hand freezes halfway to its target when Richard suddenly shifts his eyes to me.

"Some people have more money than sense," he mutters, nudging his head to the palatial mansions balancing perilously on the cliff edge. "It would be a great view, but I wouldn't be hanging around during hurricane season."

My brows stitch when his voice comes out with an amused huskiness. He is acting like we're friends on a leisurely Sunday drive, not him kidnapping me under the pretense he is helping me.

"Yeah, crazy," I mumble when his stare lingers, waiting for my reply.

Richard eyes me curiously, unable to ignore the shakiness of my voice. I plaster the best fake smile onto my face, vainly trying to pretend my stomach isn't lodged in my throat. He stares at me for several more seconds before sketchily shaking his head. I inhale my first breath in a long minute when he devotes his gaze back to the scenic view zooming by the driver's side window.

Happy he is no longer paying me any attention, I lift my knee, adjusting my position so the ball of my foot rests under my backside. To an outsider, it appears as if I'm getting comfortable, only I know I'm preparing for battle.

Once I'm satisfied I have a proper defense to fight off Richard's attack, I dive for his gun. My movement is so agile, I have the barrel of Richard's gun pointed at his temple before a single heartbeat sounds through my ears.

"Pull over," I grind out through clenched teeth, my gaze fixated on Richard.

Richard's fingers flex on the steering wheel. "There is a café a few miles out. I'll stop there," he replies, unaware of the dangerous situation he is in.

I cock back the gun's hammer. Its loud click is barely audible over the pounding of my heart. I'm so nervous, sweat is slicking my palms, making me anxious I'll lose my grip before I'm safely off Richard's radar.

After firming my hold, I demand again, "Pull over." My words are dangerously low as anger envelops every nerve in my body.

Hearing the underlying fury drenched in my voice, Richard slants his head to the side. His brows become lost in his hairline as the air in his body leaves in a brutal whoosh.

"Jesus Christ, Cleo, what the hell are you doing?" he mumbles, his undeveloped words coerced out of his mouth in a rush of panic.

The dust billowing around the car slows when he eases his foot off the accelerator. As he veers his vehicle to the side of the road, the mad beat of my heart slows to a brisk canter. Richard pulls to the very edge of the road, leaving plenty of space for vehicles to pass us before shifting his eyes to me.

"Cleo..." His tone is low and full of silent warnings.

I glare at him, soundlessly advising he isn't the only one who can issue threats with a rueful stare. After hitting him with the worst death-stare I've ever released, my eyes drop to the large collection of photos stashed in the console.

Following my gaze, Richard balks as his throat works hard to swallow. When rage floods his cheeks, I curl my finger around the trigger of his gun, bracing for his brash response.

He surprises me by muttering, "I can explain this, Cleo." He raises his eyes back to me. "Just give me the chance to explain. It isn't what you're thinking." He peers straight into my eyes, letting his seemingly direct gaze sweet-talk me.

Little does he know I've seen all his tricks, so I'm not buying the latest gimmick he's trying to sell me. The sweet, naïve Cleo he wanted to coerce into his bed five years ago is nowhere to be seen. She is long gone, buried right alongside my family.

"Unlock the doors," I request, my tone not betraying the panic thickening my veins.

Richard stares at me, his chest thrusting up and down. "You're safer in here than out there." He motions his head to the mottling of houses dotting the coastline. "People like us don't belong here, Cleo."

"I'll take my chances," I respond, glaring into his eyes with the same amount of disdain.

Richard's eyes bounce between the barrel of the gun pointed at his torso and the lock on the driver's side door as he seizes a few moments for silent contemplation.

Just when I think he will deny my request, the distinct sound of a lock unclicking booms into my ears. Bitter relief engulfs me, but I save my gratitude for a more appropriate time.

I lick my dry lips before instructing, "Now remove the keys from the ignition and hand them to me."

Richard smirks, his cocky attitude returning so swiftly the air becomes rife with a muggy stuffiness. "I won't do that, Cleo," he advises, his head shaking like my demand was merely a suggestion. "I'm not doing a single darn thing until you stop pointing that at me." He nudges his head to the gun rattling in my hand.

"Then I guess we'll be sitting here a while then," I snap, my tone telling him I'm not in the mood for his power trips. I am days away from beginning my cycle. He should not be messing with me.

"I guess we are." Richard's voice has a twang I haven't heard previously. "Until you put the gun down, we're going to sit here, wasting time like we're a couple of retirees with nothing better to do."

"Spoken like a man who doesn't have a gun pointed at him," I retaliate, my voice rising in anger. "You'll do what I tell you to do, when I tell you to do it." The little voice inside me breaks into rapturous applause, smitten by the sheer determination relayed by my stern tone.

Its standing ovation doesn't linger for long. The anger scorching my veins grows when Richard throws his head back and laughs.

"I think you have our roles reversed. Master Chains may have convinced you that participants in power play have equal rights, but we know that isn't true. The master commands. The submissive obeys." He locks his glistening eyes with me. "Since there is only one sub in this car, it's safe to say who the master is."

My pulse rings in my ears, startled at his extensive knowledge of my relationship with Marcus. I'm not talking about the obeying part of his ignorant assessment of the BDSM lifestyle, I'm talking about Marcus's involvement in the BDSM community. How could Richard know about that? There is no way he could know any of that unless he's involved in the lifestyle too...

My thoughts trail off as my eyes rocket to Richard. He winks, confirming my silent suspicions that he is familiar with the BDSM lifestyle—*very familiar*. My pupils expand in shock as various scenarios run through my brain on the real reason he suddenly arrived on Marcus's doorstep this morning. None of them are pretty.

With his arrogance at an all-time high, and his grin smug, I can easily derive his true motive. He isn't here to coax secret information from me, he is here to gloat, to ensure his superiority is showcased in the brightest light. He thinks he has the upper hand since he holds the most influential cards. What he doesn't realize is, he didn't keep his cards close to his chest. I just saw his entire hand.

"You gave Mr. Carson access to Chains. You sold out your own community just to make a profit. Your new truck, your fancy apartment—those weren't gained from working in security. You only achieved that at Chains' expense." My tone ensures he can't mistake my statements as questions. "Why would you do that, Richard? What could they have possibly done to deserve this type of injustice?"

The laughter lining Richard's face vanishes in an instant. "You don't know what you're talking about," he retorts, his voice dangerously low, exposing his rapidly surging anger. "I came here to help you." He glares into my eyes, his disdain at my accusations unmissable. "I don't know why I bothered. You're just as judging and condescending as the members of Chains."

As my back molars grind, my fear shifts to fury. Thinking he has me distracted with blatant anger, Richard lunges for the gun. I'm too well rehearsed in handling men like him that I foil his attempts before he gets within sniffing distance. I rear up my knee, ramming it hard enough into his wrist that a painful grunt emits from his lips before I yank open the passenger side door with my other hand. I land on the compacted dirt with a thud, sending pain rocketing up my arm, but it doesn't deter me in the slightest.

Rolling onto my knees, my eyes shoot in all directions, frantically searching for the gun that dislodged from my grasp during my tumble. The overgrown edging of the dirt road hinders my efforts to find the small black pistol in the grass. My poor eyesight means I can barely see as it is, let alone with fear-induced tears welling in my eyes.

When the sound of Richard's driver's side door cranking open booms into the silence, I crank my neck to the side. His black boots stomp onto the ground with a bang when he curls out of his car and races toward me.

I push off my feet with a grunt, charging for a large hedge on my right.

"Cleo, stop!" Richard yells out in urgency.

I continue with my mission to evade him, running as fast as my quaking legs can take me. The sharp prickles on the hedge scratch my forearms when I push through the bush, trying to put as much space between Richard and me as possible.

When I reach the clearing on the other side of the hedge, I boost my speed, ignoring Richard's continued pleas for me to stop. My heart is thumping against my ribs, and sweat is slicking my skin, but my pace remains unchecked.

My heart launches into my throat when my frantic pace comes to an abrupt halt. With my urge to get away from Richard my utmost priority, I nearly run straight off a cliff. I'm millimeters from plunging to my death, balancing dangerously on a crumbling cliff face with only the minutest portion of dirt left under my feet. My pupils widen, and my breathing shifts to a shallow pant as my body merges into survival mode.

Turning my eyes only, for fear of falling if I were to move, I spot Richard cautiously approaching on my left. "Cleo," he warns, his tone lowering with panic when he notices how precariously I am dangling on the brink. "Carefully step back," he instructs me, like it's the simplest thing to do.

When I attempt to follow his instructions, the unstable ground under my feet gives way. The panic curled around my throat tightens when fragments of rock topple into the waves smashing the chunky boulders below. With the weather being temperamental the past week, the ocean is showcasing its power in the most frightening way. It's an awe-inspiring yet teeth-chattering visual.

"I can't move," I gasp out, my panic so uncontained I'm not above seeking assistance from a man I've always seen more as an enemy than a friend.

Approaching me as if I am a bomb about to detonate, Richard cautiously moves closer to the volatile rock edge. "Keep your eyes on me, Cleo," he instructs when my fearful gaze shifts sideways to the scenery threatening to take me to my final resting place.

Panting, I stray my eyes back to Richard, ludicrously believing he is my safest option to get out of this situation alive. How ridiculous is that? I'm frozen in place, more afraid of plunging to my death than of a man who has hundreds of images of me in his car.

My stomach gurgles when I feel the ground shifting beneath my feet. "Stop," I breathe out. "The ground is too unstable to hold both our weight."

Richard continues moving toward me, his steps slow and without noise.

"Richard, please." A single tear glides down my cheek as the earth I'm balancing on loosens more. "It isn't safe, stay back."

Richard lifts his eyes from the ground to me. "I've got you, Cleo," he assures, the honesty in his eyes adding strength to his admission. "You've just got to trust me. Do you trust me, Cleo?"

My head shakes instinctively, the fear curled around my throat not persuasive enough to realize now is not the time for honesty.

The heavy groove of worry digging into Richard's usually smooth forehead deepens from my brisk shake. "Well, I guess it's lucky I have enough confidence for the both of us."

Before I can understand what his reply means, Richard charges for me. A zinging pain rockets up my arm when he seizes my wrist in a firm hold and yanks me backward. I crash into his body with so much force, the brutal grunt that escapes his lips fans the hairs clinging to my drenched neck. We fall to the ground with a thud a good three to four feet back from the edge, which crumbles into the ocean below like a soggy cookie being dunked in coffee.

"Oh my god," I sigh, my words barely audible.

I clutch my chest for dear life, ensuring my heart remains in its rightful spot as fear engulfs every inch of me. I'm not the only one shunted in silence by the events that just occurred. Richard lies on his back next to me, his chest rising and falling with every deep inhalation of air he takes. His eyes are arrested on the crystal clear blue sky, the first one Florida has had the past four days. It's eerily beautiful in a serene moment in time.

I join Richard in his silent stance, unable to think of an appropriate thing to say. Yes, from the multiple photos of me in his car, my alarmed response to his presence is warranted, but if his sole aim was to hurt me, why did he just risk his life to save mine?

Before a lucid thought can coalesce in my brain, the hair on my arms prickles with awareness. You know that feeling you get when you're being watched? That's what I am feeling right now.

My breathing kicks up a notch when the noise of grass crunching under feet sounds through my ears. Raising my hand to shield my eyes from the blinding afternoon sun, I crank my neck so I can identify the person sneakily approaching us.

"Shian?" *Shian lives in New York, so why would she be in Florida?*

Hesitant in her approach, Shian presses her index finger to her lips, requesting I remain quiet. Sick unease spreads through my veins like wildfire, increasing the perspiration making my skin a sticky mess. When I nod, Shian continues on her sneaky approach. Half of me wants to warn Richard, whereas the other half wants to run into Shian's arms in gratitude for her rescue.

Unsure which side of the coin I should follow, I remain quiet, unemotional and unmoved.

Once Shian is a few feet from us, she removes her gun from her holster and devotes its attention to Richard. "Keep your hands where I can see them," she instructs, the barrel of her government-issued pistol locked on the section of skin between Richard's eyes. "If you so much as blink, I'll shoot you."

Richard balks, then does as instructed. He holds his hands in front of his torso and keeps his body perfectly still. When Shian approaches Richard's left side, he turns his eyes to me. Our eyes lock and hold for several terrifying moments. Although the expression on his face displays he is a calm and collected man, his eyes are showing anything but.

"Roll onto your stomach and rise to your knees," Shian demands, her tone loud enough to break through the blood roaring in my ears.

Ignoring Shian's stern request, Richard mutters, "I didn't do what they think I did." He is so quiet, I strain to hear him. His brows scrunch as the storm in his eyes grows more rampant. "I should paraphrase it better. I didn't do what they are accusing me of. I'm not a good man, Cleo, but I'm not a monster either."

Tears prick in my eyes from the sheer uncertainty of his tone. For a man who exudes confidence by the bucket load, the shakiness of his voice has my nerves sitting on edge. They are even more unstable than the cliff's edge I was dangling on mere seconds ago.

Ignoring Shian's continuous screams for Richard to follow her instruction, I keep my eyes locked with his and say, "Okay. Just explain that, and I'm sure they will understand. Nothing bad done with good intentions can't be undone with honesty."

The corner of Richard's lips tugs high. "You've always believed there is good in everyone," he mutters under his breath, his cinnamon-laced breath fanning my mouth. "Promise me you won't let anyone ever taint that about you."

My eyes bounce between his as horrible unease settles deep in my stomach. "Richard—"

"Promise me, Cleo," he interrupts, his low voice barely heard over Shian's demand for him to kneel.

"I promise," I stammer out as fresh tears leak from my eyes. I don't know why I am crying, but Richard's swift change in composure has sent my emotions so haywire I'm beginning to wonder which way is up.

My breath snags in my throat when Richard leans over for the quickest second to press his lips to mine. I'm not the only one disturbed by his sudden movement, Shian balks as well. Her reaction isn't solely based on Richard's impromptu kiss though. It's when he stealthily rises from the ground and sprints for the cliff's edge, reaching the clearing in under two heart-thrashing seconds.

"Richard, no!" I scream at the same time Shian fires her gun. "Stop! Don't fire!"

I scramble to my knees, knowing Richard's chance of surviving his fall is practically non-existent as it is, much less with a bullet wound to contend with.

My pleas fall on deaf ears when Shian continues firing, sending the vile smell of gunpowder filtering into my nostrils. Everything slows to a snail's pace as a scene gruesome enough to incite nightmares evolves before my eyes.

My hand darts up to muffle my screams when one of the bullets dislodged from Shian's gun hits Richard in his upper left shoulder. His body jolts when he is impacted by the pain no doubt blackening his veins. He spins almost lifelessly to face me. His face is ashen, his eyes unmoving. More tears seep down my cheeks, matching the blood trickling from the side of his mouth. Unbelievably, he awards me one last cocky grin before he falls backward, plunging lifelessly into the dark, tumultuous waters below.

"No!" I shout in a blood-curdling scream.

The putrid scent of fear permeates the air as I crawl to the cliff's face on my hands and knees. With concerns for my safety in the background of my mind, I move to the very edge of the crumbling ground Richard just fell from to peer down at the ocean, which is showcasing Mother Nature's power in the ultimate light. Nothing but volatile waves breaking on sharpened rock surfaces confronts me.

Richard is nowhere to be seen.

3

A hiss of air parts my lips when a first responder dabs antiseptic ointment onto the scratches on my arm. Although tender, my body welcomes the pain, happy to use it as a distraction to the ache maiming my heart. Richard and I were never close, but I'm still baffled by the events that just occurred.

"Sorry," the handsome middle-aged medic apologizes, mistaking my grimace as him hurting me.

Faintly smiling to assure him I'm fine, I drift my eyes around my location. People are covering every inch of the café I'm sitting in. With Shian's approach so under-scaled, I had no clue about the massive police operation supporting her from the sidelines. Just in the café parking lot, there are a dozen police cruisers, three ambulances, and two unmarked black SUVs. The SUVs' tinted windows are so dark, they reflect the helicopter hovering in the distance, searching for Richard's body in the eerie waters of Bronte's Peak.

Even though it's an unpleasant winter's day, the swell of the crowd continues to grow as fast as the sun is setting on the horizon. The spectacle of a massive police hunt is too compelling to inhibit the curiosity of the locals. I can't say I blame them. I've watched events unfold from live broadcasts many times the past twenty-six years. Some I'd give anything to un-see.

My mind drifts from horrid memories when the brush of a hand down my arm draws my attention back to the present. Shian is standing in front of me with an apprehensive smirk etched on her mouth and a pair of sorrowful eyes.

"Is Marcus here yet?"

She shakes her head. "With media swarming Bronte's Peak, he's having trouble gaining entry unnoticed..." Her words taper off as she peers at someone over my shoulder.

Although the smile tugging her full lips high is a clear indication of whom she is looking at, the primitive awareness activating every nerve ending in my body truly gives away who is entering the café.

Slinging my head to the side, my heart squeezes in my chest. Marcus is standing just inside the main entranceway door of the café. He is wearing the same tailored suit he left the house in earlier, but he has removed his suit jacket. His recognizable green eyes are hidden by a cap hanging low on his head. His gaze swings to the left before veering to the right as he seeks me among the cramped surroundings. When he spots me sitting on one of the red leather-topped swivel stools stretched across the counter of the cafe, the pain scouring his beautiful face with thick lines clears away in an instant.

He pushes off his feet to make a beeline for me. I do the same. My pace is more frantic than his. I rush for him, my steps so frenetic, I clumsily trip over my feet halfway across the room. My scratched-up arms brace out in front of my body, preparing for imminent impact. My tumble to the floor is thwarted when Marcus catches me in his arms before pulling me to his broad chest. I inhale deeply, relishing in the scent of his unique smell.

"Cleo..."

One of his hands holds me close to his big, protective body, while the other one runs over me, physically inspecting me for injuries.

"I'm fine," I mumble into his erratically thrusting torso.

My guarantee appeases his worries so quickly, the tightness spread across his chest loosens before my eyes. I don't know how much time passes before he delicately draws me back by the tops of my shoulders. When his eyes drop to mine, I take in a sharp breath. The pain in his breathtakingly beautiful irises is more than I can bear. They are striking and tormented at the same time, just like our first meeting in the elevator four years ago.

When the moisture in my eyes becomes too great to ignore, Marcus cups my jaw so his thumbs can sweep away my tears the moment they fall. Once the small handful of disobedient tears has been cleared off my cheeks, he locks his eyes with mine. They express so much without a word needing to be spilled from his lips. His anguish. His relief. His disappointment. They are all conveyed by his beautiful green irises. The previously stated responses I can understand, but there is one emotion leaving me a little baffled. The deep, dark cloud of guilt. What could he possibly be feeling guilty over? I chose to leave with Richard. I was the one who put my life at risk. So if anyone should be harboring guilt, it should be me.

Before I can voice that to Marcus, Shian appears at our side. "Two local detectives want to ask Cleo a few questions," Shian advises, her dark gaze bouncing between Marcus and me.

"No," Marcus replies, answering on my behalf.

Although peeved he didn't check with me first, I'm also grateful. From the circumstances of my day, I am exhausted. Not just physically, but emotionally as well. And in all honesty, with a bombardment of emotions hammering me, I don't think I could handle any more.

Shian and Marcus continue speaking, but since I have my ear pressed against Marcus's torso, I can't hear a word they are saying. I don't need to hear

Marcus speak to know his thoughts, though, the frantic beat of his heart tells me everything I need to know. Although angry, he is more concerned about my safety than punishing my stupidity. I don't know whether I should be disappointed or pleased by that revelation.

Marcus's eyes lower to mine when I work my neck side to side, struggling to ease the knot that formed there after my earlier fall. I wouldn't necessarily say it's painful, it's more annoying than anything.

"Are you sore?" Marcus questions me as his fiercely dark eyes dance between mine.

I attempt to speak, but Shian beats me. "The paramedics checked her over. Other than a few scratches—"

Marcus cuts off Shian's reassurance that I am uninjured with a sweep of his hand through the air. His eyes remain arrested on me as he reads the response from my eyes.

Not receiving the intended message, Marcus devotes his focus back to Shian. "I'm taking Cleo home. If you or the local authorities wish to ask her any more questions, you can tomorrow morning."

Shian once again attempts to speak. Marcus once again cuts her off, this time with a rueful glare. The vibrant hum of chatter filling the room with energy dulls to a faint buzz when Marcus and Shian participate in a sweat-producing stare down. If I weren't trapped in the depths of despair, I'd be just as fascinated as the other hundred or so spectators mesmerized by the two alphas going to war.

But since I'm on the verge of collapsing from exhaustion, I harness my desires and lock eyes with Shian. "I know you don't know me from a bar of soap, so you have no reason to believe me, but I've told you everything I know. I've given you every snippet of my life that involved Richard, so can't the rest wait until the morning?"

Shian stops glaring at Marcus, her sole focus now on me. The anger radiating from her eyes simmers from a raging tornado to a summer shower when she sees the truth beaming from my sagging gaze.

"Okay," she says, nodding.

Bitter relief engulfs me.

"But you're not to talk to anyone in regards to this case. Not the local authorities, your sister, or those pesky reporters you work with," Shian advises, her tone growing snarky toward the end. "If you're even tempted to have a cry-fest confession, call me. I'm the girl for the job."

My brow arches as disbelief taints my face. Nothing against Shian—she sat by my side most of the afternoon while I sniveled nonstop about Richard and why he'd ever think jumping off a cliff was his only option—but she still doesn't seem to have the nurturing vibe.

"Hey," Shian jeers, her voice shifting from austere to playful. "I've comforted grown men in the midst of a cry-fest." Her shoulder touches her ear when she shrugs. "I may have been the cause of their tears, but that's not the point."

A giggle spills from my mouth before I have the chance to shut it down. I smack my lips together, mortified I've become such a heartless wrench, I can't even spend a few measly hours mourning the loss of a work colleague with respect. *I am a terrible person.*

Spotting my horrified expression, Shian runs her hand down my arm. "Don't feel guilty, Cleo. You did nothing wrong. Richard reacted the way he did as he didn't want to face the consequences of his actions like a real man. His choices should not be carried on your shoulders."

I'm shocked when I don't see the faintest bit of remorse in her eyes. You'd think knowing she shot Richard mere seconds before he plunged to his death would have her insides twisting, but she doesn't appear the slightest bit fazed. She either conceals her shrewdness well, or she is more coldhearted than I initially perceived. When she runs her hand down my arm for the third time in under a minute, I am assuming it's the latter. She has learned to hide her emotions well.

After bidding farewell to the two detectives wishing to speak to me with a dip of his chin, Marcus guides me to a car idling at the front of the café. A giant beast of a man with shoulders as broad as the grin on his face opens the passenger side door for me when he notices our approach. His black suit and white dress shirt showcases his impressive frame well, but I've always believed people's eyes are the windows to their souls, so the sunglasses he wears don't allow me to get an accurate read on him.

"Cleo," he greets me, my name rumbling out of his mouth in a thick purr.

I smile, hiding my unease about why he seems so familiar, yet I swear I haven't seen him before. Shrugging off my confusion as a consequence of a long day, I slide into the passenger seat of the car he is holding open for me. The ache of my weary muscles dulls when the softness of well-worn leather gently caresses them.

While fastening my seatbelt, suspicion taints my face. The interior of the car is in severe need of an upgrade. Don't get me wrong, it has nothing on my Buick, but it would be a minimum of fifteen years old. The vinyl on the dash is cracked and faded to a point it's beyond repair, the parking brake is cranked high between the two front seats, and there is a pair of fluffy white dice hanging from the rearview mirror. Although presumptuous of me to say, I highly doubt this car is from Marcus's fleet. Even Abel's car isn't as outdated as this one.

I swing my eyes to Marcus. Sensing my inquisitive stare, he finishes tugging a baseball cap down low on his head before lifting his eyes to me.

"Whose car is this?" I ask when he fails to the read the silent questions my eyes are relaying.

The twinkle in his eyes grows for every second spent staring at me in silence. "I don't know," he eventually mutters, his smooth voice cracking with concealed laughter. "But you can be assured the paparazzi didn't peer in my direction when this bad boy rolled into the parking lot."

Another inappropriate giggle leaves my mouth before I can shut it down. I know I shouldn't feel remorse about the actions of others, but that doesn't stop it from occurring. Remorse is one of those things you can't control. It sneaks up on you when you least expect, more often than not leaving you feeling more remorseful than you were to begin with.

My eyes lift from my intertwined hands when Marcus tracks his thumb along the throb in my throat. "Don't feel guilty, Cleo. As Shian already stated, the actions of a grown man should never be placed on another's shoulders, much less the woman he lured into a trap with the intent to harm her."

"I wouldn't necessarily say I'm feeling guilty, I just hate that Richard thought he had no other option than to harm himself. What could he have possibly done that was so bad suicide was his only option?" My teeth munch on my bottom lip as I struggle to hold my tears.

"This," Marcus barely whispers, rubbing at the heavy groove scoured between my lowered brows. "And this," he continues, trailing his thumb to the tears threatening to spill from my eyes at any moment. "When you hurt someone you care about, your brain doesn't function the same way. Even when your intentions are to ease their pain, most of the time you end up doing more bad than good."

My breath hitches halfway to my lungs when his eyes tell me his statement is more referring to himself than Richard. Is that what his earlier guilt was about? His actions during our week apart?

My suspicions are confirmed when the guilt in his eyes darkens as he brushes the back of his fingers over the area where my cheek used to be marked. Although the injuries from my attack five days ago are no longer visible, Marcus's memory is so fervent, he caresses the exact area that stung with pain after I was struck.

Hating the remorse his eyes are carrying, I nuzzle into his embrace. His sweet breath fans my lips when he exhales harshly, seemingly surprised by my loving gesture. His shocked response entices my nurturing nature even more. I lean across the cranked parking brake so I can press my lips against his. Our kiss is nothing more than an innocent schoolyard peck, but it soothes me more than I could ever explain.

It must have the same effect on Marcus, as the instant our lips touch, the heavy grooves on his forehead vanish. Careful not to irritate the scratches on my arms, he seizes my wrists and pulls me to sit cradled in his lap. Although it's a tight squeeze in the confines of the unknown stranger's car, nothing could dampen the comfort his tenderness awards me with. He doesn't speak. He just holds me close to his body as the warmth of his hands pacifies my shaking limbs. I'm sure our gesture isn't uncommon for this location, it appears to be the perfect setting for a raunchy rendezvous. Although I'm sure most of the couples who parked here aren't doing so to admire the scenery.

After taking a few moments to ease the pain in my heart using nothing more than his touch, Marcus locks his eyes with me. "Let's get you home."

I attempt to correct him that Ravenshoe isn't my home, but no matter how hard I try to fire the rebuttal off my tongue, my mouth refuses to relinquish it.

I've never had a fondness for lying.

4

Twenty minutes later, we pull into Marcus's residence. Since the security system is still down, Marcus parks on the far left-hand side of the driveway. After shutting down the engine, he curls out of the driver's seat and urgently strides to my side of the car. I undo my seatbelt and clamber out when he opens the passenger side door for me. My face grimaces when my muscles kick up a stink about my abrupt movements. My throbbing joints didn't appreciate the tight confines of the car as much as my heart did.

Marcus's hand stiffening on my lower back reveals he noticed my grimace, but he remains quiet, his sole focus devoted to guiding me into his residence. Silent determination beams out of him in hot, invisible waves. If brooding personalities made me nervous, his swift change in demeanor would have me sweating profusely. But since I have gotten used to his ominous moods, the sweat misting my skin isn't from fear, it's based solely on excitement.

The longer we continue with our trek, the firmer Marcus's stance becomes. The energy bouncing between us is as crackling as ever, but it's been somewhat downplayed by the rigidness thickening the air. His composure reminds me of the minutes leading up to his departure this morning. Although Marcus never mentioned what his emergency meeting pertained to, the fretful mask that slipped over his face when he advised me he had to leave had my stomach twisting in knots. Marcus is a very reserved man who guards his emotions with the same protectiveness a father uses to shield his children, but the worry his eyes held this morning was unmissable. He was the most fretful I've ever seen him—until now.

"Did you get everything sorted before you had to leave?"

"Hmm?" Marcus's gaze remains fixated on the entranceway of his property.

My brows stitch, stunned by his blasé response. Marcus is a highly intelligent man. Daftness does not belong in his repertoire.

I lock my eyes with his. "Your emergency meeting with the band? Did you get everything worked out before you had to...umm ... come get me?"

I roll my eyes, loathing my inability to leave things on the table. If I learned to reel in my annoying habit of needing to know everything, I wouldn't be subjected to the murderous glare Marcus is now directing at me. His gaze is downright furious, and it sets my pulse racing.

The beat of my heart slows when I realize his wrathful snarl isn't directed at me. He is peering past my shoulder, not into my eyes. With my heart thumping against my ribcage, I swing my eyes in the direction Marcus's are facing. The twisting sensation in my stomach moves to the base of my throat when I spot Abel standing at the entranceway. He is next to a lady wearing a fitted black pantsuit that showcases the generous curve of her hips. Although her stance is strong, even my poor eyesight can see the gleam of remorse in her eyes. It's an exact replica of the remorse Abel's are transmitting.

Panic clutches my heart when Abel's begging-for-forgiveness eyes stray to his shuffling feet, Marcus's irate gaze too much for him to bear. My back is relieved of the feverish heat pumping out of Marcus when I pace away from him. My wish to undo the mistakes I made has my speed increasing with every step I take.

Abel is taken aback when I throw my arms around his small torso and hug him fiercely. I silently thank him for the assistance he gave me earlier, while also relaying to Marcus he has no reason to be angry at him. Abel did everything in his power to stop me from going with Richard, so if anyone should be dealing with Marcus's anger, it should be me.

My assumptions about Marcus's anger are proven wrong when Marcus angrily snarls, "You assured me Richard would be arrested before he got in sniffing distance of Cleo. That was the only reason I agreed to leave. I took you at your word that you'd protect her."

"Whoa, what?" I ask, peeling back from Abel to drift my eyes between Marcus and the unknown woman he is fiercely scolding. "You knew Richard was here? What he was planning to do?"

Marcus's jaw tenses, but his lips stay snapped shut. He doesn't attempt to deny or agree with my accusations. When my eyes lock on his female companion, she mimics his stance, although her remorseful eyes are more forthcoming than Marcus's resolute gaze.

I turn my eyes to Abel, hoping the bond we've grown the past four days will be greater than his loyalty to Marcus. He rapidly blinks, fighting hard to ignore the moisture glistening in his usually forthright eyes. I say "usually" as today his eyes are as emotionless as Delilah's Christmas message in the eCard she sent last year. It was as cold and heartless as she is.

I drift my eyes back to Marcus. "Did you know Richard was in Florida?" I ask again, my stubbornness not allowing me to back down without answers.

Acting like I'm not even in his presence, Marcus keeps his furious gaze locked on the unknown African American lady I'd guess to be mid-to-late forties. Although her clipped black afro hair, beautifully clear skin, and small smattering of freckles over the bridge of her nose gives her the appearance of a gentle soul, the glare she is directing at Marcus upends her homely façade. Her narrowed gaze is just as ruthless as Marcus's.

She flinches when Marcus snarls, "Years on the force and a weasel of man like him still got away from you." My stomach flips from the viciousness of his words. It wasn't what he said that has my stomach twisted in knots, it was the way he said it.

"Please," retaliates the unnamed lady, her voice drenched in sassiness. "If you didn't bring the FBI in, this case would have closed days ago. But you had to bring in the bigwigs, who, of course, wanted to get him on more than standard stalking charges."

I back down from my stern stance, my intuition telling me I'll get more answers watching these two go to battle than Marcus could ever relay. Abel also regresses. He follows me to the edge of the patio, where we stand in silence, watching the two powerhouses go toe to toe.

"It was one agent, Regina," Marcus replies to her sneered comment, throwing his arms into the air. Even in the tenseness of the situation, my pussy pulses from his domineering gesture.

Regina spreads her hands across her ample hips. "You know as well as anyone, Marcus. It takes one person to bring down an entire team."

A blaze of anger flashes in Marcus's eyes. "If it weren't for that *one* agent, Richard could have had Cleo halfway to Mexico by now!"

Regina's curt laugh does nothing to ease the tension binding my stomach in knots. "That would have never happened if Cleo didn't leave with him. No one was prepared for that. You weren't even prepared for that. It left us scrambling."

Marcus's jaw tightens so firmly it almost snaps. As his squinted gaze drifts to me, he clenches his fists open and closed. His eyes relay his disappointment without a syllable leaving his mouth. Not trusting my legs to keep me upright, I slip my hand into Abel's sweaty palm. Within a matter of seconds, my stupidity steamrolls me into silence.

Only now am I realizing how much danger I put myself in. Who knows what would have happened if Shian's operation didn't catch up to us? My heart falls from my ribcage. The idea of being seriously injured isn't the cause, it's the idea of leaving Lexi alone and defenseless. I'm struggling to come to terms with knowing one day I'll be the last Garcia left in Montclair, I never considered the consequences for Lexi if that happened to her.

Realizing I've overachieved when it comes to punishing myself, Marcus shifts his focus back to Regina. Although they continue slinging insults at each other for the next ten minutes, my exhausted brain is too fried to absorb all their comments. I get enough snippets to gain an understanding of what their argument pertains to—Marcus is annoyed Regina didn't keep her word, Regina is annoyed I left with Richard—but not enough to ease the sick feeling twisting my gut.

My attention only snaps back to the present when the Regina says, "You should have kept your agent on Cleo's sister, then none of this would have happened."

I gulp down the bile rapidly surging to the back of my throat as I step closer to them. "What does Lexi have to do with this?" I ask as my eyes dance between two pairs of narrowed gazes gawking at me with apprehension.

Regina licks her lips, but not a word seeps from her mouth. Marcus's lips move in preparation to speak, but his eyes convey he won't tell me anything I don't already know.

"You might want to wipe the dishonesty from your eyes before that lie comes spilling out your mouth," I mutter with my eyes locked on Marcus. "Because no matter how much you try to mask shit with bullshit, it still smells like shit."

Regina's lips twitch as she struggles to hold her smile. "You were right, I don't even know her, and I already like her," she chuckles while moving to stand next to Abel.

Abel's eyes spark with mischief as he nods. My pursuit to unearth Lexi's connection to this case is temporarily impeded when my spent brain notices the similarities between Regina and Abel. Same rounded cheeks, same smattering of freckles across their identical noses, and same big, worldly eyes. The only difference between them is Regina is a good twenty to thirty years younger than Abel, and she is female.

I suck in a deep breath when reality dawns.

Noticing my gasping expression, Abel says, "Ms. Cleo, please meet my daughter, Regina, long-standing member of Ravenshoe PD." The twinkle of admiration in his eyes intensifies when he shifts them to Regina. "Regina, this is the lovely Ms. Cleo I've been telling you about, Mr. Everett's girlfriend." He overemphasizes my title with a dramatic flair I haven't heard him use the past four days.

When Regina thrusts out her hand in offering, it snaps me out of my shocked trance. Seizing the opportunity bestowed by her friendly gesture, I accept her handshake before pulling her in close.

"What does my sister have to do with Richard's case?" I ask, keeping my hand clenched around hers to ensure she understands the urgency of my question.

Although my nerves are rattled from today's tumultuous events, it isn't bad enough to snuff my overwhelming desire to protect my sister. Technically, she was the reason I left with Richard, so if Regina has knowledge that will back up my intuition, I want to hear about it. *Then maybe I won't feel so stupid about the foolish decisions I made today.*

When Regina's eyes stray to Marcus, who is standing behind my left shoulder, I step in the direction of her path, cutting off any warning he is relaying to her.

"Do you work for Ravenshoe PD or Marcus?" I query, my tone unforgiving with my snarled-in-anger words.

Regina's eyes return to me. She doesn't answer my question, her stern glare alone ensures there is no doubt where her loyalties lie. She may be like family to Marcus, but she has just as much blue blood running through her veins as she does red.

"I'm Lexi's legal guardian, so I am within my rights to request information on any matters pertaining to her," I mutter, using the same excuse I always use when meddling in Lexi's life.

Regina doesn't accept my declaration with the same amount of ease Lexi's college professors and work colleagues did. Don't get me wrong, the remorse in her eyes did double, and the tightness in her shoulders relaxed, but she holds herself firm with dignified respect.

"That may have been the case after your parents' unfortunate passing, but when Lexi turned eighteen, the rights of who she wants to be updated on her personal matters reverted to her," Regina replies, her tone repentant but to the point.

I release Regina's hand as confusion overwhelm me. What does that mean? Is she saying Lexi is aware of everything happening but requested for me not to be updated?

Reading the silent questions my eyes are asking, Regina explains, "But, in saying that, Richard's arrival in Florida clearly iterates what I've been saying all along. His focus was never on your sister. He only wanted you. Despite the numerous pictures he had of her, she was never in any danger."

If she is aiming to lessen my panicked confusion, she is doing a terrible job. I'm more frightened now than ever. My baffled eyes stray to Marcus when he runs the back of his fingers down my cheek, removing a tear I didn't realize had spilled from my eye until now.

"Is Lexi safe?" I ask Marcus even though his eyes are already conveying his answer.

The curt nod of his head sends more tears trickling down my face. These are filled with gratitude.

"Yes," he murmurs before banding his arms around my quivering shoulders. His hold is so firm, my feet lift off the ground. "Just like you, I'd never let anything happen to her, Cleo," he mutters, his assured tone boosting the confidence of his statement.

"Does she know about Richard? And the photos?" I mumble into his chest.

"Yes," he repeats. His warm breath fans the hairs clinging to my neck.

Marcus's movements are so agile, I don't realize he is moving until we arrive at his office I left in a flurry mere hours ago. My entire universe has been upended so much since then, it truly feels like a lifetime has passed in a matter of hours.

Holding me close, Marcus strides across the room, lifts the chair toppled on the floor, then sits in front of his desk. As he logs in to his computer, Regina and Abel hover by the door. Their presence is strong enough I'd never forget they were here, but not overly intrusive. My nose tingles when the computer monitor illuminates, displaying I've missed thirty-three FaceTime chat requests from Lexi the past three hours. *Oh god—she must have been panicked out of her mind.*

"She's okay," Marcus informs me, intuiting the reason for the new bout of moisture in my eyes. "She was updated on your whereabouts the instant Shian arrived on scene."

Before I can communicate my thanks, Lexi's beautiful face fills the computer.

"Cleo... Jesus, you scared me!" she scolds down the line as angry, hot tears stream down her face as freely as mine do.

5

"Another hot chocolate?"

I shake my head. "No, thank you," I reply to Abel, who is clearing away the empty plates and mugs left on the coffee table by the multiple agents filling Marcus's large living room.

I stand from the couch I've been sitting on the past two hours and make my way to the side of the room. Like he has done numerous times tonight, Marcus stops speaking to the agent he's communicating with so his eyes can track my every move. When I stop at the side of the main living space, his eyes lock and hold with mine. The worry his eyes have held the past three hours intensifies when he takes in my slumped frame and drooping eyes. I am genuinely exhausted—the most tired I've ever been.

After speaking with Lexi for nearly an hour, our call was interrupted by Shian and a handful of local and interstate FBI agents. Although she hasn't said anything, I'm relatively confident Shian caught wind of Regina's presence at Marcus's residence. Since Richard's case is being jointly investigated by interstate agents, no one was willing to wait until tomorrow morning to question me. That's means I've spent the last two hours discovering my decision to leave with Richard today was one of the silliest I've made. He's not only been stalking me relentlessly the past two years, he also bugged my work computer, landline, and my home PC. He was watching me even more than Marcus was the past three months.

I know this may categorize me as coldhearted bitch, but I'm just being honest. I thought discovering Richard was stalking me would be the most upsetting issue I'd face today. It wasn't. It was discovering Marcus brought me here under the guise he wanted me to know him, when in reality, he only brought me here as the FBI figured it was a way to force Richard to react.

By drawing Richard out of his comfort zone, Shian assumed he would make a mistake. She was right, but it doesn't lessen the devastation on my behalf. I only agreed to come here as I wanted to experience the real Marcus—the man behind the disguise he wears in front of others.

Now, I'll leave with more questions than I arrived with. Such as, how long has he known about Richard? Did he only bring me here because it was the safer option than his sub house in town? And, last, but not at all least, do I still hold the title of his girlfriend?

Deep down inside, I know why Marcus didn't tell me what was happening. I would have never left Montclair if I knew the reason he wanted me to go with him, but it doesn't stop me wondering if that's the only reason he deceived me the past four days. Was his deceit just a one-off lie? Or will it be something that will continue in our relationship? *If we still have a relationship.*

My heart-wrenching inner turmoil simmers to a dull bubble when my body's primitive awareness of Marcus's proximity activates. My body senses his nearness mere moments before he curls his arms around my waist and pulls me to his torso. Needing his comfort to soothe the hesitation prickling my spine, I melt into his embrace. The generous curve of my backside nuzzles into his crotch as my heavy head lolls onto his hard pec muscle.

"Nearly done," he mutters against my hair before he presses a kiss to my temple.

He sways his hips. His movements are so smooth, he could rock me to sleep. Witnessing him display his nurturing side in front of the dozen pairs of eyes gawking at us makes me realize the man standing behind me is Marcus—not Master Chains. Although they are technically one and the same, the past two weeks have awarded me with so much insight into Marcus's unique personality, I can confidently distinguish which person I am interacting with.

The man who finger-fucked me on his couch in his living room was Master Chains. The man who intuited my every need, want, and desire while eating pizza with his bandmates was Marcus. The man who sat at the breakfast bar two weeks ago, negotiating with me to become his sub without looking at me was Master Chains. The man who pinned me to the wall as we bartered our terms on more amicable grounds was Marcus. There are many more instances I can give that clearly define whom I was associating with at the time... all but one. The man I associated with in his playroom four days ago was neither Marcus or Master Chains. He was a little bit of them both.

Wanting to confirm my suspicions that the man making me swoon is Marcus, I pivot on my heels to face him. The air is sucked from my lungs from the sheer closeness of his exquisitely handsome face. *God, he is gorgeous.* Plump lips and soul-stealing eyes on a face carved by the world's best sculptor to bring women to their knees.

I'd give anything to pretend he brought me here because he wanted to, not because he was forced to.

When stupid tears loom in my eyes, Marcus's dark brows slant. "Cleo... don't," he mutters as his worried eyes dart between mine. "Whatever you're thinking, it isn't true. Your tired head isn't letting you see the full picture."

I stare up at him, blinking and confused. I either said my thoughts out loud, or he can indeed read my inner monologue. My attempt to interpret his riddled statement is lost when Shian arrives at our side. My eyes roll skywards, announcing my annoyance at her unfortunate timing. Any time things get interesting between Marcus and me, she appears like magic, thwarting the intrigue bristling between us. We've barely spoken more than a sentence to each other the past three hours. With our communication skills already lacking, the last thing we need is someone interfering.

My heart stops beating when Marcus asks, "Any news on Richard?"

Shian quirks her lips before shaking her head. "No. With the bad lighting, they put off the recovery until the morning."

"Recovery?" I ask, confusion evident in my tone.

Marcus only stiffens for the quickest moment, but it's long enough for me to notice. "The recovery of Richard's body, Cleo," he explains, his tone a unique mix of infuriation and anger. "The FBI isn't undertaking a rescue mission. It's a recovery mission."

The salad sandwich I consumed for dinner threatens to resurface. Although I know there is no way Richard would have survived the fall, a small part of me was hoping there was a possibility he would be found alive. Then I could have placed him into the ground myself.

I stiffen, stunned by my callousness. I'd like to say I am utterly flabbergasted by my reaction, but that would be untrue. Since the death of my parents and Tate, I've become a little bitter with matters pertaining to life and death. My parents and brother were wonderful, hard-working members of society who never stepped out of line or said a bad word about anyone, yet they were taken from me way too soon. At times, Lexi may be the bane of my existence, but she doesn't deserve the short life sentence she's been issued either. So, although the final words Richard spoke to me have been running through my mind on repeat the last two hours, all the horrid things I've learned about him are swinging the pendulum in the opposite direction it was sitting when he plunged to his death.

Don't get me wrong, I'm not saying my heart isn't pained by his decision—self-harm should never be an option—I just don't have enough tears left to shed over a man who taunted me more than he was kind to me. Furthermore, most of my tears were depleted at my parents and Tate's funeral. The rest will remain for the day I say my final goodbye to Lexi.

My tear-welling eyes rocket to Marcus when he says, "We'll discuss it more thoroughly in New York tomorrow."

The gurgling of my stomach intensifies as the despicable thoughts plaguing me the past two hours ring true. The fact Marcus wants to take me home immediately following the closing of Richard's case proves he didn't bring me here of his own free will—he was forced to.

My stomach lurches into my throat when a new reality dawns. Does he want me here now? Or is he once again being strong-armed?

Incapable of ignoring my flipping stomach for a moment longer, I step out of Marcus's hold. When he puts up a protest about my unexpected departure, I mumble, "I'm going to grab a shower." My tone is so to the point, there is no chance my declaration could be construed as a question.

My unchecked pace out of Marcus's living room is so fast, the air ripples in my wake. Ignoring Marcus and Shian's demands for me to stop, I take the stairs two at a time, my desire to get away from it all so fervent I'm practically sprinting.

I only just make it into the guest powder room before the dinner I consumed resurfaces in the ghastliest way. My back bends harshly as my body works hard to expel the products that have been swirling relentlessly the past two hours.

Once every crumb of my sandwich has been dispelled, I rest my backside on the balls of my feet. I jump, frightened beyond belief when a damp washcloth brushes my bare shoulder. It isn't the fact someone has snuck up on me unaware that has me jumping out of my skin, it's the fact they just witnessed me at my worst. Always desiring to represent the well-put-together Cleo, no one has ever seen me this disheveled.

After gathering my heart from the floor, I accept the lily-scented cloth from the wrinkled hand while raising my eyes to my savior. A grin curls on my cracked lips when the soulful dark eyes of Abel peer back at me.

"Uh-uh," Abel mutters firmly, reading my apology for what he witnessed before it has the chance to be articulated. "You have had a very rough day, Ms. Cleo. Side effects of this nature are perfectly normal."

Stealing my chance to refute his claim that my sickness is associated with Richard, he moves to the window perched above the vanity to crack it open. As cool, salty air blows into the small confines, he lowers the toilet seat, flushes the cistern, then replaces my washcloth with a new one.

Warmth blooms across my chest when he says, "Come on, let me have a look at you?"

Not waiting for me to reply, he places the back of his hand on my forehead to check for a temperature as his worldly eyes dart between mine, as if he is physically inspecting my soul for internal injuries.

"I'm not sick," I mumble, my voice showing my delight for his caring nature. "I'm just—"

"A Garcia," Abel interrupts.

The expression marring his adorable face causes a small chuckle to escape from my lips. His brow is arched high, and his nose is pointed down. He reminds me of Mr. Fitzgerald, my fifth-grade science teacher—in a less scary type of way.

As he times my pulse, Abel glares into my eyes, daring me to negate his true statement. I keep my mouth shut. Abel and I have shared many stories the past four days, most featured Lexi and my Garcia antics. Although I downplayed my influence in the stories I shared, Abel knows before my tragic loss, I was just as much a part of the antics as Lexi was.

After washing his hands in the sink, Abel gently caresses my neck with both his hands. Just him taking the weight off my tired head is a godsend.

"Hmm," he murmurs to himself before he abruptly cracks my neck to the right.

My eyes bulge as panic makes itself known. My alarm doesn't last long. Only long enough for me to realize whatever Abel just did to my neck completely erased the consequence of my tumble out of Richard's car. All the pain throbbing in my neck the past three hours has vanished, taking my thumping headache right along with it.

I lock my eyes with Abel, shock smeared on my face. "What did you do?"

He humbly shrugs. "An old trick I learned during my years of service."

My O-formed mouth shifts into a smile when he playfully salutes. "You were in the military?"

Abel gathers the two dirty washcloths from my hands to place them in the woven hamper under the vanity sink while answering, "Yes. Sergeant First Class Brown at your service, Ms. Cleo."

"How come this is the first I'm hearing about this?" I query, my tone picking up in conjunction with my attitude.

My drastic shift in mood is not surprising. Abel has the type of aura that rubs off on you. I have no doubt even someone with a heart as black as Delilah's would have a hard time ignoring his charisma.

My girly giggle jingles around the washroom when Abel does a little jig on the spot. His dance moves are similar to the ones he broke out last week when he spotted Marcus carrying me over his shoulder as he raced to show me his newly constructed playroom. For a man his age, he sure can move.

"I can't reveal all my talents, Ms. Cleo. I don't want to give Mr. Everett any more competition than he already has."

Heat blemishes my cheeks over his statement. If I'm being honest, my blushing response isn't solely based on his brazen retort, it also comes from having two people in a small space.

Suddenly, my mouth gapes as my spine straightens. "That's why you knew how to fire a gun? From your years of service?"

Abel winks, soundlessly confirming my suspicion. "Although it has been a few years since I've fired my gun, I most certainly enjoyed blowing out her old cobwebs."

I smile. "Bet that wasn't an opportunity you thought my arrival would bring you."

Abel's dance moves stop before his gaze meets mine. "You brought many things I never suspected, Ms. Cleo," he confirms, his tone laced with unchallenged gratitude.

I firm my stance, preparing for the physical blow I'm about to receive. It's lucky I trust my body's intuition, as Abel hits me with my hardest blow of the week when he says, "You brought joy to my boy I thought I'd never see before my demise. You fulfilled the wish I've been pledging to accomplish for over two decades."

Abel cuts off my rebuttal by lifting his index finger in the air. "I'm not saying I'm going anywhere anytime soon, Ms. Cleo. I am merely stating a fact. Before you, Marcus was reserved, closed off..." My shock of him calling

Marcus by his first name doesn't register before he tacks on, "…controlled. You're changing him for the better. You're making him the man he has always strived to be."

"That's not by his choice, though, Abel. He is being forced to change by influences outside of his control." I try to keep my devastation out of my tone. I miserably fail.

"You can't truly believe that, Ms. Cleo. I've seen him with you away from this." He gestures his hand to the thick door that's unable to conceal the flurry of activity happening downstairs. "The man who had me trekking all over the city to find the exact wide tooth comb your wild mane requires is not a man influenced by others. He is man persuaded by his heart."

It's the fight of my life to ignore the prickling of moisture in my eyes, but I give it my very best shot. Abel has already seen me bare my stomach to the world, he doesn't need to handle a blubbering Cleo as well.

Realizing he has me stumped for a reply, Abel takes the empty seat next to me. In his black suit and crisp white shirt, he makes sitting on a cold-tiled floor look trendy. I feel the raging beat of his heart through his hands when he curls them around mine.

"People often mistake the leaders of the community as being the most influential. I don't. Power lasts for years, but influence lasts a lifetime."

6

I stop packing Lexi's Indian hipster dress into my suitcase when the hairs on my arms prickle to attention. After my discussion with Abel, I had every intention of taking a shower and crawling into bed. It was only when I saw my suitcase sitting open on the bed in Marcus's master suite did my plans alter. I won't lie, my eyes have welled with more tears than I can count the past thirty minutes. I wanted to believe Abel's assumption that I was here via Marcus's choice, but seeing my suitcase thrusted my imminent departure back to the forefront of my mind, effectively squashing any hope of believing I am here as Marcus's guest. I am only here because he was strong-armed into bringing me here.

My sweep of the room stops when my eyes lock in on a figure standing at the end of the walk-in-closet. Although my vision is hazed with unshed tears, I don't need 20/20 sight to know who is standing there, gawking at me with a set of angry eyes. The way my breathing switched from ragged gasps to shallow pants is all the indication I need to know it's Marcus watching me.

Resting my backside on the balls of my feet, I watch him span the distance between us. Like every moment we are together, the air is fired with heady lust. The only thing dampening the electricity is the desolate glint darkening Marcus's eyes. Although his outside appearance is as well put together as it always is, his eyes show he feels just as tormented as I do right now.

I hate that I'm being so melodramatic. If I sat back and viewed the entire picture, I would have known this was bound to happen. This is the exact reason I've kept my distance from everyone the past four years, because I didn't want to feel the pain when they left. My life has had a lot of ups and downs the past seven years, but indisputably the most horrific was losing my family. That hurt beyond description. It was a pain I'd never wish on my worst enemy. One I wish I'd never have to experience again. Unfortunately, that isn't the case.

"Why are you packing?" Marcus mutters, his low timbre causing a chill to run down my spine "Abel can do that for you in the morning."

Although my heart warms at the mentioning of Abel's name, it does nothing to ease the pain. Actually, it makes it ten times worse. I'm going to miss Abel more than I can express. Four days ago, he was a stranger, today, he is family. Our interaction in the washroom this evening was brief, but compelling enough to last a lifetime. He and his smooth dance moves will always have a special place in my heart.

My eyes drift between Marcus's heavy-hooded gaze when he seizes my wrists and plucks me from the ground. The squealing protest of my muscles signals I've been packing for longer than I realized.

Remaining quiet, Marcus places his hand on the curve of my back and paces toward the master bathroom. When he did similar things the past week, sexual energy would crackle and hiss in the air. But not tonight. Don't get me wrong, our natural sexual compatibility is still there, but for once, my perception is outweighing the desires of my body.

The closer we get to the master bath, the more frantically my eyes bounce around our surroundings, vainly trying to find an excuse not to enter the bathroom. Even with my nerves balancing on a steep cliff, I know I can't trust myself alone with Marcus. I can barely control myself around him as it is, let alone in an intimate setting where clothing is not a requirement.

I roll my eyes when my fake yawn comes out sounding more like a yearning moan than a yawn. "I'm so beat, I'm going to pop straight into bed. I don't need a shower—"

"Shh, Cleo," Marcus interrupts.

His deep tone returns the energy missing mere seconds ago with a vengeance. Lust hangs so densely in the air, I can barely breathe through its vivacity.

My core tightens when Marcus mutters, "I've showered you every day we've been here, and I'll continue showering you every day once we leave."

I don't respond to his remark. I can't. The briskness of his tone and the dominating verve vibrating out of him has shunted me into heightened stupidity. I don't need to peer into his eyes to know who is standing before me.

Master Chains has arrived.

The lighting in the bathroom automatically switches on when Marcus swings open the thick Balinese door. My heart kicks into a mad beat, spurred on by an odd combination of anxiety and excitement. It grows in intensity the further we merge into the bathroom.

Once we arrive at the side of the large double shower, Marcus's hands shoot down to the hem of my shirt. His warm breath fans my heated cheeks when he whips my shirt off with a sense of urgency. My bra follows not even two seconds later. After discarding my shirt and bra on the floor, he switches his attention to the fastener on my skirt. Although him undressing me is nothing new, he's never done it with such urgency before. Usually, he takes his time, savoring every inch of my skin as if it's a gifted treasure slowly being revealed.

I remain frozen in place, shocked and incredibly turned on when he begins removing his clothes with the same anticipation he had when stripping me. Morally, I know I should stop this before it goes too far, but I also know that will never happen. I am lost to this man. I'm so far gone, I'll take any little piece he is willing to give me. I want him to sweep away my pain, to wash away the horrid thoughts plaguing me—some old, others new.

Gratitude pumps into me when Marcus helps me into the shower. Warm water glides down my cheeks, successfully concealing an annoying rogue tear that unwillingly spilled from my eye. Although angry I can't control my childish sobs, there isn't much I can do about them. My eyes have been brimming with moisture all day, so it was only a matter of time before tears would eventually fall.

As the steaming hot water conceals my tears, Marcus tugs an elastic band out of my hair, freeing my locks from their tight restraint. Once my hair falls to my shoulders, I close my eyes and lean deeper into the spray, allowing the water to wash dirt from my body as efficiently as it soothes my battered heart.

Just like he has done every day the past four days, Marcus commences nurturing me. He shampoos my hair before lathering my body with the soft heavenliness of a cashmere and seaweed shower puff. His loving nature has me double-guessing my initial assumption that I am in the presence of Master Chains. Usually, the man who showers me every day is Marcus. Master Chains only emerges in his playroom, or when mine and Abel's taunting becomes too bothersome for him.

When I pop my eyes open, I realize neither of my theories are accurate. I'm at a loss on who is standing in front of me. Although Marcus's eyes are crammed with pussy-quaking dominance, and his sharp jaw is firm and rigid, he is nurturing me in a way I've only experienced in Marcus's realm. It's like he is stuck between two parallels. He wants to dominant me and nurture me at the same time.

My thighs squeeze together as an endless stream of wicked thoughts bombards me. Images of all things I could experience being in the presence of both Marcus and Master Chains hit me so hard and fast, my tiredness soon becomes a distant memory. I'm hot and needy in a matter of seconds, my hankering impelled by not only the roughish thoughts quickening my pulse, but also the glorious visual of Marcus naked. He is standing so close to me, the heat of his flesh scorches my skin more than the sweltering water pumping out of the showerhead. Just imagine, a caring, nurturing Marcus with an edge of dominance he usually reserves for a playroom environment? Just the thought has my astuteness severely wavering, and don't even get me started on my race to climax.

When Marcus catches me staring at his impressive erection, he places his hand under my chin and raises my head. The tingling sensation hampering my sex doubles when my eyes lock with his commanding, yet hesitant gaze. He looks like a man who ordered every item on the menu, but he doesn't know which decadent piece to sample first. I don't care where he starts, he just needs to hurry before he discovers the true power he has over me. He truly is a Master. He hasn't even touched me yet, and I'm already teetering on the edge of orgasmic bliss.

With his eyes arrested on mine, Marcus rinses the shampoo from my hair. My horniness grows more rampant with every perfect massage his long, dexterous fingers inflict on my scalp. My breathing turns urgent when a few of his hearty kneads erotically tug my hair. He continues with his routine of gentle strokes and painful tugs until my hair is void of shampoo.

My eyes pop open when Marcus switches off the water faucet and steps out of the shower. Confusion overwhelms me. *This is not how our shower sessions usually end.*

Noticing I've failed to follow him out of the shower, Marcus's eyes lift from the towel he is drying himself with to me. His brow arches into his hairline as he takes in my wide-eyed appearance. I can tell the instant he reads the expression on my face. Not only does the spark of dominance in his eyes grow tenfold, but the thickness of his cock also increases.

My hope of him washing away the agony still encumbering my insides dissipates when he shakes his head. "No, Cleo. You make me too reckless, I don't trust myself." He continues shaking his head while handing me a towel.

With my hands fisted at my side, I keep my eyes arrested on him. "Please, Master Chains," I shamefully beg, leaving my dignity at the door. "You might not trust yourself, but I trust you."

I should be ashamed I've lowered myself to begging for him to converse with me, but I'm not. If this is my last chance of interacting with him in his private abode, I'm not above begging. For all I know, this could be our last encounter altogether, so I want it to be the best one we've had. Then maybe, when he returns here alone, he may think of me.

The excitement making my skin a sticky mess fades when I spot the indecisiveness in his eyes. His eyes are still blazing with unbridled hankering, but its strength isn't as great with its tinge of doubt.

"Please don't make me do this alone," I barely whisper.

The pulse throbbing Marcus's neck merges into dangerous territory when my juddering hands cup my breasts. Marcus doesn't have many weaknesses, but I know this is one of a very limited number. Fondling myself is nearly as effective as goading him when I want to unleash his dominance.

I moan when my thumb and index fingers roll the stiff peaks of my nipples. Although you could construe my throaty moan as a ploy to force him to dominate me, that isn't true. It was one hundred percent authentic. With the showerhead switched off and Marcus's heated gaze scorching my breasts, my nipples are the most budded they have ever been.

"*Cleo...*" Marcus growls out in warning, his gravelly tone a clear indication of his waning decisiveness.

"Please, Master Chains," I beg again, lowering one of my hands to toy with the hardened bud of my clit. "I need to come, but I want *you* to make me come."

Marcus's breathing is so heated, white puffs of smoke merge from his gaped mouth with every exhalation of air, but he maintains his quiet stance. If he is hoping the fury gleaming out of him will thwart my endeavor to climax, he has underestimated the power he has over me. The more his eyes rage with arrogant dominance, the wetter my pussy becomes.

My knees shake when the pad of my thumb flicks the engorged bud of my clit. My body is so sexually excited, I'm moments away from shattering in ecstasy. "If you don't want to bring me to climax, I guess I'll have to do it myself."

Staring into his eyes, I thrust two fingers into my dripping sex. My pussy clenches around my fingers, shocked by the sudden intrusion. Its pulsating clasps sync in perfect rhythm to the tick impinging Marcus's jaw. My hand cupping my breast darts out to brace myself on the steam-covered glass door when a deep growl rumbles from Marcus's hard-lined lips. The dominance beaming out of him in invisible waves has more effect on my libido than my penetrating fingers. It sends a jolting spasm rocketing through my core and causes my knees to buckle.

"Do not come, Cleo."

I reply with a grunt since my race to climax has rendered me incapable of articulating words. With how tightly my muscles are stretched with both exhaustion and sexual exhilaration, every inch of my body is caught up relishing the tingling sensation running down my spine. I groan huskily when my thumb rolls over my clit on repeat. Every perfect flick has my race to climax gaining momentum. My coil tightens and tightens over and over again until I can no longer hold it back.

Just before I topple into climax, the sweetest noise I've ever heard jingles into my ears, "If you want to play, you must first kneel."

7

I lock my brimming-with-lust eyes with Marcus as I lower to my knees. You'd think the pain of kneeling on a rigid, tiled floor would dampen my excitement. It doesn't. It ramps it up to a never-before-seen level. Not only am I once again in the presence of a man I've had multiple fantasies about the past three months, I'm also directly in front of his primed and ready-to-go cock.

I lick my lips as an infinite torrent of excitement blazes my veins. The wetness pooling between my legs intensifies when Marcus paces toward me, only stopping to gather his tie left sprawled on the floor

"What's your safe word, Cleo?"

"Pineapple," I mumble, my voice unlike anything I've ever heard. It's husky and robust, but with a dash of guilt that I've once again forced him to interact with me against his wishes.

My lips twitch, preparing to recite my safe word again as I have done every time we've played together. A tinge of vulnerability plagues me when Marcus doesn't request for me to repeat it. He merely stares into my eyes while demanding for me to intertwine my hands in front of my body. The extreme sexual connection between us hisses and cracks in the air when I do as instructed without a single qualm of hesitation.

Remaining quiet, he uses his silk tie to bind my hands together. He fastens the impromptu restraints tightly enough I'll never forget they are there, but not firmly enough to incite panic. The muscles in my thighs tense when he assists me off the floor. He steps us backwards until I am once more positioned under the large showerhead. My erratically panting chest thrusts forward when he raises my arms into the air so he can secure his tie to the showerhead dangling above my head.

When he yanks roughly on his makeshift tethers, my body is stretched to its absolute limit. One more millimeter and I'd be balancing on my tippy toes. After ensuring I'm secured firmly enough I'll have no chance to escape unaided, Marcus moves to stand in front of me. The throb of my pussy adjusts from barely contained to frenzied when the crest of his cock braces against my aching-with-desire sex. Just the thought of his thick, long, and mouthwateringly hard cock thrusting into me pushes my urge to climax back to the forefront of my mind.

"No," Marcus mutters as he places his knee between my legs, foiling my attempt to ease the uncontrollable throbbing sensation battering my pussy with a quick squeeze. "If your thighs touch at any stage, you will be punished," he warns, his tone gruff.

His threat makes my fight ten times worse, but I give it my best shot to remain obedient. I've learned many things the past four days. The most significant is that Marcus wasn't lying when he said my punishments would no longer incite pleasure. I never realized an ostrich tickler could be a torture instrument until it was placed in the hands of my Master.

My brows join when Marcus unexpectedly steps out of the shower. After closing the thick glass door in his wake, he secures a towel around his hips and pivots on his heels. A new wrinkle cracks on my forehead when he exits the bathroom without so much of a backward glance.

I still as panic roars through my body. "Master Chains?" I breathe out heavily.

Silence. That's all that greets me.

"Master Chains?" I query again, louder this time. "Are you coming back?"

Horrid alarm makes my skin a sticky mess when my words echo around the soundless room before booming into my ears. I suck in deep breaths as I strain to hear the meekest sound.

Silence. Nothing but endless silence.

"Oh god, please don't be mean," I plead, fighting against the restraints tethering me to the showerhead.

Although I'm certain Marcus's scare tactic is a ploy to curb my disobedience, my panic is rising at a rate I don't appreciate. I can barely breathe as it curls around my throat, silently asphyxiating me. I'm not just the most sexually frustrated I've ever been, I'm the most scared as well.

"Marcus?" I stammer out, not below being insubordinate to force him to respond to me. "Please don't do this. This isn't funny."

Panic grips my heart when nothing but my manic breaths are heard.

"Marcus, please come back." My words are so raw they sound like they went to hell and back before leaving my mouth.

I stop thrusting against the restraints holding me firmly when the sound of a door creaking open seeps into the room. I slump onto the balls of my feet as I struggle to calm the wild beat of my heart.

"Please don't ever do that to me again," I implore, my voice cracking with unshed tears. My panic was so strong, I was on the verge of doing something I never wanted to do again. I was nearly forced to use my safe word. "That really scared me. Silence is a hard limit for me. I thought you knew that?"

Although I am embarrassed about my childish response to a few moments of quiet, the past ten minutes saw my panic surging to a point it's never reached before. I swear, my heart is thrashing against my chest so hard, the entire town of Bronte's Peak can hear it.

Some of the panic raring through my body sails out the window when Marcus steps into the shower recess. It isn't just his captivating face and pussy-watering body that has my heart rate skyrocketing, it's the small silver instrument he is holding in his hand. *What possible use could he have for a pinwheel?*

I freeze as reality smacks into me. "I didn't come, so technically you can't punish me," I stammer out, breathless with an even amount of excitement and alarm.

Ignoring my statement, Marcus covers my eyes with one of the many blindfolds he has in his playroom. With my vision hindered, my ears pick up their slack. I'll be honest, half of the ragged pants I'm frantically sucking in are triggered by excitement, whereas the other half are crammed with fear. This isn't like Marcus. He is usually an informative talker in the bedroom. There hasn't been one incident the past two weeks where he hasn't ensured I was aware of what he was doing, and that I was comfortable with the scene we were undertaking. So to say his silence is somewhat off-putting would be an understatement—a major one.

An ear-piercing squeal rolls up my throat when the shower faucet suddenly switches on, drenching me head to toe with icy-cold water. I fight against the restraints binding me to the showerhead. My efforts are utterly pointless. The more I struggle, the firmer my restraints become.

"Oh... god...it's freezing," I mutter through clattering teeth as I give up on my endeavor to free myself.

New goosebumps bristle on my arms when an odd piercing sensation pricks the skin on my erratically panting chest. If I hadn't spotted the pinwheel in Marcus's hand, I'd be none the wiser to what's causing the weird scratching sensation to my chest. The skin around my areola pulls taut when my nipples bud painfully quickly. Although the water is beyond freezing, it isn't the cause of the weird excitement flooding my needy core. It's the pinwheel Marcus is running over my engorged nipple.

The sensation of the pinwheel pricking my skin isn't overly painful, but it's incredibly arousing. The best way I could describe it would be comparing it to the sensation I assume Marcus experiences when I rake my nails down his back in the midst of ecstasy. It's a feeling that walks the line between pleasure and pain.

When Marcus tracks the pinwheel to my left breast, he increases the pressure on the device. As the little silver prongs dig deeper into my skin, my womb tightens more. Every arousing nip builds the tension feeding the air with heady lust. It also makes me forget about the below-freezing waters numbing my toes.

Marcus devotes the same amount of attention to my left nipple as he did my right, lavishing it with a stimulating mix of both pleasure and pain. By the time he tracks the pinwheel away from my breasts, I am completely mindless, lost to the chase of climax.

My teeth catch my bottom lip when the pinwheel unexpectedly traces over my inner thighs. This is the one thing I hate about being blindfolded. Although my body can intuit Marcus's closeness, its awareness isn't precise enough to tell me exactly where he is.

My teeth munch on my lip so harshly, I'm confident I'll drawn blood when the warmth of Marcus's breath hits my throbbing sex. "Spread your legs wider, Cleo." Marcus's voice so core-clenching deep, I nearly squeeze my legs together instead of apart.

"More," he demands roughly when the sweep of my thighs isn't up to his standards.

Placing his hands on the inside of my thighs, he separates my thighs to his desired width. "Keep them there."

"Ah, god," I mumble under my breath when he unexpectedly sucks my clit into his mouth.

His unexpected devotion to my clit is so overwhelming, if I weren't bound to the showerhead, my buckling knees would see me tumbling to the ground. He licks, bites and sucks my pussy at a frenzied pace, arousing every nerve ending in my body.

My breathing turns rampant when my quivering leg brushes past Marcus's thick cock. Considering the water is a cold as the Hudson in winter, I'm surprised—and utterly delighted—by how hard he is.

After skillfully teasing my clit until I'm on the brink of ecstasy, Marcus withdraws his mouth from my tingling pussy. Before a single gripe can seep from my mouth, the jabbing sensation of the pinwheel returns full force. Its piercing touch stimulates the area just below my navel before it slowly tracks down to the erogenous zone above my heated core.

My pupils widen with each bump of the pinwheel as it moves closer to my throbbing-with-need clit, mere millimeters from an area tightened with anticipation. The desire to squeeze my thighs together nearly becomes unwinnable when Marcus increases the pressure on the pinwheel even more. I grunt, fighting with all my might to ignore the intoxicating ambience of pleasure steamrolling me into a quivering, blubbering mess.

"Do not come, Cleo. Do you understand me? If you come, I'll punish you."

What? He can't be serious, can he? This may be one of the more painful sensations I've experienced with him, but it's also one of the most outstandingly fan-fucking-tastic sexual encounters I've ever had. Imagine this—freezing cold water, the warm of Marcus's mouth on my clit, and a prickling sensation hitting every erogenous zone in my body. This is... *God.* I can't express how good it feels.

"Cleo," Marcus barks, snapping me back to the present. "Did you hear what I said?"

"Yes," I stammer out, my voice nearly a sob. I'm not on the verge of crying because he is hurting me, I'm on the brink of tears wondering what my punishment will be when I forsake his threat. My urge to climax is so strong, it's practically dangling on a very thin thread, threatening to snap at any moment.

I wrap my hands around the satin tie tethering my hands above my head when Marcus growls, "Yes, what?"

My failure to issue the correct reply increases the pressure on the pinwheel. My thighs wobble as every hair on my body prickles to attention. The sensation is so overwhelming, my safe word sits on the tip of my tongue, primed for imminent release. I'm not bowing out of our exchange because I want it to be over, it's because if he doesn't hurry up and touch me, I'm not below finishing myself. That's how desperate I am to come.

"*Cleo...*" His furious growl sends my libido into haywire.

"Yes, Master Chains, I understand," I reply when my continued silence infuriates him more. I don't need to see him to know he is angry. I can feel the wrath of his eyes scorching my skin. It's so warm, it's as if the freezing water soaking every inch of my body no longer exists.

The satin tie digs painfully into my wrists when Marcus runs the pinwheel over the hood of my clit. My nostrils flare as I resist the urge to be swept away in the tidal wave of excitement attempting to overtake me. Because Marcus toyed with my clit until it became a firm, stiff peak, the small prongs on the pinwheel dip into areas previously untouched. It's an antagonizing and amazing experience all at once.

"Please, oh god. Please, Master Chains," I cry out when the sensation becomes too much to bear. "I can't hold it back. It's too strong."

Marcus remains quiet. The only indication he heard my muffled pleas is when he drags the pinwheel over my clit again, his pace even more torturously slow than his first pass. As if the sensation of the pinwheel scouring my clit isn't enough, Marcus thrust two of his fingers inside me. My knees buckle beneath me when he hits the sweet spot deep inside my pussy.

Using my slumped figure to his advantage, he finger fucks me at a speed so fast, stars blister in front of my eyes, and my every inhibition about our exchange completely vanishes.

"Ah... Please... oh..."

The tears I've been fighting to keep at bay most of the day spring to my eyes when Marcus continues ignoring my begs for release. He works my body to the brink of snapping before he withdraws all contact. Then he does it all over again.

And again.

And again.

I don't understand why he is being so mean. What did I do wrong that I deserve to be punished? I know my earlier goading would have grated his nerves, but my desire to unleash his dominance has never backfired on me so callously before. Usually, when I tempt him, he exerts his power by showcasing how well in tune he is with my body. He ensures that by the time our session is over, I have no doubt who the master of my body is. He is.

But today he is not doing that. He is using my body against me. He is pairing off my heart and mind in a cruel battle I'm too tired to undertake.

"Why are you punishing me?" I whimper, displaying the barrage of emotions hammering me. I'm the most turned on and devastated I've ever been. "Why are you hurting me? I haven't done anything wrong."

A long, quivering moan of disappointment simpers through my parched mouth when the sound of metal clanging on tiles rings through my ears. Since I can't see, I can only assume it's the pinwheel dropping to the floor. A second wave of disappointment courses through me when Marcus removes his fingers from my clenching core.

My disappointment is pushed aside when Marcus cups my thighs so he can guide my legs around his sweat-slicked waist. My soft pants of breath shift to feral grunts when his heated flesh nestles the folds of my drenched sex. I wait for his glorious cock to impale me, loving that we've finally reached this part of our exchange.

I wait.

And wait.

And wait.

He does nothing. He remains perfectly still. Not entering me or making a single move. He just rests his sweat-drenched forehead against mine and allows the eerie quiet to speak on his behalf. His silence worries me more than him withholding my climax.

"Why are you doing this?" I ask, my words hiccupped through a sob.

He remains perfectly still, not even the sounds of his breath are audible. I'd like to say my composure is an exact replica of Marcus's. Unfortunately, that would be a lie. My breaths are so ragged, my whistling lungs overtake the sound of my pulse shrilling in my ears. My body is shaking with both anger and the effects of the freezing cold water running down my spine, and my heart is beating so fast, I have no doubt Marcus can hear it. But no matter how much my body conveys my devastation, Marcus refuses to acknowledge its silent screams for clemency.

In no time at all, his silence becomes too much for me to bear. He has my emotions on opposing teams, much like my unnatural body temperature. My outsides are frozen from the bitterly cold water pumping out of the shower-head, where my insides are still heated with lust so potent, his coldhearted demeanor hasn't dampened its excitement in the slightest.

These are two very contradicting viewpoints. The same can be said about how I view Marcus right now. Discovering he paid for Lexi's enrollment in the Kayldeco program shows how beautiful his insides are, but the man standing before me now is as cold and heartless as the water syphoning from the showerhead.

"Tell me why you're doing this or put me down," I command, my voice as weak as my demand. "You're being mean. I haven't done anything to warrant this type of punishment."

Silence. Nothing but silence greets me.

"Marcus... please."

The room is so quiet I swear I hear the first crack fracture my heart. The pain is so intense it nearly cripples me. Some people see silence as appeasing, but when you are suddenly stripped of all the noises you loved, silence can be more painful than the cruelest taunts. That's what happened to me when my parents and Tate died. My entire world was stripped of sounds I'd give anything to hear again. My dad telling my mom he loves her, Tate jeering me for using all the hot water, and the comforting words my mom would say to Lexi when she endured a tough coughing fit. Every beautiful noise I loved was gone. Stripped away. Taken in an instant. So, you may see silence as a beautiful thing. But I hate it.

"Pineapple," I murmur, my broken heart resonating in my low tone.

Marcus's statured composure doesn't falter in the slightest.

"Pineapple," I repeat, louder this time, wanting to ensure he hears me. "Pineapple. Pineapple. Pineapple!"

8

I blink back tears when Marcus yanks my blindfold off my face. It hangs in the middle of my thrusting chest, dangerously close to the area that feels like it's being torn in two. He places me on my feet before his hands lift to untie the restraints on my wrists. The muscles in my arms feel like Jell-O when they flop to my side.

Marcus catches me when my knees buckle, my shuddering body no longer capable of holding its own weight. Tears mix with the droplets of water beading on my cheeks when he draws me to his chest and strides out of the shower. I burrow my head in the towel he wraps around my shoulders, wanting to hide my tearstained face from the horribly cruel world.

The frantic beat of my heart kicks up a notch when Marcus walks us into the master suite. The feverish heat pumping out of the vent sends my suspicions into overdrive. Why would he crank up the heat to such a ghastly temperature? It truly doesn't make any sense...unless.

My eyes rocket to Marcus when the truth hits me like a ton of bricks. He was preparing for this reaction. He wanted me to use my safe word. The only thing I can't fathom is why. Why did he push me to the absolute brink so I was forced to say the one word I never wanted to say to him again? Is it an alpha-male power trip I don't understand? Or a mind game I'm too tired to participate in?

A new reality dawns when Marcus places me on the bed. Our eyes only lock and hold for the briefest second, but it's long enough for me to read all the signals his eyes are relaying. He is angry about me leaving with Richard this morning. He's mad I put my life at risk. He has no right to be angry, though. He has done as many reckless things as I have the past week. He not only endangered his personal safety by bringing me here, he also risked financial suicide. If he wants to be angry, so be it, but I shouldn't be receiving all his wrath. Some of it should be projected at himself.

"Richard was unhinged, Marcus. Who knows what he would have done if I didn't go with him. He could have hurt Abel, he could have hurt you."

"He could have killed you!" Marcus roars, startling me. His voice is so furious it ricochets off the pristine walls of his bedroom before returning to rattle my heart straight out of my chest.

I sit in silence, muted with shock by his brutal response. I've never seen him so furious. Usually, he is the calm, contrite one of our twosome.

Marcus stands in the middle of his room. His fists clench open and closed as he battles to leash his anger. It's a pointless endeavor. The tick of his jaw grows as rampant as the white-hot anger blazing out of his eyes.

"Not just today, but last week as well," he mutters when his composure simmers back to his customary level.

My heart falls from my ribcage when our eyes meet. His squinted gaze is tormented and broken.

"Why are you so goddamn stubborn, Cleo? Why do you always do senseless, idiotic things all the time? Things that could get you hurt. Things that could get you killed." He chokes out the last word.

"Because it's who I am," I fight back, rising from the bed. "He said Lexi was in danger. I believed him. That was the only reason I went with him. To protect my sister." Unlike Marcus, my voice is void of unbridled anger. I'm too concerned about the pain radiating out of his eyes to engage in a battle bigger than Ben-Hur.

"Your sister?!" Marcus fires back. "Your sister's safety has nothing to do with this!"

My breathing hitches as confusion makes itself known. I am genuinely baffled by his statement. "Believing Lexi was in danger was the only reason I went with Richard today. I had no intentions of leaving with him until he uttered her name. Clearly, it was a stupid thing for me to do, but if I have to place my life in danger to save hers, that's what I'll do, Marcus. Because when you love someone, you do everything in your power to save them." My last sentence comes out strained through clenched teeth as I struggle to hold my tears.

Not trusting my legs to keep me upright, I sit back down on the mattress. My sudden slump sends a few rogue tears spilling down my cheeks. I angrily brush them away, not wanting Marcus to spot them. My endeavors are futile. The pain in his eyes triples when he spots the moisture glistening on my cheeks.

After scrubbing his hand across his mouth that still shows evidence of my arousal, he moves to stand in front of me. Although most people would be cowering from the furious scowl etched on his handsome face, I'm not worried. Nothing could be greater than the fear I feel at the concept of losing him or my sister. That distresses me more than anything.

Marcus's hand shakes when he runs the back of his fingers down my cheek to clear away a few tears smeared there. His eyes still relay his anger, but they also expose his remorse for making me cry.

Once all my tears are taken care of, his beautifully tormented eyes meet mine. "Did he hurt you?" he asks as his heavy-lidded gaze drifts between mine.

Pain strikes my chest when I spot the hollow bleakness in his eyes. "No," I reply, shaking my head. "He never got the chance. Shian arrived before—"

"Not today," Marcus interrupts, his tone one I haven't heard before. "Last week. In his apartment. Did he hurt you then?"

My heart stops beating when the reasoning behind his anger comes to fruition. His irritation isn't only from my stupidity today. He knows about me going into Richard's apartment after my attack last week.

"No," I reply as my stomach gurgles uncontrollably. "We only went to his apartment to collect his cell phone so he had directions to drive me home. He didn't hurt me. Not today or that day."

The remorse weighing heavily on my chest eases when the torrent of pain in Marcus's eyes lessens from my confession.

A stretch of silence passes between us. Although it's crammed with palpable tension, it's a necessary requirement before we can continue with our conversation. Marcus needs a few moments to rein in his anger, while I need a few minutes to contemplate what all this means.

With everything that has happened the past several hours, much less days, I haven't stopped to consider what Richard's motives were the day of my assault. If I were to believe all the information divulged to me this evening, the knight-in-shining-armor Richard wore while assisting me last week isn't as gleaming as it once was. Was his arrival in the alleyway just a coincidence? Or was he there on purpose?

Before I can voice my queries to Marcus, he stands from his crouched position and paces to a set of drawers stacked near his closed bedroom door. After gathering a manila folder full to the brim with papers, he pivots on his heels to face me. My heart launches into my throat when I see the absolute agony radiating from his beautiful eyes. Even though he is standing before me as naked as the day he was born, that isn't the cause of his vulnerability. It's his raw, unguarded eyes stripping him wholly naked.

Now his coldness in the shower makes sense. He wanted me to experience what he felt today. The torment, the anger, the relief. I put him through the wringer, and he just replicated those exact emotions from me. He expressed himself in a manner he is most accustomed with—using my body.

Remaining quiet, Marcus paces back to me. He puts the folder on the mattress before securing a pair of boxer shorts from his bedside table for him and a cotton shirt for me.

"Thank you," I mutter when he places the shirt over my head before pulling my saturated hair out of the collar. Although my voice still showcases the chaos of emotions thickening my veins, it isn't as brittle as it was earlier.

The mattress creaks when Marcus sits down next me. I knot our shared towel around my hair before adjusting my position to face him. The gleam in his eyes tells me I should face him while he hits me with what will most likely be my hardest blow of the day.

My intuition is proven dead on point when he opens the manila folder far enough I can see the first image inside. I slap my hand over my mouth when the contents of my stomach rush to the base of my throat. My body's response is from the disturbing visual of the man who attacked me in the alleyway lying lifeless in a shallow ditch. The bullet wound between his eyes ensures there is no doubt about his fate. His eyes are as lifeless as they were when he struck me last week.

The battle to constrain my twisting stomach doubles when Marcus says, "The gun recovered at the scene today matches the caliber of weapon used to kill Stephen. Although ballistics are still a few days away, early tests indicate the bullet lodged in Stephen's skull was fired from Richard's gun." His tone grows weary at the end of his admission.

I swallow several times in a row when Marcus flicks through the photos in the manila folder until he stops on one of Stephen and Richard riding an elevator together. On closer inspection, I realize they're standing in the same elevator car I stood in with Richard last week.

"They knew each other," I mumble, more to myself than Marcus.

"Yes," Marcus answers, even knowing my declaration wasn't a question. "It's unknown if their acquaintance is recent or if they'd known each other for some time." He runs his hand over the five o'clock shadow I'm not used to seeing on his chin. "Shian also voiced speculation on your involvement in Stephen's death. Stephen's time of death is believed to have happened within two hours of you being filmed in the elevator with Richard. His apartment is only half a block from Richard's."

My eyes rocket to Marcus, shock smeared all over my face. "What?" I ask, certain I didn't hear him right.

Surely, Shian doesn't believe I'm a suspect, does she?

"You know I'd never... I couldn't... *hurt* anyone," I stammer out, unable to say the word "kill."

To an outsider, my mourning Richard's death may seem callous, but I wouldn't intentionally harm anyone. I'm may only have half a heart, but I am not entirely heartless.

"I know, Cleo," Marcus assures me, his tone giving no indication of concern or distrust. "And now, so does Shian."

My brows join, worried by his remark. Although I've only seen Shian and Marcus interact a handful of times, I know they have a unique bond. At the start, I thought it was because they have a mutual understanding—both being powerhouses in the BDSM lifestyle. But only now, after seeing anger flash in Marcus's eyes during his confession, do I realize my assumptions weren't 100% accurate. Their bond is not just based on mutual respect for a BDSM member. They are also friends.

The anger in Marcus's eyes holds firm when he rifles through the remaining photos in the folder. They replicate the ones I saw in Richard's car earlier today. They clearly show he was stalking me for years. They also display my idiocy without a smidgen of skepticism.

When I divulge my knowledge of the photos to Marcus, he works his jaw side to side as his clutch on the folder turns deadly. "He could have hurt you, Cleo," he mutters, his words displaying most of his anger resides from fear. "He could have hurt you badly."

Although I hate that my actions distressed him today, seeing him so open and raw heals some of the nicks inflicted on my heart upon discovering he only brought me here as part of an FBI sting. It doesn't entirely erase them, but it's like a band-aid. Sturdy enough to cover up the little gashes until they have the chance to fully heal.

"I know," I reply, bouncing my eyes between Marcus's. "But thankfully, he didn't. And Shian ensured he'll never have the opportunity to hurt me again." My last sentence comes out muffled, coerced through the bile sitting in the back of my throat. "I'm okay, Marcus. I promise you I am fine."

Marcus releases a deep breath, drowning out most of my assurance. My hand shakes when I raise it to rub the heavy groove between his dark brows. My heart smashes against my ribs when he closes his eyes and sucks in a sharp breath, like my meekest touch is too much for him to bear. Adoring his response, I trickle my hand down his cheek, drift it past his deliciously plump lips, then tickle the dark shadow of hair on his chin.

"This is different. I've never handled prickles before. I've only been with clean-shaven men." My voice is throaty, alluding to what we were in the process of doing before our exchange shifted from punishment to healing.

An unexpected grin tugs my lips high when Marcus opens his eyes to glare at me. Although they are still clouded with justified anger and heartache, it isn't at the same level as mere seconds ago. There is too much jealousy pumping from his envious eyes to keep his anger at bay. I know it isn't an appropriate time to goad him, but if it's the only way I can remove the tension stifling the air, I'll use it. I've never seen Marcus lose his cool like this before. Not even when Lexi had a gun pointed at him. Since I am the reason for his drastic shift in mood, shouldn't I be the person to erase it?

We sit in silence for several minutes. The air is dense with unsaid sentiments, but it also teems with silent understanding. Although Marcus has a right to be angry, he also understands the lengths I'll go to protect my sister. He knows, as he has done the same thing with his sisters. Hell, he's even safeguarding Lexi as if she is his family, and she doesn't have a drop of his blood running through her veins.

My heart squeezes when my spent brain recalls the first half of my day. Lifting my tear-welling eyes to Marcus's, I mutter, "Thank you." Although I only say two little words, my heartfelt tone relays more gratitude than my words ever could.

Marcus angles his head to the side as he peers at me, confused. "For what? I didn't do anything."

I roll my eyes. Even if I wasn't referring to what he did for Lexi, the past five days was way above and beyond "didn't do anything." He may have been forced to bring me here unwillingly, but my time with him has still been some of the best days of my life. For a man in a compromising position, Marcus made me feel welcome in his home. For that alone, I'll forever be grateful, much less what he did for Lexi.

Pushing aside the silly butterflies taking flight in my stomach, I say, "For what you did for Lexi. The Kalydeco program." My last three words are choked through a sob, still amazed he accomplished something I've wanted to do for years. I know his wealth contributed to that, but he still went out of his way to research how to have her included in the program. "That was so sweet of you to do. I don't know an appropriate way to thank you."

Marcus slants his dark brow as the expression on his face changes from worried to smug. "I can think of a few ways," he mutters, winking seductively.

I dig my elbow into his ribs, hitting him right in the tender spot between his ribcage and hip bone. All the tension hanging thickly in the air evaporates the instant his beautifully scrumptious laughter fills the room. Marcus's laugh suits him to a T. It's husky and rough but makes your insides feel gooey and warm when you hear it. It's both naughty and sweet.

My damp hair falls to my shoulders like a satin waterfall when Marcus pulls off the towel wrapped around my head. After banding his arms around my waist, he slides us up the bed until we are tucked under the snuggly warmth of his feather down quilt. When he requests for me to roll onto my hip, I do so without hesitation. Just like he has showered me every night since we arrived in Ravenshoe, he has spooned with me as well. At the start, I was surprised by his loving nature, but then I figured he had a lot of lost opportunities to catch up on.

The fine hairs on my nape stand to attention when Marcus gathers my hair to the side so he can nuzzle his chin in close to my neck. My heart sighs, loving the return of Marcus... I can't say the same thing about my aching insides. They are still coiled tight, waiting for the release Master Chains usually awards me with.

After a few moments of relishing Marcus's nurturing side, I roll on my hip to face him. Thankfully, he doesn't stop my endeavors. My muscles grow tauter when I am met with his alluring green irises. He stares into my eyes, his forthright gaze sharing a lifetime of stories without a peep seeping from his lips. The only story they don't disclose is the one I want to know the most.

Deciding there is only one way to cure my curiosity, I blubber, "Why did you force me to use my safe word?"

I know he was angry, but that doesn't explain why he wanted me to safe word. My knowledge of the BDSM lifestyle is still that of a novice, but it's extensive enough to know it's unusual for a Dom to coerce his sub to end a scene. Usually, they strive to avoid their sub safe-wording.

Don't they?

Marcus draws me in tighter, pulling me so near, the tips of our noses brush against each other. "You hurt me today, Cleo," he mutters, sending his coffee-scented breath lingering into my nostrils. "For nearly an hour, I didn't know where you were, or if you were safe. That utterly decimated me. I wanted you to feel the same pain."

His eyes dance between mine, soundlessly gauging my reaction to his confession. I remain quiet, honestly at a loss on how to reply.

"You didn't hurt me, though," I eventually reply when I fail to comprehend his riddled explanation.

"I know," he responds, "because I made you safe word."

My brow arches as my heart ceases beating. "You made me safe word so you wouldn't hurt me?"

"Yes," Marcus replies in an instant. "My desire to punish you for leaving with Richard was strong . I wanted you to feel what I felt knowing you put your life in unnecessary danger, but I couldn't do it. No matter how much I wanted to hurt you, I couldn't do it."

I still as reality dawns. That's why he stopped his campaign of punishing me the instant I said he was hurting me. I know the idea of physically hurting me sickens him, but he didn't need to worry. I didn't mean it in the physical sense, I meant he was emotionally scarring me. Although emotional abuse should never be tolerated, I don't believe that was what Marcus did this evening. He was hurting, and the only way he felt comfortable voicing his pain was by using actions. I can't fault him for that.

"You couldn't hurt me as you're not a sadist," I remind him, hating the sorrow marring his face. "You don't hurt people for your own pleasure. You instill pain for your sub's pleasure. That's not a sadist."

Marcus laughs, brittle and jam-packed with pain. "You wouldn't be saying that if you knew the thoughts I had today. Not just about Richard, you too." He tucks a strand of my hair behind my ear before locking his eyes with mine. "At one stage, I considered tying you to this bed for the rest of your life, only leaving you enough chain to reach the bathroom..." His teeth graze over his bottom lip before he mutters, "And the playroom."

The most inappropriately timed smile stretches across my face, smitten at the idea he wanted me here so badly, he was willing to go to such levels to keep me here.

My smile enlarges to a full-toothed grin when he adds, "It was only when Shian threatened to arrest me for kidnapping did I change my mind."

I don't know if he was aiming for his statement to be playful, but the smallest giggle still erupts from my mouth. His comment not only sends blood gushing to my heart, but also intensifies the throbbing sensation between my legs.

I purse my lips and arch my brow, pretending to act serious. "I don't know if the laws in Florida are the same as Jersey's, but where I'm from, you can only be charged with kidnapping if the person is held against their will."

Marcus's lips twitch as he struggles to contain his smile. "Are you saying you want to be tied to my bed for the rest of eternity, Cleo?" he asks, his tone not as playful as the twinkle in his eyes. It's a little more serious since it's lined with sentiment.

I shrug my shoulders, continuing with my nonchalant approach. "Depends?"

"On what?" Marcus immediately fires back. His two words fire out of his mouth so quickly, there is no mistaking his piqued interest.

I stare him straight in the eyes, my expression deadpan. "On what I get out of this negotiation."

A whizz of air parts Marcus's curved lips as they carve into an illustrious grin. "This isn't enough?" His tone is smug as his eyes roam around his opulent master suite.

"No." My response is curt and resolute. "But this, on the other hand," I continue, cupping my hand on his crotch. His cock hardens at my meekest touch. It immediately erases any qualms I had about my brazenness. *Thank god.* Although my libido is heightened beyond belief, I don't think my body could be subjected to another punishment from Master Chains.

"This could *possibly* persuade me."

The smirk that etches onto Marcus's handsome face sends my pulse skyrocketing. "Possibly?"

My teeth munch on my lower lip as I shrug my shoulders, acting like I need some persuading. His cock grows thicker, accepting my challenge.

Even knowing I'm about to expose my most lethal hand doesn't stop me moving my other hand to hover over his frantically beating heart. "This... I don't need any persuading about." My eyes float between his as the temperature in the room turns roasting. "I'm sorry I hurt you today. I'm sorry for not considering how it would make you feel when I left with Richard. But I'll never be sorry for protecting my sister. I've been doing it for so long, it's as natural as breathing to me. But if you can forgive me for hurting you, I promise I will always consider your feelings before I act recklessly again. It doesn't mean I won't do stupid things, but it may lessen them to the occasional mishap."

The dominance my frisky tease awakened in his eyes dampens from my admission. His response fills me with dread, panicked I've broken every one of his rules in his BDSM contact. The most important—the non-love provision.

Pretending I can't feel my insides twisting up, I scoot across the mattress, filling in the minutest portion of air left between us. "So what do you say, Master Chains? Do you accept the new terms of our agreement? Or do you have some stipulations you'd like to add?" I cringe when my voice comes out with a tremor I was hoping to conceal with light-hearted commentary.

My heart slithers into my gut when Marcus murmurs, "Hmmm." He takes his time considering his options, building the suspense until it hangs so thickly in the air, it's almost murderous.

The five o'clock shadow on his top lip tickles my mouth when he murmurs, "I accept your offer, Ms. Garcia. No further negotiations necessary."

I exhale loudly as fresh tears prick my eyes.

We seal our new deal with a kiss...and a few hours twisted beneath the sheets.

9

My hand sweeps at the handful of tears trickling down my face before I pull back from Abel's embrace. Even though I'm confident my cheeks are tear-free, the twinkle in Abel's eyes tells me he didn't miss the one or two splashes that hit the collar of his shirt.

"You'll be back soon. I just know it," Abel mutters, squeezing my hand. "Until then, you continue reminding that boy of mine that life is about noise, mess, and chaos." He nudges his head to Marcus sitting in the driver's seat of his fancy sports car. After returning his mischievous eyes to me, he continues, "And I'll enjoy the benefits of a full night's sleep without any noisy interruptions."

I swallow harshly as heat rises to my cheeks. *That's my cue to leave.*

After pressing a final kiss on Abel's elevated cheek, I slide into the passenger seat of Marcus's car. The tight pleated pencil skirt I'm wearing glides up inappropriately high on my thigh. A grin curls on my lips, loving Marcus's bug-eyed reaction to the scandalous portions of skin I'm exposing. Not a word seeps from his mouth, but the hiss of air straining through his teeth gives me the exact reaction I was hoping for.

I've never used my body as a ploy for attention before, but I'm not above using it to secure Marcus's utmost devotion. Although he spent hours last night devouring every inch of me, there is still a snippet of worry festering in my heart that things between us are about to drastically change. It probably has more to do with returning home than Marcus's quietness this morning, but I can't one hundred percent testify to that. Marcus has never been an overly talkative person anyway, so both my assumptions could be entirely off the mark.

Storing away my confusion for a more appropriate time, I fasten my seatbelt and swing my eyes to Marcus. My breath hitches when I spot him watching me, the hunger in his eyes as prominent as ever.

"You ready?"

A grin curls on my lips. "As ready as I'll ever be."

My thighs touch when he revs the engine of his expensive pride and joy. The vibration of the high horse-powered motor rumbles through my seat before clustering in my rapidly awakening core. It reminds me so much of the time we evaded the paparazzi when we were leaving the airport hangar. With the media being well-informed of the band's home base, Marcus said, any time a jet is scheduled to arrive, the paparazzi are either expecting a member of Rise Up, or a handful of the wealthy businessmen who also claim Ravenshoe as their hometown. It's their regular haunt to stalk since the band's home bases are closely guarded secrets.

My grin sags to a pout. "I didn't think the paparazzi knew about this place?" I hate that my foolishness yesterday has compromised his privacy.

"They don't." Marcus's lips curve higher than the needle on his speedometer. "But when I recalled how much you enjoyed the ride last time, I thought I'd treat you to a similar thrill."

My heart rate kicks into a canter. "The ride? Or the event that took place after the ride?" I query, my voice full of sass, loving that I'm in the presence of the carefree Marcus I've only seen a handful of times since arriving in Ravenshoe.

Marcus doesn't answer my question. He doesn't need to. His eyes relay the entire story.

A girly squeal ripples through my lips when he plants his foot to the floor. The impressive power of his engine thrusts me into my seat, while his lusty grin hits every one of my hot buttons. His car fishtails in the loose gravel of his driveway before zooming out of the recently repaired security gate. I sling my head back, aspiring to wave goodbye to Abel. Although he is covered by a dust cloud, I can't miss his bright smile beaming through the gritty fog.

By the time Marcus weaves his car through the winding roads of Bronte's Peak, the aggravation gnawing my heart is completely forgotten. I feel like I'm on a rollercoaster ride—literally. Not only is my stomach following the ebb and flow of the road surface, but so are my emotions. I don't know if it's a good thing or not, but I can't remember the last time I felt so many contrasting emotions in a twenty-four hour period. It's been crazy. A true rollercoaster ride.

My brows stitch when Marcus fails to take the exit to the private airstrip where the band's jet is housed. "Weren't you supposed to take that exit?" I ask. My words are forced through a gag, hating that I'm one of those annoying backseat drivers. They are the worst of the worst.

Marcus remains quiet. Even though he isn't looking at me, I know his eyes are on me. I can feel the heat of his gaze drifting between my barely covered thighs and my face. You can't hide the heat of desire.

With my interests piqued, I turn my eyes back to the scenery whizzing by. Just like a majority of Bronte's Peak, the panorama is breathtakingly beautiful.

Marvelous, architecturally pleasing homes scatter the shoreline, nestled amongst a coastline that stretches as far as the eye can see. I've always been a city girl, but Bronte's Peak is growing on me. It's like an oasis in the middle of a bustling world, contending to gobble up every moment of freedom. It's a reminder to stop and breathe, and maybe occasionally smell the roses. It's peaceful but not so overly quaint that you feel claustrophobic.

The further we travel, the less opulent our surroundings become. The houses go from sprawling mansions to cozy family homes I've become accustomed to in Montclair. The manicured lawns aren't as green or kept as the ones in Marcus's neighborhood, but the neighborhood has a sense of pride radiating out of it. This area may not be as wealthy as Bronte's Peak, but it's alive with a richness money can't buy. It's a community.

"Where are we?" I ask Marcus, my tone as surprised as my wide eyes.

Before a syllable escapes Marcus's lips, he pulls in front of a weather-chapped house. It's identical to many other homes on the street, except its paintwork has recently been done, and the trimmings around the windows are a beautiful sky blue in coloring. It's a cute little house full of old-world charm, but I'm still at a loss as to why Marcus would bring me here.

"Come, I want to show you something," he says, unclipping his seatbelt and curling out of his seat.

My pulse quickens, spurred on by his voice. It's brandishing the same amount of excitement it did when he had his playroom installed in his private residence. Suddenly, I freeze as the breakfast I consumed in a hurry this morning gurgles in my windpipe. *Oh god—please don't let this be his sub house.*

"Thank you," I stammer when Marcus opens my passenger door and aids me out of his car.

With his hand on the curve of my back, his eyes sweep the area, ensuring we are alone. Considering it isn't even 7 AM, the street is unsurprisingly quiet.

My worry that this is indeed the house Marcus's subs lived in grows when he removes a key from his trouser pocket and places it into the bulky lock on the front door. A damp smell hits my senses when he swings open the door and gestures for me to enter the humbly sized house.

With my heart smashing into my ribs, my eyes bolt in all directions, unsure which item to take in first. There is a small, cozy living room on my right, a spotlessly clean, homely kitchen in the far-left corner, and a well-used dining table covered with sheets of paper nestled between the kitchen and living areas.

Deciding to start at the more welcoming space, I pace into the living area. Although it's filled with furnishings similar to my home in Jersey, the musty scent lingering in the air conveys this residence hasn't recently been used. Don't get me wrong, it's the type of home that gives you the warm and fuzzies, it just hasn't been occupied enough to harbor that real family vibe a childhood home usually conveys.

My eyes rocket to Marcus when I spot a photo sitting in prime place on the mantelpiece. It's an exact replica of the picture Abel showed me last week. The one of Marcus and his three sisters. The mad beat of my heart slows as I walk over to the mantle to secure the photo in my hand. Marcus hovers close by, but remains quiet, allowing me to absorb the space at my own pace.

I shift my eyes to Marcus. "Is this your family home?"

Marcus's brows furl. "Not particularly, but it was as close to a home as I had at the time."

Although confused by his riddled reply, I can't tear my eyes away from the family treasures scattered around the living room. I love stuff like this. Nothing can replace memories, but photos are a very close second to capturing a lifetime of stories.

As I remove a small coat of dust from the frame, my eyes absorb the other pictures proudly displayed on the mantelpiece. All feature Marcus and his sisters in some light. My chin dips down low when a pair of twinkling eyes capture my attention. Even though the photo looks very well-worn, there is no way I could mistake those worldly eyes. After setting down the photo of Marcus and his sisters, I pick up the photo of Abel and another handsome African American man. Abel is wearing a full military uniform. One lapel is entirely covered with shiny medals.

"How long ago was this taken?" I ask Marcus.

Apprehension strains his face as he mutters, "Well before I was born." His mouth carves into a panty-wetting smirk. "Don't let Abel ever catch wind you were drooling over his photo. He'll never let you live it down."

I giggle. "He's very handsome."

My giggle turns into a full chuckle when Marcus playfully growls. Well, I assume he is playing, it's hard to tell from the expressionless mask he is wearing.

"Who is the man standing beside Abel?"

Marcus coughs to clear his throat before he answers, "That's my father, Josiah." His deep tone is a clear warning that I'm not to ask any more questions in regards to his father. It was stern, clipped with unbridled anger, and, if I'm being honest, pussy-quakingly delicious.

Not wanting our conversation to merge into uncomfortable waters, I place the frame back onto the mantel before pivoting around to face Marcus. Our relationship has had too many ups and downs the past week to add any more bumps in the road. We are barely holding on as it is, so I'm not willing to throw more obstacles in our path.

We stand across from each other in silence. I wouldn't necessarily say it's awkward, but there is a tinge of restlessness.

Marcus ends our tense standoff by waving his hand to a door on my far right. "In there is my real home," he informs me, his voice not as riddled with anxiety as the one he was using earlier.

Guided by my curiosity, I pace to the door. Marcus shadows closely behind me, his steps so quiet they are barely heard tapping on the well-used carpet. The smell of soot, dust and wood filters through my nose when I swing open the door. My heart goes into a tizzy when my eyes rake the room. Even if I weren't a fan of Rise Up's music, I'd still know what this room is. This is where it all began for Rise Up. This is Marcus's grandmother's garage. It's so well known, it had its own two-page spread in *Rolling Stones* magazine three years ago. Although its exact location was never disclosed, every inch of this double garage was digitally archived. It's just as important as the scraps of paper Noah and Marcus used to pen their first album. I won't lie, I'm totally chuffed he brought me here.

Striving to ignore the stupid sentimental tears looming in my eyes, I pace deeper into the room. "Is that the actual microphone Noah sang his first full-length song on?" I ask, recalling an article I read years ago that said Noah never knew he could sing until the day he belted out a tune in Marcus's grandma's garage.

"Yes," Marcus replies, his lips curling into a smirk. "And that's the drum kit Slater learned to play on."

A giggle topples from my mouth from the horrified expression on his face. From his grimace alone, I gather the rumors about Slater not having a musical bone in his body before he met Marcus must be true.

I slowly saunter around the makeshift studio, taking in all the unique details with the same set of keen eyes I used when inspecting Marcus's playrooms. In all honesty, this room is just as impressive as his playroom, because it shows who Marcus was before he became Marcus—bassist of Rise Up. I could just imagine him and his bandmates hanging out here every weekend, playing riffs and dreaming about the day they would be big stars. I wonder if they had any idea it would turn out the way it did? They not only accomplished greatness, they also proved that four men from a little no-name town in Florida can achieve anything they set their minds to. It's truly inspirational.

Rolling my eyes at my gushiness, I shift on my feet to face Marcus. "Would you look at me acting all star-struck. You must get sick of seeing stars in the eyes of your fans?"

"Never," Marcus replies without pause for consideration. His deep timbre increases the heat on my cheeks. "That's what music is about."

I laugh. "What? Making all the girls go ga-ga?"

The huge grin on my face morphs onto Marcus's. "No, it's about making them feel. That's what I love about music. The fame, the screaming fans, the groupies..."

I giggle at his disgruntled expression.

"... They aren't what started Rise Up. It was the opportunity to voice ourselves through lyrics. To express what we were never game to say out loud. It was a chance to be ourselves."

My face goes deadpan from the hurried mutter of his last sentence. I bite on the inside of my cheek, praying it will stop my immature squirming when Marcus steps closer to me, filling the small portion of air between us with his impressive frame. "I wanted to show you this when we first arrived, but the band's security detail wouldn't agree with my request—not with an unknown threat on the loose."

I attempt to interrupt him, wanting to know how long he knew I was being stalked and if they knew all along it was Richard, but before a word escapes my mouth, the entirety of his statement crashes into me.

"You wanted to show me this when we arrived? Days ago?" I ask as my widening eyes dance between his.

Marcus nods. "Yes. If I hadn't promised your sister I'd have you on the first flight home yesterday, I had many things I'd planned to show you. But since I've seen how Lexi operates when I don't adhere to my promises, that must wait until we return to Ravenshoe."

Blood rushes into my heart more quickly than it can be pumped out. "Oh, Marcus, don't ever show your fear. If Lexi gets one sniff of your hesitation, you'll be a goner." I inwardly sigh when my voice comes out sounding more risqué than the stuttering idiot I feel like on the inside. My heart is dancing with so much glee at Marcus's admission he wants to bring me back to Ravenshoe, I can't be sure I'm not having a heart attack.

The chances of merging into coronary failure territory triples when Marcus curls his hand around mine and paces us to the corner of the room while mumbling, "I'm already well past gone," under his breath.

My attention reverts from divulging the inner secrets his eyes are relaying when he says, "This was the real thing that brought Rise Up together." He nudges his head to a white electric guitar leaning on an amp at the side of a makeshift stage. "My grandma sold this guitar so she could buy me a laptop to create music with." His eyes twinkle as his lips twitch. "For years, my dad thought the school had lent me this 'fan-dangle computer' so I could improve my studies. It didn't even have a word processing program on it." The smile on his face melts away. "Shows how much attention he paid."

After running his hand over his recently shaved chin, he continues with his story, "When we were at the music store, we ran into Noah. He was there gawking at a Gibson acoustic guitar. I swear nearly every instrument he eyed that day was sitting in my grandmother's garage, collecting dust. When I told him that, he straight up called me a liar." His smile returns, stronger than ever. "I, of course, had to prove him wrong."

My heart thwacks against my chest, adoring that Marcus is sharing stories with me no one in the public knows. Although it was disclosed he and Noah met in a music store, the articles were never this in-depth.

"So how did you know Noah could sing?" I ask, tracking Marcus as he moves across the room to collect a seat from a stack of chairs leaning on the garage door.

"I didn't. I asked him to sing so I could test out the music producer my grandma had the owner of the music store download onto my laptop," Marcus answers, laughing. "I had planned on altering his voice with a high caliber voice adjustment stimulator, wanting to prove to him that anyone could be a singer with the right program." He pauses for a moment like he is recalling a fond memory. "I didn't adjust anything about his voice that day, and I never have since."

He sets the chair down in front of me, sits, then drags me into his lap like he is my own personal chair. My playful giggle switches to a moan when my backside brushes against his impressive groin. I don't know if he is hard, but try as I may, I can't ignore the heat of his thick flesh nestled on my backside. Clearly, since I grind against him not even two seconds later.

"Don't, Cleo," Marcus warns. "My grandmother may have passed, but she still lives in this house." His sweet breath tickles my earlobe when he whispers, "She isn't as forgiving as Abel."

Blood rushes to the surface of my cheeks. It doesn't last long, only as long as it takes for Marcus's brief chuckle to hit my eardrums. Although I love hearing his laugh, I swear, I'm never moaning during sex again. The little voice inside me stomps her feet before crossing her arms in front of her chest, denying my silent pledge with an edge of confidence Marcus's devotion has bestowed her with.

Dust scratches my throat when Marcus seizes his grandma's guitar from the ground and rests it on my thighs. In silence, he takes a few moments tuning it. Although he seems calm and put-together, I can feel his heart smashing into his ribs. It's so furious, it's pulverizing my back.

I jump, startled within an inch of my life when the amp at our side roars to life. Because I was so immersed in discovering why his heart was erratically beating, I failed to notice his fingers strumming the strings of his guitar. A huge grin etches on my face as I watch Marcus in his absolute element. The way his fingers flex against the guitar strings with ease, and the pure enjoyment radiating out of him, displays how much he loves his music. He is in his prime right now—just like he is in his playroom. It's a beautiful thing to witness, and I'm beyond smitten I get to see this side of him.

I listen with interest, struggling to work out what song he is playing. I'm sure it isn't one of his band's songs—I'm a diehard Rise Up fan, so I'm sure I'd recognize it. This tune has a familiarity about it, but the actual song title is slipping my mind.

I groan in frustration when I can't work out the song title. It has a long instrumental opening, one of the longest I've heard. If it's the song I'm thinking of, it was out years ago, way before Rise Up was a thing, and way before I was even conceived. I can hear the tune perfectly in my head, but I'm at a complete loss on its title... until Marcus starts signing the lyrics. When he reaches the last line in the second chorus, the song title finally clicks.

"'November Rain,'" I whisper to myself.

Marcus doesn't sing the song in the same rock grunge way Gun N' Roses does. He gives it soulful edge that has my panties moistening even faster than my heart rate is quickening. He performs it like it was personally written for him to sing. And he performs it well.

If I couldn't feel his utter happiness beaming out of him, I'd be concerned about why he chose to perform a song about couples needing time apart, but all I'm feeling is gratitude that I'm seeing a side of him I don't think many people have seen before. It's an incredibly humbling moment.

The longer his impromptu one-of-a-kind performance continues, the more my heart thrashes my ribs. My god this man can sing. His voice melts through my veins like molten lava, slicking my skin with a fine layer of sweat.

When Marcus reaches the extended guitar riff in the middle of the extremely lengthy song, I close my eyes and get caught up in the music. Every chord he plays shreds my body of negative energy, leaving nothing but a twenty-six-year-old woman head over heels in love with a rock star. God—I should pinch myself just to be sure I'm not dreaming.

When the song ends, I break into rapturous applause, not the slightest bit embarrassed I'm fawning over him like a groupie. Hell, I'm so horny, I'll downgrade my high morals to groupie standards if it gets me one step closer to Marcus touching me. His voice was...*my god.* How can I describe something so sexually satisfying it has me on the brink of ecstasy? That's what his voice does to me. I'm panting, hot, and on the verge of climax.

Marcus rests his guitar on the amp and stands from his seat, taking me with him. When he places me on my feet, I spin around to face him. Utter astonishment and glee are all over my face.

"How come I've never heard you sing before? My god—Marcus! Your albums would be double triple quadruple platinum if you sang with Noah." Goosebumps prickle my skin just thinking about their voices singing in unison.

Marcus smiles, humbled by my reply, but he remains as quiet as a church mouse. My heart rate kicks into overdrive when the slightest touch of pink graces his cheeks. *Oh. My. God—my praise embarrassed him.*

"Why in the world would you be embarrassed, Marcus?"

Marcus's eyes snap to mine. They grow in anger when he spots my leering grin. His angry glare does nothing to dampen my excitement. I made a Dom blush, tell me one other sub who can gloat about that? I freeze, disturbed by my own statement. *I'm not Marcus's sub, so why do I continually refer to myself as if I am?*

Confusing my disgusted expression as being upset over his narrowed squint, Marcus admits, "I've never sung in front of anyone before. It isn't something I generally do. I honestly can't think of one time anyone has heard me sing."

Happy to use his admission to push aside my inner conflict, I mutter, "I really like being your first."

Before Marcus can announce his disgust or pleasure over my declaration, a commotion outside the garage secures our attention. When the garage door rattles, like someone is attempting to pry it open, I stand motionless in fear.

Marcus mutters something under his breath when the distinctive noise of multiple cameras clicking breaks the silence surrounding us.

"Jesus... mother of lord." I barely hold my curse words when a large brute of a man suddenly steps into the garage. When my eyes rake the length of him, my first instinct is to arm myself with a weapon. The only reason I don't is when his smiling face registers as familiar. He is the man who opened the car door for me yesterday.

"How many are there?" Marcus asks the unnamed man, his tone clipped.

The brunette gent shrugs. "Around a dozen or so. If you want to wait thirty minutes, I can get a few guys here to move them on."

"Thirty minutes?" Marcus asks, his tone hinting at his annoyance. "You can't get them here any quicker? My plane is already on the tarmac."

"Depends." The man pauses, soundlessly building the suspense. "On how you want to explain *her*." He nudges his head to me.

Marcus's jaw ticks. I'm assuming his anger is due to the unnamed man referring to me as "her."

I feel the crazy beat of Marcus's heart through our conjoined hands when he curls his around mine. "Cleo, this is Hawke, head of Rise Up's security. Hawke, this is my girlfriend, Cleo," he introduces, his tone not as wrathful as the glare he issued Hawke moments ago.

Just for reference, hearing Marcus call me his girlfriend a second time didn't lessen the impact. It was just as magical as it was the first time.

"Nice to meet you, Hawke." I accept the hand he is holding out.

"Likewise." Hawke's twinkling-with-amusement eyes shift back to Marcus. "Girlfriend?" he queries with astonishment smearing his deep tone. "Gemma heard some talk between the boys last week, I thought they were playing tricks on her."

Marcus cocks a brow and glares into Hawke's eyes, not appreciating the ghost of a smile cracking on his twitching mouth. A tense stretch of silence passes between us. Not long enough we forget the paparazzi are moments away from breaking down Marcus's garage door, but long enough for a beading of sweat to form on my nape.

"Alright," Hawke gives in to Marcus's wrathful glare, holding his hands out in front of his body. "But maybe next time you unwillingly drag a man across a porch, you might stop to consider your actions first."

The tension drains away from Marcus's face. "Unlikely. If it weren't for Jenni and me that night, you'd still be watching Gemma from afar."

Hawke grumbles something under his breath as he steps out of the garage. He returns not even two seconds later grasping a hideous floral hat, a pair of thick-rimmed reading glasses, and a yellow raincoat with pink polka dots.

"I hope they're for Marcus," I protest before I can stop my words. I'm not a fashionista by any means, but I wouldn't let my snooping neighbor Mrs. Rachet be caught dead in that horrid ensemble, much less myself.

My eyes snap to Marcus, informing him I wasn't joking when his breathy chuckle trickles into my ears. He stops smiling as the apprehension in his eyes brews. "It's either that outfit or you travel with Hawke to the airport hangar," he informs me, wiping the smile straight off my face. "Until things cool down with Global Ten Media, we can't be seen together."

Although I should be mad Global Ten's investigation into Chains is still influencing my relationship with Marcus, gratefulness pumps into me. I've been in so much of a lust-filled bubble today, I completely forgot the world surrounding us. Thankfully, Marcus has his head screwed on straight, or who knows what type of mistakes we could have made. I'm not being facetious when I say I am lost to this man. When I'm with him, it's as if the world, and anything trying to drag me down, no longer exists.

My bottom lip involuntarily drops into a pout as I accept the horrendous clothing and accessories from Hawke. Although my mood has taken a significant nosedive, I'd rather have my picture snapped in this outfit than be separated from Marcus. For the past week, he has been my lifeline. He boosted my confidence when worry dragged it down, and reeled in bad behavior when I was being overly bratty. He truly balances me out, making me a stronger and more determined woman.

Like my crashing-back-to-reality temperament could get any shoddier, its plunge switches from a forty-five-degree decline to a heart-shattering ninety-degree descent when I pop on my disguise, huddle under the nook of Marcus's arm, then run through the gauntlet of paparazzi lying in wait for us outside Marcus's grandma home. It isn't being photographed in a pre-eighties getup that has caused my drastic decline. It's the questions the paparazzi hammer Marcus with as we weave through them that has my heart sitting in my throat.

"Marcus, are you aware of the murder of a former Rise Up bodyguard?"

"Marcus, would you like to express your condolences to Stephen's family?"

"Marcus, do you wish to comment on the rumors you were a key witness in an FBI investigation yesterday that resulted in the death of a New York resident?"

"Marcus... Marcus ... Marcus!!"

The endless stream of questions continue until I'm sitting in the passenger seat of Marcus's car. With the paparazzi pushing their lenses in close to tinted windows, vying for the money shot, Marcus's car rolls down the street at a painstakingly slow 5MPH. With the media's interests at an all-time high, even a big burly bodyguard like Hawke is having a hard time dispersing them. I keep my head down low, not just ensuring the paparazzi don't capture my image, but so I can hide my shameful face from the world.

By the time Marcus maneuvers his car into the isolated airstrip on the outskirts of Ravenshoe, my rollercoaster ride of emotions comes to an end, stopping at a devastating low. I can't believe I've become so callous the past four years that discovering two men somewhat related to me lost their lives didn't affect my composure in the slightest. I spent my night being adored by a man I'm in love with before swooning in a garage that has enormous sentimental value to him without a single smidge of remorse passing through me.

I know the power Marcus has over me is strong, but I had no clue it was so powerful, it completely wipes away my empathy.

I am a truly terrible person.

10

Remaining quiet, I shadow Marcus out of his vehicle and toward the private jet. Just like when we arrived five days ago, people scatter around us, removing jackets, handing over keys, and aiding me out of my disguise. When Marcus curls his hand around mine, his eyes drop to our intertwined fingers. My hand is so clammy, there is no way he could miss their ghastly stickiness. Forcing a smile onto my face, I ensure him I'm fine, even when I'm not. He returns my smile, although it's nowhere near as big as the one I'm used to seeing.

We climb the stairs of the private jet in silence, glide past the two attractive flight attendants with a brief dip of our chins, then stroll down the empty aisle. Although my eyes still bug in awe of the beautifully rich cabinetry and opulent leather seats of the private jet's cabin, my dour mood isn't fully registering it. It's like everything in life, the highs are awe-inspiring, but the lows are genuinely crushing.

While Marcus and Cameron discuss air nautical procedures and precipitation, I pace to a set of white leather recliners at the front of the galley. Although Marcus's flow of conversation continues without pause, he didn't need to voice his protest to my withdrawal. The fact I had to practically yank my hand out of his firm grasp is all the indication I needed he wasn't pleased with my decision.

After plunking into one of the two leather chairs at the front of the cabin, I reach for the unopened water bottle sitting on the table tray in front of the seat. Marcus's eyes drift across the room when he notices the rattle of my hand. I'm shaking so much, water sloshes over the rim of the glass I'm attempting to fill.

My glass isn't even half full when Marcus crouches down in front of me. He seizes the bottle from my grasp, fills my glass, then dispenses of the empty bottle into a waste receptacle on his right. He cautiously watches me as I take a sip on the chilled water I'm hoping will eradicate the bile sitting in the back of my throat. It does nothing to ease the fiery burn of regret.

Marcus tucks a strand of hair behind my ear before lifting my chin, accessing my soul without a word spilling from his straight-lined lips. I want to tell him I'm fine and he can continue doing pre-flight checks with Cameron, but no matter how hard I fight my mouth to relinquish my words, they remain entombed in my throat. I'm not fine, I feel horrible inside and out.

Marcus sighs heavily before he leans in to press a kiss to the corner of my mouth. His minty-fresh breath settles some of the unease swirling in my stomach. "Give me a few minutes with Cameron, then I'll get you settled in."

He waits for me to nod before he stands from his crouched position. His feet remain planted on the ground, unsure if he is coming or going. While scrubbing his hand over his chin, his eyes dance between the cockpit and me. His indecisiveness at leaving me breaks through the heavy cloud attempting to swallow me whole. I know I'm being childish, but no amount of scolding can stop the pain gnawing my chest. It's so tight, it feels like it's crushing my heart.

"Go on, I'm fine," I stammer out. "I'm just zonked after our activities last night." I inwardly cringe, praying he didn't hear my deceit as loudly as I did.

Thankfully, he doesn't. After a final kiss on my temple, he heads back to Cameron.

I snuggle deeper into my chair before securing a popular gossip magazine out of the rack attached to the bulkhead. If I can keep my mind occupied, the silence of the cabin won't let my mind stray to more gruesome thoughts.

I'm not surprised when I discover a picture of Rise Up graces the front page. Ignoring the headline screaming a possible rift between front man, Noah Taylor and his wife, Emily, I aimlessly flick through the magazine. Usually, I'd gobble up every gossip article I could find on the band, but this time I don't even bother reading the loosely factual story. I watched Emily and Noah very attentively two weeks ago, if they are close to separating, there is no help for the rest of society. They are as in love now as they were when they married six years ago.

I'm halfway through reading my eerily accurate horoscope when a deep voice booms out of the speakers. "Cabin crew, prepare for takeoff."

My brows scrunch. *That didn't sound like Marcus.*

The heavy groove marring the middle of my brows deepens when Marcus steps out of the cockpit and takes the empty seat next to me. Remaining quiet, he secures his lap sash around his waist before leaning over to strap me in. Images of him restraining me last night rush to the forefront of my mind, pushing away some of the dread festering there.

My mouth gapes opened and closed like a fish out of water when the plane lurches forward to taxi to the runway. "Who's flying the plane?" I ask, my words forced through the solid lump in my throat.

Marcus removes the magazine splayed across my thighs. He places it into the rack and curls his hand around mine. His surging pulse rages through our conjoined hands.

"Cameron will first pilot today," he explains, his neutral tone not giving me an indication of whether or not it was his choice.

"Doesn't he need a co-pilot?"

Marcus grins a smile that clears away my nerves. "No. This type of plane can easily be flown without a co-pilot."

I arch my brow and glare into his eyes, demanding further explanation. When he fails to give it, I say, "If you don't need a co-pilot, why did you have one last week?"

My heart does a weird flippy thing when Marcus growls, "Because it was a requirement Cormack had included in my contract."

"Cormack?" I query, recalling Marcus mentioning his name during our Dom/sub negotiations two weeks ago.

"He's the manager of our band." Marcus's brows furrow down low. "Well, technically he owns Destiny Records, but when we negotiated for him to remain our manager, he added his own stipulations. Hence my requirement to fly with a co-pilot."

Ignoring the snip of anger in Marcus's tone, I reply, "It's a pretty smart move. It not only ensures his talent remains safe, but it also means his company's revenue continues to improve." I elbow him playfully, hoping to lighten up our conversation. Although he'd never say it, I can tell my negativity is rubbing off on him.

He remains quiet, his focus fixated on the tarmac whizzing past the large oval windows of the jet.

"Did you not want to fly today?" I ask. My tone relays I know the reason behind his decision, but I would prefer for him to express it.

Marcus turns his eyes from the window to me. "I love flying, it's the one time my mind is void of any thoughts."

"I don't know if you should admit that to someone who has flown with you when you're behind the..." My words trail off when I can't think of what the driving mechanism pilots use is called.

"Control column," Marcus fills in.

"Yeah. Don't admit your mind is empty when you're in control of the entire plane. Or I might not fly with you again."

Marcus's brief chuckle eases some of the tension sitting on my chest. "Duly noted," he murmurs under his breath.

Another stint of silence stretches between us. I'm starting to realize bouts of silence are a necessary requirement in this bizarre kinship we are developing. It gives me time to sit back and rationally think—well, the best I can in the presence of a man with Marcus's aura. Usually, my mind strays to wickedness when he is close by, but occasionally, I can rein in the desires of my body to have an intellectual conversation. It's rare, but it still happens—sometimes.

"If you love flying so much, why aren't you flying?" I query as my eyes dance around his handsome profile. Just drinking in his carved chin, sculpted nose and soul-stealing eyes diminishes the turmoil swishing in my stomach.

Marcus takes his time configuring a response before he ultimately replies, "Something more important came up."

"Something more important than flying?" I ask, shock in my tone. When he nods, I mutter, "What could be more important than that? You love flying, you just said so."

Marcus locks his eyes with me. "Not a what, a who." He brushes his fingers down my cheek, which is damp from a rogue tear I failed to hold in during our commute to the airstrip. Then he clarifies, "You."

My stomach does a weird whooshing thing when the jet lifts off the ground. I can't be sure if it was from gliding into the air or from Marcus's confession. When the giddy feeling continues to grow as the plane soars into the scattering of white clouds, I can testify it was caused by Marcus's admission. He said he loves flying, yet I'm more important to him than that. Does that mean he cares about me just as much as flying? *Or more?*

My heart rate doubles when I connect my eyes with Marcus. Before I can pry any more information out of him than his forthright eyes are transmitting, the snooty flight attendant from last week arrives at Marcus's side. "Mr. Everett, would you or your *guest* care for any beverages before we serve brunch?"

Wow. For a lady whose face is as hard as a brick wall, her voice is strikingly pleasant... except for when she sneered "guest."

When Marcus shifts his gaze to me, I shake my head, soundlessly advising him I'm still full from the breakfast Abel made this morning. Although my late awakening saw me scarfing down three pancakes in under a minute, it was adequate enough nutrients to sustain me until lunch.

"We are both fine, thank you, Gabriella," Marcus replies, his tone as low as Gabriella's slit eyes become when he devotes his attention to me.

With a huff and a final sneaky glare, Gabriella spins on her heels and paces down the aisle as stealthily as she arrived. Her quick departure is thwarted when Marcus requests, "But can you turn down the bedding in the sleeping quarters. Ms. Garcia and I will be retreating there shortly."

Gabriella's eyes rocket to Marcus even more quickly than a bullet fired from a gun. She stares at him as if he just asked her to sacrifice her firstborn child for him. Her startled response assures me there has never been anything between them, because if she had slept with him, she'd realize sacrificing her firstborn is a small price to pay for a night with him.

Marcus dabs his thumb under my puffy, dark eyes. "Lexi may never let me steal you away again if you come back looking this tired."

Feeling Gabriella's furious gaze burning a hole in the side of my head, I reply, "I wouldn't look so tired if you knew the meaning of a quickie. But since you're so determined to spend hours testing every position known to mankind, who am I to stop you?" My last sentence comes out with so much attitude, I'm beginning to wonder if Lexi snuck into the cabin before we ascended thirty thousand feet into the air.

My tease has the effect I'm aiming for when Gabriella huffs so loud, three continents heard it. She pivots on her heels and charges down the aisle, her feet stomping with every step she takes. I fight to hold in my childish grin, but the smallest smile stretches across my face before I can shut it down. I should feel bad I've made her upset, but I don't. She deserved it. I did nothing to her, so why should I feel guilty for feeding her back the attitude she is dishing out?

"If I wasn't incredibly turned on by your cattiness, I'd be tempted to punish you for goading my staff, Cleo," Marcus utters, his timbre so low, goosebumps rush to the surface of my skin.

"If I weren't so incredibly turned on by the idea of you punishing me, I'd be tempted to apologize to Gabriella, *Master Chains*."

A wave of nausea hits me as a second dose of guilt slams into me. Although my remorse managed to hang around longer than it did this morning, it still wasn't long enough to be deemed respectable.

"What happened to Richard and Stephen was not your fault, Cleo. So why should you harbor blame for their decisions? They were grown men—both of them," Marcus declares, shifting my focus back to him.

"It isn't that I'm feeling guilty, but I should be feeling something, shouldn't I?" I reply, my voice revealing my utter bewilderment. Not just about my goat hill moods, but that Marcus can read me so easily. How is it possible he already knows me so well he can intuit the cause of my silence?

I connect my eyes with Marcus's. "Doesn't it make me a terrible person that I'm smiling and enjoying life when two people just lost their lives?"

"No." Marcus shakes his head. "Guilt isn't rational. It weighs down innocent people's hearts when the person who should be harboring it feels nothing. Don't feel guilty because of the consequences of others. Understand that when people are hurting, it was *their* guilt that made them irrational, not yours. Nothing you could have done would have changed the outcome for either of those men, Cleo, because their decision was made long before you entered the picture. You just got tangled in the wrong web."

"Me or you?" I reply, vainly trying to ignore the shakiness of my heart in my words. "Ever since you got snagged by my net, your life has gone into turmoil."

Marcus unlatches my belt, seizes my wrists, then carefully drags me across the leather seat until I'm sitting cradled in his lap. His thumbs make quick work of the unexpected tears rolling down my cheeks. Once every drop of moisture has been taken care of, he holds me close to his chest.

The wild beat of his heart answers my question, but just in case I'm incapable of deciphering what it means, Marcus says, "Just like Stephen and Richard, nothing will change the outcome of my life either. Some events in life are minor bumps in our travels, others cause huge detours, but no matter which journey your life takes, you always end up where you are supposed to be. This is where we are supposed to be, Cleo. You are supposed to be with me."

My heart warms, loving that he quoted a portion of a saying he said to me the afternoon we visited his hotel room in New York. That was when he declared he'd been looking for me the past four years. It was in that instant I knew I had fallen in love with him. Madly. Deeply. Wildly.

I pop my head off his chest and peer into his eyes. I want to tell him how he makes me feel. I want to throw down the hand I've been holding close to my chest the past two weeks. I want to smack him with straight-up honesty. But since I don't want to lose him, I don't do either of those things. Because no matter how beautiful Marcus's quote was, love is not on his agenda. He has never hidden that from me. So instead of saying the three little words sitting on the tip of my tongue, I cup his jaw with my trembling hands and seal my mouth over his, expressing every emotion coursing through me via a kiss instead of worthless words.

11

Blood gushes into my heart when Marcus pulls into the driveway of my family home. It may not be a fancy mansion surrounded by manicured lawns that have every strand of grass meticulously in place, but this is my home, and it means more to me than any monetary value ever could. My home is full of priceless memories, thankfully more good than bad.

My lazy pace out of Marcus's car turns frantic when Lexi unexpectedly appears on the front porch, "Cleo!" she shouts, her chattering teeth unmissable as a brisk winter wind whips her hair around her face.

The reasoning behind her shuddering becomes apparent when I swing open Marcus's door. Either Florida's weather spoiled me, or Montclair is going to have a white Christmas. It's below freezing.

As Lexi gallops down the six stairs of our warped porch, I charge up the cracked sidewalk. We crash into each other's arms halfway down the path, giggling and crying like conjoined twins separated at birth. Lexi's hug is so brutal, the air leaves my lungs, and my backside makes contact with the concrete. Our unladylike topple onto the ground does nothing to dampen our heart-squeezing reunion. Even seeing Mrs. Ratchet's curtains ruffling can't lessen our enthusiasm. We laugh until tears spring into our eyes and our cheeks hurt from smiling so much. Then we laugh some more.

Our hearty chuckles only stop when the quickest flash of a memory filters into my brain. The last time we were so carefree resulted in Lexi having a severe coughing attack. Although her attacks aren't uncommon, that one held my heart captive the past week. It was one of the most severe ones she's had since our parents passed.

My lips smack together as my eyes rocket to Lexi. I run my eyes over her face to check for any excessive redness before dropping them to her chest. It's thrusting at a similar rate as mine. My brows furrow as confusion engulfs me.

When my baffled eyes return to Lexi's face, she waggles her brows and nods. "I swear, I only coughed up half a lung this morning instead of my usual two," she declares, her voice similar to the one she used last year when she tried to convince me to buy a new car.

"It works that quick?" I ask, certain no drug could be so wondrous.

I use my hand to shelter the sun from my eyes when Marcus stops in front of Lexi and me and says, "Some cases have reported wheelchair-bound CF sufferers are able to ride bikes within two weeks of starting treatment."

Although his tone is informative, the glimmer in his eyes tells me he didn't miss mine and Lexi's immature greeting. They also show he isn't bothered by it, he actually looks pleased... or maybe confused? I can't say I don't understand his confusion. I went from a blubbering mess in the plane to gleaming like a cat licking the cream straight out of the carton. My emotions are truly all over the place.

I shift my eyes back to Lexi, seeking her response to Marcus's admission. It isn't that I don't believe Marcus, but Lexi can give practical statistics, not just theoretical ones. She is a walking billboard for the Kalydeco program.

My jaw falls open when Lexi nods, confirming Marcus's assumptions. "Listen," she instructs before pulling my head down to her barely thrusting chest.

I still my breathing as I press my ear into her chest. Although her heart is beating wildly, her usually wheezy and panting breaths I've become accustomed to hearing the past twenty-one years of her life are barely audible. Don't get me wrong, her lungs are still crackly, but it sounds more like chalk running down a chalkboard than a bag of chips being torn open.

Excited, I pop my head off Lexi's chest, smack my hands on each side of her face, then plant a big sloppy kiss right on her lips. Ignoring her disgusted gag, I leap from the ground to do the exact same thing to Marcus. Thankfully, he doesn't recoil at my loving gesture. In fact, he does the opposite. He draws me to his big body before slipping his tongue into my mouth, not the slightest bit concerned about the handful of teenage spectators we've obtained. I'm not sure if they recognize Marcus, or if they are envious of his sports car parked in my driveway. Either way, their curious gawks aren't strong enough to leash my desires. Pretending we are the only two people in the world, I band my arms around Marcus's neck and return his kiss with just as much passion as he is bestowing.

His kiss... *God.* A lifetime of kisses would never compare. It's tempting, hot, and toe-curlingly delicious.

By the time Marcus withdraws his sinfully delicious mouth from mine, I'm in a foggy lust haze. I feel like I'm drunk even though I haven't had a drop of alcohol in days. Lexi giggles at my unsteady footing before curling her arm around my waist to aid me in climbing the front stairs of our porch. After gathering my suitcase from his car, Marcus follows us into our house.

A pungent aroma of spices and charcoal filters into my nose when we enter the foyer. With my brow raised in suspicion, I remove my winter coat and hang it on the coatrack before popping my head into the kitchen. I don't entirely enter the stinky room. I'm too concerned about what I'm going to find to walk into a battle zone without first scoping the area.

The kitchen looks the same as it usually does, except for a large pot sitting on the stovetop. With bubbles of brown goop dripping down the side, I'm relatively sure it's the source of the horrid smell streaming through my nostrils.

I sling my head back to Lexi. "You cooked?" I ask with my brows arched high.

She bounces on her heels, her expression smug. "Yep. I made us lunch."

My stomach slips off the radar. It hasn't even sampled her latest concoction, and it's already protesting against it. "Ah... Marcus and I ate on our way here," I lie.

When Marcus's lips twitch, attempting to negate my claims, I kick him in the shins. When his eyes rocket to mine, I plead with him to follow through with my ploy. A man with an iron stomach would have a hard time consuming any meal Lexi made, let alone a man whose butler serves nothing but five-star cuisine.

While returning Marcus's narrowed glare, I suggest for him to get his senses checked. If he thinks the putrid smell in the air is appetizing, I'm vastly concerned about him and his senses. I've heard musicians can have issues with their hearing over time, but I had no clue it stretched to other sensory elements.

"Yeah, we already ate," Marcus affirms, mercifully reading my silent pleas.

"Oww!" I protest when Lexi unexpectedly hits me. I'm not talking a little fairy tap I've come to expect from my sister, I'm talking a full-on punch with closed fists, one inflicted to cause harm.

"What was that for?" I ask, my words coming out whiny.

Lexi smirks, her composure as smug as the grin on her lips. "It was either punch you or cook you lunch. On Jackson's recommendation, I tried to go the non-violent route. I told him you wouldn't fall for it, but I gave it my best shot." Her eyes swing to the side during the last half of her sentence.

Following her gaze, I spot Jackson leaning on the entranceway wall of the living room. He is wearing a low-hanging pair of jeans, a white V-neck collared shirt, and his feet are bare. Compared to Marcus's scrumptious suit-covered body, he is very casual. He wears the look well.

"Hey, Jackson," I greet him, walking over to place a kiss on his cheek. "For future reference, I'd rather the violent approach. Broken bones can heal, but my stomach would never survive Lexi's lunch," I whisper into his ear.

Although I'm certain neither Lexi nor Marcus heard what I said, Jackson throwing his head back and laughing gives an indication. Seeing him so carefree fills me with glee. The last time I saw Jackson, he'd just discovered Lexi hadn't been attending her CF physio appointments. He was truly devastated. I'm glad to see the pain tainting his eyes that day has left.

My neck cranks back to Lexi when she says, "You won't be smiling when you find out what these two have been up to." With a stern glare, she darts her index finger between Marcus and Jackson.

Sweat slicks my skin when the quickest flare of concern blazes in Jackson's eyes. Before I can ask what the cause of his worry is, a third man joins us in the kitchen, making the already cramped space even more confined. He has shoulder-length thin, blond hair pulled back in a messy man bun. His razor-sharp jawline is covered with a cropped beard, and he is wearing a pair of dark slacks and a long-sleeve shirt. His outfit is a cross between Marcus and Jackson's—borderline smart casual. I'd always wondered what that saying meant. He gives definition to the term. He is handsome, if you like your men a little more rugged.

"Cleo," the stranger greets me with a nod of his head, seemingly knowing who I am. "Marcus," he continues, thrusting his hand out in offering.

Marcus accepts the stranger's offer, but his eyes never leave mine. His uncordial response has my suspicion growing rapidly. That's very uncharacteristic for him.

The mischievous twinkle in Lexi's eyes builds and builds for every second I stare at the unnamed stranger in shock. Not noticing my watchful stare, he places a mug in the kitchen sink before helping himself to a bottle of water in the fridge. If I were standing in Marcus's kitchen, unexpected guests could be warranted, but he is standing in my home, helping himself like he is a close family member. The only thing is, he isn't a family member. He isn't even a causal acquaintance. I recall faces, his is not one I recall.

"I'm sorry, who are you?" I ask, no longer capable of harboring my curiosity.

Lexi giggles, happy I reacted precisely how she wanted me to.

"Oh, sorry," the stranger apologizes, running his hand down his trousers to remove the condensation before offering it in greeting. "I'm Brodie, Jackson's cousin."

My eyes frolic between Jackson and Brodie. I don't see any similarities between them. They have the same color hair, nearly the shame shade of eyes, but they are two very different looking men.

I cross my arms in front of my chest. "What town are you from? Caldier or Algoe? Everyone knows the Collards originated from those two areas."

When Jackson attempts to speak, I cut him off with a stern finger point. His throat works hard to swallow the rebuttal he was about to serve.

"Let the man speak," Lexi says, encouraging my interrogation. She stands beside me, her posture as stiff as mine.

After bouncing his eyes between Lexi and me, Brodie flicks them to Marcus standing behind me. Even if he hadn't sought Marcus's assistance, I still knew Marcus was there. The bristling of the hairs on my arms gives away his nearness, let alone my excited, shallow breaths.

After swallowing harshly, Brodie returns his eyes to me and mutters, "Algoe." He shrugs his shoulders like it's no big deal.

"Liar!" Lexi and I shout in sync, our loud voices bellowing around the room.

"There is no such place as Algoe. It's a fictional hamlet made up in the 1930s to copyright maps," I enlighten, my tone informative but with a hint of bitchiness.

"Is that true?" Brodie asks Marcus.

I crank my neck back at Marcus. His elevated shoulders drop the instant he catches my wrathful glare. My back molars grind together as my eyes narrow into thin slits.

"Are you going to tell us who he is, or are we going to force-feed him Lexi's lunch until it's tortured out of him," I ask, my tone half-wrathful, half-astonished. I'm so confused by my pendulum-swinging moods, my voice can't even choose which side to take.

"My cooking isn't that bad," Lexi grumbles under her breath.

Crickets are heard when no one attempts to deny her statement. Not even a squeak parts Marcus's lips. His screwed-up facial expression tells me the scent of Lexi's lunch has finally caught up with him.

Cocking my hip, my austere stare grows. Marcus's eyes twinkle in amusement as the corner of his lips pucker high. He's always found my attempts to overpower him amusing. He can be cocky. He knows he has me over a barrel.

Marcus returns my glare with just as much intensity, but instead of firing the air with tension, it sparks it with palpable lust. When he scrubs his hand over his clipped afro, my fingers twitch in envy. It's the fight of my life to keep my feet planted on the ground. I just want to mash our lips together and leave Lexi the task of unearthing who our counterfeit visitor is.

The only thing that stops me making a fool of myself is when Jackson pipes up, "Brodie isn't my cousin. He works for Marcus's security team. He was assigned to keep an eye on Lexi until we knew who was stalking you. Since Lexi was present in a lot of images the FBI obtained last week, we wanted to ensure she wasn't a target."

I sling my eyes to Jackson. "Then why not just say that?"

His brows shoot up into his hairline as the color in his face drains. "That's why." He nudges his head to a flash of red at my side.

Blood is racing through Lexi's body so hard and fast, she looks like she is about to combust. Her fists are balled at her side, and her wrathful eyes are rapt on Jackson.

"It was Marcus's idea," Jackson mumbles, attempting to weasel himself out of trouble. "I just agreed to pretend Brodie was my cousin."

If he is hoping his confession will ease Lexi's anger, he needs to come up with a new tactic. His statement only angers Lexi more.

"How many times did I ask you if Brodie was really your cousin?" Lexi asks Jackson, her tone firm. Even though she technically asked him a question, she continues speaking, denying him the chance to reply. "And how many times did you assure me he was who he said he was?"

Jackson works his jaw side to side as his hand scrapes the stubble on his chin. He looks so fretful, I'm starting to feel sorry for him. In all honesty, he didn't do anything I wouldn't have done to keep Lexi safe. If she knew Brodie was here to keep an eye on her, Lexi would have had his bags packed so quickly, his head would still be spinning three weeks later. So if Jackson felt a little white lie was needed to ensure Lexi was safe, I won't judge him for it.

"As stupid as it sounds, Marcus and Jackson had their reasons to keep this from us," I express to Lexi, prying her enraged gaze from Jackson. "I'm not saying it makes what they did right, or that it can excuse them from any punishment you'd like to instill—" *I pray her punishment will include them eating the disgusting pot of food on the cooktop.* "—but at the end of the day, they were trying to protect us, Lexi. Can we really hold that against them?"

Lexi thinks about my heartfelt pledge for all of two seconds before answering, "Ah, yeah, I can." She swings her eyes to Marcus. "You should be so grateful you picked the timid, more reserved Garcia woman." Her eyes drift back to Jackson. "You weren't so lucky."

12

Marcus and I spend the entire week hidden away from the world in my family home. We parked his car in the garage to keep suspicious eyes at bay and had a month's worth of groceries home-delivered, so we'd have no reason to leave. I know the main reason Marcus brought me here instead of his expansive New York property was because he knew I needed the comforts of home as I worked through the gauntlet of emotions bombarding me. He was right. The past week has been a rollercoaster ride in good and bad ways. Marcus has been my rock, astonishing me time and time again with his wisdom and understanding... and impeccable bedroom skills. He's been perfect, more than I could have ever hoped for.

The only downers we've faced are from outside influences.

After a short investigation, Richard's death was recorded as suicide on his death certificate even with the county of Ravenshoe still searching for his body. Although Shian shot him in the seconds leading up to his death, the coroner did not believe the bullet wound to his shoulder would have caused grave injuries. It was Richard's decision to leap over the cliff's edge that instigated his demise. The bullet that killed Stephen, the man who assaulted me in the alleyway, was matched to the bullets in Richard's gun. The shell casings and identifiable markings on the dislodged bullets were also positively confirmed as being one and the same.

Shian believes Richard and Stephen colluded my attack in the alleyway two weeks ago. When Stephen took the assault further than Richard stipulated, Richard sought his revenge in the ghastliest way. Police are under the assumption that the ten minutes Richard spent searching for his cell phone the night of my attack wasn't as innocent as it seemed. They believe that was when he orchestrated his revenge on Stephen. Allegedly, our arrival at his apartment was not to secure his phone. He was there to collect his gun.

Although I've been informed of numerous horrific things about Richard the past week, the last thing he said to me the day he saved me from the cliff plays on repeat in my mind most nights before I go to bed. He admitted he had done some terrible things, but he was adamant it wasn't as bad as what they were making it seem. Only now am I wondering if the "they" he was referring to is the FBI?

"Sorry," I mutter, my attention reverting to the present when a soft voice calls my name.

Anna, a personal assistant hired by Marcus, steps in front of me. "Did you prefer the emerald green or the mint?" She hands me two hand-sketched drawings with green satin swatches stapled in the top right corner.

For the past hour, Anna and I have been working on an extensive collection of garments, trying to find the perfect one for me to wear to a fundraising gala next week. In all honesty, I had forgotten entirely about Slater's verbal invitation weeks ago. I took his invite with a pinch of salt, assuming he was just being polite. I had no idea his invite extended to this level. I'm not only an invited guest to the Serena Scott $10,000 per plate annual Fundraising Gala, I'll be one of only a handful of attendees dressed in a one-of-a-kind J. Holt-created gown, handcrafted and sewn by none other than fashion icon Jenni Holt, wife of Nicholas Holt, lead guitarist of Rise Up.

"Umm..." I look at the two designs we've narrowed in down to, not one hundred percent convinced on either design. They are both beautiful, but they aren't the exact style I'm aiming for.

"What look are you going for?" Lexi asks from her stalking post at the edge of the living room. My scare with Richard last week shook her so greatly, she's been mothering me nearly as much as I usually mother her. Don't get me wrong, she is as painful as always, but that's one of the many things I love about Lexi, so I wouldn't have her any other way.

I was hoping Lexi could join us at the fundraiser, but with the plate fee being so high, neither of us were willing to push Marcus's generosity further than it's already been stretched. He has already done so much for us by paying for the Kalydeco program, there is no way I could ask for another dime.

I answer Lexi's question with a shrug. "I don't know? Is there such a thing as sexy and classy?"

"Uh huh," Lexi giggles before running her hand down the front of her body. She stands tall, showcasing her undeniable beauty with a hint of pompousness.

I roll my eyes. "Maybe I should wear you then?"

With a giggle, Lexi pushes off the wall and paces to me. "Eww, that's very Hannibal Lecter, Cleo." She slithers her tongue in a way no woman ever should.

After propping her backside on the edge of the chair I'm sitting on, her eyes lower to the drawings I'm grasping. She peruses them with a pair of fresh eyes. I've looked at so many sketches, they are all starting to look the same.

"Is that the mask you're wearing?" Lexi queries a short time later, nudging her head to the gorgeous silver beaded mask sitting on our coffee table.

"Yes," I reply, my love for the mask evident. The instant I saw the hand-crafted beads and crystal design, I knew it was the one I was going to wear. It's exquisite—nearly as divine as Marcus's eyes.

"That's classy," Lexi purrs, her words rolling off her tongue. "So now we just need sexy." She screws up her nose as she continues perusing the drawings. "This one," she says, pointing to the full-length ball gown sketch in my left hand.

"I was steering toward that one, but something about it doesn't feel quite right," I admit, pretending I still have some of the fashion sense my brush with designer clothing awarded me with five years ago.

Lexi purses her lips as she nods, agreeing with my suggestion. I jump in fright when she suddenly mutters, "I know!" She yanks off the satin swatch for the dress she disregarded and places it next to the sketch she has chosen.

My pupils widen as I nod. "Perfect!"

"That would be lovely," agrees Anna, joining our intimate gathering with a confidence not many women hold when trying to get between two Garcia sisters. "I'll get your selection and measurements straight to Mrs. Holt."

Accepting the sketch board from my hand, Anna removes the old satin swatch and replaces it with the one I want. "You have quite an eye for fashion, Cleo," she praises. Her eyes roll as a tsk escapes her red-painted lips. "I'd like to say the same for Mr. Everett's previous subs, but that would be pointless. Their idea of fashion never went past the lingerie department at Barney's." She laughs as if she is sharing a funny joke.

I don't find her humor amusing. Actually, I feel ill. "Umm ... I'm ... Ah."

"Cleo isn't Chains' sub," Lexi informs Anna when my words fail me. "She is his girlfriend."

Anna's pupils widen to the size of saucers. I can see her confusion twisting up from her stomach to her throat. She looks truly baffled. "Oh, I'm very sorry," she mumbles, her tone relaying the uncertainty of her reply, like she is unsure if Lexi's admission is true.

My hand darts out to calm Lexi when she rises from the couch, preparing to unleash an onslaught of verbal abuse on Anna. "It's just a title, it's not worth bickering over," I assure her in a soft tone to ensure Anna doesn't overhear me.

Reading the truth from Lexi's narrowed gaze, Anna stammers, "Certainly. Mr. Everett's girlfriend. I shall jot that down."

Lexi huffs loudly before standing from the couch. "You do that," she snarls, showcasing her lack of maturity with three tiny words.

She leaves the living room as quickly as she arrived. Her feet stomping loudly nearly drowns out Anna's muffled apology.

"It's fine, Anna. Truly."

Hating that we've made her feel uncomfortable, I stand from my seat and aid her in gathering swatches of material and hundreds of sketches she brought with her. Anna remains quiet, but her eyes relay apology after apology.

Once we have all the items packed away, I walk Anna to the door. Although my stomach is swirling from her assumption I am Marcus's sub, I can't be angry at her. Anna has been working with Marcus for years, so it's understandable she was confused about my status in his life. If Marcus hadn't spent the last two weeks worshipping me as if I am a goddess, I may have looked a little deeper into Anna's remark. But since my confidence is at an all-time high, I'll let her comment slide without a second thought. It's the right thing to do. *Isn't it?*

When we reach the front porch, Anna turns around to face me. She is a pretty lady, mid-thirties, crystal clear brown eyes and curly hair sitting just below her shoulders. Her vibrant red hair gives her aura a wildness her contained personality fails to dampen. When she first spoke, I thought she was from Britain, but she quickly corrected me that her heritage is Irish.

"Mrs. Holt will have the dress finalized by close of business Thursday," Anna informs me, her voice high in elation. "Then I'll come and assist you getting ready next weekend. You're going to look fabulous, Cleo. The belle of the ball."

Suddenly, she balks, the color in her face not as vibrant as it was mere minutes ago. She appears as if she wants to say something, but's hesitant about what my reaction will be.

"What is it?" I ask, hoping her first impression was the most accurate one. The one that displayed she is a woman of strength and honor. Even with our ages being nearly a decade apart, I could imagine us becoming close friends.

"Umm... do you think we could get ready at Mr. Everett's property?"

When I remain frozen in silence, Anna continues, "It isn't that your home isn't lovely, Cleo. It is. I just have wonderful supplies my team can access at Mr. Everett's house. With it being the first time Mr. Everett has taken a guest to this gala, I want to make you shine in the beautiful gown you've selected."

Finding out I'm the first person Marcus has taken to the gala eases some of the turmoil swishing in my stomach, but it doesn't stop me from saying, "You have supplies at Marcus's house?"

Anna nods a little overeagerly. "Yes. Some of Mr. Everett's subs were very pedantic." She rolls her eyes, the disgust on her face unmissable. "None were as pleasant as you. One... oh, I was glad to see the back of her. She was horrid ..." Her words taper off into silence before she swallows harshly. "Oh my goodness. I just did it again. I'm so sorry, Cleo. I have a terrible neurosis of shoving my foot in my mouth as it is, but since you're so easy to talk to, I'm saying things I should never be saying."

"It's fine," I advise, not needing any more apology than her remorseful eyes are relaying.

She isn't saying anything I haven't heard previously, and part of me is grateful she already feels comfortable enough around me to be herself. I also like that she thinks I'm the politest sub Marcus has had—*even if I'm not his sub.*

"It's fine," I repeat more forcefully when Anna's eyes continue to convey her sympathies. "We will get ready at Marcus's property. It's closer to the gala anyway, so it makes sense to get ready there."

"Okay. Thank you," Anna murmurs before leaning in to press a kiss on each of my cheeks. "I'll see you next week?"

I smile and nod. The silent plea for forgiveness in her eyes holds firm as she saunters down my front patio. I wait for her to slip into her expensive-looking car, wave goodbye, then shut my front door. Noticing I'm back within the safety of my home, Brodie leaves his bodyguard post at the side of the foyer and enters the kitchen.

Even though he is no longer guarding Lexi, Brodie's presence has remained in my home the past week. The only difference now is he flanks me instead of Lexi. Although Marcus would never admit it, I'm sure that only happened at his request. It's annoying having my every move watched, but it hasn't been all bad. Brodie's personality adds a whole new dynamic to our small group. He is funny, straightforward, and doesn't jump to Marcus's every command. Don't get me wrong, he strongly conveys the aura of a bodyguard, but he does it in a less knee-quaking way than I expected.

From an outsider's perspective, you'd swear he was Jackson's cousin. That's how well Brodie plays the role. The only reason he couldn't pull the wool over mine and Lexi's eyes is because we've known the Collards for decades, so we've met most of their family. Brodie's name was never mentioned. That alone was a dead giveaway he wasn't a Collard. Their family is as close-knit as mine was before it came to a tragic end.

Rubbing a kink in my neck, I pace toward the kitchen, which is bustling with noise, not wanting negative thoughts to dampen my happy mood. Although a little edgy about my conversation with Anna, I'm not utterly surprised by it. Just like me, Marcus has a past. His is just a lot more risqué than mine. Although it would be nice to live in our isolated bubble for the rest of the eternity, these types of mishaps will become more regular as our relationship blossoms.

When I pop my head into the kitchen, I spot Brodie, Lexi and Jackson huddled around our little eating nook. A grin curls on my lips when I spot Jackson giving Lexi a sneaky kiss on the nape of her neck while Brodie is distracted by a sports story in our local paper. Lexi and Jackson's disagreement last week ended the instant Jackson apologized for being deceitful. It was that exact moment I realized Lexi wasn't just in love with Jackson. He is *it* for her. Usually, her spats with ex-boyfriends have lasted days, if not weeks. Only once they groveled, begged and pleaded for forgiveness with extravagant gifts did she back down. Jackson barely mumbled the word "sorry," and Lexi was leaping into his arms to accept the rest of his apology with a steamy kiss.

"Did you see the latest injury report? I don't like the Mounties chances this year," Brodie says, backhanding Jackson's shoulder.

Jackson stops placing a peppering of butterfly kisses on Lexi's neck to peer at Brodie. "Is it true Jones is out?" he asks, his interest notable.

The evil glare Lexi directs at Brodie is so potent it could kill millions. I push off my feet and pace deeper into the kitchen, knowing Lexi well enough to know she is seconds away from full-blown psychopath mode. Brodie is either a fearless man or an idiot. I'd be hesitant to interrupt Lexi when she's being showered with attention if our house was burning down, much less for an article about our local football team.

My steps freeze halfway into the kitchen, shocked when Lexi simply slumps her shoulders before picking at a blueberry muffin sitting in front of her. This isn't right. That's not how my confident, sassy-mouthed sister would usually react.

I watch the trio for a moment, taking in their unique kinship. Although Jackson's attention reverts to Lexi as quickly as it left, it only takes a matter of seconds before Brodie once again interrupts them. Every time he does, the vibrant gleam that regularly sparks Lexi's eyes fades more and more.

Brodie's interruptions happen another two times before a solution for Lexi's predicament formulates in my muddled brain. Lexi's head lifts from her hacked muffin when I ask, "Hey, Lexi, do you mind if we skip Sunday roast night this week?"

Lexi peers at me, blinking and confused. Sunday roast night has been a regular event in the Garcia household from the week my parents were married. Although I hate breaking tradition, the thought of my sister's heart breaking pains me more. I also didn't meddle in her life for years to watch all that hard work unravel the instant the magic starts to happen.

"I'm getting a little claustrophobic being holed up here, so I thought I might head out for a few hours. Maybe watch a movie and grab some take-out?" I explain to Lexi's confused expression.

"Just you, or all of us?" Lexi waves her hand around the table she is sitting at, lingering on Brodie's half a little longer than Jackson's.

"Me and Marcus..." I trail my words off on purpose, not missing the opportunity to return some of the feistiness she always gives me.

Lexi is quiet, but I still hear her muttered whine at my reply.

Happy she has stewed long enough, I tack on, "Oh, and Brodie, since he pretty much goes anywhere Marcus goes."

Lexi vaults out of her chair, her excitement uncontainable. "Oh, yeah, sure. We can do roast night any night of the week. Who says it has to be on a Sunday?"

She mouths a silent "thank you" as she stalks across the room, her eyes growing larger with every step she takes. "I friggin love you," she mutters into my ear before wrapping me up in a huge hug. "Brodie is a great guy, and he has an ass that nearly puts Jackson's to shame, but his idea of privacy is partially closing the bathroom door when he pees."

I giggle at the last half of her statement. "Not when Marcus is here," I jest, my tone full of wit.

Lexi draws me to arm's length. "If only Marcus were here last week," she grumbles, faking a gag.

When Lexi moves to stand beside me, I catch the curious glance of Jackson. His eyes bounce between Lexi's for many heart-clutching seconds. I can tell the instant recognition dawns on his face on what our little tactic is about—the most prominent, sultry grin tugs his lips high.

"Give me twenty minutes to pack, and we'll be out of your hair for the weekend."

Mortified at the gleam of lust rapidly forming in Lexi's eyes, I shift my gaze to Brodie. "Will you be ready to leave in twenty?" I ask him.

He stands from his chair. "Yes. Will we be taking one car or two?"

My brows furl. "Umm... give me five minutes, and I'll let you know."

When Brodie nods, I spin on my heels and stroll to my room where Marcus has been detained the last two hours. From the way Lexi forced him out of the living room when Anna arrived, anyone would swear I was selecting my wedding dress, not a ball gown.

Hearing Marcus's clipped tone vibrating under the doorjamb, I knock on my bedroom door, endeavoring not to interrupt him if he's on a private call. With no pause in the conversation, Marcus unlocks my door and swings it open. His hard-lined lips tuck into the corners of his mouth when he spots me standing behind the door, but the thigh-quaking glint in his eyes remains stable. His contradicting emotions have me wondering who is standing before me. *Is he Marcus right now or Master Chains?*

With his other hand, he gestures for me to enter. "So what exactly does that mean?" he asks his caller as I pace into the room.

I feel sorry for his caller, I'm not on the receiving end of his curt tone, and my pulse still quickens from his furious undertone.

"That doesn't make any sense. You said it was adequate."

Not wanting Marcus to think I'm eavesdropping on his conversation, I saunter to my closest to gather my suitcase. Marcus's eyes track my every move as I place my suitcase on the bed before picking up his overnight bag, which is resting on my office chair. I put them side by side, advising my intentions without speaking a word.

"And the requirement for that would be?" I smile when his voice doesn't come out as stern as the one he was using earlier.

Incapable of ignoring the way his heated gaze makes me feel, I pack my more risqué clothing first, mainly the items from the top drawer of my dresser. The naughty ones I prance around in every night after a shower when I'm striving to unleash his dominance. The ones that have seen us experimenting with hot wax, freezing ice, and the sinfully wicked pinwheel we used last week. The pinwheel was just as stimulating the second time around, if not better, since Marcus didn't withhold my climax the second time.

My room has seen more action the past week than it has in its entire life. I've been spanked, bound and gagged in this room, and I've loved every goddamn minute of it. Although, I'll admit, keeping the noise level down has been a real struggle. Not only is this weekend going to be a blessing for Lexi and Jackson, it will also be a godsend for Marcus and me as well. I wasn't being facetious when I said I love Marcus's dominance, this weekend getaway will be the perfect opportunity to have it unleashed in a natural setting—his playroom.

Like he's intuited where my thoughts strayed, Marcus bands his arms around my waist and presses a kiss to my temple. Before I have the chance to nuzzle into his embrace, he retreats even more quickly than he arrived.

"What type of consequences can we expect if we chose that route?" The angry snarl of his words has my temperature rising.

A lewd smirk etches on my face when my eyes lock in on a pair of clothespins sitting on my bedside table. Aiming to brighten Marcus's surly mood, I gather two clothespins in my hand, then spin around to face him.

"Do we need these or do you have spare ones in your playroom?" I mouth, waving the pins in the air as my teeth slowly scrape my bottom lip.

Marcus's head slants to the side as he glances into my eyes. The angry cloud hindering his alluring gaze weakens with every second we stand across from each other in silence. When he reads the statement my heavy-hooded gaze relays, the temperature in the room turns stifling, fired by lust so potent it hisses and cracks in the air.

"I'll call you back," Marcus snaps into the phone.

He disconnects his call and returns his cell to the pocket of his trousers before he stealthily paces toward me. He walks slowly, building the sexual tension bristling between us with nothing but an amorous smirk.

"Are we going somewhere?" .

"Yes," I reply, my voice coming out in a lusty purr. When I spot the quickest glimmer of hesitation in his eyes, I add, "As long as everything is okay? We can stay here if you want. I just thought we'd have access to more... *equipment* at your house." There is no way he could miss the sexual innuendo laced in my reply. It's drenched in it.

Marcus scrubs his hand along his five o'clock shadow as he contemplates a response. The longer he takes replying, the more my worry surfaces. He's mentioned numerous times the last week how his creativity is being stretched only having standard household instruments to use, so I thought he'd be chomping at the bit to go to his house. That's his domain. The one place he has access to all his fancy BDSM toys and gadgets.

I take a step back, needing some distance between us so I can adequately access his eyes. I can barely breathe let alone think straight when he is standing so close. His usually forthright eyes leave me more dumbfounded. Although they are void of the suspicion they held the last two times he was deceitful, they still have my apprehension rising.

Just as I'm about to ask what his phone call was about, Marcus asks, "Where are we going?"

The excitement in his tone smoothers my curiosity, but it doesn't entirely erase it. "Why did you hesitate?" I ask, realizing the only way to get answers is by asking questions.

His tempting body and alluring eyes may make me daft when I stare at them too long, but my attempt to keep our relationship on an even keel have seen me using a more direct approach in our conversation the past week. What I said to Lexi last week was right. Marcus and Jackson had a reason they kept the details of Richard's investigation quiet, but that ruse should have ended the instant Richard plunged to his death. There was no reason for them to continue pretending Brodie was Jackson's cousin...unless there is more to the story than he is telling me?

"Was that Shian?" I ask, my tone bossy. "Was she giving you an update on Richard's investigation?"

Just like they have numerous times the past week, Marcus's eyes spark with amusement at my stern tone.

After running his index finger over my furrowed brow, he admits, "I hesitated as Anna messaged to apologize for any uncomfortableness she may have caused us. She is afraid referring to you as my sub will cause a rift between us. I assured her we will be fine. Then you started packing. Your actions had me worried you were concerned you weren't filling my requirements."

He steps closer to me, increasing the hunger for friction on my skin running rampant through my body. "You are."

If I hadn't heard the honesty in his reply, I would have probed his response further, but since he is telling the truth, I steer our conversation back onto an even playing field. "So that was Anna on the phone?" I ask, nudging my head to the pocket where his phone is.

"No." Marcus's finger glides over my forehead, removing an unruly hair stuck there. His touch is basic, but his touches are always meticulously placed. He knows I can barely withstand the temptation of his alluring eyes, so I don't stand a chance when he is staring straight at me while also touching me. "But I don't want to discuss who that was. Not yet."

His tone ensures I know his statement was not a request, it was a demand.

"Does it have anything to do with Lexi or me?" I continue to probe, my Garcia stubbornness not allowing me to stand down without a fight.

"Cleo..." Marcus growls out in warning, his eyes not holding the amusement they did mere seconds ago.

"Marcus..." I reply, sneering his name with the same intensity he said mine. "We agreed no more lying, so tell me the truth."

His stares into my eyes, his ticking jaw the only audible sound. "Fine, but we are going to negotiate first." Not giving me a chance to respond, he continues. "I want an entire week with you— alone."

Ignoring the pleas of my heart to accept his agreement without any added stipulations, I utter, "What about Brodie?"

"What about Brodie?" Marcus mimics, his tone not as high as mine. His is more gruff and menacing. "I have a week until I'm scheduled to return to the studio. I don't want our time interrupted by any outside sources."

My heart slithers into my gut. I didn't realize our private bubble had such a short expiration date. I shouldn't be surprised, though, Marcus has spent nearly every waking moment with me the past two weeks. Although he is an extremely wealthy man who can absorb the loss of production, it's selfish of me to take up so much of his time. He doesn't just have his bandmates to factor into his decision, he also has many other prominent businesses, such as Chains and Links.

My eyes snap to Marcus when he says, "Since I only have a week to convince you to come with me, I want an entire week without interruptions. Just you and me. Sunday to Sunday."

"As your sub or your girlfriend?"

Marcus's brow arches high. "Have you ever considered the possibility of having the best of both worlds?" he instantly replies, quoting part of a saying I said to him weeks ago.

I try to hide in my smile. I miserably fail. Who could in these circumstances? I'm swooning so severely, my head feels giddy.

"Okay," I agree, nodding.

The lust in Marcus's eyes grows tenfold.

"I was agreeing to spend the week with you, not to have the best of both worlds," I inform his lust-sparked eyes.

The desire in his eyes remains firm, not the slightest bit put-off by my reply. He knows as well as I do that a week of solidarity won't just be a blessing for Lexi and Jackson, it will be a godsend for us as well. There are only so many hours you can spend holed up in a tiny room before your feet get itchy with cabin fever. For a man who has traveled the world, I'm confident Marcus's feet are well overdue for a scratch.

"On one condition."

Marcus's eyes snap to me, waiting for me to continue.

"I need to attend my meeting tomorrow morning with Mr. Carson. I want to hand in my notice in person. It's the respectful thing to do," I advise his questioning expression.

"I understand." Marcus steps closer to me so he can cradle my jaw in his hands.

He isn't surprised that I'm handing in my resignation at Global Ten Media, as we have discussed it many times the past two weeks. Although I'm fearful of leaving a position that has offered me stability the past five and a half years, I'm eager to see what life has in store for me next.

My resignation in no way means I'll live the high life with Marcus as his sub—or even worse, his live-in groupie. It means I am opening up to the possibility my high distinction grades from NYU could award me with greater opportunities than the ones I had at Global Ten. I studied my ass off in college to ensure I was at the top of my class three of the four years I was there. Now I write obituaries for a living in a toxic workplace that negatively impacts me more than it encourages me to succeed. A change in career has been long overdue. With Marcus's encouragement, I'm finally going to bite the bullet and do something I should have done a long time ago.

My decision was not made lightly, but a heap of weight lifted off my shoulders the instant it was made. It will be a scary couple of months, but because I've had no social life, I have plenty of accrued paid leave to fall back on if my plans go to shit. Even if Marcus decides tomorrow morning he's reached his quota on bratty Garcia women antics, Lexi and I will survive at least six months before things get uncomfortable. There are also plenty of opportunities for me to do freelance work while searching for a new position. So, I'm confident we will be fine no matter which direction my relationship with Marcus takes—*I hope.*

Breathing out my nerves, I connect my eyes with Marcus. "One week, Sunday to Sunday with a slight intermission tomorrow morning... and I get to take you on a date when the Chains investigation blows over. A proper date."

"A date?" Marcus queries, his brow inching high on his face like it's a foreign word he's never heard before.

Giggling, I bob my head. "Yes. A date."

"You just negotiated an intermission into our agreement, you can't add a second stipulation without me first adding a term," Marcus argues, his tone a mix between playful and serious.

"Why not?" I ask, my voice as high as his bowed brows. "You do realize you're dealing with a brat? The normal rules don't apply to me."

Not waiting for him to respond, I pivot on my heels and make a beeline for my closest. The giggles shuddering my frame turn into a shiver of lust when Marcus curls his arms around my waist and draws me back into his embrace. My breathing pans out when I feel how excited my little tease made him. His cock is strained against the zipper of his trousers, struggling to break free. I sink deeper into his embrace, my brattiness evaporating faster than my scruples when the stubble on his chin drags down my neck.

"An entire week of ironing out your kinks in my playroom," he murmurs into my ear, sending a flurry of goosebumps rushing to the surface of my skin. "Where no one will hear your screams." My knees pull together when his rich, chocolatey smooth voice ramps up his efforts to seduce me. His voice is so delectable it could coerce any woman into his bed without even needing to see his handsome face.

A husky purr rumbles up my chest when his teeth graze the shell of my earlobe. His bite is hard enough for slickness to pool between my legs, but not hard enough I'm worried I just made a deal with the devil. Only one devil is standing in this room. It isn't Marcus. It's my lust-driven heart that's allowing Marcus to play its strings as well as he performed his guitar last week.

One beautiful twang at a time.

13

We climb the platform stairs of Marcus's New York residence in silence, our composure more restrained than the last time we arrived at one of his properties. That has more to do with Brodie's eagle eye watching us from the driver's seat of his car than anything. Even with Marcus's assurance he was capable of driving us to his property, Brodie tailed us the entire way, even following us into the McDonald's drive-thru we visited halfway through our trip. Brodie's watchful presence did nothing to dampen the lust sizzling between Marcus and me the past two and a half hours. Nothing could ever dampen that. It's so strong, it hangs heavy in the air, slicking my skin with a misting of sweat.

In silence, Marcus punches a six-digit PIN into the security panel at the side of his property. When a buzzer shrieks loudly into the crisp winter air, he pushes on the floor-to-ceiling glass door, then gestures for me to enter. Just as eagerly as they did the first time I was here, my eyes absorb the opulent starkness of his property. Its pristine marble tiles and floor-to-ceiling glass panels are breathtaking against the modern, slick furnishings, but it doesn't compare to his Florida property. The sheer lavishness of this estate ensures you can't mistake it's Marcus's residence, but his Florida property is his home, making them so starkly contradicting, they can't be reasonably compared.

With the air set to a warm temperature, my hands instinctively dart down to remove my coat. My pulse quickens when Marcus mutters, "Let me."

He stops in front of me, his hands moving to the buttons of my jacket as his eyes lock with mine. His gesture mirrors that of our first face-to-face meeting in this very foyer. That was only weeks ago, but it feels like a lifetime has passed since then.

Once Marcus has the three buttons of my jacket undone, I shrug it off my shoulders. When it falls to the floor, I fully expect Marcus to bob down and pick it up. He has quite the neurosis of keeping things in order, so you can imagine my surprise when he leaves it where it is, sprawled on his pristinely clean floor.

I smile, loving that he has become so caught up in the moment, his usual equilibrium has faltered. My scarf is the next article of clothing he removes. Every spin it makes around my neck coils the springs in center tighter and tighter. The air is scented with the fragrant aroma of lust, and the energy bouncing between Marcus and me is enough to power the stadiums his band regularly plays in.

"Are you hungry?" Marcus asks, his deep voice sending a cluster of excitement to my aching core.

I shake my head. "No. Not unless you're on the menu?"

Marcus doesn't reply to my bold statement, he merely curls his hand around mine and guides me to the stairs that will take us to the second story of his property.

The further we go, the greater the bristling of excitement grows between us. It's incredible how much his silence appeases me. Usually, I can't stand too much quiet, but when I am with Marcus, his silence speaks volumes. When we officially met in person weeks ago, I said, "Attraction is too tame of a word to describe standing across from Master Chains in the flesh." It truly is. There isn't a word in the dictionary that can describe how I feel standing across from him, much less beside him.

If this turns out to be nothing but a crazy lust-fueled fling, I may never recover. Could you imagine having your body worshipped as if it's a temple by a man who knows your requirement for "more" but never once judges you on it? Instead, he taught you that just because your sexual desires are unconventional doesn't make them any less worthy of exploration. Would you be able to give that up? If you answered yes, you're lying to yourself.

As we climb the spiral staircase of Marcus's grand home, the sexual tension crackling between us amplifies. It builds and builds and builds until I no longer have the strength to ignore it. The instant our feet step onto the landing of the second story of his home, I launch for him. My lips mash against his as my hands frantically fiddle with the pearl buttons of his shirt.

Marcus's needs are just as potent as mine. His tongue runs the ridge of my mouth as he yanks my skirt down my quaking thighs, shredding the material in the process. Once my now-ruined skirt is discarded on the floor, he cups my thighs and directs my legs around his waist. I purr, loving the feeling of his heavy flesh bracing the seam of my meager panties.

Air hisses out his mouth when I rock my hips forward, dragging my soaked sex up the length of his rod. My confidence catapults to an all-time high. I love that I can force little responses from him. A hiss, a guttural moan—it doesn't matter how small of a response he awards me with, I cherish every single one of them. Knowing little old me can spark a reaction out of a man as dominant as Marcus is the biggest compliment I've ever received. One I'll cherish for eternity.

Marcus's mouth only just catches my breathy chuckle when we crash into what I assume is a priceless painting halfway down his corridor. Our movements are so volatile we are staggering like two drunken sailors returning from shore leave. It probably doesn't help that Marcus's trousers are pooled around his shoes, and his eyes are snapped shut as he steals my soul with perfect lashes of his tongue and playful nips of his teeth.

I drag my mouth away from Marcus's sinful lips. It's a torturous effort. "Do you have any staff I should be worried about disturbing?"

Marcus smiles as he scrapes his lips down my neck, only stopping when he reaches the throb of my throat. "No. Aubrey left this morning for a week of paid vacation."

"Good."

I slither my hand down the rock-hard bumps of his abs, grasp the waistband of his briefs and yank them down. My eyes bulge when his erection springs out of his trunks. My god—I'll never tire of seeing his glorious cock.

"So impatient," Marcus mutters against my neck.

"Says the most impatient man I've ever met," I reply, my words breathless.

Not bothering to deny my accurate statement, Marcus pins me to the wall we've just crashed into before jerking his hips up. Because he is so hard, and I'm drenching wet, the crown of cock dips into my throbbing core, taking my panties right along with it.

Marcus groans, unappreciative of the thin material between us. My core spasms when he clasps the lace material in his hand and snaps my panties straight off my body. They float to the ground like tissue paper gliding haphazardly in the air as he impales me in one fast sheath.

I throw my head back, my chest thrusting up and down as my body struggles to accept the sudden intrusion without calling out. Not waiting for my body to adjust to the sheer girth of him, Marcus withdraws his cock to the tip before slamming back in, knowing my body relishes every rough pump of his thickened shaft.

I dig my nails into the hard muscles of his shoulders, holding on for dear life as he fucks me so furiously, his balls slap the tender skin between my pussy and my puckered hole. Tingles sweep across my stomach, growing in intensity with every perfect stroke he awards me with. He jerks his pelvis up with each pump, stimulating my pulsating clit with his deliriously mouthwatering V muscle.

"Oh... yes," I moan, my words garbled by the arousal curled around my throat.

My pants of ecstasy grow louder when Marcus yanks down the cup of my bra before trapping my erect nipple in his mouth. His tongue curls around the hardened bud, teasing and stimulating it until the tingles sweeping my stomach extend to my chest. My body is so welcoming of his frenzied pounding, my previous requirement of additional stimulation is unnecessary. With him fucking me like I've never been fucked while his impressive body pins me to the wall, all the incentive I need to orgasm is delivered with precise accuracy.

My climax is building so fast, I'm mere moments from freefalling into the haze of orgasmic bliss.

"Not yet," Marcus mutters against my breast when my pussy clenches around his cock, warning him I'm close to climax.

The whine attempting to break through my parched lips traps in my throat when Marcus lifts his eyes to mine. His dominance is at an all-time high, beaming out of his with such authoritativeness the chances of holding back my orgasm nearly become unwinnable.

Slowing the pace of his pumps, he firms his grip on my hip with one hand before the other one slithers up the sweat-slicked skin of my stomach. Air leaves my body in a brutal grunt when he curls his hand around my throat. His hold is firm enough, my lungs become panicked they're not getting enough oxygen, but not firm enough to stop an erotic moan rolling up my chest.

My nostrils flare when he stares into my eyes and tightens his grip even more. Even though my first instinct should be panic, I'm not the slightest bit worried. I trust Marcus enough I know he would never intentionally hurt me. That's why he didn't prompt me for my safe word. He is confident he can intuit my body well enough to know when I've reached my limit. And I trust he would never take our interactions to a level I'm not comfortable with. I trust my Master with my body, so, of course, I also trust him with my life.

Marcus watches me cautiously, absorbing and categorizing every expression crossing my face. As the smallest portions of air seep into my lungs from his firm hold, I take in the way my senses are heightened from his dominant grip. Every muscle in my body is pulled taut, honed by the danger associated with his hold. I feel vulnerable, but crazily aroused by the head rush the lack of oxygen is giving me. It's hard to explain, but being at Marcus's complete mercy is a thrilling and highly addictive experience. One I'd never participate in again if it wasn't him doing it.

"Good girl," Marcus breathes out, his words strangled by lust. "You're not only trusting me, you're trusting yourself and your body's desire. Now you will be rewarded for that trust."

He loosens his grip on my throat before he thrusts back into me. He rocks his hips in a rhythm matching the intensity of the throb in my throat. He starts slow, teasingly building my orgasm back to the brink with every perfect stroke.

With the combination of his erotic hold and his glorious cock pounding me to oblivion, it doesn't take long for my climax to reach fever pitch. Feeling my pussy clamping around him, Marcus's grip on my neck firms. His hold is tighter than the one he used earlier, thrusting a rush of panic to the forefront of my mind.

"Give it to me, Cleo," he mutters, his words strained through his clenched teeth.

A rush of giddiness impinges my head as the sparks in my stomach detonate. My eyes roll into the back of my head as the most furious climax I've ever endured roars to life. The hairs on my body bristle as I implode, my entire body shuddering overwhelmingly. I can't think. I can't breathe. I can't do anything but surrender every ounce of my soul to an orgasm so out of control my knees buckle and white spots dance before my eyes.

I am done.

Swept away.

Completely and utterly shattered.

"Breathe, Cleo," Marcus demands, his stern words dragging me out of an erotic trance.

My lungs snap to the urgent command of his voice, drawing in a ragged breath so urgently, my windpipe squeaks in protest. My expanding chest competes with Marcus's as I gasp for air, my body equally delighted and disgruntled it can once again breathe.

Once I have my breathing back to a safe pattern, I snap open my eyes. Bewilderment overwhelms me when I notice I'm sitting huddled in Marcus's arms on the floor halfway down his hallway. From the sticky mess on my thighs, there is no doubt I didn't reach climax alone, but I can't recall when Marcus came.

"Did I pass out?" I question breathlessly, my voice husky from his dominant hold.

Marcus removes a strand of hair from my sticky neck before answering, "No. You were conscious the whole time, you just got swept away by the sensation."

My eyes bulge. *What the hell is this man doing to me?* I've never come so hard I've blacked out before. Don't get me wrong, I'm not complaining. That was... *Whoa.* Phenomenal is the only word worthy of that experience.

I lock my eyes with Marcus's sexually satiated, yet exhausted gaze. He looks pleased by my stunned reaction. Actually—he looks smug as hell.

The cocky arrogance beaming out of him triples when I breathlessly mutter, "When can we do that again?"

14

Marcus's eyes lift from the computer monitor in front of him when he notices my presence lingering outside of his office. As his index finger jabs the home button, his eyes permit me to enter. In silence, his heavy-hooded gaze drifts over the outfit I've chosen to wear to my meeting with Mr. Carson. It's my favorite dress, even more so since its free-flowing satin skirt made it easy for Marcus to corrupt me in it. It's the Adrianna Papell whimsical dress I wore my first night at his New York property.

I slow my pace, my steps drawn out to ensure he has plenty of time to take in the polished Cleo he rarely sees. Although I haven't gone out of my way to dress up for my meeting, I've certainly ramped it up a notch from the casual Cleo Marcus has become accustomed to the past two weeks. It isn't that I want to impress Mr. Carson, I just believe you should always present a professional front when in a working environment. Considering the last time I stepped foot in Global Ten I was wearing a pair of puddle-stained jeans and a tattered coat, I figured I'd put in more effort today.

The spark in Marcus's eyes doubles with every prowling step I take, so I'd say my effort will be well-received. "Are you certain you have to hand in your notice in person?" he asks, his tone gruff with unusual arrogance.

I slip between the small portion of space left between his desk and him while nodding. "A few more hours and I'll finally be free."

I didn't realize how much working at Global Ten was negatively impacting me until I made my decision to quit. I thought a majority of the weight on my shoulders the past four years came from Lexi's health issues, only now do I realize it was only half of my dilemma. My low self-esteem and lack of self-worth were all based on my career—not my personal life.

Marcus's index finger traces the invisible seam of my lace-top stockings. His touch is so gentle it feels like a feather running along my skin, enticing a smattering of goosebumps to race to the surface. When his eyes lift to mine, I can tell he didn't miss my body's reaction to his touch. His eyes expose his sexual hunger, and a ghost of a smile cracks onto his lips.

"These are nice. Classically elegant with a touch of sexiness." He stares straight into my eyes as he says, "Just like you."

I smile, adoring that I'm privileged to see both sides of him. Last night in the hallway, he was the dominant, sexy lover who ruled my body with a command that demands respect. This morning, he is the handsome, devoted boyfriend who served me hot chocolate in bed before shampooing my hair. It's utterly surreal how contrasting his personalities can be in and out of the bedroom. I truly am getting the best of both worlds.

I love Marcus's dominance, so the idea of submitting to him in the bedroom is no longer an issue for me. My concern about being his sub lies entirely on him governing every aspect of my life. What I wear, eat, and how many hours I sleep. No, that isn't an exaggeration. Those points were stipulated in the contract Marcus drafted weeks ago. By having the contract temporarily withdrawn during our first negotiation, I secured the ultimate deal. I get the dominant, alpha male in the bedroom, and the not-so-bossy boyfriend outside of sexually strenuous activates. Don't get me wrong, Marcus's personality is still a little demanding, but I'd be lying if I said his commanding temperament wasn't a turn on for me.

When Marcus reaches the section where my stocking attaches to my suspender, a rough growl tears from his throat. "Please tell me your boss is gay?"

I screw up my nose and giggle. "From the stories I've read on Mr. Carson, printed by his own media company, I'm fairly certain he isn't gay."

My laughter halts when Marcus's eyes snap to mine. His lust-filled gaze is slit, his jaw ticking profusely. *Clearly, he didn't hear the humor in my reply.*

My smile grows. "Shouldn't that have been your first sign I wasn't the submissive for you?"

"Should what have been my first sign?" he asks as he continues his leisurely exploration of the skimpy undergarments I wore hoping for this exact reaction.

When Marcus reaches my matching black lace panties and garter belt, the vibration of his growl rumbles through my body, activating every one of my nerve endings.

"Your jealousy," I force out past the lust curled around my throat. "Correct me if I'm wrong, but from my research into BDSM, Doms don't get jealous. They like sharing their subs with other Doms. They relish their subs pleasing other men. Some even want to know all the details of their exchanges once it's over. It's a turn on for them."

My last sentence comes out as a soft purr when Marcus slips my panties to the side and slides his index finger into me in one long thigh-quivering thrust. "You think I'd ever share this," he growls, dragging his finger back out at the same torturous pace he entered with.

"No," I reply breathlessly. "Marcus wouldn't share. But I don't know about Master Chains. Maybe he likes that type of thing?"

My hands shoot out to secure a firm grip on Marcus's desk when he thrusts his finger back in, taking it so deep, he hits the little nub at the end of my cervix that drives me wild with desire.

"Marcus and Master Chains are one and the same, Cleo, so wouldn't our preferences be the same?"

My hair sticks to my neck when I shake my head, denying his claim. I'd like to articulate a more confident response, but with the pumps of his finger grinding in and out of me at a faster rate than my hazy head can contemplate, I'm at a loss for words.

With his finger-fucking me at a furious pace, Marcus uses his other hand to guide my backside onto the edge of his desk. Thank god—as my knees are so close to buckling, I won't be upright for much longer. My thrusting chest sticks out when I lean back to rest my hands on the keyboard of his computer. I can barely breathe when he scoots his chair in close and burrows his head between my legs. My loud moans of ecstasy bounce off the pristine white walls of his office before shrilling into my ears when he sucks on my throbbing clit.

As his finger commands every inch of my aching sex, his mouth teases my clit with painful nibs and pleasurable sucks. In no time at all, I'm lost to the chase of climax. All cognitive thoughts vanish as I get swept into a sensation the world's best drug couldn't replicate. This is bliss—pure, heavenly bliss.

My moans turn into grunts when the fire sparked in my belly grows so out of control I can no longer contain it. I pant through the overwhelming shudders overtaking me, knowing I must wait for Marcus to give me permission before I can succumb to the pleasure attempting to sweep me away. A plea for release sits on the tip of my tongue, but thankfully, Marcus hears the silent appeals of my body and submits to its cries before it explodes.

"Now, Cleo!" he roars, hurtling my orgasm straight over the finish line.

He licks, bites and finger-fucks me while his name is torn from my mouth in a long, shouted scream. I quiver and shake against his mouth as my sex clenches his finger, milking his thrusting digit as if I'm begging his cock for the hotness of his spawn. My orgasm is intense and prolonged, so shattering, I've barely returned from a lust-crazed cloud when I hear a zipper lowering.

My hands pull out from beneath me when Marcus grips the globes of my ass and drags me forward until my soaked sex is dangling off his desk. "Do you have a replacement for these?" he asks, his eyes arrested on a scrap of lace material he is holding to the side, erotically exposing my pussy to his avid gaze.

I shake my head. "They are my only pair." When I saw them into the bottom of my lingerie drawer, I packed them specifically for him. I assumed this type of response would have been instigated after I was freed from the restraints of Global Ten Media, not before.

Not giving me the chance to explain they are his to do with as he pleases, Marcus rocks his hips forward, dragging his engorged knob through my drenched pussy. I mew when the rim of his cock glides over my sensitive clit.

Because of my half-seated position, I can see every precise move he makes as he lubes himself with the juices of my climax, hoping it will lessen any friction.

The sexually gratifying visual is interrupted when Marcus fists my hair and yanks my head back. His beaming-with-dominance eyes arrested on me, he sheaths me one glorious inch at a time. The sensation is amazing—unlike anything I've ever experienced. Not just because his cock is filling every inch of my aching-with-desire pussy, but because he is staring straight at me while doing it, soundlessly advising that the usual D/s rules don't apply to us. We are not in his playroom, we do not have a signed contract, yet he is still commanding every morsel of me. He truly is a Master—the very best I've seen.

He pumps his magnificent cock in and out of me, over and over again. His rough yanks on my hair add to the sweeping sensation rolling across my stomach. It builds to a point every muscle in my body is taut, preparing for imminent release.

"Do you think I would share this?" Marcus grunts between pumps.

I watch a bead of sweat slide down his delicious mocha skin as I shake my head. My response pleases him, sending our leisurely office romp to a mind-hazing fuck. I curl my arms around his suit-covered shoulders as I meet him grind for grind. Knowing he was in such a frenzy to fuck me that we are both still fully clothed heightens the excitement activating every nerve ending in my body. Nothing but the two most intimate parts of our bodies are exposed as he drives me wild with desire. Just the thought of being craved so much makes a reckless wildness scorch my veins. I shudder violently as the first sparks of an orgasm catapult into me.

"I'm close," I warn, my voice bearing the immense tingling sensation overtaking every inch of my body.

Marcus jerks his hips forward faster, thrusting in and out of me at such an out-of-control speed, his desk jumps along the marble tiles of his office floor. I pant through the sensation of being thoroughly fucked—*thoroughly claimed.*

Sensing I'm on the verge of losing my battle to stave off my orgasm, Marcus demands, "Eyes."

He tugs my hair back so roughly, it's nearly too unbearable to tolerate. It's the final push I needed to freefall over the edge.

"Oh..."

I quiver and shake as every muscle in my body rides the intensity of my second earth-shattering climax this morning. My pussy clenches around Marcus's heavily veined cock, begging for the hotness of his cum to mingle with my climax as I whisper his name on repeat. The silent pleas of my throbbing sex get answered when Marcus hilts me to the very base of his cock before my name comes roaring out of his throat in a grunted moan.

The veins in his neck throb profusely as the heat of his cum lines the walls of my pussy.

"This..." He runs his eyes over my face before dropping them to scan my body. "I'd kneel before I'd share this."

15

"You ready?"

The sultry grin on Marcus's face amplifies when I run my hand down my dress, smoothing out the crinkles our impromptu romp on his desk caused to the satin material. "I'm not as put-together as I would have liked, but I guess it will have to do," I reply, my tone hinting more for liveliness than annoyance.

Marcus's lusty eyes drink in my sexually flushed face before he turns them back to the clog of traffic surrounding us. The corners of his mouth curve higher when his tongue delves out to replenish his lips with moisture. Just from the way his eyes darken and the pleats in his trousers flare, I know he can still taste me on his mouth.

I rib him with my elbow, faking annoyance at his response. I'm not annoyed. Not in the slightest. Our time together in his office was so out of this world, my face is still showcasing its gratification two hours later. Even our hour and a half commute in peak-hour traffic couldn't dampen my heated cheeks and lust-crammed eyes. I look like a woman who is sexually sated—and rightfully so.

The past two weeks have been so unreal, I'm beginning to wonder if my attack in the alleyway did more damage to my brain than first perceived. Most of the time, it feels like I'm in a paradoxical universe, one where nothing but my utter happiness is the primary focus. The only thing keeping me grounded is my contradicting emotions. Like now, I've gone from reveling in the high of orgasmic bliss to being riddled with so many nerves my hands shake. What caused the sudden shift in my composure? Marcus pulling into the driveway of Global Ten Media.

"Are you sure you don't want to drop me off a block or two over?" I offer, giving him the same suggestion I have five times the past hour. "Someone may recognize your car."

Marcus pulls his car to the curb, stopping just out of the valet's eyesight. "Our agreement was I either drive you to Global Ten or Brodie did." His eyes roam over my flustered cheeks. "I'm glad you didn't choose the latter as Brodie is a stickler for arriving early. If he had walked in on us, I would have had to fire him."

I giggle. Although his words could be construed as snappy, his tone doesn't allude to that. He is carefree Marcus right now, not Master Chains.

"Alright, then lets gets this over with," I breathe out nervously.

Marcus gives my hand a gentle squeeze before he rolls his vehicle toward the valet. I jump out of my skin when the unexpected shrill of a cell phone buzzes into my ears. The screen in the console of the car displays his call is from Shian, so you can imagine my surprise when he hits the decline button to send her call straight to voicemail. My eyes drift between Marcus and his vibrating glove compartment when the silence rapidly encroaching us is interrupted by another cell phone. This one is connected to his vehicle's Bluetooth.

"Did you want me to get that?"

"No," Marcus immediately answers, startling me with his snappish response.

"Okay," I sigh, stunned by his manic behavior.

When he stops at the front entrance of Global Ten, I swing my eyes to his. "Wish me luck," I whisper shakily.

"You won't need it," Marcus assures me before he leans over to press a kiss on the edge of my mouth. "Call me as soon as you're done, and I'll come and collect you." He drops his eyes to the brand-spanking new cell I'm clutching for dear life.

Nodding, I lift it off my thigh to place it in my purse. Its screen automatically illuminates, requesting for a lock code to be entered. My eyes snap to Marcus. He didn't disclose it required a code when he handed it to me after our tryst in his office this morning.

Spotting my inquiring gaze, he mutters, "It's the same lock code as your last phone."

I freeze for a beat before sighing. "I don't even want to know how you knew what that was," I grumble under my breath. With two valets rushing to open our doors, I don't have the time nor the patience to begin that conversation.

"Just dropping off a passenger," Marcus advises his valet through the crack in his driver's side window, his door remaining locked.

The sternness of his tone has the valet jumping to his command. "Yes, Sir, not a problem." He steps away from Marcus's car with his hands held in front of his body like he is walking away from an attack dog ready to maul him at any moment. *I'm glad to see I'm not the only one who snaps to Marcus's commanding tone.*

"Thank you," I gesture to the valet opening my door.

He dips his broad-brimmed hat, soundlessly welcoming me to Global Ten. I carefully slide out of my seat, wanting to ensure none of the Global Ten Media conglomerates gawking at Marcus's car in awe catch more than what they bargained for.

Although I could have changed my risqué undergarments after my exchange with Marcus, I didn't. When he discovered my lacy underwear was the only pair I owned, he kept them intact, proving he is just as fond of them as I am. It also feels daring wearing the garments he wanted to shred of my body in public. They are a hearty reminder of my sexual preferences, demure with a little hint of naughty, but only for those privileged enough to see it.

The dash of wickedness scorching my veins clears away some of the nerves making me a jittery mess. With my confidence boosted, I step onto the sidewalk of Global Ten with an air of dignity and grace. A handful of men eyeing Marcus's flashy sports car switch their attention to me. When the heat of their covetous gazes rakes my body, I stray my eyes away. My eyes roll skyward when they chuckle, assuming their inappropriate ogle has made me flustered. It hasn't. I'm just not interested in securing their attention. I've already secured the utmost devotion of the one pair of eyes I wanted. I don't need any more.

"Call me as soon as you're done, Cleo," I hear Marcus command just before the passenger door slams shut, trapping the angry rumble of Master Chains in the confines of his car.

Although curious what has caused the sudden shift in Marcus's personality, I give him a quick wave before heading for the large revolving doors of Global Ten Media. My steps are hurried, encouraged by the prospect of new beginnings. *The faster I get this over with, the faster the next stage of my life can commence.*

As I walk into the foyer of Global Ten Media, my eyes drink it in as if it's the first time I'm seeing it. This place has been the bane of my existence a majority of my past four years, but it's a timeless building that adds to the rich heritage of mid-Manhattan. Its architecturally designed shell successfully conceals its depressing core.

When I weave through the rotating doors, the air violently evicts from my body. There is a large floral shrine sitting to the left of the security desk Richard manned the past six years. Although most of the flowers have wilted under the unnatural setting, the display indicates mourners still regularly visit the shrine. Some flowers are so fresh they look like they arrived straight from the farm.

Although reports of Richard's death did feature on the local news, the full story of events has never been disclosed. As far as the public is aware, Richard plunged to his death in a freak accident while vacationing in the scenic hamlet of Bronte's Peak. Not a word has been breathed about the stalking, attempted kidnapping, and murder charges the FBI were planning to charge him with.

Every aspect of Richard's death has been swept under the rug just as conveniently as Stephen's murder was ignored. I can't say I don't understand the FBI's hesitation to divulge the entirety of their investigation to the media. If the media caught wind of Marcus's involvement in either case, they would have a field day. The amount of press following Marcus's every move is already insufferable, so imagine how bad it would be if they knew of his association with not one but two deaths.

Furthermore, under the circumstances, I don't believe either Stephen or Richard's family need to know the gritty details of their downfall. They are grieving, so why not give them a few days of grace before revealing their sons weren't quite the men they thought they were?

With my mood not as chipper as it was, I scan my employee ID at the security turnstiles, then head for the bank of elevators. For every floor the car climbs, the more butterflies take flight in my stomach. I'm not generally a nervous type of person, but I've never done anything like this before. When I gained an internship at Global Ten, I truly thought my every wish had come true. For the first year, it was everything I expected and more. But one mistake was the catalyst of my career, shifting it from a dream position to a nightmare I'd give anything to wake up from.

I chuckle to myself. I know it's just a coincidence that the story I approved on Marcus's bandmate was partially the cause for my fall from grace, and that Marcus just happens to be giving me the courage I need to swim back to the surface, but some parts of me wonder if it's just a coincidence, or something more significant coming into play?

Before my muddled brain can conclude its ramblings, the elevator dings open on the very top floor of Global Ten—the floor Mr. Carson's office is located on. Breathing out my nerves, I step into the bustling corridor. The vibrant hum of activity feeding the air with vibrancy dulls with every shaky step I take. My hand runs across my cheeks before dropping to my dress, confident I have a large stain the frosted mirror doors of the elevator failed to announce. Otherwise, what other reason would there be for the two dozen pairs of eyes gawking at me?

Unless... my inner monologue stops as reality dawns. They aren't staring at me in shame or disgust. They are eyeing me in awe.

"It's about time someone stood up to that witch," Katie from advertising says with a wink as she floats by me.

"Right on, girlfriend, she got what was coming," mutters Elise from her concealed cubicle on my left, holding her arms in the air like she is preaching to the Lord.

"I've watched that footage at least a dozen times," informs Brad, the lead investigator at New York Daily Express. "It doesn't matter how many times I see it, it never gets old."

My steps stop midstride. "They have footage of me slapping Delilah?"

Brad holds his stomach, like his hearty chuckle is literally splitting his insides. "Yes," he replies with a nod. "If you get the chance, watch it in slow motion. The look that crosses Delilah's face is priceless, but her grunt..." He keeps talking, but I can't hear anything he is saying through his belly-crunching laughter.

When Brad's laughter becomes too great, he sits in his chair and swivels to face his desk. The last thing I see while passing his office is him yanking tissues out of a box on his desk to dab the tears trickling from his eyes. He laughed so much he made himself cry.

My eyes lift from the ground when a soft voice greets me, "Hello, Cleo. Mr. Carson is in a meeting. If you'd like to take a seat in the conference room, I'll call you in as soon as he is done."

Emmelyn, Mr. Carson's assistant, gestures her dainty hand to the conference room. Emmelyn has the sultry Latin lover look down to a T. She has black wavy hair that sits just above her tiny waist, voluptuous curves on her hips and chest, and a face that could make grown men cry just by looking at it. Although she is rumored to have been working with Mr. Carson for the past four years, she is new to the Global Ten Media team, so I'm somewhat surprised she knows who I am.

"Would you like a cup of coffee or a glass of tea?" Emmelyn asks when we enter the empty conference room.

"No, thank you." My stomach is too twisted up to risk the chance of putting anything inside it.

"Okay. Let me know if you change your mind."

After dipping her chin in farewell, she closes the conference room door and walks to her desk. With the combination of the warm temperature and my jittering nerves, my jacket becomes unnecessary. After undoing the three buttons of my coat, I sling it off my shoulders. My first instinct is to hang it over the back of my chair, but with everything in the room being meticulously placed, my eyes seek a more suitable location to hang it.

Spotting a coat rack in the far corner of the room, I push off my feet. Although my coat isn't as elaborate as the ones hanging on the stand, it's more suitable to hide its tattiness from Mr. Carson. While concealing my jacket amongst the designer ones hanging on the coat rack, from the corner of my eye, a flurry of blonde gathers my attention. Although there is a significant privacy blind separating Mr. Carson's expansive office from the conference room, the air duct blowing warm air into the room is fluttering the blinds so much, sections of Mr. Carson's desk become exposed.

I stray my eyes away, not willing to spy on a man I am planning to scold for invasion of privacy. The only reason my eyes don't entirely stray away is that the flurry of blonde is much too long to be Mr. Carson's hair, and the person's build is also two sizes too small.

Ignoring the little voice inside me reprimanding me on my double standards, I drift my eyes back to the glass partition. Just as my two-second glance suspected, there is no doubt the flurry of blonde isn't Mr. Carson. If the glossy lock hanging halfway down a pink, dusty-colored blouse isn't convincing enough, the fact Mr. Carson is standing in front of the blonde is another reliable indication.

His hands clasp the top of the blonde's shoulders as he peers down at her sitting motionless on his desk. I can see his lips are moving, but I've never been good at lip reading, so I can't understand a word he is saying. Their gathering appears intimate, but there is a crackling of tension in the air I can feel from here.

I conceal my body into the nook in the conference room when Mr. Carson's head suddenly lifts. I suck in deep breaths, praying he hasn't detected my presence. He hasn't. He is just securing two tissues from the box on his desk to hand them to the blonde. Shocked their exchange warrants tissues, my utmost devoted attention becomes arrested on the blonde. Considering her body is shuddering like she is crying, it seems like the sensible thing to do.

Even with my head screaming at me to give them privacy, I can't tear my eyes away from their exchange. I don't know if it's my intuition advising me to keep watch, or if my investigative journalism skills have sent my moral compass way off course. No matter what it is, I continue to watch their exchange for the next several minutes, absorbing every move they make. The way Mr. Carson cups the blonde's jaw in his hand and whispers to her, how he draws her into his chest and holds her firmly when her shuddering deepens, and how he ignores his ringing cell phone and landline on his desk until every shake hindering her body dissipates.

His full attention remains devoted on her until every tiny tremor of her body has been exhausted. Once he has her returned to a somewhat calm composure, he walks her to the door. My heart stops beating when I see the forlorn look on Mr. Carson's face when he closes the door after his guest exits. He looks truly devastated, like a man who has just had his heart torn out of his chest.

My head snaps to the side when the conference room door unexpectedly opens. I dive away from the glass wall, not wanting to be busted spying on Mr. Carson's private life.

"Oh, sorry, I didn't realize anyone was in here," says a soft voice, her tone muffled by a sob.

As she begins closing the door, I catch the quickest glimpse of her profile.

"Keira?" I query, my voice relaying my uncertainty. Although I've met Keira a handful of times, I can't one hundred percent testify that the briefest preview of a tear-stained face is her.

My theory is proven when Keira stops exiting the conference room and sheepishly lifts her head from the ground to me. Pain strikes my chest when I notice how many angry tears are staining her beautiful face. The concern etched on my face doubles when my eyes drop to her dusty pink blouse and black pleated pencil skirt. *Oh, my god—she's Mr. Carson's unknown guest.*

With my mouth failing to produce the words my brain wants it to relinquish, I pace closer to Keira. I'm not even halfway across the conference room when Keira mutters, "I'm so sorry, Cleo."

My shock at her apology doesn't register when she flies out of the conference room, nearly knocking over Mr. Carson as he enters. *What in the world could she be apologizing for?*

16

"Are you sure there isn't anything I could say or do that would convince you to stay?" Mr. Carson questions, his eyes lifting from my resignation letter clutched in his hand.

I shake my head. "No. This decision is best for all involved."

He sinks deeper into his chair, sending the squeak of overworked hinges bouncing around the room. "Delilah has been given a two-week suspension with the stipulation she can only return to her position on the agreement she works with a career guidance officer and undertakes anger management counseling. Global Ten Media is doing everything in its power to correct her error in judgment last month, Cleo, so if you're concerned about any conflict, there is no reason to fret. I'm bringing Global Ten back to its glory days, I need staff like you to help me drag it back from the ashes."

I smile, pleased by his praise. Although I appreciate everything he's put in place to reel in Delilah's malicious reign over the past three years, it still isn't enough to change my mind. With Global Ten's investigation into Chains still active, my loyalties must remain with Marcus. I love him, and I'll support him while he is unjustly vilified.

Marcus is a wonderful man, and just because he is involved in the BDSM lifestyle does not give anyone cause to harass him. If I could inform Mr. Carson of that without the fear of prosecution, I would. But since I need to be legally conscious of anything I say regarding this case, I shift my investigation in a new direction.

"Can I ask you something?" I ask, prying him away from his private thoughts. His mind seems as adrift as mine today.

When he nods, giving me silent permission, I say, "When I was talking to Keira a few months ago..." Ignoring the way his spine straightens at the mentioning of Keira's name, I continue, "She mentioned that the head of media had been pushing the story into Chains for nearly a year before you agreed to investigate it."

Mr. Carson's eyes remain fixated on the glistening tabletop as he nods, agreeing with Keira's admission.

"Why did you suddenly agree to the investigation? What changed your mind?" I inwardly sigh when my voice is void of the panic clutching my throat.

Mr. Carson's tongue darts out to replenish his cracked lips as he raises his eyes to mine. My heart whacks my chest when I spot the furious gleam darkening his squinted gaze. Gone is the businessman gushing about a staff member he wants to keep, replaced with a man who climbed from the deepest depths of poverty to become one of the wealthiest men in the country.

"The owner of Chains operates his business under the guise he is helping the members of his community. He is not. He is solely operating to make a profit. He doesn't care about the members of the BDSM community. All he cares about is lining his pockets with money—"

"That's not true," I interrupt before I can stop my words. "How could you have possibly reached that conclusion?" I scoot to the edge of my chair, wanting to look him straight in the eyes so he can see the honesty relayed by mine. "Your advisors aren't giving you the correct information. Chains isn't about profit margins and money-hungry power plays. It's about giving the BDSM community a safe, sensual and sane place to express themselves. A place to play in safety."

"In safety?" Mr. Carson retaliates, his loud voice startling me. "Did you see the photos the surveillance camera took that day? Did you look at them?"

"Yes. Many times." I was mostly seeking interactions between Marcus and me, but I've viewed the surveillance images over a dozen times the past three months. "Every person in those images was at that party of their own free will. If they didn't want to be there, they wouldn't be there."

"That's not true," he argues, mimicking the tone I used earlier. He stands from his chair, his fists clenching open and closed as he struggles to reel in his anger. "What happens at those parties is wrong, it may not be illegal, but it should be, as no one should be subjected to what happens at *those* parties. It's sick and ... *inhumane.*"

I also stand from my chair, my anger too great for me to remain seated. "Every person at Chains was a consenting adult. A human being who should be allowed to express their sexual partialities without fear of judgment. Just because you don't agree with it, doesn't make it immoral or sick."

"They hurt people! They are sick, bigoted men who get off on harming those below them!" Mr. Carson's voice is so loud, it roars through the top level of Global Ten Media, silencing everyone in its path.

"Like you hurt Keira?"

He stills as his eyes snap to mine. They are blazing with uncontrollable rage. He is both angered and sickened by my question. "I didn't hurt Keira," he mutters under his breath, his words barely audible. "I'd never hurt her."

"She left your office with tears streaming down her face," I disclose, pointing to the section of privacy curtain still flapping in the breeze of the AC. "She was devastated. If you were not to blame for that, who is?"

He locks his eyes with mine. The tension radiating out of them is so palpable, it slicks my skin with sweat. "Everything that's happening to Keira is of her own doing—"

"Just like everything that happens at Chains is the members' own choice," I interrupt, using his words against him. "You can dislike their choices. Hell, you can even hate them. But you cannot tell them how to live their lives. Nobody has the right to dictate to someone else how they should feel or act. Not your boss, not your wife, and not even your Master. Those choices solely belong to the person born with them. A submissive title does *not* change that."

As I pace to the side of the room to gather my coat, I run the back of my hand under my nose, ensuring none of the contents threatening to spill have the chance to escape. After experiencing the most wondrous two weeks of my life, Mr. Carson's words cut a little deeper than I care to admit. I may not be Marcus's sub, but my knowledge of the BDSM community no longer allows me to sit by and watch someone ridicule me or anyone in the lifestyle about our sexual proclivities without reacting to their vicious words. Considering I'm seconds away from exposing how erroneous Mr. Carson's assumptions are, I need to leave, and I need to leave now.

Mr. Carson's eyes remain steadfast on me as I sling my coat around my shuddering shoulders and gather my purse from the tabletop. I keep my head held high, refusing to let him see he has rattled me. I can tell by his confused eyes he wants to say something, but his mouth refuses to relinquish his words. When his eyes track mine as I head for the door, the confusion in them grows. Just like his actions have me double-guessing why he initially agreed to investigate Chains, mine have him doubting my resignation. This is as personal to him as it is to me. He's just on the opposing team.

Just before I exit the door, Mr. Carson's hand shoots out to seize my wrist. His hold is firm enough to gather my attention, but not rigid enough to warrant panic. "Is there something you need to tell me, Cleo?"

When I shake my head, he acts like he didn't notice it. "Did I chose wrong? Did I push you into something against your will? You can tell me anything, Cleo. You have my word, anything you say in these walls will remain between us."

The absolute agony in his words softens my anger somewhat. "The only thing I have to say is, despite what society tells you, everyone has the right to be who they want to be. As long as it's safe, sane and consensual, the opinions of others shouldn't be taken into account. Perhaps you should remember that the next time you're prying into people's private lives as if their choices are less valid than your own."

With that, I exit the conference room, leaving Mr. Carson standing in the middle, muted and dumbfounded.

The tapping of my high heels on the veined marble tiles of Global Ten Media's foyer is drowned out by someone calling my name. I flinch when my shoulder is suddenly pinched in a tight squeeze. Still reeling from my exchange with Mr. Carson and the rattled nerves this building always incites, I yank away from the person accosting me.

The panic blazing my veins simmers when a voice I immediately recognize says, "Shit, sorry, Cleo. I didn't mean to scare you."

Pretending I can't feel the imprudent stare of numerous ex-colleagues, I pivot around to face the velvety smooth voice. Regret makes itself comfy in the middle of my chest when I come eye to eye with Dexter, IT consultant of Global Ten Media. His brows are stitched together tightly, and a worried cloud obscures his usually lively eyes.

Although we've only ever interacted during working hours, Dexter quickly became more of a friend than a work colleague. At the start, I thought our mutual respect was because he didn't treat me like a walking Barbie doll with a slim waist and ample chest, but it was more than that. Dexter kept his word the last time we spoke, he went out of his way to talk to Delilah in the hope it would ease her unachievable demands on me. Although his private word didn't lessen Delilah's strict regime, I appreciated the effort he put in. Not many people are willing to go up against Delilah, so recognition for valor should be given when it's due.

Smiling to alleviate the irritation marring Dexter's handsome face, I pace to stand in front of him. "Sorry, I'm a little touchy after a meeting with Mr. Carson." My voice comes out snarky, still off-balanced from my exchange with Mr. Carson.

Although I left the meeting with my head held high, I'm afraid I may have created more problems for Marcus and the members of Chains than I set out to. If Mr. Carson wasn't already wary of my involvement in the BDSM community, I'm confident he suspects it now.

A feeble smile etches on Dexter's mouth as he asks, "Is everything okay?"

"Yeah," I scoff, brushing off his interest with a wave of my hand. "Nothing I can't handle." My teeth grit when the last half of my sentence comes out shaky.

Smiling a grin that makes my heart beat a little faster, Dexter curls his arm around my shoulders and guides me outside of Global Ten Media Headquarters. "You can tell me all about your run in with Mr. Carson while you buy me lunch, I'm starving, and you owe me."

Ignoring the inquisitive glance of the security officer manning the security desk, I mumble, "I owe you?"

Dexter adjusts a tattered old laptop bag over his shoulder as he escorts me out the large revolving doors of Global Ten. "You asked me to bring you anything I found on the surveillance tape directly to you. I'm bringing it directly to you."

Sick unease spreads through me. "You...f-found something?" I roll my eyes at my pathetic reply. I'm a grown woman for crying out loud, but I am stuttering like a second grader.

Not hearing the sheer panic relayed in my low tone, Dexter replies, "Yup."

I swallow several times in a row, frantically washing away the bile creeping up my esophagus before it sees daylight.

"Do you have any alcohol in your satchel?" I query. I aim for my voice to come out playful. It was a pointless endeavor. "Because from the look on your face, I'm certain I'll need a stiff drink before I hear what you have to say."

Dexter's lips curl into a shit-eating grin. I don't know him well enough to decipher if it's a friendly smile or one from the Reaper about to claim my demise.

"When you see what I've got up my sleeve, your head will be spinning either way," he mutters with a waggle of his brows.

My lips quirk as panicked curiosity engulfs me. If he is about to serve me my last meal, would he smile while doing it? I've heard of the term "smiling assassin," but Dexter doesn't seem like two-faced man. He's always been more of a help than a hindrance.

As we continue our trek across the wondrous landscape of New York City, I keep my gaze on Dexter, hoping a slip in his composure will surrender some information about what he has unearthed from the doctored surveillance tapes. His composure doesn't falter in the slightest. He remains quiet, carefully leading me through the crowd of people mingling on the overcrowded sidewalks until we reach Toloache 50.

My eyes rocket to Dexter, shocked that out of all the restaurants in the city, he picks the exact one I dined at with Serenity three weeks ago.

Spotting my gaped mouth, Dexter asks, "Don't you like Mexican?"

Not waiting for me to reply, he places his hand on the curve of my back so he can direct me to a booth in the very far corner of the restaurant.

"If it's your first visit, I'd suggest sticking to mild."

"I've been here before. The food here is great," I disclose before handing my jacket to the smiling waiter.

"Oh, hi, nice to see you again," I greet when I realize it's the same waiter from two weeks ago.

The handsome man peers at me in confusion. His brows furl as his baffled eyes run over my face. He is utterly dumbfounded as to who I am. *Ouch, that's a sting my ego didn't see coming.*

After accepting the menu from the shunted-into-silence waiter, I slip into the chair opposite the booth Dexter has taken a seat in. I can't believe I was so idiotic I thought a waiter would remember me from weeks ago. He must see thousands of faces every week, so why in the world would he remember mine? Clearly, my run-in with Mr. Carson has startled me more than I care to admit.

When the waiter takes our orders, I ignore the protests of my grumbling stomach by only ordering an alcohol-free beverage. With my mind still a twisted mess of confusion, I'm not willing to haze it more with alcohol. Until Global Ten's investigation into Chains concludes, I need to be on my game. Alcohol has always made me a little unforgiving, so I'll push my love of a fruit cocktail to the side for the greater good.

Dexter peers up from his menu, his brow quirked in suspicion.

"I have plans for lunch with a friend," I explain. Well, he is more than a friend, but I keep that snippet of information to myself.

"I'll have two servings of *queso fundido* and a bowl of chips and salsa." The waiter jots down Dexter's order before accepting the menu from his grasp.

"Hungry?" I query. I keep my tone friendly, hoping it will ease the tension in the air. It doesn't.

Dexter's eyes shoot to my vibrating cell phone when it rattles on the tabletop, I quickly silence it and flip over the screen, ensuring Dexter won't see the sneaky picture I took of Marcus this morning that I saved as my screensaver. A sense of unease engulfs me when my quick flip alerts me I've already missed two calls from Marcus during my travels from Global Ten to Toloache. *Great.*

After swallowing down my unease, I return my eyes to Dexter. From the narrowed squint of his icy blue eyes, I worry my endeavor to hide my caller's identification was ineffective.

"Thank you," I whisper to the waiter when he places our beverages in front of us, happy to use him as a distraction from the awkwardness firing between Dexter and me.

Maybe my assumption about us being more friends than colleagues was misguided? With the sternness of his lips and the anger vibrating out of him in invisible waves, extremely uncomfortable are the only words I can use to explain our exchange accurately.

I'm grateful I didn't order lunch when Dexter asks, "Was Marcus Everett the reason you were assaulted in the alleyway outside of Global Ten three weeks ago?"

"How do you know about my assault?" I query, focusing on the less important part of his question, doing anything to draw the focus away from his knowledge of my relationship with Marcus.

After scanning the room, Dexter's hand digs into his dilapidated laptop satchel sitting on the seat next to him. My stomach winds up to my throat when he produces a folded-up piece of paper not even two seconds later. I swear, the entire world is drowned out as I watch him slowly unfold the document before handing it to me. I stare at the sheet of paper like it's a bomb set to detonate at any moment.

Exhaling harshly, I run my sweaty palms down the flare of my skirt before accepting the paper. My intuition that this is a deadly weapon is confirmed when my eyes lower to the badly granulated picture. It's an exact replica of the photo Richard showed me at Marcus's residence in Florida. The one of Marcus and me entering the hotel in Manhattan four weeks ago.

What does this mean? Did Dexter stumble upon this during his efforts to restore the tape Marcus had doctored? Is he working in cahoots with Richard? Or is he just as confused about this photo as I am? I seriously don't know what his point is for showing me this. But I do know one thing. I'm not getting lured into another trap. I barely survived the first one.

Pushing back from the table, I dump the photo onto the table so I can gather my coat the waiter hung on a rack on my right. Dexter's confused eyes bounce between mine as I hastily shove my arms into my sleeves of my trusty coat. My movements are so frenzied, the frail material of my jacket crumbles from my rough tugs.

"I won't hurt you, Cleo," Dexter mutters, his voice displaying his utter bewilderment at my eccentric behavior.

I laugh a scary witch-like cackle. "That's not the first time I've been told that the past month," I sneer through the panic curled around my throat.

I've never been more grateful for nosy nancies when my frightened laugh gains me the watchful eye of a dozen or so patrons seated around us. Their eyes track me as I race for the sidewalk, my speed so unchecked, I barrel through a group of teens entering the premises without pause for remorse.

"Cleo!" Dexter shouts as I hightail it out the main door of Toloache.

Refreshingly cool winds of a December day blast my face when I rush onto the sidewalk. My screaming lungs protesting the lack of air is the only thing that stops my brisk pace down the crammed sidewalk. Standing to the side, I splay my hands across my hips to suck in numerous breaths of air. The oxygen trickling into my lungs does nothing to ease the tightness spread across my chest. Although I've never experienced a panic attack, I'm reasonably sure that's what's happening right now.

Realizing there is only one man who can calm any storm attempting to overcome me, I change the course of my direction. I consider signaling for a taxi, but with Links only a few blocks from my current location and traffic at its worst, it would be quicker for me to walk.

Ignoring the tears threatening to spill from my eyes at any moment, I hustle through the mass gathering of people lingering on the sidewalks. New York always has an eclectic mix of people lining the streets. Food vendors, artists, businessmen and women, and tourists stretch as far as the eye can see. Usually, my eyes would drink in the marvel of my sister city, but today my panic is too great to grant my eyes' silent pleas.

Just as I'm about to cross the road as per the flashing man is indicating, my elbow is seized in a firm grip. My chest grows tighter when my gaze meets with a set of stern blue eyes I left baffled in the restaurant minutes ago. Remaining quiet, Dexter guides me into a small alley on my right. His hold isn't overly firm, I could easily shrug out of his grasp, but with the realization dawning that he knows about my relationship with Marcus, I'm acting more subdued than normal.

The smell of urine adds to the queasiness in my stomach when we travel deep into the alley. Our unexpected presence startles a group of homeless men seeking shelter from the chilly winds in the nook of an old store. When Dexter releases my elbow from his grasp, I lean my back on the brickwork to suck in some breaths. Horrid alarm is curled around my throat so tightly, it thrusts my exchange in the hallway of Marcus's home to the forefront of my mind.

After my lungs have regained the ability to breathe without fear, I lift my eyes to Dexter. He peers at me, his shock unmissable.

"What the hell is going on, Cleo?"

Bile burns the back of my throat from the desolate look in his eyes. It's the same look his eyes held when I told him about my parents and Tate's accident. Usually, I keep that type of information to myself, but since one of our impromptu meetings in the ravine of Global Tens' IT department occurred on the anniversary of my parents' death, I spilled details of my personal life I've never openly shared before. Although many of our colleagues knew of my tragic loss, not one before Dexter expressed condolences for it. Even though it happened years before we met, the words he said to me that day will forever be carried in my heart.

"Every tragedy has a lesson equal in significance to its heartbreak."

When he said it, my thoughts immediately went to the green-eyed man who offered me comfort in the elevator that horrific day. That was the first time I honestly wondered if it was something more significant bringing us together. If we were truly destined to meet that day. Now, it seems like it was true. I'd give anything to bring my parents and Tate back, but I don't know if I could give up Marcus. Is that horrible of me to say? *God—it is.* But it's also true.

I tug on the hem of my skirt, anxiously knotting it around my fingers while asking, "Where did you get that photo from, Dexter?"

Dexter works his jaw side to side before he moves to a dumpster halfway down the alley. My brows furrow when he pulls out a state-of-the-art laptop from his frayed bag. From how ratty his bag is, I never suspected he was housing computer equipment worth thousands. He rests his laptop on the dumpster lid, then fires it up. Ignoring my inner voice warning me to be cautious, I pace to stand next to him.

"Remember the doctored footage you asked me to look into?" Dexter asks as his fingers fly wildly over his keyboard.

I nod. *How could I forget it?* That's the only piece of evidence Global Ten has of Marcus's connection to Chains.

I sigh in sweet relief when Dexter advises, "As I originally assumed, whoever doctored the tape is a computer genius. I couldn't recoup a single second of the missing footage."

My deep sigh lodges in my throat when Dexter quickly adds, "But..." He pauses, building the suspense until it's nearly murderous. "Working with a restrictive timeframe can cause issues to arise for even the greatest hacker."

He brings up a photo on the screen. It's nothing more than a stream of yellow taxis. "There is an ATM across the street from the hotel Delilah secured the surveillance footage from. Although it faces west, at the right time of the day, with the right angle, it reflects images from inside the hotel foyer. They reflect off the side mirrors of any cars in the vicinity."

My pupils dilate as the color drains from my face. "You're kidding, right?"

Shaking his head, Dexter points to a taxi positioned fourth down a line of many. Squinting, I drag my face to within an inch of the laptop screen so I can access the image more diligently. I gasp in disbelief when the smallest fragment of Marcus and me is seen in the side mirror of the taxi Dexter is pointing at. Realizing I've spotted us, Dexter clicks a few times on the photo, zooming in close enough, it replicates the picture he showed me earlier.

I swallow several times in a row before locking my eyes with Dexter, "Have you shown this photo to anyone?"

Although my tone alludes to my worry about Global Ten discovering my connection to Marcus, that isn't my priority. I'm more concerned at establishing the relationship between Richard and Dexter than worrying about the possibility of being sued for breach of contract.

"I had contemplated sharing my discovery with Delilah," Dexter admits, his shoulder perking up. "Then I remembered our agreement. I said I'd bring anything I found to you first, I'm a man of my word."

"So you haven't shown this photo to anyone?" I ask with suspicion rife in my tone.

When Dexter shakes his head, I say, "Then how did Richard get an exact replica of that photo?" My voice is smeared with annoyance, angered at the continuous lies of the people surrounding me.

Dexter balks, seemingly stunned. "Richard who?"

If I didn't spot the absolute bewilderment scouring his handsome face, I'd be attempted to think he was faking surprise. "The head of security at Global Ten. The guy the shrine in the foyer at Global Ten is for," I explain to his baffled expression.

I can tell the instant recognition dawns on Dexter's face. "Richard, the jerk from security, had this photo?"

I arch my brow, shocked by his crude remark about a man who just lost his life. When Dexter remains quiet, glaring at me and waiting for me to answer, I nod.

While running his fingers through his thick mane, he curses under his breath. "He must have had more skills than he let on," he mutters more to himself than me. "That image took me weeks to find."

Remaining quiet, his hand drops from his hair to scrape the stubble on his chin. His lips twitch, but not a word seeps from his hard-lined mouth. I imitate his silence, categorizing every thought passing through his astute mind. Although our relationship isn't close, I feel like I know him well enough to read some of his thoughts. He is truly stumped by my confession. Beyond shocked.

After a beat, Dexter's dazed eyes meet with mine. "How did you know Richard had this photo?"

Shit. I didn't consider the fact my interrogation could do a complete one-eighty on me.

"Umm ... Richard showed it to me," I eventually advise, deciding honesty is always the best policy.

"When?" Dexter probes, his voice not as grilling as the one he was using earlier.

My heart slithers into my churning stomach. "Around an hour before his death," I admit, my tone low as the sluggish beat of my heart.

"You went to Florida with Richard?" Dexter sounds astonished, like he is more blindsided by my supposed relationship with Richard than he is of my actual relationship with Marcus. I guess his response isn't wholly unwarranted. My run-in with Richard three months ago was water cooler fodder at Global Ten for weeks following the incident.

"I wasn't in Florida with Richard. He came there to see me. To show me that photo," I disclose, nudging my head to Dexter's laptop screen.

"And?" Dexter presses, assuming I've not already divulged all the cards I'm guarding close my chest. "What else happened?"

"Nothing. He showed me the photo. We left. He fell." I swallow hard, fighting to eradicate the bitter taste in the back of my throat.

I balk, beyond stunned when Dexter unexpectedly curls his arms around my back so he can draw me to his torso. His erratically beating heart bellows into my ear, nearly making me miss his muttered, "Jesus, Cleo, you were there when Richard died?"

Unsure if he is asking a question or stating a fact, I nod.

"Fuck," Dexter breathes out slowly, proving he was asking a question. "I'm sorry you had to witness that, Cleo. No one should ever see that. Jesus... I don't know what else I can say to make this any easier for you."

"You don't need to say anything. I'm okay," I murmur into his chest. I try to pull out of his embrace, but his hold is too firm for me to break away from.

After squeezing the living beejeebers out of me, he gently peels me off his chest by the tops of my shoulders. As his eyes frantically scan my face, he asks, "Are you okay? Were you hurt? *Did he hurt you*?" His last question comes out with so much pain, you'd swear he'd been sucker-punched.

I shake my head. "No." *Not externally anyway.*

Dexter takes a moment to absorb the truth from my eyes. Happy I am being honest, he sighs deeply. "Good." He shuts down the screen of his laptop, then stores it back in his ratty bag.

I eye him curiously, shocked he is ending his interrogation when it has only just begun. Why isn't he grilling me for more info? Even if his interests in Richard are waning, is he not the slightest bit curious as to why I was at the hotel with Marcus?

When I ask him that, he mutters, "Not particularly." He shrugs his shoulders in the most nonchalant way.

I take a step backward, blinking and confused. "Why?"

"Why not? Don't you think you've been through enough, Cleo?"

"Yes, but..." My words fail me. I'm too stunned by his blasé demeanor to force my mouth to cooperate with the prompts of my brain. Don't get me wrong, I'm in awe he would do this for me, but I'm still flabbergasted nevertheless.

"I'm not going to add more to your plate, Cleo. You worked under Delilah for three years, you've done your time. So as far as anyone at Global Ten is aware, this picture never existed."

Bitter relief engulfs me when I read the truth from his eyes. "Oh my god, Dexter. I don't know what to say?"

He smiles a shy grin. "I'll take a thank you."

"Thank you," I express wholeheartedly while battling to ignore the tears welling in my eyes. I wrap my hands around his and squeeze them tightly. "Thank you, thank you, thank you."

"You're very welcome," Dexter replies, like it's no big deal. "But don't think our new deal gets you out of buying me lunch."

I laugh. I know I shouldn't as it is a highly inappropriate thing to do in the tenseness of our meeting, but it breaks free before I can shut it down. "I owe you a lot more than lunch."

"Be careful what you throw out in offering, Cleo. I still haven't secured a date for Global Ten's Christmas party yet."

My laughter immediately stops. "I just resigned from my position," I disclose, my tone a mix of relief and remorse. "After the run-in I just had with Mr. Carson, I doubt my invitation would still be valid even if I hadn't resigned."

"Lucky my invite has a plus one then." Dexter cockily winks.

Stealing my chance to reply, he gathers his laptop bag from the dumpster and exits the alleyway, only glancing back at me staring at him in shock once, and if I am being totally honest, with a slight smidge of admiration.

17

As I enter the main doors of Links, I hear someone calling my name. I stop sweeping the bustling space when my gaze locks with Serenity's glistening hazel eyes. I wave a greeting before removing my coat to hang it on the coatrack on my left. Compared to the freezing wind blowing outside, the temperature in Links is warm and inviting.

"Wow! Look at you all jazzed up." Serenity swoops to greet me with a kiss on the cheek. "I thought Marcus said he had to pick you up?"

With my mood still high from my exchange with Dexter, I return Serenity's hug with more gusto than usual. "When did you get back from Ravenshoe?" I ask, recalling Abel's eagerness for her return last week.

"This morning," she replies, pulling back from our embrace.

The warmth blooming across my chest grows when I spot nothing but joy radiating from her beautifully unique eyes. She is as in love with Abel just as I am.

"And already back at the helm. No rest for the wicked, hey?" I spiritedly bump her with my hip.

"Yeah, something like that," she replies with a roll of her eyes.

She tries to conceal the quickest flare of apprehension blazing through her usually vibrant eyes before I see it, but she wasn't quite quick enough. I arch my brow, demanding an explanation for her odd reaction. Just like her big brother, Serenity doesn't lack confidence, so I'm somewhat surprised by her dour response. The only time I've seen her high-spiritedness dulled by anxiety was when we had lunch together after Marcus and I broke up. So to say I'm worried about her rapid shift in composure would be a major understatement.

When Serenity fails to comply to my silent request for further information, I decide to voice it instead. "Is everything okay?" I ask as my eyes scan the area, seeking Marcus amongst the crowd.

Is he aware of Serenity's issue? I highly doubt it. Because if he was aware, he'd be standing right beside me, grilling her too.

Or maybe he is aware, and that's what caused his drastic shift in mood this morning? Worry hangs heavily on my chest as my baffled brain sorts through the events thus far today. I thought Marcus's grouchy temper was a consequence of a forced intermission in our week of reclusion. I had no clue it was something greater than that. I really need to reel in my shrewdness when I'm with Marcus, and start thinking with both my head and my heart. It won't be easy, as one glance into his eyes and all rational thoughts vanish. But if I want our relationship to withstand the test of time, I need to pay attention to all factors of our relationship. Not just the sexual elements.

My eyes return to Serenity when she murmurs, "Stop fretting, Cleo. Everything is fine...as long as I remember the mantra 'all guys are assholes.'"

Some of my panic clears away from the loathsome expression on her face. "I can't believe you nearly gave me a heart attack over some random guy."

"Not just some *random* guy," Serenity recants, her mood rising as quickly as her plump lips. "A super-hot, tall drink of water who makes my insides squeal every time he steps into the room. It's just a pity he's the bane of my existence. Hence, the 'all guys are assholes' reference."

"Not all guys are assholes. Your brother is pretty cool." I waggle my brows excessively, hoping a little bit of friskiness will lessen the anxiousness clouding her pretty hazel eyes.

It doesn't have the effect I am aiming for when her face pales. "Please shut up. I love you, Cleo, and I'm *soooo* glad you and Marcus got your shit together, but if I have to hear one more gushing compliment about either of you, I'm going to vomit." Her eccentric gag gains us the attention of a handful of Links clients keeping warm from the chilly winter day in the main rec room.

I giggle. It's the only defense I have to stop myself from asking what accolades she's heard about me. Considering no one in Links knows who I am, I'm confident the compliments she is referring to came from Marcus. It might seem conceited I want to know what he said, but after the knock my ego took during my meeting with Mr. Carson, a little boost wouldn't go astray.

"So when do I get all the juicy details about the man who has your panties twisted in knots?" I ask, once more bumping her with my hip.

Serenity returns my hip bump, her eyes void of the anxiety they held earlier. "When you get my annoying big brother off his case."

"Marcus knows who he is?" I ask, shock resonating in my tone.

Guilt darkens Serenity's eyes. "No. But he knows of him."

My brows furrow in confusion. Suddenly, the light bulb in my head switches on. "Is he a member of Chains?"

"What?! No!" Serenity shouts, clearly shocked by my assumption. She spreads her hands across her hips as she clears her face of all emotions. "But would it be so bad if he were?"

"No," I reply, dragging out the short word overdramatically. "Not for me, anyway. Your brother on the other hand..." I leave my sentence open, letting her answer it how she sees fit. Marcus is very protective of his sisters. So much so, I don't know what his reaction would be if he discovered one of them wanted to follow his footsteps into the BDSM lifestyle. I'm sure he'd support them, but it isn't a conversation I'd volunteer to participate in.

Reading my inner monologue from my eyes, Serenity says, "Now tell me again all guys aren't assholes?"

I look her straight in the eyes, my expression deadpan. "All guys aren't assholes."

Her mouth gapes. "If the purpose of your visit was solely to torture me, you're shit out of luck, Sherlock." She places her hands on my shoulders and guides me into the industrial kitchen of Links.

The small grin on my face turns massive when I spot Lexi in the corner of the room. The sleeves of her shirt are crinkled around her elbows as she scrubs a large stainless steel pot in a sink of bubbly water. When she discovered Links was seeking volunteers, she pledged to help every Monday morning before school. I'm glad to see her naughty weekend with Jackson didn't alter her obligation.

"I stupidly agreed to let your sister cook the porridge this morning. Big mistake on my behalf. The pots may never recover, and don't even get me started on the people brave enough to eat that mess," Serenity grumbles, her tone half-amused, half-mortified.

The smile on my face sags when we stop in front of three pots with bottoms so black, they thrust an image of Delilah's wilted heart into the forefront of my mind. I sling my head sideways so I can glare at Lexi with an *I can't believe you made such a mess* face.

"What?" Lexi shrugs her shoulders. "How was I supposed to know you have to stir porridge?" She leans in close to Serenity and me, ensuring we will be the only ones to hear her next sentence. "After my night, I can barely stand up, let alone move my arms. I swear muscles I didn't even know about are aching."

"Hell-to-the-yes, Sister," Serenity replies, holding her hand in the air for a high five. "I saw that sweet thing who dropped you off this morning. My god... heaven wrapped up in delicious milky skin."

My eyes rocket to Lexi when she accepts Serenity's high five while saying, "Preach. Although after he spends his morning searching antique stores for a replacement entranceway table before my neurotic sister returns home, he may double guess our next exchange."

Serenity's beautiful giggle shrills into my ears when she throws her head back and laughs. "You were right, Cleo. I do love her. She is perfect." She wraps her arms around Lexi the best she can without getting her crushed linen shirt wet. "Don't ever change for no one, girl."

When a lady shredding lettuce on our right calls out Serenity's name, Serenity raises her index finger into the air, requesting a minute before drifting her eyes back to me. "I'll let Marcus know you're here?"

Since her statement comes out sounding like a question, I nod. "Since she is my responsibility, I guess I should help clean up the mess she made," I mumble, nudging my head to the stack of burned pots.

Any reply Serenity attempts to give is doused with laughter when Lexi stuffs a handful of bubbles into my face. I cough, choking on the tingles racing up my nose from inhaling the bubbles unexpectedly. Serenity shakes her head, like she knows all too well how taxing younger sisters can be before padding over to the lady requesting her assistance.

After wiping my face with a tea towel, I shift my eyes to Lexi.

"What?" she remarks again, her tone telling me she knows exactly what my stare is referring to.

When she maintains her quiet front, I mutter, "You broke the entranceway table?"

"No," she fires back, shaking her head. "Jackson did." Her sentence is heavily muffled with laughter. "What about you? Any broken furniture I should know about?" She waggles her brows, her mood a drastic improvement from the one she had yesterday.

I wrap an apron around my waist before setting to work on the first pot. "No. All furniture was left intact." I wait a beat, fighting not to let my maturity stoop to Lexi's level. Clearly, it's a complete waste of time when I confess, "A priceless painting may never recover, though."

I shush Lexi when she loudly hollers, "I knew some of Mom's rebellion was in there someone!" She rakes her eyes down my body, her stare outrageous enough to make a hooker blush. "I thought you looked a little different today. It's a good look for you. You should wear filthy Cleo more often."

Suddenly, she freezes. "Oh, you gave your notice today, didn't you?"

I smile while nodding.

"How do you feel?" Lexi asks, even though she can read the answer from my brightened gaze.

"Brilliant." I overemphasize the word in a dramatic purr.

"Good," Lexi replies, playfully barging me with her shoulder. "You should have done it years ago."

I nod in full agreement.

A small stretch of silence passes between us as we tackle the coated-on porridge scorching the pots. The pots are so far gone, if I weren't mindful of our bank balance, I'd throw them in the trash and purchase new ones. But with me handing in my notice, my penny pinching just firmed to a whole new level. If people thought my budgeting was pedantic before, they have no idea, because it just became ten times worse.

A short time later, the hairs on my arms prickle with primitive awareness. Before my body can fully register Marcus's arrival, he bands his broad arm around my waist and draws me backward. I rest my head on his chest and inhale deeply, relishing the scent of his unique smell activating every one of my hot buttons.

With our impromptu romp in his office stretching our time a little thin, he ran out of time to shave this morning, which means the stubble on his chin scratches my neckline when he drags his mouth to my ear to whisper, "You were supposed to call me."

My pulse quickens from his stern tone. From the affectionate way he is holding me, I failed to notice the anger radiating out of him. Only now do I realize the heat warming my back isn't based on affection, it's anger.

When I attempt to spin around to face him, he tightens his grip on my waist, denying my request. "You were supposed to call me. Why didn't you call me?" he snarls viciously, sending my heartrate haywire.

"It was five blocks, I decided to walk. It's a nice day for it." I'm planning to tell him about my confrontation with Dexter, but not in the presence of the dozen or so pairs of eyes gawking at us.

Marcus's fingers flex painfully on my hip, sending a tingle of pleasure to my core. "You walked here?" he asks, his tone brimming with even more unbridled anger.

I wait a beat before cautiously nodding, mindful I'm admitting to being disobedient in a place funded by his BDSM club revenue. *Thank god we are in public, or who knows what his punishment may have entailed?*

Marcus manages to keep his furious growl in—barely. I felt it rumble up his chest, so I didn't need to hear it to know of its existence. He tugs at the cords wrapped around my waist, dumps the apron onto the scrubbed-clean pots, then clasps my hand in his. His pulse is so furious it pulverizes my hand.

"Say goodbye to your sister," he instructs me, his tone stern.

I glare into his eyes, informing him I don't appreciate his commanding tone. My pussy may be shuddering in anticipation, but for once, my astute brain is overruling my lust-driven body's desire.

"Would you rather be punished in privacy or in front of witnesses?" Marcus questions, his tone so low only those closest to us can hear him.

When I float my eyes around the room, I realize we haven't just gained a handful of spectators, everyone in the kitchen has their eyes rapt on us. Some are clutching elaborate trinkets curled around their necks as they inconspicuously peer at us through lowered lashes, where others just stare without shame, not hiding their interest in the slightest.

I drift my eyes back to Marcus. My first thought is to continue with my stubborn stance, but with my ego already dealing with two knocks I didn't expect today, I gather my purse and turn to face Lexi.

"Goodbye," I grind out through gritted teeth. "I have to go as my *boyfriend* is being an insensitive *jerk.*"

A collective gasp booms around the kitchen, revealing to me that I said my statement louder than I intended. Pretending I can't feel Marcus's irate gaze, I wrap my free arm around Lexi's shuddering-with-laughter torso and give her a quick hug the best I can since Marcus is still clutching my other hand.

"Oh, Cleo, some furniture is about to get broken."

"Furniture or body parts?" I reply, my pitch snarky. "And I'm not referring to my body parts."

There has only been one time I've wanted to cause physical harm to another human being. It was when I kneed Richard in the balls. If Marcus doesn't tread carefully, he will end up being my second slip up.

Lexi laughs. "If anyone can bring a master to heel, it will be you, Cleo," she mutters, encouraging my defiance. She gives me one final squeeze before pulling back.

After dipping his chin in farewell to Lexi, Marcus exits the kitchen, dragging me along with him.

"I recant my earlier statement," I mumble to Serenity as her wide eyes track us crossing the rec room. "All men are assholes."

My admission angers Marcus more. His grip on my hand turns so lethal, my knuckles turn a pasty white color.

"I need my coat," I advise when he takes a sharp left at the end of the rec room, heading to the back entrance of Links instead of the front.

"I'll buy you another," he mutters, his tone so low, I'm confident the devil felt its shudder.

I dig my heels into the ground the best I can in these shoes. "I don't want another coat. That's *my* coat. I want *my* coat." I know I'm acting like an immature imbecile over an article of clothing that cost me twenty dollars three years ago, but with my annoyance hackled to a record-breaking high, my astuteness has completely vanished.

Marcus muffles something under his breath. Although I couldn't testify on a Bible, I'm reasonably sure it was a curse word. Releasing my hand from his, he trudges to the entrance of Links, furiously yanks my jacket off the coatrack, then stomps back to me. In silence, we continue our trek.

The Links patrons' faces light up when they notice Marcus strolling down the corridor where the rooms are located. None approach us, though. Marcus's rueful expression is enough warning for them to stay away. I don't blame them. I love this man, but I'd give anything to have a few continents between us right now. I don't know what his problem is. Yes, I failed to call him once my meeting with Mr. Carson was over, but my head wasn't screwed on straight after my impromptu lunch date with Dexter, so a bout of forgetfulness can be excused.

Besides, I've walked the streets of New York many times the past twenty-six years. Half the time the sun wasn't even up. So if he is worried about me getting hurt, there is no need, I'm capable of taking care of myself.

When I say that to Marcus, he steps come to an immediate halt on the cracked sidewalk at the back of Links. He glares at me, his jaw ticking so profusely the entire left side of his face twitches. He looks like he wants to say something, but not a peep seeps from his lips.

"I'm not a damsel in distress, Marcus. I don't need you to rush in and save me."

Steam billows out of his nose when he inwardly grunts. "Don't push me, Cleo. Not today." His tone guarantees I can't mistake his warning as a suggestion.

After helping me into the passenger seat of his car, he throws my jacket in the back seat before running around to the driver's side. His speed out of the alleyway is so manic, he narrowly misses a homeless man rummaging through a dumpster halfway down the alley.

"Jesus Christ, slow down."

Acting like he didn't hear a word I spoke, Marcus demands, "Put your head down."

I smack my back molars together before doing as requested. The flashing of paparazzi lights commence the instant we merge out the alleyway. Although the traffic around New York is bumper to bumper, I'm thrusted into my seat when Marcus finds an opening relatively quickly. It's only when I hear beeping horns and curse words directly following his merger into traffic do I realize it wasn't a clear opening.

His engine revs as he exerts the power of his flashy sports car on the unsuspecting motorists he weaves through dangerously. The tendons in his cut arms flex with every change of the gears. Even my plummeting mood can't deny the visual of an angry Marcus is an enticing one.

Approximately five minutes later, the flashing lights stop hindering my vision.

"I lost the paparazzi," Marcus informs me, confirming my suspicion.

Lifting my gaze from my intertwined fingers, I lock eyes with him. His hands are clutching the steering wheel for dear life, the skin on top of his knuckles is void of any natural skin coloring. His jaw is pulled tight, ticking and grinding in sync with the mad beat of his heart, and his eyes are narrowed into tiny slits.

"Why are you so angry?" I ask, shocked at his sudden shift in composure.

I've become accustomed to my rollercoaster moods of late, but this is the first time I've seen Marcus exert this level of aggression. He wasn't even this angry the night he discovered Richard killed Stephen.

Keeping his gaze locked on the dense flow of traffic, Marcus sneers, "You were told to call me. You said you'd call me."

"And I decided to walk. Big deal." I roll my eyes, acting as immaturely as he is.

"Was the decision to walk made before or after you had Toloache tacos for lunch?"

I stare at him, shocked and blinking. "How do you know about that?"

He remains quiet, ignoring me.

"Do you have someone watching me?" I ask, my anger rising faster than my snarky tone.

"No," Marcus eventually grinds out. "But after today's performance, I may reconsider."

Snubbing his sneered comment, I stare straight into his eyes while asking, "Then how did you know where I went to lunch? There are thousands of restaurants in New York. There is no way you could have known where I'd eaten unless you have someone following me."

Marcus's eyes drop to my cell phone resting on my thigh. It's only a quick glance, but long enough to spill a lifetime of secrets. I call him every derogatory name I know under my breath while attempting to pry apart my cell phone. It takes me hitting it on the shiny dashboard of his car to get the back to crack open.

"Cleo..." Marcus growls in warning, his tone as feverish as the blood scorching my veins.

I ignore him and continue with my mission, not the slightest bit concerned I'm wrecking a phone I can't afford to replace. My anger is too intense to think lucidly.

My fury reaches fever pitch when I find a small black device thinner than a sheet of paper planted under the battery of my cell. Even not being friendly with computers, my years as an investigative reporter assures I can't mistake what this item is.

Fuming in anger, I peg the battery of my cell at Marcus's head. My teeth crunch when it misses its mark. It hits the driver's side window before crumbling to the floor.

"You planted a bug on my cell!" My statement is not a question, it's a declaration. "Why the hell would you do that? Did you not learn the first time what happens when you invade my privacy?"

Not waiting for him to reply, I yank on the latch of my door.

"Jesus Christ, Cleo. We're in rush hour traffic," Marcus roars, like I'm not aware we are surrounded by a sea of vehicles. I'm aware, but my desire to get away from him is more potent than concerns for my safety.

"Unlock my door."

After everything that has happened today, finding out he bugged my cell is the straw that broke the camel's back. I am beyond ropeable he did this. Being controlling in the bedroom is one thing, but taking that trust and exploiting it outside of that environment is a hard limit for me—*a very hard limit.* That's one of the main reasons I wouldn't sign on to be his sub. The idea of giving up all my power was more than I could bear.

"Unlock my door!" I shout when Marcus pretends he didn't hear my first request.

"No," he answers, his tone precise and without concern.

"Let me out!" I scream, my voice so loud, I gain the attention of the vehicles on each side of us.

When Marcus continues to deny my request, I secure anything I can and peg it at his head. My lip gloss, a set of keys, my purse, they all go sailing across the car, more hitting their target than not.

"Goddamn it, Cleo, stop it!" Marcus roars, his words so furious, they rattle my ribcage.

Even with panic overtaking my anger, I continue with my assault. My mind is too blurred with seeking revenge to stop and consider the consequences of my actions. When I run out of supplies to hurl at him, I remove my shoes and throw them across the confined space. A tinge of hesitation passes through me when the heel of my shoe hits Marcus just above his furrowed brow, leaving a scratch mark visible enough even my squinted-with-anger eyes can see it.

My body crashes into the passenger side door when Marcus unexpectedly pulls down an alley. Before I can comprehend what he is doing, he throws back the driver's seat, seizes my wrists, then drags me across the console of his car. With my head buried in his crotch and my ass perched in the air, the flare of my dress bunches around my waist. I freeze when the warmth of one of Marcus's hands yanks my panties down my thighs, while the other one pins my lower stomach to the console. The sheer lace material of my panties is no match for his strength. They crumble to my knees like sheets of tissue paper.

I suck in a shocked breath when reality dawns. *Oh, hell no, he is not spanking me now. We're in public for crying out loud!*

Before my inner monologue can be articulated, Marcus places a firm smack on my right butt cheek. I call out as fiery warmth spreads across my burning backside. His second hit is just as firm as the first. It adds to the heat turning my skin pink while also increasing the dampness between my legs. By the time he inflicts his third hit, I've stopped thrashing against him, my body too immersed in controlling the raging fire rapidly building in my core to consider the absurdity that I'm being spanked like a child.

He completes another two spanks before he switches to soothing the burn his hand made. The sound of his ragged breaths is the only thing I hear when he caresses the globes of my stinging ass with gentle squeezes and soft rubs. His pulse is raging through his body so uncontrollably, I can feel it surging through his thighs my head is resting on. He is also hard as steel, the heat of his flesh unmissable since it's pressed against my cheek.

Once the sting of his spanking fades, Marcus covers my dripping core with my dress, then sets me back down on the passenger seat of his car.

"Now sit," he instructs, staring straight into my eyes.

Subdued and muted, I merely nod.

18

By the time we are five miles out of the city, the throbbing of my core has dampened to a slight simmer, and the tick of Marcus's jaw isn't as noticeable. When I adjust my position on his smooth leather seats to ease the burn on my backside, Marcus's eyes stray from the road to me.

"Are you sore?" he asks, his tone nothing like his earlier one.

I give him a gentle smile before shaking my head. Although my backside is undoubtedly feeling the effects of his hand, it isn't a bad pain. This may sound stupid, but I was acting like a child, so Marcus treated me as if I were one. If I weren't so aroused by his spanking, I'd be disturbed by that statement, but like every moment I spend with Marcus, I'm realizing I hardly even know myself. I hated being spanked as a child, so why the hell do I love it as an adult?

My silent vow doesn't give Marcus the assurance I was hoping. The remorse in his eyes continually grows until we pull into the long weaving driveway of his New York property. He parks his car in a garage at the side of his house before jogging around to assist me out. A crisp winter breeze whips up under the skirt of my dress, soothing the heat spread across my backside as we climb the platform stairs hand in hand.

After throwing his keys into a crystal bowl on a glass entranceway table, Marcus guides me toward the curved stairwell on my left.

"I thought I was preparing our lunch." I motion my head to the ingredients I took out in preparation this morning. I wasn't being facetious when I told Dexter I had plans for lunch. Marcus and I have plans, we just aren't eating out.

"We will have lunch after I've made sure you're okay."

Hating his low tone, I mumble, "I'm fine, Marcus."

Marcus continues guiding me through his residence, his mouth tight-lipped. When we reach the master suite, he toes off his shoes and removes his suit jacket. After placing his wallet and showy watch onto the dresser on his right, we enter his opulent bathroom. My heart squeezes when he walks us to his sizeable egg-shaped tub. In silence, he commences drawing a bath, only leaving my side to pour some fragrant-smelling oils into the rapidly filling water.

After removing his shirt, trousers, and boxer shorts, he assists me in removing my dress and bra. My panties are still sitting on the floor of his sports car. Once the tub is brimming with water, he steps in and rests his back against the edge before holding out his hand for me. My toes tingle from the contrasting temperatures when I dip my foot inside. The water is as heated as the fiery cloud brewing in Marcus's dark gaze.

I don't need to peer into the large mirror next to the tub to know Marcus's handprint is on my backside. The hiss of air straining through his teeth when I spin around to sit in front of him is all the indication I need to know that I am wearing his marks.

I sink down low into the tub, loving the way the oily water slithers against my skin like the world's most treasured silk. Assuaging quiet passes between us. Usually, I hate too much silence, but I can handle it in small batches when it does more good than bad. It gives me a chance to settle my nerves enough I can try and work out what the hell happened between our tryst on Marcus's desk to him spanking me in his car. I've been known for my drastic shift in moods in the past two weeks, but I've never seen Marcus act so reckless. I know he says I make him that way, but his recklessness has always had a sense of maturity. I've never seen him lose his cool before. Usually, nothing rocks his core.

Five minutes of silence awards me with five additional minutes of confusion. Deciding there is only one person who can answer my questions, I carefully roll over to face Marcus. Water splashing over the tub surpasses the sound of his heart thrashing against his chest when I balance my chin on his sweat-slicked torso to peer up at him.

"What's going on?" I ask, my voice a nurturing purr void of any judgment. I'm not angry. I'm more concerned than anything.

Marcus's chest deflates when he exhales a deep breath. "I shouldn't have marked you," he breathes out slowly, his words choked with guilt.

"And I shouldn't have thrown my shoe at your head. We all make mistakes," I counterbid. I keep my tone low, ensuring he can hear the honesty in my reply.

I'm not upset about him marking my skin. I love wearing his marks as much as I love him. I just hate that we reached a point in our argument he had no other choice but to spank me to calm me down. We've done so much communicating the past two weeks, I thought we had reached a stage where we were comfortable enough to express ourselves without needing to lash out or act juvenile.

"I also shouldn't have walked to Links," I continue, swallowing down my absurd declaration of love before I accidentally blurt it out. I do love Marcus, but it's way too early in our relationship to admit that openly. "After everything I put you through in Florida, I should have been more courteous about how that would make you feel. I just wasn't thinking straight. Dexter caught me unexpectedly, and with my head not screwed on right, I had an error in judgment."

Marcus scrubs his hand across his tired eyes, but his lips don't move an inch. His silence worries me more than the anger growing in his narrowed gaze from the mention of Dexter's name, but it doesn't stop me from saying, "The way this works is, when someone admits they were wrong, you're supposed to acknowledge their mistake and admit your own. Such as, 'I shouldn't have bugged your cell, Cleo. That was wrong of me to do.'"

Marcus drops his hand from his face. "So I should apologize for something I'm not sorry about?" he replies.

If I didn't hear the genuine confusion in his voice, my spikes would hackle from his reply, but remembering this is all new to him, I let his snippy comment slide—this time.

"You don't have to apologize, but it would be nice if you at least explained why you thought that was appropriate." I grit my teeth when my voice comes out with more annoyance than I wanted to express.

After tracing his index finger over the faint scar on my top lip, Marcus locks his eyes with mine. "I'm trying to keep you safe, Cleo."

"No. You're trying to keep me contained. I'm not a sub, Marcus, so you shouldn't be treating me as if I am."

If the water didn't ripple, I'd be none the wiser to the sudden clench of his fists.

Pretending I can't feel the wrath of his gaze, I continue with my endeavor to keep our relationship on an even playing field. "During our negotiation, you said you couldn't give up control in the playroom. I accepted that, but you aren't keeping your end of our deal. You're trying to control our interactions both inside and outside of the playroom."

I expect him to voice anger at my admission, or at the very least, deny my accusation. He does nothing. He doesn't speak a word.

"Say something," I murmur as my eyes dance between his.

"What could I possibly say?" he snarls. "'You're so hell-bent on making sure you aren't forced into submission you're making stupid mistakes?' Or perhaps, 'I'm sorry I care enough about you that the idea of you getting hurt rips me open?' Would either of those be a suitable thing for me to say in a non-controlling way?"

My backside rests on the balls of my feet when he abruptly stands from the tub, steps out, then leaves the bathroom without a backward glance. With my heart smashing against my ribs, I rest my back on the edge of the bathtub, pretending the trickling of moisture rolling down my face is from the steam trapped in the bathroom and not tears.

I stay in the bath until the water becomes too cold to ignore. After wrapping a towel around my shuddering frame, I trudge into the master suite, my steps slow and shaky. The pain tearing me in two simmers when I notice Marcus has laid out clothing on the bed for me. They are sitting next to the bottle of ointment he used to soothe the sting of my first spanking.

After applying the ointment to the welts on my bottom, I get dressed, then make my way downstairs. With a tired headache thumping my temples, I'm tempted to crawl into bed and sleep away a few hours, but Marcus laying out clothes for me has altered the direction of my course. *He's trying to make amends, so shouldn't I put in the same effort?*

I find Marcus five minutes later in the kitchen, cooking the meal I prepped earlier. His eyes lift from the eggplant he is grilling when he senses my presence. A ghost of a smile graces his lips as he gestures with his head for me to sit at one of the stools he has set up for our meal.

My first instinct is to help him prepare lunch, but I soon realize he knows his way around the kitchen. He doesn't even follow the recipe I printed out this morning. He just mixes the garlic-cumin vinaigrette with feta and herbs before serving it on top of the grilled eggplant.

"Thank you," I murmur when he places a generous helping of eggplant onto my plate.

Once he fills our two wine glasses to the brim with crisp white wine, he takes the empty seat next to me. I cough to clear my voice of nerves before saying, "I'm—"

"Shh," Marcus interrupts, his voice firm yet void of anger. "Anything we need to say can be said after we've eaten."

Leading by example, he picks up his fork and consumes a large chunk of eggplant.

With an arched brow, he glances into my eyes, encouraging me to do the same. Not trusting my swishing stomach, my first bite is a lot smaller than Marcus's. The instant the deliciously aromatic food hits my taste buds, my hunger returns as rampant as ever.

Once we've finished our lunch, Marcus and I clean the kitchen in silence. Although worry is still hanging heavy on my heart, every little brush of his body against mine as we work in sync eases the weight. Tension is firing the air, but unlike in the bathroom, it isn't from anger. The hefty aroma of lust soothes the snip of anxiety left over from our disagreement.

The hem of my shirt rides up high on my stomach when I stretch onto my tippy toes to place the wineglasses back into their rightful spots. Whoever designed this kitchen must have been a giant, as no average-sized person could reach that cabinet without straining. I'm not tall by any means, but I'm relatively sure my five-foot-five height isn't uncommon.

After placing the wineglasses in the cupboard, I spin around to face Marcus. My steps falter halfway around when I spot his amorous stare watching me intently. The shift of tension in the air is so quick, it nearly knocks me onto my ass—literally.

"Can I show you something?" Marcus asks, his tone low.

Not trusting my voice not to crack from the unease of his words, I nod. I feel the surge of his pulse through our conjoined hands as we walk into his office. When we reach his desk, he gestures for me to sit in his leather chair. After pinching the material on his trousers, he takes a seat on the edge of his desk. Unlike his big bulky desk in Florida, this one is glass and extremely flimsy. Not flimsy enough it couldn't handle our rigorous activities this morning, but definitely not as bulky as his desk in Florida.

Marcus's voice has a snip of anger to it when he says, "The phone call I took yesterday afternoon was in regards to an incident that occurred at Links the night before. Last Wednesday, the Links hotline took a call from a woman distressed about her neighbor harassing her. The counseling staff at Links handled the call as they were trained to do. They offered the anonymous caller shelter at Links and contacted the authorities on her behalf. They did everything by the book, and it still wasn't enough."

His throat works hard to swallow before he continues, "After being questioned by police, the accused went to the complainant's house to confront her about her accusation. Their altercation ended with her fighting for her life in the ICU."

My hand shoots up to cover the shocked gasp expelled from my mouth. A rush of moisture burns my eyes when Marcus swivels the mouse on his computer, bringing up horrifyingly similar images to the ones Shian showed me last week. Nearly every inch of the dilapidated studio apartment displayed on the screen is covered with photos of a female with platinum blonde hair and dark brown eyes.

Although this level of stalking is miles above the caliber of Richard's, I can understand Marcus noticing the similarities between the two cases. There are photos of the unnamed blonde sleeping, eating, and even doing something as mundane as laundry—just like Richard had of me.

"You see my protectiveness as if I'm trying to control you. I'm not, Cleo. I'm trying to stop something like that from happening to you." The pain in his words cuts me raw.

"I'm not her, Marcus. What happened to her is terrible, but she isn't me. I'm not lying in a hospital fighting for my life." My distress for the unnamed lady resonates in my low tone.

"No, you aren't," Marcus agrees as the pain in his eyes doubles. "But you could have been. You went with Richard—willingly." His nostrils flare as his eyes dance between mine. "So did Sylvia. Her stalker convinced her if she'd just give him a chance to explain, she'd realize it was all a big misunderstanding. It wasn't. He was stalking her for years. When she didn't take the news of his infatuation as well as he was hoping, his anger went above what anyone could have predicted."

I try to think of a comeback, but I'm at a loss for words. I did go with Richard of my own free will. It may have been under the guise of protecting my sister, but it doesn't change the facts. If things didn't work out the way they did, my outcome could have been as horrendous as Sylvia's.

While Marcus shuts down his computer, I sweep my hand across my cheeks, removing a handful of tears my eyes couldn't hold in. Once my cheeks are dry, Marcus's hand catches my wrist, plucks me from my seat, then takes my place. I nuzzle my head into his broad chest so I can listen to his heart thumping, hoping it will help to ease my twisting stomach. It's so knotted up I'm afraid my lunch is about to see daylight.

No—make that *is* going to see daylight.

Diving off Marcus's lap, I sprint into the hallway. I only just make it into the washroom at the side of the living room before my lunch exits my body in the ghastliest way.

19

When the ear-piercing shriek of the microphone roars through my ears for the third time the past two minutes, I give up on my endeavor to become a rock star and exit the recording booth tucked into the corner of Marcus's home studio.

"Did you get anything decent?" I ask Marcus, who is sitting behind a massive deck of instruments and gadgets that are too technical to explain.

His face screws up. "I wouldn't quit your day job," he teases.

Well, I assume he is teasing, but his low monotone makes it hard for me to 100% testify to that.

"Too late," I reply with a waggle of my brows.

A girly giggle topples from my mouth when Marcus seizes my wrists and pulls me to sit on his lap. My laughter switches to a moan when my backside rubs his impressive groin. With my mood carefree, I grind against his crotch unashamedly. When his cock twitches from my playfulness, I do it again, and again, and again until his animalistic growl rumbles through my shuddering chest.

My internal chuckles come to an immediate halt when Marcus mutters, "Does your goading need another session in my playroom?"

I freeze as a spark of lust combusts in my sex. I'm not freezing in fear, I'm freezing with excitement. After coasting over our little bump Monday morning, things have been surprisingly smooth for Marcus and me the past four days. Our routine hasn't altered much from the one we had in Florida, except this time, we're doing it alone.

I'll be honest, I miss having Abel as a sparring partner against Marcus, but it's also nice having Marcus all to myself. I don't have to worry about sashaying past his office door stark naked when he is on conference calls with his record label, or being busted serving him breakfast with a few essential elements of my body parts on the menu. I also haven't had to keep my heightened excitement on the down low for the fear someone will hear my lusty screams. It has been perfect, better than I could have ever predicted.

The only thing I've had to worry about is reminding Marcus I am not Sylvia Broadbent from Unit 23, W. 34th Street. I am here, I am fine, and I'm not fighting for my life in the Intensive Care Unit.

You'd think that part of my obligations would be an easy fix, but it hasn't been. Marcus is in the entertainment industry, but he will never be an actor, as his acting skills are weak. Don't get me wrong, he plays the part of a Dom very well during our scenes in his playroom, but it's when he lets go of his need for control do I discover a very caring and intelligent man hidden beneath his hard outer shell.

Sylvia's incident rocked his core more than he'd care to admit. He tries to say he isn't comparing our two predicaments, but I know he is. Not just because every time he gets an update on Sylvia's condition his mood swings toward the negative, but because when he spots the very faint scar on my top lip, the pain in his eyes almost becomes too much for me to bear. Although his attentiveness is something I've always dreamed of, I'd give anything to wash the pain from his eyes permanently.

"What are you working on?" I ask Marcus, trying to keep my focus away from my sappy thoughts that will have us christening his recording studio for the third time this week.

Although I'd never deny Marcus, for the past four days, I've been striving to keep our interactions even between sexual contact and intellectual conversations. Let me tell you, it's been a very tiresome few days. Don't misinterpret my admission, Marcus is an extremely intelligent man who has no qualms participating in a range of conversations. It's me who has the problem. Just hearing him speak hits every one of my hot buttons. My attraction to him is so intense, I doubt a hundred years could dampen it.

Marcus grins a smile I've only seen on a handful of occasions. "It's a joint project that has just come to light."

"Joint? As in for you and me? Or..." I leave my sentence open for him to finalize.

"For you and me," he fills in, still smiling.

"Okay...sounds good. Although I'm not sure you should trust me with anything in this room. Computers and I aren't friends," I reply, waving my hand around his extravagant home studio.

Marcus arches his brow. "So how have you been submitting your freelance articles if you're not accustomed to computers?" he queries, knowing all too well what my answer is as he's watched me type them up on his laptop the past week.

I send out a feeler email to a few publishing houses I was offered contracts with when I finished my internship at Global Ten. Surprisingly, a handful remembered my work before I was seconded to the dungeon. After an impromptu phone interview, two have offered to screen any stories I write. If they print my story, I get paid a freelance retainer fee. Although it's a very casual employment arrangement, I'd rather have a laidback approach than none at all.

I answer Marcus's question with a shrug of my shoulders. "I just magically teleport them my articles."

Marcus tries to hold in his smile. He miserably fails. My dorky metaphors and goading nature are growing on him—*slowly*.

"So what's this joint project?" I ask, excitement in my tone.

Marcus slouches deeper into his chair, so he has an unencumbered view of my face. "What are your thoughts on writing an all-exclusive feature on an integral member of the number one band in the world?"

His showy voice gives away which band he is referring to, but I act stupid, loving his carefree attitude too much to dampen it. "Oh my god! Am I interviewing Twisted Perfection?" I falsely gush. I am a fan of Twisted Perfection's music, but none of their members hold a torch to the man in front of me.

Marcus snarls, bearing teeth, apparently not appreciating my mention of Rise Up's biggest competition. Although Rise up has had a clean sweep at nearly every award ceremony in the country the past four years, Twisted Perception gave them a run for their money this year. Rise Up may have walked away with Album of the Year at the Grammys, but rumors were it was by the skin of their teeth. Not in my books—just those pesky reporters who love filling the glossy pages of magazines with loosely based factual stories. Although, from Marcus's reaction, I'm beginning to wonder if some of the rumors of a rift between the two world-dominating rivals are true.

A hiss of air escapes Marcus's stern-snapped mouth when I swivel in my seat to face him front-on. My train of thought is lost when I feel his cock thickening beneath me. From the spark of dominance growing in his eyes, it's clear I'm not the only who has noticed his body's reaction to my accidental grind up. I smile, loving that he is a defenseless as me when it comes to this crazy lust-filled relationship we have begun.

"I don't think we should mix business with pleasure, Marcus. That will just make things complicated," I eventually murmur, my words jittery since they were forced through the lust curled around my throat.

Marcus tucks a strand of my hair behind my ear. "You don't think it's a little too late for that?" he mutters. His gravelly voice sends shockwaves straight to my pussy. "Things are already complicated."

He trails his finger down my cheek, along my collarbone, and across my shoulder blade, knocking the sleeve of my bulky sweater off my shoulder in the process.

When his tongue delves out to replenish his top lip, my insides clench. "This would be a different type of complicated." My shuddering voice gives away my excitement. "I don't write stories based on half-truths, Marcus. I write *exactly* what I see."

"And what are you seeing?" Marcus asks, standing from his chair, taking me with him.

Hundreds of buttons light up on the studio panels when he places me down on them. I try to hold my weight off the technical-looking equipment, but my efforts are fruitless when Marcus curls my legs around his waist and drags my backside closer to him. Not giving me the chance to object—*not that I was going to*—he whips my one-shoulder knitted sweater over my head. My hair falls halfway down my back in a tussle of curls when he tugs at the elastic keeping my unruly locks at bay.

"I see a man who doesn't play fair," I mumble incoherently when he places a peppering of butterfly kisses on my exposed neck. "Who knows he has me at a disadvantage and exploits it at every possibility."

Marcus smiles against my neck. "I see a beautiful woman who can't take an opportunity presented to her because she is too stubborn to acknowledge it was her talent that secured it."

"My talent?" I murmur, my words barely audible when his hand slips under my cami to cup my aching-with-desire breast. Even though there is satin material between his hand and my breast, his touch scorches my skin as if there isn't. "How would you know what writing talent I have?"

My bottom lip begrudgingly drops into a pout when Marcus pulls away from my neck. If I knew my question would cause him to retreat from lavishing me with his affections, I wouldn't have asked it.

With his sentiment-filled eyes arrested on mine, he secures his wallet out of the back of his trousers. My brows furrow when he pulls out a folded-up scrap of newspaper. Suddenly, my heart lurches into my throat. *I really hope that isn't the story I printed on Noah being in rehab.*

After carefully opening the short newspaper article, Marcus recites, "Phillis Brooks will always be remembered as a loving mother, grandmother, and pillar of the community. After retirement from the textile industry in 1990, her greatest passion merged with helping others. With four grown children, and grandchildren by the dozens, her kitchen was never closed, much like her heart. Phillis's tireless charity efforts ensure her memory will forever live on in those fortunate enough to have known her. A service will be held for Phillis at St. Augustine Memorial Chapel on August 2nd at 3 PM. If you wish, donations may be made to the Augustine Shelter Foundation, or a charity of your choice in lieu of flowers—"

"It's sad to know my story is over, but when I look back, I see more than a lifetime of memories," I quote, reciting part of an obituary I wrote nearly six months ago.

I stare at Marcus, dumbfounded and confused. Why would he carry around the obituary of little old lady who lived in some random town in Florida? It doesn't make any sense. Unless...

My breath snags in my throat when reality dawns. "Phillis was your grandmother?"

"Yes," Marcus replies, his lips curling into an apprehensive smile. "What you wrote was true. By the time she passed, she had lived the equivalent of two lives."

"I'm sorry for your loss," I sympathize. "From the little dossier I was given, she seemed like a wonderful lady."

"She was," Marcus confirms, "but no one was interested in that when she passed. Every one of her obituaries failed to mention her charity work or other family members. All they cited was her association with me—all but yours. You kept it about her—exactly as I had requested."

Nothing against the other journalists, but if that's true, it's terrible. I'm sure Phillis was incredibly proud of her grandson, but the effort she put into numerous charities the last nineteen years of her life was mammoth. She raised millions of dollars for a homeless shelter in her final two years with nothing but hard work, and I'm sure plenty of tears, so wouldn't that deserve a worthy mention in her final chapter?

After storing the cut-out of Phillis's obituary back in his wallet, Marcus locks his eyes with mine. Tears prick in my eyes when he discloses, "The verse you wrote at the end of her obituary is scripted on her headstone."

"It is?" My two short words are incapable of concealing the barrage of emotions slamming into me.

Marcus tugs a handkerchief out of his trouser pocket and hands it to me before nodding. Lucky, as I need it to catch a handful of tears rolling down my cheeks.

After waiting for me to mop up my tears, Marcus pinches my chin and lifts my head. "Is that proof enough I believe in your writing ability?"

Not wanting him to hear my snivel, I merely nod. "But I still don't think this is a good idea, Marcus. I've just stepped away from one investigation involving you, so it wouldn't be wise to dive straight into another."

The crackling of my voice displays my wariness. Although I'd never share Marcus's secret with anyone, even writing a pop-culture piece on the band's upcoming tour could stir trouble. Mr. Carson accepted my resignation without requesting a three-page dossier on the reason behind my sudden exodus from his company, but I don't see Delilah being so accommodating. Skeptical controversy will rise the instant my name shifts from the hidden depths of obituaries to a front-page exclusive on a world-dominating group.

My focus reverts to Marcus when he asks, "What if I said the hard-hitting story wasn't about me?"

My cheeks protest about the sudden incline of my smile. "Nothing against your band members, but I doubt they have any hard-hitting news left to share. Unlike you, their entire lives have been played out in the public eye. Anything I write about them will be old news before the article hits the printers."

My smile grows when Marcus doesn't attempt to negate my claims. *There is no use denying the truth.*

Marcus arches his brow and says, "Off the record?"

My interests are piqued. Accepting the hand he is holding out, I reply, "Off the record."

We've barely shaken hands when he blurts out, "Noah and Emily are having a baby in April. A son."

"What?!" I cringe when my ear-piercing squeal bounces off the soundproof walls and shrills into my ears. *Soundproof, my ass.* "I saw Emily last month, she didn't even have a bump."

I straighten my spine as memories of our one and only meeting filters into my mind. Understandably, I was dazed that night. I just discovered the man I had been conversing with online wasn't just a BDSM club owner and member of a world-famous rock group, but I'd also endured one of the most earth-shattering climaxes I've ever experienced in my life after discovering he was the man I'd been searching for the past four years, so I guess lack of attention could be excused.

I lift my baffled eyes to Marcus. "Why would they want me to write this story? Emily is their publicist, shouldn't she share their news?"

Marcus shrugs. "We figured Rise Up negatively contributed to your career, so why not let the band positively impact it as well?"

My heart warms over his admission, but I didn't tell him the story of my demise last week for career advancement. I wanted to share with him the many little connections we have. When you sit down and evaluate all our near misses, it's like the universe was aligning for us to meet, but life events we never saw coming kept shifting the timeline. Although I'd forgo years of heartache, part of me thinks we didn't meet until now as it wasn't the right time for us earlier. Neither Marcus or I would be the people we are today if we hadn't experienced the life we have.

"Rise Up didn't contribute to my fall from grace, Marcus," I admit, my pitch laced with unwarranted snark. "It was your record company's publicist."

I scrunch up my nose, hating that I'm still placing all the blame for my fall from grace on Rise Up's old publicist. Some of the culpability does belong to me. I did sign off for the articles to be printed before researching to ensure the stories were true. Although I could say my job wasn't a research assistant, with each article having my name associated with it, I should have made sure the stories were factually based—or at least partially for the glossy magazines.

"What happened to your old publicist?" I ask, failing to hide my snarl.

Although I know I shouldn't harbor ill feelings for Rise Up's ex-publicist, I'm still hoping her fall from grace was as unpleasant as mine.

A massive line of wrinkles indent Marcus's usually smooth forehead. He looks the most confused I've ever seen him. After running his hand over his clipped afro, he locks his eyes with mine. "I thought you knew, that's why I didn't say anything."

"Knew what?" I ask, confused as ever.

Marcus's throat works hard to swallow before he says, "Rise Up's old publicist was Delilah Winterbottom. Your—"

"My old boss?" I fill in, my tone shocked as hell.

Holy hell. How did I not know this?

My wide eyes dance between Marcus's when he nods.

"Is that why she is so infatuated with the Chains story? Does she know your secret?"

"No," Marcus replies, shaking his head. "I wasn't part of the lifestyle back then. I joined after she was fired by Destiny Records."

I cross my arms over my chest to ward off the iciness of his words. I watch him in silence. Although I'm tempted to prompt him for more info on his immersion in the BDSM community, I'll never push him to share anything about his personal life he isn't willing to give. I pried enough into his life the two weeks following our initial meeting at Chains, I won't invade his privacy any more than I already have.

Besides, I can barely wrap my head around another bizarre connection we have, much less the fact the lady who was the catalyst of most of my problems the past three years is partially to blame for my first fall from grace. Delilah irked me from the moment we met, now I know why.

A touch of a smile graces my lips when Marcus shrugs off his jacket and wraps it around my shoulders. Even though my sweater is mere inches from me, I accept his kind gesture, preferring to be wrapped up in his warmth.

"Do you remember the uproar four years ago when Rise Up canceled a whole heap of concerts on the West Coast?" Marcus asks as he sits in the chair in front of me.

As he snags my wrist and pulls me into his lap, I nod.

"We did that because a friend of the band passed away."

I gasp in a shocked breath. Four years ago was when the rumors of the band dismantling first surfaced. A death of a friend was never reported.

The heaviness on my chest lightens when a ghost of a smile cracks onto Marcus's lips. "You would have liked Melanie, she had a lot of similarities to Lexi. Loud. Opinionated. *Beautiful.*" He murmurs his last word.

"What happened to her?" I keep my tone low, hoping he won't see my desire to know him better as being intrusive.

"She had acute lymphoblastic leukemia," Marcus answers, his tone gruff.

"That what Kylie had, wasn't it?" I ask, recalling an article written on Slater's wife undergoing IVF because of complications associated with ALL.

Marcus nods. "Yes. Twice."

I remain quiet, too shocked to articulate words to express my condolences that Kylie had to go through that twice. Leukemia is a horrible disease no one should be subjected to once in their lifetime, much less twice.

"That's how Melanie and Kylie met, they were participants in an online ALL support group." Marcus adjusts my position, so I am facing him. His body reacts with the same amount of intensity it did the first time, but the strong sentiment in the air keeps my mind on track.

"Melanie was the one who introduced me to BDSM," he discloses, his tone low.

"Oh..." I try to think of something better to say, but I can't. My mind is spiraling with morbid jealousy to form a rational thought, let alone articulate it.

"She was the only person who saw my need for control and discipline for what it was," Marcus continues, misconstruing my silence as eagerness for him to continuing sharing. Although I'm grateful he is opening up to me, half of me wishes he would stop. My throat is closed up tightly, strangled by merciless jealousy curled around my neck.

"During a spate of concerts near her hometown, Melanie introduced me to some people in the community."

I swallow harshly, fighting hard to eradicate the bitter taste in the back of my throat.

"After one concert, we attended a club similar to Chains."

"Please stop," I breathe out heavily. "I don't want to hear any more."

I feel terrible for cutting him off, but I can't hear details of him and another woman. Just the thought of him with anyone but me feels like it's tearing my heart straight out of my chest. I know it's insane to think he wasn't with anyone before me—I have resounding proof he was—but that doesn't mean I want to hear all the ghastly details. Some things are better off being left unsaid.

I clear the nerves from my voice before saying, "I want to know everything about you, Marcus, but I don't want to know this." If the devastation in my tone isn't convincing enough I've that stepped out of my comfort zone, the expression on my face is a sure-fire indication.

When Marcus cups my quivering jaw in his hand, my eyelashes flutter excessively as I battle to hold back my tears. It's a pointless effort when he says, "Nothing happened between Melanie and me." His brows furrow as he shakes his head. "Well, we kissed, once, but that was Melanie's last stance of defiance. She knew at that stage she only had days left." His last sentence is so quiet, I'm not sure he wanted me to hear it.

"Was she too bratty for you?" I force out through the solid lump in my throat. I am hoping a little bit of playfulness will ease the tension in the air.

Thankfully, it does.

"Melanie would have been the very epitome of a brat," Marcus replies, chuckling. "If she were a submissive."

My eyes rocket to Marcus, certain I didn't hear him right. The curt nod of his head strengthens the honesty his eyes are relaying.

"Melanie was a Domme?" I ask, shock in my tone.

Marcus nods. "Not fully. She didn't immerse into the lifestyle as much as I have the past four years. She was just dabbling in it, more for recreation and fun than anything."

Confusion bombards me. "Then why did she introduce you to the lifestyle?" My words stop to make way for a long, exasperated exhale when reality dawns. "She wanted you to be her sub?!" I don't know why I am smiling like an idiot, but Melanie must have been one hell of a woman if she thought she could make a man like Marcus kneel.

Giggles shudder my frame when Marcus nods. "She misread my need for control and discipline as if I needed to be controlled and disciplined."

"Smart woman," I mutter under my breath.

Marcus angles his head to the side and arches his brow. I remain quiet, acting like I didn't say anything. With a roll of his eyes, he draws me back to his chest. I adjust my position so I can listen to the thud of his heart, loving how it thumps in the same rhythm as mine.

I don't know how much time passes before I pop my head off Marcus's chest. It's long enough my jealousy has entirely subsided, but not long enough for me to forget our conversation. "If Melanie didn't get sick, do you think you would have ever become her sub?"

Marcus shakes his head. “Melanie was beautiful, funny...” His smile enlarges. “... and crazy as hell. But there has only ever been one woman I’ll kneel for.” He stares straight into my eyes, letting them finish the remainder of his sentence.

The back of his fingers trace the invisible bruise on my cheek only he can see. "Is that what you want, Cleo? My kneeling before you?"

“No,” I reply without delay. “Loving someone is accepting them for who they were, who they are, and who they will become. It isn’t about changing them.”

My eyes drop to Marcus’s chest, panicked I’ve disclosed my feelings too early. When he places his hand under my chin to lift my head, I peer past his shoulder for a few moments, taking some time to gather my bases before drifting my eyes to his.

"Every action has a reaction, every word has a meaning, and every reason has a purpose. Just like every soul has a mate. Don't hide your feelings as though you're afraid of the repercussions, Cleo, because sometimes it's the unspoken words that cause the most harm."

20

"Are you ready, Cleo?"

Leveling my breathing to calm my excitement, my eyelids flutter against the satin material draped over them. I angle my head in the direction Marcus's voice came from before slowly answering, "Yes, Master Chains."

The shuddering of my voice gives away my heightened state. After our dinner on the balcony of the master suite was interrupted by a sprinkling of rain, we decided to have our dessert inside—in the one room that causes my insides to jitter with an equal amount of euphoria and fear. *Master Chains' Playroom.*

I am bound and blindfolded over a spanking bench similar to the one Marcus had made for me, but this one is constructed from metal instead of wood. The soft leather cushioning on the middle bar is sitting just above my aching core, and my hands and legs are secured tightly on the four little nooks. My position simulates being on my hands and knees, but I'm at least three feet off the floor. My back is level like a table, and my ass is thrust high into the air. With Marcus's intention of using my body as his dessert platter, my hair has been braided to the side to keep it away from the sticky supplies we arrived with. The spanking bench is the perfect height for Marcus to access every inch of my body.

My ears prick when Marcus asks, "What's your safe word, Cleo?"

I pant with anticipation, my mind spiraling with endless possibilities. For the past two weeks, he has only prompted me for my safe word when we are stepping outside of my comfort zone.

"Pineapple,"

"Repeat it." he commands, his clipped demand rolling through me like liquid ecstasy.

Every muscle in my body tightens with eagerness as I mutter, "Pineapple."

"Good girl," Marcus praises, his tone alone enough to tell me I'm in the presence of Master Chains. I ate dinner with Marcus. Now I get to have dessert with Master Chains. *Aren't I lucky?*

"We are going to try a few things we've been discussing the past week. If anything becomes too concerning for you, say your safe word," Marcus directs me.

I nod, advising I understand. I swear, my insides are shaking with so much excitement, I'm already on the verge of combusting.

"You're free to use your safe word at any time, Cleo, but do not use it unwisely. Do you understand?"

"Yes, Master Chains."

He groans, appreciating my eagerness to please him.

A small stretch of silence crosses between us. It enhances the crazy sexual tension firing the air with heat. Without my eyesight, my other senses pick up their slack. My hearing is super sensitive as I carefully listen to each subtle move Marcus makes, and my sense of smell is so amplified, I can taste the almond syrup drizzled over the cherries sitting in a bowl on my right.

I exhale sharply when hot, sticky goop unexpectedly trickles down my spine.

Drip.

Drip.

Drip.

Until the final drop slithers down the crevice of my erotically staged backside. The liquid pools around my puckered hole when Marcus stops it from running into my aching sex with his index finger. Excitement mists my skin with a fine layer of sweat when he rubs the sticky liquid into the sensitive skin between my ass and my pulsating sex. A stream of wicked thoughts bombard me as I recall the many things we've discussed the past week. The most dominant—my desire to experience anal play.

Although I'm apprehensive about anything penetrating an area that has been previously untouched, I'd be lying if I said I wasn't excited by the prospect. Nothing Marcus has done to me in this playroom has been unpleasant, so I do not doubt that logic will continue when we tiptoe into the unchartered waters of anal play.

Some of my wicked thoughts come true when the rough bumps of Marcus's callused finger follow the trail of sweet goodness layered on my skin. He weaves his finger past my collarbone, over the swell of my hips and along the two dimples in my lower back before gliding past an area clenched with both excitement and unease, dipping ever so slightly into the virginal hole before it continues on its journey.

"Not yet," Marcus murmurs when a disappointed huff leaves my lips before I have the chance to shut it down. "If I don't prep you, the experience won't be pleasant."

My disappointed moan switches to an excited pant when Marcus's tongue follows the same pattern his finger just took, although at a slower pace this time around. Goosebumps form in its wake as he weaves his tongue over my shoulder blade and down the bumps of my spine. When it slides between the globes of my ass, my thighs attempt to hug the metal bar braced between my legs. Unfortunately, the restraints on my ankles stop me from fully clenching my thighs together.

"Relax, Cleo" Marcus instructs, his warm breath bouncing off my goose-bump-riddled skin.

I loosen my clamped thighs at the exact moment his tongue flicks my creased hole with three quick-fired hits. I meow a throaty purr, surprised by the sheer wickedness of his briefest touch. Although his tongue soon continues tracking the almond oil drizzled on my skin, the wildfire in my stomach has reached a point it can't be constrained. It's the touch of naughtiness to our exchange making it so thrilling. You know the ones I'm talking about? Where you know you shouldn't be doing something, but you just can't help but try it. That's the best way of describing my desire to try anal play.

"I'll start small and build you up, Cleo," Marcus updates.

As his tongue gathers the sweet goodness dripping between my legs, his thumb rolls in a circular motion around my puckered hole. For every stroke his tongue makes to my soaked sex, the more pressure he places on my untouched orifice.

My wrists fight against the restraints curled around them when he sucks my clit into his mouth at the same time his thumb dips into my ass. He continues thrusting forward until the entirety of his thumb is inside me.

"Oh..." I garble, unsure if it's a moan of pleasure or pain. I think it's a bit of both.

"Don't fight the sensation," Marcus murmurs, his deep voice vibrating against the folds of my pussy. "Take in how it feels. Enjoy knowing I now possess *all* of you." My thigh muscles loosen just from the way he growls out his last sentence.

As Marcus devours my pussy with long strokes of his tongue and playful nibs of his teeth, his thumb works in and out of my no-longer-virginal hole. The sensation... I don't know how to describe it. It should feel wrong, but it feels oh-so-good.

The coils continue tightening, sweeping a cluster of excitement from my dripping core to my erratically panting chest. It grows and grows and grows until the need to climax overwhelms me. Sensing my impending orgasm, the pace of Marcus's thrusts increase, closely followed by his index finger slipping into my dripping core. From the way his thumb and finger move in sync, I wouldn't be surprised to discover they are attached to the same hand. Their rhythm is perfect, a mind-hazing combination of speed, pressure, and naughtiness.

When Marcus grips my hip to calm my dangerous rocking that could send the spanking table toppling over, my unasked question is answered. My eyes roll into the back of my head as the tingles dancing in my sex multiply. I moan huskily, fighting not to charge straight for the finish line. I want to enjoy the feeling—to relish it.

I've learned many exciting things the past few weeks, but one of the more significant is delayed gratification isn't a myth. The tension, the buildup, the absorbing every thrust, bite and lash, it equals nothing less than brilliance. The climaxes I have after letting them build and simmer time and time again are out this world. Better than I would have ever believed.

"Good girl," Marcus praises, noticing my effort to stave off my climax.

If I could control my body with one tenth of his control, I wouldn't have to put in so much effort, but considering the chances of that happening is practically zilch, I continue to grit my teeth and slowly ride the swell of the ocean instead of catching the first wave to shore like my body is demanding.

My orgasm climbs to the summit before trekking back down to the valley another three times before the sensation becomes more than I can bear. Sweat is misting every inch of my skin, and my pussy is so wet, evidence of my arousal coats the insides of my thighs.

"Please, Master Chains."

Marcus doesn't answer my voiced plea. He doesn't need to. The withdrawal of his contact is the only sign I need to hear his rejection.

Through my pulse roaring in my ears, I hear his bare feet pad across the wooden floor. I count his steps. *One, two, three, four, five.* Since he walked five paces to my left, I know he is standing in front of his chest of goodies positioned under the drawers where his D/s contracts are stored. If he'd walked eight paces, he would have reached the wall of floggers, whips, and canes. I don't want it to, but a dash of disappointment dampens my eagerness. Although the idea of being hit with a cane frightens me, I have fond memories of the times we've used the cat o' nine tales and a riding crop.

I return my focus to listening to every movement Marcus makes when the sound of the wooden chest dropping shut booms through my ears. He paces back to me, his steps quicker than the ones he used earlier.

"Normally, I reserve spankings for discipline, but since you associate spankings with both pleasure and discipline, I'm going to spank you for pleasure today, Cleo," Marcus instructs, his usually smooth voice gravelly with lust. "I'll spank you five times. On the fifth spanking, you can come. Do you understand?"

"Yes, Master Chains," I reply, my excitement unmissable. "On the fifth spank, I can come."

The air thickens with heady yearning when Marcus adjusts my position so I am erotically staged in front of him. The air-conditioning vent above my head gives cooling relief to my heated core when he thrusts my ass higher into the air. Lust hangs so densely in the air, I can taste it on the tip of my tongue. It has a rich, tangy flavor, much like Marcus's ravishing chocolate skin.

My excitement reaches fever pitch when a faint buzzing noise trickles into my ears. It's similar to the way a cell phone vibrates on a desk when in silent mode, although it's nowhere near as loud. The shuddering of my legs ramps up a gear when a cold, latex material prods the puckered hole of my rear.

"Relax, Cleo," Marcus demands as he swivels the foreign object around my clenched hole.

I lick my dry lips before doing as instructed.

"Good girl," Marcus praises as he slowly inches the unknown article inside me.

Although the device matches the width of Marcus's thumb, its vibrating sensation is so strong, it hurdles my orgasm to within an inch of the finish line. I grit my teeth and loosen the clench of my ass globes even more so Marcus can slip the pulsating instrument deeper inside me. I'll be honest, it's another unexplainably odd feeling. It's peculiar but erotically delicious at the same time.

Once the small latex toy is positioned in place, Marcus moves to stand at my side. How do I know this? I can feel the heat of his heavy flesh on my right thigh. He is thick, jutted and extended halfway up my thigh.

"Five spanks, Cleo," Marcus confirms, ensuring I remember his rules.

I've barely nodded my head when he inflicts his first slap. His hit is perfectly precise. The base of his palm smacks the vibrating plug stimulating my rear, where the tips of his fingers spank my engorged clit. My knees shudder as the crest of a wave rapidly builds in my core.

"One," Marcus says while soothing the sting heating my skin with a gentle rub of his palm.

I call out when he spanks me for a second time, loving the sensation activating every sensory outlet in my body. I've never felt something so perfect, so unreal, so out of this fucking world.

"Two." Marcus's grunts display he is enjoying this as much as I am.

My eyes pop open with his third hit. It was a little firmer than the first two. It enhances my excitement to a never-before-experienced level. My clit is throbbing with need, my breathing is ragged, and my body is heightened beyond reproach. I'm close to the edge, drunk on lust, incapable of nursing a single thought.

"Three. Say it with me, Cleo."

"Three," I mimic. I don't recognize my own voice. It's husky and raw, exposing the stranglehold of excitement blazing my veins.

"Four," Marcus growls through clenched teeth when he spanks me for a fourth time, hitting me in the exact same place his first three smacks landed. My ass clamps around the device stimulating me into an untamed, reckless mess. I'm panting so wildly, I'm practically growling like a feral animal.

"Last one," Marcus huffs, his words as breathless as my lungs.

I dig my nails into my palms in preparation for his next spank, knowing without a doubt it will be the most blinding of them all.

My intuition is proven without doubt.

A ferocious orgasm shreds through me hard and fast when Marcus spanks me for the fifth time. His slap is as perfectly placed as the four before it. My body pushes against the restraints tying me down so fiercely, I'm certain they are moments away from snapping. I quiver and shake while shouting my excitement in the lust-fueled environment without hesitation. My mind is shut down, completely oblivious to everything around me but the man dominating every morsel of my soul.

It takes numerous minutes for me to come down from orgasmic bliss.

Marcus never once leaves my side. He guides me through the blinding experience with the knowledge that displays he truly is a Master. After removing the vibrating contraption from my backside, he toys with the bud of my clit, allowing me to ride the intensity of climax with a gentler approach. He praises my willingness to try new things while explaining I'm not the only one caught off guard by the brilliance of our exchange. His words add to my excitement, extending my orgasm to a point of sheer exhaustion.

Once every orgasmic shudder hampering my body has been exhausted, I slump onto the bar designed to hold me off the ground. My body is lifeless, my mind, shut down. Marcus quickly works on removing the leather cuffs binding me to the spanking bench before gathering me in his arms and striding to the other side of the room. As he glides across the room, his pec muscles drag off the blindfold covering my eyes. It slips off my face to gather around my sweat-slicked neck by the time he is halfway across the room.

The softness of silk cools my overheated skin when Marcus lays me in the middle of his four-poster bed. I hear his feet padding across the wooden floor, but I'm too sexually sated to do something as simple as count his steps, much less move my head to see where he is going.

"Open up," Marcus croons, startling me as I didn't expect him to return so soon. "I need to refuel you for round two."

A smirk stretches across my weary face when he rubs a pitted cherry over my bone-dry lips. It's covered in almond oil, giving it a slippery feeling. It's also a swift reminder of what we were just doing.

Smiling a lusty grin, I accept the cherry, playfully nipping Marcus's fingertips in the process. When the rich flavor of cherries fill my taste buds, a muffled moan simpers through my lips. It's truly delicious, nearly as scrumptious as Marcus's mouth.

When I tell Marcus that, it ends his refueling mission in an instant.

Round two has officially begun.

21

"What do you think? Tuck it into a tight bun so it showcases those beautiful eyes and appallingly high cheekbones, or leave it draped down?"

I quirk my lips while peering at my reflection in the massive mirror in Marcus's master bathroom. Gerard, the hairdresser/makeup artist Anna hired to help me get ready for the gala tonight, is holding my wavy mess of hair off my face. There is an occasional stray tress floating down my exposed neck, but for the most part, my hair is slicked into a low, glossy ponytail that hangs halfway down my back.

Although I've never seen my hair so shiny and smooth, I'm still not convinced the slicked back look is for me. Excluding our session in the playroom last night, Marcus always requests for me to remove anything pinning my hair back, so I think he'd prefer for me to wear it down.

Before I can voice my opinion to Gerard, Marcus enters the bathroom. My pulse quickens as my eyes drink in his midnight black tuxedo pants, white pleated dress shirt, and satin vest. A black bowtie is hanging open on his impressive chest, mere inches from the two buttons of his shirt he hasn't yet fastened.

When his eyes lift from the cufflinks he is pinning to his cuffs, he catches my perverted gaze. The corners of his lips tug high when I give him a flirty wink. When the visual of his half-dressed tuxedo-covered body and lusty grin becomes too great for me to ignore, I return my eyes to Gerard. The expression on his face tells me he didn't miss my obvious ogle of Marcus's delicious body. His brow is cocked, and his lips are pursed.

"If only the rumors of him being gay were true," Gerard snickers, his gorgeous French accent on full display.

He tugs on my ponytail, announcing his annoyance with a hint of the playfulness he has shown all day. Gerard would be at least in his mid-fifties, if not sixties. His black and white peppered hair is short at the sides but has a big loop on the top. It kind of reminds me of Johnny Depp's hair in *Cry Baby*. His rich chocolate eyes are barely seen over the thick-rimmed glasses he wears halfway down his straight, prominent nose. He is handsome and an absolute hoot. I've laughed more the past three hours than I have the past three years of my life.

When Gerard first sauntered up the front entrance of Marcus's residence in a fitted black suit and an aura of authority, my initial guess was that he was Marcus's manager, Cormack. It was only when he circled me like a shark stalking its prey as his eyes absorbed my air-dried hair and makeup-free face did I realize who he was.

"Fabulous," was all he said before he looped his arm around mine and dragged me into the master bathroom where I have stayed for the past three hours being groomed, pampered and tortured.

Although Gerard hasn't said he is in the BDSM lifestyle, the wicked grin on his face when he waxed my legs has my suspicion piqued. That and the fact he called me Marcus's sub at the beginning of our exchange. Although I stuttered like a fifth grader, I handled his incorrect reference with more maturity than Lexi handled Anna's minor slip up.

My focus strays back to the present when Marcus inconspicuously slips a small purple device into his pocket. My insides clench as I recall in crystal clear detail how that tiny butt plug and Marcus's hand awarded me one of the most dramatic orgasms I've ever experienced.

I noticed the plug sitting next to the sink Marcus washed it in the instant Gerard and I entered the bathroom, but I was too mortified with embarrassment to do anything but stare. Thankfully, the truckload of makeup Gerard arrived with soon concealed the plug, which, in turn, snapped me out of my frozen haze.

I'm going to be brutally honest. I thought my session in the playroom last night would have ended the way it began—with a foreign object probing my backside. It didn't. Don't get me wrong, it concluded in the most brilliant way you could imagine, but I just assumed it would follow the path it started on.

It was only when washing the sticky almond oil off my skin did Marcus advise that we have to build up to anal sex. It isn't something you just dive straight into. Supposedly, that purple plug is one of many he has in his chest of goodies. They range in sizes and colors, going from the width of my pinkie finger to the size of Marcus's cock.

After ensuring I enjoyed my first taste of anal play, Marcus explained we would work up to the bigger, more exciting toys before he fully "claims" me as his own. Yes, that's the exact word he used. When he said that, excitement and fear quivered through me at the same time. It's not that I fear Marcus hurting me—I know that will never happen, and I can't wait to be claimed by him—but once I merge out of the haze of lust, part of me panics about how wickedly evil I am being. Like is it normal to be excited at the prospect of having anal sex with your boyfriend? If you had asked me that same question three short months ago, I would have said no. Now...I'd probably lecture you on how it's your body, and only you can decide what to do with it.

Gerard pinches my chin, drawing my attention back to him. "No gaga faces, the drool will ruin your lipstick."

He runs his eyes down the length of Marcus's body, his avid gaze way below what could be classed as acceptable. "Me, on the other hand, I can ogle all I like, I'm not wearing any lipstick."

My soft giggle secures Marcus's utmost devotion. Although he continues to have a quiet word with Anna, I can feel his eyes on me the entire time. I sit quietly staring at my reflection in the mirror as Gerard runs a wide comb through my hair, removing every kink of my curls. It feels foreign having my hair pulled back so tightly. My makeup is done in a similar palette I usually use, but my hairstyle completely alters my look. It's like an imposter is staring back at me. Thanks to my Latin heritage, I've always had voluptuous curls, so they are second nature to me. Taking away my curls is like switching Marcus's gorgeous chocolate skin to white—too odd to comprehend.

After he has finished his conversation with Anna, Marcus paces over to stand next to me. A sultry grin curls my lips high when he leans down and presses a peck to my hairline. The scent of his ravishing skin lingers into my nostrils as he lifts his eyes to Gerard.

"Leave Cleo's hair down," he instructs him, his tone ensuring there is no mistaking his request was not a suggestion.

Gerard scoffs. "You want to hide that face with a mop of curls?" he asks, incredulous. "That's ludicrous, Marcus. Oh...I thought I had taught you well." He drags his eyes down Marcus's body, his peeved expression growing for every second ticking by. "Clearly, I did not."

Ignoring Gerard's snippy comment, Marcus returns his eyes to me. "I don't want to hide Cleo's face. I want the first thing that captured my attention to frame the face that ultimately stole it."

Gerard stares at Marcus, blinking and confused. I'm not confused, I know what Marcus meant by his saying. My untamed hair was the first thing he saw when I fell into the elevator four years ago. It was also what I used to shelter my tear-stained face when he comforted me. That day was my worst day, but Marcus sees it as his best. It was the day we officially met. It was also the day he decided to become a Dom. To some, that may not seem like a big deal, but to a man who lives his life in the spotlight, it was a mammoth decision. One I supposedly helped him make.

"Fine!" Gerard huffs when Marcus's unforgiving glare becomes too much for him to bear.

He continues muttering in French as he picks out the hundred or so pins he used to contain my hair. The instant he tugs the elastic out of my hair, I shake my head, loosening the firm hold his brush made to my wavy locks. After raking my fingers through my hair, and twisting some strands around my finger, I lift my eyes to the mirror. *There's the Cleo I remember.* Uncontained. Natural. *A brat.*

Marcus must be in full agreement. Clasping his hand around mine, he plucks me from the beauty chair and makes a beeline for the door.

"Attendez! Nous sommes pas fini!" Gerard shouts in French, his voice as high as my excitement.

Marcus ignores him and continues hightailing it out of the room. His movements are so swift, air ruffles the satin dressing gown slipped around my naked body. The buds of my nipples harden more when Marcus notices the curve of my breast his hasty pace exposed. His gaze is so hot, a bead of sweat forms in the gulley of my breasts.

Marcus works his jaw side to side before lengthening his strides. "The quicker we go, the quicker we can return," he mutters to himself.

We continue moving through his property until we enter the guest bedroom positioned across from his old sub room. Anna's head shoots to the door when its creak gives away our arrival. She smiles as her eyes absorb my face and body.

"You look beautiful, Cleo."

"Thank you," I reply shyly, unaccustomed to getting compliments.

My breath catches in my throat when I spot a striking green dress hanging on a full-length mirror across the room. The daring V neckline that cinches into a rhinestone buckle in the middle adds the touch of sexiness I was aiming for, while the free-flowing skirt that leads into a modest train will hide the parts of my body I am less comfortable with—mainly my curvy hips and ass. It's a classically elegant dress you'd expect to see on A-list celebrities walking the red carpet. It's truly stunning.

"Are you ready to try it on?" Anna asks when she recognizes the excitement blazing my face.

I turn my eyes to Marcus, seeking his permission. When he nods, I follow Anna into a small dressing nook set up in the corner of the room. I'm so excited, my knees clang together with every step I take.

A tiny satin G-string the same shade as my dress sits on a small wooden chair in the corner of the nook. Wanting to maintain a small snippet of my modesty, I slip the panties up my quivering thighs before removing my dressing gown. Anna aids me into the dress before working on the tiny buttons running down my spine. I've always wondered what it feels like for a princess to get ready for the ball, I just always assumed I'd be in Anna's position when it happened.

After waiting for Anna to finish latching the back of my dress, I spin around to face her. The modest-sized train swishes on the floor as I pivot the best I can without treading on the gorgeous satin material.

The humble twinkle in Anna's eyes detonates into a blinding spark of admiration when I ask, "Does it look okay?" It feels like it fits perfectly, but with no mirror in the dressing nook, I can't be sure.

"Oh, Cleo, it suits you perfectly. You look beautiful." She clasps my hands in hers, the shudder of her arms rattles up mine. "No matter what anyone says tonight, don't ever forget that."

My brows stitch as confusion engulfs me. Before I can ask what she means by her statement, Anna gathers the train of my dress in her arms and nudges me into the main part of the room. All thoughts vanish from my mind when my eyes lock in on Marcus standing across from me. He has put on his tuxedo jacket and secured his bowtie around his neck. Even if I hadn't seen his tailor measure him earlier this week, I'd still know his tuxedo was handcrafted specifically for him. It showcases every magnificent detail of his body in panty-wetting detail. My god, he is... I can't think of just one word. Perfect. Gorgeous. Beautiful. *Mine.*

Marcus's eyes reveal a similar set of words passing through his mind as he absorbs my body with passionate devotion. They also disclose his every want, need and desire. Mercifully, I appear to be his drug of choice.

Marcus locks his eyes with Anna standing behind my shoulder. With a dip of his chin, he excuses her from the room. I mouth a silent thank you to Anna as she gathers her belongings from a dresser on my left before exiting the room.

After breathing out my tension, I drift my eyes back to Marcus. Remaining quiet, his eyes scan my face, memorizing every tiny pore. The palpable sexual friction between us builds with every silent second that ticks by.

Once he has studied every minute detail of my face, he locks his eyes with mine. "Come here."

My first step toward him is shaky, hampered by the throb hammering my yearning sex. The heat spreading through my veins like molten lava intensifies when Marcus pushes off his feet, meeting me stride for stride. The reckless hunger bristling between us is so dense, it glistens my body with a misting of sweat and sends my pulse racing.

The moisture pooling between my legs grows as Marcus places his hand on the curve of my back and guides me to the full-length mirror my dress was hanging on. Tears prick my eyes when I see my reflection for the first time. This may be conceited of me to say, but I truly look beautiful. I *feel* beautiful too.

After gathering my hair to one side, Marcus carefully removes my chain link necklace he gave me on my birthday. He places it onto a sleek glass table on his right before gathering an item out of a black velvet pouch. My lungs work hard to achieve adequate oxygen when he slips a beautiful diamond choker around my neck. The choker is made up of small brilliant cut diamonds that are four strands wide. A large circular pendant sits in the little groove of my neck, and four strings of diamonds erotically drape down the gulley of my breasts. The daring neckline of my dress showcases the stunning piece in the most brilliant light adding even more glamor to my risqué garment.

My breath snags when I notice a hidden chain link in the choker's pendant. It matches the one nestled in the O-ring of my dress. I can barely catch my breath when the cuff of Marcus's tuxedo jacket rises high enough to expose two chain links engraved on the silver cufflinks of his shirt.

I drag my teeth over my bottom lip when Marcus runs his hands down the trail of diamonds nestled between my breasts. Two of the strands are the perfect height, stopping right above the swell of my breasts, but the other two are too long, extending halfway down my stomach.

"Is that the design?" I ask, my voice relaying my sheer pleasure at our matching accessories.

Marcus smiles a grin that sets my pulse racing. "No. Let me fix it for you." He moves to stand in front of me.

Goosebumps form on the nape of my neck when he brushes my hair off my shoulders. His touch is only brief but intense enough to instigate a reckless yearning. I level my breathing to ward off my excitement, but it's a pointless endeavor when Marcus's hand slips beneath my gown. My nipples bud painfully when the heat of his hand cups my naked breast.

Smirking at my body's alert response to his touch, Marcus's other hand secures one of the strands of diamonds draped in front of my quivering stomach. My pupil widens when he lifts it high enough I can see the tiny clamp-like contraption attached to the end. The air in my lungs is brutally evicted when he secures the clamp to my throbbing-with-need nipple. Just like the clothespins weeks ago, a weird pulling sensation draws through my breasts, sparking a wild recklessness to engulf me.

Once he has the clamp on my left nipple adequately concealed by my dress, he devotes his attention to my right breast. He toys with my nipple until it's puckered as hard as its clamped counterpart. Happy it's budded firm enough to attach the clamp, he snags the second row of diamonds draped down my stomach and fastens it to my engorged nipple.

With both nipples erotically clamped, the wetness pooling between my legs becomes unmissable. I'm practically panting, my excitement too great to control.

Stepping two paces back, Marcus locks his eyes with mine and commands, "Walk."

Curious, I take a cautious step forward. "Oh...Jesus," I mumble when my wobbled stride causes the clamps to tug my nipples. It isn't a painful sensation, more an imitation of Marcus's teeth grazing over them.

Smiling at my flustered expression, Marcus takes another step backward before nudging his head for me to follow. Fighting the desire to squeeze my legs together from the dominance brewing in his eyes, I take a step forward, closely followed by another, and then another.

We continue our routine until we cross the expansive floor of his guest suite. I swear, I'm gasping so hard, anyone would think I just ran a marathon.

Stopping next to a studded suede chaise, Marcus sits down. A grin curls onto my lips when he flips off the lid of a shoe box at his side to expose a pair of gravity-defying black stiletto heels.

"Come."

He holds out the shoe for me like Prince Charming does for Cinderella. My cheeks protest about the sudden incline of my smile as I finalize the last few steps between us. Gathering my dress with one hand, I use my other to grip Marcus's shoulder for balance. Ignoring the way his muscles bunch from my meekest touch, I slip my foot into the tiny opening of my shoe.

Goosebumps follow the trail his hand makes when he runs it down my freshly-waxed leg to secure the latch at the side. After attacking the latch like a man intimate with women's shoes, he switches his attention to my other foot. A rush of excitement sparks in my core when he lingers a little longer on my left leg than my right. It starts so high, the back of his fingers brush the area begging for his utmost devotion. It's as smooth and as shimmering as my glossy legs.

"Did you wax your pussy, Cleo?" Marcus asks. His words are so deep, I feel the heat of his breath through the layer of silk and lace covering my yearning core.

I squeeze my legs together when his dark, commanding eyes lift to my face. His heavy-hooded gaze bores into mine, demanding an answer to his question. While grazing my teeth over my bottom lip, I shake my head. I'd like to articulate a more confident response, but his heated gaze has turned my brain to mush, and I can barely stand, much less speak.

"Good girl," he praises, gratefulness in his tone. "I don't know if I could have waited twenty-four-hours to tear you out of this dress."

His response awards me with a boost in confidence... and a dash of vulnerability. I'm not hesitant about him wanting to shred my dress off me. It's purely based on his extensive knowledge on the wait time after waxing. This is one of many sandbox moments I've had in our short relationship, because I'd rather stick my head in the sand than discover how he knows the stipulated wait time after waxing a sensitive area of a woman's body.

After attaching the clasp of my left shoe, Marcus stands from the chaise. With the height of my heel, we meet eye to eye. All apprehension plaguing my stomach with horrid unease calms when he runs the back of his fingers down my flushed cheek. His attentive touch continues when his hand slides down my collarbone before skimming past my clamped nipple.

"You look ravishing, Cleo," he compliments, his voice as hot as molten lava. "Ravishing enough to eat." He pauses as his eyes flick between the door and me. "If only we didn't have people waiting for us downstairs."

I angle my head to the side as I arch my brow. "People are waiting for us?"

"Yes. The band," he replies like it's common knowledge. It isn't. This is the first I am hearing of it.

"We always arrive at the gala together as a way of showing our support to Slater," Marcus explains to my baffled expression.

Warmth blooms across my chest. On paper, Marcus and Slater couldn't be any more opposites if they tried, but when you see them together, you realize they have an incredible bond. I just wish Marcus could see how much his bandmates love and respect him. Then he wouldn't need to continue leading a double life. He could be who he truly is—him!

22

Every step I take down the elaborate platform stairs of Marcus's entranceway adds another bead of sweat to my nape. It isn't capturing the devotion of one of the most prolific bands known to mankind that has me uncomfortably perspiring, it's the clamps on my nipples tugging with every shaky step I take. Marcus remains quiet, but I know he has perceived my body's response to the blissful tugs, because the corners of his lips curl higher with every harmonized step we take.

When we reach the white stretch limousine, Jenni throws her arms around my neck and hugs me tightly. "It's a perfect fit," she gushes as her eyes absorb the dress she hand-crafted for me.

"It is, thank you. You did such a wonderful job," I praise her.

Although my gushing response could be perceived as butt-kissing, I'm too grateful to care what others think. This dress took Jenni hours to create, but she refused a dime for her time. That notion alone deserves gushing praise.

I'm grateful for the chilly wind blowing in from the west when Emily follows Jenni's suit by greeting me with a friendly hug. Although her hold isn't overly firm, it's tight enough the clamps bounded to my nipples take notice of her embrace. Thankfully, the brisk evening temperatures award me with the perfect excuse as to why my nipples are so fiercely erect.

After greeting Kylie in a similar manner to Jenni and Emily, Noah gestures for us to enter the stretch limousine. When I clamber into the lavish confines, I notice all the girls are sitting on one side. Not wanting to imbalance the natural flow, I take the vacant spot between Jenni and Kylie. Once all the members of Rise Up enter the limo, we commence our hour trip into the city.

Even with the car's sumptuous interior fired with uncontainable excitement, nothing has dampened the sexual tension that brewed between Marcus and me before we entered the limo. It's so copious, every minute has the my insides clenching more. Although he's been talking to Slater the past thirty minutes, I've felt the heat of his gaze on me numerous times. His intensely provocative watch has even more command over my body than the clamps stimulating my nipples. It makes me needy and hot, and has me wishing we weren't surrounded by six of his closest friends.

"Sorry, what did you say?" I question when I realize my endeavor to secure Marcus's devotion caused me to miss the last half of Emily's sentence.

Emily, Jenni and Kylie's eyes brighten with amusement when they drink in my flushed cheeks and wide eyes. Thankfully, they don't seem upset at my lack of schmoozing ability. Actually, they appear to be enjoying every awkward second of it. The redness of Jenni's cheeks have remained stable the past thirty minutes, and Kylie and Emily's lips are always tugged high.

Spotting my suspicious glare, Kylie mutters, "We've all been there before."

"Been where?" I ask, trying to act clueless. That would be a whole lot easier to do if I couldn't feel the heat rising up my cheeks.

All three of them cozy in close, like they're about to share nationally guarded secrets.

"I bet you wish there was no one else in the limo but Marcus and you," Emily whispers, her voice laced with playfulness.

"Or you're hoping the hotel the fundraiser is being held at has vacant rooms readily available." The laughter in her words enhances the country twang of her voice.

"Or that the latch in the disabled bathroom in the ballroom has been fixed," Jenni states matter-of-factly.

Everyone's eyes snap to Jenni. Shock and disbelief are smeared all over their faces.

"What?" Jenni mumbles, her cheeks turning the color of beetroot. "I'm not the one who created the stupid rule we all have to travel everywhere together. At the last gala, I was six months pregnant and extremely horny."

Kylie laughs before nodding in agreement. "Normally, it is Slater hot on my tail. This time around, I swear, any time Penelope leaves the room, I'm tackling him to the ground." She drifts her eyes to Emily. "What about you, have you noticed any difference this time around?"

A touch of pink graces Emily's cheeks as her hand moves to caress her basically non-existent bump. I get hit with a severe bout of the warm fuzzies when Noah and Emily's eyes meet. It turns into a full-blown pandemic when Noah awards Emily's quickest glance with his famous dimpled grin.

Emily waits for Noah's attention to revert to Marcus before whispering, "My only craving this pregnancy has been pineapple. I eat it, cook it, drink it. Anything pineapple related, I'm on it."

Kylie's eyes sling to mine when I choke on my spit. With her brow arched high into her hairline, she rubs my back in a circular motion. "You okay?" she queries ever so quietly. "Aren't you a fan of pineapple?" The cheekiness in her reply has me double-guessing Slater's knowledge of Marcus's secret life.

I forcefully swallow the spit halfway down my windpipe before nodding.

"Was that a yes to hating pineapples or..." Kylie leaves her question hanging open. It replicates my dropped jaw to perfection.

After giggling at my slack-jawed expression, Kylie returns her attention to Emily. I follow in her footsteps.

Emily leans in even closer. Her voice is so quiet, my ears strain to hear her when she mutters, "That myth about pineapple making guys' cum taste sweeter... it isn't a myth."

Jenni and Kylie's boisterous giggles boom around the car's interior, startling the members of Rise Up. I laugh too, but it's more to hide my flushed cheeks from my earlier choking. I still can't believe out of all the cravings in the world, Emily had to pick pineapples.

The remainder of our trip to New York is spent in a similar fashion as the first thirty minutes. The girls continue sharing whispered secrets, while the guys watch on with curious smirks etched on their faces. I even share little tidbits of my relationship with Marcus. Well, I shouldn't really say little, considering most of their questions pertained to certain regions of Marcus's body. *There is nothing little about that.*

Honestly, even with me immaturely giggling like a high school student, the past hour and a half has been magical. When my parents and Tate died, I let a lot of people very important to me slip away. It wasn't their choice. The burden of blame solely belongs on my shoulders. But no matter how much my heart told me is was okay to move on from my grief, it just didn't feel right to be laughing and hanging out with my friends so soon after losing my family. Then before I knew it, years passed.

Jenni, Emily, and Kylie's close bond reminds me of the friendship I had with Luke, Chastity, and Michael. Back in our high school days, I didn't think anything could separate us. We were unstoppable. *I had no clue how cruel the world can truly be.*

Emily runs her hand down my arm, returning my focus to her. "Are you okay?"

"Yeah, I'm fine." I lie, loathing that I'm letting old memories taint new ones. "I'm just nervous. I've never attended an event like this before."

I can tell by the glint of empathy in Emily's eyes she knows I am lying, but thankfully, she isn't going to push me. "There is no reason to be nervous, Cleo. Unless you have a fondness for napping in public?"

As my brows stitch, I shake my head.

"Then you will be perfectly fine," she assures me.

Nervous butterflies take flight in my stomach five minutes later when the limousine pulls to the curb of an elegant, well-known hotel in mid-Manhattan. With the attendees of this event paying thousands of dollars a plate to attend, the media presence is at an all-time high.

When Hawke arrives at the side of the limousine, the paparazzi go into a frenzy. They push and shove against the barrier, vying for the prime position to capture one of the world's hottest commodities.

After securing their masks around their faces, Noah and Emily cautiously exit the limo. They stop in front of the sponsored backdrop to give the paparazzi plenty of time to capture their photo before continuing their trek down the long red carpet. The noise of the paparazzi cameras clicking is drowned out by the fans frantically screaming for the opportunity to meet their idol in the flesh. Just like I have witnessed time and time again the past five years, Noah places a kiss on Emily's cheek before he approaches the mass gathering of screaming fans to sign autographs and pose for pictures.

Once given the signal by Hawke, Jenni and Nick exit the limo next, closely followed by Slater and Kylie. My heart warms when I notice they all follow the same routine Noah and Emily undertook.

Before I know it, it's just Marcus and me left sitting in the limo.

"Are you sure you don't want to come with me?" Marcus asks, scooting across the bench to help me put on my large silver mask.

I wait for him to secure the satin straps before replying, "No, I'll be fine with Brodie." I nudge my head to the privacy partition I know Brodie is sitting behind. "It's safer this way."

Spotting a snip of anger forming in Marcus's eyes, I say, "Despite what the members of Chains believe, a mask isn't an adequate disguise. If we want to keep our relationship out of the public eye, we can't be seen in public together." I run my thumb over his slanted brow, smoothing the heavy groove settled between them. "No mask could ever hide these exquisite eyes from the world, and rightfully so, they shouldn't be hidden."

"I don't want to hide you either, Cleo," Marcus rebuts, his tone quickening in anger.

"I know that," I assure him, peering into his squinted eyes. "But this isn't just about me and you, it's about the community you built solely to protect. If your secret is exposed, Marcus, the members of Chains will most likely follow suit. Neither of us want that. So, if we have to spend an hour or two glancing at each other from across the room like star-struck strangers, that's what we will do."

When he runs his hand over his clipped afro, I know I'm breaking through his resistance. That's something he always does when he is contemplating. It's one of only a very small handful of flaws his has.

"Besides, wasn't the whole point of clamping my nipples some form of delayed gratification?" I ask, grateful my voice comes out with the hint of sexiness I was aiming for.

Marcus's eyes spark with dominance, proving my assumption is spot on.

"Then why don't we see tonight as the same thing? Two strangers denying the magnetizing allure firing the air with heat. Only to lose their battle when they share the same transport home." I stare straight into his eyes, my expression deadpan. "We do get our own limo home, don't we?"

His lips curve into a panty-moistening smirk as he nods.

"Alone?" I clarify, wanting to ensure I'm not setting myself up for disappointment.

I love the close bond Marcus has with his bandmates and their significant others, but I'm greedy when it comes to having private time with Marcus. If he didn't indicate he felt the same way, I'd try to diminish my neediness, but since he relishes our alone time as much as I do, I'll continue trying to ensure we have adequate one-on-one time.

When Marcus nods again, I say, "Get out."

He glares at me as his face lines with concealed humor.

"The quicker we get this over with, the quicker I can have my wicked way with you," I quote, using his own words against him.

Marcus throws his head back and laughs, easing the anxiety that I'm pushing his patience to a point he isn't willing to accept.

While twisting a strand of my hair around his finger, he mutters, "Lose your panties by the end of the night, Cleo. I don't want anything in my way when I discover if my theory is true."

"What theory?"

Hunger for friction on my skin burns through me like a wildfire when his hand drops from my hair to run over my budded nipple. The heat of his skin makes the coolness of the steel clamps more noticeable.

"That I can make you come with just a set of clamps and a smile."

From the way his seductive voice makes every muscle in my body clench, I have no doubt his theory will be proven accurate.

With a gleam in his eyes conveying his confidence, he slides out of the limo, straight into an onslaught of paparazzi.

23

My entrance with Brodie into the gala isn't as elaborate as Marcus's. Although this hotel is one of the top-ranking hotels in the world, it's clear the panel of judges who awarded it that title the past three years haven't seen this side of the building.

"Careful," Brodie says, nudging his head to a pile of goop on the sidewalk in front of me.

"What's that?" I ask, sidestepping the mess that looks like the concoction Lexi cooked for lunch two weeks ago.

Brodie shrugs his shoulders before leaning in for a closer inspection. When his nose screws up, I hold out my hand, advising I don't need an update on what it is.

The hissing sound of overworked boilers jingles into my ears when Brodie holds open a thick fire exit door for me. I scoot past his suit-covered body, observing a slight aroma of a manly aftershave lingering off his cropped beard.

"I thought the whole idea of aftershave was to put it on after you shave," I jest, waggling my brows.

My eyes narrow into thin slits when Brodie stands on the train of my dress, hindering my steps down the long, dingy corridor. When I spot the leering grin stretched across his face, I immaturely stick out my tongue. Although Brodie is several years older than Tate was when he died, they have very similar attributes.

We walk in silence down the hall side by side when Brodie discloses, "Lucy said it smelled nice."

"Who's Lucy?" I grill him as we enter a door that leads us into another long corridor. "Is she your *girlfriend*?"

Brodie looks like he is going to be ill at any moment. "No. She is my daughter."

I stop dead in my tracks. Not expecting my sudden stop, Brodie crashes into my back. “You have a daughter?” I ask, shock in my tone.

My heart ramps up a notch when Brodie smiles a breathtaking grin. While nodding, he digs his hand into the back pocket of his trousers to produce his wallet. Blood floods my heart when he pulls out a strip of photo booth photos. I don't know how old these pictures are, but in the photos Lucy looks to be around three or four. She has dirty blonde hair like Brodie, but her eyes are brown in color.

“She’s gorgeous.” I’m not being deceitful. She is the prettiest little girl I’ve ever seen.

Brodie nods in full agreement. "Thankfully, she is the spitting image of her mother."

“Do you have a photo of her?” I query before gritting my teeth, loathing my inability to ease people into my nosey-nancying.

Before Brodie can answer my intrusive question, his hand shoots up to his ear. He is wearing an earplug similar to the ones the Secret Service use when protecting the President.

"Tell him we're coming," Brodie comments to whomever is jabbering in his ear. "We're in hallway three... We stopped for two seconds for crying out loud! How far does he think I can get in two seconds?"

Shaking his head, he places his hand on the curve of my back and commences guiding me through the guts of the hotel, his pace quicker than our previous one.

“Seriously? ... Okay,” he snaps. His low tone causes a surge of worry to race down my spine.

Although he is extremely quiet, I don’t miss his snide remark about pedantic rock stars and their controlling behavior. Clearly, whoever is instructing him on the other end must be an employee of Marcus’s.

After weaving through numerous damp corridors and dingy rooms, we stop at a door marked “personnel.” The faint hum of a violin trickles through the crack of the door when Brodie carefully pries it open.

“If you have any concerns, I’ll be right outside this door,” Brodie informs me.

I peer at him, blinking and confused. “You’re not coming in with me?” Sheer panic echoes in my tone.

“No.” Brodie shakes his head. “I don’t belong in there.”

Not giving me the chance to voice the same concern, he barges me through the door. My unladylike tumble into the lavish room gains me the attention of an assembly of middle-aged ladies mingling at the side of an affluent-looking space—it also makes me acutely aware of the clamps holding my nipples hostage.

Smiling to ward off their inquisitive glances, I regain my footing, dip my chin in greeting, then make a beeline for a bar I spotted during my ungracious entrance.

The deeper I merge into the grand ballroom, the more my earlier hesitation surfaces. Thousands of people fill the space with a sea of black tuxedos and luxurious silks. Even if the attendees weren't dripping in priceless jewels, the wealth in the room would still be unmissable. It's so abundant, the scent of money filters through in the air.

Approximately half a dozen gala guests smile politely when I float by. The rest... let me just say, I thought Delilah's rueful glare was the worst I'd encounter in my lifetime. It isn't. If I didn't know the pleats of my dress concealed the instruments clamped to my nipples, I would have used that as an excuse for their wrathful stares. But since that isn't the case, I shrug off their prudent glares as them knowing I am not one of their kind. Obviously, the stench of the unfortunate is more potent than the scent of the rich.

Ignoring the furrowed brows and snarled glances, I continue for the bar. Halfway across the room, my steps slow as the hairs on my arms prickle with primitive awareness. As my eyes scan my location, my breathing shallows to a wheezy pant. Although I can't see Marcus, I know he is here. I can feel it deep in my bones.

It takes me scanning a sea of thousands before I spot him peering at me from across the room. Although he is standing several hundred feet from me, the heat of his gaze takes care of the goosebumps mottling my skin—it also soothes the nicks my ego is being hammered with.

I stand frozen, caught in the trance of a pair of beautifully exquisite green eyes. Noticing my frozen-in-lust stature, the curve of Marcus's lips tug higher, but his conversation with a group of men at the edge of the ballroom continues. Although they are wearing masks, I know the men he is speaking with aren't his bandmates. They all appear a decade or two older than Marcus... and a foot or two wider.

After giving Marcus a sneaky wave, I continue my endeavor to reach the bar. With his white-hot gaze provoking more excitement in my body than the restraints on my nipples, my mouth is parched. I knew our sexual attraction would be too great to ignore. There were thousands of people mingling around us, but when he glanced at me, it was if it was just him and me. Two souls destined to meet.

"Could I please grab a bottle of water?" I ask the smiling waiter manning the bar.

After dipping his chin in acknowledgment, the waiter snags a chilled bottle of water from under the bar, cracks the seal, then pours it into a wine flute. I lift the glass to my mouth, my scorching throat too dire to wait a moment longer.

Water sprays out of my mouth when the waiter says, "$13.99."

I frailly swallow the obviously gold-flecked water before connecting my eyes with the waiter. "$13.99?" I query, certain I've heard him wrong.

I didn't. His smile enlarges as he nods.

Ignoring the disdainful huff of the lady standing next to me, I dig my hand into my purse to fish out some loose notes— notes I had planned on putting toward my electric bill due next week.

"It better be made out of angel tears for that price," I grumble under my breath as I slide a twenty dollar bill to the waiter.

The waiter's hearty chuckle rumbles some of my irritation out of my body. His reaction is playful and sweet, and displays I'm not the only one out of my league tonight.

My eyes bounce between the waiter's dazzling blue eyes when he pushes my crumpled-up note back across the countertop. "It's on me."

"No, I can't let you do that," I reply, shaking my head. I lean in closer to the bar, ensuring the opulent-looking lady glaring at me won't hear me. "You could get fired."

The waiter's dark brow slants high. "It's a bottle of water they sell at my corner store for 50 cents a bottle. I'm sure they'll recoup the loss. Besides, staff drinks are on the house, and I'm mighty thirsty." He lifts the half-empty bottle to his mouth to take a hefty chug of the liquid inside.

Once all the water has been consumed, he crunches up the bottle, then throws it into a bin at his side, his aim perfect. When I remain hesitant to accept his generosity, he crosses his arms in front of his broad chest and gives me his best "don't mess with me look."

"Are you sure?" I ask quietly, hating that my stinginess could compromise his position.

When he nods without pause for consideration, I whisper, "Thank you."

"You're very welcome." His tone gives no indication he feels sorry for me. "Have fun tonight, just be wary of the tigers, some of them bite." He gestures his head to the mass of people congregating in the lavish ballroom.

I take a sip of my drink, hoping the wine flute will hide my roguish smirk. *I have a fondness for biters. Well, one man in particular.*

My efforts are utterly pointless. The instant my lips curl, the frisky spark brightening the waiter's eyes doubles. Thankfully, I am saved from answering the questions his eyes are relaying when another patron requests his service.

After gesturing to the snarling woman that he will be with her in a minute, he turns his eyes back to me. "It was a pleasure meeting you..." He leaves his question open for me to fill in.

"Cleo," I reply, offering him my hand to shake.

"Cleo," he repeats, testing my name out in a long, throaty purr as he accepts my friendly gesture. "Very nice."

"And you are?" I query when he doesn't offer an introduction.

He smiles so widely, a small set of dimples pop onto his tanned cheeks. "Andrew, but my friends call me Andy."

The patron dressed head to toe in Gucci snarls, annoyed our greeting is delaying her service.

"It was a pleasure to meet you, Andy," I say cordially.

We finalize our exchange with a smile before parting ways. Andy assists the scowling benefactor while I go in hunt for a place to sit and scope the area. Although I've always wanted to attend a ritzy party, my nerves aren't allowing me to enjoy the experience. This event would be nerve-wracking for the most confident person, much less participating in the festivities unaccompanied.

I find the perfect location at the end of the bar Andy is working. There is a vacant padded stool perched high enough I have a view of the entire ballroom.

The separation of groups is blatantly apparent from this vantage point. The band members and their wives are congregating near a small, intimate bar in the far left-hand corner, rich, middle-aged benefactors take up a majority of the dance floor, even though none of them are dancing, and Marcus and a vast group of women and men of ranging ages fill the remaining floor space.

The wealth of the people in attendance is also obvious. Designer dresses, flashy custom-made jewelry and the poignant aroma of affluence ensures I cannot mistake that this event is only for the extremely rich. It also displays how you can't categorize wealth into the one box. It's clear not everyone in this room is friendly. With the second most prominent smell being that of competition, I highly doubt many people in this room could state they are here solely to raise funds for an incredibly worthy cause.

Most are here to gloat.

24

The past hour has flowed precisely how I thought it would. Every sneaky glance, flirty wink, and prolonged stare shared between Marcus and me has increased the silly giddiness fluttering in my stomach. They have also added an edge of naughtiness to our exchange. *Like it could get any more risqué.*

"He is quite the specimen, isn't he" says a throaty female voice at my side, startling me enough I jump. Although I could have construed her statement as a question, the smoothness of her tone ensures I don't. She was stating a fact. *A very obvious one.*

After gathering my heart from the floor, I swing my eyes to the voice. My curious glance meets with a lady with stark white hair and piercing blue eyes. Her waist-length locks have been pulled back in a low side-sweeping braid, and the diamante droplets weaved throughout the intricate design are nearly undetectable with how brightly her hair shimmers under the fluorescent lighting of the ballroom. She looks to be in her mid-thirties, but the mature huskiness of her voice gives away her real age, which I'd say is closer to fifty.

"Cartier, darling. It's a pleasure to meet you," she introduces, extending her hand in greeting.

Slipping off my seat, I accept her offer, mindful not to squeeze her hand too tightly. Her translucent, wrinkle-free fingers are covered in jewels the size of rocks. I'm afraid if I press too firmly, I may harm her.

"Cleo," I reply. I inwardly sigh, grateful my voice comes out with the confidence I was aiming for.

"Come," Cartier says, waving toward a sparkling gold bar at the back of the dance floor. "Jimmy understands my desire for quality." Her eyes skim the crowd. "Thank goodness, as I need a stiff drink in my hand to tackle the high-falutin' snobs in this room."

Not giving me a chance to object, Cartier loops her arm around my elbow and heads for the bar. Shockingly, I don't put up a single protest. After waving goodbye to Andy, I allow Cartier to guide me through the throng of people swelling in size for every minute that ticks by.

Although Cartier and I appear on opposite ends of the spectrum, the twinkle in her eyes tells me her polished exterior is nothing more than a ruse. Don't get me wrong. I'm not saying her insides aren't as glamorous as her head-to-toe designer outsides, her face is just void of the disdain the other elaborately dressed patrons have been directing at me the past hour. She looks as if she sees me as a person, not judging my value on the fake diamond studs in my ears. She reminds me a lot of Marcus—in a more feminine way.

My curiosity about Cartier's true identity grows when the patrons part so she can glide across the room without hindrance. Although I still acquire the occasional narrowed glare, it isn't issued until after Cartier's focus is diverted. She is either an incredibly influential person, or she has most of the crowd running scared. From the vibes her aura privately conveys, I'd suspect it's a bit of both.

"Is Cartier your real name?" I query, jogging to keep up with her long strides.

She smiles a wicked grin. "No, darling, don't be silly. You never give them your real name. My choice in name tells them what I want to be lavished with. Last year, I was called Porsche. This year, I wanted something easier to store. Storage has always been ridiculous in New York, but last year my storage bill was outrageous."

"Them?" I ask with arched brows, starting at the most baffling part of her statement. I commute to work every day just to avoid the costly parking bills, so I'm acutely aware of the pressing issues of garage spaces in New York, it's just not something I've ever had to worry about.

When we reach the bar, Cartier runs her hand down my locks, smoothing the frazzled pieces caused by our swift cross of the room. I stare at her in utter shock—partly confused but mostly in awe. Cartier has that type of personality that just draws you to her. She is clearly wealthy, the ten-carat pink diamond nestled in the curve of her thin neck ensures there is no mistaking this, but she seems playful and hip at the same time. Even with our vast difference in age, I'd love to see her outside of this mood-suffocating environment.

After ordering two champagne glasses from a handsome African American bartender, Cartier returns her attention to me. "This is very pretty," she praises, delicately running her hand over the diamond pendant of my choker. "Your Master chose well."

My eyes bug as air traps halfway to my lungs. "Master?" I blubber out, feigning ignorance.

Wrinkles pleat the corners of Cartier's eyes as she smiles a broad grin. "He taught you well, darling." Gathering the champagne glasses the bartender just set down, she hands one to me. "Well done. You just passed your first test."

I'm tempted to rocket my eyes to Marcus to see if he has noticed my exchange with Cartier, but realizing her remark could be another test, I keep them locked on her glistening-with-mischief eyes. It's an immense struggle, even more so when she clinks her glass against mine before taking a sizeable mouthful of the aromatic-smelling champagne, seemingly relishing my deer-trapped-in-headlights stance. The expression on her face is smug, but not in an egotistical type of way. It seems as if she is happy to enjoy my awkwardness, as long as it's her making me uncomfortable.

Hoping to settle the panic flaring through me, I take a sip of my champagne. My nose screws up when the strange taste graces my taste buds. It isn't disgusting, but it certainly isn't to my palate.

"Ah," Cartier accentuates in a long, throaty purr. "I knew you weren't his standard kettle of fish." She raises her hand in the air, gaining the attention of the bartender serving patrons at the other end. "Two virgin margaritas. Hold the virgin." She drops her eyes to me. "I don't know about you, but I lost that tag a long time ago. I'm not interested in getting it back."

I smile at her immature eye roll. With her words muffled with laughter, I notice a slight accent I missed earlier. It's an odd combination. Part British with a hint of a southern slur.

When the bartender serves us our drinks, Cartier waves her hand to a scattering of booths tucked away in the corner of the room. "There will be fewer snoops over there."

Just like they did earlier, the crowd parts when they notice Cartier sauntering toward them. With every one moving out of our way, we reach the booths in record time. While sliding into my seat, I take a sip of my drink. My nostrils flare when tequila burns my nose hairs. Cartier was not deceitful when she said Jimmy understands her desire for quality. This is the most potent margarita I've ever had—and I've had a few.

The heart-warming concoction traps halfway to my stomach when Cartier straight-up asks, "How long have you been Master Chains' sub?"

I lick the salt off my lips while shrugging my shoulders. "Who is Master Chains?"

Cartier smirks, ostensibly amused by my response. "Shouldn't you be telling me? You're wearing his collar, darling." She drops her eyes to the chain link nestled in the middle of the dramatic diamond pendant Marcus draped around my neck earlier tonight. "Chain links are Master Chains' signature. Like every community, signatures are trademarked to their rightful owner. No one would dare collar their sub with Master Chains' signature. That's not only a big no-no in this lifestyle, it's highly disrespectful."

"Perhaps I work in the..." *Come on brain, think of something associated with chains.* "...fencing industry." *Really, that's the best you could come up with?*

Cartier's breathless laugh eases the panic boiling my blood. She isn't laughing because she thinks I am an idiot, she is laughing because she assumes I'm trying to be comical. I'm not—I'm just endeavoring to keep my relationship with Marcus on a strictly need-to-know basis. Cartier is lovely, but I don't know her from a bar a soap, so there is no possibility I'll share guarded secrets with her just because she purchased me an overpriced cocktail.

Spotting the conflicting emotions pumping out of me, Cartier assures,

"Darling, it's okay, truly. I am friend of Master Chains. Anything you say is safe with me."

My pupils widen to the size of saucers when she yanks one of the diamond chains my nipple clamps are attached to. My body spasms when her sharp tug sends a pulsating buzz to my needy sex. My body is already heightened beyond reproach from Marcus's flirty glances the past hour, and she just thrusted my lust-driven heart's desire to the forefront of my mind.

"No fencer I've met has a fascination with delayed gratification. Come to think of it, there is only one friend I know who believes postponed satisfaction isn't a form of atonement." Cartier connects her eyes with mine. "The darling Master Chains. My very dear friend."

The throaty chuckle her words are laced in comes to an immediate end when I blubber out, "Friend or..." I leave my question open, not having the gall to confront a woman like Cartier. She has been nothing but friendly, but she still has an aura that commands respect.

Cartier's painted red lips purse high. "You think I'm one of Master Chains subs?" she asks as her dazzling eyes dance between mine.

With my brain too fried trying to work out what she means by "one of Master Chains' subs," I merely nod.

"Oh, darling, I'm flattered you think so highly of me. But no, I've never been Master Chains' sub," she replies, her tone as adulatory as her facial expression. "Good gosh, I'm nearly old enough to be his mother." She stops talking as her hand creeps up to clutch a thin white gold necklace hidden by much chunkier ones. "I *am* older than his mother." She locks her eyes with mine, the humor in them has completely vanished. "But if you tell anyone that, even a man as protective as Master Chains won't be able to save you."

I swallow harshly.

Cartier laughs at my grim expression. "I'm joking, darling." Her firm eyes don't match her admission. She looks like a woman who wouldn't hesitate to slice me ear to ear if I shared her secret. "But I wouldn't test my patience anytime soon. I've been told my fuse is quite short."

I nod, agreeing with her recommendation.

We sip on our margaritas in silence for the next several minutes. I wouldn't necessarily say it's an awkward time, but there is undeniable tension thickening the air. I feel bad for shutting down our conversation so quickly, but I'm too overrun deciphering half the things she said to encourage more cryptic statements. Cartier has been open and honest with me, but there are snippets of our conversation that have irked me the wrong way. Like her automatic assumption I am Marcus's sub.

I sip on my recently replenished drink, hoping it will alleviate the bitterness in the back of my throat. With Cartier's presence so influential, the bar staff has resorted to table service, meaning we are rarely without a drink. It's only been twenty minutes, and the buzz of alcohol is already warming my veins.

Although the refreshing coolness of my beverages are doing wonders for the burn scorching my esophagus, it does nothing to ease the contempt swishing in my stomach. I don't know what I find more concerning. The fact Marcus collared me without permission, or that Cartier disclosed he has subs —*plural.*

Surely she meant previously—*right?*

Deciding there is only one way to get answers, I swing my eyes to Cartier. My hasty movements cause a rush of dizziness to cluster in my head.

"Did you know Serena?" I ask, gesturing my hand to one of the many banners lining the ballroom that display whom the fundraiser is for. I figure if I start at a less controversial topic, I can work my way up to more hard-hitting matters.

Cartier shakes her head, sending blonde tresses falling into her eye. "No, but I've attended every gala the past seven years." Her eyes flicker like she is recalling a memory. Clearly, that's the case when she adds, "I remember the first time I attended an event of this caliber, I was as wide-eyed as you. Oh, the smell. I'll never forget that smell. It was the smell of—"

"Money," I interrupt before I can stop my words, the alcohol in my veins making me more brazen than usual.

Cartier's poised chuckle gains us the attention of the elegantly dressed patrons around us. "No, darling. That scent you're smelling is not money. It's arrogance and entitlement. Men and women who *think* they are better than you. They are envious, because you, my dear, are the most priceless gem here. You not only captured the attention of a man with a fine eye, but you also stole it from him."

I slant my head to the side as my curiosity rapidly increases. Her saying is very similar to what Marcus said earlier tonight. About how my hair secured his attention before my face ultimately stole it. *Maybe she truly is a friend of Marcus's.*

Wanting to test the theory, I ask, "How do you steal someone's attention?"

Cartier raises her finger in the air, signaling to a gentleman at the side of the room that she will be with him in a minute before devoting her attention back to me. "When you steal a man's attention, he loses the ability to notice anyone else in the room. Look."

She gestures her hand to a gathering of women mingling at the side of the bar. Although they appear deep in conversation with one another, their constant eye movement to the other side of the room ruins their ruse. Something—or someone—has their undivided attention.

Following their adoring gazes, I spot Marcus standing at the bar speaking with the man Cartier gestured to mere seconds ago. Seemingly sensing my gaze, Marcus's head slings to the side, and his eyes lock with mine simultaneously. I smile shyly as I fight to ignore the little voice inside me shouting with euphoria. This is the first sneaky glance we've had since Cartier filled in the vacant plus one on my invitation.

Marcus's eyes bounce between Cartier and me for several heart-clutching seconds before he dips his chin in greeting. He then returns to his conversation.

"See," Cartier explains, her brow lifting higher than her black sequin mask. "It's as if they don't even exist."

Although my insides are dancing with silly giddiness, my mouth still gapes. Cartier's assessment of the situation proves she knows who Marcus is, which in turn, also proves she knows his secret. The only thing my baffled brain can't work out is why Cartier would go out of her way to associate with me. Is she welcoming me into a community she is a part of? Or is she merely being friendly as she spotted my discomfort?

Before any probing questions can be fired off my tongue, the man Cartier gestured to earlier arrives at our booth. My throat becomes scratchy when it dawns on me why he seems so familiar. He is a very well-known and respected member of Congress.

After smiling a greeting, the man holds out his hand in offering to assist Cartier from the booth.

"I am sorry, darling, I must run. Duty calls." Cartier leans in and presses a kiss to my cheek. "This one is so handsome, I might let him play for free," she whispers into my ear.

My eyes bulge as my jaw slackens more.

Loving my bug-eyed expression, Cartier cheekily winks before muttering, "Play nice, darling, I don't think Master Chains even knows what he is dealing with yet."

25

"Everything okay?"

Lifting my eyes from my intertwined fingers, I am met with the smiling face of Emily. Careful not to expose the tiny curve in her belly, she slides into the booth I've been sitting in solo the past hour.

"Yeah, everything is great."

Emily scrunches her pointed-up nose. "Really? Because Jenni, Kylie and I are bored as hell."

Her reply shocks me. I thought my boredom was because I wasn't used to attending these glitzy types of events. I had no clue it is because it's an actual snooze fest.

Spotting my shocked expression, Emily explains, "At the start, this event was about raising awareness for ALL while hoping the attendees would contribute to much-needed research into the horrible disease. Now, it's more about smooching and hobnobbing and discovering whose bank balance is the largest. Don't get me wrong, every penny donated tonight goes to a wonderful cause, it just doesn't embody what the Serena Scott Foundation is about."

"Then why did you attend?" Curiosity rings in my tone.

"To show support for one of our own. We have attended and will continue attending every single gala." She locks her nearly translucent brown eyes with mine. "Now we've just secured another poor pauper to drag along with us."

My heart warms, pleased as punch she sees my inclusion into their unique dynamic as long-term.

"Can I ask you something, Emily?"

She nods without hesitation.

"Why do you think I'm the first person Marcus has introduced to the band?"

I'm not asking her this question in the hope she will stroke my ego. I'm asking as I'm curious as to why Marcus doesn't believe his bond with his bandmates is strong enough to withstand his secret. From what I've seen, I don't know why he keeps his involvement in the BDSM lifestyle a secret from them. It's part of who he is, so why can't he be open and honest about it with the people who care about him the most?

Emily considers my question for a moment before shrugging. "In all honesty, I asked Noah the exact same thing after we met you last month. He was just as baffled as me." She licks her lips as her eyes dilate with hesitation. "Over the years, we've tried to include Marcus's family in anything the band is associated with. Our invitations have always gone unanswered. Other than meeting Serenity after a handful of concerts last year, the rest of his family remains a mystery to us."

My eyes burn from a sudden rush of moisture in them. My tears aren't just due to what Emily said, it's the way she said it. She sounds as devastated as I feel for Marcus.

"Since we are sharing, can I ask you something?" Emily questions, her words as hesitant as her facial expression.

After swallowing down my unease, I dip my chin. *I opened these cans of worms, so now I must deal with the consequences.*

"When Marcus opens up to you, can you tell him his brothers will always be there for him? To outsiders, Rise Up is just a group of good-looking guys who sing music. To people who know them, they are a bunch of misfit brothers. They will support him no matter what it is."

"I appreciate your confidence in believing he will open up to me, but I don't know if he will. I'm just as perplexed by his personality as you guys are," I reply, loathing that my voice comes out with a hint of anger. I'm not angry at my lack of knowledge about Marcus's private life, more disappointed he feels he has to keep secrets to start with.

"Don't take Marcus's private nature personally, Cleo. For as long as I've known him he has always been... *restrained.*" She grimaces on her last word, not realizing she just hit the nail right on the head.

I jump out of my skin when a sudden, "Did you ask her?" shrieks through my eardrums.

It takes all my will not to slap Jenni, who is leaning on the leather booth, grinning sheepishly at my frightened response. My interests pique when her eyes scan the room as if she is playing the part of a detective in a poorly casted movie. Actually, come to think of it, the impish gleam the gala dampened from her eyes the past two hours has returned stronger than ever. She looks outright mischievous.

"Not yet, I was building a rapport between us." Emily squeezes my hand in silent acknowledgment our private talk will remain private.

My curiosity hits an all-time high when Kylie slowly saunters over to join our impromptu meeting, her eyes floating around the vast space as eagerly as Jenni's.

"So, is she coming?" Kylie whispers, her voice barely audible over the string quartet playing on a makeshift stage to our right.

"I haven't had the chance to ask her yet," Emily confirms again.

After playfully snarling at her two friends, Emily locks her eyes with me. "We're sneaking out," she says matter-of-factly. "We want you to come with us."

My brow arches. "You're sneaking out?" I repeat, like I'm hard of hearing.

When Emily nods, I ask, "All of you?" I know I sound like an imbecile, but I want to ensure I'm getting the full picture.

Emily continues nodding.

"And the band?"

Emily stops nodding. "No. Just us girls. Nick's brother owns a nightclub half a block up. We want to go dancing, so we're going dancing."

"And the guys don't know?" I nearly roll my eyes at the sheer dimness displayed in my voice. I'm acting like the school nark ratting out the cool kids sneaking out for a smoke at school camp.

Emily shakes her head.

"We asked, their head of security shut down our request, citing it was 'too much hassle' just for us to go dancing," Jenni informs me, her pitch snarky.

"So we came up with our own solution."

If I didn't know any better from the countless news articles I've read on Noah's protectiveness of Emily, I'd swear she was excited at the prospect of being punished by Noah. She has a wicked gleam in her eyes I've never seen before—one that encourages reckless thoughts.

"So what do you say, Cleo, are you willing to take a walk on the wild side?" Kylie questions with waggling brows.

My throat works hard to swallow as I contemplate a reply. I love that they included me in their plans—it truly makes me feel like I am one of the team, but my punishment for disobedience would be much greater than what they will endure when we get caught. And I don't have any doubt we will get caught. Emily has only been sitting with me for the past ten minutes, and I've spotted Noah peering over at least three times since then. They have a matter of minutes to leave this ballroom before their ruse is unraveled.

"Maybe next time?" I reply with a grimace, praying this isn't a one-time offer. I hardly know Emily, Jenni, and Kylie, but I have a great fondness for them already.

Like a queue of kindergarten students discovering the ice cream truck just ran out of sprinkles, the girl's lips drop into a pout one by one.

"Are you sure?" Jenni's pleading eyes bore into mine.

"I'll even have Slater take the blame if Marcus gets too worked up," Kylie adds, strengthening their silent pleas. "They are best buds, so what's the worst that could happen?"

I could have my ass spanked red-raw. Or even worse, be withheld from climaxing indefinitely.

Certain I don't want either of those consequences to reach fruition, I drift my confident gaze between three sets of begging eyes while saying, "I'm sure. Besides, if you truly want a chance to dance before Rise Up's security ruins the party, you'll need someone to act as a decoy." I press my fingertip to my chest. "I'm the girl for the job."

Emily purses her lips as she considers my suggestion.

"It could work," Jenni replies to Emily's silent question. "Remember what happened last time? We only got five, ten minutes max before Hawke came storming into the club, scaring the living daylights out of the guys dancing with us."

"I don't care how many times that guy swore on his grandfather's grave, that puddle in his pants was not sweat," Kylie mutters, giggling.

When they break into rapturous laughter, I join them, finally clued in enough to get the punch line.

Once her girly laughter settles, Emily connects her glistening eyes to mine. "Are you sure?"

"One hundred percent."

"Okay, then what's this brilliant plan you have to get us out of here undetected?"

After giving the girls a brief rundown on my plan, I slide out of my booth. My steps toward the congregation of elegantly dressed ladies Cartier gestured to earlier are confident even though my insides are shaking uncontrollably. Their conversation dulls to a snicker when they notice my approach. I force a smile on my face, praying I haven't read their eagerness wrong.

"Can we help you?" the blonde in the middle of the pack snarls as her eyes rake my body. "Good god, who are you wearing?" she mutters under her breath.

"Only an original J Holt creation," I reply. My spine snaps straight, proud I replied to her rude comment with a hint of maturity. It was a hard-fought effort.

Her pupils widen as her eyes once again drink in my dress. "J Holt? As in Jenni Holt?" she queries, her voice having an edge of pompousness to it, like she doesn't believe a word I'm speaking.

When I nod, her mouth gapes. Her next stare is more lingering than her first two.

"Oh my goodness. It's fabulous," she gushes, acknowledging the personal touches Jenni adds to every dress she designs.

"Please join us," invites a brunette in a bright purple dress.

"Oh, no, I was just leaving. Thank you anyway."

They peer at me suspiciously, wondering why I've forced myself onto them only to decline their invitation.

The suspicion leaves their faces when I say, "I just noticed you peering across the dance floor most of the night." I point in the direction Marcus is standing. Although I don't turn my head in his direction, I know he is watching me. I can feel the heat of his gaze scorching my skin.

"I was just wondering if you knew who the man is that you've been gawking at most of the night." I cringe. *It wasn't supposed to come out sounding as creepy as that.*

The blonde balks, acting unaware of whom I am referring to. Her anger is quickly subdued when I say, "I was talking to my friends, and no matter how hard we try to work out why his green eyes seem so familiar, we just can't quite pinpoint who he is."

The blonde touches my arm, the anger on her face no longer existent. "How could you not recognize those eyes?" she questions, her voice relaying she thinks I'm an idiot. "That's Marcus Everett, bassist of Rise Up."

"Oh…." I state dramatically, acting as stupid as she thinks I am. "Now it makes sense why I saw Noah, Nick, and Slater earlier. They must come to these functions together?"

Sweat bubbles on my skin when six sets of lust-crammed eyes rocket to mine. "Rise Up is here? Nick, Noah, Slater? All of them?" The questions come from multiple sources all at once.

Nodding, I extend my index finger to the bar where the band has been hiding out for the past two hours. "They're over there—all alone."

"Alone?" the blonde perks up.

She checks her face as if there is a mirror in front of her before turning her massively dilated eyes to her friends. "Let's go, girls," she demands with a nudge of her head. "This is the opportunity we've been waiting for."

They mentally prep in a similar fashion to the blonde before they make a beeline for the bar I gestured to. Their hips swing so much, the ground wobbles under my feet. Once they are halfway across the room, I give Emily, Jenni, and Kylie the signal to go. With the eagerness of the blonde at a level I've never seen, I doubt the band has any clue what's about to hit them.

Emily blows me a quick kiss before she shadows Jenni and Kylie out the emergency exit I entered over two hours ago. A roguish grin curls my lips high when ear-piercing squeals of excitement bellow across the room. I don't need to swing my eyes in the direction of the noise to know what's causing the ruckus. The shrieking cries of fans gushing over their idols is all the indication I need to know my ruse just hatched.

My smile is laid to rest as quickly as it was awoken when a female voice at my side says, "It's lucky they're more confident in their relationships than you are."

My pulse quickens as I pivot around to face the lady I'd rather remain a stranger. Although she is wearing a plain black mask with an eccentric feather on the side, I'd never forget the fierce gaze I'm awarded with once I pivot around. Hell has been left to defend itself tonight. The devil is back in all her glory.

The more Delilah's beady black eyes take in my high shoulders and lifted chin, the more my confident composure cracks. She doesn't need to quote her famous saying for me to know what she is thinking. It's beaming out of her in invisible waves, as ghastly as the pretentious gleam in her eyes.

Apparently wanting to ensure I didn't miss the disdain her eyes are conveying, she mockingly whispers, "No amount of polishing can fix a cracked shell. Once it's cracked, it can never be repaired."

"What are you doing here, Delilah?" Even weeks haven't dampened my anger about our last run-in, much less her current bombardment.

The large split in Delilah's midnight black dress creeps up high on her waif-thin thigh when she steps closer to me. "Me? More like what are you doing here? I was unaware they required the help to dress up to keep up appearances."

I snarl with bared teeth but since I was raised with morals, I don't reply to her bitchy comment. Besides, I've become so accustomed to handling her wrath the past three years, her vindictive snipes barely nick my skin before they roll straight off my back.

Proving I am the better woman, I smile sweetly. "It was lovely seeing you again, Delilah. I hope you have a pleasant evening."

My desire to get away from her is so potent, I nearly trip over the train of my dress as I make a beeline for the washroom. With her gaze so fierce it scorched my skin, a splash of cold water on my face sounds like a godsend.

My quick steps halt midstride when Delilah informs me, "I did as you suggested. I researched the BDSM lifestyle with a keener eye."

Blood rushes to the surface of my cheeks when her loud comment gains me the constant stare of the patrons around us. The hiss of the woman next to me is so convincing, I wouldn't be surprised to discover she had her incisor teeth replaced with fangs.

Realizing she has me at a disadvantage, Delilah says, "It was interesting what I uncovered, quite the eye-opening experience. If you have a few seconds, I wouldn't mind sharing some pointers with you, you know, to stop you making a foolhardy move as you venture into the lifestyle."

I spin around so quickly, a rush of dizziness clusters into my head. "The only one being silly here, Delilah, is you," I whisper, struggling to shake the attention our exchange has garnered.

Delilah shrugs off my comment with a roll of her eyes. The hairs on my arms bristle with agitation when she steps closer to me. Although I know I should shut down this conversation with a sense of maturity, the alcohol lacing my veins makes me braver than usual. Don't get me wrong, I have no intention of starting a fight. But I'm also not going to cowardly run and hide in the restroom—even if it's the smart thing to do.

When Delilah stops in front of me, I lift my eyes to hers. With her height advantage, I have to crank my neck back to meet her eye to eye. She stares at my diamond choker for several uncomfortable seconds before connecting her eyes with mine.

"A collar, how fitting." Her tone is confident, ensuring I can't mistake her statement as a question. "I'm surprised, Cleo. Truly I am. I can't believe you fell into the trap. I've always said you were dimwitted, but to allow a man to collar you..." She stops talking, allowing her ghastly facial expression to relay the rest of her sentence.

"Clearly your research was ill-informed—"

"Not from where I'm standing," she interrupts, not giving me the chance to negate her claims that I've been lured into the world of BDSM. "You're at an event surrounded by people in the BDSM industry..."

My lips twitch to correct her inaccurate wording, but I keep my mouth shut —*barely.*

"...wearing a diamond collar that costs more than you'll earn in a lifetime. Either your low self-esteem has lured you into a world where begging is essential, or your budding friendship with Cartier isn't a friendship at all. It's a business opportunity."

My eyes widen. *Clearly, she's been watching me longer than I realized.*

"I guess I should be flattered?" I reply, my tone confident.

Delilah peers into my eyes, her confusion evident.

"I'm so deeply embedded in your skin, you can't help but keep tabs on me," I inform her baffled expression. "Stalking is below you, Delilah. You should stick to fabricated stories on rock stars attending rehab."

Delilah scoffs as her expression turns from confused to enraged. "Shut your mouth, you stupid little twit. I'm not here for *you.* I'm here to do the job *you* failed to do. I am here to unearth the owner of Chains." She skims her eyes over the crowd as if she is seeking Marcus amongst them.

Although her comment makes my spine bristle with annoyance, my desire to protect Marcus outweighs my need to retaliate against her name-calling. "This is a fundraising event, Delilah. Not a BDSM party. Whomever you're looking for is not here."

Her eyes missile to mine. The fury in them is so white-hot, the beading of sweat on my forehead sizzles. "What's the annual fee to be a member of Chains?" she questions with her brow arched high.

"One point two five million dollars," I reply, not needing time to deliberate. Unlike Delilah, I did my job as per Mr. Carson's specifications. I researched Chains so thoroughly, I know every detail of its business operations, which means I'm privy enough to know its clientele doesn't deserve Global Ten Media's callous investigation.

"And the current member figures stood at 241 clients last month," Delilah informs me, displaying she has increased her research the past two weeks. "That's over 300 million dollars annually just in membership fees. Then there is the entrance fee for each party, and goodness knows what else once they enter. That easily makes Chains a billion-dollar entity."

She drifts her eyes over the mass congregation of people mingling in the opulent ballroom. Her gaze lingers longer on people wearing chokers similar to mine. Although they are not quite as elaborate as mine, they do very much look like collars acceptable for subs to wear to this type of function.

"When there is an opportunity for money to be flaunted, men intimidated by real women come out in droves. I know he is here." She returns her eyes to me. "I just need you to make a mistake so I can discover who he is."

"That is never going to happen, Delilah," I reply, crossing my arms over my chest.

She smirks a vicious smile. "It will happen, Cleo. It's not a matter of *if.* It's a matter of *when*." Her tone is confident, like she has no doubt I am moments away from making a stupid mistake.

The angry glint in her eyes softens as she mutters, "It doesn't matter how strong-willed you are, deceit cuts deep. Will you be strong enough to ignore it when it happens to you?"

"Who says that will happen to me?" I ask before I can stop myself.

Delilah looks down at me, her eyes full of pity. "While monogamy still has a place in the BDSM lifestyle, casual play and polyamory are the most readily acceptable and available options. BDSM players are known for compartmentalization to ensure their BDSM lifestyle doesn't mix with their general lives," she quotes, reciting some notes I took down early in my investigation.

"Men cheat. That's not a theory or an insinuation. They cheat. The only difference between normal men and men in the BDSM lifestyle is those connected with kink don't need to seek permission to do it. It is 'acceptable and readily available' because women like you fail to see their self-worth."

If she hadn't sneered her words so viciously, I could have taken the last half of her statement as a compliment.

"Women in BDSM aren't worthless, Delilah."

"No? Then why do they sign a contract?" she interrupts, her tone firm yet piqued with interest.

"A Dom/sub contract is nothing more than a way of laying down a set of boundaries both parties agree to," I quote, reciting what Marcus said in his kitchen weeks ago when he was trying to coerce me to be his sub.

I take a step back as my stomach swishes violently. My swirling insides have nothing to do with Delilah's wrathful glare and everything to do with me recalling the last half of his statement. "It's a smart thing to do at the beginning of any relationship, as it means there will be less chance of disappointment when it ends."

When it ends. Ouch, that was a brutal fall back to reality I wasn't expecting tonight.

"And the penny finally drops," Delilah mockingly whispers.

The scent of her perfume lingers into my nose when she attempts to clasp my diamond choker in her hand. Since its hold on my throat is so firm, she can only run the tips of her fingers over it. When Cartier did the same thing, my body barely registered her touch. But since this is Delilah, my body reacts—and no, it isn't in the way you're thinking. I've never had the urge to jump into a shower and scrub my skin. I do now.

"You see this as a collar of commitment. Everyone else sees it as a sentence. Depending on how well you behave, you might get two months, or you might get six, but eventually, your term will expire, and you'll be left hunting for the next man to collar you."

Stealing my chance to reply, Delilah leans in for a quick embrace like we are lifelong friends before she saunters back in the direction she came from, soon becoming lost in a sea of black tuxedos.

26

Tired of holding the satin train of my dress off the floor, I stand from my coward's post in the women's restroom stall and gather my purse off the waist-height countertop. This bathroom is so opulent, every stall is the size of a real-life bathroom. Black speckled counters glittered with gold flecks take up an entire wall, a large artisan sink floats in the middle of the wall, and the standard paper towels have been replaced with cloth ones.

I'd like to say its pleasant surroundings are why I've spent the last twenty minutes hiding out in the restroom, but unfortunately, it isn't. I'm spinelessly hiding, giving my brain a chance to break down my conversation with Delilah. Although from experience, I know I shouldn't pay any attention to a single word Delilah utters, part of me can't help but absorb little snippets of it.

I researched the BDSM lifestyle for weeks. I know what she said is accurate, as I wrote it. That's the main reason I was adamant I'd never be a part of the lifestyle. I don't want an agreed amount of time stipulated in a contract or a set of rules to follow. I just want Marcus. But is that something I can have without the rest? His involvement in the BDSM lifestyle isn't just a slight interest. He is the very essence of BDSM. He has the respect, the wealth, and probably a long list of women vying to be his sub. Can I genuinely compete with that?

After washing my hands, I head to the black frosted glass door. My hand freezes halfway to the latch when the sound of high-pitched laughter rings through my ears. Although I don't recognize the woman's voice, her sneered comment in concert with her hearty laughter has piqued my interest.

"Did you see the size of her choker? She probably sees it as a grand gesture of his dedication, whereas we're all seeing it as a massive beacon for other Doms."

I remove my hand from the latch and take a step backward so my feet can't be seen under the door. Although I know better than to snoop, curiosity killed the cat.

Peering through the small crack in the door, I spot two females standing near a full-length mirror at the entrance of the restroom. Just like me, they are both collared.

"Do you think he'd share her?" the blonde with shoulder-length hair asks.

The redhead snaps her neck to the side so fast, I'm confident she's going to have whiplash. "Why? Are you failing in your duties so badly that your Master needs to seek other subs?"

The blonde runs her hand down the mid-length flare of her skirt. "No. It's just uncommon for Master Chains to share, so your assumption shocked me."

The redhead stops applying a new sheen of lipstick to her lips so she can glare at the blonde. Her mouth gapes as her eyes bug. She isn't the only one stumped. I can barely inhale an entire breath.

The chance of filling my lungs with air becomes a dream when the redhead snarls, "Master Chains may not share, but you know as well as I do, commitment is not his forte. That was the reason we chose our Doms. We want a long-term commitment."

"No," the blonde objects, shaking her head. "You want to get pregnant to force a wealthy man to marry you. I want..." She stops talking as the expression on her face turns neutral.

The redhead pegs her cylinder of lipstick at the blonde's head. "If you want love, you're in the wrong place. That ship sailed a long time ago."

"That's not true. Jeremy is kind and understanding. He worships me," the blonde endorses, her tone firm.

"Until your contract expires. Then you will be replaced with a new, more improved version of yourself. Live in denial all you want, but it won't change the facts. Before we know it, we are going to be Cartier, using the tricks we learned in this lifestyle to puff our pockets with money their subs aren't privileged enough to know about."

My stomach swirls when the blonde doesn't attempt to rebut her statement.

"Until then, we continue following the rules," the redhead continues, her tone not as chirpy as it was when she entered the washroom.

The swirling of my stomach ramps up a notch when the redhead bobs down to gather her lipstick off the ground and spots my feet just back from the stall door. "Oh my god, are you eavesdropping on our private conversation? Or doing a business transaction not acceptable in public?" The last half of her sentence comes out muffled with laughter.

I roll my eyes at their childish chuckles. They sound like two roosters waking a farmer at the crack of dawn.

Their girlish giggles continue until they have prepped their faces and exit the bathroom. I wait another two to three minutes before following suit. It was a pointless effort when the first faces my eyes lock in on as I exit the washroom is the unnamed redhead and blonde.

The glee lining their bright eyes grows when it dawns on them who was eavesdropping on their conversation.

"Oh my god, do you think she heard what we said?"

The redhead locks her eyes with mine. They are a beautiful aquamarine color I've never seen before. "I hope so. It may be the only way she will learn this lifestyle isn't glamorous. It's gritty and raw."

Deciding I need some fresh air before I create a scene, I graciously smile at the unknown women gawking at me. I make a beeline for the fire door Emily, Jenni and Nicole exited over thirty minutes ago, my steps hurried. When I open the heavily weighted door, I spot Brodie halfway down the hallway on my right. He has his cell phone attached to his ear. Not wanting to disturb his conversation, I veer to the left.

As I weave through the narrow halls in the heart of the elegant hotel, my agitation eases. This may be wrong of me to say, but I feel more at home here than I do in the ballroom. Although the hotel staff give me curious glances when I saunter by, they are void of the scorn the benefactors of the fundraiser had.

Needing a pick-me-up, I yank my cell phone out of my purse and text the one person always known to help me back on my feet.

Me: *Send help, the fire-breathing dragons are out in force tonight.*

Lexi's reply is almost immediate.

Lexi: *Names, Cleo. I need names. It's a little hard to kill a person if I don't know their name.*

My laughter shrills down the hallway as I type a reply.

By the time ten minutes pass, my breathing has returned to a regular pattern, and the hackles bristling my spine have sheathed. Lexi has rejuvenated me so well, I'm primed and ready for round two.

Me: *It's time to slay the dragons once again. Wish me luck, Lexi the Leech.*

Lexi: *You won't need it, Cleo the Creep, but I'll give it to you anyway. Good luck xx*

I send Lexi a goodbye text before housing my cracked cell into my purse. This is the exact phone I pegged at Marcus's head Monday morning—minus the tracking device. Marcus offered to purchase me a new one, but other than a massive crack rippled across the screen, this phone is still in perfect working order, so why do I need another? I also know this one is void of any bugging device, as it hasn't left my sight since it was returned to me in pieces Tuesday afternoon.

As I slowly mosey down the numerous corridors in the belly of the hotel, the sounds of people mingling grow louder, as does the beat of my heart. Unlike when I entered the hallway, the quickening of my pulse isn't a consequence of rattled nerves, it's my body's intuition that Marcus is close.

Allowing my body to guide my steps, I enter a door marked "restricted." Panels upon panels of computer boards and electrical instruments greet me. It appears to be the hub of the hotel's security and network center. Ignoring my rational thinking head requesting for me to leave before I get in trouble, my body's awareness of Marcus continues leading me further into the room.

As I walk down a long gangway illuminated by strips of rope lighting, the sound of people conversing jingles into my ears. One voice I immediately recognize, his smooth, velvety timbre is unmissable even when it's forced through the blood roaring in my ears. The female voice I'm confident I've heard before, but I can't pinpoint exactly where.

My shaking steps end when I reach the room from which the sounds are projecting. After a nerve-clearing breath, I peer into the room.

My body's intuition about Marcus's nearness was right. He is standing in the room caressing a blonde female in a long, elegantly flowing velvet dress. His arms are banded around her waist, and her head is resting on his chest. Although their exchange could be viewed as friendly, sick, vehement jealousy taints my blood, hating that the opportunity to sneak away for a quick cuddle wasn't awarded to me.

I give myself a mental pep talk, reminding myself that I am a confident, beautiful, independent woman who can view the facts in front of her without any outside influence. Just because the two unnamed women in the restroom and Delilah don't believe in monogamy, doesn't mean Marcus agrees with their logic. Our relationship is different. We're building something unique—unlike anything anyone in this lifestyle has seen. Right?

Right. Then why am I finding it so hard to give them the privacy their little rendezvous deserves?

Pushing aside the horrid unease twisting my esophagus, I pivot on my heels to leave. My footing stumbles halfway around when the blonde suddenly pops her head off Marcus's chest. I pant, panicked she has noticed my presence. My anxiety shifts to wariness when I recognize the face of the woman Marcus is caressing in a hidden nook. It's Keira. The same woman Mr. Carson was comforting in his office mere days ago.

With my heart twisted with suspicion, I watch their exchange for the next several minutes. I take in every little detail as sick jealousy makes it hard for me to breathe. Keira's stance, the way she keeps her eyes lowered, and the fact she never speaks unless asked a question confirms what my violent jealousy is already telling me. She is a submissive. And from the way she is glancing up at Marcus with nothing but admiration adorning her face, I'm confident she either wants to be Marcus's sub or she already is his sub.

The margaritas I downed earlier threaten to resurface when Keira's toss of her perfectly straight locks exposes even more travesty. She is a wearing a collar. Not just any collar—one with a chain link nestled in the center.

Oh, god. I'm going to be sick.

Bile scorches the back of my throat when Marcus runs the back of his fingers over the chain link pendant on her collar. His lips move, but I can't hear a word he is speaking over my pulse thumping my eardrums. Unable to leash my curiosity, I take a step into the room. The instant my heel clicks on the tiled floor, my cover is blown.

My pupils dilate to the size of saucers when Marcus slings his head to the side, his eyes locking immediately with mine. The guilt in his eyes cripples me.

"Cleo..." he growls out in warning, like I'm the one who just got busted schmoozing with another person in a hidden room, much less another sub.

"Umm... Sorry? Wrong room."

I cringe at my pathetic reply before pivoting on my heels and exiting the electrical hub of the hotel. As I clumsily pace down the hallway, my ear pricks, expecting to hear the tap of Marcus's feet scuttling across the tiled floor at any moment. All I hear is silence.

Silence is not my friend. It allows my thoughts to run wild—*to run reckless.* If he wasn't doing anything wrong, why wouldn't he follow after me to assure me of that?

Although my steps are shaky, they are surprisingly quick, having me reach Brodie in less than a minute.

"Cleo?" he queries, shocked by my gaunt expression. "Are you okay?"

I clutch at my throat as I struggle to secure a full breath. My fingertips brushing the choker curled around my neck makes my endeavor to breathe ten times harder.

"Can you remove this?" I ask Brodie, dragging my hair to the side to expose the fastener at the back of my collar. "Please, I can barely breathe."

Brodie jumps into action, removing the choker in a record-setting pace. I keep my back facing him as I tug off the nipple clamps fastened on my engorged nipples. My teeth grit, incapable of ignoring the sensation of my blood flooding back into the numb buds. It's a beautifully cruel reminder of how I felt when Marcus gifted me this collar. I thought my choker was a representation of our union, much like a wedding band. It's round because it goes on forever. *Clearly, I was wrong.*

When I pivot around to face Brodie, his eyes dance between mine. "Did you see Marcus?" He keeps his tone low, acting like he is unaware of Marcus's whereabouts. *It's a pity his eyes don't convey the same confidence his tone holds.*

"No," I lie with a curt shake of my head.

Brodie releases a deep exhalation of air. It's quickly redrawn when I ask, "But if I did, what would I have seen?"

Brodie balks as he strangles out a bunch of "Ahs" and "Umms." The guilt in his eyes matches the guilt I saw in Marcus's eyes.

Anger rushes to the surface of my cheeks, brightening them with a vibrant red coloring. "How long have they been down there?" I nudge my head in the direction I just came from.

Brodie rubs at a kink in his neck while muttering, "Who?"

I grit my teeth together before issuing him the stinkiest stink-eye I've ever given.

"Around ten or fifteen minutes," he responds, unable to withstand my fury for a moment longer. "I was supposed to ensure you didn't go down there."

I don't know if his hesitance arises from guilt, or because he is worried about what his punishment will be for failing to adhere to Marcus's request.

I realize it's the latter when he asks, "Are you going to tell Marcus about this?"

"No," I reply, shaking my head. "But when you see him again, can you give him this." I thrust my diamond collar into Brodie's chest. "And tell him to go fuck himself."

Ignoring the tears looming in my eyes, I escape into the ballroom before

Brodie can stop me. I know Brodie doesn't deserve to cop the wrath of my fury, but the fact he continued with Marcus's ruse to deceive me warrants his own form of punishment.

Snarling at the shocked faces of the two females who confronted me outside the bathroom, I weave through the dense throng of people mingling in the lavish surroundings. I have one focus on my mind. Riding the very first taxi home, crawling into bed, and forgetting about a world I don't belong in.

Halfway across the room, my elbow is suddenly clutched in a firm hold. With my body not reacting the way it usually would in Marcus's presence, I keep my retaliation to a bare minimum. A rueful glare spurred on by malicious anger.

The thin slit of my eyes widen when I realize who I'm directing my anger at. Even if his worried gaze weren't covered with a plain black mask, I wouldn't be able to mistake his icy blue eyes and ruggedly handsome face.

"You alright, Cleo?" Dexter's voice is tainted with apprehension.

He peers in the direction I've just stormed in from, seeking the person who has caused me to act so stupidly. Although I can't see Marcus, I can feel the heat of his gaze on me, so I know he is in the room.

I step into the path of Dexter's worried gaze. Even vehemently angry at Marcus, my desire to protect him still outweighs my desire to hurt him. "It was just a group of girls not appreciating my inclusion in the festivities." Because my statement is somewhat truthful, it comes out authentic.

"Okay," Dexter says, his lips pursing. "So it's not the green-eyed man whose eyes are growing even greener the longer we stand across from each other? He's becoming so green, he looks like he is about to go on a hulk-smash." The playfulness in his eyes immediately dampens my anger.

When he chuckles at my immature eye roll, I punch him in the bicep.

"Come on, Cleo, you have to admit, that one was pretty funny," he stammers out through laughter.

"That wasn't funny. It was pathetic," I retaliate, my tone relaying my words were not meant to be callous.

"No. That's pathetic," Dexter retorts, nudging his head to Delilah watching our exchange with a keen eye from the bar Andy is working behind.

Believing my stare is directed at him, Andy smiles and waves. I return his friendly gesture with a brief wave before turning my eyes back to Dexter. "Did you know Delilah was going to be here?"

"Uh huh." He nods. "Considering I'm here as her date, I can't play stupid."

"You're Delilah's date?!"

"Shh, Cleo," Dexter pleads, covering my mouth with his hand. "I don't want the whole world knowing. *Jesus.*"

His eyes dart around the room, ensuring my loud squeal didn't gain us any unwanted attention. Although our exchange encouraged a handful of new spectators, there are only two I'm concerned about—Delilah and Marcus.

"Why are you here as Delilah's date?" I ask Dexter when he removes his hand from my mouth. I flinch as my eyes widen. "Did you just call your date pathetic?"

"Sue me for honesty," he mumbles, ignoring my first question to answer the less complicated one.

My breathing turns labored when he curls his arm around my torso and leads me onto the dance floor.

"Ah, I was just on my way out."

"If you leave now, you'll give Delilah more ammunition against you." Dexter's tone is direct and to the point.

My eyes lock with his. "You know about her vendetta against me?"

His lips twist, seemingly unsure of how to reply. "She knows you're the key to discovering the man behind the Chains empire, so she is gunning for blood," he eventually answers.

Spotting the panic flaring in my eyes, he quickly adds, "But we're going to ensure her speculations remain exactly that—speculation."

He tucks a strand of my hair behind my ear before banding his arms around my waist. Although there is a good two to three inches of air between us, I swear I hear Marcus's furious growl rumble across the room. It quickens my pulse and does stupid things to my libido.

"That's why I agreed to be Delilah's date," Dexter advises, forcing my focus back to him instead of scanning the room for Marcus. "She thinks I'm dancing with you to pry information from you. My sexiness is supposed to baffle you so much, secrets come spilling out of your mouth before your mushy brain can stop them."

I laugh. If I hadn't seen the sheer cockiness beaming out of him, I might have considered another response, but with his confidence so high, I'm sure my little bout of laughter won't dent his ego too much. It was also laugh or cry —I'd prefer to save my tears until I am in privacy of my own home.

"Oh, you don't think I'm up to the challenge?" Dexter remarks when he hears my quiet chuckles, his tone as pompous as his bowed brow.

"No, I'm not saying that. I just don't know whether to be insulted or pleased by your disclosure. I'm not surprised Delilah thinks I'm such an airhead that a drool-worthy man with strikingly handsome features would turn my insides so gooey, they'd melt out of me before I could stop them. I'm just shocked you'd expose that to me. Why would you do that?"

Hoping to downplay the pain shredding my heart in two, I overemphasize my praise of Dexter's features. Although he is a very handsome man, my heart is such a twisted mess, I haven't even stopped to appraise how handsome he looks in his flawless tuxedo.

Just like last week, Dexter shrugs his shoulders like it's no big deal. "Why not? I get to rub shoulders with the people who rule this city while dancing with a beautiful woman who *unfortunately* doesn't find me attractive enough to turn her insides into goop."

I blush. Partially because the sway of our dance moves has decreased the space between us, but mainly because of his compliment that he thinks I'm beautiful. It gives my battered ego a small boost it badly needs.

We dance in silence for several moments with nothing but tension between us, it's not caused by Dexter's closeness—he has been a complete gentleman—

it's from the scene of Marcus and Keira playing on repeat in my baffled mind the past twenty minutes. My heart is begging for me to stop and properly evaluate the situation, but my brain—and Dexter's remorseful eyes—are pleading me to stop this nonsense before I get so tangled up, I'll never leave unscathed.

I'm truly at a loss on what to do. I've just had the most magical two weeks of my life blindsided by a five-minute event I'm still baffled about. Surely there must be more to this story than what I saw? Or am I so infatuated with Marcus I'm not seeing the entire picture? *Is love truly that blinding?*

Yearning to ease the pain fettering my heart, I lock my eyes with Dexter. "Do you believe people can change who they are destined to be for love?"

Dexter peers down at me as if I asked him the access codes for the nuclear weapons in Tennessee. His response is what you'd expected from a twenty-eight-year-old bachelor.

"I don't know about for love," he eventually replies, his tone cagey. "But I believe anyone can change who they are if that's what they truly want."

"What if they aren't sure if it's what they want when they're not having it?" I cringe. Even I'm baffled by my riddled statement.

Aiming to lessen the confusion marring Dexter's face, I ask my question in a simpler way. "Have you ever been so tied up over someone, you forget who you are when you're with them?"

The confusion on Dexter face vanishes as he nods.

"Is that normal?" Sheer bewilderment echoes in my tone.

A flurry of girls at our side hovers closer when Dexter smiles. "Yes, Cleo, that's perfectly normal." He stares me straight in the eyes, his expression deadpan. "It's called love."

"But isn't love supposed to build your confidence and self-worth?"

Dexter once again nods.

"Then why does it hurt so much?" I mumble more to myself than Dexter.

Dexter's fingers flex on my back so firmly, his knuckles pop. His heart thrashing against his ribs nearly drowns out his reply, "Because you're in love with the wrong person."

27

Four songs pass before Dexter and I lose most of the stares devoted to us. All but two remain. The two that put us in this predicament to begin with. Marcus and Delilah. From the whitening of Noah's face when Hawke had a quiet word in his ear, I'd say the girls' plans of dancing the night away are about to come to an end. With his fists clenched at his sides and two of his bandmates in tow, he hightails it to the front exit of the hotel, sending the paparazzi into a frenzy.

"Is there something I'm missing?" Dexter asks when he notices the grim expression on my face.

I timidly shake my head. Although Noah is without a doubt angry about Emily sneaking out, I'm confident her punishment won't be as severe as mine. *Wouldn't have been,* I mentally correct. There is no *won't* when there is no chance of it happening.

Over the charade of pretending my heart isn't bleeding out, I lift my eyes to Dexter and ask, "How much longer until I can crawl into bed and forget tonight ever happened?"

The bright gleam in Dexter's eyes dampens from my admission. "Just a bunch of girls making fun of you, hey? Chin up, kiddo, or who are the women at Global Ten going to discuss around the water cooler if they don't have their fierce-less leader to look up to?" His tone conveys he isn't goading me, he is trying to build my confidence, not tear it down. "You're tougher than this, Cleo, don't let the naysayers bring you down."

"Who said it was the naysayers? Maybe your devilishly good looks are wearing me down, making my skin thinner than it used to be." I try to make my voice come out playful, but the heaviness of my heart alters my tone.

My jaw quivers in Dexter's hand when he cups my chin. His thumb carefully brushes my cheeks, as if he is catching my tears before they fall. He doesn't need to worry, the anger still heating my veins is potent enough to stave off my desire to cry.

Smiling to soothe the sting of rejection, I pull away from Dexter's tender embrace. Although I appreciate his support, I don't need any more awkwardness to this already difficult exchange. Dexter accepts my rejection with a sense of maturity not many men his age display. He graciously acknowledges the silent pleas of my eyes with a humble smirk. The same can't be said for Marcus.

Although I keep my gaze discreet, my eyes track him as he storms across the room, his pace unchecked until he enters the door I exited fuming in anger nearly forty minutes ago. Even though his slamming of the door is soundless, it rattles my heart straight out of my chest cavity. Although I should be happy he tasted his own medicine, I don't feel happy. I feel horrible. So much so, my stomach won't stop churning.

The contents of my squishy stomach nearly surfaces when Dexter unexpectedly dips me.

"Eyes on me, Cleo," he mutters before flipping me back up so quickly, my hair falls in front of my face. "As far as anyone in this room knows, you do not know the man who just stormed out of here. You aren't here with anyone. You just came here to have a good time," he explains to my baffled expression.

He curls my arms around his neck before swinging his hips in the rhythm of the music. Since his body is plastered to mine, we move in sync. To anyone but us, we appear like an intimate couple moments away from shredding each other's clothes off. Dexter's ruse is so compelling, only the crippling pain gnawing my chest is stopping me from believing it is true. Everyone's eyes are on us—even Delilah's. That's probably because we look like idiots bumping and grinding against each other to a string quartet rendition of "Angel" by Robbie Williams.

The quartet has barely made it to the second chorus when my shoulder is tapped. "I'm cutting in," states a deep voice I don't immediately recognize.

My eyes bulge when the gentleman doesn't wait for Dexter to reply. He merely places one hand on my lower back, molds his body to mine, then foxtrots around the room like we are two ballroom dancers putting on a display for the fundraising benefactors.

Shocked by the stranger's brazenness, and stellar dance moves, I lift my eyes to the man accosting me. On the way from his thrusting chest to his eyes, I take in his white pleated dress shirt, midnight black tuxedo jacket, cropped beard and lined-with-amusement mouth.

"I thought you didn't belong in places like this?" I murmur as my eyes lock with Brodie's twinkling gaze.

"I don't." He twirls me around and around until we are out of Dexter's earshot. "But I was given unambiguous instructions that forced me into this getup." He grimaces as he drops his eyes to his outfit.

A dash of humor tinges my blood when I notice the tuxedo jacket he is wearing is at least two sizes too small. "Did you give Marcus my message?"

"Yep," Brodie replies, popping out the "P" with a hint of the cheekiness blazing in his eyes.

"And? What did he say?" I roll my eyes, hating my inability to curb my inquisitiveness.

"You can ask him that yourself." Brodie stops his marvelous dance moves as quickly as he started them.

Muted and confused, my bewildered eyes frolic between his. When he motions his head to the right, I follow his gaze. A whiz of air puffs from my mouth when I notice we are no longer on the dance floor. He twirled me into so much of a tizzy, I'm standing outside the door Marcus entered mere minutes ago. *Oh, shit, this isn't good.*

Before I can voice my concerns to Brodie, my elbow is seized, and I'm dragged into the narrow corridor. I don't need to look up to know who is clutching my arm. My level breathing and the prickling of the hairs on my nape give away who it is.

Master Chains.

Remaining quiet, Marcus guides me deeper into the corridor, away from prying eyes or ears that may be watching us. Just one touch of Marcus's hands on my skin has me wanting to forget what I saw earlier. It's genuinely astonishing how his briefest touch can switch my anger to longing instantaneously. I've gone from boiling with rage to panting in lust in under two point five seconds.

The needs of my body are thrown into the background of my mind when we enter a small room on my right, and I realize we aren't the only two members attending our gathering. Keira is standing up a few paces in front of me. With her hands splayed across her tiny waist, her twinkling-with-remorse eyes bounce between Marcus and me. Seeing her up close has my anger steamrolling back in at a rate I can't control. There is no doubt the charm in the middle of her choker is a chain link. It's as obvious as the sun hanging in the sky.

My eyes snap to Marcus. "Are you friggin kidding me? Out of all the rooms in this damn hotel, you had to bring to the one already occupied by your sub!"

He glares at me, acting like I spoke the curse words I struggled to maintain. I spin on my heel, preparing to exit the room. Since Marcus's hand is clutched around mine, I don't even get two steps away from him before he yanks me backward. I grit my teeth, fighting with all my might not to smack the egotistical gleam off his face. It's a pointless effort. The pleas of my broken heart soon become too great for me to ignore.

Raising my hand, I attempt to slap it across Marcus's face. Keira gasps loudly when Marcus thwarts my endeavor by snatching my wrist within mere inches of his face. When he draws me to his body, the anger radiating out of him mists my skin with sweat. His nostrils flare as his eyes glare into mine, warning me he has reached his limit. He isn't the only one.

After issuing me his wrath solely by using his eyes, Marcus shifts them to Keira, who is watching our exchange with reverent silence. "Would you mind giving us a minute," he commands her, his tone relaying his statement is not a suggestion.

My anger reaches fever pitch when Keira bows her head before stepping backward. Her stance couldn't be more submissive if she tried. I place my hands onto Marcus's thrusting chest and push back. I need distance between us, and I need it now. I can't think straight when he is standing so close to me, and my intuition is telling me it's vital I think rationally right now.

After exhaling a deep breath, I ask. "Is Keira your sub?" My heartache resonates in my low tone.

Ignoring my interrogation, Marcus asks, "Who was the man you were dancing with?"

"Is. Keira. Your. Sub?" I dramatically pause between each word like he's hard of hearing.

"Who was the man you were dancing with?" Marcus's tone is as low as mine.

"Is Keira your sub?!" I scream at the top of my lungs, my voice laced with an equal amount of anger and devastation.

"Keep your voice down," Marcus requests, his tone a complete contradiction to the fury radiating out of him.

"Why? Are you afraid Keira will discover she isn't the only sub on your long list of many? Or that not all your subs are as submissive as her?"

The glare Marcus directs me rams a brick into my throat, but it doesn't stop me from asking, "Is Keira your sub?"

Ignoring my question, Marcus seizes my wrist and drags me to a stack of chairs in the corner of the room. After flipping over a chair, he takes a seat. I eye him in utter shock, silenced by the calm demeanor radiating out of him as he rolls up the sleeves of his dress shirt. Confusion engulfs me. *Where did his tuxedo jacket go?* I gasp in a sharp breath when reality dawns. *Now Brodie's two-sizes-too-small tuxedo jacket makes sense.*

When Marcus unexpectedly yanks me down so I am splayed across his knees, reality dawns. *Hell no, this is not happening again.* "You're *not* spanking me to subdue my anger!"

"I'm not spanking you to subdue you! I'm spanking you so you'll calm down enough to tell me why the hell you think it's appropriate to give my staff permission to curse me."

I yank away from him, my movements so abrupt, I stumble in my heels. My face grimaces, unappreciative of the pain rocketing through my backside when I land with a hard thud. When Marcus moves to aid me off the ground, I shake my head. My anger is boiling to the point a slight sting to my backside doesn't even register.

After scrambling off the floor, I ask, "Brodie cursing you? That's really your biggest concern right now?"

Marcus doesn't answer me. He doesn't need to. The tick of his jaw answers all my questions. This has nothing to do with Brodie and everything to do with Dexter and me dancing.

"You're such a hypocrite. I discover you hiding out with another woman who is wearing your trademark, but if I dare dance with a *friend* who is trying to keep *your* secret a secret, there is hell to pay."

"A *friend?* If that's how your *friends* look at you, Cleo, you need to get new friends," Marcus responds, ignoring the most integral parts of my admission. The parts that expose Dexter is aware of his double life, and I am aware of Keira's significance in his.

"He is *not* your friend, Cleo. Friends don't look at friends like that."

"And how *exactly* was he looking at me?" Even though I'm asking a question, I continue talking as if I didn't. "Was it a similar look to the one Keira was giving you when you had your arms wrapped around her? The one that undeniably displays she has no intention of being your *friend*?"

Marcus's nostrils flare, but his lips remain pursed, proving what I said is true. He knows as well as I do, Keira isn't just his friend. I don't know if that means they have a past or a future, but I do know one thing—it causes my earlier jealousy to return stronger than ever.

"What was the point in bringing me here, Marcus? To prove without a doubt I don't belong in this lifestyle? If it was, you wasted your time. I'm already acutely aware of that fact. I told you I was never going to be what you needed me to be, but you didn't believe me. Maybe tonight will be all the proof you need."

"Goddammit, Cleo, I don't want you to be my sub. I just want you—for once—to do as you're goddamn told."

I brush away a sneaky tear that fell from my eye before Marcus has the chance to see it. "You don't want me as your sub?!"

"No!" he snaps back, his tone so low it vibrates the tips of my toes.

"Then why did you collar me as if I am?" I ask, loathing that my crackling voice exposes the catalyst of emotions pumping into me.

Marcus balks as if my words physically slapped him, but not a word seeps from his thinned with grimness lips. His silence hurts me more than his words ever could. It's by far my hardest limit.

"Because at the end of the day, no matter how much you try and deny it, you still want a submissive. I'm not a sub, Marcus. I don't know how I can make that any clearer for you."

My eyes burn with moisture when he maintains his quiet front, neither denying or agreeing with my assumption.

"If that's truly what you want, why don't we just cut our losses now before real feelings evolve?" I suggest, pretending I haven't already developed feelings for him.

The first tear trickles down my cheek when my suggestion is met with silence. Incapable of holding in my devastation for a moment longer, I spin on my heels and race for the door.

My heart shatters into a million pieces when Marcus lets me leave without protest.

To be continued...

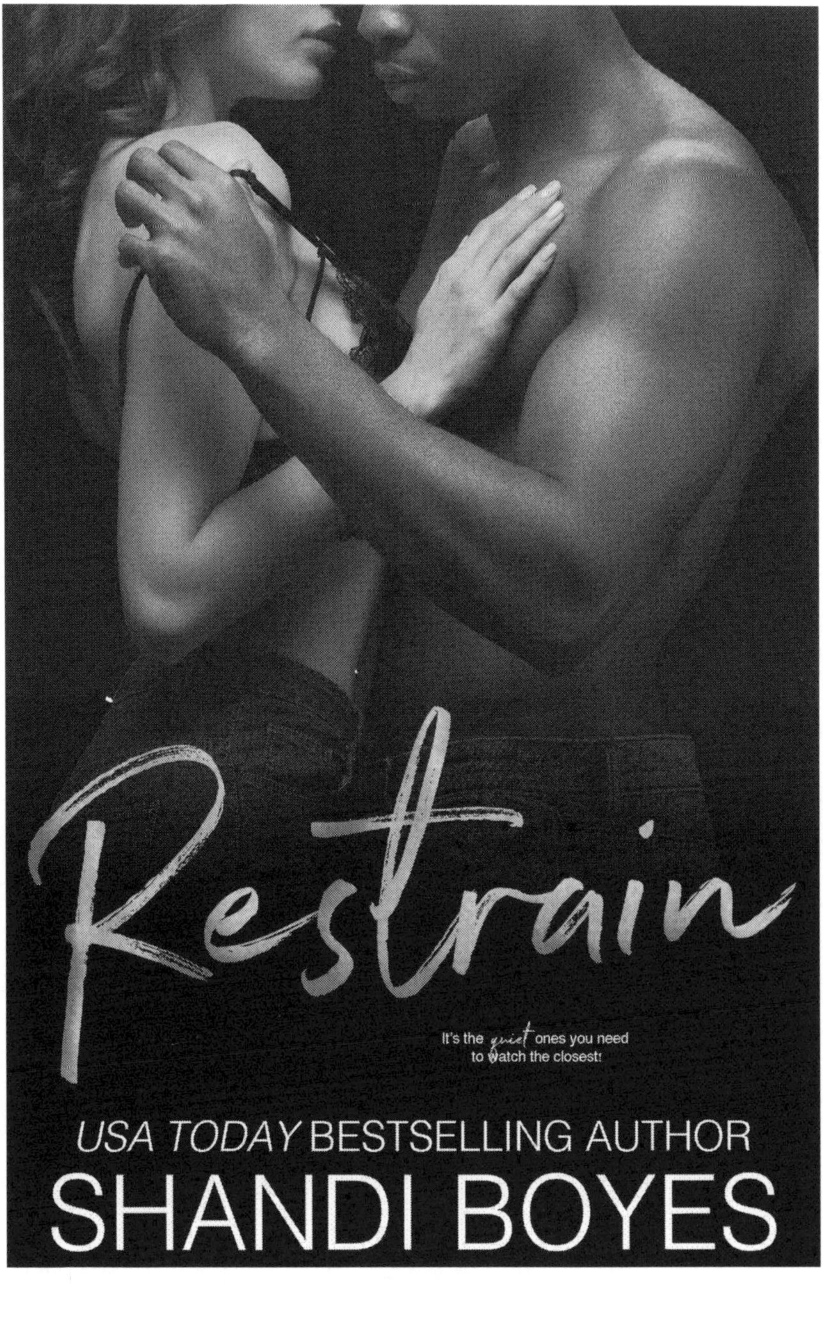
Restrain
It's the quiet ones you need to watch the closest!
USA TODAY BESTSELLING AUTHOR
SHANDI BOYES

1

The click of my heels racing down the narrow corridor nearly drowns out the deep, thick voice begging for me to stop. I don't look back. I don't need to. Although I recognize the voice, it isn't the one I want to hear. It isn't Marcus.

My speed remains unchecked as I push through the heavy door leading to the ballroom where the Serena Scott Foundation is being held. Denying Brodie's plea for me to stop, I weave through a horde of elegantly dressed people mingling in the opulent ballroom. Although I gain just as many curious gawks as I did the first time I stumbled into the foyer hours ago, not all their eyes are slit with disdain—some are doused with worry.

Pretending the moisture in my eyes is from expensive perfume burning my corneas, I continue with my trek. I keep my head held high, my shattered heart not enough of a deterrent to warrant embarrassing myself in public. My soul may be shattered, but my Garcia pride remains intact.

I'm halfway across the room when Brodie's distinct rumble sounds over the string quartet entertaining the wealthy benefactors of the Foundation. "Cleo, wait up."

I crank my neck to peer at him. Although I only met him last week, I hate that he is caught in the middle of a battle he doesn't belong in.

"I'm fine, Brodie," I assure him before continuing my effort to leave the gala before my tears fall.

The air in my lungs is brutally evicted when I spin back around and crash into a rock solid wall. Pain tingles across my face when my nose slams into an extremely hard pec. The pain is so intense, moisture floods my eyes. *At least now I have an excuse to cry in public.*

"Shit, Cleo, are you okay?"

Holding the bridge of my nose to ensure no blood trickles onto my priceless silk dress, I lift my tear-welling eyes. Dexter is peering down at me, his face lined with regret. When he spots the small trickle of blood pooling in the crevice of my nose, the worry tainting his face grows tenfold.

"Here." He clutches my elbow and guides me to the bar Andy is working behind.

Noticing our collision, Andy hands Dexter a ziplock bag full of ice. I grimace when Dexter removes my hand to replace it with the bag. It isn't pain causing my scrunched-up expression, it's the freezing coldness of the ice pressed against my flaming-with-anger face.

"I'm fine," I assure Dexter, removing the ice from my nose.

I roll my eyes at my pathetic reply. *Are those the only two words I know today? I guess if I can convince those around me that I'm fine, I might believe it as well.*

I use one of the stark white cloth napkins fanned across the bar to pat under my nose. "See?" I express when my quick dab fails to produce any blood. Although our collision was painful, it was more the shock of it happening than actual pain. Physically, I am fine, it's just my insides that look wretched.

Not getting the message, Dexter places the bag of ice on the bar then cradles my cheeks. His thumb gently pushes on my nose to make sure it's still in one piece before his fingers skim my blemished cheeks. His gentle touch as he inspects my face for damage soothes some of the nicks my argument with Marcus created. Don't get me wrong, another man's touch will never erase Marcus from my soul, no matter how long our stint of absence is, but it's nice to be rewarded with tenderness after my heart was just ripped to shreds.

The exact moment Dexter's hands drop from my face, a broad arm wraps around my waist. My idiotic heart hopes it's Marcus clutching my hips for dear life, but my body knows it isn't. It didn't react like it does when its awareness of Marcus activates. It more jumped in fear than excitement.

"Honey, how many times have I told you to watch where you're going?" asks the thick, deep voice from above—a voice I immediately recognize.

My spine snaps straight when Brodie's beard tickles my lips as he places an impromptu kiss on the edge of my mouth. Although his lips are barely touching mine, the angle of his head doesn't expose that. It looks as if we are kissing—*intimately.*

Shunted in silence, I return Dexter's baffled stare with as much confusion as Dexter is bestowing on me.

"I thought... aren't you with... hold on... What the hell is going on?" Dexter's words are as baffled as his facial expression. His jaw is hanging loose, and his eyes are wide with shock.

After running his slit gaze over Brodie for the third time, Dexter says, "You're the douchebag who just cut in while I was dancing with Cleo. One minute she was there, the next, she was gone."

"It isn't called 'whipping them away for a quickie' for no reason," Brodie fires back, not the slightest bit deterred by Dexter's name-calling.

My and Dexter's eyes rocket to Brodie in sync. He waggles his brows before cuddling me into his side. Because of his tall height, I snuggle right into the nook of his arm like I belong there. My mouth opens and closes in preparation to deny his claims, but I'm stunned into silence, my mouth won't cooperate with my brain.

When the cockiness radiating out of Brodie becomes too much for Dexter to bear, he devotes his attention back to me. This time when he drinks in my wide eyes, flustered cheeks, and disheveled appearance, the worry in his eyes doesn't grow. It dampens—*majorly.*

"You went for a quickie?" Although he is staring straight at me, I don't believe Dexter's question is directed at me. He appears as if he is talking to himself.

Dexter misses the brief shake of my head when Brodie says, "We better get going, Cleo. I'm eager to finish what we started." He looks Dexter dead set in the eyes. "If you know what I mean?" If he didn't, the arrogant wink Brodie adds to his short sentence ensures there is no misconception.

I'm taken aback when Brodie locks his lustful eyes to mine. He is playing the part so well that if I didn't know any better, I'd swear we had just returned from having a quickie. Marcus may never secure a role in a major motion picture, but if Brodie doesn't dull down his acting skills, Hollywood will come knocking.

Not giving me the chance to protest, Brodie pushes off his feet and heads for the door I fled through mere minutes ago. His hurried pace only slows when a raspy voice calls my name. Cranking my neck to the side, I see Andy holding out my purse for me. My head is so fuzzy, I entirely forgot I'd placed it on the countertop after my collision with Dexter. I'd like to say my daft behavior is based on the alcohol lacing my veins, but that isn't the case. I stopped drinking well over an hour ago, and even if I didn't, every drop would have burned off during my exchange with Marcus. That's how heated our interaction was. Potent enough to singe Satan's bottom.

When I reach out to accept my purse from Andy, my brows scrunch. Even with blood roaring in my ears, I couldn't miss the crinkling of paper when I accepted my satin clutch from his grasp. Noticing a small piece of paper Andy inconspicuously handed me during our exchange, I raise my eyes to his. He smiles softly, acknowledging the paper is for me without a word tumbling from his lips.

"Be careful, Cleo." I've never been good at lip reading, but I'm certain that's what Andy mouths before his attention reverts to a benefactor requesting his assistance.

Still jolted with shocked silence, I nod before allowing Brodie to escort me out of the gala. Since Dexter is paralyzed with astonishment, he doesn't hinder Brodie's endeavor. I don't know if I should be peeved or pleased by that notion. Considering it's the second time in under ten minutes I've failed to warrant a chase down, it bruises my ego more than I'd care to admit.

I swallow the horridly bitter taste in the back of my throat as I store the scrap of paper in my clutch. Andy seems like a great guy, but with my heart sitting in tatters, the last thing I want is more complications.

My eyes lift to scan my location. Brodie and I are moments away from reaching the emergency door I exited moments ago.

I dig my heels into the thickly piled carpet in an attempt to slow Brodie's urgent pace. My efforts are utterly fruitless, his speed is so unchecked, we finalize the last half-dozen strides in two heart-thrashing seconds. "I swear to god, Brodie, if you've lured me into another trap, Lucy will be an only child," I grumble under my breath, my words wheezy.

"I swear to god, Cleo, if you force me into this getup one more time tonight, I'll reconsider my stance on whipping women."

Even hearing a whip of edginess in his voice—*no pun intended*—I freeze in place. His tone is playful, but it was void of any confirmation that Marcus isn't lurking behind the door for me like he was last time Brodie stole my attention from Dexter.

"Are you luring me into a trap?" I stare straight into Brodie's twinkling-with-amusement eyes. "Is Marcus standing behind that door?" I point to the door we're mere feet from.

"Not even a snide remark on my whipping comment?"

I'm glad he can find humor in my situation, but I am not amused. The more my shock at his admission we got freaky in the middle of a fundraising gala subsides, the more my anger is returning.

Incapable of ignoring my rueful glare for a second longer, Brodie breathes out, "No. Marcus isn't behind the door."

I don't want it to, but disappointment slams into me.

"My instructions were to collect you, bundle you into a car, then take you home." All the humor in his voice has vanished, leaving nothing but a thick timbre hindered by a snip of regret.

"Marcus wants me to leave?" *God—expressing it out loud hurt more than thinking it.*

The knife twisting in my heart pushes deeper when Brodie nods.

"What does he think I was doing? I was leaving before you stopped me," I retaliate, my anger so wrathful, I can't stop it, even knowing it's being forced on the wrong person.

Peering at me with a set of remorseful eyes, Brodie pulls the listening contraption out of his ear and stores it in his pocket. The demands of the person squawking in his ear are loud, I hear their grumbly voice mumbling through his trousers the entire time he scrubs his hand over the cropped beard on his chin while he configures a reply to my question. His anxious response sets my nerves on edge. It isn't one I anticipated from a bodyguard left to clean up the mess of his boss. It seems more personal than that.

"What's going on, Brodie? This isn't like you. It also isn't like Marcus. I know him. That wasn't him." I mumble my last two sentences, my voice wary it's allowing my heart to speak on behalf of my head before it's had time to evaluate everything rationally.

They say love can make you blind, but that isn't the case right now. I know what I saw. *I hate what I saw.* But my gut is cautioning me not to jump to conclusions. Marcus said just last week I was fulfilling his requirements, so what has changed so drastically between now and then?

"What did I do wrong?" My words tumble from my mouth before I can stop them.

"I'm not the man you should be asking, Cleo." When he spots a glint of moisture teeming in the corners of my eyes, he mutters, "I'm just doing the job I'm paid to do. Please don't make it any harder on me." I can tell by his tone he is remorseful for my situation, but he is also being honest. He is just doing his job.

Brodie steps in front of me, engulfing me in his bottled-cologne scent. "What do you want to do, Cleo? Stay here or go home?" The brutal pain in my heart softens, encouraged by him seeking my opinion instead of forcing one onto me.

Incapable of speaking for fear of crying, I nod.

"Home?" Brodie confirms, unsure what my gesture refers to.

When I nod again, Brodie releases a deep exhalation of air. Gratefulness spreads across his face as he splays his hand on the curve of my lower back. Remaining quiet, he pushes open the emergency exit door, then nudges his head for me to enter before him. My eyes fleetingly scan the dingy hallway when I cautiously step into the mildew-scented area. Just as Brodie guaranteed, Marcus is nowhere to be seen. Half of me is grateful his pledge was spot on, however, the other half is devastated.

I have so many emotions pumping into me right now, I'm at a loss as to what the hell is going on. Marcus didn't confirm that Keira is his sub, but he didn't deny it either. Add that to the culpability his eyes were carrying during our exchange, and all the arrows point to the same conclusion—Keira is his sub. Furthermore, if he didn't have anything to hide, why wouldn't he have just been honest? What good can possibly be achieved with deceit?

The playful vibrancy bouncing between Brodie and me when we walked into the hotel hours ago has been snuffed, traded for a stuffiness that makes my stomach churn. Brodie doesn't speak until we merge onto the cracked sidewalk at the back entrance of the hotel.

"We are looking for a dark gray Jaguar," he murmurs as his eyes scan the crammed street hidden behind the hotel.

After wrapping my arms around my torso to ward off the chilly winds prickling my skin with goosebumps, I help Brodie locate our transport. With the gala attended by the wealthiest of the wealthiest, the alley is lined with expensive vehicles. It's like an auto show of the most pristine cars—some vintage, some not even scheduled for production yet. If my heart weren't a twisted mess, I'd be tempted to yank my cell out of my clutch to snap some pictures for Jackson. He has a fondness for restored classics. But since it feels like my heart has shrunk to a quarter of its size, I keep my cell stored away.

When Brodie notices me shivering, he shrugs off his jacket and drapes it over my shoulders. Before I can express my thanks, a dark gray Jaguar pulls to the curb in front of us. After ducking his chin to peruse the driver's credentials, Brodie opens the back passenger door and gestures for me to enter. My body slicks with sweat, shocked by the contrasting temperatures between the cab of the Jaguar and outside. It's like I've trekked out of the Antarctic straight into a Syrian desert. It's roasting in here.

My neck cranks to the side so fast my muscles squeal in protest when the passenger door slams shut with Brodie still standing on the sidewalk. The request for an explanation is rammed back into my throat when he cracks open the front door. *Phew! I thought he was leaving me here—alone.* I've always embraced New York's eclectic lifestyle without a second thought. But with my mind hazy from my exchange with Marcus and unexplained dizziness, I'm not as welcoming of a solo voyage as usual. I love New York—it's my sister city—but navigating my way through the craziness unaccompanied seems daunting tonight.

Panic wells inside me when Brodie fails to slide into the passenger seat. Remaining on the sidewalk, he hands the driver a yellow post-it note with an address hand-scribbled across the front. "Take Cleo to this address. Don't stop for anything. Do you understand?" he instructs, the authoritativeness of his tone shocking me.

Brodie is a bodyguard, but I've never heard his voice have this much sharpness. When the driver nods, Brodie slaps his hand on the hood of the Jaguar, soundlessly advising the driver to exit.

Anxiety grips my throat as I scoot across the sticky leather seat. Failing to notice my gaped jaw and bugged eyes, Brodie's stance stiffens. His entire composure screams of a man on watch. His shoulders broaden as his chest puffs out, his feet plant at the width of his shoulders, and one of his hands rests on the concealed gun strapped to his hip. His stature conveys a "do not mess with me" attitude.

Once Brodie's protective stance becomes nothing but a blur in the distance, I shift my confused gaze to a pair of eyes scrutinizing me via the rearview mirror. I frown in confusion as my brain racks why his eyes seem so familiar, although I'm confident we've never met.

A tiny shiver moves through me when recollection dawns on why his blue eyes are recognizable. He is the man who drove me to Marcus's residence weeks ago. The one who refused to pull over no matter how much I begged.

Incapable of ignoring the sick feeling brewing in my gut, I lock my stern eyes with the driver before asking, "What address are you taking me to?"

He peers at me, blinking and confused. Recalling that his English is poor, I ask another way, "Montclair? Are we going to Montclair?"

"No." A curt shake of his head amplifies his short reply. "This address." He taps the post-it note stuck to his steering wheel. "No Montclair."

"Please..." My petition to alter our route is barely hatched when he rolls up the Jaguar's privacy partition, denying my God-given right to make my own decisions.

Clearly, he remembers me as well as I remember him.

2

Ten minutes contemplating a way out of my predicament equals ten minutes of wasted time. Previous experience told me pleading with the driver to alter the direction of our travels would be pointless, yet I still squandered the last ten minutes begging for him to do precisely that.

Confused and a little worried, I slouch into my seat and shift my eyes to the sea of vehicles clogging the streets of New York. With traffic the densest I've seen, mere seconds pass before an idea I've been toying with fully forms in my mind. I'll walk to the closest train station and take public transport home. Although my heels are the tallest I've ever worn, I'd prefer to endure blisters than have my heart undergo another brutal beating it may not withstand. I can't take the risk—one more crack could permanently disfigure it.

When the driver stops at a red light, I curl my hand around the door handle and yank it back roughly. My teeth grit when my ploy to escape is thwarted. The Jaguar's lock mechanisms are firmly in place, leaving me trapped in the car with a man who is watching me like a hawk from the rearview mirror. His gaze is mocking, goading me without a syllable oozing from his hard-lined lips.

Unable to leash my Garcia stubbornness, my overworked brain seeks a viable alternative. It smacks into me like a ton of bricks not even ten seconds later. *Lexi.* I drop my eyes to my watch to calculate the time left on our journey. If I message her now, she should arrive at Marcus's residence within minutes of my arrival. The short delay will give me enough time to pack my belongings and meet her out front. As much as it would be nice to be heedless right now, my budget isn't flexible. Every penny I have must go towards mine and Lexi's living expenses, so replacing the clothes I have stored in Marcus's expansive walk-in-closet is out of the question.

Pretending I can't feel my heart sinking into my stomach, I lean over to snag my purse from the seat next to me. My brows furl when the faintest buzz gains my attention. Assuming it's the rattle of my hands shuddering up my arms, I snatch my purse off the seat and rummage inside for my cell. My hunt for my phone halts when I feel a second vibrating sensation moments later. Although its buzz is faint, I'm certain it isn't from my shaky composure.

I run my hands down my body, only stopping when I reach the pocket of Brodie's coat curled around my shuddering frame. With my brain in a tizzy, I completely forgot he lent me his jacket. I jump in fright when an unexpected shudder courses through me again. Since my hand is resting in the pocket of Brodie's jacket, it amplifies the strength of its vibration.

My hand slips into the right-side pocket of Brodie's jacket. My pace is so slow, you'd swear there was a nuclear weapon crammed into the small opening. Blood roars to my ears when a brisk coolness graces my fingertips. Quicker than I can snap my fingers, horrid unease thickens my blood. *Please, for the love of god, don't let it be the vibrating butt plug Marcus slipped into his pocket before we left his residence.*

I slump in my chair, eternally grateful when my hand wraps around a sleek metal material that can only represent one thing—Brodie's cell phone. With my heart thrashing against my ribs, I yank Brodie's phone out of the pocket. I'm not planning on snooping, I just want to advise his caller that he is away from his phone. I know how much I panic when Lexi doesn't answer my calls, so I'd hate to put his family through the same thing.

My heart stops beating when my eyes drop to the screen of Brodie's phone and the name of his caller displayed. *Marcus.* I stare at the phone, unmoving and confused, until his call is forwarded to Brodie's voicemail. Just as quickly as the cell stops vibrating, it commences ringing all over again. With chaotic heartache thrusting me into idiocy, I slide my finger across the screen and press the cell to my ear.

"Jesus, Brodie, what took you so long? Do you have her? Is she safe? Where are you?" Marcus's voice is so panicked, his words fire off his tongue before they're properly developed. "Did you give the driver clear instructions on where to take her?"

I don't speak. I can't. I can barely breathe, let alone advise Marcus I'm not Brodie. It isn't his molten lava voice that has me tranced into stupidity, it's the absolute panic tainting his usually calm tone.

"Brodie?!" Marcus roars through the cell so brutally, I startle. "Do you have her...?" Before the entire sentence leaves his mouth, he inhales a sharp breath. "Cleo?"

My eyes frantically search the area, certain he can see me, as there is no way he'd know it's me on the other end of the line. I'm not even breathing for the fear he would recognize my wheezy pants.

"Cleo." This time his tone doesn't come out sounding like a question. It's a confirmation.

Tears prick my eyes when he mumbles, "Are you okay, baby?" I hear a commotion sound down the line like he has muffled the phone to talk to someone before. "Where's Brodie? Is he with you?"

"No," I reply, timidly shaking my head.

He exhales harshly as if he was sucker-punched. "Do you know where he is?"

"Umm... yes. He's at the hotel."

I don't understand what the hell is going on. The man talking to me on the phone is not the same man I was arguing with twenty minutes ago. I know I said previously I can tell the difference between Marcus and Master Chains, but this is ridiculous. Surely his contrasting personalities don't extend past the bedroom. *Do they?*

"What?" I ask when Marcus's deep voice calling my name draws me back to the present.

"Where are you, baby?" His voice is a soft, nurturing purr. "Who are you with?"

My brows stitch. He has only called me a term of endearment a handful of times. The first few times was before we met in person. It was when he was wooing me to be his sub. It was more a playful tease than a term of endearment. The second time was following my attack in the alleyway. So, for him to say it to me twice in under a minute has my confusion intensifying to a point I'm not comfortable with.

"What's going on, Marcus?" Dread echoes in my tone.

"I can't update you right now, Cleo. I just need you to tell me where you are."

Even with my spikes hackled from his crass tone, I breathe out, "I'm in your Jaguar."

Marcus releases a massive exhalation of air. It's so robust, my face grimaces when it shreds my eardrums. "She's in my Jag," I hear him tell someone in the background.

I sit up straight in my seat when a mix of male and female voices react to his revelation. "Who are you with? Are you with *Keira?*" Keira's name is barely whispered since it took every morsel of my soul to articulate it.

I press Brodie's phone close to my ear when muffled voices reverberate down the line. The multiple accents are so jumbled, I wouldn't be surprised to discover Marcus is cupping the speaker of his phone.

Although it's only faint, I overhear Marcus say, "I want this wrapped up. I need to go."

My jaw tightens when a female voice replies to his request. Although I can't one hundred percent testify it was Keira, the green sludge lacing my veins doesn't hear logic. As far as my jealousy is concerned, that female voice belongs to Keira.

My heart rate races as my stomach churns. "That was Keira, wasn't it?"

There is a scrape of a chair across the ground before the thud of shoe-covered feet padding on a tiled floor booms through the cell's speaker.

"Answer me, Marcus. Was that Keira?"

"Cleo. Stop."

Angered by his continued deflection, I hit the end call button on Brodie's phone, switch it off, then send it sailing across the interior of Marcus's Jaguar. A tinge of hesitation courses through me when Brodie's phone smacks into the polished wooden trim on the back driver's side door before dropping to the floor. Neither Brodie or his cell phone deserves the wrath of my anger. That right solely belongs to the man who confuses me as much as he irritates me.

Feeling guilty that I've damaged property that doesn't belong to me, I lean over to collect Brodie's phone from the floor. I stop halfway, hindered by the buzz of my cell phone in my purse. Even knowing who is calling doesn't prevent me from yanking my phone out of my bag and peering down at the screen. Although the display screen states my caller's identity is unknown, I know who it is. Other than my sister, nobody calls my phone.

Feeling spiteful, I send Marcus's call to voicemail. Pretending I can't hear my cell phone ringing again, I fish the twenty dollar bill out of my wallet I attempted to give Andy for my bottle of water and slam it against the privacy partition. The driver slides down the window, noticing the crumpled-up note.

"We go to this address," he maintains, jamming his index finger into his steering wheel.

Although his words are firm, they also expose his wavering constraint. If I had more than small change in my purse, I'm confident I could use it to my advantage, but considering this twenty is all I have, I stick with my initial plan.

"Yes, we go to that address, but faster." I inwardly sigh, grateful when my voice comes out smooth and confident, meaning he will have more chance of understanding me.

"Fast?" the driver confirms, peering at me in the rearview mirror after lowering the partition down. His face is flushed with anger, but his bright eyes expose his interest.

When I nod, he double-checks, "This address?" The horn of the Jaguar beeps when he taps the post-it note firmly.

"Yes," I verify, leaning over the partition to hand him my note.

He smiles, exposing his slightly crooked teeth. "Okay. Thank you."

He puts my twenty in the top pocket of his short-sleeve dress shirt before increasing the pressure on the gas pedal. Happy the first stage of my plan has successfully launched, I slip back into my seat, refasten my seatbelt, then drop my eyes to my phone. If I weren't already aware of my mystery caller's identity, the four calls I've missed the past two minutes guarantees I can't be mistaken. No one I've ever met is as impatient as Master Chains.

After sending Marcus's fifth call to voicemail, I begin dialing a number I know by heart. I've only dialed two digits when the screen announces another call. Hitting the end button, I continue with my mission.

My attempts to call Lexi are impaired over and over again by Marcus's constant calling. Annoyed beyond belief, I swipe my finger across the screen and press my cell to my ear. "What!?" I scream down the phone. My voice is so loud the driver of the Jaguar raises the partition once more.

"Cleo?" queries a hesitant voice—a voice that doesn't match Marcus's.

Swamped by guilt, I sink into my seat. "Hey, Dexter. Sorry. I've just had a ..." My words trail off when I can't find an appropriate word to describe my night. It went from an awe-inspiring high to a devastating low so quickly, my head is still spinning.

"Shitty night?" Dexter fills in.

I feebly laugh. "Yeah, something like that." I lick my parched lips before saying, "I'm sorry about what happened earlier. I didn't ditch you for Brodie—"

"I know," Dexter interrupts. "Look, I'm not going to lie, Cleo. He is a damn good actor. I was truly worried at the start, but then I realized you're not *that* type of girl."

"*That* type of girl?" I mimic.

Although I'm sure he was being playful, the feminist side of me I buried two months ago is rearing her head, ready to defend the rights for any woman to do as she sees fit with her body.

Dexter's husky laugh douses my agitation—slightly. "I didn't mean it in a bad way, Cleo. I just meant you deserve more than a five-minute romp in a storage closet. But, hey, if that's what turns you on, so be it. Any man would be crazy to miss an opportunity to be with you."

It could just be my woozy head, but his last sentence sounded like it was laced with sexual innuendo.

"Thanks?" My tone makes my praise sound like a question more than a declaration. I'm not used to getting unexpected compliments, so they always thrust me into a state of idiocy when I do.

Dexter's breathless laughter switches to a belly-clutching chuckle. "I've made you embarrassed," he snickers between laughter.

"No, you haven't." I wave my hand through the air like it's no big deal, eternally grateful he can't see me, otherwise he would have noticed my inflamed cheeks and wide eyes.

Dexter's laugh tells me he doesn't believe a word I said. Rolling my eyes at the cockiness beaming down the line, I ask, "Was there a purpose to your call? Or did you just set out to make me uncomfortable?"

"So you're embarrassed?"

"Fine! I'm embarrassed. Happy?" That isn't entirely true. I'm more confused than anything. I've got too many thoughts passing through my mind to add a flirty comment into the mix.

"Very much so." His throaty purr causes the hairs on my arms to bristle. Which, in turn, adds to my confusion. "Anyway..." he breathes out heavily, like he is snapping himself out of a trance. "I have a very valid reason for my call."

Noticing the snip of unease in his voice, I straighten my slumped form. My intuition is proven dead on point when Dexter mutters, "How well do you know Keira Herrington?"

"Not very well. Why?" The swishing of my stomach resonates in my low tone.

I hear Dexter rub his hand over the scruff on his chin before he answers, "Being Delilah's date gave me more than just cooties."

I try to shut it down, but a small smile tugs at my lips before I can stop it. My grin is brief, but obviously long enough for Dexter to hear. Clearly, when he says, "Ah, that's better," as if he heard my cheeks incline over the phone.

My smile enlarges more. "I suggest a disinfectant bath with a steel sponge," I chide, hoping a bit of playfulness will settle the nerves wreaking havoc with my stomach.

My efforts have the effect I was aiming for when Dexter's boyish laughter barrels down the line. "Don't worry, I have an entire recon planned to rid me of her germs."

His reply increases the bow of my brow. *How close did he and Delilah get if he is required to don a hazmat suit after their date?*

After settling his vigorous chuckles, Dexter asks, "Do you have any plans tomorrow, Cleo? I'd rather share the information I have in person than over the phone."

I frown, panicked. "It's that important?"

"As important as breathing," Dexter fires back in an instant.

My stomach flips, loathing the disturbing images his reply bombarded me with. All were similar to the ones I saw earlier tonight, but this time around, Marcus and Keira weren't elegantly dressed. *They weren't dressed at all.*

"Yeah, I can meet you somewhere. Did you want me to come to you?" I ask through the solid lump in my throat.

"Nah." Dexter drags out the one word as if it's an entire sentence. "Isn't that pizzeria you mentioned a few months ago in Montclair?"

My brows furrow. "Villa Victoria? Yeah, it's on Park Street," I reply, shocked he remembered a restaurant I mentioned months earlier.

"I'll meet you there tomorrow. Say around two?"

Even though he can't see me, I nod. "Okay. I'll see you tomorrow at two."

"Alright." I hear his smile through the phone. "I'll see you tomorrow. Bye, Cleo."

"Bye, Dexter," I bid him farewell, confusion evident in my tone.

Just before I disconnect our call, a question pops into my head. "Dexter?"

"Yeah," he answers immediately.

My lips are dry, so I lick them before asking, "Am I going to need anything tomorrow? Like ... *tissues*?" My voice is so weak, I won't be surprised if he asks me to repeat my question.

He doesn't.

"Depends," he replies, honesty in his response.

Sickness spreads through my gut. "On what?"

My breathing stills, my heart stills. I swear, time stands still as I await his reply.

"On if you're in love with Marcus Everett," Dexter eventually replies, his tone so low I'm certain the devil heard it.

The wooziness inflicting my head swells when the air is sucked from my lungs. Hearing my unenthusiastic response, Dexter asks, "Are you, Cleo? Do you love him?" His voice sounds confused. *He isn't the only one.*

"No," I mumble, my voice cracking with emotions. I try to shake my head to strengthen my statement, but my body won't allow it.

My hand darts up to rub away a tear descending down my cheek when Dexter mutters, "Bring tissues."

3

I've barely calmed the erratic beat of my heart when the Jaguar pulls in front of the platform steps of Marcus's New York residence. My plan to have Lexi pick me up in the minutes following my arrival has been left for dust after my conversation with Dexter. I've done nothing the past forty minutes but stare at the pitch black sky, striving to untangle some of the confusion bombarding me. Forty minutes of silence awarded me with forty minutes of additional confusion.

Pushing aside my bewilderment, I accept the hand the Jaguar driver is holding out for me. With my tight dress holding my thighs hostage, it's a little harder to slip out of the car than it was to enter it.

"Thank you," I say graciously when the driver passes me Brodie's cell I sent hurling across the car earlier.

The driver dips his chin before jogging around to the driver's side door of the Jaguar and slipping inside. I wait until his taillights disappear in the distance before climbing the platform stairs. The same set of butterflies that take flight in my stomach every time I climb these stairs are still present, they just aren't based on giddy silliness. I genuinely feel ill.

My shaky steps up the stairs halt halfway when the large glass entranceway door suddenly swings open. With my poor eyesight hampered by tears, it takes me several blinks to recognize the person standing in the doorway. It's the beautiful middle-aged Hispanic lady who disappeared within minutes of my first arrival at this residence. Aubrey, Marcus's personal assistant/housekeeper.

"Come on, dear, it's cold out there." She signals with her hand for me to hurry.

I push off my feet before my brain can cite an objection to her bossy tone. When I stop in front of Aubrey, shivering from the sprinkling of rain mottling my hair, she snatches my purse, Brodie's jacket, and his cell phone out of my hands.

"I need that," I instruct, pointing to my purse when she dumps my belongings on the glass entranceway table.

Just because I've spent the last forty minutes in a daze doesn't mean my plans have altered. I'm still calling Lexi to pick me up.

"You are to be fed, showered, and sent to bed. Mr. Everett didn't state which order, so you can choose whether to eat or shower first. What do you want to do?" Aubrey's tone indicates she's not to be messed with.

I take a step back, bamboozled by her bitchiness. *Is every female in Marcus's life without a heart, or just those who work for him?*

When I ask Aubrey that, her brows stitch. She looks as bewildered by my response as I am to her affirmation she was given instructions on how to handle me. The longer she stares at me, the weaker her evil glare becomes. Apparently, the anger activating every nerve in my body is potent enough she can feel it shuddering the ground as well.

The twinkle in her eyes grows as she mumbles, "You're different than the others."

"That's because I am *not* one of them," I reply, hating that I'm once again defending my title in Marcus's life. "I am *not* Marcus's sub."

Aubrey runs her hands down the crease of her skirt, seemingly unsure of a reply. I wouldn't necessarily say she doesn't believe me. She just seems unaware of how to act in this predicament. Obviously, she is more well-equipped to handle Marcus's subs than she is his girlfriends. *Ex-girlfriend,* I mentally correct.

Wanting to switch off the washing machine in my stomach, I mutter, "Do you have any reservations about me eating in my room?"

She peers up at me with her dark eyes blinking. "No. I'll arrange for your meal to be brought there."

Smiling to issue her my thanks, I gather my purse off the entranceway table and make a beeline for the stairs. Aubrey's eyes burn with concern, tracking me the entire time. Once I hit the landing of the spiral staircase, I dig my cell out of my clutch. My hand is slicked with so much sweat, I nearly drop it while nervously fumbling for Lexi's number. She answers not even two seconds later.

"Cleo...Hi." The scrumptious laughter accompanying her greeting dulls the ache in my chest. Her girly giggle is full of vibrancy and love—a stark contradiction to the emotions pummeling me into a blubbering mess.

"Have I interrupted something?" I ask when the sound of sheets shuffling jingles down the line.

"No... Jackson, stop it," Lexi chastises him, her words muffled as she cups her phone. "You know I'm here whenever you need me, Cleo, what's up?" Her last sentence comes out in a hurry since a girly laugh quickly followed it. "Jackson...don't, it's Cleo."

"Oh, hey, Cleo," Jackson mutters down the line, his words as high as my arched brow.

I pace into the main suite of Marcus's residence. "Hi, Jackson. Is everything okay?" I ask, my tone laced with suspicion.

"Perfectly A-OK." Jackson draws out his words.

I stop frozen at the side of Marcus's bed when Lexi's faint moan is barely covered by Jackson's throaty laugh. My confusion grows when a loud yelp barrels through my phone's speaker moments later, closely followed by a manly growl. *What the hell are they up to?*

I hold my phone to my ear with my shoulder so I can gather my overnight bag from the footlocker at the end of Marcus's bed. As I enter the expansive walk-in closet, Lexi and Jackson's playful banter continues as if I'm not eavesdropping on every murmured statement. I am. I listen like a real creep, adoring the utter bliss radiating out of my baby sister's voice. She sounds so incredibly happy, tears spring in my eyes. And for the first time tonight, they are tears of happiness.

I stop stuffing clothes into my bag sprawled open on the pristinely clean floor when I catch the quickest snippet of a request Jackson makes between a peppering of smooching kisses. He was quiet, but not soft enough for my snooping ears to miss. "Say it again?"

"No." Lexi's one word is drenched with heavy sentiment. "I'm talking to my sister," she continues, revealing she is aware I'm listening in like a weirdo.

I push the phone in close to my ear, displaying the title "Cleo the Creep" Lexi gave me four years ago is still going strong when Jackson demands, "Say it again, then I'll leave you alone."

Standing frozen in the middle of the dead quiet closet, I can hear Lexi's heart thrashing against her ribcage before the faintest whisper of, "I love you," spills from her lips.

I gasp in a shocked breath as a rush of moisture floods my eyes. The satin material of my dress does a terrible job mopping up my tears when Jackson replies, "Not as much as I love you."

Not trusting my legs to keep me upright, I move to sit on the chaise Marcus spanked me on the morning following our first session in his playroom. Although devastated by the circumstances of events that has happened thus far tonight, hearing my baby sister express her love to the man of her dreams has fulfilled one of my greatest wishes.

Just like me, Lexi closed herself off after our parents and Tate died. In the beginning, I thought her reasons were the same as mine—she was afraid of people leaving her. It was only after watching her wade through breakup after breakup the past three years did I realize our logic for keeping people at arm's length was entirely different. I kept people away because I was afraid they would leave me. Lexi kept them away because she was afraid of leaving them.

Every time Lexi started a new relationship, she began immediately plotting its demise. She has often quoted she didn't want love, marriage, and a family. Where in reality, she didn't want them to suffer the heartache of losing her. I don't know if her change in mindset is based on how well the Kayldeco program is working for her, or if she just needed a man like Jackson to prove loving her will be worth the heartache of losing her. *Maybe it's a bit of both?*

Telling Jackson she loves him is a massive step for Lexi—one so significant, I'm not going to ruin it by being melodramatic.

"Lexi," I breathe heavily down the line, drawing her attention away from Jackson, who I can hear schmoozing her neck.

"Yes." Lexi voice sounds elsewhere. A faint slap bellows down the line before Jackson's hearty chuckle. "Sorry, Cleo. You *now* have my undivided attention."

A smile stretches across my face when Jackson warns, "You have five minutes, Cleo. Use it wisely." The last half of his sentence is barely audible, overtaken by the thud of feet padding against a hard floor. If my assumptions are right, it sounds like Lexi is chasing him down our hallway.

I jump, startled when a door suddenly slams moments before Lexi's breathless pants wheeze down the line. "Sorry, he's truly gone this time. I used our new reinforced door to lock him outside."

"Lexi..." I drawl out with a laugh.

"What?" I can imagine her shrugging. "He needs a moment to cool down. Hell, I need to cool down." She dramatically huffs. "Our week of solidarity is nearly up, so we're getting in as much alone time as possible, but, my god, my body is feeling it."

My theatrical gag ends when I hear Jackson pounding on our front door. "Lex, let me in. Mrs. Rachet is taking my picture."

"Smile, Jax," Lexi squeals, her voice so high she sounds more like a teen than a grown woman. "She will post that on the Montclair Neighborhood Watch website, so you better look good. Once an image is released to the world, there is no chance of removing it."

My childish giggles nearly have me missing Jackson's shouted demand, "Goddamn it, Lex. Let me in! I don't have any pants on."

When Lexi ignores Jackson's continued requests for entry, I say, "Lexi." I drag out her name in a long, warning purr. "You can't tell a man you love him, then throw him outside without any pants."

I hear Lexi's throat work hard to swallow. "You heard that?" Her voice is not as chirpy as it was.

"Yep. Every word," I confess, not the slightest bit hesitant to admit I am a creep.

Lexi huffs. I can just imagine her rolling her eyes. "Stop acting like I won valedictorian. It was only three little words, Cleo."

"Three *very important* little words."

"Whatever," Lexi grumbles under her breath.

She doesn't fool me. I heard her heart skip a beat. After a short stint of silence, the clunk of our front door lock booms into my ears, closely followed by the creek of the warped floorboards in our entranceway.

"He's in. Are you happy?"

"Very much so," I reply, smiling.

My eyes lift from my heel-covered feet when I detect another presence in the room. I don't want it to, but a dash of disappointment thickens my blood when I spot Aubrey entering the master suite. She has a white napkin curled over her forearm, and she is balancing a silver tray on her hands. With a contrite smile, she places the serving tray onto a stack of drawers on her right. My stomach grumbles when the smell of curry filters into the air. Its desolate response reminds me I haven't eaten since lunch.

Spotting that I'm on a call, Aubrey dips her chin, then exits the room, leaving the door open in her wake. My attention reverts to my cell when Lexi's soft giggle jingles down the line. It appears a few moments in the blistering cold winds Montclair is famous for didn't dampen Jackson's interest in the slightest. I don't know why, but that awards me an immense amount of pleasure. At least one of the Garcia women is feeling the love tonight.

"I love you, Lexi. I'll talk to you tomorrow," I say down the line.

Lexi shushes Jackson before saying, "Hold on one minute, young lady. You didn't just call to tell me you love me."

Warmth blooms across my chest, cherishing the fact she knows me so well she can intuit what my call is about.

"Your voice is doing that weird skittish thing it only does when you're excited or nervous. So, spill the beans, Cleo, or I'll torture it out of you."

"All the way from Montclair?" I jest.

"I'll find a way," she assures me, her tone confident.

I wait a beat, giving my body a chance to rid itself of nerves before saying, "No, you're right. I didn't just call to tell you I love you. I called to ask you something."

I hear Lexi's pulse raging through her veins as she waits for me to continue. Her thudding heart is drowned out by a fit of laughter when I ask, "Did you know pineapple makes guys' cum taste sweeter?"

4

Shame wallops me as I stand on the landing in the second story of Marcus's residence, swinging my eyes up and down his opulent home. I have my bags packed and sitting at my side, but I'm at a loss as to where I'm going. I can't go home as I don't want to interrupt what should be an uninterruptable moment between Lexi and Jackson, but I can't stay here either. Just the thought of facing Marcus head on has my stomach twisted up in knots. God—I wish I had a bundle of cash sitting in my bank account, begging to be squandered. Then I'd simply call a taxi and spend the remainder of my weekend holed up in a two-star motel on the outskirts of town. But, unfortunately, there are no hotel rooms in New York city available for three hundred dollars a night—yes, I checked. Furthermore, I can't afford the cab fare to drive me there.

This is one of those sporadic moments where I wish I didn't love my sister as much as I did, then I wouldn't have hesitated to ask her to come pick me up. Considering it's been over three hours since I left the gala, even with my forty-minute delay in calling her, we would have been long gone before Marcus arrived home.

I don't know if I'll survive seeing him again. I wasn't being dishonest when I said if this turned out to be nothing but a crazy, lust-fueled fling it would kill me. It isn't just killing me. It's gutting me alive. I haven't even left his residence yet and I already feel hollow. Imagine how much worse it will be when I build up the courage to walk out his front door?

I repeat a mantra my dad always quoted as I stoop down to gather my overnight bag from the floor. "It's time to pull up your big girl panties and show how strong you truly are."

Although he was originally talking about dealing with schoolyard bullies or clients disgruntled by the scathing article printed about them by Global Ten, it's still suitable for this occasion. Not facing Marcus would be a cowardly way of ending things. Even with my heart being held together by a thin thread, it knows confronting him in person is the right thing to do. My parents raised me to be a strong, independent woman, so I can't just push that aside when the circumstances don't fall in my favor.

My steps down the glamorous hallway are shaky and long. With Aubrey advising she was heading to bed hours ago, the entire house is plunged into eerie darkness. My heart slithers into my stomach when I open the door of a room I'd give anything not to see again. Marcus's old sub room.

If it is old.

Careful not to impact the heavenly thick wool carpet, I place my dowdy overnight bag on the ground next to the closed bedroom door, then trudge to the bathroom. Although I've already showered once tonight, I still feel dirty. It's probably more to do with this room than anything.

I take my time in the shower, ignoring how starkly contradicting it is to the grandness of Marcus's bathroom. Don't misconstrue my statement, this bathroom is a thousand times better than the one in my home, but compared to Marcus's four vanity sinks, egg-shaped tub, and large double shower, this one just looks shabby.

I huff incredulously. I've clearly allowed the opulence of Marcus's properties to spoil me. Maybe that's why I'm finding it so hard to leave? It isn't because of my confusion, it's because I don't want to give this up. God—no wonder everyone assumes I am Marcus's sub. I'm acting just like one.

Annoyed at myself, I dress in a pair of stretchy yoga pants and a long-sleeve shirt. I'm so peeved, I don't bother putting on panties or a bra. I don't even dry my hair. I'll deal with the aftermath of my decision tomorrow. For now, I just want to crawl into bed and forget the world exists.

That would be a whole heap easier to do if I weren't doing it in the bed Marcus's previous subs used. I've been tossing and turning non-stop the past forty minutes. I've never seen photos of Marcus's former subs, or been given any indication of how they look, but I'm imagining a flurry of beautiful blondes with ocean blue eyes and perfect facial features. They are gorgeous women, but their faces are horrid enough to instigate nightmares.

Realizing I'll never achieve sleep in this room, I crawl out of bed, collect my bag, then leave the room. Because the house is so unnervingly quiet, the padding of my feet is readily distinguishable. The first door I open is the room Marcus and I prepared in earlier tonight. It has too many memories for me to sleep in there. The second door is the home gym. Other than the bench Marcus lifts weights at, there isn't another flat surface. I close the door and continue my trek, knowing there are only three more doors to explore. Two I'm well acquainted with. Marcus's bedroom and his playroom. Considering I don't plan on stepping foot in either of them, it leaves me only one option. The media room.

Gratitude clears away some of the nerves fluttering in my stomach when I notice the configuration of the room. It has two rows of reclining chairs lined in front of a monstrous projection screen. Thankfully, each chair is void of the armrests found in cinemas. If it weren't for the small walkway down one side, they would extend wall to wall.

After snagging a cashmere blanket draped over a railing on my right, I dump my bag on the floor and trudge down the small staircase. The bulky chair in front of the large screen is calling my name, beckoning me to it. My steps are sluggish, weighed down by the heaviness of my exhausted muscles. I am truly the most fatigued I've ever been. Even my blinks are long as my eyes fight to stay open.

My muscles sigh in gratitude when I slump in the super comfy recliner. The leather is so voluptuous, it curves around my body, cradling it with comfort. It's so blissful, before I know it, I fall into a much-needed, yet restless sleep.

I don't know how much time passes before I am awoken by the noise of someone yelling. "Where is she?! You said she was here!"

I blink several times in a row as my body struggles to produce enough saliva to quench my bone-dry mouth. I've clearly been asleep long enough my mouth had time to gape open, but not long enough for my thumping headache to relinquish its stranglehold on my temples.

"She was, Sir. She was in your room last time I saw her."

My pulse quickens when a furious growl rumbles through my chest. "Sir? Stop calling me goddamn sir! How many times have I told you not to call me *that*?"

A rush of giddiness clusters in my head when I lurch to a half-seated position. It isn't my temples drilling my skull causing my staggering response, it's recognizing the voice shouting so loud he'll wake three continents. *Marcus.*

"I'm sorry, si—ah, Mr. Everett. It's an old habit from my previous employer," Aubrey explains, her tone as low as my heartrate.

Panic clutches my throat when Marcus mutters, "I'll be your previous employer if I hear you say it again. Do you understand me?"

"Yes, I understand," Aubrey replies dismally.

"Good. Now, where is she?" Marcus's words are smeared with so much anger, they went to hell and back before they were delivered.

"She was in your room. I swear." Aubrey's voice cracks with emotions.

"I checked in my room, she isn't there!" Marcus yells, his stern timbre shuddering through the thick paneled door between us.

"What about the subs' room, have you checked there?" Aubrey questions, confirming what I suspected last night. She is aware of Marcus's involvement in the BDSM lifestyle.

"I checked. She isn't there either!"

My brows stitch when my ears misinterpret the anger in Marcus's voice as panic.

"She didn't leave, Mr. Everett. How could she? She doesn't have access to the security codes." I can hear the sheer bewilderment in Aubrey's tone. Clearly, she has never seen this side of Marcus either. Usually, he is calm and collected. Tonight, he is anything but.

"Yes, she does. I gave them to her last week!" Marcus's tone is wrathful enough to rattle my ribcage. "I asked you to watch her until I returned. You shouldn't have slept."

Hating that Marcus is directing his anger at the wrong person—much like I did hours ago—I throw off the thin blanket draped over my shoulders and trudge up the stairs. For how heavy my muscles are, my movements are remarkably quick.

I throw open the door with so much force, it slams into the drywall. "Don't speak to her like that. Just because she is your staff does not give you the right to disrespect her. Did your father not teach you any manners?"

Marcus and Aubrey's eyes rocket to me in sync. Aubrey's are brimming with relief. I don't know if her response stems from discovering I'm still present in Marcus's residence, or because I am standing up for her. Marcus's eyes are as black as the sky, tainted and murky, much like the sludge his deceit created in my heart.

I take a step backward, startled by the blatant fury beaming out of him in invisible waves. I take another step back when I realize it isn't anger being projected from his narrowed gaze. He's panicked.

"Cleo," he sighs deeply.

I flinch when he charges for me. His movements so fast, the air ripples in his wake. My mouth gapes when he smashes his lips against mine. His tongue slides into my mouth before a smidge of hostility can be announced by my overworked brain. I didn't think any kiss would top the one he gave me in the driveway of my home two weeks ago. I was wrong. This kiss... *my god*. He kisses me with so much vigor, my brain can't formulate an objection before it's turned to mush. He kisses me until my mind is blank and my panties are wet. He kisses me until I forget my name. Then he kisses me some more.

When he pulls away, the squeal of my lungs battling to be replenished with oxygen rings over the manic thump of my heart. Marcus places me on my feet before cradling my slackened jaw with his shaking hands. His eyes go crazy, scanning every inch of my face. I return his stare, muted with shock.

"When I couldn't find you, I thought you were gone. I thought you'd left me," he mumbles under his breath, his voice drenched with uncontrollable fear, like the thought of me leaving him truly gutted him.

The pure devastation in his tone cuts me raw, but it doesn't stop me from saying, "I *am* leaving you, Marcus. Just not until tomorrow morning."

It's the fight of my life not to roll my eyes over the dimness displayed in my voice. How pathetic have I become that I can't break up with a man until after I've slept on his couch because I have nowhere else to go? I am better than this, my parents raised me better than this.

"I am leaving you," I say with more determination. "Now."

It will be a struggle, but I'll find a way to make it happen tonight, because standing across from him is more than I can bear. Seeing everything I am losing up close hurts way more than I could ever explain.

"No," Marcus says, shaking his head as his stern eyes dance between mine. "You're not leaving me, Cleo."

The anger his kiss dampened steamrolls back into me from the vicious snarl of his words. He replied as if my decision to leave him isn't my choice. Like he is the only one who has a say on the length of our relationship. Well, I have news for him.

"I'm not your submissive, Marcus, so any stipulated timeframe you force your subs..." I overemphasize the "S" on the end of "subs" to enhance my statement. "...to adhere to don't apply to me."

The rapturous standing ovation of the little voice inside me dims to a faint clap when Marcus replies, "I have plenty of resources at my disposal to restrain you here, Cleo. Don't test me."

The veins in my neck thrum, my body choosing its own response to his frisky tease. Annoyed at both Marcus and my lust-driven body, I roll my eyes, pivot on my heels, then head for the door.

"I might have stupidly thought that was sweet when you joked about it weeks ago. Now it's just disturbing," I snarl, my words wildly reckless.

My knees clang together when Marcus warns, "I'm not joking, Cleo. If you leave me, I'll hunt you down and tie you to my bed." His low tone vibrates from the roots of my hairs to the tips of my toes.

Huffing, I continue for the door. I may be head over heels in love with this man, but I am not so down on my luck I'm willing to pretend I didn't see what I see. So many women stay in relationships they should have left years earlier. I'm not going to be one of those women.

Gritting my teeth in the hope it will stop my tears from falling, I pry open the media room door. Unsurprisingly, Aubrey has made herself scarce. I don't blame her. The tension bristling the air is so dense, it has slicked my skin with a fine layer of sweat. And don't even get me started on the mess it has caused to my insides.

My angry strides into the hallway freeze when Marcus murmurs, "Cleo, please." I never knew two small words could express such agony.

After exhaling a deep breath, I pivot around to face him. He tries to tuck it away, but I see the quickest flare of emotion pass through his eyes before he entirely shuts it down. For someone who has poor acting skills, he is genuinely portraying that the idea of me leaving him is cutting him raw.

"We could have had something magical." When he endeavors to interrupt me, I continue speaking, foiling his attempt. "But you ruined what could have been the best thing of your life all because your desire to follow the rules of a BDSM lifestyle was stronger than your desire for me."

"No, Cleo," he denies, shaking his head. "Nothing is stronger than the desire I have for you. Not BDSM. Not the rules. Not a person. Nothing. I would kneel before I'd let any of those things take you away from me."

"She was wearing your collar! Your trademark!" I retaliate, loathing that my voice displays I am on the verge of tears. "You looked at her like you look at me." The anger in my voice makes way for sheer devastation. My heart smashes into my ribs so fast, it feels like it's moments away from breaking out of my chest cavity.

Confusion smears on Marcus's face before he shakes his head, soundlessly denying my accusation.

"I saw you, Marcus. I saw you with *her*!"

"You saw me comforting a friend. Nothing more."

I brush a tear from my cheek, hating that it makes me look weak. "A friend wearing a collar everyone in *your* lifestyle knows belongs to *you*. I looked like an idiot proudly prancing around in your trademark. The same one *she* was wearing." My voice is barely a whisper, doused more with shame than anger. I'm not ashamed of myself, I'm disappointed in his pathetic attempt at admitting his mistakes. I thought he was more of a man than this. Clearly, I was wrong.

"Say something. Tell me I'm wrong. Tell me everyone didn't think *she* was your sub when they saw her collar."

He remains quiet, breaking my heart even more.

"You're pathetic," I mutter under my breath, beyond devastated.

Ignoring the flare of anger detonating in Marcus's eyes from my taunt, I spin on my heels and exit the media room. I'm so rattled with sick outrage I forget to gather my bag from the floor. It can wait. I'd rather wander around Montclair naked than spend another moment standing across from a man so cowardly he'd rather lie to my face than tell the truth.

I've barely made it halfway down the hall when Marcus catches me. He seizes my left wrist in a vice-like grip and yanks me backward. Just like earlier tonight, I act before thinking. My right hand flies toward Marcus's face so wildly that I don't stop to consider the consequences of my action.

Everything slows to snail's pace when my hand connects brutally with Marcus's left cheek. My slap is so firm, his head snaps to the side as a fiery burn incinerates my palm. Although my slap was a spur-of-the-moment decision, I know Marcus had time to stop me. The blaze in his eyes moments before my hand connected with his cheek was all the indication I needed to know he could have stopped me if he wanted. I just can't fathom why he didn't?

Seizing both of my wrists Marcus slaps my hands across his face over and over again. "Hit me, Cleo. Scratch me. Yell at me. But you're *not* leaving me!" he growls between slaps.

He doesn't hold back. He uses my hands to hit him continually until the redness on his face matches mine. They aren't soft taps either. They are so potent, the sound of skin slapping skin echoes off the pristine walls before booming back into my ears. Every hit he inflicts on his face with my hands breaks my heart more.

"Stop it," I blubber through a sob. "Stop it. Stop it. Stop it."

I yank away from him when he fails to adhere to my screamed demands. The air leaves my lungs in a grunt when my sudden movement causes us to crash into the same painting we stumbled into the last time we interacted in this hall. With how much my heart is tearing in two, I'd give anything to transport back to that day.

"Stop it, Marcus! Stop it! You're hurting me," I barely murmur, my heart broken beyond repair. "Pineapple."

Marcus releases my hands in an instant, the expression on his face mortified. I don't know if his brisk response is from me using my safe word or from my declaration that he was hurting me.

I scoop my stinging hands in close to my chest as my eyes roam his red-welted face. I can hardly breathe through the pain curled around my throat when I spot the absolute agony in his eyes. He is truly devastated. His desolate eyes show his heart is breaking as much as mine.

"Why? If you didn't want me to leave, why be with *her*? Why deceive me? Do you think so little of me you thought I'd stay when I discovered you are cheating on me?"

"I didn't cheat, Cleo. I don't cheat. But even if I did, I'd *never* cheat on you." The fury of his low tone doesn't match the sentiment in his eyes.

"I saw you, Marcus!" I roar, my heartache unmissable.

He leans into me, pinning me to the painting with his impressive, suit-covered body. "You saw nothing. Your mind was playing tricks on you. I shouldn't have sustained your climax. I shouldn't have teased you. You're clearly not trained enough for that yet. I played with fire, wanting to ignite your desires, but instead, I ended up getting burned."

Even confused by his riddle, I thrust against him, striving to break free, hating that he is using my attraction to him to insult me. My efforts are utterly pointless. He is too strong for a woman of my size to contend with.

Using the only weapon I have left in my arsenal, I angrily sneer, "I'm *soooo* sorry my submissive qualities aren't up to your standards, *Master Chains*. I'll be sure to be more courteous to my next Master."

Marcus leans into me, crushing not just my body, but my heart as well. He glares into my eyes, his arrogance too haughty for my liking. His body temperature is so hot, a bead of sweat forms on the nape of my neck before rolling down my back.

My lashes blink back tears when he raises his hand to grip my throat. His hold isn't tight enough to impede my breathing, but it's firm enough for my traitorous body to respond to his touch. He curls his hand around the identical spot he did the last time we were in this hallway. I didn't know it at the time, but that was my first taste of sub space. Our exchange that night showed how much I trusted him. I didn't even flinch when my life was placed in his hands. Now he has ruined that. His deceit broke my trust, and everyone knows broken trust can't be fixed. *Can it?*

Seemingly reading my inner monologue, Marcus asks, "How can you trust me with your life, Cleo, but not your heart?" His voice sounds tormented, as if he is stuck in an alternative universe, incapable of distinguishing the enemies from the allies.

He tracks his thumb over the vein throbbing in my neck before tightening his grip on my throat. My pupils widen as a feverous current rages through my veins before clustering in my heated core. Although I should be pulling away from his hold, demanding for him to stop this instant, my body doesn't cite a single protest. Not even my eyes demand for his withdrawal.

"Trust extends much further than a playroom, Cleo. When you trust me, it's the greatest compliment. Just like your distrust is the biggest disparagement."

He bounces his eyes between mine, the anger in them simmering to a slight boil as he loosens his grip. I keep my eyes locked on him as much-needed air hisses between my parted lips.

"You either trust me or you don't, Cleo. There is no middle ground," he murmurs as he drops his hand from my neck to brush it over my budded nipple, woefully displaying my enticement by his hold. It stiffens even more from his meekest touch.

A bout of shock hits me when his eyes lift to mine. I was expecting them to be filled with smugness, reveling in my body's inability to deny his touch. They aren't smug—not in the slightest. They are as tormented as ever.

"Do you trust me, Cleo?" he asks as his beautifully haunted eyes frolic between mine.

My first instinct is to shake my head, but no matter how hard I plead for my body to respond to the prompts my brain is firing, it refuses. It trusts Marcus. So does my heart. It's just my brain begging for me not to get caught in a trap.

"Keira is a submissive," I mutter, using her name for the first time tonight, wanting to ensure he knows to whom I am referring. My voice is barely a whisper, but it's confident enough to express that my statement was not a question. It was a confirmation.

"I know." Marcus cradles my quaking jaw.

It's the fight of my life not to lean into his embrace, but I give it my best shot, still scorned by betrayal.

"She was wearing your collar."

"I know," he repeats, his voice a seductive purr that successfully conceals his bewilderment.

"Because she's your sub?"

This time there is no doubt my question is a question. Just the heartbreak resonating in my low tone makes it unmissable. My heart cracked more just voicing that admission out loud.

"No," he denies, shaking his head. He locks his eyes with mine, ensuring I can see the honesty relayed by them as he discloses, "Keira has *never* been my sub. She will *never* be my sub." My lips quiver when he presses the softest kiss on the edge of my mouth as he mutters, "I don't need anyone but you, Cleo. I will *never* need anyone but you."

"Then why was she wearing your collar? And why didn't you say she wasn't your sub when I asked you?"

My lungs suck in their first full breath in over ten minutes when Marcus draws back enough he relieves the pressure placed on them. His tongue delves out to replenish his lips as he contemplates a reply. The longer he takes deliberating, the more my anger resurfaces.

"You made me angry. First I had to send Cartier over to deflect the bartender's advances, then you danced with Dexter."

Pushing aside my bewilderment that he knows Dexter's name, I snarl, "So you collared a submissive with your trademark just to make me jealous? Real mature, Marcus."

He balks, shunned by my reply. "What? No. I didn't collar Keira. I don't even know why she was wearing a collar, because as far as I am aware, she is without a Dom."

If he is hoping his answer will subdue my anger, he needs to devise a new tactic. I'm more ropeable now than I ever was.

"She doesn't have a Dom as the one she wants is already occupied. And since we don't have an official contract, I guess she figures she'll just stand in the wings, waiting for you to have your fill." I shrug my shoulders, the expression on my face leaving no doubt I'm enraged with jealousy. "Or maybe she will turn up to a gala wearing your signature and force a permanent intermission in our relationship."

Marcus's dark brows slant together. "So I get punished for the actions of another? How is that fair?" he questions, his tone half-wrathful, half-confused.

"I'm not punishing you for Keira wearing your trademark. If she did that of her own accord, you're not to blame. I'm punishing you because you didn't ask her to remove it, and you didn't deny she was your sub."

Marcus's baffled eyes bounce between mine. "How do you know what I said to her? Did you hear a word I spoke?"

I freeze as the quickest flashback from earlier tonight runs through my tired brain. My stomach winds up to my throat when I recall I didn't hear anything either of them said. I could barely hear a thing over my pulse shrilling in my ears, much less the low tone Marcus was using.

"No. You didn't hear anything I said, did you?" You could construe his statement as snarky, but the relief in his eyes doesn't allude to that.

I shake my head. "Still doesn't explain why you didn't deny she was your sub."

"I was being stubborn. Just like you were when you refused to answer my questions about Dexter," Marcus immediately fires back, his tone laced with as much jealousy as mine. We are both being immature.

"Then why did you let me leave?" Although my words are shaky, I'm pleased they come out with the confidence I am hoping for. "You had every opportunity to stop me, but you didn't. You just let me go. That hurt me, Marcus. So much..." My sentence trails off when my words crack with emotions.

Marcus runs his hand over his clipped afro, a tell-tale sign he is worried. He peers past my shoulder for several heart-thrashing seconds before he connects his eyes back with mine. "For the past few weeks, my security team has been receiving death threats. Tonight's was more concerning than the previous ones they have investigated."

My sharp inhalation of air nearly misses the rest of his admission. "This is nothing out of the ordinary in my industry, so usually I'd just brush it off as a consequence of fame, but this time was different." He twists a piece of my humidity-frizzed hair around his index finger. "I never had anyone to protect before. *Now I have you."* He whispers his last sentence so softly, I barely heard him.

"You let me leave to protect me?" I ask, sheer bewilderment in my tone.

"Yes," Marcus answers, nodding.

His confession pushes us into resolute silence, plagued with confusion. Although I'm still angry, and my brain continually argues with my too-easy-to-forgive heart, I'm too tired to keep bickering. What I saw between Marcus and Keira was wrong—there is no doubt in my mind, but when I push aside my jealousy, and look at the entire picture, I realize their exchange could have been as guiltless as mine was with Andy. They were fully clothed, and they weren't kissing. As much as it kills me to admit, other than Keira's poor choice in accessories, their exchange was innocent. Furthermore, what Marcus said is true. When you trust someone, it should extend past the bedroom.

The same can be said for acting recklessly. Marcus doesn't just make me irrationally reckless inside the playroom, he makes me unreasonably reckless in all aspects of my life. So much so, I'm lashing out without first sitting down and evaluating the entire picture. I'm allowing my fear of losing him as a way to push him away, instead of cherishing every moment we have. Clearly, he is doing the same thing.

Instead of telling me he was worried about my safety, he let me believe the horrid notions running through my head, as he knew I wouldn't stand by and watch it happen. My desire to flee the gala was one of the most potent I've had. I guess to Marcus, it was the perfect solution to ensure my safety. It was stupid, but it was also effective.

After swallowing down my unease, I lift my eyes to Marcus's. My breath traps halfway to my lungs when I notice he is observing me cautiously. The uncontrollable rage in his eyes has entirely subsided, but the slap marks on his face are as angry as ever.

"Tell me how to fix this, Cleo. Show me what to do. I'll do anything you want, just don't ask me to give you up. I'd rather die than give you up."

God—Marcus. The pain in his voice makes it feel like an elephant is sitting on my chest.

"I can fix this," he assures me, his tone confident. "I just need the chance to do that. Give me a chance, Cleo. Trust me enough to know I'd never intentionally hurt you. Give me that much, and I'll award you with so much more."

I return his fervent gaze with equal vigor. I'm at a loss for a reply. Not just because his captivating green irises are luring me into a tangible trap from which I'll never be strong enough to break free, but because I genuinely can't think of anything he can give me than he hasn't already given. My only request at the start of our relationship was to have our D/s contract removed from our negotiation. Marcus did that—then so much more. So what more could he possibly give me?

I freeze when an idea pops into my head. It causes a rush of giddiness to hit my stomach and head at the same time. Don't ask me if it's a good or bad giddiness as I wouldn't be able to say.

Like he can sense my internal battle, Marcus places his hand under my chin and raises my head. "Tell me," he requests, his tone not wrathful or annoyed.

I swallow the brick lodged in my throat before checking, "Anything?"

"Anything," Marcus confirms while tucking a strand of my wild hair behind my ear. "I'd give up everything I have before I'll give you up."

Once the unruly curl is secured behind my ear, the back of his fingers trace my earlobe, slide down my neck, then skim over my barely exposed collarbone. His touch is brief, but robust enough to spark a fire deep in my stomach I never expected to ignite tonight. It also strengthens my determination to push our relationship onto a whole new playing field. One I'm sure Marcus has never fielded before.

Marcus's hand freezes on the collar of my shirt when I ask, "Have you ever made love?"

His Adam's apple bobs up and down before he shakes his head. "No."

"Will you make love to me? Will you give me that? Will you give me a part of you no one else has had?"

Marcus peers into my eyes, the sentiment in them growing every second that ticks by before he whispers, "Yes."

5

The tension in the air rapidly changes to lust when Marcus curls his hand around mine and paces toward his master suite. Incredulously, my hands are clammier now than they are when I kneel in his playroom. That probably has something to do with this being as foreign to Marcus as it was for me entering Chains months ago. Although I hate that I'm forcing him out of his comfort zone, I won't stop our exchange. I need this—*we need this.*

After swinging open his bedroom door, Marcus switches on the lights, then merges deeper into the room. My brows furrow when his brisk pace has us passing right by his monstrous bed sitting in the middle of the vast space.

"You don't need a bed to make love," Marcus advises my stunned expression. "You just need a place where you can worship, devour, treasure, and..." He fleetingly glances my way before muttering, "love."

My heart rate kicks into a mad beat, an awakening combination of lust and excitement when he walks us into the bathroom. The attraction crackling between us is as vibrant as ever, but it's even more powerful, encouraged by a connection more compelling than just jealousy. There are so many emotions passing between us. Mutual respect. Understanding. Silent pleas for forgiveness—not only from Marcus, but me as well. But more than anything—the most intoxicating of them all is the sentiment of desire. It's so strong, I'll confidently declare that Marcus wants this as much as I do. He wants to share this experience with me—and only me.

Marcus releases my hand to switch on the shower faucet. After ensuring the temperature is adequate, he devotes his attention back to me. He stares at me, unmoving, nonjudgmental. He just stares.

"What are you waiting for?" I'm so used to him taking charge, I'm a little stumped on how to move our exchange forward without jumping him like an out-of-control nymph.

"For you to tell me what you want," Marcus answers as a ghost of a smile cracks on his lips.

My eyes dance between his. "I want you."

"Good. That's a start." His smile enlarges. "Where do you want me? What do you want me to do?"

My brows stitch as confusion makes itself known. *Why is he handing all the power to me? This isn't what I wanted.* I gasp when reality dawns.

I connect my eyes with Marcus's. "I don't want to top you, Marcus. I just want *you* to make love to *me*. Not *me* top *you*."

"So you still want me to take charge?" he clarifies, his brows furrowing.

I smile at the unease in his voice. "Yes and no. I want you to lead, I just don't want any rules. I'm pretty sure that's the only difference between BDSM sex and vanilla sex... both participants control the exchange."

My smile enlarges when Marcus grimaces at me mentioning the word "vanilla."

The worry tainting his gorgeous face vanishes when I grip the hem of my shirt and whip it over my head. Air hisses through his teeth when my naked breasts fall heavily to my chest. Obviously, he was unaware I am naked beneath my clothing.

Keeping my eyes locked with his, I shimmy my yoga pants down my thighs. His avid gaze raking over my body boosts my confidence. I've never felt more desired than I do right now. "So beautiful, Cleo," Marcus murmurs more to himself than me.

I brazenly step toward him, my desire to undress him as potent as my need to taste him in my mouth. Usually, I'd have to wait for him to permit me to touch him, but since our exchange is happening on neutral territory, my body can express its desires without fear of repercussion.

As I fiddle with the buttons on his fancy dress shirt, Marcus gathers my hair to the left so he can ravish my neck. I lean into his embrace, adoring the smattering of kisses he places along my jaw and down my throat. Each soft nib and suck adds to the twinge inflicting my throbbing sex. My body heats up when one of his hands lowers to the curve of my back to draw me in, where the other cups my breast to toy with my erect nipple.

Because I'm so caught up in calming the furious storm brewing in my core, it takes me nearly five minutes to undo the last button of his shirt. I feel Marcus smile against my neck when his shirt drops to the floor in a heap. As my hands work on the belt wrapped around his waist, Marcus toes off his shoes. Warm water glides down my face when he steers us into the shower, his impatience meaning he isn't even undressed yet.

I pull back from his embrace. "So impatient," I tease, inwardly sighing when my voice comes out with the hint of sexiness I was aiming for.

Any reply Marcus is planning to give is rammed back into his throat when I lower myself to my knees and glance up at him. I lick my lips when the glorious image of his thick cock bracing against the zipper of his trousers is thrust into my vision.

When I brush my hand over his massive bulge, Marcus mutters, "I thought I was supposed to worship you?"

"Oh, believe me, this will be just as fulfilling for me as it is for you," I guarantee while sliding down his zipper.

I squeeze my thighs together when his glorious cock springs free. He is thick, long, and jutted. My mouth waters when I spot a bead of pre-cum pooling at the top of his engorged knob. Loving that I don't need to wait for permission, I wrap my hand around his thickened shaft before my tongue makes quick work of the salty goodness. Marcus's groan rolls down his chest until it vibrates on my tongue.

Once I lap up every drop of his excitement, I lower my mouth down his densely veined shaft. I sink my lips as far down as possible, only stopping when it's physically impossible for me to take any more.

"God, Cleo," Marcus sighs, his tone announcing it's more a sigh of pleasure than disappointment. "I love the way you suck my cock, all greedy and eager."

His praise encourages my pursuit. I run my lips up and down his magnificent manhood on repeat as my hand works the section missing out on experiencing the warmth of my mouth. I may have no gag reflex, but that doesn't mean I can deepthroat Marcus. The girth of his cock is already a challenge, let alone the length of him.

"Slow down, Cleo, I don't want to cum in your mouth," Marcus advises me a short time later, his tone laced with lust. "I want to be wrapped in the warmth of your pussy before I cum."

I continue my pursuit, acting like I didn't hear what he said.

"Cleo..." Marcus growls out, his tone as unforgiving as my pumps on his cock. "Slow down."

Although his growl is clearly a warning, my speed remains unchecked. My tongue gathers every bead of pre-cum seeping out of his knob as my mouth sucks urgently on his shaft. I'm so dying to taste him, my cheeks hollow painfully with every suck.

When I peer up at him, advising him I have no intention of stopping, his grip on my hair loosens, and the strain marring his beautiful face fades.

"Good boy," I mutter through a mouth full of cock.

If I hadn't seen the quickest smirk etch onto his mouth, I'd be worried about my brazenness, but since the spark of admiration in his eyes is making me the most confident I've ever felt, I continue my mission to unravel him without pause.

Approximately five minutes later, my dedication is awarded in the most glorious way. The strong, brackish taste of Marcus pumps onto my tongue in raring spurts as he grunts my name in a guttural moan. My throat struggles to swallow every delicious drop of his spawn, but I give it my best shot, not willing to waste a single morsel of his cum.

Once every scrumptious drop has been consumed, I lift my eyes to Marcus. He peers down at me. Shock and admiration are smeared all over his face. My kneecaps pop back into place when he aids me into a standing position. I sway slightly, intoxicated by lust. In the past few weeks, I've only been allowed to suck his cock twice. Once was in the playroom when I wasn't allowed to touch him, and another was when I woke him three days ago at 3 AM in the most glorious way. Although stunned by my brazenness, excitement soon pushed aside his anger.

Marcus's big hands swallow my cheeks as he cups them before sealing his lips over mine. His tongue slides into my mouth, not the slightest bit concerned that his cum was just inside my mouth. Just the thought of him tasting a smidge of himself has my thighs touching. He kisses me until the dizziness causing me to sway like a leaf in the breeze becomes uncontrollable.

Keeping his hands on my shoulders to ensure I don't succumb to the giddiness clustered in my head, Marcus kicks his drenched pants to the side, then moves to stand behind me. Although he just came, the heat of his erect cock scorches my back when he bands his arms around my waist and draws me into his body, stilling my swaying movements simultaneously. The cushy softness of my backside can't take away from the sheer girth of his cock. He is even thicker than he was when I had him in my mouth.

My head lolls to the side when the softness of cashmere scrapes over my aching breasts, down my quivering stomach before scrubbing ever-so-slightly over my throbbing clit. Marcus delivers an additional three gentle rubs over my pussy before he moves the shower puff back to my torso. I try to hold in my whine. I miserably fail.

"Who's impatient?" Marcus mutters, his voice so tempting, a gathering of goosebumps race to the surface of my skin.

Once every inch of my torso has been thoroughly lathered with fragrant body wash, Marcus takes a step backward. Although disappointed by his lack of contact, the gentle sweeps of the heavenly soft shower puff on the weary muscles in my back keeps my disappointment at bay. His touch is gentle enough to know he is nurturing me, but firm enough to knead out the tension of my night.

After washing the suds off my torso and back, Marcus moves to stand in front of me. The excited butterflies in my stomach drop to my sex when he glances into my eyes and lowers himself to his knees. The reasoning behind his submissive stance becomes apparent when he lathers my legs with the same amount of attention he gave to my torso and back. Although my pussy was well-cleaned previously, it's awarded a second lot of attention when he slides the shower puff from my left leg to my right.

My breathing turns labored when the tips of his fingers extend past the shower puff to graze ever-so-slightly over my throbbing clit. The chances of securing an entire breath are lost when Marcus snags the extendable showerhead from the middle of the pole to remove the suds from the lower half of my body. The heated water pumping onto my pulsating sex adds to the tingling sensation sweeping across my stomach. He pulls it in close, ensuring every inch of my pussy is rid of bubbles.

I groan a low, raspy moan when Marcus peers up at me while replenishing his top lip with moisture. His eyes tell me he knows how desperate I am for him to touch me, but he remains entirely still, wearing nothing but an amorous smirk on his gorgeous face. The longer he stares at me, the stronger my desires grow. I'm so damn desperate for him to touch me, I'm not above being disobedient. Any punishment he wishes to instill will be worth it if he'll just touch me. I'm so close to the brink, I'm confident one sweep of his thumb over my clit will have me freefalling over the edge.

Suddenly, my spine snaps straight. *I don't have to fear discipline. Not tonight.*

Marcus's throaty laugh is muffled by the dampness pooling between my legs when I grip the back of his head and mash it with my pussy. I moan a throaty purr when the tip of his tongue grazes my throbbing clit. My hands shoot out to brace against the foggy shower door when his tongue slides up the folds of my aching sex before rolling around the bud of my clit.

"Yes," I hiss through gritted teeth when he suckles my clit into his mouth.

Although the lashes of his tongue and the nips of his teeth are more reserved than I am used to, they aren't weak enough to stave off my desire to climax. I try to hold it back. I fight with all my might to ignore the tidal wave crashing into me, attempting to drag me away. But the sensation is too intense. Within seconds, I'm swept into the current, unable to breathe, move, or have a single lucid thought.

"Give it to me."

I inhale a sharp breath, overcome by the sensation carrying me away. My orgasm is so strong, my vision blurs, and my entire body quivers and shakes as it rides the awe-inspiring intensity. The orgasmic shudders coursing through me turn me into a quivering, blubbering mess. I'm shaking so uncontrollably I lose my grip on the shower wall, and my knees buckle.

"I've got you," Marcus guarantees as he firms his grip on my ass to keep me upright.

Once every blissful shudder has been exhausted from my body, Marcus stands from his knelt position, gathers me in his arms, then strides out of the bathroom. My damp hair fans across the silky soft bedspread covering his monstrous bed when he lays me down in the middle of it. The thermostat is set to a pleasant temperature, but it doesn't stop goosebumps racing to the surface of my skin since neither Marcus or I dried off upon exiting the shower.

Beads of water roll off his afro and drip onto my stomach as he places a trail of kisses from my neck to my still throbbing core. I girlishly giggle when he presses the quickest peck to my tingling sex. His touch is only brief, but strong enough to ignite a new fire deep in my stomach.

With his lustful eyes fixated on me, he kneels between my legs before carefully raising my backside off the bed. My breathing levels when the crest of his cock braces the seam of my soaked pussy.

I graze my teeth over my bottom lip when he attentively asks, "Are you ready?"

I nod, too overcome with emotions to express words.

My back arches off the bed and my eyes snap shut when he slowly inches inside me. The sensation is overwhelmingly sweet and toe-curlingly delicious at the same time. My sex ripples around him, coercing him deeper until every inch of his glorious cock is hilted. I purr softly, adoring the heaviness of him inside of me.

The past two weeks we've had sex a minimum of two to three times a day, and every single time awards me with an entirely new sensation. Today is no different. With my pussy well-prepared for his intrusion and happily accepting it, the pain usually associated with taking a man of his size isn't present.

When my eyelids slowly flutter open, they are met with the most alluring pair of dazzling green eyes. Marcus watches me carefully, ensuring not an ounce of pain crosses my face as he slowly drags his cock back out. My vagina hugs him, massaging every perfect vein feeding his magnificent manhood. After pulling out to the tip, Marcus rocks back into me, his pace not as slow as his first pump, but a nice speed that guarantees he is not fucking me, he is making love to me.

Goosebumps follow the track his lips make when he moves them between my neck and breasts. His mouth adores the top half of my body while his cock worships the rest. I feel cherished, I'd even go as far as saying loved.

When I asked Marcus to make love to me, I truly thought it would be an hour or two filled with awkwardness. Although he has never explicitly said it, making love is not Marcus's forte. He is a man who likes to fuck, and he fucks well. But not seeing a snick of hesitation on his face as he worships my body is a treasured memory I'll never forget. This experience expresses way more than words ever could. I feel admired, cherished, respected, and Ioved.

Striving not to cornily express my undying love during our activity, I grip the round globes of Marcus's perfect ass and enjoy the sensation. He rocks in and out of me, over and over until the unmistakable signs of an orgasm awaken within me. Although his speed is a lot slower than we usually go, the rim of his cock hits the sweet spot inside me with every grind.

As he continues driving me to the brink with nothing but a mouthwatering smirk, a leisured speed, and a contented face, I work through my bewilderment at how quickly my climax is cultivating. Usually, I need... *more,* but I can't deny the tingling sensation sweeping across my core. It's so strong, I feel like I'm mere moments from climaxing.

No, make that I *am* climaxing.

My nails dig into Marcus's ass as a furious wildfire roars through my body. I'm not the only one caught off guard by my climax, Marcus is just as shocked as me. He stills for a mere second before he continues grinding into me, forcing me to ride the intensity of my soul-stealing climax. His muscles contract and release with each perfect pump his cock does as he uses every inch of his body to make love to me. I shiver and shake as I whisper his name on repeat, adoring that I achieved the unachievable. *I came during sex.*

My orgasm is long and exhaustive, one of the strongest I've ever had. It feels like hours pass before I can garner the strength to open my eyes. When I do, I spot Marcus staring down at me, smiling and uncontained. His eyes are the rawest I've ever seen them, so open and honest. Tears well in my eyes when I read the sentiment in his heavy-hooded gaze. He isn't just happy he accomplished greatness, he is as smug as hell.

"Shut up," I murmur while throwing a fist into his rock-hard abs.

I growl a hungry grunt when he flexes his cock. That one little flex thrusts me to within an inch of the finish line. My god—the power this man has over my body is truly astounding. Even when he is making love, he is still a Master.

"I'm not laughing at you, Cleo. I'm smiling. Missionary has never been my position of choice, but after seeing the way your face flushes with ecstasy as your pussy milks my cock, I might have to alter my opinion on that humble position. That was by far the sexiest thing I've ever seen."

The tears looming in my eyes nearly roll down my face when Marcus unexpectedly flips over. Since he is still hilted inside me, I follow his movement. I purr like a kitten when the hard muscle of his Apollo belt grinds against my clit in the process.

Loving my reaction, Marcus jerks his hips upwards. A husky moan tears from my throat when his cock inches even deeper inside me at the same time his pelvis stimulates my clit. Wanting to return his tease, I defy my Jell-O thighs by raising myself onto my knees. A blistering of stars twinkle in front of my eyes when I slam down hard, taking Marcus's cock to the very base.

A grunted moan roars through Marcus's lips as his grip on my hips turns deadly. "Jesus Christ, Cleo. We're supposed to be making love."

My hands shoot out to lean on his sweat-slicked torso as a surge of excitement spasms in my pussy, loving the curtness of his tone. I also need a minute to catch my breath. Because we've never done this position, the change in angle is truly breath-stealing.

"We've already made love. Now I'll prove you can make love without needing to go slow," I whisper breathlessly. "It's the emotions displayed during the exchange that differentiates sex from making love."

Marcus's teeth grit when I swivel my hips in a circular motion. "It's the reactions you force from the one you're worshipping." When I tighten the walls of my vagina around his twitching shaft, he thickens even more. "It's expressing your every want, need, and desire without using words."

Marcus's eyes bounce between mine for several seconds. I can tell the instant he reads the honesty from my eyes, as he releases my hips from his firm grasp and places his hands behind his head. Although his eyes are still raging with naturally engrained dominance, they are also sparked with agreement. They permit me to do as I please without a word needing to be passed through his quirked-with-amusement lips.

"Show me, Cleo. Tell me what you want to say but are too afraid to speak," he commands.

I do exactly that. I express everything he means to me without a syllable escaping my mouth. I tell him how much I love his dominance, his caring nature, his bossiness. But more than anything, I express those three little words I'll never be game to say out loud.

I tell him that I love him—over and over again until we collapse from exhaustion.

6

"Remember, Brodie goes where you go, Cleo," Marcus instructs from the driver's seat of his car, the deep hum of his voice persuasive enough for a flock of birds nesting in the tree at the side of his residence to take flight.

I roll my eyes, faking annoyance to his unyielding demand. I'm not annoyed. Although at times, his protectiveness hackles my spine, after years of going it alone, it's nice having someone care enough about me they are worried about my safety. I'm also too exhausted to take on the stress denying his command would instigate. Last night smoothed some of the kinks in our relationship, but there are still many other bumps that need ironing out.

"I know, Marcus. I've already brought Brodie a studded collar and lead. Since he is shadowing me like a puppy, he may as well dress the part," I jest, my tone high-spirited.

Marcus's deep growl rumbles through my chest before clustering in my throbbing sex, which is still reveling in the aftermath of our lovemaking that proceeded until the wee hours of this morning. Resisting the desire to squeeze my thighs together from his scrumptious growl, my eyes stray to Marcus. He peers up at me, exuding anger and silent expectations. The absoluteness of his gaze sends a chill down my spine.

"What?" I murmur, questioning myself more than Marcus.

Although stumped by his response, I have no doubt he is angry. Blatant jealousy pumps out of him in enraged spurts, and his gaze is so hot, the brisk winter winds aerating my damp hair become a distant memory.

The cause of his sudden shift in composure comes to light when Marcus mutters, "I thought your knowledge of animal play was minimal?"

My eyes bulge when the quickest flash of a memory sparks in my spent mind. I'm held captive as I recall the lady standing in front of me, lowering herself onto her hands and knees to crawl into Chains at the heel of her Dom.

When I snap out of my trance, I try to hold in my laughter that Marcus is fretful of Brodie kneeling at my heel. The more I struggle to contain my childish giggles, the harder my fight becomes. I don't know what's more amusing. The fact Marcus thinks Brodie would heel, or that Marcus is so blinded by jealousy, he can't see that I care for Brodie as if he is family. Brodie is a great guy, but there isn't an ounce of attraction between us.

Marcus's eyes thin when my dainty laughter trickles into the dew-filled air. "It isn't funny, Cleo," he grinds out through clenched teeth.

Snubbing the way his narrowed glare hits every one of my hot buttons, I bend down, slap my hands on each side of his cheeks, then plant a big sloppy kiss on his hard-lined lips. My excitement mounts when Marcus growls as I fail to open my mouth at the request of his lashing tongue.

"Our shared shower already has you behind schedule," I mumble against his lips before pulling back. "You don't want to leave Cameron waiting on the tarmac even longer, do you?"

The quickest flare blazes through Marcus's eyes. Although I'm confident I've seen it before, the nanosecond between its arrival and departure is too fast for me to decipher what it means.

Marcus's hand tightens around his steering wheel as his eyes roam my face, categorizing every fine feature with detailed accuracy. When his eyes land on my faintly blue-tinged lips caused by the nippy mid-December temperatures, he asks, "Where is your coat? Why didn't Aubrey get your jacket as I requested?"

When his hand curls around the door latch, preparing to exit his vehicle, I bump my hip against the driver's side door, keeping him trapped in his car. "Aubrey gave me my coat as per your request, I left it on the entranceway table. I'm feeling a little warm."

The concern Marcus's eyes have been carrying all morning doubles. "Are you unwell? Are you sick?" His eyes thoroughly inspect me with the same attentiveness Abel had weeks ago. "Should I stay? Do you want me to stay?"

"No, I'm fine. I'm just a little warm after our *strenuous* activities this morning. Who wouldn't be after that exchange?" I fan myself, acting all flustered. My inflamed cheeks aren't a ploy to lessen his worry. Our exchange went above and beyond my wildest dreams. "Last night was wow, Marcus. Like... *whoa*!"

The worry clouding Marcus's usually vibrant eyes dulls from my confession when he reads the honesty on my face. Last night was out of this world. Not only is my heart still beating at triple the speed, but my muscles are screaming from exhaustion. *Who knew making love was such an arduous experience?*

I lean into the open driver's side window so I can place my hands on each side of Marcus's recently shaved jaw. The contrasting temperatures between my hands and his face are staggering. Come to think of it, his cheeks are just as heated as mine.

"Call me when you land, okay?" I try to keep the worry out of my voice. I fail. Marcus is a very skilled pilot, but that doesn't mean I'll not freak every time he's in the air.

"Alright," Marcus agrees before he nibbles on my lips. "Stay safe, baby."

His kiss is brief but wondrous enough to cause a rush of dizziness to cluster in my head. After taking one last whiff of his delicious scent, I regretfully withdraw from his scrumptious mouth and take a step back from his car. The loud rumble of his engine breaks through the uncomfortable silence bouncing between us when he cranks the ignition of his sports car and revs the engine. The pout on my lip switches to a smile when he playfully revs his engine a few more times for good measure, ensuring our exchange is ending with fond memories instead of sad ones.

"That's better," Marcus murmurs when he spots my smile. "I'll see you soon, Cleo."

Not trusting my mouth to hold back the heavy sentiment I feel, I broaden my smile and idiotically wave. Marcus winks before increasing the pressure on his gas pedal. From the way I stand on the stoop of his stairs, watching his car roll down the asphalt, you'd swear he was leaving for war, not spending the week laying down tracks on another no doubt record-breaking album.

I wait for the taillights of Marcus's car to disappear on the horizon before pivoting around and climbing the platform stairs. "Come," Aubrey says from the entranceway. She gestures her hand in the same manner she did last night, but this time, her tone is void of any annoyance.

Earlier this morning, when Marcus was submitting his flight manifest for his trip to Ravenshoe, I had a quiet word with Aubrey. It was awkward, but one hundred percent necessary. I wouldn't say it was unnecessarily awkward for Aubrey—I was the only blubbering idiot in our conversation—she handled it with the maturity awarded by her age.

Although I pathetically used my argument with Marcus as an excuse for my appalling behavior, Aubrey graciously accepted my apology before issuing one of her own. Our bond started on unstable ground, but with us both being mature enough to admit our wrongdoings, I think all previous awkwardness will now be avoidable. Once I'm satisfied that's been achieved, I'll begin working on her relationship with Marcus. It's clear before last night they had an amicable working relationship, but their exchange in the hallway has added some obvious cracks I'll strive hard to repair, since part of the blame for their spat lands on my shoulders.

Aubrey drapes a large blanket around my shuddering frame before running her hands up and down my prickled arms. Once she is satisfied my body temperature has returned to an acceptable level, she curls her arm around my shoulders and guides me into the living room. A grin curves on my mouth when I spot a large mug of hot chocolate sitting on the coffee table. It's positioned right next to my recently loaded Kindle.

"I'll get fat if I keep consuming sugar-laced drinks while sitting on my backside reading," I grumble under my breath.

"It's Sunday. Besides, from what Mr. Brown told me this morning, I don't think you need to worry. Mr. Everett isn't planning on being gone long." Aubrey's usually smooth voice is hindered by the crack of hilarity.

When my eyes sling to hers, the hue of pink on her cheeks shifts to a vibrant red coloring. "You've been talking to Abel?" I question, happy to deflect the conversation away from my vigorous sex life.

Like her face could get any redder, Aubrey's cheeks blaze even more. "Yes," she replies with a faint smile.

I step into the living room and slide onto the comfy couch, inconspicuously snagging my Kindle and hot chocolate off the coffee table on my way by. "Did you and Abel talk to plan Marcus's visit, or..." I leave my question open, letting my waggling brows speak on my behalf.

The heat on Aubrey's cheeks ascends halfway down her neck. "Our call was not in regards to Mr. Everett."

She stands still, frozen by my shocked stare. Before I can configure a response to her admission, Aubrey mumbles something under her breath before she pivots on her heels and exits the living room without a backward glance. Since our relationship is still wading in murky waters, I store her flustered response away as ammunition for when I'm next wrangling Abel.

After switching on my Kindle, I snuggle into the couch Marcus defiled me on weeks ago and get caught up in the fictional world of my all-time favorite author.

I've been reading for nearly two hours when the buzz of a cell phone interrupts me. Unable to tear my eyes away from the super-hot sex scene of a detective and his long-lost love, I continue reading as my hand aimlessly searches the coffee table for my cell. When I find it, I dash my eyes between my Kindle and the screen of my phone. Noticing it's a message from an unknown caller, I rest it against my thigh. With my utmost attention devoted to the story melting my Kindle more prominent than my need to be persuaded by a telemarketer, I ignore my caller.

"Damn," I murmur to myself when the storyline merges into wicked territory. The tension between the two characters is so hot, it would fog up my glasses if I were wearing any.

When my cell phone buzzes again and again, I place my Kindle on the coffee table with disappointment and read the messages. The second helping of hot chocolate I guzzled down with a set of homemade scones gurgles in my stomach when I read the first message.

Unknown Caller: *Are we still meeting today? Dexter xxx*

The contents of my stomach wind up to my throat when I read his second and third message.

Unknown Caller: *Don't forget the tissues.*

Unknown Caller: *Actually, bring two boxes just in case.*

Riddled with worry, my eyes shoot to the clock hanging in the middle of the blank wall of the living room. It displays it's nearly noon. With traffic, it will take me almost an hour and a half to get to Montclair. That leaves me half an hour to get ready, so I have no excuse not to meet with Dexter. *Dammit.*

Although Marcus and I worked through a lot of my concerns last night, I still have a lot of unanswered questions. And although I'd donate a kidney to ease the confusion muddling my mind, shouldn't I seek answers from the man who is the source of them?

After a few moments of deliberation, I fire back a quick message to Dexter, notifying him that our meeting is still on. Worry slows my strides as I weave through Marcus's residence, seeking Brodie. I know he is here, as he was the first person Marcus called when he discovered his trip to Ravenshoe had been moved up a day.

I find Brodie twenty minutes later in the room I couldn't sleep in last night. Marcus's old sub room. His brows are furrowed together, and he has a confused expression etched on his face. When he spots me standing in the doorway, he drifts his eyes to me. "Do I want to know what this room is?"

From the scratchiness of his tone, you'd swear he was standing in the middle of Marcus's playroom, not his guest bedroom. Although his question is highly warranted, I quirk my lips and shake my head. Brodie's brows stitch together even more from my blasé response.

While running my sweaty palms down my jeans, I pace deeper into the room. "Will you be ready for a trip to Montclair in twenty minutes? If not, I can take myself, then you can continue unpacking." It's the fight of my life not to roll my eyes over the dimness in my voice. I sound like a child asking a parent for a cookie while dinner is being served.

Brodie stands from the bed before shifting to face me. "Marcus said he wanted us to stay here for the week."

"We are, I just have plans with a... *friend* for lunch." I grimace at my poor choice in tone. If Brodie wasn't already suspicious of my motives, I'm certain his interests are now piqued.

"Who's your friend?" Brodie's tone is similar to one you'd expect a detective to use when grilling you for murder charges, not a bodyguard protecting you because your boyfriend is worried about overzealous fans.

"Is your friend a male or female?" Brodie continues to probe when I fail to answer his first question.

I cock my hip and spread my hands across my waist. "Does it matter? A friend is a friend, no matter what their gender is."

Brodie's lips curve high enough I can see the pegs of his white teeth. "So it's a male friend."

I cross my arms in front of my chest, but don't negate his claim. *Lying has never been my forte.*

"Does Marcus know you're meeting a *male* friend?"

I squint my eyes at his smug expression. He laughs off my attempt to snarl at him, finding it more humorous than dangerous. His brutish response unleashes my Garcia fighting spirit.

"Does Marcus know you helped remove the nipple clamps from my breasts last night?"

Brodie's eyes widen to the size of saucers as he takes a step back, shocked by my brazenness. "I didn't touch you. I might have noticed the clamps on your necklace when you shoved it into my chest, but I sure as hell didn't remove them for you."

"Marcus doesn't know that," I fire back, my tone relaying I'm not joking.

I stare at Brodie, praying he won't see the truth in my eyes. My desire to talk to Dexter is strong, but not strong enough to throw Brodie into the deep end without a life jacket.

When his malevolent glare intensifies, the take-no-shit expression on my face grows. It feels like the moon circles the earth three times before Brodie shakes his head. As a sneaky smirk cracks onto his lips, he snags his jacket from the bed he is standing next to.

"He has no fucking clue what he's dealing with," he murmurs under his breath as he curls his arm around my shoulders.

When he drags me into the corridor, I mumble, "I was planning on taking a shower and getting changed before we leave."

"I was planning on masturbating on a floral bedspread while watching porn, but I guess plans change."

My eyes rocket to Brodie. Disbelief—and if I am being honest—a little bit of impishness is lining my face. As I said to Marcus earlier, there is no spark of attraction between Brodie and me, but even a blind woman couldn't deny Brodie is a handsome man. Not as attractive as Marcus, but that would be a hard feat for any man to conquer, so just the thought of him getting a little handsy with himself has my pulse rising.

Spotting my slack-jawed expression, Brodie assures me, "I was joking, Cleo."

I stare at him, my suspicion uncontainable. His eyes aren't expressing mischievousness. Actually, they aren't revealing anything.

My disbelief is proven on point when Brodie mumbles, "I wasn't planning on watching porn."

7

"I've been to this pizzeria many times before. There is no back exit. All clientele must walk in and out that door." I point to the glass door of Villa Victoria. Brodie and I are parked just a few spaces up from here.

When Brodie continues to protest about my request for privacy, I snap out, "You're a bodyguard, Brodie, not a watchdog. This will be a very long week if you don't occasionally learn to heel." My spine straightens over my poor choice of words, but the sternness on my face remains firm.

Brodie studies me, drinking in my determined resolution. "Jesus, and here I was thinking Lexi was the bossy one in your dynamic." Although his tone is a little snarky, the laughter in his voice dampens the snappiness of his reply.

"Who do you think she learned her bitchiness from?" I query with a bowed brow.

Brodie doesn't answer my question. It's a smart decision on his behalf. Clearly, he isn't just a handsome man, he is a shrewd one as well.

"Give me your phone." A stranger may construe his statement as a request, but I didn't. It was a demand.

After handing him my cracked cell, he unlocks the screen without requesting my access code, then scrolls to my contacts to add a number to my frequently called list. If he had slapped my face he couldn't have shocked me more.

Snubbing my disapproving glare, Brodie advises, "This is my cell number. If you so much as sniff an ounce of trouble, call me. I'll be in that pizzeria faster than a crack dealer running from the police."

He tilts my cell toward me, not relinquishing it from his tight grip until I give him my wholehearted agreement that I'll call him at the first sign of trouble. Storing my cell in my purse, I slide out of Brodie's car and head into the pizzeria. Although my insides are bristling with annoyance, I realize Brodie is just doing the job Marcus pays him to do. So, if anyone is going to cop the wrath of my anger for my privacy being invaded, it should be the man leading the helm. Mr. Marcus Everett.

Inane butterflies take flight in my stomach when I swing open the thick glass door of the pizzeria and enter. The smell of garlic and melted cheese smacks into me, forcing a rampant grumble to gurgle in my hungry tummy. With it being late in the afternoon, the crowd isn't as heavy as the ones I've come to expect during evening rush hour, but there are still a good number of people mingling in the space.

My head slings to the side when a distinctive voice calling my name rings through my ears. Dexter is sitting at a table on my right, just in front of a large painted mural. He is dressed down today compared to last night, wearing a pair of well-fitted jeans and a light blue long-sleeved shirt rolled up to his elbows.

After placing my jacket on the coatrack on my left, I pace over to greet Dexter, taking in a set of tattoos on his arms I didn't know he had.

"Hey, Cleo," he greets, rising from his chair to place a kiss on my cheek. "No tissues?"

I force a smile on my face, vainly portraying his playful comment didn't cause a stabbing sensation to my heart.

After returning his greeting in a similar manner, I take a seat across from him. A flustered waitress arrives at our side not even two seconds later. She informs us of the specials, then takes our drinks order. Wanting to get our festivities over sooner rather than later, I order my main meal at the same time as my drink. Thankfully, Dexter follows suit. It isn't that I don't want to spend time with Dexter, I just don't want Brodie left sitting in his car longer than needed. It may not be snowing, but with the temperature beyond freezing, I'd say there is only a matter of days before Montclair is covered by a blanket of white.

Dexter waits for the waitress to gather our menus and leave before locking his eyes with mine. The light blue color of his shirt makes his icy blue eyes more prominent than usual, and the scruff on his chin adds a manly edge to his usually boyish looks. He is already the rightfully-titled resident hottie at Global Ten, but if the women from Accounting could see him now, I doubt they'd continue running their yearly poll. He'd be the hands-down winner time and time again.

"Did everything work out okay last night? You sounded pretty rattled when I talked to you on the phone," Dexter queries, genuine concern echoed in his tone.

I smile when inappropriate images of my rendezvous with Marcus this morning flash before my eyes. "Yeah, everything is fine. I was just overreacting," I assure him, waving my hand through the air like it's no big deal. "You know us girls, dramatic and all."

I cringe, loathing that I used the weakest excuse known to mankind for my pitiful behavior. I also shouldn't be lying, Dexter saved my hide more times than I can count last night. And how does he get awarded for his gallantry? By me lying to his face.

"What about you? How did your date with Delilah end?" Although I'm chomping at the bit for Dexter to disclose the real reason behind our sudden lunch date, it's more polite to ease us towards that conversation than hammer him with the big questions straight up.

Dexter waits for our waitress to finish serving us our drinks before answering, "Not quite how she was hoping."

The churning of my stomach ramps up a gear. Delilah is attractive—if you can look past her narrowed eyes and near-constant abhorrent facial expressions. Even if Dexter wasn't accustomed to her taxing personality, it doesn't take more than a few minutes for a stranger to discern that Delilah is as satanic as her nearly pitch-black eyes.

Dexter dips a corn chip the waitress left on the table into a spicy salsa mix while saying, "If I were interested in financial gain, the circumstances of my night would have altered significantly. But since I've never had an interest in money, her proposal didn't tickle my fancy in the slightest."

If I push aside his odd choice of words, his reply doesn't shock me. If he were money-hungry, he could have pocketed millions by exposing Marcus's secret. Considering that idea never crossed his mind assures me he isn't meeting with me for financial incentive.

With my interest piqued on Delilah's motives last night, I lock my eyes with Dexter and ask, "Delilah propositioned you?"

A faint grin stretches across his face before he nods. I can't tell if it's an expression of mortification or satisfaction.

"For sex or something else?" My low tone reveals my embarrassment at asking such an insensitive question. After everything he has done for me, I'm definitely starting to consider Dexter more of a friend than a work colleague, but I'd have a hard time questioning Lexi in this manner, much less an attractive male.

Thankfully, Dexter doesn't seem the least bit worried about my imposing question. He just pops a corn chip into his mouth before muttering, "Honestly, sex was never mentioned, but I had a feeling she believed it was part of our negotiations."

"Negotiations?" I ask, my interest unmissable.

My eyes lift when a plate of steamy, aromatic food is set down in front of me. Even though I gorged on scones mere hours ago, the delicious scent lingering into my nostrils has my stomach grumbling like it's never been fed.

"Thank you," I murmur to the pretty waitress serving me.

After placing Dexter's meal in front of him, she skedaddles away from our table. Her eagerness to leave has me wondering if she caught wind of our conversation, or if she is hoping Dexter won't see how flustered her cheeks got when he thanked her for her hospitality with a flirty wink. When she continually glances over at us while serving the patrons sitting behind us, I realize it's the latter.

"You have a fan," I say to Dexter, nudging my head to the waitress.

When Dexter cranks his neck to peer at her, the heat on her cheeks grows. "She's cute. But I don't do blondes."

"You don't *do* blondes?" My voice is snarled with a hint of bitchiness. "Does that refer to dating or..." I leave my question open for Dexter to answer how he sees fit.

Dexter smiles a shit-eating grin before shaking his head. "I don't date. So..." He leaves me hanging, much to my dismay.

Disgusted by his nonchalant avoidance of women of a particular hair color, I grab a handful of the corn chips he's been munching on and peg them at his head. His smile enlarges to a full-toothed grin as he snags a rogue chip clinging to his shirt to consume it. Its loud crunch is barely audible over his concealed laughter. I shake my head in disbelief before tackling the scrumptious meal in front of me.

After settling down his boyish chuckle, Dexter locks his eyes with me. He only stares at me for a minute, but the heat of his gaze is as blistering as standing on the sun. When his stare becomes too great to ignore, I arch a brow, requesting a reason for his prolonged gaze.

"You do realize Delilah won't quit hounding you until you give her the identity of the man at the helm of Chains, don't you?" he responds to my silent interrogation.

"Yeah, I'm aware of that, but it doesn't change anything. The people she is hounding don't deserve to be harassed, so until that stops, I'll continue deflecting her ruses," I reply, my tone indicating to my shock at our quick change in subject.

"You speak like you're one of them, Cleo." Dexter peers into my eyes, his concern unmissable. "Are you?"

I forcefully swallow a chunk of chicken in my mouth. Its greasy goodness now feels as dry as a rock. "Would it bother you if I were?"

Dexter leans back in his chair as his dark brows incline. He takes his time configuring a response. I can't help but stare at him, wondering if he is weirded out by my question. His face is void of the disgust I expect people to hold when I voice an interest in BDSM, but it isn't pleasant either. He looks genuinely confused.

By the time he replies, the hot meal he was served has turned stone cold. "It's not my place to judge. I just didn't realize you were in so deep, Cleo."

"I'm not." Well, not in the way he is suspecting. I'm in deep as I am in love with Marcus, but I'm not a submissive as Dexter is assuming.

I place my fork on my plate, my earlier hunger vanished. "When you asked me to meet you here, you mentioned Keira. What does she have to do with any of this?"

My stomach gurgles when Dexter replies, "I'm beginning to suspect a lot more than you realize."

He scrubs a napkin over the stubble on his chin before snagging his dowdy satchel off the floor. With a nudge of his head, he summons me to his side of the table. Swallowing down the concern his worried eyes have instigated, I move to sit in the chair next to him instead of across from him.

"Do you remember when Keira joined Global Ten? The ruckus about her getting a senior position when she wasn't qualified for it?" Dexter queries as he fires up his laptop.

Recalling the snarky comments circulating the water coolers the days following her arrival, I dip my chin.

"Do you remember when that was?" Dexter asks when he spots my agreeing gesture.

My lips quirk. "Around four months ago?" I answer, my interest highly notable.

Dexter nods in agreement. "Before that, her time was shared between a vast number of volunteer organizations. She'd never actually worked for payment before Global Ten."

With two clicks of his mouse, he brings up photos of Keira in front of numerous reputable charity organizations. Some I recognize from articles in prominent newspapers, others are more personal. The most notable photo shows Marcus to her far left.

"So you spotted suspect number one and two," Dexter remarks as he watches my throat work hard to swallow. "What about number three?"

My confused eyes dance between Dexter's for several moments before I return them to the photos on the screen. It takes me scanning the images an additional four times before I locate the face of the person Dexter is mentioning.

"Mr. Carson?" I question, my tone unsure even though I'm certain it's him. Although his face is barely distinguishable since it's the size of a tack head, there is no doubt that's his handsome profile. I recall faces, his is one I recall with ease.

When Dexter nods, my stomach flips. I've hardly had the chance to settle my twisting stomach when Dexter brings up another set of photos. These are more stomach-churning than his first two. They appear to be a part of a police file, and the polaroids are dated June thirteenth—exactly two days before Keira joined Global Ten. The set of eight polaroid photos display injuries to a female victim's back, thighs, and chest. The extent of her injuries range from small scratches to bruises the size of an orange.

"Who is that?" I ask Dexter, my voice quivering with nerves. Even with my vision hazy from a rush of moisture flooding my corneas, my intuition is warning me I'll not like unearthing the mysterious blonde's identity.

My eyes rocket from the medical report hidden behind the scattered polaroid photos to Dexter when he says, "By the medical report, she is Jane Doe."

My hand shoots up to cover my mouth. "She's dead?"

"No," Dexter quickly responds, appeasing my dread in an instant. Although I feel horrible about her injuries, I'm sure she would much rather be injured than dead.

"That's just what the treatment clinic marked her down as when she refused to give them her real name," Dexter informs me.

My brows join together. "Why would she do that?"

Dexter shrugs his shoulders. "I'm assuming to protect the identity of the man who assaulted her?"

Ignoring the barrage of silent questions my eyes are issuing him, Dexter's fingers fly wildly over the keyboard of his state-of-the-art laptop. My eyes sneakily scan our surroundings to ensure no one is eyeballing us when Dexter hacks into a government website. He moves through the site with ease, exposing this isn't the first time he's hacked their servers.

When Dexter brings up the screen he is searching for, he nudges me with his elbow, stealing my attention from a man gawking at me from the far corner of the restaurant. Although most of his face is covered by the newspaper he is reading, the top half of his sunglass-covered profile seems familiar.

My suspicion on his familiarity is pushed to the back of my mind when a video begins playing on Dexter's laptop. It's from one of those fancy private medical centers in the middle of Manhattan, one someone like me could never afford. If I were to believe the rumors, just getting a simple flu shot in an establishment like that costs thousands of dollars.

The air sucks from my lungs when the quickest flurry of blonde captures my attention. The curve of Dexter's lips tells me he noticed my breathless response to a blonde scurrying out of the main entrance of the medical center to slide in the back seat of the heavily tinted Escalade.

"That was Keira." Even though my tone is low, there is no way Dexter could construe my response as a question, it was a declaration.

Dexter swivels in his seat to face me front on. "Did you notice the timeline on the video?"

Unable to speak, I merely nod.

"That was within an hour of these pictures being taken." He points to the polaroids of the lady with the badly bruised back. "These photos were taken at the same medical center Keira exited," he discloses, his tone forthright.

My eyes snap to his. "Are you sure?" I ask with panic smeared in my tone.

Dexter nods as he zooms into one of the images on top of a stack of papers. My heart lurches into my throat when in the far right-hand corner of the picture the name of the medical center becomes visible. It matches the business name marked above the entrance Keira dashed out of.

I slouch into my chair, unsure where my loyalties lie. Although I know the injuries Keira sustained can be normal for some subs, there is a sick, twisted feeling in my stomach warning me that isn't the case. The way she responded to Marcus last night leads me to believe she's a demure sub, one who would rather please her Dom than suffer the consequences for discipline. Furthermore, the pain etched on her face increased with every step she took in the surveillance video. Opposed to me, Keira seems to balk from pain. I'm the only idiot who relishes it.

My eyes lift from my intertwined fingers when Dexter says, "I ran the license plate of the car that picked her up. It registered to a car service in lower Manhattan."

Dexter's ruffling through a stack of papers in his bag stops when I ask, "Always On Time Limousine Service?"

"Yeah, how did you know that?" His shock is uncontained.

"That's the limousine service Chains uses for its clients," I explain.

Although I should feel guilty exposing that, I don't. The limo service Chains uses is a well-known fact to every member of the Daily Express Team investigating Chains, so it would have only been a matter of time before Dexter knew himself. Besides, I kept the most important part of my knowledge concealed, the knowledge that the fleet of Escalades used on a day-to-day basis by Always On Time Limousine Service is reserved solely for the use of Chains' VIP clientele. The fleet of Escalades is what transports Chains' submissives to hair appointments, shopping expeditions, and spa treatments. It's also their chosen mode of transport when sharing subs with other Doms. But since my extensive knowledge of Chains' protocol was awarded personally, it doesn't feel right to share that information with Dexter.

My hand rattles when I secure a glass of water off the table to take a sip. My mouth is so parched, I down half the glass before my scorching throat feels any relief. Once I set my water back down, Dexter advises, "It took me a few hours, but I tracked the Escalade through the city."

My lips quiver when I begin to speak, "Where did it go?"

Even though Marcus guaranteed me last night that Keira has never been his sub, I pray he doesn't mention Marcus's New York residence.

When Dexter's silence becomes too unbearable for me to ignore, I plead, "Please, Dexter."

"I'm just making sure you're ready for this, Cleo," he murmurs, amplifying the giddiness twisting my stomach.

"I'm ready," I reply, even though I am anything but.

My silent prayers are answered when Dexter says, "It went to an abandoned warehouse on the corner of Coulson and 42nd street."

He brings up Google maps and zooms in to the address he mentioned. It shows a similar landscape you'd come to expect from the commercial industry in New York. Although most old warehouses have been converted into trendy apartments, some have been abandoned as investors wait for the prime opportunity to either convert their project or sell it on to another investor.

"I ran the address through the database, and it led me to a foreign investor company from Nepal," Dexter informs me, his voice confident but with a smidge of hesitation. "I followed the company's legal paper trail the past three days. I've got nothing. I'm guessing whoever is operating their security is the same person who doctored the surveillance image from the hotel."

My eyes snap to Dexter. "You think the warehouse is owned by the same entity as Chains?"

"I'd put money on it." Dexter nods. "That's why Keira went there. The bruises on her body weren't from being assaulted, they were placed there during a party at Chains."

He shuffles through the small stack of papers in his satchel. His eyes grow wider when he finds the article he is looking for. My heart leaps in my chest when my eyes drop to the elegant calligraphy on the paper. It's a replica of the invitation Mr. Carson handed me months ago when he put me undercover at a Chains party.

"A Chains party was held the night before Keira sought assistance for her injuries." Dexter hands the invitation to me, proving what he is saying is true. "That party is reported to have been held only two blocks from the medical center Keira was taken to. Although medical reports state she arrived alone, surveillance images do not corroborate that. She was dropped off by this gentleman."

The miniscule portion of my lunch threatens to resurface when Dexter hands me a photo. Although the image appears to be nothing more than a man sitting in a flashy dark gray sports car, it's the make, model, and license plate causing the fierce response from my body. It's Marcus's car. The exact car he drove me to Global Ten Media in earlier this week, and the exact car he drove away from me in mere hours ago.

Spotting my ghastly expression, Dexter says, "Now you can see why I'm worried about you, Cleo. I don't want anything like that to happen to you."

"Just because Marcus helped Keira doesn't mean he hurt her," I mumble through my sob, my voice half-confused, half-devastated.

I don't know what warrants more devastation. The fact someone hurt Keira when she clearly displays she isn't into that type of play, or the fact Marcus failed to inform me of the real connection he has with Keira. If he helped her through this, that's clearly more than just a simple friend-helping-friend situation. When people go through a crisis together, it either gives them an unbreakable bond or tears them apart. There is no middle ground.

Dexter gives me a moment to settle some of the confusion pumping into me before he hits me with even more bewilderment. "Mr. Carson approved the investigation into Chains the Monday morning following the incident. Keira started working at Global Ten that same day."

"Woah... what?" I know I sound like an imbecile, but his admission just blindsided me. "Are you saying there is a connection between Keira being assaulted and Mr. Carson approving the investigation into Chains?"

"Look at the evidence, Cleo. Would you see it any other way? *Someone* at Chains hurt Keira."

He doesn't need to say Marcus's name for me to know who he is accusing when he sneers "someone."

"Mr. Carson took offense, and now he's determined to ruin whoever did it."

I remain quiet as my brain processes all the information Dexter has handed me thus far. When I add it to seeing Mr. Carson comfort Keira in his office, the evidence is damning. Mr. Carson's fierce reaction Monday morning reiterates that the Chains investigation is personal to him, much like Keira did when she bombarded me in the elevator weeks ago. The only thing that baffles me is why are two opponents associating with each other? If Mr. Carson cares enough about Keira he wants the blood of the person who hurt her, why would he hunt a community she is clearly a part of and respects? It truly doesn't make any sense. Unless...

My eyes rocket to Dexter. "I'm really sorry, but I have to go."

Not waiting for him to reply, I stand from my chair and gather my purse from the tabletop. Dexter mumbles out an excuse for me to wait. His words trap in his throat when I lean over to place an impromptu kiss on the edge of his cheek. When he suddenly moves, my lips brush the edge of his mouth. The smell of garlic and tomatoes lingers into my nostrils when I pull back, panicked strangers will construe my friendly peck as more than friendly.

"Thank you," I graciously praise, peering straight into Dexter's wide blue eyes. "I owe you big time."

"You still owe me lunch!" is the last thing I hear Dexter shout as I race across the restaurant, secure my jacket, then stumble onto the sidewalk outside.

With my focus devoted to deciphering the information bombarding me, I accidentally bump into a gentleman exiting at the same time as me.

"Sorry," I mumble as I sidestep the man wearing a dark drench coat, black cap, and a pair of sunglasses, so I can hotfoot it to Brodie's car. My eagerness is so apparent, I'm practically sprinting.

"That's okay, Cleo," replies the stranger.

My steps halt midstride when the deepness of his voice registers as familiar. After taking a moment to clear the confusion from my face, I spin on my heels to face the person I bumped into. My eyes dart in all directions, seeking his dark coat. He is nowhere to be found.

8

Lexi's head lifts from the newspaper sprawled across her and Jackson's intertwined legs when our front door's creak announces my arrival. The confusion etched on her face grows when she spots me entering the main entrance of our home. Her shock switches to happiness when she spots Brodie trailing closely behind me. Her response startles me. Although Lexi's temperament is friendly most days, it's unusual for a person to compel such a response from her, much less a man who usually hackles her spikes more than he soothes them.

After hanging mine and Brodie's coats, I pace into the living room. The apprehension twisting my stomach eases when I spot a brand new entranceway table sitting in the position our old table used to be. Although its super shiny lacquer doesn't match the rest of the outdated furniture, it's a beautiful piece that adds a touch of class our house has been missing the past four years.

"You like?" Lexi stands from the couch and paces toward me.

"It's very nice," I greet her with a hug and a peck on the cheek.

My brows stitch when she holds on to me a little longer than normal.

"Did you miss me?" My melting heart echoes in my tone.

Lexi scoffs before drawing back. "Not exactly." She rolls her eyes at my waggling brows. "Alright. Fine. I missed you. Okay?"

"Okay," I reply with an equal amount of sassiness. "I've missed you too."

After checking that Jackson is occupied talking with Brodie, Lexi returns her eyes to me. The worry in them has my nerves sitting on edge. Anxiety has never been a problem for Lexi, she has confidence by the bucket loads, so I'm somewhat surprised by the concern her eyes are holding.

"Can I talk to you for a minute?" She nudges her head to our kitchen.

I nod before pacing into the funky-smelling space. Lexi shadows closely behind me, acting like she can't smell her disastrous culinary skills. Some of the nerves making me a jittering mess dull Lexi secures a saucepan from the drawer under the oven and fills it with milk before placing it onto the stovetop. She adds all the ingredients for her famous hot chocolate before spinning around to face me.

"What did you do?" I accuse. She doesn't usually make me hot chocolate unless she is sucking up. Actually, come to think of it, the last time she made me hot chocolate was when she drew a gun on Marcus.

"This isn't about me." Lexi's tone is apprehensive. "This is about you and Chains."

Not trusting my legs to keep me upright, I take a seat in one of the chairs at our small eating nook. I truly don't know if my brain can handle any more information than it's currently tackling. The ten-minute trip from the pizzeria to my house was a complete blur, not just wasted trying to work out the connection between Marcus, Mr. Carson, and Keira, but also struggling to identify the stranger I bumped into. Although years ago, I was regularly confronted by Montclair locals wishing to express their condolences for my loss, the stranger's voice didn't seem to be the right age for that. His voice was smooth and alluring—like a man in his mid to late twenties.

My attention drifts back to the present when Lexi places a large mug of hot chocolate in front of me. Horrid unease twists up my throat when I notice two marshmallows floating in the rich, sweet goodness. Lexi doesn't believe hot chocolate needs any more sweetness, so her Garcia stubbornness means she usually serves mine without the puffs of sugar.

"Spit it out, Lexi. I'm dying here."

She sits on the chair across from me. After tucking her feet under her bottom, her big brown eyes stray to mine. For the quickest second, all I see is our mom reflecting back at me. *God, I miss her.*

"Hit you straight up?" Lexi queries, wanting to ensure I know she isn't going to hold back.

"Straight up," I confirm, nodding.

She takes a sip of her hot chocolate before placing it on the tabletop. I'm tempted to follow suit, but chose to wait, unsure if I can trust my churning stomach with liquid.

"I thought the whole idea of your week with Marcus was for him to have time to convince you to go with him to Ravenshoe?" she asks, her tone low and without judgment.

"It was," I verify, recalling Marcus saying that during our negotiations in our room last week.

I pick up my mug, feeling that I've overreacted to the worry on her face. Maybe it's more exhaustion than apprehension?

"Then why are you here?" Her tone is so forthright, if I didn't know her better, I'd swear she was annoyed by my visit.

My mug freezes halfway to my lips as my brows stitch in confusion. I was too busy battling through disappointment that Marcus had to leave earlier than expected, I haven't stopped to consider what altered his prior arrangement.

My eyes lift to Lexi when she squeezes my hand. "Did something happen that changed his plans? Or..." She leaves her question open for me to fill in.

"Nothing really happened... Well, we did get in an argument last night. But that was resolved before he left this morning," I answer, my words as unconvincing as my facial expression.

Lexi's eyes dance between mine. "Are you sure? As he was adamant last week he wanted you to return to Ravenshoe with him. That's why he kept begging for you to hand in your notice at Global Ten. He wanted to make things official between you."

I nod. It isn't a confident nod. "He said he'd see me soon. He did seem a little edgy before he left, but that's just the way he is." My voice softens at the end of my statement as worry makes itself known. "What do you think it means?"

Lexi shrugs as the concern in her eyes doubles. "I don't know what to think. When I first saw you walk in the door, I was worried. Then I saw Brodie, so I figured I had nothing to worry about. Why would he keep protection on you if he didn't care about you?" She grazes her teeth over her bottom lip before she quickly mumbles, "Then I got close enough to see the worry in your eyes, and it had me doubting everything." She locks her eyes with mine, the mayhem in them unmissable. "I'm so fucking confused."

I laugh. It isn't my usual full-hearted laughter, but you work with what you have. "Welcome to the club. I've been like this for months."

Lexi smiles. It isn't as bright as her usual smile either. "Alright, I hit you with straight up honesty. Now you need to do the same."

Lexi giggles, gags, and grimaces during my recount of the events that occurred from the time Marcus and I negotiated a week of solitude until I walked through the front door. She also threatened Marcus's life on more than two occasions when I reached the parts that included Keira. The only thing that kept her backside planted on her seat and not rummaging through the safe bolted in my parents' closet, was when I disclosed Mr. Carson's involvement in the bizarre circumstances I find myself in.

Once I've finished relaying the entire story, nearly an hour has passed on the clock and we've consumed two mugs of hot chocolate.

Lexi slumps into her chair before raising her eyes to me. "Okay. First of all, I understand your confusion. Woah!" She waves her hands in front of her head like her brain is exploding. "Second, you're evil. It was only a few weeks ago you argued that being spanked wasn't natural, then you go and do *that*..." She doesn't need to express what her "that" is referring to. Her face shows the entire picture.

"I didn't tell you everything so you could judge me—"

"I'm not judging you, Cleo. I'm in friggin' awe. Kudos to you—seriously."

If I couldn't see the honesty in her reply, I'd be tempted to recant her statement.

"So what's the look on your face about?" I query.

I stand from my chair to place our dirty mugs in the sink. Lexi waits for me to turn around to face her before she says, "There are parts of your story that don't make sense."

"I know. That's why I'm here, seeking answers," I agree, crossing my arms in front of my chest.

Lexi rises from her chair and paces to stand next to me. "But the person you should be seeking answers from isn't here, Cleo. He is over a thousand miles away somewhere in Florida."

Even though I know whom she is referring to, I bounce my eyes between hers, pretending I don't.

"If you want your questions answered, you need to ask Chains," she suggests, her tone revealing she wasn't buying my attempts of acting clueless.

"And how am I supposed to do that?" I hate that I'm acting so cowardly that I want my baby sister to pull me out of the quicksand trying to swallow me whole.

"What did Daddy always say?" Lexi queries with her brow arched high.

"Most conversations start with a hello," we quote in sync.

"I'd probably start there," Lexi suggests, her tone more mature than her twenty-one years.

"Good point. I'll give it a go."

Lexi runs her hand down my arm before she exits the kitchen. Her girly giggle shrills through my ears not even ten seconds later. "Jackson Josiah Collard, we have guests."

Even from the kitchen, I'm not buying her scold. She needs to remove the absolute bliss from her voice if she wants anyone to believe her reprimand. Ignoring the mortified expression crossing Brodie's face as he watches Jackson and Lexi play tonsil hockey, I gather my cell from my purse on the entranceway table and saunter into my room.

The worries I held yesterday about being spoiled by the opulence of Marcus's properties are proven unfounded when I pace into my childhood bedroom. Although it isn't as grand as Marcus's bedroom, it has much more sentimental value than money could buy. I've lived in this room my entire life. No price can be placed on that.

After carefully closing my bedroom door so it doesn't give out a squeak, I move to my bed to sit down. My brows furrow when I notice the stuffed rabbit I came home from the hospital with is sitting between the ruffled pillows on my bed. It's usually housed on the shelf above my desk.

Placing my cell down, I lift Mr. Bunny from my bed, give him a quick squeeze, then put him back in his rightful spot. Just the smell of his mottled fur flashes images of my parents to the forefront of my mind, inciting tears to prick my eyes.

I take a moment to settle my nerves before striding back to my phone and dialing Marcus's number. He answers not even two seconds later.

"Hey," I greet him. My voice is confident, but it also gives a hint to the torrent of emotions pumping through me.

"Hey, Cleo. Everything okay?" Marcus's tone is laced with worry.

I smile, loving that he detected my apprehension when I only spoke one little word.

"Yeah, I'm fine. Just a little worried. I thought you were going to call me once you landed?" Since most of my statement is true, it comes out sounding honest.

"Ah. Yeah. Umm. Our departure got pushed back." My heartrate kicks up from the uneasiness in his reply. He usually exudes confidence by the bucket loads, so his skittish response is odd.

"You're still in New York?" I query, excitement echoed in my tone. This conversation will be ten times easier if I can do it in person, as more times than not, Marcus's eyes relay more than his words ever could.

"Ah. Yeah, but we're flying out soon," Marcus answers, his words flying out of his mouth in a flurry.

Disappointment slashes through me. "Oh... that's a bummer." I roll my eyes. I sound like a fifth-grader.

"Cleo, is this important? I could listen to your voice all day, but I'm a little busy right now," Marcus discloses, his tone sharper than usual.

"Oh, okay. Sorry," I reply flimsily, muted into stupidity by his admission he likes listening to me talk. I've always thought my voice was a little nasally and high.

I press my cell in close to my ear when I hear a female in the background greeting Marcus. Her voice is high and bouncy, the type you'd expect from someone in the twenty-one to thirty-year age bracket. I hear Marcus shush her before he muzzles the phone with his hand. Although they continue talking, I can't understand any of their words. It probably doesn't help that my hearing is affected by the rush of jealousy roaring through my body. Jealousy was never a horrid neurosis of mine...until Marcus came along.

After what feels like an eternity, Marcus's attention returns to me. "I have to go, Cleo. I'm sorry, baby. I'll talk to you soon. Okay?"

"Okay." I'd like to articulate a better response but I'm left a little dumbfounded, but the chance to respond is lost when Marcus disconnects our call.

I stare at my phone, blinking and confused. Our conversation went nothing like I had predicted. Before we officially met, Marcus and I communicated on the phone for hours every night, so to have our call ended in under a minute is truly shocking. His abrupt reply can only mean two things. He truly is busy, or he doesn't want to talk to me. With how badly my stomach is twisting up I have a horrible feeling it's the latter.

I jump, startled, when Lexi asks, "What did he say?"

She has her shoulder propped up on my door. I stare at her with as much confusion as my call with Marcus created. . *How did she get my door open without it creaking?*

Misreading the expression on my face as contempt, Lexi pushes off her feet and saunters into my room. "Did he give you any answers?"

I shake my head. "I never got the chance to ask any. He hung up on me."

"He hung up on you?" She sounds as shocked as I feel. My mattress squeaks in protest when Lexi flops onto the overused springs. "So what are you going to do now?"

I take a minute to consider a mature response. It's clearly a waste of a precious minute when I reply, "I'm going to yank my head out of the sandbox and start using the brain our parents hard-earned money went toward developing."

Lexi peers up at me as confused as ever.

"Do you know where my box is?" When Lexi's confusion grows, I ask, "The box I left Global Ten with? The one with all my work on Chains?"

"Should be by the entranceway where you left it. I don't touch your stuff."

I'm halfway down the hall before the entire sentence leaves Lexi's mouth.

My box is where she said it would be, tucked between our coatrack and our new entranceway table. Jackson and Brodie's heads lift from the sports highlight program broadcasting on the TV so their eyes can track me dragging the heavy box into the formal dining room. Although the box isn't overly heavy, with my muscles still weak with exhaustion, it feels like I'm dragging a Mack truck.

Like a perfectly timed skit, Lexi enters the dining room at precisely the same time I'm struggling to lift the box onto our large oval table. "Jesus. What have you got in here?" she grunts while assisting me, realizing the strain crossing my face wasn't fake.

I flip off the lid of the box, allowing the documents inside to answer on my behalf. Lexi's eyes bug as they wander over the hundreds of pictures I printed out after my night at Chains.

"Holy shit. You were right. Seeing it in the flesh doesn't match what you imagine when you're reading it."

She picks up the photos of a lady hanging from a steel-like contraption wearing nothing but rope for clothing. "That takes a lot of trust," Lexi mumbles under her breath.

"It does," I agree wholeheartedly. "That's one of the biggest things in the BDSM world. Trust."

Lexi places the photo onto a bunch of ones displaying Marcus's mask-covered face. "Then why are you re-opening your investigation into Chains? I know Marcus owes you some explanations, but *investigating* him? This doesn't feel right, Cleo. It's something I'd do, but this isn't you. You bring the smarts, I bring the looks. You bring the understanding, I bring the suspicion. You bring the creep, I bring the—"

"Leech," we say in sync.

The rigidness in the air evaporates when our conjoined laughter fills the room.

I wait for her laughter to dim before saying, "I'm not investigating Marcus, I'm investigating Chains."

Lexi rolls her eyes. "They are one and the same, Cleo," she fires back as a cloud of chaos overtakes the glint of happiness in her eyes.

"Not Chains the person. Chains the company," I inform her. I move my hand to the pocket of my jeans to dig out the photo I sneakily borrowed from Dexter on my brisk exit of the restaurant.

Lexi inhales a sharp breath when I hand her the printout of Keira's bruised back. "Are those whip marks?" Lexi runs her index finger along the welts in Keira's back.

I commence answering her question with a shrug. "I think so. The pattern is unusual, though. I've never come across that type of pattern during my research."

Lexi raises her panicked eyes to me. "Are her injuries typical for people in the BDSM lifestyle?"

I quirk my lips while taking a moment to contemplate a response. I want to be honest with Lexi, but I don't want her to panic either. "Depends. Some people need... *more,* where others need a lot more," I eventually answer. When panic flares in Lexi's eyes, I confess, "I researched the lifestyle for weeks, and from what I've seen, this seems extreme. But it never would have happened without the submissive's permission. There are very strict rules to ensure nothing like this happens without prior consent. It may seem cruel, but some people need that type of stimulation to feel whole."

Lexi remains as quiet as a mouse. It's an uncomfortable three minutes filled with awkward tension.

"Say what you want to say, Lexi. I'm a big girl, I can handle it," I express, loathing the concerned look she is issuing me.

Lexi's tongue delves out to replenish her lips before she asks, "Do you need that much...*more,* Cleo?"

Relief floods her eyes when I shake my head. "No. After last night, I'm beginning to wonder if my desires for more are based around the lifestyle or the man associated with it."

Lexi continues with her silent stance, forcing me to say, "Last night was the first time I climaxed without additional stimulation. That should mean something, shouldn't it?"

"Yeah, it should." The color in her cheeks returns. "It means I want what you're having." She excessively waggles her brows.

I inwardly sigh, grateful her playful response killed the tension hanging thickly in the air.

After placing the photo of Keira into the box next to numerous surveillance images of Marcus, Lexi spreads her hands across her tiny hips. "Okay, let me check we're on the same page?"

She waits for me to nod before saying, "Her injuries happened at Chains?" She points her index finger at Keira's photo. Although her eyes are showing her relief, I can tell she is still rattled, as her slim finger is incapable of hiding the tremor of her hands.

I nod. "There is a match in timelines between a Chains party and her seeking medical assistance."

"And she is the reason Global Ten Media is investigating Chains?"

"Yes. Well, I'm assuming that's the case. My intuition is warning me she is somehow involved, I just need to work out how." I pull out a chair from the dining table and sit down.

"Easy," Lexi replies as if it's the simplest solution in the world. "She wants revenge on the Chains community for what happened to her, so she sold them out to Global Ten."

Lexi's eyes drop to mine when I reply, "No. Although her assault seems to be the premise of the investigation, she didn't initiate it."

"How do you know that?" Lexi questions, shock smeared in her tone.

I swivel in my chair to face her. "She isn't against the members of Chains, she is working in cahoots with them."

Lexi looks the most confused I've ever seen her.

"Remember me telling you about Keira bombarding me in the elevator the morning I was called into Global Ten for an emergency meeting? How she pleaded for me to write my story on Chains based on facts, not a sugarcoated pop culture piece? She defended the BDSM lifestyle and the rights for its members to choose their own sexual proclivities."

Lexi crosses her arms over her chest as she nods, her interest unmissable.

"That was her." I point to the photo of Keira.

Lexi gasps in a shocked breath as her pupils dilate to the size of saucers. "That doesn't make any sense. The evidence clearly shows she was the reason the Chains investigation commenced, so why would she then defend them?"

"That's what I am endeavoring to find out. Keira is the link between Chains and Global Ten. If I can work out why, I might be able to work out how to end the investigation before Marcus or any of his clientele get caught in the crossfire."

My eyes track Lexi when she spins on her heels and makes a beeline for the door. "Where are you going?"

She cranks her neck to peer at me over her shoulder, but her pace remains unchecked. "We need wine before we tackle this head on."

"We?" I retort, pretending I can't read the excitement on her face.

Lexi freezes halfway out the room, cocks her hip, then glares at me. "Yeah, *we*. Do you really think I'll let you do this without backup? I'm your little sis. We Garcia women stick together through a crisis."

She strengthens her stance as the gleam of cheekiness in her eyes turns calamitous. "Besides, if you're going to take down a billion-dollar company with those grainy images, you'll need someone without shitty vision to help."

I glare at her with my mouth gaped open. "Then you better get your glasses," I tease when she fails to acknowledge the threat in my glare.

Lexi stares at me, her confidence at an all-time high. "I was planning to—right after the wine."

9

"I never said that, Professor. I may think your breath smells like dog doo, but I'd never say it out loud."

Lexi springboards into a half-seated position when I throw a kernel of caramel-coated popcorn at her head. Is it wrong of me to admit I know who she is talking about even though I've never attended her college? Her physics professor is a lovely man, but my god, the times I served him at our local gas station during summer holidays my senior years of high school, were unpleasant enough for the memory to stick. I've always believed a scent is the quickest way to trigger a memory. That's one of the reasons I was so baffled about the mysterious stranger I bumped into yesterday. I swear I've smelled his scent before.

My attention drifts back to the present when Lexi's bewildered eyes roam around the dining room. She has a massive gob of dried drool in the corner of her mouth, and the papers she was sleeping on have creased her cheek. Guilt makes itself comfy in the middle of my chest when I spot the dark rims circling her eyes. She looks exhausted, which is understandable considering it's 5 AM.

"Did I fall asleep again?" Lexi queries, her words muffled by a tiger-like yawn.

"Only for a few minutes," I lie. She's been out nearly two hours. "We should probably call it a night anyway. You've got your volunteer session at Links tomorrow before school."

"Today," Lexi corrects, grimacing.

"Sorry," I apologize, hating that I've put her natural body clock out of whack.

She waves off my worry. "It's okay. I have exams the next two weeks."

Guilt slams into me.

It doesn't last long when Lexi quickly adds, "But I don't have any today. Thank god."

"Thank god, indeed."

Lexi gingerly stands from her chair to aid me in gathering the documents and photos we have sprawled across the table. Although we can confirm without a doubt that Keira is a member of Chains, we are not any closer to discovering the connection between her and Global Ten. This will make me sound like the most horrible person in the world, but I'm just being honest. I don't know what I find more concerning. The photos of Keira's bruised back, or the dozens upon dozens of images of her gawking at Marcus from the surveillance pictures gathered from my night at Chains. Although Keira was wearing a simple silver mask, her platinum blonde hair, small facial features, and prominent blue eyes guarantee her identity can't be hidden. She was in multiple shots, and as I had suspected, her eyes were always firmly rapt on Marcus, proving her fascination with him is more than just friendly.

"Oh, hold on," Lexi says when her stack of papers tumble onto the mouse of the laptop, awakening its monitor. "Do you remember how we searched for Mr. Carson and Keira?"

Nervous butterflies take flight in my stomach as I nod.

I breathe out slowly when Lexi says, "We finally got a match."

"What month is it? Around June/July?"

She shakes her head. "No. It was in September."

"Around the time the Chains investigation started?" I'm shocked as the first searches done were based on the prior six months, so why didn't it come up then?

"Not September this year," she clarifies, drawing my attention back to her. "September fifteen years ago."

"What?" I ask, certain my lack of sleep is playing tricks on my spent brain.

Lexi spins her laptop around to face me. There is a picture of a teenage boy and a girl I'd guess to be around the age of ten. It's a newspaper article about a local baseball charity game played in Jersey. All benefits from the game were donated to a domestic violence shelter the community was endeavoring to get off the ground.

"That looks like Keira," Lexi summarizes.

I nod in full agreement. Although she is much younger, she has the same eyes and hair color. "It's either Keira or her twin sister."

"Is that Mr. Carson?" Lexi points to the handsome teen in the photo who has his arm wrapped around Keira.

I lean in to inspect the photo more thoroughly, not wanting speculation to run wild in my mind. The teen's cheeks are shiny since they are covered in sweat, his eyes are as wild as the messy mane of inky black hair on his head, and his jaw is stiff and rigid, even though he'd be barely over the age of fifteen. He is Mr. Carson. I am certain of it. I was so fascinated by the local boy from Jersey who turned into a self-made billionaire, I gobbled up every article I could find on Mr. Carson when I was younger. This picture matches ones I've seen of him in his teen years.

"That's Mr. Carson," I confirm to Lexi.

"So they've known each other for fifteen years, as this photo is way too chummy for a random stranger pic," Lexi says as shock replaces the tiredness in her eyes. When I nod, she asks, "Where do we go from here?"

I scroll through the additional images attached to the article Lexi discovered, striving to devise what this new information could mean for my investigation. This changes everything, because not only are Keira and Mr. Carson well-known to one another, but unlike this photo, they are playing on opposing teams. Is that what their confrontation was about in his office last week? Maybe Keira thought using tears was a way to break through Mr. Carson's stern resistance? *Much like she used a chain-link choker as a way of capturing Marcus's attention.*

Suppressing my jealousy before it gets the better of me, I click through articles matching the story on the charity baseball game. Just thinking about Marcus being intimately connected with another woman triggers feverish jealousy, but I've got too much on my plate to add anything else.

My manic clicking stops when I stumble upon a picture of a lady with a broad smile and vibrant eyes. It takes several minutes staring at the familiar-looking brunette's face before I realize how I know her. Just as quickly as recognition surfaces, so does the familiarity of her surname.

With my heart sitting in my throat, I do a quick internet search on the brunette's name, but instead of using her whole name, I focus on her surname. My eyes go crazy when they are bombarded with hundreds and hundreds of responses for my search. Newspaper clippings, arrest warrants, photos, everything and anything you could imagine is displayed in front of me. It's exciting and stomach-churningly worrying at the same time.

I remain quiet, struggling to join each piece of the puzzle to the right section. It's a complex puzzle that comes together surprisingly quickly when all the main players are exposed.

When the final piece locks into place, shock hits me so hard and fast, I'm nearly knocked onto my ass. I connect my eyes with Lexi. "Do you need a ride to Links today?"

My words are hurried as I jump up from my seat to gather all the documents sprawled across the desk at a more frantic speed than the one I was using earlier.

"I was going to catch the train. Why, are you going that way?" Lexi answers, watching me with bewilderment etched on her face.

The fettering of her brows increases when I nod. "I have a brunch date I completely forgot about. Get dressed, I'll update you in the car."

Several hours later, I'm mingling in the lobby of an extremely elegant apartment building located across from Central Park. That smell of wealth I whiffed at the fundraising gala two days ago is as blatant in the building as the scent of taxi fumes in Times Square.

After running his eyes down mine and Brodie's body for the tenth time the past twenty minutes, the pompous-looking receptionist says, "Yes, Ma'am. I'll send them straight up." He is talking into the small black device lodged in his ear canal.

With a snarl, he gestures his hand to the mirrored glass elevator banks behind his station. "Penthouse floor. George will show you the way."

A gentleman in a dark burgundy suit and top hat dips his chin in greeting before waving his hand to the elevator banks. When he pushes off his feet, Brodie and I shadow him. I've always felt out of place around the wealthy, but my neurosis has been pushed aside today because Brodie's discomfort is strong enough for the both of us.

Our ride in the elevator with George happens in silence. I'd like to say resolute silence, but with elevator music filling the void, it isn't entirely silent. My eyes rocket to Brodie when he whistles along to the tune. If it isn't bad enough my ears are being subjected to torture from the elevator music, having him whistling along makes it ten times worse. I don't hate many things, but whistling is on my concise list of dislikes.

"You should sleep more. You get grumpy when you're tired," Brodie snickers as we follow George out of the elevator, straight into the lavish foyer of an opulent home.

A large crystal vase full of fresh lilies and pussy willow branches sits on an antique round table in the middle of the vast space. The extravagant floral arrangement fires the air with a refreshing scent of pollen, ridding it of the wealth its maplewood wainscoted walls and tiled marble floors convey. After scrubbing his polished shoes on the bristled mat, Brodie places the box we arrived with at the side of the glistening space before joining me in soaking up the lifestyle many dream of but will never achieve.

I stop appraising an original Monet when the distinct rumble of Cartier rolls through my ears. "Darling, if I had known you were coming, I would have seen my guest out earlier."

She floats across the room like an angel gliding over a cloud. She is dressed more casually than she was when I saw her Saturday. Her fit body is covered with a floral kimono cinched so dangerously loosely at the waist, Brodie is mere moments away from inspecting *precisely* what she is wearing under her satin gown.

A grin curves on my lips when Cartier greets me with two air kisses to each of my cheeks. The unique scent of flowers and spices lingers in her wake when she welcomes Brodie in the same fashion. My grin enlarges to a full smile when the beard covering Brodie's chin can't hide his smirk from Cartier's friendliness.

My brows bow when a handsome man in his mid-thirties struts into the room. From his disheveled hair and rumpled clothing, it isn't hard to decipher what he was doing, but his peacock attitude is a good give away. After smirking a greeting to us, he leans in to whisper something into Cartier's ear. I slap Brodie's arm at the same time Cartier hits the unknown man's chest.

"Do you recognize him?"

"HBO?" Brodie mouths, acknowledging my suspicion he is one of the lead actors who stars in a popular sitcom on HBO.

When the dark-haired man finalizes his conversation with Cartier, he shifts his gaze to Brodie and me. We both stand a little straighter, trying to act like we weren't just spying on their exchange. It's a woeful effort. The instant his highly recognizable eyes lock with mine, I know he is precisely whom I suspected, which makes me grin like an idiot. I'll be honest, I'm a little starstruck right now.

Cartier waits for her guest to leave with George before drifting her eyes back to me. "Look at you, just as ravishing in casual clothing as you are in designer dresses. I understand Marcus's beguilement." Every R she pronounces rolls off her tongue with a throaty purr.

"Come, let's get something to drink." She pivots on her heels and saunters into a room on our left.

"It's not even 10 AM," I grouse, shadowing her into the massive living room.

My jaw slackens in an unladylike manner when the wonderment of silk, gold, and maplewood bombards me. At least my response was more subdued than Brodie's. He didn't hold in his curse word.

This room is massive, stretching the entire length of the apartment. The views of Central Park from the floor-to ceiling-windows are breathtaking. This would have to be one of the most valuable properties in New York City. Nothing could replicate this view—*not a single darn thing.*

Cartier giggles, adoring our slack-jawed expressions. I guess she has become accustomed to the awe she wakes up to every morning. Arriving at a bar on our right, Cartier offers us a drink. I kindly refuse. I've never been fond of drinking so early in the morning, and my lack of sleep last night has already given me a severe case of dizziness, so I don't need anything to add to it. Brodie also refuses her request, citing, "I don't drink while on the job."

After pouring herself a three-finger serving of fancy whiskey in a crystal glass, Cartier takes a seat in one of the four voluptuous sofas in her living room. Brodie and I also sit, but on the couch across from her.

"I thought Marcus said you were a journalist?" Cartier queries, peering at me with a set of suspicious eyes.

"I am," I confirm, nodding.

"Then why do I get the feeling I'm sitting across from two detectives?" She holds her hands out in front of her body like she is pleading innocence. "I swear, Officers, I don't know anything. I'm a good girl."

Brodie's throaty laugh rumbles my nerves out of my stomach. While kicking his shoe with my heel to halt his immature response, I mumble, "I'm not here to interrogate you, but I did come here to ask you something in confidence."

Cartier reads the honesty from my eyes before her dazzling gaze shifts to Brodie.

"This is the first I'm hearing of it," Brodie advises her questioning glare.

"He didn't know we were coming here until he pulled into the valet," I inform Cartier when her suspicion remains high.

Cartier shifts her eyes back to me. "How did you even know where *here* is, darling?"

"This," I reply, scooting to the edge of my chair to show her the article I saved on my phone during our hour commute.

She gasps in shock when she recognizes the image reflecting back at her. It's a photo snapped of her when she was cutting the ribbon at a domestic violence shelter in New Jersey nearly twenty years ago—the same shelter Keira and Mr. Carson were raising funds for fifteen years ago. Although Cartier is decades younger, and her hair is as dark as the storm looming in her eyes, I have no doubt it is her. The modern fashionista smiling at the camera is wearing a replica of the small thin necklace she hides under her big bulky ones. I only caught the quickest glimpse of the collar she was fiddling with Saturday night, but its infinity eight design was captivating enough for me to remember. It's simple but classically elegant.

Since the photo was snapped years before Cartier began using nicknames to hide her true self, her full name was displayed—Phoebe Annabella Gottle, wife of the suspected mob boss of New York City. Although I was unaware of Mr. Gottle's influence in New York when he arrived at my home with Marcus after he was arrested last month, my impromptu internet search of him this morning unearthed more information on him than months of investigative journalism could ever locate on Cartier. Unlike his wife, Mr. Gottle's personal life isn't personal.

"The Gottle surname is not unique... except in New York." My eyes wander around the affluent surroundings. "I knew the exact building to find you as Henry looks after his family members very well."

Brodie's eyes snap to mine at the same moment Cartier's do. His eyes are wide, and his mouth is gaped. Cartier's expression isn't as shocked as his. Her plump lips have scoured into a thin line, and her eyes have narrowed.

"I am not his family, darling. I was nothing more than his whore." Her words are hurled off her tongue like daggers, but it does nothing to hide the massive sentiment dangling on her vocal cords.

"A whore who happens to still carry his last name?" I query softly, my confidence lacking from the dubious glare she is directing at me. "Please correct me if I am wrong, but how can the title of 'wife' be misconstrued as 'whore?'"

Cartier straightens her spine before her eyes drop to the diamond chain-link pendant nestled in the groove of my neck. "Some things are more valuable than titles. If you lose that, you lose them. Simple. A last name means nothing, and neither does the piece of paper stating it does. The law doesn't tell you whom you belong to, darling, your heart does."

My heart breaks from the pure agony in her words. This was not my intention. I didn't come here to drag down her eminent personality I adore. I just want answers to questions I know she can provide.

When I explain that to Cartier, she stops peering at my pendant to look at me. "Does Marcus know you're here?" .

Missing a backbone, I shake my head.

I thought my admission would pain her more. It doesn't. The faintest smile creeps across her face as she says, "Oh, darling, you remind me so much of myself at your age. You revel in defiance. I'm just grateful you learned in weeks what took me years to work out."

"Learned what?"

Brodie tries to deflect his curiosity with a sizeable yawn, but I'm not buying his attempts. He is not only listening to every word Cartier and I speak, but he is also digitally categorizing it for future use. Although interested in learning what he is planning to do with the information, my primary focus must remain on the task at hand. If I juggle too many balls, some will eventually fall. Considering every ball I'm juggling has immense sentimental value to me, I'm not willing to let one topple from my grasp. So, for now, I'll push aside Brodie's interest as purely inquisitiveness until each ball is safely placed back into my pocket.

Cartier licks her lips before replying, "Rebelliousness keeps the flame flickering longer. Don't ever lose that, darling, because when you do, the remains of an overinflated balloon are never as pretty as they once were."

I'm shunted into silence, confused by her statement. Brodie appears just as baffled as me, but instead of keeping his bewilderment to himself, he asks, "What does that mean?"

Cartier shifts her eyes to Brodie. "Have you ever had someone who makes you feel so wonderful, you believe nothing could ever bring you down?"

Brodie nods.

"Imagine every compliment or precious thing they did for you was the equivalent of pumping air into your balloon. Once the balloon is at its greatest, there are only two things that can happen. It either pops or they let it float away. To some, popping the balloon you've worked so hard to inflate seems cruel. The balloon may have an opposing opinion. Why spend years growing something to its best only to let it float away the instant it reaches greatness?"

When Cartier toys with the thin necklace I referred to earlier, I blurt out, "Did Henry give you your necklace?" before I can stop my words.

Cartier's hand drops from her neck at a faster rate than my plummeting heart slithers into my stomach. The devastation brewing in her eyes with a rueful smirk cuts me raw. It's the same turmoil Marcus's eyes held when he noticed my cut lip after I was assaulted in the alley weeks ago.

"I'm sorry, I didn't mean to pry," I apologize with sincerity in my tone.

Cartier accepts my apology with an air of grace. "Intellectual curiosity is the forefront of knowledge, Cleo, but idle gossip is the first step to hell. Perhaps you should remember that when you're prying into people's lives."

"I am *not* prying," I assure her, stunned by her statement.

"You're a reporter arriving at my home with a vault of old news that was buried faster than it was built," Cartier fires back. "Is that not prying?"

I nod, agreeing with her. She seems shocked by my obliging response. She shouldn't be. Everything she said was true, so why would I deny it?

"Yes, I am a reporter, and I did disrespectfully present myself to you this morning as if I am here as your guest. But you can be assured, I am not here to break a story, Cartier, I'm here to stop one unjustly being broken. One I believe is very dear to your heart."

A tense stretch of silence passes between us. I wouldn't necessarily say her silence is off-putting, it's more like she is generating her own reason for me arriving unannounced by reading the truth from my soul-baring eyes instead of listening to the words I spoke.

Realizing there is only one way to gain her trust, I expose my most lethal hand. A spark of curiosity blazes in Cartier's narrowed gaze when I take the printout of Keira's injuries from my purse. The heat of Brodie's body blooms across my chest when he leans in intimately close to my side as I carefully open the folded-up piece of paper.

"Where the hell did you get that?" Brodie asks at the same time an exasperated gasp escapes Cartier's O-formed lips.

Ignoring Brodie's question, I keep my focus fixated on Cartier. "That's Keira Herrington, a founding member of Chains."

Cartier remains quiet, neither denying or agreeing with my accusation. She doesn't need to speak for me to hear the words she is saying, though. Her forthright eyes reveal the truth.

"This is also Keira." I hand her the fresh printout I printed minutes before leaving my home—the one that shows Keira volunteering at one of the many charities Cartier founded.

"And so is this one." I hand her the final photo of Keira and Mr. Carson when they were younger. Cartier gasps with even more shock over this image.

"I don't know how, but I know these two are linked in some way." I gesture my hand between the photo of Mr. Carson and Keira and the single ones of Keira. "If my hunch is right, Keira's injuries were the catalyst behind Global Tens' investigation into Chains. I just haven't worked out that link yet. I was hoping you'd help me."

I sheepishly lift my eyes to Cartier. She is glancing straight at me with shock and dread tainting her beautiful face. "Chains is being investigated?" Her tone is high with disbelief.

Shit. I assumed her extensive knowledge on Marcus Saturday night meant she was aware of the investigation. I had no clue I would be the one breaking the news.

After swallowing down the unease lodged in my throat, I mumble, "Yes."

I'm expecting Cartier to sigh in disappointment, or at the very least voice anger about people's right to privacy, and how they shouldn't be judged or ridiculed because of their sexual proclivities. She does nothing of the sort. She merely looks me straight in the eyes and says,

"Give me everything you have. All of it, Cleo. By the end of today, there will be no story."

10

"I've got it," says Cartier, her voice sounding more like a ticket hackler in Yankee stadium, than showing the refinement it usually holds. "I don't know how I bloody missed it, but now it's as clear as day."

The past several hours of research must be taking its toll on Cartier. From her dark-ringed eyes and gaunt expression, I'd say I wasn't the only one burning the candle at both ends last night. She looks as wretched as I feel. Even Brodie appears exhausted. He is slumped on a body-hugging chair, basking in the rapidly setting sun. If I didn't hear his faint snoring, I'd be none the wiser that he was napping.

My aching muscles squeal in protest when I stand from my seat to take up the vacant spot next to Cartier. She has numerous print outs of the Chains' event I attended last week, but the one she is holding in her hand is the group photo of Marcus, Keira and Mr. Carson taken at a charity event over twelve months ago. Following the direction of her gaze, I realize her eyes aren't rapt on Marcus nor Mr. Carson, her gaze is firmly fixated on Keira.

Stumped as to why she believes this is the key to unlocking our confusion, I lift my eyes to her and say, "You're going to need to fill me in. I'm a little lost."

Cartier's beautiful chuckle jingles into my ears, warming my heart and awakening Brodie. After scrubbing the back of his hand over his tired eyes, Brodie moves to join my intimate gathering with Cartier. I'm glad she and I managed to costar over the massive barrier I lodged between us this morning without too much drama. Cartier's warranted unease only lasted the length of time it took for her to hear my quiet grumblings about Global Tens' investigation into Chains while I was unpacking my box of goodies I took from my office when I was placed on suspension for striking Delilah.

"Look, darling. It's Lauren Schwartz," Cartier says, handing the photo to me.

I drop my eyes to scan the image once more, searching for the woman Cartier is referring to. "Who is Lauren Schwartz, and what does she have to do with this investigation?"

Cartier laughs harder. "Not Lauren Schwartz the person, Lauren Schwartz the thing. A wonderful thing only a small number of people can afford."

She extends her overly manicured index finger to a shimmering of glitter on a hand resting on the edge of Keira's small-framed hip. Although the image is bright enough to see the enormous diamond engagement ring nestled on a tiny finger, it does not indicate to whom the hand belongs as the owner has been cut from the photo.

"That's a one of a kind platinum ring encrusted with an Asscher-cut 18-carat diamond, specially designed by Lauren Schwartz," Cartier explains.

"How can you be so sure?" I drag my face to within an inch of the image to inspect it properly. "There is no doubt that's a spectacular rock, but how do you know it belongs to Lauren Schwartz?"

Cartier cranks her head to the side. Her glare is so roasting, even if we were in the Antarctic, a coat would not be necessary. "I know my jewelry, darling. I was only researching new names last week. Lauren has a nice ring to it—no pun intended."

I giggle before handing the photo to Brodie as per his silent request. "Okay, so we know someone schmoozing Keira is extremely wealthy, but that doesn't bring us any closer to discovering the link between Mr. Carson and Keira. Everyone at the charity campaign is wealthy."

"But you wouldn't cut just anyone out of a photo," Brodie mutters more to himself than Cartier and me. "This was done on purpose."

Brodie spins the photo around to face me before he glides his finger down a blurry section of the picture. "Someone used Photoshop to remove the person standing next to her. This photo would look more legitimate if they removed the hand curled around her waist."

"Exactly!" Cartier overemphasizes. "They assumed removing her face from the photo was stripping her of her identity, but they couldn't be any more wrong. That piece of jewelry is as identifying as a set of greasy fingerprints. We just need the right person to crack the code."

My pulse hastens when she secures her diamond-encrusted cell phone out of the pocket of her kimono and dials a number I know will haunt her for months to come.

"Phoebe," Henry Gottle answers not even two rings later. His deep, raspy voice bounces around the room on speakerphone. His voice is a flawless display of what you'd expect from a mob boss—sexy and dangerous. "It has been too long, my love. How are you?"

"Cut the crap, Henry. You know as well as anyone, Phoebe died a long time ago," Cartier snaps down the phone, her tone forthright but jam-packed with emotions.

"Is that why you won't sign the divorce papers, because you're dead?" Henry retorts, his tone so low it spurs a smattering of goosebumps to race to the surface of my skin.

"No." Cartier shakes her head, sending a rustle of blonde curls into her eyes. "It's to stop any other fool making the same mistake I did."

"Mistakes have consequences—"

"And consequences have actions. I've heard it all before, Henry. I don't need to hear it again," Cartier interrupts.

Henry sighs. If I hadn't read the many horrendous things he has done the past forty years of his life on the commute to Cartier's, I'd swear he was a man harboring a broken heart. "What do you want, Cartier?"

Cartier tries to snuff the flare of disappointment raring through her eyes from him addressing her by her infamous nickname, but she wasn't quick enough to entirely shut it down before I saw it. "I need the name, address, and contact details for a woman wearing a Lauren Schwartz ring."

"Seeking prospective gifts?" Although Henry only utters three words, the disdain in them made his sentence appear much longer.

"If I said yes, would you give me the information?"

Henry takes his time configuring a response before he replies, "Have I stopped you yet?"

This time, Cartier sighs. "Can you get me the information I need, Henry? Or shall I contact someone from the Pop—"

"I'll get you the information you need," Henry snarls down the line, cutting Cartier off midsentence. "Give me everything you have, and one of my guys will call you in five minutes."

Henry kept his word. Within five minutes of Cartier relaying the dimension, cut, and size of the stone in the Lauren Schwartz ring, one of Henry's crew, Cooper, emailed Cartier the name, age, and address of the vanishing lady. Marissa Schulte, a forty-five-year-old native from the Upper West Side.

"That's only half a block from here," Cartier explains when I pull out my iPhone to look up her address.

Remaining quiet, Cartier continues scrolling through the email as Brodie and I peer over her shoulder. Cooper's dossier is so detailed, page after page of text on Marissa's day-to-day life flies by in an instant. If any of it's relevant, I wouldn't know, as Cartier's eagerness to get to the numerous image attachments in the bottom of the cryptic email is stronger than my ability to speed read.

"Words are deciphered solely on how the reader chooses to translate them. Photos capture unsaid words. A look, a feeling, a moment in time no words could ever express. If you ever want to see someone's true feelings, don't ask them to articulate them, ask them to express them," Cartier responds to my private grumbling.

I stop trying to unjumble her statement when an image of Marissa pops up on the screen. The first few photos were from years ago when Marissa was married. They are seemingly uninteresting... until Cartier continues clicking. Not only does Marissa and Mr. Carson's relationship become exposed in the timeline of photos, so does my knowledge of why Marissa's face registered as familiar.

"I could be wrong, but I swear Marissa is the lady I met when Mr. Carson propositioned me to investigate the Chains story. She was the unnamed blonde who convinced them to have a set of eyes in the room." I lock my eyes with Cartier. "Did Cooper's dossier list an occupation?"

Brodie shakes his head, answering on behalf of Cartier. "From what I read while Cartier was scrolling, Marissa has been a stay-at-home mother since the birth of her daughter twenty-five years ago. She is on the board of numerous charities, but husband number three's significant earnings ensure she doesn't have to lift a finger if she doesn't want to."

"Have you met her, Cartier?" I ask, knowing she is a benefactor for hundreds of charities founded around the New York region.

"No. She must be new to the area. With her bank account that large, highfalutin' snobs around here would have paraded her around for society to see if she's been here longer than six months," Cartier answers, nudging her head to a printout exposing Marissa's net worth.

I choke on my spit, stunned by the number of zeros attached to the first three digits. "There is a decimal point there somewhere, right? My vision is just too poor to see it?"

Cartier remains quiet, but Brodie's response is less reserved. His chuckle rumbles out of his cracked lips before it bounces off the luxurious wallpapered walls to shrill into my ears.

My attempts at nipping his laughter in the bud with a quick kick are thwarted when my toe jabs into the thick wooden chair Cartier's silky derriere is sitting on.

"Ah… crapola," I scream, wishing I could articulate the string of curse words running through my mind without fear of prosecution. "That... *friggin* hurt."

"You really want to swear right now, don't you?"

Gritting my teeth, I nod.

"Then, why don't you?"

Because Marcus has rules in place to discourage my love of profanity. Rules I don't want to break since they all include some form of sexual deprivation.

Instead of expressing what I really want to say, I shrug my shoulders. Brodie peers at me as if I said my private thoughts out loud. Before a single accusation can be fired off his tongue, our attention reverts to Cartier when she says, "Here is the link you've been searching for, darling."

"No way. That can't be true," I murmur as I peer at a photo of Marissa, Mr. Carson and Keira taken at the end of last year. "Mr. Carson only turned thirty last year. This can't be right. There must be a mistake. There is no way Keira is Mr. Carson's niece."

I aim for my tone to come out firm and to the point, but the nerves jittering my stomach are uncontainable, coating every word I spoke with the quiver of panic. I'm fiercely protective of Lexi because she is my blood, so I have no doubt Mr. Carson's protectiveness of Keira is just as intense. Now his response last week makes sense. He saw the medical report on Keira's injuries. That's why he agreed to the Chains investigation. He's protecting his niece from what he assumes are monsters.

My eyes swing to Brodie when he says, "According to Cooper's report, Marissa and Jack Carson have the same mother but different fathers. Marissa's father passed away in a workplace incident when she was eight. Her mother remarried five years later. Two years after that, she gave birth to a baby boy. Jack Carson."

"So there is a fifteen-year gap between siblings?" I query, my brain too spent absorbing all the information I'm being handed to do simple math.

Brodie nods. "Marissa gave birth to Keira a few months shy of her twenty-first birthday. Jack was only five at the time. Keira is his niece."

"Then why is that not common knowledge? None of the articles we have read the past five years mention that Mr. Carson has a niece."

Cartier stands from her chair, her movements effortless and harmonious. After running her hand down my frazzled hair, she locks her glistening eyes with mine. "There is no rhyme or reason for the way people live their lives, which also means there is no motive for judgment either. They could have a very good reason why they kept their relationship out of the public eye."

When I attempt to interrupt, Cartier continues speaking, foiling my chance. "Look at you, darling, you're exhausted because you're working so hard to protect Marcus." She runs her index finger over the heavy bags under my eyes the best she can without gouging my eyes out with her chunky rings. "When you love someone, your sanity fluctuates between manic and frenzied, and sometimes the only way to calm the agitation is by concealing it. That logic doesn't just extend to partnerships, it's for everyone you love. Mothers, fathers, siblings..."

"Nieces," we say at the same time.

"Yes," Cartier agrees with a faint smile. "Now you just have to decide what you're going to do with the information you've unearthed."

I wait a beat, hoping a solution to my predicament will smack into me. It never comes.

"I don't know what to do, Cartier. What would you do?" I ask, loathing that I'm leaving an important decision to a woman who was a stranger mere days ago, but adoring that we've created such a strong bond in a short period, I feel comfortable asking her this.

"Only you can make that decision, darling." Cartier's eyes dance between mine. "But let me say one thing. Love is when another person's happiness is more important than your own. When you truly love somebody, sometimes it takes big mistakes to figure that out. Then it often takes an even bigger mistake to fix the first mistake."

My brow furrows as confusion stirs in my gut. "Why do I get the feeling our conversation just shifted away from Keira and Mr. Carson and reverted to Marcus and me?"

Cartier smiles sweetly, but it's the anxiety in her eyes causing my biggest worry. "Because no matter which path you choose to walk, controversy will follow you."

"Why?" I query, genuine confusion echoed in my tone.

Warmth blooms across my chest when Cartier skims the back of her nearly translucent fingers over my cheek in the exact area Marcus always does. If I didn't know any better, I'd swear she knew about my attack weeks ago.

"The most crucial mistake I made was when I was your age. I fell in love with a man whose heart belonged to another." She intertwines her fingers in front of her body before locking her glistening eyes with me. "My second was believing I could force him to love me even if his heart didn't belong to me. He married me to prove his devotion. He left me to verify mine."

"I'm so sorry, Cartier," I express, hating the absolute agony in her eyes. Although I don't know what I am sympathizing with, the pain radiating from her beautiful eyes warrants acknowledgment. "You're a beautiful person who deserves the world." I wave my hand around her opulent home. "You deserve even more than this."

"Thank you, darling." She accepts my praise in a manner I'd hoped.

I do not mean to suck up, I just hate that my visit has caused a ripple in her previously calm waters. She was airy and carefree in the minutes leading up to my disclosure of her true identity. Now her eyes are so dull, it feels like I've sucked the life straight out of them.

Reading the guilt in my eyes for what it is, Cartier says, "Don't feel bad, Cleo. My conversation with Henry was short but long overdue. Just knowing it helped Marcus immensely outweighs any negativity associated with it. It means more to me than any gift I've been given." She takes my hands in hers and squeezes them. "Now I'll award you with the same respect you bestowed upon me by trusting me to help you."

Horrid unease twists from my stomach to my throat when she says, "Tread carefully, darling. Your heart is in the right place wanting to protect your Master, but that also means you're placing it in the line of fire. Have you ever heard of the saying, 'To keep a secret is wisdom, but expecting others to keep it's madness?'"

I peer at her, blinking and confused when she hands me the printout of Keira's injuries from months ago. She stares at me, unmoving and unspeaking. Her eyes are soul-baring, but the worry in them doesn't weaken their usual forthrightness. It feels like her silent warning is more based on Marcus and me than my fight against a man equally as powerful as the one I'm striving to vindicate.

"Look closely, darling. All the evidence you need is in your hands."

After tapping the printout in my hand, she spins on her heels and exits the living room as quickly as she entered, leaving Brodie and me to devise our own way out.

11

"You alright, Cleo?"

After dragging my seatbelt over my erratically panting chest and clicking it in place, I raise my eyes to Brodie. He is watching me with the same set of worried eyes he's been directing at me the past hour. Although I could see a broad range of questions filtering through his eyes as we packed my belongings sprawled throughout Cartier's living room, these are the first words he has spoken to me since we unearthed the connection between Keira and Mr. Carson. He didn't even utter a syllable when our mad dash through a sprinkling of rain to his car drenched us head to toe. I expected a curse word—or the very least a grumble—he said nothing. His silence worries me more than the glint of anxiety in his eyes.

"Yeah, I was just thinking," I answer when the worry in Brodie's narrowed gaze grows from my delay in responding.

A gathering of wrinkles pleat the corners of his eyes when he screws up his nose. "That's your thinking face?"

His playfulness has the effect he was aiming for when I lean across the middle console to pop my fist into his thick bicep. I regret my decision when the thick ridges of his arm cause more damage to my hand than to him.

Grimacing, I cradle my injured hand with my uninjured one. "My god, did you pack rocks under your shirt this morning?" Unexpected laughter hinders my question.

Brodie's brow cocks high into his hairline as a ghost of a smile cracks onto his lips. "I aim to please."

I smile more broadly, equally loving and hating his cocky attitude.

I wait for him to finish latching his belt before mumbling, "Can I ask you something, Brodie?"

He runs his hand along the scruff on his chin, gathering the stubborn drops of rain still clinging to the bristles of his beard before replying, "As long as it's a question I can answer, sure, shoot." His tone is as hesitant as his facial expression.

Surprised by his anxious reply, the question sitting on the tip of my tongue rams into the back of my throat. Taking my silence as the end of my interrogation, Brodie shrugs, cranks the ignition on his car, then begins to back up. His foot glides from the gas pedal to the brake when the shrill of a cellphone rings through my ears. My heart beats triple time when I register the ringtone as familiar. A grin curls on my lips when Brodie's cell phone starts hollering not even two seconds later. My smile doesn't last long, only long enough for a terrifying notion to bombard me. Usually, bad news is delivered in quick succession.

My panic subsides when Brodie mumbles, "It's Lucy."

He nudges his head to the cell I'm clutching for dear life, enquiring my caller's identity, his eagerness unmissable. I lower my eyes, just as eager to discover who my caller is. My smile returns when I spot Lexi's scowling face stretched across the screen. She wasn't impressed when I snapped a sneaky picture of her last week.

My smile must answer Brodie's questions as he drifts his eyes back to the road before activating the bluetooth device in his ear. I follow his suit, minus the bluetooth part.

"Miss me?" I query into my cell, not bothering to issue a greeting.

Lexi gags. "Only a lunatic would miss your snoring ass."

"Whatever," I force out with a laugh. "I'm not the one who talks in her sleep. 'I swear, professor. I might think your breath smells like dog doo, but I'd never say that out loud.'"

I giggle even more loudly when my confession has Lexi stumped for a reply. My insides do a little jig, pleased as punch I've finally shocked her into silence. This is the first time I've succeeded what I previously thought was an unwinnable achievement.

When Lexi's silence lingers longer than anticipated, I ask, "Is everything okay, Lex?" I use Jackson's nickname for her, conscious it may catch her off guard enough to disclose whatever the problem is.

"Yeah... umm ... Never mind. I've just realized why the microwave isn't working. It wasn't switched on." She huffs loudly, feigning stupidity. Her tone is so convincing, if I didn't know her as well as I do, I might have believed her.

"What's going on, Lexi?" My worried pitch is strong enough to gain the attention of Brodie. He disconnects his call, houses his cell in his jacket pocket, then devotes his eyes to me. When I catch sight of the time on the dashboard of Brodie's car, my worry intensifies. "Why aren't you with Jackson? I thought you guys were going out tonight?"

"I'm fine." She's lying—don't ask me how I know, I just know she is.

"And I'm not with Jackson as he got called into work. His schedule is all over the place." Now she is telling the truth.

I stare at Brodie, speechless. I know Lexi is lying, but I can't just call her out, can I? Brodie must spot the apprehension in my eyes, as the instant he gets a clearing in traffic, he completes a U-turn, altering our course from Marcus's residence to Montclair.

"Brodie and I are coming, we're around forty minutes away."

Lexi breathes slowly down the line, attempting to drown out the expletive curse word that quickly follows it. "I'm not at home," she discloses after a stretch of uncomfortable silence. "I'm in New York."

I grit my teeth. I knew she was lying. If I had just called her out on it, we could have saved two minutes driving in the wrong direction. When I advise Brodie of her location, he dangerously veers into oncoming traffic. Thankfully, the motorists driving on the other side of the road are vigilant, meaning we avoid getting into a collision.

I brace my hand on the ceiling to lessen the crazy bounces hammering my body from Brodie's manic maneuvers. "Where *exactly* are you, Lexi?" My tone is unforgiving.

If she lies to me again, I'm not above disciplining her. I don't care that she is twenty-one, she is still my baby sister. My worry could be unwarranted, but being deceitful isn't Lexi's forte, so for her to lie to me, I know it's for something significant.

All noise ceases to exist when Lexi replies, "I'm at Toloache."

"Why are you at Toloache?" Panic roars through my body.

Hearing my question, Brodie increases the pressure on his gas pedal.

"This is where the note told me to come," Lexi answers, her tone relaying that she feels stupid.

I push aside my desire to agree with her assessment for a more appropriate time. "What note, Lexi?"

"A card. It was on my bed when I woke up from a nap this afternoon. I thought it was from Jackson, but he just messaged me. It wasn't from him. He's only just got out of surgery, he's been in their since midday. Cleo, something doesn't feel right. I've only just arrived, but my intuition is warning me something is off."

Jesus Christ. I lock my panicked eyes with Brodie as dread chills my spine. "Please, hurry."

Nodding, Brodie flattens his foot on the gas pedal. We weave in and out of traffic with more stealth than bees swarming a honeypot.

"Lexi, are you there?" I query, panicked by the eerie silence coming down the line.

"Yeah." My heart leaps in my chest from the sheer panic relayed in her tone.

"Can you leave?"

"Uh huh."

"Okay. Leave. Now. Please." Wheezy breaths separate my words.

I hear a chair scrape across the ground before a male voice filters down the phone. The panic curled around my throat lessens when I realize it's the waiter checking in on Lexi. After assuring the server she is okay, Lexi accepts her coat then leaves. I've never been more appreciative to hear the buzz of traffic as I am right now. Hearing noise tells me Lexi is okay. It's silence I don't want to hear.

"Take a right as you exit, Links is a few blocks over. I'll meet you there."

"Okay," Lexi croaks out, her voice shattered by anxiety. "Cleo?"

"Yeah," I reply.

"Will you stay on the phone with me as I walk?"

I brush away a tear rolling down my cheek from her panicked tone. "Yes, of course I will.

I do precisely that for the entire ten-minute journey that usually takes twenty-five. We don't speak, we just listen to each other breathe, both grateful for the lack of commotion.

Brodie has barely pulled to the curb at Links when I throw off my seatbelt and race into the foyer. Even with my top lip dotted with sweat, I keep my jacket on, too motivated to find Lexi amongst the hundreds of patrons who use Links every day. I close my eyes and sigh loudly when I spot her standing at the side of the rec room with a wide-eyed Serenity. Not even caring that I'm in public, I let my tears flow freely, beyond grateful she is uninjured.

"Do you recognize this man?" Shian slides a photo across the desk I've been sitting behind the past two hours.

Although Lexi was uninjured, Brodie suggested we report the incident to the authorities. The fact someone was in my house when Lexi was alone warranted my agreement, but instead of calling Montclair PD as I had expected, Brodie called Shian.

Not looking at the picture, I crank my neck to Lexi. She shakes her head, acknowledging she's unaware of the man's identity. "Shian showed me his picture earlier, I've never seen him before," Lexi discloses, her voice not as haunted as it was earlier. Lexi acts tough, but her insides are a little squishier than she'd care to admit.

After running my hand down her arm, soundlessly assuring her she is fine, I lower my eyes to the picture. The longer I glance at the mug shot, the closer my brows join.

"That's Andy. He was working behind the bar at the fundraiser I attended Saturday." My gaze dances between Shian's worried eyes. "Why do you have his photo? What does he have to do with this?"

Shian plucks the photo out of my hand. "We believe he is the man who left the note for Lexi."

"Why? Lexi said she's never seen him before, so why would he do that?" I cringe when my voice comes out snarky. I do not mean to be short with Shian, I'm just lost on what this all means.

Bile gurgles in my throat when Shian slides a second picture across the table. I curse the day I was born when I recognize the faces projecting back at me. It's Richard and Andy standing side by side. From the way they are clutching each other's shoulders and smiling broadly, it's as obvious as the sun hanging in the sky they know each other well.

"Andy thought Lexi was me," I murmur under my breath, answering my own question.

Shian nods, even though I didn't need her confirmation. "We couldn't comprehend why we were still intercepting messages in regards to your stalker case after Richard's death. Now we have a better understanding. These two are like brothers," she says, pointing her index finger between Andy and Richard. "They did everything together."

Clearly.

"Can you stop this from continuing? Will Andy be held accountable for this? He broke into our house. Into my sister's room..." My words stop as I fight to hold in my sob.

Shian licks her lips, her eyes hesitant. "The fact Andrew was detained sitting in the booth he reserved to meet with you aids in our case, but with how fickle the justice system is, I never make guarantees anymore. With no fingerprints at the scene or on the note, our evidence is minimal at best."

"He broke into our house!" I stand from my chair, my anger too great to inhibit. "You need to make him confess, Shian. He knows what he did wrong, force him to admit that."

"It isn't that easy, Cleo—"

"Bullshit!" I interrupt, shaking my head. "Look him in the eyes and force him to kneel. You're a Domme for crying out loud! How can you not make a pathetic man like him kneel?"

Ignoring Shian's flaming-with-anger face, I make a beeline for the door. Legally, Shian can't force a confession from someone, but I sure as hell can.

I'm shocked as hell when the first door I fling open in the long corridor is the one Andy is sitting in. *Andrew,* I correct myself. *He is not my friend.*

"Cleo," he says, shocked, adjusting his slumped position. "What are you doing here? Did you read my note?"

"It's a bit hard to read when you gave it to the wrong person," I reply, my words a vicious snarl.

Andrew's brows crimp as his lips purse. "What?" he asks, confused as ever.

"That was my sister's room. The note you left for me was placed on my baby sister's bed!" I roar, sending my loud voice bouncing off the stark white walls before booming back into my ears.

Andrew's eyes bounce between mine, his confusion unmissable. "Woah...hold on a minute. I didn't give your sister a note. I gave you a note. Remember?"

"You gave it to the wrong person, you dipshit!"

My brisk charge across the room is thwarted by the FBI agents sitting across from Andrew. They dive out of their seats, halting my endeavor to smack the confusion right off his face. I kick and wail against them, acting like a woman possessed. Going after me is one thing, but endangering the life of my sister intensifies my anger to a whole new level. Nothing gets in the way of me protecting my sister—not even two burly FBI agents.

Using their distraction of Shian's reprimand to put me down, I shrug out of their hold and charge for Andrew. Although the handsome blond agent curls his arm around my waist before I can reach Andrew, his firm hold leaves my arms unrestrained, meaning I can strike Andrew across the face. Since the agent yanks me back at the same time my hand sails wildly through the air, nothing but my sharp nails connect with Andrew's face.

Air hisses through his teeth when my nails drag across his face, leaving three significant scratches embedded in his nearly perfect skin. "What the fuck, Cleo? What the hell are you doing?"

He appears genuinely shocked, like he is appalled at the level I will stoop to protect my sister. He has no idea. If I weren't being subdued by a man the size of a bear, the scratches on his cheek would be the least of his worries.

"Tell them the truth," I implore as the FBI officer drags me out of the room.

"What the fuck do you think I'm trying to do?" Andrew yells through the rapidly closing interrogation room door.

"Read the note, Cleo!" I hear him scream as I'm hauled down the corridor, suddenly panicked I'm about to face my own prosecution. "It will explain everything. Just read the note!"

12

I carefully drape a cashmere blanket over Lexi's sleeping frame before tiptoeing out of the spare room of Marcus's residence. Warmth flourishes in my heart when my quiet exit from her room has me passing by a man I know she's been dying to see. *Jackson.*

"How is she?"

I crank my neck to peer back at Lexi sleeping before returning my drooping eyes to Jackson. "She is good. She wanted to wait for you to arrive, but Aubrey's hot chocolate is more lethal than she realized."

Some of the heaviness on my chest clears away when Jackson's bright white smile lights up the faintly lit room.

"Go on," I say when his eyes relay he is chomping at the bit to check on her himself.

My cheeks incline when he places a quick peck on the edge of my mouth before ambling to her bedside. Lexi stirs, her body recognizing Jackson's presence even in her sleep. Her groggily saying his name is the last thing I hear when I enter the hallway, closing their door behind me.

I jump, startled to within an inch of my life when I spot a shadowy figure propped up halfway down the hall. Although I'm grateful for the smiling assassin's eagle watch, he still isn't the person I was hoping to see.

The whole "Andy" incident happened over six hours ago, and I still haven't heard from Marcus—not even a text asking if I am okay. I'm not going to lie. Even with his house filled with people I care about, I'm devastated by his lack of contact.

"Did Andy confess?" I ask Brodie, hoping he will have an update from Shian.

My hopes are dashed when he shakes his head. "Not yet, but the DA is holding him on remand a few days, we'll see if a few nights in solitary can rattle a confession out of him."

"Hopefully that works. If not, I wouldn't mind another attempt."

Brodie smirks before shaking his head. "You're lucky Shian likes you, Cleo. If anyone else pulled that stunt, you would have been eating Christmas turkey behind bars."

A stretch of silence passes between us. It's plagued with awkwardness.

I'm the first to break the silence when I ask, "Have you heard from Marcus?" My words come out quietly.

Brodie scrubs his hand across his chin while muttering, "Yeah."

"Yeah?" I question, certain I heard him wrong. I didn't. The guilt in Brodie's eyes grows tenfold when hundreds of silent questions from mine bombard them.

"What did he say?" I eventually ask when Brodie doesn't crumble under the pressure of my eyes.

Brodie half shrugs. "Not much." He breathes heavily, exposing he hates being stuck in the middle of Marcus and me. "It was the same stuff he always says. Make sure you're eating, sleeping, etc." He lifts his eyes from the ground to me. "To make sure you're safe."

Even annoyed Marcus didn't call me himself, heat blooms across my chest from Brodie's admission. "Did he say when he was coming back?"

Brodie nervously shifts on his feet before shaking his head. "He didn't mention anything to me."

"Alright," I breathe out slowly, my disappointment revealed by my short response. "Well, I'm going to go to bed." I don't know why I felt the need to update Brodie on my happenings, it just occurred before I could shut it down.

Brodie nods. "Okay. I'll see you in the morning?"

Since his statement comes out sounding like a question, I nod.

Just before I enter the master suite, Brodie calls out of my name. "Marcus did say one thing that baffled me."

He waits a beat, unaware he is torturing me, before adding on, "'Tell Cleo if she is cold, she can borrow my jackets. Navy blue is my favorite color.'"

"What does that mean?" Shock is evident in my tone.

Brodie's shoulder touches his ear when he shrugs. "I don't know."

After a final shrug showing his confusion, Brodie gallops down the stairs, disappearing into the blackness of Marcus's residence in three heart-thrashing seconds.

While showering and preparing for bed, I contemplate what Marcus's riddled statement could mean. Minutes of deliberation award me even more confusion. Shrugging off my perplexity as the effects of an exhausting week, I crawl into bed, wanting to forget the world exists.

I don't know how much time passes before I'm startled by someone slipping in between my sheets. The panic surging through my veins simmers when the unique scent of Marcus lingers into my nostrils. He scoots across the mattress until the heat of his naked torso warms my cami-covered back. A grin tugs on my weary face when he curls his arms around my waist and draws me back until he is cocooning me. It's incredible how well he eases my agitation. Every worry I've had the past forty-eight hours disappeared the instant he wrapped me up with his warmth.

"Hey," I greet him, my words barely a whisper since I'm half asleep.

"Hi, baby." Marcus presses his lips to my temple. "Go to sleep. I just want to hold you for a minute."

Blood floods my heart. "You flew all the way here just to spoon me?" I try to conceal the sheer delight doubling my heart's size. I miserably fail. I'm as smitten as hell he is here.

"Yes," he replies, his tone shocked. "I'm sorry it took me so long to get here. I was tied up convincing a friend not to arrest my girlfriend for battery."

I bite on the inside of my cheek to ward off my smile. When I attempt to roll over to face Marcus, he holds on tightly, refusing my request. I pout, even though the room is so dark he can't see me.

"How did Cameron handle the news of you wanting to fly out again so soon?"

Marcus stiffens for the quickest second before he murmurs, "He is paid well enough he knows his opinion doesn't count." His reply is nearly drowned out by the sizeable yawn breaking free from my mouth.

"Go to sleep, Cleo," Marcus demands, his bossy tone sending the thump of my temples to my aching sex.

"I'm not tired," I lie. I'm so exhausted, I'm finding it hard to keep my eyelids open.

When I grind along Marcus's thickened rod, which is braced against my panty-covered backside, his deep growl rolls through my ears. I yelp when his teeth unexpectedly sink into my earlobe. His bite is soft enough for excitement to cluster in my core, but firm enough to divulge its execution was more for punishment than pleasure.

After lavishing the sting of his teeth with the lash of his tongue, Marcus repeats. "Go to sleep, Cleo, or your disobedience will require punishment. And it won't be in the way you're hoping."

Hearing the snip of danger in his warning, I stop grinding against him and nuzzle deeper into his embrace. With his closeness warming both my heart and my body, mere seconds pass before I fall blissfully asleep.

Several hours later, I wake up startled, disoriented, and confused. As one of my hands rubs the sleep from my eyes, my other creeps along the warm bedding in search of Marcus. I sigh when my exploration comes up empty. The bed is void of another soul. I scoot up the mattress to rest my back on the headboard, muted with confusion. Marcus was here last night, wasn't he?

Leaning over, I switch on the lamp on the bedside table. Once the room illuminates with unnatural lighting, I scan my eyes over the expansive space, ensuring I am alone. It's a replica of how it was left hours ago. The only difference is I'm tucked under the comforter instead of sleeping on top of it. That isn't unusual for me. As a child, I often fell asleep on the floor only to awake hours later in my bed. I assumed it was my dad moving me, but I guess now that isn't the case.

Baffled by the empty room, I snag the pillow next to me and lift it to my face. I inhale deeply, relishing the scent of Marcus's skin on the pillow. There is no doubt he was here. His scrumptious smell is too fresh and invigorating to have been left days ago.

Squealing with excitement, I fling off my comforter and race into the bathroom to get ready. I'm so eager to see Marcus again, I throw my hair into a messy bun on top of my head as I frantically scrub my teeth and gums with a toothbrush. Happy my breath is minty-fresh, I exit the bathroom. Although my pace is brisk, it isn't fast enough to miss a small card tucked into the edge of the last vanity mirror. As my brows stitch with suspicion, I pace toward the card and pluck it from its inconspicuous hiding place.

My eyes lift to scan the room, certain that card wasn't there when I showered last night. Everything in the bathroom is meticulously in place—as expected for any residence in Marcus's realm. Ignoring the rattle of my hands, I drop my eyes to the rectangular card. My breath snags halfway to my lungs when I read the handwritten note.

The most beautiful smiles hide the deepest secrets,
the most dazzling eyes hide the number of tears they have shed,
and the kindest heart is usually the most broken.
Actions always prove why words mean nothing.

I flip the card over, seeking any indication as to whom the message is from. Although my heart swears the note is from Marcus, receiving this card the morning following Lexi receiving one has my worry intensifying. There are no identifiable markings on the postcard. It seems as if it magically appeared, thwarting my panic at the same time it triggers it.

Seeking answers, I push off my feet and exit the bathroom. I gallop down the stairs two at a time, not stopping until I crash into a wall of hardness —literally.

"Whoa, Cleo, slow down. Did you take too many vitamins this morning?"

Lifting my eyes from the ground, I'm met with the twinkling gaze of Brodie. He has a mug of steamy hot coffee in his hands and is sporting a set of tired bags under his eyes, which is surprising since he went to bed hours before me. The suspicion tainting my blood grows when I notice how rumpled his clothing is. I swear that's the same outfit he was wearing last night. Has he not showered since yesterday?

I splay my hands across my cocked hip. "Why are you wearing the same clothes you had on last night?"

My rigid stance eases when Brodie replies, "Lucy had a fever last night. Although I couldn't be there in the physical sense, I could morally. I stayed up with her, retelling her favorite fairytales." His last handful of words are muffled by a massive yawn.

"Oh..." I'd like to say more, but guilt has stolen my words.

"Is she okay now?" I ask once I've regained the ability to talk.

Brodie's hand scrubs his tired eyes as he nods. "Yeah, probably just a virus of some sorts. Kids are full of germs."

Smiling at his screwed-up expression, I say, "I can only imagine."

My hand splayed on my hip slithers to my back when Brodie nudges his head to the card I'm clutching. "What's that?" he asks with interest.

"Umm ..." I graze my teeth over my bottom lip as I contemplate a reply. It's a very long minute.

Realizing Brodie could aid in un-riddling my confusion, I pull the card out from my back and hand it to him. I watch him in silence, categorizing every expression that crosses his face as he reads the small message scripted on the card. His eyes blaze with a similar range of emotions I felt while reading the card for the first time.

Brodie connects his eyes with mine. "Who gave you this?"

I answer his question with a shrug.

"Do you recognize the handwriting? Is it Marcus's?" he continues to interrogate, his words hurried.

Concerned by the worry in his tone, I once again shrug.

"You need to give me more than shrugs as answers, Cleo," Brodie chastises, his tone void of any amusement. "I'm not a fucking mind reader."

"I don't know who it's from. I woke up to it lodged in the bathroom mirror." Ignoring the apprehension in Brodie's eyes which has exploded to full-blown worry, I confess, "I believe it's from Marcus, though."

"Why?" Brodie snaps, shocking me with his curt tone.

"Who else would it be from?"

Brodie glares at me, his stare anything but pleasant.

"Marcus came home last night. He snuck into my bed around 2 AM. Putting two and two together, it's pretty obvious who the message is from. *Let alone your disheveled appearance.*" I mumble my last sentence under my breath, but the look crossing Brodie's face tells me he heard it.

Acknowledging I can't dig my hole any deeper than it is, I ask, "Was Lucy really sick last night? Or was a pedantic rock star the real cause of your tiredness?"

Not taking the time to absorb my snippy comment, Brodie says, "Meet me in the foyer in five minutes." His curt tone ensures I can't mistake his demand as a question.

"But I want to see Marcus."

"I just finished sweeping the house. Marcus isn't here. Five minutes, Cleo."

Snubbing my slack-jawed expression, he takes the stairs two at a time, disappearing before I have the chance to articulate one of the many gripes running through my brain.

Nearly two hours later, Brodie pulls into a cute little double story house in a community east of New York. He hasn't even clambered halfway out of his car when the cutest little squeak of, "Daddy!" roars through my ears. I recognize the flurry of blonde galloping down the stairs from the photos Brodie showed me Saturday night. It's his daughter, Lucy.

Excited squeals bellow out of Lucy's mouth when their meeting halfway down the painted sidewalk results in her being twirled into the air. Her gleeful giggles make fond memories of my dad greeting Lexi and me the same way rush to the forefront of my mind. *God, I miss my family.*

Lexi must be feeling the same sentiment, as the angry mask she's been wearing since I begrudgingly dragged her out of bed clears away the longer she watches Brodie and Lucy interact. Nothing can compare to the love a parent has for their child. You can love someone with every ounce of yourself, and it still wouldn't represent the love parents have for their children. The love from a parent isn't the same as the love you crave from a spouse. They are unique and special in their own right.

At Brodie's request, Lexi and I unlatch our seatbelts and climb out of his car. The frigid breeze rattling my bones does nothing to lessen my excitement when Lucy greets me by wrapping her tiny arms around my thighs and squeezing me tightly. When she releases her death-like grip, I bob down to face her eye to eye.

"Hi, Lucy," I greet while running my hand down her hair to smooth the pieces floating in the wind from Brodie's robust twirls. "It's a pleasure to meet you. Are you feeling better?"

Lucy nods her adorable head. "Yes, thank you." Her words are so undeveloped, I swear she said, "Spank you" not thank you.

Shocked by my disturbing thoughts, I stand from my crouched position so I can watch Lucy greet Lexi in the same manner. Smiling, I accept the hand Lucy is holding out, then follow her into the quaint home where I stay for the next three hours, learning all aspects of Brodie's life.

I'd like to say the stories shared were full of rainbows and lollipops, but unfortunately, that isn't the case. Brodie's wife, Caroline, passed away when Lucy was six months old. Although Caroline has a large family, as far as Brodie is concerned, Lucy is the only family he has. With Brodie's hours being sporadic, he has a live-in nanny who aids in raising Lucy. Ms. Mitchell has a heart of gold, and her fondness for Lucy is unmissable. Her children are grown, but she is not yet a grandmother, so she has plenty of time to devote her motherly attentiveness to Lucy. It's the perfect predicament. One I hope will last for many years to come.

After bidding farewell to Ms. Mitchell with a kiss on the cheek and promising Lucy we'll come back to visit soon, Lexi and I shadow Brodie to his car. Heat blooms across my chest when I see the indecisiveness in Brodie's eyes. I can see how much he hates leaving Lucy without a word needing to spill from his hard-lined lips.

"Why do you do it?" I latch my belt.

Brodie starts his ignition and reverses from the driveway of his family home before locking his eyes with mine. "Do what?"

"This." I gesture my hand around his car, hovering more on Lexi and me. "There are plenty of positions that wouldn't require overnight stays, so why do it?"

Brodie takes his time configuring a response. I don't know whether he is stumped or doesn't appreciate me analyzing his choices. I'm not at all judging his parenting. I saw him interact with Lucy, she is a well-adapted four-year-old who is well-taken care of and loved. I'm just trying to understand why he'd work in a field where they are forced to be apart.

My eyes lift from my intertwined hands when Brodie says, "I did consider a change in career when Caroline passed away. I even took an extended leave of absence from my position, but this type of industry is hard to give up. Once it's in your veins, you can never fully remove it."

His response seems more heartfelt than one you'd expect from a bodyguard. Don't get me wrong, I've always believed in having pride in your position, but his response seems more than just pride. His job is important to him.

Before any more interrogating questions can filter from my mouth, the shrill of a cellphone rings through my ears. Brodie taps on the device in his ear before saying, "Shian, did you find anything?"

My suspicion piques when Brodie continues with his conversation. If I'm not mistaken by the snippets of his reply, he didn't introduce Lexi and me to Lucy to prove she was unwell, he needed us out of Marcus's residence. The only thing I can't fathom is why.

My silent questions are answered when Brodie disconnects his call and locks his eyes with mine. "The card you found in the bathroom wasn't from Marcus." The swirling of my stomach doubles when he says, "The handwriting matches the card Lexi received yesterday. Whoever broke into your house yesterday was in Marcus's house last night."

"But you said Andy is in custody," Lexi interjects, leaning forward to join our conversation.

"He is." Brodie nods.

"Then who sent the card?" Shock is in my tone.

Brodie shrugs. "I don't know, but until we find out, you're going to become well accustomed to this space." He gestures his hand between the small portion of air sitting between us. "I've just become your new best friend, Cleo."

He wasn't joking. He did precisely that for the next four days.

13

My eyes lift from an article on the rapid advancement of technology's effects on diversity when a commotion at the door gains my attention. Lexi has her shoulder propped up on the entrance of Marcus's office. Her lips are facing down, and her eyes are dull.

"If I spend another moment cooped up inside, I'll go bonkers," she mutters, her words enunciated with an exaggerated huff.

I peer at her over the screen of Marcus's laptop when she moseys into the room, her steps sloth-like. "I thought you were studying?"

"I am, I did, I conquered. Can we please do something more invigorating today? I'm bored out of my fucking mind."

Lexi and my eyes missile to the door in sync when the distinct rumble of Aubrey sounds over the quiet. Although there are a good dozen or so feet between us and the cookie-smelling room Aubrey is baking in, I'm confident she heard Lexi's curse word. Just like Marcus, Aubrey is not a fan of derogatory comments, sneered words, or any mention of God's name attached that isn't a prayer.

Over the past four days, Lexi has been learning the hard way that swearing isn't acceptable in this residence. Although her punishment hasn't been as spine-tinglingly delicious as the course I endured last week, she is quickly learning disobedience limits rewards, whereas obedience doubles them.

"Great, there goes my afternoon snack," Lexi grumbles under her breath.

She props her backside onto Marcus's flimsy desk before dropping her eyes to the document on my screen. "What are you working on?" Although she is asking a question, she keeps talking, foiling my reply. "Snoozefest. Why are you writing about that? Magazine articles are no different than novels. If you want to sell stories, write what you read."

"I like reading about this stuff, it's interesting," I argue with an immature roll of my eyes.

Lexi makes snoring noises, cutting off any further replies I was planning to give.

"Oh, is that Chains?" she asks when an email notification pops up on the screen.

My pulse quickens as I drop my eyes to the monitor. Although Marcus's messages have been more sporadic than usual the past three days, I still cherish every one I get. His messages and phone calls are brief but sweet enough to cause a toothache.

Not wanting Lexi to snoop on my private conversation, I minimize the screen on my laptop and click on the email. Realizing it's a message from the security company Marcus hired to install a state-of-the-art security system in my home in Montclair, I return the screen to its original position.

Lexi tries to hide it, but I see the quickest flare of excitement blaze in her eyes when it dawns on her she is mere hours away from returning home. Although I've pleaded and begged for her to stay with me at Marcus's house until the culprit of the notes is apprehended, she is refusing my requests. She is siding with Jackson, believing both notes were delivered before Andy was arrested, and my poor eyesight is the cause for me not noticing it earlier. Considering we haven't had any dilemmas the past four days, my apprehensions are beginning to swing in the opposite direction as they did days ago.

"So can we go out?" Lexi drags my focus back to the present.

Confused by her question, my brows furrow. "Go where, exactly?"

"To lunch," Lexi questions as her legs swing wildly in the air.

I eye her suspiciously, shocked by her blasé response. She usually only acts skittish when she is hiding something.

"I don't think it's a good idea, Lexi," I say, unable to read the prompts her eyes are relaying.

Lexi drops her bottom lip and gives me the biggest puppy dog eyes she's ever issued. "Please, Cleo. Why can't we go out?" Her whiny voice makes her sound more like a teenager than a twenty-one-year-old woman. "Shian said Andy's bail hearing isn't until Monday, so there is no reason for us to hide out. *Please*.... I really really *really* want to get out of this house."

Her whining stops when my cell phone buzzes and vibrates on Marcus's desk. Like every time it dings announcing a message, my hopes kick into overdrive that it's from Marcus. Unfortunately, my dreams are left for dust when the screen displays the message.

Unknown number: *What's a girl got to do to get a lunch date around here?*

If I hadn't recognized the tone of the message, the shit-eating grin on Lexi's face would have disclosed my caller's identity either way.

"Are you and Serenity conspiring against me?" I ask Lexi, swiveling the screen of my phone to face her.

"No," Lexi lies, nodding.

I try to hide my smile from her double-meaning reply. It's a hard-fought battle. "Yes or no, Lexi, which one is it?"

"We aren't conspiring against you. We're just colluding so you'll join us for lunch," she states matter-of-factly.

"Conspiring and colluding are the same thing," I mumble, laughter in my tone.

Lexi crosses her arms in front of her chest as she shakes her head. "No, it isn't. Conspiring is when you're doing something evil. Colluding is when you work together for the greater good."

My eyes roll skywards. Her excuse is as weak as the one Marcus used when arguing that negotiating and comprising are separate entities. They are the same damn thing.

"Come on, Cleo. Serenity is hungry, I suggested lunch as a solution for her hunger. She thought it was a great idea," Lexi continues to plead.

I glare into her eyes, knowing there is more to the story than she is sharing. Her eyes frolic between mine, the plea in them growing in intensity for every second that ticks by. "If you're worried about Marcus being angry, don't be. I'll talk to him. We'll even take Brodie with us. *If we must.*" She mumbles her last sentence.

She continues pleading until she breaks through the protective wall I built around us the past four days. Then she proceeds chipping away at the panic curled around my neck until its tight grip is loosened enough I can reluctantly nod. I never could deny her, so I don't know why I bothered resisting her request.

My nod was brief, but not curt enough for Lexi to miss it. "Yes!" she screams, throwing her arms into the air. Anyone would swear she just won the lotto.

Her eyes track mine when I push the office chair away from Marcus's desk and stand. "Let's do this."

Not giving me the chance to change my mind, Lexi wraps her arm around the nook of my elbow and drags me out of Marcus's office. Her pace is so unchecked, she barrels into Aubrey, sending cookies and milk flying into the air.

"Sorry," she apologizes with a grimace before continuing our trek, her excitement too high to stop her.

Fifty minutes later, our coats are hung by the beautiful hostess at an elegant restaurant where I've only dreamed of dining. Not wanting to be the odd man out, Brodie is holed up in his car with a bag of greasy takeout and a few sports magazines. I finalize my risqué text to Marcus, ensuring his understanding of our desire to eat out will be rewarded upon his return tonight, before storing my cell into my clutch.

My leisured steps into the elegant-smelling space quicken when my sweep of the room has me stumbling upon a familiar face sitting across from Serenity. *Cartier.*

"Hello, darling," she greets, rising from her seat to place air kisses on each of my cheeks. After greeting Lexi in the same manner, she says, "I don't need to ask whom you belong to."

I smile. "Lexi, this is a friend of mine, Cartier. Cartier, this is my baby sister, Lexi." I try to keep the muckiness out of my voice during my introduction, my attempts are borderline. I can't rein in my pride when it comes to Lexi.

Lexi cordially greets Cartier with a smile. Her embrace of Serenity is a little friendlier. They act like lifelong friends as they wrap their arms around each other and bounce on the spot, giggling like teen girls on the way to prom.

"Thank you," I gesture to the waiter when he fans a white napkin over my lap after I take a seat across from Cartier. "I wasn't aware you knew each other," I say to Cartier as my eyes drift between her and Serenity.

The twinkle of fondness in Cartier's eyes grows when she locks them with Serenity. "It's a recently formed relationship. We have one man we both care very much about." I assume she is talking about Marcus until her hand caresses the thin necklace hidden behind her bulky ones. "Speaking of men I care about, how are things with you and Marcus? Everything okay?"

Cartier's hand drops from her neck when I gush, "Umm... Great. Actually, it's wonderful."

Cartier smiles, but it's more reserved than her usual smile. It was more like she had to force it onto her face than it being there of its own will. "Stop acting so damn happy or people will get the wrong impression," she snickers under her breath.

"Are you sure it's the wrong impression they'd be getting?" I ask with a waggle of my brows. I indeed need to limit my time with Lexi, her maturity is starting to rub off on me—and not in a good way.

Wrinkles crease my nose when Cartier rolls her eyes. "Gosh, if I didn't know any better, I'd swear you're acting like a love crazy imbecile."

I graze my teeth over my bottom lip, incapable of denying her snickered claim.

The happiness making my head a giddy mess drifts into abyss when Cartier requests, "Please tell me you haven't expressed..." Her words trail off as she assesses my face. "Whatever this is..." she swirls her hand around my loved-up expression, "...to Master Chains."

If it weren't for the dire expression on her face, I might have laughed at her statement. But since her gaunt appearance is relaying nothing but panic, I leash my childish response and briskly shake my head.

Cartier sighs deeply. "Thank god," she murmurs frailly.

"Would it really be that bad if I did?" I ask before I can stop my words.

Cartier's tongue delves out to replenish her lips before she swivels in her seat to face me. She waits, soundlessly building the suspense until it's nearly murderous. Just when I think she isn't going to speak, she says, "I like to believe I know the true Marcus, the one beneath the Master Chains mask he regularly wears, but even I can't guarantee what his reaction would be if you declare your *love* for him." She whispers the word "love" as if it's a curse word. "I thought I knew Henry, and look how that turned out."

Ignoring the swirling in my stomach induced by her peculiar reply, I accept the wine list from the waiter, happy to use it as a distraction while unravelling Cartier's puzzling statement. I've barely scanned the first page of cocktails when the menu is plucked from my grasp.

Keeping her eyes locked on the waiter, Cartier says, "We will have sparkling water, thank you."

My bottom lip drops into a pout. With nearly every drop of alcohol in Marcus's house potent enough to knock me on my ass with one sip, I was very much looking forward to a fruity cocktail. And, if I'm being honest, I was hoping to lace Cartier's veins with alcohol to loosen her lips.

"Alcohol ages you," Cartier snickers, her voice as mortified as my facial expression.

"Says the lady downing margaritas last week like they were apple juice," I scold, my playful tone dulling down my snappy reply.

Cartier's chance to reply is lost when Serenity and Lexi's prolonged greeting comes to an end. My eyes roam Lexi's face when she plops into the chair next to me. Her face is red with exertion, but no signs of air struggle are notable. It's indeed amazing how much the Kalydeco program has been a godsend for Lexi. If I didn't already love Marcus with every morsel of my soul, Lexi's new lease on life would have soon taken care of that.

Don't get me wrong, I'm not saying I love Marcus because of what he can give me. I love him for how generous and kind he is. His kindness extends way beyond monetary value. I believe even if he weren't a wealthy rock star and BDSM club owner, his charity efforts would still be as strong as they are today. His grandmother left him a lasting legacy, one that will live on for years after he is gone.

Feeling giddy, I snap open my clutch to check for a return message from Marcus. Regretfully, my screen is void of any messages or missed calls. After accepting the menu from the grinning waiter, Lexi swaps seats with Cartier as per Cartier's request.

I raise my eyes from the menu to Cartier, taking in her flawless designer-clothed body on the way. When our eyes meet, she asks, "Have you talked to Marcus about what you unearthed Monday?" Her tone is more friendly than the one she used earlier, but it still has a hint of antagonism associated with it.

I shake my head. "No. I want to do it in person."

Cartier stills from my confession but remains quiet. I can understand her reservation. I've had plenty of opportunities to discuss my findings with Marcus the past four days, but every time I prepare to expose the connection between Keira and Mr. Carson, my words clog in my throat. I don't know why. I think part of my worry stems from the protectiveness Marcus displayed to Keira Saturday night, and the other half is concerned about what his reaction will be when he discovers I've been investigating him.

I'd like to say my investigation into Chains ended the instant Cartier unearthed the link between Keira's assault and Mr. Carson's agreement to investigate Chains, but that would be a lie. Although it isn't as rampant as it was days ago, I've still spent a minimum three hours a day seeking further information on their connection. Mr. Carson and Keira's family association is buried by so much legal propaganda, that one photo Lexi discovered Sunday morning is the only photo I've found of them together. It's as if they are total strangers.

I stop twisting my napkin around my fingers so tightly they are void of natural color when Cartier places her hand over mine. She peers at me like she wants to say something, but not a syllable escapes her lips.

Dying for her to articulate the secrets her eyes are struggling to conceal, I ask, "Have you talked to Marcus about what I discovered? About *Keira*?" I whisper her name since my hackles are still bristled from last weekend.

I feel sorry for what happened to Keira months ago, but I'm still angry at her wearing Marcus's trademark. There is only one reason she did that—she wanted Marcus's attention. And, unfortunately, that's precisely what she got. Marcus is a smart man, but he fell straight into Keira's trap last weekend. The fact she unarmed a man as guarded as Marcus has me truly worried about the influence she has on him. I have no doubt Marcus feels guilty for Keira's injuries if they were sustained against her wishes while she was a patron at his club, but unless her injuries were placed there by him, it's unnecessary guilt. If Keira genuinely cares for Marcus, as her eyes relayed last weekend, she should relinquish him from his guilt, not encourage it.

A wisp of blonde hair falls into Cartier's face when she shakes her head. "No, darling. It's not my place to tell him. It's yours. Relationships are enough work without third-party influences butting in."

"Ain't that the truth," I mutter to myself.

I realize my quiet summarizing wasn't as discreet as I was aiming for when Lexi and Serenity's heads lift from their menu to peer at me. Although their gazes drop back to the menu seconds later, I can feel the heat of their eyes on me. It isn't the warmth of friendliness, it the heat of worry.

"When you get the chance, you really need to talk to him, darling," Cartier requests, tapping my hand with hers. "I know he is swamped, when I saw him yesterday, he was run off his feet, but the information you found could be critical for many people very dear to him. You must tell him what you discovered, Cleo. It's the right thing to do."

I swallow the bitter taste in the back of my throat before murmuring, "You saw Marcus yesterday?" Although I wholeheartedly agree that I need to inform Marcus of my findings, my primary focus is on Cartier's admission she saw Marcus yesterday.

A twinkle of fondness flares in Cartier's eyes as she nods.

"You went to Florida?" Shock smears my high tone.

The glimmer in Cartier's eyes dulls before she timidly shakes her head. "No, darling. Why would I go to Florida?" she asks, sounding disgusted at the idea.

"Because Marcus is in Florida," I object, my words laced with unwarranted bitchiness. When Cartier balks from my admission, I ask, "He is in Florida, isn't he?"

For the first time, Cartier looks genuinely fearful. She forcefully swallows before her eyes drift to Serenity and Lexi, who are once again eyeballing our exchange in silence.

"You must have gotten your dates mixed up, Cartier. You saw Marcus last week, remember?" Serenity's attempt at lying is as woeful as mine usually are. I hardly know her, and I still know she is lying, that's how bad her effort was.

"Oh, yes, that's right. It was last week," Cartier agrees with her squinted gaze locked on Serenity.

Because I can't see her eyes, I can't 100% proclaim she is lying. Her vocals were higher than usual, indicating deceit, but since we met mere days ago, it doesn't feel right to call her out as a liar.

Cartier sighs loudly when our waiter magically appears at her side, demonstrating that she too felt the uncomfortable awkwardness plaguing our small gathering.

By the time everyone's orders have been jotted down, any opportunity to grill Cartier and Serenity further are lost. They are buried in discussion with Lexi about a man named Ricci.

Over the next hour, I try to participate in the conversation being held around the table, but with my mind elsewhere, my responses are lackluster, missing the Garcia spark. Lucky Lexi's personality makes up for my deficiency in schmoozing. I know the cause of my absentmindedness. While unjumbling the complexity of my conversation with Cartier, many theories ran wild in my mind—*none of them were pleasant.*

Accumulating my knowledge of Marcus and Keira's connection, the link between Mr. Carson and Keira, Marcus's sudden decision to return to Ravenshoe alone, and Cartier's admission she saw Marcus as recently as yesterday has bombarded me with a severe case of nausea. I feel sick—*incredibly unwell.*

Excusing myself, I snag my clutch off the table and make a beeline for the washroom. Although my first thought was to splash some water on my face, when I'm in the safety of the stall area, I yank my cell phone out of my purse. After kicking down the toilet seat in the vacant stall in the far back corner, I dial Marcus's number. His cellphone rings on repeat—over and over again.

All six of my calls sent to voicemail amplifies the sick gloom creating havoc with my chest. I sit in silence, assuring myself repeatedly that Cartier was mistaken, that she didn't see Marcus yesterday, and that Marcus isn't accepting my calls as he is in the process of flying home.

Several minutes of reassurance awards me with nothing but additional butterflies in my churning stomach. Why would a woman as intelligent as Cartier get something so simple wrong? She wouldn't have, would she? And although Marcus is flying, wouldn't advances in technology mean he could still answer my call if he wanted to?

I run my hand across my cheek, gathering a stupid tear descending down my face when Lexi calls out, "Cleo? Everything okay?" From the way her voice is projecting, it sounds like she is standing right outside of the stall.

"Uh, yeah, just an aversion to the clams." I cringe, loathing my inability to think on the spot.

"Eww. Alright. Buzz me if you need assistance."

She waits for me to respond before she leaves me in peace. I take a few more minutes to settle the restlessness on my face before dumping my tear-gathering napkin into the bowl and flushing the cistern. My brisk pace to the vanity to wash my hands slows to a snail's pace when my eyes lock in on a shimmering of blonde standing next to the only sink in the room. I calm the unnatural beat of my heart, confident the world wouldn't be so cruel to throw me another curveball right now. I've been dodging so many balls this week, one will eventually hit me square in the guts.

A timely reminder of how cruel life can be hits fruition when the blonde pivots on her heels to snag a paper towel from the muted washroom attendant dressed entirely in black on her right. Seemingly unaware of my gawking glance, Keira thoroughly dries her hands before placing a selection of bills onto a gold tray in the corner of the room. I suck in a grateful breath when she heads for the door without so much as a sideways glance in my direction.

The air I've just drawn in is brutally evicted when her swayed steps stop. She turns her head to face me, her movements stiff and robotic. "Cleo?" she greets, her tone apprehensive, like I'm a mirage standing before her.

Realizing I'm not an illusion, she paces two steps toward me. "What a pleasure to see you again." Her tone is so convincing of her gratuity, I may have believed her if the quickest flash of annoyance didn't blaze through her eyes.

"Hello." I'd like to express more, but vehement jealousy has stolen my words.

Even though her exchange with Marcus last week could be construed as innocent, I hate that she interfered in our relationship at all. What she did last week was wrong. If I weren't fearful of airing my dirty laundry in public, I'd tell Keira precisely how disgusted I am about her ruse. But since I was raised better than that, I dip my chin, finalizing my greeting, then hightail it to the sink.

Keira doesn't utter a syllable as I wash my hands at a record-setting pace before heading for the washroom door.

"Cleo, wait," she calls out as I glide into the corridor.

I hear her apologize to the washroom attendant in Spanish before she shadows me down the corridor separating the restrooms from the main seating area of the restaurant. "I really didn't want everything to come to this. What I said to you in the elevator months ago was true. I do genuinely like you. It's just... just..."

"Just what, Keira?" I spin on my heels to face her. "I'm nice, but not nice enough for you to respect me? Or am I only convenient to associate with when I'm not occupying the time of the Master you want?"

She tucks her fancy clutch under her arm as her eyes fleetingly float around the room. "You need to keep your voice down." Her tone is more mature than her twenty-five years.

"Why? Are you afraid people will discover you aren't as innocent as you portray?"

Keira's eyelashes flutter as she struggles to blink back her tears. My throat tightens, hating that I'm allowing my jealousy to turn me into a vindictive, malicious person.

Lessening the severity of my wrath, I take a step closer to her. "If you were honest with your uncle, all of this could have been avoided."

"*All* of this?" She retaliates, her voice quickening with anger. "What's happening is not my fault. I've done everything in my power to stop Global Tens' investigation into Chains."

"Have you tried being honest?" I fire back, my tone just as stern as hers.

"Yes!" she answers, her word hissing out of her mouth like venom.

"So you told your uncle everything? You explained that the bruises and whip marks you sought medical assistance for were put there by your own choice?"

She balks as her pupils turn massive. Clearly, she is unaware how deep my investigation into Chains has gone. As quickly as her tears appeared, they vanish. She realigns her slouched pose before the glint in her eyes turns evil. She glares at me, issuing a stare so chilling, it reminds me of my many run-ins with the devil herself.

Not willing to back down without a fight, I take a step toward Keira. We are standing so close, the gold trim of her clutch digs into my chest. "I saw the devastation on your uncle's face firsthand when he disclosed the reason he agreed to the investigation into Chains. He thinks they are monsters, Keira."

She stares at me, blinking and mute. Her silence confirms my suspicions. She is a part of the BDSM lifestyle but unwilling to admit it. I don't know if her hesitation stems from shame or because her views on the lifestyle are as negative as Delilah's.

"Weeks ago you implored me to look at the BDSM lifestyle from the angle of a person intrigued by it but not guided by society's opinion of it, yet you're doing the exact opposite. You're letting a community you love take the fall for your cowardice. I know it's hard to express yourself, Keira. I fully understand what it's like to crave things society doesn't deem acceptable, but I'd never let those I care about be caught in the crossfire. Be honest with your uncle. Tell him those bruises and marks on your back were put there by your own free will. If you care about Marcus at all, save him from being unjustly vilified."

"Why? So he can ride off into the sunset on a white horse with you?" Keira's hackling tone shocks me. "I'm sorry things didn't work out for you and Marcus, Cleo, but that doesn't mean I'll disgrace my family name just so you can claw your way back into his good graces."

"What?" I ask as my eyes dance between her. If she failed to hear the confusion in my tone, the expression on my face is unmissable. I am more confused than ever.

"We all make mistakes. Mine is keeping my inclusion in the BDSM lifestyle from my family. Yours is believing you can make a man like Master Chains kneel. Dominance is who Marcus is, he doesn't know any different, so the instant you forced vanilla on him, you lost him. Be angry, Cleo. Lash out. But remember the blame for the demise of your relationship lies solely on your shoulders—not mine."

My lips twitch, dying to rebut her false statement, but not a word spills from my mouth. I don't know why, I just can't get a syllable out no matter how hard I fight. It probably has something to do with the fact Keira knows Marcus and I made love. How could she know that...unless.

My eyes missile to Keira. "When did you last see Marcus?"

The egotistical gleam in her eyes doubles, enhancing my hesitation as she replies, "We had brunch yesterday." She scans her eyes over our location before she advises, "In this very restaurant."

She locks her eyes with mine, ensuring I can't miss the honesty in her reply. "As I said, Cleo, I like you. You're kind-hearted, eager to please, and you'd make a wonderful submissive, you're just not the right sub for Master Chains."

"And let me guess, you are?" I snarl, my words vicious.

She remains quiet, but the smirk on her face answers all my questions. Her confidence is at an all-time high, and way too smug for my liking.

Her abhorrent smile is wiped straight off her face when I sneer, "You have until Monday to tell Mr. Carson the truth about your injuries, or I'll expose your secret."

"You wouldn't dare," She mutters under her breath as she clutches the vein throbbing furiously in her delicate neck. "That would not only jeopardize your freedom, it will also undermine any chance you have of winning back Marcus. I know Marcus's worth, so I know there is no way you'd risk it. I know from experience one taste of him is never enough."

I take a step closer to her. The veins in her neck thrum even more violently when I snarl, "I've never been one to back away from a dare, Keira, so please feel free to test me. I dare you."

14

With it being early on a Friday afternoon, the city is thrumming with activity. Taxis clog the streets in a stream of yellow as people cram onto the sidewalk. With winter arriving a week earlier than usual, my love of people watching has been downgraded to designer coat admiring. It's probably for the best. With my mood still edgy from my exchange with Keira, I'm not in the best frame of mind to absorb my sister city in the true glory she deserves.

I trust Marcus, but Keira's remark—"one taste of him is never enough"—is an accurate description I'd expect from any woman who has been bedded by him. He is like a drug—so potent one taste makes you an addict.

My eyes drift from the hotdog vendor serving a lady wearing a five-hundred dollar pair of couture shoes when Lexi asks, "Are we still going?"

The stitch of her brows deepens when I reply, "Hmm?"

Lexi swivels her phone around to face me, allowing the email she just received to speak on her behalf. It's an email from my ex-boyfriend Luke, advising that the location of his birthday party tonight has changed to his parents' sprawling mansion. From the photos attached to his email, it appears as if the party is already in full swing. This is not surprising for Luke.

"It seems Mr. Popular is still as popular out of high school as he was in," Lexi murmurs as she returns her phone to face her.

I nod. Luke was the equivalent of the popular jock. He had the looks, the brains, and was the beloved captain of the basketball team. He was the very epitome of every teen girl's high school crush. He was a great boyfriend. He was just too... *sweet* for me.

If I hadn't met Marcus, I would have never understood why my relationship with Luke didn't work. I needed *more* than he could give me. Don't construe my confession the wrong way, I'm not saying I broke up with Luke because he was too perfect. It was because I would have never felt comfortable expressing my true desires to him. And, in all honesty, even if I did suddenly grow a backbone, I don't think Luke would have fulfilled my wishes the way Marcus can. He wouldn't hurt a fly, much less spank my backside until it's red raw.

Ignoring the chill of duplicity running down my spine, I return my focus to Lexi. "What did you reply?"

Her eyes dance between mine. "I didn't reply. It's not a replying type of email."

I glare at her. "You have to reply. It's the polite thing to do."

"Then you do it. You're CC'd in the email."

Fighting hard not to roll my eyes at her snappy mood, I snag my cell phone out of my purse and log in to my email. Although I pretend I didn't notice the absence of any message or missed calls from Marcus, the stabbing pain maiming my heart foils my endeavors.

It takes a few moments for my emails to download, but when they do, I freeze, paralyzed by a horrendous attack of jealousy sluicing my veins. It isn't Luke's mass email to the hundred plus recipients that has me sweating like I've run a marathon, it's an email from a private company, informing me of the location of the latest Chains' party being held tonight.

I didn't realize when I logged in to the server months ago I'd be added to their mailing list for future parties. This is a significant gaffe by Marcus's company. If members aren't paying the extreme annual dues to be a member of Chains, shouldn't emails like this be revoked to ensure privacy is maintained for paying guests?

I startle, scared out of my mind when my cell phone suddenly buzzes in my hand. I level my breathing before dropping my eyes to my phone. The endeavor of my heaving lungs doubles when I realize who is calling me... Marcus.

After reminding myself that I trust him—*over and over again*—I connect his call and push my cell close to my ear.

"Hello," I greet, my tone apprehensive.

"Hey," Marcus greets, his tone more pleasant than mine. "Sorry I missed your call. My phone was on silent."

My heart reprimands my brain for being too quick to judge when he asks, "Are you ready for me to come home tonight? It's been a long week."

"Yes," I reply, smiling. Because my reply is honest, it's echoed in my tone. "What time are you arriving?" Although I'm asking a question, I continue talking, thwarting his chance to reply. "Because I completely forgot I accepted an invitation to attend a friend's birthday party months ago. I was hoping we could attend together? *As a couple.*"

"Who's this friend?" Marcus queries, his interest uncontained, proving he didn't miss the dip in my pitch when I said the word "friend."

Loathing he didn't have a response to my admission I wanted our relationship to go public, I reply, "Umm... he's an ex-boyfriend of mine."

I cringe as I wait for his reply. Thankfully, he doesn't keep me waiting long.

"How old of a relationship are we talking, Cleo?" He tries to keep jealousy out of his question, his efforts are borderline. There was a slight snip of envy left dangling in the air at the end of his question.

"A very long time ago," I answer, happy I'm not the only one who struggles to rein in my jealousy in this bizarre relationship we are endeavoring to get off the ground.

I hear Marcus scrub his hand over his clipped afro as he mutters, "Okay."

"You'll come?" I query, excitement laced in my words.

"Yes," he chuckles, appeasing every nick my confrontation with Keira caused to my heart. "When is it?"

"Tonight." My one word fires off my tongue in a hurry, my glee unbridled.

"Tonight?" Marcus confirms, his tone high with reservation. "I can't do tonight, Cleo." He sounds genuinely remorseful.

"Why? I thought you said you were coming home tonight?" I can't help but sound disappointed.

"I am," he answers after sighing heavily. "I'm just not arriving until late this evening."

I struggle to ignore my brain's repeated pleas for me to grill him for information. It's a waste of time. "Why are you arriving back so late? Can't you bring your flight forward an hour or two? You're the pilot, you can do whatever you want."

Marcus sighs again, this one more grim than his first. "I haven't got time to discuss this right now, I'm swamped, but I'll see you tonight. Okay?"

I remain quiet, unsure how to reply. I also don't want to open my mouth for the fear the sick gloom hammering my stomach will attempt to see daylight.

"I know you're disappointed, but I promise I'll make it up to you. Okay, baby?" Marcus asks, coercing me to bend to his will by calling me a term of endearment, which he rarely does.

"Okay." I despise that I've become so desperate for his attention, I'm letting my heart win every argument against my intelligent mind. "I'll see you tonight."

As I'm dragging my cell away from my ear, Marcus calls my name. "Make sure you take Brodie with you." This time, he doesn't attempt to hide the jealousy smeared in his low tone.

After agreeing to his unbendable demand, Marcus disconnects our call. It's a pity his eagerness to end our call wasn't quick enough for me to miss hearing a female voice call his name. I'm not talking about the name on his birth certificate, I'm referring to a name only a handful of people know him by Master Chains.

My teeth graze my bottom lip as I lower my cell from my ear. The turmoil making my stomach a horrid mess ramps up when my phone illuminates the email from Chains, notifying the location of tonight's party.

"What's wrong?" Lexi asks, intuiting my forlorn look. "Change of plans?" Her voice sounds as devastated as I'm feeling. She knows I've been counting down the hours until Marcus's return, so seeing me end our call on a sour note has her worry piquing.

"No, he's still coming home tonight, he's just not getting in until late." I keep my voice upbeat, hoping to lessen the worry lines marring her forehead.

"So what's with the pouty lip?" Lexi twangs my bottom lip with her thumb.

Her playfulness makes me smile. "It's... umm...I don't know. It's nothing. I'm just being stupid."

"Cleo." She only says one word, but her eyes express so much more.

"It's nothing. Truly. I've just got a million things running through my head right now." I huff, portraying my best worrywart impression.

Lexi rolls her eyes. "You'll learn to slow down one day."

I can tell she wants to say more, but thankfully, after a reassuring bump of her shoulder against mine, she drifts her eyes to the scenery whizzing by the window.

The remainder of our trip to Marcus's New York property is made in silence. Quiet is a rare commodity when you're in Lexi's presence. Even Brodie continually peers at us via the rearview mirror, shocked by our tightlipped composure. Usually, he can't get a word in between us.

With our late lunch stretching into the earlier afternoon, it's a little after six PM when Brodie's vehicle rolls to a stop at the platform stairs of Marcus's house. Lexi curls out of the car at a record speed before galloping up the stairs. When she reaches the landing, she cranks her neck back to peer at me. "I'm going to grab a shower before getting ready. Jackson packed all my dresses, so if you need to borrow one, help yourself."

My brows stitch. "Why would I need to borrow a dress?"

Although my poor vision makes Lexi appear as nothing more than a blur, I swear I saw her eyes roll. "Luke's party. Drrr. Be ready to leave at nine. That way we are fashionably late, but not annoyingly late."

Not giving me the opportunity to protest that I don't feel like going out, she charges in the house, stealing my chance to reply.

I drift my eyes to Brodie, who is peering at me in the rearview mirror when he says, "At least she's regained her bounce."

Smiling, I nod, although I'm still suspicious about what caused her sudden change in temperament. I'm beginning to wonder if I am the only Garcia to have a run-in with Keira today? Lexi is as fiercely protective of me as I am of her, so I don't doubt if she discovered Keira was dining in the same restaurant as us, nothing would have stopped her from having a quiet word with her. By quiet word, I mean, severe threat.

Shutting down my inner monologue before it causes the contents of my stomach to see daylight, I mimic Brodie's departure from his now stationary vehicle. We trudge up the steps in silence, both our shoulders weighed down by a difficult day. Even the slight sprinkle of rain dotting our hair with glistening drops doesn't increase our pace.

The slight creak of the front door announces our arrival to Aubrey, who is sitting in the living room watching a Spanish soap opera show. The glee on her face is doused when she spots my downcast head. Switching off the program, she stands from her seat and moseys toward us. I've barely yanked my coat halfway off when she arrives to my side with a towel in one hand and a pair of thick socks in another. My brows stitch. *Where did she get them from?*

After using the towel to pat sporadic sprouts of curls dry, I kick off my shoes and replace them with the heavenly comfort of the socks Aubrey handed me. My confusion grows when I shift on my feet to face Brodie, preparing to offer him my towel to dry himself. He is nowhere to be seen.

Acting like it's perfectly reasonable for people to vanish into thin air, Aubrey curls her arm around my shoulders and guides me into the kitchen. Although I ate mere hours ago, my stomach grumbles when an alluring smell of spices and curry lingers into my nostrils. Abel's specialty is breakfast treats, any scrumptious morsel of food you could imagine consuming before midday was sampled by me during my five-day stint in Bronte's Peak. Aubrey's cooking specialty fills in the remainder of the day. It's lucky Marcus's staff members don't follow him to each location, or I'd end up the size of a house.

Actually, come to think of it, I could really use Abel's advice right now. Although Abel has never said it, I'm reasonably confident he is aware of Marcus's preferred bedroom activities. If he weren't, the sudden arrival of a playroom in the residence he calls home would have been an odd moment for all involved. But Abel took it in his stride, neither expressing condemnation or praise, so it displays he has an open mind—one I need to possess if I want any chance of working through the confusion debilitating me.

After sitting down on the stool I sat in when Marcus attempted to coerce me into being his sub, I lock my eyes with Aubrey. She is standing in front of the stovetop, serving a large helping of coconut curry chicken onto a bed of jasmine rice. The ladle freezes halfway between the pot and the bowl in her hand when I ask, "How many of Marcus's subs have you served this dish to?"

After taking a beat to clear the panic on her face, Aubrey spins on her heels to face me. "None," she says confidently as she paces toward me to set down the bowl of steamy goodness.

I arch a brow as my eyes silently assess the truth in her eyes. I'm taken aback when nothing but genuine honesty reflects back at me.

"How can that be true?" I question, more to myself than Aubrey.

She gathers a fork from the top drawer, wraps it in a napkin like a fancy restaurant, then sets it down next to my bowl. "Can I be honest?" she queries, her pitch hesitant.

Not trusting my voice not to crack with emotions, I nod.

"The entire time I've worked with Mr. Everett, he's had stringent rules. How I could interact with his subs, what they could wear, and what food they ate." She drops her eyes to the bowl of scrumptious chicken calling my name, begging to be consumed. "Any products laced with creamy goodness were not on his list of prepared meals."

"Prepared?" I query, my tone confused.

Aubrey nods. "He had a list of meals I was to prepare for each night of the week. I worked Saturday through to Sunday preparing the meals for the following week."

"Then what?"

"Then I worked from home the remainder of the week." She paces to a stack of drawers at the side of the kitchen. After gathering a sheet of paper, she returns to her original position and hands the document to me.

I breathe out my nerves before dropping my eyes to the sheet of paper. The concern blackening my blood is unwarranted. The list is nothing more than a grocery list with a set of meals made up for each day. Although the meals appear lavish with the inclusion of salmon and poached chicken, they are also bland, with every meal complemented by steamed vegetables or a side salad minus any condiments. There is also not a dessert mentioned in the entire document.

My spine straightens when reality dawns. Raising my eyes from the paper, I lock them with Aubrey's glistening gaze. "Today is Friday, isn't it?" I scan the kitchen, expecting the date to appear before my eyes magically.

“Yes,” Aubrey agrees with a giggle.

"Then why are you here?" I cringe when my high tone makes my voice come out rude. I’m not trying to sound obnoxious, because all I'm feeling is gratitude. Even more so since my stomach’s focus hasn’t veered away from the fragrant dish in front of me to cite an objection about Aubrey’s disclosure that Marcus preferred his previous liaisons to be uninterrupted.

Aubrey taps the piece of paper I'm clutching for dear life. "Because Mr. Everett said none of this applies to you. In fact, he didn't even give me a list of meals he wanted prepared this week. I was told to make you feel as if you're in your own home."

I grind my back molars together as I fight to ignore the tears welling in my eyes. Not trusting myself not to blubber, I quickly reply, “You’ve done exactly that. Thank you.”

A flare of happiness sparks in Aubrey's eyes before it makes way for a dusting of tears. I'm glad to see I'm not the only one incapable of ignoring the substantial sentiment in the air.

“Now grab a fork and take a seat. If I eat all this chicken, Marcus will force us to eat that rubbish,” I mumble, nudging my head to the paper I’ve dumped on the countertop.

With a smile, Aubrey does as requested. We spend the next several moments sitting side by side, consuming the dish I'm sure took her hours to make. The chicken is so tender it melts in my mouth the instant it hits my tongue. Aubrey discloses that the recipe has been handed down by her family for generations. It's so old, she doesn't even recall where it originated from.

Although Aubrey and I are separated in age by around two decades, we talk as if we are friends. I discover she is the eldest of eleven children, ranging between the ages of 17 and 54. Her parents still live in Mexico, along with half of her siblings, and she is unmarried with no children of her own.

“Did you not want children, or was the timing never right?” I query, praying she won’t see my question as being nosy. I’m so genuinely interested in her life that I blurted out my question before I could stop my words.

"A little bit of both. With so many younger siblings, by the time I reached thirty, it felt like I had already raised my children." She slips off the stool and moves to the sink to commence clearing away our dishes. "It may be selfish, but I wanted some *me* time."

"That's not selfish." I join her at the sink. After accepting the dish she is holding out, I continue, "Selfish would have been leaving your parents to raise your siblings alone."

"Hmm. I guess." She shrugs her shoulders. "I've always grown up believing it takes a community to raise a child, not just its parents. It's unfortunate that logic isn't as strong as it used to be."

"If my dad were still around, he'd 100% agree with you. He always said 'it is the free-range parents' fault for raising a generation of entitled people.' Don't get me wrong, he wanted his children to achieve greatness, he just didn't want us to become self-centered and undeserving while doing it. 'Everyone wants the glory, but no one is willing to climb their way to the top anymore' was another one of his favorite sayings."

Aubrey giggles. "My papa calls them the 'silver spoon generation.'"

The rest of our dishes are done in silence. It isn't uncomfortable, but the silence does allow my thoughts to run wild. At least this time, not all my thoughts are reckless—like Aubrey's disclosure that Marcus's sub rules don't apply to me. But for every question I answer, another one pops up. Like is Marcus's negligence of the rules a good or a bad thing for our relationship? Before me, Marcus hadn't even frolicked with a sub outside of the playroom, let alone made love to one. I adore that I have that special part of him, but part of me worries I'm drawing him too far out of his comfort zone. Marcus doesn't instill punishment for pleasure, but what Keira said is true. The BDSM lifestyle is all he knows. If my desire for him to give that up became stronger than my need to be dominated, could Marcus walk away from the BDSM lifestyle?

I'd like to say yes confidently, but if I did, that would be a lie. I truly don't believe Marcus's desires for me are stronger than his need for power and control. He has never hidden the fact he craves control, so why would that logic suddenly change? *It wouldn't.*

I thank Aubrey for dinner and our chat when I hear my cell phone vibrating on the glass entranceway table. Because the residence is quiet, every buzz it makes adds to the quickening of my pulse.

My lungs take stock of their oxygen levels when I lift my cell and discover three unread messages from an unknown number. The first message is a simple one-line text.

Unknown number: *I'm here if you need me.*

The next two messages are picture files. Although the image of an elegantly dressed couple wouldn't usually instigate a horrid epidemic of nausea, it's recognizing the two people in the image that has my stomach churning out of control.

The first photo is a snap of Marcus and Keira standing at the front an industrial-looking building. Marcus has his arm wrapped around Keira's waist, and his nose is tucked into her neck, hiding his alluring green eyes from the person snapping their photo unaware. They are both wearing masks—similar to the ones I saw Chains patrons wearing three months ago.

The second photo is a little harder for me to decipher. It's so pixelated even someone with perfect eyesight would have a hard time decrypting it. It's only when I flick between the two images numerous times do I realize what the second photo is. Both photos are identical, but one is zoomed in to display the bare skin on Keira's right shoulder blade. Because her shoulder is mottled with faint bruises and red welts, the image is barely identifiable. It also doesn't help that her welts are a circular pattern... My inner monologue trails off as I'm held captive by a terrible notion. Those marks on Keira's shoulder look oddly familiar to ones I've seen before. They are nearly an exact replica to the strands on a flogger I saw in Marcus's playroom at Chains months ago.

No, they couldn't be...Marcus wouldn't cheat on me. *He doesn't cheat.*

I nearly drop my phone onto the marble floor when a deep voice asks, "What's that?"

I take a moment to settle the mad beat of my heart before connecting my eyes with Brodie. If he keeps scaring the living daylights out of me, I'm going to put squeakers on his shoes. My god—I can barely breathe with how hard my heart is thudding my chest.

My brain demands I act on these photos immediately. I twist my phone to face Brodie, who removes my cell from my grasp so he can appraise the images more diligently. Initially, his brows stitch, but I know the exact moment it dawns on him what he is looking at. His jaw quivers as his eyes rocket to mine.

"Who sent you those pictures?" he queries, his tone direct.

I shrug. "Does it matter? What's captured in the photo should be more concerning than who took them, shouldn't it?"

Brodie's lips twitch, preparing to speak, but I beat him to it. "What do you think caused the marks on Keira's shoulder?"

Brodie's throat works hard to swallow as he scrubs his hand over his chin. He remains as quiet as a church mouse. He doesn't need to answer my question, though. His eyes tell the entire story.

I angrily shake my head, sick of the constant deflections of my questions. If someone would just answer one goddamn question without skirting it, I wouldn't be so consumed by confused rage right now. It's the constant feeling of being left in the dark that's driving me more crazy than Keira's acknowledgment she wants Marcus to be her Master. Yes, these images are as innocent as the ones I witnessed in person last week, but they'd be a whole heap easier to handle if there weren't a shadow of doubt placed on every question I ask.

Realizing there is only one man who can give me answers, I snatch my cell out of Brodie's hand and head for the stairs, wanting privacy for what should be a private conversation. I'm halfway up the curved stairwell when Brodie shouts, "Just because you received these photos tonight doesn't mean they were taken tonight. They could be from months ago."

"It still doesn't change the facts, Brodie. Although more ghastly than last week, Keira is once again wearing Marcus's trademark in public."

Brodie replies, but I don't hear a word over the roaring of blood to my ears. After running my sweaty hands down the flare of my skirt, I dial Marcus's number. I command on repeat for my body to calm down, it never listens. It's a lot harder feigning ignorance than I realized.

Marcus's cell rings eight times before it connects to his voicemail. I stand from the bed to pace a track into the plush carpet fibers of Marcus's master suite. My brain is warning me not to act so irrational—he could merely be flying home—but my heart is enlarged with worry, certain Marcus's silence is more dire than my brain realizes.

When my heart's pleas ring louder than my brain, I scroll through my list of contacts, stopping when I find a number I stored in there weeks ago. My hand shakes when I press my cell phone close to my ear. I count the rings—*one, two, three, four*—praying I don't reach eight before my call is answered.

Gratitude pumps into me when the distinctive clip of a landline shrills into my ears on the seventh ring.

"Hello," greets a thick husky voice I immediately recognize.

"Hi, Abel," I address, hating that I've allowed the pleas of my foolish heart to put him in the middle of my confrontation with Marcus. "I'm sorry to bother you, I am just seeking Marcus. He isn't answering his cell, so I thought I'd check and see if you knew when he was scheduled to fly out."

"Fly out? Ah... I'm confused as to what you mean, Ms. Cleo."

The panic in his tone also shocks me. "He was scheduled to fly out earlier today, but his departure was delayed. Is he still there? Can I talk to him?"

Abel's heavy sigh obscures the tapping of his feet on the wooden floorboards of Marcus's Florida home. He coughs to clear his throat before he mutters, "Umm... Ah ..."

"He is there, isn't he?" I interrupt, my tone crammed with suspicion.

My suspicions amplify when Abel replies, "No. I haven't seen Mr. Everett today, Ms. Cleo."

The room spins around me as I'm overwhelmed with dizziness. Not trusting my legs, I sit on the edge of Marcus's huge bed.

"When did you last see him?" I ask, my voice half-panicked, half-laced with unbridled jealousy. I'm frankly stumped on which emotion to honor. I feel panicked and enraged with anger at the same time.

Horrid unease twists in my stomach when Abel replies, "I haven't seen him since he left with you weeks ago." His voice has a whip of edginess to it, like he too is annoyed by Marcus's lack of contact.

I remain quiet, unable to speak through the terrible feeling twisting my stomach. Marcus said he was returning to Ravenshoe, so why wouldn't he stay at his residence while he was there? Not unless he stayed elsewhere...

I'm freed from my sickening thoughts when Abel asks, "Ms. Cleo, are you there?"

"Ah, yes," I reply, my voice as low as my heart rate. "If you hear from Marcus, can you tell him I need to talk to him?" I roll my eyes, loathing that the confidence I built the past three months was sideswiped in one afternoon.

"Yes, Ms. Cleo, I most certainly will." Some of the dread scorching my throat eases from Abel's guarantee.

After apologizing again for disturbing him, I bid farewell to Abel, then disconnect our call. I don't know if I'm just being spiteful, or merely striving to spark a reaction out of Marcus, but I send him a cryptic text message.

Me: *How's the weather in Florida? Be sure to rug up before you return home because things are getting mighty cold here. By the way, Abel says hello.*

I glare at my phone for the next twenty minutes, yearning for it to ring, buzz, vibrate—to do anything!

It does nothing.

15

I angrily swipe at a tear on my cheek when a brief tap sounds on the door of Marcus's bedroom. Not waiting for me to give permission to enter, Lexi cracks open the door and saunters inside. I slowly suck in a lung-filling gulp of air as I drink in her perfectly made-up ensemble. She is wearing a thick wool skirt with a dangerously high slit kept modest by three strategically placed chunky diaper pins. Her long-sleeve white shirt accentuates every perfect curve of her body, and her hair has been curled in a crazy, rock-chick style. With her vibrant brown eyes shadowed with a glittering of midnight black powder, her red-painted lips really pop off her face. She has taken the requisite 80's Rock 'n Roll dress code on Luke's invitation and given it her own edge. She looks so sexy, I'm afraid shoulder pads and teased-up bangs are about to become all the rage again.

Noticing I'm still wearing the same outfit I wore at lunch, Lexi checks the time on her watch. "It's 9 PM, Cleo," she states as if I am unaware of the time.

"I know," I reply, rising from my slumped position. "I'm not going. I called Jackson, he'll be here to collect you soon."

"No," Lexi responds, spreading her hands over her cocked hip. "You RSVP'd for both of us. That means we're *both* going."

She tosses aside my furious glare as if it's as weightless as a piece of lint before padding into the walk-in closet I share with Marcus. I can hear her grunting and moaning as she digs through my minuscule collection of clothes. She arrives at my bedside two minutes later holding a ghastly bright fluorescent pink slip dress I forgot I owned with a pair of glossy navy blue heels.

"Tease out your curls and cake some blue eyeshadow on your eyes, and you'll be good to go." Lexi throws the dress at me.

"Come on, Cleo. Chop, chop. There is such a thing as too late," Lexi bickers when I fail to move my sloth-like form.

“I don’t want to go out. I’m tired,” I grumble when she grasps my arms and drags me from the bed.

Ignoring my childish whine, she whips my shirt over my head before wrangling with the zipper on my skirt. I freeze when her nose digs into my armpit. She inhales two quick whiffs in rapid succession before murmuring, "Good enough." She yanks my dress off the coat hanger and drags it over my head before I can blink.

“You don’t understand, Lexi. I have a very legitimate reason why I don’t want to go out.”

"I know," Lexi sighs, cutting me off. "I ran into Brodie in the hallway."

Great. The last thing I want is people talking about me behind my back.

“It’s not like that, Cleo,” Lexi replies to my private thoughts. “Brodie wasn’t gossiping about you. He’s just worried. I assured him you’ll be fine. You’re a Garcia. We survive anything.”

She swirls an eyeshadow brush in her makeup kit I didn’t notice she was holding until now. Happy she has an adequate amount of blue eyeshadow on the brush, she sets to work on doing my makeup.

I remain quiet, running her declaration through my mind on repeat. I am a Garcia, and I’ve survived much worse than this, but I don’t know if I’ll survive losing Marcus. Just the thought of not having him in my life has my stomach twisting up in knots.

After applying enough makeup to my face to conceal my devastation, Lexi locks her eyes with mine. "When the game is ending sooner than you like, you force the opposition into the penalty box," she recites a quote our dad mentioned numerous times in our teens. I've never understood its logic. Tonight is no different.

I begrudgingly slip on my heels, gather my cell, then shadow Lexi into the hallway. Although I’m not the best company, being surrounded by old friends will remind me I’m stronger than I realize. Just as I’m about to take the first step of the stairwell, Lexi seizes my elbow. My eyes bounce between hers when she continues clutching my arm until she has dragged me to the very end of the hallway.

“Brodie is downstairs,” she whispers like it's a treasured secret.

“Yeah... so?”

The hallway is dimly lit, but it isn’t dark enough for me to miss Lexi’s eye roll. “You can’t force penalty time by colluding with the umpire,” she grumbles.

Chilly winter winds whip my hair into a frenzy when Lexi cranks open the window we are standing next to. After thrusting her purse and cell into my chest, she clambers out the window.

“Are you insane? We’re grown women, for crying out loud. We don’t need to sneak out.” Half of my sentence is muffled by a bout of childish giggling. My reaction can’t be helped. With Lexi’s super tight skirt, watching her scoot along the tree branch her legs are wrapped around is extremely entertaining.

“If I get a splinter in my snatch, you’re digging it out,” Lexi warns, her pitch drenched with cheeky innuendo.

"If you're wearing panties, you won't have to worry..." The remainder of my sentence gets lodged in my throat when Lexi suggestively waggles her brows.

"Lexi! You're..." I can't think of an appropriate word to call her. "You're bad," I settle on.

"Obviously not since you're only just realizing this." She grunts when she lands on the dew-covered ground with a thud, her years of cheerleading awarding her the perfect dismount.

After throwing down her purse and our cells, I hike my skirt up high on my thighs and climb out the window sill. My ovaries shrivel up when the freezing cold temps outside have me wishing I could dart downstairs to retrieve my coat. It's as thin as my patience is right now, but it would be better than nothing.

"Come on, Cleo." Lexi encourages me to hurry. "Jax has the heat on in his truck."

I grimace when the tree bark digs into the smooth skin high on my thighs. My dismount isn't as graceful as Lexi's. It isn't a lack of cheerleading skills causing me to fall to the ground like a sack of potatoes, it is hearing Brodie calling my name. For how loud he is, I'm confident he is on the second level of Marcus's house.

My assumptions are proven correct when Brodie's torso leans out of the window I just climbed out not even two seconds before. His wide eyes dart between me and Lexi standing frozen on the manicured turf, the confusion in them doubling for every second that ticks by.

"Don't you dare!" he warns in a gravelly tone when he realizes what we are doing.

"Never dare a Garcia, Brodie, because you'll never win." Lexi curls her arms around my elbow and bolts toward Jackson's truck idling at the end of Marcus's driveway, lugging me behind her. For a woman who weighs ten pounds less than me, she hauls me across the grounds without even breaking into a sweat.

"Cleo, you have five seconds to get back here!" Brodie shouts from the top floor.

When his demand is met with a bout of laughter, he roars, "Goddamn it!"

Lexi increases her pace when Brodie disappears from the window. With how eerily quiet the night is, I can hear the thuds of his steps as he gallops down the stairs. He takes the last steps just as we reach Jackson's truck. Lexi throws open the door so forcefully, the truck's hinges squeal in protest.

"Go, go, go," Lexi requests, squealing when we dive into the roasting hot cab. Lexi wasn't joking, Jackson has the heat up high.

Jackson's truck glides down the asphalt at the exact moment Brodie sprints down the platform stairs. "You know he'll just jump in his car and force Jackson to pull over," I inform Lexi, my words wheezy from our mad dash.

"Bit hard without these."

Swinging my eyes from Brodie chasing us on foot, I spot Lexi dangling a set of car keys on her index finger—keys that don't belong to her.

"And it isn't like he can just show up to Luke's, since the venue of his party changed." Her smile is the largest I've seen. "I deleted Luke's email from our servers too, just in case you were wondering."

I don't know whether to hug her or strangle her right now. My exhausted body is welcoming the surge of adrenaline from our risky breakout, but there is still a smidgen of doubt blackening my blood.

Some of my dread dampens when Jackson seizes Lexi's wrist and drags her across the bench until she is nuzzled under the nook of his arm. After pressing a kiss to her temple, he whispers three little words I'd give anything to hear right now. "I love you."

The past week has been hard on them. I wouldn't necessarily say it's been any harder than it has been on Marcus and me, but there is no doubt "absence makes the heart grow fonder" is not a theory they're interested in testing again anytime soon.

Unsurprisingly, we've barely exited Marcus's street when my cell starts hollering. Surprisingly, the call isn't from Brodie. It's from Marcus. Taking matters into her own hands, Lexi snatches my cell phone out of my hand, declines Marcus's call and silences my phone. I eye her curiously when her fingers tap wildly over the screen. The swoosh of a message being sent sounds through my ears, closely followed by Lexi's phone buzzing, indicating she has received a text message.

She drops my cell into her lap before picking up her phone. I peer over her shoulder, watching her configure a two-sentence email.

If you want to talk to my sister, you'll have to go through me first. And there is NO chance of that happening until you explain these, dipshit.

Her lips quirk as she attaches the two photos the anonymous messenger sent me earlier tonight. Her message has barely left her inbox when her cell starts ringing. I don't need to peer at the screen to know it's Marcus. I can feel it deep in my bones.

My brows scrunch when Lexi denies Marcus's call before returning her cell to her purse. "Never negotiate with terrorists," she explains to my baffled expression. "How many hours did you spend sniveling in your room tonight waiting for him to return your call?"

Jackson's gaze strays from the road to me. His worried glance is discreet, but strong enough to make me feel ashamed.

"I wasn't sniveling," I lie, loathing the sorrow-filled glances being directed at me.

Lexi arches her brow and glares at me, acting like she didn't hear a thing I said.

"Around two hours," I mumble, knowing she'd eventually read the truth from my eyes.

Lexi checks her watch. "So at eighteen minutes past midnight, Chains' can have his questions answered. Until then, he can suffer in his jocks."

"He can what?" I ask, confused.

"Suffer in his jocks," Lexi confirms, grinning. "I heard Cartier say it earlier today. It has a nice ring to it."

Snubbing my slack-jawed expression, she devotes her attention to Jackson.

I spent the first half of our commute unscrambling everything that has happened thus far today. You'd think my primary focus would be on learning when the photo of Marcus and Keira was taken, but it isn't. With Lexi's mention of Cartier, my prime focus has centered around her concern about me expressing my love to Marcus. Is it just a coincidence his withdrawal of contact directly follows my request for him to make love to me?

Cartier has said numerous times the desire to be loved was the conundrum that unraveled her relationship. Can the same be said for Marcus and me? I didn't hold anything back last week when we made love. I expressed everything he meant to me using my body instead of the words I really wanted to say. So maybe that is the cause of his lack of contact? Perhaps he doesn't see our relationship heading in the direction he desires, and this is his way of ending things amicably.

I know it's extreme to think this way, but what other reason could he have for pretending he was in Florida? Although I don't have proof, my intuition is telling me he's been in New York the entire time. Unlike Keira, Cartier has no motive to lie about seeing Marcus. She saw him yesterday—in New York, and she spoke as if he has been here the entire time, so I believe her. And Abel seemed just as concerned by Marcus's lack of contact as I was.

Panicked alarm slams into me when reality dawns. I feel sick— so horribly ill. *Is Marcus breaking up with me because he hated vanilla sex?* If he is, he doesn't need to be worried. I enjoyed making love to him—it was beautiful and special —but I *love* being dominated by him. If I knew my request for him to make love to me would have such an adverse reaction, I would have never asked him to do it. I just wanted a piece of him that no one else had. I wanted to claim him as my own—much like he did by placing his collar around my neck. I never wanted it to end us.

Lifting my eyes from my intertwined fingers, I lock them with Jackson. "Pull over," I stammer out, my words choked by the bile surging to the base of my throat.

"Pull over," I demand more assertively when my first request is met with silence.

Seeing the panic on my face, Jackson pulls his truck to the curb. I've barely scampered out of the cab when the coconut chicken I ate at dinner resurfaces in the ghastliest way. It's nowhere near as appetizing the second time around.

Once the heaving racks hammering my body ease, Lexi hands me a wad of tissues from the glove compartment.

"Can I please have my cell?" I plead while wiping a remnant of vomit from my bottom lip.

"Please, Lexi," I beg when she puts up a silent protest to my request. "*Please.*"

She huffs before leaning into the cabin of the truck to fish out my cell phone. The shake of my hand is obvious when I accept it and dial Marcus's number. Although I'm a skittish bag of nerves, my determination remains resilient. This phone call is long overdue.

Marcus answers not even two rings later. "Cleo, where the hell are you? I told you to take Brodie with you. Why did you leave without—"

"Did I break us?" I interrupt, my voice displaying I'm on the verge of tears but mighty pissed off. My eyes are brimming with so much moisture, I'm certain they are moments away from bursting, but the anger roaring through my veins is keeping them at bay.

"I didn't mean to break us. I like what we did, but if I knew you were going to hate it, I wouldn't have asked you to do it." My words are forced out my mouth so fast, they're nothing more than a blubbering string of nonsense.

A chair scrapes across the ground before the stomps of shoe-covered feet bellow down the line. "Cleo... baby, please don't cry." Marcus's words are jutted like he is pacing. "You haven't done anything wrong. I swear to God, we're okay." His voice is a stark contradiction to the fury radiating down the phone. He sounds equally panicked and wrathful.

His term of endearment forces a stray tear to topple from my eye, but my broken heart is not crippled enough to stop me seeking answers. "Why are you lying to me, Marcus?"

"I'm not—"

"Stop, Marcus! I *know* you're in New York. I *know* you never went to Florida. I *know* you've seen *her*. How much more proof do you need?" Anger quickly overtakes my heartache. "If you didn't want to be with me anymore, you could have just said. You didn't have to go to such lengths to get rid of me. We don't have a contract, so you don't owe me a specific amount of time. You owe me nothing but honesty."

I hear his hand run over his clipped afro as he curses softly. "Cleo, I need you to stop talking and listen to me." His demeanor is calm and controlled, an absolute contradiction to the woman he is talking to. I'm shaking so much, my teeth are chattering as if I'm standing in the middle of the arctic, and my shuddering response has nothing to do with the freezing winter temps curling around my body.

"You need to trust me. Remember, being trusted is a compliment greater than being loved," Marcus implores, using the same pleas he made the last time he lied.

"Just like the smallest lie encourages doubt in the biggest truth. A lie, no matter what size, cracks the foundation trust is built on. You lied to me, Marcus. Over and over again," I reply, my tone devastated yet firm.

Suddenly, my spine snaps straight when a male voice says, "I've got a trace on her cell. She is on highway 32, half a mile down from off-ramp 12."

Before I can register my disgust that he tracked my cell, Marcus says, "Stay where you are, Cleo. I'm coming to get you, then I'll explain everything." His words are breathless as if he is running.

I push my cell in close to my ear when a faint tune sounds down the line. Although the music isn't overly familiar, I'm confident I've heard it before, I just can't recall exactly where.

Air evicts from my body in a brutal grunt when recollection dawns. The soft, ambient music has me recalling a time when the pleasantry of the tune didn't match the explicit scenes unfolding before my very eyes. Scenes only attendees at an exclusive invitation-only gathering would see. It's the same music that was playing the night I was a guest at a BDSM club in lower Manhattan. It's the music played in Chains.

Lexi gasps when I suddenly question, "Are you at Chains?"

A string of garbled words leave Marcus's mouth. Although I'm certain he is speaking English, I'm only listening for two words. Yes or no.

When I fail to hear either of those words, I snarl, "Answer the goddamn question, Marcus! Are you at Chains?!" My voice is so loud a pack of dogs start howling in the distance, startled by my brittle tone.

Marcus waits a beat before he breathes out, "Yes, but—"

The rest of his sentence is lost when my phone slips from my grasp, shattering into a million pieces when it collides with the asphalt. I close my eyes and raise my head to the sky, struggling to hold back the tears threatening to spill down my cheeks at any moment. It's a pointless effort when the cool breeze blowing across my face contrasts against the fat, hot tears sliding down my cheeks.

I count backward from thirty, giving my heart the chance to mourn the end of my relationship before returning my chin to its normal position and fluttering open my eyes.

"I need a drink... or fifty," I instruct Lexi, who is staring at me with worry.

Remaining quiet with sheer alarm tainting her beautiful face, she nods before aiding me back into Jackson's truck. After cocooning my shuddering frame with her tiny body, she signals for Jackson to continue our journey, leaving my shattered cell on the edge of the road looking as mangled as my heart feels.

16

The first two hours of Luke's party flies by. I bounce between guests, acting as if the last six years of my life never happened. But like all alcohol-induced happiness, my wine-inspired social butterfly routine is nipped in the bud even more quickly than it began. For the past hour, I've floundered around, willfully moving from group to group, hoping to feel welcomed in one of the cliques parties like this always attract. Unfortunately, just like my night at Chains, I don't belong here either. It isn't that I don't feel welcome, it's just no amount of idle chit-chat and warm alcohol can cure debilitating heartache.

Needing some fresh air, I weave through the partygoers bumping and grinding on the makeshift dance floor in the middle of Luke's parents' house until I merge onto the wooden deck at the back of their sprawling property. I shake my head in disbelief when I spot a handful of birthday guests swimming in the pool—barren of any clothes. Although the pool is heated, no amount of alcohol-fueled bravery would have me stripping down in front of hundreds of guests for an impromptu swim. I've never been overly audacious. That's why I'm so surprised at how much I loved Marcus's dominance. I've always said I am a strong-willed and determined young lady. Clearly, that isn't the case. Just my miserable attempt at enjoying the celebration of a dear friend shows how pathetic I've become.

Not anymore. This miserable Cleo act ends tonight.

The familiar giggle of Lexi sounds through my ears when I reach the pool room at the back of manicured grounds. Considering Lexi's laughter came from the direction of the pool, I keep my gaze front and center, not trusting my sister's wild antics. The last thing I need is to see her in the buff once more.

I inhale deeply when the scent of Luke's aftershave he wore in college lingers into my nose. Back in the day, this used to be Luke's bedroom. He wanted privacy, and supposedly a detached dwelling mere feet from the principal residence was the perfect solution for his predicament. I feel a rush of heat creep across my cheeks when I recall some of the events that took place in this room. This is the very room I lost my virginity in. It was a highly awkward and stumbling time. Thank god Luke was also a virgin, so he was just as ill-informed on the probability of orgasming during sex as I was. He never once voiced a concern that I didn't climax during sex, because he didn't know I was supposed to.

My pupils widen when my trip down memory lane is interrupted by the man I was thinking about. Luke walks out of a steam-filled bathroom with nothing but a thin towel wrapped around his drenched hips.

Allowing the alcohol lacing my veins to get the better of me, my eyes drink in his carved body, veined arms, and glistening pecs unashamed—not once, but twice!

"Cleo," Luke greets, shocked when he spots me standing at the side of his bed, obsessively ogling him.

"Hey." I cringe, loathing my lack of elegance. "Sorry. I was just seeking a place of solitude. It's getting a little rowdy out there."

Luke smiles a grin that makes him look younger than his twenty-six years. "It is. It reminds me a lot of our high school parties. Although I don't recall the pool being quite that cold."

When he peers out to the pool, I follow the direction of his gaze. As I suspected, Lexi is in the pool. Thank god my eyesight is poor enough I can't tell if she is naked or not. Not that I can see either way since her tiny body is swamped by Jackson's large frame.

"She is very much like you," Luke laughs when he spots Lexi sucking face with Jackson.

I fiddle with the hem of my dress to stop myself from rolling my eyes like a fifth grader. "Only ten times wilder."

My eyes snap to Luke when he throws his head back and chuckles. "You keep telling yourself that, Cleo, then maybe one day people might believe it."

"I wasn't that bad, was I?" My eyes widen in shock when my voice comes out all throaty as if I'm a little sex kitten purring at his heel, begging for him to stroke my back.

I'm not the only one who noticed the change in my vocals. Luke's eyes blaze with excitement as his towel fails to conceal his impressively stiff manhood. I bite on the inside of my cheek, vainly trying to hold the snippet of modesty I have left as I divert my eyes away from his erect cock.

"Oh shit," Luke grumbles as he snags a pair of jeans off a rumpled bed to yank them up his thighs. "I swear to God, Cleo, if you blush, you're not leaving this room with your virtue intact."

I giggle as heat blooms across the shallow blackness in my chest. "You can't use the same line years later, Luke. It's just tacky."

Luke's laughter warms my chest even more, soothing some of the nicks Marcus's betrayal caused. "Why not? You're acting like you've never seen my cock. We both know you sure as hell have."

"It's different now." I twist my head to the side to ensure he is dressed before shifting on my feet to face him. He is clothed. Well, if you consider wearing a pair of jeans commando as dressed, he is. "You were only a boy back then, so things could have changed."

I'm disgusted with myself when my eyes drop to the zipper of his jeans as I chew on my bottom lip. Marcus's betrayal hurt, but two wrongs never make a right.

Pretending I wasn't just eyeballing him with suggestion, I pick up a throw cushion scattered on the floor and peg it at Luke's head when he grabs his crotch and asks, "Did you want to check?"

"You're disgusting," I mumble, faking annoyance. I'm not annoyed. It's great bantering with him again. I feel like I've flashed back to my teen years. I'm just peeved at myself. I'm acting like a harlot with no morality.

Sensing my thoughts have veered toward the negative, Luke says, "And you're the prettiest girl I've ever seen." He wraps his arms around my waist before drawing me into his bare wet torso. "I'll lasso the moon if you want me to."

"If you do, I'll throw it straight back, because out of all the stars in the sky, none will shine brighter than you," I quote my half of our shared declaration from our two-year courtship.

Luke smiles, appreciating that I remembered the saying he created. "So what's all this about?" His worried gaze dances between mine. "I've never seen your eyes so lifeless, Cleo, not even after..."

He doesn't need to finish his sentence. I know what he is referring to. And no, it isn't about the demise of our relationship. Although I incited our break up, our relationship ended on amicable terms. Luke and I were great together, we just weren't perfect.

I don't know if it's the alcohol warming my veins, or the fact I don't have any girlfriends to talk to, but over the next twenty minutes, I share every detail of my relationship with Marcus with Luke. By everything, I mean *everything*. BDSM included. The only part I leave out is Marcus's true identity. Luke listens intensively, only butting in to ask the occasional question.

Once I've spilled my guts, Luke locks his eyes with mine and says, "You need to tell him how you feel, Cleo."

I throw my arms into the air. "Did you not just hear a word I spoke? He's at a BDSM club."

"Did you hear a thing you said?" Luke fires straight back. "He *owns* a BDSM club, Cleo. It's his business. I'm not sure what your ideas on running a business entail, but I sure as hell don't run my pharmacy from home. I have to rock up occasionally." The playfulness in his tone eases some of the sting his brutal honesty caused. "Chains never lied about owning a BDSM club. You knew that about him when you agreed to meet him, so you can't throw it in his face."

"What about all the other stuff? The photos? Collaring other subs? Him pretending he is in Florida when he isn't?"

"Come on, Cleo. I thought you were the mature one in our group. That's all high school shit. Remember when Stacey Coulter found a love letter in her locker, and she told you it was from me? You didn't talk to me for three days. It was only after asking her for proof did you realize the note wasn't from me."

"Because she spelled your last name wrong," I admit, recalling our first real fight.

Luke's wet blond hair flopped on his head barely moves when he nods. "Instead of asking me straight-out, you cut all ties with me for days. It fucking killed me, Cleo. I loved you, yet you wouldn't give me the time of day." He locks his eyes with the diamond chain pendant I haven't worked up the courage to remove. "You're doing the exact same thing to him. I was lucky I knew where you were. I camped under your bedroom window every night during our breakup. Chains isn't so lucky. He has no clue where you are."

Moisture wells in my eyes. "When did you get so smart?" I jest, hoping a little bit of playfulness will stop my tears from falling.

I lose any chances of holding back my childish sobs when Luke replies, "When I lost the girl of my dreams because she didn't feel confident enough to talk to me like she just did."

He plucks two tissues out of a box next to the couch we are sitting on, then hands them to me. After mopping up the handful of tears on my cheeks I was unable to contain, I mumble, "Why aren't you mad?"

"Why would I be mad? A much-needed lesson was learned when I lost you. Now another lucky schmuck is reaping the benefit of my heartache."

When my bottom lip drops into a pout, Luke mutters, "Just like some lucky schmuck is reaping the reward of me discovering you have no gag reflex."

I slap my hand over his mouth as my eyes scope the area, wanting to ensure no one overheard his admission. Happy we are void of prying eyes, I slowly remove my hand from his mouth. "That isn't common knowledge," I whisper as if I am sharing guarded secrets. "Besides, it was a banana that ultimately discovered that skill."

Luke scoffs. "A banana might have started the investigation, but my cock ended it. Also, I guarantee you everyone in this house is aware of the fact you have no gag reflex. I was a teenage boy, Cleo, that was bragging rights."

He chuckles even more loudly when I smack him on his bare chest. "Go and put some clothes on. I'd hate for people to get the wrong idea."

"Too late," he murmurs under his breath as he stands from the couch.

I watch him in silence as he grabs a clean shirt out of a basket of laundry on the ground and slips it over his head. Luke has a fit, athletic body with perfect clumps of muscles to drive women crazy. His hair is a little longer than I remember, and his eyes are wiser, but he is still the same boy I thought of more as a best friend than a lover. I think that's where our relationship went wrong. We had the sexual attraction, but it arrived much later than our friendship did. We probably should have stayed friends instead of seeking an attraction that needed to be sparked. Sexual connection should come naturally and without effort. *Shouldn't it?*

"Call him. Text him. Email him," Luke suggests, nudging his head to a desk covered with paperwork. "If you don't want to be with him, tell him. But put him out of his misery, Cleo, as you know as well as anyone what it feels like being left in the dark."

I pick at a ball of lint on my dress as I nod, too ashamed to look Luke in the eyes. Those three hours between expecting my parents to arrive home, and the police arriving on my doorstep to inform me of their accident were the longest three hours of my life. I called my parents on repeat, leaving message after message. It was pure torture. Luke understands it as I called him in a state of panic numerous times in those three hours.

Luke's warm breath flutters my hair when he leans down and places a quick kiss on my temple. "I'll wait for you outside with a bottle of tequila and a tub of ice-cream. You just tell me which one you need the most."

I wait until I hear the door latch click into place before raising my downcast head. My legs shake when I stand from the couch and pace to the desk Luke nudged to. I first consider calling Marcus, but remembering how one-sided our conversations have always been, I decide to write to him instead. That way I can express everything I want to say in one fell swoop. It will be out there, exposed for the entire world to see.

When I sit behind the desk, the desires of my answer-seeking brain overrule my lust-driven heart. Instead of logging into my email account as predicted, my fingers type a web address I haven't used in weeks. Although I haven't used the Chains' chat forum in months, my login details remain active. I type a name into the search engine before removing my hands from the keyboard, needing a few moments to ensure I'll be strong enough to face the possible outcome my snooping may unearth.

Realizing no amount of time will lessen my devastation, I tap the enter key. I inwardly curse when my search returns a match. Master Chains' account is once again active. Even my too-forgiving heart releases a few choice curse words as I click on his account and open a messenger box.

Over the next ten minutes, I type every thought passing through my mind. My disappointment that he wasn't man enough to tell me I was no longer what he wanted. My anger at being betrayed. My annoyance at the constant lies I've been told. But most importantly, I express how angry I am that he wooed me so intensely, I couldn't help but fall in love with him.

I hate that you're so easy to love.
I hate that I fell in love with you even when my brain begged me not to.
I hate that you'll never love me back.
But more than anything, I hate that I can't hate you because I love you too much.

After signing the bottom of my message, *from the one who wants the best of both worlds,* I hit send before I can talk myself out of it.

The room spins around me when three eclipses trickle across the screen not even a second later, advising that Master Chains is in the process of typing a reply. With how quickly his message is delivered, it's evident he didn't read my entire message.

Master Chains: *Stay where you are, I'm coming to get you.*

17

Panic wells when I spot a flashing red light blinking in the middle of the laptop screen. I snap down the screen, mortified I'm being watched. My eyes swing around the space, seeking any identifiable markers Marcus could use to unearth my location. My breathing halts when reality dawns. He doesn't need to find recognizable pinpoints. He'd just have someone track Luke's IP address. *Shit. This won't end well.*

I push back from the desk with so much force, the large leather office chair I'm sitting in sails backward, only stopping when it crashes in the bathroom door Luke exited nearly an hour ago. Bopping down, I gather my heels I kicked off during our heartfelt chat. I hop across the room on one foot as I slip my feet into the tight confines of my shoes. Either my feet are swelling, or my shoes shrunk, as it takes more effort than it should to slip them on.

A frigid breeze prickles my arms with goosebumps when I swing open the glass door of the pool house and step onto the paved footpath. My eyes frantically search the area, seeking Lexi and Jackson amongst the scantily clad pool crowd that has swelled in size the past hour. I spot them huddled together under a cabana on my right. They are clothed—barely.

"We need to go," I notify Lexi, hurling Jackson's jeans I gathered off the AstroTurf during my travels into their smooching faces. "Marcus is on his way here."

Luke's high school parties were famous for the number of attendees he could cram into one space, tonight is no different. The entire residence is jam-packed with partygoers, I'd easily say the figure is in the mid to high hundreds, so the chances of someone recognizing Marcus is immense. We had enough trouble evading the dozen paparazzi at his grandmother's residence weeks ago, so I don't like his chances of escaping the clutches of drunken fans by the dozen.

Even with her dramatic moves dampened by her inebriated state, Lexi jumps into action. She thrusts her legs into her skin-tight mini skirt before wiggling it up her goosebump-riddled thighs. Although I'm overcome with panic, a dash of gratitude pumps into me when Jackson shelters Lexi's half-dressed frame with the large beach towel they were snuggled under. His stern gaze is enough to retain most of Lexi's modesty, but an additional finger point is required to warn some lurkers to look away.

After pulling her shirt over her head, Jackson commences getting dressed. His jeans are barely covering his drenching wet boxer shorts when Lexi curls her arm around his elbow and drags him toward the house. Music blares into our ears when we enter. It doesn't take me long to realize my initial guess about Luke's guest count was way off. There would be a minimum of a thousand people taking up every inch of his family home.

Our efforts to leave are hindered by a large group of people lining the front porch, waiting to enter. You'd swear we were at the latest nightclub hotspot by the eagerness spread across their face.

I've just dodged a lady losing her biscuits in a hedge when I hear someone calling my name. Spinning around, I spot Luke standing at the foot of his front porch. Just as he promised, he has a tub of ice cream in one hand and a bottle of tequila in the other.

"I'm sorry, I have to go," I shout, aiming to project my voice over the deafening roar of partygoers.

Luke holds the bottle of tequila to his ear, soundlessly acknowledging he can't hear me.

"I'll call you," I mouth as I mimic making a call with my thumb and pinkie against my ear.

Luke holds his finger in the air, requesting a minute. I nod before turning my panicked gaze to Lexi. Although my intuition is screaming blue murder at me, the kindness Luke bestowed on me tonight deserves more than a minute of my time, so at the very least I should bid him a proper farewell.

"I'll meet you guys in Jackson's truck," I advise Lexi, whose eyes are bouncing between me and Luke's rapidly approaching frame.

"Tread carefully, Cleo," Lexi warns, her tone surprisingly smooth for how dilated her eyes are. "You're only supposed to aim for additional game time, not be sidelined for the rest of your career."

Stealing my chance to reply, she dashes to Jackson's truck, giggling the entire trip. I wait for Jackson to have her safely latched in the passenger seat before swinging my eyes back to Luke. Our long strides have us meeting in the middle of the sidewalk in two heart-thrashing seconds.

His eyes drift over my face as he stops to stand in front of me. "Hey, I thought we had plans?" he says, waving the scrumptious goodies in the air.

My nose scrunches up as guilt burrows into the black crevice in my heart. "I'm sorry, I need to take a raincheck. Maybe next week?"

Luke nods, graciously accepting my guarantee I'm not once again going to become a stranger, even though we've been out of touch for so long.

His heart-cranking eyes dance between mine for several moments before he asks, "It's him, isn't it? That's why you're fleeing?"

"Yeah," I whisper, embarrassed I'm acting like a coward. "He knows I'm here."

Luke's brows scrunch for the quickest second before recognition dawns. "He tracked you?" When I slant my head, he adds, "You did say he was possessive. I didn't realize it extended this far, though." His last sentence is hampered by a dash of worry. "You're not running as you're afraid of him, are you, Cleo?" Now there is no doubting his concern. His words were drenched with worry.

I shake my head. "Not at all. Marcus would never hurt me. Not physically, anyway." I stiffen the instant I realize I said Marcus's real name.

Luke stares at me, unmoved by my disclosure. I shouldn't be surprised by his nonchalant reaction. I'm sure there are millions of men in the world named Marcus.

After promising I am in no way in fear for my safety, I say goodbye to Luke with a brief kiss on his cheek and a rub of his arm. "I'll call you. We'll do lunch next week," I assure him.

Luke smiles. "Great. Then I'll have the perfect opportunity to tell you about Rachel."

My heart swells to double its size when I see the twinkle of admiration in his eyes. If I still know Luke as well as I used to, it's the twinkle of love. "Rachel Dion? That has a nice ring to it." I run my hand down his forearm before walking back down the sidewalk. "Thanks for tonight. I can't wait to hear all about Rachel."

Luke rolls his eyes at the exaggerated waggle of my brows. When I reach the end of the sidewalk, I spin on my heels to face Jackson's truck. Luke waits for me to disappear behind a large bush before he returns to his house overrun by rowdy partygoers.

My quick strides to Jackson's truck slow when a sense of awareness washes over me. I curl my arms around my torso to ward off the icy chill running down my spine as my wide gaze floats around the space. Even though drunken guests have spilled out of the house and onto the front lawn, there is a weird, spooky feeling enveloping me. It reminds me of the times I've allowed silence to overwhelm me, but I'm surrounded by noise this time, and it's still spine-chillingly creepy.

The reason for my body's odd response comes to light when I return my eyes front and center. Even my poor vision can't encumber my recognition of the dark sports car parked two spots behind Jackson's truck. It isn't spotting Marcus's vehicle that has my heart slipping into my queasy stomach, it's detecting a flurry of blonde walking away from his passenger side door that makes me sick.

Keira is wearing a dress matching the one in the photos sent to me earlier tonight. The grin on her face is mocking and contrite, and her eyes are blazing with lust. Believing I'm stuck in a jealous trance, I tilt to the right, wanting to ensure I have correctly identified Marcus's car. I have. Not only does the license plate leave no doubt in my mind, the stern green eyes glaring at me from the driver's seat corroborate my findings.

Returning my body to its original position, I lock my eyes with Keira. Realizing I've spotted her advancing frame, her cheekbones incline before the most pig-headed smirk I've ever seen stretches across her face. She looks like a woman who not only baked the cake, but she also got to eat it too. Her arrogance is at an all-time high, sending my anger skyrocketing to a point I can no longer ignore.

Gritting my teeth, I spin on my heels and head it the opposite direction. I don't know where I'm going, but it's anywhere but here. The fact Marcus arrived to collect me with Keira in tow has my anger reaching fever pitch. I've never been so furious.

In the process of racing down the red cup-lined sidewalk, I spot Brodie approaching me from my left. His gaze is as stern as Marcus's. I change the direction of my course, hoping the throng of drunken guests bouncing on the lawn like they are at cheerleader tryouts will conceal me long enough to derive an appropriate action plan. I can barely breathe through the anger curled around my throat, much less think straight.

With my vision blurred with tears, I bump into more people than I skirt. I apologize on repeat as I continue for Luke's poolroom I can see on the horizon. My frantic steps stop when my forearms are suddenly clutched in a vice-like grip. My back molars grind together as I fight to be released from the person's firm grasp.

My wailing stops when a distinctly male voice says, "Hey, Cleo, I didn't realize you knew the Dions?"

Although the man's voice comes out with a slur of someone who has a few drinks under their belt, I still recognize who it is. *Dexter.*

"Damn, Cleo. Look at you. Always beautiful, no matter what the century." If I weren't so enraged, I could kiss him for his compliment. My ego is so battered I'd even accept a wolf-whistle from a bunch of dirty construction workers.

As Dexter bobs down to plant a greeting on my cheek, my eyes frantically dart between his hazy gaze and Brodie's rapidly approaching frame. I don't know why I do it. It could be a state of panic or a last-ditch effort to maim Marcus as painfully as his deceit gutted me, but before I can stop myself, I curl my shaking hands around Dexter's bristly jaw, tilt my head to the side to better align our lips, then seal my mouth over his.

The instant my lips brush Dexter's, I know I've made a stupid mistake, but there's no turning back when Dexter drops the bottle of beer in his hand so he can weave his fingers through my wild mane. He slides his tongue along my gaped lips before plunging it into my mouth. His hand holds me hostage as his tongue explores every inch of my mouth.

I don't return his kiss, but the patrons surrounding us can't tell. They call out and wolf-whistle, encouraging Dexter to deepen our kiss even more. His exploration of my mouth only comes to an end when an arm wraps around my waist, and I'm forcefully dragged back. Dexter's hold on my head is so firm, the roots of my hair pull from my scalp when Brodie yanks me away from him.

Before my body registers the pain rocketing through my scalp, my heart is hit with a much worse jab. Marcus arrives out of nowhere, his fist swinging as forcefully as his stern gaze pins me in place.

The strength of Marcus's unexpected hit is so strong, Dexter stumbles backward, landing on the ground with a sickening thud. Partygoers using the lawn as a dance space squeal while dashing out of the way of a red-faced Marcus. He fists the collar of Dexter's shirt before planting a second hard knock to his chin, sending his head flying to the side with a sickening amount of force.

"Marcus, stop!" I scream when his fist rears back to hit Dexter for the third time.

Thrusting out of Brodie's hold, I scramble closer to them on my hands and knees, only stopping when Dexter uses Marcus's distraction to lunge forward and head butt him in the nose. The fury lining Marcus's face matches the blood oozing out of his nose from Dexter's unexpected attack. The sound of cracking booms into my ears when the two well-built men slam onto the concrete sidewalk like a ton of bricks. They continue brawling like street fighters, going punch for punch, ignoring everyone's pleas for them to stop—mine included.

I stare at them, shunted into silence. Marcus's impressive fighting skills are expected since he is fueled by jealousy, but Dexter's have completely blindsided me. Most men would have been knocked out after Marcus's first swing, but Dexter holds his own, issuing several of his own blows to Marcus's unprotected body.

Hating that they could get injured because of my stupidity, I drift my eyes to Brodie and demand, "Stop them."

After taking a second to register my request, Brodie nudges his head to Jackson, who is standing on the sidelines of the large group watching the fight like they're at a private MMA match. Brodie drags Marcus off Dexter at the same time Jackson curls his arms around Dexter's wildly thrusting body. Once they have been pulled apart, Dexter and Marcus stare at each other with nothing but disgust radiating out of their narrowed gazes. It infuses the air with tension so thick I can taste it on the tip of my tongue.

With Marcus's composure more controlled than Dexter's, Brodie relinquishes him from his grip, but with Dexter continually fighting Jackson, Jackson remains holding on to him tightly, showcasing his impressive strength. Tears stream down my face as I stand muted, bouncing my eyes between the two furious men. Dexter's eye is already swelling so badly, it's nearly sealed shut, and Marcus has blood gushing out of his nose and mouth.

After running the back of his hand under his nose, Marcus drifts his eyes to me, exposing his recognizable face to the crowd standing behind me. It takes a matter of seconds for their chants for more to turn into murmured hums and excited whispers. The dozen or more camera phones capturing the fight double as the sizeable crowd swarms, hoping to get up close and personal with an idol.

Sensing he is moments away from being swamped by overzealous fans,

Brodie locks his eyes with Marcus and says, "We've got to go." The sound of police sirens wailing in the distance amplifies his suggestion.

Marcus continues glaring at me, his eyes unforgiving, his fists clenched. Guided by the pleas of my aching heart, I pace to stand in front of him, my legs wobbling with every step I take. When my hands lift to cradle his blemished cheeks, he pulls away from my embrace, adding a brand-new nick to my already faltering heart.

Dropping my hands to my side, I advise, "You need to go."

Marcus stares at me for mere seconds, but it feels like the moon circles the earth a thousand times. His eyes are dark and full of torment, matching the sludge sitting in my chest where my heart used to belong. A tear rolls down my cheek when he pivots on his heels and stalks back to his car. Although the crowd shows their excitement at seeing a famous rock star in the flesh, none approach him, his rueful glare compelling enough to dose their enthusiasm to ask for an autograph.

When Marcus disappears within the crowd, Jackson releases Dexter from his hold. Mumbling a string of gibberish under his breath, he fixes his crumpled clothing. Once his clothes are sitting right, he locks his eyes with me, spearing me in place. I've never seen him so angry.

"I'm sorry," I murmur, wishing I could offer him more than useless words.

Ignoring the snickered comments murmured by mainly female guests, I weave my way through the hundred or so party invitees camped on the front lawn. Unlike Marcus, the crowd doesn't part when they see me coming. I get elbowed and barged no matter which direction I take. When each jab into my ribs is made with a bitchy remark, I realize they're intentionally hitting me.

Noticing my struggle, Brodie's naturally engrained protective demeanor kicks into gear. He curls his arm around my shoulders before using his other hand to push people out of the way. The crowd grumbles when his rough approach knocks several cameras out of my face. Although I don't want him to damage equipment I can't afford to replace, I keep my mouth shut, grateful to get away from glares so heated they're burning me alive.

"Out of all the men in the world, you had to kiss that one," Brodie murmurs under his breath, nudging his head to Dexter, who is watching my escape from the sidelines. Brodie's question was quiet enough the people lurking around us didn't hear, but not soft enough for me to pretend I didn't. "Marcus is... I don't know, Cleo. Fuck."

"It was a stupid thing to do, but I wasn't exactly thinking straight when I noticed he arrived with *her*," I reply, my plummeting mood not enough to surrender the jealousy blackening my blood. "I might have kissed Dexter, but it was nothing compared to how Marcus deceived me."

Brodie stops walking when we reach the passenger door of Jackson's truck. I can feel the heat of Lexi's baffled gaze drilling into my temple, but I can't take my eyes off Brodie. He may not be speaking yet, but his forthright gaze is warning me to listen carefully to what he is about to tell me. It gives me this horrid feeling that my entire universe is about to be upended.

"Are you talking about Keira?" Brodie queries with scrunched brows. "The blonde watching your every move?"

When I crank my neck in the direction Brodie's eyes are peering, he pinches my chin and yanks my head back to him. "The first thing you need to learn about recon is don't let your target know you've spotted them." His eyes dance with mine before he glances back over my shoulder. "Is she wearing a satin dress just like the one in the photos you received earlier tonight?"

When I nod, Brodie's deep exhalation of air is unable to conceal the string of curse words that follow it. "Marcus didn't turn up with Keira. He spent the last three hours with me searching every street in Montclair for you. Keira was already here when we arrived. When she recognized his car, she came over to talk to him."

"What?" I ask, confident I've misheard him. "Marcus was at Chains—with Keira. That's why she was wearing his marks in the photos. They are together."

Brodie shakes his head. "Marcus was at Chains earlier tonight." My eyes rocket to his as horrid unease twists in my stomach. Spotting my flaming-with-anger face, he quickly adds, "With investors. He is selling Chains."

"What? Why would he do that?" I barely whisper. "Keira was wearing his marks, you saw them, Brodie, you know what they are."

My argumentative tone loses steam when Brodie shakes his head.

"That's what I was coming to tell you when I busted you sneaking out. The photos sent to you were photoshopped. Those marks on Keira's back weren't real. They were added recently. That photo was from a fundraising event over a year ago. A five-second Google search told me that."

I stare at Brodie, wishing he was lying while also incredibly grateful for his admission.

"For two people who work with words for a living, you're both shit at communicating," he chastises, his tone forthright.

"Then why did he pretend he was in Florida when he wasn't? That doesn't make any sense."

Brodie stares me straight in the eyes. "Once again, I'm not the man you should be asking. If you want answers, you have to go in there and get them." He jerks his chin to Marcus's car idling two spots up from where we are standing. "If you want to walk away and pretend today never happened, your chariot awaits." He opens the passenger seat of Jackson's truck.

I drift my eyes between Brodie, Lexi, and Marcus for numerous heart-clenching seconds. My first thoughts are to push off my feet, fall to my knees at Marcus's heel, and beg him for forgiveness. The only thing stopping my feet from moving was the way he rejected my touch earlier. Maybe I am too late? Perhaps the choice no longer belongs to me?

Seemingly reading my inner monologue, Brodie says, "He wouldn't still be sitting there if he weren't waiting for you, Cleo."

"How will you get home?" I query, mindful Marcus's car only has two seats.

"We'll take him," Lexi offers, the slur of her tone reminding me she is still intoxicated.

I peer at Brodie, gauging his reaction to Lexi's offer. He nods before requesting for Lexi to scoot.

I wait for Jackson to climb into the driver's seat before shifting on my feet to face Marcus. I fiddle with the hem of my dress before plucking at a ball of lint, doing anything to delay the inevitable. Once I've worked up the courage to survive his dismissal, I push off my feet and pad to his car.

His car remains stationary until I slide into the passenger seat, then all hell breaks loose.

18

My fingernails bend harshly when I secure a tight grip on the leather seat of Marcus's sports car. His speed is so furious, when we hit a small dip in the driveway, his tires lose traction on the asphalt, and we go airborne. He whizzes out of Luke's parents' property so fast, Jackson's truck no longer tails us within a matter of seconds. An oncoming motorist honks his horn, unappreciative of Marcus's frantic swerve between cars when he illegally overtakes a sedan driving the designated limit.

"Please slow down," I request, fearful his anger will lead to a wreck. "You're scaring me." My voice displays my sheer horror. I'm not worried about me being injured as much as Marcus getting hurt.

Marcus's grip on the steering wheel turns deadly before his pressure on the gas pedal eases. Although his speed is still well above the limits marked on the side of the road we're careening down, it's a hell of a lot slower than it was initially.

Because he is gripping the steering wheel so tightly, the unnatural coloring of his hand is even more prominent. "Are you hurt?" I scoot to the edge of my seat to inspect his hand more diligently.

When my fingertips brush the bruised skin angrily stretched over his swollen knuckles, he yanks his hand away as if he was burned by my touch. "Don't."

I stare at him, my stomach churning with both fear and regret. He keeps his gaze on the road, his jaw clenched, his eyes dark and lifeless. I want to express my sorrows nearly as much as I want to seek answers to my questions, but I do nothing. I just sit, gawking at him, willing him to speak, to say something. He says nothing. Not a thing. He just stares into the black abyss of a stormy night, unblinking and unspeaking.

I balk twenty minutes later when the sudden shrill of a cell phone rings through my ears. Marcus answers his call before the second ring.

"They increased the offer, but not to the amount you're requesting," says a thick, husky voice with a hint of maturity to it. "I'll continue squeezing them. They say they have reached their limit, but I know they have a few more millions up their sleeves."

When recognition dawns on what their negotiation is for, I close my eyes and count to ten, doing anything to ward off the tears threatening to spill at any moment. He is selling Chains just like Brodie said. *Oh my god, I'm a terrible person.*

My eyes pop back open when the gentleman on the phone says, "Mr. Everett, are you there?"

Air snags halfway down my throat when I comprehend the reason for Marcus's delay. He is watching me, his gaze intense and heated with an equal amount of anger and lust. The pain in his eyes triple when he drops them to my kiss-swollen lips. With his gaze white-hot, my tongue instinctively darts out to soothe the burn of his glare. A brutal pain stabs the middle of my chest when I taste the beer Dexter was drinking on my lips.

Ashamed, I twist my neck to the side and peer out the window, successfully hiding the handful of tears toppling from my eyes.

Even more tears glide down my cheeks when Marcus says, "Let them have it."

"That's not wise, Mr. Everett. They're still ten million away from your reserve. If you give me a few more hours, I can get them to the figure you're seeking—"

"I don't care about the money. Accept the terms," Marcus interrupts, his tone ensuring his caller is aware his decision is not negotiable.

I hear his caller gulp loudly before he mutters, "Okay, if you're sure?"

Ignoring his sneaky question, Marcus asks, "How long until handover can be finalized? I want this wrapped up as soon as possible."

His caller "ums" a few times as the noise of papers ruffling sounds down the line. "I've never sold a business of this manner before, so there isn't a specific time frame recommended. If the buyers are happy to move forward quickly, handover could be as early as Monday morning."

I peer at Marcus over my shoulder, my eyes expressing that I don't want him to do this. Chains is a part of who he is, if he sells it, he will lose a part of himself.

Not noticing the silent pleas of my eyes, Marcus's gaze remains locked on mine as he says, "Email me the contracts, I'll have them authorized and returned by 6 AM."

He disconnects his call, foiling his caller's ability to reply.

"Why would you sell Chains? It's a part of you, Marcus. It's also a part of Links," I blurt out before I can stop my words.

Marcus acts like he didn't hear a word I spoke, but I know he heard me, as the veins in his neck thrummed the instant I mentioned Links. Although I don't know the entire story behind Links, I know Marcus well enough to know how important it is to him. Chains' profits fund Links and many other worthy charity projects. Marcus's band is wealthy, but I doubt any rock group could amass the wealth Chains has the past three years. It's a sad but true notion—privacy is the most valuable commodity you own—only second to love.

"I'm sorry, Marcus. I'm sorry for hurting you. I'm sorry for everything I said—did—will do, but I don't want you to sell Chains. I'll do anything you want. I'll sign our contract. I'll publicly expose Global Tens' unwarranted investigation into Chains. I'll do anything you want if you'll reconsider your decision to sell Chains. I do *not* want you to sell Chains."

I angrily swipe at a tear rolling down my cheek when Marcus snarls, "That's no longer your decision to make." His eyes drift from the roadside to me before he viciously sneers, "Any of them."

His confession ends our conversation in an instant.

Marcus's speed slows while he fields numerous calls from his lawyer, allowing Jackson, Lexi and Brodie to catch up to us twenty minutes later. They pull into Marcus's property not long after us. Detaching his cell from Bluetooth, Marcus clambers out of the driver's seat and climbs the stairs of his residence without so much as a glance in my direction. His conversation with his lawyer continues without pause as Aubrey assists him out of his coat.

I remain sitting in his car, sickened with grief. I may not have acted like it tonight, but I am an adult who can accept the consequences of her actions, but the people who rely on Links aren't as lucky as me. Most of Links' patrons are children stuck in a debilitating world of domestic violence. They don't deserve for my stupidity to ruin their chance of a normal upbringing.

I run my hands over my cheeks, collecting my tears when a brief tap sounds on my driver's side door. The outside temperature is so cold, white air puffs out of Jackson, Lexi and Brodie's mouth as they stand by the passenger side door of Marcus's car waiting for me to exit.

"Do you want me to stay?" Lexi asks when I peel out of the car to stand next to her.

The worry in her eyes grows immensely when I shake my head. "No. I created this mess, now I must fix it." I lock my eyes with Jackson. "Can I ask a favor before you leave?"

When Jackson nods, I ask, "Can you check Marcus's hand? I think the fight may have done some damage to the ligaments in his hand. It could be nothing, but he has a world tour scheduled next month, so I'd rather be safe than sorry."

"Yeah, no worries. I have my bag in my truck," Jackson replies, nudging his head to his vehicle.

Lexi, Brodie, and I wait in the living room of Marcus's residence for nearly an hour before Jackson merges from Marcus's office. My chest grows heavy from the gaunt expression on his face. If he wants to become the world-renowned surgeon he is striving to be, he needs to alter his facial expression. If he confronts his patients' families to update them on their condition after surgery like he is approaching me now, I have no doubt they would fall to their knees and howl. He has the same look on his face the surgeon did when he advised us Tate didn't survive surgery.

"He damaged his hand?" I ask, even though the truth is projected by his direct gaze.

Jackson nods. "I'm fairly sure he has broken the capitate and scaphoid bones in his hand. He has also done extensive ligament damage. I won't know the full picture until he has a set of x-rays done in the morning."

"Will he need surgery?" Lexi's words are as low as I'm feeling.

Jackson shrugs. "I won't know until I get the x-rays, but at a guess, I'd say no."

"Can he play guitar?"

Jackson's remorseful eyes peer into mine before he shakes his head.

"Jesus Christ," I mumble under my breath. "Like this night could get any worse. His band will cancel their tour."

Although I'm murmuring to myself, Lexi says, "Don't panic until you know the actual results, Cleo. His hand might not be broken. It could just be swollen."

When she peers up at Jackson, wanting him to back up her theory, he unconvincingly nods, making my guilt ten times worse.

After numerous assurances that I'll be fine, I bid farewell to Lexi, Jackson, Brodie, and Aubrey. My nerves don't fully kick in until the taillights of Brodie's car disappear over the horizon. It isn't just the eerie silence playing havoc with my emotions, it's the chaos equally numbing my heart and brain.

My steps down the hallway separating Marcus's office from the central living space are shaky and drawn out. I am exhausted, but my sluggish actions have nothing to do with tiredness. Marcus's head lifts from his desk when he detects my presence. I prop my shoulder on the doorjamb of his office, waiting for him to give me permission to enter.

My heart rate quickens to a brisk canter when he stands from his office chair and paces toward me. Although he has his cell phone pressed up against his ear with his taped hand, he doesn't speak a word. I close my eyes and inhale deeply when his unique scent overtakes the stench of desecration leeching out of my pores. My eyes snap open when a spark of electricity surges through my top lip. Marcus's touch is only brief but strong enough to fill me with hope.

The pain in his eyes turns lethal when he stares at my lips while roughly scrubbing them with his thumb as if he is trying to remove Dexter from my mouth. He scrubs and scrubs until my mouth reaches a point of blistering from his feverish touch.

When he steps back, I peer up at him, issuing silent apology after silent apology for my idiocy. When his hand moves toward me, I pray it's to pull me into his body and comfort me until the moisture leaking from my eyes stops running. I've always said I'm saving my tears for my darkest day—this is my darkest day.

My hopes are dashed when Marcus says, "You need to shower. You still smell like him." He then shuts his office door with me standing on the other side.

I stand frozen, staring at the white frosted door, confident the male scent on me doesn't belong to Dexter. Not wanting to stir any more trouble, I keep my mouth shut and wait for his shadow to disappear from behind the door. When it does, so do I. I don't go far, only to the bathroom in his master suite. I know running would ease the sting of his rejection, but I won't run. I'll face the consequences of my actions with a maturity I did not hold tonight. I just need to work out what that appropriate outcome is.

After taking a shower hot enough to hide the tears staining my cheeks and incinerate Luke's cologne scent from my skin, I pad into the massive walk-in closet. Although my clothes are stacked in a neat pile on my right, I veer to the left, allowing my heart to guide my steps. I dress in one of Marcus's bland white undershirts and a pair of his cotton boxers. Since the waistband of his boxers are too loose for my female frame, I roll them up until the cuff is sitting high on my thigh.

My toes grip the plush woolen carpet as I slowly pace out of the room. Instinctively, my hand darts out to run over Marcus's suit jackets hung in sequence of their color. I've done the same thing every day the past weeks, because even though his clothes have been laundered, they still smell like him.

My brows furrow, leaving a substantial groove in the middle of my head when I notice a folded-up piece of paper sitting on top of one of many black polished dress shoes. Bending down, I gather the note. I swallow away the bile burning my throat as I slowly unfold the unknown document. My heart stops beating when I read the handwritten message scripted inside.

A relationship can weather any storm
if the couple continues standing under the one umbrella.

I miss you.

Marcus xx

I search the note for any indication of whom the message was written for, it's void of any clues. The sluggish beat of my heart doubles when I stand mute, staring at the group of freshly pressed navy blue suits hanging in the closet.

Recalling the message Brodie shared last week, my jaw gapes. "Tell Cleo if she is cold, she can borrow my jackets. Navy blue is my favorite color."

In a hurry, I check the pocket of the first navy blue jacket I stumble upon. I find a matching folded-up piece of paper in the breast pocket. This note leaves no doubt whom the messages belong to. They belong to me.

The name Cleo is of Greek origin, it means "Glory."
Glory can mean many things: a victorious triumph, an award.
But for me, it recalls magnificence and great beauty.
That's what you are to me.
Wait for me, Cleo.
The storm will soon be over.
Marcus xx

I find another four notes hidden in Marcus's suit jackets, each one placed in one of his beloved navy blue suits. They all follow a similar tune—that we are stronger than the storm striving to overcome us. God—what I would have given to find these messages sooner, then maybe I wouldn't have acted so recklessly. I thought I was losing him, little did I know he was fighting to save us.

I sit on the edge of his bed for several minutes, my stomach churning, my mind at a loss on how to move us past this. Marcus is sacrificing everything, yet I've given up nothing. I've always maintained that I want our relationship on an even playing field, shouldn't that refer to both sides of the team?

I inhale a sharp, quick breath when an idea pops into my brain. There has only ever been one thing Marcus has requested during our negotiations—he wants me. If he still desires that, I can give him that—wholly and without reservation.

I stand from the bed and race across the master suite. My steps are weightless since all the heaviness on my shoulders lifted the instant I made my decision. That's how much I want this—not even my brain can cite an objection. I gather a fancy treasure chest-like key out of the wooden box sitting on top of a stack of drawers before exiting the main suite.

I pace across the hall, reaching the door of Marcus's playroom within two heart-thrashing seconds. The boom of the lock sliding out of place bellows down the hall when I shove the key into the door and twist. I move through the playroom in a flurry, wanting to have my ducks lined up in a row before the noisy clank of the lock mechanism announces my intentions to Marcus.

Remembering the rules associated with this room, I remove my clothing, fold them into a neat stack, then place them on a woven laundry basket on my left. The coolness of the air vents prickles my skin with goosebumps as I head for the trunk of goodies Marcus and I spent a week working through before our separation.

My hand rattles when I pry open the singular drawer above the chest, but I push aside my shaky response, knowing it's more based on exhilaration than fear. I place a new D/s contract on top of the drawer before hunting for a pen. Failing to find one, I dash back into the main room and gather one from in there.

I freeze halfway into the playroom when I hear Marcus climbing the stairs. With his shoulders still weighed down by my betrayal, his steps are clunky, sending every one of them booming down the hall. I race for the blank contract, flipping it over until I find the most significant section I need to fill in—my signature.

After scrawling my name across the bottom of the document, I set it square in the middle of the drawer before adopting a submissive stance. I lower to my knees, bow my head and rest my hands on my bare thighs, palm side up in an offering position. With my hair still wet from my shower, it clings to my naked back. I am exposed and utterly raw with nothing but remorse blanketing me.

I level my breathing before pricking my ears so I can listen to every step Marcus takes. I count his steps. *One, two, three, four, five,* until they stop just outside the playroom door. The hairs on my nape stand to attention, announcing his arrival, but I keep my head down low, waiting for my Master to issue any punishment he sees fit.

I wait.

And wait.

And wait.

19

My muscles grow weary as I wait for Marcus to respond. Although the pain in my aching joints tells me I've been kneeling for some time, I know Marcus is still with me. Even strangled by remorse for my betrayal, my body's awareness of his closeness is still primitive. She knows her mate, and she knows him well enough to hear all the thoughts running through his mind right now. He is torn, stuck between wanting to punish me and wanting to walk away. His indecisiveness kills me more than believing Keira was his sub. I've laid myself bare to him, yet he is still considering walking away from me. That hurts—a lot.

I shut my eyes to ward off my tears at the exact moment Marcus steps into the room. With my head still bowed, I watch his feet slowly pace across the room behind a set of lowered lashes. He stops in front of the chest moments before the sound of paper sliding across wood trickles into my ears. I don't breathe—I can't, every muscle in my body is reserved for listening to any prompts Marcus may give when he realizes I've signed on to be his sub. A sigh. A murmur. I'd even take a grumbled curse word.

He does nothing. He remains perfectly silent.

I pull my chin in close to my chest when he spins on his heels to face me. Every stride he takes to lessen the bridge between us has my pulse quickening. His steps are slow, as if they are purposely torturing me. My hair falls from my face when he grips my chin and raises my head. He has my recently signed contract in his hand, his hold so firm it has a massive crinkle down the middle of it.

"This space may be known as a playroom, but you do not play games in here," Marcus mutters, his tone a stern warning that I'm no longer in the presence of Marcus. *Master Chains has arrived.*

"I understand, Master Chains." My quivering voice gives away the emotions pumping through me.

"Then why did you sign this?" He thrusts the contract to within an inch of my face.

I angle my body to the side so I can look him in the eyes. "Because I wanted to. I want to be yours. I want to be your sub. And I want you to punish me for the wrong I did."

"Disobedience does not get rewarded," he snarls, assuming I'm using my idiotic decision to kiss Dexter as a way of forcing him to dominate me.

That's not what I'm doing. I want him to punish me so we can move past this. If my research into the BDSM lifestyle is correct, once a punishment has been issued, the reason for the punishment is no longer valid. So once Marcus punishes me, he'll have no reason to be angry anymore. I'll also happily suffer through the pain my disobedience will bestow upon me, as I doubt it will be anything close to the ache gnawing at my chest.

"I was wrong, I deserved to be punished, and I'm willing to accept any punishment my Master sees fit." My words come out strong, hiding the turmoil brewing in my stomach from Marcus's rueful glare.

When he releases my chin from his firm grip, I return my head to its bowed position. My entire body quakes uncontrollably as I wait for him to make his decision. I don't know what I'll do if he walks away from me. This is the furthest point I can reach to display my devotion to him, I can't do any more than this.

I sneakily run my hand under my nose to gather the contents spilling from it when Marcus pivots on his heels and paces away from me. To begin with, I'm panicked, assuming he has decided he is done with me and my Garcia antics.

I suck in a grateful breath when I realize my assumptions are wrong. "Because this is the first time, you, the sub, will be punished purely for pain instead of pleasure, I will allow you to choose your punishment and the severity of it." His voice is monotone and flat, unlike anything I've ever heard.

I nod, incapable of speaking through the heartache of him referring to me as "the sub" instead of my real name. He has always called me Cleo in the playroom. He has never addressed me as if I am not a real person.

When he moves back to stand in front of me, I notice his feet are now bare, but his trousers remain in place, acknowledging that our session in the playroom is not about pleasure. If it were, he wouldn't be clothed.

"Look at me."

I swallow away my nerves before peering up at him. He has removed his suit jacket and tie, and his business shirt is undone at the front. Even with my mood suffocated by fearful guilt, my eyes can't help but drink in his smooth skin pulled tightly over the impressive ridges of his stomach and torso. His body is truly a masterpiece—one I'll do anything to make mine.

"First, you will choose what instrument you want to be punished with. Then you will choose the severity of your punishment. But be warned, if I do not believe the punishment equates to the level of your disobedience, our session will end, and your contract will be void. Do you understand?"

"Y-y-yes, Master Chains," I reply, idiotically stuttering like a fifth grader. It isn't panic about the pain I'm no doubt about to experience that has me stammering my words, it is the sheer darkness of Marcus's eyes. He looks like he's lost his soul. I hate that I've caused him so much pain his usually vibrant eyes are dull and lifeless.

"Choose your punishment, C—" He stops himself before saying my name.

Following the direction of his gaze, I take in his wall of floggers, whips, and canes. When I first entered his playroom in Chains, I was shocked by the apparatus I assumed would be as unpleasant as they looked. But the more weeks I spent with Marcus, the more I understood that in the right hands, even something as tortuous as a whip with pronged ends can be used to entice pleasure.

None of the toys Marcus has used on me ever solely caused pain. They walked the fine line between pleasure and pain, awarding me enough courage to try many of the floggers and whips in his collection. The only thing I haven't been brave enough to face is the canes. I don't know why, but they scare me. So much so, they are the perfect instrument to prove to Marcus I am taking this seriously. I understand the severity of my disobedience, and I am willing to face the consequences of my actions.

"I choose the cane, Master Chains," I advise. My voice comes out with so much confidence, anyone would assume I'm choosing a dessert.

For the quickest second, Marcus's stern mask slips, exposing an emotion his face hasn't held tonight—panic. As quickly as his mask slipped, it returns. He paces to the wall, his steps fast and with purpose. After gathering the cane sitting in the middle of a stack of three, he moves back to stand in front of me.

"Now the severity."

I peer down at my hands, trying to devise an appropriate number of strikes. I'm reasonably certain the cane will be painful, so the first number that pops into my head is deficient. But not wanting Marcus to null our contract, I continue racking my brain for a more appropriate number.

Once I have a number settled in my head, I lift my eyes back to Marcus. His face is stern, but his eyes show he is as bewildered as I am right now.

"I choose seven strikes, Master Chains," I advise, hoping the seven strikes will erase the seven seconds I kissed Dexter.

Seven may not seem like a high number, but when I realized seven seconds was all it took to unravel something magical, I'm hoping seven strikes with the cane will absolve my betrayal.

"Very well." Marcus nods. "Stand from your position and move to the spanking bench."

I bob my head, acknowledging I've heard him before doing as requested. The ache in my muscles grows with every step I take. It isn't just exhaustion causing their taut response, it's my body preparing for the next stage of our exchange.

Once I'm bent over the spanking bench where I received my first taste of anal play, Marcus moves to stand beside me. He leans the cane against the

Saint Andrew's cross so he can adjust my position. His freezing cold hands are a stark contradiction to the heat roaring through my body. Our bodies seem on opposing sides of the spectrum—much like the massive sentiment bouncing between us. The uninhibited lust that always surges between us is still in effect, but it's stultified by anger and regret.

Happy I am positioned correctly, Marcus takes the cane in his hand. "What's your safe word, sub?" His voice is barely a whisper when he reaches my horrid nickname.

I fight back tears before murmuring, "Pineapple."

"Repeat it."

"Pineapple," I choke out through a sob.

He waits for what feels like an eternity before reiterating, "If at any time you want me to stop, say your safe word. Do you understand?"

"Yes, Master Chains," I reply, nodding.

There is no chance of that happening. If I don't go through with the punishment I instigated, our contract will be void. I'll never let that happen. Nothing would be more painful than losing Marcus—not even seven strikes with a cane.

"I want you to count each strike. When we reach seven, this will be over, and tonight will never be mentioned again. Do you understand?"

"Yes, Master Chains," I repeat, thankful for his pledge that my punishment is in line with the severity of my deceit.

"This is going to hurt," Marcus warns under his breath as he raises the cane into the air, preparing to strike. "But it will be nothing compared to the pain I felt seeing you kiss another man."

I grit my teeth when the cane lands hard across my backside. Just as I had anticipated, the hit is intense, ten times worse than any I've been given in this playroom. Tears spring to my eyes in an instant as I cry out in pain. It's a sharp bite to my skin, one I'm certain I'll never relish.

I wait for the burn of his strike to release its grip on my throat before muttering, "One."

Marcus's second hit is just as brutal as the first—if not more severe. The tears looming in my eyes are so plentiful, they have no option but to slide down my cheeks and drip onto the floor near Marcus's bare feet.

I suck in mass gulps of air, fighting to breathe through the pain roaring inside my body. It does nothing to ease the agony spreading across my butt cheeks. This pain is the worst I've ever endured.

My body's big shakes echo in my tone when I stammer out, "Two."

I'd give anything for that number to be seven right now. I don't know if I'll survive another five strikes of that caliber. It burns so much, it feels like my skin is on fire. I wouldn't be surprised if my ass is bleeding by the time we reach seven strikes.

When Marcus fails to strike me with the cane for the third time, I angle my head to the side and peer at him from under the veil of my hair which has fallen in my eyes. From the expression on his face, anyone would swear it was him being hit by the cane. His beautiful eyes are tormented and full of pain, his jaw open and quivering.

When he spots me peering at him, he murmurs, "Say it." His voice is so soft I barely hear his request over the thumping of my heart against my ribcage.

"Say it," he repeats louder, ensuring I can't mistake his request.

More tears fall from my eyes when I shake my head. "No."

"Goddamn it, Cleo! Say your safe word!" he shouts, his loud words vibrating in my heart.

"No," I reply, shaking my head more fiercely. "I kissed him. I deserve to be punished. I hurt you. Punish me. Make me pay for my mistake, then we can move on from this."

The last half of my sentence is muffled by a whimper when Marcus strikes me for the third time. His hit isn't as firm as his first two, but with my backside still struggling with the agony of his first two strikes, it feels just as intense.

I try to ride the crest of pain, hoping to shift the fine line between pleasure and pain to a satisfying experience. It's a pointless effort. The endorphins pumping through my body from his strikes are curtailed with so much pain, I can't trick my brain into believing it's an enjoyable experience.

Swallowing down the bile scalding my throat, I murmur, "Three." I hiccup through a sob before whispering, "Four more to go."

Marcus stands next to me with his broken hand clenched so firmly, the tape Jackson wrapped around it is cracking and crumbling to the ground. His eyes frantically dart between my weeping face and my aching backside as he requests, "Say your safe word. You've reached your limit. Say it."

Hating the sheer agony in his tone, more tears roll down my cheeks. "No."

"Say it!" Marcus roars, scaring the living daylights out of me. "Stop being so goddamn fucking stubborn and say it!"

I balk at his rare use of a curse word before shaking my head. The pain shredding across my backside is brutal, but it's nothing compared to the pain his eyes held when he peered at me in the moments leading up to him hitting Dexter. I won't say my safe word, no matter how much he begs. Four more strikes and tonight will be forgotten.

I can live with that.

When I continue shaking my head, Marcus lifts the cane high into the air. I squeeze my eyes shut and grit my teeth, praying I'll be strong enough to endure another four strikes. I just want this over so we can move forward.

The bamboo sluicing the air breaks through my pulse raging in my ears. It's the sound of pure pain, equally evil and haunting. A loud crack booms around the room, it's the loudest one so far. I wait for pain to quickly follow it.

It never comes.

I crank my neck to the side, shocked and confused. I've only experienced subspace once before, and I'm certain this isn't it. I was barely lucid last time, this time I'm very much coherent.

I inhale a sharp breath when I spot the cane lying at Marcus's feet, snapped in two. It's as broken and mangled as Marcus's beautifully tormented eyes staring at me in shock. He shakes his head before spinning on his heels and exiting the room without so much as a backward glance in my direction.

It's only when I hear him murmur the word "pineapple" as he gallops down the stairs of his palatial residence do I realize the man striking me with the cane wasn't Master Chains—it was Marcus.

20

I wake up several hours later, curled in a ball in the middle of the four-poster bed in Marcus's playroom. This is where I crawled to and cried when the sound of Marcus's engine roaring to life echoed into the room within minutes of him fleeing. I had planned on taking a few moments to gather any dignity I had left, but I guess exhaustion eventually overwhelmed me.

I scoot down the bed, pretending I can't feel the sting of my naked backside when it glides along the smooth, satin sheets. A blanket I don't recall being there falls from my shoulders when I swing my legs over the bed and stand. My muscles squeal, unappreciative of taking the weight of my body. Unlike every other time I've walked out of this room, this time they aren't protesting from exhaustion, they are aching from dehydration. I swear every ounce of moisture in my body was shed last night—that's how much I cried. Losing something you love is never easy, whether it's by death or their choosing. Last night proved that.

Upon entering the main suite, I drift my eyes to Marcus's bed. I'm not surprised to notice it hasn't been slept in. The house has a dead-quiet feeling, like the entire world has vanished. I pace to the landline phone on my left and snag the cordless handset from its dock. While dialing a number I know by heart, I gather my suitcase from the foot of Marcus's bed and move into the walk-in closet.

"Hey, Cleo, you okay?" Lexi asks weakly, her weak voice exposing I've woken her up.

"Yeah, I'm fine," I lie, my tone low with guilt. "Umm ... can you come pick me up?"

Lexi sucks in a sharp breath. "Of course I can." Her voice cracks as if she too is struggling to hold in her tears. "I'll be right there, okay?" I hear the shuffling of sheets before the sound of bare feet padding on tiles booms into my ears.

When I fail to answer Lexi's question, she asks, "Do you want me to stay on the line with you until I get there?"

Heat blooms across my chest, warming some of the black sludge sitting in the crevice where my heart used to belong. "No, it's okay. I'm going to take a shower, then pack."

"Alright," Lexi replies, her tone low. "If you change your mind, you know how to reach me. I'll be there as soon as I can, Cleo."

"Thanks." I'd like to express more, but the substantial sentiment in Lexi's tone isn't allowing it.

My hand rattles when I place the phone back onto the deck. Although I just told Lexi I am going to shower, I veer to the left instead of the right. Although Marcus didn't touch me very much last night, I can still smell his unique scent on my skin, and I'm not willing to wash it away just yet.

Nearly an hour later, I descend Marcus's curved staircase. The clatter of my suitcase wheels thumping down each step announces my arrival to Aubrey. I balk, shocked by her presence. The house was so padded-cell quiet, I assumed I was alone. After placing my bag at the edge of the entranceway, I shift on my feet to face Aubrey.

"Is Marcus here?" My heart may be shattered, but if he is home, I refuse to be a coward who leaves without saying goodbye.

"No," Aubrey replies with a curt shake of her head. "He is attending a press conference to announce the cancellation of Rise Up's world tour."

"His hand is broken?"

Aubrey smiles a reserved grin before nodding. "He had x-rays earlier this morning. He won't be able to play an instrument for eight to ten weeks."

I scan the room, seeking any type of clock. With Lexi's drowsy reply and the tired headache thumping my skull, I assumed it was still early. I startle, stunned by how high the sun is hanging in the sky. Without seeing a clock, I can quickly tell it's nearly noon.

"Come and have something to eat before you leave," Aubrey says, gesturing her head to the kitchen. "I have a fresh pot of hot chocolate waiting for you on the stove top."

My stomach churns. Its squishy response has nothing to do with the quality of Aubrey's hot chocolate and everything to do with her acknowledgment that I am leaving. She's acting like she is aware of my departure as if someone updated her hours before my decision. My stomach flips even more violently. Clearly, Aubrey and Marcus's relationship is more stable than I first perceived.

Aubrey's steps into the kitchen stop midstride when the sound of a doorbell ringing fills the silence bristling between us. When she heads for the door, I quickly mutter, "I'll get it." *It's for me anyway.*

Aubrey peers at me, reading the rest of my statement my mouth failed to produce from my eyes. With a shy grin, she dips her chin before continuing her trek to the kitchen. Her speed is so unchecked, anyone would swear her backside was as burning as mine. I wait for her to enter the sweetly aromatic room before heading for the door. Although I'm stunned by Lexi's quick arrival, I am also grateful. Every minute I spend in Marcus's house adds to my grief.

"I'll pay any speeding tickets you received in your travels," I mumble, swinging open the large glass door.

My breath traps in my throat when the vibrant chocolate eyes of my sister I was expecting to see have been replaced with the eyes of the devil. Satan has returned with a vengeance, her snarl as vicious as the sharp cut of her bob hairstyle.

"I'll be sure to take you up on your offer... *when hell freezes over,*" Delilah retaliates before sauntering into Marcus's property without waiting for permission.

"Hell has already frozen over, Delilah, otherwise, why would you be here?"

Delilah accepts my snotty remark without protest as she removes her elaborate black fur coat. Considering how evil she is, I'd say that's the skin of a real animal—no fake fur for a woman as wicked as Delilah. She folds her coat over her rake-thin arm before moving to the edge of Marcus's entranceway. She inspects his property with the eagle eye of a person who is accustomed to wealth. From my research, I know she and money are close friends. That's probably because she leeched herself onto one of the wealthiest families in New York City. The Gottle's.

"You have five seconds to tell me what you're doing here, or I'll use the olive branch Mr. Gottle extended to me last week." My statement is a complete lie. Although Mr. Gottle assisted in my investigation of Keira last week, I've never personally spoken with him.

Delilah's utter stupidity rings true when she replies, "When you speak with Henry, be sure to tell him I said hello." She is clearly ludicrous. No one in a right frame of mind would taunt a mob boss.

She scrubs her hands together as if she is ridding them of dirt before locking her eyes with me. "Now that we have the idle chitchat out of the way, why don't we get down to business?"

My pulse quickens when she takes a step toward me. Because her strides are so long, she reaches me in one fluid march. "I knew it would only be a matter of time before you exposed Chains' identity. I was right. I just had to be patient."

She thrusts a folded-up newspaper into my chest. The paper has been so recently rolled through the printers, the ink is still sticky.

Air brutally sucks from my lungs when my eyes scan the headline on the front page.

Rise Up's Golden Boy Not So Golden

In a state of panic, my eyes frantically speedread the document. Every nightmare I've had the past three months comes true when detail after detail of Marcus's involvement in the BDSM community is presented before me. His ownership of Chains, its connection to Links—it even has reports from supposed ex-subs "brave enough to recount their horror of living with a sadist."

"None of this is true," I snarl, lifting my eyes to Delilah. "He is not a sadist or masochist. He doesn't instill pain for his own pleasure. He does it for his subs' pleasure. You're going to ruin a good man all because you're a vindictive two-faced bitch who steamrolls anyone who dares to have a different opinion."

Delilah shrugs off my admission, but the quickest blaze in her eyes exposes that some of my words cut deeper than she'd care to admit. "You should be privileged you were awarded the first copy. I thought it was the least I could do since you were the source of the story."

Horrid unease scorches my veins when her finger points to the byline under the scathing headline. Although I've dreamed of having my name printed on the front page of the New York Daily Express, I don't want to achieve it like this.

"You can't run this story, Delilah," I plead, my words the sincerest I've ever used with her. "I'm imploring for you to just once listen to the little voice inside of you telling you this is wrong. You know this is wrong. Please don't do this."

"It's too late," Delilah advises, spinning on her heels and heading for the door. "The special online edition is scheduled to be released at noon. The print edition will follow an hour later."

The mirrored frame hanging in the entranceway rattles furiously when she slams the front door of Marcus's property with force. I stand frozen, muted and confused. My paralyzed stance doesn't linger for long, only long enough for me to see it's three minutes past eleven. I might not be able to stop the story from going to print, but I can warn Marcus of its arrival, then maybe his media team will have a chance of mitigating the shit storm that's sure to follow.

I charge into the kitchen, startling Aubrey, who is standing near the stovetop. The brush of her hand across her wet cheeks is quick, but not fast enough for me to miss it. Although concerned about what has caused her to cry, my utmost priority must remain Marcus.

Snatching the phone from the cradle, I dial Marcus's cell phone number. It rings and rings and rings until his voicemail eventually picks up.

"I know I'm the last person you want to speak to right now, but please call me. It's urgent."

I hang up and redial his number.

When my calls reach his voicemail another three times, I place the telephone back on the cradle before my eyes stray to Aubrey. "Do you have a car?"

She barely nods before I trudge around the kitchen and curl my arm around her shuddering shoulders. "Do you know where Marcus's press conference is being held?"

Aubrey once again nods.

"Good, show me where it is."

While driving into the city, I borrow Aubrey's cell phone to update Lexi of my change in location. She warns me against approaching Marcus in public, but I shove aside her caution, mindful that things can't get any worse than they already are. I set up a google alert on Aubrey's phone for any articles mentioning Marcus's name with the inclusion of BDSM in the search field before calling his number on repeat.

Thankfully, no pings are received during my travels.

With me expressing the absolute urgency of my plea, Audrey's car circles the block of the hotel Marcus's press conference is being held at within a record-breaking forty-five minutes.

"Pull over anywhere, and I'll walk the rest of the way," I demand when traffic becomes so congested near the hotel, pedestrians are moving at a faster speed than vehicles.

"Thank you," I say to Aubrey when she maneuvers her car to the furthest lane.

I place a quick peck on her cheek before snagging her cell and my purse from the middle console.

"I'll get it from you later," Aubrey advises when my panicked eyes lock on her cell clutched in my hand. "Just go."

I nod before closing the door. The love I have for my sister city is tested when I push and barge my way through the mass of people mingling on the sidewalks. New York streets are always crammed with people, but with having one of the most prolific bands of all time gathered in one place, the swell of the crowd has doubled.

"Excuse me. Pardon me. Sorry," I continue to plead as I shove my way through the clog of paparazzi standing by the exit of the hotel.

The scene inside the hotel is nearly as frantic. Gushing guests, squealing fans, and over a dozen security officers line the foyer of the elegant hotel. My eyes scan the room, unsure of what direction to take. When I spot a man I've met before, I head for him.

"Hey, Hawke. I'm not sure if you remember me—"

"Cleo, right?" he greets as his face stretches into a welcome smile.

"Yeah. That's right," I reply, smiling. "I need to speak with Marcus. I've been calling his cell nonstop, but he isn't answering."

"That's not surprising, Emily makes the guys hand in their phones before every press event or meet and greet. She wants them interacting with real-life people, not an electronic device."

He places his hand on the curve of my back before guiding me to conference room number three. Upon opening the door, a massive brute of a man with a shaved head and an angry snarl drops his gaze to me.

"This is Cleo. Marcus's girlfriend," Hawke quietly advises the snarling unnamed man.

In an instant, the sheer terror radiating out of him in invisible waves disappears. He smiles, softening the harsh lines on his face before gesturing for me to enter.

"Thank you," I whisper to Hawke before merging deeper into the room.

He nods before spinning on his heels and returning to his original position.

Since the press conference is well underway, I move to the far edge of the room, then skedaddle to the row of tables Marcus and his bandmates are sitting behind. Spotting my sneaky approach, Kylie and Jenni wave a greeting before gesturing to the empty seat next to them. I shake my head before continuing my mission.

The confidence Marcus generally exudes by the bucket load isn't present today. His chin is tucked in close to his chest, and his uninjured hand is cradling his bandage-covered one. He doesn't even lift his eyes when a reporter asks for details on how his hand was injured. He leaves Emily the task of responding, citing it was the result of an "error in judgment."

The only time his eyes lift from his hands is when I reach the edge of the table he is sitting at. His narrowed gaze doesn't swing around the room. They lock straight onto me, proving he can sense my presence as easily as I detect his. I chew on the inside of my cheek when I see the pure devastation radiating out of his beautiful green irises. They are as cold and blank as they were in his playroom last night.

Before I get the opportunity to request to speak with him, the loud ding of a cellphone shrills from my pocket. I suck in a deep breath, conscious it could be my last chance to breathe before digging Aubrey's cell out of my pocket. The prompts of my body are proven accurate when the screen displays 138 alerts on my search of Marcus Everett and the BDSM lifestyle.

Just as quickly as my eyes rocket to Marcus's, the buzz of numerous cell phones sounds through the room. It's a tidal wave of horror, swelling in size and intensity with every beep. The quiet snickers are the first to arrive, closely followed by the hammering of paparazzi questions. Marcus leaps from his chair and lands in front of me as if magic.

He snatches Aubrey's cell phone from my hand before dropping his eyes to the screen. The more he scrolls through the dozens of stories on his hidden BDSM lifestyle, the firmer his jawline becomes.

His eyes missile to mine when he reads the name of the lead reporter of the investigation.

"I didn't do this. You know I didn't do this," I stammer out, my words choked by devastation.

"You're an investigative reporter?" Marcus questions, the roar of his words enough to silence everyone in the conference room.

"Yes." The brief nod of my head sends tears toppling down my cheeks. "But you know this. I told you I work for Global Ten Media." Unlike Marcus, I keep my voice low, striving to lose the attentive ear of the hundreds of reporters surrounding us.

"You told me you worked for Global Ten. You never mentioned you were an investigative reporter! You write obituaries for a living for fuck's sake! I've never seen your name in print," Marcus shouts, his voice so loud, I hear his screamed statement twice since it bounces off the stark walls before echoing back into my ears.

I stare at him, shocked and confused. I don't understand what he is saying.

I never explicitly said I was an investigative journalist, but that was because I didn't need to. He knew about the Chains investigation. He knew I couldn't discuss the particulars of the case for fear of being prosecuted, so I don't understand why he is acting as if he doesn't know. He knows I'm an investigative journalist. *Doesn't he?*

"How many more coals do you want to drag me over, Cleo?" Marcus's words are as broken as his slit gaze. "First you cheat on me, and now this? Is nothing sacred to you?"

The crowd sighs in sync, just as stunned by Marcus's revelation as I am.

"I didn't cheat. Kissing isn't cheating," I deny, hating that I'm being forced to defend myself in front of hundreds of people watching my every move, much less doing it with the most pitiful excuse I've ever used.

Marcus takes one step toward me. He stands so close, the furious heat of his body dries the wetness on my cheeks. "Yes, it is," he snarls viciously.

The hotness of his breath bounces off my lips when he murmurs, "You should have packed an umbrella, as you never know when the next storm is about to brew."

As his eyes dance between mine, his hand slides into the pocket of his trousers. Two seconds later, he presents a folded-up piece of paper. My stomach flips when I realize what he is holding. It's the D/s contract I signed last night—the one thing still tethering us together.

I recoil when Marcus rips the contract in half, not stopping his onslaught until each section crumbles to the floor like rubbish. Once our agreement has been destroyed beyond recognition, Marcus sneers, "We're done. I never want to see you again. Do you understand?"

Incapable of speaking for fear of sobbing, I nod.

"Good. Goodbye, Cleo," he bids me farewell, his tone flat and without hesitation.

With that, he spins on his heels and exits the conference room via a back entrance. His stunned bandmates soon follow him, leaving me defenseless against a bunch of ravenous journalists, desperate to unearth any tidbit of information on his recently exposed secret.

21

The paparazzi go manic. I'm bombarded within seconds. Cameras and microphones are shoved in my face as an endless stream of questions pummel into me. I raise my hand to shelter my eyes from the blinding camera lights as I endeavor to locate the door I entered mere minutes ago. The swarm of the paparazzi is so strong, for every step I take forward, I'm knocked back three paces. My full name, address, and date of birth are shouted between journalists eager to share their knowledge with the hope it will be returned full-circle when I pick which media company I'll award an exclusive to. That will never happen. Even stunned by what just occurred, I'll never share my story.

My endeavors to reach the exit are impaired when my hips are suddenly grabbed by a firm hold. The terror thickening my veins dulls to a slight boil when I recognize the smell of the man clutching me.

"Keep your head down," Brodie instructs, altering the direction of my course so we head toward the set of doors Marcus and his bandmates entered earlier.

I step on numerous black dress shoes and expensive high heels as Brodie guides me out of the hair-raising situation I find myself in. Although the shouted questions continue when we enter a thin corridor of the hotel, the brutal elbows and shoves end.

As I gulp in deep breaths to quell the anxiety making me a clammy mess, Brodie pushes his finger to his ear and says, "Yeah, I've got her."

"Marcus?"

Brodie begrudgingly shakes his head. "It's Lexi. She's waiting for you outside."

I've barely recovered from my first brutal blow when I'm hit with another. Marcus is standing at the end of the corridor with his blazing-with-anger eyes firmly locked on me. When I take a step toward him, the curt shake of his head pins me in place, freezing me with both fear and remorse.

His eyes dance between Brodie and me for several heart-thrashing seconds before he angrily mutters, "Brodie, let's go."

Brodie's lips twitch, preparing to issue a reply, but his words stay entombed in his throat when Marcus shouts, "Now."

Brodie lowers his eyes to me, the remorse in them uncontainable. "Lexi is just outside those doors."

I swing my head in the direction he is facing. It looks like an emergency fire exit you'd expect celebrities to use when avoiding the paparazzi. When I return my moisture-filled gaze to Brodie, the tears ramp up a gear. Marcus is nowhere to be seen.

"I'm really sorry about all of this, Cleo," Brodie murmurs before he pushes off his feet and heads in the direction Marcus was standing.

Nursing my bruised ego the best I can, I make my way to the emergency exit door. I've barely merged onto the cracked sidewalk when the smell of rotten tomatoes streams through my nose. Lifting my eyes, I catch sight of a flurry of red charging toward me.

I dodge the soaring tomato, forcing it to land on my shoulder instead of my chest where it was aimed.

"Skank. Whore. Cheater." Numerous teenage girls scream from the other side of the alley as they continue pegging rotten food products at me. "You don't deserve a man like Marcus Everett. You're nothing but trash."

They throw hurtful words as if they are grenades as I race down the street to my baby poo Buick parked halfway down the alley. Hearing their taunts, Lexi emerges from our car, her face as red as the tomatoes being thrown at my head. When one lands on her stomach, she bends down and picks it up before pegging it back at the jeering teens.

"You better run," Lexi yells when her thrown tomato smacks one of my tormentors right across the face.

While she retaliates to their childish taunts with equal maturity, I slide into the passenger seat of my car and use my shirt to clear smears of egg yolk from my hair.

I've scarcely removed the eggshells from my hair when Lexi returns. She grumbles angrily under her breath as she snags her seatbelt and yanks it across her chest. Because she is tugging on the latch so hard, the seatbelt mechanism locks into place, foiling her endeavors.

"Goddamn motherfucker shit-box cock-sucking piece of crap!" Lexi yells, saying every curse word she was forced to hold back this week.

I don't know how I muster the strength, but a hearty giggle spills from my lips before I can stop it. It's another one of those cry or laugh moments. Considering I cried so much last night that I'm fresh out of tears, I must laugh.

Upon hearing my laughter, Lexi cranks her neck and peers at me. She stares at me like I am insane, which only makes me laugh even more. My laughter must be contagious, as Lexi soon follows suit. We laugh so much our car vibrates as if her rusted engine has been cranked. We laugh until our bellies ache, and our eyes fill with happy tears, then we laugh some more.

When my laughter loosens up my devastation, I slump into my seat. The deep sigh I release ruffles a strand of hair that has fallen in my face. "I royally fucked up," I murmur, more to myself than Lexi.

"No." The shake of her head amplifies her short reply. "We fucked up."

I peer at her, confused by her statement. *What does she have to do with any of this?* She might have encouraged me to sneak out last night, but I'm an adult who could have said no at any stage. She also didn't kiss Dexter, the blame for that idiocy solely belongs to me. As much as this kills me to admit, Delilah was right. She knew my insecurities would get the best of me. By doing that, I not only exposed Marcus's involvement in the BDSM community, I also sacrificed our relationship.

Not reading the questions my eyes are relaying, Lexi picks a chunk of eggshell from my hair, dumps it into the cracked vinyl console between us, then fires up the ignition. When the radio begins broadcasting breaking news, she leans over and switches it off. Hating the silence as much as I do, she commences whistling.

When she hears my disgruntled moan, she murmurs, "It's either face the music or listen to my whistling. Pick your team, Cleo?"

She whistles the entire hour journey home.

When Lexi pulls our rusted old Buick into the driveway of our family home, my eyes go crazy, frantically searching the hands of the dozen or so teens camped out on the sidewalk of our house. Thankfully, they are void of any molded fruit and vegetables.

"I know gossip on social media spreads like wildfire, but how did they discover my involvement so quickly?" I query, stunned.

Lexi unlatches her seatbelt before gathering my hands in hers. "The press conference was recorded live."

My pupils dilate. "They broadcasted my fight with Marcus." Although I appear to be asking a question, I'm not. I'm summarizing. "That's why they called me a whore. They heard what he said to me?"

Lexi's brows furrow before she nods. "They've also seen the video of Chains and Dexter fighting last night. They know the real reason his hand is broken," she discloses, her voice low with worry about how I am going to take her news.

"I'll be eaten alive. You know how crazy the Rise Up fans are," I mumble under my breath.

Lexi nods in agreement. "I also know how quickly things like this blow over. You've just got to keep your head down for a few days and weather out the storm."

"What's with all the storm metaphors lately?"

Lexi shrugs. "You've got to ride out a storm to see the rainbow at the end?"

Stealing my chance to reply, she cranks open her driver's side door and exits our Buick. Mercifully, the angrily snarls of Montclair locals aren't as vociferous as those in New York City. Things dampened down considerably celebrity-wise after Justin Bieber moved into town a few years ago. Hopefully, the fanatic teen fans continue camping out on his doorstep. It's the smart thing to do considering the chances of Marcus arriving at my property are slim to none.

As per Lexi's request, I spend the remainder of my week hiding away from the world. With her final exams ending Tuesday afternoon, we've spent a majority of our time watching Netflix and splurging on the occasional Passionflix movie. I haven't heard from Marcus at all the past six days. Honestly, I didn't think I would. He made it extremely clear during the press conference that he doesn't want to see me. And if that wasn't evident enough, the arrival of my packed suitcase via a courier company within the hour of me arriving home Saturday afternoon was a sure-fire indication.

Unsurprisingly, the news of Marcus's involvement in the BDSM community hasn't dampened the band's appeal in the slightest. If anything, it has made their fans more rampant. The press is going crazy, vying for exclusive interviews with anyone in the industry associated with Marcus, and the band's popularity has soared to a level no one expected. My social media accounts were always filled with Tweets and Facebook posts about teens idolizing the members of Rise Up, now, it's not just teen girls posting those declarations. If I had a dollar for every time I read a post from a grown woman begging for Master Chains to spank her, I'd be a very wealthy lady.

The media and the public's reaction to Marcus's scandal proves I'll never understand this bizarre thing we call life. His secret may be exposed, but public awareness of the BDSM lifestyle has grown tenfold. Unlike Delilah, most reports have conveyed both sides of the coin. It truly is a win-win for Marcus. The band's albums from years ago are once again at the top of the charts, and the dialog about individuals having the right to choose their own sexual prerogatives has been established. I'd give anything to go back and alter the decision I made last Friday, but since I can't, I'll take comfort in the fact the heartache I've endured the past six days has made it easier for women who are battling between their desires to be both feminist and submissive. Maybe now they'll realize they can have both.

I shut the screen of Lexi's laptop, hiding my umpteenth rejection letter for the week. Before Marcus's scandal broke, I was struggling to keep up with the number of stories my freelance journalism career had offered me. Now I am getting rejection letter after rejection letter. Although every rejection arrives with a letter of offer for me to do an exclusive interview about my relationship with Marcus, none have accepted the stories I penned in the hope of moving my name away from Marcus's.

"Another rejection?" Lexi paces into the living room.

I curl my feet under my bottom while nodding. Accepting the mug of hot chocolate she is holding out for me, I gently blow on the steamy goodness. "They increased their offer on an exclusive, though. If the rates keep climbing like they have the past six days, I'll reach seven figures soon."

Lexi timidly shakes her head. "If only you were interested in Chains solely for his money."

"Would you be tempted?" I ask Lexi, curious of her reply.

She considers my question while sipping on a glass of tea. "I don't know. Maybe?" She places her tea on the coffee table before swiveling her torso to face me. "If it were Chains, yes, I'd sell his story."

I peer at her, shocked by her admission. She's never been money-hungry before.

"But if it were Jackson, no, I wouldn't," she explains to my bewildered expression. "That's why you don't have to defend your decision not to make a profit out of this, Cleo. I may not have as many brains as you, but I get why you're remaining quiet. You loved him, so you'll protect him no matter what."

"I love him," I correct before I can stop my words.

Moisture looms in my eyes as my hand darts up to the pendant wrapped around my neck. Although I could use the chain's light weight as a reason for my constant checking, I know that isn't the case. Just like Cartier, I've resorted to seeking courage from a piece of jewelry instead of the man who gave it to me.

My stomach churns as I am plagued by another severe bout of nausea. The past six days have followed along a similar tune. I pretend the world doesn't exist until something shoves me back into reality. When the pain of my existence becomes too much for me to bear, the contents of my stomach reenter the world in the ghastliest way.

"Not again," Lexi mutters when I springboard from the sofa and race into the bathroom.

I've barely skidded to my knees in front of the toilet when the sweet brown goodness I enjoyed earlier resurfaces. Just like every time I've vomited the past week, its return isn't as pleasant as its consumption.

Once my stomach is void of any nutrients, I stand from my kneeled position, then move to the sink to wash my hands. While splashing fresh water on my face, I catch sight of Lexi's worried expression. The concern on her face stretches to mine when I notice she has my tattered old coat in her hand and a set of keys. "Are you going somewhere?"

"No. We are."

When I peer at her, blinking and confused, she paces into the bathroom to assist me into my coat. "A broken heart doesn't make you nauseated," Lexi informs me while pulling my hair out of the neckline of my coat. "But babies do."

"What? Don't be ridiculous. I'm not *pregnant*." I murmur my last word, fearful speaking it out loud will cause it to come true.

"Then you'll have no reason to deny my request for you to pee on a stick," Lexi fires back, her tone dead serious.

A trickle of doubt entered my mind earlier this week when I recalled my period didn't arrive on my return from Ravenshoe. But with Richard's death and the stress of the investigation, I pushed it aside as an effect of the strenuous strain placed on my body. The week following our return was a roller-coaster ride of emotions that plagued both my mind and my body. I never figured my soaring moods had anything to do with being pregnant until the bouts of vomiting arrived.

When I fail to shadow Lexi out of the bathroom, she cranks her neck back to peer at me. Her eyes convey that her suggestion of purchasing a pregnancy test isn't up for negotiation.

"We shouldn't spend our money willy-nilly," I mumble, using any excuse I can not to face the truth. "After my disclosure on national television that I breached my contract with Global Ten, I can't be guaranteed Mr. Carson will pay the remainder of my salary as we negotiated. He might hold over that monetary amount until his legal team advises their next move."

"It's six bucks, Cleo. Stop being so cheap," Lexi replies, grumbling.

"It's not six dollars," I continue to argue, my Garcia stubbornness not allowing me to back down without a fight.

"It's when you know the pharmacist, and he gives you a *we used to fuck* discount."

My eyes bulge as the rest of my argument lodges in my throat. Using my frozen stature to her advantage, Lexi seizes my wrist and yanks me out of the bathroom.

After wading our way through a contingent of media still hounding me for an exclusive and a handful of teens still hoping to spot Marcus, we arrive at the drugstore Luke owns twenty minutes later. Just locating Luke's truck in the parking lot has my nerves hitting an all-time high.

"I can't do this, Lexi. I can't face Luke, and I also don't want to confront the truth. If I'm pregnant, nothing will change. I can't tell Marcus—"

"Why not?" Lexi interrupts, her tone high in shock.

"The media would tear me apart—even more than they already are. They will have a field day saying I trapped Marcus and am after his money. That gauntlet we just ran, it will double in size for every month of my pregnancy, then it would turn crazily stupid when the baby was born. I can't put a baby through that any more than I could do that to you or Marcus. This is my life, Lexi. It's not a circus."

Lexi flicks a rogue tear from my cheek before locking her eyes with mine. "What if I get it? I'll tell Luke it's for me."

"Then what?" I ask, loathing how heavily I'm relying on others to dig me out of the bottomless pit I'm in.

"Then we'll put one foot in front of the other until we work out which path you want to take." Her glistening eyes bounce between mine as she murmurs, "You don't need a test, do you? You already know."

I nod. "Life likes to display just how fucking cruel it can be, so why not throw another curveball into the mix?"

22

The pregnancy tests go precisely how I predicted. But instead of being baffled with color charts and a box of instructions, Luke gave Lexi top of the line pregnancy tests—three of them. All I had to do was pee and wait, then I discovered I'm six to eight weeks pregnant. *My fucking god.*

I place the third positive test back on the cracked vanity before resuming my frozen stance on the toilet. Lexi's nerves are so evident, Jackson joins our pity party in the bathroom, making the cramped space even more so. When his eyes lower to the positive tests, my first thought is the hide them before he reads the results, but I'm so lost right now, I'll happily accept advice from anyone.

"Are these tests yours?" Jackson peers at me.

Although relief crosses his face when I nod, I swear a small dash of disappointment also filters through his eyes.

"The good news is you're only six to eight weeks, so you've got plenty of time to decide what you want to do," Jackson says, using his surgeon voice I've only heard a handful of times.

A whizz of air parts his mouth in a rough grunt when Lexi backhands him in the stomach.

"What?" he asks when she glares at him.

"Cleo is not having an... *abortion*." She whispers her last word as if it's a curse word.

"I wasn't suggesting one. I meant for telling Marcus. With miscarriage statistics so high, doctors recommend you wait a minimum of twelve weeks before announcing a pregnancy. This will give you a few weeks to clear the fog from your head."

"I need a lot more than a few weeks," I grumble under my breath.

Jackson smirks, proving he heard my private mumble. "Do you have a preferred obstetrician you'd like to see?"

I roll my eyes before shaking my head. "I haven't been to the doctor's since the mandatory health check Global Ten employees get."

"And she wonders how she ends up pregnant," Lexi snickers.

She connects her eyes with mine, the angry cloud in them growing with every second that ticks by. "Did Marcus know you weren't on the pill?"

I shrug. "I don't know. He never asked, and I honestly forgot to mention it." When the storm in Lexi's eyes triples, I add, "I know, I know. Very stupid. But I'll be okay. From the way his D/s contracts were worded, it's clear his previous subs had a full medical exam before any contact, so I don't have to worry about diseases or anything."

"No, just one that requires food, shelter, and clothes for at least the first twenty-one years of its life," Lexi retorts.

"Alright, Lex, I think Cleo's got enough on her plate without us adding to it." Jackson's assurance lessens the severity of Lexi's glare, but it doesn't fully douse it. "There is a local obstetrician in Montclair, but I'd rather refer you to a specialist in Queens." He hands me a tattered card from his wallet. "I've worked with her a few times, she comes highly recommended."

The rueful glare Lexi is directing at me reverts to Jackson. Her gaze is white-hot, adding to the horrid mugginess of so many people in the small space.

"She is also fifty-eight," Jackson announces, understanding the meaning of Lexi's suddenly cold demeanor. "If I didn't love your jealousy, Lex, I'd be pissed about your mistrust."

"I'm not the one who slept with half the interns during residency," Lexi fires back, shadowing Jackson out of the bathroom. "How am I to know if she is one on a long list of many?"

"Lexi, if we start this conversation, I'll mention my run-in with not one, but two of your ex-boyfriends at Luke's birthday party last week."

Their jealous bickering continues until they enter Lexi's bedroom. Their argument doesn't last long. I've barely hidden the pregnancy tests in the top drawer of my desk when the sound of shouted words is replaced with needy moans.

Not wanting another dash to the toilet, I snag my old cell phone off my desk and trudge to my bed. My phone is over four years old, but it's in perfect working order. Its extensive playlist has been a godsend the past six days. Although seeing Lexi deliriously happy with Jackson has made my heartache stronger, I'm also glad my foolish decision hasn't impacted them too significantly.

Another benefit of my outdated iPhone is its iCloud capabilities. All the sneaky photos of Marcus I took during our brief fling are stored on my phone. Although seeing what I've lost adds to the endless pit in my chest, I've perused our photos numerous times the past six days. I always start my trip down memory lane from the beginning of our relationship—at the snaps I took of Marcus with his bandmates the very first night we met. Tonight is no different.

The slideshow of photos goes from our first night together until the morning Marcus left for his supposed trip to Ravenshoe. They display that our time together was brief, but jam-packed with memories.

I still haven't worked out the reason for Marcus's deception on his location. The only person who can answer my questions is the same man who is avoiding me like I have the plague. Even Lexi has been unsuccessful in reaching him. If his face weren't splashed across every news program and article in the world, I'd assume he vanished.

When the montage of our brief relationship ends on a sneaky video I took of Marcus singing in his recording booth, I scroll back to the only photo I have of us together. It's a corny selfie I made him take in the minutes leading up to our dinner on the patio being disrupted by a sprinkling of rain, but it's a perfect representation of our relationship—fire-sparking and intense.

As I stare at our contrasting skin tones and eye coloring, I daydream about what features our baby could get from each of us. I wonder if he or she will have Marcus's alluring eyes—part of me hopes they will, whereas the other half wants the brown-eyed Garcia gene to reign supreme—then I can keep a part of my family history continuing even years after I'm gone.

When the creak of my bedroom door breaks through my pulse shrilling in my ears, I scrub away a rogue tear the curve of my lips is caressing. The pain crippling me dampens when Lexi slips into the bed and curls her body around mine, like she has done the past six days. I don't know if my quiet sobs aren't as silent as I aimed for, or if she just knows me well enough to know when I'm having a low, but she arrives at precisely the right time every single night.

"Shh. I've got you, Cleo," she guarantees when the shivers racking my body become too great to ignore.

The following morning, Lexi prances into the kitchen, her steps as upbeat as my mood. "Is that waffles I'm smelling?" she asks as she paces to the fridge to snag one of the many vitamin waters Jackson stacked in the fridge last night.

"Uh huh," I reply, accepting the bottle of vitamin water from her hand. "Jackson knows these are a waste of money, right?"

Lexi shrugs. "He thinks they'll help with your nausea. He also wrote down a list of vitamins he wants us to pick up for you today."

"Are you going out?"

Lexi waits for me to check on the waffles before answering, "Yeah. I have a follow-up appointment with Dr. Spencer. He wants to see my results firsthand."

Ignoring my heartstrings painfully tugging, I smile. Dr. Spencer has been Lexi's CF specialist since the day my parents discovered she had CF. Dr. Spencer fought for years to get Lexi included in the Kalydeco program when the drug was first discovered, but his requests went unanswered. I'm certain if he didn't have four sons he was putting through medical school, he would have personally funded Lexi's inclusion in the program.

"Thank you." Lexi's eyes blaze with excitement when I carefully pluck two waffles out of the waffle maker and pop them onto the plate she is holding out. "I haven't had your waffles in years, Cleo. I'm dying to discover if they still taste as yummy as they used to."

She wasn't lying. She doesn't even add any condiments before taking a sizeable bite of the still steaming waffle. "Sooo good," she mumbles through a moan.

Happy the first part of "Operation Get Cleo Back" has been hatched, I pour another batch of mixture onto the waffle machine. I've had an entire week to mourn Marcus, and as much as I wish I could continue hiding away from the world, it's time for me to get my wheels back in motion. I'd like to say discovering I am pregnant is the catalyst for my new and improved attitude. Unfortunately, that would be a lie. It was waking up to find my bank account void of the salary I was expecting to be wired in there overnight.

If my accounting skills are correct, I have approximately fourteen days to find employment or I'll be homeless. With not just having Lexi's health to factor into my dilemma, any mourning must be pushed aside until I've dug myself out of the massive, ceaseless pit I'm sitting in.

My eyes swing to the side when Lexi asks, "Are you alright, Cleo?" Her words are mumbled by a syrup-slathered waffle.

"Yep" I reply, enunciating the P to add extra emphasis to my false statement.

Lexi's brows inch together as her eyes dart between mine. For the first time in a week, my weary gaze must portray the screamed prompts of my brain, as Lexi smiles before returning her focus to tackling her breakfast.

I place the final plate in the kitchen cupboard when the distinct noise of knocking sounds from my front door. Snagging a tea towel off the drying rack, I apprehensively pace out of the kitchen. Although the brazen attempts of reporters have dulled down the past three days, I still receive the occasional cold calls from eager media companies vying for an exclusive interview.

"I'll get it," Jackson says, coming out of Lexi's room.

He throws a shirt over his shaggy hair as he bypasses me standing mute in the hallway. Jackson has been a godsend the past week. Even with his mother facing a terminal illness, he has been by my and Lexi's side during this entire ordeal. The tumor in the base of Janice's skull hasn't shrunk, but the optimism of her family has increased tenfold the past two months, as it hasn't grown either. Their family is proof that a positive attitude can sometimes be the only drug you need.

As much as I'm grateful for Jackson's assistance, I'm also worried he will burn out. His residency requirements at the hospital are already crazy, let alone handling creepy stalkers obsessing over how a plain-Jane member of society snagged a rock star and journalists who are inept at taking no for an answer.

I never thought I'd say this, but I'm really missing Brodie. He may pee with the bathroom door hanging wide open and tell crude jokes as if he is Kevin Hart performing on stage, but he is a great guy. I guess Brodie's disappearing act should have been my first clue that things were truly over between Marcus and me. For weeks, Brodie shadowed my every move. Then, suddenly, poof, he was gone. What Lexi said last week was true. Knowing Marcus had Brodie tailing me meant he still cared. Just like withdrawing his contact implies the opposite.

I snap my thoughts back to the present before they put a dampener on my recently formed go-get-'em attitude in just enough time to see Jackson open the door. My brows stitch when our expected caller's frame is covered by a large hamper of goodies. It's only when I hear the unique rumble of a recognizable male voice do I push off my feet and head into the foyer.

"Hey, Dexter," I greet, my tone apprehensive.

I haven't seen Dexter since our kiss last week. I did send him a quick text earlier in the week to apologize for my appalling behavior. When he replied saying I had nothing to apologize for, I ended our conversation. It wasn't that I was ungrateful for him loosening the guilt wrapped around my throat, I just had too much going on to factor in another person's feelings. My priority was nursing Marcus through his scandal—albeit unnecessary, but I didn't know that at the time.

When Jackson's wide eyes shift to me, asking if I'm okay to be left alone with Dexter, I nod. Dexter is harmless. *Although my scalp still tingles from his rough hold.*

Dexter waits for Jackson to enter Lexi's room before drifting his dazzling eyes to me. "I wanted to get you flowers, but I've always thought they were pointless. They cost a fortune, they last a matter of days, then they end up as compost." He hands me the massive basket filled to the brim with food. "I thought this was more practical."

"It's great. Thank you, Dexter." My high tone relays the sentiment in my voice. After my calculations this morning, this food basket means way more than I can express.

I mosey into the kitchen. Dexter follows behind me, indiscreetly taking in my home on the way. "Your home is nice, Cleo. It has a real family vibe to it."

I set down the basket on the kitchen table before spinning around to face him. "Thank you. It has a lot of my mom and dad embedded in its bones."

"They bought this when they got married, didn't they?" Dexter removes his coat and slings it over the chair I am sitting next to.

I smile. "Yeah, they did. I can't believe I mentioned that to you." I'm usually more reserved with sharing information about my personal life.

I step into the hallway so I can see the heart of the home. "It was rundown, but while my mom sampled cakes and organized the seating chart, my dad spent his hours bringing her back to her glory days. My dad carried my mom over the threshold the night of their wedding."

My small smile increases when I recall how beautiful the molded-wood features look after a coat of paint. That's the first thing I'll do once I get settled. I'm going to return my home to a state my parents would be proud of.

One I'll be proud to raise my family in.

"How come you're not at work?" I query, praying Dexter won't see the stupid sentimental tears looming in my eyes.

He chews on the corner of his lip. "I'm on leave." He rocks back and forth on his heels, his nerves clearly evident. "Didn't feel like explaining my black eye and chipped tooth to my supervisor."

My pupils grow as guilt engulfs me. I don't know how I missed it earlier, but now that he pointed it out, his right eye is still wearing the effects of his fight with Marcus.

"You chipped your tooth?"

Dexter runs his tongue along his teeth before saying, "Yeah. Not that you can tell now. My dentist is a genius."

I cringe, loathing what his bill to have a chipped tooth repaired was.

"I don't have much, but if you're willing to accept installments, I'll pay your dentist bill."

My steps to gather my checkbook halt midstride when Dexter says, "I didn't come here to hand you my medical bills, Cleo."

I spin around to face him. He has his arms crossed in front of his broad chest and an amused smirk etched on his face.

"You didn't?"

When Dexter shakes his head, I stammer, "Then why are you here?"

"To see if you're okay. I thought we were friends?" He shrugs his shoulders as if it's no big deal. "I wanted to come last week, but decided to wait for the craziness to die down." His neck cranks to peer at the kitchen wall facing the front of my house. "But from what I saw out there, things are still pretty hectic."

Some of the heaviness on my chest lifts from him calling us friends. I was worried my stupidity last week damaged our recently formed friendship. "I'd like to say I'm surprised by the media's tactics, but we both know all too well the tactics reporters stoop to for a story."

"Hey," Dexter says, holding his hands out in front of his body. "Don't shove me into that cesspool. I might work for Global Ten Media, but I sure as hell ain't one of them." He nudges his head to the wall he was looking at earlier.

"Thanks for the sneaky stab at my career, Dexter," I grumble under my breath.

He barges me with his hip. "You might be a reporter, but I don't see you pitching a tent on someone's front lawn so you can harass them day and night."

I remain quiet, unsure how to reply. What he is saying is true, but if my career didn't nose-dive after the false story I approved on Noah in rehab, would I be one of them? Morally, I'd like to say I was raised better than that, but I can't one hundred percent certify that. My career was my life until it came tumbling down, so who's to say what I would have done for the story of the century?

The fact I attended an underground BDSM nightclub wearing nothing but a satin slip proves the lengths I will go to for a story. The only reason that ruse is more acceptable is because I continually told myself it was for my sister's well-being. Although part of me wonders now how true that was. Maybe I'm not as saintly as I like to portray. Perhaps I am just like Keira, displaying one façade to the world while poorly hiding another.

"Talking about jobs, have you decided what you're going to do yet?" Dexter questions, guiding me away from my negative thoughts.

"Honestly, no. I don't have a clue." Realizing there are products that require refrigeration in the basket, I pry open the saran wrap and gather them in my hands. "I'm going job hunting this morning," I advise, pacing to the fridge.

"Around Montclair?"

I place the orange juice and cream into the fridge before spinning on my heels to face him. "Anywhere, really. A job is a job. I'll take what I can get."

Dexter scrubs his hand over the stubble on his chin as he stares into space. Not wanting to interrupt his train of thought, I start packing away the items in the basket. Although most are products I've previously used, they are much fancier brands than the ones my grocer stocks.

I've just finished stacking the banana and walnut muffin mixture in the pantry when Dexter asks, "You studied personal relations, right?"

I screw up my nose. "Yeah, but just as a filler class as the creative writing course was full. I wasn't overly good at it."

"Did you pass?" Dexter asks with an arched brow.

I giggle before nodding. "Just."

Dexter checks his watch before questioning, "Do you have any plans next Friday?"

"Christmas eve?" I ask, certain he has his dates confused.

He doesn't.

"Yeah, my father's lifelong friend is attending Global Tens' Christmas Eve ball. I think he is someone you'd *really* like to meet."

My brows scrunch from the ambiguousness of his reply. It isn't what he said, it's the way he said it. It was showy and teeming with attitude, very unlike Dexter.

"Thanks for the offer, but I'm not interested in attending a function overrun with reporters." *That's the last thing I need.*

"Why not? The opportunity would be immense, Cleo. You could be walking away from something—"

"I'm not interested, Dexter," I interrupt, my tone stern and to the point. "I appreciate you looking out for me, but I don't want to work in that industry anymore. I can't handle the stress right now."

Even with my worry at an all-time high that I'm weeks away from being homeless, I'm not so desperate I'll fall to my knees and beg the people responsible for the demise of my career and relationship for any scraps they're willing to throw me. I'd rather scrub toilets for a living than lower myself to those standards. Furthermore, discovering I'm pregnant ensures I need to limit my stress. My baby doesn't deserve to be bombarded with out-of-control hormones and soaring emotions. If I don't lower my stress, the poor baby will have a mental breakdown before it's even born.

Dexter's lips twitch as he struggles to hold back further debate. I issue him a glare, warning him I've reached my quota on our conversation.

"Alright," he eventually breathes out. "But if you change your mind, I'm only a phone call away."

"Thanks, but there is no chance of that happening."

I lied.

23

"No luck?"

I shake my head before closing our front door, blocking out the nagging questions from the paparazzi still following my every move. After placing my portfolio on the entranceway table, I sling off my coat and pad into the living room Lexi is gawking at me from. My steps are slow, weighed down by the intense amount of pressure I'm under.

I slump onto the sofa next to Lexi so I can pry my stilettos off my aching feet. Air whizzes from my thin, grim lips when I spot the mountain-sized blister on the back of my heel. I knew trekking the streets of Montclair in a pair of heels would be a tortuous feat for my ego, but I had no clue it would cause physical pain as well.

"Ouch. I'll get the iodine," Lexi offers, rising from the couch.

I've barely skimmed off my second shoe when she reenters the room, clutching a bottle of iodine and a box of Band-Aids.

"I think it's time to devise a new tactic," she suggests, handing me the items she gathered.

Before I can announce a protest to her suggestion, she continues talking, foiling my attempt. "I'm not saying you have to accept Dexter's offer, but I think you should use his invitation as a way of confronting Mr. Carson. Your leave is not negotiable, Cleo. You earned those hours by working your ass off for his company the past five years. The least he could do is hear you out."

At Jackson's suggestion, I reached out to Mr. Carson after contacting my bank to ensure there wasn't an error processing my paycheck. There wasn't. I was informed by Mr. Carson's PA that he will be unavailable until next year, so I spent my week job hunting. I've yet to secure a position. It isn't because the companies believe I lack the skills for the job, nor am I overqualified, they just don't want the stigma attached to my name to negatively impact them. I can't say I blame them. Having a prospective employee arrive at an interview with half-dozen paparazzi in tow would have to be a major deterrent for any employer.

"When this dies down, come back and see me," is a quote I've heard on repeat the past five days. Little do they realize by the time the media's interest in me ends, I'll be homeless.

"Mr. Carson is on leave, so I doubt he'll be attending the gala," I reply, issuing any excuse to avoid being lured into agreeing to this plan.

Lexi leaps off the couch, startling me. "If the news printed by his own company is right, he'll be at that gala."

She hands me a front-page article on Mr. Carson and a mystery blonde he was seen with at a racetrack event last month. Although the blonde's face in the photo is anything but pleasant, Mr. Carson's hold on her implies they are more than friends. He is holding her like a groom would when carrying his bride over the threshold.

"Rumors are they'll be attending the event together."

I peer at Lexi, stunned by her snoopiness.

"What? My nosey-nancying is encouraging the media to shift their focus away from Marcus... which in turn will shift their focus away from you as well."

My heart rate turns calamitous when I flip over the paper to discover Marcus's handsome frame. With the recovery time of his hand being critical, he has been photographed entering and exiting a well-known physical therapist's office in lower Manhattan the past week. If the gossip articles are anything to go off, the band will resume their world tour as early as late January.

Lexi removes the article from my hand, practically prying it from my death-clutch hold. I'd like to say as the days roll on, my grief over losing Marcus is fading. It isn't. I miss Marcus just as much now as I ever have. I always thought the saying "absence makes the heart grow fonder" was a crock of shit. Now, I'm a believer. I miss Marcus for every second of every hour of every day. Years will pass, and I don't see that logic changing.

My eyes lift to Lexi when she hands me my cell phone. "Accept Dexter's offer."

My brisk headshake slows when Lexi suggests, "Or I'll sell my Kalydeco medication on the black market."

I stare at her, blinking and confused. "You can't do that. It's illegal."

"Yes, I can," she confirms, her tone firm. "With the price being so high, people are desperate. But you don't need me to tell you that, do you, Cleo? As you already know the steps people will take to protect the ones they love."

I huff. "I only considered it once. It was still out of my price range," I admit, unashamed. I'm not deceitful when I say I'll do anything to protect my sister, even going as far as risking prosecution for purchasing medication on the black market.

I lick my dry lips before accepting my cell from Lexi. My hands shake uncontrollably when I punch Dexter's number into the screen from the business card he handed Lexi last week. As the sound of ringing buzzes in my ear,

I stand from the couch and pace to the front window to peer outside. The media's numbers have halved the past week and a half, but their presence is still highly notable.

"Cleo," Dexter greets, proving he has my number stored in his phone. "How are you? Good? I hope you're calling to accept my offer?"

I wait a beat to ensure his interrogation is over before replying, "Hi, I am good, thank you for asking, and in regards to your offer, if your plus one is still available, I'll happily tick the box." My words come out in a flurry, spurred on by the nervous butterflies taking flight in my stomach.

"But just as friends. I'm not ready for anything more than a friendship right now," I clarify, wanting to ensure he doesn't mistake my acceptance of his olive branch as a date.

Dexter chuckles. "That's understandable. It's not every day you're dumped during a live broadcast, so I don't blame you for being turned off at the idea of dating again." Although his tone comes out playful, it doesn't stop his words from brutally stabbing my heart.

"So...umm ..." I cringe at my inability to produce words. Dexter's laidback approach to my public humiliation has me a little stumped for a reply. "What time do you want me to meet you there?" I force out through the unease gripping my throat, silently asphyxiating me.

"I'll come pick you up around 6 PM."

"Oh, no that's not necessary. You live in New York. I'll come to you. It will be easier this way."

"Come on, Cleo, the gas prices are astronomical at the moment, let alone the parking fees. Are you sure that's an expense you want the day before Christmas?"

My ego absorbs his brutal maiming without a smidge of hesitation. "Fine. I'll see you at 6." Stealing his chance to reply, I disconnect our call. *Okay, maybe my annoyance was late to the party.*

Riddled with guilt that I'm being a cow to a man who deserves nothing but my admiration and respect, I quickly send Dexter a message.

Me: *Sorry, bad reception. I'll see you Friday at 6. Thanks for the invite.*

Dexter replies not even two seconds later.

Dexter: *I look forward to making you smile. That's one asset void of a monetary value, but also the most priceless.*

His reply has my worry sitting on edge, but I shut it down, too overrun with hormones to decipher cryptic riddles.

Me: *I look forward to once again smiling, thank you for taking up the challenge.*

My phone buzzes, indicating another message, but I ignore it, my mind too busy unscrambling why I feel so guilty. I have nothing to feel guilty about, but there is no doubt that was the emotion thickening my blood during my phone call with Dexter.

"Done?" Lexi queries, glancing up at me.

I give her an unenthusiastic nod. "Yes. Now I just have to find something to wear and work out a way to convince my heart it isn't wrong to go out with the man who aided in ending my relationship." A loud grumble spills from my lips as I flop onto the couch. "Oh, god, this isn't a good idea, Lexi. Maybe I shouldn't go? This will look bad."

"Bad to who?" Lexi argues, straightening her spine. "You've seen the articles, Cleo. Marcus has been on more dates the past two weeks than he has the past two years."

I grab one of the cushions from the couch and mash it into her face, muffling her heartbreaking words. Although everything she says is true, I still don't want to hear it. I'd rather keep my head stuck in the sand than believe the rumors circulating about Marcus's new playboy status. The idea of him with previous subs was an uphill battle, but it's nothing compared to seeing him night after night on *E News* with a new beautiful woman on his arm.

"I swear on our parents' graves, if he attempts to have our little boo-boo call one of those bimbos Mommy, I'll cut his balls off," Lexi warms, nudging her head to the TV broadcast of an exclusive interview with a woman whom Marcus went on a date with last week.

My heart swells and painfully squeezes at the same time. I love that Lexi calls my baby "our little boo-boo." She has done it numerous times the past five days—even Jackson caught on to the trend. But the gouging sensation inflicting my heart is from her admission that another woman could be a part of my child's life. That wouldn't really happen, would it? Stepmothers and fathers only enter the equation if the child is an orphan, right?

Right. So why is a horribly bitter taste scorching the back of my throat?

"Oh no," I mumble, fighting to hold back the sludge in my stomach racing to my lips.

Realizing I have no chance of ignoring the ghastliness of Lexi's admission, I slap my hand over my mouth before I go running into the bathroom for the third time today.

"Do you have wet wipes and mints?" Lexi queries.

I stop rummaging through my tiny purse and peer up at her. "Why would I need either of those things?"

Lexi rolls her eyes before gathering breath mints from the vanity cabinet in the bathroom and wet wipes from under the sink. "You vomit a minimum three times a day, Cleo. Today you're only at two. Breath mints are essential."

I arch a brow. "And the wet wipes?"

"Who wants to dance with a girl with vomit on her chin?" A big shake hampers Lexi's tiny frame. At first I think it's caused by laughter, but I soon realize it's vileness. Lexi can't stand the word vomit, much less actual vomit.

"I need a bigger clutch," I mumble, glancing down at the tiny black sequin purse I'm holding.

Lexi nods in agreement while pacing to the clutches stacked in my closet. "What's he doing in here?" Lexi twists her body so I can see Mr. Bunny clutched in her hand.

"I don't know. I swear he has a mind of his own lately." I remove him from her grasp and place him back on his rightful spot on the shelf above my desk. The dust circle where his fluffy backside sits reveals he hardly moves from my shelf, but I've noticed him in weird locations the past two weeks.

Shrugging off my confusion as Jackson playing tricks on me, I help Lexi hunt for a clutch to match the dress I'm wearing to the Global Ten Media Christmas function. My pulse accelerates when she pulls out a plain black clutch from the very back of my closet. I shoved it in there, hiding it from the world as I wish I could my face. It's the purse I used at the fundraising gala I attended with Marcus.

"It's just an accessory, Cleo, it has no sentimental value whatsoever," Lexi assures my mortified expression.

"Here. Look." She clicks it open and yanks out all the crap hiding inside. Most is the standard accessories every girl has—lip gloss, compact powder, a few loose notes, tampons, and an emergency condom stash that's so outdated it expired two years ago.

"Guess you won't be needing these anymore." Lexi jeers, turning the clutch upside down to dump the dreaded products without having to touch them.

In the flurry of dumping my possessions, a burst of white captures our attention when it flutters haphazardly in the air. Our eyes follow a folded-up piece of paper as it slowly floats in the air, its pace so whimsical it has trance-like qualities.

When it lands on the ground, Lexi's eyes rocket to mine. "What's that?"

"I completely forgot about it," I admit, bending down to gather the item. "It's from Andy."

Lexi's brows stitch. "Andy? As in Andy who broke into my room when I was sleeping Andy?" she queries, her voice fretful. "The same Andy who broke into Marcus's house? What ever happened to him?"

I shrug. "I don't know. I never got an update. I'm assuming we'll be informed of his hearing date when his case goes to court, but other than that..." I stop talking, having no real explanation to give.

"What does the note say?" Her interest is notable.

My lips quirk. "I never read it."

Lexi snatches the paper out of my hand before hotfooting it to the other side of the room. I don't bother chasing her. I can barely walk in my heels, let alone chase down my barefoot and more energetic sister.

My eyes swing to the side when Lexi sighs heavily.

"His phone number?" I've hardly dated the past four years, but I never have any trouble gaining a collection of phone numbers when I do go out.

"No," Lexi replies, shocking me. "It's some sort of riddle."

Peering down, I read the note.

The master commands. The submissive obeys.
Look closer, Cleo.
The people surrounding you aren't who you think they are.

There is an address for a property in East Village scribbled under the handwritten quote.

"That's not a riddle. I've heard that before." I stop talking, giving my brain time to summarize. The air brutally sucks from my lungs when reality dawns. "Richard said that to me in the hours leading to his death."

"Something like this?" Lexi only speaks three words, but her eyes aren't as reserved. They hammer me with questions so hard and fast I'm nearly knocked onto my ass.

I shake my head. "No. He said exactly that."

"What does it mean? Shian said Richard and Andy were as thick as thieves, do you think he is playing games? Or..." Lexi leaves her question open, hoping I can fill it in. I can't. I have no clue what this message means. I'm assuming the address at the bottom doesn't belong to either Richard or Andy, as they lived in the same apartment building in East Harlem, so I'm truly at a loss about what this means.

"Maybe you should cancel tonight. Something about this doesn't feel right," Lexi discloses.

Before I can reply, the sound of knocking booms into my room. I drop my eyes to my watch, it's three minutes to six.

"It's too late to cancel now," I mumble, grabbing the clutch from Lexi's grasp and harshly shoving my belongings inside.

Although my intuition is screaming as loudly as Lexi's, my curiosity is also piqued. With Global Ten's function being held in the financial district, with a little persuading, I may be able to convince Dexter to detour past the address on the note Andy handed me.

My fast strides out of my room are halted by Lexi seizing my wrist. No words spill from her mouth, but her eyes issue her doubts.

"I'll be fine," I assure her before wrapping her up in a big hug.

24

With traffic at its absolute worst, my request to alter the direction of our course is never relinquished by my tongue. We've been sitting in standstill traffic for nearly an hour. It's probably best Dexter hired a limousine company to transport us to the function, or I'm confident his patience would be wearing thin. Driving in New York is already a challenge, much less on Christmas Eve.

"No, thank you," I reply when Dexter offers me a drink from the small crystal bar tucked under the windowsill of the stretch limousine. My mouth is parched, and I'd love a drink, but considering any liquid in the bar is alcohol-based, my quenching my thirst must wait until we arrive at the Christmas party.

After Dexter fills his glass with a generous serving of whiskey, he sinks back into his chair, cautious not to spill any liquor on his expensive tailor-fitted suit. When I swung open my front door to greet Dexter, my eyes bugged out of my head. Compared to my simple satin long-sleeve dress and plain black pumps, Dexter was dressed to the nines in a tailored suit and bowtie. Mortified I'd mistaken the dress code, I rushed back into my room, hoping to glam up the bland design of my dress with a few intricate pieces of jewelry and a new take on my hairstyle.

Although time was against me, I wrangled my wavy locks into a twisted French braid that slides down the right side of my neck. Although Dexter's appearance still screams wealth, my hasty mini makeover compliments his sophistication.

"Do you know if Mr. Carson is attending tonight?" I aim to keep the hopefulness out of my voice. My attempts are borderline.

Dexter's brows bow high into his hairline. "Yes. Since he hasn't attended the past five years, a conscious effort was made to assure he was at tonight's event."

"A conscious effort? By whom?"

Dexter shrugs. "That's just the gossip around the water coolers."

"Any other gossip I've missed out on?" I twist to face him. Even though the main purpose of our date is to make contact with Mr. Carson, I don't want to be rude. Dexter has made an effort to impress me tonight, and it would be ill-mannered of me to pretend I haven't noticed.

"Hmm," Dexter murmurs, his voice giving the hint he guzzled his whiskey too quickly. It's raspy and thick, and if I am being totally honest, pulse-quickening. "Keira and Delilah no longer work at Global Ten.

"Oh." I'd like to say more, but my words are trapped in my throat.

"No one knows why or how, Keira just failed to turn up the Monday morning following..." He locks his eyes with me. "... you know."

Still unable to talk, I nod. He is referring to the night we kissed.

"And Delilah hasn't been seen since she was seconded to a secret assignment the start of last week. She didn't even pack her office. It's like she has vanished off the face of the planet."

My brows furrow. "She's probably torturing a whole new set of defenseless interns at another Global Ten office?" I don't know why my reply comes out sounding like a question. Delilah is the bane of my existence, but I'm still shocked by Dexter's nonchalant disclosure of her supposed disappearance.

"Did you know Keira was at the party the night we kissed?" Dexter queries, placing his empty glass on the bar.

I wait for him to refill his drink before answering, "Not at the start, but I spotted her as I was leaving."

"Figured as much," he murmurs under his breath before taking a sizeable gulp of the brown liquid inside. He screws up his face, unappreciative of the burn of liquor rolling down his throat. "I don't know what burns more. The whiskey or knowing you only kissed me to get back at him."

"Dexter... I... ah." I can't formulate words as every one I try to force out of my mouth is a lie. I did kiss him to get back at Marcus, but I never figured I'd be confronted by his honesty.

"Don't feel bad," Dexter demands, plonking his half-consumed whiskey on the bar. "I can think of much worse ways to be used. Hell, you're welcome to use me anytime you like."

I elbow him in the ribs when he waggles his brows excessively.

"I just hope you aren't seeing me in the same shady light you're seeing him. Our kiss might have added ammunition to the failure of your relationship, but that couldn't have been the only downfall." His voice softens at the end, a unique mix of confusion and regret.

"Our kiss didn't help, but there were a lot of misunderstandings before that," I admit before I can stop my words.

Dexter runs his fingers through his thick hair as he returns his eyes to mine. The unease in his gaze sets me on edge, but I hold my ground, acting like I am still the strong-willed Garcia my parents raised to me be.

"Can I speak freely?" Dexter asks, his tone forthright.

Appreciating him seeking permission, I reply, "Yes. Please."

"Marcus embarrassed you in front of millions of viewers, sat by and watched the media call you every vulgar name known to mankind, then paraded around town as if you were nothing more than a blip on his radar, yet, you still wear his trademark. Why? Did he knock your confidence so low you can't see how much you're worth, Cleo? Despite what you're thinking, you're better than this. You deserve better than *that*." He nudges his head to the chain link pendant curled around my neck.

My hand instinctively darts up to cover my pendant, protecting it from the harshness of his slurred words. Although everything he says is true, it doesn't make it any easier to hear.

"It's complicated," I murmur, using the same excuse my heart has argued with my brain over and over again the past two weeks.

The remainder of our trip is made in silence, our conversation as barren as the bottle of whiskey Dexter emptied during our two-hour trip. When we arrive at the gala, I force a smile onto my face before following Dexter out of the limousine. Thankfully, with Dexter attached to my side, it takes the paparazzi glancing in my direction three times before they realize who I am. By then, it's too late. Dexter and I have already entered the lobby where the Christmas function is being held, and they are trapped outside by the big burly bodyguards manning the doors.

A flurry of black in the corner of my eye gains my attention when Dexter moves through the crowd of people gawking at us. Although the stranger's glance is one of hundreds directed at me right now, my body is responding differently. His gaze seems familiar—*hauntingly familiar*.

While Dexter chitchats with a man and an elegantly dressed lady, my eyes scan the crowd, seeking the person who set my heart rate rocketing with a single glance. It takes me several moments to lock in on a razor-cut jawline concealed by a turned-up trenchcoat collar. I hold my breath when his head shifts in my direction. For the quickest second, time comes to a standstill. I'm certain I've seen that face before, only now it belongs to a ghost.

"I need to use the washroom," I advise Dexter as my eyes follow the black blur careening through the crowd as if he is panicked by my wide-eyed glare.

Dexter loosens his grip enough I can slip my hand out of his grasp, but not quite enough to not project his disappointment I'm fleeing his company so early. When his eyes lower to mine, a stabbing pain hits my chest. His eyes are teeming with remorse and silent pleas. They nick my heart, but don't diminish my naturally engrained inquisitiveness. My desire to hunt down the man mere moments from evading me is so strong, nothing could stop me—not even Marcus.

"I'll be right back," I assure Dexter, loathing how many people I've made feel terrible the past three months.

I wait for Dexter to nod before dashing in the direction the suit-covered man went. My pace quickens when the man I'm chasing peers back at me, pinning me in place with his murky blue eyes. My frozen stance comes to an end when he darts down a concealed corridor at the edge of the hotel foyer. I take off after him, my fear overrun by curiosity. Even with a cap hanging low on his head, I'm certain I recognize those eyes.

When I reach the entrance of the eerily black corridor, I glance over my shoulder, back to the large gathering of people lingering in the foyer. My intuition is screaming at me to spin on my heels and return to Dexter, but no matter how loudly it pleads, my inquisitiveness reigns supreme.

Exhaling a deep breath, I step into the dingy and cramped space. My heart rate doubles when my poor vision locks in on a blob of black halfway down the hall.

"Richard?" I query, my voice equally scared and hopeful. "Is that you?"

Ignoring my interrogation, he shuffles further down the dingy corridor. The hiss of overworked boilers adds to the squealing in my ears as I cautiously step down the brick-lined corridor. Murmured voices sound over the creaking of old water pipes when I stop at a T intersection halfway down the corridor. I glance in three directions, unsure which way to go.

My head snaps to the side as my heart smashes against my ribs. Something just darted past the hallway on my right, scaring the living daylights out of me.

"Hello?" I call out, praying I'll not be front page news again tomorrow—its headline more horrendous than the ones I've endured the past two weeks. "Is anyone down here?"

My shouted questions stop the murmured voices in an instant while adding to the sweat slicking my skin. I pivot on my heels, preparing to leave, too paralyzed by the fear scorching my veins to continue my mission. Just before I exit, I spot a man halfway down the corridor wearing a black trenchcoat. I push off my feet and race down the hall before my brain can cite an objection.

"Richard," I mumble in disbelief as I grip the man's shoulder and spin him around to face me.

I take a step back, frightened. The man I've approached isn't Richard. It's Mr. Carson.

"Cleo?" I don't know why, but his greeting sounds like a question. "What are you doing down here?"

"Oh. Um. I was looking for a friend. Have you see anyone else down here?" When the nape on my neck prickles, I straighten my spine and take a step back, moving out of Mr. Carson's hold. When I leaped in fright, his hands must have shot out to stop me from falling, otherwise what other reason would he have for holding me?

"No, there isn't anyone else down here. You shouldn't be down here either, Cleo. It isn't safe." Not giving me a chance to reply, he places his hand on the curve of my lower back and directs me toward the foyer. The way he moves us through the dimly lit corridors with ease exposes he is familiar with the floorplan of this establishment.

"Is this one of your properties?" I inwardly gag, hating my obsessive need to know everything.

"Yes," Mr. Carson answers, his tone direct and to the point.

"That must be nice."

He drops massively dilated eyes to mine, seeking silent clarification on my riddled statement.

"Having enough money to buy half of New York."

He smirks. "Not quite half, but I'm getting there."

"By forcing people out of their homes they've lived in their entire lives? Who said chivalry was dead?"

Mr. Carson's long strides come to an immediate halt. The glare he directs at me would make grown men shiver in their boots, but I hold my ground. All my nerves were so rattled out of me while chasing ghosts down dingy corridors that I'm fearless.

"What are you talking about?" Mr. Carson queries.

"Where shall I start?" I murmur, tapping my finger on my pursed lips. "The fact you didn't keep your pledge to pay for my sister's health and schooling for the remainder of her life? Or the part about how you increase your bank balance by swindling your ex-employees out of their rightful entitlements?"

"A check for your sister's full tuition was mailed over a month ago. I addressed the envelope myself," he replies, his tone giving no indication of deceit. "And in regards to your entitlements, your salary was paid this morning, along with the other twenty-eight thousand employees I pay every week."

"Unless some money-hungry dust bunnies came in and cleared out my account, both this week and last week's salaries were not deposited into my bank account." If I wasn't being swarmed by embarrassment, I'd not hesitate to whip out my phone to show him how dire my bank account is. It's the lowest it's ever been.

When Mr. Carson glares at me with confusion etched over his face, I push aside my embarrassment and hunt for my phone in my clutch.

"I don't need proof," he assures me, stopping my manic rummaging by placing his hand over mine. "Your eyes are the only proof I need."

I snap my clutch back together, hoist it under my arm, then lift my eyes to Mr. Carson, using my soul-baring eyes to my advantage. Tears prick in my eyes when he nods before guiding me into an office at the end of the hall so he can secure a checkbook from the top drawer. I watch him in silence, too stunned to do or say anything. He writes a check for ten thousand dollars before handing it to me.

"That's way too much. My weekly salary is only—"

"We'll work out the details Monday morning. Until then, take that as collateral and my word as your guarantee. I've never backed down from a pledge. I am a man of my word, so you can be assured I'll find out who caused this error, and I'll personally fix it," he promises, staring straight into my eyes.

Incapable of speaking for the fear of crying, I store the check in my clutch, dip my chin in thanks, then spin on my heels. I may have shamefully bombarded him outside of working hours, but my pride is too great to allow him to see my tears.

"And Cleo?"

I force a neutral expression on my face before cranking my neck back to peer at him.

"I didn't get to the position I am in by sitting on a perch and shitting on those below me. I used to be one of those unknowns on the bottom rung, so I understand the struggle it takes to reach the top." I smile when some of his Jersey boy heritage rings true in his voice. "My offer from weeks ago is still valid. I need people like you to bring Global Ten back to its glory days."

I shake my head, knowing no amount of agony will ever have me working for a company that so hideously invades people's right to privacy.

Spotting my disagreeing gesture, Mr. Carson says, "I don't need an immediate answer, Cleo. Think about it over the weekend, a week, a month. Take as much time as you need. My offer will remain as long as it takes for you to realize mistakes were made, but I'm doing everything in my power to fix them."

"Okay," I agree, accepting his guarantee with the confidence his eyes are relaying. "I'll consider your offer if you'll consider one of my own."

He stores his check book in the drawer before pacing around the desk to stand in front of me. "Hit me with it," he says, crossing his arms over his broad chest.

"Talk to your niece."

He balks as his pupils dilate to the size of dimes.

"I don't know why you're keeping your lineage a secret, but I have a feeling even you don't know the entire story. Any good journalist will tell you there is only one way to get answers—"

"By asking questions," we say in unison.

"Exactly," I confirm, nodding. "I know the importance of protecting your family, but there comes a point where you need to make sure the people you're protecting are being shielded for the right reason. I saw the photos of Keira. I understand how hard they would have been for you to see. But the voice of the majority is no proof of justice."

With that, I exit his office, my steps more spirited than the ones I took earlier.

25

Needing a few moments to settle my erratic heart, I slip into the women's restroom at the side of the foyer. With most of the guests in the main ballroom, a peaceful silence has fallen over the elegant space. I do my business in one of the vacant stalls before heading to the sink to wash my hands. Thankfully, this time I'm not bombarded by any unwelcomed guests.

As I wash my hands in the sink, I take in the way the little secret nestled safely in my womb has added to the rosiness of my cheeks. My eyes are wide and bright, spurred on by both excitement and fear, and my hair is extra glossy thanks to the overload of vitamins Jackson has been feeding me the past week. Although my insides feel like they're in a million pieces, my outside appearance successfully conceals their shattered remains.

After tucking a few strands of rogue hairs back into my braid, I trail my fingers down my cheek, stopping once they reach the diamond pendant sitting in the little groove of my neck. While I stare at the necklace, I recall what Dexter said in the limousine. Although his sneered statement hurt to hear, every word he grinded out was true. I've been slaughtered in the media, called names I'll never speak. I lost my job, my freedom, and my right to privacy the instant Marcus ridiculed me in front of not only millions of viewers, but his fans and bandmates as well, yet I'm still wearing a gift that symbolizes I am his. This needs to stop—the pain, the anger, the remorse—it all needs to stop.

I feel the shudder of my hands up my arms when I slide them around my neck to release the white gold latch on my nape. I exhale deeply when my necklace descends down my chest, puddling around the neckline of my dress. Gathering the thin chain in my grasp, I fist it tightly before placing it in the hidden nook of my clutch.

I peer back at the mirror, feeling oddly naked. The necklace was thin, but its significance was immense. "You've got this," I declare to the stranger staring back at me.

I hold my head high as I weave through the throng of people mingling in the opulent space. My ruse of using the washroom took longer than I anticipated, and the mood of the crowd has greatly improved since I left. Not only is alcohol enticing a carefree sentiment amongst the cheerful group, so is the beloved Christmas bonus disbursed in every Christmas card Mr. Carson awards. From the gleaming smiles of numerous partygoers, this year's bonus must have improved over last year's.

I find Dexter sitting at a bar at the side of the dance floor. His expensive suit jacket has been removed, and his bowtie is draped around his slumped shoulders. I quicken my pace, eager to discover what has caused his low composure.

"Hey. Sorry it took me so long. I got lost." I don't know why I lie. It just came out of my mouth before I could stop it.

"Cleo?" Dexter peers at me like I am a ghost. I understand the look he is giving me as I just wasted twenty minutes I'll never get back chasing a ghost. Perhaps that's why I lied to Dexter? As it wasn't an utter lie? I did get lost—chasing pipedreams. "I thought you'd left. That I pushed you too hard, and you decided to leave."

"No," I reply, shaking my head. I place my clutch on the bar before facing him. "What you said hurt, but it was true. See?" I brush my hand down my naked neck.

The dark gleam in Dexter's eyes clears away as he drinks in my bare neck. "It's gone," he murmurs, running the backs of his fingers down my neck.

"Yes," I answer, barely choking back a sob.

Dexter's glassy gaze bounces between mine. "You're free of him!"

It's the fight of my life not to lower my hand to the non-existent bump in my stomach. What Dexter said is a lie. My baby guarantees I'll never be fully free of Marcus. But with time, and assistance from my family and friends, I'll eventually be okay with that. *I hope.*

"I'm so proud of you, Cleo."

When Dexter leans in to place a kiss on my lips, I crank my neck to the side, forcing his lips to land on my cheek. Dexter doesn't protest my snub of his contact. I don't know if it's because he's encircled by women fluttering their excessively long lashes and pursing their lips as they strive for his attention, or because he is too drunk to notice it. Either way, I'm glad to have dodged another bullet directed at me tonight.

"Come on, we better work off some of this whiskey lacing your veins before you end up in bed with Meeka from Classifieds," I mumble, helping Dexter from his chair.

"What's wrong with Meeka?" he answers, winking suggestively at Meeka, who is giving him kissy gaga faces.

I curl my arm around his waist and guide him to the dance floor. My initial thoughts about his intoxication ring true when he sways and stumbles with every step we take. "One, she's married. Two, she's married. And, three—"

"She's married?" Dexter chimes in.

"Bingo."

Dexter laughs, forcing the flock of women circling him to hover closer.

"If you laugh again, you're on your own, Mister."

Dexter hiccups. "Mister, hey? I like the sound of that."

It takes nearly an hour of dancing before the excessive alcohol Dexter consumed burns off. You'd think dancing someone back to sobriety would be a torturous endeavor, but it has actually been a lot of fun. For once, I just let go. I shimmy and shake my caboose without a concern in the world, realizing that no matter what I do, or how well I behave, it won't change people's opinions of me.

Even before I precariously tiptoed into the world of BDSM, I was ridiculed and mocked by people I thought were better than me. Only now do I know that nothing will alter people's desires to ridicule one another. We live in a world full of judgmental people who speak before they consider how their mockery will be absorbed by the person they are taunting. It's unfortunate, but true.

"I need a drink," I shout, ensuring Dexter can hear me over the music booming out of the speakers hanging above our heads.

Dexter's eyes bounce between mine. "Do you want me to come with you?"

"No, I'll be fine. Do you want some water?"

When he cups his ear, signaling he can't hear me, I move in closer. "Do you want some water?"

"I'd rather have whiskey, but if water is all you're offering, I guess I'll take it." His husky voice sends a flurry of goosebumps racing to the surface of my skin. Although his lips brushed the shell of my ear with every word he spoke, I'm still shocked by my body's response. My body has only ever reacted like this with one man—that man isn't Dexter.

Since I'm numb and in a trance of confusion, I don't notice the rapid advancement of Dexter's lips until it's too late. His kiss is brief—only swift enough for his tongue to slide halfway across my mouth—but long enough to consume me with horrid grief.

Yanking back, I muster a fake smile on my now whiskey-scented lips. "Water. I'll be straight back."

I pivot on my heels. Not trusting my stomach, which is flipping with unwarranted guilt, I race for the washroom instead of the bar. When my black pumps step off the makeshift floor, the reasoning behind my body's peculiar response to Dexter's closeness comes to fruition. Marcus is standing at the edge of the dance floor with his heavy-hooded gaze firmly rapt on me. He is wearing an impeccably tailored suit that showcases every perfect ridge of his mouthwatering body. The dark circles around his alluring eyes display his sleep the past two weeks has been as lacking as mine, but he is still the most handsome man I've ever seen.

My brain signals for me to look away before I get stuck in a trance by his tempting eyes, but it's too late. I'm frozen, dazed by the thick sentiment firing the air with heat. The tension bristling between us is so hot, it hisses and crackles over the loud roar of guests mingling between us. It switches my flipping-with-unease stomach to somersaulting-with-excitement.

I can't believe even after weeks of absence, the attraction between us is still so intense. It feels like we stepped back in time, back to the night we officially met. God—what I'd give to go back to that day. To forget the furious storm raging between us—to fix the mistakes I made.

The pleas to forget the world around us fall on deaf ears when a polished blonde intimately drapes her arm over Marcus's broad shoulders—a blonde who looks remarkably identical to Keira in every way.

When Keira snootily glances into my eyes while whispering in Marcus's ear, I grit my teeth, then spin to face the opposite direction. She looks so cozy with him, like they are perfect for one another.

After breathing out my despair, I head back to Dexter. The anger boiling my blood has made quick work of the nausea twisting my stomach, meaning I no longer need to use the washroom.

"We need to leave," I tell Dexter, stopping at his side.

Dexter stops dancing with a curvy brunette. The angry glare she is directing at me extinguishes when I say, "I need to leave. Thank you for tonight. I'll call you tomorrow."

Before I get two steps away, Dexter grips my elbow and pulls me backward. The more his worried gaze roams my face, the closer his brows stitch together. Seemingly reading the blatant fury pumping out of me for what it is, he lifts his eyes in the direction I came from. His jaw gains a quiver when he spots the cause of my sudden fury.

He returns his eyes to me. "If you leave now, you're letting them win."

"No," I deny, shaking my head. "If I leave now, I'm letting them live," I snarl through clenched teeth.

The unnamed brunette waiting for the return of Dexter's attention snickers over my bitchy remark. I'm glad she can see the humor in my situation. I am anything but amused.

A girly squeal topples from my lips when Dexter bands his arms around my back and unexpectedly dips me. Dizziness clusters in my brain just as quickly as confusion clouds me.

He flips me back up while saying, "You want him to feel what you're feeling? Give him a taste of his own medicine."

He plasters his body to mine, allowing me to feel every inch of him—*every inch*. He draws me in so vigorously, we share the same breath. He grinds his pelvis against mine, his moves as surprisingly fluid as his fighting skills.

While feeling the heat of Marcus's gaze scorching my skin, I close my eyes and meet Dexter's dance moves step for step. We move together glibly, like two people who know each other intimately well.

I don't know how much time passes before I lose the heat of Marcus's gaze. It's long enough for my thirst to become dire, but not long enough for my anger to be fully subdued.

When my eyes slowly flutter open, I inconspicuously scan them around my surroundings. Marcus is nowhere in sight.

My eyes stray back to Dexter. "If I didn't know any better, I'd swear you've played these games before."

He doesn't agree or dismiss my claims, he merely smirks before guiding me off the dance floor so I can satiate my parched throat. While unscrewing a bottle of water, Dexter peers past my shoulder. The color of his overheated cheeks drains to the soles of his shoes as his throat works hard to swallow. I glance over my shoulder, seeking the person who has caused his gaunt appearance. My first thought is it must be Marcus, but I soon realize that his peacock feathers fan out whenever Marcus is in his presence—they don't cower away.

Unable to spot the cause of Dexter's worry, I drift my heavy-lidded gaze back to him. I forgot how tiring dancing can be. I'm truly exhausted. His eyes frolic between mine for several moments before he asks, "Will you be okay if I leave you here for a minute? I've just seen someone from a past life I'd like to buy a drink for."

"Sure," I reply, placing my half-guzzled bottle of water on the counter.

Relieved by my agreeing gesture, Dexter presses a quick kiss to my cheek before ambling in the direction he was looking.

When I return my baffled gaze to the bar, I notice he has left his wallet on the counter. "Dexter, you forgot your wallet."

I twist my torso to face him. I can't pinpoint him in the sea of black. "It's a little hard to buy someone a drink without any money," I mumble to myself.

After using my crumpled-up twenty-dollar note to pay for my and Dexter's water, I push off my feet and head in the direction he went. There are only two bars in the room, so he couldn't have gone far.

My unsteady pace grows more wobbly when my elbow is suddenly clasped and I'm dragged into a room concealed by a thick curtain. My screams are cut off when a hand clamps over my gaped mouth, stealing my pleas for help.

As quickly as my panic rises, so does my anger. Not only do I recognize the scent of the man accosting me, my body is also activating with primitive awareness of its mate. *Marcus.*

I attempt to spin around to face him. His clutch on my hips firms, foiling my endeavor. My spine straightens when he burrows his nose into my hair and inhales deeply.

"God, I've missed your smell."

The scent of hard liquor filters through my nose, displaying he is heavily intoxicated.

"Let me go," I sneer, my words choppy, clogged by the inane lust curled around my throat.

I'm appalled by my body's reaction to his meekest touch. He is only conversing with me as he is drunk, yet I'm clammy and hot, and don't even get me started on the improper thoughts running through my mind.

Marcus complies with my request by loosening his grip on my right hip, but instead of dropping his hand to his side, he slides it up the planes of my quivering stomach before cupping it around my breast. My disloyal nipples bud, adoring his touch after weeks of absence.

"Don't." My one word is barely audible since it was forced out of my mouth against my body's wishes.

"You know what to say if you truly want me to stop," Marcus murmurs into my ear before he places a peppering of kisses down my neck.

"I don't need a safe word, remember? I'm not your sub."

My knees shake when he rolls my nipple between his thumb and index finger. His pinch isn't overly painful, but my body responds as if it is. When he twists them for a second time, this time more firmly than the first, my clutch and Dexter's wallet falls to the floor with a clatter.

"Always so responsive," Marcus mutters, revealing he is aware of my body's silent pleasure in his meekest touch.

As his fingers uncoil the tight weaves of my braid, his lips glide down my exposed neck. My core spasms when he sinks his teeth ever so slowly into my shoulder. My nostrils flare as I fight with all my might not to give any indication to the fire raging in my stomach. I can't believe how treasonous my body is. I am boiling with unbridled anger and lust at the same time. *How is that even possible?*

I yank away from Marcus, sickened that I've become so lust-crazed I've lost all my marbles. He splays his hand across my stomach and yanks me back. I shamefully moan when our rough collision allows me to feel how aroused he is. His cock is thick and long, straining against the zipper of his trousers, dying to break free.

"You seem to have a dilemma. Do you want me to fetch Keira for you?" I viciously snarl, my words doused with so much jealousy they're drowning in it.

"Why would I want Keira when everything I need is right in front of me?" My breathing turns manic when his hand splayed on my left hip drops to my aching sex. "You're saturated, and no matter what you say, I know every drop of this goodness is for me. Your pussy doesn't ache with need when *he* grinds up against it, your neck doesn't flush when *his* lips brush past it, and your heart doesn't race at triple the speed when *he* walks into the room. Those prompts of your body belong to me. They've always belonged to me. *They'll always belong to me.*" He growls out his last sentence in a thick and raspy groan.

I remain quiet, incapable of denying his egotistical remark since every word he spoke was true. Even when Dexter kissed me, my body didn't react with a tenth of the intensity it did when Marcus clutched my elbow. Marcus owns my body—and he knows it.

"Stop," I plead through a quiver when he slips my panties to the side so he can run his finger through the folds of my soaked sex.

"No," he mutters into my ear, his one word sharp and precise. "That's not the right word."

A wave of excitement rolls over my stomach when he slips his finger inside me. I mew, overwhelmed and heightened beyond belief. My pussy ripples around his stationary digit, encouraging the continued defiance of my adulterous body.

"Tell me what you want, Cleo," Marcus commands. His hot breath hitting my neck causes a smattering of goosebumps to form in its wake.

I remain quiet, too conflicted to form a response. After the two weeks I've endured, I should be demanding for him to release me from his clutch this instant. I should be marching out of this room and announcing I'm perfectly fine living my life without him in it. I should be doing anything but whispering, "I want you."

Marcus growls, pleased by my response. His husky groan sends my libido into overdrive. I'm panting and hot, crazed by an emotion like no other. The desire to be loved.

A cluster of dizziness rushes to my head, making me giddy, when he suddenly spins me around. Any concerns of me crashing to the ground are a forgotten memory when he cups his hands around my thighs to band my legs around his waist. My back braces against one of the many shelves lining the small room we are cavorting in. Leaning me back, he lowers the zipper of his trousers.

While he frees his hard cock from his trousers, I pry open the buttons of his dress shirt to expose the rippled abs and firm pecs I've missed ogling the past two weeks. Our movements are frantic—almost possessive. I feel like I'm drunk, even though I haven't had a drop of alcohol in weeks.

With his eyes locked on mine, he snaps my panties off my body and pockets them in his trousers, which are hanging dangerously off his hips. I throw my head back and moan in delight when he impales me with one ardent thrust. The pain of taking a man his size without preparation is excruciating, but I welcome the pain—I relish it.

I claw at his back with my nails as he pumps in and out of me at a furious speed. My pussy adores every crazed thrust, meeting him grind for grind. I use the sturdy shelving as a tether to keep me upright so I can slam down on his barely exposed cock over and over again. We are fucking so manically, industrial products topple off the shelves I'm braced against, landing around Marcus's feet.

He rolls his hips with every precise thrust of his magnificent cock, ensuring his pelvic bone stimulates my throbbing-with-desire clit. The sensation is overwhelming—unlike anything I've experienced. I moan on repeat, incapable of caring if anyone can hear me. I've wanted this for weeks, so I'm not going to let anything stop me from cherishing every perfect sound.

A brutal tidal wave crests at my stomach before plunging into my tightened coil. I can feel my orgasm growing, and growing, and growing until it reaches a point I can no longer hold it back.

"Give it to me, Cleo," Marcus demands, showing he is as intuitive with my body as ever.

My eyes snap shut as I quiver and shake. I grunt a string of indecipherable words, loving that we've reached this stage of our exchange without any additional stimulation needed. When the exhausting shudders wreaking havoc with my body fade, I tighten the walls of my vagina around Marcus's densely veined cock, begging for the heat of his spawn, wanting him as unraveled as me.

He thrusts into me another four times before answering the silent pleas of my body. He stills as the hotness of his cum roars out of him in raring spurts. With his eyes tightly shut, he growls my name in a feral grunt, pushing me into my second climax—this one more powerful than the first. I clench the walls of my pussy around him, graciously milking every drop of his cum as I shout his name on repeat.

After coating the walls of my throbbing sex with his cum, Marcus opens and locks his eyes with me. He rests his sweat-drenched forehead on mine as his beautifully tormented gaze bounces between my lust-crammed eyes.

After reviving my heart with nothing more than an amorous glance, he carefully places me back on my feet. I brace against the shelves since my legs are wobbling like Jell-O on a plate. We remain quiet for several moments, struggling to regain our breath.

After curling a piece of my wild hair around his finger, Marcus bends down to gather his trousers, which are furled around his shoe-covered feet. My bottom lip slumps into a pout when he tucks his cock, still firm and glistening with my arousal, back into his boxer shorts. Air snags in my throat when he returns his eyes to me, they appear more haunted than mere minutes ago. I pant, panicked he is already regretting his decision.

My knees curve inwards as his index finger gathers the moisture my full-to-the-brim pussy couldn't contain. With his wide gaze dancing between the hum of activity outside and me, he drags his cum-covered finger across my neck. I remain still, motionless and in shock when he follows the same routine another two times.

Once his cum is smeared in the exact position my diamond collar used to sit, he locks his dark gaze with mine. My heart breaks from the desolate look in his eyes. He appears truly broken. I hate that our exchange has filled him with remorse when all I'm feeling is euphoria.

His sweet breath fans my lips when he mutters, "This is one collar he'll never be able to remove. Even if he can't see it, he will smell it."

After one last prolonged glance of my flushed and disheveled appearance, he spins on his heels and stalks to the door.

"Marcus?" I ask, dazed.

He acts like he doesn't hear me as he continues his trek without pause. His long strides have him crossing the room in two heart-thrashing seconds. I stand frozen, unmoving and unspeaking. My muted stance doesn't last long. Only as long as it takes for my anger to steamroll back in. Who does he think he is that he can treat me in such a way? I'm not a worthless whore he can dispose of like trash. I'm going to be the mother of his child, for crying out loud.

Fuming with out-of-control rage, I grab one of the many toilet paper rolls knocked down during our exchange and peg it at Marcus's rapidly retreating frame. "I hate you!" I scream, my voice hoarse from my previous erotic cries.

I continue throwing insult after insult at him, telling him I don't need him in my life, and I never want to see him again. Every word I scream is a lie, but I'm praying one will nick his gigantic ego enough to force him to retaliate.

None of them work. He just exits the room without so much as a sideways glance in my direction. Then I slump to the ground and cry.

26

My hand furiously scrapes across my cheek to gather my tears when the clunk of a lock sliding out of place booms into my ears. I still as my body seeks signs of the trespasser's identity interrupting my private sulk. Failing to hear any signs, I lift my eyes from the ground to see Dexter is entering the room. His brows furrow, and his lips quirk when he spots me sitting on the ground.

"Are you okay, Cleo?"

I rise from the ground, my legs still shaky from the mind-hazing climax I endured minutes ago. The squares of toilet paper I used to wipe some of Marcus's cum off my neck drop to the floor like feathers floating in a warm summer breeze. "Um. Yeah. I just needed a minute."

Dexter remains quiet. He doesn't need to speak for me to know what he is thinking, though. The room reeks of sweaty, lust-fueled sex. It's so pungent, even if Marcus hadn't smeared his cum on my neck, I'm confident Dexter would still know what occupied our hour apart.

Embarrassed by him catching me getting down and dirty in a storage room, I tuck my chin in close to my chest, not just hiding my flaming red cheeks from Dexter, but my grossly collared neck I was only halfway through cleaning up when he arrived. My slumped posture has me catching sight of my purse and Dexter's wallet dumped in the middle of the room.

"Let me," Dexter says when I bob down to gather the articles off the floor.

He swoops down and collects the items before a syllable can escape my lips. "Thanks," I murmur when he hands me my clutch.

My brows stitch when his hand rummages through his wallet, as if he wants to assure nothing is out of place.

"I didn't touch anything," I assure him, equally shocked and appalled he'd think I'd steal from him. I may have been close to homeless before bumping into Mr. Carson, but I'd never resort to such levels of stealing just to put food on the table. There is desperate, then there is *desperate*. I'm still on the first step of desperate.

"It's not you I'm worried about," Dexter mutters under his breath, his words so soft I'm not sure he wanted me to hear them.

Happy his wallet is in its original condition, he slides it into the pocket of his trousers. His change in position conveys even more wariness.

"I take it the person you wanted to buy a drink for was a woman?" My voice is smeared with relief that I'm not the only one who struggled to be respectful in public. He has a large red smear on the collar of his dress shirt. If my hunch is right, it appears to be vibrant red lipstick. For how high on his collar it is, it could have only been put there one way.

Dexter's wide, confused eyes bounce between mine for several heart-clutching seconds before he shrugs, indicating he is unaware what my question refers to. I'm not buying his innocent act. His pupils expanded to the size of saucers the instant I insensitively probed, plus the quiver in his jaw tripled.

"The lipstick on your collar? Unless Meeka cornered you unaware, I can't think of another way that mark could have gotten there." I waggle my brows, happy to use his gasping expression to detract from the awkwardness of him finding me sitting on the ground bawling in a storage room in the middle of Christmas Eve celebrations.

His cheeks turn a hue of pink as his hand darts up to his neckline. When his fingers immediately graze the area I am referring to, my assumption is proven dead on point. "It was an interesting opportunity I'd be a fool not to take advantage of," he murmurs, his tone laced with innuendo.

Stealing my chance to chastise him further, he bands his arm around my sweat-drenched back and guides me out of the storage room. I flinch, expecting him to react to the sticky mess on my body. My worry is unwarranted. He doesn't even notice my change in hairstyle, much less that every inch of my skin smells like Marcus. That probably has to do with the fact his own skin is a sweaty, sticky mess.

My long strides out of the storage room come to a dead halt when my eyes lock in on a pair of alluring green eyes across the room. Just like earlier tonight, Marcus doesn't hide his skin-roasting glance. He just stares at me, unashamed and without remorse. While Keira blubbers nonstop in his ear, he sips on a glass of whiskey. My throat feels scratchy when his other hand slides into his trouser pocket—the same pocket he stuffed my shredded panties in.

I can tell the exact moment his fingertips graze the damp material, as his nostrils flare, and the lust-incited gleam in his eyes doubles.

Sickened that he is thinking of me while he has Keira plastered at his side, I break out of Dexter's hold and head for the door. I can't handle this anymore. My hormones are too out of whack to continue with this rollercoaster ride. I *want* to get off. I *need* to get off. I thought I was strong enough to handle this, but I'm not. Marcus doesn't just rule my body, he rules my heart as well, and every day I spend without him shrivels it more and more.

If I don't stop this crazy ride soon, there isn't going to be any of me left to love. Our baby deserves better than a heartless mother. *My* baby deserves the world, so if I must cut ties with its father to give him or her that, so be it. Just like Lexi, I'll do everything in my power to protect my baby. Even denying my heart its greatest wish.

"Cleo, wait!" Dexter shouts, following me onto the sidewalk. "He is playing games with you, and you're letting him win."

I angrily wipe at the tears streaming down my face, loathing that they're making me look weak. Once all my tears are cleared away, I spin around to face Dexter. "I'm not letting him win. I'm forfeiting the game. It's different."

"No, it's not. You're giving him all the power, letting him play you like a pawn."

I viciously shake my head. "No, I *gave* him all the power. Now I'm taking it back."

"Until he corners you in another storage closet for a cheap fuck," Dexter roars, the viciousness of his words shocking me.

My nostrils flare as my eyes rocket to Dexter. "Until you've walked a day in my shoes, you have no right to judge me. That was *not* fucking—"

"Then what was it?" Dexter interrupts as his wild eyes dance between mine. "Because you sure as hell look like you've just been fucked. Real classy, Cleo. Arrive at an event with one guy to wander off and fuck another."

"Oh, how convenient for your ethics to arrive now. Where were they when you were guzzling down whiskey as if it was water? Or when you got lipstick on your shirt?!"

The hushed whispers of those around us advise that our little spectacle is gaining us unwanted attention, but unable to back down without having the last word, I take a step closer to Dexter and sneer, "It's not classed as fucking when it's with someone you love."

He snarls, bearing teeth. "He treats you like a whore. That's not love, Cleo. That's treating you how you're acting."

"Whatever," I immaturely retaliate, flicking off his cruel comment as if it's a piece of lint. Nothing he could say will pain my heart any more than its already hurting. "Maybe one day you'll understand the difference between fucking and love. Until then, stick to what you know, Dexter. As a man who won't date women with a certain hair color shouldn't be giving relationship advice. "

When I spin on my heels, Dexter grabs my wrists and drags me back. Air whizzes through my gaped lips when he yanks me into his raging-with-anger body. If it weren't for our hands stuck between us, we would be plastered together even closer than we were when dancing.

"I already know the difference between fucking and love. But since I'm foolishly chasing a woman who can't see her worth, I have to sit by and watch her make mistake after stupid mistake."

My eyes bounce between his as shock makes itself known. Although he didn't directly name names, his blazing eyes tell the entire story. He wants me.

"Dexter... I..." Of all the times for words to fail me, I wish now wasn't the time. "I'm sorry. I like you, but we will never be a couple—"

"Why?" he interrupts, his anger growing. "Because I'm not a billionaire rock star with a fucked-up obsession with kink? Or because I don't treat you like a whore? What the fuck has he given you that I can't?"

My lips twitch, but I remain quiet. I can barely breathe, let alone speak. I've never been confronted with such a furious glance as the one Dexter is giving me. Not even when I was assaulted in the alleyway months ago.

"Give me a reason, Cleo! One fucking thing he's given you that I can't, and I'll drop my entire campaign. I'll walk away, knowing the better man won," Dexter yells, sending his loud voice roaring into the eerie quiet.

"A baby," I murmur before I can stop my words. "He gave me a baby."

Dexter balks but remains as quiet as a monk on a vow of silence. I would have assumed he missed my snapped comment if he wasn't clenching his fists opened and closed.

"You're pregnant?" he queries, his tone high. "With *his* baby?" His voice sounds disgusted when he sneers "his."

Before a syllable is fired off my tongue, I'm slammed with a barrage of personal questions. I'm not just talking about a handful of Global Ten Media employees assuming we are a prime example of an office romp gone wrong, I'm talking about the dozen or so paparazzi absorbing and categorizing my every move.

"Did she say 'baby?' He gave her a baby?"

"Is the baby Marcus Everett's?"

"Can you repeat your pregnancy confirmation louder?"

"Cleo, would you like to confirm reports you're the reason for Rise Up's latest world tour cancellation?"

Ignoring the screamed questions being thrown at me left, right and center, I lock my eyes with Dexter's brimming-with-disappointment eyes. "I'm sorry," is all I murmur before pushing through the throng of paparazzi cramming the sidewalk to signal for a taxi. Thankfully, one pulls to the curb almost immediately, saving me from the onslaught of painful elbow jabs and even more probing questions.

"Are you famous?" the driver asks when I slide into the backseat and beg for him to go.

"No, just a case of mistaken identity," I assure him before connecting my pleading eyes with his in the rearview mirror. "Please go."

The gentleman's eyes glisten, then he pulls away from the curb. "I'll still get your signature just in case," he murmurs before throwing a used napkin and pen over the partition.

My scribbled signature didn't save me the exorbitant fee for the cab ride from New York to my home in Montclair. If I didn't catch sight of Mr. Carson's handwritten check in my purse while rummaging for a non-maxed out credit card, I might have cried when the driver announced the fee.

"Thank you," I say to the driver, paying his tip with the last of the crumpled-up bills in my purse.

He smiles softly before unlatching the locks. Although annoyed at his belief I was going to stiff him on his fare, I can also understand his hesitation. I spent the entire trip with my head resting on the chilly window while peering out at the starless sky. With my mind in a state of panic on how I'll dodge the latest scandal engulfing me, the expression on my face no doubt displayed my desire to flee.

I can't believe I blubbered out my news like that. If it isn't bad enough I've shared my pregnancy with everyone before Marcus, I did it in front of a group of reporters. I'm not only going to be slain by the media, but the diehard Rise Up fans as well. They already hate me after watching the video of Marcus and Dexter fighting. There are even shirts being sold in local stores emblazoned with "I wouldn't kiss Cleo for a million dollars" or "Who said pirating was the demise of music? It was a woman named Cleo." Now they will hunt for blood. It's my fault, though. If I had just kept my mouth shut, none of this would be happening.

I take a deep breath, mentally preparing for my second run through the shards of hell before cranking open the taxi door. Although the media has been camped out on my lawn the past two weeks, their presence has tripled from when I left earlier this evening. Clearly, gossip circulates even more quickly than a taxi ride from Manhattan to Montclair.

The questions thrown at me are oddly similar to the ones in New York, but instead of asking me to repeat my confirmation, they're requesting for me to confirm the rumors that Marcus is denying the paternity of our baby.

I keep my head down and my lips clamped shut as I struggle to push my way through the media. How can this be legal? They are trespassing on private property, yet when I called the police to complain, I was treated as if I were the criminal.

Their crushing onslaught continues until I enter the foyer of my home. Taking a minute to clear my nerves, I lean my back on the entranceway door and suck in lung-filling gulps of air. I pretend the wetness glistening my cheeks is sweat from the blinding paparazzi lights scorching my skin as I made the trek from the sidewalk to my front porch.

My heart rate doubles when the crazed frenzy outside the door replicates ones heard inside. Pushing off my feet, I pace into the living room, gathering an umbrella out of the nightstand on the way. The reasoning behind the ruckus comes to light when I see the program Lexi is watching on TV. It's a live broadcast of my arrival home, slightly delayed as per national standards.

Lexi cranks her neck to peer at me. "I knew something was wrong the instant the media swarm grew in size. I wanted you to tell Marcus you're pregnant, Cleo, but not like this." She nudges her head to the TV.

Before I can request for her to switch it off, she rewinds the footage until it stops outside the building I fled from an hour ago. I dump the umbrella I gathered to defend myself before taking the empty seat next to Lexi. Just like I was, Marcus is swamped by the paparazzi as he leaves Global Ten's Christmas function. Although my heart is still in tatters, I take comfort in the fact he is minus the blonde he had plastered to his side most of the night.

Lexi takes my hand in hers when Marcus and his lawyer stop in front of the media. His lawyer—a man matching the picture Marcus showed me after my attack in the alleyway—advises he will be releasing a brief statement. I scoot to the edge of my chair, wanting to ensure I can hear what he has to say.

Standing to the side with his head held high but his eyes elsewhere, Marcus allows his lawyer to speak on his behalf. "As per speculations, Mr. Everett has recently become aware that an old acquaintance of his, Ms. Cleo Garcia, has announced she is pregnant."

The media go crazy, nearly drowning out the rest of his statement. "Although Mr. Everett wishes Ms. Garcia well, until such time as her pregnancy is confirmed and DNA tests are arranged, Mr. Everett will act under the assumption Ms. Garcia's child is not his. Any further questions in regards to the alleged pregnancy and paternity should be directed to my office." He hands a bunch of business cards to the media contingent in the front row before gesturing for Marcus to leave before him.

The paparazzi follow Marcus down the stairs, asking question after question until he slides into the back seat of a blacked-out SUV. Lexi switches off the TV as her wide, shocked eyes stray to mine. Her lips twitch, but not a peep escapes her mouth. I'm just as dumbfounded. Although I hate that Marcus was informed of my pregnancy via the media, his denial is shocking.

"How can he deny little boo-boo is his?" Lexi asks, reading my private thoughts.

I shrug, a better reply above my comprehension.

"That's bullshit, Cleo. That—"

"Hurts," I stammer out, my one word muffled by a sob. "I saw him tonight," I admit, not caring that my tears are falling freely. "We..." The horrified expression on my face speaks on my behalf.

"Tonight?" Lexi asks, certain she heard me wrong.

"The building he was standing in front of was the location of Global Ten's Christmas party. He was there as Keira's date." My voice displays my disgust in myself. Even though I had him first, tonight I technically became the other woman. That's one label I've never wanted.

"I tried to stop our exchange, but I'm defenseless when it comes to him," I blubber while running the back of my hand under my nose. "I still love him, even when he is tearing my heart in two."

"Oh, Cleo..." Lexi murmurs while pulling me into her arms, where I stay for the next several hours, crying about a man I love, but never wholly owned.

27

The clatter of a chair scraping across the floor awakens me from my restless sleep. Rubbing my tiredness from my eyes with the back of my hand, I crank my neck to peer at the clock on my bedside table. It's 4:17 AM. I've been lying in bed the past six hours, but have barely slept two. I slump back onto my pillow, hoping to block out the world long enough to ease the thumping of my temples.

My endeavor to get more sleep fails when the softest tickle of fur brushes my forearm. I jackknife to a half-seated position, sending a flurry of dizziness to my head. My hands shoot up to my temples, circulating them to soothe the nausea roaring to my throat.

Once the desire to vomit has eased, I drift my eyes to the cause for my startled response. Mr. Bunny is lying at my side, tucked into the blankets. He wasn't there when I went to sleep. I'm certain of it. I stop staring at Mr. Bunny when a second scuff-like noise booms into my ears.

Slipping out of bed, I pad to the door. My footing is unsteady, shocked by Lexi's early awakening. She hasn't seen the sun come up since the day Jackson dragged her to *Fosterfields Living Historical Farm*.

I lighten the tap of my feet when a male moan breaks through the sound of my pulse shrilling in my ears. I clutch at my chest, equally revolted and relieved. My darn sister and her propensity to get naughty in any spot other than her bedroom nearly gave me a heart attack.

Not wanting to bust Jackson and Lexi in a compromising position, I tiptoe backward. "Shit," I grumble when I crash into something halfway down the hall.

"Cleo, what the hell are you doing sneaking around so early?" Lexi's voice is groggy as if she has just woken up.

Lexi's drooping eyelids pop open when a painful grunt echoes down the corridor.

"Where's Jackson?" I don't know why I whisper my question, but my intuition is screaming at me to remain quiet.

"He was called into surgery a few hours ago," Lexi answers, her voice as shallow as mine. "Something about a mass casualty..." She ends her sentence with a shrug.

Our eyes rocket to the kitchen entrance when a second groan resonates into the corridor, this one sounding like a man in pain.

"Go into Mom and Dad's room and lock the door," I instruct, shoving Lexi down the hall.

"No, Cleo. I'm—" The rest of her sentence is drowned out when I cup my hand over her mouth.

My desire to keep her safe fuels me with so much strength, I drag her down the hall without breaking into a sweat. Throwing open our parents' bedroom door, I roughly push her inside. With adrenaline thickening my veins, my shove is more powerful than I anticipated. Lexi lands on her backside with a sickening thud. I grimace, hating that I've hurt her, but determined to keep her safe, I tuck away that flare of emotion.

Lifting my finger to my lips, requesting she remain quiet, I quickly scamper out of my parents' room, shutting their thick wood door behind me.

My hand rattles out of control when I twist the key, locking Lexi inside. She bangs on the door, her hits loud enough for me to hear, but not sufficient enough to stop the man in our kitchen from groaning once more.

"Cleo, let me out," Lexi begs, her voice breaking into a sob.

I place my hand over the area her banging is coming from before whispering. "Call the police. Tell them we have an intruder and stay on the phone with them until they arrive. Do not come out of this room for anything. Do you understand me?" My last sentence is laced with worry.

"Cleo, please."

"I love you, Lexi the Leech." *So much so, I'll never let anything bad happen to you.*

With my stomach lodged in my throat, I spin on my heels and head toward the man groaning. My heart thrashes against my chest with every step I take down the eerily black corridor. I keep the lights off, knowing the floorplan well enough to use it to my advantage. The hairs on my arms stand to attention when I stop at my bedroom door to collect the stainless steel baseball bat I keep hidden behind my door.

You know that feeling you get when someone is watching you? It's overwhelming me right now. I freeze, paralyzed with fear when I lean on my bedroom door too hard, hurtling its loud creak down the hall.

Straightening my spine, I pull the bat behind my back when a large shadow fills the entrance to my kitchen. From the build alone, I can tell it's a male, much less the overpowering testosterone sucking oxygen from the air.

"Cleo," gargles a voice I've heard many times before—of one who plunged to his death weeks ago.

I take a step backward, crashing into my door when Richard steps out of the alcove, allowing the street lights beaming in the living room to illuminate half of his face.

"It was you? At the gala tonight?" I ask, hating that my quivering voice exposes the nerves making my skin a sticky, clammy mess.

"Yes." Richard nods weakly. "And the pizzeria. And Toloache. And the fundraising gala--"

"And the notes in my room," I interrupt, my words as bewildered as my facial expression.

Richard locks his eyes with mine before shaking his head. "No, those notes were not from me. I only left you one note. The one Andy gave you."

I gingerly shake my head when he steps closer to me, bringing the knife he is clutching to within striking distance. My fear could be unwarranted since he is fisting the knife at his side, but the fact he is approaching me in my house, armed, and weeks after his supposed death has my panic surging to an alarming level.

He lowers his eyes to my stomach. "Are you pregnant like the reports said?" he questions as his Adam's apple bobs up and down.

A tear falls from my eye when I timidly nod. *Is that what caused his sudden reappearance? News of my pregnancy*?

Richard returns his eyes to mine, the worry in them uncontainable. "Why didn't you read my note, Cleo?" he asks as his massively dilated gaze bounces between mine.

"I did," I reply, pulling the bat out from behind my back to display I'm armed.

Although his eyes are tainted with dread, there is a gleam in them warning me of impending danger. He looks more fearful now than when I was dangling precariously off a cliff months ago, but instead of looking like a man who is seconds away from rescuing me, his composure is exuding a man who is about to wreak havoc on another.

A ghost of a smile cracks onto Richard's mouth when he spots the bat clutched in my hand. "Good girl," he murmurs, sounding pleased. "I've got you. We'll get out of this together. You've just got to trust me. Do you trust me, Cleo?" Half of his confident declaration is lost to a wheezy bout of coughing.

He stumbles down the hall, bracing himself against the wall as if he can't walk without support. My panic surges to an all-time high when my vision clears enough to see large droplets of blood on his chin and the neckline of his shirt.

"Do you trust me, Cleo?" Fear clutches my throat when I notice his teeth are smeared with blood. "We won't get out of this alive if you don't trust me."

My head instinctively nods, causing tears to roll down my cheeks. I don't know if it's panic forcing me to cowardly nod, or the plea in his massively dilated gaze. Just like the minutes leading up to his death, his eyes are open and raw, exposing he is a man I should trust, not fear.

"Good. Then run!" Richard roars, startling Lexi so much she furiously bangs on our parents' bedroom door over and over again. "Run, Cleo, and don't look back!"

He pivots on his heels and charges down the hall with the large knife held out in front of his blood-stained body. His steps are more furious than the ones he used mere seconds ago.

Paralyzed with fear, I watch him tackle a second man I didn't see hiding in the shadows. The concealed man grunts when he crashes into the entranceway table, Richard's hit was so firm, he knocked him nearly twelve feet.

"Run, Cleo, Run!" Lexi screams at the top of her lungs.

Her frantic scream pushes me into survival mode.

Spinning, I race down the hall as fast as my shuddering legs can take me. I fumble over my feet when a loud boom echoes down the hall two seconds later. "That one was in his stomach, the next one will be in his head."

The audible click of a gun's hammer freezes my heart. "What do you want? I don't have much, but I'll give you everything I have."

A chill of dread runs down my spine when a familiar voice replies, "I want you. I've always wanted you."

Through a wobbly pair of knees, I turn around to face a man who just became a stranger to me. Even cloaked in darkness, I am confident my rattled brain has identified the man standing before me. I'm so sure, I'll boldly confirm he is the man I was dancing with mere hours ago without even seeing his face.

"Dexter, what are you doing?" I lower my panicked eyes to Richard, who is slumped on the floor. Although he is motionless, I seek comfort in the fact his chest is rising and falling.

"No," I plead when Dexter emerges from the shadow to yank the knife out of Richard's grasp, not caring that he slices his hand in the process. "He isn't a part of this, Dexter. He has nothing to do with anything happening between us."

My chin quivers when Dexter lifts his eyes to me. They're almost lifeless, black and hollow. "No? Then why did he give you this?" A piece of crumpled paper floats across the floor before landing at my bare feet. It's the slip of paper Andy handed me at the gala three weeks ago. He must have stolen it out of my purse when he gathered our belongings off the floor in the storage room.

"It's just a riddle, it doesn't mean anything."

Dexter laughs. It's the laugh of an evil man. "A riddle with my love's address and phone number on it means nothing?! Don't treat me like an idiot!" he roars before backhanding me.

The bat falls to the floor with a clatter when I raise my hands to protect my face from another blow. My first instinct is to fight back, but the lights beaming through the glass paneling on the side of my entranceway door ensures I can't mistake what Dexter is aiming at me. He has a gun pointed at my stomach.

"I *know* Richard went to Florida to show you want he found. I *know* he's been sending you sneaky messages." My roots pull from my scalp when he fists my hair and yanks me to within an inch of his face. "And I *know* he wants to make you his." His sneer covers my throbbing cheek with spit.

I painfully hit the wall when he throws me backward as if I am as light as a feather. "The only thing he hasn't worked out is, you don't belong to anyone but me. I suffered the loss. I endured the pain. I get the reward for years of heartache. Not Richard. Not Marcus. Not the fucking man who stole the love of my life. Me! I get it! He took the woman I love, so, in return, I get to take his."

I flinch when he crouches down in front of me to curl his hand around my throat. "An eye for an eye. A death for a death. A love for a love. That's how life works, isn't it?" He drags the barrel of the gun down my cheek, his pressure so firm, a trail of blood follows its wake. "Now there's just one problem I must take care of first. If he had just followed the rules as I had instructed, all of this could have been avoided."

His eyes stray to Richard, who is gagging on his own blood. "But since he is too pathetic to do as asked, I must take care of business myself. You think Stephen's death would have warned him I do not appreciate being double-crossed. Richard was supposed to fix the error made while I watched from the wings like I did the night you were attacked in the alley."

My chin quivers when he returns his evil eyes to me. They're dark and lifeless, but also display what he is saying is true. "Stephen was supposed to rattle you until I arrived as your savior. I didn't give him permission to touch you the way he did. But be assured, my sweet Cleo, your face was the last thing Stephen saw before I sent him to hell for touching what is mine. Nobody touches what is mine! Nobody!" he roars through gritted teeth.

His nostrils flare as anger lines his face. "He should have walked away as instructed, then I wouldn't be forced to fix his mistakes." I assume he is still talking about Richard until he replaces his gun with the knife he took from Richard as mumbling, "If my research on the female anatomy is correct, right about here will fix the errors Marcus made while keeping your vital organs intact."

My eyes widen when the coolness of a blade digs into my lower stomach. My pleas for clemency trap in my throat when he tightens his grip, stealing my ability to breathe, much less talk.

As his eyes frolic between mine, the evil in them grows. "Sit still. I don't want too much damage done, as you never know, one day we may want children of our own."

I spit in his face, my last fighting defense since his hold on my neck has me drifting in and out of consciousness. My vision blurs as white spots dance in front of my eyes. I slump against the wall, floating into darkness when he tightens his hold around my neck even more.

My eyes bulge when the searing pain of a knife slicing my skin forces me back into consciousness. The pain is intense, ten times worse than anything I've experienced. I don't just feel the pain in my stomach, but in my heart as well.

Dexter stares into my eyes, enjoying watching the life inside me vanish with every inch of the blade he painstakingly slants into my stomach. My hands wrap around his, willfully fighting to stop him harming my unborn baby, but I'm too weak to compete against a man his size. I'm barely conscious, much less lucid enough to comprehend that the more I fight, the further his knife inches in.

I wheeze uncontrollably as sticky, warm liquid covers my hands. I drift between blackness and light as Dexter whispers in my ear, updating me on all the places we'll visit during our relationship, and how happy I'll be now that I've stopped fighting him. He apologizes for hurting me before expressing his undying love for me, and how in time, I'll understand why he went to such lengths for our relationship.

"When you love someone, no one stands in your way. In time, Cleo, you'll thank me for what I did. I've saved your bastard child from a lifetime of misery, like my parents should have done for me."

My head slumps forward when he releases my neck from his grip. My lungs fight to fill with oxygen but the blood oozing out of my stomach hinders their efforts. Feeling the blackness rolling in, I lift my head and stare into Dexter's eyes. My first lot of words are garbled by the bile sitting in the back of my throat. They are incoherent and breathless.

Realizing I'm trying to talk, Dexter tilts his head to the side. My blood-stained lips tickle his earlobe when I whisper, "I'll never be yours."

He rears back suddenly, stunned by the callousness of my sneered words.

Wanting him to feel the pain searing my heart in half, I wheeze out, "I hate you."

Happy my Garcia stubbornness has reigned supreme, I allow the blackness to take over.

28

"Requesting assistance to 160 Valley Road, Montclair. We need a trauma unit and multiple first responders. Officer down. I repeat, officer down."

A ragged groan expels from my lips when someone pushes hard on my stomach. My eyes pop open as a furious pain scorches my veins. I thought having my wisdom tooth extracted without anesthesia was painful. This is ten times worse. It's not just the pain of the knife still stabbing my stomach causing tears, it's wondering if my baby and sister are safe.

Seeking an update, my lips move. Nothing but painful grunts escape my blood-stained mouth. Fear clutches my heart, stricken with grief my unborn baby has been seriously injured by the knife still stabbed in my stomach.

Suddenly panicked I'm still in Dexter's presence, I attempt to sit up, my desire to protect my sister and unborn baby more dire than dealing with the pain swallowing me whole.

"Stay down, baby, an ambulance is on its way."

I slump back onto the floor where I'm sprawled, certain I'm dreaming, as that voice sounded remarkably like Marcus.

I'm not dreaming. The ashen face of Marcus enters my peripheral vision not even two seconds later. "Stay awake, baby. Keep your eyes open and on me," he pleads, staring at me with hollow, black eyes. "You're going to be okay. Both of you. Just stay with me. Alright?"

Weakly nodding, I do as requested, gasping through the pain striving to overwhelm me. My breathing is garbled, weakened by the panic curled around my throat, and my vision is hazy from an incalculable number of tears swamping my eyes. The pain in my heart is as horrendous as the stab wound to my stomach. I can't believe this is happening. Nothing makes any sense.

Other than foolishly kissing Dexter two weeks ago, I haven't done anything to warrant this type of retaliation, much less my innocent unborn baby.

Seemingly reading my inner monologue, Marcus mumbles, "The battleline between good and evil runs through the heart of every man, some just aren't capable of ignoring the temptation." The pain in his words cut me raw. They are tinged with regret, sorrow, and remorse. His voice is the most devastated I've ever heard.

Before I can issue him silent comfort with my eyes, Shian drops at his side. "How is she?" Her gaze dances between Marcus and me. Her dark eyes are as wide as Marcus's, and they are also brimming with as many tears.

"Losing too much blood, where are the paramedics?" Marcus's voice is laced with uncontrollable worry.

"They're on their way." The sound of sirens wailing in the distance strengthens Shian's assurance.

"Brodie?"

I feel like an angel floating on a cloud, both woozy and free. Attacks of dizziness are as regular as breathing for me the past three weeks, but this feels different, it almost seems unreal.

Shian swallows harshly before replying, "He got shot three times. One in the arm, one in the spleen, and one in the chest. Fellow agents are working on him. He is still with us—*barely*."

I swallow the horrid taste in the back of my throat before forcing out, "Lexi?" My one word is so garbled I can hardly understand what I said.

Thankfully, Marcus can read the silent plea in my eyes. "Lexi is okay, she is safe and uninjured," he assures me.

Shian jerks her chin up at someone across the room. Two seconds after her nod, Lexi appears at my side. Her face is marked with hot, ugly tears, and her entire body is quaking. I realize how frighteningly cold I am when she gathers my blood-stained hands from my stomach to rest them in her lap.

"You silly, silly, girl. You should have locked yourself in the room with me," Lexi chastises, her voice more a plea than an angry snarl. "Don't ever do that to me again!"

Before I can reply, two first responders arrive at my side. One replaces Marcus's hands with his own while the other searches for a vein in my arm. The mumbled request for an immediate blood transfusion sounds through my ears as the white spots dancing in front of my eyes double in size.

"Please be careful, she's pregnant with my baby," Marcus advises them, his eyes drifting between the first responders and me. "She's due August 29th."

I peer up at Marcus, blinking and confused. How could he know my due date? I haven't even been to the doctor's yet, so I have no idea the date our baby is due. But he just blubbered it out like he is so in tune with my body, he knows precisely the moment we conceived.

I inwardly snort. *He probably does.*

My confused eyes drift to one of the first responders when he chuckles under his breath, "I guess we know what you were thankful for Thanksgiving weekend." He spiritly winks before jotting down the information Marcus handed him in my file.

Marcus glares at him, stunned by his cheerful demeanor. I also stare, but I'm not startled by his response. I know he's attempting to ease the tension thickening the air by using his charismatic personality. I'm just glancing at him in bewilderment, wondering how he knew what Marcus and I were doing Thanksgiving weekend.

Noticing he has me baffled, he places down my file, then explains, "The 29th of August is exactly 40 weeks following Thanksgiving weekend. Obviously, someone gifted you something you'll always be thankful for."

My pulse skyrockets as my eyes snap back to Marcus. Not expecting my rushed movement, my woozy head cites an objection to my unannounced crusade. My eyes roll into the back of my head as I'm overcome by a severe bout of nausea. I feel like I'm floating, even though the rigidness of the tiled floor is digging into my aching back.

"Cleo, keep your eyes open, baby," Marcus demands, his tone indicating the arrival of another savior at my side, this one more demanding than any before him. *Master Chains has arrived.*

I try to do as my Master requests. I try to instill the obedience our time in his playroom taught me. But no matter how hard I fight—no matter how much I beg for my body to listen to its Master—the blackness comes steamrolling in so hard and fast, I don't have a chance of stopping it.

As I'm swept away by a bright white cloud, my thoughts stray to my first sexual encounter with Marcus.

"You make me so reckless," he said that morning. "You make me irresponsible and careless. I don't know whether I should punish you for making me reckless or punish myself."

When I told him I could handle any punishment he wanted to give, he said, "Be careful what you wish for, Cleo."

No... he wouldn't have purposely forgone protection, otherwise why did he deny our baby earlier tonight? He doesn't want me so much he is willing to tie himself to me for eternity. *Does he?*

"Cleo, stay with me, baby," Marcus demands, gently shaking my shoulders, dragging me back to the present. "Keep fighting. Fight for our baby, Cleo. Fight for us."

I struggle against my heavy eyelids, wanting to peer into Marcus's eyes so I can read the truth from his forthright gaze. But no matter how hard I fight, I can't keep my eyes open.

"Our baby. You want our baby?" I murmur, my words barely audible as my veins are deprived of adequate oxygen.

"Yes. Always," is the last thing I hear as I fall into unconsciousness, closely followed by,

"Move, she's flatlining!"

29

Marcus

What started out as a dream, turned into a nightmare.

I lift my burrowed head from my hands when the creak of a door sounds through my ears. I'm not Cleo's family, but I refused to leave the waiting room for next of kin attached to the operating room she was wheeled into three hours ago. I keep my eyes locked on Jackson as he cautiously approaches Lexi and me, refusing to look at the amount of red blood covering his white scrubs. His face is as gaunt as mine and his eyes as glistening.

When he shakes his head to my silent question, a part of me dies. The hope, the optimism the world couldn't be so cruel to one person—it vanishes in an instant. I drop my head back into my hands, denying the vultures of the media to get one more picture of me with tears streaming down my face. Although Lexi's sobs drown out the incessant clicking of their long-range cameras, I know they're still there.

People often believe that members of the BDSM lifestyle are sick, worthless people. This past few weeks, I've witnessed more unspeakable behavior than I've ever seen in my club. Not only did I see the woman I love lying lifeless on the floor, cradling the blood-soaked area our baby was nestled safely in mere hours earlier, I also saw vultures more concerned about getting an image worthy of the front-page news than letting the first responders do their job. The scum of the paparazzi would rather a woman and unborn baby die than miss out on the opportunity to harass me one more time. They'd rather watch a man fall to his knees and howl than offer him comfort. They are pathetic human beings, not me or anyone in my lifestyle.

Overwhelmed with anger I've been harboring for months, I stand from my chair before sending it hurdling across the room. Incapable of holding in the rage tearing my heart out of my chest, I do the same with the chair standing next to me. I did what he asked. I let her go so she'd be safe, yet he still hurt her.

If I knew weeks ago what I know now, I wouldn't have been so goddamn stupid.

Upon arriving at Stephen's house to question him for the assault on Cleo, police stumbled onto a crime scene. Although a body wasn't discovered in the vicinity, it was apparent it would only be a matter of time before one was found.

When police linked a connection between Stephen's murder and a series of death threats I had received for Cleo two days earlier, I panicked. After filling Lexi in on the investigation, she packed Cleo's belongings, and I shipped her off to Florida.

The initial plan was for me to stay with Cleo in my sub house in Ravenshoe, but I couldn't do it. No matter how many times I fought my hands to turn left when we exited the airport hangar, I turned right. Cleo wasn't my sub, and I wasn't going to treat her as if she were. Don't get me wrong, I did fill in a contract months ago, I wanted her to be my sub, but that was because I feared losing her more than anything.

I know BDSM, I don't know relationships, so having a piece of paper guaranteeing Cleo was mine for a stipulated amount of time was almost everything I could have wished for. There was only one thing I wanted more—*her.*

When the local law enforcement office in Ravenshoe caught wind of Richard knowing Cleo's location, they hatched a plan to catch him red-handed. It took the guarantee of Abel and his daughter, Regina, that they would keep Cleo safe for me to leave that morning. I thought seeing Cleo leave with Richard would be my worst day—it's nothing compared to how I am feeling now.

When Richard plunged to his death, the FBI assumed the death threats I'd been receiving for Cleo would cease. They did for the first week, but the morning of Anna's arrival to fit Cleo for a dress to wear at the Serena Scott Fundraising Gala brought the arrival of new threats—these more gruesome than the first.

Her stalker was clever—generally one step ahead of the FBI with every move he made. Although stumped by his caliber of computer knowledge, the agents working the case believed the evidence was clear-cut. Richard's body was never found, so their focus remained on him and anyone associated with him—i.e. Andy.

I'll admit, I overreacted the day Cleo walked to Links after dining with Dexter, but with my security team receiving images of her entering and exiting Toloache within seconds of Serenity advising me of her arrival, panicked anger was my first emotion. The pictures didn't contain a threat like the other correspondence I had received, but they still displayed Cleo was being watched.

The night of the gala was the first time I received a digital threat firsthand. Usually, they'd go through the servers at Chains, but that one came directly to my cell phone. That threat not only warned of ill-harm to Cleo, it also had a picture of her sitting at the bar where she lingered the first hour of her arrival. The threat gave statistics on how it would only take a few drops of poison to kill a woman of Cleo's size, and that all I had to do to save her was walk away and never look back. Since that was something that seemed impossible for me to do, my security team launched into action.

As my men worked behind the scenes, Cartier moved Cleo to a safer location. Although the booths were in the far corner of the ballroom, Cleo was flanked by undercover FBI agents and members of my security team. She was safer that night than anyone else in the country.

When Keira called me to advise she had information on a man at her work harassing Cleo, I should have requested for her to give me the details over the phone. Unfortunately, I've always had a weak spot for Keira. Not because I want her to be my sub, but because of injuries she sustained in my club during my watch.

I created Chains so members of my community would have a safe, sane, and consensual place to play. My guarantee was voided the day Keira's Dom failed to acknowledge her repeated use of her safe word. I still recall the look in her eyes when she stumbled into my office, draped in a blanket and crying. The horrified cloud in her eyes that night nearly haunted me as much as seeing Cleo's face the night of her assault. They are two images added to many I'd give anything to forget.

Keira didn't extend any more information on the man threatening Cleo than I already knew. She advised of the exchange between Cleo and Richard months earlier and mentioned them meeting up in Florida. With her knowledge lacking, it soon became apparent Keira had staged a ruse to secure my utmost attention. Conscientious of her mental well-being, I endorsed caution while handling the matter.

Although shocked at discovering Keira was wearing a chain link pendant, upon further questioning, I believed her reasoning behind it. Still rattled by her exchange at Chains only weeks earlier, she believed wearing my trademark would ensure no other Dom would approach her. It's a logical action, but one I'd rather not explain to Cleo. I hated keeping Cleo in the dark, but the confidential indemnity I guarantee my clients ensured I was unable to update her on all the details regarding my exchange with Keira. *Now I wish I wasn't so damn stubborn.*

Just as they had done throughout the night, my security team kept me updated via a transmitter device lodged in my ear. During my argument with Cleo in the computer facility room of the hotel, my security team received another credible threat. Although watching Cleo walk away from me with her face etched in devastation, it was my safest bet to ensure she'd leave the gala uninjured, as just like all the other threats the prior two weeks, this one was adamant Cleo would be safe as long as she wasn't with me.

The night I returned home and thought Cleo had left me...that was one of my hardest days. I don't know what you call the weird fluttering thing my heart does every time I'm with her—the one I've never experienced with anyone before her—but it was thumping to an entirely different beat that night. *It's pumping a similar rhythm now.*

I'll be upfront. When Cleo asked me to make love to her, I felt threatened. Not because I didn't want her to know what she meant to me, but because I'd never done it before. My confidence exudes in a playroom environment. I know my strong points, and I exploit them during scenes, but making love was a whole new ball game for me. I'm not saying I didn't enjoy it, but it was unlike anything I've ever experienced before.

While Cleo was recovering from our night of lovemaking, Shian introduced me to an FBI profiler who specialized in the type of stalking Cleo had endured the past year. He discovered a distinct pattern with her stalker's tendencies, proving this was something he had done before. On his advice, I left Cleo in New York while I pretended to return to Ravenshoe, hoping her stalker would believe we had separated.

Little did we know at the time, Cleo had arranged to meet her real stalker the day of my departure, and during their conversation, she exposed that our relationship was still going strong. So, as much as I believed my absence would diminish the threats to Cleo's life, her stalker's rage grew, angered by my attempts to defraud him.

Although I firmly believe in Chains and what it represents for members of the BDSM community, my reasoning behind selling it far outweighed my desire to keep it. With the FBI's investigation into Richard being the most in-depth Shian has conducted, several missing pieces of a puzzle started falling into place. *Well, so it seemed at the time.*

The Dom who assaulted Keira is believed to have been Richard. Although he used an alias to initially gain access to Chains, when his annual membership application wasn't endorsed by the party member who invited him, Chains' staff took extra precautions to ensure the safety of its party members.

Richard was the only Dom suitably matched to Keira the night she was allegedly assaulted. Their compatibility test scores were shockingly similar, making them ideal D/s candidates. Wanting to discover if my assumptions were accurate, I met with Keira for brunch the week of my separation from Cleo. Although Keira denied knowing the identity of her Dom due to being blindfolded, her eyelashes excessively fluttered when I showed her an image of Richard I'd found on the Chains servers.

But with Keira's continued request for anonymity, and the lack of cameras in the playrooms, my assumptions were merely hearsay. Believing it was my decision to cut Richard from the Chains community months ago as the reason for Cleo's death threats, selling Chains felt like the right thing to do at the time. I wasn't lying when I said I'd kneel before I'd give up Cleo. I'll give up everything I have before I'll lose her.

Have you ever had an out of body experience? That's what it felt when I was standing in the playroom with Cleo while punishing her for kissing Dexter. I was there, but I wasn't. I've struggled many times the past few months with aspiring to exert my power over Cleo, while also wanting to cherish her at the same time. I suffered the same torture that night.

I watched Cleo kiss another man, knowing it was the perfect ploy to lessen the severity of her stalker's threats. But instead of embracing the opportunity, I let it eat me alive. I should have manned up. I should have absorbed my anger with the steel rod my father lodged in my back since the day I was born. I should have been a man. Instead, I acted like an idiot.

I never knew what blinded by love meant, but if I had known the identity of Cleo's stalker the night she kissed Dexter, and I had a weapon capable of issuing him the torment I went through, I would have killed him. I would have made him suffer as horrendously as I did. That's how much it cut me raw seeing Cleo kiss another man. I've traded subs. I've walked away from women kneeling at my feet, begging to be loved the instant the flare in their eyes told me they were getting too close. But never in all my life have I experienced the pain I felt seeing Cleo kiss another man.

I thought the kiss would be the ultimate proof to her stalker that Cleo and I were no longer together, but do you know what happened? The threats worsened—instantly. They were so horrific, even Jackson had a hard time stomaching them when he caught the quickest glimpse of one on my computer monitor when he was checking my hand. I struck Dexter hard—*now I wish it were even harder*—but my hand isn't broken. It merely presented the perfect opportunity for me to walk away from Cleo once and for all.

Going against the advice of my lawyer, I anonymously released my story to the public before organizing a press conference I knew would allow me to shame Cleo in front of millions. Cleo is a stubbornly beautiful opinionated woman I knew wouldn't stand by and watch a person she cared about be slaughtered without first trying to intercept her attacker's play. But instead of embracing Cleo's determination, I used it against her.

I tore her heart out for the world to see, then I let her be ridiculed and called horrid names no one with a soul as beautiful as hers should ever be associated with. I gave her up to save her, yet it was my inability to fully let her go that has brought us here today.

I never went to Global Ten Media's Christmas function with the intentions of doing what I did. When Cleo removed her collar, Shian needed another wireless tracker placed on her. Knowing where Cleo was at all times was our only chance of keeping her safe. I knew I could get close to Cleo. And I did. But my desire for her was even stronger than I could have anticipated. For just an hour, I wanted to believe I could save her from anything. I wanted to raise two fingers in the air and tell the world to get fucked. I wanted Cleo to be mine and only mine. Now, I ruined everything because I thought right would always triumph over wrong. I should have known better—my childhood shows that isn't the case.

Deep down inside, I know I'm not entirely to blame for today's outcome. Dexter caught everyone by surprise. He disarmed Shian's usually guarded persona by giving her unlimited access to Global Ten's servers when she was investigating Stephen's assault of Cleo and Richard's stalking case. He befriended Brodie by hacking into the security servers at the hotel where the gala was held when Brodie believed he saw Richard in attendance. He even called in a possible sighting of Richard at Global Ten's function last night. He embedded himself in every aspect of Cleo's life by befriending those closest to her.

The only person he failed to woo was me.

I knew something wasn't right with Dexter the moment I saw him enter the fundraising gala. He had his arm wrapped around Delilah a majority of the night, but his eyes never left Cleo. He watched her all night, often moving positions to ensure he could surveil her from afar. But he was clever, purchasing his drinks with cash, and familiarizing himself with the location of the security cameras around the ballroom.

That was his first downfall. I know from experience, only men who have something to hide shield themselves. My security team's prime focus that night was Dexter. Their attention was only diverted because a facial recognition scan of the area received a positive match to a man the FBI had been searching for the prior two weeks. Richard.

Richard was trying to help Cleo, but more often than not, his assistance had the opposite effect, because instead of looking at the main players, the FBI was constantly chasing a ghost. Their focus was sidetracked from the man they should have been watching.

Dexter is obsessed with Cleo, there is no doubt about that. The only thing we can't work out is why. The FBI profiler said there is usually some deep-seated connection that triggers stalking cases of this caliber. Although it's still early, no credible link has been found as to why Dexter is so obsessed with Cleo.

I get his fascination—any red-blooded male would. Cleo is a beautiful woman with a heart of gold, but what makes a man hurt someone he claims to love? What drives him to such a brink of insanity that he believes it's acceptable to stab a knife into a pregnant woman's stomach without fear of prosecution? What society do we live in that a story is worth more than a life?

Exhausted from throwing chairs across the room as if they are tennis balls, I crouch down on the floor and suck in ragged breaths. My body is slicked with sweat, successfully concealing the two tears my brimming eyes couldn't contain. The little flutter my heart makes every time Cleo is in my presence has been doused, leaving a hollow, empty space in its place.

My eyes raise from the ground when a familiar scent lingers in the air. Same brown eyes, same straight nose, and same angelically beautiful face meet my curious glance. Cleo and Lexi are so similar, the only thing that separates them is their scent. Cleo's smell is refreshing and clean, where Lexi's is wild and carefree—much like their personalities.

"Jackson said we can go and see Cleo if we want. I think you should go first," Lexi murmurs, her usually smooth voice choked by tears. "Do you want to see her?"

Not trusting my voice not to break, I nod, then stand. I tug Lexi to my side before placing a quick peck on her hairline. When I first arrived on scene at Cleo's attack, Lexi was standing at the end of the hall with a loaded gun uncontrollably shaking in her hands. Her need to protect her sister and unborn nephew was revealed when I saw how poorly the door she was standing in front of was splintered. Lexi is tiny, a little smaller than Cleo, but the adrenaline surging through her body saw her kicking open a thick wooden door before firing at the man assaulting her sister.

Her first shot missed, but her second hit of Dexter's shoulder was a through and through. If Shian and I hadn't arrived when we did, I have no doubt Lexi would have killed Dexter. She had a fire in her eyes that mimicked mine to a T. She wanted him dead as much as I did. The only thing that stopped both of us was when Cleo suddenly gasped in a wheezy breath, exposing she was still alive. That led us to where we are right now—to the hospital where Jackson works.

No matter how much my heart is breaking, I know Jackson did everything in his power to help Cleo. He loves Cleo as much as he loves Lexi, so I was sure he would take care of her when Lexi suggested him as the surgeon to operate on Cleo. He did everything in his power. I know this, and I will continue telling myself this as I face my darkest day.

"I'll be back soon," I assure Lexi, knowing how difficult it's for her to let me see Cleo first.

I follow Jackson into the hallway of operating rooms, my heart rate lowering with every stride I take. They have Cleo in a private suite in the west wing. She is lying in a large hospital bed that makes her appear much younger than her twenty-six years. Her hair has been brushed straight, stopping just below the swell of her breasts. She looks peaceful and rested, even with only sleeping a few hours every night the past three weeks. Although Cleo isn't aware, I was with her every night the past month. Maybe not in the capacity she needed, but in spirit I was with her every night.

"I'll be in the hall if you need anything," Jackson advises before exiting Cleo's room, leaving me alone with her.

I stand at the side of her bed with my hands, which are itching to touch her, balled at my side. She has been through enough today I don't want to risk hurting her anymore.

"I'm so sorry, baby," I whisper, my voice barely audible over the beeping of machines. "I was trying to protect you when I should have been protecting us. All of us." I peer down at her flat stomach, sending a flood of moisture back to my eyes.

Unable to withstand the desire to touch her, I run my index finger down her exposed forearm—the one without tubes and wires. When the hairs on her arms bristle from my touch, my heart stops beating. I lift my eyes to her face, then take a step back, stunned. Cleo's eyes are open and peering straight at me.

"Hey. How are you?" It's a stupid question to ask, but I'm too shocked to articulate more.

As Cleo's hand slowly creeps down to her stomach, her eyes silently question the results of her surgery. Cleo was assaulted by Dexter fifteen days ago, since that day, our baby has been hanging on by a thread. The knife wound Cleo sustained during her attack did significant damage to her uterus. Although our baby was unharmed, the wound still threatened its life. Doctors were adamant Cleo would eventually miscarry. Today was our last ditch effort to save our baby. We knew the odds were against us, but both Cleo and I agreed to try was better than sitting by and doing nothing. Unfortunately, our hopes were dashed, leaving us both devastated.

Although the tears streaming down Cleo's face tells me she read the answer from my eyes, I murmur, "I'm sorry, baby, Jackson did everything he could, but the damage was too much. Our baby didn't make it."

Cleo's entire body quakes as fresh tears roll down her cheeks unchecked. Although Jackson was upfront about the chances of our baby surviving, we were both optimistic that life couldn't be so cruel to one person. *How wrong were we?*

Careful not to agitate her still-healing body, I slide into the bed next to Cleo and gather her in my arms. She nuzzles her head into the groove of my chest, using my shirt to catch her tears. For every tear she sheds, I issue her a silent promise that it will be one of her last. I've seen her cry more the past two months than I ever wanted to witness. If I see her cry again in this lifetime, it will be too soon.

After the shudders wracking her tiny frame have eased, I gently pull her back by her shoulders. Balls of moisture are beaded on the top of her extremely thick lashes, and her cheeks are white. I kiss away her tears before scooting down the bed to meet her eye to eye.

"Heaven may have held our baby before us, but it's just keeping him safe until we meet him again."

Her brief nod sends more tears trickling down her face. I let these stay, knowing they are a part of her grieving process. We all grieve in our own way. Cleo shows her grief on the outside, in the tears she sheds and the pain etched on her beautiful face, where my pain is felt on the inside. No matter which way you show it, it doesn't make it any less significant. Grief is grief.

I pull Cleo in close to my chest, careful not to cause her any more harm. "Every tragedy has a lesson equal in significance to its heartbreak. We will work through this, and hopefully find the reason behind it in the near future."

Cleo draws her head off my chest so her eyes can bounce between mine. She looks both confused and horrified. I slant my head to the side, silently reading her soul-baring eyes. I come up stumped as to why she looks so panicked.

"What's it?" I ask, deciding a more direct approach is needed.

Her lips quiver as she begins to speak, "That saying you just said, have you heard that before?"

"Yes," I reply, smiling softly. My heart thwacks my chest as I prepare to share a snippet of my life I don't often tell. "My grandmother regularly said it after events in my childhood. Why? Have you heard it before?"

"Yes." She gently nods. "Dexter said it to me after I told him about my parents' accident. He said the exact same quote."

Her admission mystifies me. Although I've heard similar quotes before, I've never heard it quoted in the exact manner my grandmother used to say it.

As I sit in silence with Cleo safely wrapped in my arms, my mind drifts back to the first day we met. The beautiful brunette who stole my attention with one glance of her angelic face wasn't the only person I comforted that day. When I was leaving the hospital, I spotted a man in the parking lot, mumbling and cursing to himself. Although he was angry, his grief was also clearly visible. I shared that quote with him that afternoon, hoping the words I failed to say to Cleo could help another.

That couldn't have been Dexter—*surely.*

Cleo has often quoted how intermingled our lives have been the past four years, but it wouldn't extend this far.

Would it?

30

Two years later….

Cleo

Resolute silence falls over the large gathering of people surrounding me when I step out of the alcove I'm standing in. Although I'd like to say their gaped-mouth expressions are due to the one-of-a-kind J Holt creation I'm wearing, that isn't the case. It's the soulful voice of Marcus breaking through the hum of chatter. Our guests sit in silence, marveled by a voice that can make me swoon and scream in ecstasy at the same time. My smile beams as I glance at the two men standing on each side of me, both silenced in awe by Marcus's acoustic serenade. When he proposed, Marcus said he would sing at our wedding. I just had no clue he would do it in front of a hundred of our closest family and friends.

Abel's eyes twinkle with moisture as he walks me down the white rose petal aisle with another man I've always seen as family. Miguel dips his chin at his wife's appreciative ogle of his suit-covered body. Although two years ago the world proved how cruel it can be to one person, I'm glad that logic hasn't come true for Miguel and Janice. Her tumor hasn't just stopped growing, it's shrinking in size as well. Doctors still caution Miguel not to get his hopes up, but optimism has always been his strong point.

As we continue slowly pacing down the aisle, my ears drink in every perfect syllable of Marcus's beautiful voice as my eyes absorb our guests. Shian, forever the rebel, is sitting in the very back row. Although her tailored pantsuit gives her a tough exterior, the glistening moisture in her eyes softens her not-to-be-messed-with persona.

I arch a brow at Richard, who is sitting a few spots up from Shian. His cocky attitude is beaming out of him as brightly as ever. Even two bullet wounds within a month couldn't squash his peacock demeanor. Although it took the FBI several months to solve the riddle of a man as psychotic as Dexter, when they did, they also discovered that Richard, although arrogant, isn't a murderer nor a stalker. I don't even believe he is a Dom who doesn't understand he needs to stop when being given a sub's safe word.

When Marcus confronted Richard about any prior exchanges with Keira, Richard never denied his interaction with Keira the night of Keira's alleged assault. He agreed they did act out a scene that night at Chains, but he refuted not stopping when she safe-worded. He's adamant she never spoke a word, much less something as important as a safe word.

Although new to Chains, Richard had been in the BDSM lifestyle three years before his exchange with Keira. He openly expressed an eagerness to gag his subs, but assured Marcus he never muzzled a sub until he had extensive knowledge of her limitations. Trust is a significant factor in the BDSM lifestyle, so casual playmates rarely perform scenes that require an immense amount of trust.

When Richard's account of events is stacked with Keira's desire to be Marcus's sub, doubt of Keira's accusations surfaced several months ago. Although Keira could have been assaulted by another Dom that same night, I highly doubt it. I don't believe Keira was the victim of wrongdoing at all. I believe her entire ruse was solely devised to get her close to Marcus. She knew how important a safe, sane and consensual environment was for him, so guilt hit him hard when she was allegedly assaulted in his club. It's just lucky Marcus is a shrewd man who saw past the ruse—albeit a little later than I would have liked.

Considering Richard is an invited guest of both Marcus and me, I'd say I'm not the only one who doubts Keira's claims. Marcus must believe Richard is innocent, or he wouldn't be here. Admitting he was wrong is a massive step for a man as dominant as Marcus, but just like the FBI, he is discovering not everything is always as it seems.

After going to such lengths to protect me, the FBI looked further into Richard's alleged stalking and murder charges. They soon realized all the evidence they had on Richard was planted by Dexter. Even the image of Richard and Stephen together in the elevator was discovered to be fraudulent.

Although Richard went about it in the wrong way, he was trying to help me the morning he arrived at Florida. His impressive hacking skills that he remarkably kept under wraps had him unearthing Dexter's ruse faster than Shian's skilled team. Unfortunately for all involved, Dexter was always a few steps ahead of everyone.

The quote Marcus said to me the day we lost our baby was the final piece of the puzzle to understanding Dexter's obsession with me.

Overwhelmed with grief, I never considered the consequences for anyone else involved in my parents' car accident. From the police report, I knew when my dad hit a section of black ice, he veered into oncoming traffic. What I didn't know was that his car struck another, killing a twenty-three-year-old San Francisco native who had recently moved to New York. After further investigation, it was discovered that Shelly Christian had moved to New York to escape the clutches of her manic stalker. She did everything the police had requested—doctoring any contact they had, filing for a restraining order, changing her phone number and address. When nothing worked, Shelly became so desperate, she drove to the other side of the country. Her stalker was just as determined as she was. He never gave up. His name was Dexter Elias.

Dexter—believing he'd lost the love of his life—took vengeance on the person he felt responsible—my dad. The desire to get back what he lost made him move to New York and seek employment at the same company of the person he sought vengeance on. Me. His plans to make my life miserable stayed on track the first few months... until we met in person. The FBI believes that's when Dexter's revenge shifted to obsession. Shelly and I have a lot of similarities. We were both of Latin heritage, both orphans, and we were both looking for a break in life. Shelly never got hers—I found mine in Marcus.

Some believe if I'd just denied Mr. Carson's request to go undercover at Chains all our heartache would have been avoided. I don't believe that's true. If I hadn't gone to Chains, I would have never met Marcus again. He would have never paid for my sister's inclusion in the Kalydeco program, and I would have never felt as loved as I do right now having him serenade me in front of our guests.

Marcus's grandmother's quote is true. Every tragedy has a lesson equal in significance to its heartbreak. I'd give anything to lessen the pain I endured losing my family and our unborn baby, but I'd also give anything to keep Marcus in my life. He is my reward for years of unhappiness, as I am his.

When I reach the end of the aisle, the crowd breaks into rapturous applause, as appreciative of Marcus's singing talent as I was the first time I heard him sing. Miguel and Abel place a kiss on my cheek before handing me to the groom, who is waiting next to his long line of groomsmen. Unsurprisingly, Marcus's bandmates all have a prime spot at the end of the aisle, just as their wives—my very dear friends—have a place on my side of the church.

There are also two extra inclusions on Marcus's side that wholeheartedly deserve to be there. The man who saved me when I nearly bled out on the floor of my living room, and soon-to-be husband of my baby sister, surgeon extraordinaire, Jackson Collard. And Brodie, the man who took three bullets for me when Dexter lured him out of the safety of his patrol car by telling him Richard had broken into my home. I knew Brodie's love of his job was more deep-seated than a standard bodyguard. I just had no clue he was an undercover FBI agent. I shouldn't be surprised—his acting skills are the best I've seen.

"Hi," I greet Marcus when I stop to stand in front of him.

His eyes dance between mine as the back of his fingers run down my cheek before faintly hovering over the scar in my top lip only he can see. After the loss of our baby two years ago, Marcus pledged me a lifetime of happiness. He has strived to achieve that every day since. The rollercoaster ride we endured the first two months of our relationship has been just as thrilling the past two years, but instead of having soaring highs and devastating lows, we are on a ride that never stops gliding.

The past two years have been magical, unlike anything I could have imagined. The death of our unborn child was a horrible experience I'd give anything to change, but our loss also brought us closer together, bonding us in the same way I'm sure our son would have if he had survived our attack. Although our baby never had the chance to take his first breath, he will always be a part of our lives. Marcus and I even have his date of conception and due date tattooed on our wrists.

Sensing where my thoughts have drifted to, Marcus runs his index finger over the Roman numerals etched on my wrist, drawing my eyes to his.

"Hi," he greets me.

He only says one word, but he doesn't need to say more. His eyes express everything his mouth fails to articulate. As Marcus quoted the day we lost our baby, heaven may have held our baby before we did, but they are keeping him safe until we meet again.

Marcus's lips curve when a loud squeal breaks the silence encompassing us. I giggle before following his amused gaze to our six-month-old daughter Tatum, wooing the crowd with her adorable black ringlet curls and unique hazel eyes. Although Tatum's pregnancy was an unexpected surprise, even more so considering the significant damage Dexter did to my uterus, news of her impending arrival was handled more pleasantly than our unborn baby.

I still get the occasional gripe on social media about trapping Marcus by getting pregnant, then using his grief to sink my nails into him more deeply. But for the most part, the media and fans have welcomed me into the Rise Up family with open arms—*mostly.*

Marcus's obvious grief the two weeks following my attack was broadcast around the world. The loss of our unborn baby hit him harder than he'd ever admit, but his relief that I was spared any life-threatening injuries was also visible. Just like our first meeting, it was a beautifully tormented moment in time.

The media played out the entire charade like some sort of morbid re-telling of Cinderella. I was cast the part of Cinderella and Marcus was Prince Charming. The fans gobbled it up, adoring that a modern-day harlot could have a prince whisk in and rescue her from her miserable, decrepit life. Although my feminist side hates the idea of being cast as a damsel in distress, I'll never express my disdain out loud, preferring headlines full of half-truths than ones entirely based on fiction.

Realizing she has captured the attention of her daddy, Tatum blows a loud raspberry—her way of awarding him kisses from a distance. After scrunching up her nose and snarling a toothless grin, she attacks the silver spoon Aubrey gifted her with unbridled fury. Her teeth have been giving her hell the past week. No. Correction. Her teeth have been giving *us* hell the past week. Unlike her mother, Tatum doesn't appear to be a fan of pain, which is very well, because that's one conversation I'd prefer to avoid in the future.

Although I am an orphan, and Marcus has no contact with his parents,

Tatum doesn't notice the absence of her grandparents. Miguel and Janice, as well as Abel and Aubrey, have stepped into the roles so well, Tatum will never miss cherished family memories.

I met Marcus's parents the month following my near-death experience. It wasn't a pleasant meeting, one I'd prefer not to share on the happiest day of my life, so it must wait for a future story. Serenity keeps them updated on events in Marcus's life, but I'd expect to see pigs fly before a reunion occurs between Marcus and his parents.

"Are you ready, Cleo?" Marcus asks before pivoting on his heels to face the wedding celebrant.

"Uh huh," I answer, smiling a grin that displays my utter joy.

Although our wedding is occurring nearly a year after Marcus wanted, I'm glad I held my ground and adjusted the dates. I wanted to ensure I had time to lose my baby weight before squeezing into the gorgeous satin and lace gown Jenni handcrafted for me.

While handing my bouquet of white roses to Lexi, I playfully wink at Serenity, soundlessly revealing I didn't miss her bug-eyed expression regarding the hottie seated three rows back when we arrived at the church. Serenity rolls her eyes before sticking out her tongue. Her nonchalant approach is blown out of the water when her wide gaze immediately returns to the man she hasn't taken her eyes off the past ten minutes.

"Try not to scare this one off," I playfully chide to Marcus, moving to stand next to him.

"If he grasps how to treat a lady like a lady, I won't have to scare him away." Marcus's tone is a unique mix of commanding and nurturing.

I smile, adoring his protectiveness of his sister, while also feeling sorry for Tatum when she reaches dating age. When Marcus slips his hand over mine, my smile enlarges. His palm is clammy and wet—he is just as nervous as I am.

When I shift my eyes to peer at him, his massively dilated gaze meets mine halfway.

"Are you ready to have the best of both worlds, Master Chains?"

Marcus's eyes flare as the corners of his lips curve high. He looks happy, intrigued, and if I'm being totally honest, smug as hell. The reason behind his pompous attitude comes to light when he slides his spare hand into his pocket to activate the tiny device he has hidden inside. My knees curve inwards as a ferocious wildfire ignites in my stomach. I stand perfectly still, praying our guests are clueless to the vibrating jolt turning my sex into a sticky, heated mess.

Happy I'm on the brink of orgasm, Marcus switches off the device before drifting his eyes to me. "As ready as I'll ever be," he croons, his voice causing even more dampness to puddle between my legs.

There he is. The man I fantasize about every night.

Master Chains has arrived.

EPILOGUE

Marcus

"Slow down, anyone would swear you've been away from home for a week."

I sling my arm into the air, too eager to return home to bother bantering with Cameron about my obvious excitement. I've been away from Cleo and Tatum for a week, I am well past eager. As I gallop down the stairs of my private jet, the flashing of bulbs in the distance flicker in the droplets of rain falling from the pitch-black sky. Unlike the Florida temperatures I've become accustomed to the past seven days, the night is cool and summer is now a distant memory.

"Thanks," I say to Tripp, one of the many men who work at the private airstrip I own on the outskirts of Montclair, when he throws a set of keys across my expensive pride and joy.

My muscles sigh when I slide into the driver's seat, appreciating the way the vibrating leather pads Cleo had installed relieve the tension of a long week. The past week has been the longest week of my life. In the past three years, I've never been away from Cleo more than a night, so to spend seven nights without her by my side, I'm not only restless, I'm extremely fatigued.

With modern technology, I kept in contact with Cleo and Tatum as if they were right in front of me—but there is one thing missing no technology can replicate. Their smell. Just like every other sensory outlet in my body, my sense of smell has improved since I met Cleo. Smell has a direct link to the limbic system. The limbic system is responsible for the processing of emotions and memory. That's why when I smell the scent of pollen on a dew-crisp morning, I can recall Cleo in crystal clear form. Her beautifully plump lips, the generous swell of her breasts, her alluring curves that capture the attention of every man when she walks into the room. One smell and I'm trapped, caught between a man wanting to parade his most valuable asset in public for the world to see, and the Master who wants to possess every inch of her so thoroughly, she'll feel me with every breath she takes.

Tonight, I'm not stuck. I know exactly what I want.

My tires lose traction on the wet asphalt when I increase the pressure on the gas pedal. I go whizzing toward the exit manned by a four security guard-strong team. Paparazzi rush toward the exit when they spot my sports car gliding down the pavement. I flash a grateful smile to the two security officers braving the wet weather to clear a path through the media circling me. With my family's time equally shared between Montclair and Bronte's Peak, the paparazzi isn't as dense as normal.

I'm thrusted into my seat when I spot a clearing between the flashing lights. My engine roars to life, showcasing its power with a grunt every man loves. There is only one purr more intoxicating than the rumbling of my high-powered engine. My wife's.

My excessive speed has me eluding the paparazzi by the time I'm halfway home. I lower my speed to a more appropriate level, but it remains above the designated limit marked on the road, my eagerness too powerful to contain.

As I roll down the curved driveway of our family home, my eyes scan our palatial mansion for any signs of life. With a live-in nanny, a housekeeper, and two bodyguards, I'm surprised to find my residence plunged into blackness. I can't often escape the constant bustle that has become my life the past three years. Silence is a hard limit for Cleo—meaning I am forever surrounded by noise. I'm not going to complain. After living the first sixteen years of my life restrained with silence, I relish every beautiful sound. The whispered I love yous, the screams of ecstasy torn from my wife's mouth, and the coos of my daughter when she covers my chin with slobber. I cherish every perfect noise. To me, they are more beautiful than any song I've produced.

I park my car at the edge of our entranceway, my patience too thin to park my vehicle in the garage. Dots of rain fall on my suit-covered shoulders as I climb the stairs of the home I bought in the months following Cleo's recovery. It's a large estate nestled in a gated community of Montclair. This town is my wife's home, it was her refuge after having all the sounds she loved cruelly torn from her, so it was the right place for her to recover after the loss of our unborn baby.

As I toss my keys on the wooden table in the entranceway, my eyes catch sight of the Roman numerals on my wrist. "One day, little man, one day," I murmur to myself, reminding our son we will meet again one day.

The tapping of my feet as I take the stairs two at a time booms into the eerie silence filling my house. Years ago, I would have panicked about a lack of fanfare for my arrival home, but now, I appreciate that Cleo has her hands full chasing a toddler and manning all the charity organizations she boards as part of Chains' charity efforts.

As per Cleo's request, I remain the sole owner of Chains. Except now, instead of having one BDSM club cloaked by secrecy, I have fifteen well-represented clubs dotting the coastline from New York to Florida. The exclusivity and guarantee of privacy are still two of the utmost priorities of my clubs, but having a safe, sane, and consensual place for people of my community to play will always be my number one focus.

My brisk speed down the dark corridor of the main residence of my property slows when I stride past a fluorescent pink-painted door. Although I'm dying to smell my wife's indescribable scent, I carefully pry open the ghastly-colored door and step into the room. Tatum is sleeping in the top corner of her crib, sucking on her thumb. She stirs softly when I run my hand over the sprout of black curls on top of her head. Other than her angelic face, Tatum is the perfect mix of both Cleo and me. She has her mom's curls and my black hair. Her skin tone is a mix of us both, and her eyes are the perfect combination of Cleo's and mine. She truly is the best of both Cleo and me mixed into one adorable little package.

I snag the fluffy rabbit Cleo arrived home from the hospital with when she was a baby and tuck it under Tatum's arm before exiting the room. Eager to slip into bed with Cleo, I remove my suit jacket and tie as I finalize my strides down the end of the hall. My steps halt midstride when a surge of adrenaline roars through my veins. I stop just outside our bedroom door when a flicker of light in the corner of my eye garners my attention.

The heat thickening my veins migrates to the lower half of my body when I turn my head in the direction the light is coming from. There are four small candles dancing around a room that makes my chest puff with smugness every time I enter it. Although the candles are dim, they are bright enough to erotically showcase the visual of my naked wife kneeling at the entrance of our playroom. Her chin is tucked into her chest, and her hands are resting on her bare thighs, palms side up in offering. Although she is perfectly still, I know she has sensed my presence as the hairs on her nape are prickling with attention.

When I pace into the room, my eyes swing sideways. Just as I had suspected, Tatum's baby monitor is sitting on the drawers above the chest of toys and gadgets we've made good use of the past three years.

My cock thickens painfully as I turn around to close our playroom door, not only blocking out noises from outside, but also locking Cleo's erotic screams inside the soundproof walls.

As I remove my clothing, my eyes drink in every delectable curve of my wife. The smug grin on my face turns into a genuine smile when I spot a splatter of paint on the ball of Cleo's foot. Although I offered to have an interior designer return Cleo's family home to its prior glory, Cleo was adamant she wanted to do it herself. Because it's a feat of love more than a chore, she has spent the last year sanding and painting every wall herself. Her love of her family shines through in that property, as it does with our daughter's name. Tatum is named after Cleo's little brother, Tate.

If security wasn't an issue, I would move us in into Cleo's family home the instant Cleo finishes her renovations, but with her and Tatum's safety my utmost priority, my dream must remain precisely that—a dream.

Once my clothes are removed, folded and sitting on top of Cleo's nightgown, I move to stand in front of her. She is kneeling next to a cart Aubrey generally serves breakfast on every Sunday, but instead of it being covered with scrumptious savories, it's filled with even more delicious products. Nipple clamps, vibrating butt plugs, a riding crop, and a pinwheel are a small handful of the instruments she has laid out.

Placing my hand under her downcast chin, I lift her head. The thrill of the hunt scorches my veins when her beautiful chocolate eyes lock with mine. Cleo's eyes are the reason I've grown an obsession with blindfolding her. They are my eternal weakness, potent enough to unravel me with a single glance. I've learned to limit my need for control outside of this environment, but in, this room, there is no compromise. Although Cleo continually breaks the boundaries outside of this domain, she is well aware of the rules associated with this room.

Cleo hates the title of submissive, but she has many submissive qualities. She loves being dominated and pleasing her Master. She is cautious of the rules and is eager to explore the BDSM lifestyle, and she challenges me to be the best Master I can be. She is the perfect submissive—the best I've ever had, even without the official title.

"What's this?" I ask, my voice throaty as I struggle to ignore the heat of her lust-filled gaze hardening my cock even more.

Cleo licks her lips as she follows my gaze to the instruments laid out on the cart. "We only got halfway through our list last night, so I thought we could finish it tonight, Master Chains." I feel the soft purr of her voice to my balls.

"We are well overdue to adjust your hard and soft limits, but that's not usually done while utilizing the instruments associated with them."

"Why not?" Cleo questions, returning her eyes to me. "It will be more fun this way."

"Eyes," I demand when her amorous smirk instigates a wild recklessness to run through me.

Only Cleo can make me throw caution to the wind. I've never been as heedless with another woman as I am with her. I have had subs who went above and beyond to please, ones who never wanted to leave my side, and ones who would bend to any will to keep me as their Master. But there has only ever been one woman I altered the rules for. She was the one who walked into my world and amazed me with her strength and determination. She was the one who truly proved I can have the best of both worlds. She is my wife.

A husky growl rolls up my chest when Cleo drops her eyes to her hands the instant my command leaves my mouth. *See—perfect submissive.*

"Because I am feeling generous, I will approve your request." I don't need to see her face to know she is smiling. I can feel it deep in my bones. "But be warned, I am restless, so my patience is thin. Today is not the day to test me. Do you understand?"

"Yes, Master Chains," Cleo replies without delay.

Her agreement makes me want to pull her into my lap and ravish the mouth I've been dying to taste all week, but I won't. The day I became her husband, I not only promised to love and cherish her every day of my life, I also promised that every time we stepped into this room, her every desire, wish, and craving would be fulfilled. Cleo loves being dominated, so much so, I'll push aside my need to fuck her hard and fast on the floor she is kneeling on to ensure she is dominated in the way she needs.

"Very well. Move onto the Saint Andrew's Cross."

"Yes, Master Chains."

Keeping her head tucked into her chin, Cleo stands from her kneeling position and moves to the Saint Andrew's Cross in the middle of the room. Her pert tits lift high on her erratically panting chest when she stretches out her arms to rest them on the polished wood. Her legs soon follow suit. After gathering a blindfold from the chest on my right, I pace toward her, my strides purposely slow so she has plenty of time to see how hard she has made me.

Just as she has done every time I stand before her naked, Cleo's eyes run over my body, categorizing and memorizing every inch of me as if it's the first time she has seen me naked. Her attentive gaze makes me even harder. For every step I take, the shimmer between her legs becomes more apparent. She is so wet, her arousal glistens on her thighs.

My hands twitch to touch her when I stop to stand in front of her, but I keep them balled at my side—barely. Cleo's eyes remain arrested on mine as I shackle her wrists and ankles with the leather cuffs on the cross. I restrain her tightly enough her skin gets the pinch she loves, but not firmly enough to hinder the little squirms she makes. Happy she is safely locked in, I crank the handle on the cross until she is inclined to a forty-five-degree angle.

I take a step back to appreciate the beauty of my wife bound and erotically staged in front of me. The Saint Andrew's Cross is the perfect instrument to expose every inch of her gorgeous body. The rosy pinkness of her nipples, the beautiful little ripples in the bottom of her stomach from growing our daughter, and the angry scar that reminds me every day of how lucky I am to still have her in my life. She is undoubtedly beautiful—perfect in every way.

Incapable of waiting a minute longer to touch her, I move to stand in front of her. Cleo's minty breath fans my hungry lips when I slide a blindfold over her ravishing eyes, dampening the firm grip she has on my balls and throat.

A trail of goosebumps follow in my wake when I track my finger down her blemished cheek, then over the chain link nestled in her neck, before dropping it to the swell of her breast. Her thighs squeeze together when my fingers' trek over her body has me reaching the bare mound of her glistening pussy.

"Spread your legs wider," I demand as my finger glides through the wet folds of her soaked sex.

The pants of her breath grow as she does as instructed. "Good girl," I praise as I slowly inch my index finger inside her.

The walls of her vagina ripple around me, silently begging me to lose control. I push into her so deep, I hit the little nerve inside her that drives her wild. Cleo braces against the restraints holding her tightly as a throaty purr simpers through her lips.

I pump my finger in and out of her as I gather one of the instruments she left out in offering off the silver cart. With her mind stuck in a lusty haze, the air leaves Cleo's body in a hankering grunt when the unexpected intrusion of latex replaces my finger. She stills for the quickest moment before her husky growl advises me she is aware of the instrument I am priming. For a woman who had never experienced anal play before me, my wife has become obsessed.

After coating the anal plug with Cleo's arousal, I move it to the crevice only I have claimed. I circle the plug around her puckered hole before slowly inching it inside.

"Stop squirming," I demand, using my voice that only belongs in this room.

I swivel the anal plug, stretching her more, as I sink it deep inside her. Cleo moans when I flick on the switch at the end, sending a pleasing vibration over every inch of her body. When I slide my fingers back into her pussy, she squeezes around me. She is even tighter now—clenched with arousal. Her soaked sex is hot and begging to be consumed. Unable to deny myself for a moment longer, I lower my mouth to her clit.

"Oh...yes..." Cleo hisses when my tongue circles her throbbing bud before I suckle it into my mouth.

She quivers against me as her delicious arousal engulfs my taste buds. I roll my tongue down her pulsating sex before plunging it inside. Her pussy clenches around my tongue as she fights to stave off her orgasm. She has trained well the past three years, learning that orgasms released after an immense battle are often the most rewarding.

"Do not come until I say," I warn, ensuring she is aware of the rules. My domain. My say. "If you come, I'll punish you."

Her frustrated grunt thickens my cock even more.

After driving her to the brink of climax three times, I pull my mouth away from her aching-with-need pussy. She whines softly. She isn't the only one disappointed. I could eat her greedy cunt all night long.

Her disappointed moan switches to an animalistic grunt when the leather tassels on my favorite flogger run over the taut skin on her stomach. I flick the handle of the flogger slowly, preparing her skin for the sting of its touch before increasing the pressure of my taps.

Her nipples harden to the point of cutting diamonds when the leather cracks against her puckered buds. Her nipples have always been responsive and nursing our daughter hasn't altered that fact.

I work the cat o' nine tales over the skin on her stomach, breasts, and inner thighs until they are covered with gorgeous pink welts and her cries of ecstasy have reached a stage of begging. "Please, Master Chains. I can't hold it back much longer."

"Not yet," I reply, placing the flogger down to secure another instrument.

I continue working through each of the items until the desires of my body can no longer be ignored. Watching Cleo orgasm three times ensures I've played my role of Master well, so there is no need for me to continue depriving myself. The paddle I'm grasping drops to the floor with a clatter as I line my engorged knob with the entrance of my wife's saturated pussy.

"Wait, please," Cleo demands softly.

Our chests compete against one another when I'm stilled by her request. Usually, Cleo follows the rules of the room to a T, trusting my ability to read her needs, she's never had to voice her desires before. I tug her blindfold off her forthright eyes, fearful I've misread the signals of her body. I did have her gagged until mere minutes ago, so maybe she wanted to safe word but couldn't.

She blinks several times in a row as her eyes adjust to the brightness of the room. "Hey," she greets me with a grin, her lips curving upwards.

"Hi," I reply, shocked by her carefree response.

Although her eyes reveal her exhaustion, they're brimming with so much love, I'm tempted to re-cover them.

I secure my first full breath in over a minute when she says, "Sorry for stopping you. I know it's against the rules. I just..."

She lowers her eyes, fearful she'll be punished for disobedience. Her glossy black hair falls from her face when I lift her chin to its original position.

"What is it?" I ask, reminding both myself and her that she isn't my sub—she is my wife.

Her throat works hard to swallow before she whispers, "I just really want to touch you. I haven't touched you in a week, so I'm dying to feel your skin against my hands." She swivels her restrained wrists to enhance her request. "Please," she frailly begs, equally turned on and panicked by the idea of being punished.

Her deep exhalation of air fans my sweat-drenched face when I say, "Okay." It's quickly redrawn when I add on, "But first we're going to negotiate."

Cleo stares into my eyes, her gaze unreserved and without fear as she replies, "I do not need to negotiate. I'm willing to accept any terms my Master sees fit."

See—the perfect submissive.

One I'll happily command for the rest of my life.

The End...

AFTERWORD

I hope you enjoyed Restrain as much as I enjoyed writing it. I am planning on writing a book from Marcus's POV. He has so much to tell.

The next book in the Bound Series is Dexter.
His story is called The Misfits.

Facebook: facebook.com/authorshandi

Instagram: instagram.com/authorshandi

Email: authorshandi@gmail.com

Reader's Group: bit.ly/ShandiBookBabes

Website: authorshandi.com

Newsletter: https://www.subscribepage.com/AuthorShandi

If you enjoyed this book - please leave a review.

ACKNOWLEDGMENTS

Thank you to all the wonderful people who have supported me in my new endeavor. I'm incredibly grateful to have been blessed with such wonderful family and friends.

The time and effort it takes in writing a book are immense. You sacrifice your family, your hobbies, and yourself to produce a book that you hope your readers will enjoy. If you have enjoyed this book, please leave a review. A review is the only way you can truly thank an author for all the effort they put in.

Not many people are aware, but I'm a mother of five. I have four boys and one little daughter. I'd never be able to produce these books without the support of my husband. He comes home from working ten hour plus days to shower the children and get them ready for bed, never once saying a negative word. He is my rock, my inspiration, and my everything.

Also thanks to my mum Carolyn, for reading and assisting me when I call you crazily saying a scene isn't working. I appreciate everything you do. And last, but not at all least, my editor, Krista. Thank you for making my manuscripts extra sparkly. I appreciate everything you do!

Once again, thank you for your support and messages. I read every single one received. Please leave a review, and I'll see you on the flip side.

Cheers Shandi xx

ALSO BY SHANDI BOYES

Perception Series

Saving Noah (Noah & Emily)

Fighting Jacob (Jacob & Lola)

Taming Nick (Nick & Jenni)

Redeeming Slater (Slater and Kylie)

Saving Emily (Noah & Emily - Novella)

Wrapped Up with Rise Up (Perception Novella - should be read after the Bound Series)

Enigma

Enigma (Isaac & Isabelle #1)

Unraveling an Enigma (Isaac & Isabelle #2)

Enigma The Mystery Unmasked (Isaac & Isabelle #3)

Enigma: The Final Chapter (Isaac & Isabelle #4)

Beneath The Secrets (Hugo & Ava #1)

Beneath The Sheets(Hugo & Ava #2)

Spy Thy Neighbor (Hunter & Paige)

The Opposite Effect (Brax & Clara)

I Married a Mob Boss(Rico & Blaire)

Second Shot(Hawke & Gemma)

The Way We Are(Ryan & Savannah #1)

The Way We Were(Ryan & Savannah #2)

Sugar and Spice (Cormack & Harlow)

Lady In Waiting (Regan & Alex #1)

Man in Queue (Regan & Alex #2)

Couple on Hold(Regan & Alex #3)

Enigma: The Wedding (Isaac and Isabelle)

Silent Vigilante (Brandon and Melody #1)

Hushed Guardian (Brandon & Melody #2)

Quiet Protector (Brandon & Melody #3)

Bound Series

Chains (Marcus & Cleo #1)

Links(Marcus & Cleo #2)

Bound(Marcus & Cleo #3)

Restrain(Marcus & Cleo #4)

Psycho (Dexter & ??)

Russian Mob Chronicles

Nikolai: A Mafia Prince Romance (Nikolai & Justine #1)

Nikolai: Taking Back What's Mine (Nikolai & Justine #2)

Nikolai: What's Left of Me(Nikolai & Justine #3)

Nikolai: Mine to Protect(Nikolai & Justine #4)

Asher: My Russian Revenge (Asher & Zariah)

Nikolai: Through the Devil's Eyes(Nikolai & Justine #5)

Trey (Trey & K)

K: A Trey Sequel

The Italian Cartel

Dimitri

Roxanne

Reign

Mafia Ties (Novella)

Maddox

Demi

Rocco

Clover

Smith

RomCom Standalones

Just Playin' (Elvis & Willow)

Ain't Happenin' (Lorenzo & Skylar)

The Drop Zone (Colby & Jamie)

Very Unlikely (Brand New Couple)

Short Stories

Christmas Trio (Wesley, Andrew & Mallory -- short story)

Falling For A Stranger (Short Story)

Coming Soon

Skitzo

Made in the USA
Coppell, TX
20 August 2023

20567940R00444